Acclaim for the
Brides of the Bloodstone trilogy

CAPTURED BY YOUR KISS

"Passionate, engrossing. . . . *Captured by Your Kiss* is a book to lose yourself in, falling into the intense emotions of the characters, and the harshness of the setting and time period, and letting the complex threads of the plot hold your attention until the last page."

—The Romance Reader

"Great depth, drama, and action. . . . A very strong novel that will satisfy readers of the series. You'll be captivated and completely engaged with the myth, the magic, and the romance Ms. Holling has so beautifully created."

—*Romantic Times*

"Sure to captivate. . . . A trilogy full of love and adventure. All three [are] sure to thrill those who enjoy a good medieval tale."

—Romance Reviews Today

"Ms. Holling creates a romantic tale with characters who stay in your heart long after their story is over. *Captured by Your Kiss* is a gem of a book, and not to be missed."

—The Word on Romance

"It was hard to catch my breath as I galloped through the pages of *Captured by Your Kiss*. Ms. Holling's plots are so skillfully written that each book of the trilogy seems to melt into the other. The readers feel right at home in the period, enjoying the company of friends, some old, some new."

—Rendezvous

"*Captured by Your Kiss* is a fantastic conclusion of this fascinating trilogy. There is adventure, danger, and a beautiful love story."

—Reader to Reader

TAMED BY YOUR DESIRE

"Time stands still as the reader is caught up in the conflict and experiences, and the excitement of this romantic tale."

—Rendezvous

"The clash of wills and biting and dynamic repartee are reminiscent of Shannon Drake's Scottish romances."

—*Romantic Times*

TEMPTED BY YOUR TOUCH

"A tender triumph that tempted me to keep reading all night long."

—Teresa Medeiros, *New York Times* bestselling author of *Yours Until Dawn*

ALSO BY JEN HOLLING

MY
IMMORTAL
PROTECTOR

JEN
HOLLING

POCKET BOOKS
New York London Toronto Sydney

Pocket Books
A Division of Simon & Schuster, Inc.
1230 Avenue of the Americas
New York, NY 10020

This book is a work of fiction. Names, characters, places, and incidents either are products of the author's imagination or are used fictitiously. Any resemblance to actual events or locales or persons, living or dead, is entirely coincidental.

First Pocket Books paperback edition March 2008

POCKET and colophon are registered trademarks of Simon & Schuster, Inc.

For information about special discounts for bulk purchases, please contact Simon & Schuster Special Sales at 1-800-456-6798 or business@simonandschuster.com

Designed by Jill Putorti

Cover design by John Vairo, Jr.

Manufactured in the United States of America

10 9 8 7 6 5 4 3 2 1

ISBN-13: 978-1-4165-2585-1
ISBN-10:   1-4165-2585-8

MY
IMMORTAL
PROTECTOR

Prologue

⸻⸻⸻

STRATHWICK, SCOTTISH HIGHLANDS
1597

It was another troubled night for Deidra. Her father blamed it on the storm—the screaming wind, the driving rain, the rumbling thunder. But it wasn't the storm; at least not entirely. The storm made the creatures restless and frightened. And when they were afraid, Deidra didn't sleep.

William MacKay sat on his daughter's bed in the candlelit room. He'd already checked under the bed and behind the screen and deemed them animal-free. Deidra believed him. She would know if creatures were in the room. She knew it was all very strange to her father. There had been a time when Deidra had been more comfortable with animals than with people, a time when the thoughts and feelings of creatures had comforted her.

Now they haunted her.

Her cries of terror had brought her father rushing to her room. He sat with her now, gazing down at her with furrowed brow. Rain danced against the shutters.

Her new stepmother, Rose, stood in the doorway, red hair streaming over her shoulders, pale brow creased with concern.

"What is it, sweeting?"

Tall dog, tall dog, tall dog. The frantic chant filled her mind, pressing out other thoughts. She slapped her hands over her ears just as Billy, the large mastiff, nosed past Rose, searching for its master. Once it saw that William MacKay was in Deidra's room, relief poured from the dog. He crossed the room to sit at William's feet. Unfortunately the chant continued, but now it was filled with adoration and hope of table scraps later.

Deidra couldn't stand it. She wanted them out of her head. Her body went stiff, eyes screwed shut and teeth clenched. *Get out! Leave me alone!*

Her father's hands circled her wrists. "Deidra? What is it?"

Rats were on the move, in the walls, heading for the kitchens, excited at the prospect of rummaging through the rushes for dropped food.

Something growled in her head, rumbling in her chest and growing louder, filling her like the thunder. *No more, no more, no more.* Her father took her shoulders and gave her a hard shake.

"Deidra! Look at me!"

"She's growling," Rose whispered, her voice hushed with concern.

Deidra twisted, hands gripping the sides of her head. "Make them stop, Da, I pray you!"

Her father gathered her close, arms wrapped around her. "What is it? The animals?"

The rats, the dogs, even the horses, all of their thoughts filled her mind like a roar. She had no thoughts of her own; she was nothing but a container they filled.

"Aye," she whimpered. "Make them stop, please, Da, please, please, *please!*"

Her father's arms tightened. He didn't say anything, and, young as she was, Deidra understood why. There was nothing he could do. Nothing anyone could do. They were witches, and this was their lot. They could not undo what they were. When you were born a witch, you died a witch.

"Why, Da, why? I don't want to be a witch anymore. Why are we this way?"

He inhaled deeply, his eyes shifting inward with thought. "My mother told me it was a *baobhan sith.*"

"A blood witch?" Rose asked quizzically, approaching the bed.

William sat back and nodded, his hand still on Deidra's back. She liked it there; it was warm and strong and comforting. When he was with her, she felt mayhap she could bear the thoughts, mayhap even learn to ignore them one day.

She swiped at the tears that leaked from her eyes and tried to focus on what her father was saying. It was easier to ignore the animals when she had something else diverting her attention. She asked, "What's a *baobhan sith?*"

He smiled at her. "A witch that drinks blood and has many special powers. They derive power from the moon. My great-great-grandsire made a pact with one many years ago."

"I thought they killed men," Rose said. "All the stories I've heard tell of them luring young men with their beauty and dancing, then draining their blood. You can *talk* to them?"

William shrugged and ran a careless hand over his graying hair, leaving it in disarray. He wasn't an old man, but his black hair had a metallic sheen to it from all the silver strands.

"Aye, apparently so," he said.

Rose sat on the end of the bed. "What sort of pact?"

"I don't really know, exactly. His son was dying . . . he asked for the magic to heal him . . . and the *baobhan sith* made him a witch," he said as he smiled down at Deidra, "a healer like Rose and I." He shrugged. "And we've had witches in the family ever since."

"A pact," Deidra whispered with wonder. It was so simple.

Her father rubbed his hand over her head. "Aye, lass. That's from whence MacKay magic springs." He stood, planting a kiss on the top of her head. "You'll be fine now?"

Deidra didn't know if she would. She still heard the animals, but now she had something to ponder, something to distract her from all the noise in her head. She nodded, since she knew it would please him.

Rose and her father bid Deidra a good night and left her alone in the darkness. She closed her eyes and listened to the rain tapping against the shutters. Animals chattered in her head, and she thought about pacts and *baobhan siths*.

Her situation had seemed hopeless before. But suddenly she had options, possibilities.

If pacts could be made to create witches . . . perhaps they could be made to take magic away.

Chapter 1

*F*or a while, Deidra thought Luthias had actually forgotten about her.

Hoped. Prayed.

But she did not possess such blessings. Apparently he'd been no more than distracted, busy hunting other witches. Word had reached her of a spectacular witch trial and hanging in the lowlands—complete with torture and dunkings. The images it brought to mind made her want to crawl under her bed and hide like she had when she'd been a wee bairn. No doubt Luthias's stink was all over those trials.

Luthias Forsyth was a witch-pricker, a man well versed in the torture and execution of witches. The past few decades had been very prosperous ones for Luthias and very dangerous ones for Scotland's witches . . . and women. That was the difficulty with being a woman in Scotland. One did not have to be a witch to burn for witchcraft. One merely needed breasts.

That had changed for a time in 1597, when King James had rescinded his edict that had allowed witches to be hunted and killed like wild game. But King James ruled England now, too, and the Presbyteries had control of Scotland. Witch hunting was regaining popularity. Today, it had come to Strathwick. Again.

For the past three days Deidra had hid in the tower room of Strathwick, her family's home. It had been a while since she'd been forced to hide out in this manner. So long, in fact, that she'd begun to hope that perhaps the hiding was finally over.

She stretched out on the bed, reading by candlelight a chapbook about Saint George slaying the dragon. When she was younger, she had loved these stories, but the older she'd grown the less likely the stories had seemed. She had read her father's histories and attempted to read her mother's journals and herbals, but she couldn't stay awake while reading any of them. She had read and reread their translations of the Greek myths. There was nothing left to read but these chapbooks, and they just made her roll her eyes. She shut the book with a sigh.

A dog had followed her upstairs and now sat beside the bed, staring at her. When she turned even slightly in its direction it whined softly and shifted from foot to foot.

Deidra ignored it.

She never knew how long Luthias would nose around the village, asking questions about her, making sure she wasn't practicing magic. Checking up on her. Once, when he'd come, she had not hid. She'd been eighteen and feeling very idealistic and full of the need to cure injustice. She had imagined how, when he came sniffing around her, she would give him a flaying about all the innocent women he had murdered. She'd thought that somehow she would be able to make him see the error of his ways. . . .

It hadn't turned out the way she'd planned. By the time he'd found her, she'd been surrounded by animals—dogs, cats, sheep, chickens. It had been difficult to explain them away when he'd asked why all the animals in the village migrated to Goodwife Anne's house, where Deidra assisted in the shelling of peas.

She had started out strong, telling him it meant nothing; they were pets, that *he* was the monster, not the girls he killed. His long angular face had hardened to granite, and he'd started in on her, calling her a foul witch who communed with the animal spirits, quoting the Bible and how she was a blemish on humanity. In the end, she had run away, more frightened and confused than ever. He had followed, harrying her home, promising that soon she too would pay, as all witches did.

Her father had run him out of the village and threatened to kill him. He'd stayed away for a time, but of course he'd come back. He always came back, and when he returned he brought reinforcements. From that day forward, when he'd brought a guard of mercenaries with him, rendering her father powerless. The only thing Deidra had been able to do was hide.

He was so persistent, so intent on her. She hadn't practiced any sort of witchcraft in more than a decade, and yet still he was obsessed with her. She didn't understand why he couldn't just forget, move on, hunt other witches. And she supposed he did in the time between visits, but he never forgot about her. Every year he returned, as reliable as the seasons, and stayed for several days. But this time nearly two years had passed with no sign of him, and she'd begun to hope.

There was a tap on the door. Deidra closed her book and twisted toward the door. "Aye? Come in."

Her stepmother, Rose, peeked her head around the edge of the door. "Are you hungry?"

Deidra swung her legs over the side of the bed and sighed. "Not really."

Ignoring this, Rose entered, balancing a tray, and crossed the room. The warm smell of herbs wafted to Deidra and her stomach rumbled. Rose set the tray on the bed.

"I heard that," she admonished. "Stop being a wee fool. You will eat my soup." Rose rarely took no for an answer. A strong woman, made of steel and as beautiful as a well-honed sword. Deidra wished she could be more like her. She doubted Rose would hide from Luthias.

Rose smiled as she uncovered a dish to reveal a savory bean soup, warm bread with jam, and dried fruit. All of Deidra's favorites.

Deidra sighed but gave her stepmother a grateful smile. Rose was an amazing woman and had more than made up for the years Deidra had been motherless. She had married William MacKay twelve years ago. She was still a relatively young woman—in her thirties—but her hair had turned almost completely white. Her face still held a youthful beauty, but neither William nor Rose could resist using their healing magic at every opportunity, and it aged them both. Yet another reason Deidra hated this witchcraft curse—it would eventually take away everything that mattered to her. It had already altered her father and Rose's life in ways they'd not anticipated.

After they'd married, Rose had borne William a son, Ross. And had miscarried every pregnancy since. It was the healing magic; something about it made her different, made her unable to bear any more than Ross. And now Ross was gone, sent to King James's English court to learn English ways so he would not be a heathen like his parents.

Luckily, thus far Ross had shown no signs of magical ability. It appeared he might be like William's brother, Drake. Deidra envied him.

"Is Luthias still in the village?" Deidra asked.

Not meeting Deidra's gaze, Rose fussed with some currants that had spilled out of the little bowl.

"What is it? It's been three days and he's *still* here?"

Rose straightened and planted her hands on her hips. "I think you're just going to have to show yourself. He knows you're here somewhere and he's not going away until he sees you." Her voice and face softened. "It'll be just as it always is. He'll see you are not doing any magic and go away."

Deidra dropped her chin on her fist and glowered at the wall. She did not want to show herself. A dozen years had passed since the incident that had sparked Luthias Forsyth's obsession with her, and Deidra was no longer a child but a woman . . . and yet she still trembled in his presence. She felt eight years old again, terrified and wanting to bury her face in her father's shirt.

"I should go away," Deidra murmured. "It brings danger to you and Da when he comes here searching about for witchcraft. There is plenty to find here. One day he will strike against you for sheltering me. I feel it." She shook her head, fear gripping her shoulders tight. "I bring danger on us all."

"What foolishness. Don't be ridiculous." Rose pushed the tray at her insistently. "You know we won't hear of it. You will stay here with us until you marry and that's the end of it."

Deidra chose to ignore that and picked at the currants instead. No man would ever marry her. She was one and twenty, and not a single offer had been made for her. Her parents took her to gatherings, but the men she met did not seem to find her looks pleasing or her person interesting. It was her hair. Wild and woolly, like a sheep's. She'd heard what the other lasses said about her. She was ugly and a mute, raised by animals. No, she would never find a man with such references.

She snatched a roll off the tray and stood, pacing the room. "I will live in the mountains, somewhere far away from here, on the Continent perhaps . . . the Alps, in a remote chalet where he'll never find me and I bring danger to no one."

Rose made a dismissive sound and waved a hand. "That kind of behavior never brought anyone any happiness. Remember you Stephen Ross?" She raised her copper brows. "We all loved him well, but he was so miserable he couldn't see it. So away he went and now everyone thinks he's a monster, living in the mountains. No friends or family. People fear him."

Deidra did remember Stephen Ross. He'd been a young man when she'd been a child. Crippled in an accident, he'd tried to live among friends and family, but the pain and bitterness over what had happened to him had cankered his soul and made him unpleasant. Eventually he'd moved to one of his estates in the far north to live in isolation.

"People say he is a *baobhan sith*," Rose said. "That he traps unsuspecting travelers and drinks their blood. Would you like them to say that about you?"

Rose was clever, playing on Deidra's need for acceptance and approval. Deidra disliked the taint of witchcraft. But she ignored the question and slid Rose a dubious sidelong look. "I thought blood witches were all women."

Rose shrugged. "I suppose they can be either men or women. I know not." Rose smiled slyly. "Perchance Mr. Forsyth could tell you more about them. Go see him and find out."

Deidra scowled and returned to the bed, where Rose sat. "Is it true? Is Stephen Ross really a *baobhan sith*?" She still remembered the tale her father had told her as a child, about how her great-great-great-grandsire had made a pact with a blood witch. She'd always found the story compelling but not particularly useful. After all, she'd assumed the *baobhan sith* were not real. A story told to children to keep them close to home.

When Rose didn't reply, Deidra pressed, "So . . . do you believe in the *baobhan sith*? Do you really think there is such a thing?"

Rose gave her a mildly condescending smile. "If you grew up in my family . . . and married into such a family as I did . . . well, you would understand that anything is possible."

This was true. Rose's sisters were both powerful witches. Rose herself had married a witch. And Deidra was a witch, though she hadn't used her magic in years. At least not intentionally. To be precise, she had become proficient at ignoring it, and it didn't trouble her overmuch these days. But that mattered little in Mr. Forsyth's world. He *knew* what she was capable of. He had seen it with his own eyes. And even now, though she might deny her magic to herself and to others, the animals knew and would never allow her to forget it. They sensed it in her and flocked to her. Most of them did not have the capacity for reason. They did not understand that she would never speak to them again. They all wanted something, so they kept trying.

"Drake went to a blood witch."

Deidra nearly dropped her bread. Her jaw did drop. "Uncle Drake?"

Rose nodded, the corners of her mouth tight, her gaze turned inward. She obviously wasn't certain she should be speaking of this, but she had decided to anyway. "Do you recall when Ceara was ill? And your father and I could not cure her?"

Deidra remembered well. Aunt Ceara's deadly ailment was what had turned her parents' hair white through their constant attempts to heal that which not even magic could cure.

"He took her to the blood witch."

"*And?*" Deidra prompted, breathless.

Rose shrugged. "I know not. Ceara is dead. Drake is . . . different. But he did say that he saw her. So there must be such a thing."

The *baobhan sith* was real after all. Deidra was intrigued. Perhaps another path lay open to her, one she had not previously considered. However, the visit had not benefited Ceara. Perhaps she should go to the source, find out what had really happened.

Her mind turned to Stephen Ross. She'd not known him well. He'd been a good friend to the MacDonells, Rose's family. He was the illegitimate nephew of an earl and very wealthy. He could afford to live off in some remote castle, far away from the stares. She remembered the way he'd limped, the lines pain had drawn in his youthful face. He'd not been born crippled, but Deidra had not known him when he'd been a whole man.

What Deidra remembered most of all when she recalled Stephen Ross was that he'd been beautiful. She'd found him angelic in countenance and particularly enchanting when he'd smiled, which had been rare. He'd never paid much attention to her, except once, when her animals had bothered him. He'd bellowed like a baited bear, terrifying her. She'd cut a wide swath around him after that.

But that had been a very long time ago. She was not a little girl but a woman, and he did not scare her.

Much.

Rose patted her knee. "Think about showing yourself, aye? Maybe then he'll go away."

Deidra smiled wanly. Even if Luthias did go away, he'd just come back. He would keep coming back until she could prove she was not a witch.

When Rose was gone, Deidra gathered up the rest of the currants and bread, wrapped them in a napkin, then stuffed the napkin into a canvas satchel. She placed the bowl on the floor. The dog preempted its instinctive rush forward and sat back, staring at her with pleading eyes, flanks quivering with hope.

"Go ahead," she said.

The dog's nose disappeared in the bowl.

Deidra crossed the room to her clothespress and threw open the doors. Scanning the interior, she grabbed fresh stockings and a clean shift. She started to close it then ran a hand over her wild, unruly curls. She snatched up her comb and stuffed it in the satchel with everything else before closing the doors.

She hesitated, standing in the center of her room, satchel in hand. She wanted to leave immediately, to get as far away from Luthias Forsyth as possible. She crossed to the bed and sank down on it. It would be unwise to leave now. Someone might observe her leaving and report back to Luthias.

It would be a few more hours yet before the castle went to sleep.

So she waited.

The dog finished eating and stared at her expectantly, trying to communicate with her. She could feel it pushing at the membrane of her thoughts, but she would not allow it entrance. She walled it out, just like she did all creatures. It had a name, but she refused to use it, refused to acknowledge it.

She lay back on the bed and stared at the ceiling, the weight of time and her task pressing on her soul.

Luthias had grown tired of this little hamlet. Year in and year out he came here, keeping track of the animal whisperer. He slept in smelly crofts with the rustics, who stank and fed him food unfit for animals. He had never married, and he had no family save a sister he hadn't spoken to in a lifetime. His was not a life for a family man. He lived like a nomad. Still, he had a house in Edinburgh, and it would have been nice to have had a woman waiting for him there.

But it was not his lot. God had handed him this calling, this gift of rooting out witches, and he was obligated to use it in His name. Still, there had been a time when a wife and family had been possible. That was before the MacKays. Before Deidra.

Tonight he slept on a cramped mattress stuffed with heather and probably crawling with fleas, which he had paid far too much for. His men had found stables around the village, though one slept outside this croft, protecting him. A blanket hung between Luthias and his hosts, but that did not block out the sounds of the smith rutting on his wife. They thrashed about, grunting and huffing and whimpering. He couldn't remember the last time he'd lain with a woman, but he was certain that when he had, it hadn't been nearly so noisy.

Jen Holling

The blanket stirred, and a moment later a small face peeked around the side of it. The smith's son. Luthias glared at the lad and the face swiftly disappeared . . . but seconds later he was back, staring with wide, serious eyes, all the while the tanner strained and groaned on the other side of the blanket.

Luthias thought he might go mad.

He threw back the itchy wool blanket and struggled off the mattress, grabbing his cloak and rushing out of the croft into the cool night air.

He stood under the waning moon and inhaled deeply of the crisp air, thick with peat smoke. His legs twitched from agitation, and he jigged his foot impatiently.

He would leave in the morning. The witch hid from him and would not show herself. He usually did not back down from a challenge. He'd smoked witches out before, but this one's family was different. They were white witches. Luthias had long subscribed to the notion that the only good witch was a dead one, but that had been before he'd witnessed William MacKay heal a dying man. That could not have been the devil's work, for the man had been William's enemy—and that enemy had been doing God's work, trying to end William MacKay's life. True evil would have let him die. True evil would have relished in the revenge. True evil such as Deidra MacKay.

She had been the murderer that day. She had set her hellhounds on the man, a whole horrifying snarling pack of them, and they had ripped the man's throat out while she'd looked on with approval. And she'd only been eight years old.

The image of such a small lovely child committing such a vile, inhuman act had haunted Luthias for twelve years now. God had made him witness to that horror for a reason. God haunted him with nightmares of the child for a reason. Every day since he had walked away from Deidra, he had regretted it. He had tried to comfort himself with the knowledge that trying a child was illegal and he'd honored the law. But he knew in his heart it had just been an excuse. God's law superseded any law created by man. He was God's servant, and Deidra MacKay offended God. It was his calling to keep her from committing any further horrors and to punish her if she transgressed. She was not a child anymore; had not been for some time. It was past time for him to set things to rights.

He took his calling very seriously.

The twitching stopped, but he didn't want to go back inside. He didn't think he could sleep in that croft tonight anyway. He crossed the dark yard and lowered himself onto a log. It was too dark to travel in such terrain, plus his men needed their sleep. Tomorrow they had a long journey ahead of them. He'd caught word of another witch in the lowlands. This one heard the voices of the dead and used her magic to find lost objects. Evil. He shuddered just to imagine the kind of evil that raised the dead for profit. He would come back to Strathwick and seek another opportunity.

As he sat contemplating his next assignment, he became aware of movement in the distance, near the castle. He sat very still, watching. A lone figure moved silently through the darkness. But he was wrong; he soon saw that it was not alone. In the distance behind it followed an entourage of figures low to the ground. Dogs, it appeared, or mayhap wolves.

Luthias recoiled inside, his lips curling.

The animal whisperer, out skulking about after everyone else was asleep. As he watched, he noted she carried a satchel. She disappeared into the stables, then reappeared moments later leading a horse. He watched her until she was gone.

She was leaving Strathwick.

He felt an unfamiliar tugging at the corners of his mouth and realized it was a smile. He'd finally smoked her out.

A change of plans was in order. He would not be heading directly to the lowlands after all. God had finally rewarded his patience with opportunity. It was time to set things right.

Chapter 2

———— ✣✣✣ ————

Bráighde Pele crouched upon a jagged black mountaintop. The castle was not far from MacKay lands, but it still took Deidra two days to reach it. Its name meant "hostage tower," and it was no mystery why the castle had acquired it. Craggy rocks and a thick forest surrounded it on all sides. The overgrown rubble of an abandoned kirk blocked the way to the south. This was dangerous and difficult terrain to traverse, discouraging all but the most determined.

An odd choice for a cripple . . . but not for a _baobhan sith_. In fact, it was the perfect lair for a blood witch—away from prying eyes. Deidra's pulse stepped up a few beats with hope and excitement. The idea that her life could soon be transformed from nightmare to normal was almost too much to contemplate. It swelled inside her, threatening to overtake her and make her reckless. The horse felt the excited trembling in her thighs and wanted to understand. It probed at her. She blocked it, her jaw set, shutting her mind against it.

It had been a difficult journey for Deidra. She loathed sleeping outside. Animals sensed her presence somehow and flocked to her, all wanting something.

Unlike most people, she had nothing to fear from even the most dangerous beast, but that mattered not. She would rather fear them than be stalked by them.

The tower rose before her, reaching high above the castle walls. Many years ago—even before Deidra's father had been born, when the castle had been nothing more than a simple tower—it had been owned by the MacKays and used to hold pledges. When the MacKay lairds had kidnapped enemies and held them for ransom, they'd locked them up in the tower and forgotten about them until the ransom was paid. Sometimes it had been a very long time before that happened. Often, the hostages hadn't lived to see release, and so the ransom had had to be returned . . . or fought over. It was a place of death and darkness, and it made Deidra's chest heavy with dread.

The Rosses of Irvine had purchased the castle and the land around it many years ago and built the tower up into a grand estate. Stephen owned it now and had moved into it nearly a decade ago. Few had seen him since, though he did send occasional letters to family and friends.

As she drew closer, the sky seemed to grow thicker and darker above the castle. It was no more than her imagination, but the place exuded dread, as if cursed and forgotten. Deidra pulled her wool araisad closer to her neck. She didn't understand why anyone would choose to make such an unpleasant and isolated place their home—unless they had something to hide. A *baobhan sith*. He *had* to be one.

It was late afternoon by the time she rode beneath

the portcullis and into the courtyard, tired and hungry. She'd been forced to dismount and walk the horse the last few miles. She couldn't guess what kind of hospitality to expect from Stephen Ross. In the Highlands, it was expected of a laird to extend hospitality to those of rank, regardless of the laird's circumstances. But Stephen Ross was not normal.

It didn't take long for Deidra to find out what kind of welcome she would receive. Servants rushed at her seconds after she entered the courtyard. Men crowded around her, grabbed her, and hauled her away from the horse. Her nervous excitement transformed into panicked confusion. She pushed at them, her skin crawling. Their hands were all over her body, patting her down as they searched for weapons. They confiscated the knife she'd strapped to her thigh.

"I'm here to see Stephen Ross," she said over and over, but her words elicited no response—not even eye contact. It was as if the men were mutes.

Her horse was led away, and one of the men gripped her upper arm in a firm hold, leading her forcefully across the courtyard and into the castle. Her heart hammered in her throat, her breath coming in small gasps as terror tightened her chest. *Baobhan siths* murdered people—ripped their throats out and drank their blood. She had not told anyone where she was going. No one knew where she was. She could disappear and no one would ever suspect she'd come here.

Foolish. Foolish. Foolish. And impulsive.

The men led her to an enormous room, its high ceilings carved with dragons and griffins. A huge chair, its back to Deidra, crouched before a blazing fire. A bear skin draped the back of it, and more skins covered the arms.

The men shoved Deidra until she stood before the chair, her back to the fire. Sprawled in the thronelike monstrosity was Stephen Ross, but not the Stephen Ross Deidra remembered from her youth.

Even as a cripple Stephen Ross had not been a small man. He'd not been over-tall, but he had been broad and thick with muscle. The man that sat before her was enormous. He wore a white shirt that hung open, exposing a muscled chest furred with light blond hair that traveled down a hard abdomen, disappearing beneath a thick leather belt.

Pale blue eyes regarded her without emotion. His blond hair had grown long and hung loose over his shoulders and down his back. He was still an exceedingly handsome man, but pain had deepened the lines beside his mouth and eyes, showing the passage of years. Pale whiskers stubbled his chin and upper lip. He looked disreputable and dangerous. Not at all like a harmless cripple.

His arms rested on the chair arms, and he gripped a tankard in one of his hands. He stared at her beneath dark blond brows. The men exited the room, leaving them alone. Deidra stood mutely before Stephen Ross, trembling uncontrollably. The blasting heat from the fire at her back did nothing to dispel the chill fear that gripped her.

He took a long, thoughtful drink from his tankard, his gaze remaining fixed on her. Then he said, "I know you."

His presence overwhelmed her. She couldn't form a coherent thought. She trembled from the inside out. Her mouth opened and closed, but nothing came out.

He lowered the tankard to rest on the chair arm. His gaze scanned her from head to toe. "Are you from the village?"

Deidra managed a small shake of her head.

"What do you do?"

She blinked. "I—I don't understand."

He sighed with studied patience. "What do you do?" Each word was enunciated, as if she were an addlepate. "Do you work magic with your hands? Your body? Your mouth? What will it be tonight?"

Though innocent in experience, Deidra was not innocent in knowledge of what went on between men and women. Nevertheless, his comment struck her as so inconceivable that her mind scrambled for some meaning other than the one his words conveyed. He hadn't just assumed she was a common village trull. He *couldn't* have.

His brow lowered into a frown. "You'd think you would have cleaned up a bit first." He waved a hand at her, encompassing her travel-stained attire and ending with a baffled wave at her head. "Or combed your hair and removed some of the foliage." He slurred his words slightly, indicating that he'd drunk more than one tankard. He took another deep drink, watching her all the while.

Heat rushed to her cheeks. She patted at her hair self-consciously and felt the leaves stuck in there. She pulled them out, dropping them surreptitiously to the floor.

He wiped a hand across his mouth. "You'd better be impressive, sweet, or I'm not paying full price, not for a wench that wilna even pick the leaves from her last tumble out of her hair."

And with *that* bit of crudeness, there was no doubt what he inferred. Her jaw unhinged as she stared at him in stunned silence. It had been a very long time since she'd last seen Stephen Ross, and even then, she'd been a child and had not actually known him. Nevertheless, this was not what she remembered. In her memory he'd been a charmer, not a whoremonger.

He reached a hand out to her, strong fingers curved invitingly. "Come closer, wee dustball. Let us put that sweet mouth to good use."

She gaped at his hand. "You think I am a whore? That I came here to . . . to . . . to . . ." She was so appalled that she couldn't even say it. Her lip curled in disgust. "You make me sick."

He lowered his hand but didn't look terribly surprised at her indignation.

She swept her arm out to encompass the room. "Is this what you've become? A pathetic cripple, lying around drunk, paying whores to make you feel good for a few moments?"

His eyes narrowed to pale blue slits. "I assure you, lassie, it will take more than a few moments."

Deidra rolled her eyes. "You cannot help me. I can see that now. You are no *baobhan sith*. You are just a sad lonely man who has to pay for companionship."

He leaned back in the chair, rubbing his fingers over his lips. "And when she speaks, she spews forth poison."

"At least I don't spew forth whisky fumes."

He glowered at her for a moment, then his mouth curved. A second later he chuckled. He raised his tankard in a salute to her.

"You are Rose and William's bairn."

This surprised Deidra. After a second she nodded, though inwardly she recoiled at being referred to as a child.

"I thought I recognized the eyes and the hair." He raised his finger as if to trace her features, then dropped it heavily so that his hand rested again on the fur-covered chair arm. "But it was the mouth that gave away your heritage. Only Rose has such a gimlet tongue."

"She is my stepmother, not my mother."

"She raised you since you were a wee thing." He held a hand out to indicate a child's height. "You obviously learned your razor wit from her."

Deidra loved her stepmother and normally would be proud to be compared to her . . . if the comparison had been made by anyone else. How dare such a waste of flesh pretend to know her? He knew *nothing*.

She crossed her arms over her chest. "The earl of Irvine is a well respected man. You obviously did not learn to be a sot and a lecher from him."

He feigned a scowl. "I sense disappointment. What is it you said before? I am no *baobhan sith*? What is that?"

Deidra sighed and looked heavenward. He didn't even know what a *baobhan sith* was. This was a wasted, useless journey. "A *baobhan sith*? A blood witch? Surely you jest. I thought everyone had heard the tales of the blood witches."

"No, not everyone." He shifted in his chair and glanced to his right. Another, smaller chair was beside him. He indicated it with a careless wave. "Pray, have a seat and enlighten me."

Deidra remained rooted to the spot. She had not forgotten his rudeness. She was still insulted.

He stared up at her, his pale eyes probing. "You're still in a chuff, aye? Well, I apologize. How's that? Smooth your fur any?"

Deidra's lips tightened and her arms folded closer to her chest.

Stephen sighed. "Come now. Accept my apology . . . or at least pretend to. What else will you do? It's late, you're in the middle of nowhere, and I offer you a hot meal and soft bed. Indulge me."

He had a point. Deidra didn't really want to, but it *was* late and she *was* stuck here for the night. She sank into the chair. The bone-deep ache from two days of hard travel and fitful sleep on a hard ground throbbed through her. Every muscle pulsed with exquisite pain as she relaxed in the chair. It was a fine, well made chair, just like everything else she'd seen in the castle thus far. The soft pillow she sat on had been skillfully embroidered, and a skin hung over the chair back and arms, cushioning the wood and making the seat extremely comfortable.

"Hungry? Thirsty?" Before she could answer, he gave a harsh shout. Seconds later, a man entered the room. "Fetch our guest some food and drink, and prepare a room for her."

The man bowed out and Stephen turned his attention back to her. He cocked his head slightly as he regarded her. "Deidra . . . aye?"

She nodded and he smiled, pleased with his memory, which apparently had not been impaired by the excess of spirits.

"Good. Deidra—tell me now the tales of the *baobhan sith* that I was deprived of in my youth."

Deidra leaned back in the chair with a contented sigh and looked skyward in thought. Truth be told, she was glad for a reason to sit and talk to someone about the *baobhan sith*. It wasn't as if she could tell anyone back home what she wished to do. But what did Stephen Ross care? And even if he wanted to, it was doubtful he could stop her.

"Well, the most common tale sings of four young lads on a hunting trip. They shelter for the night in an abandoned cottage. They are sitting around the fire, talking and singing, when one of them wishes for women to keep them company. Immediately women appear. They are beautiful women—"

"Like you?"

Deidra's mouth opened to respond negatively when she suddenly realized what he'd said to her. Her mouth snapped shut. His elbow rested on the arm of his chair, and his chin sat on his fist as he stared at her as if enraptured by her tale. Or by her.

Heat flooded her cheeks. Did he jest? She knew she was not beautiful. She had wild, unruly hair that she had given up on a long time ago. And as for her shape, she had none. She was small and unwomanly—straight as a lad. She was also considered strange and unfriendly by most people.

He was jesting . . . or drunk. Or both. Either way, she would not participate in the game.

She forced herself to speak, shaking her head and swallowing convulsively. "No, no, of course not. They . . . they were womanly . . . with long flowing hair, and fine shapes . . . womanly shapes. And voices sweet as nightingales."

He arched a blond brow as if he didn't believe her, but he said nothing.

"So," she continued, tearing her gaze away from his rapt stare. Her voice became strange and uneven, difficult to squeeze through her constricted throat. "The men danced and sang with the beautiful women . . . but soon the dancing became lascivious and wild. Then suddenly the women changed. Their eyes became catlike and they grew fangs and claws. They tore into the men, ripping out their throats and drinking their blood. One of the men was a papist and wore his rosary. The witch touched it and screamed an inhuman shriek. He took that opportunity to escape from her. She pursued and caught him. But he was canny this time and threatened her with the rosary, warding her off until morning. When the sun came up, the blood witch had disappeared."

Stephen's servant appeared with a tray laden down with food and drinks. He set it on a table between their chairs.

"The ale is mulled. Have some." Stephen waved at the tray.

Deidra hesitated, then took the ale. She was hungry and thirsty. She drank deeply of the warm, spicy brew, then chose a bannock from the tray and bit into it, sighing deeply at the rich, warm taste.

He smiled, but there was strain around his mouth. He leaned toward the tray slowly, like an old man, and took the bottle of whisky, grabbing the throat of it and falling back heavily in his chair.

So he was still in pain. She hadn't been certain, as he looked well enough, but then again, he hadn't moved from the chair since she'd arrived.

"You traveled all of this way," he said. "A woman, alone, because you thought I might be a blood witch. And yet, by your own description, they are evil, dangerous creatures." He drank whisky straight from the bottle and wiped a hand across his mouth. "You want something only a *baobhan sith* can give you. And it is extremely valuable to you. Indeed, it is so valuable you are willing to risk your life for it. If I were a *baobhan sith*, I would be ripping your lovely throat out right now, aye?"

Deidra's hand crept to her neck. "Aye, I suppose so."

"It seems . . . oh . . ." He raised a shoulder and looked skyward, as if searching for words. "Mayhap a trifle stupid? And here I'd always believed you to be an intelligent lass."

Deidra smiled ruefully. "You don't know me at all, and you certainly have no idea what I left behind. Maybe a *baobhan sith* would be welcome in comparison."

He raised both brows thoughtfully and nodded. "Aye, I hadn't considered such a thing, sheltered as you are by both the MacDonells and the MacKays. They love their own, cosset and dote on them. But you're still unhappy." He inhaled deeply, leaning to the side to contemplate her. "So you left something bad behind you. What if it followed you? Did you think for a moment that I don't want your trouble? Why do you bring it to me?"

Deidra opened her mouth in protest, then snapped it shut. She supposed he had a point, and that had not occurred to her. "He didn't see me leave. I escaped without anyone's knowledge. Besides, he's after a witch . . . and you're obviously not one."

Stephen nodded. "You're the animal whisperer, aye? I remember that."

Deidra grimaced. "Not anymore. I stopped talking to them over a decade ago. Unfortunately, they haven't stopped talking to me."

"So the animals still talk . . . you just stopped listening."

"That's right."

He studied her. "Interesting."

Deidra shrugged. "Not really."

"Clearly, someone back home finds it fascinating. They know you're still a witch and will not let it go."

He was pretty sharp for a sot. She continued to reevaluate whether or not he was actually drunk, but he kept pouring the whisky down his throat and slurring his words. It was very confusing.

His gaze narrowed. "But why a *baobhan sith*? What can a blood witch do for you?"

Deidra smiled without humor. "You'll never know, will you, since you know nothing about them."

He smiled back, but his was full of mirth. "That's not entirely accurate, sweeting. I said I'd never heard of a *baobhan sith*, but once you explained what one was, I realized that of course I knew of them. I'd just heard them called other names."

"Really." Deidra's lips flattened. She felt strangely irritated that he was not ignorant of blood witches. "Such as?"

"On the Continent they are called *strigoi*. They are witches who died and came back to drink the blood of their families. Then there are the *dearg-dul* and *deamhain fhola* in Eire. Bloodsuckers both, but not terribly threatening, since a pile of stones atop their grave keeps them put." He shrugged as if bored by the subject. "And there are other names and stories." He rubbed his fingers over the stubble beneath his lips. "But I had not heard of a *baobhan sith* before today. So . . . you believe these stories, aye?"

Deidra hesitated. "I believe the story of the *baobhan sith*. Of these other creatures you tell of . . . the red thing and whatnot . . . well, I know nothing of them and cannot say one way or the other."

He kept rubbing at his lips, but she could see it was more to hide his smile than aught else. "But you have some proof of your bloodsucker, aye? Pray tell, if it pleases you."

She lifted her chin and squared her shoulders. "What care you? You've already made up your mind that I am foolish and empty-headed."

His hand dropped and his eyebrows flew up in astonishment. "What?"

"Aye, I am no addlepate. I can see your smirk."

"I am not smirking." He recomposed his face to grave seriousness. "I do not think you are foolish and empty-headed. You are clearly a thoughtful and intelligent woman. And I vow that I am truly, deeply curious about your quest."

She didn't believe him. At least not entirely. She didn't think he cared one whit about *baobhan siths* or any other form of blood witch. However, he had to be rather lonely, sitting in his big room, drinking himself into a stupor and comforting himself with whores. She supposed he wasn't quite ready to lose her company. And for some reason, she felt reluctant to retire just yet.

"Very well." She sighed dramatically, as if it were much more trouble than it actually was. "I know because my uncle Drake met a *baobhan sith*."

Stephen frowned dubiously at her. "Drake, you say? I know Drake."

"It is true. He did."

Stephen's frown deepened. "Tell me."

"You remember his wife, Ceara?"

He nodded gravely.

"She was very ill . . . like your back." Deidra lowered her eyes, unable to hold his gaze when speaking of his injury. She remembered how bitter Stephen had become when neither her father nor Rose had been able to heal his back. It had been a caustic dram to swallow. After all, that's what the MacKays did. They healed with magic, and yet they'd done naught for him. It was sometimes that way. They could heal many things, but not everything. Preexisting conditions, such as a ruined back that had already mended incorrectly—such a thing could not be undone because it had already healed. The fact that it had healed wrong didn't make it any less healed.

"I seem to remember Ceara being ill, not a cripple."

Deidra glanced up. "No, she wasn't cripple, but still, there are ailments that are similar in the fact they cannot be healed. My father and Rose were able to help her temporarily, but it always returned. We suspected witchcraft but could find no evidence of that, even with Aunt Isobel and Aunt Gillian's help." She shook her head. "My parents did all they could. They healed her over and over . . . She is the reason they are both completely white haired. She was killing them. Finally, one day, she told them to stop. . . ."

Stephen nodded thoughtfully but did not respond.

"There is a story about how the MacKays got their magic. My great-great-great-grandsire made a pact with a blood witch. Uncle Drake thought maybe he could make a pact with a blood witch, just like our ancestor did." She shrugged. "But I guess it didn't work out, because Ceara died anyway and Uncle Drake has shut himself up in Creaghaven for years . . . just like you. People say you're a *baobhan sith,* because you close yourself up here. No one sees you . . . stories circulate . . ." She gave him a sheepish smile. "Bráighde Pele is on my way to Creaghaven . . . so I thought I'd try."

He smiled back, but it didn't reach his eyes. "I'm sorry to disappoint. But I am just a man, and not even a whole one at that. If I were a *baobhan sith,* you wished to make a pact with me?"

"I thought if the *baobhan sith* can give magic, mayhap it can take it away."

"And your uncle's failure tells you nothing? Such as maybe there is no such thing as a *baobhan sith*? Or if there is, she doesn't grant wishes?"

Deidra's lips thinned mutinously.

"Why not go to your uncle? Find out what his experience with the blood witch was?"

"Well, that is what I plan to do tomorrow."

He propped his chin on his fist. "Well, I am glad for your mistake. Had you chosen another route, I would not have had the pleasure of your company this evening."

Deidra tried to take a drink of mulled ale to hide the trembling of her lips, but her throat closed up and she coughed and sputtered. At the moment, she was glad, too.

This was the Stephen Ross she remembered. The handsome charmer she'd been completely enamored of as a child. She found that she was not as immune as she had assumed she would be. She had a terrible time speaking to most men, but something about this evening, or about Stephen, had made it easy for her to talk. Until now. Her tongue knotted up again.

She reminded herself that he was doing nothing more than making do with what he had available to him tonight. And now he was being flirtatious and charming in hopes that she would finish out the night giving him for sweet words what he would have paid coin for otherwise.

It was rather insulting when she considered it logically.

She found her tongue again. She set her tankard down and stood. "Thank you for your hospitality, but I must start out early in the morning."

He contemplated her from his seated position. His expression was enigmatic, strange, as if he found her the puzzling one. She squeezed her hands together to stop herself from wringing them. She wanted to say something but felt it was better for her to leave it at that. He must understand what she meant. She had made it clear that she was not here for his amusement.

After a long moment he braced his hands on the arms of his chair. His face set into hard, uncompromising lines. Then he hauled himself up. The muscles stood out on his arms and his jaw grew rigid.

He was even more formidable standing than he had been sitting. He stood nearly a head taller than her and twice as wide in breadth. His shirt still hung open, giving her an eyeful of tense, hard muscle. She swallowed and quickly averted her eyes to stop herself from staring.

When he stood, he let out the breath he'd apparently been holding. "I'll show you to your room."

He limped across the room. Deidra hesitated, then followed.

Outside his chambers, he led her down a corridor to a flight of steps. A lantern sat in a deep depression in the wall, giving them a dim, wavering light to see by. A rope banister was bolted into the stones. He took the stairs a bit slower, but still, Deidra was impressed with his mobility.

"You get along quite well," she commented. "I'd

imagined you bedridden or some such, not nearly so . . . mobile." And muscular. In her experience, cripples were often wizened and weak. Stephen looked quite robust.

"Aye, I suppose, for half a man."

Bitterness edged his voice as he gripped the rope railing. She understood why muscle layered his arms and chest. He used his upper body to compensate for the weakness in his lower limbs.

At the top of the stairs he paused, palm pressed against the wall. Deidra reined in the urge to place her hand on his back and ask if he needed her help. He wouldn't want it, she knew that.

He recovered quickly and led her to a door at the end of the corridor. He pushed it open, then stood aside so she could enter.

It was a huge chamber. The enormous bed was the centerpiece, draped with silk curtains. Her eyes slid past the bed to seek out the windows. There were two, and the shutters were open, allowing the cool breeze in.

"Will this be adequate?" he asked.

She turned toward him, nodding. "Oh, aye. It's very nice. If I don't see you in the morning, I wish to give my thanks again, and to wish you well."

He inclined his head. When he stood like that, tall and straight, it was hard to believe he was crippled, but then he turned and limped toward the door.

"Good night, Deidra." He didn't look back as he shut the door behind him.

As soon as he was gone, she rushed to the windows and closed the shutters up tight. The room was practically perfect. She turned a circle, pleased she was up so high. This was how her room was back home. She sometimes had problems with birds, but for the most part the height kept away any beasts that thought to trouble her.

She collapsed on the bed and closed her eyes. Tomorrow, it was off to see her uncle. She hadn't seen him in years and wasn't relishing the confrontation. She didn't know what she would say to him and couldn't imagine how he would react. She was discouraged by her meeting with Stephen, but she reminded herself that his being a blood witch was nothing more than a rumor. The information she had on her uncle was more solid, as he had actually seen and spoken to a blood witch.

Still, it was difficult to sustain real disappointment. Somehow, her evening with Stephen had left her with a pleasant warmth, as if she had finally met someone who had somehow managed to see past the animal whisper to the woman beneath.

Stephen returned to his drawing room, but didn't sit. Lounging in front of the fire with a bottle of whisky no longer held the same appeal as it had just a few hours earlier. He imagined Deidra in his tower room. Her slight, feminine body, the wild, wonderful curls, her large, clear blue eyes. He'd seen many beautiful women in his life, and she wasn't one of them. She was not homely—far from it—but she was not a beauty either. She was intriguing, adorable, delightful. She would leave in the morning, possibly before he was even out of bed, and he would not see her again. Maybe never.

That was unacceptable.

She had come to *him,* sought help from *him,* and now he regarded her with a sense of ownership and responsibility. Logically, he knew she was not his responsibility and would never be his in any manner. But it didn't diminish the feeling.

Deidra MacKay had barged in and disrupted his uncomfortable but routine life. It was not a particularly happy life, but he managed. The monotony of it had lulled him into a sensation of being carried on a sea of inevitability, of fate. But not anymore. Deidra the animal charmer had swept the cobwebs from his eyes and revealed how empty his life really was.

He thought about the task she'd set for herself. Finding a *baobhan sith.* Upon initial examination it seemed absurd. But when he considered the matter more closely, it was not at all foolish. One would assume the stories of blood witches were naught but tales told to frighten children, but Stephen knew better. He had seen magic in his lifetime, in both his own family and his friends'. He'd grown up surrounded by witchcraft and magic, and it had never touched him. He'd remained immune.

And he was sick to death of it. If there was such a thing as a *baobhan sith* and there were pacts to be made, by God he wanted his share of the magic for once. He was weary of being a cripple, weary of the pain. Even now it dug and twisted in his back, like a stake rammed deep. For years he'd feared they'd somehow left the bullet deep in his spine, but both Rose and William MacKay had assured him there was no bullet in there—merely a spine that had healed crooked, causing him to suffer endless agony.

He snagged the neck of the whisky bottle and took several long swallows. It did little to dull the pain these days. He might be forced to resume taking the poppy juice. He hated the poppy juice—or, more aptly, he hated himself when taking it. The whisky didn't do him any favors either, but at least he could think straight when imbibing. When he took the poppy juice, he was not himself. His thoughts scattered and grew muddled. Sometimes he would write things, and when he read them later, they were senseless babblings.

He took the whisky to his bedchamber and called for a servant to ready him for bed. He could dress and groom himself, but a woman came in each night to work his back hard with her fingers and fists. It was blissful agony, exhausting him, but eventually it lessened the pain and usually helped him sleep.

Tonight it just hurt. Her hands were sharp little rocks, digging into his muscles and making the pain worse rather than better.

"Stop!" he finally bellowed, frightening her so that she backed away, hands clasped under her chin.

She was a big woman, with strong hands and arms, but she had an odd, feminine wilting-flower disposition completely at odds with her stout physique.

"I'm so sorry, sir. What did I do wrong?"

He slumped back onto the bed and buried his head in his forearms. "Nothing—just leave me."

He heard her scurry out of the room. He lay

motionless on the bed, face pressed into his arms. The whisky dragged at him, pulling him down. He fought at the oblivion tonight. If he gave in to it, he would not wake early.

He pushed himself off the bed, teeth grinding, back screaming. He gathered some personal items, some poppy juice and whisky, then thought that perhaps he might need food, too. In the kitchen he wrapped bannocks in a napkin and tossed in dried meat and apples. He wrote a short missive and addressed it to Rose at Strathwick.

He went to the stables. There he told the groom he would be leaving in the morning and asked him to inform the steward. Before the boy left, Stephen gave the groom the letter to Rose, then sent him to sleep elsewhere. Stephen found a soft pile of hay, rolled up in a blanket, jammed another rolled-up blanket behind his back, and waited for the throbbing in his back to subside. It did, incrementally.

The groom would tell everyone how their master eschewed his grand soft bed to sleep in the stables, and they would all think he'd finally gone over the edge. Stephen didn't particularly care. This was the only way he could be certain she wouldn't leave without him.

Judging by her response to him that evening, she would not want his company. Too bad for her. She would get it anyway. He might be crippled, but he was not an invalid. He could function quite well through the pain. Sometimes he was useless the next day, but that would likely work to his advantage as well. She was a compassionate sort and would not leave him to suffer.

He finally drifted off to sleep. It didn't seem as if he'd been asleep long when a soft voice drew him from his slumber. The dim stable swam in and out of his vision, and his stomach lurched. His back had locked into position. There would never be any jumping out of bed in the mornings for Stephen Ross. During sleep, his back tended to freeze. The next morning, getting out of bed was a nightmare. But it was a nightmare he'd grown accustomed to. There had been a time when he'd toyed with the idea of actually becoming an invalid. Putting himself through the misery of moving every single morning for the rest of his life had been almost too much to bear. But in truth, the longer he didn't move his back, the worse the pain grew. Daily activity, along with the rubs and exercise, had minimized the pain as much as possible. That and liberal doses of alcohol. He supposed the human body wasn't much different from any tool—regular use and the application of a lubricant kept it functional.

His stomach still heaved, and his head felt thick and foggy. He only hoped he didn't need to bock. It would be quite unpleasant, since he wouldn't be rising from the hay anytime soon. Lying in his own vomit was not an experience he enjoyed.

He lay still, listening to the voice, willing his mind and body to calm.

"*Leave me alone.*" The words were ground out softly, steel girding every word. "You have a groom to tend you and besides, *I don't care!*"

A horse blew and stomped a hoof.

Was she leaving already? Stephen lay helpless, and

slightly panicked, wondering if he could force himself out of the hay before she left. He was reluctant to begin thrashing about or call for help. He knew she already saw him for what he was—a cripple—but there was no need to rub his ailment in her face. He did have some dignity.

"Be silent!" she hissed.

Stephen could only imagine that she was speaking to the horses, since he had not said a word, nor had he heard anyone else in the stable. Her voice had taken on a hysterical edge, so he decided it was time to lighten the mood.

"Forgive me," he said. "I must have been talking in my sleep."

He heard a frantic scrambling, then she shrieked. "Who's there?"

"It's just me."

"Where? Where are you?"

"Over here in the hay, trying to get some sleep . . . and not having much luck with all the arguing."

She came into view, legs apart, hands on hips. "You've been spying on me."

Stephen's head was beginning to clear. His stomach had finally settled. He shifted, getting an arm beneath him. His back gripped and he decided that was far enough for the moment.

"Hardly. I was here first, and I was asleep until you came in."

She scowled down at him. She had cleaned up since he'd seen her earlier. Her clean, scrubbed face was porcelain smooth, her cheeks pink with emotion. Her wild curls had been somewhat tamed and hung to her shoulders in soft corkscrews. Still, a few pieces of hay stuck in her curls, making her look as if she'd just had a tumble. His groin tightened at the sudden image of her in the hay, beneath him.

"I thought you didn't talk to animals anymore," he said.

"And I thought rich men slept in beds."

He smiled. "I suppose we both have some explaining to do, eh?"

"Humph." The sound was very derogatory.

In the hopes of encouraging her to talk to him, he decided to be honest with her.

"I came out here to sleep because I didn't want you to leave before I woke."

She blinked and took a step back. Her eyes narrowed suspiciously. "Why?"

"Well . . . I thought you might need some company on your journey—a companion. After all, you're a woman alone, and such an undertaking isn't safe."

She folded her arms over her chest and leaned back slightly, brows raised. "And you think you can protect me?"

He was accustomed to such insults. Nevertheless, coming from her, it still stung. But just a twinge.

"Well, aye. I may be crippled, but I'm not an invalid. I can travel and I can protect you."

She shook her head. "No, I don't need some rich man and his entourage. It will frighten the blood witch. And as a witch myself, I don't travel with anyone I am not sure of. I don't know your people."

"As you wish. They will remain behind." That would be inconvenient, but he really hadn't expected anything else. "You can trust me."

"I don't know you."

"Aye, you do. I remember you when you were but a wee thing, talking to dogs and rats and whatnot. And your family, they know me and trust me. The Mac-Donells, they love me. Sir Philip is like a brother to me. My uncle is an earl. Really, need you better reference than that?"

Her mouth curved into a smirk. "That was before."

"Before what?"

"Before you squirreled yourself away on your estate, hiding so that everyone believes you to be a *baobhan sith*. No one really knows you anymore."

He didn't like her answer . . . mostly because there was some truth to it. Not much, but mayhap a wee bit. "I still see family and friends. And I write to them frequently." His back had relaxed, so he chanced pushing himself up farther. It locked again, but he was sitting now. He fought to keep the pain from showing on his face. He didn't think he was entirely successful. She was canny, and he noted that she studied his expression closely.

"Why do you *really* want to come with me?"

"Your family would cripple me for good if they knew I let you set off on your own."

She shook her head. "No. I don't believe you really care about me or them."

Now Stephen was taken aback. "There's where you're wrong, lassie. I care whether you come to harm and I care very much about Rose and William."

"You hate my parents."

Her words brought him up short. Pain knifed through him from the sudden movement, but he ignored it. "From whence did you get such a notion? Surely not from them."

She shook back her curls with a superior air. Hay fluttered to her shoulders. "You are bitter and angry that they could not heal you. So much magic and yet none for you."

His brow lowered. He *had* felt that way, but it hadn't mattered then and it didn't matter now. He was past that. Some things ran stronger and truer—and he knew that if Rose or William could have healed him, they would have. Just as they had aged themselves prematurely trying to heal Ceara.

No, he did not blame them. This was his lot. He'd been an outsider even in his own family. The bastard son of a bastard who'd died ignominiously, it was inevitable, he supposed, that his own life would end in a similar manner. The sins of the fathers and all that. At least his father had had the decency to die well.

"You have some strange thoughts, lass. I hold no grudge against your family. I love Rose like a sister, and William the same."

Her arms dropped to her sides and lines creased her forehead, but she didn't appear entirely convinced. "Then why? Why would you undertake such a journey?"

Stephen sighed. "For the same reason you do."

She frowned. "To get rid of magic?"

"Not the *exact* same reason. I want something. If

there is such a thing as a *baobhan sith*, then I want some of the magic too."

"But the blood witch didn't cure Ceara."

"Ceara was ill, not cripple." He shrugged. "At least I can come with you to Creaghaven and see what Drake has to say about it."

Deidra considered him, her head tilted to the side. "You're sure you can sit a horse?"

"Oh, aye—for hours," he lied.

She chewed her bottom lip, contemplating the hay-scattered floor. Finally, she sighed. "Very well. You may come. But if you cannot keep up"—she pointed a threatening finger at him— "then I will leave you behind."

He snorted, standing with as much dignity as he could muster. He was pleased that he had convinced her, but that didn't mean he fancied the manner in which she spoke to him. He could hold his own. She would see. He might need some whisky and a wee bit of poppy juice to manage it, but she would eat her words before their journey was over.

Chapter 3

————◯◯◯◯————

*A*lready he slowed her down and they hadn't even left Bráighde Pele. She should never have agreed to let him accompany her. She'd made a huge mistake. She berated herself as Stephen limped back into his castle, insisting they eat an enormous breakfast before they set off. She gritted her teeth and agreed, acquiescing only because it might be some time before they ate such a hearty meal again.

Finally, as the sun rose, they mounted up and set off. It was good weather for travel. In May, the weather was warm and the trees were brilliant—every shade of green and white and yellow blossoms blooming over trees and shrubs.

Deidra watched Stephen warily from the corner of her eye. He had limped from the castle to the stables, insisting on carrying all his own gear, but now that he was mounted, he moved as naturally as anyone else. Perhaps this wouldn't be as terrible as she'd feared. That is, if it hadn't been for the irritating beast he rode.

The horse was insistent. It was an unusually intelligent beast and sensed that she was different. It continued to query her tirelessly, becoming agitated as she ignored it, blowing and shaking its head with frustration. Just like all animals, this one wanted something. Something about another horse, but Deidra understood nothing else as she blocked it out.

Stephen frowned down at the horse as it pranced. He gripped the reins tightly. "What's the matter with her?" he murmured.

"How should I know?" Deidra snapped. She worried that the horse would toss Stephen off and she would be forced to somehow get him home not just crippled but unable to even walk.

Stephen raised a brow at her. "I was talking to the horse, lass."

A dog barked in the distance. The morning was cool and foggy; the air was thick and damp. A gossamer layer of sparkling dew covered Stephen's blond hair.

He frowned, turning his head as if to look over his shoulder, but his range of motion was limited. The barking gradually grew louder.

"Damn," he said under his breath.

Before Deidra could ask what he swore about, a small black bear burst from the underbrush. It bounded around Stephen's horse, barking and whining. Not a bear, but a dog. Black and huge and shaggy, its breed was unidentifiable.

"Och—down, Duke, down! You'll spook Countess!"

The dog continued to bark and bounce hysterically. Its excitement at discovering its master was palpable to anyone, she imagined, but she could feel more from it. It had a reason to be deliriously happy. Duke had thought Stephen was leaving never to return and now they were reunited. She felt a pang of sympathy for the dog, then angrily shoved it away. She was usually better at blocking the animals, but the infernal horse refused to leave her alone.

"Duke? Countess?" she snorted. "What did you name your cat? Princess?"

He scowled at her but didn't answer.

She let out a surprised laugh. "You did, didn't you?"

Stephen ignored her. "Go home, Duke!" He held his arm out straight, pointing back in the direction they had come from. "Go home!"

Duke ignored his commands and continued to dance ecstatically around the horse.

"Why won't he listen?" Stephen stared at the dog with consternation, then shifted his gaze to Deidra. "And you won't do me the quick favor of sending my dog home?"

Deidra returned his stare levelly. "I told you, I don't do that anymore."

He cocked his head slightly. "That's not true. You spoke to Countess last night."

Her jaw tightened and her gaze narrowed. "No, I did not."

"You did. I heard you." He considered her, lips pursed. "You hear the animals, you just don't respond. Interesting. How does it feel, running from what you are?"

"At least I can run." As soon as the words passed her tongue, shame flooded her, but she bit it back.

His brows shot up, but rather than become angry at

her barb he appeared impressed. "Well, I guess if you can run, then you should, aye? I cannot argue with that."

She thought that would be the end of it, but it wasn't. "What if," he said, hand out and a shoulder raised, "your father's beloved dog was on its deathbed. You are the only one who can save it by communicating with it."

Deidra shook her head. "That would never happen. My father could heal it."

"What if he couldn't? What if it was some ailment beyond him—like your uncle's wife?"

She shrugged. "Then there is nothing I could do. We knew all of Ceara's symptoms and it did us no good. There was nothing she could tell us that could help us to help her."

His brow lowered. "All right. Let us just *pretend* that your father cannot heal. The same situation."

"I cannot imagine such a thing."

He gave her a tight smile of strained patience. "Try. It's called pretending. You don't know how to imagine or pretend? I know you were a little girl once—I saw you."

Deidra rolled her eyes. "Why would I want to pretend? What foolishness. This is my life. There is no point in pretending it's not."

He shook his head at her, as if she were some odd creature he'd never encountered before.

She let out an exasperated breath. "Oh, very well. If such a thing was to happen, and my father had no healing magic, I still would not speak to the dog."

"But it's your father's beloved dog! He will mourn it dreadfully. It would cause him deep, deep unhappiness. And you have the power to prevent that, to bring him joy."

It was a simplistic argument and she shook her head at him, disappointed he thought she would cave to sentimentality. "Everything dies. That is a fact of life. Even my father can't keep a person alive forever. Magic can't subvert God's will. It is around us, always. It is the spider that traps and eats the fly, the kine that eats the grass—and you then butcher and eat the kine. That is life. It is not for me to meddle with and change. I am a witch. I would be changing the natural course of events. If the dog is meant to die, it will die. Anything else would be the devil's work."

He didn't even blink. Duke had calmed somewhat and now kept pace with them, stopping occasionally to sniff at things on the ground.

"I never thought to hear such a speech from a member of the MacKay clan. Do you also believe that it is good and right to burn a witch? God's work?"

"No, I never said that."

"So you believe that your father and Rose do God's work."

She hesitated, then nodded.

"But you hold yourself to a different standard."

"Because I am not the same as my father and Rose. They do good work. They heal the sick. That is Christ's gift."

He shifted in his saddle, his forehead creasing with discomfort. "What about the MacDonells? Isobel can see into people's minds. Gillian speaks with the dead."

"That's different. Gillian speaks to lost souls and

directs them to the light. Isobel's visions bring families together and help others to find objects lost to them."

"But the dead are dead and the lost are lost. Isn't that God's will as well?"

"You speak nonsense," Deidra said, cross with him. He confused her and made her belly uneasy. His arguments were too logical. She knew she was right. Why else did Luthias Forsyth plague her so and yet leave the rest of her family alone? He believed he did God's work and had deemed her evil.

Stephen looked skyward and rubbed the underside of his chin thoughtfully. "I seem to remember a Bible passage—Numbers, is it? In which an angel speaks to a donkey and it speaks back. So the conclusion I would draw from that is that angels are the ones who speak to beasts, not mere humans and certainly not demons."

"When beasts speak, they are possessed by devils." Saying it out loud, it sounded absurd. She didn't believe Countess was a demon. Intelligent, mayhap, but not maleficent.

"Huh." Stephen gripped the saddle horn with both gloved hands but said nothing else.

As the silence drew out, Deidra's shoulders drew up tight. She didn't like talking about the animals. It made her uncomfortable. It brought Luthias Forsyth near, as if just speaking of it conjured him and now he was on her heels, following her. Reminding her that one slip, one single misstep, and he would be there to catch her.

Stephen's silence felt like a judgment, but how he judged her was a mystery. He didn't agree with her, but why? It pressed at her chest, the wanting to know. She slid him side glances, hoping to see some sign of his thoughts in his eyes or expression.

He pondered something as he gazed off in the distance, his eyes as pale blue as a clear Highland sky. His body rocked gently in time with Countess's walk. Deidra saw him then as he truly was—a man, whole and strong, not *bacach*.

And he was a fine one. Broad and strong, fine of feature. His nose was straight, his mouth full and wide, made for smiling. She remembered his smile, too. She'd received it a few times since she'd arrived at Bráighde Pele. He would have had dozens of bastards if he'd been a whole man. He might have them yet. She wondered if his back kept him from lying with women. . . .

As if sensing her intense scrutiny, he turned his head and caught her stare.

Her cheeks blazed and she quickly looked away— then turned back, the words bursting out of her, unbidden. "What? You think me faithless to my family for holding such beliefs? Faithless to my true self?"

After a moment he nodded. "Aye, I do. But more than that, I wonder who put such words in your mouth. They sound nothing like William or Rose, and they certainly do not sound like you."

"They are God's words, given to me by God's messenger."

"God's messenger!" Stephen covered his mouth, his eyes wide with shock. "Here? On earth? And who might that be?"

Deidra's eyes narrowed at his mocking. "God's messengers here on earth are pastors, reverends, the like, you addlepate."

"Oh." He let out a huge sigh of relief, then grinned at her sour look. "So you were told this by a pastor. No doubt a witch-hunting one."

"Aye." She sighed deeply. "He sees the evil in me."

"A witch hunter sees evil in a wean who crawls by kine if it stops giving milk. That's what they do. They hunt witches—that's why they're called witch hunters. And they wouldn't be very good at their chosen occupation if they never found any, so they see witchcraft in everything."

She shook her head. "No. This man is different. He has witnessed my father and Rose heal and knows it is the work of God. He does not want to burn them. And he has spared me for so long out of some odd courtesy to them. But he knows I am different. That I am not good as they are."

Stephen sighed and frowned at her. "You are wrong, lass. But I can see you're deaf to sense, so I'll not waste any more breath trying to convince you."

That stung. It didn't matter that he was right; he couldn't convince her, and the more he tried, the more she would argue her case. What bothered her was his lack of interest in trying. He didn't really care, not if he would give up so easily.

She closed her eyes and shook the foolish notion from her head. Why should he care? She didn't care about him! Again she regretted her foolish decision to allow him to join her. Not only would he slow her down but now he was making this journey miserable with his tiresome conversation.

She decided that she wouldn't listen to any more of it. She would shut him out as surely as she shut the animals out.

Stephen longed to stop for the night, but he refused to suggest it. He knew what Deidra thought. He was dead weight, slowing her down. And she was right. Fortunately he didn't particularly care what she thought. Still, he was determined to prove her wrong, which meant she would be the one to decide when to stop for rest and sleep.

Unfortunately, she had stopped talking to him. He must have annoyed her by telling her she was not evil and now she looked anywhere but at him, her mouth a thin line.

He prayed she would decide to stop soon and not make him break the silence. His back screamed. His belly cramped. The agony made him queasy, and he had nothing but whisky in his belly to boch. He had been dosing himself liberally from a leather flask he'd brought, but it was not helping.

Duke wasn't doing well either. At first he had run ahead, diving in bushes and chasing birds. But now he walked behind them, tail sagging and tongue lolling.

Stephen noticed that as the sun sank, Deidra's shoulders drew up tighter. Her gaze scanned the barren landscape around them, eyes wide and wild. It dawned on him with sudden sickening horror that she was not going to stop. She feared something, and if he didn't find out what, they might ride all night. The thought made him light-headed. He gripped the saddle horn hard, willing the nausea to pass.

"Deidra? Is something amiss?"

"No," she said too quickly, pushing curls off her forehead. They fell right back.

"The horses are tired. Perhaps we should stop for the night."

Her gaze darted around nervously. "I want to find a cottar . . . a sheiling . . . something."

They hadn't passed a cottage in miles, and though it had been years since Stephen had ventured this far from home and even longer since he'd been this far north, he still recalled it being sparsely populated. In fact, he was relatively certain they had little chance of passing a cottage in the next couple of hours. He wanted to sprawl over his horse's neck with fatigue and disbelief, but his back would never allow such an extravagant range of movement.

He cleared his throat. "I think that's unlikely, Deidra."

She gave him a sharp look. "Why do you say that?"

"Because there isn't much out here. We haven't passed anything in hours."

"That only means that we're due to come across one." She desperately scanned the gloaming, her voice growing shrill.

She knew better than that. It meant nothing of the sort. Stephen frowned at her. There was something here he was missing. There was a reason the idea of stopping without a shelter made her so anxious.

"No, that's not what it means. A man could travel for days out here without seeing a soul."

Her mouth flattened. "There are *things* out here."

What *things*? Understanding dawned. She didn't want to sleep out in the open where anything could get at her. She claimed to ignore the animals, but she couldn't, at least not all of the time. She must be vulnerable when she slept—that was what had brought her to the stable last night. Countess shook her mane and snorted, eyes rolling toward Deidra. Deidra pointedly looked away.

He would wager his last drop of whisky that she didn't want to sleep anywhere near the horses. Things were suddenly much clearer and even more dire than he'd feared. Would they ride all night if they didn't find shelter? Stephen didn't think his back could bear it.

"Deidra, we have to stop."

She didn't respond; instead, her head turned, eyes scanning the horizon, skin pulled tight over cheekbones.

"Deidra, listen to me. We cannot just ride all night. The horses must rest. Duke is exhausted. *We* must rest."

She swung toward him, eyes wild, lips thinned. "No! I didn't invite your dog along. *You* are the one who must rest. *I* could ride all night." Hysteria edged her voice. Her chest heaved as she sucked in deep breaths.

"Peace. Just stop for a moment. Not for the night."

Her jaw hardened and he thought she might refuse. Then her shoulders sagged as if she could no longer hold up under the weight of this cross she bore. She drew rein. "Very well."

Stephen didn't relish dismounting in front of her,

but there was nothing for it. He'd known the cost when he'd decided to make this journey.

He pressed the ball of his foot into the right stirrup. Pain lanced up his thigh, stabbing at the base of his spine. His mouth went dry and he couldn't swallow. He forced his left leg to swing over the horse's back. Pain slashed through him, shoving every other thought from his mind, removing shame and pride. His fingers curled into the saddle and he clung to it, hanging on so he didn't crumple to the ground. He pressed his face into the horse's withers. Sparks of light danced behind his eyelids. He couldn't move, couldn't breath, couldn't see.

Vaguely, in the distance, he heard a voice speaking his name. Hands touched his waist, urging him to the ground.

"No," he ground out into a mouthful of sweaty horse hair.

"Let go." Her voice was firm and her fingers wrapped around his, trying to pry them from the saddle.

He didn't feel like fighting. He released his grip and sagged backward. She grunted, catching his weight and keeping him from falling. She lowered him to the ground.

"A blanket," he gasped.

She scurried away. Soft whining and a wet nose pressed to his ear. Duke. He licked Stephen anxiously.

"Shoo—go away," Deidra said, returning a second later with Stephen's rolled-up blanket. Duke whined plaintively, but the wet tongue disappeared.

"Inside," he gasped, "there is a bottle."

His eyes squeezed shut, so he didn't see what she

did. He couldn't hear much either over the pain screaming through him and his heart thudding in his ears. Every rock on the ground dug into his side. His back locked rigid with pain, breaking and twisting.

"I have it," she said.

"I need to drink some."

The smooth, cool lip of the bottle pressed against his lips. Thick, bitter liquid dribbled over his tongue and down his throat. He drank it greedily, then choked and fell into a coughing fit that nearly made him faint.

He heard Deidra's voice over him as if from a distance, tight and angry. "Damn you, Stephen Ross— you knew this would happen!" She still held him. She sat on the ground, one leg stretched out, his back resting on her thigh, her arm around his shoulders. He let his head fall against her shoulder. Soft curls pressed to his forehead. It soothed him, her arms, the soft texture of her hair, her breathing as her chest rose and fell.

Slowly, he began to feel his back again. At some point it had ceased to be an individual body part and had just been a screaming ball of knotted muscles. It still hurt like hell, but he could feel it: a spine lined with muscle, hips and buttocks. All accounted for and in agony.

She still harangued him angrily, but he found it comforting.

"I knew you would slow me down, but I let you talk me into this foolishness and now you cannot even move."

Stephen cleared his throat. "Calm yourself. And I will be able to ride just fine tomorrow."

She gave a short, sarcastic laugh of disbelief.

"Aye, I told you, I'm crippled, not invalid. However, I cannot keep abusing my back all day and night without resting it for a tic, aye? So let's stay here tonight."

Her body stiffened, but she didn't say a word. She had to know they couldn't move, not in his current condition. If he'd been with someone else he might have cursed his injury, but the way he saw it, his current pain was her fault. Even she couldn't be immune to the effects of their day in the saddle. She just hid it better.

The poppy juice worked its magic, making him loose and languid. "You ken," he said, "had you allowed me to bring servants, we would have had tents and camp beds and hot food. And tonight I'd have a woman to massage liniment into my back. But no, you cannot have anyone else along. Now see what happened?"

"You're blaming this on me!" She yanked out from beneath him, and his head slapped the ground. Pain jarred through him. He grunted and cursed.

"I can't believe you are trying to put the blame on me!"

"It was a jest, lass—a jest."

"No, it wasn't. Aye, you're right—we would have had all of that. And I am sorry, but if you need all of that you shouldn't have come along. You should have stayed in your castle where you would be safe and fed and pampered."

He lay on his back, staring at the stars piercing the sky. "Everyone needs to rest, lass. Even you."

She sniffed. "I'm fine. I could have ridden on for days."

Stephen shook his head slowly, a small smile pulling at his lips. She was stubborn. The poppy juice didn't make the pain disappear, but it made it easier to bear. Waves of lethargy swept over him. Duke belly-crawled to Stephen's side and lay his head on Stephen's thigh. Stephen rested a hand on the dog's head. He started to drift off to sleep when a small, cool hand slid beneath his neck. A folded blanket slipped beneath it to pillow his head.

He opened his eyes. Deidra leaned over him, her smooth skin smudged with road dust. "Would it help if I rubbed the liniment into your back?" she asked softly, blue eyes wide and anxious.

Her question stunned him. That was the last thing he'd expected her to offer. Was this some sort of poppy-induced hallucination? He'd had a few of those before, and they had prompted him to stop taking it.

Whatever it was, reality or fantasy, he meant to play along. He found his tongue quickly enough.

"Aye, that would be of great help in getting us on our way quicker in the morning."

She gave him a brisk nod. "Where is the liniment?"

He told her where she could find it. When she returned, she stood over him, staring down.

"You need to roll over, don't you?"

He grinned. "After you help me remove my shirt."

Her eyes narrowed, as if evaluating whether he was capable of lechery. Apparently deciding she had no choice, she shooed Duke away again and dropped to her knees where she set to work unhooking his leather jack. He helped her pull it off his arms, then she went to work untying the bottom laces of his shirt.

"There," she said, sitting back on her heels. "Now you can just push it up in the back."

He hid his smile by struggling to roll onto his stomach. He rested his head on his bent arm. She pushed his shirt up and gasped. He didn't have to look at her face to know what she viewed with horror.

"Did it hurt?" she asked in a hushed voice. Before he could answer, she answered herself. "What am I asking? Of course it hurt."

Her fingers touched the healed but mangled skin gently, tracing over the ragged edges of the scar. He shuddered with intense pain-pleasure, and she drew her touch away. The strong medicinal scent of the liniment tingled the inside of his nose. Her fingers, gloved in the greasy cream, dug into his back. He bit back a grunt of pain and squeezed his eyes shut. It always hurt at first. Her fingers worked at his knotted muscles, pressing and kneading, forcing the muscles to loosen.

She started to use her fists. His teeth bit into his bottom lip until he tasted blood. She was stronger than she looked. He imagined her in his mind, working at his back, sleek, slender muscles standing out on her arms, mouth grim, curls damp and clinging to the sides of her fine-boned face. She was beautiful, exotic, strange. He decided he wanted her, to taste and feel her. It had seemed a rather unlikely proposition at first, but here she was massaging his back. She was unpredictable.

Her hand rested on his hip. "Roll onto your side." She sounded out of breath.

He realized he was aroused, and he hesitated but

did as she bid, pushing himself onto his side. His back was definitely improved from her ministrations.

She started in on his hip. This time he couldn't suppress his cry of pain when she ground her knuckles into the tight muscles. Pain radiated from his back and down both legs, and she was attacking it right where it hurt the most.

"With hands like yours, I can't believe you're not married."

She gave a short laugh. "What man would marry a woman for her hands?"

"I would."

She laughed again, but this time it was edged with bitterness. "It's not as if you have much of a choice."

His eyes sprang open. Had she just insulted him? A smile tugged at the corners of his mouth. "You think I can't get a worthy woman."

"Well, you are a cripple. And a bastard."

"I'm also rich and pretty."

Her fingers dug hard into the muscles of his side.

"Ouch!"

"Forgive me," she said with false humility. "Unbuckle your belt."

His heart skipped a hopeful beat. "What?"

"So I can pull down your trews and rub the thigh."

"Oh." He did as she bid. If she noticed the state of his erection, she said nothing at all. He was surprised he could be so excited, considering the amount of pain he'd been in, but he was. He wanted her quite badly.

"So," he said as she worked the muscles of his thigh. "Why aren't you married?"

"Who'd have me?"

"Lots of men. You're fetching."

She snorted but said nothing.

He twisted his neck to look at her. Her cheeks had flushed dusky in the dark. She pointedly kept her gaze on her work.

"Are you telling me no man has offered for you?"

"Who would? I'm a witch."

"The MacDonell women are all witches and they had no problem finding good men."

"Aye, well, they're beautiful," she snapped, her fingers growing rough and careless.

He considered whether he should leave her alone—she could end up really hurting him if he continued baiting her. But he decided it gave him too much pleasure to forgo.

"And so are you," he said, meaning it. The more time he spent with her, the more fetching she became. She was lovely and smart and strong, and she had a kindness to her that she tried to hide but could not deny.

Her mouth pinched tight. "I pray you—false flattery out of pity is insulting."

"It's not false. You are very bonny."

The pressure her fingers exerted lessened momentarily. "Roll to your other side," she said.

He rolled onto his back, then toward her. Instead of moving around behind him, she pushed his shirt up and his trews down on his left side and started kneading the muscles.

She was very good. Much better than the woman

back at Bráighde Pele. And not nearly as modest as he would have imagined. He could see many benefits to keeping her around. Of course, if she was right about the blood witch, he would have no need for a massage very soon.

He studied her face as she worked his flesh, her eyes intent, her face grave. She had huge eyes, with long, heavy lashes. They gave the illusion of softness and delicacy, when she was really anything but. As if feeling his gaze on her, those thick lashes raised, and her gaze met his.

His breath caught on the look: smoky, indefinable.

"Who ever told you that you weren't beautiful?" he asked softly.

She held his gaze for a long moment, her lips slightly parted, then she shrugged and returned her gaze to her work with a swallow that drew her neck tight. "No one."

"Then why?"

Her lips curved into a bitter smile. "No one ever told me I was, either."

"I just told you."

She rolled her eyes and let out an exasperated breath.

He grabbed her wrist. "I suppose that means nothing coming from a cripple, but I have known many beautiful women."

She stared at her wrist, enclosed in his hand. She tugged at it. She was so small and yet quite strong. But not as strong as he was. He held fast to her wrist.

Her lips thinned. "I think the massage is over."

"But this conversation isn't."

She pushed off her knees and sat on her heels, glaring poison at him. "What do you want me to say? I remember you. You are a lecher. You pour out flattery like old wash water. It is meaningless."

There was some truth to what she claimed. He was known to give extravagant flattery—but he wasn't this time.

"Why would I lie to you?" he asked, his grip on her wrist tightening. "What would be my purpose?"

She yanked on her arm, but rather than loosing his hold, it set her off balance and she fell to her knee. "I know not—mayhap you mean to flatter your way to more back rubs?"

He pulled on her wrist, bringing her down closer to his level. "I didn't ask you to rub my back."

She strained away, the cords of her throat standing out in panic. "Then—then you think it's some warped way of thanking me."

He arched a brow. "If I wanted to thank you, I could think of a better way."

She was so close he could smell her. Her skin, her sweat, the sweetness of apple on her breath. And lust flooded him, all at once, powerful. Her pulse thudded wildly at her throat, her eyes locked on his. She saw the change. The rate of her breathing increased.

"Let go of me." She ground the words out between clenched teeth, but her eyes were wide, the whites shining in the gloaming.

He considered letting her go. He was not the type of man to ever force himself on a woman, but she nettled him. She thought she was above him somehow. *Better.* And maybe she was, in a sense. She was whole. Had painless use of her body.

But she was a witch, an outcast, too. They were more alike than she cared to admit.

His other hand slid around behind her neck and drew her in. He didn't apply enough pressure to her neck to stop her from breaking away if she really wanted to. Apparently she didn't. She resisted, leaning back, but not enough to stop him or even slow him. His lips touched hers, gently at first, testing and tasting.

She exhaled softly, as if surprised, and her lips trembled. She tasted wonderful, sweet and warm. His mouth moved over hers, feather kisses. When her lips relaxed, he slid his hand to the side of her neck. The skin there was as soft as down and he rubbed at it, wallowing in the exquisite sensation. She shivered and tilted her head but still didn't pull away.

Her lips parted and he kissed her deeper. His original purpose in kissing her now eluded him. He wanted more. He wanted her body, warm against his. Skin to skin. He tried to draw her closer. She came to him at first, sweet and willing, then suddenly the muscles in her neck wired tight and she jerked backward.

He opened his eyes and looked up at her, surprised to find himself breathing hard. His body ached now— not with pain but with arousal cut short.

She stood on her knees, the back of one hand pressed against her mouth, her eyes wide with horror.

"Deidra," he said, reaching a hand toward her, his voice rough and cracking slightly.

Black curls bobbed as she shook her head, mute, throat working. She scrambled to her feet and turned away, walking rapidly until she disappeared into the darkness.

Stephen sighed, supremely irritated with himself, and sank back to the ground. Duke returned to his side and stretched out, pressing warmly against his side. Kissing her had been a huge mistake. Certainly not the first he'd made, but in such a situation as they were in, it was one of the stupider ones. He hoped she planned to return.

Deidra paced in the darkness, torn between her fear of the dark and her reluctance to return to the camp with Stephen. She kept the fire she'd built in sight and paced a wide circle around it. She didn't really understand what had happened earlier. The entire episode—his back giving out, her inexplicable offer to rub it, and the subsequent kiss—was incomprehensible to her. She didn't know what to think or do; in fact, she hadn't been able to think or reason at all. So she had run.

Putting distance between them had given her the ability to review what had happened. In retrospect, she realized that regardless of what he'd said, the only reason he had kissed her was that he'd wanted something. Not the obvious thing a man wanted from a woman. He wanted something more from her.

Crippled or not, he was a rich, handsome man, accustomed to having his way in all things. And what he currently wanted was Deidra MacKay at his service. She had made his life difficult by denying him the comforts of home—no servants, no comfortable bed, no hot food or woman to rub his back. All of it was Deidra's fault.

But she was here, able-bodied and fully capable of supplying him with the things he was accustomed to. He knew she would never do it for money, but she might do it if she was smitten. Did he really believe she was a silly girl who would lose her head over a bonny face?

The idea made her pace faster, hands on hips and mouth tight. The moon hung high above her, and a chill wind cut through the thin material of her dress. She pulled her araisad closer, turning back in the direction of camp. She wondered if he'd been able to get a blanket to protect him from the biting wind.

Her mouth drew tighter the moment the traitorous thought crossed her mind. She widened her circuit around the camp. Why was he doing this? Did he really believe there was a blood witch and that the blood witch could heal him? Or was this something else? A game because he was bored?

Well, she was not the smitten, silly fool he thought she was. At least, not entirely. So she had temporarily lost her head, but it was back now, firmly on her shoulders. The kiss had been unexpected, that was all. Never in her imaginings had she expected to feel his warm lips pressed to hers, nor had she expected them to be so soft and supple. And his hand, when it had gripped and caressed her neck, had scattered shivers down her spine. It was as if he'd found touching her irresistible. She shuddered, and her jaw locked in irritation.

It wouldn't happen again—she knew that much for certain. She knew what to expect now and would not behave with such wanton abandon. Now that she better understood what had caused her to respond in such a manner, she felt better—well, enough to return to the camp. She squared her shoulders and marched back to where she'd left him.

He had settled them into the camp, unsaddling the horses and building up the fire. Her strong stride faltered. She had expected him to still be lying on the ground where she'd left him, but he wasn't. He sat upright, eating a bannock and tossing pieces of dried meat to Duke.

She did not meet his gaze as she crossed to where he had put her things, near his. She moved them farther away.

She prepared a bed for herself using a thick wool blanket and a leather satchel for a pillow. She could see him out of the corner of her eye, watching her every move. It felt like a touch almost, making the hair stand along her neck and arms. But when she chanced a quick look, he was not looking at her at all. She scowled at him as he dug through a sack.

"Are you hungry?" he asked, pulling out more dried meat and dried fruit.

Her stomach rumbled. "No." She rolled herself up in the blanket and put her back to him.

"You haven't eaten all day."

"So?"

He made a soft sound of exasperation. "You have to eat."

"I don't *have* to do anything."

"Och, is that what this is? You're starving yourself to spite me because I kissed you? Surely you can think of a better way to get your revenge."

Her teeth clenched. She didn't want to admit even to herself that he was right, so she grumbled, "I *am not* hungry." This time her stomach rumbled loud enough to be heard from where he sat.

He laughed. "Fine, then. You're not hungry."

She did not respond. She lay there, her back to him, mouth drawn tight. She listened to him move around, eating and then preparing for bed. Her belly cramped with hunger. She was being a stubborn fool and she well knew it, but there was no help for it now. She willed sleep to come so she could wake up refreshed and finally get a chance to eat, but sleep was elusive. Her mind refused to rest. Witticisms shot through her mind—things she wished she had said to him earlier. Worry also plagued her. What would happen when she fell asleep? She was outside. There were creatures in the darkness—and that annoying horse. They pressed at her now. She felt them, in the wood around her. They had been aware of a presence for some time and were edging closer to investigate. She tried to ignore them, but it was hard when they frightened her.

As she lay there wide awake, a plan nagged at her. She should wait for Stephen to fall asleep, then sneak food. He would soon be oblivious from taking the poppy juice, if he wasn't already.

So she waited, straining to hear any sounds from him in the darkness. At some point she must have worried herself to exhaustion, because she did fall asleep.

Her dreams were vivid and strange, full of light and movement. Stephen was there and he kissed her. It was exciting at first. Her heart pounded in her throat and her head was muzzy and dreamy, but then something went wrong. She sensed it. He held her too hard, his mouth felt strange and wet. She jerked back to look at him. He was no longer a man at all but a hideously disfigured monster, and just like all the beasts, he wanted something from her. He held her by her shoulders and shook her, demanding in a strange, wet language, which she somehow understood, that she *hear* him.

She screamed and struggled to escape his iron hold but he held her fast, repeating, "Talk to me, Deidra, hear me," over and over and over in his monster voice.

Wolves surrounded them, watching, waiting, sniffing at the air eagerly. They whined and crept closer, tails between their legs.

Deidra fought against their thoughts, threw up a wall to block them, but she was vulnerable during sleep. She wanted to shout at them with her mind, so loud it would terrify them into silence. She knew she could, she'd done it before many years ago—but that would only open her mind to them. She shook her head, eyes burning with fear and confusion. The air sparked around her, acrid smoke blocked her nostrils and filled her throat. A murmur grew around her, uneasy. *Hot, hot, bad, bad, fire. Move.*

A fire.

Deidra woke with a start. Her chest heaved as she

fought to draw in clean air, not the dream fug of smoke and soot. Damp hair clung to her forehead and temples. She lay very still, afraid to move, staring at the moon and trying to calm her racing heart. She strained to hear over its liquid thudding in her ears. Were they around her, the wolves? Or had it really just been a dream? And what of Stephen? The memory of his monster mouth sent the hair prickling all along her back and arms.

She turned her head to the right. A large velvet muzzle was in her face. It blew hot and wet against her cheek.

Fire. Must go.

Deidra let out the breath she'd sucked in and shoved Countess's nose out of her face. It was just the stupid horse. She rolled onto her side, putting her back to the irritating creature.

But Deidra wasn't a fool. She tested the air, lifting her head and smelling. The air was clean and crisp— no trace of smoke. Nothing more than a dream.

She crawled over to her leather satchel, glancing over her shoulder at Stephen. He was a wool-covered lump a few feet away. A rolled plaid was jammed into his back. She wondered how he'd accomplished that without assistance. A pang of guilt stabbed her. She should have helped him get situated for the night. Instead she'd sulked like a child and left him to himself.

She stiffened her spine to the thought. She was not his servant, nor would she be. He had shown himself perfectly capable of caring for himself.

She returned to her bedroll with her satchel and rummaged for food.

Countess batted her in the head with her muzzle. Deidra tried to ignore the horse, but she kept knocking her nose against Deidra's head periodically. The horse was most insistent, trying to communicate the danger of a fire.

Deidra stood and walked the perimeter of the camp, but there was no orange glow on the horizon, nor was there the faintest scent of smoke. She wanted to convey this to the horse, but that would have required speaking to the animal, and Deidra would not do that.

She returned to her bannocks and apple. Countess whinnied and stamped her forehoof. Stephen mumbled and moved. Deidra froze, bannock halfway to her lips, her breath held until he lay still again. She glared at the horse and haughtily gave the beast her back.

But it didn't matter. The horse could not read her body language, and even if it could have, Deidra doubted it would care. Countess continued to harass her, batting at Deidra's head with her muzzle and blowing at her. Deidra didn't know how much more she could take. She wanted to scream and pull her hair in frustration, and worse—she wanted to talk to the horse, to tell it to *leave her alone*.

She didn't want this—she had never wanted any of it. Not Stephen's troubles and kisses, or his horse's determination to make her miserable and make her an outcast and murderer again.

Deidra stared blankly into the darkness, rocking rhythmically every time Countess knocked her in the head, wondering why she was doing this. Why had she agreed to let Stephen Ross tag along? She couldn't even remember now. She looked over at him, sleeping. He was far more able-bodied than she had expected. He'd also assured her he would be fine by morning. In addition, he had managed to unsaddle and hobble the horses all by himself.

He didn't need her.

And that made what she had to do next easier. She stood and quietly gathered her things together. Countess grew agitated and tried to follow, but Deidra secured her to a tree. She released her own much quieter and more docile horse and, without a backward glance, crept away into the night.

Chapter 4

———— ⚬⚬⚬ ————

$\mathcal{I}$t was still dark when Stephen woke. His back didn't hurt as long as he lay still. He listened for Deidra but heard nothing, only the soughing of the wind in the trees. He tucked in his chin and rounded his back, hissing through his teeth at the pain that clamped around his tailbone. He closed his eyes and exhaled, working his back with slow stretches to warm it and wake the muscles.

There was still no sound from Deidra. He hoped she was asleep. He did not want her to witness his waking ritual. He imagined her watching him, wondering what the devil he was doing. He supposed it was unavoidable that she would see him doing this at some point, but he hoped it would be later, rather than sooner.

When his back felt sufficiently limber, he sat up, immediately looking over his shoulder. Countess was tied to a tree. He frowned, scanning the clearing.

Deidra was gone. No horse, no things, no Deidra.

She'd left him.

The idea struck him dumb for a full minute, and he found himself searching the camp again, wondering if he'd somehow missed something in the dark. But no, she was really gone.

He rubbed a hand over his forehead and laughed ruefully.

So he shouldn't have kissed her.

Damn it. His hand curled into a fist and he pressed it into his forehead. He knew better. He'd known it had been a bad idea at the time, for too many reasons to count, but none of those reasons had included being abandoned.

In truth, he hadn't contemplated such an outcome. He hadn't believed she had it in her.

Obviously, he'd been wrong. He dropped his hand and shook his head, smiling again. It was amusing, really. Had she expected him to be so dejected by her defection that he would run home with his tail between his legs? Or maybe she didn't care at all—she just wanted to be quit of him.

As he got to his feet, his smile faded from the stiff pain momentarily paralyzing his lower back. He forced himself to breathe through it. A few deep twists and he worked the worst of the pain out. But only temporarily. A few hours on horseback would bring the gripping pain back, and no amount of exercise would get rid of it. Only the deep massages that another could provide would alleviate a modicum of the pain, but that wouldn't happen anytime soon. It didn't matter. He was going anyway. A chance to be free of this pain forever—even a slim chance—was worth trying. And at least now he would be able to travel at his own pace. He could stop whenever he needed to, to rest and work some of the tightness and cramping out of his back. He told himself that if he could bear it just a little while longer, he might be free of it forever. He refused to contemplate failure. He'd been down that road before and would deal with that if it occurred. But for now he just had to keep moving.

He gathered his things together, still somewhat amused by Deidra's flight. He knew where she was going. *She* knew that he knew. He might be a cripple, and therefore slower than she was, but they were both going to the same place. So she had surprised him. He'd underestimated her.

But then, she'd underestimated him, as well.

The sun rose before her, warming the chill from her bones. She thought of Stephen back at the camp and wondered if he was awake yet and what he had thought when he'd realized she'd deserted him.

She felt horribly guilty about leaving him behind. It didn't help a bit that he had been right last night. She had gone miles without seeing a single sign of life. It was only as the sky lightened that she began to see indications of human activity. A peat bog, with a long trench dug in it. The peat was stacked to dry farther along her route. And not far beyond that were a dirty-faced boy and his dog, set to watch the peat. He stared at her as she rode by but didn't say a word.

She wished she could stop thinking about Stephen. She regretted not having woken him before leaving—to say good-bye and to see if there was anything he needed.

And to give him the chance to talk her out of going on alone.

No, no, no. She'd done the right thing by leaving as she had. Perhaps it had been cowardly, but was it not said that discretion was the better part of valor? She was probably twisting that adage to assuage her own guilt, and it did little to comfort her.

She came to the top of a rise and reined in her horse. A village crouched in the glen below; the largest concentration of cottages clustered about the loch. Relief rushed through her, and the tightness in her shoulders lessened the slightest bit. She was glad to finally find a safe haven to rest in for a while where she wouldn't have to fear the creatures in the wild.

She tapped her horse's side and rode along the top of the rise until she reached the road. A crossroad loomed in the distance, marked with a huge blackened pile of rocks. The air smelled foul—like soot and burned meat. It reminded her of her dream from the night before. A spring wound tight behind her breastbone.

As she rode closer, she realized the blackened pile was not rocks, as she'd first assumed. It had been kindling, piled high around a stake. The spring wound tighter, making her gasp to catch her breath.

There *had* been a fire last night. The scent of it still burned her nostrils, though the smoke was long gone. And Countess had been right. The fire had been a danger to her. What she didn't understand was how the horse had known about it.

As Deidra passed the stake, a wind rose and blew

across the tumbled, blackened wood, sending ashes spiraling through the air to clog her throat and burn her eyes. Her vision swam in and out as moisture built behind her eyes.

The village had burned a witch last night. Her blackened skeleton was tied to the stake still. It seemed strange to Deidra that the witch's clothes and hair and skin had all burned away but the rope that had strapped her to the stake, though blackened, still held fast, keeping her upright for all who passed to see. Her head tilted back, her bony jaw open in a silent scream.

The spring in Deidra's breast wound so tight that she feared it would burst. It squeezed her heart, made her struggle for air. Her stomach lurched as she rode past the horror, hating the sight but unable to avert her eyes.

She reined her horse in, staring at the distant village with trepidation. Should she go around it? This was no safe place. But finally the urge to rest won out. How much trouble could she get in at the inn, asleep? She would not stay long.

A somber atmosphere lay over the village like a thick fog. The people she passed on the street watched her with tight lips and grim eyes. Deidra felt as if everything about her screamed *witch*, even though she knew that was impossible.

Food first, then sleep.

She came to a common house that served ale and food, and she tethered her horse in front of it. A fire blazed in the center of the dwelling; long tables were situated around it. She sat at an empty one and was brought mulled ale and barley stew as soon as she showed her coin. The brew was warm and the food felt good in her empty belly. She sighed deeply as she emptied her bowl and asked for more.

Her server was a large woman, but kindly, and brought her a slice of dark bread with the next bowl and charged her nothing more. Deidra supposed she looked pathetic, small and thin and starving.

A dog wandered inside. Every rib showed through its scraggly brown fur. Its droopy ears cocked, and it scanned the room. Deidra thought of Duke, which reminded her of Stephen, and the spring in her breast, which had been loosening, wound tight again.

She turned away. A moment later the dog appeared beside her, whimpering up at her. It laid its head on her thigh, and she jerked away. So it lay at her feet.

She tried to ignore it, continuing to shovel down the last spoonfuls of stew. But in the end she sopped up the juice with her bread and dropped it on the ground without looking at the dog. She heard it swallow the bread in a single gulp.

She sighed. She was a lodestone wherever she went, attracting any stray animal that happened to be wandering about.

She was nearly finished with the rest of her bread when a shadow fell across the table, blocking out the firelight. Deidra looked up from her meal. Her heart jumped up into her throat, making her choke on the food she attempted to swallow. She coughed and gasped, her eyes bulging and her legs tense with the instinct to run.

"Deidra MacKay. Fancy meeting you here."

At the sound of his voice, paralysis gripped her. She hadn't been truly alone with him without the protection of her family in twelve years, and it had been her dearest wish never to be again. But here she was, alone with Luthias Forsyth.

She went dumb, unable to speak or move, only able to stare at him in horrified silence. How was it he was *here*, when she had left him at Strathwick?

He seemed taller than she remembered. He hadn't been a young man when they'd first met, but neither had he been old. Frighteningly, he didn't appear to have aged a single day since that long-ago day when he'd tortured her father, then tried to burn him. He had less hair on either side of his shiny pate, and he was still tall and thin, but somehow he was not weak at all. He looked powerful and fearsome. He stared down at her with intense gray eyes that seemed to see straight to her soul.

"What's the matter, Deidra? Cat got your tongue?" He looked down at the dog that lay patiently at her feet. "Or should I say dog?"

Evil, evil man to say such a thing. But the reminder of all that was suddenly at stake galvanized her to action.

She shook off the shocked stupor. "Of course not," she snapped.

"Ah, she speaks. And what are you doing so far from home, Miss MacKay?"

Deidra swallowed and tried to appear nonchalant. "Just passing through."

"On your way to . . . ?" His thin gray brows rose in question, wrinkling his high forehead.

She wanted to tell him to stay out of her business, but she didn't dare anger him. Instead she said, "On my way to see my uncle."

"All alone?" He drew back in scandalized shock. "It's dangerous for a woman to be traveling alone."

"I can take care of myself better than most men."

He smiled as if he'd caught her in a trap. "I can attest to that!"

Her lips hardened, but she did not respond to his taunt. The dog at her feet whined but didn't otherwise move.

Luthias tilted his head to study her. "Few fathers would allow their daughters to travel alone and unprotected. I do not believe your father is one of them."

He was right, of course. William MacKay was probably frantic, wondering where his daughter was. In fact, he was probably searching for her. But Deidra didn't think it was wise to admit anything. Luthias obviously assumed she was alone and unprotected, but he didn't *know*, and she didn't intend to confirm his suspicions.

When she didn't answer, he pulled out the bench opposite her and sat down, adjusting his immaculate black robe. He looked so out of place in this rustic common house, surrounded by crude furniture and smoke from the lard lanterns. He was obviously not the common laborer that frequented this establishment, or even a villager. This was a city man, a lowlander with means.

"How long will you be here?" he asked, his voice smooth and pleasant.

Deidra swallowed, her mind racing ahead, trying to decide the best response to get him to leave her alone. She most assuredly did not want to remain in this village any longer than necessary, and yet leaving no longer felt safe. She would be all alone and unprotected. But to stay here was to also put herself in danger. This village had just burned a witch and now she understood why. Luthias was in town. If anything went amiss while she was here, fingers would point and Luthias would be more than happy to tie her to a stake.

What continued to confuse her was how he'd managed to get here so quickly. When she'd left Strathwick, he'd been in the nearby village. He must have left when she had and come straight here. Had he come here because he'd known there had been a witch inhabiting this little hamlet? Or had he just lucked upon her?

"Who was she?" Deidra asked, hoarse, as if she'd been screaming, but the screaming was only in her head.

Luthias smoothed a finger over his eyebrow. "Who?"

"The woman you burned last night," she hissed through clenched teeth.

"Oh, her. She was a witch."

And he dismissed a woman's life just like that. *Just a witch.* No name. Fear and anger mixed inside of Deidra to create something reckless.

"By whose definition?" she pressed.

His thin lips curved condescendingly. "Whose do you think, Deidra?" He shook his head, as if deeply disappointed in her. "Do you truly believe I am the one to make these laws? It is God's law, enforced by the kirk and king."

"The king lives in England now, and I have heard that there they do not burn witches so zealously."

His smile became genuine. He leaned forward slightly. "We're not in England."

Deidra started to stand, but he stopped her, placing his hand on her arm to hold her in place. The touch of his hand went through her like a knife, cold and repellant. She was too appalled to move away.

"I have been waiting for this for a very long time."

"Waiting for what?" she asked, her voice rising shrilly. A handful of villagers was scattered about the common house, but not one of them intervened. They all watched surreptitiously, none of them daring to stare openly. Luthias had obviously put the fear of God's cleansing fire into them.

The dog sat up, whimpering and thumping its tail. Luthias shot it a narrow look. "Is this your hellhound? Will it try to rip my throat out?" He didn't look terribly frightened by that possibility.

"No—I know not. It's not my dog. I don't know what it wants."

He snorted dubiously. "I have men ready to snap its neck if it so much as growls."

Deidra's throat tightened. She wanted to send the dog away, but she feared it would only become more protective if she finally acknowledged it.

"What have you been waiting for? Why not just burn me and get it over with?" Deidra asked, successfully distracting his attention from the dog.

"Surrounded by your MacKays, protecting you? No, I had to bide my time and be patient. I knew God would eventually reward me. He would not put me through such tests for no reason."

Her stomach dipped. This was his reward? "Let me go." She tried to pull her arm away, but he held it flat on the table. He had her, away from family and aid, and he didn't mean to let her escape.

Memories from a dozen years ago flooded her. Her father's hand clamped to a table as Luthias beat it with a mallet until it was a bloody pulp, the crack of bones, the gush of blood, the pain that distorted her father's face. Luthias had been righteous and excited while he'd tortured her father. He loved his work and believed in it.

To her, he had been terrifying, monstrous. Even though her father had healed completely, seeing him beaten in such a way had affected her. She'd had nightmares for a long time. Sometimes when she looked at her father, all she saw was a mangled hand, even though his was whole. She had thought the old wounds had healed, but she could see now they'd only scabbed over. And here was Luthias Forsyth, pick, pick, picking at the scab.

Her breathing grew shallow. Her hand tightened into a fist. "What do you want?" she whispered, appalled at the whimper in her voice.

"Justice," he said with no malice, only confidence and faith in his beliefs. Justice for the long-ago day when a mere eight-year-old had held him hostage with her magic. She had called the animals to rescue her and her father, but she had given them no direction.

However, they had felt the intensity of her fear. They had seen her as a deity of sorts—a divine leader—and had been willing to kill and die for her. And that day they had done just that.

It had sealed her fate with Luthias forever.

Deidra wrenched away, yanking her arm from his grasp and stumbling backward. The bench toppled over, and she came down hard on her shoulder, knocking her head against the floor.

She was momentarily dazed, but she was free.

She rolled to her feet. He rushed around the table in pursuit. Deidra spun around to run the other way, but a man appeared at the door, arms crossed over his chest, blocking her way.

Heart throbbing in her throat, she tried to dart to the side as Luthias snatched at her. The dog was there, standing beside her, hackles puffed out, making it appear twice its size. It growled, loud and menacing, lips peeled back to expose wicked, sharp teeth.

Deidra reared back in surprise as it leaped at her. She flung her hands up to protect her face, but it flew past her, catching Luthias's arm between its jaws. Dog and man crashed to the floor.

"No!" Deidra shrieked. In her panic she couldn't even remember how to speak to the dog so it would understand—she had not done it in so long. "No! Leave him alone!"

Men appeared—the same men he had threatened her with earlier—and converged on the growling, slathering melee on the floor. They drew enormous knives from their belts and hacked at the dog.

It yelped and went silent. *No!* The scream rose in Deidra's chest but did not pass her lips. She stared at the bloody, hairy mass on the floor, hands clamped over her mouth, muscles rigid with horror. *Why? Why? Why?* She hadn't asked it to protect her. She hadn't wanted its help. Now it was dead and Luthias's belief in her wickedness had been validated.

Luthias still sprawled on the ground, dusty robes askew and torn, face flushed. He looked at his arm, at the torn, bloodstained sleeve, and then back at Deidra. His brow lowered and his lips thinned into an uncompromising line.

He got to his feet and straightened his robes, his dignity restored. "Take her into custody."

His thugs grabbed her arms. She struggled to escape, though she knew it was futile. "What did I do? I didn't do anything!"

"You set your hellhound on me. You tried to murder me through witchcraft."

"It's not my dog! I've never seen him before today." She writhed and twisted, but it was no use. He was deaf to her protests. The men dragged her from the common house and shoved her through the streets before tossing her unceremoniously into a hole behind a large house.

It was dark and damp in the hole. A grate was dropped over the top, creating a patchwork pattern of light on the ground. As her eyes adjusted, she realized she was in a cellar. Barrels lined the wall, and crates were stacked beside them. Deidra sat on a crate, shoulders slumped, and stared into the darkness.

She had denied her magic for so long, for no other reason than to avoid this very situation she now found herself in. She couldn't quite comprehend how she'd managed, in spite of her very best efforts, to end up this way. Luthias was right. It must have been God's plan for her all along. He *was* working through the witch hunter.

A voice in her head taunted that she should never have left Stephen. But really, what could he have done to prevent this? He was a cripple. And besides, the true root of the thought was that she had never felt so alone in her entire life. And for a little while, with Stephen, she had not been alone. Though she had rejected his company, he had wanted hers. It hurt now to admit it, but she regretted leaving him, regretted her stubborn streak of independence. No, not independence. Isolation. She was no better than he was, walling herself off and driving away those who tried to tear down the walls.

But those were selfish, self-pitying thoughts. Stephen was an innocent. Better he not get caught up in her mess. She was the witch. If she was to be punished for it, she must face it alone.

Chapter 5

———— ∞∞∞ ————

Stephen was relieved to arrive at the village, even if the welcoming committee was a charred corpse strapped to a stake. He knew Deidra had come this way because he'd tracked her. He doubted she'd stopped anywhere for the night, so he looked for the telltale signs of fresh horse dung. And Duke was an excellent bloodhound, too, keeping him on track. He wondered what Deidra had thought when she'd seen the corpse at the crossroads. Coming as she did from a family of witches, it must have been troubling. He wondered if her desire to sleep in a village had over-ridden her misgivings about the dead witch.

Only one way to find out.

The town was subdued as he entered on foot. It had been at least a mile since he'd been able to sit a horse. At the point where it had begun to feel as if a white-hot rod had been rammed up his spine, he'd dismounted to walk it out.

Unfortunately, walking was only a temporary solution. He leaned heavily against Countess as he limped into the village. Jagged teeth had sunk into his spine and held there. Pain radiated down both legs.

He tried to greet folks he passed on the dirt main street, but no one would meet his eyes. He stopped outside a cottage that was obviously inhabited by a tanner, judging by the skins hung to dry all over the walls.

A man stood before a skin stretched tight over two beams. He scraped rhythmically at it with a curved knife and was so engrossed in his work that Stephen had to clear his throat several times before the man turned.

"I'm witch hunting, my friend, and was told there was a *baobhan sith* out this way."

The man's brows drew together and his mouth snapped shut. After a moment he shook his head. "I know not of that matter." Before Stephen could say another word, the man walked purposefully into his cottage and shut the door.

Stephen glanced around. There were few people out and about, and he decided that mayhap it wasn't the best time to be asking about witches, not with a burning still fresh in their minds. It might somehow be misinterpreted and go badly for him, and he was in no condition to be running for his life.

He limped on, leaving the tanner's cottage behind. Farther down at the end of the dirt lane sat a long house with a sign out front depicting a crude drawing of a large cup with a white substance overflowing the top. The alehouse. He would have more luck in there, he hoped.

The murky interior stank of lard candles and barley stew. His belly cramped in response. He was hungry, but not for that. The pain in his back had managed to conceal his hunger, but now it would not be ignored.

He slid onto a bench and grunted, head cradled in his hands as the tension ebbed and throbbed painfully out of his spine. He breathed in and out, slowly, and focused on the sensation and sound of his breathing. He sat that way, knuckles pressed into the hollows of his eyes, concentrating on his breathing until the pain became manageable again.

He raised his head. A stout, red-faced woman stood before him, hands on hips and hairy brows raised expectantly.

"What's there to eat?"

"Soup and ale."

And that was it, he supposed, since she gave no further options.

She trudged away, returning moments later with a big bowl of barley stew, a tankard of ale, and a crust of bread. The stew looked better than it smelled. He wanted to dive into it, but first he needed some answers.

As he dug through his bag for his spoon, he asked, "Has a young woman been through the village recently?"

She gave him a sharp look and her thick chin raised a notch. "Now, what would a young woman be doing traveling all alone?"

Stephen's brow arched. "I don't recall specifying that she was alone?"

The woman was not so easily trapped. "You didna say she weren't either. And ye asked aboot no one else."

He inclined his head. "Very well. Has a young woman with dark curly hair—*traveling alone*—passed through here recently?"

The woman's brows drew together into a single furry line. "Why would a young woman be traveling alone? 'Tis just not safe."

Stephen was growing mildly irritated at how she avoided answering the question. Her avoidance also indicated that she probably *had* seen Deidra but didn't want to tell him. That could mean nothing good.

"She's daft, a wandering idiot. Well. Not usually. We try very hard to keep her from wandering."

She stared at him blandly. "Or maybe she's running away from something."

Stephen shrugged. "Mayhap aye . . . mayhap no."

"Mayhap she's not daft. Mayhap she's running from you. It wouldna be kind of me to be giving up a woman on the run. Mayhap you'll knock her around a little for *wandering* off, or kill her."

"Mayhap she's my wife or daughter? Then by rights I own her and can do whatever I please."

The woman snorted and planted a hand on her hip. "You're too young to be her father, and—"

"Ha!" Stephen pointed at her and laughed with victory. "You *have* seen her! Where is she?"

The woman's lips pursed, her expression sour. She crossed her arms over her chest and said grudgingly, "We're not to speak of it."

Stephen's heart skipped. That sounded very bad. Worse than he'd feared if the whole village had been instructed not to speak of it.

Working to keep the urgency from his tone, he asked, "Why is that?"

Her mouth pursed even tighter, becoming a thin, wrinkled slash. But her throat worked as if she was about to burst with the desire to spill everything she knew.

Stephen removed his purse and dumped the contents on the table. The woman's eyes grew round at the sight of the pile of shiny coins. It was probably more coin than she had seen in her whole life.

He met her gaze, his own serious and steady. "What happened to the woman?"

The woman looked from the coins to Stephen and licked her lips. When her eyes met Stephen's again, they held, and he could that see she was about to give him the information he sought. But then something changed. Her gaze rose to look at something above his head. Her face closed. She lowered her eyes and mumbled something, then turned away and left him.

Stephen sighed grimly and glanced over his shoulder, scooping up his coins. A tall, narrow man stood in the doorway, his shiny bald head brushing the top of the doorframe. Cold gray eyes fixed on Stephen. Chips of dirty ice. Stephen met the man's gaze, then noticed the rough-looking men who had entered before him. Mercenaries. They situated themselves strategically around the room.

A knot of foreboding formed in Stephen's gut, but he was no stranger to such situations. It had been awhile, back when he'd been a whole man, but there had been a time when he hadn't been able to stay out of trouble no matter how hard he'd tried—and the odds had never been good. Of course, that's what had gotten him cripple. Lousy odds.

He located his spoon. This might be his last good meal for a while, and he was not about to let it go to waste. He turned his attention to his food and, after taking a deep pull of ale, began spooning down the thick soup.

Within minutes the robed man circled the room, coming to stand in front of Stephen. Stephen continued to eat, acknowledging the man only with a nod. He knew his dismissive attitude would not dissuade the man, but he nevertheless continued to ignore him until he had finished his meal.

As he washed his coarse bread down with a swig of ale, the man said, "Are you finished?"

Stephen slammed his tankard down with exaggerated force. "Aye."

The man did not appear intimidated. No doubt it was his lurking mercenaries—either that or he knew Stephen was a cripple—because Stephen knew that he was formable sitting down. He continued to keep his body in the best condition possible, focusing primarily on his upper body, for if his legs finally went, that would be all he would be left with.

"You've been looking for someone," the man said.

Stephen wiped his mouth with a handkerchief. "Aye. What care you?" But before the man could answer his query, Stephen added, "And who are you, eh?"

The man smoothed a hand over his black robes, clean and crisp and entirely out of place in this Highland hamlet. Impossibly, the man squared his already square shoulders and announced, "I am Luthias Forsyth, a visitor to this village. And you are?"

"Stephen Ross. A visitor also."

"Ah, good." The man smiled, a perfunctory stretching of thin lips, completely devoid of any real feeling. "We are both strangers here. We should be friends."

Stephen glanced over at Luthias's thugs, who were unsuccessfully trying to blend into the shadows at the back of the room. "You have enough friends, methinks."

Luthias's smile grew, but it was still empty. Stephen imagined that it hurt him to smile that way, as if his lips would split from the strain.

"One can always use more friends," Luthias said through his smile, "when doing the Lord's work."

Stephen considered Luthias, more uneasy than ever. By words and attire the man was clearly a holy man of some sort—or at least imagined himself to be. Stephen's dealings with holy men were generally disastrous. They didn't agree on much past the idea that there was a god, and that's where any similarity in philosophy ended.

Nevertheless, with a blackened corpse on the crossroad and Deidra's whereabouts still a mystery, Stephen couldn't dismiss the man as he'd like to.

He waved a hand at the bench opposite him. "Have a seat then, friend."

Luthias slid onto the bench across from Stephen. "I was told you are a witch hunter."

"News travels fast," Stephen murmured. The tanner must have run straight out his back door to tattle as soon as Stephen was out of sight.

"It's a small village and they feel particularly . . . indebted to me today."

"That was your handiwork at the crossroads, aye?" Stephen queried.

Luthias inclined his head.

Stephen thought he was beginning to understand Luthias's interest in him. Perhaps this wasn't as dangerous as he had initially assumed. If he played the man right, he would get out of this with his skin intact, and a bit of information to boot.

He kept his expression bland. "Am I encroaching on someone's hunting grounds?"

Luthias held up a placating hand, his chin dipping as if to protest, but Stephen pressed on.

"I am not hunting a typical witch—not the kind that sours milk or causes crops to fail. No, I am hunting a rare breed. The *baobhan sith.*"

Luthias's smile returned, but this time it was not entirely dead. There was a spark of something in his eyes. Interest. "I am not concerned, friend. I welcome more warriors in God's army. I only wish to assure myself we are both achieving the very best results for the Lord. The only way to be certain is to share information."

Stephen narrowed his gaze. "What sort of information?"

Luthias spread his palms on the tabletop. "A witch is a complex creature. They can disguise themselves and appear quite normal. Because of this one must have a care not to inadvertently harm the innocent."

Stephen nodded, rubbing at his chin thoughtfully. He could no longer guess where this conversation might lead. Since when was a witch hunter concerned with the innocent? It set him off balance, and he didn't like that.

Luthias continued. "I have spent more than a score of years educating myself, and honing my knowledge of witches and their ways. But I freely admit that there are areas where my expertise is sorely lacking. I'm sure the same applies to you, Mr. Ross. I would very much like to learn more about the *baobhan sith*. If you are willing to share, that is."

Stephen frowned, continuing to rub at his whiskered jaw. He thought it unwise to appear eager. After a long moment he said, "So you want me to teach you what I know?"

Luthias gave a dry, humorless laugh. "Well, aye. But more important is what I can teach you."

Stephen smirked. "You believe there is actually something you know that I am ignorant of?"

"Most assuredly." Luthias glanced around them, then leaned forward slightly and said in a low voice, "I am writing a book . . . a sort of . . . supplement to *Malleus Maleficarum,* if you will."

"A book, eh?" Stephen was mildly amused. But this man's knowledge could be useful on many levels, and since he was clearly the source of the villagers' odd, subdued behavior, he was likely the only one who would actually tell him Deidra's whereabouts.

Stephen nodded slowly, as if the decision had been a weighty one to consider. "Very well. Show me what you've got."

Stephen didn't know what to expect of Luthias's "teaching." Considering the subject matter and the tavern wench's reluctance to talk about Deidra, he feared the worst.

They stepped out into the cool, moonlit night. Duke rose from where he had been waiting patiently and danced around Stephen's legs, yipping. Stephen scratched his head and crossed to Countess. He removed his ebony cane from where he'd tied it to the saddle.

"Where are we headed?" he asked, leaning on the cane.

Luthias surveyed him critically, his gaze lingering on the cane. "I do not believe a walk to the crossroads would be wise tonight. I can gather the ashes tomorrow."

Stephen couldn't fathom what he meant by that, but he was glad he wouldn't be forced to hike back to the crossroads tonight. It was cold, and his back throbbed angrily. What he really wanted was some whisky and a bed—and maybe a whore willing to rub the knots from his back for the right price.

They made their way slowly down the dark, dusty street. Luthias kept pace with Stephen's slower, limping gait. Stephen considered asking about the ashes but decided against it. Luthias assumed he was also a witch hunter, which meant he expected Stephen to be knowledgeable in matters of the hunt. Since Luthias offered no further explanation on the gathering of ashes, Stephen could only conclude it was a common aspect of witch hunting and not worthy of comment. He would only reveal himself as a novice or, worse, an imposter, if he asked about it.

"What brought you here?" Stephen asked. "Yon witch at crossroads?"

"Not precisely," Luthias said. He strolled beside Stephen, tall and ramrod straight. "I actually came for another witch but did not find her immediately." He held up an instructive finger. "However, God always provides. He made my visit purposeful. He placed another witch in front of me to detain me here, keeping me in the path of the one I sought."

The uncomfortable uneasiness returned to Stephen's belly. Whatever it was that Luthias wanted to show him would not be pleasant. "How do you mean?"

"I arrived here to find that several local rustics had fallen ill with a strange malady. Strange because it was unlike aught I'd witnessed before—"

"You're a physician, too? Have you seen a great many ailments?"

Luthias hesitated, frowning with disapproval at the interruption. "No," he answered, drawing out the single syllable. "I am not a physician, but I have seen much illness and death in my life."

Caused it, no doubt.

"The victims' eyes were swollen shut and their entire bodies had swollen like bladders." His lip curled. "It was really quite disgusting."

"What led you to believe this was an act of witchcraft?" Stephen pointed the tip of his cane toward the crossroads, invisible in the darkness.

"I questioned one of the victims, then others, and discovered that all of the men had fornicated with the witch. During the questioning it was revealed that she had bewitched them—"

Stephen put his cane out, stopping Luthias. "These men were all married, correct?"

Brow furrowed, Luthias stared down at the cane held across his chest, then fixed his gaze on Stephen.

"Aye."

Stephen lowered the cane.

"Why do you ask?"

Stephen smiled. "I have found that married men are unusually predisposed to bewitchment."

Luthias nodded wisely. "Aye, I have noted this too."

And yet the witch hunter had drawn no other conclusion than believing that the men must have been telling the truth. They couldn't possibly have been lying to keep their wives from gelding them.

Stephen limped forward. "How did you discover the fornication?"

"The witch attempted to bewitch me during the interrogation, but I am immune to such magic. So I inferred that she had done so before. When I probed deeper, I found that aye, it was so." His narrow chest puffed out when he said the last.

Stephen raised his brows and nodded appreciably. "Immune, eh? Interesting. Once she realized you were immune, she then told you everything?"

"Aye—and with a wee bit of help from the Lord."

"Prayer?"

"Ah, no." Luthias seemed confused by Stephen's question. Apparently prayer was not an aspect of witch hunting.

Stephen stopped in his tracks. "What then, if not the Lord's word?"

"I never said that I didn't use the Lord's word—just not that alone. I also dunked her in the loch and laid stones on her chest." He cocked his head to the side. "Do you use prayer alone?"

Stephen nodded. "Naught else works on the *baobhan sith*. You see, you cannot harm them. They heal rapidly and do not die. So torture is useless. But they are evil, and God's word curdles their blood."

They stood beside a large house, the largest in the village. On the ground at their feet was a wooden grate. Luthias stared down at it, deep in thought, and too late Stephen realized the error of what he'd said.

"Blood witches have healing magic?" Luthias asked in a tight voice, his eyes locked on the grating.

Stephen gritted his teeth, but there was no turning back now. To recant would only introduce suspicion.

"Aye," he answered faintly.

Luthias's nostrils flared. He was breathing hard, impassioned. "What you are about to see is the culmination of more than a decade of work. The final chapter in my book."

Stephen nodded at the grating. "That? In there?"

"Aye, I was a godly man before I became a witch hunter, but I found my calling when our parish became infested with witches and I was recruited to help smoke them out. I realized then I had a gift. God would not give me such a gift, then not expect me to use it in his service. But one day I was presented with a dilemma, something that in all my years of interrogating witches I had never encountered. White witches. Until that day I would never have believed such a thing existed. But their child . . ." His gaze turned back to the grate. "Their child was the spawn of evil. It taunted me, tried to kill me. But God protected me. Saved me so that I could keep the evil in check. Brought me here so that I could finally smote it out."

He gestured into the darkness, and three of his mercenaries materialized. "Bring her up. It's time for a little talk." One of the men reached for the grate, but Luthias held up a hand. "First lock up the dog."

Duke sat beside Stephen's cane and looked up at them, as if he knew he was being discussed.

One of the mercenaries looped a rope around Duke's neck. The dog's lip immediately curled, and a low growl emanated from his chest as he set his haunches to resist.

Stephen placed a hand on Duke's head to soothe him. "It's all right, laddy—go on."

Duke whined but let the man lead him away.

The other two men descended into the hole. Stephen's jaw grew rigid. If Luthias's story hadn't convinced him, the removal of Duke made it clear that the witch being held captive in the hole before them was Deidra. This might go very bad for them both if she recognized him.

His pulse sped up as he waited for the men to emerge from the hole with Deidra. Though he schooled his expression to show nothing, his mind played out various scenarios. In his mind he was able and quick: heroic. But he knew the truth. In every scenario he could imagine they both ended up dead because he was a cripple.

The ladder creaked as they ascended. His mouth dried out when the first head appeared. One of Luthias's men crawled out of the hole. He turned and grasped a pair of delicate wrists, forcibly hauling a slight woman out of the hole and setting her on her feet in the moonlight.

It was Deidra, looking as skittish as a rabbit. She shrugged the man's hands off her and turned, her gaze passing over Stephen to Luthias before jerking back, eyes wide with shock and recognition.

Stephen's heart sank. He turned to gauge the damage, but Luthias had not been watching Deidra. His gaze was on Stephen.

"It calls itself Deidra MacKay. Have you heard of the Strathwick MacKays?"

Stephen nodded, frowning. "Aye, I have . . . In fact," he said, getting an idea that he hoped would buy them some time, "I've seen this woman before."

Luthias drew back, looking from Stephen to Deidra with suspicion. "You *know* her?"

Nothing showed on Deidra's face now except fear. She huddled back against the man who held her, watching Luthias.

"I don't know her. I've seen her before. Her father is a healer, known throughout the Highlands. I went to him to cure my mangled back, but, as it turned out, he was naught but a charlatan."

He hoped that his statement would fix any damage he'd done to the MacKays by his earlier careless remarks, as well as explain Deidra's recognition of him.

"Charlatan?" Luthias said dubiously. "I don't understand why William MacKay could not heal you, but I have seen the MacKay magic with my own eyes. It is not false."

"Really?" Stephen said, and this time it was his voice that held doubt and disbelief, though in reality he was dismayed. "Hmmm . . . are you certain of what you saw? Some frauds are gifted in the arts of chicanery."

Luthias shook his head. "No. I *saw* it. With my own eyes. Do you not believe me? Do you think I do not know what magic looks like? What do you think it is I spend my life doing?"

Stephen didn't know how to respond, especially since the witch-pricker was beginning to sound offended. He glanced at Deidra. She watched him, her face clear of aught but wariness. *Good girl.*

Stephen rubbed at his jaw meditatively. "If he was a witch, why did you not try him? I don't think I comprehend."

Luthias's lips drew into a thin line, and he lifted his chin slightly. "Because he is the one I believed was a white witch, or some sort of saint."

Stephen raised a brow, not liking the sound of that. "Your opinion has changed?"

Luthias nodded. He was looking not at Stephen but at Deidra, his intense gaze fixed on her, his eyes narrowed.

She shrank farther back from him and looked as if

she'd bolt if not for the two enormous men who held her captive between them.

"I did not know of the *baobhan sith* until today. I had heard of them, but I'd thought it was a story, not real. You have shown me much today, Mr. Ross. I fear I have been deluded all of these years. The MacKay was no saint at all but a *baobhan sith*."

That was *not* what Stephen had intended. Before he could say a word, Deidra screamed, "Falsehoods!" She surged forward, straining against her captors as if she would attack Luthias. "My father is a great man! And he is good, unlike you. You are an evil murderer, doing the devil's work, and you don't even know it. *You* are the one bewitched."

"She speaks," Stephen said lightly, smiling. He turned to Luthias and was chilled by the hatred and hunger he saw in the other man's countenance as he gazed upon Deidra. This went beyond duty to the Lord; he *wanted* her. She was his obsession, the thing he had worked for. And this was his moment, the one that made all the waiting worthwhile. Stephen understood that there was nothing short of his or Deidra's death that would stop this now that it had started.

Stephen looked between the two of them, trying to stem his rising anxiety. He wanted to snatch her away, get her as far from this place and this man as possible. But that would not be happening, of course. He was a cripple, and nothing but his wits would save them tonight . . . which didn't leave him feeling particularly optimistic about their chances.

"I have met the MacKay," Stephen said, "touched him, in fact. He is no blood witch."

Luthias turned to face him. "How can you be so sure? He was able to heal himself, as you claim blood witches do."

"Blood witches have many characteristics. She is his daughter, correct?" Stephen moved to stand before her and touched a lock of her curling chestnut hair where it brushed against her cheek.

"Aye."

"Then she would be a blood witch, too." This was not something he knew at all. Did blood witches reproduce in the traditional way? He didn't think so, but then again, he didn't know. He knew, however, that Luthias did not know, so he could fabricate whatever he wished where blood witches were concerned.

Luthias's brow furrowed. "You are sure of this? How does one identify a blood witch? Dunking?"

Stephen shook his head and waved a dismissive hand. "No. Torture has no effect on them. She may cry and scream like a mortal woman, but it is all an act."

"That is no different from other witches." Luthias stared at Deidra, deep in thought. "If traditional methods do not work, what does?"

"Prayer. Holy objects."

"Idolatry," Luthias hissed, scandalized. "Heresy."

Stephen raised a shoulder. "Sometimes God chooses to work through these instruments. But primarily it is his word."

Luthias considered Deidra carefully, his jaw working. Finally he said, "Let us try my way first."

Stephen's muscles went rigid as the whites of Deidra's eyes flashed at him, but he just shrugged. *Damn.* He'd hoped to save her from this, to buy them some time so he could think of a better plan.

Luthias gestured to the mercenaries to lead her away, then followed more slowly, keeping pace with Stephen.

"What manner of witchcraft does this woman do?" Stephen asked.

To Stephen's surprise, the thin man shuddered. "She has the devil's own powers to command beasts to do her bidding."

"Truly? Why doesn't she call on them now to aid her?"

Luthias tapped a finger against his temple and smiled. "Because I am wiser this time. She nearly killed me the last time I trapped her. She had me surrounded by wolves, and the only thing that saved me was a knife to her throat."

Stephen asked, aghast, "She was only a child then, aye?"

Luthias snorted. "A demon in disguise. I do not make the same mistakes twice. All the beasts in this village have been restrained. I have men surrounding the hamlet, ready to kill any wild creature that dares to enter."

Stephen forced a smile. "You have certainly prepared for this moment."

They stopped in front of a stone cottage. Luthias's gaze fixed on some faraway point, and he inhaled deeply. "Aye, I have. I feel as if God has been preparing me for this my whole life."

Looking into the man's passion-glazed eyes, Stephen said a silent prayer for them both. They were well and truly trapped.

Deidra had been stuck down in that hole for hours and had hated every single moment . . . and yet she had been nauseated with fear anticipating when Luthias would finally come for her. When the men had finally come, she'd fought them, terrified and confused. It had been too soon! She hadn't been ready yet! Memories of her father's interrogation had crashed through her mind, fresh and vivid as if it had just happened yesterday instead of twelve years ago. She saw his hand, trapped in the pilliwinkes as Luthias drove wedges into the device with a mallet—the bright red of his blood, the wet crunch, the smell of his sweat and grunts of pain. She had been the reason for his suffering because he'd been so afraid of what Luthias would have done to her if he hadn't submitted.

And so she'd fought Luthias's men with mindless panic, knowing she couldn't win, but fighting the inevitable anyway. She'd known what came next; everyone knew. Torture and death. If you were lucky, they might strangle you before they burned you. The men had laughed at her ineffectual struggles until she'd landed a good kick in the fat one's crotch. So he'd backhanded her, dazing her enough to shove her up the ladder and into the cool night air.

Luthias had been waiting for her there, and he'd not been alone.

Stephen was here. A painful arrow of hope shot

through her. But how could he possibly help her without incriminating himself? It was hopeless. Luthias was too powerful.

And yet, *he came, he tried.* He gave her hope. Her heart seemed to swell with hope and something else—affection for him.

After her initial shock, she'd managed to mask her surprise, but Stephen had seen it and played it off beautifully. She wanted to throw her arms around him and kiss him.

She was shoved into a small cottage reminiscent of the one Luthias had tortured her father in while she'd cowered behind his chair. Panic seized her again, gripped her by the throat. She turned and tried to duck beneath their arms, but they shoved her across the room.

She crouched on the floor of the small dark cottage with the two guards, waiting for Stephen and Luthias to join them. One of the men went around the room lighting lanterns. The yellow light did nothing to dispel the shadows from the corners. It lent a dingy hue to the rough table and benches that inhabited the sparsely furnished room. A blanket strung from a rope served as a screen dividing the room into sleeping and living quarters.

Deidra clasped her hands together in an attempt to quiet her uncontrollable trembling, but it did no good. By the time Luthias and Stephen entered, she had to clench her teeth together to hide their chattering. Stephen's grim countenance—tight jaw, averted gaze—did nothing to improve her shaking.

She had broken with her conscience while imprisoned in the damp hole. She had called to the animals. And they had not answered. Perhaps it had been too many years and they no longer understood her. She didn't know the reason. She knew they still talked to her, that they still sensed something in her, because even though she had worked most of her life to ignore them, she was still sometimes unsuccessful. But it had been more than a decade since she had talked back. Maybe she had forgotten how.

Nevertheless, they'd always been there, a dull noise in the back of her mind, but now there was nothing but silence. They had abandoned her, just as she had abandoned them.

"Have a seat, Miss MacKay." Luthias gestured to a bench against the wall.

Deidra didn't move. Her gaze fixed on the bench across the room, just like the one where her father had once sat. She scanned the room, her gaze falling on the table a few feet away. A towel was spread on the table, concealing something beneath, but she could see the outline of long implements—knives and other instruments for poking and cutting.

She was rooted to the floor, her gaze fixed on the table, her heart throbbing in her throat. Her breath wheezed out of her as if her throat was too small, and her knees weakened.

Hands grabbed at her arms, dragging her to the bench. Panic unfolded in her chest, its wings beating frantically. Her gaze fell on Stephen as the men's hands pressed on her shoulders, forcing her to sit. *Do something.* But what could he do?

"No!" she cried and fought against them, twisting so that instead she dropped to her knees. "No!"

Stephen watched, face expressionless, hands clasped behind his back. He could not help her now. Perhaps he could later, but to do something now would be foolhardy and the death of them both. They both knew she would not die from whatever Luthias did to her today. And if the result of the torture was bad, and they could get her to her father before the wounds healed, she could be as good as new.

But that was a big *if*.

She swallowed hard and rose to her feet. She was about to obey Luthias's command to sit on the bench when she caught the almost imperceptible shake of Stephen's head. She hesitated, uncertain of what that negative head shake meant. Was he telling her to disobey? To continue her defiance?

She turned her attention to Luthias, who watched her patiently, his chin raised slightly. He assumed obedience.

They were stronger than she was, every one of them. They could force her to do anything they wanted . . . if she was cognizant. *If she was cognizant.* They couldn't make her do a single thing if she was unconscious.

She made her decision. They couldn't very well interrogate her if she was insensible. But Luthias was a savvy man and would not easily be fooled. Pretending was too dangerous and would probably net her more harm. So rather than even try, she released the thread of control that had held back the flood of panic threatening to overwhelm her.

She thrust herself backwards, away from the bench as the men shoved her forward. They grasped her arms and tried forcing her to the bench. She went wild, screaming, kicking, scratching, biting. She let the fear and wildness take her. There was nothing she wouldn't do now that she'd released it. The men yelled at her. Luthias yelled at her. She understood nothing over the roaring in her ears. She fought so violently that she hurt herself. Pulled so forcefully, she felt a pop, and then her body hung bonelessly between the men. A scream of pain rose in her throat, choking her and mixing with helpless cries of fear.

Her limp worm-arm was yanked. Her head exploded with pain, enveloping her in a black, hot cloud, pushing it all away and sending her sinking into blissful unconsciousness.

Chapter 6

Stephen, Luthias, and the two mercenaries stared down at the woman on the floor, all of them equally stunned by what had just transpired.

Stephen had known Deidra was an exceptionally bright woman. She had read him well. *Too* well. He had wanted her to fake a faint, but she'd done far more, rightly assuming a man like Luthias could tell the difference and would test it if he was uncertain. So she dislocated her own shoulder, collapsing into a heap and leaving her captor to stand there holding her arm awkwardly. It was all Stephen could do to stop himself from shoving the man out of the way.

But he held back, staring dumbfounded with the rest of them at the crumpled woman on the floor. Her hair was wild, her face scratched and bleeding. She looked the part of the crazy village witch.

"Jesus God," Luthias muttered. "Methinks she has a bit of the beast in her."

Stephen rubbed a hand over his face and let out an amazed breath. "There'll be no interrogation tonight. Is there a healer who can tend to her arm?"

Stephen noticed the look the mercenaries exchanged. Luthias's lips pursed together as he shook his head.

Stephen raised his brows. "Och, was that her? At the crossroads? You burned the village healer?"

Luthias's brows lowered. "She was a witch and would have done us no good anyway. *Healer.*" He spat out the word. "A pretty word to hide what they truly do—poison their innocent victims with evil."

Stephen sighed, but he didn't feel exasperated at all. God rest her soul, but the healer's death was the best thing that could have happened to Stephen and Deidra.

"Carry her to the cot," Stephen ordered the men.

One of the men obeyed without question, picking her up and carrying her across the room to where a blanket hung.

Luthias crossed to a table Stephen hadn't noticed and threw back a towel. Silver instruments gleamed in the faint lantern light. Knives, pointed rods, clawlike implements. Luthias examined them, his brow wrinkled in thought, then selected a long, pointed pick.

Stephen clenched his fist, his chest tightening, but only asked, "What are you doing?"

"Making certain," Luthias murmured. He approached the cot and stood over her. Without warning, he jabbed Deidra in the thigh. She didn't move. Stephen bit the inside of his mouth, his muscles rigid. *That's enough.* Luthias jabbed again.

"I think she's out," Stephen said conversationally, though in truth he was ready to toss the man across the room.

Luthias watched her a few seconds longer before nodding and taking a step back. "Aye, you're right."

"Leave her," Stephen said. "If she's a blood witch, the shoulder will heal itself in a day or so. If she is not, it will swell. She'll be in such pain that a mere touch will cause her excruciating agony." He shrugged. "Should make interrogation effortless."

Luthias nodded thoughtfully. "We'll set a guard on her." He extended an arm toward Stephen, open-palmed. "Come, let us find a meal and a bed and take up where we left off on the morrow."

Deidra's eyes opened to thick blackness. She did not know where she was or how she'd gotten there. No lanterns were lit. Her entire body—*nay,* her entire world—had been reduced to the screaming pain in her shoulder. Her stomach heaved and she tried to roll to her side, afraid she would choke on her own vomit, but she couldn't move without pain exploding throughout her body like a shock.

She lay still, drifting in and out of delirium. Animals inhabited her mind, small ones. They came to her, inquiring, feeling her presence. She heard them scuttling beneath her cot. Most had busy, senseless thoughts, focused on food and predators. But there were other, more intelligent thoughts interspersed with the mindless. The rats.

When she was a child, rats had been secret companions to Deidra. They were intelligent animals. Curious and friendly, with good memories. She had shut them out for so long that it was a comfort to hear their thoughts in her head again.

She asked them if men were near. The answer came quickly enough—a man stood outside, in front of the cottage. Deidra's head rolled to the side. She tried to think of how she could use the rats, but the pain was too much; she could barely think. The rat scratched at the cot legs, trying to climb up to her. She warned it away and it dropped back to the ground.

She drifted again into the fog of pain. Time had no meaning. She sensed so many different animals now that her mind was wide open. Some were aware of her, others were just there, and her mind marked them, though they were not aware of her. Duke was near. Her horse, which had a name, but she did not know it. Countess was here also, securely tied and hobbled. When their minds touched, the horse grew excited.

Deidra's mind was wandering aimlessly through a confused fog when a familiar voice suddenly brought it all back into focus.

"Deidra."

Her eyes fluttered open. It was still dark. A blanket hung between her cot and the rest of the room, shutting out all of the windows and blocking any light.

"Stephen?" She tried to say his name but it came out a croaking mumble through her cracked and dry lips. Her tongue seemed too large for her mouth.

"Here, drink this," he whispered near her ear.

A cup pressed to her bottom lip and a cool beverage slid down her dry throat. She sucked at it greedily. It soothed her parched tongue. He pulled it away too soon. The drink left behind a bitter taste, but she didn't care—she felt better already.

"Let it settle," he whispered. "I'll give you more in a moment, when I know you won't bring it right back up."

She was almost giddy from the sound of his voice, the exquisite comfort she felt from his mere presence. It almost made the pain and fear bearable.

"How are you here?" she asked, her voice cracking on every word. "He'll discover us. It can't be safe."

"The guard offered me twenty minutes alone with you for two crowns. I gave him five. He won't bother us."

A jolt of shocked disgust shot through her. "*What?*"

"Aye, sick bastards, but it is common enough, and it is why I must get you out of here tonight. Believe me when I say that I will not be the last he makes the offer to."

Deidra squeezed her eyes shut, a new horror entering her world. Men would pay to rape her before they burned her. That man out there would make profit off of her violation when she was helpless. It was vile. She thanked God for Stephen. Thanked him for sending her to him first before she started this foolish quest. She wanted to ask him why he'd come for her, why he was doing this when she'd abandoned him, but she was afraid of his answer.

For her father, for her family. Not for her.

His hand slid beneath her neck, tilting her head up. "Here, drink some more."

She sipped at the drink. Whatever it was, it was drugged. She tasted it now, but she didn't care. Anything to take the edge off her agony.

He withdrew the cup again and she asked, "Will there be more men after you leave?"

"No." He ground the word out in such a way that the single word was infused with so much conviction, such arrogant knowledge, that she almost smiled. He added, "You won't be here anyway."

Her heart sped and she reached for him with her good arm. He caught her hand in the darkness and brought it down to rest on her belly, enveloped in his. He was an anchor. She felt grounded with him here, beside her, holding onto her.

"How?" she whispered. "I'm not even sure I can walk."

"You'll be able to run when I'm finished with you." She heard a smile in his voice. "Drink more."

She did as he bid. Her body relaxed as the drug took effect. Her pain began to recede. His fingers were warm around hers, strong and reassuring. She trusted him completely, she realized. She would do whatever he asked of her right now. It felt strange and foreign to give her trust away so thoroughly, but nevertheless she was.

Her head was thick and pleasantly fuzzy, so without a thought, she said, "Stephen, I am afraid."

Before tonight, she would never have admitted such a thing to anyone. But now it seemed natural to share such things with him.

"I know," he said. "But I won't let anything happen to you. I vow it."

His voice, his promise, caressed her ears, the most beautiful thing she'd ever heard. His breath feathered against her cheek, his lips pressed a kiss to her forehead. She tilted her head so that his lips brushed her nose. He paused. His breath was uneven against her face. He didn't ask what she was doing, or what she wanted. He knew. His mouth touched hers, warm and inviting, and she drank him in, deeper than the drug that loosened her limbs.

His kiss was long and deep, tasting and probing. She made a soft sound, a moan of longing. It came from deep in her chest. He pulled away too quickly.

She wanted to whimper and plead, but she did not.

He sighed deeply, regret in his exhalation. "This is going to hurt."

Before she could ask what he meant, he took her wrist in one hand and placed the other on her shoulder. He gave a push and a twist, and it felt as if her shoulder had been skewered with a red-hot poker. Pain radiated through her body, all encompassing. She couldn't suck in enough air, and she lost consciousness.

When she woke it was still dark. She blinked and turned her head toward where she'd last seen Stephen.

"I'm here," he said, as if reading her mind. "Try moving your shoulder."

Her jaw tightened. The memory of the pain she had experienced before fainting came flooding back. She didn't want to move it. It would hurt too much. But she knew he'd only done what he'd felt necessary, so with a small grunt, she forced her arm to move.

And was astonished when it did. It hurt, quite badly still, but it was not beyond movement. In fact, at the moment the pain was completely bearable.

"You fixed it," she breathed, pushing herself to a sitting position. "How did you fix it?"

"It matters not now. Listen very carefully. We are running out of night, and darkness is our only friend. When I distract the guard I want you to quickly slip out the door and around the side of the cottage. From there you must tread carefully. Luthias has locked away most of the village's animals to protect himself from you, but there might still be some animals that could give away your presence." His hand closed over hers, hard and urgent. "You must speak to them, Deidra, let them know you mean no harm and they must be quiet."

She nodded.

His hand continued to grip hers firmly. "Get as far away as you can before dawn. I don't care how you manage it—steal a horse if you must, run all night—it matters not, just move fast and do not stop. No rests. Continue northwest until you arrive at Drake's lands. Only then should you rest. Once—"

"Wait!" Deidra hissed, overwhelmed by his insistent instructions. "Were will you be? Must I do this alone?"

His hand tightened on hers. "Aye, you must. I will stay here and send Luthias's witch hunt in the opposite direction. Away from you."

Panic streaked through her. She grabbed his arms, clinging to him. "No! I'm not leaving you. The guard will tell—I don't care how much you paid him. I'm a witch and you're the last one with me before I escape. Luthias will torture him and he will tell."

"No, he won't. He will disappear tonight, never to be seen again. They will assume you did it, some sort of witchcraft." He paused. "Besides, you didn't have any problem leaving me before."

Her eyes burned and her breath caught. She released him abruptly, angry and hurt that he would throw that in her face, yet knowing he was right. "That was different," she said, her voice a choked whisper.

He let out a rueful breath. "No, it was just the same. I slowed you down then and I still will. Nothing has changed. I am a cripple."

"I'm a cripple now, too."

His soft laugh was bitter. "You're hardly a cripple. Even with a sore shoulder you can move twice as fast as I can." His tone changed, deeply serious. "Make no mistake. Your shoulder feels better now, but it will swell and stiffen. Willow bark is the best thing for it; have Drake brew you some. But you must keep moving; it will keep the stiffness at bay, for a while at least."

Her eyes burned, her face felt hot and tight. Terror froze her limbs. She didn't want to leave him, to do this alone.

He gripped both of her hands. "You're strong and smart and beautiful, Deidra MacKay. You'll be fine. You do not need me or any other man."

She sniffed. That might or might not be true, but she still wanted one—she wanted this one. "What will you tell them?" she asked.

"When it is discovered you've escaped and the guard disappeared, I will tell them that I was correct—you are a blood witch. You healed yourself, then transformed your guard and yourself into animals to escape."

"Can blood witches do that?"

"I know not—but neither do they."

Deidra shut her eyes tightly, her heart contracting painfully in her chest. His boots scraped as he stood.

"Let's go."

He helped her to her feet. Pain radiated through her shoulder, but it was contained to her shoulder and she could move. She was no longer immobilized with pain. She became aware of a burning in her thigh. She lifted her skirt and touched the top of her thigh. It was crusted and tender.

"What happened to my leg?"

"Luthias stabbed you . . . to be sure you were truly insensible. You'll need to take care of it as soon as you're safe."

She dropped her skirt. She wanted to protest, to insist he come with her, but he was safer this way. If caught aiding her, he would be tried with her. And his idea to send them in the wrong direction was an excellent one. Perhaps when they didn't find her quickly he would be able to leave and join her at Drake's.

He led her to the door. She noticed that his limp was more pronounced, and guilt stabbed her afresh. No doubt her predicament had put additional strain on him. When had he last slept? He was right; he truly would slow her down.

Oddly, that knowledge did nothing to dampen her desire to be with him. It was strange that she had formed such a strong attachment to him. In spite of his back, he made her feel safe and cared for: wanted. It moved something deep in her chest that he'd gone to so much trouble for her, placed himself in such danger.

He cracked the door, and a sliver of moonlight limned his profile, strong and handsome. What had he been like before the accident? As a whole man, he would have been beyond the reach of someone like Deidra MacKay, but now, altered as he was, he saw her and cared for her.

He closed the door and turned to her. "Are you ready?"

She closed the distance between them and placed her palm against his chest. He went very still. She lifted onto her tiptoes and pressed her lips to his. For a single heartbeat he did nothing. He didn't move or breathe. Then his arms came up around her, pulling her into him, his mouth warm and soft. She clung to him with her good arm, fear and lust twisting into something sharp in her belly. She was afraid of what would happen next, of losing this man and this feeling. His hands moved up her back as he kissed her, his tongue sliding warmly against hers. She shuddered, the sensations whipping through her, new and delicious.

When his hands cupped her shoulders, pain seared through her like a jagged piece of glass. She turned her head with a small cry, ending their kiss as she buried her head in his shoulder.

His whispered apologies ruffled the curls at her temple. His arms still held her, but delicately now, as if she were fragile as an eggshell.

"I'm fine," she said when she regained her breath. And she was—at least in comparison to how she'd felt earlier.

He set her away from him, his hands still rubbing her shoulders gently.

"You should go before the joint swells any more. Go to Drake and all will be fine. He can protect you." He pressed a fervent, lingering kiss to her forehead. Her heart reached out to him. What if she never saw him again?

As if reading her thoughts, he said, "I will see you again, Deidra, I vow it."

She nodded. She choked on the words; they stuck in her throat. There was so much she suddenly wanted to say to him, but there was no time.

He turned back to the door. After another brief peek outside, he opened the door wider.

"Now go," he said in an urgent whisper. "Around the west side of the cottage—and do not stop until dawn."

He pushed her in the center of her back, breaking her inertia. She was out the door and moving quickly but silently around the side of the house. Her steps were inaudible in the soft grass.

She trusted him to take care of the guard, trusted him so much that she never even looked back. She turned the corner of the house and headed north. The cottage was on the edge of a cluster of cottages. She only had to pass two more unseen, and then another hundred yards to the fields, where the wheat was tall enough to hide her if she bent low. And beyond that, the wood.

When she was at the last cottage, pressed against the outer wall, she finally looked back. But not because she was afraid or worried; because of the longing that tugged at her heart. She didn't want to go on without him. What would happen if Luthias figured it out? What would he do to Stephen?

So intense was the worry and longing that she almost turned back, but she stopped herself. He had gone through a great deal to help her. Her return could ruin everything.

She believed in his promise to see her again. She took a deep, cleansing breath and braced her shoulder with her hand—then ran as fast as she could toward the wheat and freedom.

Chapter 7

⊗⊗⊗

Wake. Wake. Danger. Hide.

Deidra's eyelashes fluttered.

Wake. Now.

She came awake immediately and lay very still. The moon hung low overhead, visible between a gap in the trees. She turned her head toward her companion.

The wolf stood just outside the pale light of the moon. She watched Deidra, eyes gleaming yellow.

Deidra had decided, while hiding in the waist-high wheat, breath sawing in and out of her burning lungs, that since she was suffering for magic she didn't even use, there was no more sense denying it. She was damned no matter what she did, so she might as well embrace it. Then, at least, if she burned for it, they would be justified.

She asked the wolf where the danger lay.

Animals did not communicate as humans did. There was no east or west to them; they did not perceive direction in such concrete terms. The wolf communicated senses and thoughts to her. This wolf sensed danger from the direction of the village she'd escaped from the night before. They were after her.

Time to move.

She was on her feet, but unafraid. As long as she remained aware of her surroundings, she could stay one step ahead of the danger. The animals would help her with that.

The wolf turned and disappeared into the trees. Deidra followed. The wolf had come to her last night, in a dream, and when she'd awakened, there had been her new friend, sitting nearby, watching her. It didn't frighten her at all. Such things happened to her frequently. In the past she'd ignored it, which had puzzled the animals, since she had communicated with them in her sleep.

The wolf had a keen sense of direction and was able to understand where Deidra wanted to go. It had led her all day yesterday and had even fed her, bringing her a dead hare as an offering. Deidra normally did not eat flesh, but she made an exception out of respect to the wolf and uncertainty about her next meal. It had apparently watched over her all night.

Deidra didn't want to imagine what Luthias would make of this new development. Nothing that he didn't already believe, she supposed. It was too late to even care. She'd made her decision, and there was no going back.

Leaves and twigs crunched and cracked underfoot, sounding obscenely loud in the silent forest. Her wolf companion tread silently, not a single sound coming from her soft padding. Deidra paused, suddenly aware of how odd the absolute silence was. No a single sound, not even the soft buzzing of insects, broke the quiet. She scanned her surroundings cautiously, over-whelmed with the sensation of being watched. She looked at the wolf, but her friend had disappeared.

Deidra's heart leaped, and she called out to the wolf in her mind, panicked at being alone. A branch snapped loudly to her right. Deidra whirled toward the sound.

A boy appeared from the trees and froze the moment he sighted Deidra. His eyes widened so that the whites glared at her and his mouth opened and closed, though no sound issued forth.

Deidra shook her head frantically. "No, no. *Shhh!*"

But the boy paid her protest no mind—he was working up a scream. He dropped the bow he held and opened his mouth, his chest rising in spasmodic gasps as he prepared to let loose. But before a single sound issued forth from his lips, the wolf flew out of the trees and knocked the boy off his feet.

A shock reverberated through Deidra, almost as if the wolf had attacked her, and she rushed forward. *No,* her mind screamed at the wolf, but it was too late. The boy had never had a chance. His feet twitched, then went still.

Deidra froze, hands clapped to her mouth. *No, no, no, oh, God no.* The scream rose in her mind, spiral-ing around so that she thought she might be sick. How could she have been so arrogant, so foolish? *This* was why she'd stopped communicating with animals all those years ago. They thought she was one of them; one of them, but more. A leader, a god, and they pro-tected her as such. Her fingers curled into her face. Did she really think anything had changed? She could not control the beasts.

Her feet were rooted to the ground, her heart squeezing in her chest as she stared at the boy, at his still feet, and the wolf feeding on him, ignoring her pleas to *stop, stop, stop, please stop*. It was ruled by the bloodlust now.

"Adam?" The voice rang out through the trees.

The wolf's bloody snout jerked up, its ears pricked forward. *Danger.*

Run, Deidra ordered. The wolf darted into the trees. This time Deidra touched the creature's mind as it left, assuring herself that it was not just hiding for a new attack. She implored it to keep moving and wait for her somewhere ahead, then prayed that it would obey her this time.

She tried to look away from the lad, from his bloody rended throat glistening wetly in the moonlight. The wolf had done that to protect her. A lone wolf did not attack without provocation. Although she was repulsed, she also knew the wolf was not to blame. It was *her* fault. She had not made her wishes clear.

This . . . this senseless death was what happened when she meddled with things she couldn't control.

"Adam!" The call came again, forcing Deidra to move.

She ran blindly into the wood, following the wolf. Branches slapped at her face, brambles and roots caught at her feet. The sound of her heart and her breath heaving in her chest filled her ears. Her foot caught on a rock and she went down hard.

She lay on the ground, the horror of what she was responsible for wringing sobs of revulsion from her. She didn't have the energy to go on, to even move, so she cried there, face in the dirt, tears wetting the ground until there were no more. And when they finally dried up, she just lay there, exhausted, not having the strength of heart to do any more. She didn't care if they caught her. She deserved it. Perhaps she should go back and give herself up.

A wet, cold nose nuzzled at her hair, and she shrank away. She came to her feet and wiped the wet grime from her face. Yellow eyes stared back at her. Though the wolf could not articulate its thoughts in language, it understood what she contemplated and chastised her for a fool by sending her an image of herself engulfed in flames. The wolf was right; she didn't want to burn.

Time to move again.

After lying motionless on the cold ground, her shoulder and thigh protested movement. She gritted her teeth and ran after the wolf through the night. Her sides ached, her chest burned, her shoulder and arm were one blazing limb of fire, and the wound in her thigh throbbed, but she didn't stop until the black towers of her uncle's stronghold were in sight.

Creaghaven was an ancient keep, destroyed and rebuilt over the years. It sat on a man-made motte and was surrounded by a sea of jagged creags jutting up out of the ground on every side. Even a well-shod horse could not easily make it to the gates, at least not with any speed. And forget about maneuvering siege machines anywhere near the walls. The price of such safety, however, was isolation.

She picked her way wearily through the forest of rocks, limping slowly and wincing when she stepped on a sharp stone protruding from the ground. There was no sign of life outside the castle or on its walls— not even a lit torch. No doubt her uncle had few visitors to this remote and barren location and saw no point in wasting the fuel. She had arrived from the east, through the forest rather than the main road. She'd had to walk the berm and circle the curtain wall before arriving at the front gate. Perhaps they just hadn't seen her.

She pulled the rope that dangled down beside the portcullis. A sharp clang shattered the quiet. She rang twice, then waited.

It was evening; he should be up and about. Even if he wasn't, he had servants who would be.

It seemed a very long time before the porter's window opened in the door beside the gate. An unfamiliar face peered at her from beneath thick brows. It was night, but the moon was bright. Still, they were in the shadows, and his eyes looked like empty black holes burned into his head.

"Whot?" he snapped.

"I am here to see my uncle, Drake MacKay."

The thick brows lowered. "Uncle, eh?" His head moved as he scanned her from head to toe. She didn't imagine he could see much more of her than she could of him. "Your name?"

"Deidra MacKay."

The window slammed shut, and Deidra was left to wait again.

The exercise of travel had kept her warm, but now, waiting in the darkness, the chill seeped through her clothes. She shivered, running her hands up and down her arms.

Drake had always been very different from her father, but he'd never been the "odd" one. No, that had been reserved for William MacKay, a witch. Drake had been born perfectly normal and nonmagical. But nevertheless he had not been able to escape the family's legacy of oddness. It had happened seven years ago, when his wife had died. It had been an unusual situation for many reasons—the first being that friends and family of the MacKays died infrequently. In fact, far less frequently than everyone else. They tended to live to ripe old ages, usually ailment free.

Except Ceara.

Drake had been distraught over his brother's failure. So he'd taken her to a blood witch to make a pact. No one knew anything past that. Whatever had happened, Ceara had died.

Drake had not been the same afterward. His visits had become infrequent and had finally stopped altogether. He'd retreated to this stronghold in the more remote area of the Highlands, and the rumors had flourished. *Drake kept the dead body of his wife preserved in salt and he still searched for a cure. He was mad and didn't realize she was dead. He dressed her corpse and conversed with it.* Deidra didn't believe the stories.

A great amount of time passed while Deidra paced

outside the gate, trying to stay warm and growing increasingly concerned. She was about to ring the bell again when the slide of the latch made her straighten. The door swung open with a creak.

Her uncle filled the doorway, staring down at her as if she was a ghost.

He had changed—so much so that she could only stare at him in astonishment. The first and most remarkable thing that she noted about his appearance was his beard—full and lush and black, it hung down his chest in a tangled riot of curls. His hair had grown long too. He tied it at his nape, but locks of curls escaped to hang beside his face.

They stared at each other for a long moment before Deidra broke the silence with a tentative, "Uncle Drake? Is that you?"

He blinked as if coming out of a dream. "Deidra? What are you doing here?" His voice was rough and cracked when he spoke, as if he didn't do it very often.

Deidra's mouth opened, but nothing came out. She didn't know where to start. Finally she said, "I'm in trouble."

Drake stepped back and opened the door wider so Deidra could enter. She hurried in, the fear and watchfulness falling away like a cloak. She felt safe for the first time in days.

"Are you being followed?" he asked.

"I know not . . . but I don't think so."

He gestured to someone on the walls, and moments later a handful of men appeared. "Secure the perimeter around the castle."

The wolf was still outside the castle. It had become alarmed at her entrance into the curtain walls. Deidra soothed it with her mind and urged it to go out on its own. She warned it about the men and told it to get far away from here. She didn't know if it obeyed.

Drake led her into the keep. It was an old structure, built many years ago. Rather than fireplaces lining the walls like the more modern structures, fire pits ran up the center of the great hall, all of them currently cold.

From the great hall he led her to a staircase. They climbed to the next level. At the top of the stairs was a large room hung with colorful tapestries. Fur rugs covered the floor, and a fire blazed in a new stone fireplace, obviously built within the past decade.

He sat at a long wooden table and gestured for her to do the same. She winced when she sat, and he asked sharply, "You are hurt?"

"My shoulder. Dislocated. Stephen reset it . . . but it still hurts."

Drake nodded and gestured to someone across the room. "A willow bark infusion, posthaste."

The woman returned a few minutes later with a small pot and a cup. She poured the infusion for Deidra and handed her the cup. Deidra smiled gratefully, wrapping her hands around the warm clay and sipping the healing beverage.

"So," he said when she was finally settled in the chair opposite him. "What sort of trouble are you in?"

She recounted the whole story, beginning with Luthias sniffing around Strathwick and ending with her escape from the village.

Drake listened pensively to her tale, combing some of the tangles from his beard with his fingers. His eyes narrowed, and he pointed a finger at her.

"There is something else—something you left out."

How could he know that? Her gaze dropped to her hands, wrapped around the cup. She feared it was all there anyway, all of her sins, written in her eyes. "I . . . I killed a boy."

When he didn't respond, she looked up. His hand had paused in its combing.

"You killed a *boy*? How did such a thing occur?"

She swallowed, eyes downcast again, fixed on the empty bottom of the cup. "I am speaking to the animals again." Her voice was soft, barely above a whisper. "A wolf led me through the forest . . . helped me . . . protected me . . . then killed for me."

"Ah . . ." The word was released on a breath of understanding. "You ordered the wolf to kill the boy."

She shook her head vigorously. "No, never."

"So the wolf killed the boy without your consent?"

Her head jerked up, her mouth a thin line. "I did not give my consent, but I may as well have given the order."

"But you didn't. And you wouldn't have, would you?"

Her mouth grew tighter, harder. When she didn't answer him, he smiled grimly.

"No, of course you wouldn't. You're not like me. I'd kill for much less."

Deidra sat back in her chair, taken aback by his admission. He did not elaborate.

"Stop being a martyr and move past it. It wasn't your fault. Trial and error—this is the way of all learning, and you, my dear niece, are relearning your gift."

"It's a life, not an error," she said through gritted teeth. "That boy is *dead*."

Drake smiled back, his white teeth bared in his black beard. "Aye, and we are the MacKays; we play with life and death. That is what we do. So move past it, lass, or you will never make it in this world."

Deidra's lips trembled with anger and guilt, but she said not another word.

After a moment Drake exhaled a loud sigh. "We have two problems. Stephen Ross's safety and your nemesis, Luthias Forsyth. Assuming Stephen is as clever as I recall—"

Deidra nodded confidently. He was very clever. "Oh, he is."

Drake's brow twitched before he continued. "Then he is probably still safe and Luthias thinks they are the very best of friends." He looked skyward, fingers toying with the hair beneath his bottom lip. "There is really only one thing to do. Luthias Forsyth must disappear. Forever."

Deidra swallowed hard and nodded. He was right. She didn't relish the idea of murder, but in this case, if she didn't, he would kill her. And from the way he'd spoken, he no longer had any qualms about coming after her parents. He was a danger to all of them now.

"What about this other notion—of the *baobhan sith*? Have you given up on it now that you're communing with beasts again?"

Deidra sighed and shrugged. "I know not. Stephen is more determined than ever to find the blood witch."

Drake frowned slightly. "What has that to do with you?"

"Well, I . . . I . . . ," she stuttered on for a moment before clamping her lips shut.

He watched her patiently with raised brows.

She exhaled impatiently through her nose and continued, "I don't see what a blood witch could possibly do for him."

"A great deal," Drake said. "End his pain, for one. His back injury—he doesna fake that for sympathy, Dee-dee." He leaned forward, dark blue eyes intense, mouth a grim line in his beard. Only her father and Drake had ever addressed her by that endearment, and she shrank a little in her chair, feeling like a child again. "Do you know what it's like to live alone, to suffer in silence because no one cares?"

Deidra shook her head. "What are you saying? Many people care about Stephen. He is the one who chose to live a recluse, shut away from the love of—"

"Love?" Drake's voice rose angrily. "Pity is *not* the same thing. Do not confuse them."

Pity. Deidra's brows lowered in confusion. They were clearly not speaking only of Stephen.

"Who are you talking about, Uncle Drake? No one pities you. *You* choose to stay away."

He sat back in his chair and looked to the side. "That's because no one understands. No one can ever understand until they live it."

Deidra certainly didn't understand. He was comparing his situation to Stephen's, yet their situations were nothing alike.

"How is becoming a blood-sucking night crawler a good alternative to being a cripple?"

Drake's mouth flattened. "It's better than a half-life or no life at all."

"So you think he should go to the *baobhan sith* and become one?"

Drake turned back toward her, the tight set of his shoulders relaxing as the fight drained out of him. "I know not without talking to Stephen. But it matters not. It would not serve him. She will not help anyway."

The breath left Deidra in a rush. "So the *baobhan sith* is real?"

Drake hesitated a moment before shrugging. "I assume so. In truth, I saw no proof that she was a blood witch. But the surrounding villagers believed she was and left offerings to her."

"Offerings?" Deidra frowned dubiously. "That sounds primitive. Why would they tolerate a witch in such a climate as ours? They could easily have her killed with no repercussions."

Drake smiled. His gaze was fixed on something above and beyond her. "Aye, you'd think. But she has them scared. They said they'd tried it before and it had ended badly for the leaders of the revolt. So now they are obedient wee sheep."

This worried Deidra. It was not safe for Stephen to travel so far and into such treacherous country. Especially if it was all for naught.

"We should try to stop him," Deidra mumbled.

Her uncle gazed at her, his brows drawn together in a perplexed frown. "Methinks, lass, you have more important things to worry about. For instance, how we're going to make Mr. Forsyth disappear."

Deidra's cheeks flamed. She raised her chin and said, "Of course. I thought you had a plan already."

"Well, nothing so solid as stone yet. We need your father. And mayhap Philip Kilpatrick. The earl of Kincreag would be useful too."

Deidra shook her head. "There's no time for that."

"Does your father even know you're here?"

Deidra cast her gaze downward. She had tried very hard not to think of her father. She knew he was worried sick and probably angry that she had not trusted him. She did trust him, but she didn't want him involved with Luthias. She didn't want Luthias's obsession to encompass her father. But it was too late, and the only way to protect her father was to kill Luthias.

"He doesn't know."

Drake cursed under his breath and stood. "Well, we cannot do aught until we send him word and he arrives."

"No." Deidra stood too, palms on the table. "Luthias wants him and Rose now, too. We must leave them out of it. I pray you."

She saw the concern in her uncle's eyes and knew she had won this round.

He nodded thoughtfully. "Whatever we do, we will have to use you as bait."

"Me?" Deidra sagged back in her chair, dread settling on her chest. "Why?"

"Because he is obsessed with you. You are the elixir that frames his existence. He wants you badly enough to do something foolish if he thinks it will gain your capture."

He was correct, of course, though she hated to admit it. "So how do we do that? He doesn't travel alone anymore. He has guards, mercenaries. I don't know how many."

Drake waved this away as insignificant. "I have men, too. I am not worried about his mercenaries. But we do need him somewhere remote. We do not want witnesses."

Deidra felt unclean, sitting here plotting a man's death. But there seemed no other alternative. It was him or her, she reminded herself, so she must get past the guilt. It certainly didn't seem to faze her uncle. He looked thoughtful but not the least bit disturbed.

The boy from the woods appeared in her mind, his face, trying to scream. She squeezed her eyes shut, trying to force the image away, but it was burned in her mind. Maybe she deserved whatever Luthias Forsyth wished to do to her.

Drake stood. "Come, you are tired, no doubt, and in need of a bath and a meal, and more willow bark tea. Once you are clean and fed and get some sleep, your mind will be clearer."

Deidra sighed and rubbed her hands over her face. He was right. She hadn't slept well in weeks. Her shoulder did feel somewhat better, but sleeping in a comfortable bed would speed the healing process more than anything else.

She blearily followed her uncle as he led her through the keep. He deposited her in a small but comfortable room, and moments later a woman came in with soup and bread and fresh water to wash with.

With a full belly and clean face and ears, she slid beneath the fur blankets and tried to sleep. Her eyes burned with exhaustion, her head hurt, but sleep eluded her. The boy . . . had his body been discovered? Did Luthias suspect it was her? Of course he did. And where was Stephen? Was he safe? Or was he paying for helping her with his life? How would she even know?

She touched her mouth, remembering that last kiss and how she'd wanted to cling to him. She sent up a prayer. *If there is a God and He listens to witches, please don't let that be our last kiss.*

Stephen had meant to follow Deidra the very next day. Unfortunately, all that exercise had done nothing for his back. It was stiff and aching, and when he woke that morning he could barely walk without knives of pain shooting down his thighs. There would be no travel for him today.

No, his first priority was laudanum. He had given the last of his stash to Deidra when he'd reset her shoulder. Unfortunately, in a village such as this, there was none to be had, and with the healer gone, there was no one to treat him with the local fauna. In lieu of poppy juice, he usually medicated with whisky, but he couldn't take the chance of acting foolishly and talking out of turn.

There was precious little he could do but bear up

and wait it out. He had expected some questions from Luthias about Deidra's disappearance, but losing the guard had been a stroke of brilliance on Stephen's part. Luthias had assumed her escape had been a product of magic or the guard's treachery. Either way, Stephen was in the clear.

Stephen currently lodged at the baker's, paying a king's ransom for a heather mattress on the floor and as much bread and ale as he cared to eat. Luthias visited him there the next morning.

With the help of the baker's wife, a rolled blanket was pushed beneath Stephen's back so that he could sit. Duke reclined on the floor beside the bed, but when Luthias appeared, the dog got to his feet and trotted out.

Luthias didn't seem to notice. He pulled up a stool and seemed uncharacteristically unaware of his surroundings. He rubbed his hands together, his lips a thin, harsh line, gray eyes darting about the room. His leg jigged nervously.

"You say that the *baobhan sith* are capable of such rapid healing? What of the guard?"

Stephen shrugged. "I know not. Perhaps she turned him into one."

Luthias's head turned sharply as he pinned Stephen with a surprised look. "She can do that? Transform humans into blood witches?"

Stephen nodded.

"And does one then bow to her wishes? Become her slave?"

"Slave?" Stephen considered this. Why not? He was

creating this fiction as he went along anyway. "Aye, though slave isn't exactly how I would term it. They have a will of their own, but they see her as their creator and owe her a debt."

Luthias's slate eyes slanted right and left with alarm. "She could create armies of blood witches, all under her command."

Stephen watched him, trying not to reveal his unease. It seemed everything he said led Luthias to some unanticipated and very unhelpful conclusion. Luthias was becoming genuinely anxious, and in such a man, anxiety led to only one thing: action.

Stephen had to get out of here.

"No doubt she returned to her home, the seat of her power." He would send word to the MacKays, warn them to dispose of this nuisance of a human once and for all, while he found Deidra and went on to the blood witch.

Luthias's gaze focused on something far away. His brows furrowed. "Mayhap not. She can surround herself with underlings and animals any time she pleases. She has no need to go home." He rubbed a hand over his face. "No, I don't believe she has gone far. My men are searching the surrounding wood. I will let you know if we find something."

And he left. The man's obsession irritated Stephen. He would never give up. He would stalk Deidra until one of them was dead. Stephen would make sure it was Luthias.

He prayed she was on her way to Drake's and would soon be safe. In fact, it surprised him to realize how fervently he wished for her safety. She had come to depend on him, and to someone like Stephen that meant a great deal. He would not fail her.

He cursed his back and decided to hell with it—he was going anyway. This was too important. It couldn't wait on his damned back. He packed his things, moving as fast as his pain would allow, and fetched Countess. He was beginning to think they would make it out of the village unharassed when the sound of pounding hooves made him draw rein and bring Countess around to see who followed.

It was Luthias, with a handful of men behind him.

Stephen mentally braced himself but gave the witch hunter a pleasant look. Duke, however, was not inclined to fake it. The dog lowered his front paws and barked incessantly at Luthias.

"Leaving so soon?" Luthias said, nearly shouting to be heard over the din of Duke's barking. "We haven't even found her yet."

Stephen gave Duke a sharp command and the dog fell silent. He lay on his belly, head erect, watching Luthias closely.

"Aye, but I have my own theories. Methinks she returned to her family, so that's where I am headed. And if not . . ." Stephen shrugged. "You said her family is blood witches, too—so I find what I search for either way."

"I wouldn't recommend going there alone."

"I can handle them."

Luthias shook his head, a small smirk on his lips. "Write me if you have any success. I'll add it to my book."

He turned his horse neatly on its hocks—a move that hurt Stephen's back just watching it—and returned to the village with his men.

MacKay lands were actually in the opposite direction from where Stephen really wanted to go. But he couldn't chance leading Luthias toward Drake and Deidra. So he went several miles out of his way before heading west. It would take him longer this way, but there was no help for it.

By the time he stopped for the night, he felt as if he had made no progress at all past killing his back. All he'd done was circle the town—south, then west, and finally north again. He stared into the fire, wondering if it was possible to stop Luthias, wondering if he should turn back now and kill the man with his bare hands. Duke whined and curled closer, as if sensing Stephen's violent thoughts. Stephen sighed and lay back, imagining Deidra's hands on him, rubbing the ache from his muscles and then laying with him, her body pressed close to keep him warm.

They'd gotten lucky this time. Luthias would not be so easily fooled again. And the only way Stephen stood a chance against him was by being a whole man. More than whole.

A *baobhan sith.*

Chapter 8

—∞∞∞—

Two days had passed at Creaghaven, and Deidra was growing restless. Her shoulder had improved. Drake had kept a steady infusion of the willow bark in her belly and urged her to rest. As she had nothing better to do while waiting for Stephen, she complied without argument. Her shoulder still ached and it was a bit tender, but she didn't feel it would hamper travel. If not for Stephen, who knew what condition her shoulder might have been in? That made her laugh. If he had not rescued her, her shoulder would have been the least of her worries. She probably would not even be alive.

Her humor faded in her concern for him. She had spent the morning on the curtain wall, gazing out over Drake's lands as far as the eye could see, searching for Stephen. Was he alive? And if he was, would he come here? Or go straight to the *baobhan sith*? He had vowed that he would see her again. *Vowed*. She believed him. She just didn't know *when* he planned to see her again.

That thought gnawed at her belly. As the day wore on, Deidra grew anxious for action, certain that while she idled about, he'd gone off to see the blood witch without her. That's when she remembered something she had done as a child—a game of sorts. She sent her mind out like a net, touching the minds of animals near and far, trying to determine if they had been startled by a stranger nearby. Not even the most intelligent animal could identify Stephen without having known him before, but they could acknowledge that someone new was nearby.

She was about to give up when a hawk replied with an image of a man on horseback, a black dog trotting along beside them.

Stephen.

And he didn't look well. Countess moved very slowly, and Stephen slumped forward in an unnatural position. She touched Countess's mind and found the horse distressed by her master's behavior. Countess knew something was wrong.

Heart pumping and breath coming in short gasps, Deidra hurried down the ladder and into the stable, crashing into her uncle. He grabbed her shoulders to steady her.

"Ho, now. What is it, lass?"

"Stephen! He's here. And he looks hurt." She wrenched away from him and led her horse from its stall.

Drake grabbed her again. "Wait just a tic, lassie. What mean ye to do? Carry him on your back?"

She tossed curls out of her eyes. "If I must."

"Just calm yourself. Let me get a wagon and we'll go fetch him."

"Get the wagon and meet me." She yanked her arm away amidst his irritated cursing and slid onto the horse's back, saddleless. Hands wrapped in the mare's mane, Deidra tapped her sides and told her where to go.

Since she had begun speaking to animals again, she'd become acquainted with her mount and had even named her. Blue Bonnet, or Blue for short. The horse had a fascination with eating flowers. Deidra found riding so much easier when the horse could communicate with her about weight shifts and what was more comfortable. Currently, Blue didn't care for being ridden bareback but understood the urgency of the matter.

Deidra slid off the horse's back the moment she spotted Stephen. He didn't look nearly as poor as he had from the bird's-eye view; in fact, he was surprised to see her, straightening in the saddle and drawing rein.

"Deidra! Greetings." He extended a hand to her, pleasure lighting his pale eyes.

She clasped it in both of hers. Duke danced and yipped around her legs. With her mind, she asked the dog to calm down, and he immediately sat down on his haunches.

"How are you?" she asked. "Are you well? Uncle Drake is bringing a wagon for you to ride in the rest of the way."

The pleasure disappeared from his eyes and his brows lowered. "What is this? A wagon?" His jaw tightened and the skin of his neck flushed. He pulled his hand away from hers. "Why don't you just bring a litter for me to lie in?"

Deidra hesitated. He did not seem pleased by her concern. "Would that have been better?"

"Do I look like I need a wagon?"

Deidra's brows raised nearly to her hairline, uncertain how to answer him. She *knew* how the ride had worn on him. She *knew* he was in pain, regardless of how he currently looked.

He studied her face and his mouth hardened. "I told you I could make this journey and that I would be fine."

Deidra took a step back. "But you weren't that first night—"

The sound of hoofbeats and the creak and crunch of wagon wheels approaching drew their attention. Duke started to stand, an excited bark rising in his chest, but again Deidra stayed him. He was growing unhappy with her interference.

Drake rode on horseback beside a narrow wagon driven by an old man. It was slow going with such treacherous terrain.

When Deidra looked back at Stephen, his face was an emotionless mask. He gave her one last empty stare and tapped Countess's sides. He rode right past Drake without a word. His posture was erect, and Deidra could only imagine the pain it caused him to maintain it. Loyalty won out and Duke raced after him.

Drake and the wagon driver stopped and watched Stephen's retreating back before turning back to Deidra.

Deidra slowly walked toward her uncle, though her gaze remained on Stephen.

"He looks well enough to me," Drake said.

"He hides his pain." Deidra's chest hurt. She was

confused. He was angry, she could see that, and he was in pain, and somehow it all felt like her fault.

Drake stroked at his beard. "Do you think he recognized me?"

Deidra shrugged, remounting Blue. She returned to the castle, riding beside her uncle. "I think he is vexed with me."

"You think?" Drake said, his tone dry.

"You agree with his ire?"

"Well, I ken I would be a bit irritated if I was treated like an invalid by a bonny woman when I'm clearly not."

Deidra let out an exasperated breath. "What do you mean? I was showing concern for him. I was trying to help."

"It doesn't feel too manly when you have to be carted about like a wean. Especially if your woman thinks you're so weakly."

Deidra's face flushed. "What?" Her voice cracked on the high warbling note, and she averted her eyes from his perceptive stare. "I am not his woman. And I don't think he's weakly. He's very strong. It's just his back . . . it hurts him."

When she glanced back at her uncle, he smiled slyly at her in his beard. "You're right, lassie. You'll never be his woman if you keep coddling him."

Deidra's throat tightened and her cheeks flamed. She kept her gaze straight ahead the remainder of the ride. But what Drake said had struck a nerve and rubbed it raw.

His back felt as if a swarm of angry bees had stung him over and over and over again—were in fact still trapped in his shirt, stinging and stinging. But he bore up through it all. The castle gates were still open and he passed through without harassment, riding Countess straight to the stables. He had a few minutes alone there, and he intended to use every second dismounting without an audience.

He was standing beside Countess, face pressed into the saddle, still waiting for the throbbing pain to abate just the slightest bit, when they entered. He forced himself to straighten.

He couldn't even look at Deidra. He'd thought about her every step of the journey, worried about whether or not she had arrived safely and how her shoulder fared. And then she'd ridden out to meet him. It had surprised him, pleased him excessively . . . until she'd informed him of the wagon on the way to fetch him.

He had hoped, after all that had transpired between them, that when she looked at him again she would see something other than a cripple. Unfortunately, nothing had changed. Except now, instead of being impatient with him, she pitied him, felt a sense of responsibility.

He unsaddled Countess with rough movements, ignoring how every movement sent pain lancing through his back. They all worked in silence. Drake and his servant unhitched the horse from the wagon. Deidra and Stephen brushed the horses and gave them fresh hay and water. Deidra sent him furtive looks the whole while. She knew he was upset, but he wondered if she even knew why. He wasn't about to tell her now.

He could barely think through the pain. He needed rest before he could contemplate anything else.

Thankfully, Drake said, "You must be hungry."

The three of them had gathered near the stable door.

"Aye, I am," Stephen said. "But it's been a long ride. A bed would not be unwelcome."

"I'll get you some food. Deidra? Why don't you find him a bed?"

Stephen barely managed not to groan. Now he would have to be alone with her and she would want to *talk*. He had nothing to say to her now, not when he used every last ounce of energy to hide the fact that the bones of his spine were rubbing together like gravel. He followed her into the keep, keeping his face stoic and emotionless to discourage conversation.

"How did you get away from Luthias?" she asked.

"I just left."

She glanced at him over her shoulder. Concern filled her huge blue eyes. She was so beautiful it almost hurt his eyes to look at her. Her hair was clean and springing with dark curls, her fine-grained skin glowing with health, her bottom lip red and swollen from gnawing on it with worry. He wanted to take that lip between his teeth—

"He didn't suspect anything?" she asked, tearing him from his fantasy and back into the world of pain.

"No," he said, scowling at her. "I told you I could handle it, that it would all be fine. Do you not believe me capable?"

Deidra shook her head. "No, that's not it at all. I was

just worried. I don't know what I would have done without your help."

"Burned."

She swallowed hard, hand on a door latch. Quite suddenly the anger hit him like a fist in the gut. Once he had been strong. No one had doubted what he was capable of. But now he was pitied and forced to accept help from people that by all rights should need him. And she *did* need him. She would have burned if not for him, would be dead now, and yet still she treated him like a mewling child. He was sick of it. Not just from her but from everyone. It was why he had retreated to Bráighde Pele. He wanted to grab her and shake her and show her exactly what he was capable of. Instead he brushed past her as she swung the door open and dumped his things on the floor.

The room was small, in keeping with the rest of the keep, but well tended. A large, comfortable-looking bed sat in the corner, and a table and chairs were placed against the wall near the door. Deidra lit the brazier next to the bed to warm the room.

"This will do." It would more than do. He gazed longingly at the bed, wanting her gone so he could collapse onto it. Hopefully, a woman would come with his food and he could entice her into a deep back rub.

As if reading his mind, Deidra suggested tentatively, "I could rub your back."

The muscles around his spine contracted painfully at the very thought. God, he wanted her to. She was good at it—better than good, sinful. But no. She offered out of pity and the need to repay him for what he'd done. He'd had his fill of pity.

"Just leave."

He kept his back to her, to hide the pain contorting his face. *Leave. Just leave.*

She didn't leave immediately, and he nearly growled at her again to go when he heard the quiet latch of the door as she shut it.

His shoulders sagged and he let his head drop forward. God, he hurt. He trudged to the bed and knelt on it.

"Here, let me help you," Deidra said as she grabbed his boot.

He did whirl then, startled and angry. He'd thought she was gone, but she'd stayed, damn her. "I told you to leave!" His words came out harsh and angry because the move had wrenched his back.

She didn't back down but stood before him, chin thrust out. "You need me. You need help."

He leaned forward so that his nose nearly touched hers. "Not how you think, lass. You stay and you'll get more than you wagered for."

"You're all threats."

The fury bubbled up inside him. She was partly right, and that's what chafed. He was full of steam and threats, and she knew that he was in too much pain to carry them out. But damn it, that's what made him so angry. She thought she knew him. Thought she knew all he was capable of because he was crippled. She knew nothing.

The anger throbbing in his temple dulled the pain

in his back, sent power to his limbs. He grabbed her shoulders and pulled her hard against him. A small, satisfying gasp of surprise escaped from her lips before he crushed them with his own.

She was stiff with surprise, her palms pressed against his chest. He worked her lips, kissing and nuzzling, pressing into her mouth with his tongue. Her body softened, her lips parting for him, letting him in.

A groan of pleasure rumbled through him and his hands slid down to stroke her back, to press her in closer to his aching erection. He could do this and more, just as well as any other man. Her arms wrapped around him, slim fingers sliding beneath the leather of his jack, cool through the linen of his shirt. His pain faded to a small ache, and he thought he might die if he couldn't be inside her, whatever the cost to his back later.

Using his fingers, he pulled her skirt up until his fingers brushed bare thigh. He slid his hand up over her skin, open palmed. It was soft as silk, and firm. She whimpered, her breathing coming faster. When he cupped her bottom, her leg came up, wrapped around his thigh, and he couldn't wait another moment.

He backed her toward the bed, tasting her small, perfect chin, the smooth line of her throat. The backs of her thighs hit the bed, but before he could push her backwards, she gripped his biceps hard and pulled back.

"Wait," she said, gazing up at him with lust-hazed eyes.

His fingers slid between her legs, stopping her

thought instantly. He saw her eyes go blank as he stroked at her. Her fingers dug into him, and the leg wrapped beautifully around him tightened and flexed. Ah, yes, he could see that she had forgotten he was a cripple, or anything else. She only knew that he could make her feel wonderful, just as she sometimes made him feel. And for this one small moment, that was enough.

He slid a finger inside her and burrowed his other hand under her skirt to rub at her nub. Her body contracted around his finger and her head fell back. She cried out, her head snapping back to bury against his chest as her body climaxed. She shuddered against him for a moment before raising her head and blinking dazedly at him.

He kissed her again. She was ready for him now. He wanted to be inside her, those legs wrapped tight around him. His cock ached in anticipation. He would take her hard and quick the first time, but then . . .

He started to ease her back on the bed, but she stopped him again.

"Wait, Stephen."

He sighed with strained patience. "What is it, sweet?" He kissed the corner of her mouth, the tip of her ear. He stroked at her thighs, showing her it wasn't over—it was just beginning.

She swallowed hard and said, "What about your back? Surely this will make the pain unbearable . . ."

And she twisted the knife in his pride, making him less again. He released her abruptly and moved away, raking a hand through his hair. He felt sick with anger and disgust. He could tell her the truth—that there were ways to make love that would not hurt him at all. But that would involve admitting that he had to take certain precautions because he was a cripple. He would *not* do that. Not with her.

"Get out, Deidra."

"But Stephen—"

"Get out." He ground the words through his teeth, cutting off any protest from her. "And Lord help me, if I turn around after that door closes and still find you here, I cannot be responsible for what I might do."

He waited, hands on hips, and a second later the door closed. He turned, the anger and frustration still built up in his chest, making it feel too tight.

This time she was gone.

Chapter 9

———❦❦❦———

$\mathcal{D}$eidra woke to a flood of shame and anger the next morning. She lay on her bed, eyes closed, the day before playing out over and over again behind her eyelids. She still was not certain what exactly had happened. She pressed her cold palms to her hot cheeks, but it did nothing to cool the burn in her body.

She had only been trying to help him. Why couldn't he see that and understand? Everything she did to help only seemed to make him angrier. And what really confused her was the fact that he had allowed her to rub his back once before. He had quite enjoyed it then. What had changed? Now her offer only infuriated him.

She sensed her companions before she actually saw them. When she sat up, they were clustered around the room—animals. Duke had found his way into her room and now sprawled at the end of her bed. His pleasure at her finally being awake was palpable. He licked the air, then belly-crawled across the fur blanket to her so she could scratch his ears.

Another dog lay on the floor near the door, along with several cats and a bird. Deidra knew there would have been even more if there hadn't been so many predators gathered in one place. The small ones hid.

The other animals reacted to Deidra's rousing, sitting up, tails wagging, approaching the bed. The bird, a small brown-and-yellow thing, chirped and bounced on the windowsill.

They usually wanted nothing more than to be close to her. It had pleased her as a child that they'd thought of her as some kind of mother god. It distressed her as an adult. Too frequently, she had to guard her thoughts because the animals would act on them without her making any requests at all.

She washed and dressed, and the dogs and cats followed her downstairs. Drake and Stephen were already at a long table in the great hall, breaking their fasts. Drake watched her approach, shaking his head the whole while.

"This is how I remember her as a bairn, surrounded by animals like some wood sprite."

Deidra studied Stephen surreptitiously as she joined them. "I don't invite them to follow me around. They do it of their own accord."

"Duke," Stephen said with a good-natured reprimand in his voice. "I was wondering where you'd gone."

Duke trembled with happiness as Stephen vigorously rubbed his hand over the dog's ears and back.

"You look like hell, Dee," her uncle said, eyes narrowed on hers. "Did you sleep at all last night?"

Deidra's mouth flattened, irritated that her uncle had called attention to the dark half circles under her eyes. "I slept fine." Which was a lie. The animals had been in her head last night, all night. And then of course there had been the incident with Stephen. She had left him, aroused and hurt and confused—none of which had been conducive to sleep.

Stephen watched her but said not a single word. Her eyes met the question in his, then darted away. Being near him made her suddenly and excessively nervous. She took a piece of bread from the basket and tore off the crust.

"So, uhm . . . what are we going to do?" she asked, nibbling on the bread crust.

"I told you," Drake said. "We have to lure Luthias here or somewhere near, at least. Then kill him."

Stephen rubbed the back of his hand against his chin, and it rasped along the whiskers. The memory of those same whiskers chafing the sensitive skin of her face, of those hands slipping between her thighs, made her face flame, and she prayed he did not notice. She had to look away, down at her bread. She tore off several more pieces, but her stomach was too knotted to actually eat them.

Stephen said, "The witch hunter is obsessed with her. So long as he knows Deidra is here, he will come." He paused. "I can send him word that I'd heard you came this way."

He was addressing her directly. She glanced up, found that pale blue gaze on her, and looked right back down at her bread.

She was grateful when Drake spoke—something nonthreatening to look at. "No, a letter is no good. Someone else might read it. It could get lost or left behind. If discovered, the finger could be pointed at either one of you—or both, if they know you are . . ." Drake's brows raised, and he sat back in his chair. "Well, whatever the two of you are."

Deidra looked quickly between Drake and Stephen, stunned and embarrassed that her uncle had said such a thing. Stephen only watched her closely, his own face expressionless.

When Deidra could finally speak, she sputtered, "What do you mean? We are nothing . . . er, friends. That is all."

Her statement was met with silence from both men. She searched frantically for something to say, her mind dwelling on the interlude with Stephen last night, his mouth, his hands . . . hardly the marks of mere friendship.

Her uncle placed a hand over hers, stopping her frenzied bread shredding. "It's only a piece of bread, Dee, have mercy on it."

Deidra sat back in her chair, an idea occurring to her. "The animals. I could send animals to fetch him."

"Fetch him?" Stephen said dubiously. "Seems rather obvious. He's not stupid. And methinks he is not overfond of beasts, thanks to your tutelage."

Deidra shrugged. "Still, I think the animals can help. Perhaps I could send some to do something suspicious . . . such as watch him, follow him . . . but they would be conspicuous. Naturally, he would think it was my doing and follow the animals."

Stephen nodded appreciably. "Aye, she's right." His gaze turned to Drake. "What will you do when he's near?"

"Ambush him and his men." Drake scratched at his chin, deep in his beard. "After that, you'll have no more worries, m'dear." He patted Deidra's hand.

Deidra wanted to skip over that part in her mind and get to the part where he was no longer a thorn in her side.

Stephen slapped his hands on the table and stood. "Very good, then. It looks like all is in order here." He inclined his head to Drake. "Thank you for your hospitality. I hope you'll come to Bráighde Pele one day so I can return the favor." He turned to Deidra. "And it was good seeing you again—alive, that is. Prithee, listen to your uncle and try to stay that way."

His smile was completely and utterly false. Deidra searched his face, confused by this speech that appeared to be a good-bye.

"What . . . ? Are you leaving?"

"Aye. I vowed to see you again, to be certain of your safety. And I see you are in excellent hands. It's now time for me to be on my way."

He limped away from the table, Duke trotting beside him. Deidra stared after him, slack-jawed. She looked at her uncle, perplexed.

Drake watched her meditatively. "Didn't expect him to leave, eh?"

Deidra let out a confused breath. "Why would I? I thought he came to help."

Drake bit his bottom lip and shrugged. "Not much he can do, crippled as he is. I wager we'll manage without him."

A lump of indignant anger rose in Deidra's throat.

"You'd be surprised at what he could do. I would not be alive right now if not for him."

"Hmmm" was all Drake said.

Deidra stewed for a moment, picking at her piece of bread before standing decisively and following Stephen. She found him in his chambers, stuffing his things into a leather sack.

"Why are you really leaving?" she asked.

He continued what he was doing without even looking at her. "I came for the blood witch, remember? I am a cripple. I'm of no use here."

"Drake says he doesn't believe the blood witch will even help you."

Stephen shrugged. "I'd like to find that out for myself."

"I thought we were going together."

"Was that why you snuck away in the middle of the night?" His face was bland, his stance slightly challenging.

She stepped toward him, fists clenched. "I was afraid. But I'm not anymore." *Because of you.* But she couldn't say it, not when he looked at her so uncaringly.

"Good. Then mayhap you'll step up and do what is necessary. Kill Luthias and stop running from yourself. For myself, I'm going to see a witch about my back, and I dinna intend to return half a man."

What did that mean? Her heart jumped a little at the implication. If the blood witch couldn't help him, would he return at all?

She reached for him. "Stephen, I know you hurt, but—"

He threw down the boot he held and said through clenched teeth, "My God, spare me your compassion and just *leave me the hell alone.*"

She recoiled as if he'd slapped her. He might as well have. It took her a moment to catch her breath from the shock and hurt of his words. His face was twisted, lip curled, brows lowered. It was as if he hated her, couldn't stand the sight of her.

She backed away, out of the room, and left him.

After getting directions from Drake, Stephen set out, heading north. Drake had been skeptical of Stephen's quest, warning him that the blood witch would not help him. But Stephen had no intention of giving up until he tested the theory for himself. Though he had not seen Ceara for himself before she'd died, it sounded as if something horrible had ailed her, and no doubt the *baobhan sith* had wanted nothing to do with plagues even a witch could not cure. And besides, Drake was not known for his charm. No doubt he'd ordered charity at sword point and offended the blood witch. Stephen thought that with a bit of charm, he might have a better chance at convincing her.

He had nothing to lose. He'd already lost everything the day the bullet had lodged in his back. It had not been an accident. The man who'd shot him couldn't have cared less if he'd lived or died—he'd just wanted Stephen out of the way. Stephen had been protecting his best friend, Philip Kilpatrick. He had failed at protecting his friend that day, but his strong constitution had kept him alive long enough to send help and Philip survived.

But part of Stephen had died that day. His back had been ruined, and there had been nothing anyone could do to change that. Not for lack of trying, however. Stephen's uncle was a powerful earl who had used his power and position to bring every healer of renown to Stephen's bedside. But none had been able to help him. Not with witchcraft or with science.

Stephen had given up trying long ago. This was his last hope, and he couldn't think past it, couldn't let himself contemplate another failure.

And so he kept on, focused on his goal and nothing else.

The terrain only grew more difficult the farther north he traveled and the weather grew colder. He wore a plaid as the Highlanders did, wrapped around him and pinned to his shoulder, with woolen trews beneath. It helped to appear local, and besides, the Highlander style of dress suited their environment. It kept him very warm.

Small game was plentiful—badgers, squirrels, hare, deer. He managed to snare a hare with his latch, the small crossbow that hung from his saddle. He thought of Deidra as he skinned and cooked it, wondering if she was able to eat the creatures she communed with. It seemed rather morbid when he considered it that way—cannibalistic almost—and he nearly lost his appetite. But he needed his strength and didn't know when he might snare another, so he finished his meal, throwing the bones to Duke.

The next day he had to cross the mountains. He did not relish it, but at least he could go at his own pace and stop as needed. Attempting to go around the mountains would add days, maybe weeks, to his journey. He was muscling through the pain because it was necessary, but he knew there would come a point when he simply could not go on. He hoped to get to the blood witch before he reached that point.

He rode Countess as far as he could, then dismounted and led her up the treacherous slope. It was slow going, as there was no road or trail this way. He had to find their trail through the jagged rocks rising higher and higher. Duke led the way, running ahead for a while, then coming back to walk with Stephen for a short while before scouting ahead again.

On more occasions than he cared to count, Stephen found himself immobilized with pain while in a precarious position—pressed against a cliff side, or maneuvering around a jutting creag with a narrow lip of rock that dropped off in a sheer drop. He was beginning to wonder if this had been a really bad idea. Maybe he should have gone around the mountain—at least then he might make his destination alive.

Eventually he had to cut Countess loose and hope she would find her way home or back to Deidra, but the way was no longer safe for her. He looked back once to see that Countess was trying to follow. She had come to two jutting rocks, and the only way forward was between them—a tight squeeze for a man, but impossible for a horse. He tried to ignore the tug of guilt as her eyes followed him until he was out of sight. He wished for Deidra's gift then so that he could explain it all to her, but she probably wouldn't understand anyway.

He continued on foot, keeping an eye out for hares and other small game. Duke had run off ahead so long ago that Stephen was starting to worry that he had fallen or hurt himself. There was nothing he could do about it unless he actually came upon the dog.

He managed to shoot another hare on his downward descent. It continued to bound, arrow quivering from its ribs, disappearing between two sharp rocks stabbing upward through the ground. Stephen followed, peering around the stones. The hare had come to rest on the edge of a crevice in the rock. He stared at it, lips compressed with displeasure. There was no way to retrieve the hare except by circling the rim. If Duke had been here, he could have sent the dog to fetch the hare. He called out to the dog and waited, but Duke didn't come.

He held on to the sides of the rock as best he could, though there were no depressions or handholds, and slid around between them.

The hare had stopped moving. The sides of the rock were concave and slick from a small mountain stream that trickled down the mountain and emptied into the crevice, where it traveled onward.

Stephen stood beside the rock, listening to the soft bubble of water, considering how badly he wanted the hare. Wildlife had grown scarce now that he was in the mountains, and once he reached the bottom of the mountain there would be several miles of barren moorland. He needed this hare.

He unstrapped his satchel and sword from where they were buckled across his chest and tossed them to the ground.

He braced himself and edged along the narrow ledge, his back and palms pressed to the wall behind him. Slow and steady, he crept along the ledge until the hare was almost within reach.

When he was within arm's length of the animal, he braced himself and bent his knees, crouching and reaching for the carcass. And just as he feared, his back seized as his fingers grasped the arrow jutting out. He clenched his teeth and froze. He kept his weight back against the stone behind him to keep from toppling into the crevice.

But he was strong. This was the reason he worked his body so hard, so that when necessary, he could muscle through any situation. He stayed there, head pressed hard against the stone, back twisted in anguish. He heard a far-off crack but couldn't think enough to care what it was.

He didn't know how long he stayed there, jagged knives impaling his back and holding him prisoner, but at some point the pain lessened and he thought he could move.

He opened his eyes and tried to straighten. A weight in his hand moved. He looked down. He had broken the arrow in his clenched fist. The hare, impaled on the arrow, dangled from the thin piece of bent wood that held the broken arrow together. Stephen only hoped it held until he made it to the other side of the crevice and safety.

In increments, he straightened, grunting and groaning until he stood again. He edged along the ledge, the hare jiggling each time he took a step. He was almost to the other side and safety when the thin strip of wood snapped and the hare fell. Stephen reached for it reflexively—a very bad move—throwing off his balance. His foot slipped on the slick rock and he was falling, slipping down the slope. He twisted, fingers scrabbling for a handhold, trying to catch himself through the pain, but he crashed to the bottom of the crevice, landing on his side and arm.

Though he was not unconscious, the pain from the fall did render him insensible for a time. It radiated through his body and down his legs. Sparks of light flashed behind his eyelids. His stomach lurched and he imagined that soon he would be laying in his own vomit.

Slowly, coherent thought returned and he feared he had done serious damage to his back again—perhaps broken it. And damned if those MacKay witches were too far away to help. Again.

He laid his head against the damp stone and closed his eyes. If he lost the ability to move, then that was it for him. It was over. He gave up. He would just die here without a fight.

But eventually the twisting sword of pain diminished to a manageable throb, and he pushed himself up. His arms shook. The hare was an arm's length away, but any supplies for skinning and cooking it were up at the top of the crevice in his satchel.

Gingerly, he climbed to his feet and peered upward at the eye of fading light above him.

The lip of the crevice didn't seem that far away. A normal man, with a normal, functioning back, should be able to climb out of the hole, albeit with difficulty.

Unfortunately Stephen was not normal, nor did he have a properly functioning back. Nevertheless, he had overcome bigger obstacles than this.

He slid his hands all over the rock face in front of him, even standing on his tiptoes, searching for some kind of handhold. There was nothing. The walls bowled in all around him. He had fallen into a hole with nothing but a dead hare and a small puddle to keep him company.

Hands on his hips, he stared hard at the fading light above him. If he could just jump high enough, he could grab the lip of the crevice and pull himself up. Unfortunately, jumping was not something he'd been able to do for a very long while.

He prepared to try anyway, his heart speeding with anticipation of the pain to come, teeth clenching. He bent his knees and thrust upward, arms extending.

He felt it immediately in his back. Pain wrenched it, streaking down the backs of his thighs. His fingers brushed something, but he couldn't see or hear or make his fingers curl around it. He landed on his feet, but they collapsed beneath him, and he crashed to his knees.

The cold stone bit through the wool of his trews. Head lowered, he heard a rumbling sound, like a wounded animal, and realized it was him—moaning deep in his chest at the pain racking his back and thighs.

He didn't think anything would be able to bring him to his feet anytime soon.

But he was wrong.

A voice called down to him, "Stephen? Are you down there?" It was both the sweetest sound he'd ever heard and poison to his heart.

He opened his eyes. Blocking the light was a riot of curls gilded to golden fire by the light behind them. The face was dark and shadowed. But he knew the voice, the hair, the curve of her face like he knew his own heart.

Deidra.

Chapter 10

───◦◦◦◦◦───

$\mathcal{D}$eidra knew her behavior was irresponsible and that Stephen might never forgive her. Still, it didn't matter—she would rather he be alive and angry with her than dead with foolish pride intact. Certain that something terrible would befall him, she had fretted nonstop since he had left. So as a precaution, she'd kept in contact with Countess and Duke. She had not liked the route he'd taken north, but as long as Countess had reported nothing amiss, Deidra had not become alarmed.

Meanwhile, Drake had sent out a scout to discover the current whereabouts of Luthias. The scout had just returned with the information when Countess's thoughts had changed.

The horse had been alone and distressed. Stephen had left her behind, and she hadn't known what to do. She'd tried to follow but hadn't been able to and was currently wandering around the mountain.

It had been rather surprising to discover there really was no anguishing over what to do, no indecisiveness. It had required no thought at all. She'd packed a bag and left just as Drake had been formulating a plan of attack.

She hadn't told Drake she was leaving—he would only have tried to talk her out of going or perhaps even physically stopped her. She'd left a letter, explaining to him that she would be back soon, but she needed to be sure Stephen was safe.

Luthias would still be here when she returned. Stephen's safety took precedence over everything else.

And now, she was nearly weak with relief that she'd been so decisive. She'd met up with Countess and left her with Blue, some oats, a half dozen apples, and instructions to head back to Creaghaven. Then she'd followed Duke's thoughts.

The dog had been ecstatic to see her, leaping in the air and almost knocking her off her feet.

Take me to him, she'd ordered Duke, and they'd been off, racing up the treacherous mountainside. Duke had been surefooted, leaping among the creags like a mountain goat. Deidra had followed much slower, though they'd remained connected mentally the entire time.

She had been climbing for more than an hour when she'd come upon Duke, sitting beside a leather bag, a sword, and a latch. The dog had stood, tail wagging, at her appearance.

"Stephen?" she'd called out, hurrying to the paraphernalia.

There had been no answer. A few feet away, from a crevice in the rock, rose the sound of a man moaning in pain. Her heart had squeezed convulsively.

"Damn," she muttered, dropping to her knees at the edge of the crevice and peering down into the cave.

"Stephen?" she called again.

The sun streamed down into the cave in a single shaft of light, and everything outside the oval-shaped shaft was too dark for her to see.

She heard a scraping, and then into the light limped Stephen, head tilted back to peer up at her. He was dirty and scraped. His long hair had come loose from the cord he'd used to tie it back, and tangled, blond locks fell over his shoulders. Still, he was the most beautiful sight she'd seen.

"Damn you, woman," he growled. "What are you doing here?"

"Countess told me you'd left her. I was worried."

The tight squeezing of her heart relaxed. He was well. By the tight set of his face, she could see he was in a great deal of pain, but he was standing, and that was reason enough to rejoice.

"We have to get you out of there."

He shook his head. "Not tonight, lass. My back will not tolerate another attempt."

"What do you want to do?"

"There is rope in my bag. Take it out and then throw the bag down to me."

Deidra did as he instructed.

"I have a blanket, liniment, and some laudanum your uncle gave me in here." He held the sack up. "I need to rest a bit, and then you'll have to tie the rope to something that will hold my weight. I'll climb up it."

Deidra didn't want to wait. She wanted him out of that hole now so that she could rub the pain from his back, but he was right. Trying to get out now, when he was probably in excruciating pain, was rash and stupid and would only make things worse.

"What about food and water?" She grabbed her bag and started rummaging through it. She had brought extra for him.

"I have that in here. Fash not. Get some sleep yourself, and we'll try again in a bit."

Deidra sighed. She wasn't really tired, but she unrolled her blanket anyway. Duke lay down beside her, his body warming her. He was concerned for his master. He didn't understand why Stephen stayed down in the hole. He wanted Deidra to do something. Deidra communicated to the dog that Stephen couldn't come up right now and that they would help him out later.

The dog whined, distressed, staring down at his master.

"I'm fine, laddy," Stephen called from below.

At the sound of his voice, Duke barked.

"Deidra, let him know I'm fine."

Deidra tried to communicate this to Duke, but she wasn't entirely successful, as the dog felt her anxiety. He did quiet down to lie on the lip of the crevice, his snout hanging over the side so he could watch over Stephen. His body was tense, ready to spring into action at one word from Deidra or Stephen.

Sleep didn't come. Deidra lay on her back, scanning the rocks around her to determine the appropriate one to secure the rope to.

"Deidra? Are you awake?"

Deidra rolled to her side. "Aye."

"What about Luthias? I thought you and Drake were going after him. Does Drake even know you're here?"

Deidra hesitated. "I left him a letter explaining . . . and Luthias isn't far. He is still looking for me. We can do it when I get back."

"Providing he doesn't find you first."

"He won't. The animals, they warn me of intruders."

"Deidra." The single word drifted up to her, full of exasperation and affection.

Her heart contracted painfully at the sound. She asked, "What will you do if the blood witch refuses to help you?"

"I don't know. I cannot think of that now."

Her heart sank. Deidra didn't know what she had hoped he would say, but that wasn't it.

"What will you do if she *can* help you?"

Her heart tripped into the silence as she waited for his response.

And waited.

In fact, he was silent for so long that she thought maybe he had fallen asleep.

"Stephen?" she said in a loud whisper, not wanting to wake him if he was asleep but desperately wanting to hear his answer. If he was whole again, what would he do?

"Aye, I'm here."

That didn't answer her question. She bit her lip, wanting to ask again, but feeling foolish and transparent. Her feelings must be obvious to him; she was a moon-eyed puppy following him about.

"There are so many things I would do, Deidra. More than I can count." His voice was wistful, a great weight in it.

"Is it really so different? Is there really so much that you cannot do?"

"Aye, lass, it is." The silence ensued again.

Deidra curled on her side, her heart heavy. She couldn't have him either way, it seemed. It was hopeless.

"For example," he said, continuing their conversation. Her heart jumped, surprised, but she didn't move or say a word.

"The other night, at your uncle's. We would not have stopped with the kissing."

The air left Deidra in a rush. The memory of that night fired her cheeks and sent lust spiraling to her core. She closed her eyes on a shuddering breath, instantly aroused.

"I shouldn't have stopped then," he said, his voice musing. "You think I am a cripple, incapable of the simplest feats, but I assure you, that is one we can still carry out."

Deidra's breath came short, her hand sliding down to press against the ache between her legs. She had thought a great deal about that night. Relived it in her mind, wondering what would have happened if she had just kept her mouth shut.

"No, we could have both slept well that night. But if not for this back that you love throwing in my face, I would have had you on that bed and made you scream my name."

Her mouth was dry, eyes now gazing sightlessly into the gloaming. "Really?" she asked hoarsely.

She hadn't realized she'd said the word loud enough for him to hear until he replied, "Aye, really."

Her heart tapped rapidly in her throat, making thinking difficult. She scooted closer to the edge of the crevice. He didn't say any more, but she didn't want this conversation to end. She'd been haunted by that night in his room when he had kissed her and touched her. She had tried to touch herself as he had, tried to re-create the sensations coursing through her body, but it hadn't been the same without that one important ingredient: Stephen.

Maybe it was the dark, or the fact that he was in a hole and therefore she wouldn't have to look him in the eye, but something made her bold. Bold enough to ask, "How would you do that?"

She swore she heard his sharp intake of breath, even from her perch above him.

"That's a dangerous question. When I get out of this hole, I'll show you."

A smile tugged at her lips. "Tell me now."

After a long, heavy silence, he said, "I'd start by looking at those pretty breasts this time. I regret neglecting them before. I felt them pressed against me, and they're perfect, methinks. Round and soft. Your nipples are probably pink and taste sweet, so I would kiss them next."

Desire knifed through her, sharp. She closed her eyes and rubbed at the ache with one hand, felt the weight of her breast with the other, imagining how they felt to someone else, and imagining how it would have felt if it had been his hands cupping it.

"It will be hard to tear myself away from them." His voice had grown deeper, rougher, and it sent a thrill of excitement through her.

"I know this already," he continued, "but your mouth will be calling to me—and not just with words, though I plan to make you forget every word but my name. The memory of their taste would bring me back to them."

She swallowed hard and whispered, "Aye, I remember that, too."

"What, sweeting?" he said. "You'll have to speak up if you wish me to hear you."

Did she? This lewd talk frightened her a bit. She was a virgin, had done little more than exchange a few kisses with a village boy, and now she talked about things a man only did with his lover. It both frightened and exhilarated her, and she realized she wanted more.

"I said, I remember that too . . . when you kissed me."

"I'll do it again and again, don't fash on that. Then I will kiss other places."

Her breath caught as her heart tripped in her chest. Though he'd not been specific, the image of his mouth pressed to other parts of her body caused her legs to go weak and her lashes to flutter.

"Where?" She realized she'd said the word so softly that he couldn't possibly have heard her, so she cleared her throat and repeated herself. "Where?"

He made a deep sound, a soft laugh, but a lecherous

one, as if he was as eager to carry out his scenario as she was to hear it. "Everywhere, sweet. Your neck and the porcelain skin of the insides of your arms . . . your smooth belly, your thighs . . . and between them."

Her fingers pressed harder as her body clenched. She shut her eyes, unable to believe that his voice and his words made her body spasm with pleasure. She gasped, rubbing harder and faster.

"Stephen . . ."

"Aye, sweet—I wish I were there, too."

When the sensations coursing through her faded, she turned her hot face into her blanket, mortified. He had known what she'd been doing. Had known and encouraged it.

"Deidra?" His voice floated up to her.

She didn't want to answer now, for she was too embarrassed. But she couldn't ignore him, so she said, "Aye?"

"I meant every word. But now I must sleep so I can get out of this hole."

She bit her bottom lip, smiling with eagerness. Her body was languid and loose now and she was surprised that sleep slowly crept up on her. The last thought to occur to her as she drifted off was that he had never truly answered her question. She still didn't know what he would do, past ravishing her, if the blood witch could make him whole again.

After a fitful night, Deidra was up with the sun looking for a rock to which she could secure the rope and still have enough slack to reach Stephen.

"How are you feeling this morning?" she asked as she tossed the rope down to him.

"Better," he said, but the word was short and clipped, indicating that though he might be better, he was still in pain.

She peered down over the edge of the crevice and watched as he looped his sack over his shoulder, gripped the rope in both hands, and pulled himself upward.

For Deidra, it would have been easier to hold the rope and use her feet to climb, but apparently Stephen's legs were not necessary. He lifted his weight solely with his arms. Veins stood out along his thick forearms, and in no time he hooked the edge of the crevice with his forearm and lifted himself out with a grunt, rolling onto the rocks beside Deidra. Duke immediately licked his master's face, whining excitedly. Deidra told the dog to stop. He moved a few feet away and sat, watching Stephen with barely restrained joy.

Stephen lay on his back, staring up at the sky and breathing hard. Deidra did a visual inventory of him as he lay there. Some scrapes and bruises, but it didn't look as if he was seriously harmed.

As she sat there, waiting for him to recover himself, awkwardness settled over her. After what had happened the night before, she suddenly had no idea what to say to him. Her face flushed at the memory, and her belly dipped.

She got to her feet and gathered up the rope, keeping her face turned away from him. Once it was coiled, she turned back toward him to find him sitting up, watching her.

"Are you ready?" she asked, hoisting her own bag over her shoulder.

He continued to stare at her, a bemused smile on his face. "Where are we going?"

Deidra exhaled with exasperation. "To see the *bao-bhan sith,* of course."

He scratched at the thickening whiskers on his jaw. "I thought you'd changed your mind about that."

She shrugged. "I don't know."

He smiled ruefully. "Coming along to dandle the cripple? Make sure he doesn't do anything stupid and kill himself?"

Deidra's mouth tightened and her eyes narrowed. Essentially what he said was true—except the stupid part—but he put such an unpleasant spin on it. What did it matter if she did care? So he'd injured his back and needed a bit of extra care. She *wanted* to give it to him. Why did he have to be so difficult about it?

"I know you're not stupid; you're very clever. Mishaps on such treacherous terrain can happen to anyone, Stephen, cripple or whole. That is why most people prefer not to travel alone."

"You have chosen to travel alone on more than one occasion in recent weeks. How do you manage not to have such mishaps?"

"The animals help me."

He got to his feet with a grunt and a grimace, and sighed. "I suppose the company would be welcome."

She let out the breath she hadn't realized she was holding and waited for him to join her.

"Is it far?" she asked. "It seems a long way to go on foot."

"No, once we cross the moors at the base of the mountain it's only a few miles. The *baobhan sith* lives off the coast, on a small island."

"Are you well enough to travel?" she asked hesitantly, not wanting to further irritate him but wanting to make sure he was ready and able to travel. "Would you like to rest for a while first?"

He raised a brow and gave her a long, reproachful look. "Let's go." He limped past her. Duke bounded ahead, up between the rocks, and Stephen followed.

Deidra sighed and readjusted her bag. This would prove to be a long trip if he didn't accept her help. But at least he wasn't going it alone.

Chapter 11

───∞∞∞───

*T*wo days later they reached the base of the mountain, then took two more days to cross the moor before arriving at the fishing village on the coast. Stephen wanted to fall to his knees and cry with joy. It had been a very long time since he had experienced such agony. After climbing out of the crevice four days ago, his back was still rife with pain, but he was loath to let Deidra see his suffering. She had seemed impressed with the way he had climbed out, and he wanted to continue to seem strong and capable to her—especially after the emasculating experience of being rescued by a woman. At least all he'd needed from her was a rope. It would have been far worse if he'd needed her to pull him out.

The past four nights, when they'd stopped to rest, she'd offered to rub his back with liniment. There was nothing he'd wanted more than her fine hands working the knots of pain from his muscles, but his pride had made him refuse. All he could think of was the way he'd kissed her and touched her, and the questions she'd asked him while he'd been trapped in the crevice, too far away to lay hands on her. He'd talked big then, and though he was sure he could follow through eventually, he didn't know if it was possible in his current condition. Now that they were finally here, and he stood within arm's length of her, she watched him with that anxious look on her face, the one that made him furious that he warranted it.

No, he did not want her pity. He was not some wounded animal that needed nursing. But his pain was too great to do what he really wanted to do—kiss away that concerned look on her face, make love to her until she forgot there was anything wrong with him.

They had both grown quiet these past few days, hardly speaking past necessities. He knew Deidra didn't know what to say to him after what had passed between them, and he didn't want to do or say anything to break that spell that he'd created and make himself seem weak to her. Soon he would be a man, a whole one, and things would be different.

So he'd refused her offer and taken too much laudanum to dull the pain. When he'd woken each morning, his head had felt fuzzy and thick and his belly queasy. But he'd been able to sleep, which had made continuing on the next morning possible.

And they had finally made it. Tomorrow morning he would go to the *baobhan sith* and end this hell on earth forever, God willing.

They found an inn with a room for rent. He felt Deidra's gaze on him as they ate in the common room. The fare was mutton and turnips—warm and filling, and so much better than dried fruit and hard bannocks. Deidra ate the turnips and bread but didn't touch the mutton he'd ordered for her.

"Is something wrong with your meal?" he asked without looking at her.

"No."

"Then why aren't you eating your meat?"

When she didn't respond, he looked up to see her staring at him with wide eyes.

"What?"

"I rarely eat meat. Only when nothing else is available. It's difficult when I can hear them."

Stephen nodded. "I had wondered about that." His own mutton suddenly seemed a little less appealing, but he continued shoveling it in. "When did you stop eating meat?"

"I've never really eaten it. My parents said I refused to eat meat as a child. I suppose I knew even then, though I don't remember."

He eyed her critically, wondering if the lack of meat affected her adversely. She stared back at him with clear blue eyes. Though pale, her color was still good, pink in the cheeks. She was rather small, though. Still, many cottars rarely ate meat and they survived, though smaller than most chieftains and clansmen.

She said, "I'm very healthy and strong . . . for my size."

He'd felt her body. It was strong; slender, but strong. He cleared his throat. "If you're finished, you can wash up and go to bed. I'll be up in a bit."

She shook her head. "No, no—you take the bed. I'll sleep on the floor."

He gave her a slow smile. "Who said anyone was sleeping on the floor?"

Deidra's mouth opened, but no words came out. As she stared at him, a blush rose up her neck to stain her cheeks. "I see," she finally said, her voice cracking.

He laughed softly. "It's hardly different from the past few nights, aye?"

They had lain near each other, wrapped in their own blankets. But somehow they both knew that sleeping together in a bed was different. Intimate.

She broke eye contact and her eyes darted around the room, as if looking for escape.

He doubted he was truly capable of anything lascivious tonight, but it was a pleasure to see her so flustered at the thought of sharing a bed with him.

She stood. "Well, uhm. I . . . uh, guess I'll head up then." She turned, still not looking at him, and scurried away.

He ran a hand over his chin and jaw, staring after her. And amazingly, there was a stirring down below. He had truly thought he was in too much pain to even think about lying with a woman, even one he wanted as much as he wanted Deidra, but damned if he'd been wrong.

He downed the rest of his ale, still staring contemplatively at the doorway where Deidra had disappeared. No matter how much he wanted it, this back was going to give him a problem. The tavern wench came by his table, inquiring if he wanted another tankard. Her hands were strong, forearms muscled from carrying platters of food to the patrons. And she had a look about her that said she did some extras on the side for the right amount of coin.

Stephen smiled at her. She smiled back and shifted a hip out. She placed a hand on her hip and thrust her bust forward so he could get a good look at her ample cleavage.

"Or mayhap there's something else ye'll be wanting?" she asked, a red brow arched.

Stephen jingled the purse at his waist with a smile. "Aye, I think there might be."

Deidra had lain awake for more than an hour, alternately terrified and excited. But as the time had dragged by and Stephen hadn't come, she'd begun to grow concerned. Was he hurt? Maybe he couldn't come upstairs? She was close to throwing back the blanket and going back down to look for him when the door opened. Duke padded in first and flopped down beside the bed.

A war raged between her mind and her body. She wanted to ask him where he'd been, what had taken him so long, but she couldn't move, couldn't speak, could only lay paralyzed, waiting for him to come to bed. What would happen next?

The room was dark, but her eyes were squeezed shut anyway. Her ears strained, listening to him moving around the room. The mattress shifted beneath his weight and her breath hitched. *He was on the bed.* His hand was on her shoulder, warm and wide.

"Are you afraid, Deidra?" he whispered.

She couldn't lie. Duke sensed her agitation and

came to stand beside the bed, whining and shifting from paw to paw, his claws making a soft, scraping sound on the floorboards.

"Aye," she said.

"Don't worry," he whispered. "I won't touch you. Do you wish me to sleep on the floor?"

She turned quickly and put her hand on his arm. "No, no, I'm fine. You can sleep here, if you want."

"I want." His voice was low and rough, with an undertone that said he wanted more than just to sleep beside her.

She turned back toward the wall. Her heart hammered wildly, her body weak. She wanted, too. He stretched out beside her and placed a hand on her hip. She felt it throughout her body, like fingers of lightning, streaking through her. She tried to force a swallow past her constricted throat.

She coughed, then found her voice. "You seem much improved."

He sighed deeply. "Aye, I am."

She frowned and sniffed, catching a pungent scent. "Is that liniment I smell?"

"It is." His hand moved, stroking her hip. His hand was large and strong, and her body melted like butter next to a flame. Her head fell back. She drew in a shuddering breath.

His breath warmed her neck. In her mind, she imagined his mouth, a hair's width from her skin, so close, almost touching. She trembled inside, waiting, wanting.

The clean scent of him, along with the sharp scent of liniment, filled her nose.

"You didn't have to put it on yourself," she whispered. "I would have, had you just asked me."

"I didn't." The words blew across her skin, followed by the feather touch of his lips gently kissing. Her loins loosened as she sank deeper into the bed.

"I know you didn't ask me. But you should have."

"No, no, I mean I didn't put it on myself."

She froze, brows drawing together. "Then who did?"

He still kissed her, soft lips on her jaw and ear. "The woman downstairs, Anne is her name, I believe."

Deidra's stomach plummeted and nausea rose. She had seen this Anne. That woman looked like a whore. Deidra doubted very seriously that the only thing she'd done had been to rub his back. And now here he was, in bed with her. His breath tickled her neck again, and her skin crawled. She slapped at the skin on her neck, trying to wipe away the sensation. Her curled fingers collided with his mouth. He jerked away with a muffled grunt.

"What the hell was that for?" he asked. He'd moved his head back, but his hand was still firmly planted on her hip, holding her in place.

"Why didn't you just ask me?" Deidra's face burned with indignation. The more she thought about it and imagined it—that woman, rubbing her hands all over him—the more her belly twisted. She feared she might be ill.

Before he had a chance to reply, she continued, her voice too loud, trembling slightly, "I've offered over and over again and you refuse. All I want to do is help and you won't let me. Instead you hire a whore to do it. What else did she do?"

He said nothing, only held very still.

Deidra turned, anger making her movements exaggerated, and pushed at him. "Get off me."

His hand held her hip tighter. She tried to climb out of the bed, but he held her down. It was too dark to see.

"Let me up," she ground out through clenched teeth.

"No." He pressed with his palm, surprisingly still holding her in place. He was very strong. "She did nothing more than rub liniment into my back. I knew you were tired. I didn't want to ask you to do that."

"Liar! You just don't want me to touch you. You'd rather lay with that . . . that . . . *woman* with the breasts. I am the strange woman, the animal woman with crazy hair and no breasts—that's why—"

His hand moved from her hip to cup her breast. She inhaled sharply, her thoughts scattering like dropped pebbles. His fingers kneaded, palm sliding beneath and holding her breast, as if weighing it.

Deidra couldn't seem to catch her breath. She had just been sick with anger, but now she couldn't remember what had made her so angry.

"They feel like breasts to me," he murmured. "And very fine ones, so your babbling makes no sense."

Her response was a shuddering exhalation. The ache from the other night was back, throbbing between her thighs. But her memory was also back—he had hired a whore to rub his back.

"You shouldn't have," she whispered.

"Maybe not, but I wanted us both rested."

Her belly dipped and she immediately forgave him.

His hand left her breast, only to reappear on the strings holding her shift closed. He pulled slowly on each one until the air cooled her hot skin.

His hand slid inside, over her bare skin. Deidra's eyes closed and she bit her lip.

"What was it I said I would do?" When she didn't answer, he asked reproachfully, "You don't remember?"

Oh God. She remembered every word he'd said that night, imagined it over and over again until she'd ached with unsatisfied lust.

She swallowed hard, trying to find some moisture in her mouth. "You said . . . you said you'd kiss . . . *them.*"

"Them?" he asked quizzically. His thumb rubbed lazily over her hardened nipple. Each time it swept across her, it was as if he strummed an instrument between her thighs. "Oh, you mean *these,*" he said.

Even though he couldn't see her, she nodded vigorously. He must have heard the sound of her hair against the pillow, because he asked no more questions. The bed shifted slightly, and then his tongue replaced his thumb.

She made a sound in her throat, part choke, part gasp. It felt so good, but she wanted more. Her back arched so that she pressed her breast hard into his mouth.

"Mmmm . . . ," was all he said and sucked harder.

Yes. That was what she wanted. Her body ached and throbbed. She felt swollen down there, as if she was about to burst. Her hips moved against his leg. His hand touched her bare calf, then slid upward, under her shift, pushing it up as he went.

Oh God. Yes, touch me there. She was afraid to say it aloud, afraid to hear her voice, heavy and strained with excitement, but she wanted him to know, know like the animals knew her thoughts.

His hand slid up her thigh to her belly, barely brushing the curls. Her legs had loosened for him, knees falling apart. She made a frustrated noise.

He released her nipple with a soft chuckle.

"What did I say I would do next?" His breath blew cold across her damp nipple and she shivered.

"Kiss me," she whispered.

His mouth covered hers, tongue meeting hers. She gripped his neck, holding him to her as she met his tongue, explored his mouth. Her leg hooked over his, pressing closer.

He pulled away. His labored breath feathered the side of her mouth. She panted now too, ready to explode. She needed him to do something, to touch her, to be inside her.

"What next, Deidra?"

Her mind was blank, she could barely think. She shook her head.

"Think, sweet, you must remember."

"Uh . . . you said you'd kiss me . . . everywhere."

He made a deep sound of appreciation, then kissed her jaw. The tip of his tongue teased her ear, drew the lobe between her teeth.

She gasped, desire stabbing her low.

He kissed her neck and her collarbones.

"Everywhere?" he whispered.

"Aye, yes, I pray you!" The words burst out of her, urgent, pleading.

He pushed her skirt up farther so that it was gathered around her chest, and then his lips, warm and soft, pressed to her belly. The muscles quivered beneath his mouth. He kissed and licked as his hand slid between her thighs, pushing them open.

Please, please, please. The refrain cycled over and over in her mind, and she didn't even know what she begged for. All she knew is she needed him lower, touching, inside . . . and then he was, his fingers stroking between her lips, opening them, then his tongue licking at the nub.

She gasped, light flashing behind her eyes, her hips pressing up. Pleasure made her heart and belly tremble. She didn't know if she could stand much more, but it was wonderful, impossible, her body felt barely able to contain the sensations. His finger slid inside her and his tongue continued to lick. The air left her lungs. She gasped. Her body convulsed. The pressure that had been building reached a crisis and she cried out as it washed over her, over and over again.

And when the strange squeezing pleasure lessened, she let out a shuddering laugh. Her body felt heavy and loose, tiny shocks of pleasure still radiating from her core.

"You found that amusing?" he said, humor in his voice.

"No . . . no . . . just . . . I do not have the words."

He laughed softly. "We're not finished yet."

No, she didn't suppose they were. She knew there was more to lovemaking than what they had done thus far, even though that seemed like quite a lot. She lay there, her skin damp, her body weak, waiting.

He rolled heavily onto his back. "That was quite a lot for my back, lass. If you want me to finish, and I know I do, let's do this."

His hands spanned her waist, and he pulled her on top of him. Her leg snaked over him so she straddled him. He slid one hand along her lower back to her bottom, pressing her into his erection. And unbelievably, the lust stirred in her again. His other hand gripped the back of her neck, pulling her mouth to his.

He pulled her up so that his cock pressed into her, stretching her, filling the ache that had reappeared. She felt a moment of pain, and her body stiffened. He held her, whispered to her and kissed her chin and mouth and neck. When he moved again, the pain was gone. She relaxed. She pushed against his chest so that she was nearly sitting up. His hands pressed her hips down so that he went deeper, filling her.

And then he lifted her, pulling out halfway, then thrusting up into her. She moaned, catching his rhythm and matching it. His cock rubbed against something inside her, and each time it did, the pressure wound tight and tighter. She rocked against him, working him deeper with each stroke, their bodies moving like one sinuous animal.

Stephen groaned, his hands stroking up her ribs to rub at her breasts. She covered his hands with hers, loving the way he felt inside her and all over her. She shifted and pressed, the pleasure winding tighter and tighter. Stephen cried out suddenly, his hands sliding around to her back and pulling her onto his chest. His mouth covered hers and her body tightened around him as they both climaxed, bodies and mouths locked.

She collapsed on his chest, head resting beneath his chin. The sensations pulsed through her in waves, centering in her core and radiating outward. She couldn't think or see; she could only lie there, completely wrung out. She was asleep within minutes.

She woke sometime later, her body chilled. Stephen had pulled her shift down over her body, and his hands traced lazily along her shoulders and back.

"Am I keeping you from sleeping?" she asked, rolling off of him so she could lie beside him.

"No, I wasn't tired."

"Liar."

"I mean it . . . tomorrow . . . everything changes."

His words were like a door slamming in her heart. Though she hadn't expected him to change his mind, she had managed to forget about it for a while. She turned her back on him and faced the wall. This was why they had come. The only reason. And if the blood witch agreed to change him, everything would change.

His hand rested on her arm. "It will be fine," he said, stroking her skin. "I promise not to do anything stupid."

"I don't care what you do. I was only making sure you got here safely." The words were out of her mouth before she could even think about them. *Stupid, stupid.*

Of course she cared. She would not be with him in this bed if she didn't.

"If you do not care, then why do you care whether I'm safe or not?"

"I don't," she hissed. "At least not anymore."

He sighed, his hand dropping away. "Very well. We'll talk about it later, then."

She bit her lip to stop herself from saying anything else.

"Are you coming with me?" he asked.

Her vision blurred. She didn't know what she wanted anymore—except that she didn't want this to change. Not him, not the way they had felt together tonight. Now that she spoke with the animals again, she was reluctant to give it up. It didn't matter to Luthias whether she actually did or not. He believed what he believed, regardless of proof otherwise, so why should she give up the one advantage she had?

After a long moment she said, "I will wait here."

He sighed again but didn't say another word.

They lay the rest of the night in silence. Deidra's thigh muscles ached, his seed still damp between her thighs. Uneasiness filled her. Change was in the air, she felt it. She feared that the change was Stephen and that his changes would leave no room for her.

Chapter 12

—∞∞∞—

Stephen didn't think Deidra was asleep as he prepared to leave the next morning. He hadn't slept much, and he didn't believe she had slept at all. He stood over the bed, staring down at her small figure curled away from him.

Duke sat beside him, whining.

Stephen shook his head at the dog. "No. You cannot come with me."

Duke lay on his belly, nose between his paws, and didn't make another noise. Stephen suspected Deidra had spoken to the beast. He usually wasn't so well behaved.

Stephen wanted to say good-bye to her, but she was strange to him suddenly. This had been her quest. Now that she had changed her mind, it seemed she expected him to as well. But their problems were nothing alike. She was a still a whole woman whether she spoke to animals or not. He loved her. He wanted to be the man she deserved—a whole man. She would see when he returned that it would all be well.

He turned to leave when her voice stopped him. "I left something for you on the table, by the door. Take it with you." Her voice was flat, emotionless.

He crossed to the table. A simple wooden rosary lay upon it. He lifted it, puzzled. "Papist idolatry?"

"In the stories, it is the only thing that will protect you against a blood witch."

His hand curled around the rosary as he looked back at her. More protection. It angered and touched him at the same time. He didn't know what to do with this woman. He only wanted to be a man, and she continued to mother him. Still—who knew what would happen next? He took her offering and left without a word.

The village sat on Scotland's northern coast. The *baobhan sith*'s island was a few miles out. Unfortunately, there were many islands to the north. He would need directions and a vessel. The wind blew hard, cold, and salty coming up off of the water, pushing up high, jagged sea caps. Fishermen at the water's edge prepared their vessels to head out, regardless of the rough water. Stephen didn't want to ride with a fisherman. He wanted his own boat. And besides, he doubted many people visited a blood witch.

He walked along the shoreline, inquiring, until he found a fisherman with a boat to rent.

The man scratched at his head, tan and shiny, a sharp contrast to his face, which resembled a walnut. "Ayuh," he said. "I hiv a skiff. Whot hiv ye for barter?" He looked Stephen over dubiously, apparently thinking he couldn't have much worth trading in his single leather satchel.

Stephen removed the leather purse from his waist and shook several coins out in his palm. "How is this?"

The man's gray and wiry brows rose as he contemplated the coins. "Ayuh. That'll do."

Stephen turned over the coins, and the fisherman led him to a small skiff.

"Have a care," the man said. "The sea is angry today. Where are ye headed?"

"To see the *baobhan sith*."

The man drew back, eyes wide, as if Stephen had drawn his weapon.

"You jest?" he hissed, voice low.

"Nay. Does she not receive visitors?"

The man barked an incredulous laugh. "Visitors? By God, no. Not unless they are not coming back." He wiped a hand over his mouth and looked around him at the other fishermen. He turned back to Stephen with a considering look. "Ye ken, ye'll not likely be coming back from there yourself."

Stephen shrugged, climbing into the skiff and setting on the cross-boards gingerly. His back ached, protesting last night's activities. Stephen wouldn't trade that ache for anything. It reminded him of how he'd finally possessed Deidra. And soon enough the pain would be over forever.

"Which island is it?" Stephen asked, looking out to the dozen islands both near and far in the distance.

"That one." The man pointed to a small rocky island several miles away.

Stephen stared at the tiny island, a pebble in the vast sea. He had a lot of rowing ahead of him.

"Gude luck to ye!" The fisherman pushed Stephen's skiff away from the shore. "But if ye meet with only foul luck, ye canna say I didna tell ye so. So I'll not mourn ye."

Stephen laughed softly. "Aye, well, it'll be my own fault."

The fisherman stood on the shore and waved, grinning now, a blackened, crooked smile. "Aye, lad, that it will. That it will."

The man's behavior did not bolster Stephen's confidence, but he had come this far. He was not stopping now. If he didn't come back, maybe it was for the best. His life had been purposeless, aimless until Deidra had shown up at Bráighde Pele with her stories of the blood witch. He didn't want to go back to that. He'd rather die.

Deidra. The thought of his death after her warnings made him feel a little ill. He redoubled his efforts on the oars. The skiff cut through the water. The salt and damp clung to his lips and hair. Seals dipped and bobbed past his skiff, heading for an island farther out.

His shoulders ached by the time he reached the little island. He dragged the skiff ashore and climbed the rocky slope. There were no trees on this island, only rocks and grass. At the top of the rise he was confronted with more rises . . . and a lamb.

The black-faced lamb bleated at him and trotted away, up and over another rise. Stephen followed. As he climbed the rise, he grew aware of a sound that grew with each step he took. Bahhing and bleating. It waxed and waned with the wind, but nevertheless grew stronger.

At the top of the next rise he looked down over a flock of woolly black-faced sheep, their horns curled like seashell ears. Past them was a house built into the hillside. The door was currently shut.

The lamb he followed reached the bottom of the hill. Instead of joining the rest of the sheep, it disappeared into the hillside.

The hill Stephen currently stood on housed the stable. Stephen continued down the hill, twisting and stretching his aching back the whole way.

The entrance to the stable was twice as wide as the door to the house. The fence was open so the sheep could come and go as they pleased. Stephen stepped inside and waited for his eyes to adjust to the gloom.

It smelled musty inside, of hay and dirt and dung. The interior of the stable was much larger than it looked from the outside. Two long troughs separated the room into halves. Near the back, scattered hay led to a large pile.

The lamb had gone to this pile. A full-grown sheep lay there on her side, her distended stomach heaving with labored breaths. She was giving birth.

Stephen crossed to her and knelt beside her, placing his hands on her belly. There was movement beneath his hands. The sheep raised her head slightly to briefly look at him, then rested it back in the hay.

Odd business for a blood witch to be in. Or so he assumed. He didn't really know all that much about blood witches. He supposed they needed a source of income just as everyone else did.

He straightened with a grunt and left the stable, crossing the open valley. The grazing sheep gave way for him, bleating their annoyance at his trespassing.

When he stood in front of the door in the hill, he knocked sharply. "Hello! Is anybody there?"

It would be a lie to say that he was unafraid. The little farm was not what he had expected, and it made him uneasy—that, combined with the lack of response from his knock. There was no door latch on the outside of the door. He pushed against it and knocked again, but there was no response.

Stephen turned to survey the valley and sheep and stable, scratching at the whiskers on his jaw. He could sure use Deidra right now, to talk to these beasts. Maybe they knew something.

He didn't fancy breaking the blood witch's door down. That would no doubt set them off on the wrong note. And besides, he thought, glancing back at the door, it looked pretty solid. It might do more damage to him than he could do to the door.

With a sigh he continued his inspection of the island. He found nothing of note. There was another grassy hill behind the one with the door, and beyond that, sea.

More islands were visible in the distance. Stephen wondered if she had left for the day. But when he squinted up at the sun, he recalled that blood witches didn't fancy sunlight, and it was a bright day.

He turned quickly back toward the hill. She was here—inside the hill-house. Mayhap she locked herself in and the sun out during the day. It did not behoove him to hammer at her door anymore. It might anger her. He returned to the stable.

The sheep was straining now and blowing harshly through her nose. Stephen knelt beside her, hands spanning over her stomach again.

He was no farm boy. He had been raised by his uncle, an earl, and treated as if he'd been his son, even though he had been conscious every day of his life, since his father had died, that he was not the son of an earl but the bastard son of a bastard living on charity. Nevertheless, he had not been expected to work in the stables. Stephen didn't know if the sheep was in distress or if her state was normal. It would certainly reflect well on him if the blood witch woke to find he had helped birth one of her lambs. He built the hay into a bed and lay near the sheep, to watch over her until the *baobhan sith* awakened.

Deidra lay in bed for a long time after Stephen left, waiting. What she waited for she wasn't entirely certain. She knew all he wanted was to be "whole." But suddenly she couldn't stop replaying the stories from her childhood over and over again in her head. Blood witches were cunning, bloodthirsty. They enticed the unknowing, then ripped their throats out. How did you make a pact with an animal? If Deidra knew anything, she knew animals, and one did not reason with bloodthirsty ones.

At noon the ostler banged on the door, demanding that she either pay for another night or get out. She packed her things and left the inn, Duke at her heels.

She couldn't sit here all day, not with these thoughts. She would go to the beach and wait.

She took the long way, walking through the main village lane, searching for Stephen's distinctive limp and long blond hair among the other people milling through the streets, but he was not to be found. She sat by the water's edge, Duke at her side, and scanned the coastline, watching all the boats that came in with a hopeful heart, only to slump dejectedly when they did not contain Stephen.

She waited until night fell, but there was still no sign of Stephen. With a heavy heart, she stood. She might miss his return in the dark. Or he might not even return until morning, since rowing alone at night was risky.

She returned to the inn to wait there. The ostler was busy talking to a tall, balding man. Deidra's heart stopped. The ostler noticed her and pointed. The man turned, and her suspicion was confirmed.

Luthias Forsyth.

Duke sensed her fear at the sight of the man and hunkered low, snarling and barking. Luthias's eyes narrowed on Duke. With a gesture, men appeared beside her with raised clubs.

Run, Duke, run! Deidra screamed in her mind. The dog spotted the men and heard her demand. He leaped back when the first club smashed down, barely escaping a crushing blow. He bounded out the door and raced away.

The men grabbed her arms as Luthias approached. "Miss MacKay. Fancy meeting you here. And look at you, completely healed, as if your arm had never been broken."

That wasn't entirely true. Her shoulder still ached from time to time, but it was much better. Instead of addressing this, she said, "You've been following me."

Luthias smiled, hands steepled before him. "But of course. What came as a surprise to me is that you're here with a man . . . the same man who duped me into believing he was a witch hunter." He leaned in closer to her. "Where is he, Miss MacKay?"

She yanked on her arms, fear bubbling up in her chest. Oh God, she shouldn't have returned. They would have thought that she and Stephen had left town and they would have followed; now they would wait around to trap Stephen.

"Who?" she said, still struggling. "I don't know who you speak of. I travel alone."

"Oh, come, Deidra, do you really think me stupid?" He waved a dismissive hand at her. "Never mind. We will find him and he will be tried as your accomplice."

"My accomplice? I have no accomplice!"

"He set you free when I had you in my hands." He curled his raised hand into a fist and shook it at her.

Her heart squeezed in her chest as she shook her head frantically. "I don't ken what you're talking about."

He motioned to several more men stationed around the room. "Search the building and village for him. He might have seen us and is hiding. Have a care—the 'crippled man' was likely an act. He is probably much stronger and faster than he lets on."

He turned his gaze on Deidra. "Come with me, Miss MacKay. I have a few questions for you."

He turned, walking deeper into the inn. Deidra's captors pushed her along after him. Deidra gave the ostler a pleading look as she was shoved past him, but he averted his eyes and turned away.

She was all alone.

Stephen slept the day away. He woke once and saw that the sheep had given birth to a lamb. He lay there in excruciating pain for a while, staring at lamb and mother, breathing in the odor of hay and manure. He contemplated getting up, but instead he fell back asleep.

When he woke again he sensed immediately that something had changed. He was not alone. But it wasn't the presence of animals he sensed. It was something else, something dangerous.

It was dark; no light illuminated the stable. He blinked into the darkness, his heart thudding with fear and pain. His back felt as if a spike had been jammed into the base of it.

Slowly his eyes grew accustomed to the dark, and he could make out shadowy figures. A pale lump—the sheep and lamb; darker shadows in the center of the room—the troughs; and something very dark and dense just to his right.

"Good evening," said a soft, feminine voice.

The surprise snatched at his heart. He squeezed his eyes shut, trying to push back the pain and remember why he was here. The pain, that was why.

His heart beat overtime. "You are—you are the *baobhan sith*?"

"You know that I am. Who are you?"

"I am Stephen Ross. I came for your help."

"Help?" She laughed softly. Her voice was rough, husky. "Not many come to me for help. And they are all disappointed."

Stephen bit the inside of his lip as he forced himself to a sitting position. Her hand on his shoulder stopped him.

"Stay. You are hurt. I am not a healer. I cannot fix this ailment. I've heard of some that might. The MacKays of Strathwick. They might be able to help you."

Stephen let out an incredulous breath, then laughed. The irony was such that laughing seemed the only alternative. The derisive humor bubbled upward and he laughed harder, wondering what Deidra would think when he told her. He laughed until it hurt his belly and back.

When the pain finally dulled his humor, he sighed, resting his forehead on the floor.

"You have humor," she mused. "And you're comely. Your body is strong." Her hand ran over his arm and shoulder. "Despite this . . . weakness."

He tensed, the hair along his neck stiffening. He wanted to shrug her off but didn't dare.

"You can see me?" he asked warily.

She laughed now, a knowing, sensuous laugh, but she didn't answer. "Maybe I *can* help you, Stephen Ross. Come."

"One moment, prithee," he said, and readied himself to make another attempt at standing. But before he could even try, she lifted him, effortlessly, it seemed, until he stood, then pressed his back against the wall.

His eyes screwed shut and he let out a broken cry of pain.

"Can you walk now?" she asked.

He pressed the back of his head to the dirt and rock wall. *No, not yet.* He shook his head. She waited, still supporting him with a fist wadded in his jack, pushing him against the wall.

She was unnaturally strong.

Stephen took a few deep breaths, then pushed at her hand. She released him and he slumped forward, remaining upright under his own power.

"I'm fine."

"Good, follow me."

He sensed rather than heard her movement away from him. He guessed that she was leaving the stable. This was confirmed when he saw her silhouette standing in the stable's open doorway. Tall and shapely she stood, waiting. The breeze moved her hair that hung loose to her waist and the bottom of her thin dress.

Stephen limped after her. He had lied—he wasn't fine. His back and legs were stiff with sharp spikes of pain radiating from his spine down the backs of his legs. Each step felt like a mallet driving the spikes deeper into his hips.

He joined her in the fresh night air and inhaled deeply to clear his head. In the moonlight she was beautiful. Red hair hung in a glistening waterfall over her shoulders and down her back. Large, dark eyes stared at him from an expressionless, heart-shaped face. Her skin was pale and fine, unmarked, and the dress she wore, made of gossamer or some such thin material, left little to the imagination. She was well made, too.

They traversed the valley. She adjusted her speed so that she didn't get too far ahead of him. He wanted to fall to his knees and praise God when they made it to the open door at the other end of the field. She disappeared inside, and seconds later a candle was lit. He stood just inside the doorway and watched as she circled the room, lighting candles until the entire room was lit with a circle of them. She was clearly not lacking in luxuries.

Despite being built into a hillside, it was a comfortable house. It appeared to be a single room, but Stephen couldn't be sure, as parts of it were in complete darkness beyond the candles. The floor was dirt and spread with rushes, and her candles were beeswax, not lard. A long table against the east wall held nothing but a salt cellar. An enormous curtained bed was at the far end of the room, and a stool sat to the west of the bed, with a tapestry loom before it. Not far beyond that was a chair with a blanket and a book on the seat.

"So, Stephen Ross." The *baobhan sith* turned, blowing out the long thin flint match she used to light the candles. "What is it you believe I can do for you?"

She was a beautiful woman. She approached him slowly, her steps measured and flowing—gliding almost. When she stood an arm's length away, he saw that her eyes were a deep green, her skin flawless.

"I have heard that you do magic in return for certain . . ." He rotated his hand at the wrist to indicate his inability to pin a good word on it and finally finished, "*obligations.*"

Her brows drew together in confusion. "Obligations? Magic? This is very strange. What sort of . . ." She waved her hand in an exaggerated parody of his fumble for words. "*Obligations?*"

"The MacKays—it is said that a *baobhan sith* made them witches. Many generations ago a MacKay came to a *baobhan sith* seeking aid. His son was dying. He made a pact with the blood witch. In return for his son's life she made him a witch, and it is carried in his line to this day."

Her smile was small and condescending. "I don't know of this pact you speak of, but I assure you, your story is mangled."

Stephen's mouth drew up into a tight smile. "I assure *you,* I have not made this story up. I know the MacKays, and they *are* witches."

"I believe you, Stephen. Peace. But we are not demons. I am not Satan with whom you can sign a bloody contract."

Stephen's brow arched and he glanced around the room. "Do you call on him, then?"

She threw her head back and laughed. It was a full, throaty, feminine sound. "You are very amusing, Stephen. I shall like having you around."

Her words sent a chill through him, especially when he recalled that she had lifted him from the ground with one hand and no effort. He did not want to stay around. He had plans.

"Why am I amusing?"

"You think *I* know Satan?" She pointed to her breast as she turned away from him. She crossed the room, hips swaying, and disappeared into the shadows.

Stephen stood nervously, waiting. His back still hurt, but it wasn't so bad. He had some laudanum, but he would not take it when his situation was so uncertain.

When she didn't reappear, he called, "Miss . . . er . . ." He realized then that he had never gotten her name. *"Baobhan sith?"*

He started to follow her into the dark shadows where she had disappeared when a cold wind stirred his hair from behind. He turned.

She stood behind him with a tray laden with cheese, dried fruit, sweet meats, and nuts. He startled violently at the sight of her there. He had not even heard her approach.

"Eat," she purred. "You must be hungry."

"Where were you?"

She lifted the tray higher. "Fetching this for you." She brushed past him with the tray, set it down on the long table, then pulled out two chairs. He followed and sat down. After a second's hesitation he began to eat greedily.

"Why do I amuse you?" he asked again when she sat across from him.

"Because you think I know Satan" She gave a silent, derisive laugh. "That I would even know him." She tilted her head to the side. "You have ingested all of the witch propaganda, have you not? All witches consort with the devil. What of the MacKays? Have you seen them commune with Old Nick?"

"No. They are not evil."

She sat up straighter, palms on the tabletop and brows raised. "But I am?"

Stephen lifted a shoulder. "I don't know that yet, do I?"

Her brows lowered and her mouth flattened. "What do you want? Hmm? What favor do you ask of me?"

He could see he was not charming her. He tried to give her a winning smile without overdoing it. "I am willing to become a witch, if it will make me whole."

She stared at him as if she expected him to say more. When he didn't, she frowned and gave a little shake of her head, as if confounded. "That's it? How does this benefit me?"

Now Stephen was confused too. "What do you want? I thought you would name your price. Give me your terms."

"What do you have that I would want?"

"I am a wealthy man. I can give you lands or money."

She spread her hands to indicate their surroundings. "I have a whole island . . . and what would I do with money?"

Stephen ran a frustrated hand through his hair. "Then you tell me. What do you want? If I don't have it, I can probably get it for you."

She licked her bottom lip and surveyed him appraisingly. The way she looked at him, like a horse for sale, made him uneasy. He wondered if she would want him to lay with her. She was a beautiful woman, and normally the idea of being with someone like her would be a welcome distraction, but not anymore.

It felt . . . well . . . *wrong*. Such a thought seemed absurd on the surface, but when looked at deeper, it went back to Deidra. It felt like a betrayal. She was the one he wanted—not in some illicit affair, but as his wife.

But he didn't want to be with her if he was only half a man. He would do anything to be whole again, and sleeping with a beautiful woman was a small price to pay.

"The only thing I am lacking is a companion. I am alone on this island, except for the occasional weeping sacrifice the villagers send over. Halfwits, all of them, sent because they want to be rid of them." She laid a palm on her breast. "What am I to do with them? They are as useless to me as they are to them."

Stephen asked, "So . . . what do you do with them?"

Her slow, enigmatic smile made his throat tighten.

"I cannot tell you that . . . at least not yet. So, what do you say?"

"You want me to find you a companion? What are you looking for?"

Her look was condescending. He was not that dull; he knew who she wanted, but he didn't want to volunteer for the job.

"A man . . . comely, intelligent, amusing, able to satisfy a woman." A perfectly shaped red brow arched suggestively. "And just such a man is here, in my home, wanting something from me."

Stephen's heart sped up. She was going to do it. She would grant him his wish if he would stay with her. He would never be with Deidra either way, it seemed. If he had to go on without her, he'd rather do it without the excruciating pain.

"Before you make your decision," she said, leaning back slightly and giving him a view of her breasts— the thin material of her gown did not camouflage her jutting nipples the slightest bit, "let me tell you a bit about what it means to be a *baobhan sith*." She reached across the table and chose a piece of cheese, turning it in her fingers while looking at it. "This cheese has no taste for me. When I eat it, it tastes like dust . . . just like everything else." She dropped it back on the tray with an air of disdain. "I can smell it better than you can smell. It smells delicious. And if I force myself to eat it, it gives me no sustenance. My body rejects it."

Stephen shook his head. "Rejects it?"

"I bock it up."

Stephen picked up the cheese she'd dropped and examined it thoughtfully before popping it in his mouth. He shrugged. "It's not that good. Not worth the price of a good back."

Her smile was small and wistful, her eyes far away. "That's what you think now, lad. But there might come a day when the crisp bite of a fresh apple in autumn seems an elixir of the gods. The memory more powerful than the love of a child or a good man." She opened her palms and looked down at them. "And right there, in your hands when child and man are both dust." Her eyes met his and her smile twisted ruefully. "Not that I would know about either."

"If that's all there is to being a *baobhan sith*, then I willingly give it up."

"No, that's not all there is . . . there is the matter of the sun."

"The sun?" Stephen remembered the story Deidra had told him that first night she'd shown up at his home looking like a dustball. The beautiful women with voices like nightingales. They entranced men, then fell on them, ripping their throats out and drinking their blood. One man survived—because of a rosary and the sunlight. Stephen's belly tightened. It was night. He was suddenly thankful for the good-luck charm Deidra had given him before he'd left. He unhooked the front of his jack and casually scratched at his chest. The bulge of it in the pocket sewn into the inside of his jack brushed the back of his hand and reassured him.

"Aye, the sun," she said. "A blood witch is very strong . . . the sun saps our strength, whereas the night fuels us. We are strongest—and hungriest—when the moon is full."

Stephen let out an internal sigh of relief that the moon was currently not full. "All right. So that is why you locked yourself into your home during the day?"

She smiled and nodded. "Aye, I sleep during the day."

"But you can go about during the day?"

She inclined her head. "Aye, a *baobhan sith* can live amongst others . . . the great lords do well as *baobhan siths.* They drink and carouse all night, then merely seem incapacitated from the night's activities. No one thinks a thing about them lying abed all day. Women, however, don't do so well. They can seem invalids during the day, but at night, when they are strong and"—her eyes scanned him with increasing interest—"hungry, people get suspicious."

Stephen stared back at her. "It seems a small price to pay for strength and wholeness."

"To be hunted? To live long after all you have loved has passed away? To subsist on nothing but living blood? To feed like an animal?" She shook her head. "You show your ignorance." She smiled and leaned across the table. "You think I am a fool, do you not? You think I will change you and then let you leave? You will be mine." She leaned back in the chair and shrugged nonchalantly. "You're mine either way. You will not leave this room without my blessing."

"What do you mean, I'll be yours?"

Her mouth curved into a smile. "Mine to do with as I wish." She touched her neck, trailing her fingers from neck to bosom. "My blood will be in you. You will be stronger, aye, but not as strong as me. Your mind will be mine."

Stephen frowned at her. "And who do you belong to?"

Her head tilted slightly. "You are clever." She nodded slowly. "Aye, I had a sire once, but she is dead now, so I am released of her."

Stephen contemplated what it meant. To be an animal that lusted for blood, but to be strong and pain free. This woman didn't seem animal-like. She retained thought and intellect and, judging by the loom and books, an interest in life. She wasn't some walking dead, a monster. But he would be bound to her. He would have to give up Deidra unless he killed this blood witch. He had thought that he didn't want to be with Deidra unless he was a whole man, but the thought of never being able to hold her again, or touch her . . . or even talk to her made his chest feel as shoveled out as an empty grave. He thought of the rest of his life stretching out before him without her. Empty, pointless.

And suddenly, when it came down to the choice between his back and Deidra . . . he finally knew what he wanted more than anything else.

But he was here and the blood witch was dangerous. He could keep her talking till morning, but he didn't know how many hours away dawn was. The island was small and he was slow. Even if he could get away he couldn't row back to the mainland in the dark.

It didn't look good for him.

"I see you are thinking a great deal, Stephen." She smiled. "I can see the cogs turning behind your eyes."

"There is much to think about . . . such as how do you know you want to spend the rest of your life with me?"

Both thin red brows rose nearly to her hairline. "Rest of my life? My goodness, that is not what I had in mind."

"What do you have in mind?"

"Until I am bored of you."

"That could take forever," he said with a smile.

She laughed. "Oh, you have a high estimate of yourself. You *will* amuse me."

"I certainly hope so." Stephen didn't think they could keep up this banter the whole night, so he decided the best way to stall for daylight was to ask her questions. "Why all the sheep?"

"I trade their wool for goods and money. And they are food as well."

Stephen raised a brow. "Food? I didn't think you ate."

"I do not eat their meat. I drink their blood. And I have guests, the people I trade with . . . you, that I feed. It is wise to have such things on hand."

"I thought you drank human blood."

Her lips curved again. "Blood is like wine . . . there are many flavors and qualities. The blood of a healthy child is like the finest Pinot Noir, whereas, say . . . a rat is vinegar—and then there is every variety in between. But they are all sustenance, and we consume what is available and what is safe."

"What about me?" Stephen asked. "What kind of wine would I be?"

She tilted her head to examine him. "You're not an old man, but pain has taken its toll on you . . . you are healthy though, your body is strong, but I have never enjoyed biting through tough muscle . . . The poppy juice you drink and the whiskey you consume to dull the pain taint your blood. You're no better than an old wife's honey mead, methinks."

That sounded promising. He apparently wasn't a very appetizing meal. Perhaps he would be safer if he just told her he'd changed his mind. Still, daylight was too far away to reveal that yet.

"What do you think, Honey Mead?" She watched with a small, interested smile reminiscent of a cat toying with her meal.

"I have a choice?"

"One would assume your journey here represented a choice already made."

"That was before I knew I could never leave."

She pushed the curtain of red hair over her shoulder. "I never said you couldn't leave. In fact, I would very much like to leave this island. With a companion. Perhaps relocate to France. There are many *baobhan siths* there and no one suspects a thing. Or Rome."

"I don't really want to leave Scotland."

She shrugged. "Edinburgh, then."

Stephen smiled. "Can I bring a lass I fancy?"

She leaned forward with a wide smile and he saw a flash of them then—sharp incisors that gleamed in the candlelight. His innards shriveled at the sight, and he swallowed hard.

"Only if you share," she whispered.

Stephen stood. There was a lantern in the skiff. He could read the stars. He didn't particularly care. He had not thought this through properly. Or, more accurately, he had, but then he'd fallen in love with Deidra. Before her, such an offer would have been more than acceptable—but now, he'd rather die.

"I think I'll be going," he said, backing toward the door, feeling the weight of the crucifix in his pocket.

She didn't move, and her expression did not change.

"Where will you go? It's the middle of the night and you're a cripple on an island."

"I've sailed before. I can navigate by the stars."

He reached the door and fumbled behind him for the latch. His hands were unsteady, so he turned to see what he was doing. He opened the door, and it immediately slammed shut in his face.

Stephen whirled around. She was right there, palm on the door, holding it closed. He had heard nothing—not a single sound—and yet here she was. His heart thundered in his chest as he reached inside his jack.

She caught his wrist. "What have you in there, Honey Mead, aye?"

He tried to jerk his hand away, but she was strong, her grip like iron.

"You didn't think I could just let you leave, did you?" She shook her head as if he was such a little fool. "So you could bring them back for me?"

He brought his other hand up and grabbed her wrist, trying to pull her hand away. Her other hand snaked around behind him and grabbed his hair, pulling his head to the side.

"You wouldn't really leave without giving me a little taste, would you?" Her green eyes, so intense they nearly glowed, fixated on his bared neck. Her mouth opened, incisors sharp and gleaming. She was so unnaturally strong that she immobilized him. Her teeth sank into his neck and he groaned as pain seared him. She pressed her body against him, sucking at him.

He didn't want this. He wanted Deidra. A fog clouded his mind as she sucked at him; his legs grew weak, as if drugged. He felt his body going limp. Soon he would be lost, her slave. He abandoned the idea of the crucifix and instead released her wrist and snapped his dirk from his belt. He jammed it into her stomach.

Her scream was inhuman. She ripped her teeth from his neck and pushed him aside. Stephen slumped against the door, panting and scrambling for the crucifix. She stared down at the dirk hilt protruding from her stomach. Blood stained her gown, slick and wet, and dripped from her mouth.

Her screaming stopped. "You thought this would stop me?" she asked, yanking the dirk from her body. She tossed it aside. "Now you've made me angry. I won't change you now, I'll just drain you dry and throw your body to the fish."

She came at him again. He pulled the rosary out and held it before him. She reared back, lips curled and hissing.

"Not evil, eh?" Stephen wheezed. His neck hurt, but his mind was starting to clear. "Not of the devil? Then why does this blind you?" He took a step forward and she stepped back, hands rising to ward him off.

Stephen slowly began to back away. She stared at him, bloodied lips closed. He opened the door and limped into the darkness. Sheep bleated around him, and the wind blew across the grasses. He shivered, the cold cutting him bone-deep, unnatural.

He drew the rosary beads over his head so the crucifix hung over his heart, and he limped across the island as fast as his crippled legs would take him. Too slow. He cursed his damn back for bringing him to this and now making escape impossible. She could just walk fast and catch him.

Fortunately, she didn't even follow.

He looked behind him constantly, blood roaring in his ears, but there was no pursuit.

It wasn't until he was a safe distance from shore that he dared stop and light the lantern on the skiff. He stared back at the island but saw nothing. He lowered his head into his hands and let out the shuddering breath he'd been holding. God's blood, that had not gone well.

Home. That's all he wanted anymore. To fetch Deidra and take her home.

Chapter 13

———⌒∞∞∞⌒———

*D*rake stood in the shadows of a large fishing vessel, watching as Stephen rowed in slowly in the wee hours of the morning. The sun had not risen, and only the earliest risers were out preparing their vessels for the morning catch. Stephen stopped rowing when he was about fifty feet from the shore; from there he just drifted.

As Drake watched him drift, he became increasingly concerned. There was no movement from the slumped figure in the skiff. He ran around to the shoreline and cupped his hands over his mouth. "Stephen!"

Stephen was illuminated by the lantern that hung on the stern of his boat; it circled him like a halo. His head rose. Drake couldn't make out his face, but he imagined Stephen peering at him.

"Stephen! It's Drake."

It seemed as if the effort of looking at Drake was too much for Stephen and he began to sway. To Drake's horror, he swayed so far that he toppled to the side, splashing into the sea. Drake stared, dumbfounded for a heartbeat before ripping off his boots, throwing off his sword and dag, and diving into the water.

He swam hard, his panic increasing when Stephen's

head didn't reappear. When Drake was close to the skiff, he dove beneath the surface. The water was too dark to see anything, but he reached in front of himself as he swam, feeling for Stephen until he touched wisps of hair. One more stroke and he grabbed the leather of Stephen's jack.

He curled his fingers into it and kicked upward, dragging him along until they broke the surface. Drake took a gasping breath, pulling Stephen's head above the water, then immediately began swimming back to shore, one arm hooked around Stephen's neck. He was dead weight, dragging at Drake.

"God damn it, Stephen, wake up!" Drake ground out, a band of fear crushing his chest.

They were nearly to the shore when Stephen coughed and sputtered, and the fear crushing Drake's chest finally eased.

"Get your feet under you," Drake said, struggling to stand himself without dropping Stephen into the thigh-high water.

Stephen managed to stand, still coughing and leaning heavily on Drake's shoulder. They struggled the rest of the way to the rocky shore, where Drake lowered him to the ground. Stephen coughed and panted, blinking blearily.

"What happened?"

Stephen shook his head, rubbing at his eyes. "I know not . . . how did you get here?"

"I followed you and Deidra. Did you see the blood witch?"

Stephen nodded, rubbing a hand over his face. Obviously it hadn't gone well.

"Damn it," Drake cursed, and the anger flooded him fresh, as if it had just happened, as if he'd just rowed his dying wife across the water. "She probably isn't even a real witch. . . ."

Stephen pulled his collar aside, revealing two ragged puncture wounds in his neck. The leather of his jack was stained dark, as was his shirt beneath. He had lost a lot of blood.

"Jesus . . . ," Drake breathed. His stomach churned as he imagined how Stephen had gotten such odd wounds. "What the hell happened?"

"She's a *baobhan sith*." He touched the puncture wounds on his neck. "She—It . . . is a monster . . . like the tales. She is beautiful . . . and unnaturally strong. She drinks blood . . . and the rosary stopped her." He grabbed the rosary in his fist and held it tight.

Drake's gaze narrowed as he stared into the darkness where the far-off island lay. So she was a *baobhan sith*. She could have saved Ceara yet had chosen not to.

Bitch.

"How is Deidra?" Stephen asked.

"I know not. I've been here, waiting for you since yesterday."

Stephen slowly got to his feet with a grunt. Drake stared back at the sea. The need to go to the *baobhan sith*'s island *now* pulled at his chest. But he had preparations to make first—and Deidra's problem to take care of. The blood witch would wait. But she had much to answer for.

Drake followed Stephen's slow progress to the inn, where they were greeted exuberantly by the innkeeper.

"Oh, aye, she's still here," he said, nodding enthusiastically to their query about Deidra. "Would you like to go up and see her?"

Drake thought the ostler's behavior odd, but Stephen didn't seem to notice. He limped wearily toward the stairs.

Drake stopped him with a hand on his arm. He was sure he was not needed for their little reunion—and besides, Stephen would need rest and recovery before they could continue on.

"You go on up and get some rest. I have some business to take care of. Let's plan on leaving tomorrow morn, aye?" That gave Drake nearly twenty-four hours to do what he needed to do.

Stephen stared at him uncomprehendingly. In fact, it was as if he'd been listening to something else. Drake glanced around the room, but it was empty except for two other patrons, and they were not speaking.

After a moment, Stephen nodded. "Aye, tomorrow."

"Can I have that rosary?"

Stephen's hand slid inside his jack, and he pulled the black wooden beads over his neck, dropping it in Drake's hand. Without another word he turned and continued on up the stairs.

Drake watched his friend, concerned by his bizarre behavior. It was as if he'd been walking in his sleep. He'd lost a lot of blood and was probably in pain. Tomorrow, after some rest and food, he would better . . . and hopefully Drake would have some very good news for him.

What surprised Stephen the most was that there was very little pain. In spite of all he had just been through, as well as the probable strain he'd put on his back by rowing, his back hurt no more than usual. More than anything else, Stephen felt numb and stiff. He also felt like he'd taken too much laudanum. The steps before him stretched on and on. As he dragged himself upward, only one thought kept him climbing. Deidra was somewhere at the top.

Something was different, and Stephen didn't understand what it was. *He* felt different. It was the blood loss, no doubt. Though the wound to his back had happened twelve years ago, he still remembered the pain and the weakness from the blood loss. Nevertheless, it had not been like this. Or so he remembered. He had been completely incapacitated that time, unable to walk. And the blood fever had gotten him for a time.

Perhaps that's what it was. The blood witch had infected him with something. His head seemed to be in a tunnel, sounds came to him from far away. Walking was strange, too, as if there were a buffer between his feet and the steps as he climbed the stairs.

And he heard things: a voice in his head—thoughts, really, but they weren't his own. The voice told him to return, go back to the island and to the blood witch. Each time the thought drifted through his mind, it exerted a physical pull over his body, dragging him down, making each step harder than the last. Pulling him back to the island.

But he kept on. *Deidra.* He had to see her, had to hold her and talk to her. At the top of the stairs he realized something was wrong. He'd been so preoccupied with his own strange state of mind that he hadn't paid much attention to aught else. But now he felt it.

He was being watched.

He turned and frowned down the stairs. The ostler stood at the bottom of the stairs watching his progress. The moment Stephen caught him watching, the ostler smiled and nodded and waved Stephen up.

"Can I bring you something to break your fast, sir?"

Stephen started to refuse, for he wasn't hungry. In his recollection, the ostler had not been nearly so hospitable when he was here before, but he realized he needed to feed his blood, regain his strength.

"Meat. Bring me meat—and don't overcook it."

The ostler nodded and backed away.

Stephen continued down the narrow corridor until he reached the room where he and Deidra had stayed the night. He knocked briefly before pushing the door open.

His mind was such a thick muddle that it took him a moment to comprehend the scene before him.

Deidra was tied to a chair beside the bed, arms bound behind her, ankles bound to the chair legs, her mouth gagged. Something was wrong with her head . . . her wild curls were wilder than usual, and a red band marked the clear smooth skin of her forehead.

Luthias Forsyth stood beside her, turning at Stephen's entrance. A rope dangled from one hand.

"Stephen Ross! So good to see you. Did you find your blood witch?"

Stephen's mind struggled to grasp what was happening, to find a quick and effective solution for this predicament, but he could not focus on anything except Deidra. Something shifted in his chest; the leaden feeling made way for something dark and primal.

His eyes fixated on her forehead, the raw wound. The rope in Luthias's hand.

She'd been thrawed.

And the strange lethargy that had gripped him broke. He ran at Luthias, grabbing the front of the man's robes and throwing him across the room.

It was clearly the last thing the witch hunter had expected from a cripple, judging from the stunned look on his face as he crashed into the wall and crumpled to the floor.

Stephen reached for his dirk, but it was gone. He'd left it in the blood witch's belly. He went to Deidra's chair, some part of his mind wondering at his diminished—though not absent—pain. He fumbled with the gag at the back of her head.

Luthias started bellowing. "Kyle! Boyd! Get up here!"

The clamber of boots on the stairs meant Luthias's henchmen were coming for him. Stephen's fingers tugged urgently at the knot. He finally worked it loose and removed the gag. Deidra gulped a deep breath and blurted out, "Your back! It is better!"

He had no time to respond. Luthias attacked him from behind, clasped fists slamming down across his back. Stephen barely felt it. He whirled and backhanded the witch hunter, who stumbled back into a wall.

The door burst open and four men crowded into the room.

"Get him!" Luthias cried.

The men rushed Stephen and knocked him to the floor. Once he was down, they kicked him. He was again surprised that he didn't feel more. He heard Deidra crying and begging them to stop, but that seemed far off, in the distance. The blows kept coming—to the back and ribs and head—until his odd, altered consciousness finally slipped away.

Chapter 14

*D*eidra's eyes squeezed shut and tears streamed down her face as she called out to every animal that could hear her. *Help me.* Her forehead stung, the skin raw from the rope Luthias had wrapped around her head and twisted tighter and tighter until the rough hemp had broken the skin. A thrawing was not much, considering, and she knew there was far worse to come.

Luthias was on his feet again, rubbing his jaw gingerly and wincing. "Drag him downstairs and put him in the wagon."

Deidra opened her eyes to see the men dragging Stephen out of the room. "Stephen," she whispered, but he was past hearing. He had returned to her only to die. She should have stayed at the beach. She should not have come back. Luthias would not still be here and Stephen would be safe.

But there was no point in dwelling on *what-ifs*. She had done none of those things, and now they were both in serious trouble.

Luthias watched her, saw that she still gazed at the empty doorway. They were alone in the room. Rage filled her heart as she stared up at the man who systematically destroyed her life.

"You can't save him now," he said. "And you can't save yourself this time."

She only stared, her eyes narrowing.

"There it is," he mused, gazing down at her but keeping his distance. "There is the evil I knew lurked behind those angelic eyes. You want to kill me."

"One doesn't have to be a witch to want you dead. One has only to know you, and know what a flat-minded man you are."

"Hmm . . . I'm not so sure about that."

There was no sense in talking to him. He heard what he wanted and twisted all else to fit his warped view of the world.

She sat up as straight as she could, tied to a chair, and met his gaze directly. "What will you do with Stephen?" she asked, keeping all fear and uncertainty from her voice.

He paced away, fingers steepled in front of him. "In many ways, Miss MacKay, he is worse than you are. He aids and abets a witch using trickery and lies. You were born evil. Perhaps you cannot even help what you are. Mr. Ross, however, made a conscious choice. He *chose* evil."

She shook the stray curls out of her eyes and raised her brows for effect. "Maybe I bewitched him."

He nodded thoughtfully. "Aye, that is possible. That is what we shall find out."

She gave him a narrow stare. If cursing was in her power, she cursed him now. *Let all you do to others be visited upon you.* "If you hurt him, I vow you will be sorry."

"You think I am stupid? I *know* you. I have watched you for twelve years. If not for your creatures, you are as powerless as any other woman. And I would never be so stupid as to allow an animal around me when you are near."

Deidra was well aware of that. She had called to the animals, but they had not come. She felt them, but they were not near and they could not come near, though some tried. Duke lurked outside the inn, waiting for his opportunity, but a man with a club guarded the inn, and he swung it hard every time Duke came near.

It seemed hopeless. She wanted her father, who seemed invincible. She wanted him to hold her while she cried, then make it all better, but she was alone and beyond tears, at the brink of a hollow cavern of despair that she was tempted to fall into. This man had made her his life, made it his lifelong purpose to destroy her and everything she loved. *He* was the evil thing. Ubiquitous, destructive, driven by hate. And he couldn't even see it.

One of the men clomped back up the stairs. His eyes bounced off Deidra, afraid to meet the witch's gaze.

"Untie her," Luthias ordered.

The man shuffled forward and knelt beside her chair. His fingers worked the knots at her ankles, his gaze watchful, as if he expected her to leap at him even though her wrists were still bound behind her. He circled the chair and untied her wrists. She stood and backed away, rubbing the circulation back into her cold, numb hands.

The man grabbed her arm and pushed her out the door. "Where are you taking me?" she asked.

"To trial," Luthias said behind her.

"Here? How can you try me here? No one knows me! Who will testify?"

"You'd be surprised. You've had contact with a handful of people since you've been in town."

She tried to look over her shoulder incredulously, but the man shoved her harder, and she almost fell down the stairs. "And what would they testify to?"

"I cannot reveal my case. If I take you home, your blood witch parents will try to kill me. And unlike you, they might succeed. But worry not; they are next once I'm through with you."

Fresh panic clawed at her chest. This idea that her parents were blood witches was preposterous, and yet, just like his obsession with her, he seemed married to it, unable to see reason or logic. "What have William and Rose ever done to you? They've never harmed you and have helped so many!"

Downstairs the ostler averted his gaze. The other patrons kept their heads down, but Deidra felt their stares as they passed.

"They offend God," Luthias answered. "So they offend me. It is unnatural. Those people they allegedly healed are not truly healed; they are now the devil's servants. Witches just like them."

Outside it was cool, the smell of salt and fish strong in the air.

"Then you have much work before you, because they have healed hundreds of people."

"Aye," he said, his voice taking on a deeper tone. "It is a war I and other God-fearing men fight. I have always known God created me for something great, some important task, and it has finally become clear to me in these past weeks."

They stopped at a wagon. Stephen was sprawled in the back, still unconscious. A horse was harnessed to the wagon. Deidra considered her options. Duke was nearby; she felt him. The horse was not intelligent, but it was wise to her. It would do whatever she ordered. Tail swishing, the horse turned her head to look at Deidra. Men stood on either side of the animal, holding its reins and harness. It was old, a nag, and just getting free from the men, if it was possible, would no doubt injure Stephen. And if the horse did get away and was caught, it would no doubt be killed. No, Deidra needed to wait for something that had a chance of success.

Luthias watched her closely, as if he anticipated an escape attempt. Deidra climbed into the wagon beside Stephen. She lifted his head into her lap and pushed his hair out of his face. After a moment the cart moved, taking them through the village.

He was so pale, and his skin was cold. Her heart contracted with the sudden intense fear that he had died. She put her fingers to his throat. There was a pulse. The band squeezing her heart eased, leaving her skin feeling odd and prickly and her limbs shaky.

She brushed his hair back, wondering what had

happened on that island to make him so ill. Was he hurt? Then she saw the marks on his neck. Two circular scabs. They looked like a bite—jagged and red around the edges. She touched them, wondering if they would infect his blood. He felt far from feverish, though.

The wagon halted in front of a building.

"Get out," Luthias snapped.

Deidra started to remove Stephen's head from her lap when he groaned, his brow furrowing and his head turning to the side.

"Stephen," she whispered, placing her palm against the side of his face. "Stephen, can you hear me?"

His hand came up, touching hers. "Your forehead . . ."

"It's fine." And it was, for now at least. She was so overwhelmed by all that was happening that her forehead was the least of her concerns. "I'm going to get us out of this."

He gazed up at her, eyes so pale and blue as he said, "I love you, Deidra. I came back because I love you."

She wanted to respond but couldn't. Her throat thickened, clogged with tears, and she couldn't squeeze the words past. She managed a tremulous smile and mouthed, *I love you, too,* but then her arms were seized and she was yanked from the wagon. Stephen's head hit the bottom of the wagon with a thump.

Her mind scanned the area, but there was nothing of use to her. Some cats and rodents. All of the dogs were locked up. All of the large beasts had been herded out of town or were locked up in barns and paddocks.

This horse and Duke were all she had. She would find a way to make use of them.

They dragged Stephen out of the wagon. He was able to get his feet beneath him, though he seemed unstable. Luthias's men pushed them both into the building.

It was a meeting house of some sort. A long table sat at the front of the room, and benches filled the rest of it. Two men with long, square beards were already seated at the table, and they stood when Luthias entered. Two other men and a woman sat in the "audience."

A black robe lay over one of the benches. Luthias picked it up and swung it around his shoulders, becoming official. He lovingly smoothed his palms over the robe and picked a piece of lint off the front before going to the center chair at the table.

"We are here today to review the matter of Deidra MacKay's complicity with the devil in witchcraft and the involvement of Mr. Stephen Ross," he intoned. He took his place at the table, and the bearded men sat when he did.

Stephen and Deidra were brought forward.

"Miss MacKay, how do you plead to these charges against you?"

"I ken not of the devil, sir. I am a Christian woman."

His eyes narrowed on her. He turned his sharp gaze on Stephen. "And you, Mr. Ross?"

Stephen swayed like a reed in the wind. He squinted across the room for a long moment, then said, "What was the question?"

Luthias's mouth thinned in irritation. "Are you Miss MacKay's accomplice in carrying out the devil's work?"

Stephen scratched his head, as if confused. "I do not understand the question."

Luthias rolled his eyes. "You are not a dunce. Prithee stop acting one; this part is not nearly so convincing."

"She just said she did not know of the devil," Stephen protested. "So how could I help her do something that she knows nothing about? You see? Your question is what makes little sense when looked at logically."

Luthias gestured to someone in the audience. A woman came forward and stood close to the table. She was an older woman, her graying black hair pulled back into a tight chignon at the base of her neck. Her lips and the skin on her throat were drawn tight, as if she was very nervous, and her hands contributed to this impression by being clasped very tightly in front of her.

Luthias said in his most polite and interested voice, "Tell me, Dona, what you saw when Miss MacKay came to town."

"Well, sir," she said, turning her body so she faced Luthias and no one else. "That woman came into town with that man. I was catching a chicken to prepare for dinner when they passed my house. All of the chickens went mangit, racing after her and squawking in such a manner ye wouldna believe. I called my dog to go out and herd them back, but he were already gone, racing after the couple. My cat left, too."

"You are saying that with the appearance of this woman"—Luthias pointed to Deidra—"all of your normally obedient and well-behaved creatures showed signs of dementia by racing after her."

The woman nodded without even looking at Deidra. "Aye. When we finally rounded them all back up, they were outside of the inn, as if waiting for her."

"Were yours the only animals outside of the inn?"

"Oh, no, sir. There were many. In fact, many found themselves there that day, rounding up beasts and bringing them home."

Luthias nodded to the woman, and she scurried back to the benches. "What have you to say to that, Miss MacKay?"

Deidra shrugged. "I didn't notice." Of course she had noticed. But she had no other explanation for the phenomenon other than the truth, and that, of course, would have been a bad thing to admit.

"It's my fault," Stephen said.

Luthias raised a skeptical eyebrow. "Yours?"

"Aye . . . I rub bacon fat into my boots to keep the water out. The animals smell that and come running."

Luthias's mouth compressed as if bored and annoyed. "I was not aware that chickens ate bacon."

"Och, they do not, but I had a hole in my bag and bannock crumbs were falling out of it."

Luthias gave him a long-suffering smile. "I see. Can you also explain why Mr. Keith's horses broke out of their stable to set up vigil beneath your window? Or why Mr. Elliot's sheep were found sleeping outside the inn?"

Deidra turned to look at the two men, who both nodded gravely.

Stephen spread his hands. "Why when men cannot control their own animals does it become a case of witchcraft?"

"Because, Mr. Ross, this is not an isolated event. This happens everywhere Miss MacKay goes. She speaks to the animals, commands them, and they obey her."

Not really. Deidra wished they would obey her now. Duke was not alone . . . she didn't know who was with him, but it was someone familiar, someone he felt safe with, and he didn't want to leave. And the horse was just stupid. Every time it tried to obey her and walk forward, it felt the wagon harnessed to its back and stopped, puzzled.

What good was this gift if the animals were too stupid to be of use?

Stephen had grown silent—no witty comeback to Luthias's latest accusation. Deidra looked over at him and saw him swaying on his feet. His skin had gone ashen. He dropped to his knees and then onto all fours. Deidra tried to drop down beside him, but the men grabbed her arms and held her back.

Stephen's breathing was loud and labored. Deidra felt her breath growing short, as if in sympathy. What would she do if he died? Her parents were not here to heal everyone. They didn't even know where she was now. Even if they searched for her, how would they guess she had come here? She had, in fact, never lost anyone close to her. Her mother had died during childbirth, so she had never known her. She didn't know if she could bear losing Stephen.

Luthias unfolded his long body and circled the table, eyeing Stephen warily. He placed a shoe on Stephen's shoulder and pushed. Stephen's arms and legs collapsed, and he fell to his side. Luthias knelt beside him and lifted an eyelid, peering into Stephen's eyes. Stephen shook his head and weakly tried to push Luthias's hand away.

Luthias rested his forearms on his knees. "Take them both to the back room. Secure her and keep a guard on her at all times." He stood. "Methinks this one is ready to confess."

It was daylight by the time Drake reached the island. Good. He wanted her weak. He grabbed his ax out of the bottom of the skiff and jogged across the little island, memories of the last time he was here slamming through him. His wife, so frail and weak. His begging. That monster's cold refusal. And now this. She had not only denied Stephen but she'd also tried to kill him. To eat him. Drake wouldn't leave her for the witch hunters.

She was his.

The sheep bleated fearfully and stumbled away as he raced through them, the black cloud of fury building each time his boots thudded on the rocky ground. He realized he was smiling, but there was no humor in his smile—just an angry baring of his teeth. When he reached her door, he didn't stop to knock; he swung the ax with a grunt of pleasure. It slammed into the wood with a satisfying *clump*, and wood chips flew.

He hacked and hacked at the door until the boards busted inward. He kicked them until they cracked in, then reached his hand through the hole he'd made, feeling for the latch. A deafening blast sent him reeling away from the door. He yanked his hand out, scraping his arm. There was a new hole in the door.

The bitch had a dag. Luckily she'd missed him. His fury mixed with excitement at the chase, and he started hacking at the door again with new vigor, staying well away from the exposed holes. She'd had plenty of time to reload, and since he doubted she planned to miss him this time, he made certain he hacked that door to pieces. It was easier than he'd imagined. His body was flooded with strength, like some mad berserker. All he wanted was to kill this creature that murdered his loved ones.

When he felt as if the door was sufficiently weakened, he took several steps back and came at it at a run, shoulder first, head tucked. He barreled forward, crashing into the door. His momentum paused only momentarily as the door gave way and he crashed forward. The gun exploded again, deafening him. He fell to the ground and rolled, immediately coming to his feet, ax in one hand, dirk in the other.

He scanned the room, doing a mental inventory of his body. He was pleased to note that she'd missed again. Part of the wall had been blasted out next to the door.

He spotted her near the back of the room. She

didn't look like a monster at all but like a terrified little girl. Long, red hair hung wild around her shoulders. She held a long-barreled dag in both hands; it hung in front of her gown, barrel drooping toward the ground. The gown snagged his attention, disturbing him. It was stained a rust color. Dried blood.

She seemed pale and weak. She dropped to her knees, the dag thumping to the ground.

Drake advanced cautiously. It was probably a ploy to gain his sympathy.

"Get up."

She stared up at him but didn't move. Her eyes seemed enormous, too big for her face.

"What's the matter with you?" he growled.

"Kill me." Her voice was empty, devoid of emotion. "I can't fight back. Just make sure you cut off my head and burn it. I do not want to come back to this life."

Was this supposed to elicit his sympathy? He wasn't stupid. "So you want to die now, aye? Likely story. *Get up*. Or I swear I'll make living painful."

She stood slowly, her large green eyes unblinking. She left the dag on the ground.

"Turn around and put your arms behind you."

She did as he requested, going so far as to cross her wrists so he could tie them together with ease.

He turned her back around and frowned down at her. She stared back, unblinking. The front of her gown was stained with dried blood. He pulled it away from her body and saw the hole in the material Stephen's dirk had made when he'd stabbed her. He peered through the hole and saw that the skin of her belly was marred—but not with a fresh wound. This wound looked as if it had happened weeks ago and was healing.

He released her gown as if it had been on fire. When he met her gaze, a single fine red brow was arched.

"I should kill you now," he said, his voice low as the anger welled in his heart again.

"You'd better do it now, because come night, you won't be able to." She smiled, sly and unpleasant. "And I will not be so merciful this time."

So she remembered him. He wondered if she had. He wasn't afraid of her. A person had to have a reason to live to fear for their life, and his reason was about to be served.

He grabbed her elbow and pulled her toward the door. She stumbled along after him. He noticed she didn't have any shoes on.

"Where are your shoes?"

"I don't wear them."

He studied her placid expression. "Do you feel anything? Are you dead inside?"

The smile she gave him was slightly sad. "I feel everything—more than you could possibly comprehend."

A snide remark slid to the end of his tongue but went no further. Something about the joyless curve of her lips stopped him. It immediately irritated him that he would feel any measure of sympathy at all for such a *thing*, so he dragged her out the door and down to the skiff with a bit more force than was necessary.

He took extra precautions in the little boat, tying

her hands to the plank she sat on so she couldn't attack him while he was rowing. She didn't fight him or speak at all.

She watched him as he rowed, never taking her eyes off him, hardly even blinking.

"What?" he finally barked, unnerved by her stare. "Are you cursing me?"

"We will not make it."

"What are you blathering about?"

"We are too late already."

Her words created a knot in his gut, but he kept rowing as if unfazed. "Too late for what?"

"Your friend Stephen Ross. He has found trouble that he is not equipped to handle."

Drake stopped rowing. "How do you know?"

"His blood is my blood now. I hear his thoughts and he hears mine . . . well, the ones I want him to hear. He is in trouble. He and another."

Deidra. Stephen and Deidra were in trouble. If anything happened to Deidra, her father would kill him. He had sent William word. Told him not to worry, that he would take care of Deidra and keep her safe.

"What is it? What's wrong?"

She shrugged carelessly. "I know not. Our link is weak. He hasn't tasted my blood."

Drake rowed harder, glaring at his prisoner. Her words disgusted him. "You will fix this."

"What am I supposed to do? I am weak. The sun saps my power."

"I don't know!" he yelled, fury and despair exploding in his chest. "But this is your fault—all of it, ever since you killed my wife, and *by God* you will fix it or I will make you pay."

Her green eyes narrowed. "You can't do—"

"*Do not* even say it. Because blood witch or not, I will make you pay for destroying my life. I will extract it from your sorry, useless hide if I have to."

Her mouth snapped shut. After a moment she sighed and shook her head. "I will help you, but you should know, I do nothing for free."

The pressure crushing his heart eased. "I can pay you. I told you that before, and you didn't want my money."

She smiled, slow and strangely satisfied. "Oh, it's not money I want."

Chapter 15

—⧉—

$\mathscr{S}$tephen wasn't certain what was happening to him, why he felt so oddly detached from his body and the events occurring around him. *Loss of blood, loss of blood.* His body had grown very cold. It was not a typical chill that one got from being out in the damp cold overlong, but a bone-deep cold, past shivering. Another blanket or a pair of warm wool hose would not remedy this. It was in his marrow, chilling him from within. He'd fought to think clearly throughout the mock trial, but a fog had settled over his mind and he'd no longer been able to sift through it.

One thing kept him going when the voice in his head urged him to give in to the lethargy threatening to overwhelm him: Deidra's presence. He was hyper-aware of her in a way he'd never been before. Surely he imagined it, but it seemed so real. He could smell her, the musky scent of her skin, the blood that flowed beneath it. He could feel her, the heat from her body, though they didn't touch. And strangest of all, he could *hear* her. Not her voice, since she did not speak, but her breathing, her heart, pumping blood through her body.

And he smelled her fear—a sharp scent, cold, unnatural sweat, the accelerated pumping of her heart. She needed him. He could not give in to this.

They sat him in a chair. He was too weak to hold himself up for more than a few seconds, and he slumped forward, sliding onto the floor. His body crashed gracelessly. It should have hurt all over, but most especially his back. And yet it did not. He felt no pain, just a cold numbness.

The men hoisted him up off the floor and replaced him in the chair. This time one man held him upright while the other wrapped a rope around his chest, securing him to the back of the chair. His head hung down, his chin resting on his chest. With enormous effort, he managed to raise it, his eyes seeking Deidra.

She was across the small room. Two men held her arms. She stared back at him, her eyes enormous and wild, the color drained from her face.

They started with his hands. His chair was dragged to a nearby table, where one of Luthias's thugs held his arm down. Luthias removed his robe and hung it on a peg near the door. He approached the table and chose a small hammer, suitable for crushing stones.

"Mr. Ross," he said in a pleasant voice, tapping the hammer against his open palm. "Tell me, did you assist Deidra MacKay in escaping from my custody a sennight ago?"

"Aye," Stephen said, unable to take his eyes off Deidra.

She stood across the room, watching him. Her heartbeat increased, racing now, so that he feared for her. Her breathing had grown shallow. It amazed him that he could sense all of this. Visually she was alarming as well. Her eyes were large and round, but she didn't seem to be seeing him. She looked right through him.

"And you did it under her command."

Stephen shook his head. "No, I did it because it was the right thing to do. She is no witch."

Luthias's eyes narrowed, his thin lips becoming thinner. But Stephen knew more, he saw so much more now, and Luthias was not displeased, though he'd have liked everyone to believe he was. Perhaps he even believed it on some level, but Stephen knew better. Luthias wanted to hurt Stephen and Deidra. He was glad Stephen was being difficult.

The hammer came down, crushing Stephen's pinky. Stephen's detachment broke. It hurt. He cried out but quickly clenched his teeth closed, hissing through them. His smallest finger, and all the way up his hand, felt as if it had been ripped off, as if it were still being ripped off.

"*God.*" The curse tore out of him, long and drawn out and full of agony.

Deidra's lips drew back, but no sound came from her. She only stared at Stephen's hand. His own anguish drowned out all the other things he had just been sensing, but he was aware that her heart skidded along even faster. She was having a hard time breathing.

Luthias's voice came to him from far away. "I'll ask you again, Mr. Ross, did she command you to aid her?"

Stephen took a deep breath, bracing himself. "No, she did not."

The hammer came down again on his pinky—the same one. The crushing pain twisted his body, but this time he made not a sound, just bit at his lips as agony throbbed and stabbed through him. He was aware of nothing else now, could sense nothing except the black-red pain that blinded him, shutting out everything else.

He waited for the intensity of the pain to subside, but it seemed to go on forever. His vision swam, refusing to focus. Slowly, after what seemed a very long time, the pain lessened incrementally.

Luthias paced back and forth between Deidra and Stephen. When he noticed Stephen blinking blearily at him he asked, "Mr. Ross, are you in league with the devil?"

"The devil, you say?" Stephen slurred. "I know not—do we have a pact, you and I? Because if so, then aye."

Luthias narrowed his gaze on Stephen. A voice spoke in Stephen's head, urging him to keep pricking at the witch hunter, infuriate him so that Luthias would just kill him. All that stopped him was Deidra. He wished he could spare her this. She slid down the wall, knees to her chin, enormous blue eyes staring at his bloodied hand.

Luthias moved in front of Stephen's chair so that he could no longer see Deidra. Stephen closed his eyes and kept her in his mind. His head fell forward. *So very tired.*

Luthias grabbed a wad of Stephen's hair and yanked his head back. "Have you witnessed Deidra MacKay communing with animals?"

Stephen bared his teeth. "No."

Luthias hit him in the face with the hammer. Stephen's head snapped back, pain spiking through his cheek to his nose and skull. He felt and heard the crack of his cheek. A dull ringing filled his head. He tried to think, to remember what he was supposed to do next, but all he could think was defiance.

"No!" he yelled again, through the pain blinding him, clouding all thoughts from his head. His voice sounded strange and thick.

"Liar!" Luthias screamed, pulling harder on his hair.

"No! No, no, no, no!"

The hammer came down again, cutting off his garbled shouts, and again, hammering coherent thought from his head until blissful nothingness finally superseded the pain.

Breathing had grown impossible for Deidra. It was as if her chest had crumbled inward, restricting the movement of internal organs. She wheezed, eyes fixed on the man in the chair. He hung to the side—the only thing keeping him upright were the ropes binding his torso to the back of the chair.

Blood dripped from his fingertips to the ground. But that wasn't the only place leaking blood. It dripped from his face . . . or what should have been his face. Luthias had beaten it unrecognizable.

Her hands gripped her throat, as she tried to suck in more air, but her vision clouded at the edges. The scene before her wavered and merged with another scene, an older scene, but one just as gruesome. Her father secured to a chair, his hand clamped into the pinni-winks as Luthias crushed every bone in his hand. Blood flowed down the table, pooling on the floor beneath him . . . beside her. She had crouched on the floor behind her father's chair, hands over her ears, trying to block out his grunts of pain and Luthias's shouted questions. But when she would open her eyes, she saw it anyway, her father's blood sliding across the floor. Growing into a puddle. Soon it would overtake her, drown her.

Then she was back in the room with Stephen.

Stephen was not her father. Stephen could not heal himself. She didn't want to struggle to breathe anymore, didn't want the burning throat and lungs. She wanted to be strong and brave, like her father and stepmother. And Stephen.

Luthias stood to the side of Stephen, bloody hammer still gripped in his fist. He looked down at his handiwork then turned to Deidra, huddled on the ground, wheezing pitiably.

"He gave his life for you, witch. Your magic is strong to command such obedience."

Magic? No, not unless love was magical. And she supposed it was. It was love that had given Stephen the strength to die for her. She would rather him not love her at all than die in such a manner for her.

She didn't want to go on like this, hunted, everything she loved cut down because of her. If she must die, then she would die well, on her own terms. She let her head fall back, eyes shutting, and she stopped struggling for her next breath. Within moments, the tightness in her chest loosened and the air came easier.

But as her head cleared, the impact of Luthias's words penetrated her mind. *Dead.* Stephen was dead. Luthias had killed him. Beaten him with a hammer.

Rage built, black and faceless, like her love. There was nothing left for her now. He had crushed her future, her love, her heart into nothing. Dead.

She opened her mind and her soul and felt them. They were here, in town. They had always been here. Luthias had moved them to the outskirts of town or restrained them, but they were still there, waiting. She had felt them all along, but her reluctance to use them, to put any life in danger, had built a wall, a restraint that had kept her apart from them.

But she was past worries and guilt and fear. Power flooded her as she heard them all, felt them all. Was one with all of them. Each and every creature within miles lifted its head and waited. If she asked, they would die breaking free from their restraints and kill their captors. Just to obey her.

She called them all, her eyes locked on Luthias.

And he saw something, saw the change, because his eyes narrowed and he walked toward her, raising his hammer. "Now, lass. It's just you and me." That wasn't entirely true—his mercenaries were still in the room, watching. "Do you commune with the animals?"

"Aye," she said, and it wasn't her voice that spoke— it was the creatures, speaking with her, through her. She was more than Deidra MacKay, greater, stronger. "I do. And you'd better run."

His head tilted to the side, her unexpected confession setting him momentarily off kilter. Then he straightened, his eyes darting around the room, though he did not move his head.

"Why?"

The answer came, in the form of growling outside the door. Luthias jerked around, wide eyes fixed on the door. A cacophony of barks and snarls of dozens of dogs. It sounded like hell was outside, crazed to get in. The door shook as the dogs launched themselves against it, snarling like rabid animals.

Luthias's entire body jerked with each heavy thump at the door.

"Make it stop." His voice shook, spittle flew out of his mouth. "Make it stop now!" He came at her, hammer raised.

She forced her numb limbs to move, and she rolled to the side. Glass shattered, and the snarling took on a viscous quality. The iron windowpanes held, keeping the beasts out, but jaws snapped through the open spaces where glass used to be.

No one guarded the door. Luthias's men stood back from the doors and windows, weapons held at the ready, looking around them in baffled terror. They were far more concerned with what was outside the doors than what was inside. Deidra darted for the door.

"Stop her!" Luthias shouted.

The men started to obey until the low roar of thunder stopped them all. It rose from all around them, shaking the table so that Luthias's metal instruments trembled and clinked.

Luthias's head whipped around as the thunder grew.

A smile pulled at Deidra's mouth, hysterical, pleased. She must look like a true witch now, evil and maniacal. He was terrified. She wouldn't be surprised if he had pissed himself. She had finally lived up to his inflated opinion of her. And it felt *good*. Evil witch? She would show him evil. She would call up the animals to maul him to death, and she would laugh and dance on his grave.

The thunder peaked with a crash against the wall. The stone and wood of the building groaned and creaked. It reverberated through her bones and chest. Dust sifted down on them from the rafters.

"Stop it," Luthias ordered.

Deidra ignored him, so intent was she on the magic she created. *Keep coming, keep coming, I'm in here, I need you.*

"*Stop!*" Luthias's voice rose, high and wavering. "In God's name I order you to stop!"

The Lord was apparently not listening to the pleas of witch hunters today. Luthias's face had gone ashen, and he had lost his hammer. The thunder grew, and the animals crashed against the wall again. This time stones tumbled from the wall.

"Do something!" one of the men shrieked. "Make them stop!"

Luthias fell to his knees, hands clasped before him, and he began to pray, exhorting God to save them, to stop the evil witch's villainy.

The crash came again, and this time the wall gave way. Deidra ran to Stephen and wrapped her arms around him, shielding him with her body as the

roof tumbled in and livestock stampeded into the
building.

Dust choked the room, laying over Deidra and Stephen like a blanket. She squeezed her eyes shut and
coughed. She only dared to raise her head when she
felt animals pressing against her. The dust had settled
somewhat, though there was still a haze to the air. Animals—sheep, kine, horses, and goats—filled the small
room. They surrounded her, making it impossible for
Luthias or his men to get near.

Luthias, his balding head covered in dust, a red
slash across his forehead, gazed about the room in
bewilderment. Two of his men picked themselves up
off the ground, but the other two that had been in the
room with them were nowhere to be seen—they'd
either been trampled or they'd slipped away.

Luthias shook off his bewilderment and tried to
cross to her anyway. He pushed at the beasts, trying to
move them. "You cannot get away with this."

Growling and snarling brought him up short. The
dogs had found their way in. Deidra held them back
with her mind. They were dogs, not wild animals, and
therefore easier to control.

Luthias turned toward the sound, his throat working.

"I think," Deidra said, "that I already have gotten
away with it."

He turned his head slightly so that he could see her
while still keeping an eye on the dogs.

"Take your men and leave, or I will loose them on
you," she said calmly.

He raised his hands, open-palmed, in a placating

manner. "You only make things worse for yourself. We have an entire town of witnesses now."

He was an obstinate, stupid man. Of course she had made it worse for herself. There was no getting out of this one. She was a witch, and everyone knew it. But what he didn't understand was that she no longer cared.

She let the dogs advance closer—they rushed forward and stopped, as if restrained by an invisible leash. They growled and snarled with renewed enthusiasm.

Luthias tried to back away from the threatening beasts, but the livestock bunched around him made movement impossible.

"Very well," he said. "Until next time."

And there would be one, of course. He would not stop until one of them was dead. She should kill him now, let the dogs loose to rip his throat out. But she couldn't. The rage had drained from her body, and she gave him safe passage. As long as he left, she would honor her word. She might be a witch, but she was not false.

So she watched him and his men leave.

And when they were gone, she finally dropped her guard. Surrounded by the warm comfort of the animals, she sank to her knees beside Stephen's chair, laid her head against his thigh, and wept. She wept for the man in the chair who had sacrificed so much for her only to die. Her heart wept for love and future lost, all dust and ash. And most of all she wept because of her own culpability. If not for her cowardice, Stephen would not have died. If she had not been so afraid, she could have called the animals sooner and stopped this before it ended so tragically.

She clutched at his legs, the grief ripped from her chest in painful sobs. *She* had done this to him. He had come back to her, and she had killed him.

"Deidra!" The shout brought her head up. "Deidra . . . Stephen? Oh my God."

It was her uncle.

"I'm here," she called out, her voice wavering and strained.

Her shoulders were grabbed, and she was yanked to her feet and into a tight hug. The contact, warm and strong, brought fresh tears to her eyes, and she sobbed harder.

"I ken, Dee-dee, I ken, but you must bear up now. We cannot stay here."

"B-b-but Stephen—"

"I ken." Drake said to someone else, "Is he dead?"

"Aye," a female voice answered.

A new wave of anguish washed over Deidra. Even though she'd known Stephen was dead, having it verified by a third party shredded her heart anew. Drake held her tighter.

"Will that matter?" he asked.

"Nay," the woman said, her voice smoky and deep, but feminine. "It's better that way."

Deidra lifted her head, rubbing the tears from her eyes with her sleeve. "What are you talking about?"

"Later," Drake said. He gently set Deidra aside and circled Stephen's chair. He untied him, then hoisted him up and over his shoulder. "Let's go—*now*."

Drake led the way out of the destroyed building. The woman with him was striking. Pale skin, long red hair that hung loose down her back. She wore a filthy stained chemise, and over it a man's shirt and araisad.

Four horses were hobbled outside the building, where a fearful crowd had gathered. When the four of them appeared, a collective gasp rippled through the crowd. Several villagers actually turned and ran back the way they'd come.

"Aye," the red-haired woman called out, "that's right. Get your arses back inside. Not a thing to see here." More of the townsfolk dispersed, all of them averting their eyes.

Deidra mounted one of the horses. Drake came to her and laid Stephen's body across the front of her saddle. "Here—we haven't time to tie him to the other horse, and you're the smallest." He gave her an apologetic look. "It won't be long, I vow it."

She nodded, her throat thickening. His body weighed heavily against her. She clutched his belt in one hand and the reins in the other and spurred her horse forward. They rode for at least a mile, Deidra fighting to keep Stephen's body across her horse. When they were a good distance from the town, Drake drew rein and moved Stephen's corpse to the fourth horse, tying it securely to the saddle.

Deidra couldn't seem to stop crying, couldn't seem to stop staring at Stephen's lifeless body. Her eyes and her head hurt. Her body felt weak and drained. It seemed impossible that she still had so much water in her body, but it was true. The tears just kept leaking out of her.

They headed west for several miles until the sky began to darken. Drake led them into a stand of trees, then dismounted. He untied Stephen from the horse and laid him out on the ground.

The woman approached Stephen's body slowly, and Drake took several steps backward.

"We have an accord, you and I?" she said in that deep husky voice, her head tilted inquiringly.

Drake nodded.

She removed her araisad, then knelt beside Stephen. Deidra came to stand beside her uncle.

"What is happening?"

Drake nodded to the woman. "The *baobhan sith*."

Deidra's eyes widened and her heart stumbled as she fixated on the woman pushing up her shirt sleeve.

Like a fist, hope gripped her heart. "Will she . . . Stephen?"

Drake nodded. "She says she can." His mouth flattened grimly. "We'll see."

The woman withdrew a dirk that had been strapped to the inside of her arm. Deidra recognized it as Stephen's. She drew the sharp edge of the blade along the inside of her forearm, cutting herself.

Blood welled up, spilling over her arm. She pressed her open wound to Stephen's mouth, sliding her other hand under his neck and tilting it so that his mouth and throat opened.

The scene before her was so grotesque and obscene that Deidra had to look away.

"What is she doing?" Deidra asked hoarsely, keeping her eyes averted.

"Vampires subsist on blood. She is . . . feeding him." Drake's voice was thick with distaste, but he did not look away.

After several minutes Deidra chanced a look back. The woman pulled her hand away and wrapped the sleeve of the shirt around her wound. She rose to her feet gracefully and turned to face them.

Drake looked from the woman to Stephen's still body. "Well? He still looks dead to me."

"Patience. Come, start a fire and let us sit and rest. We must talk."

Drake gave Deidra a look that said he didn't trust this woman, but then he shrugged and began walking around the clearing, picking up kindling.

Deidra did the same, all the while stealing glances at Stephen. Her eyes deceived her, sending her heart leaping when she thought she saw his chest rise, only to realize it was all in her mind. The *baobhan sith* had restored hope to her heart, yet Deidra was afraid of what would happen next. Nothing? Would he remain dead? Or would he wake as something terrible? She tried to imagine Stephen subsisting on blood, and the idea—so contrary to her own life— was repellent.

When a fire crackled, the three of them sat around it in silence. Drake ate bread and cheese and dried meat, while Deidra picked at a bannock. The *baobhan sith* ate nothing.

"When he wakes," she said, breaking the silence with no preamble, "he will be hungry. He will not know himself, and he will not know any of us."

Drake stopped chewing and stared at her. "What are you saying?"

"I am saying that you both are potential food for him. He will not touch me." The woman's large green eyes turned on Deidra. "I sense that you love him very much. Will you make this sacrifice for him?"

Deidra's mouth dropped open. It closed and opened several more times before she could form a coherent sentence. "You mean . . . let him feed on my blood?"

"Are you insane?" Drake shouted, standing up, hands fisted, body leaned forward as if ready to strike.

The *baobhan sith* rolled her eyes. "Sit down. I do not mean that she must die. She can simply let him partake of some of her blood. Or she can become one of us."

Deidra closed her eyes, her stomach turning at the idea of drinking blood every day.

"Don't look so disgusted, child. You would be able to be with him forever."

The woman's expression did not match her tone. She looked bitter and disillusioned, her smile more of a smirk. She didn't believe her own words.

"I don't really know that living forever is such a good thing," Deidra said carefully.

The woman's lips curved appreciably. "You are clever. It does have its drawbacks."

She raised her brows quizzically, looking from Deidra to Drake. "So what are we to do? He needs blood and soon."

"Will animal blood work?" Drake asked.

She nodded. "So long as it is fresh. *Very* fresh."

Drake stood and grabbed his latch and arrows. "I'll be back." He disappeared into the trees.

Deidra wrapped her arms around her knees. She was so weary. Her eyes burned from all the crying. Her mind buzzed, overstimulated. She'd passed the point of exhaustion and wouldn't have been able to sleep or relax now even if she'd wanted to. And she didn't want to. She needed to be awake when Stephen woke.

The woman stared at Deidra with such frank curiosity that Deidra felt her face flushing. She laid her cheek on her bent knees, hiding her face. The woman was beautiful, even as filthy and road-worn as they all were. Deidra felt like a dustball.

She rolled her head so that her chin rested on her knees. "What's your name?" she asked the woman.

The woman straightened, surprised and wary. "My name? Why?"

"Because I don't know what to call you."

This seemed to give her pause. "Why not call me what everyone else does? Vile witch. Blood sucker. Filthy leech. Dead thing."

Deidra managed a weak smile. "I'd rather not."

"Well then, you can call me Hannah."

"Hannah. That doesn't sound Scots."

"No. I'm Irish. It probably doesn't sound Irish either. My name is Aedammair. It means 'fire.' But I haven't been called that in . . ." She scanned the sky, as if it held the answer, then shrugged. "In a very long time."

Deidra could see that. *Fire.* Her hair was such a brilliant red that it looked like a sunset. It caught the light from the fire like metal.

"How long?" Deidra asked.

"Too long."

"Why Hannah? That sounds nothing like Aedammair."

Hannah sighed heavily, as if the thought of unloading such a story wearied her. "Some other time, mayhap. Your lover is waking."

Deidra's heart jerked, her head swiveling to the ground where Stephen still lay. She saw nothing at first, just the dark oblong shape of him, lying motionless. Then a groan and the shape shifted.

The frantic fluttering of Deidra's heart brought her to her feet. "Stephen?" She took a step forward. She needed to see him, to touch him, to know she had not killed him.

Hannah rose in one graceful move and put a hand out, stopping Deidra. "Do not go any closer."

Deidra's belly knotted. She laced and unlaced her fingers, eyes locked on the moving darkness. He had just been dead and now he wasn't. It was a miracle.

"Where is Drake?" Hannah muttered, eyes scanning the trees around them.

"What's the matter?" Deidra asked. Hannah's unease transferred to Deidra, making the lacing of her fingers change to a twisting.

"He's waking and Drake has not returned. This is not good."

"Is he dangerous?" Deidra asked, straining to see Stephen in the darkness.

Hannah's mouth flattened. "You may get to be a blood witch whether you wish to or not."

A shock went through Deidra and she took a step back, hands to her throat. "What?"

Something rustled and moaned in the darkness. This time it sounded anguished, as if he was in terrible pain.

Deidra stepped forward again, concerned. "What is the matter with him? He doesn't sound well."

Hannah turned to her, her eyes grim. "He's not. He's just been dead, remember? But he will be fine, so long as he doesn't do anything he later regrets."

"What the hell!" Stephen shouted from the darkness, then moaned again. He sounded hurt and confused, and it tugged at Deidra. She wanted to go to him, to help him.

The dark shape rose from the ground. He was on his feet. Hannah moved in front of Deidra.

"You," he said, his voice low and menacing. Stephen but not Stephen. "What did you do to me?"

Deidra was confused, too. How could he see anything in this darkness? She couldn't make out any more of him than a darker shape in the darkness. But he apparently saw and recognized Hannah.

"Stay back, Stephen," Hannah said. "Someone is returning with something that will make you feel better."

"You did this to me," he growled furiously. "Make it stop. Now!" His breathing was loud and deep as he continued to advance. "What is that behind you? It smells sweet—*oh God*, I can almost taste it."

Deidra's chest squeezed like a fist, and she grabbed the back of Hannah's shirt in panic. The longing and hunger in his voice unnerved her. That was *not* her Stephen.

"Stephen," Hannah said, her voice full of authority, "that is not for you."

And suddenly he was right there beside them. Deidra had not seen him move, had heard nothing. Startled, she sucked in a gasp and stumbled backward, dragging Hannah along with her.

Hands grasped at her and Deidra fought, pushing and slapping. In the firelight she saw fangs, animal-white and sharp. Hannah's body stood between them, blocking his access. Deidra put her hand up, shoving his chin away, trying to keep his fangs as far from her flesh as possible, but she knew that he would over-power Hannah and then kill her.

And then his hands were gone. Deidra fell onto her backside and scrabbled backward like a crab.

Stephen and Hannah stood in the firelight. Her arm was out between them, as graceful as a swan's neck, her fore and middle finger pointing to a spot between his eyes.

"Do not move," Hannah commanded. Deidra did not know whom she spoke to—her or Stephen—but she froze.

Stephen did not move either. He stood, stonelike, his face strained and pale, his eyes fixed on Hannah. Deidra gasped. His face. It was marred by dried blood and a red wound, but it was no longer ruined.

Deidra's eyes scanned the trees, her mind going

out to the animals, looking for information on her uncle. She had avoided contact with them, her mind shying away; Drake needed to kill one, and she couldn't in good conscience lead the prey to him, though that would likely happen anyway once they sensed her.

Drake was coming. The animals had all fled, smelling the hunter, but he had captured something, and it was alive and in pain. It wanted her help.

She heard footsteps, then Drake burst into the clearing, a red fawn draped across his arms like a child.

It lifted its head toward Deidra. She blocked its thoughts, just as she used to before this mess. There was nothing to be done for it.

"Bloody hell," Drake muttered, his gaze on Stephen. He approached slowly. "What's wrong with him?"

"Take the fawn, Stephen," Hannah said, ignoring Drake's question.

Stephen reached out and took it from Drake.

Hannah dropped her hand, her shoulders sagging, and Stephen blinked, looking around as if he'd just woken from a dream. His eyes scanned them all, registering no recognition. Then his gaze dropped downward to the dying animal in his arms. His face distorted into a ravenous snarl.

He fell to his knees, burying his face in the fawn's neck. Deidra turned her face away, hand clamped over her mouth. She was sickened beyond belief. Her stomach heaved, and she was glad she had not eaten anything. But the animal felt almost no. ing—a moment of fear, some mild pain, then its mind dulled, as if clouded with drink.

Drake's hand rested on Deidra's shoulder. "How are you, Dee-dee? Did he hurt you?"

Deidra shook her head, unable to remove her hand from her mouth. No, she was not hurt—not in any way that could be seen with the human eye, at least. Her heart felt battered, possibly damaged. *This* was not the Stephen she had fallen in love with. She didn't know what this was—a predator, an animal—but it frightened and disgusted her.

"This is only temporary," Hannah said, joining them outside the firelight.

"What the hell is wrong with him?" Drake asked in a loud, angry whisper. "He's like a beast, inhuman. *That* is not normal."

"His blood has been drained; he must replenish it. So long as he feeds regularly, he is no different from me. A *baobhan sith* only becomes feral when they do not feed."

Feral. A word used for animals gone wild. Animals that must be killed.

"There is much for him to learn and understand." Hannah rubbed a hand across her eyes. "Is there a safe place we can go?"

Drake nodded, distracted. His frowning gaze was fixed on Stephen. "When can he travel?"

"When he's finished he'll be disoriented, but he should be able to ride a horse." Hannah's gaze scanned Drake from head to toe and apparently found him lacking. "Better than you, no doubt."

"Does he know who we are?" Deidra asked tentatively.

"He knows who I am," Hannah said. "You both he probably recognizes, but is confused . . . cannot find a name to match the faces. Fash not, it will all come back eventually. He was dead, after all."

Deidra tore her gaze away from Stephen to look at Hannah. "This happened to you once?"

"It was a very long time ago." She studied Deidra's expression. "Can you love him this way?"

It was a bald question, one Deidra did not have an answer for. She opened her mouth and closed it. She turned and looked at the man hunched near the fire, drinking animal blood. The fawn was dead now. It had been a painless death. Stephen had somehow drugged the animal as he'd fed on it. Deidra looked back at Hannah's knowing eyes, then at her uncle, who averted his gaze to the ground.

"I know not," she finally admitted.

Hannah let out a soft, breathy laugh. "Well, at least you're honest."

Deidra's throat tightened.

Hannah tilted her head to the side. "You regret I did this? Because I can kill him. Now is the best time. After tonight he only grows more powerful."

Deidra shook her head vigorously. "No, no, that's not what I want."

Hannah still studied her, as if gauging the validity of that statement, then her eyes shifted behind Deidra. "And there he is," she said softly.

Deidra turned. Stephen sat beside the fire. It limned his face in black and red, the blood-black smudges on his mouth. He stared down at the fawn he had just mauled. He dropped it, as if it had burned him, and stared at his bloody hands. He stood abruptly, leaning back on his heels and straightening. It was a fluid movement, something that Stephen's back never would have allowed him to do.

Deidra's mouth hinged open. Stephen seemed to realize this at the same time she did, because one of his hands went to his back.

"Stephen," Deidra gasped, coming to her feet and taking a step toward him. "Your back—it's healed."

He turned, his eyes scanning the three of them. He showed no signs of recognition until his eyes rested on Hannah, and then they narrowed. He held his bloody hands out to her.

"What the hell have you done to me?"

"You wanted this." Hannah's voice changed when she spoke to him; it became firm, commanding. A master addressing a servant.

He shook his head. "I don't remember that."

Hannah stood and smiled, as if he was a forgetful child. "Well, Stephen, you do not remember much, do you?"

His eyes moved to the side as he searched his mind. After a moment his gaze moved to Deidra. "I know you."

Deidra's hand went to her neck, her heart fluttering. "Aye," she said softly. "You do."

His gaze lingered on her a moment longer before he took a deep breath and looked down at his hands again. "I need to wash."

Drake came to life from his silent and motionless state. He stood. "Come with me. There is a burn not far."

Drake glanced at Hannah, one brow raised in question.

She inclined her head. "He is safe. For now."

Chapter 16

⧫⧫⧫

$\mathcal{S}$tephen followed the bearded, black-haired man away from the campsite. The women watched him silently as he passed. He felt strange and exposed in his current condition, drenched as he was in blood. It sickened him, and at the same time the taste of it was still in his mouth, warm and delicious.

His mind was fuzzy, a fog he couldn't quite sift through. There were hazy images. The woman with the black curly hair and large blue eyes. A dog. A tall man with a hammer. The memory of pain flashed through him, throbbing in his hand.

He lifted his hand. It was covered with blood, but not his own. It was whole and functional. He bent each finger to test it. Red marks marred the skin, but they were old and healed. And yet the memory of excruciating pain spiking through his hand was fresh. He dropped his arm and looked around. The man had led him to a burn.

The bearded man stood beside it watching Stephen cautiously.

Stephen felt as if he should know the man, and yet

he could not locate a memory associated with him. But it was there. Somehow he just knew. Like a curtain he could pull back and all would be revealed . . . except he couldn't find the curtain. He knelt beside the burn and scrubbed his hands in the water, plunging them into the soft sand and pebbles along the bottom and using that to scrub the blood off. When his hands were clean, he did the same to his face.

He sat back on his heels and looked upward, blinking the water from his eyes like tears. He was so confused. The one thing he was sure of was that *he* was what had changed. Everything around him had stayed the same. He also knew that he was stronger than he had ever felt. And that he had been crippled before. He had lived a useless life; he had been weak and angry. Now he was whole and strong.

He felt good. Amazing. And that woman . . . the black curls, the beautiful eyes, they excited him. He'd wanted to taste her, drink her blood. That was wrong. He knew that now, but such a thing had not even entered his mind before. He'd been so hungry. It had been unlike any hunger he could ever remember. As if his stomach had shriveled into a currant, dry as ash. It had hurt, so that all he'd been able to think of had been easing the pain.

He took a deep breath and looked up at the man beside him.

The man had never taken his eyes off him. He was watchful, curious. His hand rested on the dirk at his waist. "You look well, Stephen."

Stephen said nothing. His gaze turned to the water.

The man tapped his fingers on his dirk hilt. "Do you know who I am?"

Stephen shrugged. "I know I should."

"My name is Drake MacKay. And aye, you do know me. Very well."

That sounded right to Stephen. He nodded slowly. "The woman, the one with the curls . . ." He touched his hair when he said the last. "I know her very well, too."

"Aye," Drake said. His voice was low and full of meaning, making Stephen wonder if she was perhaps his wife. That felt right, too. He wanted to ask, but that somehow seemed disrespectful. If she was his wife, surely he would *know* that on some level.

Drake said, "She is my niece. Her name is Deidra." He watched Stephen closely, then said, "She is a witch."

Stephen nodded meditatively. "Aye . . . and she is hunted."

Drake snorted. "You will both be hunted when they get a look at you."

Stephen looked up at him quizzically.

Drake slapped him on the shoulder. "You died, man."

Stephen searched his memory, but he had no recollection of dying. Of course, he had no recollection of much of anything.

Drake laughed. "Och, aye, man. You are a witch, too. The walking dead."

Stephen got to his feet, surprised by this information. This, of all the things that had occurred tonight, felt wrong.

Drake turned and walked back toward the fire glinting faintly through the trees.

"Fash not on it. You're in good company here."

Luthias left the coastal village immediately after the witch had called upon her hell beasts to trample him. Running away with his tail between his legs had not been his first instinct. His nature was to stay and fight, to regroup. But he'd remembered the thunder and the animals and the broken bodies of two of his men, and he'd decided that here, so far from his resources, was not the proper place or time to take another stand.

So he retreated. She had merely won a skirmish. God would never let such a creature win the war. This was only a test of Luthias's resolve, and he would not fail. The decisive battle was yet to come. He had preparations to make.

This time he took witnesses—villagers. They had not wanted to come. They'd been argumentative, complaining about crops and livestock and other responsibilities they'd felt were more pressing than God's calling. Luthias had managed to persuade them by reminding them that he did the king and kirk's work and if they were not cooperative, then both king and kirk would be informed. This had motivated them to set aside their obligations and travel with him.

They traveled south. It took nearly a week, but Luthias had no choice—the nearest lowland city of sufficient size was Sterling, and he very much needed the aid of real Scots, not these Irish hybrids that wore women's skirts. He needed real God-fearing men, not bare-legged papists.

In Sterling he sought out a kirk session to state his case. He was fortunate. The king was in one of his witch-hating periods. King James had done several policy about-faces in the past decade, all of which had affected Luthias's fortunes. His fortune was currently on an upswing. And even better, the king was strongly anti-Highlander. He hated them. In fact, he insisted that the Highland chieftains' firstborn sons be sent to the lowlands or England for schooling so as not to be poisoned by vulgar Highland ways.

Luthias and his witnesses stated their case to the elders. Witches had infested the Highlands. It was anarchy. He needed reinforcements, and he needed to get to the root of the problem. Strathwick was a nest of evil and it was growing, spreading throughout the region.

The root of the evil were the MacKays. Luthias then told them about the blood witch. Again, his witnesses were useful in testifying to the presence of a blood witch in their village, enumerating her attributes and confirming that she was in league with the MacKays.

It was then that Luthias made his most audacious and dangerous accusation—that the head of the Strathwick MacKays was nothing less than a blood witch, as was his wife. And that they must be exterminated before spawning any more witches.

This was not welcome news to the elders. The MacKay was not a lord, but neither was he a commoner. He was a landowner who commanded many men. What was more, the king looked upon him favorably, in spite of his being a Highlander. His firstborn son was currently at the English court in London, and it was said the king was fond of the boy because of his fair countenance.

The elders murmured amongst themselves for some time. When still they seemed undecided, Luthias drew his trump card. He brought the broken bodies of his men forward and showed them what the animals had done.

The elders were moved.

They issued a warrant for William MacKay and his daughter, Deidra. The elders stressed that a man of MacKay's stature must be questioned by the king. Luthias was only to apprehend him. There would be no independent investigations.

That was all Luthias needed to draw Deidra to him. With her lover broken, he suspected she was headed south anyway, bringing him to her home to have him healed. Though Luthias had told Deidra that Stephen Ross was dead, at the time he hadn't really known. It wasn't as if he'd had the opportunity to hold a spoon to his mouth. In fact, he doubted Stephen had actually died. He had seen men live through far worse than what he'd dealt Stephen Ross. If alive, he wouldn't be for long, and there was only one place where he could be made good as new.

Strathwick.

Chapter 17

———— ∞∞∞ ————

$\mathcal{D}$rake led them all back to Creaghaven. They made the journey in record time, in spite of the fact that they took an easier, yet longer, path through the mountains. Stephen and Hannah could ride without stopping, showing no signs of fatigue. Deidra and Drake pushed themselves just to keep up with their grueling pace. They did not need to stop for the night, and Drake thought it best that they just keep moving. They took short sleep breaks during the day but otherwise pressed forward.

Deidra dreaded the *baobhan siths'* feeding time, dreaded seeing Stephen become feral again, but it never came. Neither Stephen nor Hannah ate anything at all on the journey, and they didn't seem worse for it. Perhaps they were not like humans and didn't require daily sustenance. She didn't ask.

She did not know if Stephen even remembered her. He *recognized* her, but that wasn't the same as remembering her. His behavior gave away nothing. He was quiet most of the time. He did not eat the food that Drake offered him. He did not talk except when necessary. And worse, he seemed to be avoiding her. She did find him watching her sometimes, but the sensation unnerved her, making her feel like an animal being stalked. Then she recalled how he'd tried to attack her, and she found herself unable to meet his gaze for more than a few seconds.

She felt as if she'd lost him all over again. Now that he was a "whole man," she didn't matter . . . except as food. It was worse than what she'd feared. She wanted to be happy for him, because he was clearly cured. He was no cripple now. But it was difficult when he didn't seem to be the same person.

When they arrived back at Creaghaven, Duke, Countess, and Blue were all there waiting for them. Deidra was relieved that they had found their way home. She'd told them all where to go, but even humans lost their way, and with domesticated animals it was not always certain they understood.

The animals were all pleased to see them, but when Stephen called Duke to him, the dog tucked his tail between his legs and tried to slink away. This alarmed Deidra more than anything that had happened since Stephen had woken. The dog was frightened. He knew it was his master that called to him, and yet his master smelled all wrong, like a predator. Stephen called the dog again, this time with steel command in his voice. The dog belly-crawled to him and lay flat, nose to the ground, while Stephen patted him. Stephen stood to frown down at the dog, and Duke took the opportunity to run over to Deidra and press his head into her leg.

Deidra put her hand on Duke's head and tried to

soothe him. Stephen frowned at the dog in wounded confusion.

Well, he remembered his dog.

His gaze rose from the dog to meet Deidra's eyes. His own were accusatory, as if she had had something to do with Duke's defection. Then he turned and followed Drake into the keep, where they all went to their respective chambers.

Deidra was so very tired and dejected that she longed for the obliviousness of sleep, but when she closed her eyes, her sleep was troubled with vivid dreams of Stephen kissing her, his lips warm and hungry. Her heart swelled with bittersweet joy that she was in his arms again and he touched her and loved her; that he was not lost to her . . . and yet some part of her understood that this was fleeting, not real.

Still, she took it, grasped the moment with both hands, wrapping her arms around him. He pushed her backward, onto the bed, his hands sliding up her thighs, raising her shift as his body pressed between her legs. *Yes, oh yes.* Her body ached and throbbed for him. She wanted him deep inside her, to give her surcease. She wrapped her thighs around him and moved against him, waiting for him to penetrate her, to end this wanting, but he didn't.

He kissed her deeply, his hips thrusting into hers, driving the ache deeper until she moaned from it, but it did not satisfy, it only made it worse, made her frenzied. His mouth moved over her chin, to suck on her neck, and then she felt it, the sharp piercing of his teeth, sinking deep.

But rather than hurt, it sent her over the edge. She cried out. Her body shuddered and convulsed as his teeth sank in deeper. Waves of ecstasy flowed over her as he sucked, and as he did, he finally pushed inside her, and she screamed.

She woke with a start, body still throbbing with unfulfilled desire. She lay staring at the ceiling, her hand clamped to her throat. Her hair was damp, her breathing labored. She had never had such a dream before. Was that what it meant to be with a blood witch? Pleasure and pain? She rolled onto her side and curled her legs up, willing the gnawing deep in her belly to subside. She still wanted him. But she didn't think he wanted her anymore. He had the beautiful Hannah, and they were exactly alike.

Eventually Deidra's racing heart slowed and her breathing evened out. The calm brought clarity of thought, but no answers to her dilemma. The longer she lay there, the worse she felt. She loved Stephen Ross no matter what he was. It was the who he'd become that troubled her. She didn't even know if this was the same man.

Though it wasn't yet morning, she rose from the bed and dressed. Duke stood, tail wagging happily. He had officially defected, refusing to go near Stephen and sticking to her side like a leech.

She led the dog through the castle and out into the small garden behind the kitchens. The squat stone well stood in the center of the herb and vegetable garden. She dropped the bucket over the side and hauled up water. Duke nosed around in the bushes but came running when she signaled *water* to him in her mind. She leaned against the stone well, staring up at the stars, while the dog drank. As soon as he had his fill, he raced away again. The mild scent of garlic and onion filled the air, making her stomach rumble.

She had been standing there for several minutes, her body still humming from the residual sensations and emotions the dream had left behind, when she suddenly realized that she was not alone in the garden.

She turned abruptly.

And saw nothing. She searched the grays and blacks of the garden. If someone was there, they could easily hide in the darkness beside the castle walls. She felt exposed. She started back toward the door that led back into the castle, calling out to Duke in her mind. She was even more disturbed when Duke's response was an unequivocal refusal to return to the garden.

Stephen was here.

Deidra swallowed, excited and fearful. She wanted to see him, to speak with him alone. But she couldn't seem to get the memory of his attack out of her head.

She turned in a slow circle, scanning the shadows around her. "Stephen?" she said, cursing the tremor in her voice. "I know you're here."

She waited, heart pounding so loudly that she was sure he could hear it. Her gaze jerked from left to right. Panic built in her throat. She felt as if she were being stalked. She was about to call out again when the darkness near the corner shifted. Her heart jumped as a figure moved forward, into the moonlight.

Für wen dieses Buch geschrieben ist

Dieses Buch ist geschrieben für alle, die sich, aus welchen Gründen auch immer, ehrlich und aufrichtig informieren wollen, um was es im Christentum, im Christsein eigentlich geht.

Es ist auch geschrieben für solche,
die nicht glauben, aber doch ernstlich fragen,
die geglaubt haben, aber unzufrieden sind mit ihrem Unglauben,
die glauben, aber in ihrem Glauben sich verunsichert fühlen,
die zwischen Glauben und Unglauben ratlos sind,
die skeptisch sind gegen ihre Glaubensüberzeugungen, aber auch ihre Glaubenszweifel.

Es ist also geschrieben für Christen und Atheisten, Gnostiker und Agnostiker, Pietisten und Positivisten, laue und eifrige Katholiken, Protestanten und Orthodoxe.

Gibt es nicht viele Menschen auch außerhalb der Kirchen, die sich in den grundlegenden Fragen des Menschseins nicht zeitlebens mit vagen Gefühlen, persönlichen Vorurteilen, scheinbaren Plausibilitäten begnügen wollen?

Und gibt es heute nicht auch in allen Kirchen viele Menschen,
die nicht beim Kinderglauben bleiben möchten,
die mehr als ein Repetitorium von Bibelworten oder einen neuen konfessionellen Katechismus erwarten,
die an unfehlbaren Formeln der Schrift (Protestanten), der Tradition (Orthodoxe), des Lehramts (Katholiken) keinen letzten Halt mehr finden?

Alles Menschen freilich,
die trotzdem kein Christentum zu herabgesetzten Preisen wünschen, die den kirchlichen Traditionalismus nicht durch eine konformistische Anpassungskosmetik ersetzt haben wollen,
die vielmehr beeindruckt von kirchlichen Lehrzwängen zur Rechten und ideologischer Willkür zur Linken den Weg suchen zur unverkürzten Wahrheit von Christentum und Christsein.

Nur eine neue Adaption eines traditionellen Glaubensbekenntnisses oder auch eine auf alle alten oder neuen Streitfragen Antwort wissende Miniaturdogmatik soll hier nicht geboten, allerdings auch kein neues Christentum propagiert werden. Wer die traditionellen Glaubenssätze dem heutigen Menschen noch besser verständlich machen kann als der Verfasser, der ist hochwillkommen. Nichts, was sich verständlich machen läßt, soll hier abgelehnt werden. Insofern bleiben alle Türen für die größere Wahrheit offen. Hier soll nur ohne Bekehrungseifer und theologische Lyrik, ohne altbackene Scholastik und ohne modernes Theologenchinesisch von einem, der von der Sache des Christentums überzeugt ist, eine sowohl sachgemäße wie zeitgemäße Einführung versucht werden:

Ins Christ*sein:*   nicht nur in christliche Lehre oder Doktrin, sondern ins christliche Sein, Handeln, Verhalten.

Nur Einführung: denn Christ sein oder nicht Christ sein kann jeder nur selber ganz persönlich.

Eine Einführung: eine andere oder anders geartete wird nicht exkommuniziert, dafür aber auch ein wenig Toleranz erwartet.

Was also will dieses Buch, das nun faktisch doch so etwas wie eine kleine »Summa« des christlichen Glaubens geworden ist?

Es will mitten im epochalen Umbruch kirchlicher Lehre, Moral und Disziplin nach dem Bleibenden suchen: das von den Weltreligionen und modernen Humanismen Verschiedene und zugleich den getrennten christlichen Kirchen Gemeinsame. Der Leser hat einen Anspruch darauf, daß ihm zugleich historisch-exakt und doch aktuell, auf neuestem Forschungsstand und doch verständlich das Entscheidende und Unterscheidende des christlichen Programms für die christliche Praxis herausgearbeitet wird:

was dieses Programm *ursprünglich,* noch nicht bedeckt mit dem Staub und Geröll von zweitausend Jahren, bedeutet hat und

was dieses Programm *heute,* neu ins Licht gestellt, einem jeden für ein sinnvolles, erfülltes Leben bedeuten kann.

Kein anderes Evangelium,

doch dasselbe alte Evangelium

für heute neu entdeckt!

Der Verfasser hat das Buch nicht geschrieben, weil er sich selber für einen guten Christen, sondern weil er Christsein für eine besonders gute Sache hält. An einem Buch wie diesem könnte und müßte man eigentlich bis zum Lebensende arbeiten. Aber man wäre auch dann damit nicht fertig. Soll es jedoch in der gegenwärtig schwierigen Situation von Kirche und Gesellschaft – gleichsam als positives Pendant zum Buch über die Unfehlbarkeit – eine wegweisende Funktion wahrnehmen, so muß es jetzt und nicht erst in drei oder dreißig Jahren erscheinen.

A. Der Horizont

I. Die Herausforderung der modernen Humanismen

Ganz direkt gefragt: *Warum soll man Christ sein?* Warum nicht Mensch, wahrhaft Mensch sein? Warum zum Menschsein auch noch Christsein? Ist Christsein mehr als Menschsein? Überbau? Unterbau? Was soll überhaupt Christsein, was soll Christsein heute?

Christen müßten wissen, was sie wollen. Nichtchristen müßten wissen, was Christen wollen. Ein Marxist wird auf die Frage, was Marxismus will, eine bündige, griffige – wenn auch heute nicht mehr unumstrittene – Antwort geben können: die Weltrevolution, die Diktatur des Proletariats, die Vergesellschaftung der Produktionsmittel, der neue Mensch, die klassenlose Gesellschaft. Was aber will Christentum? Die Antwort von Christen bleibt vielfach schwammig, sentimental, allgemein: Christentum will Liebe, Gerechtigkeit, Lebenssinn, Gutsein und Gutestun, Menschlichkeit ... Aber wollen solches nicht auch Nichtchristen?

Die Frage nach dem, was Christentum will, was Christentum ist, hat sich ohne Zweifel drastisch verschärft. Heute sagen andere nicht einfach anderes, sondern oft das Gleiche: Auch Nichtchristen sind für Liebe, Gerechtigkeit, Lebenssinn, Gutsein und Gutestun, Menschlichkeit. Und oft sind sie es in der Praxis noch mehr. Wenn nun aber andere das Gleiche sagen, wozu dann noch Christ sein? Das Christentum steht heute überall in *doppelter Konfrontation:* mit den großen Weltreligionen einerseits, andererseits mit den nichtchristlichen, »säkularen« Humanismen. Und selbst den bisher in den Kirchen institutionell abgeschirmten und ideologisch immunisierten Christen drängt sich heute die Frage auf: Ist das Christentum – verglichen mit den Weltreligionen und den modernen Humanismen – etwas wesentlich anderes, wirklich etwas Besonderes?

Diese Frage kann nicht nur rein theoretisch, nicht nur allgemein beantwortet werden. Sie muß so konkret und praktisch wie möglich im Horizont unserer Zeit, unter Beachtung der Erfahrungen und Bedingungen unseres Jahrhunderts, unserer gegenwärtigen Welt und Gesellschaft, des heutigen Menschen untersucht und beantwortet werden. Nicht um eine umfassende Zeitanalyse kann es freilich in diesem ersten Teil gehen. Wohl aber um eine kritische Sichtung des Christentums selbst im Zusammenhang konkurrierender Ideologien, Strömungen, Bewegungen: Es soll also nicht die heutige Welt und Gesellschaft in sich selbst beschrieben und analysiert werden; dafür gibt es eine uferlose Literatur. Wohl aber soll das Christentum in seinem Bezug zu dieser heutigen Welt und Gesellschaft neu ergründet und bestimmt werden. Die heutige Welt und Gesellschaft ist somit nicht der direkte Gegenstand, ist freilich auch nicht der abzuwertende Gegenpol, sondern vielmehr der ständig präsente Horizont oder Bezugspunkt unserer Untersuchung.

1. Wende zum Menschen

Täuscht man sich, wenn man wider allen Anschein der Meinung ist, daß die Entwicklung gerade der *modernen Welt selbst,* ihrer Wissenschaft, Technik und Kultur die Frage nach dem Menschsein heute in einer Weise aufwirft, daß die Antwort auf die Frage nach dem Christsein eher erleichtert als erschwert wird?

Täuscht man sich, wenn man wider allen Anschein der Meinung ist, daß im Zug dieser modernen Entwicklung die *Religion* keineswegs ausgespielt hat, die letzten Fragen des Menschen weder gelöst noch gar liquidiert wurden, daß Gott weniger denn je tot ist, daß bei aller Unfähigkeit zu glauben ein neues Bedürfnis zu glauben aufbricht?

Täuscht man sich, wenn man wider allen Anschein der Meinung ist, daß die von den vielen Krisen des Menschengeistes miterschütterte *Theologie* keineswegs am Ende ihrer Weisheit, keineswegs bankrott, sondern aufgrund der gewaltigen Arbeit der Theologengenerationen zweier Jahrhunderte heute um vieles besser als früher darauf vorbereitet ist, die Frage nach dem Christsein neu zu beantworten?

Säkulare Welt

Der Mensch will heute vor allem Mensch sein. Kein Übermensch, freilich auch kein Untermensch. Ganz Mensch in einer möglichst menschlichen Welt. Ist es nicht erstaunlich, wie der Mensch die Welt in den Griff bekommen hat, wie er den Sprung ins Weltall ebenso wie zuvor den Abstieg in die Tiefen seiner eigenen Psyche gewagt hat? Daß er somit vieles, ja beinahe alles, wofür früher Gott, übermenschliche und überweltliche Mächte und Geister zuständig waren, in eigene Regie genommen hat und wahrhaft mündig geworden ist?

Das ist doch gemeint, wenn man von einer »säkularen«, weltlichen Welt spricht. Früher war mit *Säkularisierung*[1] zunächst nur – juristisch-politisch – die Überführung kirchlicher Besitztümer in den weltlichen Gebrauch von Menschen und Staaten gemeint. Heute aber erscheinen nicht nur einige Kirchengüter, sondern ungefähr alle wichtigen Bereiche des menschlichen Lebens – Wissenschaft, Wirtschaft, Politik, Recht, Staat, Kultur, Erziehung, Medizin, soziale Wohlfahrt – dem Einfluß der Kirchen, der Theologie, der Religion entzogen und in die direkte Verantwortung und Verfügung des so selber »säkular« gewordenen Menschen gestellt.

Ähnlich meint das Wort »Emanzipation« ursprünglich rein rechtlich die Freilassung des Kindes aus väterlicher Gewalt oder des Sklaven aus der Macht des Herrn. Dann aber meint es im übertragenen politischen Sinne die bürgerliche Gleichstellung aller derer, die in einem Abhängigkeitsverhältnis zu anderen stehen: gegenüber der Fremdbestimmung nun die Selbstbestimmung der Bauern, Arbeiter, Frauen, Juden, nationalen, konfessionellen oder kulturellen Minderheiten. Schließlich meint so das Wort »Emanzipation« die Selbstbestimmung des Menschen überhaupt gegenüber blind geglaubter Autorität und nicht legitimierter Herrschaft: Freiheit von Naturzwang, vom gesellschaftlichen Zwang und vom Selbstzwang der noch nicht mit sich selber identischen Person[2].

Beinahe zur gleichen Zeit, da die Erde aufhörte, Mittelpunkt der Welt zu sein, lernte der Mensch, sich selbst als den Mittelpunkt der von ihm erbauten Humanwelt zu verstehen. In einem jahrhundertelangen komplexen Prozeß, wie ihn bahnbrechend der große Religionssoziologe Max Weber[3] analysiert hat, trat der Mensch dann seine Herrschaft an: Erfahrungen, Erkenntnisse, Ideen, die ursprünglich vom christlichen Glauben her gewonnen wurden und an ihn gebunden waren, gingen in die Verfügung der menschlichen Vernunft über. Die verschiedenen Lebensbereiche wurden immer weniger von einer Überwelt her gesehen und normiert. Aus sich selber heraus wurden sie verstanden, aus ihrer eigenen immanenten Gesetzlichkeit erklärt. Nach ihr und nicht nach überweltlichen Instanzen richteten sich immer mehr die Entscheidungen und Gestaltungen des Menschen.

Ob man es beklagt oder begrüßt, so oder anders deutet: Selbst in den traditionell katholischen Ländern erscheinen heute die Restbestände des christlichen Mittelalters weithin liquidiert und die weltlichen Bereiche der Vorherrschaft der Religion, der Kontrolle der Kirchen, ihren Glaubenssätzen und Riten, aber auch der Deutung der Theologie weithin entzogen.

Ob die Emanzipation freilich der rote Faden der Menschheitsgeschichte ist, ob diese Welt in ihren Tiefenschichten wirklich so säkular, so weltlich ist, wie sie an der Oberfläche scheint, ja ob sich für das letzte Viertel des 20. Jahrhunderts nicht wieder eine neue geistesgeschichtliche Wende und ein neues Bewußtsein, eine vielleicht etwas weniger rationalistische und optimistische Einstellung zu Wissenschaft und Technik, Wirtschaft und Erziehung, Staat und Fortschritt abzeichnet, ob also der Mensch und seine Welt nicht doch komplexer sind, als Experten und Planer der verschiedenen Bereiche dachten, ist eine offene Frage. Hier interessiert zunächst die Frage: Und die Kirchen? Und die Theologie?

Erstaunlich genug: Kirche und Theologie haben sich nicht nur – schließlich – mit dem Säkularisierungsprozeß abgefunden: sie sind vielmehr recht energisch – besonders in den Jahren seit dem Zweiten Vatikanischen Konzil und der Neuorientierung des Weltrates der Kirchen – auf ihn eingeschwenkt.

Öffnung der Kirchen

Diese säkulare Welt also – früher als »diese« Welt, als die böse Welt par excellence, als Neuheidentum betrachtet – wird heute in der Christenheit nicht nur zur Kenntnis genommen, sondern weithin bewußt bejaht und mitgestaltet. Gibt es doch kaum eine größere Kirche oder eine ernstzunehmende Theologie, die nicht in irgendeiner Form beanspruchte, »modern« zu sein: die Zeichen der Zeit zu erkennen, die Nöte und Hoffnungen der heutigen Menschheit zu teilen, an der Lösung der dringenden Weltprobleme aktiv mitzuarbeiten. Die Kirchen heute wollen – zumindest in der Theorie – nicht mehr zurückgebliebene Subkulturen, Organisationen des ungleichzeitigen Bewußtseins, institutionalisierte Tabuierung von Wissen und produktiver Neugierde sein; sie wollen aus ihrer Selbstabschließung ausbrechen. Die Theologen wollen die traditionalistische Orthodoxie hinter sich lassen und es mit der wissenschaftlichen Redlichkeit auch den

Dogmen und der Bibel gegenüber ernster nehmen. Den Gläubigen wird einiges an neuer Freiheit und Offenheit zugemutet: in Lehre, Moral und Kirchenordnung.

Zwar sind die verschiedenen Kirchen mit manchen ihrer eigenen *innerkirchlichen* Probleme – Überwindung des römischen Absolutismus in der katholischen Kirche, des byzantinistischen Traditionalismus in der östlichen Orthodoxie, der Auflösungserscheinungen im Protestantismus – nicht fertig geworden. Zwar haben sie trotz endloser »Dialoge« und zahlloser Kommissionen für manche relativ einfache *zwischenkirchliche* Probleme – gegenseitige Anerkennung der kirchlichen Ämter, Abendmahlsgemeinschaft, gemeinsamer Kirchenbau, gemeinsamer Religionsunterricht, andere Fragen von »Glauben und Kirchenverfassung« – keine klaren praktischen Lösungen gefunden. Um so leichter sind sie sich bezüglich der meisten *außerkirchlichen* Probleme, in ihren Forderungen an die Gesellschaft, einig geworden. In Rom wie in Genf, in Canterbury, Moskau und Salt Lake City dürfte man, wiederum zumindest in der Theorie, folgendes humane Programm unterschreiben: Entwicklung des ganzen Menschen und aller Menschen; Schutz der Menschenrechte und der Religionsfreiheit; Kampf zur Beseitigung von wirtschaftlichen, sozialen und rassischen Ungerechtigkeiten; Förderung der internationalen Verständigung, der Rüstungsbeschränkung; Wiederherstellung und Wahrung des Friedens; Kampf gegen Analphabetentum, Hunger, Alkoholismus, Prostitution und Rauschgifthandel; ärztliche Hilfe, Gesundheitsdienst und andere soziale Dienstleistungen; Hilfe für Menschen in Not und die Opfer von Naturkatastrophen . . .

Sollte man sich über diesen kirchlichen Fortschritt nicht freuen? Selbstverständlich, und manchmal darf man sogar ein wenig lächeln. Auch für päpstliche Enzykliken wie Dokumente des Weltkirchenrates gelten anscheinend die Regeln der klassischen Politik: Entlastung der sehr unbequemen und oft ergebnislosen kirchlichen »Innenpolitik« durch angestrebte Erfolge in der bequem erscheinenden »Außenpolitik«, die weniger von sich selber als von anderen fordert. Wobei manche Inkonsequenzen in der offiziellen kirchlichen Haltung – progressiv nach außen, gegenüber den anderen; konservativ bis reaktionär im eigenen Bereich – nicht ganz verborgen bleiben: Der Vatikan etwa, der nach außen energisch soziale Gerechtigkeit, Demokratie und Menschenrechte verteidigt, übt nach innen noch immer autoritären Regierungsstil, Inquisition, Verwendung öffentlicher Gelder ohne öffentliche Kontrolle. Und der Weltkirchenrat tritt mutig für Freiheitsbewegungen im Westen, aber nicht für solche im Sowjetbereich ein, konzentriert sich auf Frieden in fernen Landen, ohne Frieden im eigenen Bereich, nämlich zwischen den Kirchen herzustellen.

Und doch wird man die Öffnung der Kirchen gegenüber den großen Nöten der heutigen Zeit aufrichtig bejahen. Zu lange hatten die Kirchen ihre kritische Funktion als moralisches Gewissen der Gesellschaft vernachlässigt, zu lange das Bündnis zwischen Thron und Altar und andere unheilige Allianzen mit den herrschenden Mächten aufrechterhalten, zu lange als Hüter des politischen, ökonomischen und sozialen Status quo gewaltet. Zu lange verhielten sie sich ablehnend oder reserviert gegenüber allen gründlicheren Änderungen des »Systems«, unter Demokratien wie Diktaturen sehr oft weniger um die Freiheit und Würde der Menschen als um die eigenen institutionellen Positionen und Privilegien besorgt, selbst bei Millionenmorden von Nichtchristen klaren Protest scheuend. Nicht die christlichen Kirchen, auch nicht die der Reformation, sondern die in den Büchern der Kirchen- und Profanhistoriker oft als »flach«, »trocken« oder »seicht« apostrophierte Aufklärung hatte ja schließlich die Menschenrechte durchgesetzt: Gewissensfreiheit und Religionsfreiheit, die Abschaffung der Folter, die Beendigung der Hexenverfolgung und andere humane Errungenschaften. Sie hatte im übrigen auch schon für die Kirchen – in der katholischen Kirche erst vom Vatikanum II zur breiten Auswirkung gebracht – einen verständlichen Gottesdienst, effektivere Verkündigung und zeitgemäßere Seelsorge- und Verwaltungsmethoden gefordert. Die großen Zeiten gerade der katholischen Kirche aber waren, wenn man den kirchengeschichtlichen Handbüchern glauben will, die Zeiten der Re-aktion auf die moderne Geschichte der Freiheit: die Gegen-Reformation, die Gegen-Aufklärung, die Restauration, Romantik, Neoromanik, Neogotik, Neogregorianik, Neoscholastik. Eine Kirche also in der Nachhut der Menschheit, in Angst vor dem Neuen immer unter dem Zwang nachzuziehen, ohne eigene schöpferische Anregung für die moderne Entwicklung.

Nur vor dieser reichlich dunklen Vergangenheit läßt sich die gegenwärtige Entwicklung richtig verstehen. Es geht in diesem konkreten Eintreten gerade auch konservativer Kirchen für mehr Menschlichkeit, Freiheit, Gerechtigkeit, Würde im Leben des Einzelnen und der Gesellschaft gegen allen Rassen-, Klassen-

und Völkerhaß um eine teilweise sehr späte, aber doch äußerst bedeutungsvolle *Wende zum Menschen.* Und was noch sehr viel bedeutungsvoller ist: Mehr Menschlichkeit wird nicht nur durch Proklamationen von Kirchenleitungen und Theologen von der Gesellschaft gefordert. Sie wird an ungezählten Plätzen der Welt von ungezählten Unbekannten in aller Unscheinbarkeit geübt und gelebt. Geübt und gelebt auf der Linie der großen christlichen Tradition, aber doch zugleich mit einer neuen Wachheit von all diesen zahllosen anonymen christlichen Botschaftern der Menschlichkeit, Seelsorgern und Laien, Männern und Frauen in manchen gewöhnlichen und auch sehr ungewöhnlichen Situationen: im nordöstlichen Industriegebiet Brasiliens, in den Dörfern Süditaliens und Siziliens, in Missionsstationen des afrikanischen Busches, in den Slums von Madras und Kalkutta, in den Gefängnissen und Gettos von New York und mitten drin im sowjetischen Rußland und im islamischen Afghanistan, in zahllosen Krankenhäusern und Heimen für alle Nöte dieser Welt. Niemand kann es leugnen: Im Kampf für die soziale Gerechtigkeit in Südamerika, für den Frieden in Vietnam, für die Rechte der Neger in den Vereinigten Staaten und in Südafrika, aber auch – nicht zu vergessen – für die Versöhnung und Einigung Europas nach zwei Weltkriegen waren aktive Christen führend. Während die größten Schreckensfiguren unseres Jahrhunderts – Hitler, Stalin und ihre Statthalter – programmatische Antichristen waren, so waren umgekehrt notorische Friedensstifter und Hoffnungszeichen für die Völker bekennende Christen: Johannes XXIII., Martin Luther King, John F. Kennedy, Dag Hammarskjöld, oder zumindest vom Geist Christi inspirierte Menschen wie Mahatma Gandhi. Doch vielleicht wichtiger als sie alle mögen dem Einzelnen jene wirklichen Christenmenschen gewesen sein, die ihm persönlich in seinem Leben begegnet sind.

Alles dies und manches andere an positiver Bewegung in der heutigen Christenheit hat auch viele kirchlich nicht engagierte Menschen aufmerksam werden lassen. Und konstruktive Diskussionen wie praktische Zusammenarbeit zwischen Christen einerseits und Atheisten, Marxisten, Liberalen, säkularen Humanisten verschiedenster Prägung andererseits sind heute keine Seltenheit mehr. Mag sein, daß Christentum und Kirchen doch nicht die quantité négligeable sind, für die sie von einigen, nur um technologischen Fortschritt der Menschheit besorgten westlichen Futurologen gehalten werden. Über »das Elend des Christentums«[4] zu schreiben, ist zwar für bestimmte nachchristliche

Humanisten noch immer ein Bedürfnis, wie denn Christen ihrerseits so oft wie möglich die Gelegenheit genutzt haben, genüßlich über »das Elend des Menschtums« zu schreiben.

Nun hängt allerdings das *Elend des Christentums* mit dem *Elend des Menschtums* zusammen. Nur unernsthafte Christen haben je bestritten, daß es im Christentum menschlich, sehr menschlich zugeht. Sie haben höchstens die Menschlichkeit bei menschlich-allzumenschlichen Skandalen und Skandälchen in der Christenheit – meist ohne viel Erfolg – zu verdecken und zu vertuschen versucht. Umgekehrt sollten eigentlich auch nachchristliche Humanisten nicht bestreiten, daß sie, zumindest verdeckt, noch immer von christlichen Wertvorstellungen bestimmt sind. Weder kann die Säkularisierung nur als die legitime Folge des christlichen Glaubens verstanden werden, wie das Theologen gerne tun[5]. Noch auch kann sie, wie das von Philosophen versucht wird[6], nur aus ureigenen Wurzeln erklärt werden. Weder ist etwa die moderne Fortschrittsidee nur eine Säkularisierung der endzeitlichen Geschichtsdeutung des Christentums, noch ist sie nur aus eigenen philosophischen Ansätzen heraus entstanden. Die Entwicklung geschah vielmehr in dialektischer Auseinandersetzung. Nicht nur das christliche, auch das nachchristliche kulturelle Erbe ist ja nicht einheitlich. Und was eigentlich menschlich, human ist, ist – wie auch noch die jüngere grausame Geschichte zeigt – ohne das Christliche im Hintergrund nicht immer leicht zu bestimmen. Und so werden denn auch nur unernsthafte Humanisten bestreiten, daß der moderne nachchristliche Humanismus bei allen anderen Quellen (besonders den Griechen und der Aufklärung) unendlich viel dem Christentum verdankt, dessen humane Werte, Normen, Sinngebungen oft mehr oder weniger stillschweigend übernommen und assimiliert worden sind, ohne daß dies immer gebührend anerkannt wurde. Das Christentum ist in der westlichen (und damit weithin auch in der globalen) Zivilisation und Kultur, ihren Menschen und Institutionen, Nöten und Idealen allgegenwärtig. Es wird »miteingeatmet«. Chemisch reine säkulare Humanisten gibt es nicht.

Als vorläufiges Resultat mag somit festgehalten werden: *Christentum* und *Humanismus* sind *nicht Gegensätze;* Christen können Humanisten, und Humanisten können Christen sein. Später aber soll begründet werden, daß Christentum nur als radikaler Humanismus richtig verstanden wird. Doch schon jetzt ist klar: Wo immer nachchristliche Humanisten (liberaler, marxistischer,

positivistischer Provenienz) einen besseren Humanismus praktiziert haben als die Christen – und sie taten es durch die ganze
Neuzeit hindurch recht oft –, da ist dies eine Herausforderung
für die Christen, die nicht nur als Humanisten, sondern auch als
Christen versagt haben.

2. Ausverkauf des Christlichen?

Das Christentum ist durch den modernen nachchristlichen Humanismus nicht nur faktisch herausgefordert. Es geht um eine
grundsätzliche Frage, die theoretisch wie praktisch von größter
Brisanz ist und die klar ins Auge gefaßt werden muß.

Die Seele verloren?

Wenn die christlichen Kirchen, mindestens in der Theorie, so
human geworden sind oder zu werden versuchen, wenn sie sich
für alles Menschliche einsetzen, wofür sich auch andere Menschen einsetzen, dann stellt sich die Frage: Warum nicht *ganz*
offen sein in der Überwindung aller sektiererischen Abgeschlos-
senheit? Das ist doch der Zug der Zeit: Zahlreiche »katholische«
Gewerkschaften, Sportvereine, Studentengruppen haben in der
nachkonziliaren Zeit ihr gesondertes Dasein aufgegeben. Aus
»katholischen« Parteien sind »christliche«, aus »christlichen«
Parteien »demokratische« geworden. Warum also überhaupt
eine Kirche, die innerhalb der Menschheit etwas Besonderes zu
sein beansprucht? Wenn schon so modern, fortschrittlich, aufgeklärt, emanzipativ, warum dann noch irgendwo konservativ,
traditionalistisch, jedenfalls versteckt der Vergangenheit verhaftet? Kurz und deutlich: *wenn schon so human, warum eigentlich
noch christlich?*

Das ist eine bedrängende Frage für viele innerhalb der Kirchen:
Beständige Fundamentalisten und ängstliche Pietisten in den
protestantischen Kirchen fürchten für das Ende des Christentums. Konservative Katholiken und insbesondere Enttäuschte
aus der Generation des Montini-Papstes sehen bereits »das trojanische Pferd in der Stadt Gottes«[1] und sinnieren wie der thomi-
stische Philosph Jacques Maritain trübselige ›Gedanken eines
Bauern von der Garonne‹[2]. Aber auch offene und kenntnisreiche

katholische Theologen mahnen: zurückhaltend H.U. von Balthasar[3] und geistreich-sarkastisch den ›Verfall des Katholizismus‹ analysierend Louis Bouyer[4]. Wem jedoch selbst das keinen Eindruck machen sollte, der sei darauf aufmerksam gemacht, daß auch kühle Beobachter außerhalb der Kirche fragen, wohin die Christenheit heute treibt. Der nicht unbedingt konservative Herausgeber des ›Spiegel‹ schrieb schon längst vor seinem Jesus-Buch einen Leitartikel[5], welcher in der Frage gipfelt: »Wozu dann Kirche?« Nach ihm haben die Konservativen jedenfalls ein Argument für sich, das ihnen kein noch so scharfsinniger Fortschrittler entkräften könne: »Ist es wahr, was die aktivsten Neuerer behaupten, so werden die christlichen Kirchen nicht nur liquidiert im Sinne von ›verflüssigt‹ (Friedrich Heer), sondern überflüssig.« Diese Frage ist meines Wissens bisher von keinem Reformer gründlich beantwortet worden.

Die sehr ernste Frage wäre somit, ob die ganze Modernisierung und Humanisierung des Christentums nicht schließlich und endlich doch – gegen die besten Intentionen ihrer Vorkämpfer – zum Ausverkauf des Christlichen führen muß. Wobei bei Ausverkäufen die Fassaden – zur Reklame gebraucht – zunächst intakt bleiben, ja den Eindruck eines sehr guten Geschäftsganges vermitteln, nur daß eben die *Substanz verkauft* wird.

Also karikierend gefragt: Tendiert das alles nicht auf ungemein *aufgeschlossene Kirchen,* die statt beten handeln, die überall in der Gesellschaft aktiv mitmischen, alle Manifeste mitunterschreiben, sich mit allen möglichen Aktionen solidarisieren und wenn möglich, zumindest mit Worten aus der Ferne, mitrevolutionieren, währenddessen in der Nähe ihre Räume sich immer mehr leeren, die Predigt umfunktioniert und das Abendmahl noch mehr vergessen wird und so der Gottesdienst der Gemeinde – entliturgisiert und enttheologisiert – zur sozialpolitischen Diskussions- und Aktionsgruppe oder aber zum Konventikel einer »Kerngruppe« degeneriert? Alles in allem eine Kirche, in der zwar noch immer, wenn auch etwas weniger, Steuern bezahlt und Spenden entrichtet werden, in der sich aber schließlich kaum noch jemand versammelt; die eine »Agglomeration« für sich lebender Christen ist, aber kaum noch »Kirche« (= Ekklesia = Gemeinde = Versammlung) genannt werden kann?

Und nun kongenial zu einer derart aufgeschlossenen Kirche vielleicht eine ähnlich *fortschrittliche Theologie?* Wiederum karikierend verdeutlicht: Statt der abgestandenen neuscholastischen Denzinger-Theologie aus dem vorigen Jahrhundert, deren

Kraftlosigkeit spätestens im Vatikanum II erwiesen wurde, jetzt so etwas wie eine angepaßte, modern gemixte Cocktail-Theologie, die auch nicht mehr christliche Substanz aufweist? Eine Theologie, die mehr hilflos als planmäßig in alle Richtungen zugleich vormaschiert, sich um alles kümmert und die Enttäuschten aller Konfessionen zu vereinigen vermag? Also: Katholische Neuscholastiker, der Exegese mittelalterlicher Theologen und päpstlicher Enzykliken überdrüssig geworden, genießen als nachträglich späte Auch-Psychologen, Auch-Soziologen, Auch-Ökonomen, Auch-Ökologen das Neuheitserlebnis humaner Wissenschaften!? Früher moderne Existentialtheologen, frustriert von einer weltvergessenen und zukunftsblinden Worttheologie, politisieren ihr Denken, zeigen ihr soziales Interesse, richten sich auf Zukunft aus und üben sich nach dem Jargon der rechten Eigentlichkeit nun in dem der linken Uneigentlichkeit!? Und die Abkömmlinge protestantischer Pietisten, von Biblizismus übersättigt, konvertieren zur nachidealistischen Ideologiekritik und fordern antiautoritär Parteilichkeit für soziale Aktion und zumindest verbale Revolution!?

Eine solche Theologie – freilich die traditionelle mit all ihren merkwürdigen Glaubens- und Sittensätzen in einem Fachjargon für Eingeweihte ebenso wie diese moderne mit all ihrem Bemühen um die »Welt« – stände im Zeichen der *Dezentralisierung:* »Zentrifugismus« wäre ein unschönes Wort für eine unschöne Sache, falls jemandem an Etikettierungen gelegen ist. Aber nicht daß man die Augen offen hält und die Menschen, die Welt, die Gesellschaft, die Gegenwart oder eben auch die Vergangenheit, die Überlieferung, die Geschichte ganz genau anschaut, ist das Übel – täte man es nur besser, gründlicher, konkreter, realistischer. Sondern daß man sich in der Welt ver-schaut, die kritische Distanz aufgibt, vergißt, wo man steht, die Mitte verliert, das ist die Gefahr. Dann eben treibt die Theologie, wie Karl Barth es immer mit Recht genannt hat, »Allotria« – womit in Athen »andere Dinge« und in Basel die »Fasnacht« gemeint ist: ein »Carnéval des animaux (théologiques)«, dem allerdings meist der musikalische Humor eines Saint-Saëns abgeht. Solche Theologie redet zerstreut, unkontrolliert, unkonzentriert gerade dort, wo sie von *anderem* reden muß, von anderem reden *muß.* Sie weiß dann nicht, warum überhaupt, wozu überhaupt, woher überhaupt sie redet. Und aus der »Theo-logie« – der im Blick auf Mensch, Welt, Gesellschaft, Geschichte geübten »Rede von Gott« – wird ein modernes oder traditionelles, ein gelehrtes und manchmal auch recht naives »theologisches« Gerede von allen möglichen Dingen: eine zur Ideologie degenerierte Theologie, die von allem »Relevanten«, nur nicht von Gott redet, die mehr »konkret« nach »Welt« als nach der Wahrheit sucht, sich mehr um das Zeitbewußtsein als um die Heilsbotschaft müht und statt einer Selbstbehauptung eine Selbstsäkularisierung betreibt.

Sollte es also doch stimmen, was manche vermuten? Selbstentfremdung der Theologie im Zeichen der Aufklärung, der Aktualität, der Interdisziplinarität, der Human- und Geisteswissenschaften? Selbstliquidation der Kirche im Zeichen der Anpassung, der Modernität, des Dialogs, der Kommunikation, des Pluralismus? Selbstaufgabe des Christentums im Zeichen der Weltlichkeit, der Mündigkeit, der Säkularität, Solidarität und Humanität? Ein langsames Ende ohne Schrecken?

Natürlich stimmt es nicht. Und es wird, so hoffen wir, auch in Zukunft nicht stimmen. Doch auch Karikaturen sagen Wahrheit aus. Und sollte man vielleicht, nach rechts problemblind, solche und ähnliche Fragen aus Furcht, nicht genügend modern, gar konservativ zu erscheinen, dem Papst und den Konservativen überlassen? ›Has the Church lost its soul?‹ Dies war der Titel einer gut begründeten Newsweek-Analyse von 1971[6]. Hat die Kirche ihre Seele, ihre Identität verloren? Die Frage galt der katholischen Kirche, die unter Johannes XXIII. und dem Vatikanum II den kühnsten Kurswechsel der neueren Kirchengeschichte vollzogen hat, in der nachkonziliaren Zeit aber unter einem Vakuum an geistiger Führung in Rom und im Gesamtepiskopat leidet, der an die Reformationszeit erinnert. Diese selben Fragen werden sich indessen in dieser eher wirren Zeit des großen Übergangs alle christlichen Kirchen stellen müssen, die mehr progressiven wie die mehr konservativen. Denn eine Kirche kann ihre Seele verlieren dadurch, daß sie progressiv in allem Verändern nicht bleibt, was sie ist, *oder* aber daß sie konservativ in allem Unveränderlichbleiben nicht neu wird, was sie sein soll. Man kann durch Überarbeitung, durch Bewegung ohne Ruhe sein Leben gefährden, aber auch durch Übersättigung und Ruhe ohne Bewegung.

Kein Zurück

Man wird also das Gesagte nicht mißverstehen können. Wir nehmen nichts nachträglich zurück. Eine Wende zum Menschen, zur »Welt«, zur Gesellschaft, zu den modernen Wissenschaften war überfällig. Auch konservative Christen können nicht daran vorbeisehen, wie gerade die Kirche der Neuzeit die christliche Botschaft in wachsendem Ausmaß kompromittiert und verstellt hat. Anders als in früheren Epochen ohne kritisch-schöpferische Mitarbeit an der Gestaltung der Zeit, antwortete die Kirche auf neue Entwicklungen vor allem denunzierend, reagierend und wenn möglich restaurierend. Sie trennte sich dadurch immer mehr von jenen Menschen, die die moderne Geschichte zu größerer Freiheit, Vernünftigkeit, Menschlichkeit vorangetrieben haben: eine sich gegen die Moderne abkapselnde und einigelnde Kirche, verflochten mit den herrschenden Mächten nach außen, traditionalistisch, autoritär und oft totalitär nach innen. Man mag das programmatische *Wort* »politische Theologie«[7] – von Konstantin bis Carl Schmitt[8], dem Wegbereiter des Führerstaates, theologisch und politisch belastet und mißverständlich – als ungeeignet ablehnen; der weniger programmatisch als funktional zu verstehende Terminus »gesellschaftskritische Theologie« ist vorzuziehen. Aber den *Intentionen* der »politischen Theologie« muß nachdrücklich zugestimmt werden: wenn sie nämlich den inneren Gesellschaftsbezug der christlichen Botschaft herausstellen und dabei deutlich machen will, daß die Kirche als geschichtlich-gesellschaftliche Erscheinung schon immer politisch wirksam war und ihre vorgegebene Neutralität und Abstinenz von öffentlichen Stellungnahmen in vielen Fällen nur die bestehenden bedenklichen politischen Allianzen verschleierte. Die theoretische Auseinandersetzung mit den Humanwissenschaften war und ist ebenso dringlich wie der praktische soziale Einsatz – beides gerade von jungen Theologen trotz aller Schwierigkeiten von rechts und von links in vorbildlicher Weise geübt. Sosehr die Kirche in der Gesellschaft Ort großer Tradition bleiben wird, sosehr muß sie es ablehnen, einfach Hort des Bestehenden zu sein. Ein Großteil der Schwierigkeiten gerade in der katholischen Kirche und Theologie stammt heute aus dem Problemüberdruck, den eine jahrhundertelange autoritäre Stauung erzeugt hat. Ein Großteil der Verwirrung gerade im Kirchenvolk kommt nicht von der theologischen Kritik, die nur aufdeckt, was ist. Sie kommt von den Kirchenleitungen und ihren Hoftheologen, die seit langer Zeit das Kirchenvolk nicht auf die ständig notwendigen Reformen in Lehre und Praxis vorbereitet, sondern es dagegen systematisch immunisiert haben, die die Menschen nicht in die kritische Freiheit eingeführt, sondern ihnen immer nur mit Emphase Einheit, Gebet, Demut und Gehorsam gepredigt haben.

Die *Wende* also gerade derjenigen Kirche, die wohl mehr als andere Kirchen noch in unseren Jahrzehnten im Namen von Dogmen und Rechtssätzen gegen Mitmenschlichkeit und Solidarität gesündigt, den Dialog Christen, Nichtchristen und vor allem ihrer eigenen »loyal opposition« versagt, die Resultate der Natur- und Geschichtswissenschaften verurteilt, unterdrückt und vernachlässigt hat, die Wende also gerade der katholischen Kirche zur »Welt«, zum Menschen, zur Gesellschaft war nicht – wie in Rom noch immer einige meinen – ein Zufall, ein zum Teil mit dem »guten Papst Johannes« zusammenhängendes Mißgeschick. Sie war schlicht eine *geschichtliche Notwendigkeit:* grundgelegt in einer völlig veränderten Gesellschaft, vorbereitet durch eine ganze Generation nicht verzagender Theologen und Laien, ausgelöst durch einen großen ebenso menschlich wie evangelisch gesinnten Charismatiker, schließlich in Gang gesetzt durch eine Kirchenversammlung von Bischöfen, die damals, von Theologen beraten und inspiriert, viel vom Wehen des Heiligen Geistes sprachen, bevor sie unter einem anderen Papst in ihre alte Umgebung zurückkehrten und die päpstliche Kurie versuchte, die Fehler des Vorgängers zu korrigieren und ihre wankende Herrschaft über das Imperium Romanum wieder neu zu festigen.

Angesichts des nicht unerwarteten nachkonziliaren »backlash« wäre es schade, wenn allzuviele, die die Wende vorbereitet und mit herbeigeführt haben, nun älter geworden in Fortschrittlichkeit stehen blieben, statt ihre Fortschrittlichkeit im Fortschreiten zu bewähren. Die Kirchengeschichte geht ohnehin weiter, und auch die Theologie des Vatikanum II und seiner Interpreten wird die letzte nicht sein. Eine Rückkehr aber zur vorkonziliaren Kirche ist nicht mehr möglich. Soviel hat sich in der nachkonziliaren Zeit gezeigt: the point of no return ist erreicht, und die Alternativen fehlen. Anders als im 19. Jahrhundert stellt ein romantisch verklärtes Mittelalter, stellen Neoromanik, Neogotik, Neogregorianik, Neoscholastik, Neoultramontanismus keine verführerischen Ausweichmöglichkeiten mehr dar. Dies alles wurde durchgeprobt, und zu leicht befunden. Auf die Dauer kann auch die katholische Kirche unmöglich zum Ergötzen einiger kirchlicher und nichtkirchlicher Ästheten und Philanthropen als Museum des Abendlandes (museal mit lateinischer Kultsprache, byzantinischem Zeremoniell, mittelalterlicher Liturgie und Gesetzgebung und nachtridentinischer Theologie) dienen. Sie wird sich auch heute nicht als Kultkirche domestizieren lassen dürfen.

Wir bleiben also dabei: Auf der ganzen Linie, wie hoffentlich in diesem Buch deutlich werden wird, eine unvoreingenommene *Offenheit für die »Moderne«*, das Außerchristliche, Nichtchristliche, Humane, und schonungslose Kritik der eigenen Positionen, Distanzierung von allem kirchlichen Traditionalismus, Dogmatismus, Biblizismus. Aber trotz allem *kein* unkritischer kirchlicher oder theologischer »*Modernismus«*. Liebhaber und Verächter des Christlichen unter den Gebildeten dürften es schätzen, wenn hier von allem Anfang an unmißverständlich zum Ausdruck gebracht wird: Eine Humanisierung der Kirche war notwendig und bleibt notwendig, aber unter der einen Bedingung – ohne Ausverkauf der christlichen »Substanz«[9]! Der Diamant soll nicht verschleudert, wohl aber geschliffen und wenn möglich zum Strahlen gebracht werden. Das Christliche ist bei dieser Wende zum Menschlichen nicht verschwommener, sondern präziser, sachlicher, entschiedener zur Geltung zu bringen, mit Augenmaß und kritischer Distanz gegenüber *allen* Bewegungen unserer Zeit, gegenüber den säkularen Utopien, Illusionen, Konformismen von rechts *und* links. So ist denn auch der Titel dieses Abschnittes – Herausforderung der modernen Humanismen – aktiv und passiv zu verstehen: Die herausfordernden modernen Humanismen sind selber herausgefordert.

3. Keine Verabschiedung der Hoffnung

Zu lange haben Theologen die Welt schlecht gemacht, als daß sie jetzt nicht die Versuchung verspürten, alles auf einmal gutzumachen. Manichäische Weltverteufelung – jetzt abgelöst durch säkulare Weltverherrlichung: beides Zeichen theologischer Weltfremdheit. Sehen nicht untheologische »Weltmenschen« die Welt oft differenzierter, realistischer bezüglich der positiven wie der negativen Weltaspekte? Illusionslose Nüchternheit ist angebracht, nachdem auch in unserem Jahrhundert allzuviele Theologen sich vom Zeitgeist blenden ließen und sogar Nationalismus und Kriegspropaganda wie dann auch totalitäre Parteiprogramme schwarzer, brauner und schließlich auch roter Färbung theologisch untermauerten. So werden Theologen selber leicht zu

31

Ideologen, zu Verfechtern von Ideologien. *Ideologien* hier nicht wertneutral, sondern kritisch verstanden: als Systeme von »Ideen«, Begriffen und Überzeugungen, von Deutungsmodellen, Motiven und Handlungsnormen, die – meist durch bestimmte Interessen gesteuert – die Wirklichkeit der Welt verzerrt wiedergeben, die wahren Mißstände verschleiern und rationale Begründungen durch den Appell an Emotionen ersetzen.

Ist die einfache Berufung auf das Menschliche, das Humanum, die Lösung? Auch *Humanismen* wechseln rasch. Was ist noch übriggeblieben vom klassischen griechisch-abendländischen Humanismus nach den großen desillusionierenden Demütigungen des Menschen: der ersten durch Kopernikus (des Menschen Erde nicht Zentrum des Alls), der zweiten durch Marx (des Menschen Abhängigkeit von unmenschlichen gesellschaftlichen Verhältnissen), der dritten durch Darwin (des Menschen Abstammung aus dem untermenschlichen Bereich), und der vierten durch Freud (des Menschen geistiges Bewußtsein gründend im Triebhaft-Unbewußten)? Was ist bei den so verschiedenen Menschenbildern der Physik, der Biologie, der Psychoanalyse, der Ökonomie, der Soziologie, der Philosophie noch übriggeblieben vom früheren einheitlichen Menschenbild? Der aufklärerische Humanismus des »honnête homme«, der akademische Humanismus der »humaniora«, der existentialistische Humanismus des ins Nichts geworfenen individuellen »Daseins« – sie alle haben ihre Zeit gehabt. Ganz zu schweigen von dem sich anfänglich ebenfalls human und sozial gebenden und von Nietzsches Übermenschen faszinierten Faschismus und Nazismus, dessen wahnwitzige Ideologie von »Volk und Führer«, »Blut und Boden« die Menschheit eine noch nie dagewesene Zerstörung menschlicher Werte und Millionen menschlicher Leben gekostet hat.

Kann man angesichts dieser Lage nach all den vielen Enttäuschungen eine gewisse Skepsis gegenüber den Humanismen nicht verstehen? Die Arbeit vieler säkularer Analytiker in Philosophie, Linguistik, Ethnologie, Soziologie, Individual- und Sozialpsychologie beschränkt sich heute vielfach darauf, der Unlogik des verworrenen, widersprüchlichen und unverständlichen Materials dadurch einen Sinn abzugewinnen, daß man auf Sinngebungen überhaupt verzichtet, daß man sich vielmehr wie in den Naturwissenschaften auf die positiven Gegebenheiten (Positivismus) und die formalen Strukturen (Strukturalismus) beschränkt und sich mit Messen, Kalkulieren, Steuern, Program-

mieren und Prognostizieren der einzelnen Abläufe zufrieden-
gibt. Die Krise des säkularen Humanismus, die schon früh in der
darstellenden Kunst, in der Musik und in der Literatur signali-
siert wurde, zeigt sich aber vielleicht am deutlichsten dort, wo er
sich bisher am stärksten erwies und über eine breite Massenbasis
verfügte: im technologisch-evolutionären Humanismus und im
politisch-sozial-revolutionären Humanismus. Nachdem wir die
Lage der christlichen Kirchen einer schonungslosen Kritik unterzogen haben, wird man es uns nicht als ideologische Voreingenommenheit auslegen, wenn wir uns zur Klärung der eigenen
Situation um eine ebenso schonungslose zeitkritische Analyse
der heute herrschenden Ideologien bemühen. Keine pessimisti-
sche Kulturkritik ist die Absicht, wohl aber eine realistische
Einschätzung der Gegenwart, die in West und Ost zahllose
Impulse zum Besseren enthält, aber vielleicht doch entscheidende Anstöße benötigt, um eine wirklich bessere menschliche Gesellschaft heraufzuführen.

Humanität durch technologische Evolution?

Erschüttert scheint die *Ideologie einer von selbst zur Humanität
führenden technologischen Evolution.* Man hat ausgerechnet[1],
daß wir im Blick auf 50 000 Jahre Menschheitsgeschichte und
einem Durchschnittsalter der Menschen von 62 Jahren jetzt im
800. Lebensalter stehen, von denen die Menschheit rund 650 in
Höhlen verbracht hat: erst seit 70 Lebensaltern gibt es Kommunikation zwischen den Generationen durch das geschriebene
Wort, erst seit 6 für Massen von Menschen das gedruckte Wort,
erst seit 4 exakte Zeitmessung und erst seit 2 einen elektrischen
Motor. Die allermeisten aber der heutigen Gebrauchsgüter wurden erst in diesem einen 800. Lebensalter entwickelt, so daß der
Umbruch unseres Lebensalters als der zweite große Einschnitt in
der Menschheitsgeschichte nach dem ersten – der Erfindung des
Ackerbaus in der Jungsteinzeit und dem Übergang vom Barba-
rentum zur Zivilisation – zu betrachten wäre. In unserem Zeitalter nun hat die Agrikultur, welche für Jahrtausende die Basis der
Zivilisation ausmachte, ihre Vorherrschaft in einem Land nach
dem anderen verloren. Und zugleich wird auch das vor 2 Jahrhunderten begonnene Industriezeitalter überwunden: Die mit
Handarbeit Beschäftigten werden in den fortschrittlichen Ländern aufgrund der Automation ebenfalls sehr rasch zu einer

Minderheit, und eine nur in Umrissen erkennbare Super-Industrie-Kultur erscheint am Horizont. Soll so vielleicht von selbst in Erfüllung gehen, was der geschichtsphilosphische Optimismus der französischen Enzyklopädisten, was Lessing mit seiner ›Erziehung des Menschengeschlechts‹, Kant mit seiner Vorstellung eines »ewigen Friedens«, Hegel mit seiner Geschichtsauffassung vom »Fortschritt im Bewußtsein der Freiheit«, Marx mit der Utopie der »klassenlosen Gesellschaft«, Teilhard de Chardin mit der Evolution zum »Punkt Omega« gedacht und erhofft hatten?

Der Fortschritt der modernen Wissenschaft, Medizin, Technik, Wirtschaft, Kommunikation, Kultur ist beispiellos: er übertrifft die kühnsten Phantasien Jules Vernes und anderer früher Futurologen. Und trotzdem: diese Evolution scheint vom Punkt Omega noch weit entfernt und scheint oft noch weiter von ihm wegzuführen. Auch wer die Totalkritik der Neuen Linken am gegenwärtigen gesellschaftlichen »System« nicht mitmacht und nicht alle seine Hoffnungen auf eine Totalumwandlung der fortgeschrittenen Industriegesellschaft setzt, kommt je länger desto weniger um die beunruhigende Feststellung herum, daß in diesem phantastischen quantitativen und qualitativen Fortschritt irgend etwas nicht stimmt. In kurzer Zeit ist das *Unbehagen* an der technischen Zivilisation allgemein geworden, wozu viele Faktoren – hier nicht zu analysieren – beigetragen haben.

In wachsendem Ausmaß bezweifelt man gerade in den fortschrittlichsten westlichen Industrienationen jenes Dogma, an das man lange Zeit geglaubt hat: daß Wissenschaft und Technik der Schlüssel zum allgemeinen Glück der Menschen seien und der Fortschritt unvermeidlich und gleichsam automatisch erfolge. Es ist nicht mehr die noch immer sehr reale, aber durch das politische Arrangement der Supermächte geminderte Gefahr einer atomaren Zerstörung der Zivilisation, die am meisten beunruhigt. Es sind die große Welt- und Wirtschaftspolitik mit ihren Widersprüchlichkeiten, die Lohn- und Preisspirale und die weder in Amerika noch in Europa zu bändigende Inflation, die schleichende und oft auch akute Weltwährungskrise, die wachsende Kluft zwischen reichen und armen Völkern, alle die Probleme auf nationaler Ebene, die den Regierungen über den Kopf wachsen und eine mangelnde Stabilität auch westlicher Demokratien – von den Militärdiktaturen in Südamerika und anderswo nicht zu reden – anzeigen. Es sind erst recht die Probleme an Ort und Stelle, wie sie sich etwa in einer Stadt wie New York als drohende Zukunft für alle städtischen Agglomerationen zeigen: hinter der imposantesten Skyline der Welt eine anscheinend grenzenlos sich ausbreitende Stadtlandschaft von immer mehr verschmutzter Luft, verdorbenem Wasser, verrotteten Straßen, verstopftem Verkehr, mangelndem Wohnraum, überhöhten Mieten, Verkehrs- und Kulturlärm, gesundheitlichen Schädigungen, steigenden Aggressionen und Verbrechen, zunehmenden Gettos, sich verschärfenden Spannungen zwischen Rassen, Klassen und Volksgruppen. Jedenfalls nicht gerade die »secular city«, wie sie sich Theologen zu Beginn der sechziger Jahre erträumt haben!

Sind die negativen Ergebnisse der technologischen Entwicklung nur Zufall? Wohin man kommt – in Leningrad und Taschkent ebenso wie in Melbourne und Tokio und selbst in den Entwicklungsländern, in New Delhi oder Bangkok, zeichnen sich dieselben Phänomene ab. Sie können nicht einfach als die wohl unvermeidlichen dunklen Seiten des großen Fortschritts verbucht und in Kauf genommen werden. Manches geht zweifellos auf Kosten von Kurzschlüssen und Mißbräuchen. Alles zusammen aber hängt doch offensichtlich an diesem so sehr herbeigesehnten, herbeigeplanten, herbeigearbeiteten *ambivalenten Fortschritt selbst:* ein Fortschritt, der, wenn er so weitergeht, die echte Menschlichkeit zugleich entwickelt und zerstört. Die früher so positiven Kategorien des »Wachstums«, der »Vermehrung«, »Progression«, »Größe«, des »Sozialprodukts« und der »Steigerungsraten« sind ins Zwielicht geraten. Denn sie drücken nun ein unabdingbares Muß, einen Zwang zu immer größerem Wachstum (der Produktion, des Konsums, des Verschleißes) aus. Ein Gefühl der Unfreiheit, der Unsicherheit und der Zukunftsangst breitet sich gerade in den hochentwickelten Wohlfahrtsstaaten aus. Erst jetzt scheint der technologische Prozeß seine ganze Vehemenz erreicht zu haben und dabei zugleich jeglicher Kontrolle – gerade auch der oft umständlich operierenden demokratischen Systeme – zu entgleiten. Das Versprechen einer »Great Society« (L. B. Johnson) – als ob der Mensch von Natur aus gut sei, wenn nur die Umwelt gut ist, und diese gut wird, wenn die Regierung nur genügend Geld einsetzt – erwies sich selbst für die Vereinigten Staaten als unerfüllbar. Und dies auch unabhängig vom unmenschlichen Vietnamkrieg! Die bekannten düsteren Computer-Analysen eines M.I.T.-Teams[2] im Auftrag des »Club von Rom« über das (nicht nur lineare, sondern exponentielle) Wachstum und die Folgen für Rohstoffschrumpfung, Überbevölkerung, Lebensmittelverknappung und Umweltverschmutzung stellen nicht nur soziale Unruhen und den Zusammenbruch der Industrie, sondern geradezu den Untergang der Menschheit spätestens für das Jahr 2100 in Aussicht. Obwohl Datenbasis und einzelne Extrapolationen fraglich sind, neu auftretende technologische Entwicklungen, geplante Gegenaktionen und überhaupt künftiges menschliches Verhalten vernachlässigt werden und die Gesamtprognose folglich umstritten bleibt, wurde sie doch recht allgemein als Warnung verstanden: daß die Katastrophe zwar nicht kommen muß, aber zumindest kommen kann.

Und so jagen sich denn heute die apokalyptischen Buchtitel: ›Das Selbstmordprogramm – Zukunft oder Untergang der Menschheit‹; ›Die geplante Verwirrung‹; ›Nach uns die Steinzeit. Das Ende des technischen Zeitalters‹; ›Kein Platz für Menschen. Der programmierte Selbstmord‹; ›Todeskandidat Erde. Programmierter Selbstmord durch unkontrollierten Fortschritt‹; ›Gefährdete Zukunft‹[3]. Autoren wie Karl Steinbuch, die noch 1968 mit ›Falsch programmiert‹[4] die technologische Euphorie förderten, verlangen 1973 eine ›Kurskorrektur‹: eine »bewußte Klärung der Normen unseres Zusammenlebens«, womit der Verfasser freilich nur »eine anspruchslose Einigung, nach welchen Grundsätzen wir zusammenleben wollen«, meint[5]! Aber auch Verhaltensforscher vom Rang eines Konrad Lorenz rechnen uns ›Die acht Todsünden der zivilisierten Menschheit‹ vor: Überbevölkerung, Verwüstung des Lebensraumes, der Wettlauf mit sich selbst, Wärmetod des Gefühls, genetischer Verfall, Abreißen der Tradition, Indoktrinierbarkeit, die Kernwaffen[6]! Für manche hat schließlich die Erdölkrise (1973) mit allen ökonomischen und politischen Auswirkungen die schlimmsten Befürchtungen bestätigt und gezeigt, wie leicht das ganze wirtschaftlich-soziale System des Westens im großen wie im kleinen erschüttert werden und wie rasch das Ende der Überflußgesellschaft kommen kann.

Die *neomarxistische Gesellschaftskritik* an diesen Zuständen, insbesondere die der »Kritischen Theorie« der Frankfurter Schule (T.W. Adorno, M. Horkheimer, Herbert Marcuse), aber auch Ernst Blochs hat sich mit dem Scheitern des »Prager Frühlings« und der Studentenrevolutionen offensichtlich nicht erledigt[7]. Dies ist das Bild, welches sich zeigt[8]: Eine stets reichere, größere, bessere Gesellschaft von überwältigender Leistungsfähigkeit und sich ständig erhöhendem Lebensstandard. Aber doch zugleich, ja gerade deshalb auch eine Gesellschaft perfektionierter Verschwendung, der friedlichen Produktion immenser Zerstörungsmittel. Ein technologisches Universum mit der Möglichkeit totaler Vernichtung und so noch immer eine Welt voller Mangel, Leiden, Elend, Not, Armut, Gewalttätigkeiten und Grausamkeiten. Der Fortschritt muß beidseitig betrachtet werden: mit der Abschaffung alter Abhängigkeiten (von Personen) neue Abhängigkeiten (von Dingen, Institutionen, anonymen Mächten). Mit der Befreiung oder besser »Liberalisierung« der Politik, der Wissenschaft, der Sexualität, der Kultur eine neue Versklavung durch den Zwang des Konsums. Mit steigenden Produktionsleistungen die Integration in einen riesigen Apparat. Mit vervielfältigtem Warenangebot die Maximierung der individuellen Konsumwünsche und ihre Steuerung durch Bedürfnisplaner und die geheimen Verführer der Werbung. Mit rascherem Verkehr eine größere Hetze des Menschen. Mit verbesserter Medizin Zunahme der psychischen Krankheiten sowie ein verlängertes und doch oft nicht sinnerfülltes Leben. Mit wachsendem Wohlstand mehr Verschleiß und Vergeudung. Mit der Naturbeherrschung die Naturzerstörung. Mit perfektionierten Massenmedien Funktionalisierung, Verkürzung, Verarmung der Sprache und Indoktrinierung großen Stils. Mit wachsender internationaler Kommunikation mehr Abhängigkeit von multinationalen Konzernen (und bald auch Gewerkschaften). Mit der sich ausbreitenden Demokratie mehr Gleichschaltung und soziale Kontrolle durch die Gesellschaft und ihre Mächte. Mit der raffinierteren Technik die Möglichkeit raffinierterer (unter Umständen sogar genetischer) Manipulation. Mit der durchgreifenden Rationalität im einzelnen der mangelnde Sinn des Ganzen.

Ja, die Liste ließe sich beinahe beliebig fortsetzen, und die Schlagworte sind bekannt: »Kultur als Maschinerie«, »Kunst als Ware«, »Schriftsteller als Produzent von Texten«, »Sex als Marktwert«, »Technik als Verdinglichung«. Eine »hominisierte«, aber keineswegs humanisierte Welt in einer mehr als merkwürdigen Harmonie von Freiheit und Unterdrückung, Produktivität und Zerstörung, Wachstum und Regression, Wissenschaft und Aberglaube, Freude und Elend, Leben und Tod. Doch diese knappen Andeutungen, die jeder aus seinen Erfahrungen reichlich belegen kann, dürften genügen, um sichtbar zu machen, wie sehr die Fortschrittsideologie einer von selbst zur Humanität führenden technologischen Evolution erschüttert ist: ein Fortschritt, der zerstörerisch wirkt; eine Rationalität, die irrationale

Züge trägt; eine Humanisierung, die zum Inhumanen führt. Kurz: ein evolutiver Humanismus, dessen nichtgewollte, faktische Konsequenz die *Entmenschlichung des Menschen* ist.

Schwarzweißmalerei? Offensichtlich nicht. Wohl aber Weiß- *und* Schwarz-Malerei, und das Resultat ist eine graue, unsichere Zukunft auch für den, der von Haus aus nicht zum Pessimismus neigt. Ein Buch wie ›Der eindimensionale Mensch‹ Marcuses ist gerade dann, wenn man letztlich damit nicht einverstanden ist und nicht wegen der Unmöglichkeit der Revolution zur Resignation neigt, ein erschütterndes Buch. Seine Faszination für die in Fortschritt und Überfluß groß gewordene jüngere Generation ist nur dem unverständlich, der es nicht gelesen hat und es doch diskutiert (wie bei berühmten Büchern oft der Fall) oder der selber in dieser herz- und hilflosen Welt so herz- und hilflos geworden ist, daß er den Protest der Jugend nicht mehr zu verstehen vermag (womit er selber zum Beweis für Marcuses These wird). Dieser bewußt anklagenden Wissenschaft kommt man nicht bei mit einer aufs Private ausgerichteten Existenz- und schließlich Seinsphilosophie im Stil des früheren oder späteren Heidegger. Auch nicht mit einer alles verstehen wollenden, aber nichts entscheidenden und ändernden philosophisch-theologischen oder historischen Hermeneutik (Wissenschaft des Verstehens). Und vielleicht auch nicht mit einem naturwissenschaftlich geprägten Positivismus oder mit einem »kritischen Rationalismus« (K. Popper, H. Albert), welcher sich als Alternative zwischen einem autoritär-dogmatischen und einem anti-autoritären radikalen Denken anbietet, der aber mit seinem durchaus dogmatischen Vertrauen auf eine universal angewendete naturwissenschaftliche Rationalität zusammen mit der Sprachanalyse und ihren formalen »Sprachspielen« als der wissenschaftliche Hauptverantwortliche für die Eindimensionalität des menschlichen Daseins angeklagt erscheint[9]. Die Frage ist, ob die »Kritische Theorie« der Neuen Linken selber über die Eindimensionalität hinausführt.

Doch soll mit der Ideologie auch die Hoffnung verabschiedet werden? Das Kind soll nicht mit dem Bad ausgeschüttet werden. *Aufzugeben* ist der technologische *Fortschritt als Ideologie*, die, von Interessen gesteuert, die wahre Wirklichkeit der Welt verkennt und pseudorational Illusionen von Machbarkeit erweckt: Aufzugeben ist nicht die Bemühung um Wissenschaft und Technologie und damit um menschlichen Fortschritt. Aufzugeben ist nur der *Wissenschaftsglaube* als *Totalerklärung der Wirklichkeit*

(»Weltanschauung«), die *Technokratie* als allesheilende *Ersatz-religion!*

Nicht aufzugeben ist also die *Hoffnung auf eine meta-technologische Gesellschaft,* eine neue Synthese von gebändigtem technischem Fortschritt und einem von den Fortschrittszwängen befreiten menschlichen Dasein: eine menschlichere Arbeitsweise, mehr Nähe zur Natur, ein ausgeglicheneres soziales Gefüge und die Befriedigung auch der nichtmateriellen Bedürfnisse, jener menschlichen Werte also, die das Leben erst lebenswert machen und sich doch nicht in Geldwert quantifizieren lassen! Die Menschheit ist in jedem Fall für ihre eigene Zukunft voll verantwortlich. Sollte sich hier nichts ändern lassen? Vielleicht durch eine radikale, gar gewaltsame Veränderung der gesellschaftlichen Ordnung, ihrer Repräsentanten und Werte: also durch Revolution?

Humanität durch politisch-soziale Revolution?

Erschüttert scheint auch die *Ideologie einer von selbst zur Humanität führenden politisch-sozialen Revolution.* Diese Einsicht bildet den Kontrapunkt zu der eben entwickelten. Wie es im vorausgegangenen Abschnitt nicht darum ging, Wissenschaft, Technologie, Fortschritt von vornherein abzuqualifizieren, so geht es im folgenden Abschnitt nicht darum, etwa den Marxismus als die wirkmächtigste revolutionäre Gesellschaftstheorie von vornherein als undemokratisch, unmenschlich und unchristlich zu deklarieren.

Auch Christen müssen erkennen und verstehen, welches *humanistische Potential* gerade im *Marxismus* steckt. Dies gilt nicht nur, wie manche meinen[10], für den jungen Marx der philosophischen ›Frühschriften‹[11], der unter Hegels und Feuerbachs Einfluß eine humanistische Terminologie (Mensch, Menschheit; Entfremdung, Befreiung und Entwicklung des Menschen) gebraucht. Es gilt auch für den anders sprechenden reifen Marx des sozial-ökonomischen ›Kapital‹[12], der unwirksame humanistische Worte und Phrasen meidet. Die humanistische Intention hat sich durchgehalten: Gegen die unmenschlichen Verhältnisse der kapitalistischen Gesellschaft sollen wahrhaft menschliche Verhältnisse geschaffen werden! Also keine Gesellschaft mehr, wo große Menschenmassen erniedrigt, verachtet, verelendet, ausgebeutet sind. Wo der höchste Wert der Warenwert, der wahre Gott das

Geld (als die Ware der Waren) und die Motive des Handelns Profit, Selbstinteresse, Eigennutz sind, wo also faktisch der Kapitalismus als Religionsersatz fungiert. Sondern eine Gesellschaft, wo jeder Mensch wahrhaft Mensch, ein freies, aufrechtgehendes, würdiges, autonomes, alle seine Möglichkeiten realisierendes Wesen sein kann: Ende der Ausbeutung des Menschen durch den Menschen.

Die Menschlichkeit der Verhältnisse, der Strukturen, der Gesellschaft und somit des Menschen selbst: dies und nichts anderes ist nach Marx der Sinn der proletarischen Revolution durch Aufhebung der Arbeitsteilung, Abschaffung des Privateigentums und Diktatur des Proletariats. Dies und nichts anderes ist das von Marx nur in Umrissen vorsichtig angedeutete Wesen der klassenlosen kommunistischen Zukunftsgesellschaft: Nicht ein irdisches Paradies und ein Schlaraffenland ohne existentielle Probleme. Wohl aber ein Reich der Freiheit und der menschlichen Selbstverwirklichung, wo es bei allen individuellen Besonderheiten keine prinzipielle Ungleichheit und Unterdrückung von Menschen, Klassen und Völkern gibt und die Ausbeutung des Menschen durch Menschen ein Ende hat, so daß der Staat seine politische Funktion als Kontrollmacht verliert und die Religion überflüssig wird. Alles in allem also ein sozialisierter und demokratisierter Humanismus.

Soweit das Programm[13]. Es dürfte bezüglich seiner Verwirklichung gut sein, nicht sogleich nach Moskau oder Peking zu schauen. Vielleicht wurden die ursprünglichen Marxschen Intentionen von bestimmten jugoslawischen oder ungarischen Theoretikern besser bewahrt und weiterentwickelt[14] als von den großen orthodoxen (marxistisch-leninistischen) Systemen, die sich faktisch durchgesetzt haben und als die mächtigen offiziellen Träger des Marxismus den Lauf der Weltgeschichte mitbestimmen. An diesen muß sich der Marxismus heute in demselben Maße messen lassen wie das Christentum an der Verwirklichung des christlichen Programms durch die großen geschichtsbestimmenden christlichen Kirchen. Das Programm kann ja von seiner Wirkungsgeschichte nicht völlig getrennt werden, auch wenn sich kritisch von der Wirkungsgeschichte und den daraus hervorgegangenen Institutionen auf das ursprüngliche Programm zurückfragen läßt. Schlechte Verwirklichung widerlegt noch nicht ein gutes Programm. Konzentriert man sich sogleich auf das Negative, so übersieht man leicht, was etwa Rußland (im Vergleich zu dem von Kirche und Adel gestützten zaristischen Regime) Lenin verdankt, was China (im Vergleich zum vorrevolutionären chinesischen Gesellschaftssystem) Mao Tse-tung, ja, was die ganze Welt Karl Marx verdankt. Wichtige Elemente der Marxschen Gesellschaftstheorie sind auch im Westen allgemein übernommen worden. Oder wird heute nicht ganz anders als im liberalen Individualismus der Mensch in seiner Gesellschaftlichkeit gesehen? Konzentriert man sich nicht ganz anders als im idealistischen Denken auf die konkret zu ändernde gesellschaftliche Wirklichkeit, auf die faktische Entfremdung des Menschen in unmenschlichen Verhältnissen, auf die Notwendigkeit der Bewahrheitung jeder Theorie in der Praxis? Wird jetzt nicht die zentrale Bedeutung der Arbeit und des Arbeitsprozesses für die Entwicklung der Menschheit gesehen und der Einfluß der ökonomischen Faktoren auf die Geschichte der Ideen und Ideologien bis ins Detail untersucht? Wird die weltgeschichtliche Relevanz des Aufstiegs der Arbeiterklasse im Zusammenhang mit sozialistischen Ideen nicht auch im Westen erkannt? Wurden nicht auch Nichtmarxisten für die Widersprüche und die strukturellen Ungerechtigkeiten des kapitalistischen Wirtschaftssystems sensibilisiert und benützen nicht auch sie für ihre Analysen das von Marx bereitgestellte kritische Instrumentarium? Und wurde in der Folge der uneingeschränkte Wirtschaftsliberalismus, für den die Bedürfnisbefriedigung Mittel zur eigennützigen Gewinnmaximierung ist, nicht schließlich durch sozialere Wirtschaftsformen abgelöst?

Wo immer Freiheit der Kritik besteht und der Marxismus nicht als dogmatisches System herrscht, anerkennt man heute freilich auch die *Schwächen* der Marxschen Gesellschafts- und Geschichtstheorie, insofern sie wie leider in allen kommunistischen Staaten eine Totalerklärung der Wirklichkeit sein will. Es sind keine »bürgerlichen« Vorurteile, wenn man einfach sachlich feststellt: Marx täuschte sich in der Grundannahme, daß die Lage des Proletariats ohne Revolution nicht verbessert werden könne. Bei aller Akkumulation des Kapitals auf der einen Seite hat sich die Vorstellung von einer Proletarisierung einer riesigen Reservearmee von Arbeitern, aus der im dialektischen Umschlag die Revolution als Übergang zum Sozialismus, dann zum Kommunismus und zum Reich der Freiheit notwendig hervorgehen sollte, in der Praxis nicht bewahrheitet. Die dieser Vorstellung zugrundeliegende Theorie vom Mehrwert (vom Arbeiter erarbeitet, vom Kapitalisten abgeschöpft), zumindest für den Vulgärmarxismus der Eckpfeiler der Marxschen Ökonomie, wird von orthodoxen Marxisten zwar noch repetiert, von anderen marxistischen Ökonomen aber beiseitegeschoben und von nicht-marxistischen überhaupt abgelehnt. Die Theorie vom Kampf zweier Klassen hat sich als Interpretationsschema für den Ablauf der Menschheitsgeschichte und erst recht für die Analyse der komplexen Gesellschaftsschichtung der Gegenwart (Verbürgerlichung des Proletariats, Mittelklassen) als zu einfach erwiesen. Die Geschichtsauffassung des historischen Materialismus beruht zu einem nicht geringen Teil auf nachträglichen künstlichen Geschichtskonstruktionen und falschen Voraussetzungen.

Der von Marx zuerst für 1848, dann für die fünfziger, dann für die siebziger Jahre erwartete und schließlich von Engels für die Jahrhundertwende prophezeite Zusammenbruch des kapitalistischen Systems gerade in den höchstindustrialisierten Ländern (England und Deutschland), aus welchem die kommunistische Produktionsweise im dialektischen Sprung hervorgehen sollte, ist nicht eingetreten. Im Gegenteil: Die sozialistische Revolution konnte sich bezeichnenderweise nur in zurückgebliebenen agrarischen Ländern durchsetzen. Der Kapitalismus aber hat sich als in hohem Ausmaß korrigierbar erwiesen. Er hat nicht nur die empirische Sozialanalyse und damit ein System von Kontrolle und Korrektur geschaffen, sondern zugleich weittragende soziale Reformen vom Kinderarbeitsverbot bis zur gesetzlichen Altersversorgung und verschiedenartigen Formen von Mitbestimmung verwirklicht. So konnten weiteste Bevölkerungsschichten vom Armutsdruck befreit und zu einem relativ gesicherten, ja früher unvorstellbaren materiellen Wohlstand geführt werden. Bisher wurde denn auch weder im Westen noch im Osten, weder in der wissenschaftlichen Theorie noch in der politischen Praxis ein anderes Wirtschafts- und Gesellschaftssystem entwickelt, das die Mängel des Kapitalismus beseitigte, ohne andere, schlimmere Übel zu erzeugen. Weder die orthodoxe zentrale Planwirtschaft noch eine Rätedemokratie, noch erst recht kurzlebige und kurzgeschlossene ökonomische Leer- und Wunschformeln einzelner Radikaler haben den Nachweis erbracht, daß sie besser Freiheit und Demokratie, Gerechtigkeit und Wohlstand zu garantieren vermögen[15]. Nirgendwo zeichnet sich am Himmel die Heraufkunft der klassenlosen freien kommunistischen Gesellschaft ab. Vielmehr droht in noch ganz anderer Weise als im Westen die Übermacht des Staates: durch die Identifikation von Staat und Partei ein sozialistischer Etatismus auf Kosten der arbeitenden Bevölkerung. Die Individuen werden mit Berufung auf ein fernes künftiges Glück der Menschheit vertröstet und in einem unbarmherzigen System und mit harten Arbeitsnormen auf die Steigerung der Produktionsziffern verpflichtet.

Es bleibt dabei: Ein gutes Programm wird durch schlechte Realisierung noch nicht widerlegt; sie hätte auch anders erfolgen können. Aber man kann sich fragen, ob es nicht auch am Marxschen Programm liegt, wenn die marxistische Realisierung so problematisch ausfällt. Durch nichts wurde die Marxsche Theorie mehr desavouiert als durch jenes etatistische System, das sich am meisten auf sie berief: der *Sowjetkommunismus*. Je länger, desto weniger konnte die Sowjetunion, die schon unter Stalin den Übergang vom Sozialismus zum Kommunismus proklamiert hatte, linken Gesellschaftskritikern als leuchtendes Beispiel im Geist des marxistischen Humanismus dienen[16]. Als eigentlicher Sündenfall wird auch von überzeugten Sozialisten die Glorifizierung der mit dem Staat identifizierten Partei und ihrer oligarchischen Führung angesehen und damit verbunden die Ontologisierung und Dogmatisierung der Marxschen Doktrin. Dieser heute als Stalinismus angeklagte orthodoxe Kommunismus, für den Lenin mitverantwortlich ist, und die imperialistische Politik gegenüber den sozialistischen »Bruder-Völkern« offenbaren ein hochorganisiertes System der Herrschaft von Menschen über Menschen, das mit einem humanistischen Sozialismus nichts zu tun hat, und eine Unterdrückung der Freiheit des Denkens, Redens und Handelns von Magdeburg bis Wladiwostock, wie es die Weltgeschichte bisher nicht gekannt hat: totalitäre, bürokratische, staatskapitalistische Diktatur nach innen, nationalistischer Imperialismus nach außen. Der Sowjetkommunismus erscheint als neue Entfremdung des Menschen mit einer »neuen Klasse«[17] von Funktionären, mit »religiösen« Zügen (Messianismus, Absolutheit der Opfer) und »kirchlichen« Aspekten (kanonische Texte, quasiliturgische Formeln, Credo, unfehlbare Hierarchie, Bevormundung des Volkes, Inquisition und Zwangsmaßnahmen), wie sie sich auch im chinesischen Maoismus zeigen. Ein halbes Jahrhundert nach der Oktoberrevolution müssen noch immer Todeszonen über Hunderte von Kilometern verhindern, daß nicht Millionen aus diesem »Paradies der Werktätigen« (mit Konzentrations- und Gefangenenlagern) fliehen, währenddem bei allen strukturellen Parallelen zwischen westlichem und östlichem Etatismus für eine Massenflucht von West nach Ost keine Gefahr besteht. Die Reaktion der Sowjetregierung schließlich auf die Veröffentlichung von Alexander Solschenizyns ›Archipel GULAG‹ (1974) zeigt in betrüblicher Weise, daß dieses ökonomisch, sozial und ideologisch unbewegliche System bei aller Entspannungspolitik nach außen für die Freiheit des Menschen im Inneren in nächster Zeit nichts Entscheidendes zu ändern gedenkt[18].

Wenn die christlichen Kirchen eine autoritäre oder totalitäre Gewaltherrschaft aufgerichtet und Menschen verbrannt und dem System geopfert haben, standen sie eindeutig – wie auch ihre Gegner feststellen und man nicht genügend betonen kann – im unbestreitbaren direkten Widerspruch zum christlichen Programm, zu Jesus von Nazaret. Steht aber auch eine kommunistische Partei im Widerspruch mit dem kommunistischen Programm, mit dem Kommunistischen Manifest und mit Karl Marx selbst, wenn sie massiv Gewalt anwendet, die Diktatur der einen Klasse und Partei aufrichtet, alle Gegner unbarmherzig liquidiert und »Konterrevolutionen« ohne Rücksicht auf Opfer niederschlägt?

Im selben Jahre 1968, da der Versuch eines humanistisch-pluralistischen Marxismus in der Tschechoslowakei an einem orthodoxen Marxismus-Leninismus scheiterte (die Tragödie des »Sozialismus mit menschlichem Antlitz«), der keine solche Pluralität zulassen kann und der für die Auflösung der etablierten Machtstruktur seines Imperiums fürchten mußte, wurde im Westen der Neomarxismus auch durch die Studentenrevolten – zuerst in Amerika, dann in Europa und Japan – in eine tiefe Krise gestürzt. Unter den beschriebenen Bedingungen der hochindustrialisierten Länder des Westens, die freilich auch immer mehr die des Ostens werden, und unter der katalysatorischen Wirkung des Vietnamkrieges war es nicht verwunderlich, wenn der Neomarxismus seine Faszination auf die mit der bürgerlichen Gesellschaft unzufriedene Jugend ausübte[19]. Man hatte erkannt: nicht mehr einfach durch Verarmung entstand die Entfremdung des Menschen wie zu Zeiten von Marx, sondern durch die Zwänge der gegenwärtigen Wohlstandsgesellschaft.

Die Führer der Studentenrevolten hatten sich dabei wesentlich durch die Theorie der Neuen Linken (Marcuse, Adorno, Horkheimer, Habermas) inspirieren lassen. Doch hatte die Kritische Theorie die doppelte Aufgabe, die sie sich selbst stellte, nicht sehr ungleich wahrgenommen? Sie verstand gut zu bezeichnen, was in der Gesellschaft geändert werden, aber nicht ebensogut, was erhalten bleiben soll. Auch blieb die Zielbestimmung der Veränderung vage. Als es dann zu dem von den Lehrern nicht vorgesehenen Übergang vom Begriff der Revolution zur revolutionären Praxis kam, fühlten sich die Lehrer mißverstanden und mußten gegen die »unbedachte und dogmatische Anwendung der Kritischen Theorie auf die Praxis in der veränderten historischen Realität« Stellung nehmen (M. Horkheimer[20]). In Vorworten, Nachworten, Fußnoten, Interviews mußten sie nachträglich klarstellen, ihre Theorie der »negativen Dialektik«, der »qualitativen Änderung«, der »katastrophalen Umwandlung«, der »praktischen Emanzipatorik« hätte niemals die direkte Umsetzung in die Praxis und vor allem nicht die unmittelbare revolutionäre Gewalt impliziert. Die Studenten kamen sich durch diese Distanzierungen verraten vor, antworteten mit dem Vorwurf der »Abstraktion«, »Folgelosigkeit«, »Veränderungsfeindlichkeit« und scheuten selbst Gewalt gegen ihre Lehrer nicht.

Damit aber war deutlich geworden: Trotz ihrer grundlegenden Einsichten geriet die neomarxistische Philosophie, insofern sie Ausweg aus Herrschaftslogik, Leistungsgesellschaft und technologischen Sachzwängen sein wollte, selber in Ausweglosigkeit. Hatte sie ihr zentrales Problem, die Vermittlung von Theorie und Praxis, von Wahrheit und Handeln, Erkenntnis und Entscheidung, Rationalität und Engagement, die Versöhnung von gegenwärtigen Fakten und zukünftigen Möglichkeiten gelöst? Testfall war die Frage der Anwendung von *Gewalt:* Gewalt im Klassenkampf war von Marx (damals im Namen des Proletariats als der »ungeheuren Mehrzahl«) und von Lenin (jetzt im Namen einer Minderheit als des »höheren Typus gesellschaftlicher Organisation der Arbeit«) und auch von der späteren Rosa Luxemburg (die Lenins Terror freilich ablehnte) bejaht und dann besonders von Stalin und Mao unter Millionen von Opfern geübt worden. Gewalt als »Gegengewalt« gegen die »strukturelle Gewalt« des gesellschaftlichen Systems, subversive oder offene Gewalt, Gewalt gegen Sachen oder Gewalt gegen Personen usw. – das war auch bald die große Frage der Studentischen Bewegung. Man berief sich auch dafür auf Marx, nach welchem die Revolution nur immer so gewaltsam sei wie der Widerstand von seiten der herrschenden Klassen gegen die Revolution.

Eine *Ernüchterung* trat ein, als den Gewalttätigkeiten von beiden Seiten die ersten Todesopfer folgten und als vor allem in Frankreich und zum Teil auch in den Vereinigten Staaten die Studentenrevolten mit Polizeigewalt erstickt wurden. Es setzte sich bei einer großen Zahl von Studenten die Einsicht durch, daß die marxistisch-leninistische Auffassung keine Rechte für den

Klassenfeind und bis zum Untergang der einen Klasse auch keinen Pluralismus und keine Toleranz zuließe und daß folglich ein pluralistischer und gewaltloser Marxismus im Widerspruch zu Marx und Lenin stand, was in Prag bestätigt wurde. Die soziale Empörung teilte man, die Politisierung des Denkens bejahte man. Aber die – mit Berufung auf ein elitäres Erkenntnisprivileg (»wahres Bewußtsein«) und die dogmatische Parteilichkeit des Denkens geforderte – blinde Autoritätsgläubigkeit, antipluralistische Intoleranz, undemokratische und letztlich totalitäre Gesinnung lehnten der Großteil der Studenten und die demokratische Öffentlichkeit ebenso ab wie ihre Realisierungsversuche in Gewalt und Terror. Nur kleine Gruppen, deren politisches Credo mehr von Michael Bakunins Anarchismus, von südamerikanischen Stadtguerillas, palästinensischen Befreiungskämpfern und Vietkong-Taktiken als von Karl Marx bestimmt war, rutschten in den Terrorismus ab, aus Verzweiflung, politischem Irrtum und ideologischer Verblendung; sie mußten als Kriminelle abgeurteilt werden. Die große Mehrzahl der Aktivisten aber trat den »langen Marsch durch die Institutionen« an, dessen Ende noch nicht abzusehen ist.

Was am Anfang über das bedeutende humanistische Potential des Marxismus gesagt wurde, bleibt unbestritten. Aber auch vielen überzeugten Sozialisten war durch die Entwicklung deutlich geworden: Nicht nur der im Osten zu Tode gerittene orthodoxe Marxismus-Leninismus, sondern auch der »revolutionäre Humanismus« (Habermas) des westlichen Neo-Marxismus scheiterte, sofern er als Totalerklärung der Wirklichkeit die Gesellschaft revolutionieren wollte. Auch er vermochte die so sehr proklamierte Humanisierung der Gesellschaft und die bessere Welt ohne Ausbeutung und Herrschaft bisher nirgendwo zu realisieren. Ganz abgesehen davon, daß die Vernachlässigung der ökonomischen Problematik zugunsten ideologischer und ästhetischer Erörterungen eine eher dürftige konkrete Programmatik erbrachte: die Frage der ökonomischen, sozialen, politischen Realisierbarkeit der Theorien blieb unbeantwortet, und die Idee einer durch revolutionären Umschlag und die Entwicklung vom Sozialismus zum Kommunismus heraufgeführten herrschaftsfreien Gesellschaft blieb so vage wie bei Marx selbst und geriet mehr denn je unter Ideologieverdacht.

Doch man mag Theorie und Praxis der verschiedenen Marxismen positiver beurteilen. Die vielfältigen Möglichkeiten, die kritische Denkhaltung und die humanistischen Impulse des Sozialismus für eine bessere Gesellschaft zu realisieren, dürfen jedenfalls nicht unterschätzt werden. Unsere (notwendigerweise gedrängten) Ausführungen, die jeder wiederum aus seiner eigenen Kenntnis der politischen Lage leicht ergänzen kann, sollten nur zeigen, wie sehr auch die Ideologie einer von selbst zur Humanität führenden gewaltsamen politisch-sozialen Revolution erschüttert ist: Ist es nicht doch eine Kritik, die destruierend sich selber aufhebt, eine Theorie, die sich nicht in die Praxis überführen läßt, eine Praxis, die durch Gewalt und Unterdrückung ihre eigenen Ziele verrät, eine Revolution, die sich als »Opium des Volkes« erweist, eine Humanisierung also, die wiederum zum Inhumanen führt? Kurz auch hier: ein revolutionärer Humanismus, dessen nichtgewollte, faktische Konsequenz die *Entmenschlichung des Menschen* ist?

Natürlich sehen auch die Neuen Linken selbst die Schwierigkeiten. Marcuses – keineswegs grundsätzlich antitechnische – Analyse und Anklage ist deshalb so erschütternd, weil er selber im Blick auf den Westen und den Osten in letzter Ehrlichkeit zugibt, »kein Heilmittel bieten« zu können. In resignierter »Hoffnungslosigkeit« bekennt er sich am Ende seines Buches zur »Negation in der politisch ohnmächtigen Form der ›absoluten Weigerung‹« und zur »Treue« zu jenen, »die ohne Hoffnung ihr Leben der Großen Weigerung hingegeben haben und hingeben«[21]. Und ähnlich Jürgen Habermas, der neuerdings jede theoretische Rechtfertigung einer revolutionären Klassenkampfstrategie ablehnt, weil es für ihn keine Theorie geben kann, die die möglichen Opfer einer Revolution von vornherein einkalkuliert und den Tod von Menschen in die Theorie einplant. Bezüglich der Schicksalsschläge, die jedes menschliche Leben treffen können, zeigt sich diese Theorie noch ohnmächtiger: »In Anbetracht der individuellen Lebensrisiken ist freilich eine Theorie nicht einmal *denkbar,* die die Faktizitäten von Einsamkeit und Schuld, Krankheit und Tod hinweginterpretieren könnte ... Mit ihnen müssen wir, prinzipiell trostlos, leben.«[22]

Doch ist auch hier zu fragen: Soll mit der Ideologie auch die Hoffnung verabschiedet werden? Auch hier soll nicht das Kind mit dem Bad ausgeschüttet werden. *Aufzugeben* ist die *Revolution als Ideologie,* die mit Gewalt den gesellschaftlichen Umsturz betreibt und ein neues System der Herrschaft von Menschen über Menschen aufrichtet. Aufzugeben ist nicht jeglicher Marxismus oder jede Bemühung um eine grundlegende Änderung der Gesellschaft. Aufzugeben ist der *Marxismus* als *Totalerklä-*

rung der Wirklichkeit (»Weltanschauung«), die *Revolution* als allesheilende *Ersatzreligion!*

Nicht aufzugeben ist also die *Hoffnung auf eine meta-revolutionäre Gesellschaft* jenseits von Stagnation und Revolution, unkritischer Hinnahme des Gegebenen und totaler Kritik am Bestehenden! Wäre es nicht oberflächlich und gefährlich, die Einsichten des Marxismus und Neomarxismus mit dem Scheitern eines humaneren Marxismus in Prag oder dem Versickern der Studentenrevolten als erledigt anzusehen? Es genügt nicht, nur gleichsam historisch den Ideen der revolutionären Bewegung bei den geistigen Vätern nachzuspüren, auf die sich die Jugend im Westen zu Recht oder zu Unrecht berufen hat. Hier ist doch etwas sehr Bestimmtes laut geworden: die große Enttäuschung über den so sehr gepriesenen Fortschritt, eine soziale Empörung über die alten und neuen ungerechten Verhältnisse, ein Aufbegehren gegen die Zwänge des technologisch-politischen Systems, ein tiefes Bedürfnis nach wissenschaftlicher Analyse und Aufklärung. Ja, geradezu ein Schrei nach einem wirklich befriedeten Dasein, einer besseren Gesellschaft, einem Reich von Freiheit, Gleichheit und Glück, einem Sinn im eigenen Leben und einem Sinn in der Geschichte der Menschheit.

Daraus ergibt sich die ernste Frage: Soll auf die »Große Weigerung« der avancierten Jugend mit einer »Großen Weigerung« der Etablierten geantwortet werden? Soll die Antwort auf die Revolution der Status quo sein? Soll das Unbehagen weiter verdrängt, der Fortschritt weiter gehätschelt, das System wieder nur ein wenig verbessert werden? Sollen also Freiheit, Wahrheit und Glück weiterhin vor allem Werbeslogans für fragwürdige Konsumgüter der fortgeschrittenen Industriegesellschaft bleiben? Oder sollte es doch Möglichkeiten geben, das sinnlose Leben von Mensch und Gesellschaft in ein sinnvolles zu verändern? Eine qualitative Veränderung, die nicht erneut Gewalt, Terror, Zerstörung, die Anarchie und das Chaos hervorrufen?

Um es ganz deutlich zu sagen: Es sollte in den beiden vorausgegangenen zeitkritischen Analysen nicht insinuiert werden, der »fortschrittsbegeisterte« Technokrat könne nicht Christ sein oder der »revolutionäre« Marxist (oder gar Sozialist) könne nicht Christ sein. Es kommt darauf an, wie man Wissenschaft und Technologie ortet und wertet: und vor allem, was man damit macht. Es kommt darauf an, was man unter Marxismus (und erst recht Sozialismus) versteht: Gerade der Marxismus wird manchmal auch einfach als eine der Tendenz nach positive Sozialwissenschaft oder als ethischer, wirtschaftlicher, gemeinschaftlicher, wissenschaftlicher und in diesem Sinne »revolutionärer« Humanismus verstanden, der Glaube an Gott keineswegs ausschließt. So kann denn ein Christ unter Umständen (kritischer!) »Marxist« sein, wenn auch freilich nicht nur der Marxist Christ sein kann[23]. Und es kann ein Christ unter Umständen (kritischer!) »Technokrat« sein, wenn auch freilich nicht nur der Technokrat Christ sein kann. Christ wird wohl nur derjenige »Marxist« sich ernsthaft nennen dürfen, für den in Fragen wie Gewaltanwendung, Klassenkampf, Friede, Liebe nicht Marx, sondern der christliche Glaube letztlich den Ausschlag gibt. Und Christ wird wohl auch nur derjenige »Technokrat« sich ernsthaft nennen dürfen, für den in Fragen wie Technologie, Organisation, Wettbewerb, Manipulation nicht wissenschaftliche Zweckrationalität, sondern der christliche Glaube der letztlich bestimmende Maßstab ist.

Es gibt zahlreiche Technokraten, die Wissenschaft und Technologie keineswegs zu ihrer Religion machen. Und es gibt auch immer mehr Marxisten im Westen und selbst im Osten, die ihren Marxismus nicht zur Religion machen. Je länger desto deutlicher zeigt sich: Die Totalverwerfung *oder* Totalannahme der technologischen Evolution, aber auch die Totalverwerfung *oder* Totalannahme der politisch-sozialen Revolution sind falsche Alternativen! Ruft nicht auch die Entwicklung der Gesellschaft im Westen und im Osten nach einer neuen Synthese? Läßt sich in einer ferneren Zukunft nicht vielleicht doch beides verbinden: die Sehnsucht eines politisch-revolutionären Humanismus nach einer grundlegenden Änderung der Verhältnisse, nach einer besseren, gerechteren Welt, einem wirklich guten Leben – und zugleich die Forderungen eines technologisch-evolutiven Humanismus nach konkreter Realisierbarkeit, nach Vermeidung von Terror, nach einer problemoffenen pluralistischen Freiheitsordnung, die niemand zu einem Glauben zwingt? Hätte dazu nicht gerade der Christ etwas Entscheidendes beizutragen?

Zwischen Nostalgie und Reformismus

Angesichts der erschütterten großen Ideologien ist es nicht leicht, sich in einer widersprüchlichen und sich ständig wandelnden Gegenwart zu orientieren. Die Moden wechseln so rasch, daß es gar keine Mode mehr gibt, weil man alles gleichzeitig tragen kann, auf Leib und Seele. Wer kann sagen, was morgen ist? Wer kann überhaupt sagen, was heute ist? Da hat selbst der gegenwartsnahe Historiker – und es gibt wenige so kenntnisreiche und so zeitbewußte wie Golo Mann – Mühe, sich zurechtzufinden: »Wir leben in einem Zeitalter der Kapitulation. Wir lassen uns aufschwatzen, was immer ein paar Gescheite oder doch ein gescheites Vokabular Handhabende uns aufschwatzen wollen. Ich habe nun schon ein paar historische Epochen aufmerksam durchlebt, was man so ›Epochen‹ nennt, aber noch keine, die so von oberflächlichen geistigen Moden beherrscht worden wäre wie die unsere. Auch: in der man so emsig an den Ästen gesägt hätte, auf denen man sitzt. Poeten gegen die Poesie, Philosophen gegen die Philosophie, Theologen gegen die Theologie, Künstler gegen die Kunst und so Historiker oder Exhistoriker oder Soziologen gegen den Geschichtsunterricht[24].«

Auf die Große Revolution folgte im vergangenen Jahrhundert die Epoche der Romantik. Sie hielt lange an. Im letzten Drittel unseres Jahrhunderts nun folgt der Welle der Revolten eine Welle von Nostalgie. Für wie lange? Fin de siècle, fin de millénaire? Einfach eine erneut übersättigte, überfeinerte, dekadente und skeptische Stimmung am Ende unseres Jahrtausends wie damals am Ende des vergangenen Jahrhunderts? Jedenfalls wieder viel Stimmung: Vernünftigkeit überspielt und überspült von Empfindsamkeit. Nicht mehr Aufklärung der Gegenwart, von der man genug bekommen hat, als vielmehr die *Verklärung einer Vergangenheit*, von der man kaum genug bekommen kann. Ein neues Biedermeier, zum Teil sogar von »links«? Oft schon eher schier Resignation. Und bis zu Vertretern der Kritischen Theorie Sehnsucht nach dem, was nicht mehr da ist. Bereits spottet man über diejenigen, die vor Jahren fortschrittlich die Fahrkarte zur Revolution gelöst haben und nun feststellen müssen, daß der Zug in eine andere Zukunft abgefahren ist.

Es ist durchaus begreiflich, daß in einer Epoche tiefgreifender Umwälzungen aller Lebensbezirke sehr viele sich nach Frieden und Sicherheit, nach den scheinbar stabileren Zeiten von früher zurücksehnen. Daß in einer technokratischen, durchrationalisierten Welt und einer unerhörten seelischen Verarmung das Heimweh aufkommt nach der scheinbar ungetrübten »guten alten Zeit«, insbesondere den »goldenen Zwanzigerjahren«: in Mode und Frisur, in Film und Literatur, in Illustrierten und Magazinen, Werbung und Wohnung, Möbeln und Musik, alten Platten und alten Sachen. Statt Utopien nun Melancholien, statt politische Aggressivität unpolitische Sentimentalität, statt perfektionierte Technik Geschmack an Krimskrams, statt Revolutionäres Museales.

Mitten im Vietnamkrieg war Segals ›Love Story‹ das erste Anzeichen eines in sich sehr verständlichen Umschwungs gewesen, von ›Time‹ bis ›Spiegel‹ aufmerksam registriert und genüßlich propagiert. Anstelle von Protesten und Friedensmärschen die Idylle privaten Glücks. Bis in die modernste Literatur zeigen sich wieder alte Neigungen: zum Erzählen, zur Biographie und Autobiographie, zu Geschichten überhaupt. In Theater und Oper kehren nach aller Kulturrevolution, Agitation und Provokation, Publikumsbeschimpfung und Publikumsvertreibung langsam die alten Stücke der großen Autoren wieder, ohne respektlose Aktualisierung und aufgepfropfte sozialkritische Kalenderweisheiten für Unmündige. Überwindung der Theaterkrise? Gleichzeitig hat man wieder einmal alles durchgeprobt: vom Tango, alten Hits und Stars und zahlreichen Symbolen eines früher scheinbar heiteren Selbst bis zum Marilyn-Monroe-Kult, zu Yoga und Aberglauben, Drogen und transzendentaler Meditation. Und über allem ein Hauch von Religion. Die Bewußtseinsindustrie ließ sich wie üblich keine Gelegenheit zur Vermarktung nehmen: von Sentimentalität und alten Sehnsüchten. Gefühle als Ware, und Verklärung als Verpackung. Das Geschäft mit der Nostalgie floriert. Wie lange?

Alle diese Moden, Wellen, Attitüden sollte man nicht zu ernst nehmen, auch nicht die Sehnsucht nach der Vergangenheit. Könnten wir nicht, ohne dem Konservativismus zu huldigen, etwas mehr Kontinuität brauchen? Etwas mehr Verbindung mit der Vergangenheit in einer Zeit der oft krampfhaften Zurückdrängung von Geschichte in Schule und Gesellschaft: als Ausgleich des eklatanten Defizits an historischem Bewußtsein, das man vergeblich auszugleichen versucht mit einem Übermaß an aktueller Ideologie, die mit dem Anspruch von Allwissenheit auftritt?

Warum also nicht eine unromantische, ernsthafte *Besinnung auf die Vergangenheit?*

Könnte sie nicht helfen, etwas bescheidener, weniger arrogant modern und unfehlbar allwissend zu sein, etwas Distanz von der Gegenwart zu gewinnen und sich umsichtig zu orientieren?

Könnte sie nicht helfen, die Phänomene der Gegenwart von ihrer Herkunft her zu verstehen und Einsichten und Kategorien zu gewinnen zum Verständnis der Möglichkeiten und Grenzen politischen Handelns, des Ablaufs von Koalitionen und Konflikten, der Ambivalenz von Entscheidungssituationen, des Unterschieds von persönlichen Absichten, sachlichen Zwecken, Nebenfolgen und Fernwirkungen?

Könnte sie nicht helfen, die Beständigkeit und Widerstandsfähigkeit, aber auch zugleich die Wandelbarkeit und Wandlungsfähigkeit der Gesellschaft trotz aller Sachzwänge zu erkennen, um rücksichtslose technokratische Entwürfe ebenso zu vermeiden wie wirkungslose radikale Proteste, die Totalkritik ebenso wie die leicht daraus folgende Totalresignation?

Könnte sie also nicht helfen, die Tages- und Parteipolitik etwas distanzierter und differenzierter zu sehen, sich aus so vielen erstarrten Fixierungen zu lösen, sich weniger zu wundern über die Jugend, die nur scheinbar noch nie so schlecht war, und sich in realistischer Hoffnung für eine neue Zukunft offenzuhalten, um so den falschen Alternativen und Polarisierungen der heutigen Gesellschaft zu entgehen, in die wir vielfach ungewollt hineingeraten sind und die uns zahlreiche unnötige Konflikte bescheren?

Kurz und gut: Geschichte, historische Erkenntnis nicht wie im letzten Jahrhundert als die primäre Orientierungsbasis oder gar stabilisierende Ersatzreligion der Gebildeten. Sondern als eine sehr wichtige Orientierungshilfe für die Gegenwart und Aufklärung im besten Sinn des Wortes, um zu konkreter Einsicht und konkretem Handeln zu kommen, zu jener effizienten Politik, die nach Max Weber ist: »ein starkes langsames Bohren von harten Brettern mit Leidenschaft und Augenmaß zugleich[25].«

Damit ist aber nun auch bereits überdeutlich geworden, daß die Besinnung auf die Vergangenheit gerade *nicht* eine neue modische Form privatistischer Geschichtslosigkeit sein darf: nicht eine sentimentale Rück-Sicht auf die Vergangenheit, die einen *Rück-Zug aus der Gegenwart* zur Folge hat. Sollte es auf Dauer möglich sein, einfach nur von den alten Lagerbeständen zu leben? Kann man sich in die Vergangenheit verkriechen, wenn man zu einer neuen Zukunft herausgerufen wird? Die massiven Probleme der Gegenwart und Zukunft lösen sich kaum in Luft auf dadurch, daß man ihnen den Rücken zukehrt. Es gilt, ihre Herausforderung anzunehmen. Keine Wehmut der Welt kann je den Wagemut ersetzen.

Auch alle Schwärmer für Nostalgie kommen also nicht darum herum, das Leben heute zu leben und in irgendeiner Form aktiv zu bewältigen. Der Aktionismus aus den revolutionären Jahren ist zwar nicht mehr gefragt. Aber vor aktiven *Reformen* innerhalb der bestehenden Ordnung wird man sich kaum drücken können. Zwischen nostalgischen oder auch einfach konservativen System-Bewahrern und revolutionär-illusionären System-Zertrümmerern haben die System-Reformer in der Gesellschaft von heute wieder mehr Chancen, gehört zu werden. Es muß ja doch etwas geschehen. Was?

Die meisten sind heute froh, wenn überhaupt irgend etwas geschieht. Und einige stellen zusammen, was alles geschieht oder zumindest geschehen könnte. Und dies ist auch schon tröstlich. Freilich, ob der gute Wille des Menschen ausreicht, um – wie etwa der frühzeitig ahnende Verfasser des Buches ›Die Zukunft hat schon begonnen‹[26] meint – eine Umkehr, eine neue Gesellschaft, ja gar den »Jahrtausendmenschen«[27] heraufzuführen? Nichts gegen neue Lebensformen, erprobt in Wohngemeinschaften, Großfamilien, experimentellen Schulen, neuartigen Berufsgemeinschaften bei Architekten, Theaterleuten, Jungfilmern, Sozialhelfern, landwirtschaftlichen und industriellen Kommunen. Nichts gegen Kreativitätsforschung, die verschüttete Quellen der Phantasie in jedem Menschen zu entdecken vermag. Nichts gegen Gruppendynamik mit ihren neuen Einsichten in die menschliche Interaktion. Und nichts gegen die Systemanalyse, die uns wieder die Ganzheit erfassen lehrt, ohne das Einzelne zu übersehen.

Aber man wird doch fragen müssen: Kann denn der Mensch wirklich als von Natur aus gut angenommen werden angesichts all des Wahnsinns und der Grausamkeit im großen wie im kleinen, zu denen er sich bis in die Gegenwart hinein ständig als überaus fähig erwiesen hat? Oder zumindest als gut-willig, so daß er seine Menschennatur verbessern kann? Kann das der Einzelne, kann das eine Regierung, kann das die Gesellschaft? Oder müssen die Veränderungen nicht in einer ganz anderen Tiefe erfolgen, wenn Emanzipationen nicht erneut schieflaufen sollen: Eine Emanzipation von der umgebenden Natur, die zu ihrer Ausbeutung wird? Eine sexuelle Emanzipation, die zu einer Pornowelle denaturiert? Das Bemühen um eine herrschaftsfreie Gesellschaft, das Chaos und Terror zur Folge hat? Experimente des Zusammenlebens in Kommunen, die zu Psychosen oder aber zum frühzeitigen Abbruch führen? Emanzipierte Hippies, die in einer Entziehungskur oder als Bettler in Katmandu enden?

Doch man schlägt so oft nur Kompromisse vor. Zum Beispiel etwa angesichts einer fehlenden überzeugenden Alternative zum kapitalistischen Wirtschaftssystem: einen Kompromiß zwischen *traditionellem* Kapitalismus und *reiner* Demokratie, in welchem weder das eine noch das andere Prinzip *ungetrübt* realisiert werden kann[28]. An einer solchen realistischen Auffassung ist zweifellos richtig, daß die Kritik der Gegenposition oder die bessere Darstellung des eigenen Standpunktes nicht ausreichen, daß gegen alle Extremismen Kompromisse möglich und notwendig sind, daß es zu einem praktischen Ausgleich zwischen Kapitalismus und Demokratie auch in der Wirtschaft kommen muß. Ein gerechter Kompromiß also: zwar nicht die volle Gerechtigkeit, aber ein Mehr an Gleichheit; zwar nicht die Mitbestimmung aller bei allen Angelegenheiten, aber die erweiterte Mitwirkung an den Arbeitsplätzen; zwar nicht die Beseitigung des Privateigentums, aber seine weitere Beschränkung; zwar nicht die Kollektivierung der Produktionsmittel, aber eine bessere Balance zwischen privater Produktion und öffentlichen Diensten. Daß sich in einer solchen Sicht auch die Vorstellung von den Aufgaben, der Verantwortung und Eigeninitiative des Unternehmers ändern muß, wird vorausgesetzt.

Aber – und das ist der entscheidende Einwand – die Motive für eine solche Änderung bleiben dieselben wie eh und je: schlicht der Egoismus (in diesem Fall der Unternehmer)! »Ausgerechnet diejenigen, die in ihren rein wirtschaftlichen Funktionen in der Tat Spezialisten des Eigennutzes sind, handeln außerhalb ihrer eigentlichen wirtschaftlichen Funktionen nicht eigennützig genug – nicht aus Selbstlosigkeit, sondern aus Unaufgeklärtheit. Ich glaube, sie sollten sich klarmachen, daß das Selbstinteresse, und nicht eine edle moralische Norm es gebietet, sich den zunehmenden Gleichheitsforderungen in einer auch der anderen Seite gerecht werdenden Form zu stellen, ihm durch praktische Maßnahmen entgegenzukommen ... Daß es bei solcher Vorwärtsverteidigung um Interessenwahrnehmung und nicht um Edelmut geht, lehrt die Geschichte[29].« Der alte Egoismus also, diese traditionelle Einstellung des Menschen, das Profitdenken im weitesten Sinne des Wortes, wie es keineswegs auf die Arbeitgeber beschränkt ist.

Hat man hier nicht bei aller Betonung der gesellschaftlichen Dynamik die Hoffnung auf eine Änderung des Menschen aufgegeben? Treibt man mit all den vielen Reformen nicht eine Oberflächenkosmetik, die den Ursachen des Übels nicht auf die Spur kommt? Weniger die notwendige radikale Reform als jener betriebsam aufgeregte *Reformismus,* der in verschiedenen Lebensbereichen (Universität, Wirtschaft, Kirche, Erziehung, staatliche Gesetzgebung) viel Änderung und wenig Besserung gebracht hat. Jedenfalls keine Änderung des Menschen selbst, keine andere Grundeinstellung, keinen neuen Menschen. Darf man sich aber angesichts der ganzen menschlichen Misere zwischen untätiger Sehnsucht und unwirksamer Reformlust mit weniger zufriedengeben? Müßte man sich über die Lage des Menschen nicht ganz anders nüchtern Rechenschaft geben: angesichts des Menschseins mit all seinen Abgründen, wie sie oberflächliche Nostalgiker und Reformisten kaum ahnen?

Die Resignation hat manche Fronten verschoben. Liberale Reformer und enttäuschte Revolutionäre treffen sich am Grab ihrer Erwartungen. Für manche ist das »Prinzip Hoffnung« Ernst Blochs vom »Prinzip Verzweiflung« – in verschiedener Form und verschiedenem Ausmaß – abgelöst worden. Wie soll man nach dieser großen Verschwendung von Hoffnung unter den geänderten Bedingungen noch an Umkehr, Änderung, Widerstand denken können, nachdem sich die Veränderungsmöglichkeiten des Einzelnen als mühsam, die der Menschheit als unmöglich und die der Strukturen als aufreibend erwiesen haben?

II. Die andere Dimension

Bleibt von den großen Ideologien des technologischen Fortschritts und der politisch-sozialen Revolution, zu denen weder Nostalgie noch Reformismus eine echte Alternative bieten, schließlich nur Richtungslosigkeit übrig? »Die Welt hat ihre Richtung verloren. Es sind jedoch nicht die richtungsweisenden Ideologien, die fehlen. Sie führen nirgendwo hin«, bekannte Eugène Ionesco, der Begründer des absurden Theaters, bei der Eröffnung der – anschließend dann wie immer in altem Glanz und Glorie durchgeführten – Salzburger Festspiele 1972[1]. »Im Kreis gehen die Menschen im Käfig ihres Planeten, weil sie vergessen haben, daß man zum Himmel aufblicken kann ... Weil wir nur leben wollen, ist es uns unmöglich geworden zu leben. Sehen Sie doch um sich[2]!« Ist das richtig? Vielleicht zur Hälfte.

1. Zugang zu Gott

Müssen wir also jene Hoffnung auf eine meta-technologische Gesellschaft, die den Fortschritt gebändigt hat und ein von Fortschrittszwängen befreites lebenswertes Leben in einer problemoffenen pluralistischen Freiheitsordnung ermöglicht, doch aufgeben[3]? Aufgeben auch jene Hoffnung auf eine meta-revolutionäre Gesellschaft, die ein wirklich befriedetes Dasein in einem Reich der Freiheit, Gleichheit und Gerechtigkeit, einen Sinn in der Geschichte der Menschheit schenkt[4]?

Transzendenz?

Man will heute nicht nur im Kreise gehen. Ein befreiendes Über-Schreiten (»trans-scendere«) über die *»Eindimensionalität«* unseres modernen Daseins ist durchaus gefragt. Das Wort Marcuses von der Eindimensionalität beschreibt sehr gut das Dasein des modernen Menschen, dem die echten Alternativen fehlen. Der technologisch-evolutive Humanismus – durch die radikale Kritik der Neuen Linken überhaupt erst seiner Eindimensionalität bewußt geworden – hat das Problem erst gesichtet, aber bisher keine Alternative entwickelt. Der sozial-revolutionäre Humanismus zeigt ein permanentes Problem- und Krisenbewußtsein, hat aber bisher weder im Osten noch im Westen einen gangbaren Weg der Befreiung aufgezeigt[5].

In beiden Fällen bleibt der Mensch – als Individuum und als Gesellschaft – der Mensch, der seine Welt nicht bewältigen kann, weil er mit so vielem, nur nicht mit sich selber fertig wird! Ein Mensch, der im gleichen Ausmaß, in dem er die ganze Welt gewinnt, seine Seele zu verlieren droht: in Routine, Betriebsamkeit, Geschwätzigkeit, in Richtungslosigkeit und Sinnlosigkeit. Mit der Bosheit des Menschen oder bestimmter Menschen hat dies nur bedingt zu tun. Die gesetzlichen Zwangsmäßigkeiten der technokratischen Gesellschaft selbst, so haben wir gesehen, sind es, die die personale Würde, Freiheit und Verantwortung des Menschen zu erdrücken drohen.

Offensichtlich genügt es nicht, sich von allen kirchlichen und theologischen Dominanzen zu emanzipieren, das Zuständigkeitsfeld weltlicher Instanzen auszuweiten, Lebensplanung und Handlungsnormierung statt religiös nun autonom zu fundieren und zu leiten, um damit die Menschlichkeit des Menschen zu retten. *Echtes Transzendieren* in Theorie und Praxis wäre nötig: ein echter qualitativer Überstieg aus dem eindimensionalen Denken, Sprechen und Handeln in der gegebenen Gesellschaft hinaus auf eine reale Alternative.

Aber gerade dieses Transzendieren ist in unserer Situation nicht in Sicht, bestätigen resigniert auch seine Theoretiker. Ja, deutlicher hat es der Lauf der neuesten Geschichte gemacht, daß ein lineares und womöglich revolutionäres Transzendieren aus der Eindimensionalität nicht hinausführt. Man ist vielmehr wie in anderen Utopien in Gefahr, innerweltliche, endliche Größen für die endgültige Emanzipation einzusetzen, was dann die totalitäre Herrschaft von Menschen über Menschen zur Folge hat: jetzt zwar nicht mehr »die Nation« oder »das Volk« oder »die Rasse« oder gar noch »die Kirche«, wohl aber »die Arbeiterklasse«, »die Partei« oder, nachdem man sich nicht mehr mit der (verbürgerlichten) Arbeiterklasse und der (totalitären) Partei identifizieren kann, »das wahre Bewußtsein« der kleinen elitären Gruppe von Intellektuellen. Und immer wieder neu wiederholt sich auch hier die Erfahrung, daß der Mensch gerade von den Kräften und Mächten, die er in seiner Mündigkeit und Autonomie entbunden hat, zuletzt abhängig wird: daß also seine Freiheit von der von ihm befreiten Welt und ihren Mechanismen gefangengesetzt wird. In dieser eindimensionalen Welt der Unfreiheit ist der Mensch – der Einzelne wie die Gruppen, Völker, Rassen, Klassen – immer wieder gezwungen zu mißtrauen, sich vor anderen und vor sich selber zu fürchten, zu hassen und so unendlich zu leiden. Gerade keine bessere Gesellschaft, keine Gerechtigkeit für alle, keine Freiheit für den Einzelnen, keine wahre Liebe.

Darf es also angesichts dieser Lage der Menschheit – etwa mit ehrfurchtsvoller Beschwörung des Schrecks vor aller »Metaphysik« – ausgeschlossen werden, daß auf der Ebene des Linearen, des Horizontalen, des Endlichen, des rein Menschlichen die *wirklich andere Dimension* nicht gefunden werden kann? Setzt echtes Transzendieren nicht echte Transzendenz voraus? Ist nicht vielleicht doch eine neue Offenheit für diese Frage vorhanden?

- *Die* Kritische Theorie, *ausgehend von ihrem Verständnis der gesellschaftlichen Widersprüche und der Erfahrung von unabwendbarem Leid, Unglück, Schmerz, Alter und Tod im Leben des Einzelnen, das sich nicht einfach begrifflich fassen und aufheben läßt (»negative Dialektik«), thematisiert die Frage nach der Transzendenz und damit die Frage nach der Religion nur indirekt: aber doch zum Teil sogar im Sinne einer »theologia negativa« als Hoffnung auf vollendete Gerechtigkeit, als unerschütterliche »Sehnsucht nach dem Anderen*[6]*«.*
- *Im* Marxismus-Leninismus *beginnt man die Fragen nach Sinn, Schuld, Tod im menschlichen Leben differenzierter zu diskutieren. Die gängigen orthodoxen Antworten: Sinn, Glück, Erfüllung des Lebens lägen allein in Arbeit, kämpferischer Solidarität und dialogischer Existenz*[7]*, können die bedrückenden »privaten Fragen« progressiver Marxisten in Ost und West nicht zum Schweigen bringen: wie es ist um individuelle Schuld, persönliches Schicksal, mit Leid und Tod, Gerechtigkeit und Liebe des Individuums. Das Sinnpotential der Religion wird von daher neu erschlossen*[8]*.*
- *In den* Natur- und Humanwissenschaften *erkennen heute manche besser die Unzulänglichkeit des materialistisch-positivistischen Weltbildes und Wirklichkeitsverständnisses und beginnen, den Absolutheitsanspruch ihrer eigenen Methodologie zu relativieren*[9]*. Verantwortliches wissenschaftlich-technisches*

Handeln impliziert die Frage nach Ethik, Ethik aber die Frage nach Sinnfindung, Wertskala, Leitbildern, Religion[10].

– Die Tiefenpsychologie hat die positive Bedeutung der Religion für die menschliche Psyche, ihre Selbstfindung und ihre Heilung entdeckt[11]. Neuere Psychoanalytiker konstatieren einen signifikanten Zusammenhang von Rückgang der Religiosität und zunehmender Orientierungslosigkeit, Normenlosigkeit und Bedeutungslosigkeit, den charakteristischen Neurosen unserer Zeit[12].

Doch nicht weniger wichtig als die Neuorientierungen in Wissenschaft und Kultur sind die Bewegungen, die sich in der jungen Generation abzeichnen und auf deren religiöse Manifestationen noch zurückzukommen sein wird. Ost und West überschneiden sich hier: Den Forderungen progressiver Marxisten wie Machoveč gegenüber dem orthodoxen Parteimarxismus nach »moralisch-inspirierenden *Idealen, Modellen und Wertmaßstäben*«[13] entsprechen die Forderungen, die etwa Charles A. Reich für die junge Generation gegenüber dem kapitalistischen System formuliert hat. Wie immer man die empirische und systematische Stimmigkeit einer Unterscheidung zwischen »Bewußtsein I und II und IIII« im heutigen Amerika beurteilt[14], niemand kann leugnen, daß hier die großen Probleme der heutigen Gesellschaft angesprochen sind, für die die bisherigen Lösungen nicht ausreichen. Und sosehr Reich in seiner Analyse des Bewußtseins der »neuen Generation« die Züge der Gegen-Kultur[15] überbewertet haben mag, so haben doch die von ihm kritisierten Liberalen und radikalen Revolutionäre das Entscheidende zur Lösung der Probleme vernachlässigt, was das größte und dringendste Erfordernis unserer Zeit ist: ein neues Bewußtsein der *Transzendenz!* Mitten in dieser technologischen Welt ein befreiendes Überschreiten aus den gegebenen Verhältnissen durch die Wahl eines neuen *Lebensstiles*: zur Bändigung der technologischen Maschinerie die Entwicklung neuer Fähigkeiten, einer neuen Unabhängigkeit und persönlichen Verantwortung, der Sensibilität, des ästhetischen Gefühls, der Liebesfähigkeit, der Möglichkeit, in neuen Formen miteinander zusammenzuleben und zusammenzuarbeiten. Und mit Recht fordert Reich deshalb eine *Neubestimmung der Werte und der Prioritäten* und damit auch eine Neubesinnung auf die Religion und die Ethik, damit ein wirklich neuer Mensch und eine neue Gesellschaft möglich wird: »Die Macht des neuen Bewußtseins ist nicht die Macht, Verfahren zu

manipulieren oder die Macht der Politik und der Straßenschlach-
ten, sondern die Macht neuer Werte und eines neuen Way of
Life[16].«

Die Zukunft der Religion

Manche hatten im 19. Jahrhundert und zu Beginn des 20. Jahrhunderts das Ende der Religion erwartet, erhofft, verkündet.
Aber niemand hatte diese Erwartung, Hoffnung, Verkündigung
als begründet aufgewiesen. Und die Proklamation des Todes
Gottes wurde ja nicht wahrer dadurch, daß man sie immer wieder neu wiederholte. Im Gegenteil: das ständige Wiederholen
dieser Prophezeiung, die sich offensichtlich doch nicht erfüllte,
hat selbst unter Atheisten viele skeptisch gemacht, ob das Ende
der Religion je herbeigeführt werden könne.

Der britische Historiker Arnold J. Toynbee: »Nach meiner
Überzeugung können Wissenschaft und Technologie die geistigen Bedürfnisse, für die alle möglichen Religionen zu sorgen
versuchen, nicht befriedigen, wiewohl sie einige der traditionellen Dogmen der sogenannten Hochreligionen zu diskreditieren
vermögen. Historisch gesehen kam die Religion zuerst, und die
Wissenschaft ging aus der Religion hervor. Die Wissenschaft hat
die Religion nie ersetzt, und es ist meine Erwartung, daß sie auch
nie ersetzt wird ... Wie können wir zu einem beständigen Frieden kommen? Für einen wahren und beständigen Frieden ist eine
religiöse Revolution, dessen bin ich gewiß, eine conditio sine qua
non. Mit Religion ... meine ich die Überwindung der Egozen-
trik, in den Individuen wie in den Gemeinschaften, indem wir
Gemeinschaft erlangen mit der geistigen Wirklichkeit hinter dem
Universum und indem wir unseren Willen in Harmonie mit ihr
bringen. Ich meine, daß dies der einzige Schlüssel zum Frieden
ist, aber wir sind ferne davon, diesen Schlüssel zu ergreifen und
zu nützen, und so wird, bis wir dies tun, das Überleben des
Menschengeschlechtes weiterhin im Zweifel bleiben[17].«

Daß so viele Atheisten von der religiösen Problematik nie
loskamen, daß die radikalsten Atheisten, Feuerbach und Niet-
sche, die sich durch die offene Proklamation des Atheismus
befreit glaubten, bis zum sehr menschlichen Ende ihres Lebens
auf Gott und die Religionsproblematik geradezu fixiert blieben:
dies alles scheint – auch wenn man hier gar nicht triumphieren,
sondern nur nüchtern feststellen will – weniger für den Tod als

für eine merkwürdige Lebendigkeit des so oft Totgesagten zu sprechen.

Am deutlichsten aber wurde Marx mit seiner von Feuerbach inspirierten Utopie eines »Absterbens« der Religion nach der Revolution desavouiert, nämlich gerade durch die Entwicklung in den *sozialistischen Staaten*:

1. Ohne Vertrauen in das automatische »Absterben« der Religion wurde der militant-aggressive Atheismus in die Doktrin des (nicht gerade absterbenden) Sowjetstaates aufgenommen und Religion und Kirchen dem auf Ausrottung zielenden stalinistischen Terror und der nachstalinistischen Repression ausgesetzt.

2. Bald 60 Jahre nach der Oktoberrevolution und unbeschreiblichen Verfolgungen und Schikanen gegenüber Kirchen und einzelnen ist das Christentum in der Sowjetunion eine eher wachsende als abnehmende Größe: Nach neuesten (vielleicht überhöhten) Angaben soll jeder dritte erwachsene Russe (Russen stellen etwa die Hälfte aller Sowjetbürger) und jeder fünfte erwachsene Sowjetmensch praktizierender Christ sein[18].

Doch auch im Westen haben sich manche Prognosen als irrig erwiesen. Der *Säkularisierungsprozeß* – man wird sich jetzt auf eine Einschränkung ganz am Anfang des Buches besinnen[19] – wurde sowohl von Soziologen wie von Theologen überschätzt, beziehungsweise zu undifferenziert gesehen[20]. Theologen der religionslosen Säkularität, die der »Gott-ist-tot-Theologie« das Präludium schrieben, bekennen sich heute wieder zur Religion und gar zur Volksreligion[21]. Oft stand hinter einseitigen Theorien nicht nur eine mangelnde kritische Distanz zum Zeitgeist und seinen Verführungen, sondern auch ein sehr bestimmtes ideologisches Interesse: entweder die Sehnsucht nach dem Goldenen Zeitalter (Verfallshypothese) oder die utopische Erwartung eines kommenden Zeitalters (Emanzipationshypothese). Oft wurden anstelle von exakten empirischen Untersuchungen großzügige apriorische Theorien entwickelt.

Aber selbst für Futurologen erwies sich die Extrapolation der Entwicklung des Phänomens Religion als schwieriger denn die in anderen Bereichen. Was läßt sich hier (zum Beispiel in der Praxis des Glaubens und Betens und der Handlungsmotive) messen und zählen, das letzte schlüssige Auskunft über die Religion gäbe? Die historisch ausgeprägte und sozial objektivierte religiöse Wirklichkeit, diese Summe von Doktrinen und Riten, Verhaltensweisen, Gewohnheiten, Lebensrhythmen und sozialen Strukturen ist ja nur die Spitze des Eisberges Religion. Die »Gesamtwirklichkeit Religion« mit all ihren Impulsen und Inspirationen, ihren Überzeugungen und Haltungen, ihrer Sinnstiftung und Integrationskraft, dem sie ermöglichenden Glauben, Hoffen und Lieben ist unendlich viel mehr. Und die Religion, so alt wie die Menschheit selbst, hat durch alle Jahrtausende hindurch den Menschengeist immer wieder neu zu fesseln vermocht. Gewiß, es können alte Riten und Gewohnheiten ihren religiösen Sinn einbüßen. Sehr oft schaffen sie jedoch zugleich Raum für neue Formen religiösen Verhaltens: alte Tugenden etwa verschwinden und machen dadurch neuen und zuerst als solchen gar nicht erkannten Tugenden (Anständigkeit, Sachlichkeit, Fairneß, Verantwortungsbewußtsein, Kritik, Solidarität) Platz[22]. Nach allen bisherigen Erfahrungen ist jedenfalls gegenüber der Zukunft spezifischer Arten von Irreligiosität mindestens soviel Skepsis angebracht wie gegenüber der Zukunft der Kirchen.

Verschiedene Interpretationsmodelle des Säkularisierungsprozesses haben sich somit als undifferenziert erwiesen: Darf Säkularisierung mit Entkirchlichung verwechselt werden? Es gibt doch den ganzen Bereich der nichtkirchlichen, nichtinstitutionalisierten Religion. Oder mit rationalisierender Entzauberung? Rationalisierung in einem Lebensbereich schließt den Sinn für das Nicht-Rationale oder Mehr-als-Rationale in einem anderen Bereich nicht aus. Oder etwa mit Entsakralisierung? Religion reduziert sich keineswegs auf das Sakrale.

Grundsätzlich sind heute *drei Prognosen* über die Zukunft der Religion *möglich*[23]:

1. Die Säkularisierung ist revidierbar, sei es durch religiöse Restauration oder durch religiöse Revolution: Die Irreversibilität des Säkularisierungsprozesses ist nicht bewiesen, und eine solche Entwicklung kann, da es keine überraschungsfreie Zukunft gibt, nicht von vornherein ausgeschlossen werden. Aber sie ist in der gegenwärtigen Lage wenig wahrscheinlich.
2. Die Säkularisierung geht ungebrochen weiter: Die Kirchen werden dann immer mehr zu kognitiven Minderheiten. Diese Prognose ist wahrscheinlicher, aber es gibt, wie zu sehen sein wird, starke Gegenargumente.
3. Die Säkularisierung geht modifiziert weiter: Sie zerlegt das religiöse Spektrum in immer neue, bisher unbekannte soziale Formen von Religion, kirchlicher oder außerkirchlicher. Diese Prognose hat vielleicht am meisten Wahrscheinlichkeit für sich.

Die wirklichen Fachleute in Religionssoziologie, von Max Weber und Emile Durkheim angefangen bis zu den heutigen, stimmen überein: Es wird – so wie Kunst – auch immer Religion
geben. Und Religion wird in allem Wandel für die Menschheit
von grundlegender Wichtigkeit bleiben: sei es mehr als Integra-
tionsfaktor der Gesellschaft im Sinne von Durkheim (Zugehörigkeit zu einer Gemeinschaft), sei es mehr als sinnstiftende und
wertrationalisierende Größe im Sinn von Weber (Eingebettet-
sein in ein Deutungssystem); sei es in weniger sakralen Formen
mehr für die persönlichen, zwischenmenschlichen Beziehungen
(Thomas Luckmann, Peter Berger), sei es ohne Aufgabe der
sakralen Formen und indirekt auch für die gesellschaftlichen
Institutionen und Strukturen (Talcott Parsons, Clifford Geertz),
sei es in Verbindung von integrierender und sinnstiftender Funktion durch die Bildung von fortgeschrittenen Eliten in den pluralistischen Gesellschaften (Andrew Greeley).

Bisherige religionssoziologische Untersuchungen waren oft
auf statistisches Material über Gottesdienstbesuch und andere
religiöse Praktiken fixiert. Ein anhaltendes Interesse an Religion
sogar unter anscheinend religionsfernsten Schichten kann aber
nicht bezweifelt werden und wurde – gegen manche unkontrol-
lierte Vermutungen und Vorurteile – durch neues Zahlenmaterial
bestätigt[24]. Zweifellos hat die extensive Kontrolle durch die Religion abgenommen: Die Religion hat auf Gebieten wie Wissenschaft, Erziehung, Politik, Recht, Medizin und Volkswohlfahrt
immer weniger direkten Einfluß. Aber kann daraus geschlossen
werden, daß der Einfluß der Religion auf das Leben des Einzelnen und der Gesellschaft überhaupt abgenommen hat? Anstelle
der extensiven Kontrolle und Vormundschaft kann ein mehr
intensiver und indirekter moralischer Einfluß getreten sein. Der
stillschweigende moralische Einfluß der Religion auf die großen
ökonomischen, politischen und erzieherischen Institutionen
etwa der Vereinigten Staaten war von Soziologen schon länger
untersucht worden. Der neuartige Einfluß der Kirchen auf die
Bürgerrechts- und Friedensbewegungen und die Bewegungen in
der Dritten Welt vor allem im Kampf gegen die Armut, im
Kampf für die nationale Unabhängigkeit in Afrika und Südamerika, hat manche überrascht. Daß die Jugendkultur in einem
nicht geringen Ausmaß durch eine neue Religiosität bestimmt ist,
wird noch zu zeigen sein: Das gilt für die Jesus-Movements
ebenso wie für die Tendenzen zur orientalischen Religiosität und
Mystik. Unter negativem Vorzeichen zeigt sich auch viel ver-

drängte und in den Untergrund abgesunkene Religiosität: von den harmlosen Formen der Astrologie über Aberglauben aller Art bis hin zum immer wieder neu virulenten Teufelsglauben.

Die *Ideologie des Säkularismus* versuchte aus der echten und notwendigen Säkularisierung eine glaubenslose Weltanschauung zu machen: das Ende der Religion oder zumindest der organisierten Religion oder auch nur der christlichen Kirchen sei gekommen. Aufgrund der eben beschriebenen neueren Entwicklung betrachten die Soziologen den Säkularisierungsprozeß im Gegensatz dazu sehr differenziert. Mehr als vom Niedergang der Religion spricht man von ihrem *Funktionswechsel:* Man erkennt, daß die Gesellschaft immer komplexer und differenzierter geworden ist und daß es nach der ursprünglichen weitgehenden Identität von Religion und Gesellschaft zu einer Trennung der Religion von den anderen Strukturen kommen mußte. Deshalb spricht Th. Luckmann von einer Lösung institutioneller Bereiche aus dem Kosmos religiöser Sinngebung, T. Parsons von einer evolutionären *Differenzierung* (Arbeitsteilung) zwischen den verschiedenen Institutionen. Ähnlich wie die Familie, so wurde auch die Religion (beziehungsweise die Kirchen) durch die fortschreitende Differenzierung von zweitrangigen (etwa wirtschaftlichen und erzieherischen) Funktionen befreit und könnte sich nun auf ihre eigentliche Aufgabe konzentrieren. Insofern bedeutet diese Säkularisierung oder Differenzierung eine große Chance. Durch das Christentum sind im System der Welt- und Selbstdeutung des Menschen neue große Fragen nach der Herkunft und Bestimmung des Menschen und nach der Totalität der Welt und der Geschichte aufgeworfen worden. Diese großen Fragen nach dem Woher und Wohin sind seither nicht mehr zur Ruhe gekommen und haben die ganze Folgezeit grundlegend bestimmt. Dieser Problemschub und Problemdruck hält auch in der säkularen Neuzeit unvermittelt an. Und wenn es auch nicht eine Kontinuität der Antworten gab, so doch zumindest eine Kontinuität der Fragestellungen. Doch haben sich die säkularen Wissenschaften des modernen Menschen bei all ihren Erfolgen in der Beantwortung dieser großen Fragen notorisch als insuffizient erwiesen[25]. Die reine Vernunft scheint hier überfordert zu sein.

Ohne weiter auf die Prognosen einzugehen, die der Religion für die Zukunft gestellt werden, wird man sagen können: Die Ablösung der Religion durch Wissenschaft hat sich nicht nur nicht bewahrheitet, sie ist eine methodisch ungerechtfertigte Extrapolation in die Zukunft aufgrund eines unkritischen Glaubens an die Wissenschaft. Bei der gewachsenen Skepsis gegenüber dem Fortschritt von Vernunft und Wissenschaft dürfte es mehr denn je fraglich sein, ob die Wissenschaft die Rolle des Religionsersatzes spielen kann und wird.

Damit ist aber der Gottesglaube noch nicht begründet: Die Frage nach Gott ist eine offene Frage. Der Gottesglaube ist herausgefordert, über den Realitätsbezug seiner Aussagen begründet Rechenschaft abzulegen und das Problem der Verifikation nicht zu umgehen.

Gottesbeweise?

Hier scheinen wir rasch in eine Aporie, eine ausweglose Situation hineinzugeraten: *Entweder* kann der Glaube an Gott bewiesen werden: wie ist er dann noch Glaube? *Oder* er kann nicht bewiesen werden: wie ist er dann noch vernünftig? Das uralte Dilemma zwischen Vernunft und Glaube gerade in der Gotteserkenntnis, das die einen zugunsten des Glaubens und die anderen zugunsten der Vernunft lösen, oder eben nicht lösen[26].

1. Die *einen* sagen: der Mensch erkennt Gott nur, wenn sich Gott zu erkennen gibt, also sich offenbart. Gott hat die Initiative und begegnet mir allein im Wort der *biblischen Offenbarung.* Also keine Gotteserkenntnis des sündigen Menschen ohne Gottes gnadenhafte Offenbarung: kein menschlicher Gottesbeweis, sondern nur Gottes Selbstbeweis. Vom Menschen wird keine neutrale Kenntnisnahme, sondern vertrauender Glaube auf Grund der Botschaft erwartet: ein »credo ut intelligam«, ein »ich glaube, um zu erkennen«.

Das ist – auf dem Hintergrund der Skepsis Luthers gegenüber der verführerischen »Hure Vernunft« – die Position der *»dialektischen Theologie«* Karl Barths[27] und in dieser Frage auch Rudolf Bultmanns[28] samt ihrer großen Gefolgschaft in der evangelischen Theologie[29]. Sie möchte die Göttlichkeit Gottes und seiner Offenbarung gewahrt wissen: gegen alle »natürliche Theologie« des römischen Katholizismus und des anthropozentrischen Neuprotestantismus nach Friedrich Schleiermacher. Zwischen dem Menschen und dem ganz anderen Gott ist eine unendliche Distanz, die nur von Gott selber her durch seine Offenbarung »dialektisch« vermittelt werden kann. Deshalb also keine Bedürfnistheologie, in der das Wort Gottes nach den Bedürfnissen des Menschen zurechtgemacht wird.

Aber werden da manche fragen: Soll das Gespräch über Gott nicht grundsätzlich mit jedem Menschen geführt werden können? Sollen die Erfahrungen des Gesprächspartners nicht einbezogen werden können? Soll die Wahrheit des Gottesglaubens eine bloße Behauptung bleiben? Wo setze ich erfahrungsmäßig an, um Gott bewahrheiten zu können? Soll denn Gott beinahe magisch beschworen werden? »Offenbarung« – eine unbegründete Voraussetzung und so vielleicht doch nur eine Illusion oder ein ideologischer Überbau? Oder auch einfach nur ein äußeres Gesetz, das der Mensch, verstanden oder nicht, schlicht zu akzeptieren hat? Soll ich mit meiner Vernunft einfach abdanken, meinen Verstand einfach opfern (»sacrificium intellectus«)? Diese Fragen, diese Forderungen nach Bewahrheitung des Gottesglaubens scheinen berechtigt:

– *Kein blinder, sondern ein verantworteter Glaube: Der Mensch soll nicht geistig vergewaltigt, sondern mit Gründen überzeugt werden, damit er eine verantwortete Glaubensentscheidung fällen kann.*
– *Kein wirklichkeitsleerer, sondern ein wirklichkeitsbezogener Glaube: Der Mensch soll nicht ohne Verifikation einfach glauben müssen. Sondern seine Aussagen sollen im Kontakt mit der Wirklichkeit, im Erfahrungshorizont des Menschen und der Gesellschaft von heute sich bewahrheiten und bewähren und sollen so durch die konkrete Erfahrung der Wirklichkeit gedeckt sein.*

2. Deshalb sagen nun aber die *anderen*: Der Mensch kann nur an Gottes Offenbarung glauben, wenn er zunächst mit seiner Vernunft Gott erkannt hat. Gottes »übernatürliche« Offenbarung im Wort der biblischen Verkündigung setzt die »natürliche« Offenbarung Gottes in der Schöpfung voraus. Die Geschöpflichkeit der Welt wird zwar nicht (wie man oft meint: im Zirkelschluß) bereits vorausgesetzt, um die Existenz des Schöpfers zu erkennen. Aber eine Reflexion über die Welt, wie sie ist, läßt Gott als Ursache und Ziel aller Dinge klar aufweisen. Also rationale Gottesbeweise aus der Wirklichkeit der Welt.

Das ist – auf dem Hintergrund der Theologie des Thomas von Aquin[30] – die Position der »natürlichen Theologie« der katholischen Neuscholastik und zurückhaltend auch des Ersten Vatikanischen Konzils 1870[31]. Während Thomas von Aquin die grundsätzliche Beweisbarkeit Gottes vertritt[32], so das Vatikanum I freilich nur die grundsätzliche Erkennbarkeit Gottes (nur eine »Möglichkeit«, eine »potentia« der Gotteserkenntnis). Diese *»natürliche Theologie«*[33] möchte vermitteln zwischen einem Rationalismus, der den Glauben auf Vernunft reduziert (Ablehnung alles »Übernatürlichen«), und einem Fideismus, der alle Vernunft auf Glauben reduziert (Ablehnung aller »natürlichen« Gotteserkenntnis). Zwischen Gott und Mensch gibt es nach dieser Auffassung trotz aller Unähnlichkeit eine Ähnlichkeit, eine Analogie, die einen Analogieschluß – affirmieren, negieren, transzendieren – auf Gott ermöglicht. Also eine doppelte Erkenntnisordnung: »Über« dem »natürlichen« Bereich, der durch die Vernunft erkannt wird, gibt es einen »übernatürlichen« Bereich, der durch den Glauben erkannt wird: eine Zwei-Stockwerk-Theorie, die es ermöglicht, sowohl dem Phänomen der Philosophie (und besonders der Religionsphilosophie) wie auch dem Phänomen der Religion (und besonders der Weltreligionen) gerecht zu werden. Eine Theorie, nach der Widersprüche zwischen der »natürlichen« und »übernatürlichen« Ebene, zwischen Vernunft und Glaube ausgeschlossen sind. Keineswegs auch hier eine Bedürfnistheologie: die Bedürfnisse des Menschen dürfen nicht der alles beherrschende Gesichtspunkt, wohl aber der methodische Ausgangspunkt sein. Die Erkenntnisordnung, in der der Mensch am Anfang steht, ist nicht einfach identisch mit der Seinsordnung, in der Gott am Anfang steht.

Aber auch gegen diese Konzeption werden manche Fragen angemeldet. Lassen wir hier die spezifisch theologischen Einwände beiseite: daß vom gnadenhaften Handeln Gottes abgesehen und der eine Gottesgedanke in einen »übernatürlichen« und einen »natürlichen« Gott aufgespalten wird; daß so nicht der eine wahre christliche Gott, sondern ein Götze, die Projektion der weltanschaulichen Fantasie des Menschen, erkannt wird. Gegen Gottesbeweise werden heute ganz allgemein Einwände erhoben:
a. Kann ein *Beweis* Gott beweisen? Kann man in eigentlichen Lebensfragen operieren wie in fachlichen, technischen oder wissenschaftlichen Fragen? Kann man in Lebensfragen mit einer rein rationalen Gedankenfolge, die durch logische Verbindung bekannter Sätze ein Unbekanntes erschließt, überhaupt etwas erreichen? Läßt sich durch logisch schlußfolgernde Denkschritte gerade die Existenz Gottes anbeweisen, so daß am Ende die nicht nur wahrscheinliche, sondern logisch zwingende Einsicht in die Existenz Gottes steht? Wird ein

solcher Beweis nicht bestenfalls eine ingeniöse Gedankenkonstruktion für philosophische und theologische Fachleute, die aber für den Durchschnittsmenschen abstrakt bleibt, undurchschaubar und unkontrollierbar, ohne Überzeugungskraft und Verbindlichkeit?

b. Kann in einem Beweis Gott noch *Gott* sein? Wird Gott durch ein solches Schluß-Verfahren nicht zu einem beliebigen Ding erniedrigt, das mit etwas menschlichem Scharfsinn er-schlossen, ent-deckt werden könnte? Ein »Ob-jekt« also »entgegen-gesetzt« dem Subjekt, uns äußerlich und durch eine logische Schlußkette gleichsam aus dem Jenseits herbeizuholen? Ist ein derart verobjektivierter Gott überhaupt noch Gott?

c. Kann die *Vernunft des Menschen* so weit reichen? Hat sich seit Kants Kritik der reinen Vernunft die Erkenntnis nicht weithin durchgesetzt, daß die Reichweite unserer theoretischen Vernunft beschränkt ist? Bleibt sie nicht an den menschlichen Erfahrungshorizont gebunden, so daß sie nur illegitimerweise über die Grenzen der möglichen Erfahrung hinausgreifen kann? Sind mit Kants methodischer Kritik des ontologischen, kosmologischen und teleologischen (physiko-theologischen) Gottesbeweises der theoretischen Vernunft nicht die Beweise für die Existenz Gottes aus der Hand geschlagen worden? Ist die Vernunft in dem – von Kant nicht geleugneten – metaphysischen Bereich zu mehr fähig als zu regulieren und zu ordnen, ohne die Wirklichkeit selber erschließen zu können? Hier liegt tatsächlich die eigentliche Problematik der Gottesbeweise, wie sie bei Platon und Aristoteles grundgelegt, von Augustinus in der christlichen Theologie beheimatet, von Thomas von Aquin umfassend systematisiert, von Descartes, Spinoza, Leibniz und Wolff im Anschluß an den »ontologischen« Neuansatz bei Anselm von Canterbury neu durchdacht, aber dann schließlich von Kant allesamt radikal in die Krise geführt und bei Fichte und Hegel spekulativ umgedeutet wurden.

Man kann sich diesen Einwänden kaum ganz verschließen und wird zugeben müssen:

– *Wie sich in der Auseinandersetzung mit dem Nihilismus zeigen läßt*[34], *gibt* es keinen evidenten Unterbau *der Vernunft, auf welchem sich der Glaube gründen ließe: Der Zweifel ist nicht erst bei einem »übernatürlichen« Überbau möglich. Er setzt schon bei der Fraglichkeit des menschlichen Daseins und der Wirklichkeit überhaupt ein.*

– *Die Wirklichkeit Gottes, wenn er existieren sollte, ist in der Welt jedenfalls* nicht unmittelbar gegeben: *Einen Gott, den es »gibt«, gibt es nicht! Er gehört nicht zu den in der Erfahrung problemlos vorfindbaren Objekten. Eine direkte Erfahrung Gottes ist nicht gegeben. Auch nicht eine unmittelbare Intuition* (»*Ontologismus*« *N. Malebranches, V. Giobertis, A. Rosminis).*

– *Ohne* Rückgriff auf die empirische Erfahrung (= a priori), *allein aus dem* Begriff Gottes *(als eines notwendigen oder absolut vollkommenen Wesens)* läßt sich nicht seine notwendige Existenz *erschließen: Der »ontologische« Gottesbeweis (Anselm von Canterbury, Descartes, Leibniz), der den Umweg über die Selbst- und Welterfahrung vermeidet, setzt einen ungebrochenen Begriffsrealismus voraus.*

– *Bei allen* Gottesbeweisen *aus der* Erfahrung (= a posteriori) *fragt es sich immer, ob sie den Überschritt vom »Sichtbaren« zum »Unsichtbaren« in die Transzendenz jenseits der Erfahrung schaffen: sowohl die verschiedenen Varianten des kosmologischen (Gott als Wirkursache) wie des teleologischen (Gott als Finalursache) Gottesbeweises, lassen Zweifel aufkommen, ob sie wirklich zu einem letzten, mit Ich, Gesellschaft und Welt nicht identifizierbaren Grund oder Ziel gelangen (beziehungsweise den Regreß ins Unendliche ausschließen).*

– *Der Glaube an Gott kann nicht unter Vernachlässigung der existentiellen Komponente einem Menschen anbewiesen werden, so daß dieser vom Glauben dispensiert statt zum Glauben herausgefordert wäre: Eine rein rationale Demonstration der Existenz Gottes, die allgemein zu überzeugen vermöchte, gibt es nach den bisherigen Erfahrungen nicht.* Gottesbeweise *erweisen sich faktisch – wie immer man über die abstrakte »Möglichkeit« der Gotteserkenntnis im Sinne des Vatikanum I denkt – als* nicht für jedermann zwingend. *Kein einziger Beweis wird generell akzeptiert.*

Gibt es denn keinen Ausweg aus der Aporie? Gibt es denn keinen Weg zwischen einer rein autoritativen Behauptung Gottes im Sinne der »dialektischen Theologie« und einem rein rationalen Beweis Gottes im Sinne der »natürlichen Theologie«?

Mehr als die reine Vernunft

Auch *Kant*, der »Zertrümmerer« der Gottesbeweise, ist keineswegs der Meinung, Gott existiere nicht. Und müßte Kant nicht zumindest in dem Sinne zugestimmt werden, daß ein mittlerer Weg zu suchen ist? Ein Weg zwischen einer dogmatischen Behauptung und einem Beweis der theoretischen Vernunft, auf deren Ebene die Existenz Gottes nach Kant nicht bewiesen, aber auch nicht widerlegt werden kann?

Wie kommt nun Kant zur Existenz Gottes? Kant appelliert dabei grundsätzlich zu Recht nicht an die »reine«, sondern an die »praktische« Vernunft, die sich im Handeln des Menschen manifestiert: Es geht nicht um reines Erkennen, sondern um das Handeln des Menschen. Kant argumentiert aus dem Selbstverständnis des Menschen als eines sittlichen, verantwortlichen Wesens. Zum Unterschied von den rein rationalen Gottesbeweisen lehnt Kant es also zu Recht ab, den menschlichen Existenzvollzug für den Fortgang des Beweisgedankens zu neutralisieren. Deswegen spricht er vom »Postulat«: Gott – »postuliert« aus der (unbedingt gebotenen) Sittlichkeit und dem (damit auszugleichenden) Glückseligkeitsstreben, »postuliert« als deren Möglichkeitsbedingung, einsichtig nur der praktischen Vernunft. Kant spricht in diesem Zusammenhang von »Glauben«, »reinem Vernunftglauben«[35]. Auch in der Kritik der praktischen Vernunft wendet Kant freilich den Blick nicht mehr »hinaus« oder »hinauf« in ein Jenseitiges (ein »Transzendentes«), sondern hinter sich selbst zurück nach innen (das »Transzendentale«): die Bedingung der Möglichkeit von Sittlichkeit und Glückseligkeit. Gott gehört mit Freiheit und Unsterblichkeit zu den drei großen Ideen, welche kein rationaler Beweis erreicht und die doch schlechthinnige Voraussetzungen des sittlichen Handelns sind..

Die transzendentale Argumentation Kants ist freilich auf begründete Kritik gestoßen, in zweifacher Hinsicht. Zum *ersten* Pfeiler seiner Argumentation: Kann man legitimerweise von einem unbedingten Sollen, von einem kategorischen Imperativ ausgehen? Gilt denn das unbedingte moralische Gesetz nicht nur dann, wenn der Mensch sich die Frage nach dem rechten Verhalten bereits gestellt hat? Muß man wirklich das Faktum einer unbedingten moralischen Verpflichtung in uns annehmen, die als solche die Existenz Gottes (= eines höchsten Gutes, das Sittlichkeit und Glückseligkeit vereint) postuliert? Setzt die Annahme eines apodiktisch gewissen moralischen Gesetzes in uns, wie es im kategorischen Imperativ (»Du sollst!«) seinen Ausdruck findet, nicht bereits den moralischen Impetus, die Frage nach der Moralität oder sogar den Entschluß zu einem moralischen Leben voraus, der doch – wie Nietzsche beweist – auch negativ ausfallen kann? Argumentiert hier Kant also nicht in einem Zirkel: Wird nicht schon die Unbedingtheit der Verpflichtung des »Du sollst« postuliert und somit das Postulat der Existenz Gottes auf einem anderen Postulat begründet?

Und zum *zweiten* Pfeiler seiner Argumentation: Das Streben nach Glückseligkeit ist gewiß allen Menschen eigen. Aber woher kann man voraussetzen, daß Pflicht und Neigung zur Übereinstimmung kommen müssen? Warum muß dem, der dem moralischen Gesetz gehorcht, unbedingt Glückseligkeit zukommen?

Der Begriff des »Postulates« verweist selbst darauf hin, daß der Rückschluß auf Gott theoretisch nicht voraussetzungslos vollzogen werden kann, sondern daß Gott vorausgesetzt werden muß, sofern man überhaupt sinnvoll sittlich leben will. Es ist – mitten im neuzeitlichen Säkularisations- und Emanzipationsprozeß – ein großer Gedanke Kants, daß Gott als die Möglichkeitsbedingung sittlicher Autonomie verstanden wird. Zu Recht lehnt er es ab, die Widersprüchlichkeit, die Antinomien der reinen Vernunft in den Bereich menschlichen Existenzvollzugs einbrechen und den Menschen ins Bodenlose der Absurdität versinken zu lassen. Aber ob hier nicht doch weiter ausgeholt und breiter angesetzt werden müßte?

Hier soll jedenfalls nicht bereits eine moralische Verpflichtung, ein unerbittliches moralisches Gesetz in uns, ein rigoroser kategorischer Imperativ vorausgesetzt werden. Vielmehr soll wie bisher von der ganzen Wirklichkeit der Welt und des Menschen, wie sie konkret erfahren werden, ausgegangen und nach der Bedingung der Möglichkeit dieser ganz und gar fraglichen Wirklichkeit gefragt werden. Kant hat die Gottesbeweise als zwingende Beweise zerschlagen. Aber ihren religiösen Gehalt hat er nicht liquidiert. Es soll keine deduktive Ableitung Gottes aus dieser erfahrenen Wirklichkeit der Welt und des Menschen durch die theoretische Vernunft versucht werden, um die Wirklichkeit Gottes in logischen Schlußfolgerungen (Syllogismus) rational zu demonstrieren. Wohl aber soll induktiv die einem jeden zugängliche Erfahrung der Wirklichkeit ausgeleuchtet werden, um so – gleichsam auf der Linie der »praktischen Vernunft« – vor eine *rational verantwortbare Entscheidung* zu stellen, die eben mehr als nur die reine Vernunft, die vielmehr den ganzen Menschen beansprucht. Also keine rein theoretische, sondern eine durchaus praktische Aufgabe der Vernunft: eine die konkrete Erfahrung der Wirklichkeit begleitende, aufschlüsselnde, ausleuchtende nach-denkliche Reflexion mit praktischer Absicht. Sollte es nicht möglich sein, eine der Kritik standhaltende Rechenschaft vom Glauben an Gott angesichts dieser konkreten Wirklichkeit von Welt und Mensch zu versuchen? Eine Rede von Gott, die durch die konkrete Erfahrung der Wirklichkeit gedeckt ist und sich an ihr als richtig erweist, um so glaubwürdig zu sein? Alles im Bewußtsein, daß manch einer durchaus echt an Gott zu glauben vermag, auch wenn er dies nicht in gleicher Weise rational zu verantworten versteht?

2. Die Wirklichkeit Gottes

Die Frage, ob Gott existiert, ist in den bisherigen Darlegungen offen geblieben. Sie soll – in zwei Phasen – beantwortet werden, um so zugleich den neuzeitlichen Frage- und Begriffshorizont für das spezifisch christliche Gottesverständnis zu gewinnen[1]. Eine gewisse »Anstrengung des Begriffs« können wir dem Leser, der sich auf eine solche Fragestellung einläßt, gerade weil in knappster systematischer Form geantwortet werden muß, nicht ganz ersparen. Wem jedoch die Existenz Gottes eine Gewißheit des Glaubens ist, der wird auf diesen mehr philosophischen Gedankengang leicht verzichten können.

Was Gott ist, kann heute weniger denn je – unter Atheisten und unter Christen – als bekannt vorausgesetzt werden. Zunächst bleibt uns gar nichts anderes übrig, als von einem Vorverständnis, einem *Vorbegriff* von Gott auszugehen, der erst in der Analyse selbst – in einem bestimmten Ausmaß – geklärt werden wird; die Fragen des Daß und des Was hängen ja innerlich zusammen. Der Vorbegriff von Gott ist das, was man gemeinhin unter Gott versteht und was verschiedene verschieden ausdrükken: der geheimnisvolle, nicht zu erschütternde Grund für ein trotz allem sinnvolles Leben; die Mitte und Tiefe des Menschen, menschlicher Gemeinschaft, der Wirklichkeit überhaupt; die letzte, höchste Instanz, von der alles abhängt; das unverfügbare, Verantwortung begründende Gegenüber.

Die Hypothese

Die letzten Fragen, in denen sich nach Kant alles Interesse der menschlichen Vernunft vereinigt[2], sind auch die ersten, sind auch

Fragen des Alltags: Was kann ich wissen? Fragen nach der Wahrheit. Was soll ich tun? Fragen nach der Norm. Was darf ich hoffen? Fragen nach dem Sinn. »Funktionale« und »wesentliche« Fragen, Technisch-Rationales und Gesamthaft-Personales – das alles läßt sich unterscheiden, hängt aber im konkreten Leben zusammen. »Rechnendes« Denken, das im Sinne Heideggers auf Machbares, Berechenbares, Richtigkeiten bezogen ist, läßt sich im Alltag nicht völlig trennen vom »besinnlichen« Denken, das auf Sinn und Wahrheit aus ist. Nur können die wesentlichen Fragen nach Sinn und Wahrheit, Norm und Werten – unter dem einschläfernden Einfluß der Wohlstandsgesellschaft mehr denn je – verdeckt und verdrängt werden, bis sie durch Reflexion oder noch mehr durch »Schicksal« im großen oder kleinen wieder geweckt werden.

Es muß nun zur Beantwortung der Frage nach der Existenz Gottes vorausgesetzt werden, daß der Mensch zu seiner eigenen Existenz und zur Wirklichkeit überhaupt grundsätzlich Ja sagt: daß er also diese zweifellos zutiefst fragliche Wirklichkeit (und besonders seine eigene zutiefst fragliche Existenz) nicht von vornherein für sinnlos, wertlos, nichtig hält, wie dies der Nihilismus behauptet. Daß er diese Wirklichkeit trotz ihrer Fraglichkeit vielmehr für grundsätzlich sinnvoll, wertvoll, wirklich hält. Daß er also – was in seiner Freiheit steht – der Wirklichkeit nicht ein fundamentales Mißtrauen, ein Grundmißtrauen, sondern ein fundamentales Vertrauen, ein *Grundvertrauen* entgegenbringt[3].

Auch für den, der so im Grundvertrauen sein Ja zur Wirklichkeit von Welt und Mensch sagt, bleibt nun freilich die durchgängige Fraglichkeit der Wirklichkeit in ontischer, noetischer und ethischer Hinsicht bestehen: Durch das Vertrauen zu ihr verliert die fragliche Wirklichkeit nicht ihre radikale Fraglichkeit. Und hier setzt die Gottesfrage ein: Die Wirklichkeit, die ein Grundvertrauen zu begründen vermag, erscheint selber in rätselhafter Weise unbegründet, als haltende selber haltlos, als sich entwickelnde dennoch ziellos. Eine rätselhafte Faktizität der Wirklichkeit, die sich in einer fundamentalen Grundlosigkeit, Haltlosigkeit und Ziellosigkeit manifestiert. Sie läßt die Frage nach der Wirklichkeit oder Unwirklichkeit, dem Sein oder Nichtsein, dem Grundvertrauen oder dem Nihilismus jederzeit neu aufbrechen.

Grundsätzlich ausgedrückt geht es um die eine Frage: *Von woher* soll die durchgängig fragliche Wirklichkeit erklärt werden? Was macht sie möglich? Was also ist die *Bedingung der*

Möglichkeit dieser fraglichen *Wirklichkeit*? Also nicht allein die Frage: Was ist die Bedingung der Möglichkeit dieser durchgängigen *Fraglichkeit*? Eine solche Fragestellung vernachlässigt die Wirklichkeit in aller Fraglichkeit[4].

Will der Mensch auf ein Verstehen seiner selbst und der Wirklichkeit überhaupt nicht verzichten, so müssen diese letzten Fragen, die zugleich die ersten sind und die unausweichlich nach Antwort rufen, beantwortet werden. Dabei steht der Glaubende im Wettbewerb mit dem Nichtglaubenden, wer denn die grundlegenden menschlichen Erfahrungen überzeugender deuten kann.

1. Von der ganz konkreten Erfahrung der Unsicherheit des Lebens, der Ungewißheit des Wissens und der vielschichtigen Angst und Orientierungslosigkeit des Menschen, die hier nicht konkret beschrieben werden muß, stellt sich die unabweisbare Frage: *Woher* diese zwischen Sein und Nichtsein, Sinn und Sinnlosigkeit schwebende, sich in der Haltlosigkeit haltende, ziellos sich entwickelnde, also radikal *fragliche Wirklichkeit*?

Auch wer nicht glaubt, *daß* Gott existiert, könnte zumindest der *Hypothese,* die freilich noch nicht über Existenz oder Nichtexistenz Gottes entscheidet, zustimmen: *Wenn* Gott existierte, dann *wäre* eine grundsätzliche Lösung für das Rätsel der fraglich bleibenden Wirklichkeit angegeben, *wäre* eine grundsätzliche Antwort, die selbstverständlich entfaltet und gedeutet werden müßte, auf die Frage nach dem Woher gefunden. Um die Hypothese in knappster Form zu umschreiben:

- *Wenn Gott existierte, dann wäre die gründende Wirklichkeit selbst nicht mehr letztlich unbegründet. Gott wäre der* Ur-Grund *aller Wirklichkeit.*
- *Wenn Gott existierte, dann wäre die sich haltende Wirklichkeit nicht mehr selber letztlich haltlos. Gott wäre der* Ur-Halt *aller Wirklichkeit.*
- *Wenn Gott existierte, dann wäre die sich entwickelnde Wirklichkeit nicht mehr letztlich ziellos. Gott wäre das* Ur-Ziel *aller Wirklichkeit.*
- *Wenn Gott existierte, dann wäre die zwischen Sein und Nichtsein schwebende Wirklichkeit nicht mehr letztlich der Nichtigkeit verdächtig. Gott wäre das* Sein selbst *aller Wirklichkeit.*

Diese Hypothese läßt sich positiv und negativ präzisieren:
a. Positiv: Wenn Gott existierte, dann wäre zu verstehen:
Warum in aller Zerrissenheit letztlich eine verborgene Einheit,

in aller Sinnlosigkeit letztlich eine verborgene Sinnhaftigkeit, in aller Wertlosigkeit letztlich eine verborgene Werthaftigkeit der Wirklichkeit vertrauend angenommen werden kann: Gott wäre der *Ursprung, Ursinn, Urwert* alles Seienden;

warum in aller Nichtigkeit letztlich doch ein verborgenes Sein der Wirklichkeit vertrauend angenommen werden kann: Gott wäre das *Sein* alles Seienden.

b. Negativ: Wenn Gott existierte, dann wäre auch umgekehrt zu verstehen:

Warum die gründende Wirklichkeit aus sich selbst letztlich unbegründet, die sich haltende Wirklichkeit in sich selbst letztlich haltlos, die sich entwickelnde Wirklichkeit für sich selbst letztlich ziellos erscheint;

warum ihre Einheit bedroht ist durch Zerrissenheit, ihre Sinnhaftigkeit bedroht durch Sinnlosigkeit, ihre Werthaftigkeit bedroht durch Wertlosigkeit;

warum die zwischen Sein und Nichtsein schwebende Wirklichkeit letztlich der Unwirklichkeit und Nichtigkeit verdächtig ist.

Die grundsätzliche Antwort ist überall dieselbe: Weil die fragliche Wirklichkeit selbst *nicht Gott* ist, weil das Ich, die Gesellschaft, die Welt nicht mit ihrem Urgrund, Urhalt und Urziel, nicht mit ihrem Ursprung, Ursinn und Urwert, nicht mit dem Sein selbst identifiziert werden können.

2. Im Hinblick auf die besondere Fraglichkeit des *menschlichen Daseins* wäre eine hypothetische Antwort wie folgt zu formulieren: *Wenn* Gott existierte, dann *wäre* auch das Rätsel des fraglich bleibenden menschlichen Daseins grundsätzlich gelöst! Man kann es wie folgt präzisieren: Wenn Gott existierte,

- *dann könnte ich begründeterweise gegen alle Bedrohung durch Schicksal und Tod die Einheit und Identität meines menschlichen Daseins bejahen: Gott wäre ja der erste Grund auch meines Lebens;*
- *dann könnte ich begründeterweise gegen alle Bedrohung durch Leere und Sinnlosigkeit die Wahrheit und Sinnhaftigkeit meines Daseins bejahen: Gott wäre ja auch der letzte Sinn meines Lebens;*
- *dann könnte ich begründeterweise gegen alle Bedrohung durch Schuld und Verwerfung die Gutheit und Werthaftigkeit meines Daseins bejahen: Gott wäre ja dann auch die umfassende Hoffnung meines Lebens;*

– dann könnte ich begründeterweise gegen alle Bedrohung durch
das Nichts das Sein meines menschlichen Daseins vertrauensvoll bejahen: Gott wäre ja dann das Sein selbst gerade des
Menschenlebens.

Auch diese hypothetische Antwort läßt sich negativ testen:
Wenn Gott existierte, dann wäre auch bezüglich meines Daseins
zu verstehen, warum Einheit und Identität, Wahrheit und Sinnhaftigkeit, Gutheit und Werthaftigkeit des menschlichen Daseins
bedroht bleiben durch Schicksal und Tod, Leere und Sinnlosigkeit, Schuld und Verdammung, warum das Sein meines Daseins
bedroht bleibt durch das Nichts. Die grundsätzliche Antwort
wäre immer die eine und selbe: weil der Mensch *nicht Gott* ist,
weil mein menschliches Ich nicht mit seinem Urgrund, Ursinn,
Urziel, dem Sein selbst identifiziert werden kann.

Summa: Wenn Gott existierte, dann wäre die Bedingung der
Möglichkeit dieser fraglichen Wirklichkeit gegeben, ihr »Vonwoher« (im weitesten Sinn) bezeichnet. Wenn! Aber: aus der
Hypothese Gott läßt sich nicht auf Gottes Wirklichkeit
schließen.

Die Wirklichkeit

Soll uns hier kein Kurzschluß unterlaufen, so müssen wir erneut
schrittweise vorangehen. Wie sind die Alternativen zu beurteilen, und wie können wir zu einer Lösung kommen?

1. Eines muß dem Atheismus von vornherein zugegeben werden: ein *Nein zu Gott* ist *möglich*! Der Atheismus läßt sich nicht
rational eliminieren: Er ist unbewiesen[5], aber er ist zugleich auch
unwiderlegbar. Warum?

Es ist die Erfahrung der radikalen *Fraglichkeit* jeglicher Wirklichkeit, die dem Atheismus genügend Anlaß gibt, um zu behaupten und aufrechtzuerhalten: Die Wirklichkeit hat gar keinen
Urgrund, Urhalt, Urziel. Jede Rede vom Ursprung, Ursinn,
Urwert ist abzulehnen. Man kann das alles gar nicht wissen
(Agnostizismus). Ja, vielleicht ist doch Chaos, Absurdität, Illusion, Schein und nicht Sein, eben das Nichts das Letzte (Atheismus mit Tendenz zum Nihilismus).

Also: gegen die *Unmöglichkeit* des Atheismus gibt es tatsächlich keine positiven Argumente. Es kann nicht positiv widerlegt

werden, wer sagt: Es ist kein Gott! Gegen eine solche Behauptung kommt weder ein strenger Beweis noch ein Aufweis Gottes letztlich an. Diese unbewiesene Behauptung beruht letztlich auf einer *Entscheidung*, die mit der Grundentscheidung zur Wirklichkeit überhaupt in Zusammenhang steht. Die Verneinung Gottes ist rein rational nicht zu widerlegen.

2. Umgekehrt aber kann nun der Atheismus die andere Alternative auch nicht positiv ausschließen: Wie ein Nein ist auch ein *Ja zu Gott möglich*. Warum?

Es ist die *Wirklichkeit* in aller Fraglichkeit, die genügend Anlaß gibt, um nicht nur ein vertrauendes Ja zu dieser Wirklichkeit, ihrer Identität, Sinnhaftigkeit und Werthaftigkeit zu wagen, sondern zugleich auch ein Ja zu dem, ohne das die Wirklichkeit in allem Begründen letztlich unbegründet, in allem Halten letztlich haltlos, in allem Sichentwickeln letztlich ziellos erscheint: ein vertrauendes Ja also zu einem Urgrund, Urhalt und Urziel der fraglichen Wirklichkeit.

Also: es gibt tatsächlich kein schlüssiges Argument für die *Notwendigkeit* des Atheismus. Es kann auch nicht positiv widerlegt werden, wer sagt: Es ist ein Gott! Gegen ein solches von der Wirklichkeit selber her sich aufdrängendes Vertrauen kommt der Atheismus seinerseits nicht letztlich an. Auch die unwiderlegbare Bejahung Gottes beruht letztlich auf einer *Entscheidung*, die auch hier mit der Grundentscheidung zur Wirklichkeit überhaupt im Zusammenhang steht. Auch sie ist deshalb rational unwiderlegbar. Die Bejahung Gottes ist freilich auch nicht rein rational zu beweisen. Ein Patt?

3. Die Alternativen sind deutlich geworden. Und hier genau liegt nun – jenseits von »natürlicher«, »dialektischer« und »moralisch-postulierender« Theologie – der entscheidende Knoten zur Lösung der Fragen nach der Existenz Gottes:

– Wenn *Gott ist, ist er die Antwort auf die radikale Fraglichkeit der Wirklichkeit.*
– Daß *Gott ist, kann aber weder stringent aufgrund eines Beweises oder Aufweises der reinen Vernunft, noch unbedingt aufgrund eines moralischen Postulats der praktischen Vernunft, noch immer allein aufgrund des biblischen Zeugnisses angenommen werden.*
– Daß *Gott ist, kann letztlich nur in einem – in der Wirklichkeit selbst begründeten – Vertrauen angenommen werden.*

Schon dieses vertrauende Sicheinlassen auf einen letzten Grund, Halt und Sinn der Wirklichkeit wird im allgemeinen Sprachgebrauch zu Recht als »Glauben« an Gott bezeichnet (»Gottesglaube«, »Gottvertrauen«). Ein »Glauben« in einem durchaus weiten Sinn, insofern solcher Glaube nicht notwendig von der christlichen Verkündigung provoziert sein muß, sondern auch Nichtchristen möglich ist. Die Menschen, die sich zu einem solchen Glauben bekennen, werden zu Recht, ob Christen oder Nichtchristen, als »Gottgläubige« bezeichnet. Demgegenüber erscheint der Atheismus, insofern er Verweigerung des Vertrauens zu Gott ist, wiederum im allgemeinen Sprachgebrauch durchaus zu Recht als »Unglaube.«

Also: Nicht nur bezüglich der Wirklichkeit als solcher, sondern auch bezüglich ihrem Urgrund, Urhalt und Ursinn kommt der Mensch um um eine freie, wenn auch nicht beliebige *Entscheidung* keineswegs herum: Da sich die Wirklichkeit und ihr Urgrund, Urhalt und Ursinn nicht mit zwingender Evidenz aufdrängen, bleibt Raum für die Freiheit des Menschen. Der Mensch soll sich entscheiden, ohne intellektuellen Zwang. Atheismus wie Gottesglaube sind ein Wagnis – und ein Risiko. Alle Kritik an den Gottesbeweisen zielte darauf: Glaube an Gott hat Entscheidungscharakter, und umgekehrt: Entscheidung für Gott hat Glaubenscharakter.

Um eine Entscheidung also geht es in der Gottesfrage, die freilich eine »Stufe« tiefer liegt als die angesichts des Nihilismus notwendige Entscheidung für oder gegen die Wirklichkeit als solche: Sobald diese letzte Tiefe für den Einzelnen aufbricht und sich die Frage stellt, wird die Entscheidung unumgänglich. Auch in der Gottesfrage gilt: Wer nicht wählt, wählt: er hat gewählt, nicht zu wählen. Stimmenthaltung in einer Vertrauensabstimmung zur Gottesfrage bedeutet Vertrauensverweigerung.

Doch leider stehen die »Tiefe« (oder »Höhe«) einer Wahrheit und die Sicherheit ihrer Annahme durch den Menschen in umgekehrtem Verhältnis: Je banaler die Wahrheit (»Binsenwahrheit«, »Platitude«), um so größer die Sicherheit. Je bedeutsamer die Wahrheit (etwa im Vergleich zur arithmetischen die ästhetische, moralische, religiöse Wahrheit), um so geringer die Sicherheit. Denn: Je »tiefer« die Wahrheit für mich ist, um so mehr muß ich mich für sie erst aufschließen, innerlich bereiten, mich mit Intellekt, Wille, Gefühl auf sie einstellen, um zu jener echten »Gewißheit« zu kommen, die etwas anderes ist als abgesicherte »Sicherheit«. Eine für mich äußerlich unsichere, von Zweifeln bedrohte *tiefe* Wahrheit, die ein tiefes Engagement meinerseits voraussetzt, kann viel mehr Erkenntniswert besitzen als eine sichere oder gar »absolut« sichere *banale* Wahrheit[6].

Doch aus der Möglichkeit des Ja oder Nein folgt auch hier nicht die Gleichgültigkeit des Ja oder Nein: Das Nein zu Gott bedeutet ein letztlich *unbegründetes* Grundvertrauen zur Wirklichkeit (wenn nicht schon überhaupt Grundmißtrauen). Das Ja zu Gott aber bedeutet ein letztlich *begründetes* Grundvertrauen zur Wirklichkeit. Wer Gott bejaht, weiß, *warum* er der Wirklichkeit vertraut. Von einem Patt, das soll gleich deutlicher werden, kann also keine Rede sein.

4. Der *Atheismus* lebt – wenn schon nicht aus einem nihilistischen Grundmißtrauen – so jedenfalls aus einem letztlich *unbegründeten* Grundvertrauen: Im Nein zu Gott entscheidet sich der Mensch gegen einen letzten Grund, Halt, ein letztes Ziel der Wirklichkeit. Im agnostischen Atheismus erweist sich das Ja zur Wirklichkeit als letztlich unbegründet und inkonsequent: ein frei treibendes, nirgendwo verankertes und deshalb paradoxes Grundvertrauen. Im weniger oberflächlichen, konsequent nihilistischen Atheismus ist ein Ja zur Wirklichkeit wegen des radikalen Grundmißtrauens überhaupt nicht möglich. Der Atheismus vermag jedenfalls *keine Bedingung der Möglichkeit* der fraglichen Wirklichkeit anzugeben: Er läßt deshalb eine radikale Rationalität vermissen, was er freilich oft verschleiert durch ein rationalistisches, aber im Grund irrationales Vertrauen zur menschlichen Vernunft.

Der Preis, den der Atheismus für sein Nein zahlt, ist offenkundig. Er setzt sich der Gefährdung durch eine letztliche Grundlosigkeit, Haltlosigkeit, Ziellosigkeit aus: der möglichen Sinnlosigkeit, Wertlosigkeit, Nichtigkeit der Wirklichkeit überhaupt. Der Atheist setzt sich, wenn er sich dessen bewußt wird, auch ganz persönlich der Gefährdung durch eine letzte Verlassenheit, Bedrohtheit und Verfallenheit aus mit den Folgen des Zweifels, der Angst, ja der Verzweiflung. Dies alles natürlich nur, wenn Atheismus Ernstfall und nicht intellektuelle Attitüde, snobistische Koketterie oder gedankenlose Oberflächlichkeit ist.

Für den Atheisten bleiben jene letzten und doch zugleich nächsten und durch kein Frageverbot zu verdrängenden ewigen Fragen des menschlichen Lebens unbeantwortet, die sich nicht nur an den Grenzen des Menschenlebens, sondern mitten im persönlichen und gesellschaftlichen Leben stellen. Wenn wir uns an die Fragen Kants halten:

Was können wir *wissen*? Warum gibt es überhaupt etwas? Warum ist nicht nichts? Woher kommt der Mensch und wohin geht er? Warum ist die Welt, wie sie ist? Was ist der letzte Grund und Sinn aller Wirklichkeit?

Was sollen wir *tun*? Warum tun wir, was wir tun? Warum und wem sind wir letztlich verantwortlich? Was verdient schlechthinige Verachtung und was Liebe? Was ist der Sinn von Treue und Freundschaft, aber auch der von Leid und Schuld? Was ist für den Menschen entscheidend?

Was dürfen wir *hoffen*? Wozu sind wir da? Was soll das Ganze? Was bleibt uns: der Tod, der am Ende alles sinnlos macht? Was soll uns Mut zum Leben und was Mut zum Sterben geben?

Also alles Fragen, die aufs Ganze gehen: Fragen, nicht nur für die Sterbenden, sondern für die Lebenden. Nicht nur für Schwächlinge und Uninformierte, sondern gerade für die Informierten und Engagierten. Nicht Ausflüchte vor dem Handeln, sondern Anreiz zum Handeln. Gibt es etwas, was uns in all dem trägt, was uns nie verzweifeln läßt? Ein Beständiges in allem Wandel, ein Unbedingtes in allem Bedingten, ein Absolutes bei der überall erfahrenen Relativierung? Alle diese Fragen bleiben im Atheismus letztlich unbeantwortet.

5. Der *Gottesglaube* lebt aus einem letztlich *begründeten* Grundvertrauen: im Ja zu Gott entscheidet sich der Mensch für einen letzten Grund, Halt, Sinn der Wirklichkeit. Im Gottesglauben erweist sich das Ja zur Wirklichkeit als letztlich begründet und konsequent: ein in der letzten Tiefe, im Grund der Gründe verankertes Grundvertrauen. Der Gottesglaube als das radikale Grundvertrauen vermag also die *Bedingung der Möglichkeit* der fraglichen Wirklichkeit anzugeben. Insofern zeigt er eine radikale Rationalität, die freilich nicht einfach mit Rationalismus verwechselt werden darf.

Der Preis, den der Gottesglaube für sein Ja erhält, ist ebenso offenkundig: Weil ich mich statt für das Grundlose für einen Urgrund, statt für das Haltlose für einen Urhalt, statt für das Ziellose für ein Urziel vertrauensvoll entscheide, vermag ich nun begründeterweise bei aller Zerrissenheit eine Einheit, bei aller Sinnlosigkeit einen Sinn, bei aller Wertlosigkeit einen Wert der Wirklichkeit von Welt und Mensch zu erkennen. Und bei aller

Ungewißheit und Ungesichertheit, Verlassenheit und Ungeborgenheit, Bedrohtheit und Verfallenheit auch meines eigenen Daseins ist mir vom letzten Ursprung, Ursinn und Urwert her eine letzte Gewißheit, Geborgenheit und Beständigkeit *geschenkt*. Gewiß nicht einfach abstrakt, isoliert von den Mitmenschen, sondern immer in einem konkreten Bezug zum menschlichen Du: Wie soll der Mensch erfahren, was von Gott Angenommensein heißt, wenn er von keinem einzigen Menschen angenommen ist? Ich kann mir die letzte Gewißheit, Geborgenheit und Beständigkeit nicht einfach selber nehmen oder schaffen. Es ist die letzte Wirklichkeit selbst, die mich in verschiedenster Weise dazu herausfordert, zu ihr Ja zu sagen, bei der sozusagen die »Initiative« liegt. Die letzte Wirklichkeit selber ermöglicht mir, daß bei allem Zweifel, aller Angst und Verzweiflung die Geduld im Blick auf die Gegenwart, die Dankbarkeit im Blick auf die Vergangenheit und die Hoffnung im Blick auf die Zukunft letztlich begründet ist.

So erhalten jene letzten und zugleich nächsten und durch kein Frageverbot zu verdrängenden religiös-gesellschaftlichen Fragen des Menschen, von denen gerade eben unter den Leitfragen Kants die Rede war, eine zumindest grundsätzliche Antwort, mit der der Mensch in der Welt von heute leben kann: eine Antwort aus der Wirklichkeit Gottes.

6. Inwiefern also ist der Gottesglaube *rational verantwortet*? Der Mensch erscheint nicht indifferent gegenüber der Entscheidung zwischen Atheismus und Gottesglaube. Er findet sich vorbelastet vor: An sich möchte er die Welt und sich selbst verstehen, möchte er auf die Fraglichkeit der Wirklichkeit antworten, möchte er die Bedingung der Möglichkeit der fraglichen Wirklichkeit erkennen, möchte er um einen letzten Grund, einen letzten Halt und ein letztes Ziel der Wirklichkeit wissen.

Doch auch hier bleibt der Mensch frei. Er kann Nein sagen. Er kann mit Skepsis alles aufkeimende Vertrauen zu einem letzten Grund, Halt und Ziel ignorieren oder gar ersticken: Er kann, vielleicht durchaus ehrlich und wahrhaftig, ein Nichtwissen-Können bezeugen (agnostischer Atheismus), oder gar eine durchgängige Nichtigkeit, eine Grund- und Ziellosigkeit, Sinn- und Wertlosigkeit der ohnehin fraglichen Wirklichkeit behaupten (nihilistischer Atheismus). Ohne Bereitschaft zur vertrauenden Anerkenntnis Gottes, die praktische Konsequenzen hat, gibt es keine rational sinnvolle Erkenntnis Gottes. Und selbst wenn der Mensch Ja zu Gott gesagt hat, bleibt das Nein eine ständige Versuchung.

Schließt sich jedoch der Mensch nicht ab, sondern öffnet er sich der sich ihm öffnenden Wirklichkeit ganz, entzieht er sich nicht dem letzten Grund, Halt und Ziel der Wirklichkeit, sondern wagt er es, sich dran- und hinzugeben: so erkennt er, *indem er dies tut, daß er das Richtige, ja das »Allervernünftigste« tut.* Denn: was sich *im voraus* nicht zwingend beweisen oder aufweisen läßt, erfährt er *im* Akt des anerkennenden Erkennens selbst (rationabile obsequium im Vollzug): Die Wirklichkeit manifestiert sich in ihrer letzten Tiefe. Ihr letzter Grund, Halt, Ziel, ihr Ursprung, Ursinn und Urwert tut sich ihm auf, sobald er sich selber auftut. Und zugleich erfährt er in aller Fraglichkeit eine letzte Vernünftigkeit seiner eigenen Vernunft: das grundsätzliche Vertrauen zur Vernunft erscheint von daher nicht als irrational, sondern als rational begründet.

Das alles besagt also *keine äußere Rationalität,* die eine abgesicherte *Sicherheit* verschaffen konnte: Die Existenz Gottes wird nicht zuerst vernünftig und zwingend bewiesen oder aufgewiesen und dann geglaubt, was so die Rationalität des Gottesglaubens garantierte. Nicht zuerst rationale Erkenntnis Gottes und dann vertrauende Anerkenntnis. Die verborgene Wirklichkeit Gottes zwingt sich der Vernunft nicht auf.

Es besagt vielmehr *eine innere Rationalität,* die eine grundlegende *Gewißheit* gewähren kann: Im Vollzug, in der »Praxis« des wagenden Vertrauens zu Gottes Wirklichkeit erfährt der Mensch bei aller Anfechtung durch Zweifel die Vernünftigkeit seines Vertrauens: gegründet in der erfahrbaren letzten Identität, Sinn- und Werthaftigkeit der Wirklichkeit, in ihrem aufscheinenden Urgrund, Ursinn und Urwert. Dies also ist das rational verantwortete Wagnis des Gottesglaubens, durch welches der Mensch gegen alle Zweifel in eine letzte Gewißheit eingeht, die er gegen alle Zweifel stets neu bewähren muß, aus der ihn aber auch. in Grenzsituationen keine Angst, keine Verzweiflung, kein agnostischer oder nihilistischer Atheismus ohne seine Zustimmung je heraustreiben kann.

7. Der *Zusammenhang zwischen Grundvertrauen und Gottesglauben* ist nun offensichtlich: Obwohl sich – material gesehen – das Grundvertrauen auf die Wirklichkeit als solche (und auf das eigene Dasein) bezieht und der Gottesglaube auf Urgrund, Urhalt und Ursinn der Wirklichkeit, so zeigen Grundvertrauen und

Gottesglauben (»Gottvertrauen«) formal gesehen eine analoge Struktur, die im materialen Zusammenhang (bei allem Unterschied) von Grundvertrauen und Gottesglauben ihren Grund hat. Wie das Grundvertrauen, so ist auch der Gottesglaube

– eine Sache nicht nur der menschlichen Vernunft, sondern des ganzen konkreten lebendigen Menschen: mit Geist und Leib, Vernunft und Trieben, in seiner ganz bestimmten geschichtlichen Situation, in der Abhängigkeit von Traditionen, Autoritäten, Denkgewohnheiten, Wertschemata, mit seinem persönlichen Interesse und seiner gesellschaftlichen Verflochtenheit. Von dieser »Sache« kann der Mensch nicht reden und sich selber aus der »Sache« heraushalten;
– also überrational: Wie für die Wirklichkeit der Wirklichkeit, so gibt es auch für die Wirklichkeit Gottes keinen logisch zwingenden Beweis. Der Gottesbeweis ist so wenig wie die Liebe logisch zwingend. Das Gottesverhältnis ist ein Vertrauensverhältnis;
– aber nicht irrational: Es gibt eine von der menschlichen Erfahrung ausgehende und an die freie menschliche Entscheidung appellierende Reflexion über die Wirklichkeit Gottes. Der Gottesglaube läßt sich gegenüber einer rationalen Kritik rechtfertigen. Er hat einen Anhalt an der erfahrenen Fraglichkeit der Wirklichkeit, die letzte Fragen nach der Bedingung ihrer Möglichkeit aufgibt;
– somit eine nicht blinde und wirklichkeitsleere, sondern eine begründete, wirklichkeitsbezogene und so im konkreten Leben rational verantwortete Entscheidung: Ihre Relevanz wird an der Wirklichkeit der Welt und des Menschen für die existentiellen Bedürfnisse wie die gesellschaftlichen Verhältnisse ersichtlich;
– im konkreten Bezug zum Mitmenschen vollzogen: Ohne die Erfahrung eines Angenommenseins durch Menschen scheint die Erfahrung eines Angenommenseins durch Gott schwierig zu sein;
– nicht für alle Fälle gefaßt, sondern stets neu zu realisieren: Nie ist der Gottesglaube gegenüber dem Atheismus durch rationale Argumente unangreifbar und krisenfest abgesichert. Der Gottesglaube ist stets bedroht und muß gegenüber den andrängenden Zweifeln stets in neuer Entscheidung realisiert, durchgehalten, gelebt, errungen werden: der Mensch bleibt auch gegenüber Gott selbst in den unaufhebbaren Gegensatz zwi-

schen Vertrauen und Mißtrauen, Glauben und Unglauben gestellt.

8. Was also »hilft« – wenn wir auf das Entwickelte zurücksehen – dem Atheisten? Nicht ein rational stringenter Gottesbeweis, nicht der Appell an ein unbedingtes »Du sollst«, nicht eine intellektuell zwingenwollende Apologetik, nicht eine von oben dekretierende Dogmatik. Sondern:

Zunächst – zumindest wo eine Berufung auf die biblische Botschaft direkt nichts fruchtet – die *solidarische Reflexion* über die Wirklichkeit der Welt und des Menschen anhand gemeinsamer Erfahrungen in Hinblick auf jene letzten und ersten Fragen: also nicht nur die Menschen dort, wo sie stehen, ab- und herausholen, sondern mit ihnen verweilen und zuerst ihre Welt bedenken und erschließen, in den Alltagsfragen die großen Lebensfragen entdecken, alles nicht in Belehrung, sondern im Gespräch.

Zugleich – und vielleicht wichtiger – das *vorpraktizierte Vertrauen*, welches zum Vertrauen auffordert, das gelebte Wagnis als Einladung zum selben Wagnis: ein Vorspringen ins Wasser, welches die Möglichkeit des Getragenwerdens praktisch »beweist« und zugleich zum Nachspringen aufruft: also ein durch die Praxis gedecktes Zeugnis für den Gottesglauben.

Schließlich – und im Grund allein – das *eigene Wagnis des Vertrauens*: Schwimmen kann man nur selber lernen. Wie andere Erfahrungen ist auch diese Grunderfahrung erst im Nachvollzug einsichtig.

Vieldeutigkeit des Gottesbegriffs

Will man dem, was hier mit Urgrund, Urhalt und Urziel, mit Ursprung, Ursinn und Urwert bezeichnet ist, einen Namen geben, dann wird man auf *das Wort »Gott«* nicht verzichten können. »Gott« ist zwar, wie Martin Buber in seinen bewegenden Betrachtungen zur »Gottesfinsternis« ausführt, »das beladenste aller Menschenworte«[7]: Keines ist so mißbraucht, besudelt, zerfetzt: die Menschen haben es in Religionsparteiungen zerrissen, haben dafür getötet, sind dafür gestorben: kein vergleichbares Wort, um das Höchste zu bezeichnen, und doch so oft Tarnung für die übelsten Gottlosigkeiten. Aber gerade weil es für den Menschen – und auch für die Atheisten, die ja nicht irgend etwas, sondern Gott ablehnen – so viel bedeutet, kann es nicht aufgegeben werden. Wer es vermeidet, ist zu achten; das Wort kann nicht reingewaschen werden. Aber vergessen läßt es sich auch nicht. Es kann vielmehr aufgehoben werden und – mit Konsequenzen für den Menschen – neu bedacht und selbstverständlich auch mit anderen Worten umschrieben werden. Also statt nicht mehr von Gott zu reden oder statt in gleicher Weise von Gott zu reden, käme heute alles darauf an, behutsam in neuer Weise von Gott reden zu lernen! Wenn eine Theologie nicht Logos von Gott wäre, sondern nur vom Menschen und von Mitmenschlichkeit redete, wäre sie ehrlicherweise – wie bei Ludwig Feuerbach – Anthropologie zu nennen.

Freilich: Auch für den Gottesglauben im beschriebenen Sinne bleibt das Wort *»Gott« vieldeutig*. Auch dem Gottesglauben ist Gott nirgendwo in unvermittelter Direktheit und gegenständlicher Ausdrücklichkeit gegeben. Nur wider den Augenschein der Welt, untergründig und ungegenständlich scheint Gott für den Glauben in den vordergründig erfahrbaren Phänomenen von der Tiefe her auf und bleibt dabei der Unbegreifliche. Jedenfalls ohne augenscheinlich feststellbare Eindeutigkeit: nicht nur leicht zu übersehen oder zu bestreiten, sondern auch sehr verschieden zu interpretieren. Auch wenn der Glaube eine ganzheitliche erfahrungshafte Einsicht ist, so läßt sich diese Einsicht in der Reflexion doch außerordentlich verschieden begrifflich auslegen. Und um die Ergänzung, Klärung und Absicherung der lebendiggefüllten, aber vielleicht auch oberflächlichen und oft einseitigen Glaubenserfahrung durch die gedankliche Reflexion mußte sich der Mensch immer wieder bemühen. Erst in der denkenden Reflexion wird die ganzheitliche Erfahrung begrifflich expliziert, wird sie logisch durchschaubar und damit auch anderen begrifflich klar mitteilbar gemacht. Die Reflexion lebt von der Erfahrung. Aber die Erfahrung bedarf der kritisch erhellenden und absichernden Reflexion.

Die ganze *Philosophie* von den Vorsokratikern bis Hegel, aber auch noch die darauf folgenden Anti-Theologien von Feuerbach und Marx, Nietzsche und Heidegger kreisen um die Gottesfrage, die, wie W. Weischedel ausführlich dargelegt hat, die zentrale Problematik der Philosophiegeschichte ausmacht[8]. Dabei wird deutlich, wie unter dem Namen »Gott« zwar sehr Verschiedenes, aber doch nicht völlig Disparates, sondern etwas Verwandtes verstanden wird: »Das Göttliche der frühen griechischen Denker in seiner unmittelbaren Anwesenheit in der Welt ist nicht das gleiche wie der Schöpfergott der christlich bestimmten Philosophischen Theologie. Der Gott als letztes Ziel alles Strebens in der Wirklichkeit, wie ihn Aristoteles konzipiert, unterscheidet sich von dem das Sittengesetz und die Glückseligkeit garantierenden Gott Kants. Der in der Vernunft ergreifbare Gott des Thomas von Aquino oder Hegels ist von dem ins Unnennbare sich entziehenden Gott des Dionysios Areopagita oder des Nicolaus von Cues verschieden. Und auch der bloß moralische Gott, den Nietzsche bekämpft, ist nicht das die Wirklichkeit haltende höchste Seiende, als das Heidegger den Gott der Metaphysik versteht. Und doch ist immer und überall unter dem Namen ›Gott‹ etwas Verwandtes gedacht: das, was alle Wirklichkeit, als durchwaltendes oder überragendes Prinzip, bestimmt[9].«

Der allgemeine Gottesbegriff ist ambivalent, vieldeutig. Die Philosophiegeschichte selber ruft nach Klärung. Aber sie selber weckt Zweifel, ob sie diese Klärung zu schaffen vermag. Es scheint zum Wesen dieses so erkannten Gottes der Philosophen zu gehören, daß er *letztlich unbestimmt* bleibt.

Insofern wollten denn die *Religionen* immer mehr als Philosophie sein. Religion entspringt gewiß nicht einem streng geführten rationalen Gottesbeweis und überhaupt nicht der noch so umsichtigen gedanklichen Reflexion. Freilich kommt die Religion auch nicht nur aus den irrationalen, geistfremden psychologischen Schichten des Menschen. Vielmehr gründet sie, wie die Religionspsychologie deutlich macht, in einer erfahrungsmäßigen Einheit von Erkennen, Wollen und Fühlen, das nicht als eigene Leistung, sondern als eine Antwort auf eine wie auch immer geartete Begegnung mit Gott oder eine Erfahrung von ihm verstanden wird. Die meisten Religionen berufen sich auf ein Erscheinen des an sich verborgenen und so vieldeutigen Gottes. Und insofern führt nun unsere Betrachtung von selbst auf die Betrachtung der konkreten Religionen hin, die versuchen, auf die Frage nach dem Verständnis Gottes und dem Verständnis des Menschen eine konkrete Antwort für Theorie und Praxis zu geben.

Freilich dürfen wir bei einer solchen Zuwendung zu den konkreten Religionen nicht hinter die Aufklärung, die nach Kant »der Ausgang des Menschen aus seiner selbst verschuldeten Unmündigkeit« ist[10], zurückfallen, dürfen wir das aus der Auseinandersetzung mit der neueren Religionskritik Resultierende nicht vergessen. Wenn von Gott in der heutigen Zeit ehrlich geredet werden soll, dann jedenfalls unter Berücksichtigung des *neuzeitlichen Horizonts,* der Glaubenden wie Nichtglaubenden eine Läuterung und Vertiefung des Gottesverständnisses ermöglicht und der hier nach Heinz Zahrnt zusammenfassend umschrieben werden soll[11]:

a. Heutiges Gottesverständnis setzt die neuzeitliche *wissenschaftliche Welterklärung* voraus: Wetter und Schlachtensiege, Krankheiten und Heilungen, Glück und Unglück der Menschen, Gruppen und Völker werden nicht mehr durch den direkten Eingriff Gottes, sondern durch natürliche Gründe erklärt. Diese Zurückdrängung Gottes aus der Welt bedeutet eine *Chance*: weil damit deutlicher wird, was Gott *nicht* ist, daß er nicht einfach mit Natur- und Geschichtsvorgängen gleichgesetzt werden kann. Erkennen wir den Auszug aus den Zweitursachen als die mögliche Voraussetzung für eine persönlichere, innere Gottesbegegnung? Oder betreiben wir nach der aufklärerischen Entgötterung der Natur nur eine Wiedervergöttlichung von Endlichem in neuen Formen?

b. Heutiges Gottesverständnis setzt das neuzeitliche *Autoritätsverständnis* voraus: Es wird keine Wahrheit am Urteil der Vernunft vorbei nur auf die Autorität der Bibel oder der Tradition oder der Kirche hin, sondern immer nur in kritischer Prüfung angenommen. Die Tatsache, daß der Gottesglaube aufgehört hat, eine nur autoritative Setzung, eine traditionelle oder konfessionelle Angelegenheit und damit eine weltanschauliche Selbstverständlichkeit zu sein, bedeutet eine *Chance*: weil der Mensch so, wie es seiner Würde und Gottes Ehre entspricht, nun wieder neu zur persönlichen Aneignung des Glaubens der Väter herausgefordert wird. Nützt man den für die menschliche Autonomie freigewordenen Raum so, daß die Menschen Gott statt als willenlose Knechte, welche wider ihre Vernunft für wahr halten, jetzt als Mündige mit ganzem Herzen vertrauen? Oder liefert man sich nach der aufklärerischen Entmythologisierung der Autorität vielleicht nur anderen Mächten aus?

c. Heutiges Gottesverständnis setzt die *Ideologiekritik* voraus: Aufdeckung des gesellschaftlichen Mißbrauchs der Religion durch Staat oder Kirche, rationale Bloßlegung des Interesses von Personen oder Gruppen bei der Inanspruchnahme des Herrgotts zur Begründung des Gottesgnadentums großer oder kleiner Herren, als Hüter und Garanten der bestehenden weithin ungerechten Ordnung. Auch diese Ausklammerung Gottes aus der Verquickung mit den politisch-gesellschaftlichen Machtverhältnissen bedeutet eine *Chance*: daß der Mensch wie vor den politischen Machthabern so auch vor seinem Gott ohne unwürdiges Buckeln aufrechten Ganges seinen Weg gehen darf: als Partner, nicht Untertan. Hat der heutige Mensch die aufklärerische Götterdämmerung so verstanden, daß Gott tatsächlich nicht ein Entwurf des Menschen aus eigensüchtigen Bedürfnissen, sondern der wirklich Andere ist? Oder versucht er doch wieder, Gott in irgendeinen Weltprozeß ideologisch einzuordnen?

d. Heutiges Gottesverständnis setzt die neuzeitliche *Bewußtseinsverschiebung vom Jenseits zum Diesseits* voraus: Durch den Säkularisierungsprozeß wird die Eigenständigkeit der diesseitigen Ordnungen (Wissenschaft, Wirtschaft, Politik, Staat, Gesellschaft, Recht, Kultur) immer mehr nicht nur theoretisch erfahren, sondern auch praktisch verwirklicht. Aber gerade diese Verabschiedung der reinen Vertröstung auf ein Jenseits und die verstärkte Konzentration auf das Diesseits bedeuten eine *Chance*: daß das Leben, welches vielleicht an Tiefe verloren hat, nun doch an Dichte gewinnen könnte. Haben wir erkannt, wie Gott damit dem Menschen gerade in diesem Leben gleichsam näher auf den Leib rückt, ihn jetzt mitten in seiner Profanität herausfordert? Oder haben wir simpel die Säkularisierung zum Säkularismus verweltanschaulicht und Gott aus dem Sinn verloren als den, der uns in diesem Leben jederzeit unbedingt angeht: der immanent Transzendente?

e. Heutiges Gottesverständnis setzt eine neuzeitliche *Ausrichtung auf die Zukunft* voraus: Der Mensch richtet heute seinen Blick nicht so sehr sehnsüchtig nach oben und auch nur historisierend nach rückwärts, sondern möglichst nach vorn. Die bewußte Erziehung der Zukunftsdimension, die aktive Planung und Gestaltung der Zukunft, bedeutet eine *Chance*: weil so die Zukunftsdimension auch der christlichen Verkündigung neu entdeckt und ernstgenommen werden kann. Wird Gott als der Kommende und als die wahre Zukunft des Menschen und der Welt ernstgenommen? Oder kommt es vielleicht zu einem völligen Vergessen der Vergangenheit, zur Preisgabe der Erinnerung an Entscheidendes in der Geschichte und damit zur Orientierungslosigkeit in der Gegenwart?

Die Gefahren der neuzeitlichen Entwicklung müssen also gesehen, aber zugleich ihre Chancen entschieden genutzt werden. Nimmt man die Geschichte der Aufklärung der Menschheit ernst, wird man jedes künftige Gottesverständnis vor folgendem Horizont sehen müssen:

- *Keine naiv-anthropologische Vorstellung: Gott als ein im wört-lichen oder räumlichen Sinne »über« der Welt wohnendes »höchstes Wesen«.*
- *Keine aufgeklärt-deistische Vorstellung: Gott als ein im geisti-gen oder metaphysischen Sinn »außerhalb« der Welt in einem außerweltlichen Jenseits (Hinterwelt) wesendes, verobjekti-viertes, verdinglichtes Gegenüber.*
- *Sondern ein einheitliches Wirklichkeitsverständnis: Gott in dieser Welt, und diese Welt in Gott. Gott nicht nur als Teil der Wirklichkeit ein (höchstes) Endliches neben Endlichem. Son-dern das Unendliche im Endlichen, das Absolute im Relativen. Gott als die diesseitig-jenseitige, transzendent-immanente wirklichste Wirklichkeit im Herzen der Dinge, im Menschen und in der Menschheitsgeschichte.*

Von diesem Horizont her wird schon jetzt für das später zu betrachtende *christliche* Gottesverständnis deutlich: Jenseits von einem primitiven anthropomorphen Biblizismus oder aber einer nur scheinbar überlegenen abstrakten theologischen Philosophie hätte christliches Gottesverständnis darauf zu achten, daß der »Gott der Philosophen« und der christliche Gott nicht billig und oberflächlich (wie bei den alten oder neuen Apologeten und Scholastikern) harmonisiert, aber auch nicht (wie bei den philo-sophischen Aufklärern oder den biblizistischen Theologen) dis-soziiert werden. Sondern daß christliches Gottesverständnis den »Gott der Philosophen« im christlichen Gott nach bestem He-gelschem Sinn des Wortes – negative, positive, supereminenter – *aufhebt*: kritisch negierend, positiv bejahend, überbietend über-steigend. Auf diese Weise würde dann der in jeder Weise *vieldeu-tige* Gottesbegriff des allgemeinen Menschenverstandes und der Philosophie im christlichen Gottesverständnis unmißverständ-lich und unverwechselbar *eindeutig*.

Dies freilich erfordert von der christlichen Theologie erheb-liche Anstrengungen.

Die Aufgabe der Theologie

»Eins möchte ich den Theologen sagen, etwas, das sie wissen und die anderen wissen sollten: Sie bewahren die einzige Wahrheit, die tiefer reicht als die Wahrheit der Wissenschaft, auf der das Atomzeitalter beruht. Sie bewahren ein Wissen vom Wesen des

Menschen, das tiefer wurzelt als die Rationalität der Neuzeit. Der Augenblick kommt immer unweigerlich, in dem man, wenn das Planen scheitert, nach dieser Wahrheit fragt und fragen wird! Die heutige bürgerliche Stellung der Kirche ist kein Beweis dafür, daß die Menschen nach der christlichen Wahrheit wirklich fragen. Überzeugen wird diese Wahrheit, wo sie gelebt wird.« So sagt der Physiker und Philosoph Carl Friedrich von Weizsäcker an die Adresse der Theologen[12].

1. Wir blicken zunächst zurück auf den Weg, den wir theologisch bis hierher gegangen sind. Die komplexen Fragen theologischer Methodik können hier nicht behandelt, wohl aber – zumindest für den theologisch Interessierten – einige Abgrenzungen vollzogen werden. Man wird uns bei allen dialektischen theologischen Aussagen *nicht* vorwerfen können, daß wir – gleichsam senkrecht von oben – im traditionellen Sinn »*dialektische Theologie*«[13] betrieben haben: Methodisch wurde möglichst konsequent immer wieder neu der Ausgang »von unten« gesucht, von den nächsten Fragen des Menschen, von der menschlichen Erfahrung her. Alles im Hinblick auf eine rationale Verantwortung des Glaubens heute. Denn:

– *Angesichts des Nihilismus darf die Fundamentalproblematik der Fraglichkeit der Wirklichkeit überhaupt und des menschlichen Daseins nicht mit Hilfe der Bibel übersprungen werden.*
– *Angesichts des Atheismus darf die Wirklichkeit Gottes nicht mit Hilfe der Bibel bloß behauptet werden.*

Die Phänomene der Religion, der Philosophie, des allgemein menschlichen Vorverständnisses erforderten eine adäquate Antwort. Natürlich ist das nicht unsere ganze Antwort: Was von der menschlichen Erfahrung her analysiert wurde, kann und muß später theologisch von der christlichen Botschaft her kritisch gedeutet werden.

Aber haben wir nun nicht mit all dem »natürliche Theologie« getrieben? So können wohl nur Theologen, in diesem Fall besonders protestantische Theologen fragen. Trotz unseres Einsetzens bei den natürlichen Fragen und Bedürfnissen des Menschen haben wir *nicht* – gleichsam im unteren Stockwerk – im traditionellen katholischen Sinn »*natürliche Theologie*«[14] getrieben. Denn:

– *Es wird keine autonome Vernunft angenommen, die stringent Fundamente des Glaubens demonstrieren könnte, welche mit dem Glauben selbst nichts zu tun haben. Vielmehr wurde aufgezeigt, daß auch schon die Vorfragen des christlichen Glaubens – die Wirklichkeit der fraglichen Wirklichkeit und die Wirklichkeit Gottes – nicht mit bloßer Vernunft, sondern nur in einem gläubigen Vertrauen oder einem vertrauenden Glauben (im weiten Sinn des Wortes) erkannt werden können.*

– *Es gibt also keinen kontinuierlichen, stufenweisen vernünftigen »Prozessionsweg« des Menschen zu Gott. Sondern es handelt sich um ein stets neues Wagnis und Risiko des Vertrauens.*
– *Es wird auch keine Eigenmächtigkeit des Menschen behauptet, in der der Mensch sich Gottes bemächtigt. Vielmehr wird vom Menschen ein Sichöffnen gegenüber der Wirklichkeit, ein Antworten auf ihren Anruf und Anspruch, ein Empfangen ihrer Identität, Sinnhaftigkeit und Werthaftigkeit, ein Anerkennen ihres letzten Grundes, Haltes und Zieles erwartet.*
– *Also alles in allem keine »Praeambula fidei« als rationalen Unterbau der Dogmatik aufgrund einer rationalen Argumentation der reinen Vernunft. Sondern ein Aufsuchen »des« heutigen Menschen an dem Ort, wo er tatsächlich lebt, um die Kunde von Gott in Beziehung zu setzen, zu dem, was ihn bewegt.*

Auf diese Weise können wir den verschiedenen faktisch nun einmal gegebenen »weltanschaulichen« Positionen der Nichtchristen kritisch gerecht werden, ohne sie theologisch umzudeuten: sowohl der Position des nihilistischen Atheisten wie der des nicht-nihilistischen (agnostischen) Atheisten wie schließlich auch der des nichtchristlichen Gottgläubigen, sei es im säkularen Kontext, sei es in dem der Weltreligionen.

Auch in der hier vorgesehenen theologischen Deutung – dies sei vorausgreifend bemerkt – wird Gott den Primat behalten und das Evangelium für den Christen das entscheidende Kriterium bleiben. Von der christlichen Botschaft her wird deutlich werden:

a. In der Wirklichkeit der Welt wird Gott als wirklich erfahren, weil er sich selber erschließt. Gott hat verborgen die Initiative: Gott zu erkennen ist möglich, weil Gott sich zu erkennen gibt. Gottesbegegnung ist, wo und wie immer, Gottes Geschenk. Des Menschen »Aufweis« von Gottes Wirklichkeit gründet immer in Gottes Selbsterweis in der Wirklichkeit für den Menschen.

b. Vom Menschen wird keine neutrale Stellungnahme erwartet,

sondern ein Erkennen im Vertrauen auf die sich ihm eröffnende Wahrheit Gottes: Insofern ist jegliches glaubende Vertrauen des Menschen, wo und wie immer, eine Wirkung des in der Wirklichkeit der Welt wirkenden Gottes. Und dies bedeutet für den Menschen stets eine Art Umkehr: Abwendung von seinem Egoismus, Zuwendung zum ganz Anderen.

c. Das Evangelium wird das entscheidende Kriterium bleiben: Es gibt nicht einfach Antwort auf unsere menschlichen Fragen, sondern verändert schon unser menschliches, oft allzu menschliches Fragen. Es ist Antwort auf diese veränderten Fragen. Insofern ist es Kritik, Reinigung und Vertiefung der menschlichen Bedürfnisse. Christliche Theologie ist so in jedem Fall mehr als Bedürfnistheologie.

2. Braucht bei solcher Beachtung des neuzeitlichen Horizonts noch betont zu werden, daß Theologie *keine Totalerklärung der Wirklichkeit* anstreben darf, welche die anderen Wissenschaften überspielt, wie dies etwa Vertreter des »Kritischen Rationalismus« – allergisch gegen das »theologische Erbe der Philosophie«, »Erlösungslehren«, Theologie überhaupt – fürchten[15]. Auf solche Befürchtungen ist zu antworten:

Nichts gegen die naturwissenschaftlichen Ideale der Exaktheit, Präzision und Effizienz, solange man nicht die naturwissenschaftlichen Methoden allzu unvermittelt von den Uhren und Computern auf den Menschengeist ausdehnt, der keine Uhr und kein Computer ist.

Nichts gegen die Objektivität, Neutralität und Wertfreiheit der Wissenschaft, solange man ihre Voraussetzungen wie ihre sozialen Verpflichtungen und Folgen nicht verkennt und Engagement nicht ausschließt.

Nichts gegen Mathematisierung, Quantifizierung und Formalisierung der Probleme, solange man nicht humorlos meint, man hätte auf solche Weise auch schon Phänomene wie Humor, Liebe und Glaube umfassend erklärt.

Nichts selbstverständlich gegen die Naturwissenschaft als Grundlage nicht nur von Technik und Industrie, sondern auch des modernen Weltbildes überhaupt, solange man zugleich die eigenen Methoden anderer Wissenschaften, etwa der Sozial- und Kulturwissenschaften und vielleicht sogar die der Philosophie und der Theologie gelten läßt.

Kurz, nichts gegen kritische Rationalität in der Wissenschaft überhaupt und in der Theologie insbesondere, wenn damit nicht ein bestimmter »Kritischer Rationalismus« – eine gegen sich selbst unkritische Rationalität – gemeint ist: ein Rationalismus also, der das Rationale mystifiziert, der alle Fragen der Politik, der Ästhetik, der Moral und der Religion nur nach dem methodischen Stil der Naturwissenschaften traktiert haben möchte und der gerade so, trotz aller Betonung von Fehlbarkeit und Revidierbarkeit bezüglich einzelner Problemlösungen, insgesamt eine dogmatische Totaldeutung mit kritischem Anspruch vertritt, die er gern der Theologie vorwirft und die nun ihrerseits wahrhaftig nicht weniger unter Ideologieverdacht steht.

Dürfen sich nicht auch Theologen der »Tradition kritischen Denkens«[16] verpflichtet wissen? Die kühnsten unter ihnen in Altertum, Mittelalter und Neuzeit haben nicht wenig Anteil an der Aufklärung der Menschheit gegenüber Mythologien, Ideologien und Obskurantismen aller Art. Doch halten sie auch wenig von einer Mystifizierung der Vernunft. Auch nach Adorno-Horkheimers ›Dialektik der Aufklärung‹ sind gerade die ach so vernünftigen Gesellschaftsingenieure alles andere als die wahren Aufklärer. Sie haben aus dem Denkprinzip der Aufklärung das Instrument der gesellschaftlichen Organisation gemacht und führen mit ihrem Instrumentalismus jenes technologische Zwangssystem herauf, in welchem das, was die Aufklärung als Freiheit, Gleichheit und Glück intendiert hatte, sich selbst negiert. Beizufügen wäre, daß die großen Initiatoren der Aufklärung – Philosophen wie Descartes, Spinoza und Leibniz, aber auch Voltaire, Lessing und Kant, dann Naturwissenschaftler wie Kopernikus, Kepler, Galilei und Newton – nie darauf verfallen wären, eine andere Dimension als die der mathematisch-naturwissenschaftlichen Vernunft schlechthin zu leugnen. Insofern werden diese großen Rationalen – keineswegs Angehörige einer professionellen Subkultur, die es auch gibt – zu Unrecht »Rationalisten«, Vertreter eines Ismus mit Scheuklappen gegenüber der ganzen Wirklichkeit, genannt.

Der »kritische Rationalismus« übersieht die Vielschichtigkeit der Wirklichkeit: »Wirkliches kann in ganz verschiedener Weise begegnen und demgemäß auch einen ganz verschiedenen Charakter tragen. Die Wirklichkeit des Atomphysikers ist eine andere als die des Platonikers, die Wirklichkeit des Alltags eine andere als die der religiösen Erfahrung. Inhaltlich betrachtet ist also die Wirklichkeit zerklüftet: sie differenziert sich je nach dem Blickpunkt, unter dem sie erscheint. Es gibt offensichtlich nicht *die* Wirklichkeit, sondern es gibt viele unterschiedliche Wirklichkeitsebenen. Das aber besagt: Man kann und darf nicht einen bestimmten Aspekt auf die Wirklichkeit verabsolutieren; denn dann rebellieren die anderen Aspekte[17].«

3. Selbstverständlich bedeutet die Entwicklung der säkularen Welt und Wissenschaft eine ungeheure *Herausforderung für die Theologie*: eine Herausforderung zur kritischen theologischen Selbstbesinnung. Die Aufgabe heute, die die Möglichkeiten einer Theologengeneration übersteigt, ist nicht leichter als die der griechischen und lateinischen Väter des 2. und 3. Jahrhunderts oder der mit dem Aristotelismus konfrontierten Scholastik des 13. Jahrhunderts oder der Reformatoren des 16. Jahrhunderts. Auch heute kann sie effektiv nur geleistet werden, wie hier angestrebt, vor dem Horizont dieser Welt, wie sie wirklich ist, mit Hilfe der Wissenschaften und Erfahrungen dieser Zeit, mit dem Blick auf die Praxis des Einzelnen, der Kirche, der Gesellschaft. Je mehr somit der Theologe von dieser Welt weiß, durch die Naturwissenschaften, die Psychologie, Soziologie, Philosophie und – heute weniger denn je zu vergessen – die Historie, aber vielleicht am meisten durch seine eigenen Erfahrungen, um so besser wird er seine theologische Aufgabe erfüllen können.

Ernsthafte Theologie beansprucht keinen elitären, privilegierten Zugang zur Wahrheit. Sie beansprucht nur, wissenschaftliche Reflexion über ihren Gegenstand mit einer diesem Gegenstand angemessenen Methode zu sein, deren Tauglichkeit wie in anderen Wissenschaften die Resultate erweisen mögen. Theologie kann sich auf keinen Fall mit der gnädigen Duldung in einem merkwürdig unexakten und unverbindlichen Sonderbereich – »religiöse Wahrheit« ähnlich wie »dichterische Wahrheit« – zufriedengeben. In der theologischen Wissenschaft gelten nicht grundsätzlich andere Spielregeln als in den übrigen Wissenschaften. Als ob etwa hier Irrationalität, unbegründbare Stellungnahmen, subjektivistische Entscheidungen erlaubt wären: Abschirmung gegen Argumente, Informationen, Fakten; unbedingte Legitimation bestehender geistiger und sozialer Tatbestände; parteiische Rechtfertigung bestimmter Glaubenssätze, ideologischer Konstruktionen, gar gesellschaftlicher Herrschaftsformen. Ernsthafter Theologie geht es nicht um Prämierung des schlichten Glaubens oder die Zementierung eines kirchlichen Systems, sondern – immer und überall – um die volle und ganze Wahrheit.

Andererseits beansprucht ernsthafte Theologie keinen vollen, totalen Besitz der Wahrheit, kein Wahrheitsmonopol. Sie beansprucht nur, wissenschaftliche Reflexion über ihren Gegenstand unter *einem* bestimmten Blickwinkel zu sein, der allerdings ein *legitimer* Blickwinkel neben anderen ist. Theologie kann auf keinen Fall ein umfassendes und bis ins kleinste festgelegtes Weltanschauungssystem sein, das die weiteren Überlegungen der Soziologen, Psychologen, Ökonomen, Juristen, Mediziner, Naturwissenschaftler letztlich überflüssig machen würde. In der theologischen Wissenschaft kann man nicht mit Berufung auf irgendwelche Autoritäten auf die Beachtung kritischer Argumente verzichten, der Konkurrenz der Ideen ausweichen, die Anfechtungen des Zweifels unterdrücken, die Möglichkeit des Irrtums bei bestimmten Personen oder in bestimmten Situationen ausschließen. Keine Wissenschaft – die Theologie ebensowenig wie die anderen Wissenschaften – hat *alle* Aspekte menschlichen Lebens und Handelns zum Gegenstand. Aber wenn es anderen Wissenschaftlern, die sich ebenfalls primär um den Menschen kümmern, mehr um die Analyse von Daten, Fakten, Phänomenen, Operationen, Abläufen, Energien, Normen geht, so dem Theologen um die Fragen *letzter* Sinndeutungen, Zielsetzungen, Werte, Ideale, Normen, Entscheidungen, Haltungen. Die oft quälenden, aber vielleicht doch befreienden Fragen nach einem letzten Warum und Wozu, Woher und Wohin lassen sich nicht, wir sahen es, mit Emotionen als illegitime Fragen deklarieren. Die Fragen der Theologie betreffen deshalb nicht nur einen *Ausschnitt* aus dem, was die Menschen sind und treiben. Sie betreffen den fundamentalsten *Aspekt* von *allem*, was Menschen sind und treiben. Unter diesem *einen* Aspekt untersucht die Theologie *alle* Schichten menschlichen Lebens und Handelns: unter dem einen grundlegenden Aspekt kann *alles* zur Sprache kommen, muß sich die Theologie *allen* Fragen stellen.

Von dieser Aufgabe darf sich der Theologe von niemandem abhalten lassen, auch nicht von der Leitung seiner Kirche, der er sich loyal verpflichtet fühlt. Katholische Theologen werden bei umstrittenen Fragen gerne auf das kirchliche »Lehramt« verweisen, beinahe so wie Diplomaten für bestimmte Stellungnahmen auf das »Auswärtige Amt«. In der Tat hat dieses kirchliche »Lehramt« in der neueren Zeit gerade von Rom aus mit Berufung auf den Heiligen Geist zu allen möglichen Fragen und mit Vorliebe zu Sünden und sehr speziellen Dogmen unfehlbar oder fehlbar Stellung genommen. Darüber wurde an anderer Stelle gesprochen[18]. Wenn aber dieses »Lehramt« meist von vornherein und ohne allzuviel Studium wußte, »was nicht geht«, so doch meist nur sehr allgemein und abstrakt positiv, »was geht«. Zur zentralen Frage jedenfalls, was Christentum eigentlich will, was christliche Botschaft eigentlich besagt, ist im letzten halben Jahrtausend – um nicht weiter zurückzugehen – ebensowenig eine feierliche römische Lehräußerung ergangen wie etwa zur Mafia oder zur Geltung des siebten Gebots im eigenen Land. Um bestimmte Dinge kümmert man sich offenkundig weniger als um andere, darf man mit Humor feststellen, wenn man mit seinen Büchern von Anfang an so viel römische Aufmerksamkeit erfahren durfte.

Der Theologe seinerseits kann nur, wie es seine Pflicht und Schuldigkeit ist, in ernsthaftem Studium unprätentiös um eine Antwort ringen, die er vor Kirche und Gesellschaft verantworten kann. Dies soll er in Freiheit unerschrocken tun, auch wenn er dabei einmal mehr von seinem Hauptquartier statt Hilfe Rükkenschüsse – nur früher waren sie tödlich – erhält. Er geht diesen seinen Weg nicht, wie ältere Prälaten immer wieder befürchten, »allein«. Auch wenn der katholischen Theologie einige »lonely woolfs« nicht schaden könnten, so fehlt dem Verfasser dafür die nötige Bissigkeit. Er möchte »Vorhut«, nicht »Außenseiter« sein: solidarisch mit seiner Gemeinschaft, verpflichtet ihrer großen Tradition, verbunden ihren Leitern und ihren Lehrern. Gerade so wird es ihm immer mehr um »die Sache«, die große Sache des Christentums gehen, ohne daß er für sich je Unfehlbarkeit beanspruchen könnte.

In dieser Grundhaltung müssen wir nun den Horizont noch erweitern: nach der Herausforderung durch die modernen Humanismen wollen wir uns zuerst der Herausforderung der Weltreligionen stellen, bevor wir dann vor dem Gesamthorizont der heutigen Welt die *christliche* Botschaft im Hinblick auf das Christsein heute herausstellen.

Christentum will nicht einfach »Religion« sein. Energisch haben christliche Theologen im Gefolge Karl Barths und der »dialektischen Theologie« gegen das Verständnis des christlichen Glaubens als »Religion« protestiert und sogar wie Dietrich Bonhoeffer eine »nicht-religiöse« Interpretation der biblischen Begriffe gefordert[1]. Daran ist vieles richtig, wie sich in unserer Darlegung der neutestamentlichen Botschaft zeigen wird. Aber wie immer man sich zur theologischen Frage stellt, religionswissenschaftlich betrachtet erscheint das Christentum als eine Religion unter Religionen: als eine – so ließe sich der wegen der Verschiedenheit der Religionen kaum eindeutig definierbare Begriff vielleicht umschreiben – bestimmte soziale Verwirklichung einer Beziehung zu einem absoluten Sinn-Grund, zu einem allerletzten Anliegen, zu etwas, was mich unbedingt angeht.

1. Außerhalb der Kirche Heil

Zum erstenmal in der Weltgeschichte kann heute keine Religion mehr in einer »splendid isolation« leben und die anderen Religionen ignorieren. Mehr denn je ist heute auch das Christentum in die Begegnung, die Diskussion, die Konfrontation mit den Religionen gestellt. Zur Erweiterung des religionsgeographischen Horizontes am Beginn der Neuzeit ist in unserem Jahrhundert eine ungeheure Erweiterung des religionshistorischen Horizontes hinzugekommen.

Aufgewertete Religionen

Die großen Weltreligionen werden heute in der Christenheit als Faktum zur Kenntnis genommen: als zumindest vorläufig bleibendes Faktum. Das ist nicht selbstverständlich. Aber das Scheitern der christlichen Mission in den Ländern der asiatischen Hochreligionen – entscheidend mitverursacht durch katastrophale, quasi-unfehlbare und Jahrhunderte zu spät verschämt korrigierte Fehlentscheide Roms, aber auch durch jahrhunderte-langen protestantischen Absentismus – hat es nach dem Zweiten Weltkrieg den unermüdlichen christlichen Missionaren der nachkolonialistischen Zeit von Nordafrika bis Korea grausam zum Bewußtsein gebracht: Leider wird es vorläufig bei den minimalen Prozentzahlen von Christen vor allem in Asien (in China und Japan wohl nur ein halbes Prozent, in Indien etwas mehr als zwei Prozent) bleiben!

Stimmt es nicht: Je bedeutender die Religion des Landes, um so unbedeutender war der Missionserfolg? Je größer von neuem das politische Gewicht eines Landes, um so schwieriger dort die christliche Mission? Sollten diejenigen Asiaten doch recht haben, die die 400 Jahre christlicher Mission in Asien – der Heimat aller großen Religionen – als eine Episode in der mehrtausendjährigen reichen Geschichte dieser hochbegabten Völker ansehen? Möglich geworden durch den Bund des Christentums mit den Kolonialmächten in einer Zeit politischer und kultureller Schwäche? Vorbei nun mit dem Ende der von den Kirchen zum Teil schamlos ausgenützten westlichen Kolonialherrschaft und den politischen, wirtschaftlichen und rechtlichen Privilegien der christlichen Missionare[2]? Auch die neueste Entwicklung gerade der mit dem Christentum verwandten Hochreligionen läßt für die nächste Zeit kaum sensationelle Fortschritte erwarten: So heftig sich die Moslems und Juden politisch befehden, so wenig sind sie deshalb dem Christentum näher gekommen. Und die gewaltige politische Aufwertung, die sowohl das neue Indien Nehrus wie besonders das China Maos und schließlich im Gefolge der Ölkrise auch die arabischen Staaten erfahren haben, machen die christliche Mission im Nahen, Mittleren und Fernen Osten noch schwerer und zum Teil überhaupt unmöglich. Erst jetzt wird deutlich, wie die epochalen Fehlentscheidungen (in Liturgie, Theologie, Kirchendisziplin) und Fehlentwicklungen besonders in der katholischen Kirche – gegen die bessere Einsicht der damaligen Jesuitenmissionare – beinahe irreparabel sind. Wäre die damalige Christenheit nicht so engstirnig westlich gewesen, hätte man noch die Freiheit der ersten christlichen Missionare im hellenistischen Imperium Romanum gehabt, so wäre die Geschichte Asiens und seiner Religionen ein klein wenig anders verlaufen. Der katholische Japaner Shusaku Endo stellt in seinem Roman ›Silence‹[3] die ganze Problematik der Mission im 17. Jahrhundert anhand der historischen Apostasie des Führers der japanischen Missionare und Jesuitenprovinzials Christovao

Ferreira dramatisch vor Augen. Mit dem Fazit: der Baum einer hellenisierten Christenheit kann nicht einfach aus Europa herausgerissen und in den »Sumpf« Japans, welches eine völlig verschiedene Kultur hat, umgepflanzt werden. Erstaunlich, wie dies in der japanischen Christenheit noch heute heftig diskutiert wird!

Unterdessen hat sich im Christentum doch – insbesondere mit dem Vatikanum II[4] und der missionarischen Neubesinnung im Weltkirchenrat[5] – bezüglich der Weltreligionen, freilich ohne besondere Reue und Schuldbekenntnisse, manches zum Positiven gewendet: statt der früheren Verachtung zumindest grundsätzlich die Hochschätzung, statt der Vernachlässigung das Verstehen, statt der Werbung Studium und Dialog. Mehrere Hundert Jahre zu spät versucht man nun mit offiziellem Segen, das Christentum von seiner europäisch-amerikanischen, lateinisch-römischen Verpackung zu befreien: jetzt endlich möglichst einheimischer Klerus und Bischöfe, jetzt endlich angepaßte Seelsorgemethoden, jetzt endlich Volkssprache im Gottesdienst, afrikanische Messen, Gottesdienste mit Gebeten islamischer Sufis, indischen Tanzformen. Freilich scheint dies alles in der kirchlichen Praxis besser zu gelingen als in der Theorie: Verkündigung und Theologie sind bisher weder den Chinesen chinesisch, noch den Japanern japanisch, noch den Indern indisch geworden. Doch ist unübersehbar: von Rom und Paris bis Bangalore, Calcutta, Colombo, Tokio und Canberra bemühen sich Einzelne und ganze Arbeitsgruppen, den wahren Ansatz, die großen Anliegen, den Reichtum des Islams, des Buddhismus, des Hinduismus, des Konfuzianismus und Taoismus zu entdecken, zu würdigen, für christliche Verkündigung und Theologie fruchtbar zu machen.

Die theologischen Ergebnisse des Umdenkens sind offensichtlich. Man wertet neu die universalen Perspektiven der Bibel (in Genesis, Römerbrief, Apostelgeschichte, Johannesprolog): daß Gott der Schöpfer und Erhalter aller Menschen ist, daß Gott überall wirkt, daß er mit der ganzen Menschheit den Bund (Noach-Bund) geschlossen hat, daß er nach dem Neuen Testament ohne Ansehen der Person das Heil aller Menschen will und auch Nichtchristen als Täter des Gesetzes gerechtfertigt werden können[6]. Heil also faktisch außerhalb der Kirche! Neben der besonderen sieht man die allgemeine, universale Heilsgeschichte[7].

Die anderen Religionen waren früher Lüge, Werke des Bösen

und bestenfalls spurenhafte Wahrheit. Jetzt gelten sie als eine Art (»relativer«) Offenbarung, durch die ungezählte Menschen der Vorzeit und der Gegenwart das Mysterium Gottes erfuhren und erfahren. Früher erschienen sie als Wege des Unheils. Jetzt anerkennt man sie als – »außerordentliche« oder »ordentliche«, darüber streiten sich die Gelehrten – Wege des Heils für Ungezählte, ja vielleicht für die Mehrheit der Menschheit. »Legitime« Religionen also, die in einer bestimmten gesellschaftlichen Situation faktisch die einzige religiöse Möglichkeit darstellen, deren Glaubens- und Kultformen, Begriffe und Werte, Symbole und Ordnungen, religiöse und ethische Erfahrungen eine »relative Gültigkeit«[8], »ein relatives providentielles Existenzrecht«[9] haben.

Reichtum der Religionen

Wer hier als Christ und besonders als streng evangelischer Theologe Einwände hat, überlege in Ruhe: Jede Religion ist in concreto gewiß ein Gemisch von Glauben, Aberglauben und Unglauben. Aber kann ein Christ übersehen, mit welcher Hingabe und Konzentration die Menschen in den Weltreligionen die Wahrheit unermüdlich gesucht und auch gefunden haben? Gehen nicht alle Religionen – wenn nicht die Naturreligionen, so zumindest die ethischen Hochreligionen – von denselben ewigen Fragen aus, die sich hinter dem Sichtbar-Greifbaren und der eigenen Lebensspanne eröffnen: Woher die Welt und ihre Ordnung, warum sind wir geboren und müssen wir sterben, was bestimmt das Schicksal des Einzelnen und der Menschheit, wie erklärt sich das sittliche Bewußtsein und das Vorhandensein ethischer Normen? Und wollen nicht alle Religionen über die Weltdeutung hinaus auch einen praktischen Weg ermöglichen aus der Not und Qual des Daseins zum Heil? Und betrachten sie nicht alle Lüge, Diebstahl, Ehebruch und Mord als sündhaft und vertreten als allgemein gültige praktische Richtschnur so etwas wie eine »goldene Regel« (was du dir selbst nicht wünschest, das tue auch keinem anderen)? Wer auch nur die geringsten Kenntisse von den Weltreligionen hat, kann nicht bestreiten[10]:

– *Nicht nur das Christentum, auch die Weltreligionen sind sich der* Entfremdung, Versklavung, Erlösungsbedürftigkeit des Menschen *bewußt: sofern sie nämlich wissen um die Einsamkeit, Verfallenheit, Verlorenheit, Unfreiheit des Menschen,* seine abgrundtiefe Angst, Sorge, seine Egoismen und seine Masken; sofern sie bekümmert sind um das unsägliche Leid, das Elend dieser unheilen Welt und den Sinn und Widersinn des Todes; sofern sie deshalb harren auf ein Neues und sich sehnen nach der Verwandlung, Wiedergeburt, Erlösung und Befreiung des Menschen und seiner Welt.

– Nicht nur das Christentum, auch die Weltreligionen erkennen die Güte, das Erbarmen, die Gnädigkeit der Gottheit: sofern sie nämlich wissen, daß die Gottheit bei aller Nähe fern und vorborgen ist, daß die Gottheit selbst Nähe, Gegenwart und Offenbarsein schenken muß; sofern sie dem Menschen sagen, daß er sich der Gottheit nicht selbstverständlich im Vertrauen auf seine Unschuld nahen darf, daß er der Reinigung und Versöhnung bedarf, daß er zur Tilgung der Schuld das Opfer braucht, daß er nur durch Sterben hindurch zum Leben kommt, ja, daß der Mensch sich letztlich nicht selber erlösen und befreien kann, sondern auf Gottes umfassende Liebe angewiesen ist.

– Nicht nur das Christentum, auch die Weltreligionen hören zu Recht auf den Ruf ihrer Propheten: insofern sie nämlich durch ihre großen prophetischen Gestalten – Vorbilder in Wissen und Wandel – Inspiration, Mut und Kraft empfangen zum Neuaufbruch in größere Wahrheit und tiefere Erkenntnis, zum Durchbruch auf Verlebendigung und Erneuerung der überlieferten Religion hin.

Der einseitige Vergleich gerade der großen Gründer und Reformer der Weltreligionen mit dem Christentum ist ungerecht. Nur der Vergleich mit der von ihnen vorgefundenen religiösen Lage läßt ihre reformerischen und neubegründenden Leistungen im richtigen Licht sehen. Dann erscheint der hinduistische Brahmanismus als »reformierter« vedischer Polytheismus, der Buddhismus als reformierter Brahmanismus, der Islam als reformierter arabischer Animismus. Und es kann sich dann schon einmal die Frage aufdrängen: Waren Buddha, Kung-futse, Lao-tse, Zarathustra, Mohammed nicht doch von denselben letzten großen Fragen und Hoffnungen umgetrieben, auf die wir gerade hingewiesen haben? Ja, suchen die Hindus im Brahma (*das* Brahma, nicht *der* persönliche Einzelgott Brahma), die Buddhisten im Absoluten, die Chinesen im Tao und die Moslems in Allah vielleicht doch das eine und selbe Geheimnis der Geheimnisse, die eine und selbe allerletzte Wirklichkeit? Selbstverständlich hat dabei jede Relgion ihren eigenen Charakter und ihren eigenen – von den Christen oft gar nicht zur Kenntnis genommenen – Reichtum. Ein paar Andeutungen mögen wenigstens einiges davon bewußt machen[11]:

1. Die von *Indien* ausgehenden Religionen – vor allem Hinduismus und Buddhismus – sind durchdrungen von einer Urerfahrung und Urhoffnung dieses bei allem Reichtum so unsäglich armen und katastrophenreichen Subkontinents: daß das Leben Leid ist, und neues Leben neues Leid erzeugt, und daß doch eine Überwindung des Leids, eine Befreiung und Erlösung möglich sein muß.

Der *Hinduismus:* Die »ewige«, nicht gestiftete, sondern gewachsene alte einheimische Religion Indiens, der man keinen bestimmten Gott zuschreiben kann. Imponierend in ihrer mystischen Grundhaltung, in ihrer grenzenlosen Offenheit und Toleranz, in ihrer Anerkennung und Assimilation fremder Ideen, in ihrem Unendlichkeitsstreben und ihrer Entwicklungsfähigkeit, die neben primitiver mythologischer Vielgötterei und orgiastischen Ritualen auch strengste Askese und Meditation (Yoga) und hochgeistige Philosophen wie die Shankaras hervorgebracht hat. Ein offenes, wachsendes religiöses System: eine lebendige Einheit in einer erstaunlichen Vielfalt von Anschauungen, Formen und Riten. Und dies alles ohne feste, allgemein gültige dogmatische Lehrsätze über Gott, Mensch und Welt, auch ohne Kirche und Mission, und doch von ungebrochener Kontinuität und anscheinend unzerstörbarer Lebenskraft. Das durch vielfältigste Formen der Askese und Meditation angestrebte Ziel ist: Erlösung aus dem Kreislauf der Geburten in einem Hinüberfließen des Ich ins All oder die Einheit mit dem Absoluten.

Der *Buddhismus:* Wohl die stärkste Gegenposition zum Christentum. Seit 500 v. Chr. in Indien, jetzt aber vor allem außerhalb in großer Vielfalt von Ceylon bis Japan, wo er den shintoistischen Staatskult durchdringt. Anders als der Hinduismus beeindruckend als der »mittlere Weg« zwischen den Extremen der Sinnenlust und der Selbstquälerei, zwischen Hedonismus und Asketismus. Buddhas »vier edle Wahrheiten« – Kernpunkt der Predigt von Benares – wollen zur Einsicht führen, warum man leidet, um dadurch die Ursache des Leidens und das Leiden selbst aufzuheben. Die Ursache des Leidens ist nichts anderes als die Selbstsucht, die Selbstbehauptung, der Lebensdurst, der von Wiedergeburt zu Wiedergeburt führt. Durch Erkenntnis und

Ausrottung dieses Lebensdurstes kommt es zur Überwindung des Leidens, welche das Leben ausmacht. Unbekümmert um Fragen wie die nach dem ersten Anfang der Welt soll der Mensch den achtfachen Pfad zur Aufhebung des Leidens gehen: rechte Anschauung, rechtes Wollen, rechtes Reden, rechtes Tun, rechtes Leben, rechtes Streben, rechtes Gedenken, rechtes Sichversenken. Nicht nichts soll der Mensch tun, sondern von allem, was er tut oder erlebt, unberührt bleiben. Statt der hinduistischen Askese die Einsicht ins Nichts. Auf diese Weise ist Erlösung möglich: Erlösung von der Selbstsucht, Selbstbehauptung, Blindheit, Erlösung deshalb vom Leiden durch bewußtes Nichtsammeln von positiven oder negativen Lebensdaten (karma). Erlösung schließlich aus dem endlosen Geburtenkreislauf der Scheinwelt des Lebens durch Verlöschen oder Befreiung im Unendlichen. So will also selbst der vom westlichen Standpunkt her zu Recht oder Unrecht »atheistisch« genannte ältere klassische Hinayana-Buddhismus – das »Kleine Fahrzeug« der Erleuchtung zur vollen Befreiung von Leid und Leidenschaft – letzte Fragen des Menschen beantworten, Heilsweg sein. Allerdings hat er dieses Heil – in ehrfürchtiger theologia negativa – nur als Nirwana (»Verlöschen«) zu denken vermocht. Ein Nichts, insofern es eine Befreiung von allem Leiden, aller Sinnlichkeit, aller Beschränkung bedeutet. Eine bildlose und wunschlose Leerheit, die spätestens im Mahayana-Buddhismus – dem »Großen Fahrzeug« – einen positiven theologischen Inhalt bekommt und mit dem Absoluten und Glückseligkeit identisch ist, so daß ein stärkeres Bewußtsein von Transzendenz, ein reicherer Kult und wohl auch eine vollkommenere Meditationsart möglich wird. Eine mönchische Weltverneinung, die sich nicht selten als Weltbeherrschung erwies, wie die großen kulturellen Leistungen des Buddhismus in Indien, Indonesien, Japan zeigen.

2. Die *chinesische Religion:* Seit Beginn unseres Jahrhunderts wird sie oft chinesischer Universismus genannt, weil im Zentrum die Harmonie des Universums steht. Sie gabelte sich ebenfalls um 500 v. Chr. in zwei Äste: Konfuzianismus und Taoismus, repräsentiert durch die beiden gegensätzlichen Philosophen Kungfutse und Lao-tse, beides angeblich Zeitgenossen des Buddha. Heute ist die chinesische Religion, sofern sie sich im maoistischen System überhaupt halten konnte, ein synkretistisches Gebilde aus konfuzianischen, taoistischen und buddhistischen Elementen.

Der aus der frühen chinesischen Religion herausgewachsene, mehr pragmatische, auf die zwischenmenschlichen Beziehungen konzentrierte *Konfuzianismus* spricht wenig von den Beziehungen zu einem Suprahumanen und wird oft als purer Humanismus verstanden, dem nur an der Pflege der menschlichen Werte – besonders Liebe (Wohlwollen = jen), aber auch Ehre, Pflicht, Takt, Geschmack – und der weltlichen Ordnungen gelegen sei. Doch die Voraussetzung seiner Verwirklichung einer natürlichen Menschlichkeit, die Grundlage seiner nüchternen rationalen Ethik und der Sinn aller moralischen Vorschriften ist: In seinem ganzen Tun soll sich der Mensch der ewigen Weltordnung einfügen. Er soll sich dem kosmisch-sittlichen Gesetz harmonisch anpassen: ein Moralgesetz *im* Menschen, in welchem sich der »Weg« (tao) des Himmels kundtut. Der Mensch vereint in sich die polaren Kräfte der Welt: yang und yin, männliches und weibliches Prinzip, welche Himmel und Erde repräsentieren. Die fünf menschlichen Grundbeziehungen zwischen Fürst und Untertan, Vater und Sohn, älterem und jüngerem Bruder, Mann und Frau, Freund und Freund werden besonders bedacht. Ethische Grundhaltung muß die Pietät sein. Und auch die Kardinaltugenden (Wohlwollen, Redlichkeit, Schicklichkeit, Weisheit und Aufrichtigkeit) sowie die »goldene Regel« – alles ist also schon in dieser vorchristlichen Ethik bekannt. So hat die konfuzianische Auffassung von der Harmonie des Menschen mit dem Himmel doch tiefe theologische Implikationen. Weisheit besteht in dem Erkennen des Willens des Himmels. Ehrfurcht soll der Edle empfinden nicht nur vor großen Männern und den Worten der Heiligen, sondern in erster Linie vor den Befehlen des Himmels. Der Konfuzianismus weist denn wie Hinduismus und Buddhismus auch alle äußeren Kennzeichen einer Religion auf: Opfer an die Götter und Ahnen und eine Fülle sakraler Handlungen für das Wohl des Menschen. Der Staat selber erscheint als religiöse Einrichtung und der Herrscher als Beauftragter des Himmels (Kaiserkult). Der Himmel aber wird als Personifikation der kosmischen und sittlichen Weltordnung und als höchste geistige Macht, welche die Geschicke der Menschen lenkt, verstanden und als »oberster Herrscher« auch mit personalen Zügen umschrieben. Eine päpstliche Bulle indessen verbot im »Ritenstreit«, der sehr viel mehr als ein Streit um Riten war, den frühen Jesuitenmissionaren, den »Himmel« oder den »obersten Herrscher« mit Gott gleichzusetzen.

Während jedoch die humanistische Ideologie des Konfuzianismus faktisch stark den Menschen zum Maß aller Dinge macht, indem sie ihn aus der Natur heraushebt, fordert der *Taoismus* gegenüber dem Konfuzianismus – seine Überlegenheit an metaphysischer Tiefe betonend – die Integration des Menschen in den Kosmos. Eine Haltung, die kosmologisch-ontologische ebenso wie naturwissenschaftliche Fragestellungen förderte und zugleich Ontologie und Ethik eng verband. Statt der fortgeschrittenen Kultur, der patriarchalischen Gesellschaft und des selbstsicheren Wissens die Rückkehr zur unverfälschten Natur, Spontaneität, Mystik, zu den Idealen von Kung-futses aufgeklärter Epoche. Der Mensch soll wieder seine natürliche Größe oder Kleinheit finden, und das Maß des Kosmos soll wieder Maß auch des Menschen sein. Gerade auf diese Weise wird der Mensch den Tod überwinden. Philosophische Spekulation und Regeln für Lebensverjüngungspraktiken (Atemübungen, Diätetik, Sexualregeln) vermischen sich hier. Schließlich wird die Persönlichkeit ins Formlose zurücktauchen und ewiges Leben haben. Taoismus und Buddhismus fanden sich in China, sind aber heute mit dem Konfuzianismus zusammen weithin – endgültig? – überdeckt vom Maoismus, der vielfach Züge einer Ersatzreligion trägt.

3. Der *Islam:* In den riesigen Räumen zwischen Marokko und Bangla Desh, den Steppen Zentralasiens und der indonesischen Inselwelt herrscht die Religion Mohammeds. Die jüngste, einfachste, aber auch am wenigsten originelle der Weltreligionen, entstanden im Arabien des 7. Jahrhunderts nach Christus. Und doch mit der formenden Kraft eines Glaubens, der wie kaum ein anderer seine Bekenner zu einem einheitlichen Typus hat werden lassen. Ein einfaches – vom Judentum und Christentum abhängiges – Glaubensbekenntnis ist Gegenstand der islamischen Dogmatik: Es gibt keinen Gott außer Gott, und Mohammed ist sein Prophet! Fünf einfache Grundpflichten oder »Säulen« des Islam sind Gegenstand der höchst ausgebildeten islamischen Rechtswissenschaft: neben dem Glaubensbekenntnis das tägliche rituelle Gebet, die Armensteuer, das Fasten im Monat Ramadan und eine Wallfahrt nach Mekka. Eine alles durchdringende Ergebenheit in Gottes Willen, als dessen unabänderliche Entscheidung auch das Leid hinzunehmen ist: »Islam« besagt »Unterwerfung«, »Hingabe« an Gott. Aus all dem resultiert eine grundsätzliche Gleichheit der Menschen vor Gott und ein übernationales muslimisches Gemeinschaftsgefühl: eine Brüderlichkeit, welche die Rassen und sogar die indischen Kasten mindestens grundsätzlich

zu überwinden vermochte. Abgesehen von der Spaltung in der Generation nach Mohammed in drei, heute noch zwei Konfessionen (die überwältigende Zahl der Sunniten und die kleine Zahl der Schiiten besonders in Persien), hat der Islam in seiner langen und umkämpften Geschichte zum Unterschied von anderen Religionen keine bedeutenden Auf- oder Abspaltungen und auch keine neue konkurrierende Religionsstiftung – allerdings wie jede Weltreligion seine Rückschläge (in Spanien, Sizilien, Osteuropa) – erlebt. Das alles bestärkt die Moslems im Anspruch, die letzte und endgültige Religion zu sein, die mit anderen zusammen Abraham, Mose und vor allem Jesus als Propheten anerkennt, deren letzter und größter jedoch Mohammed als das »Siegel der Propheten« ist. Große Leistungen in der Theologie, Mystik, Poesie und Kultur der Vergangenheit (im Mittelalter) und außerordentliche Missionserfolge in der Gegenwart (in Zentral- und Ostafrika) kommen dazu. Ohne Sakramente, Kultbilder und Musik, ohne geistliche Weihen und eine unfehlbare Zentralinstanz eine leicht faßliche Religion von erstaunlicher Widerstandskraft (Sowjetunion), Kohäsion (Araber) und Expansion (bereits über die Hälfte der Afrikaner sind Moslems). Eine Religion, mit der auch politisch zu rechnen ist: gerade in der nationalen Wiedergeburt der arabischen Staaten.

Das ist die Welt der Religionen: Die Religion ist wirklich nur in den Religionen. Und die Religionen sollte man kennen, wenn man über Religion sprechen will. Doch brechen wir hier ab: Was könnte man schon vom Christentum sagen, wenn man nur wenige Zeilen darüber schreiben dürfte! Unsagbar sind Tiefe und Reichtum der religiösen Erfahrungen der Menschheit, wie sie in den großen Religionen mit ihren zahllosen Formen, Gestaltungen und Ideen zum Ausdruck kommen. Wir können weder die einzelnen Religionen in ihren verschiedenen Stadien (Stiftung, Entfaltung, Stabilisierung, eventuell Auflösung) umschreiben, noch – religionswissenschaftlich wichtiger – ihre Konvergenzen, Affinitäten, Begegnungen, Beeinflussungen und Vermischungen auch nur andeuten.

2. Verwirrende Konsequenzen

Für das neue Selbstverständnis des Christentums ist charakteristisch, daß man heute bereit ist, dieses unermeßliche Meer zur

Kenntnis zu nehmen, zu erforschen, ja in ihm nicht nur Wege ins Verderben, sondern, wie wir sahen, bedingt Wege zum Leben, ja, zum umfassenden definitiven Wohl des Menschen, zum »Heil« zu finden. Manche, und nicht nur christliche Missionare, aber fragen besorgt: Wenn die anderen Religionen Heilswege zumindest sein können, was sind dann die Konsequenzen für den einen Heilsweg des Christentums? Sind diese Konsequenzen nicht verwirrend und gefährlich?

Anonymes Christentum?

Noch fünfzig Jahre vor der Entdeckung Amerikas hatte das ökumenische Konzil von Florenz (1442) die nach Origenes und besonders Cyprian traditionell gewordene Lehre vom »außerhalb der Kirche *kein* Heil«[1] definiert. Und zwar mit den starken Worten des Augustinus-Schülers Fulgentius von Ruspe: »Die heilige römische Kirche ... glaubt fest, bekennt und verkündet, daß ›niemand außerhalb der katholischen Kirche, weder Heide noch Jude noch Ungläubiger oder ein von der Einheit Getrennter – des ewigen Lebens teilhaftig wird, vielmehr dem ewigen Feuer verfällt, das dem Teufel und seinen Engeln bereitet ist, wenn er sich nicht vor dem Tod ihr (der heiligen römischen Kirche) anschließt[2]‹.« Alle also, die draußen sind, sind eine »massa damnata«, ein verlorener Haufen, ausgeschlossen vom Heil.

500 Jahre später, und wahrhaftig nicht zu früh, gewährt das Zweite Vatikanische Konzil Religions- und Glaubensfreiheit. In einer eigenen Erklärung lobt es die Weltreligionen und bekennt in der Konstitution über die Kirche, daß alle Menschen guten Willens, daß nämlich auch Juden, Moslems, Angehörige anderer Religionen, ja sogar Atheisten (»die ohne Schuld noch nicht zur ausdrücklichen Anerkennung Gottes gekommen sind«) zumindest grundsätzlich »das ewige Heil erlangen können[3]«. Früher konnten nur getaufte und praktizierende Christen das Heil erreichen. Dann gestand man einzelnen nichtchristlichen Individuen eine Heilschance zu. Jetzt können anscheinend sogar die Religionen als solche Weg zum Heil sein.

Vergleicht man die alte und die neue Lehre, so muß man einen Umschlag von epochalem Ausmaß bezüglich derer außerhalb der »heiligen römischen Kirche« feststellen. Was ist hier geschehen? Nicht viel, beruhigen manche katholische Theologen, nur eine neue »Interpretation« des unfehlbaren alten Dogmas: »Kirche« meint jetzt nicht mehr wie noch in Florenz, »die heilige römische Kirche«, sondern meint »eigentlich«, »richtig verstanden«, »im Grunde«: *alle* Menschen guten Willens, die alle »irgendwie« zur Kirche gehören. Aber wird hier nicht elegant die ganze gutwillige Menschheit über die dünne Papyrusbrücke einer theologischen Konstruktion durch die Hintertür in die »heilige römische Kirche« eingeführt, so daß kein Gutwilliger »draußen« bleibt? Außerhalb der Kirche kein Heil – die Formel stimmt wie eh und je, weil nämlich alle schon von vornherein drinnen sind: als nicht formelle, aber »anonyme« Christen[4] oder – wie man eigentlich konsequent sagen müßte – »anonyme römische Katholiken«.

Ist das Problem gelöst? Marschieren die Massen der nichtchristlichen Religionen nicht nur im Kopf des Theologen in die heilige römische Kirche ein? In Wirklichkeit jedenfalls bleiben sie, die Juden, Moslems, Hindus, Buddhisten und alle die anderen, die selber sehr wohl wissen, was sie, völlig »unanonym«, sind, draußen. Sie wollen auch gar nicht drinnen sein. Und kein methodischer Trick wird sie je zwingen können, gegen ihren Willen und gegen ihr »Votum« Aktiv- oder Passivmitglied dieser Kirche zu werden, die ja noch immer eine freie Glaubensgemeinschaft sein möchte. Der Wille derer, die draußen sind, ist nicht nach eigenen Interessen zu »interpretieren«, sondern schlicht zu respektieren. Und rund um die Welt wird man keinen ernsthaften Juden, Moslem oder Atheisten finden, der die Behauptung, er sei ein »anonymer Christ«, nicht als Anmaßung empfände. Eine solche Vereinnahmung des Gesprächspartners beschließt den Dialog, bevor er überhaupt angefangen hat. Eine Scheinlösung, die nur ein schwacher Trost ist: Kann man einen Verein, der an Mitgliederschwund leidet, dadurch sanieren, daß man auch die Nichtmitglieder zu »verborgenen« Mitgliedern erklärt? Und was würden die Christen sagen, wenn sie von den Buddhisten gnädig als »anonyme Buddhisten« anerkannt würden?

Es durfte nicht verschwiegen werden: Mit scheinorthodoxer Zerdehnung christlicher Begriffe wie Kirche und Heil nimmt man die Herausforderung der Weltreligionen nicht an. So weicht man ihr aus und wird leicht selber vom Rücken her eingefangen. Gerät man so nicht, ohne es zu merken, in die Gefahr, die Sache des Christentums anzutasten, nur um eine unfehlbare Formel zu retten? Macht man so nicht, ohne es zu wollen, die Kirche der Welt, die Christenheit der Menschheit gleich? Wird das Christentum so nicht zu einem religiösen Luxus und das christliche

Ethos überflüssig? Wird nicht schließlich aufgrund einer solchen Konzeption Jesus allzuleicht für die Hindus zum Avatara, für die Buddhisten zum Boddhisattva, für die Moslems zu einem der Propheten? Alles Fragen so vieler älterer Missionare, die von fortschrittlichen jüngeren und ihren Lehrern nicht immer beantwortet werden. Wobei nebenbei auch dies einmal illustriert ist: Auch sich fortschrittlich gebende Ansichten dürfen nicht kritiklos übernommen werden. Parteidenken und Fraktionszwang sind in einer Theologie, der es um die Wahrheit geht, fehl am Platz. Und haben die Konservativen in der Kirche nicht immer recht mit ihren Antworten, so doch sehr oft mit ihren Fragen.

Vornehme Ignoranz?

Die Herausforderung bleibt: Was alles über die Religion positiv und mit Recht gesagt wird, darf nicht nachträglich zurückgenommen und durch eine methodische Manipulation der Kirche oder den Kirchen verbucht werden. Außerhalb der Kirche Heil: warum es nicht ehrlich zugeben, wenn man es doch schon de facto behauptet? Nur so nimmt man die anderen Religionen wirklich ernst, nur unter dieser Voraussetzung sieht man die Problematik realistisch.

Allerdings hat sich damit die Hauptfrage nur um so klarer herausgeschält: Wenn die christliche Verkündigung heute anders als früher statt der Armut die Reichtümer der Religionen feststellt, was hat sie dann noch selber zu bieten? Wenn sie überall offenbares Licht erkennt, inwiefern will sie »das Licht« bringen? Wenn alle Religionen Wahrheit enthalten, warum soll gerade das Christentum *die* Wahrheit sein? Wenn schon Heil außerhalb von Kirche und Christentum, warum überhaupt Kirche und Christentum?

Auch nach dieser Richtung gibt es Scheinlösungen. Hier darf nicht nur behauptet werden. Hier darf erst recht nicht nur – wie auf den Spuren Luthers der jüngere Barth[5], Bonhoeffer[6], Gogarten[7] und weniger radikal E. Brunner[8] und H. Kraemer[9] – ohne nähere Kenntnis und Analyse der wirklichen Welt der Religionen in dogmatischer »dialektischer Theologie« dekretiert werden, Religion sei nichts anderes als »natürliche Theologie«, selbstmächtiger sündiger Aufstand gegen Gott und Unglaube schlechthin, und das Christentum sei keine Religion, weil das Evangelium das Ende aller Religionen sei. Es darf das gesamte

Problem auch nicht, wie es andere protestantische Theologen tun, mit einem vornehmen Ignoramus abgewiesen werden, als ob uns das nichts anginge. Wenn die christliche Theologie auf die Frage nach dem Heil des Großteils der Menschheit keine Antwort weiß, darf sie nicht verwundert sein, wenn die Menschen heute wie schon Voltaire ihren Hohn über die Anmaßung der »alleinseligmachenden« christlichen Kirche ausgießen oder sich mit einem aufgeklärten Indifferentismus zufriedengeben wie weiland Lessing mit seiner Fabel von den drei für echt gehaltenen Ringen, von denen vielleicht keiner der echte Ring des Vaters ist. Allzuleicht läßt sich die Behauptung der »dialektischen Theologie«, die Weltreligionen seien nur menschliche Projektionen, umdrehen, und gerade das Christentum als reine Projektion, Ausdruck eines absolutistisch-exklusiven Wunschdenkens, erklären.

Die Verschärfung der Problemstellung ist unverkennbar: Die Weltreligionen waren seit der Entwicklung der riesenhaften neuen Kontinente vor allem eine äußere, quantitative Herausforderung für die Christenheit. Jetzt aber sind sie nicht nur für einige Aufklärer, sondern für die christlichen Kirchen selbst zu einer inneren, qualitativen Herausforderung geworden. Nicht mehr nur das Schicksal der Weltreligionen steht in Frage wie in der kolonialistischen Epoche. Das Schicksal des Christentums selbst steht in Frage.

Damit ist freilich auch bereits die andere Seite der Problematik mit angesprochen. Herausforderung der Weltreligionen: das ist aktiv *und* passiv zu verstehen. Denn auch die Weltreligionen selber sind herausgefordert.

3. Herausforderung gegenseitig

Die Lage der Weltreligionen ist durch die neuzeitliche Entwicklung nicht etwa einfacher geworden. Auch dies ist in aller Nüchternheit zu sehen. Das Christentum darf andere Religionen nicht klein machen, um selber groß dazustehen. Doch auch eine Idealisierung der Weltreligionen – aus der Ferne eher möglich als aus der Nähe – kann der Klärung nicht dienen. Unsere schematische Skizzierung des Ansatzpunktes der verschiedenen Religionen darf ihre negative Seite nicht übersehen lassen: welches ihre ganz konkreten Mängel, Schwächen, Irrtümer sind; wie weit sich die Religionen in Wirklichkeit von ihrem ursprünglichen Ansatz entfernen; wie sie oft sehr gemischte und widersprüchliche Gebilde darstellen: ein Islam mit massiver Heiligenverehrung und Amuletten, ein Vulgärtaoismus mit Magie, Alchimie, Lebenselixieren und Unsterblichkeitspillen, ein chinesischer Jahresfestkreis aus archaischen, konfuzianischen, taoistischen und buddhistischen Elementen, ein Hinduismus, in welchem ungefähr alles möglich ist.

Keine Nivellierung

Parallelen zwischen den verschiedenen Religionen stellt die Religionsphänomenologie[1] oder eine Universalhistorie im Stil von Arnold Toynbee[2] selbstverständlich in Massen fest: in Lehre, Ritus und Leben. Und auf das konkrete Leben kommt es vielleicht noch mehr an als auf die abstrakte Lehre. Wenn man zum Beispiel als »Götter« alle diejenigen Wesenheiten bezeichnet, die durch Anrufung und Darbringung von Gaben verehrt werden, dann wird man nicht nur in anderen Religionen, sondern auch im Christentum einen praktischen Polytheismus konstatieren müssen. Oder darf man etwa von vornherein mit zwei verschiedenen Maßstäben messen? Darf man auf der einen Seite nur das hohe Ideal und auf der anderen nur die hinter dem Ideal zurückbleibende Wirklichkeit sehen? Im märchenhaften Goldenen Tempel der Sikhs zu Amritsar, am heiligen Ganges zu Benares, im buddhistischen Kandy oder gar Bangkok ist man als Christ zwar beeindruckt, aber gewiß kaum versucht, zu einer nichtchristlichen Religion zu konvertieren. Aber sollte umgekehrt der shivistische Hindu in einer neapolitanischen oder bayrischen Barockkirche oder auch im römischen Petersdom einen Appell zum Christentum als einer götterstürzenden »monotheistischen Revolution«[3] verspüren? In der kleinsten nordafrikanischen Moschee am Rand der Sahara verspürt man mehr davon.

Aber bei allen Parallelen im Positiven und Negativen lassen sich die *Unterschiede* schon rein phänomenologisch nicht einebnen, wie es besonders am Anfang die verständliche Versuchung der vergleichenden Religionswissenschaft war. Auch der Religionsphänomenologe unterscheidet grundsätzlich zwischen einer primitiven und einer hochentwickelten, zwischen einer gewachsenen und einer gestifteten, einer mythologischen und einer aufgeklärten, und vor allem zwischen einer erklärt monotheistischen und einer erklärt polytheistischen oder aber pantheistischen Religion. Im konkreten Vergleich von Parallelen und Vorstufen wird zwar oft in vorschneller Entdeckerfreude nur die Ähnlichkeit und nicht auch die Widersprüchlichkeit herausgestellt. Aber gleiche Begriffe (»heiliges Mahl«, »Taufbad«, »heilige Schrift«) täuschen, und Allgemeinbegriffe verschleiern. Der Stellenwert des Phänomens (»Prophet«, »Heiligenverehrung«) im Ganzen ist entscheidend. Weihrauch und Sandelholz mögen für weniger feine Nasen ähnlich angenehm oder unangenehm riechen, Bibel und Koran sich von außen gleich anfassen, ein Opfer mag ein Opfer sein. Aber der allgemeine Opferbegriff ist äquivok und bringt völlig Unähnliches – Erhabenstes *und* schauderhaftes menschliche Verirrung, uneigennützige Hingabe für andere *und* unsinniges Hinschlachten anderer – unter einen Hut. Und daß man beim Lesen der Bibel die Hände nicht waschen muß, macht einen höchst bedeutsamen Unterschied zum Islam aus: das Christentum ist letztliche keine »Buchreligion«. Und für Juden und Christen war der Jordan nie ein heiliger Fluß wie für andere Religionen Nil, Euphrat, Tigris oder Ganges. Auch kennt das Christentum nicht im gleichen Sinne eine heilige Stadt wie die Juden Jerusalem oder die Moslems Mekka. Die christlichen Kreuzzüge waren nicht nur unchristlich, sondern unnötig.

Und wie verschieden sind über die Äußerlichkeiten hinaus die vielen »Propheten« der Völker: ein Asket in Indien oder ein wandernder Denker in China, ein Philosoph in Griechenland oder ein Nabi in Israel. Wie verschieden die Vorstellungen von einer letzten Befreiung und Erlösung: Aufschwung zur Idee oder Versenkung in Meditation, Erfahren des Nirwana, Einklang mit dem Tao oder aber Hingabe an den Willen Gottes. »Menschenliebe« ist nicht dasselbe bei Meister Kung oder beim Meister von Nazaret. Und selbst der böse Geist ist nicht derselbe bei Zarathustra (Mazdaismus, indischer Parsismus) und im Alten und Neuen Testament. Von den Unterschieden zu primitiven Religionen ganz zu schweigen: Daß die so liebenswürdig friedlichen Fidschi-Insulaner in diesem Jahrhundert nicht mehr wie im vergangenen Menschen essen, dürfte zumindest für die Inselbesucher nicht unwesentlich sein. Allzu oft übersieht man jedenfalls gerade da die Unterschiede, übersieht man, ob dem ins Auge fallenden Versagen der christlichen Mission und etwa der Auflösung alter Stammeskulturen zum Beispiel in Afrika[4] jene immense Aufklärung und Befreiung von Dämonenangst, Magie, Naturzwängen, Irrationalität, Grausamkeit, unpersonaler, unsozialer und ungeschichtlicher Haltung, welche die christliche Mission gebracht hat: zweifellos eine Entmythologisierung und Entdämonisierung, eine Verinnerlichung und Vermenschlichung großen Stiles.

So sollte denn bei aller Anerkennung der Wahrheit anderer Religionen nicht bestritten werden: Es bestehen wesentliche Unterschiede zwischen den furchtbaren Götterfratzen der wunderbaren Götterinsel Bali und einer Ikonenwand orthodoxer Heiliger in Sagorsk, zwischen sakraler Tempelprostitution und christlicher Jungfrauenweihe, zwischen einer Religion, deren Symbol der im selben Tempel tausendfach reproduzierte Linga (Phallusstein), und einer anderen, deren Symbol das Kreuz ist, zwischen einer Religion des heiligen Krieges gegen die Feinde und einer Religion der programmatischen Feindesliebe, zwischen einer Religion der Menschenopfer (mindestens 20000 Menschenopfer in vier Tagen bei der Weihe des Haupttempels in Mexiko 1487) und einer Religion der alltäglichen Selbsthingabe für die Menschen. Selbst die Grausamkeiten der spanischen Conquistadores und die römischen Ketzerverbrennungen – dem christlichen Programm eben nicht entsprechend, sondern widersprechend, nicht christlich, sondern eindeutig unchristlich! – heben diese Unterschiede nicht auf.

Bei allem Respekt also vor dem großzügig toleranten Reformhinduismus Sarvepalli Radakrishnans, Indiens erstem Staatspräsidenten, der ebensoviel vom theologischen Liberalismus des europäischen 19. Jahrhunderts als vom Vedanta beeinflußt war: alles ist nicht letztlich eins, und alles ist nicht einfach gleich! Wer die konkrete Wirklichkeit Indiens kennt oder auch nur Berichte über den verderblichen Einfluß der konkreten Hindu-Religion auf die Lage des Subkontinents liest – die noch heute katastrophalen ökonomischen und gesellschaftlichen Auswirkungen des auch von Gandhi befürworteten Kuh-Kultes, des durch keine Gesetzgebung zu überwindenden Kastensystems, des erschrekkenden Aberglaubens und der Scharlatanerie vieler Gurus und manches andere[5]: der kann ein wenig ahnen, was für eine Aufklärung und Befreiung, Entmythologisierung und Entdämonisierung, Verinnerlichung und Vermenschlichung christlicher Glaube bedeuten kann. Angesichts der radikalen Widersprüchlichkeiten zwischen den Religionen dürfte es eine zu einfache Vorstellung sein, daß alle Religionen nach alter vielzitierter buddhistischer Parabel wie blinde Bettler denselben Elefanten betasten, der eine ein Bein greift, und es für einen Baumstamm, der andere ein Ohr und es für ein Palmblatt, der dritte den Schwanz und ihn für ein Seil hält, keiner aber von allen den ganzen Elefanten[6]. Und wenn einer blind einen Baumstamm für einen Elefanten hält? Mit Recht stellt Radakrishnan mit anderen in der unbegrenzten Vielfalt der Religionen, ihren Vorstellungen, Formen und Sprachen eine echte innere geistige Erfahrung des Absoluten (spiritual experience) fest, mit Recht auch eine verborgene Übereinstimmung, welche eine tiefgehende geistige Kommunikation unter den verschiedenen Religionen ermöglicht. Doch darf die Übereinstimmung nicht simplifiziert, dürfen die Unterschiede nicht nivelliert, darf die durchaus vieldeutige innere religiöse Erfahrung nicht verabsolutiert werden, als ob alle artikulierbaren religiösen Aussagen, alle Offenbarungen und Bekenntnisse, Autoritäten, Kirchen, Riten und Erscheinungen gegenüber dieser inneren religiösen Erfahrung gleichgültig seien.

So tolerant kann Radakrishnan nur sein, weil es sich wie bei allen Synkretismen um eine durchaus qualifizierte, eben spezifisch hinduistische (auf der Autorität des Vedanta gründende) Toleranz handelt. Östliche, vorwiegend mystisch orientierte Religionen wie Hinduismus und Buddhismus, für die das menschliche Erlebnis der Versenkung im Mittelpunkt steht, vertreten auf ihre Weise durchaus auch einen Ausschließlichkeitsanspruch: insofern sie nämlich anders als die prophetischen Religionen (Judentum, Christentum, Islam), für die das Offenbarungsgeschehen und Gottes Autorität im Mittelpunkt stehen, alle übrigen Religionen nicht aus-, sondern einschließen[7]. Der Hinduismus absorbiert alle anderen Religionen. Der Buddhismus, als höchste Heilslehre, akzeptiert andere Religionen als niedere Stufen für den gewöhnlichen Menschen: eher ein gelassenes Hinnehmen und Dulden als ein echtes Geltenlassen von Lehren, die zu den eigenen im Widerspruch stehen. In einer späteren Existenz hat der im Irrtum Befangene noch ungezählte Chancen, zur richtigen Überzeugung zu kommen.

Unbestreitbar hat es in der Geschichte der Menschheit mehrere »maßgebende Menschen« gegeben. Nach Karl Jaspers haben Buddha, Kung-futse, Sokrates, Jesus (nicht Mose, dessen Wirkung zu begrenzt, und nicht Mohammed, dessen Originalität zu gering war) letzte menschliche Möglichkeiten geoffenbart und damit für das Menschsein unumstößliche Maßstäbe gesetzt, so daß sie durch Jahrtausende auf die innere Haltung von Menschen in außerordentlichem Umfang und in außerordentlicher Tiefe gewirkt haben[8]. Unbestreitbar beziehen sich ihre Fragen und Antworten sachlich aufeinander; Gemeinsamkeiten lassen sich aufzeigen bezüglich ihrer Verkündigung und ihrer Lebensführung, bezüglich ihres Verhältnisses zu Menschen und Welt, aber auch bezüglich ihrer Mythisierung im Zusammenhang ihrer Geburt, Berufung, Versuchung sowie ihrer »Erhöhung« nach dem Tode. Doch ebenso unbestreitbar ist, daß sich diese verschiedenen »maßgebenden Menschen« nicht einfach als Teile in ein Ganzes der Wahrheit integrieren lassen: »sie stehen auch disparat nebeneinander als unvereinbar in einem einzelnen Menschen, der etwa alle ihre Wege zugleich ginge[9]«. Nur naive Unkenntnis der Tatsachen läßt die besonderen Qualitäten eines jeden übersehen oder nivellieren. Einer Entscheidung läßt sich kaum ausweichen.

Jegliches billige Überlegenheitsgefühl oberhalb aller Religionen und ihrer angeblichen Haarspaltereien – nicht nur bei Philosophen, sondern auch bei Theologen möglich – führt bei denjenigen, denen die zentralen Inhalte des Glaubens abhanden gekommen sind, zur völligen Gleichgültigkeit. Bei den anderen aber führt es zur re-aktionären Versteifung in ihrer traditionellen Glaubenshaltung. Alles Nivellieren, Abstrahieren, Generalisieren bringt uns nicht voran. Die Vernebelung der Unterschiede in einem religiösen Dachverband aller Religionen ließ bisher die verschiedenen Religionen völlig unberührt. Zu viel wissen wir von den einzelnen Religionen, als daß ein christlicher Dogmatiker noch ungeschützt behaupten dürfte, sie seien nur eigenmächtige menschliche Konstruktionen, oder ein Hindu-Universalist, sie seien im wesentlichen alle gleich, oder ein säkularer Humanist, sie seien alle nur Opium des Volkes.

Können wir uns die geistige Auseinandersetzung – in möglichst nüchterner, ansprechbarer allseitiger Bescheidenheit – ersparen? Nicht nur unter den Religionen des Westens, sondern auch denen des Ostens läßt sich die *Wahrheitsfrage* nicht ausklammern oder verharmlosen. Die jahrhundertealte, zum Teil recht grausame und heute wieder neu virulente Rivalität zwischen Hinduismus und Islam (Indien und Pakistan), zwischen Hinduismus und Buddhismus, Buddhismus und Neu-Konfuzianismus bestätigt dies. Auch in den asiatischen Religionen ist keineswegs alles gleich-gültig.

Gewiß, Wahrheitsfrage und Heilsfrage sind nicht, wie in der christlichen Theologie früher, zu vermischen. Die heutige christliche »Theologie der Religionen« hat recht: In anderen Religionen können Menschen das ewige Heil erlangen; insofern können sie mit Grund Heilswege genannt werden. Aber die Heilsfrage macht die Wahrheitsfrage nicht überflüssig. Wenn heute von der christlichen Theologie bejaht wird, daß alle Menschen, auch die in den Weltreligionen, gerettet werden können, so bedeutet dies keineswegs, daß alles gleich wahr ist. Gerettet werden sie nicht wegen, sondern trotz Polytheismus, Magie, Menschenopfer, Naturzwängen. Gerettet werden sie nicht wegen, sondern trotz aller Unwahrheit und allen Aberglaubens. Insofern können die Weltreligionen nur bedingt – nicht einfach pauschal und in jedem Fall – Heilswege genannt werden. Soviel Wahrheit sie im einzelnen auch aufweisen, was von den Christen zu bejahen ist: *die* Wahrheit bieten sie für die Christen nicht. Der Christ könnte es nicht verantworten, ebensogut Buddhist, Hinduist, Konfuzianist oder Moslem zu sein. Wo etwa Yoga oder Zen-Buddhismus vom Christen akzeptiert wird (»christliches Yoga« oder »christliches Zen«), dann nicht im Sinne einer Religion oder letzten Glaubenshaltung, sondern einer Methode oder eines Weges der »Erleuchtung«: ein von den religiösen Grundlagen losgelöstes Zen, anziehend für viele moderne Menschen durch den Akzent auf dem Nicht-Intellektuellen und einer keineswegs weltflüchtigen Mystik, auf Ruhe und Stille, auf dem dynamischen Aufbruch der Tiefenschichten des menschlichen Geistes, ebenso interessant für Theologen und Philosophen wie für Psychiater und Psychotherapeuten[10].

Freilich ist mit all dem noch nicht positiv gesagt, was für Christen die Wahrheit ist, wohl aber ist jene kritisch-selbstkritische Auseinandersetzung mit den Weltreligionen gefordert, deren Kriterium nicht das Mitleid, sondern nur die Wahrheit sein darf: eine prüfende Diagnose der Weltreligionen, die nicht richten, sondern helfen will.

Helfende Diagnose

So sind auch die Weltreligionen heute herausgefordert, im Toynbeeschen Sinn von challenge and response: aufgerufen zur Antwort. Die Begegnung mit dem Christentum bedeutet für die asiatischen Religionen einen Anstoß von unabsehbarem Ausmaß: zur kritischen Selbstbesinnung, zur Reinigung und Vertiefung der eigenen Glaubensgrundlagen, zur Befruchtung mit christlichen Ideen und Entfaltung keimhafter Ansätze. Für andere Religionen gilt analog, was man für den Neo-Hinduismus im Vergleich zum klassischen Hinduismus analysiert hat: jetzt Verstärkung des Monotheismus, Zurückdrängen der Idolatrie und Beseitigung grober Entartungen, Ethisierung der Religion, Eintreten für soziale Reformen und ein modernes Erziehungssystem, Neuinterpretation der Upanishaden und der Bhagavadgita, sogar Interesse an der Figur Jesu, wenn auch losgelöst von der geschichtlichen Erscheinungsform (mystische Interpretation des Johannesevangeliums), und Ernstnehmen der in der Bergpredigt verkündeten »ewigen Prinzipien[11]«. Man denke auch an den Einfluß der christlichen Friedensidee – beim Versagen der christlichen Friedenspraxis! – auf die neue Friedenspropaganda des Buddhismus (Friedenspagoden in Rangun und Hiroshima). Der ganze Prozeß der Reform und Erneuerung und das heißt der Konzentration, Vertiefung, Verinnerlichung und gerade so zugleich der Öffnung und Einigung, in welchem heute die Christenheit in weitesten Teilen begriffen ist, stellt eine beträchtliche Herausforderung an jene Religionen dar, die aufs Ganze gesehen – trotz allem neuen Selbstbewußtsein in den neuerwachten Nationen, trotz allen buddhistischen Weltkonzilien, panislamischen Konferenzen und manchen Vertiefungen und missionarischen Gegenvorstößen – keine ähnliche geistige Dynamik zu entwickeln vermochten (von den afrikanischen Stammesreligionen ganz zu schweigen).

Für eine fruchtbare Auseinandersetzung auf gleicher Ebene wäre dringend zu wünschen, daß die Weltreligionen im neuzeitlichen Sinn wissenschaftliche Theologien entwickelten, die das Niveau der christlichen Theologie erreichten: nicht nur eine überhöhende Meditation, sondern eine selbstkritische Reflexion. Die christliche Theologie ist die erste, die das moderne methodisch-wissenschaftliche Denken aufgenommen, ja zu einem erheblichen Teil mit hervorgebracht hat. Nur aufgrund einer echten Pluralität von Theologien aber kann es zu einem echten Dialog kommen. Nicht als ob das Christentum unmittelbar eine wissenschaftliche hinduistische, buddhistische, konfuzianische, taoistische oder islamische Theologie fördern sollte oder auch nur könnte. Aber das Christentum kann durch eine unvoreingenommene sachlich erarbeitete Religionsgeschichte, Religionsphänomenologie, Religionspsychologie, Religionssoziologie und Religionstheologie zur ernsthaften Auseinandersetzung provozieren[12]. Zur Kontroverstheologie zwischen den christlichen Konfessionen muß eine Kontroverstheologie zwischen den verschiedenen Religionen kommen. Ober besser: eine ökumenische Theologie im weitesten Sinn des Wortes.

Die Weltreligionen versuchten sich vielfach der Auseinandersetzung mit dem Christentum durch geistige Abkapselung zu entziehen. Während im Westen eine erbarmungslose Analyse der religiösen Krise vorherrscht, so im Osten noch immer die apologetische Selbstbehauptung. Sind aber Isolierung und Demarkation bei den neuen Verkehrsverbindungen und Kommunikationsmitteln nicht je länger desto weniger unmöglich? Die geistige Unbeweglichkeit und oft jahrhundertealte Erstarrung auch der großen asiatischen Religionen war in ruhigeren Zeiten vielleicht nicht so gefährlich. Aber heute werden diese Religionen, ob sie es wollen oder nicht, nicht nur in die Auseinandersetzung mit dem Christentum, sondern zugleich in die mit der rasanten modernen säkularen Entwicklung hineingezogen. Eine Entwicklung, wie sie aus Amerika, Europa und der Sowjetunion auf tausend Wegen mit ihrer ganzen Faszination und Suggestion unaufhaltsam die Länder des Nahen und Fernen Ostens ergreift und sie, wie im Falle Chinas und Japans, bereits überschwemmt hat in Wirtschaft, Wissenschaft, Kultur, Technik, Politik. Das bedeutet in vielfacher Hinsicht eine Profanisierung des Religiösen, aber oft auch eine neue Sakralisierung des Profanen – Voraussetzung für Ersatzreligionen oder »Quasi-Religionen«: jene Verabsolutierung der Nation, der sozialen Klasse oder der Wissenschaft oder auch einer Person, die den Völkern und dem Einzelnen kaum Glück bringt. Insbesondere steht der atheistische dialektische Materialismus in der Form des missionarischen Kommunismus – Marxismus-Leninismus oder Maoismus, als »Wissenschaft« deklariert – in universaler Konkurrenz aber doch auch in nicht unfruchtbarem Gespräch mit Christentum *und* Weltreligionen. Das vielfache Versagen des Christentums *und* der Weltreligionen bei der Vermenschlichung des Menschen, beim Einsatz für Gerechtigkeit, Friede und Freiheit und ihr mehr trennender als einigender Einfluß auf die Gesamtmenschheit bilden den dunklen Hintergrund, vor dem sich die ganze Entwicklung abspielt.

»Modernität« bedeutet für alle diese Länder nicht nur eine Flut wirtschaftlicher und gesellschaftlicher Strukturveränderungen, sondern eine völlig neue Form von Bewußtsein. Dabei ist nicht so wichtig, daß dieser Entwicklung zwangsläufig einige »heilige Kühe« und andere religiöse Spezialitäten, gegen die bisher selbst der allindische Kongreß weithin machtlos war, zum Opfer fallen.

Verhängnisvoll wird die Entwicklung erst dort, wo die betroffenen Religionen, von Einzelversuchen wie etwa im indischen Reform-Hinduismus oder japanischen Zen-Buddhismus abgesehen, auf die grundlegenden neuen Fragen, schicksalshaft für die Zukunft des Einzelnen wie der Völker, kaum überzeugende Antworten entwickelt haben. Um auch in dieser Richtung wie bisher konkret zu reden, soll im Sinne der helfenden Diagnose – selbstverständlich wiederum ohne jeglichen Anspruch auf religionsgeschichtliche Vollständigkeit und Gründlichkeit – auf einige kritische Punkte hingewiesen werden, die zumindest als Fragen ernstgenommen werden müssen und die ein eingehendes Gespräch mit dem Christentum erfordern[13].

a. Selbst der am Judentum und Christentum orientierte Islam denkt ähnlich wie Hinduismus und Buddhismus in bezug auf die ihm eigene Offenbarung völlig *ungeschichtlich*. Der Koran, seine Grundlage, ist von der ersten bis zur letzten Sure direkt nach dem im Himmel aufbewahrten Buch dem Propheten von einem Engel diktiert worden: Er ist bis aufs Wort inspiriert (Verbalinspiration) und deshalb in jedem Satz unfehlbar (Inerranz, Infallibilität). Und damit ist der Grund angegeben, weswegen vor der Lektüre ganz anders als bei der Bibel die Hände zu waschen sind: Der Koran ist in keiner Weise Menschenwort, sondern unmittelbar Gotteswort. An der Stelle Christi steht im Islam das Buch, anstelle der Christologie eine Koranologie.

Doch die Frage, die man auch auf die heiligen Schriften des Hinduismus oder Buddhismus anwenden könnte: Wird sich der Islam auf längere Sicht den Ergebnissen der intensiven westlichen Koranforschung verschließen können: daß der Koran, was wohl nicht nur in Afghanistan kein Gelehrter öffentlich sagen darf, sehr viel späteres und zufälliges Material enthält und eben auch eine sehr menschliche Geschichte umschließt? Hat es dann aber noch einen Sinn, die ganze moderne Entwicklung bis zur Elektrizität, den Mikroben und den Satelliten im Koran, der wegen Gottes absoluter Allmacht eigentlich gar keine Naturgesetze zuläßt, vorgezeichnet zu finden, ja, sich sogar an der Eroberung des Mondes – das heilige Symbol des Islam, allerdings relativ jungen türkischen Ursprungs – zu stoßen? Haben nicht die wissenschaftlich-technische Entwicklung und die staatliche Autorität (allen voran in der Türkei) schon zu Beginn des Jahrhunderts den Koran als Rechtsbuch weithin außer Kraft gesetzt und eine vielschichtige Anpassung der Religion – man denke an die Stellung der Frau und den Harem und überhaupt an das Zivil- und Strafrecht – erzwungen? Wie soll der Islam bei seiner im Mittelalter hochentwickelten, aber jetzt unproduktiv gewordenen Theologie die nicht aus ihm hervorgegangenen neuzeitlichen wissenschaftlichen, technischen, wirtschaftlichen, kulturellen, politischen Errungenschaften in sein System einbauen können? Müßte dann nicht die islamische Gleichsetzung des Willens Allahs oder des Koran mit der weltlichen Gesetzesordnung aufgegeben werden? Müßten dann nicht das Recht, die Natur-, Geschichts- und Gesellschaftswissenschaften unabhängig von einer Begründung im Koran entwickelt werden, auch wenn dies eine gewaltige Erschütterung der maßgebenden Tradition bedeutete? Müßten dann nicht aus den islamisch geführten und geprägten Staaten (arabische Staaten, Pakistan, Afghanistan) religiös neutrale Staaten (wie Indien im Sinne Nehrus) werden und die »heiligen Kriege« aufhören? Kann also die innere Unruhe und tiefe Anpassungskrise, die den Islam wie andere Religionen erfaßt hat, auf die Dauer durch starre Abwehr, konservative islamische Renaissance und Berufung auf die Leistungen der eigenen Vergangenheit überwunden werden? Wären hier nicht auch eine neue geistige Anstrengung und eine neue Auseinandersetzung mit der eigenen Geschichte, mit der gesamten westlichen Kultur und damit auch dem Christentum notwendig?

b. Die großen Religionen des Ostens, insbesondere Hinduismus, Buddhismus und auch der indische Dschainismus, denken im Kreis: sie haben ein *zyklisches Weltbild,* nach welchem alles, der Lauf der Welt wie das Leben des Einzelnen, vorbestimmt ist.

Aber auch hier die Fragen: Ist nicht diese Überzeugung der Grund für jenen individuellen Fatalismus und gesellschaftlichen Determinismus, die ein Haupthindernis darstellen für die soziale Besserstellung der Massen gerade in Indien? Werden sich die asiatischen Völker bei der Übernahme und Verarbeitung der modernen Wissenschaft und Technik der selbstkritischen Auseinandersetzung mit der Auffassung von einem linearen beziehungsweise dialektischen Fortschreiten der Geschichte entziehen können, wie sie von der jüdisch-christlichen Tradition, dann vom Islam und schließlich überhaupt vom neuzeitlichen Bewußtsein, auch vom Marxismus, vertreten wird? Eine Geschichtsauffassung, welche ganz anders als diese Religionen die individuelle Person in ihrer Einzigartigkeit, ihr Leben und ihre Arbeit völlig ernstnimmt? Was soll heute eine üppig phantastische Kosmogonie, Welthistorie und Mythologie? Was sollen immer neue Wiedergeburten nach dem Gesetz des Karmas, des »Tuns«, der automatischen Vergeltung aller Lebenstaten – Lehren, die von Buddha als selbstverständliche Dogmen aus dem Upanishaden-Brahamanismus übernommen worden waren?

c. Mit der Auffassung von Wiederkehr und Wiedergeburt ist für den Hinduismus (eigentlich ein Bündel von Religionen) die *religiöse Kastenordnung* verbunden, die allerdings vom Buddhismus und vom Sikhismus (einer monotheistischen indisch-islamischen Mischreligion) schon immer entschieden abgelehnt wurde. In die Kaste – es gibt in Indien an die 3000 innerhalb von vier Grundtypen – bleibt der Mensch für sein ganzes (diesmaliges) Leben hineingeboren. Von der Kaste wird ihm Berufstätigkeit, Ehepartner, die ganze Lebensform grundsätzlich vorgeschrieben.

Die Fragen: Ist eine solche Auffassung nicht im glatten Widerspruch zu der sich überall auf der Welt durchsetzenden Auffassung von der grundlegenden Gleichberechtigung aller Menschen? Ist die anscheinend unausrottbare Kastenordnung in Indien, obwohl gesetzlich insbesondere für die »Unberührbaren«, die kastenlosen Parias, beseitigt, nicht noch immer zusammen mit dem ökonomisch und sozial verheerenden Kuh-Kult die größte Belastung für das neue demokratische Indien? Ist sie nicht der Grund, warum der Hinduismus anders als der Buddhismus, abgesehen von Sonderfällen, auf Indien beschränkt blieb? Steht sie nicht im Widerspruch zum modernen Geist der Mobilität im Berufsleben, wo man nicht einfach mehr ist, was und wo man ist, sondern sich alles, auch der Wohnsitz der Menschen, ändern und wieder ändern kann? Ist also die religiöse Kastenordnung – der bisher schützende und stützende Rahmen der verschiedenen synkretistischen Religionsformen – in den großen Städten wie Bombay, Delhi, Madras und Calcutta nicht in Auflösung begriffen und kann das ohne schwerwiegende Rückwirkungen auf das religiöse Bewußtsein bleiben?

d. Nach der ursprünglich mönchischen Auffassung (Vorrang der Mönchsgemeinde, Bindung der Laien an die Klöster), wie sie zusammen mit dem strengeren Buddhismus auch die einflußreichste Hindu-Philosophie, Shankaras klassisches Vedanta-System vertritt, ist die irdische Wirklichkeit, ist das Leben, die Freude, Liebe, die Persönlichkeit, das Ich, ist die Welt überhaupt letztlich nichts anderes als wesenloser *unwirklicher Schein* (maya).

Frage: Wie soll eine solche Auffassung von der unwirklichen Welt in einer technokratischen Zivilisation glaubwürdig gelebt werden können: von Menschen in der sehr wirklichen Welt der Drehbänke, Fließbänder, Laboratorien, Computer, Verwaltungsgebäude? Kann man durch die Lehre von der doppelten Wahrheit der Wirklichkeit, wie sie ist, entgehen? Und wird der aus der Wandelbarkeit und Nichtigkeit alles Irdischen folgende weitgehende kosmische *Pessimismus* des Buddhismus – weshalb er schon immer vom chinesischen Neu-Konfuzianismus kritisiert wurde – und die ebenfalls damit verbundene beträchtliche *Indifferenz gegenüber den sozialen Nöten* der Menschen eine Antwort sein können auf die neuen Hoffnungen der im Aufbruch begriffenen Völker Ostasiens? Wird sich der Buddhismus in seiner Propaganda für Frieden und Gerechtigkeit dem weltlichen Geschehen, beziehungsweise den ursprünglich christlichen Parolen nicht noch mehr anpassen müssen? Und ist dieselbe ethische *Passivität* nicht auch der schwache Punkt in der individualistisch-quietistischen Mystik des chinesischen Taoismus, für den eine spekulative Naturphilosophie und das begierdelose, stille Sichversenken in den Ursprung der Dinge wichtiger ist als alle sozialen Tugenden? Dürfte die rühmenswerte passive östliche Toleranz je so weit gehen, daß sie das prophetische Nein gegenüber rohen und abergläubischen Religionsformen, gegenüber Verunreinigung und Entartung des Gottesglaubens, gegenüber gesellschaftlichen Mißständen und unmenschlichen Verhältnissen nicht mehr aufbringt?

e. Der chinesische Konfuzianismus betont im Gegensatz zu Buddhismus und Taoismus den Vorrang der Ethik vor metaphysischer Spekulation. Obwohl im Neukonfuzianismus (seit dem 12. Jahrhundert), der den Himmel im Menschen sucht, die Ethik metaphysisch und die Metaphysik ethisch wird, blieb der Konfuzianismus doch die vielleicht »säkularste« Religion des Ostens, die mehr an der Harmonie der Menschen untereinander und mit dem Kosmos als an einem Jenseits oder Nirwana interessiert ist. Sollte vielleicht der Konfuzianismus die religiöse Zukunft Asiens sein können?

Aber auch hier stellen sich Gegenfragen ein: Huldigen nicht gerade Konfuzianismus und Neukonfuzianismus einem kaum überbietbaren *Traditionalismus:* Ahnenkult, Überbewertung des Alters, Vorrang der klassischen Bildung, Aufbau von Staat und Gesellschaft nach dem Vorbild der patriarchalischen Familie? Entgegen der ursprünglichen Pluralität im chinesischen Denken die ideologische Stütze eines starren Sozialsystems von einzigartiger Dauer? Geradezu die fortschrittsfeindliche Staatsideologie des »Reiches der Mitte«, des isolierten alten China: eine der konservativsten Ideologien der Weltgeschichte, welche man die Kodifizierung der Ordnung der Unterordnung genannt hat? Ist nicht deshalb der mit dem Kaisersturz (1912) geschwächte chinesische Konfuzianismus – ähnlich wie 1917 der traditionellste Zweig der Christenheit, die ebenfalls mit dem früheren politischen System engstens verbundene russisch-orthodoxe Kirche – 1949 unter das Gericht des Kommunismus gekommen und seither zusammen mit dem Taoismus als Feind allen Fortschritts von den Kommunisten in seinen Wirkungsmöglichkeiten so weit als möglich eingeengt worden? Ja, wurde nicht für viele der Maoismus unter Auswechslung des religiösen durch den marxistischen Gehalt faktisch Nachfolger des Konfuzianismus: insofern er bei allen positiven Intentionen und echten Errungenschaften das System der Staatsorthodoxie übernahm und zeitweise auch den alten chinesischen Isolationismus und das Gottkaisertum in neuer Form zum Leben erweckte[14]?

4. Nicht Ausschließlichkeit, sondern Einzigartigkeit

Ungeschichtlichkeit, Im-Kreis-Denken, Fatalismus, Weltlosigkeit, Pessimismus, Passivität, Kastengeist, soziales Desinteresse, Traditionalismus: diese Andeutungen dürften genügen, um unsere diagnostischen Fragen an die Weltreligionen im Rahmen des hier Möglichen zu konkretisieren. Nur dürfen diese Fragen nicht als Entlastungsfragen für das Christentum verstanden werden! Das amerikanische Rassensystem, insbesondere von sehr bibelfesten Protestanten vertreten, ist für die meisten Soziologen nur eine Variante des Kastensystems. Und die notorische soziale Rückständigkeit katholischer Länder und ihre Anfälligkeit für den Kommunismus wird man nicht gerade dem konfuzianischen Traditionalismus zuschreiben wollen. Das christliche Europa, welches nach Ghandi nur dem Namen nach christlich ist und in Wirklichkeit den Mammon anbetet, und die Aggressivität, die Herrsch- und Profitsucht christlicher Länder in Asien, Afrika und Südamerika haben auf lange Zeit hinaus die christliche Botschaft kompromittiert. Doch werden wir auf die Probleme der

Christenheit immer wieder neu stoßen. Hier indessen sollte zur Klärung der Situation der Christenheit herausgestellt werden, daß die großen Weltreligionen sich heute nicht weniger, sondern mehr in Frage gestellt sehen als das Christentum: Ganz anders als damals die Länder des europäischen Frühkapitalismus stehen heute die Länder Asiens und Afrikas unter dem Zwang eines möglichst raschen Übergangs von der vorindustriellen Kultur zur modernen Industriegesellschaft. So rasch als möglich werden wegen des erschreckend niedrigen Lebensstandards und den noch immer zunehmenden Massen, werden wegen der internationalen Konkurrenz und der nationalen Unabhängigkeit das Produktionsniveau verbreitert und gehoben, folglich Industrialisierung und technische Schulung vorangetrieben und die vortechnischen Formen beseitigt. Ein neues Bewußtsein, eine unumgängliche Säkularisierung ist die Folge und damit auch eine Zerstörung religiöser Traditionen, Werte, Institutionen, deren Entweihung kaum eben angefangen hat.

Christsein als kritischer Katalysator

Alles dies heißt nicht, daß die traditionellen Religionen verschwinden müssen. Auch sie wandeln sich und können sich langsam anpassen. Die Absorptionskraft der östlichen Religionen ist ungeheuer, und vielleicht muß man wie in den arabischen Staaten eher als mit dem Zerfall mit einer beschränkten »Renaissance« der Weltreligionen im postkolonialistischen Zeitalter rechnen. Vielleicht auch mit missionarischen Vorstößen außerhalb Asiens, die freilich wie schon bisher kaum großen Erfolg haben dürften. In der europäischen Renaissance und Klassik gab es eine Affinität zur griechischen Antike, in der Aufklärung zum konfuzianischen China. Heute gibt es bei manchen eine bestimmte (immer selektive!) Wahlverwandtschaft mit der indischen Geistigkeit (wie schon in der Romantik), bei anderen mit dem japanischen Zen-Buddhismus. Aber die Bedeutung solcher Phänomene – zum Teil Modeerscheinungen – ist keineswegs zu übertreiben. Für die Zukunft ist sehr viel wichtiger, daß die Weltreligionen in einer bisher noch nie dagewesenen Gefährdung stehen: bei traditionalistischem Versagen ignoriert, beim Versuch des Widerstands bekämpft, in jedem Fall aber innerlich ausgehöhlt und äußerlich manipuliert zu werden (etwa der Islam als nützliches Instrument panarabischer oder zumindest antiisraelischer Politik). Soll unter solchen Umständen überhaupt der religiösen Indifferenz (besonders in Ländern beginnender Industrialisierung wie Ägypten und Indien), der inneren Aversion (bei vielen Gebildeten im hochindustrialisierten Japan) und der äußeren Aggression (im kommunistischen China) begegnet werden, so werden auch nichtchristliche Religionen um eine grundlegende Neubesinnung und damit um eine erneute, ganz anders ernsthafte Auseinandersetzung mit dem Christentum nicht herumkommen[1].

Westliche Wissenschaft und Technik bergen von ihrer Geschichte her viel zu viele Elemente aus der jüdisch-christlichen Tradition, als daß es so einfach wäre, westliche Wissenschaft und Technik zu übernehmen, ohne die eigenen religiösen Positionen in Frage zu stellen. Wir sahen: Der Einfluß der westlichen Kultur führte zu tiefgreifenden Änderungen des Hinduismus und Buddhismus insbesondere bezüglich der materiellen Güter, der sozialen Gerechtigkeit, des Weltfriedens und des Sinns der Geschichte. Aber die Bedeutung der Geschichte, des Fortschritts, der Welt, der Bedeutung der einzelnen Person, der Frau, der menschlichen Arbeit, der individuellen Freiheit, der fundamentalen Gleichheit, des sozialen Engagements: über diese und so viele andere die nichtchristlichen Religionen bedrängenden Fragen hat sich die christliche Theologie durch die ganze Neuzeit hindurch methodisch und systematisch Gedanken gemacht. Gedanken, die für die anderen Religionen, deren moderne wissenschaftliche Theologien noch alle im Anfangsstadium stecken, nicht weniger nützlich sein könnten, als es die Errungenschaften westlicher Naturwissenschaft und Technik für die Industrialisierung und kulturelle Entwicklung ihrer Länder sind. Vielleicht wird das auch in diesem Buch, ohne daß ständig auf die anderen Religionen direkt Bezug genommen wird, ein wenig aufscheinen.

Was also sollen wir nach den Ergebnissen dieser gedrängten Analyse vom Christentum her anstreben?

– Nicht *die arrogante* Herrschaft einer Religion, *die missionarisch exklusiv die Freiheit verachtet; diese ungewollte Gefahr droht im Gefolge der dogmatischen Verdrängung des Religionsproblems durch Karl Barth und die »dialektische Theologie«. Ein borniierter, eingebildeter, exklusiver Partikularismus, der die anderen Religionen global verdammt, ein Proselytismus, der unlauteren Wettbewerb betreibt, denkt zu gering nicht nur von den Religionen, sondern auch vom Evangelium.*

– Nicht *die synkretistische* Vermischung aller *unter sich so widersprüchlichen* Religionen, *die harmonisierend, reduzierend die Wahrheit unterdrückt; diese wiederum ungewollte Gefahr droht bei der liberalen Lösung des Religionsproblems durch Toynbee und manche Religionswissenschaftler. Ein lähmender, zersetzender, agnostisch-relativistischer Indifferentismus, der undifferenziert die anderen Religionen billigt und bestätigt, wirkt vielleicht zunächst befreiend und beglückend, aber in seinem Einerlei schließlich doch quälend, weil er alle festen Maßstäbe und Normen aufgegeben hat.*

– *Vielmehr der eigenständige, uneigennützige christliche* Dienst *an den Menschen in den Religionen. Und zwar aus jener Offenheit heraus, die mehr ist als herablassende Akkommodation; die die eigene Glaubensüberzeugung nicht verleugnet, aber auch keine bestimmte Antwort aufzwingt; die die Kritik von außen zur Selbstkritik macht und zugleich alles Positive aufnimmt; die nichts Wertvolles an den Religionen zerstört, aber auch nichts Wertloses unkritisch einverleibt. In dialektischer Einheit also von Anerkennung und Ablehnung soll das Christentum unter den Weltreligionen seinen Dienst leisten: als* kritischer Katalysator und Kristallisationspunkt *ihrer religiösen, moralischen, meditativen, asketischen, ästhetischen Werte.*

In solcher Perspektive hätte christliche *Mission* einen Sinn: Christliche Mission wüßte dann immer, daß sie es nicht nur mit Religionen, sondern mit Gläubigen zu tun hat. Aber sie wäre deshalb nicht in erster Linie auf möglichst zahlreiche Einzelkonversionen ausgerichtet. Vielmehr auf den echten Dialog mit den Religionen insgesamt in gegenseitigem Geben und Nehmen, in welchem die tiefsten Intentionen der Religionen sich erfüllen könnten. So käme es nicht wieder zu einem sinnlos fruchtlosen Zusammenprall, in welchem der Christ selbstsicher, aber ohne Erfolg die Überlegenheit des Christentums beweist. Es käme zu einer echten und fruchtbaren Begegnung, in welcher die anderen Religionen angespornt würden, ihr Bestes und Tiefstes zu sagen. Die Wahrheit der anderen Religionen würde anerkannt, geehrt, gewürdigt, und doch das christliche Bekenntnis nicht relativiert und auf allgemeine Wahrheiten reduziert. Also kurz: Weder ein arroganter Absolutismus, der nichts anderes gelten läßt. Noch ein fauler Eklektizismus, der von allem ein bißchen gelten läßt. Sondern ein inklusiver christlicher Universalismus, der für das Christentum *nicht Ausschließlichkeit*, wohl *aber Einzigartigkeit* beansprucht.

Gemeinsame Suche nach der Wahrheit

Von einer solchen kritisch-konstruktiven Begegnung könnten die in der Geschichte mehr isolierten Religionen Asiens gewiß sehr viel lernen. Umgekehrt aber könnte auch der christliche Glaube nur gewinnen. Zum Beispiel wenn er sich bei der Überkompliziertheit seiner Dogmatik und der vielfachen Vorliebe christlicher Frömmigkeit für Nebensachen und gar Nebengötter beeindrucken ließe von der strengen Einfachheit des Islam, von seiner beharrlich-unerschütterlichen Konzentration auf das Entscheidende des Glaubens: der eine Gott und sein Gesandter. Oder wenn der christliche Glaube seine oft allzu anthropomorphen Vorstellungen vom Vatergott korrigieren ließe durch das ehrfürchtige mehr transpersonale (besser als: unpersonale) Gottesverständnis der asiatischen Religionen, wie es auf Goethe, den deutschen Idealismus, Schopenhauer, Jung, Huxley und Hesse nicht zu Unrecht nachhaltig gewirkt hat. Oder wenn der oft noch immer zu »jenseitig« orientierte christliche Glaube sich von der tiefen und konkreten Menschlichkeit chinesischen Denkens beeindrucken ließe, vom Glauben an die Perfektibilität und Erziehbarkeit des Menschen, der vom Konfuzianismus in den Maoismus übernommen wurde. Oder wenn er für die Lösung des Rassenproblems und den klugen Umgang mit primitiven Völkern wiederum vom Islam lernte. Vergleiche wie der zwischen dem christlichen Reich Gottes und dem buddhistischen Nirwana, zwischen dem Ethos hier und dort könnten sehr fruchtbar sein.

Wie immer: Christianisierung dürfte jedenfalls nie mehr Latinisierung, Romanisierung, Europäisierung, Amerikanisierung heißen. Das Christentum ist nicht einfach die Religion des Abendlandes. In der Frühzeit der christlichen Kirche gab es ein palästinisches und griechisches, römisches und afrikanisches, koptisches und äthiopisches, spanisches und gallisches, alemannisches und sächsisches, armenisches und georgisches, irisches und slawisches Christentum. Nach der christlichen Theologie des 2. (besonders Justin) und 3. Jahrhunderts (besonders die

Alexandriner Klemens und Origenes) wirkte der göttliche Logos (logos spermatikos – das als Samen wirkende Wort) überall und von Anfang an. Wenn aber schon die Heiden Platon, Aristoteles und Plotin oder für andere auch Marx und Freud »Pädagogen« zu Christus hin sein konnten, warum nicht auch die philosophischen und religiösen Denker anderer Völker? Bietet der Osten nicht Denk- und Gestaltungsformen, Strukturen und Modelle an, in denen das Christentum ebenso gedacht und gelebt werden könnte wie in den westlichen[2]? Ist Jesus nicht, worauf Gandhi aufmerksam macht, eine östliche Gestalt, die vom Osten vielleicht kongenialer interpretiert werden könnte? Wird die Gestalt Jesu nicht von bedeutenden nichtchristlichen Denkern in Indien intensiv studiert und neu gedeutet[3]? Müßte nicht grundsätzlich und praktisch unterschieden werden zwischen dem für Christen inakzeptablen religiösen und dem durchaus akzeptablen kulturellen Hinduismus, Buddhismus, Konfuzianismus, Taoismus, Islam? Haben bestimmte Formen des Hinduismus, des Buddhismus, der islamischen Mystik die neutestamentlichen Wahrheiten der Gottesliebe, der Gnade, des stellvertretenden Leidens, ja der Rechtfertigung durch den Glauben (Amida-Buddhismus) nicht ungleich tiefer erfaßt als die Griechen oder auch die ›Kritische Theorie‹? Könnte somit all das, was sonst vielleicht vereinzelt und verstreut, fragmentarisch und sporadisch, verzerrt und verunstaltet gegeben ist, nicht im Christentum zur vollen Geltung gebracht werden: ohne eine falsche antithetische Exklusivität, vielmehr in schöpferischem Umdenken eine neue inklusive und zugleich kritische Synthese. Was also sind die Forderungen für ein Christentum der Zukunft?

- *Wir brauchen ein echtes indisches, chinesisches, japanisches, indonesisches, arabisches, afrikanisches Christentum.*
- *Wir brauchen eine Ökumene nicht mehr nur im engen konfessionell-kirchlichen, sondern in einem universal-christlichen Sinne: gründend nicht in missionarischer Eroberung der anderen Religionen, sondern in der christlichen Präsenz unter den anderen Religionen, hörend auf ihre Anliegen, solidarisch mit ihren Nöten und zugleich lebendig Zeugnis gebend vom eigenen Glauben in Wort und Tat.*
- *Wir brauchen eine Mission, die bei aller Wachsamkeit gegenüber synkretistischer Gleichgültigkeit Toleranz einschließt: bei allem Anspruch auf unbedingte Geltung bereit zur Revision*

des eigenen Standpunktes, wo immer er sich als revisionsbe-dürftig erweist.

Die Kritik der Religionen schließt also – dies übersieht man oft – eine Selbstkritik des Christentums ein. Der englische Übersetzer und Herausgeber des genannten japanischen Romans ›Silence‹ macht auf die Gegenseitigkeit des theologischen Nehmens und Gebens aufmerksam: Wenn das Ohr Japans einen neuen Ton in der weiten Symphonie der Wahrheit auffängt, dann wird auch der Westen aufhorchen, auf der Suche, wie er ist, nach neuen Klängen, die auf seine erwachenden Sensibilitäten antworten[4]. In manchen Punkten kommt heute die selbstkritische Reflexion der christlichen Theologie solch einem gegenseitigen geistigen Austausch bereits weit entgegen: so in der Kritik einer massiv hellenistisch-physizistisch verstandenen Gottessohnschaft Jesu – für die Moslems schon immer ein Stein des Anstoßes. Oder in der Kritik der seit Augustin in der Westkirche verbreiteten mythologischen Vorstellung von einer durch physische Zeugung vererbten Sünde, was ein an das Gute im Menschen glaubender Konfuzianist nie richtig verstehen konnte. Oder in der Betonung einer »Hierarchie der Wahrheiten«, die das Zentrum des Glaubens als Zentrum und periphere Aussagen (wie die vier vatikanischen Dogmen über Maria und den Papst) als periphere heraustreten läßt.

Es verdient deshalb mit Nachdruck unterstrichen zu werden: Viele Probleme im Dialog mit den nichtchristlichen Religionen liegen in der christlichen Theologie selbst. Es ist natürlich begreiflich, daß alle die verdienten Spezialisten für Islam, Taoismus, Caodaismus, Dschainismus, Hinayana-, Mahayana- und Matrayana-Buddhismus und die noch zahlreicheren Hindu-Systeme nicht mit gleicher Intensität die neuen und oft recht raschen Entwicklungen der christlichen Theologie verfolgen können. Aber trotz aller Schwierigkeiten, daß der Theologe normalerweise nicht auch Spezialist in Religionswissenschaft sein kann und umgekehrt der Religionswissenschaftler nicht auch noch Spezialist in systematischer Theologie, muß doch daran festgehalten werden: Will man im Dialog zwischen Christentum und Weltreligionen nicht von vornherein aneinander vorbeireden, will man sich wirklich begegnen, so muß man bei allen Vergleichen und Konfrontationen *stets beide Vergleichsgrößen einer kritischen Prüfung unterziehen.* Anstatt sich also beispielsweise in einem Vergleich der »Dreifaltigkeit« nur bei der genauen

Interpretation der Hindu-Trimurti (Brahma als Schöpfer, Vishnu als Erhalter, Shiva als Zerstörer) oder der »Trinität der drei Reinen« im religiösen Taoismus aufzuhalten, müßte man zugleich die christliche Trinitätslehre kritisch befragen: ob denn die griechische und insbesondere lateinische Dreieinigkeitsspekulation – die psychologische Interpretation Augustins, verfeinert durch die Relationenlehre des Thomas von Aquin, mit dem Dreieckssymbol aufgrund der »einen Natur« – den biblischen Aussagen über die Beziehungen von Vater, Sohn und Geist, auf die sie sich beziehen will, überhaupt entspricht. Vielleicht ließe es sich nach einer derartigen beidseitigen Befragung auch leichter mit einem allzu toleranten indischen Polytheisten als mit einem strengen arabischen Monotheisten reden. Ähnliches gilt von Vergleichen bezüglich Inkarnation, Jungfrauengeburt, Wundern, ewigem Leben.

So bliebe denn auch die Christenheit auf ihrem eigenen Felde *nicht* einfach im *Besitz* der bekannten Wahrheit, *sondern auf der Suche* nach der immer größeren und so immer wieder neu unbekannten Wahrheit: in freier Diskussion, der eigenen Tradition verpflichtet, aber ohne dogmatische Fixierung für jedes gute Argument offen. Gerade so könnte die Christenheit leichter zurückfinden zur einfachen Größe ihrer Botschaft in ihrer Einzigartigkeit. Mit dieser Botschaft hat sie am Anfang die Welt überzeugt, und sie wird heute wieder neu von ihr gefordert.

Man wird aber bei allen Vergleichen, bei allen Bemühungen sowohl um ein Verständnis der anderen Religionen wie um ein wahrhaft ökumenisches Christentum eines nicht vergessen: es geht *mehr um Menschen* und ihre gelebten Erfahrungen *als nur um Begriffe, Ideen, Systeme.* Das bedeutet für die Praxis:

a. Die heutigen Weltreligionen dürfen nicht archaisierend *nur* von den klassischen Texten her verstanden, beziehungsweise rekonstruiert werden. Sie können nicht einfach auf das fixiert werden, was in ihrer Tradition steril nach rückwärts weist. Heutige Religionen müssen zugleich vom heutigen Selbstverständnis her verstanden werden, nach welchem zum Beispiel die meisten Asiaten Gott sehr viel weniger unpersönlich denken, als das nach den alten Systemen Shankaras und anderer erwartet werden könnte. Religionen sind nicht historische Denkmäler, die nur von Gelehrten anhand von Texten studiert und verstanden werden können. Sie sind lebendige Glaubenshaltungen, die von wirklichen Menschen im Fluß der Religionsgeschichte immer wieder neu gelebt werden. Sie sind deshalb nach vorne zu interpretieren. Sie sind neuen Fragen zugänglich und stellen selber immer neue Fragen.

b. Ein wahrhaft indisches, chinesisches, japanisches, indonesisches, arabisches, afrikanisches Christentum läßt sich nicht am Schreibtisch ausdenken. Die europäisch-amerikanische Theologie würde ihre Möglichkeiten weit überschätzen, wenn sie meinte, durch ihre gelehrte Reflexion, durch ihre exegetischen, historischen und systematischen Analysen und Vergleiche auch die konkrete Übersetzung der christlichen Botschaft in andere Kulturen hinein leisten zu können. Dafür braucht es, wie schon bei der Übersetzung in die Welt des Hellenismus hinein, die gelebten Erfahrungen konkreter Menschen aus diesen Kulturen selbst[5]. Ohne solche Erfahrungen ist ein schöpferisches Umdenken nicht möglich, bleibt eine neue ökumenische Synthese reine Theorie und ein wahrhaft universales Christentum ein schönes Postulat. Die europäisch-amerikanische Theologie kann für eine solche Übersetzung freilich Voraussetzungen schaffen: Sie kann durch eine selbstkritische, wissenschaftliche Reflexion der eigenen Tradition im Hinblick auf andere Traditionen klarzumachen versuchen, was vom Ursprung her nicht wesentlich christlich und was wesentlich christlich ist. In diesem Sinn soll dieses Buch im Folgenden einen bescheidenen Beitrag auch zum Gespräch mit den Weltreligionen leisten: einerseits durch die dogmatisch unvoreingenommene, historisch möglichst genaue Erfassung der Gestalt Jesu und der ursprünglichen christlichen Botschaft, andererseits durch Hinweise, die zum oft vernachlässigten Vergleich mit anderen großen Gestalten der Religionsgeschichte anregen sollen.

Und so wollen wir nun, nachdem wir den Horizont des heutigen Christentums so gut wie in Kürze möglich abgeschritten haben, uns der zentralen Frage zuwenden, die wir bisher weithin als beantwortet vorausgesetzt haben: Wenn es schon einen Unterschied zwischen dem Christentum und den Weltreligionen sowie den modernen Humanismen geben soll, worin besteht dann dieser Unterschied? Christlich – was ist das eigentlich?

B. Die Unterscheidung

I. Das Besondere des Christentums

1. Der Christus

»Christlich«: weniger ein Schlagwort heute als ein Schlafwort. Christlich ist so vieles, zu vieles: Kirchen, Schulen, politische Parteien, kulturelle Vereine, und natürlich Europa, der Westen, das Mittelalter, ganz zu schweigen vom »allerchristlichsten König« – ein Titel von Rom verliehen, wo man im übrigen andere Attribute vorzieht (»römisch«, »katholisch«, »römisch-katholisch«, »kirchlich«, »heilig«), um sie ohne alle Umstände mit »christlich« schlicht gleichzusetzen. Wie jede Inflation führt auch die Begriffsinflation des Christlichen zur Abwertung.

Gefährliche Erinnerung

Ob man sich überhaupt noch erinnert, daß das nach der Apostelgeschichte in Antiochien aufgekommene Wort[1], als es zuerst in welthistorischem Zusammenhang gebraucht wurde, eher ein Schimpfname als ein Ehrenname war?

Damals, als um 112 der römische Gouverneur in der kleinasiatischen Provinz Bithynien, Gajus *Plinius II.*, bei Kaiser Hadrian anfragte wegen der vieler Verbrechen angeklagten »Christen«, die nach seiner Nachprüfung zwar dem Kaiser den Kult verweigerten, aber sonst anscheinend nur »Christus als einem Gott« Hymnen sängen (= Glaubensbekenntnisse vortragen?) und sich auf gewisse Gebote (nicht stehlen, rauben, ehebrechen, betrügen) verpflichteten[2].

Damals, als ein wenig später ein Freund des Plinius, Cornelius *Tacitus*, an einer Geschichte des kaiserlichen Rom arbeitend, verhältnismäßig genau vom großen Brand Roms 64 berichtet, den man allgemein Kaiser Nero selber zugeschrieben habe, der aber seinerseits die Schuld auf die »Chrestianer« abgeschoben habe: »Chrestianer«, hergeleitet von einem unter Tiberius durch den Prokurator Pontius Pilatus hingerichteten »Christus«, nach dessen Tod dieser »verderbliche Aberglaube« wie schließlich alles Schändliche und Gemeine seinen Weg nach Rom gefunden und nach dem Brand sogar eine große Menge Gläubiger gewonnen habe[3].

Damals, als wenig später und viel weniger genau der Kaiserser-Biograph *Sueton* davon berichtet, daß Kaiser Claudius die Juden, die auf Veranlassung des »Christus« beständig Unruhen erregten, aus Rom ausgewiesen habe[4].

Damals, als – frühestes jüdisches Zeugnis schon um 90 – ebenfalls in Rom der jüdische Geschichtsschreiber dieser Zeit, Flavius *Josephus*, mit offensichtlicher Reserve die 62 erfolgte Steinigung des Jakobus, des »Bruders Jesu, des sogenannten Christus« erwähnt[5].

Soweit die frühesten heidnischen und jüdischen Zeugnisse: Es wäre schon viel erreicht, wenn man sich auch heute erinnern würde, daß Christentum offensichtlich nicht irgendeine Weltanschauung oder irgendwelche ewigen Ideen meint, sondern irgend etwas mit einem Christus zu tun hat. Aber *Erinnerungen* können peinlich sein, das erfuhr schon manche Partei, die ihr Parteiprogramm revidieren wollte. Ja, Erinnerungen können sogar *gefährlich* sein. Darauf macht uns heutige Gesellschaftskritik erneut aufmerksam: nicht nur weil Generationen von Toten uns reglementieren, jede unserer Situationen mitbestimmen und der Mensch insofern durch Geschichte prädefiniert ist[6], sondern auch weil die Erinnerung an die Vergangenheit Unabgegoltenes und Unerfülltes hochkommen läßt und jede in ihren Strukturen erstarrte Gesellschaft die »subversiven« Inhalte des Gedächtnisses mit Grund fürchtet[7].

Christen, christliche Kirchen ohne Erinnerung? Es scheint gerade umgekehrt: Die christlichen Kirchen scheinen der Vergangenheit verhaftet. Wenn sie schon Geschichte unterdrücken, dann eher die stets unheimliche Zukunft zugunsten einer kirchlichen Gegenwart, die sich ewig gibt, in Dogma, Kult, Disziplin, Frömmigkeit. Die heimelige Vergangenheit jedoch, wiederum zur Stütze der Gegenwart, kultiviert man geradezu in den Kirchen. Kultivieren im allgemeinen Sinn: Man »pflegt« das Alter, ehrt das Alte, die Alten, die Ältesten, verehrt die Tradition und die Traditionen, restauriert Kirchen, Kapellen, Figuren, Bilder, Lieder, Theologien. Kultivieren aber auch im besonderen Sinn des Kultus: Christlicher Kult ist wesentlich Erinnerung. Liest man nicht deshalb seit beinahe 2000 Jahren immer aus demselben Buch vor? Feiert man nicht deshalb in ununterbrochener Kette – wie offensichtlich schon dem Plinius berichtet wurde – dasselbe Mahl, welches seit ältester Zeit »Anamnesis« (Erinnerung, Gedächtnis), »memoria Domini« (Gedächtnis des Herrn) genannt wird und an dem noch immer jeden Sonntag Millionen auf der ganzen Welt teilnehmen?

Aber merkwürdigerweise hat oft gerade dieser Gedächtniskult nicht unwesentlich dazu beigetragen, das Gedächtnis zu verwischen: Man las die Texte vor, oft murmelnd oder singend in unverständlicher alter Sprache und ohne jegliche Deutung, um den alten Brauch fortzusetzen und einer Pflicht nachzukommen. Man feierte das Mahl, unter dem pompösen Zeremoniell oft kaum erkenntlich, um religiöse Bedürfnisse zu befriedigen. Man hätschelte die Vergangenheit, um sich nicht mit der Herausforderung der Gegenwart und der Zukunft beschäftigen zu müssen. Man lobte die große Tradition und verwechselte sie mit den gerade überkommenen Ideen. Man ehrte die Alten und vergaß die Jungen, schätzte das Antike und vernachlässigte das Moderne, man restaurierte und degenerierte – oft ohne es zu merken. Man staubte Papierblumen ab, wo man hätte Rosen züchten können.

An sich wäre die Erinnerung eine große Chance, ein Sprungbrett, federnd, mit freiem Ende zum weitreichenden Sprung. Die Erinnerung kann mahnend vergangenen Schrecken, sie kann, gefährlicher, unerfüllt gebliebene Hoffnungen wachrufen. Die Erinnerung kann gegen die überstarke Macht des Faktischen angehen, kann den Druck der gegebenen Tatsachen abfangen, kann die Wand des Wirklichen, des Gewirkten durchstoßen, kann von der Gegenwart freimachen und auf eine bessere Zukunft hin öffnen. Sie kann das, einfach *kommemoriert,* zumindest für kurze Augenblicke. Sie kann es, wirklich *aktiviert,* auch auf Dauer. Sie kann es besonders hartnäckig dort, wo sie unabgegolten geblieben ist.

Christentum – *Aktivierung der Erinnerung.* Aktivierung – wie J. B. Metz zu Recht im Anschluß an Bloch und Marcuse einhämmert – einer »gefährlichen und befreienden Erinnerung«[8]. Das war doch ursprünglich mit der Lesung der neutestamentlichen Schriften, das war mit der Feier des Gedächtnismahles, mit dem Leben in der christlichen Nachfolge, mit dem ganzen vielfältigen Einsatz der Kirche in der Welt gemeint. Erinnerung *an was?* Von dieser offensichtlich beunruhigenden Erinnerung zeugen schon die eben vernommenen ersten heidnischen und jüdischen Nachrichten bezüglich des Christentums, Zeugnisse aus der Zeit der spätesten neutestamentlichen Schriften. Von diesen die Welt verändernden Erinnerungen berichten vor allem die christlichen Zeugnisse selbst. Erinnerung *an was?* Diese grundlegende Frage stellt sich für uns heute vom Neuen Testament wie überhaupt von der christlichen Geschichte her.

Erstens: Man betont oft und zu Recht die Verschiedenartigkeit, Zufälligkeit, teilweise auch die Widersprüchlichkeit der in der Sammlung des *Neuen Testaments* enthaltenen Schriften: Ausführliche systematische Lehrschreiben, aber auch wenig geplante Antwortschreiben auf Fragen der Adressaten. Ein Gelegenheitsbrieflein, kaum zwei Seiten lang, an den Herrn eines entlaufenen Sklaven, und die eher langatmige Beschreibung der Taten der ersten Generation und ihrer Hauptfigur. Evangelien, die vor allem von Vergangenem berichten, und prophetische Sendschreiben, die der Zukunft gelten. Die einen im Stil gewandt, die anderen eher ungepflegt; die einen nach Sprache und Gedankenwelt von Juden stammend, die anderen von Hellenisten; die einen sehr früh, die anderen beinahe 100 Jahre später geschrieben ...!

Die Frage ist wahrhaftig nicht unberechtigt: Was eigentlich hält die so verschiedenen 27 »Bücher« des Neuen Testaments zusammen? Die Antwort? Sie ist nach den Zeugnissen selbst erstaunlich einfach: Es ist die Erinnerung an einen Jesus, der im neutestamentlichen Griechisch »Christos« (hebräisch »maschiah«, aramäisch »meschiha«: Messias = Gesalbter) genannt wird.

Zweitens: Man betont ebenso oft und zu Recht die Risse und Sprünge, die Kontraste und Widersprüchlichkeiten in der Tradition und überhaupt der *Geschichte der Christenheit:* Jahrhunderte der kleinen Gemeinschaft und Jahrhunderte der Großorganisation, Jahrhunderte der Minorität und solche der Majorität: die Verfolgten werden die Herrschenden und wiederum nicht selten auch die Verfolgenden. Jahrhunderte der Untergrundkirche abgelöst durch die der Staatskirche, Jahrhunderte der neronianischen Märtyrer und Jahrhunderte der konstantinischen Hofbischöfe. Zeitalter der Mönche und Gelehrten und – oft ineinander verschlungen – solche der Kirchenpolitiker; Jahrhunderte der konvertierenden Barbaren im Aufgang Europas und Jahrhunderte des von christlichen Kaisern und Päpsten neu begründeten und auch wieder ruinierten Imperium Romanum; Jahrhunderte der Papstsynoden und Jahrhunderte der auf die Päpste zielenden Reformkonzilien. Das Goldene Zeitalter christlicher Humanisten wie säkularisierter Renaissancemenschen und die kirchliche Revolution der Reformatoren; Jahrhunderte der katholischen oder protestantischen Orthodoxie und Jahrhunderte der evangelischen Erweckung. Zeiten der Anpassung und Zeiten des Widerstandes, saecula obscura und das siècle des lumières, Jahrhunderte der Innovation und Jahrhunderte der Restauration, solche der Verzweiflung und solche der Hoffnung ...!

Die Frage wiederum erstaunt nicht: Was eigentlich hält die so wunderlich kontrastierenden 20 Jahrhunderte christlicher Geschichte und Tradition zusammen? Und wiederum gibt es auch hier keine andere Antwort: Es ist die Erinnerung an einen Jesus, der auch durch die Jahrhunderte »Christus«, Gottes letzter und entscheidender Gesandter genannt wird.

Damit aber sind wir bereits bei einer ersten, gewiß sehr vorläufigen und umrißhaften, aber wegen dieser seiner Person doch schon ungemein konkreten Beantwortung unserer Ausgangsfrage angelangt. Und nachdem wir bisher die christliche Position vor Kritik nicht verschont und mit eigenen Antworten eher gezögert haben, wird man jetzt vielleicht doch erwarten, daß die positiven christlichen Aussagen mit ebenso großer Deutlichkeit erfolgen. Selbstkritik ist ja kaum interessant, wenn sie ein bescheidenes Selbstvertrauen vermissen läßt; und gerade dies ist es, was vielen Christen bei ihrem betonten Gottvertrauen abzugehen scheint, wiewohl es auch und gerade die Andersdenkenden von ihnen erwarten.

Die Begriffe beim Wort nehmen

Die Umrisse werden später zu füllen sein. Aber in einer Zeit auch theologischer Vermischung und Vernebelung der Begriffe ist eine klare Sprache notwendig. Der Theologe leistet weder Christen noch Nichtchristen einen Dienst, wenn er die Dinge nicht beim Namen nennt, wenn er die Begriffe nicht beim Wort nimmt.

Christentum ist heute – so sahen wir[9] – konfrontiert mit den *Weltreligionen,* die ebenfalls Wahrheit offenbaren, Weg zum Heil sind, »legitime« Religionen darstellen, ja, die auch von der Entfremdung, Versklavung und Unerlöstheit der Menschen wie von der Nähe, der Gnade, dem Erbarmen der Gottheit wissen können. Die Frage drängte sich auf: Wenn dem allem so ist, was ist dann noch das Besondere des Christentums?

Die noch umrißhafte, aber doch genau treffende Antwort muß lauten: Nach dem Zeugnis des Anfangs und dem der gesamten Tradition, nach dem Zeugnis der Christen und der Nichtchristen ist das Besondere des Christentums – und wie wenig banal und tautologisch diese Antwort ist, wird sich zeigen – dieser *Jesus selbst*, der in alter Sprache auch heute noch *Christus* genannt wird! Oder stimmt es vielleicht nicht: Keine der großen oder kleinen Religionen, sosehr sie ihn unter Umständen auch in einem Tempel oder ihrem heiligen Buch mitverehren mögen, würde ihn als letztlich entscheidend, als ausschlaggebend, als maßgebend für des Menschen Beziehungen zu Gott, zum Mitmenschen, zur Gesellschaft ansehen. Das Besondere, das Ureigenste des Christentums ist es, diesen Jesus als letztlich entscheidend, ausschlaggebend, *maßgebend* zu betrachten für den Menschen in diesen seinen verschiedenen Dimensionen. Und gerade dies war mit dem Titel »Christus« von Anfang an gemeint. Nicht umsonst ist schon damals dieser Titel mit dem Namen »Jesus« gleichsam zu einem Eigennamen zusammengewachsen.

Christentum ist heute – so sahen wir auch[10] – zugleich konfrontiert mit den *nachchristlichen Humanismen* evolutiver oder revolutionärer Art, die ebenfalls für alles Wahre, Gute und Schöne sind, die alle menschlichen Werte und mit der Freiheit und Gleichheit auch die Brüderlichkeit hochhalten und die sich oft effektiver für die Entwicklung des ganzen Menschen und aller Menschen einsetzen. Andererseits wollen auch die christlichen Kirchen und Theologien wieder in neuer Weise menschlich und mitmenschlich sein: modern, aktuell, aufgeklärt, emanzipatorisch, dialogisch, pluralistisch, solidarisch, mündig, weltlich, säkular, kurz: human. Die Frage war unausweichlich: Wenn dem allem so ist, oder zumindest so sein sollte, was ist dann noch das Besondere des Christentums?

Die wiederum nur umrißhafte, aber doch schon völlig präzise Antwort muß auch hier lauten: Nach dem Zeugnis des Anfangs und der gesamten Tradition ist das Besondere wieder dieser *Jesus selbst*, der immer wieder neu als *Christus* erkannt und anerkannt wird. Man mache auch hier die Gegenprobe: Keiner der evolutionären oder revolutionären Humanismen, sosehr sie ihn unter Umständen als Menschen respektieren und gar propagieren, würde ihn als letztlich entscheidend, ausschlaggebend, maßgebend für den Menschen in allen seinen Dimensionen ansehen. Das Besondere, das Ureigenste des Christentums ist es, diesen Jesus als letztlich entscheidend, ausschlaggebend, *maßgebend* für des Menschen Beziehungen zu Gott, zum Mitmenschen, zur Gesellschaft zu betrachten: in abgekürzter biblischer Formel als »Jesus Christus«.

Aus beiden Perspektiven ergibt sich: Will das Christentum für die Menschen in den Weltreligionen, will es für die modernen Humanisten relevant sein, neu relevant werden, dann jedenfalls nicht einfach dadurch, daß es nachspricht, was die anderen vorsprechen, nachmacht, was die anderen vormachen. Solches Papageien-Christentum wird für die Religionen und die Humanismen nicht relevant. So wird es irrelevant, überflüssig. Aktualisierung, Modernisierung, Solidarisierung *allein* tun es nicht. Die Christen, die christlichen Kirchen müssen wissen, was sie wollen, was sie selber sich und den anderen zu sagen haben. Sie müssen bei aller unbeschränkten Offenheit für die Anderen – das ist hier nicht erneut zu betonen – ihr Eigenes zur Sprache, zur Geltung, zur Auswirkung bringen. Also: Das Christentum kann letztlich nur dadurch relevant sein und werden, daß es, wie immer in Theorie und Praxis, die *Erinnerung an Jesus* als *den letztlich Maßgebenden* aktiviert: an Jesus den Christus und nicht nur einen der »maßgebenden Menschen«[11].

Wenn also heute der vor allem mit Psychologie, Soziologie, Politologie befaßte nordamerikanische Theologe, wenn der christlich engagierte Intellektuelle in Frankreich, Spanien, Deutschland oder Holland, wenn der Sozialrevolutionär in Südamerika, wenn der Studentenseelsorger im islamischen Djakarta, der Missionar in Afrika oder Indien, oder auch eine katholisch erzogene römische Contessa ratlos fragen, was eigentlich christlich ist, was überhaupt das Christentum von anderen Religionen oder Quasi-Religionen, Philosophien oder Weltanschauungen unterscheidet, so liegt das daran, daß sie die Antwort abstrakt in irgendwelchen Grundsätzen, Begriffen, Prinzipien, Ideen suchen. Dort aber können sie sie nicht finden, weil das Christentum, wie schon sein Name sagen könnte, letztlich nicht auf irgendwelche ewige Ideen, abstrakte Prinzipien, menschliche Haltungen zurückgeführt werden kann. Das ganze Christentum hängt in der Luft, wenn es losgelöst wird von dem Fundament, auf das es gebaut: diesem Christus. Ein abstraktes Christentum ist auch für die Welt belanglos. Im Grunde müßten das die Christen wissen. Aber sie setzen oft mit erstaunlicher Selbstverständlichkeit voraus, daß sie auch bereits wissen, wer und was dieser Jesus Christus ist. So erwarten sie von ihm her keine Antwort. Sie suchen sie anderswo: in irgendeiner Philosophie oder Weltanschauung, in der Jugend-Kultur, in der Black-culture, in Indien, in einer romantischen Dritten Welt oder irgendeinem anderen kulturellen oder ideologischen Refugium der Moderne, in der Psychoanalyse oder in der Soziologie, in Kybernetik, Linguistik,

Verhaltensforschung, der gerade neuesten Wissenschaftswelle. Gegenfrage: Woher weiß man denn so sicher als Christ, wer und was dieser Jesus Christus ist? Ist vielleicht gerade er in der Christenheit und außerhalb der Unbekannte, der das Christentum selber zu einem bekannten Unbekannten macht?

Vorläufig sei wiederum ganz umrißhaft angedeutet, daß allein von diesem Christus her die dringenden rundum gefragten Fragen der Christen und Nichtchristen nach der *Unterscheidung des Christlichen* beantwortbar erscheinen. Als Test einige Beispiele.

Das erste: Ist eine in tiefem Gottesglauben vollzogene Mahlfeier von Christen und Moslems in Kabul, bei der Gebete aus christlicher und aus sufitischer Tradition gebraucht werden, eine christliche Eucharistiefeier? Antwort: Eine solche Mahlfeier kann ein sehr echter, ja sehr lobenswerter Gottesdienst sein. Eine christliche Eucharistiefeier jedoch wäre sie nur dann, wenn in ihr spezifisch dieses Jesus Christus gedacht würde (memoria Domini).

Das zweite: Ist ein in Benares am Ganges in letzter Hingabe vollzogenes gottgläubiges Tauchbad eines Hindu gleichzusetzen mit der christlichen Taufe? Antwort: Ein solches Tauchbad ist ein religiös gewiß sehr bedeutsamer und heilsamer Reinigungsritus. Zur christlichen Taufe jedoch würde es erst dann, wenn es auf den Namen Jesus Christus hin geschähe.

Das dritte: Ist ein Moslem in Beyrouth, der alles im Koran von Jesus Gesagte – und das ist vieles – hochhält, bereits ein Christ? Antwort: Er ist ein guter Moslem, solange für ihn der Koran verbindlich bleibt, und er mag auf seine Weise sein Heil finden. Christ aber wird er erst dann, wenn nicht mehr Mohammed *der* Prophet und Jesus sein Vorläufer ist, sondern dieser Jesus Christus für ihn maßgebend wird.

Das vierte: Ist das Eintreten für humanitäre Ideale, Menschenrechte und Demokratie in Chicago, Rio, Auckland oder Madrid christliche Verkündigung? Antwort: Dies ist ein für den einzelnen Christen und die christlichen Kirchen dringend gebotenes soziales Engagement. Zur christlichen Verkündigung jedoch wird es nur dann, wenn in der heutigen Gesellschaft praktisch und konkret das von diesem Jesus Christus her zu Sagende zur Geltung gebracht wird.

Unter Voraussetzung der im ersten Teil bereits erfolgten Klärung und der in diesem zweiten, im dritten und vierten Teil zu erfolgenden Konkretisierung können und müssen zur Vermeidung von Konfusion und unnötigen Mißverständnissen ohne alle

Diskriminierung folgende nüchternen Markierungen – überzeugt, aber nicht überzogen – gewagt werden:

- Christlich *ist nicht alles, was wahr, gut, schön und menschlich ist. Wer könnte es leugnen: Wahrheit, Gutheit, Schönheit und Menschlichkeit gibt es auch außerhalb des Christentums. Christlich darf jedoch alles genannt werden, was in Theorie und Praxis einen ausdrücklichen positiven Bezug zu Jesus Christus hat.*
- Christ *ist nicht jeder Mensch echter Überzeugung, ehrlichen Glaubens und guten Willens. Niemand kann es übersehen: Echte Überzeugung, ehrlichen Glauben und guten Willen gibt es auch außerhalb des Christemtums. Christ dürfen jedoch alle die genannt werden, für deren Leben und Sterben Jesus Christus letztlich ausschlaggebend ist.*
- Christliche Kirche *ist nicht jede Meditations- oder Aktionsgruppe, nicht jede Gemeinschaft engagierter Menschen, die sich zu ihrem Heil um ein anständiges Leben bemühen. Man hätte es nie bestreiten dürfen: Engagement, Aktion, Meditation, anständiges Leben und Heil kann es auch in anderen Gruppen außerhalb der Kirche geben. Christliche Kirche darf aber jede größere oder kleinere Gemeinde von Menschen genannt werden, für die Jesus Christus letztlich entscheidend ist.*
- Christentum *ist nicht überall dort, wo man Unmenschlichkeit bekämpft und Humanität verwirklicht. Es ist einfach wahr: Unmenschlichkeit bekämpft man und Humanität verwirklicht man auch außerhalb des Christentums – unter Juden, Moslems, Hindus und Buddhisten, unter nachchristlichen Humanisten und ausgesprochenen Atheisten. Christentum ist jedoch nur dort, wo die Erinnerung an Jesus Christus in Theorie und Praxis aktiviert wird.*

Nun, dies alles sind zunächst Formeln der Unterscheidung. Aber diese *Lehrformeln* sind *keine Leerformeln.* Warum?
Sie beziehen sich auf eine sehr konkrete Person[12].
Sie haben den christlichen Beginn und die große christliche Tradition hinter sich.
Sie bieten zugleich eine klare Orientierung für Gegenwart und Zukunft.
Sie helfen also den Christen und können doch auch die Zustimmung der Nichtchristen finden, deren Überzeugung auf diese Weise respektiert, deren Werte ausdrücklich affirmiert wer-

den, ohne daß sie auf dogmatischem Schleichweg für Christentum und Kirche vereinnahmt werden.

Gerade dadurch, daß die Begriffe für das Christliche nicht verwässert oder beliebig gedehnt, sondern präzise gefaßt werden, gerade dadurch, daß die Begriffe beim Wort genommen werden, ist beides möglich: Offenheit für alles Nichtchristliche zu wahren und zugleich alle unchristliche Konfusion zu vermeiden. Insofern sind diese Unterscheidungsformeln, so umrißhaft sie vorläufig erscheinen müssen, von großer Wichtigkeit. In aller Vorläufigkeit dienen sie der Unterscheidung des Christlichen!

Gegen alle oft gutgemeinte Zerdehnung, Vermengung, Verdrehung und Verwechslung des Christlichen sind die Dinge ehrlich beim Namen zu nennen: Das Christentum der Christen soll christlich bleiben! Es bleibt jedoch christlich nur dann, wenn es ausdrücklich an den einen Christus gebunden bleibt, der nicht irgendein Prinzip oder eine Intentionalität oder ein evolutiver Zielpunkt ist, sondern eine – wie noch sehr genau zu sehen sein wird – ganz bestimmte, unverwechselbare und unauswechselbare Person mit einem ganz bestimmten Namen! Das Christentum läßt sich schon von seinem Namen her nicht in ein namenloses, eben anonymes Christentum einebnen oder »aufheben«. Anonymes Christentum ist für den, der bei beiden Worten etwas denkt, eine contradictio in adiecto: ein hölzernes Eisen. Gutes Menschtum ist eine honorige Sache, auch ohne kirchliche Segnung und theologische Genehmigung. Christentum jedoch besagt Bekenntnis zu diesem einen Namen. Und auch christliche Theologen dürften sich die Frage nicht schenken: was, wer verbirgt sich eigentlich hinter diesem Namen?

2. Welcher Christus?

Der Christus der Frömmigkeit?

Philosophen haben sich mit den platonischen Dialogen mehr Mühe gemacht, um herauszufinden, was Sokrates eigentlich war und wollte, als manche christliche Theologen mit den originalen christlichen Dokumenten, um zu erforschen, was sich hinter dem Namen Jesu Christi verbirgt. Dies, meinen sie, dürfe man doch wohl in der Christenheit als bekannt voraussetzen. Dies brauche man nur noch spekulativ zu vertiefen, praktisch anzuwenden, für Mensch und Gesellschaft heute neu relevant zu machen. Warum, woher können sie das so – muß man schon sagen – naiv als bekannt voraussetzen? Wenn wir vorläufig vom unreflektierten Verständnis der Bibel absehen: vor allem von der christlichen Frömmigkeit und dem christlichen Dogma her.

Die christlichen Erfahrungen jedoch des einen Christus können sehr verschieden sein. Und dieselben Erfahrungen können für die einen der Grund sein, weshalb sie den christlichen Glauben bewahrt, und für die anderen, weshalb sie ihn aufgegeben haben. Da gibt es Christen, die Christus schon früh als den frommen, immer freundlichen göttlichen Heiland kennengelernt und sich nie mehr von diesem »dolce Gesù« getrennt haben, so daß der sozialkritische Jesus von Pasolinis ›Il Vangelo Secondo Matteo‹ in ihnen bange Fragen wachruft. Andere haben ihn, vielleicht in der Jugendbewegung zwischen den beiden Weltkriegen, als den großen Führer kennengelernt und singen noch heute mit derselben Begeisterung ›Mir nach, spricht Christus, unser Held‹, auch wenn das Wohin heute nicht immer sehr klar ist. Wieder anderen hat es sein sanftes und demütiges Herz angetan, so daß »Herz Jesu« für sie zum Eigennamen wurde, worauf Theologen eine sublime Theologie von der »Personmitte« entwickelten. Sehr viele denken bei seinem Namen ihr Leben lang besonders an die Weihnachtstage und an den Knaben im lockigen Haar, welche alljährlich fromme Zeit spätestens mit der Silvesternacht jeweils wieder als abgeschlossen betrachtet werden darf. Wieder andere denken bei seinem Namen einfach an Gott auf Erden und nehmen nicht zur Kenntnis, daß der Vater nicht der Sohn und der Sohn nicht der Vater ist. Und wieder andere denken bei seinem Namen an den göttlichen Sohn einer sehr viel menschlicheren, uns näheren, liebenswürdig-jungfräulichen Mutter, die dann so wichtig werden kann, daß sie wie in Lourdes auch ohne ihren Sohn auf den Altären steht.

Man könnte weiterfahren, aber es sollen hier wahrhaftig keine heiligsten Gefühle verletzt werden. Auch der Verfasser feiert gerne Weihnachten und singt ›Stille Nacht, Heilige Nacht‹ ohne größere Hemmungen. Er ist nicht unpoetisch. Nur, meint er, sollte man Poesie und Wirklichkeit nicht verwechseln. Das gilt nicht nur, wie in unserem kosmischen Zeitalter besonders eklatant, vom Mond, es gilt auch von jenem, der neuerdings wieder mehr als zuvor von recht verschiedenartigen Sängern als der Stern, ja Superstar des Lebens besungen wird.

Ungezählt sind die Lieder, die man seit 2000 Jahren in allen Sprachen der Welt gerade ihm, und ihm wohl mehr als irgendeinem, gesungen hat. Ungezählt die *Bilder,* die man von diesem Einen auf tausend Weisen gemalt, geschlagen, geschnitzt, gegossen hat. Das ist wahrhaftig das Geringste nicht, was man von ihm sagen kann. Und doch gibt gerade auch die Vielfalt individueller Bilder, die sich nicht wie beim immer ähnlichen Buddha auf einige ganz wenige stilisierte Grundstellungen zurückführen läßt, zu denken: Welches Christusbild ist denn das wahre[1]?

Ist es der bartlose, jugendlich menschenfreundliche Hirte der altchristlichen Katakombenkunst *oder* ist es der bärtige, sieghafte Imperator und Kosmokrator in den Bildformen des spätantiken Kaiserkultes, in höfisch-steifer Unantastbarkeit und drohender Majestät vor dem Goldgrund der Ewigkeit? Ist es der Beau-Dieu von Chartres *oder* der deutsche Miserikordien-Heiland? Ist es der am Kreuz thronende Christkönig und Weltenrichter der romanischen Portale und Absiden *oder* der grauenvoll realistische Schmerzensmann in Dürers »Christus im Elend« und in der letzten noch erhaltenen Kreuzigung des Grünewald? Ist es der leidlos Schöne der Disputa Raffaels *oder* der menschlich Sterbende des Michelangelo? Ist es der Erhaben-Leidende des Velásquez *oder* der Gequält-Zuckende des Greco? Sind es die glatt aufklärerischen Salon-Porträts der Rosalba Carriera und eines Fritsch vom eleganten Popular-Philosophen Jesus *oder* die sentimentalen Herz-Jesu-Bilder des katholischen Spätbarock? Ist es im 18. Jahrhundert Jesus der Gärtner oder Apotheker, der Tugend-Pulver verabreicht, *oder* dann der klassizistische Heiland des Thorwaldsen, der seinem dänischen Mitbürger Kierkegaard wegen der Eliminierung des Kreuzes-Skandalons ein Ärgernis war? Ist es der kraftlos-sanfte menschliche Jesus der deutschen und französischen Nazarener und der englischen Prä-Raffaeliten *oder* der in ganz andere Dimensionen weisende Christus der Künstler des 20. Jahrhunderts, der Beckmann, Corinth, Nolde, Masereel, Rouault, Picasso, Barlach, Matisse, Chagall?

Und nicht weniger verschieden sind die *Theologien,* die hinter den Bildern verborgen sind. Welche Christologie ist denn die wahre?

Ist es im *Altertum* der Christus des Bischofs Irenäus von Lyon *oder* der seines Schülers Hippolyt (Gegenpapst von Calixtus), ist es der des genialen Griechen Origenes *oder* der des wortgewandten lateinischen Juristen Tertullian? Ist es der Christus des konstantinischen Hofbischofs und Historiographen Eusebios *oder*

der des ägyptischen Wüstenvaters Antonius, der des größten Theologen im Westen, Augustin, oder der des bedeutendsten Papstes der ersten fünf Jahrhunderte, Leo? Ist es der Christus der Alexandriner *oder* der der Antiochener, derjenige der Kappadokier *oder* der der ägyptischen Mönche?

Ist es im *Mittelalter* der Christus des spekulativen Neuplatonikers Johannes Skotus Eriugena *oder* der des scharfsinnigen Dialektikers Abaelard, derjenige der vielkommentierten Sentenzen des Petrus Lombardus *oder* der der Hoheliedpredigten des Bernhard von Clairvaux? Ist es der Christus des Thomas von Aquin *oder* der des Franz von Assisi, derjenige des mächtigen Innozenz III. *oder* der von ihm bekämpften ketzerischen Waldenser und Albigenser? Ist es derjenige des grübelnden Apokalyptikers Joachim von Fiore *oder* der des kühnen Denkers und Kardinals Nikolaus von Kues, der der römischen Kanonisten *oder* der der deutschen Mystiker?

Ist es in der *Neuzeit* der Christus der Reformatoren *oder* der römischen Päpste, der des Erasmus von Rotterdam *oder* der des Ignatius von Loyola, der der spanischen Inquisitoren *oder* der von ihnen verfolgten spanischen Mystiker? Ist es der Christus der Theologen der Sorbonne und der französischen Kronjuristen *oder* der Christus Pascals, ist es der der spanischen Barockscholastiker *oder* der der deutschen Aufklärungstheologen, der der lutherischen und reformierten Orthodoxie *oder* der der alten oder neueren protestantischen Freikirchen? Ist es der Christus der Philosophen-Theologen des deutschen Idealismus, Fichtes, Schellings, Hegels, *oder* ist es der des Antiphilosophen-Theologen Kierkegaard? Ist es der der historisch-spekulativen katholischen Tübinger Schule *oder* der der neuscholastischen Jesuitentheologen des Vatikanum I, der der protestantischen Erweckungsbewegungen im 19. Jahrhundert *oder* der der liberalen Exegese des 19. und 20. Jahrhunderts, derjenige Romano Guardinis *oder* der Karl Adams, der Karl Barths *oder* der Rudolf Bultmanns, der Paul Tillichs, Teilhard de Chardins *oder* Billy Grahams?

So viele Köpfe, so viele Christusbilder? Auch heute noch antwortet die Frömmigkeit in verschiedenster Weise auf die Frage: Welcher Christus? Was bedeutet er für mich? Wie neueste Umfragen[2] durch alle möglichen Schichten, Berufe, Konfessionen zeigen: Die einen bekennen ihn im Raum der Kirche in Gebet und Akklamation, Sakramenten und Liturgie als Sohn Gottes, Erlöser, erhöhten Herrn und Stifter der Kirche. Anderen begegnet er in der Mitmenschlichkeit, im Alltag »draußen«, im sozialen Engagement als Freund, großer Bruder, Vorkämpfer, Anstifter von Unruhe, Enthusiasmus und wahrer Menschlichkeit. Persönlichen Bekehrungserlebnissen, spontanen Bekenntnissen zu ihm stehen dogmatische Formeln, reproduzierte Glaubenssätze gegenüber, Katechismushaftes, Erstarrtes. Für die einen bedeutet er Liebe, Sinn, Halt, Grund im Leben und ist er Inbegriff von Glück, Ruhe und Trost auch in Enttäuschungen, in Verzweiflung und Leiden. Für die anderen ist er harmlos, bedeutet er wenig, kann er nicht helfen. Und fordert er die einen zu Nachdenken, Meditation, verehrender Betrachtung heraus, reagieren andere lapidar oder auch gereizt, ausweichend, ja hilflos.

Der Christus des Dogmas?

Es soll hier nicht etwa der Eindruck erweckt werden, es sei an diesen Bildern, Theologien, Auffassungen, Erfahrungen von Jesus alles gleich wichtig oder gleich richtig, oder gar, es sei dies alles nicht richtig oder nicht wichtig. Es soll nur deutlich gemacht werden, daß man anscheinend doch nicht so einfach und naiv aus der christlichen Frömmigkeit, Literatur, Kunst, Tradition als bekannt voraussetzen kann, was sich hinter dem Namen Christi verbirgt. Zu viele verschiedene und wenn möglich noch retouchierte Fotografien von der einen und selben Person erschweren die Detektivarbeit. Und Detektivarbeit – eine oft äußerst spannende und anspannende Entdeckungsarbeit – ist christliche Theologie immer wieder zu einem recht erheblichen Teil.

Gerade dem aber würde wohl der eine oder andere Theologe widersprechen. Was es bezüglich dieser Person zu entdecken gäbe, sei ein für alle Male entdeckt worden, und Privatdetektive seien hier nicht gefragt. Es gehe hier um mehr als die christliche Frömmigkeit, Erfahrung, Literatur, Kunst, Tradition. Es gehe um die *Lehre der Kirche,* genauer: die offizielle Lehre des kirchlichen Lehramts[3]. Der wahre Christus sei der Christus der Kirche. Hier gelte, wenn auch vielleicht nicht das »Roma locuta«, so doch das »Conciliis locutis«: was nämlich die ökumenischen Kirchenversammlungen zwischen dem 4. und 8. Jahrhundert gegen Häresien von rechts und links ausgesprochen, de-finiert, ab-gegrenzt haben. Wer also wäre darnach der wahre Christus?

Jedenfalls auch nach den Konzilien nicht einfach: »Gott«. Zwar ist »Jesus = Gott« – unter dem Einfluß eines unpädagogisch einsetzenden, oberflächlichen Religionsunterrichtes, einer überhöhenden Liturgie und Kunst – leider sehr oft die Antwort von Gläubigen und (deswegen) Ungläubigen. Und wie oft erlebt man es, daß ein Kind auf den Kruzifixus zeigt und sagt: »Gelt, da hängt der liebe Gott am Kreuz!« Aber sosehr es sich hier um Auswirkungen kirchlicher Lehrdefinitionen handelt, die Jesu Göttlichkeit betonen, es sind Mißverständnisse: die so wohl durchdachte und abgesicherte Lehre der alten Konzilien in nicht mehr zu verantwortender Verdünnung, Verflachung, Simplifizierung, ja häretischer Einseitigkeit. »Gott in Menschengestalt«: das ist Monophysitismus. »Gott leidend am Kreuz«: das ist Patripassianismus. Kein altes Konzil identifizierte je einfach Jesus und Gott, wie sich dann etwas später die Germanen vom Gott Wotan zum Gott Jesus bekehrten und aus demselben Grund Jesus in dem fränkisch-römischen »Confiteor« der Messe fehlt und in anderen Gebeten ohne Bezug zum Vater direkt angesprochen wird.

Aber schon nach dem ersten ökumenischen Konzil von Nikaia (325 in der kaiserlichen Sommerresidenz) ist Jesus nur »gleichwesentlich mit dem Vater«[4]. Und nach dem ausbalancierenden Konzil von Chalkedon (451 bei Konstantinopel) ist er »gleichwesentlich mit uns Menschen«: Eine Person (= eine göttliche Hypostase), in welcher unvermischt und unveränderlich und zugleich ungeteilt und ungetrennt zwei Naturen, eine göttliche und eine menschliche, vereint sind[5]. Dies ist die klassische Antwort von der »hypostatischen Union«, vom »Gottmenschen«, wie sie seither in ungezählten theologischen Textbüchern und Katechismen der verschiedenen Kirchen des Ostens und Westens wiederholt wird.

Und trotzdem: ist es so einfach? Am Anfang haben die ökumenischen Konzilien, wie Athanasios, der führende Kopf in Nikaia bezeugt, keine Satzunfehlbarkeit in Anspruch genommen[6]. Diese ehrwürdige konziliare Geschichte ist nicht ohne Schwankungen und zum Teil auch Widersprüche. Wenigstens wenn man Nikaia I und II, Ephesos I und II, Konstantinopel I, II, III, IV nicht nur aus den theologischen Schulbüchern kennt[7]. Und gerade das große Konzil von Chalkedon war auch der Anlaß zur ersten großen bleibenden, noch heute nicht überwundenen Kirchenspaltung (zwischen den chalkedonischen Kirchen und anderen, die sich auf das vorausgegangene Konzil von Ephesos beriefen). Chalkedon hatte denn auch die Frage keineswegs auf die Dauer gelöst. Wenige Jahre nachher brach mit ungewöhnlicher

Heftigkeit der Streit um die in Chalkedon ausgeklammerte zentrale Frage aus, ob Christus, beziehungsweise Gott überhaupt leiden könne. Und dieser »patri-passianische, theo-paschitische Streit« beherrschte von da an das ganze 6. Jahrhundert und ging im 7. Jahrhundert in den »mono-theletischen Streit« über (ein Wille oder zwei Willen in Christus, ein göttlicher und ein menschlicher?)[8].

Das Problem liegt für uns heute noch tiefer. Nur zu oft erblickt man hinter dem Christusbild der Konzilien das unbewegliche, affektlose Antlitz des Gottes Platons, der nicht leiden kann, vermehrt um einige Züge der stoischen Ethik. Die Namen jener Konzilien zeigen, daß es sich ausnahmslos um griechische Konzilien handelt. Der Christus aber war nicht in Griechenland geboren worden. Es handelt sich also bei diesen Konzilien wie bei der Theologie, die dahintersteht, um eine fortgesetzte Übersetzungsarbeit: Die ganze sogenannte Zwei-Naturen-Lehre ist eine in hellenistischer Sprache und Begrifflichkeit formulierte Interpretation dessen, was dieser Jesus Christus eigentlich bedeutet! Die Wichtigkeit dieser Lehre sei nicht verkleinert. Sie hat Geschichte gemacht. Sie drückt eine echte Kontinuität des christlichen Glaubens aus und liefert bedeutsame Leitlinien für die gesamte Diskussion und auch für jede künftige Interpretation. Aber andererseits dürfte auch nicht der Eindruck aufkommen, als ob die Botschaft von Christus heute nur mit Hilfe dieser damals unvermeidlichen, aber ungenügenden griechischen Kategorien, nur mit Hilfe der chalkedonischen Zwei-Naturen-Lehre, nur mit Hilfe also der sogenannten klassischen Christologie ausgesagt werden könnte oder dürfte. Was soll ein Jude, Chinese, Japaner oder Afrikaner, was aber auch der heutige durchschnittliche Europäer oder Amerikaner mit jenen griechischen Chiffren anfangen? Schon die neueren katholischen wie evangelischen christologischen Lösungsversuche unseres Jahrhunderts weisen weit über Chalkedon hinaus[9]. Und das Neue Testament selbst ist unendlich viel reicher.

Die chalkedonische Formel muß danach, nach einem berühmten Wort Karl Rahners, mehr als Anfang denn als Ende gesehen werden[10]. Nur kurz sei zusammengefaßt, aus welchen Wurzeln die verschiedenen *Einwände* gegen die traditionelle Lösung der christologischen Frage – zwei Naturen in einer (göttlichen) Person – erwachsen[11]:

a. Die Zwei-Naturen-Lehre wird mit ihren von der hellenistischen Sprache und Geistigkeit geprägten Worten und Vorstellungen jedenfalls *heute* nicht mehr verstanden. Sie wird denn auch in der praktischen Verkündigung tunlichst umgangen.

b. Die Zwei-Naturen-Lehre hatte schon *damals,* nach dem Zeugnis der nachchalkedonischen Dogmengeschichte, die Schwierigkeiten nicht gelöst. Sie hat vielmehr in immer neue logische Aporien hineingeführt.

c. Die Zwei-Naturen-Lehre ist gerade nach der Auffassung vieler Exegeten keineswegs identisch mit der *ursprünglichen* Christusbotschaft des Neuen Testaments: Manche sehen sie als Verlagerung oder teilweise gar Verfälschung der ursprünglichen Christusbotschaft, andere als zumindest nicht ihre einzig mögliche oder gar optimale Interpretation.

Durchaus ähnliche Einwände ließen sich freilich auch gegen die traditionell-protestantische, von Calvin ausgestaltete und später von der katholischen Theologie übernommene Drei-Ämter-Lehre machen: Daß Jesus gerade Prophet, Priester und König sei – ist das in so verkürzter Systematik im Neuen Testament begründet? Und sollen gerade diese drei Titel für den Menschen unserer säkularisierten Gesellschaft noch verständlich sein[12]?

Gewiß: Der christlichen Tradition in Frömmigkeit, Literatur, Kunst, Theologie und Dogma ist zu verdanken, daß die Erinnerung an diesen Christus lebendig blieb, daß er selber nicht zu einem Monument der Vergangenheit wurde, sondern sich immer wieder neu als Faktor der Gegenwart erwies. Ohne die Kontinuität der Glaubensgemeinschaft – etwa nur mit einem Buch – gäbe es keine lebendige Christusbotschaft und keinen lebendigen Christusglauben. Jede Generation machte sich die alte Erinnerung an ihn in neuer Gestalt zu eigen. Und kein Theologe wird ungestraft die große Tradition vernachlässigen. Es hat Sinn, daß noch heute die Glaubensbekenntnisse der alten Konzilien – gleichzeitig abbreviative Zusammenfassungen wie defensive Abgrenzungen – in Ehre gehalten werden. Sie sind nicht nur Antiquitäten und Kuriositäten. Sie sind Zeichen der Beständigkeit des durch die Jahrhunderte sich wandelnden christlichen Glaubens. Es ist später auf sie zurückzukommen.

Doch zugleich ist nicht zu übersehen: Diese große Tradition ist von überraschender Komplexität. Sehr verschieden, kontrastvoll, oft disparat und widersprüchlich sind die Zeugnisse vom einen und selben Christus. Und Wahrheit und Dichtung bedürfen gerade in diesem Zentrum theologischer Sichtung. Auch traditionell gesinnte Theologen müssen zugeben: Alles in dieser

Tradition kann nicht gleich wahr sein, alles kann nicht gleichzeitig wahr sein.

Auch die große konziliare Tradition stellt also die Frage: Welcher Christus ist der wahre Christus? Und gerade wer eine dann als exklusiv orthodox erklärte christologische Tradition in Theologie und Frömmigkeit kultiviert, wird sich fragen müssen, ob nun gerade dieser, vielleicht in einer sehr schönen Kirche einquartierte, hospitalisierte, domestizierte »orthodoxe« Christus der wahre Christus ist. Denn nicht nur Staub, auch zu viel Gold kann die wahre Gestalt verdecken.

Christliche Botschaft will verständlich machen, was Jesus Christus für den Menschen heute bedeutet, ist. Wird aber dieser Christus für den Menschen heute wirklich verständlich, wenn man einfach dogmatisch von einer etablierten Trinitätslehre ausgeht? Wenn man schlicht die Gottheit Jesu, eine Präexistenz des Sohnes voraussetzt, um dann nur noch zu fragen, wie dieser Gottessohn eine Menschennatur mit sich verbinden, annehmen konnte, wobei Kreuz und Auferstehung vielfach nur noch als eine aus der »Menschwerdung« sich ergebende Konsequenz erscheinen? Wenn man den Titel Gottessohn einseitig favorisiert, Jesu Menschlichkeit möglichst verdrängt und ihm das menschliche Personsein abspricht? Wenn man Jesus mehr als Gottheit anbetet, statt ihm irdisch-menschlich nachzufolgen? Wäre es den neutestamentlichen Zeugnissen und dem mehr geschichtlichen Denken des heutigen Menschen nicht vielleicht angemessener, wie die ersten Jünger vom wirklichen Menschen Jesus, seiner geschichtlichen Botschaft und Erscheinung, seinem Leben und Geschick, seiner geschichtlichen Wirklichkeit und geschichtlichen Wirkung auszugehen, um nach dieses Menschen Jesus Verhältnis zu Gott, seiner Einheit mit dem Vater zu fragen? Also kurz: weniger auf klassische Manier eine Christologie spekulativ oder dogmatisch »von oben«, sondern, ohne die Legitimität der alten Christologie zu bestreiten, eine dem heutigen Menschen mehr entsprechende geschichtliche Christologie »von unten«: vom konkreten geschichtlichen Jesus her[13]?

Der Christus der Schwärmer[?]

»Gesucht wird: Jesus Christus, alias Der Messias, Sohn Gottes, König der Könige, Herr der Herren, Fürst des Friedens etc. Berüchtigter Führer einer Untergrund-Befreiungsbewegung.

Äußere Erscheinung: typischer Hippie – langes Haar, Bart, Robe, Sandalen. Er treibt sich gern in Slums herum, hat einige reiche Freunde, verkriecht sich in der Wüste. Achtung: Dieser Mann ist äußerst gefährlich. Für seine heimtückisch-zündende Botschaft sind besonders jene jungen Leute anfällig, denen man noch nicht beigebracht hat, ihn zu ignorieren. Er verändert die Menschen und beansprucht, sie frei zu machen. Warnung: Er läuft noch immer frei herum.« So der weithin bekannt gewordene Steckbrief einer christlichen Untergrund-Zeitung in den Vereinigten Staaten.

Charismatische *Jesus-Movements* am Rande oder außerhalb der etablierten Kirchen hat es zu allen Zeiten gegeben: nonkonformistische Appelle gegen den von den Kirchen vereinnahmten Christus an den ursprünglichen wahren Christus. Schwärmerische Bewegungen, oft wild revolutionär, aggressiv, gewalttätig, oft sanft, introvertiert, mystisch. Schon in der Alten Kirche die verschiedenen apokalyptischen Enthusiasten. Dann die Spiritualen, Geißlerbewegungen und Apostelbrüder des Mittelalters, die Schwärmer und Täufer der Reformationszeit. Später der radikale Pietismus in Deutschland, die Independenten, Quäker und Plymouth-Brüder in England, die verschiedenen Revivals in den Vereinigten Staaten. Schließlich die Pfingstbewegung, die nach dem Vatikanum II in durchaus orthodoxer Weise auch in der katholischen Kirche Eingang gefunden hat. Alle möglichen Arten von charismatischen Bewegungen[14].

Oft waren es auch einfach *Einzelgänger,* die ihrem eigenen oft wenig orthodoxen Christus nachgingen, ebenfalls in der früheren, mittleren und späten Christenheit: in ihren Schriften, Pamphleten, Romanen, oft auch einfach in ihrer Lebensweise. Lang würde die Liste derer, die ihre Kirche ignorierten, aber ihren Christus liebten: merkwürdige Geistesmänner, Theologen, Schriftsteller, Maler waren darunter. Jesus-Jünger, -Narren, -Käuze, -Gammler (Jesus-Freaks) in toller Buntheit und jedenfalls nicht so langweilig wie die orthodoxe lateinische und griechische Christologie des zweiten Jahrtausends nach dem Abschluß der großen Kontroversen im Osten. Der auch in allen Kirchen anerkannte Jesus-Narr unseres Jahrtausends: Franziskus von Assisi!

Den Kenner der Geschichte braucht somit nicht unbedingt zu überraschen, daß auch heute, nach so vielen Reden von Säkularität, Evolution und Revolution wieder dieser Jesus populär geworden ist, und zwar, scheint es, für säkulare Evolutionäre und

Revolutionäre zugleich. Und nachdem in Amerika selbst der »Tod Gottes« rasch gestorben wird und Jesus nach beinahe 2000 Jahren auch noch die Ehre zuteil wurde, zweimal im gleichen Jahr die Cover-Story von Time-Magazin zu »machen«[15], stellten jene so zeitbewußten christlichen Theologen, die immer gern die letzte Welle reiten, um, wie sie meinen, an ein neues Ufer zu gelangen, fest, daß der Wind wieder einmal gedreht hat: von der Säkularität zur Religiosität, von der Öffentlichkeit zur Innerlichkeit, von der Aktion zur Meditation, von der Rationalität zur Sensivität, vom »Tod Gottes« zum Interesse am »ewigen Leben«. Vieleicht daß sie es nun als Christen doch *noch* wichtiger finden, sich nach Marx, Freud, Nietzsche und anderen Heilbringern unserer Tage mit Jesus zu beschäftigen.

Die gegenwärtige Neuorientierung dürfte auch für die Zukunft lehrreich sein. Wie lange oder wie kurz solche religiöse Bewegungen jeweils anhalten mögen: Man sollte sie von kirchlicher Seite nicht gegen die revolutionären Bewegungen ausspielen. Sie sind vielfach auch ein Protest gegen den in den Kirchen domestizierten Gips-Christus, der weder Schmerzen fühlt noch fühlen läßt. Nicht immer sind sie Zeichen der Bürgerlichkeit und Kirchlichkeit. Zu viele Impulse aus der revolutionären Bewegung haben sich durchgehalten: die Haltung des Protestes gegen das Karriere- und Wohlstandsdenken, die Konsum- und Leistungsgesellschaft, die technologisch automatisierte und manipulierte Welt, den unkontrollierten Fortschritt, auch die etablierten Kirchen. Dann in manchem der expressionistische Stil, der Zug zur Romantik, der vielfache Irrationalismus. Was wir früher zur Kulturkritik des revolutionären Humanismus gesagt haben[16], ist somit keineswegs überflüssig geworden.

Auch die Ausgangsschwierigkeiten der Jugendlichen dürften auf lange Zeit dieselben bleiben: abgesehen von der allgemeinen Situation der Gesellschaft die Probleme mit Eltern, Lehrern, Vorgesetzten, die oft stumpfsinnige Arbeit und alle möglichen zweifelhaften und zweifellosen Vergnügen bis zur inneren Leere, Langeweile und Verzweiflung. Aber die Zielrichtung des Suchens hat sich für manche wieder geändert. Manche suchen nicht mehr sosehr die politisch-revolutionäre Aktion als vielmehr, nach all den Unruhen, Manifestationen und Provokationen, den inneren Frieden, die Geborgenheit, Fröhlichkeit, Stärke, Liebe, den Sinn des Lebens. Charles Reichs ›Consciousness III‹[17]: Es geht um mehr als um flüchtige Gefühle von Blumenkindern und Verehrung eines Mitrebellen. Es geht um ein anderes Bewußt-

sein, um die Transzendenz der Maschine, den befreienden Überstieg aus den gegebenen Verhältnissen; es geht um die Wahl eines
neuen Lebensstiles, die Entwicklung neuer menschlicher Fähigkeiten, einer neuen Unabhängigkeit und persönlichen Verantwortung; es geht um die Neubestimmung der Werte und Prioritäten, um einen neuen Menschen und gerade so um eine neue
Gesellschaft. Nur bleibt das bei den Jesus-Begeisterten nicht eine
so abstrakte Forderung wie in ›Bewußtsein III‹. Die Scheu vor
»Religion« haben manche dieser Kurz- oder Langhaarigen verloren, auch die Scheu, Ihn beim Namen zu nennen. Nachdem man
alles durchgeprobt hatte – Sex und Alkohol, Haschisch, Marihua-
na, LSD und andere »bewußtseinserweiternde« Drogen – erscheint manchen Jesus als der »größte Trip«. »Die Beatles sind
populärer als Jesus Christus«; nach diesem überheblichen Dik-
tum des Beatle John Lennon 1966 der Song ›My sweet Lord,
I really want to know you‹ des Ex-Beatle George Harrison 1971.
Bibel, Beten, ja gar Taufen sind »in«, mindestens vorläufig.

Alles also in seiner Bedeutung nicht zu übertreiben: viel Mode,
viel Geschäft, viel Kitsch, viel Aufbauschung durch newsgierige
Massenmedien und profitgierige Manager sind immer dabei. Es
liegt im System, daß jeder Protest gegen die Kommerzialisierung
selber kommerzialisiert wird. Immerhin: Wenn Rauschgift für
die amerikanische Polizei nach wie vor das größte Problem darstellt (mehr als die Hälfte der Vermögenskriminalität ist auf
Rauschgift zurückzuführen), ist man nicht unglücklich, wenn
sich wenigstens für einige der vielleicht 100000 (überwiegend
jugendlichen) Süchtigen allein in New York eine Rettung gefunden hat[18]. Christentum, von Jesus her verstanden, ist gewiß kein
Drogenersatz; es sollen nicht die Opiate durch ein »Opium des
Volkes«, nicht eine Ekstase durch eine andere ersetzt werden.
Aber offensichtlich *kann* das Christentum, von Jesus her verstanden, für manche Drogenverfallene oder überhaupt am Leben
Verzweifelnde eine verläßliche Chance sein, welche Lähmung
überwindet und neue Aktivität ermöglicht.

Kritiker jedoch fürchten bei solchen religiösen Wellen die
Naivität, Romantik, Verachtung der Vernunft, rügen kindliche
Wundergläubigkeit, missionarischen Enthusiasmus, politische
und soziale Apathie und Eskapismus, ja erkennen Reaktion,
Restauration und Gegenrevolution. Das alles kann tatsächlich
mitspielen. Fragt sich nur, warum? Wenn solche religiöse Bewegungen von rechts zu Unrecht vereinnahmt werden, dann von
links zu Unrecht verdammt. Sie sind beiden Seiten nah und fern.

Auf Jesus berufen sich nach wie vor auch viele Revolutionäre. Doch wichtiger ist: Solche religiöse Trends sind ein Zeichen dafür, daß weder die bürgerliche Fortschrittsideologie noch eine oberflächlich revolutionäre Gesellschaftskritik diese Jugend zu befriedigen vermochte. Nicht die Wohlstandskultur und nicht die Gegenkultur, nicht der Zivilisationsrummel und nicht der Drogentaumel, nicht die evolutionären und nicht die revolutionären Humanismen. Und auch jene oberflächlichen »Liberalen«, die in der bloßen »Liberalisierung« das Allheilmittel sehen, müßten zumindest verstehen, daß diese liberalisierte Jugend nun auch wissen möchte, wozu eigentlich liberalisiert wurde. Vergebens eskapieren jene von der Frage nach dem Sinn des Ganzen und des Einzelnen und sind dann noch maßlos erstaunt und verärgert, daß die Jugend, bereits an eine völlig enttabuisierte Literatur gewöhnt, nun auch die Obszönitäten – nicht jeder ist ein Henry Miller oder D. H. Lawrence – langweilig findet, sich Segals ›Love Story‹ oder wieder einmal neu Hermann Hesses ›Steppenwolf‹ oder ›Siddharta‹ zuwendet und, institutionsfeindlich, aber nicht religionsfern, die Suche nach Glück in anderer Richtung aufnimmt.

Vor diesem ganzen Hintergrund ist und bleibt es jedenfalls ein erstaunliches Phänomen, daß auch im letzten Drittel des 20. Jahrhunderts nach all den sich überstürzenden Moden – nicht zu vergessen neben Psycho- und Sensitivitytraining die Wende zur fernöstlichen Mystik – immer wieder neu dieser Jesus aktuell ist, aktuell wird: faszinierend anscheinend wie eh und je. Und zwar Jesus nicht mehr ausschließlich als Genosse der Rebellion im Kampf gegen Krieg und Unmenschlichkeit. Sondern Jesus auch gesehen als das von allen mißbrauchte Opfer, als das beständigste und zugänglichste Symbol für Reinheit, Freude, letzte Hingabe, wahres Leben. Und so merkwürdig manches für satte Bürger klingen mag – Jesus-Revolution, Gottestrip, Taufe oder Therapie des Heiligen Geistes: könnte es nicht vielleicht doch neuer Ausdruck einer uralten Sehnsucht der Menschheit sein? Eines auf die Dauer nicht zu verdrängenden Hungers nach wahrem Leben, wahrer Freiheit, wahrer Liebe, wahrem Frieden?

Ja, wer hätte gedacht, daß die säkulare Schlußbotschaft des Musical ›Hair‹ – »Das Leben kann von innen neu beginnen. Laßt die Sonne, laßt den Sonnenschein in euch hinein« – gerade auf diese Weise aufgegriffen würde? Jesus kam dort nur am Rande vor: »Mein Haar, wie Jesus es trug. Halleluja; ich habe es gern … Maria liebte ihren Sohn, warum liebt mich meine Mutter nicht?«

Ist es so überraschend, daß manche der Jüngeren meinen, das in jenem Sonnengesang so viel besungene »Leben« sei – angesichts fehlgeschlagener Revolten und angesichts nur zu gut gelungener Orgien und Hippie-Morde – ohne eine andere Art von Innerlichkeit und Brüderlichkeit, sei ohne Uneigennützigkeit, Reinheit des Herzens und jene Liebe, die mehr ist als Sex, nicht sinnvoll zu leben? Die Frage nach dem *Sinn* des Lebens, nach einem gelingenden, glückenden, glücklichen, erfüllten und deshalb richtigen Leben, kann nicht verdrängt, kann weder durch Analyse der Psyche noch durch Veränderung der Gesellschaft aus der Welt geschafft werden. So manche sind heute neu überzeugt, daß sie gerade bei Jesus jene Frage beantwortet finden, die in ›Hair‹ so formuliert ist:

> »Wo geh ich hin?
> Folge ich dem Herzen?
> Weiß meine Hand, wohin ich geh?
> Warum erst leben, um dann zu sterben?
> Ich weiß nicht recht,
> Ob ich das je versteh.
> Wo komm ich her?
> Wo geh ich hin?
> Sagt, wozu?
> Sagt, woher?
> Sagt, wohin?
> Sagt, worin
> liegt der Sinn?«

Aber nochmals: Bei allen positiven Aspekten von charismatischen Jesus-Bewegungen muß dringend davor gewarnt werden, die Zukunft des Christentums an irgendwelche Moden oder »Wellen« zu hängen, gar auf Emotionen, Hysterien oder Rauschideologien zu gründen. Auch religiöse Schwärmerbewegungen – oft Symbiosen von rebellischer Gegenkultur und konservativem Biblizismus – sind ambivalent. Manchmal sogar im selben Individuum ein Gemisch von zweifelhafter Religiosität, echter Religion und – nochmals etwas anderes – christlichem Glauben. Sie haben ihre Zeit, wandeln sich, und oft bleiben von ihr nur Spuren. Enthusiastische Bewegungen verehren ihren Christus und vereinnahmen ihn zugleich. Und der wahre Jesus Christus ist jedenfalls doch nicht der »Superstar«, der sich beliebig »machen«, »aufbauen«, »komponieren«, schließlich »inszenieren« und dann auch »konsumieren« ließe. Christentum darf nicht mit einem Schau- und Rauschgeschäft verwechselt werden.

Nichts gegen die Verbindung von Christentum und faszinierender Musik; wie fruchtbar sie ist, zeigt die Geschichte von der Gregorianik bis zu Igor Strawinsky, Krzysztof Penderecki und den Spirituals. Nichts insbesondere gegen die Vertonung biblischer Themen in Beat- und Rockrhythmen. Was sich indessen aus den Rolling Stones, Beatles, Serge Prokofjew, Carl Orff und Richard Strauss alles mixen läßt, dessen Qualität mögen andere beurteilen. Aus den Evangelien jedenfalls läßt sich für die sieben letzten Tage Jesu – auch nach Einführung durch des hochverdienten Bischof Fulton J. Sheens ›Life of Christ‹[19] – nicht alles mixen. Und wenn der Devotionalien-Christus einer christlichen Frömmigkeit und der Gott aus dem Jenseits eines christologischen Dogmatismus von den Evangelien nicht gestützt werden, so wird es doch auch nicht das allzu irdische Idol von Ekstatikern und Süchtigen. Nichts gegen die Autoren des Songs, dann der Langspielplatte, dann des Musicals und schließlich noch des Films ›Jesus Christ Superstar‹, die jungen Engländer Lloyd Webber und Tim Rice, die sich vom »unglaublichen Drama« der Jesus-Geschichte faszinieren ließen und für die stupend-raffinierte Broadway-Inszenierung der einträglichen Rock-Oper den clever sich wandelnden Direktor von ›Hair‹ (T. O'Horgan: »The swing is back to the superrational consciousness«) gefunden haben. Wenn man dort hören konnte, diese Leute verständen nichts von Religion und Jesus, so lautet die Gegenfrage, ob diejenigen, die mehr davon verstehen, es auch für andere und jüngere verständlich zu machen verstanden. Und wer urteilt, in solchen und ähnlichen Stücken würde die Geschichte Jesu unfromm vergewaltigt, überlege, wie oft sie vorher fromm verharmlost worden war. Wer kritisiert, hier würde nur Jesu Menschheit gezeigt, überlege, ob in den Kirchen nicht allzuoft nur seine Gottheit gezeigt wurde. Wer beklagt, hier würde die Auferstehung ausgelassen, überlege, wie sehr die Kreuzigung in manchen Theologien zwischen Menschwerdung und Auferstehung nur als bedauerlicher Zwischen-Fall erschien.

Jedenfalls gibt ›Jesus Christ Superstar‹ mit manchem ähnlichem zusammen für sehr viele Menschen Gelegenheit, mehr über diesen Jesus nachzudenken, was sicher auch nicht schlechter ist als eine Reflexion über ›My fair Lady‹, ›Hallo Dolly‹ oder ›The Man of La Mancha‹. Zudem, darf man vertrauensvoll hoffen, ist die »superb story« dieses Christus stark genug, um selbst durch das multi-mediale Geglitzer eines vulgär-ingeniösen Broadway-Spektakels sein eigenes Licht durchscheinen zu lassen. Und was ist dieses Licht?

Der Christus der Literaten?

»Wenn jemand mir bewiesen hätte, daß Christus nicht in der Wahrheit ist, und wenn es mathematisch bewiesen wäre, daß die Wahrheit nicht in Christus ist, so würde ich trotzdem lieber mit Christus bleiben als mit der Wahrheit.« So kurz nach seiner Entlassung aus dem Zuchthaus Fjodor Michailowitsch Dostojewski[20]. Gemessen nicht nur am Niveau Dostojewskis, sondern am hohen Ernst der Jesus-Problematik in der modernen Literatur überhaupt, machen die Jesus-Songs der Beatles und anderer, aber auch das Musical ›Jesus Christ Superstar‹ und sogar das sehr viel tiefergehende ›Godspell‹ (= gospel) einen recht harmlosen Eindruck.

Was ist *charakteristisch* für die Einstellung der zeitgenössischen Literatur zu Jesus von Nazaret[21]? Zunächst: daß man zwar die Religion der Kritik unterzieht und die Kirche weithin ignoriert und ablehnt, aber die Gestalt Jesu auffällig »schont«, so daß eine ausdrückliche Ablehnung – wie etwa bei Gottfried Benn und beim späten Rainer Maria Rilke[22] nach vorausgegangener Nietzsche-Lektüre verständlich – verhältnismäßig selten vorkommt. Und vor allem: daß man gleichsam vom Rande her versucht, sich an die Gestalt Jesu heranzutasten, nur sehr indirekt und beinahe scheu von ihr redet. Wie die Höhlenbewohner in Platons Gleichnis nur die Silhouetten sehen, die die Sonne zeichnet, so sehen die modernen Literaten Jesus mehr in den Schatten, die er wirft, als ihn selbst im Licht des Tages. Jesus steht im Widerschein. Er wird beobachtet in den Wirkungen, die er auslöst, in den Menschen, die von ihm betroffen sind. Jesus wird nicht beschrieben, nicht mit Prädikaten versehen, mit Titeln ausgezeichnet. Man nähert sich ihm, indem man den Platz ausspart, an dem er steht: in sehr, so hätte man früher gesagt, »keuscher Annäherung«. Das alles – nicht mißzuverstehen – Zeichen eines ungeheuren Respekts, einer höchst eigentümlichen Reverenz vor dieser Gestalt.

Diese neue Orientierung der Literatur bedeutet nun freilich auch: die Zeit der mehr oder weniger orthodoxen, *konventionellen historisierenden und psychologisierenden Jesus-Darstellungen ist vorbei!* Das wird man vielleicht bedauern, wenn man in seiner frühen Studentenzeit Giovanni Papinis poetische ›Storia di Christo‹ (1924)[23] und, begeisterter, die ebenfalls in beinahe zahllosen Auflagen erschienenen einfühlsamen 24 Nikodemus-Briefe des Polen Jan Dobraczynski unter dem Programmwort ›Gib mir deine Sorgen‹ (1952)[24] gelesen hat, wo Jesu Gestalt aus der Perspektive eines an der Krankheit seiner Frau selber kranken jüdischen Schriftgelehrten gesehen wird und die Hiobsproblematik mit der Kreuzesproblematik sich verschlingt und zugleich löst. Auch wenn man an Pär Lagerkvists ›Barrabas‹ (1946)[25] denkt: den schuldig gewordenen, zweifelnden, suchenden Menschen, der von dem an seiner Stelle hingerichteten Jesus nicht loskommt. Oder an des Juden Max Brod (Kafkas Nachlaßverwalter) ›Der Meister‹ (1952)[26], wo Jesus aus der wachsenden und doch letztlich distanzierten Sympathie eines griechischen Beamten in der römischen Verwaltung von Jerusalem zwischen dem nihilistisch-existentialistischen Jason-Judas und der beinahe marienhaften Ziehschwester Schoschanna (Susanna) geschildert wird: auf der Linie der großen jüdischen Propheten und der wahren Menschlichkeit.

Alle diese dichterischen Jesusdarstellungen wie auch einige frühere um die Jahrhundertwende[27] waren von nicht geringer ästhetischer Qualität und theologischer Tiefe. Nicht zuletzt dann, wenn sie von Autoren außerhalb oder am Rande der Kirche stammten. Aber sie beruhten auf einer naiven, wortwörtlichen Lektüre der Evangelien: Unbelastet von der neueren exegetisch-historischen Problematik wurde geistvoll mit literarischer Phantasie, moderner Psychologie und mehr oder weniger versteckter Aktualisierung hineingelesen, was aus den Evangelien selber nicht herausgelesen werden kann. Man benützte die evangelischen Zeugnisse als ergänzungsbedürftige Chroniken und schrieb historisierend, psychologisierend, ästhetisierend so etwas wie eine fiktionale Biographie[28]. Aufs Ganze gesehen: die poetischen Gegenbilder zu den historischen Leben Jesu der liberalen (oder orthodoxen) Exegeten des 19. und beginnenden 20. Jahrhunderts.

Wenn die heutigen Schriftsteller sich Jesus nur indirekt nähern, haben sie die theologische Einsicht hinter sich, daß die Evangelien so etwas wie eine Biographie Jesu nicht hergeben und sie überhaupt nicht unreflektiert als historische Quellen benützt werden können, worüber hier noch eingehend zu reden sein wird. Und zugleich ist zweifelhaft, ob die literarischen Stilmittel und Methoden überhaupt ausreichen, um das Leben Jesu, Person und Sache, Göttliches und Menschliches vermittelt in einer geschichtlich konkreten Person, sprachlich in den Griff zu bekommen.

Nun wollten freilich schon die konventionellen Jesus-Romane mehr sein als Historie: über Jesus läßt sich nur schwer neutral-unparteiisch schreiben. In dieser oder jener Weise waren sie religiöses Zeugnis ihrer Verfasser. Schon hinter den konventionellen Jesus-Darstellungen stand meist das Interesse, den göttlich überhöhten, weltfernen und damit irrelevant gewordenen Christus des Dogmas, der Liturgie und Theologie auf die Erde herabzuholen, ihn »von unten« menschlich wieder verständlich, herausfordernd, einladend zu machen und damit zugleich auch die eigenen individuellen und sozialen Probleme zur Sprache zu bringen.

Während jedoch die konventionellen Jesus-Romane bei allem religiösen Interesse mehr poetischen Charakter hatten, so die *neuen Jesus-Darstellungen* einen primär kritischen. Dies gilt besonders von jenen poetisch-realen Jesus-Darstellungen, wo der Bezug zum neutestamentlichen Kontext wenigstens von ferne gewahrt bleibt und Jesus als Person namentlich, wenn auch verfremdet, auftritt. Jesus ist hier durchgängig in Person die radikale Kritik an den verschiedensten Formen von Jesus-Kitsch und falscher Jesus-Frömmigkeit. Die Mauern kirchlicher Sakralität erscheinen gesprengt und bewußt eine Entdivinisierung und Entkultisierung der überhöhten Christusfigur angestrebt: Jesus soll aus der Erstarrung von Dogma und Kult gelöst und zu den Menschen befreit werden. Als Exempel authentischen Menschseins bis hin an die Grenze des Häßlichen, Grausamen und Brutalen. Der neutestamentliche Befund spielt dabei anders als bei den früheren Jesus-Dichtern eine geringe Rolle. Man setzt beim Erfahrungshorizont des heutigen Menschen ein und beabsichtigt gar nicht, ein authentisches Jesus-Bild zu liefern.

Es ist vor diesem Hintergrund nicht verwunderlich, daß es, abgesehen etwa von den beiden 1970 erschienen Romanen ›Jesus in Osaka‹ von Günter Herburger und ›Das große Gesicht‹ von Frank Andermann[29], kaum noch Jesus-Darstellungen in literarischen Großformen, in Romanen und Dramen gibt, wo Jesus ausdrücklich als »Held« im Mittelpunkt des Geschehens steht. Dafür aber sind die literarischen *Formen* sehr *vielfältig*: eine Fülle von Gedanken, die formal öfters religiöse Gattungen aufgreifen und inhaltlich meist auf die »Knotenpunkte« des Lebens

Jesu bezogen sind: auf Geburt, Passion, Tod, Auferweckung. Das zeigt gerade die Lyrik: beeindruckende Beispiele bei Peter Huchel und Paul Celan[30]. Dann aber auch kurze Erzählungen, etwa von Friedrich Dürrenmatt und Peter Handke, Theaterstücke wie des Spaniers F. Arrabals ›Autofriedhof‹ und kurze Prosastücke wie etwa in Günter Grass' Roman ›Die Blechtrommel‹[31].

So vielfältig die literarischen Formen, so *vielfältig* die literarischen *Techniken:* Wie auch sonst in der zeitgenössischen Literatur erscheint die herkömmliche Erzählperspektive abgelöst, abgelöst sind auch die traditionellen Vers- und Strophenformen der Lyrik. Dafür Spiegelungen, Verfremdungen, Brechungen, Parodien, Travestien, Assoziationen, Evokationen, Übertragungen bekannter Sprach- und Vorstellungsmuster in einen disparaten Kontext oder schließlich Montagen von Sprachformen verschiedener Provenienz[32]. Drei auch inhaltlich bedeutsame Beispiele:

Vergegenwärtigung in vielfacher Brechung bei Walter Jens: Jens gibt das Romanzitat seines Autors A. (von A. nachträglich gestrichen) wieder, das Sätze aus der Jesus-Analyse des Romanhelden »Herr Meister« enthält: »Ihr trugt seinen Schritt, euch berührte sein Schweiß; ihr habt seine Blutspur gerochen und das schreckliche Stöhnen gehört; erst weit entfernt, dann näher kommend, rasselnd und laut, dann, von den Straßenschreiern oder dem Gebrüll der Fenstergaffer übertönt, sich langsam entfernend. Und wenn ihr nicht zuschauen wolltet, mußtet ihr doch – im Zimmer verborgen, in Kellern und Höfen versteckt – seinen Schatten vorbeigleiten sehen. Die Sonne warf das Kreuz an die Wand, die Mauern wurden Augen, alle Wände fingen sein Spiegelbild auf, und es ist nichts verlöscht.«[33]

Spiegelung in den Betroffenen bei Ernest Hemingway: Drei römische Soldaten an einem Freitag spät abends leicht angetrunken in der Kneipe, brutal und doch tief beeindruckt, berichten davon, wie sie ihn annagelten und hochhißten: »Wenn ihr Gewicht an ihnen zieht, das ist der Moment, wo's sie packt.« – »Manche packt's verdammt schlimm.« – »Hab ich sie denn nicht gesehen? Ich hab 'ne Masse gesehen. Ich sag euch, der hat sich heute da recht ordentlich benommen.« Ein Satz, der in der Geschichte wie ein Refrain ein halbes Dutzend mal wiederholt wird[34].

Verfremdung durch Übertragung in einen anderen Kontext bei Wolfgang Borchert: Ein Soldat mit dem Spitznamen Jesus muß sich zur Probe in Gräber legen, damit sie für Gefallene paßgerecht gemacht werden. Er verweigert trotz Befehl plötzlich den

Dienst, »macht nicht mehr mit«: »Warum heißt er eigentlich Jesus …? Oh, das hat weiter keinen Grund. Der Alte nennt ihn immer so, weil er so sanft aussieht. Der Alte findet, er sieht so sanft aus. Seitdem heißt er Jesus. Ja, sagte der Unteroffizier und machte eine neue Sprengladung fertig für das nächste Grab, melden muß ich ihn, denn die Gräber müssen ja sein[35].«

So vielfältig die literarischen Formen und Techniken in der heutigen Jesus-Darstellung, so *vielfältig* schließlich auch die literarischen *Themen und Motive.* Durchgängig durch alle literarischen Epochen des Jahrhunderts hält sich freilich der Topos des wiederkehrenden Jesus (»Jesus redivivus«), angefangen bei Balzac und Dostojewski über Hauptmann und Rilke bis zu Ricarda Huch und Günter Herburger[36]. »Warum kommst Du, uns zu stören?«: dieses Wort von Dostojewskis Großinquisitor könnte man über so ziemlich alle diese zeitgenössischen Jesus-Darstellungen setzen. Überall werden die Zeitebenen so ineinandergeschoben, daß Jesus als Störfaktor ersten Ranges für die gegenwärtige kirchliche und gesellschaftliche Ordnung erscheint: mag er nun wie bei Dostojewski als Verteidiger der menschlichen Freiheit in der Kirche auftreten, oder wie bei Hermann Hesse, beim frühen Rilke und bei Bert Brecht als Bruder und Freund der Armen und Unterdrückten[37]. Oder bei anderen, vom Naturalisten Arno Holz über den linken Expressionismus eines Carl Einstein bis hin zu Erich Kästner, als Sozialrevolutionär[38]. Oder wie bei Andermann als Widerstandskämpfer, oder wie wiederum bei Dostojewski, Hauptmann und den Expressionisten als Leitbild für alle Narren, Komödianten und Irren, die Leidenden und Gottverfolgten.

Von hier führt eine direkte Linie zu der uns bereits bekannten Pop-Szene: Jesus – Randfigur und Outcast von Kirche und Gesellschaft, Vorläufer aller Gammler und Hippies, Traum- und synthetische Kunstfigur heutiger (von Marx, Freud und Marcuse gespeister) Sehnsuchtprojektionen nach Befreiung von jeglicher Form von Zwang, zu einem unbeschwerten glücklichen Leben. So etwa bei Herburger der demokratische »Jedermann«-Jesus in allseitiger Emanzipation (gegenüber einem japanischen Konzern, einem Zen-Meister, dem Papst, einer Fernseh-Theologin, dem reichen Mann der kapitalistischen Gesellschaft). Das popige Lebensgefühl einer kommenden Generation? Jedenfalls vieldeutige utopische Zukunftsentwürfe ohne eindeutiges Resultat. Schon beim Dadaisten Hugo Ball fand sich der Jesus, der die Menschen wieder zu Kindern werden läßt, wie dann bei Herburger der Jesus, der sich am Ende mit den Kindern, Kinderpartisanen, solidarisiert. Ein Jesus vom Kreuz herabgestiegen – um sich mit den Menschen zu identifizieren!

Der Gekreuzigte – oder das leere Kreuz? Hier wird ein Zentralproblem der modernen Jesus-Literatur aufgenommen, wie es sich schon früh in Jean Pauls Schreckensvision einer »Rede des toten Christus vom Weltgebäude herab, daß kein Gott sei« (im ›Siebenkäs‹ 1796/97)[39] in der Form einer freilich nur hypothetischen Warnung angekündigt hatte. Doch ihr Einfluß zeigt sich in der Romantik bei allen möglichen »Mönchen des Atheismus« (Heinrich Heine) bis zu Dostojewskis ›Dämonen‹. Für Dostojewski insbesondere bedeutet die Gestalt gerade des leidenden, gekreuzigten und verlassenen Christus eine ungeheure Anfechtung. Nach seiner Flucht aus Rußland nach Basel, kam er bei der Betrachtung von Hans Holbeins totem Gekreuzigten nur knapp an einem epileptischen Anfall vorbei[40]. Im ersten Teil des ›Idioten‹, drei Monate später in Genf geschrieben, spielt dies Bild eine große Rolle. Erschrocken ruft Fürst Myschkin aus: »Aber vor diesem Bild kann manch einem der Glaube vergehen.«[41] Der ›Idiot‹: das frühe klassische Beispiel einer nicht mehr direkten, sondern indirekten, poetisch-transfiguralen Jesus-Darstellung, bei welcher das Jesus-Geschehen gleichsam als das verborgene Grundmuster hinter einer Person, einer Handlung, einer Konstellation oder einem Konflikt sichtbar wird. Der ›Idiot‹, von welchem Heinrich Böll bekennt : »...ich weiß immer noch keine bessere literarische Jesus-Darstellung.«[42] Dostojewski hat das geplante Buch über Jesus Christus nicht geschrieben. Aber im Sterben bat er seine Frau darum, das Evangelium, das ihn seit seiner Entlassung aus dem Zuchthaus kaum mehr verlassen hatte, aufs Geratewohl zu öffnen und ihm eine Seite daraus vorzulesen. Seiner Frau hatte er sein letztes und größtes Werk, die ›Karamasoff‹ gewidmet. Es trägt als Motto, was Dostojewskis Vermächtnis ist:

»Wahrlich, wahrlich ich sage euch:
Wenn das Weizenkorn, das in die Erde fällt,
nicht stirbt, so bleibt es allein,
stirbt es aber, so bringt es viele Frucht.«[43]

Gegen die »Dummköpfe« unter den Kritikern seiner ›Karamasoff‹, denen ein »Gespür für die unerbittliche Gottesverleugnung, welche ich in der Legende des Großinquisitors und in dem

darauffolgenden Kapitel meines Romans dargestellt habe«, abgeht, sagt Dostojewski: »... in Europa gibt es keinen atheistischen *Ausdruck* von solcher Gewalt und hat es *nie gegeben.*
Folglich glaube ich an Christus und bekenne ich mich zu diesem
Glauben nicht wie ein Kind, sondern mein Hosianna ist durch
das große *Fegefeuer der Zweifel* hindurchgegangen, wie in meinem letzten Roman der Teufel von sich sagt[44].«

Vielleicht daß also der psychologisch und theologisch unheimlich Hellsichtige auch hier wieder einmal tiefer gesehen hat.
Tiefer in diesem Fall als Andermann, der, für einen Juden nach so
viel Leid der Kriegs- und Nazizeit ergreifend, Jesus noch lebend
vom Schandkreuz herunterholen läßt. Tiefer auch als Herburger,
nach welchem der emanzipierte Jesus nicht sterben will, demon-
strativ vom Kreuz heruntersteigt und es verbrennen läßt, um
ununterscheidbar ganz einer von den Menschen zu sein. Dem
Topos des »leeren Kreuzes« entspricht in der Literatur der Topos der »Auferstehung in uns« oder des »immerwährenden Ge-
kreuzigtseins« (bei Marie-Luise Kaschnitz, Kurt Marti, Kurt
Tucholsky)[45]. Hier könnte deutlich werden, wie sehr Jesus für
das in letzter Radikalität gelebte und gelittene Menschsein steht
und wie die Knotenpunkte des Lebens Jesu sich auch als die
Knotenpunkte der eigenen Existenz begreifen lassen. So wie
etwa im Roman ›Christus wird wieder gekreuzigt. Griechische
Passion‹ des Nikos Kazantzakis[46], dessen Leben und Werk vom
Zwiespalt zwischen religiöser Theorie und kirchlicher Praxis in
Griechenland geprägt blieb: die Darsteller eines Passionsspieles
beginnen, sich ihren unchristlichen Dorfpopen und eingetroffe-
nen elenden Flüchtlingen gegenüber mit ihren Rollen, Aposteln
und Christus zu identifizieren und werden dafür selber geschlagen und gekreuzigt.

Die Christus-Jesus-Antithetik ist vielfach zu einer Jesus-
Gott-Antithetik geworden: Dem dunklen, grausamen, oft unbegreiflichen Gott steht Jesus als der Mensch und Bruder gegenüber. Nicht zuletzt damit hängt es zusammen, daß Jesus, wie
eingangs dieses Abschnittes bemerkt, bei aller radikalen
Theo-kritik und Religionskritik geschont wird und sogar mitten
in aller Rede vom Tode Gottes in der Literatur wieder zu neuem
Leben erwacht ist.

Braucht nach dieser kurzen Übersicht noch betont zu werden,
wie sehr die Literatur helfen kann, das Jesus-Geschehen zu
verstehen? Sind die Literaten nicht oft wacher, hellhöriger, fein-
spüriger als die Theologen? Dichtung erschließt Bereiche der

Sprache und der Bilder, die das Jesus-Geschehen neu übersetzen, transponieren, verstehen lassen. Sie eröffnet neue Möglichkeiten, um unsere menschlichen Erfahrungen mit der Botschaft von diesem Jesus Christus zu konfrontieren und zu vermitteln. Sie ermöglicht den »fremden Blick«, um das, was nicht fremd ist, befremdlich und das, was gewöhnlich ist, unerklärlich zu finden.

Ein Schriftsteller will gar nicht ein objektives, historisch genaues, sachlich umfassendes Jesus-Bild zeichnen. Er will vielmehr eine Linie, die ihm wichtig scheint, ausziehen, verstärken, eine Thematik einkreisen, einen Punkt überscharf beleuchten. Die subjektive Pointierung ist Stilprinzip. An historisch exakter Forschung ist der Literat als solcher nicht interessiert. Der Theologe aber muß es sein, um angesichts der vielen Christusbilder nicht nur der Konzilien, der Frommen und der Schwärmer, der Theologen und der Maler, sondern eben auch der Literaten die Frage beantworten zu können: Welches Christus-Bild ist das wahre? An welches soll man sich in der Praxis halten? Deshalb ist die Frage am Ende dieses Kapitels noch mehr als am Anfang: Welcher Christus ist der wirkliche Christus?

II. Der wirkliche Christus

Es ist allen Nachdenkens wert, woher es kommen mag: Offensichtlich ist nach dem Sturz so vieler Götter in unserem Jahrhundert dieser an seinen Gegnern Gescheiterte und von seinen Bekennern durch die Zeiten immer wieder Verratene noch immer für Ungezählte die bewegendste Figur der langen Menschheitsgeschichte: ungewöhnlich und unbegreiflich in vielfacher Hinsicht. Er ist Hoffnung für Revolutionäre und Evolutionäre, fasziniert Intellektuelle und Antiintellektuelle. Er fordert die Tüchtigen und die Untüchtigen. Theologen, aber auch Atheisten ist er ständig neuer Anstoß zum Denken. Den Kirchen Anlaß zur ständigen kritischen Selbstbefragung, ob sie sein Grabmal oder seine lebendigen Zeugen sind, und zugleich ökumenisch über alle Kirchen hinausstrahlend bis ins Judentum und die anderen Religionen hinein. Gandhi: »Ich sage den Hindus, daß ihr Leben unvollkommen sein wird, wenn sie nicht auch ehrfürchtig die Lehre Jesu studieren.«[1]

Um so drängender wird jetzt die Wahrheitsfrage: Welcher Christus ist der wahre Christus? Auch die einfache Antwort »Sei freundlich, Jesus liebt dich« tut es nicht. Jedenfalls nicht auf die Dauer. Das kann leicht unkritischer Fundamentalismus oder Pietismus im Hippie-Gewand sein. Und wo man auf Gefühle baut, kann der Name beliebig gewechselt werden: statt Che Guevara im Jesus-Look jetzt Jesus im Guevara-Look, und wieder umgekehrt. Gestellt zwischen den Jesus des Dogmatismus und den Jesus des Pietismus, gestellt zwischen den Jesus des Protestes, der Aktion, der Revolution und den Jesus der Gefühle, der Sensitivität, der Phantasie, wird die Wahrheitsfrage so zu präzisieren sein: Der Christus der Träume oder der Christus der Wirklichkeit? Der *erträumte* oder der *wirkliche* Christus?

1. Kein Mythos

Was kann verhindern, daß man einem nur erträumten, einem von uns dogmatisch oder pietistisch, revolutionär oder schwärmerisch manipulierten und inszenierten Christus folgt? Jede Manipulation, Ideologisierung, ja Mythisierung Christi hat ihre Grenze an der *Geschichte!* Der Christus des Christentums ist – dies kann nicht genügend gegen allen alten oder neuen Synkretismus betont werden – nicht einfach eine zeitlose Idee, ein ewig gültiges Prinzip, ein tiefsinniger Mythos. Über eine Christusfigur im Götterhimmel eines Hindutempels können sich nur naive Christen freuen. Der gnädigen Aufnahme ihres Christus in ein Pantheon haben schon die frühen Christen mit allen Kräften widerstanden und oft genug mit ihrem Leben dafür bezahlt. Eher ließen sie sich Atheisten schimpfen. Der Christus der Christen ist vielmehr eine ganz konkrete, menschliche, geschichtliche Person: der Christus der Christen ist niemand anders als *Jesus von Nazaret.* Und insofern gründet Christentum wesentlich in Geschichte, ist christlicher Glaube wesentlich geschichtlicher Glaube. Man vergleiche die synoptischen Evangelien mit der weitestverbreiteten (großartig vor dem nächtlichen Tempel von Prambanan/Java und auf ungezählten Tempelfresken zur Darstellung gebrachten) hinduistischen Dichtung Ramayana, die in vierundzwanzigtausend Sanskritstrophen beschreibt, wie der hochgesinnte Prinz Rama (= der inkarnierte Vishnu), dem seine Gattin Sita vom Riesenkönig Ravana nach Ceylon entführt wurde, mit Hilfe eines Heeres von Affen, die eine Brücke über den Ozean bauten, seine ihm treu gebliebene Gemahlin befreit und schließlich doch verstoßen hat: und man erkennt den ganzen Unterschied. Nur als geschichtlicher Glaube hat sich das Christentum schon am Anfang gegen alle die Mythologien, Philosophien, Mysterienkulte durchsetzen können.

In Ort und Zeit

»»Und Christus?‹ Kafka neigte den Kopf. ›Das ist ein lichterfüllter Abgrund. Man muß die Augen schließen, um nicht abzustürzen.¹«« Aber wenn auch ungezählte Menschen in Jesus übermenschliche, göttliche Wirklichkeit erfahren haben und wenn auch schon von Anfang an hohe Titel von ihm gebraucht wurden, so ist doch kein Zweifel, daß Jesus für seine Zeitgenossen wie auch für die spätere Kirche immer als ein *wirklicher Mensch* galt. Nach allen neutestamentlichen Schriften – und sie sind abgesehen von den genannten wenigen und unergiebigen heidnischen und jüdischen Zeugnissen unsere einzigen verläßlichen Quellen, auch Talmud und Midrasch fallen dafür aus – ist Jesus ein wirklicher Mensch, der zu einer ganz bestimmten Zeit und in einer ganz bestimmten Umgebung gelebt hat. Aber hat er wirklich gelebt?

Die *historische Existenz* Jesu von Nazaret wurde ähnlich wie die Buddhas und andere scheinbar unbestreitbare Tatsachen auch schon einmal bestritten. Die Aufregung war groß, wenn auch unnötig, als im 19. Jahrhundert Bruno Bauer das Christentum als eine Erfindung des Urevangelisten und Jesus als eine »Idee« verstand. Und noch einmal, als Arthur Drews, 1909, Jesus als reine »Christusmythe«[2] interpretierte (ähnlich auch der Engländer J. M. Robertson und der amerikanische Mathematiker W. B. Smith). Aber extreme Positionen haben ihr Gutes. Sie klären die Situation und heben sich meist selber auf: die geschichtliche Existenz Jesu wird seither von keinem ernsthaften Forscher bestritten. Was selbstverständlich unernsthafte Schreiber nicht gehindert hat, über Jesus weiterhin Unernsthaftes zu schreiben (Jesus als Psychopath, als Astralmythos, als Sohn des Herodes, als im geheimen verheiratet und ähnliches mehr). Ein wenig betrüblich ist nur, wenn ein Philologe seinen Ruf damit ruiniert, daß er Jesus als Geheimbezeichnung für einen halluzinogenen Fliegenpilz (Amanita muscaria) deutet, der angeblich in den Riten der ersten Christen verwendet wurde[3]. Ob man etwas noch Originelleres finden wird?

Wir wissen von Jesus von Nazaret unvergleich mehr historisch Gesichertes als von den großen asiatischen Religionsstiftern:

mehr als von *Buddha* († um 480 v. Chr.), dessen Bild in den Lehrtexten (Sutras) auffällig stereotyp bleibt und dessen stark systematisierte Legende weniger einen historischen als einen idealtypischen Lebensablauf wiedergibt;

mehr erst recht als von Buddhas chinesischem Zeitgenossen *Kung-futse* (Meister Kung, † vermutlich 479 v. Chr.), dessen zweifellos reale Persönlichkeit trotz aller Bemühungen wegen der Unzuverlässigkeit der Quellen nicht exakt zu erfassen ist und die erst nachträglich mit der chinesischen Staatsideologie des »Konfuzianismus« (einem im Chinesischen unbekannten Wort; sachgemäßer: »Lehre oder Schule der Gelehrten«) verknüpft wurde;

mehr schließlich als von *Lao-tse*, dessen Gestalt von der chinesischen Überlieferung als real angenommen, wegen der unzuverlässigen Quellen biographisch überhaupt nicht faßbar ist und dessen Lebensdaten je nach Quellen ganz verschieden im 14., 13., 8., 7. oder 6. Jahrhundert v. Chr. angesetzt werden.

Der kritische Vergleich ergibt in der Tat erstaunliche Unterschiede:

Die Lehren *Buddhas* sind durch Quellen überliefert, die wenigstens ein halbes Jahrtausend nach dessen Tod niedergeschrieben wurden, als die ursprüngliche Religion bereits eine weitgehende Entwicklung erfahren hatte.

Erst seit dem 1. Jahrhundert v. Chr. wird *Lao-tse* als Autor des Tao-te-king bezeichnet, jenes klassischen Buches von »Weg« und »Tugend«, welches faktisch eine Kompilation aus mehreren Jahrhunderten ist, dann aber für die Formulierung der taoistischen Lehre entscheidend wurde.

Die wichtigsten Überlieferungstexte von *Kung-futse* – die ›Biographie‹ von Szu-ma Chien und die ›Gespräche‹ (Lun-yü: eine den Schülern zugeschriebene Sammlung von Aussprüchen Kungs, eingebettet in Situationsberichte) – sind 400 Jahre, das zweite gegen 700 Jahre von der Lebzeit des Meisters entfernt und kaum zuverlässig; authentisch gesicherte Schriften oder eine authentische Biographie Kung-futses gibt es nicht (auch die Chronik des Staates Lu stammt kaum von ihm).

Aber auch wenn man nach Europa blickt: Die älteste uns erhaltene Handschrift der Homerischen Epen stammt aus dem 13. Jahrhundert. Der Text der Sophokleischen Tragödien beruht auf einer einzigen Handschrift des 8. oder 9. Jahrhunderts. Für das Neue Testamtent[4] aber ist der Abstand von der Urschrift um vieles kürzer, sind die erhaltenen Handschriften zahlreicher, ist ihre Übereinstimmung größer als bei irgendeinem anderen Buch der Antike: Sorgfältige Handschriften der Evangelien gibt es bereits aus dem 3. und 4. Jahrhundert. In jüngster Zeit aber hat man vor allem in der ägyptischen Wüste noch sehr viel ältere Papyri entdeckt: das älteste Fragment des Johannes-Evangeliums – des letzten der vier Evangelien – liegt heute im Original in der John-Rylands-Bibliothek in Manchester, stammt aus dem Beginn des 2. Jahrhunderts und weicht mit keinem Wort von unserem gedruckten griechischen Text ab. Die vier Evangelien haben somit bereits um das Jahr 100 existiert; mythische Erweiterungen und Umdeutungen (in den apokryphen Evangelien usw.) finden sich vom 2. Jahrhundert an. Der Weg führte offensichtlich von der Geschichte zum Mythos und nicht vom Mythos zur Geschichte!

Jesus von Nazaret ist kein Mythos: seine Geschichte läßt sich *lozieren*. Sie ist keine Wanderlegende wie – betrüblich genug für manchen treuen Eidgenossen – der Schweizer Nationalheld

Wilhelm Tell. Sie spielte gewiß in einem politisch unbedeutenden Land, in einer Randprovinz des römischen Reiches. Aber immerhin stellte dieses Land Palästina ältestes Kulturreich im Kern des »fruchtbaren Halbmondes« dar: Bevor sich das politisch-kulturelle Gewicht auf die beiden Spitzen des Halbmondes – Ägypten und Mesopotamien – verlagerte, vollzog sich dort etwa im siebten vorchristlichen Jahrtausend die große jungeiszeitliche Revolution, in der die Jäger und Sammler sich als Ackerbauern und Viehzüchter niederließen, sich damit zum erstenmal in der Menschheitsgeschichte von der Natur unabhängig machten und sie selbständig produktiv zu beherrschen begannen, bevor es dann beinahe vier Jahrtausende später auf den beiden Spitzen des Halbmondes – Ägypten und Mesopotamien – zum nächsten revolutionären Schritt, nämlich der Schaffung der ersten Hochkulturen und der Erfindung der Schrift, und weitere fünf Jahrtausende später zum vorläufig letzten großen revolutionären Schritt, dem Griff nach den Sternen kam. Das in der Parabel vom barmherzigen Samariter genannte und in neuerer Zeit wieder ausgegrabene Jericho kann man die älteste stadtartige Siedlung der Welt (zwischen 7000 und 5000 v. Chr.) nennen. Als schmale Landbrücke zwischen den Reichen am Nil und an Euphrat und Tigris schon immer leicht Kampffeld der Großmächte, stand Palästina zur Zeit Jesu unter der Herrschaft der von den Juden gehaßten römischen Militärmacht und den von ihr ernannten halbjüdischen Vasallen-Herrschern. Jesus, den manche in der nationalsozialistischen Zeit gerne zum Arier gemacht hätten, stammte zweifellos aus Palästina: genauer aus der nördlich gelegenen Landschaft Galiläa mit einer rassisch freilich nicht rein jüdischen, sondern stark gemischten Bevölkerung, die aber anders als das zwischen Judäa und Galiläa liegende Samarien Jerusalem und seinen Tempel als zentrales Kultzentrum anerkannte. Ein kleiner Wirkungsbereich in jedem Fall: zwischen Kafarnaum am lieblichen See Genesaret im Norden und der Hauptstadt Jerusalem im gebirgigen Süden nur 130 km Luftdistanz, von einer Karawane in einer Woche zu durchqueren.

Jesus von Nazaret ist kein Mythos: seine Geschichte läßt sich *datieren*. Sie ist kein überzeitlicher Mythos von der Art, wie sie die ersten Hochkulturen der Menschheit geprägt haben: Kein Mythos des ewigen Lebens wie in Ägypten. Kein Mythos der kosmischen Ordnung wie in Mesopotamien. Kein Mythos der Welt als Wandlung wie in Indien. Kein Mythos des vollendeten Menschen wie in Griechenland. Es geht um die Geschichte dieses einen Menschen, der in Palästina zu Beginn unserer Zeitrechnung unter dem römischen Kaiser Augustus geboren und unter dessen Nachfolger Tiberius öffentlich aufgetreten und schließlich durch dessen Prokurator Pontius Pilatus hingerichtet wurde.

Unsicheres

Anderes bezüglich der genauen Lozierung und Datierung bleibt fraglich, ist aber sachlich von geringerer Bedeutung.

a. Welcher *Herkunft?* Der Geburtsort Jesu – von den Evangelisten Markus und Johannes nicht angegeben, nach den in den näheren Angaben voneinander abweichenden Mattäus und Lukas vielleicht aus theologischen Gründen (davidische Abstammung und Prophezeiung des Propheten Micha) Betlehem, nach der Vermutung mancher Forscher Nazaret – kann nicht eindeutig bestimmt werden. Jedenfalls ist, wie im ganzen Neuen Testament belegt, die eigentliche Heimat des »Nazareners« oder »Nazoräers« das unbedeutende Nazaret in Galiläa. Die Stammbäume Jesu bei Mattäus und Lukas treffen sich zwar bei David, gehen aber sonst so weit auseinander, daß sie nicht zu harmonisieren sind. Nach heute wohl allgemeiner Auffassung der Exegeten haben die in manchem legendär ausgeschmückten Kindheitsgeschichten ebenso wie die nur bei Lukas überlieferte erbauliche Geschichte vom Zwölfjährigen im Tempel einen besonderen literarischen Charakter und stehen im Dienst der theologischen Interpretation der Evangelisten. In den Evangelien wird zum Teil ganz unbefangen von Jesu Mutter Maria, seinem Vater Josef wie auch seinen Brüdern und Schwestern gesprochen. Seine Familie ebenso wie seine Heimatstadt haben sich gegenüber seiner öffentlichen Tätigkeit nach den Quellen distanziert verhalten.

b. Welches *Geburtsjahr?* Wenn Jesus unter Kaiser Augustus (27 v. Chr. bis 14 n. Chr.) und König Herodes (27–4 v. Chr.) geboren wurde, dann war sein Geburtsjahr nicht nach 4 v. Chr. Aus dem Wunderstern, der nicht mit einer bestimmten Gestirnkonstellation gleichzusetzen ist, läßt sich ebensowenig etwas ableiten wie aus der Schätzung des Quirinius (6 oder 7 n. Chr.), die für Lukas vielleicht als Erfüllung einer Weissagung wichtig war.

c. Welches *Todesjahr?* Wenn Jesus nach Lukas im 15. Jahr des Kaisers Tiberius, also 27/28 (oder 28/29 n. Chr.) von Johannes dem Täufer getauft wurde, was allgemein als historische Tatsache angenommen wird, wenn er bei diesem ersten öffentlichen Auftreten nach Lukas ungefähr dreißig Jahre alt war und nach der gesamten Überlieferung (auch Tacitus) unter Pontius Pilatus (26–36) verurteilt worden war, dann muß er rund um das Jahr 30 den Tod erlitten haben. Für den genauen Todestag, der von den drei ersten Evangelisten und von Johannes verschieden überliefert wird (15. oder 14. Nisan), läßt sich auch im Rückgriff auf den aufgefundenen Festkalender der Qumrangemeinde am Toten Meer keine eindeutige Gewißheit erlangen.

Wenn sich somit die Daten des Lebens Jesu wie viele Zeitpunkte der alten Geschichte nicht mit letzter Genauigkeit errechnen lassen, so ist es geradezu denkwürdig, daß in jenem genügend bestimmten Zeitraum ein Mensch, von dem es keine »offiziellen« Dokumente, keine Inschriften, Chroniken, Prozeßakten gibt, der bestenfalls drei Jahre (nach den bei Johannes berichteten drei Passafesten), aber vielleicht auch nur ein einziges Jahr (bei den Synoptikern ist nur von einem Passafest die Rede) oder gar nur wenige dramatische Monate zumeist in Galiläa und dann in Jerusalem öffentlich gewirkt hat, daß also dieser eine Mensch den Lauf der Welt in einer Weise geändert hat, daß man nicht ohne Grund die Weltjahre nach ihm zu datieren begonnen hat – den Herrschenden der Französischen Revolution ebenso wie denen der Oktoberrevolution und der Hitlerzeit nachträglich ein Ärgernis. Keiner der großen Religionsstifter hat in einem so engen Bereich gewirkt. Keiner hat so ungeheuer kurze Zeit gelebt. Keiner ist so jung gestorben. Und doch welche Wirkung: Jeder vierte Mensch, rund eine Milliarde Menschen werden Christen genannt. Das Christentum steht – zahlenmäßig – mit Abstand an der Spitze aller Weltreligionen.

2. Die Dokumente

Der christliche Glaube redet von Jesus, aber auch die Geschichtsschreibung redet von ihm. Der christliche Glaube ist an Jesus als dem »Christus« der Christen interessiert. Die Geschichtsschreibung an Jesus als geschichtlicher Figur. Aufgrund des neuzeitlichen wissenschaftlichen Denkens und der Entwicklung des historischen Bewußtseins ist der moderne Mensch mehr als der des Mittelalters oder der Antike daran interessiert, die menschliche Person Jesu, wie sie wirklich war, kennenzulernen. Inwiefern aber ist Jesus von Nazaret der Fragestellung und Forschung des Historikers zugänglich? Kommt der Historiker überhaupt an ihn heran?

Mehr als eine Biographie

Eine Einsicht hat sich – trotz zahlloser romanhafter Jesus-Bücher – durchgesetzt: So leicht sich Jesu Geschichte lozieren und datieren läßt – eine *Biographie* Jesu von Nazaret läßt sich *nicht* schreiben! Warum? Es fehlen dafür einfach die Voraussetzungen.

Da sind die frühen römischen und jüdischen Quellen, die aber, wie wir sahen, über die Tatsache der historischen Existenz hinaus von Jesus kaum etwas Brauchbares berichten. Und da sind neben den in der Kirche von alters her offiziell akzeptierten Evangelien noch die erheblich später, mit allerlei seltsamen Legenden und fragwürdigen Nachbildungen von Jesus-Worten ausgeschmückten, öffentlich nicht benützten, »apokryphen« (= verborgenen) Evangelien, die, abgesehen von ganz wenigen Jesus-Worten, ebenfalls nichts historisch Gesichertes über Jesus beibringen.

So bleiben denn jene *vier Evangelien,* die nach dem ›Kanon‹ (= Richtschnur, Maßstab, Liste) der alten Kirche als ursprüngliches Zeugnis des christlichen Glaubens für den öffentlichen Gebrauch in die Schriftensammlung des ›Neuen Testaments‹ (analog zu den Schriften des ›Alten Testaments‹) aufgenommen wurden: eine Auswahl, die sich – wie der neutestamentliche Kanon überhaupt – in einer Geschichte von 2000 Jahren aufs Ganze gesehen durchaus bewährt hat. Doch diese vier »kanonischen« Evangelien liefern nicht den Ablauf des Lebens Jesu in seinen verschiedenen Stadien und Ereignissen. Über die Kindheit wissen wir wenig Gesichertes, über die Zeit dann bis zum dreißigsten Lebensjahr gar nichts. Und das Wichtigste: In den vielleicht nur wenigen Monaten oder bestenfalls drei Jahren der öffentlichen Tätigkeit läßt sich gerade das nicht feststellen, was Voraussetzung für jede Biographie wäre: eine Entwicklung.

Zwar wissen wir im allgemeinen, daß der Weg Jesu von seiner galiläischen Heimat in die judäische Hauptstadt Jerusalem, von der Verkündigung der Nähe Gottes zur Auseinandersetzung mit dem offiziellen Judentum und zu seiner Hinrichtung durch die Römer führte. Aber an einer Chronologie und Topologie dieses Weges waren die ersten Zeugen offensichtlich nicht interessiert. Und ebensowenig an einer inneren Entwicklung: an der Genese seines religiösen, insbesondere seines messianischen Bewußtseins und seinen Motiven, oder gar an Jesu »Charakterbild«, »Persönlichkeit« und »innerem Leben«. Insofern (und nur insofern) scheiterte die liberale Leben-Jesu-Forschung des 19. Jahrhunderts mit ihrem Versuch einer Periodisierung und Motivierung des Lebens Jesu, wie dies Albert Schweitzer in seiner klassischen Geschichte der Leben-Jesu-Forschung[1] feststellt: Eine äußere und insbesondere eine innere psychologische Entwicklung Jesu läßt sich aus den Evangelien nicht heraus-, sondern bestenfalls hineinlesen. Woher kommt das?

Auch für Nichttheologen ist wichtig und nicht uninteressant zu wissen, wie die *Evangelien* in einem Prozeß von ungefähr 50 bis 60 Jahren *entstanden* sind[2]. Lukas berichtet in den ersten Sätzen seines Evangeliums davon. Erstaunlich genug: Jesus selber hatte ja kein einziges schriftliches Wort hinterlassen und hatte auch nichts für die treue Weitergabe seiner Worte getan. Die Jünger gaben seine Worte und Taten zunächst mündlich weiter. Wobei sie selber, wie jeder Erzähler, je nach Charakter und Zuhörerkreis verschiedene Akzente setzten, auswählten, interpretierten, verdeutlichten, erweiterten. Von Anfang an dürfte es ein schlichtes Erzählen vom Wirken, Lehren und Schicksal Jesu gegeben haben. Die Evangelisten – wohl alles nicht direkte Jünger Jesu, aber Zeugen der ursprünglichen apostolischen Überlieferung – sammelten alles sehr viel später: die mündlich überlieferten und nun zum Teil bereits schriftlich fixierten Jesus-Geschichten und Jesus-Worte, wie sie nicht etwa in Gemeindearchiven Jerusalems oder Galiläas aufbewahrt worden sind, sondern wie sie im gläubigen Leben der Gemeinden, in Predigt, Katechese, Gottesdienst verwendet wurden. Alle diese Texte hatten einen bestimmten »Sitz im Leben«, hatten bereits eine Geschichte hinter sich, die sie mitgeformt hatte, wurden bereits als Botschaft Jesu weitergegeben. Die Evangelisten – zweifellos nicht nur Sammler und Tradenten, wie man eine Zeitlang meinte, sondern durchaus originelle Theologen mit eigener Konzeption – ordneten die Jesus-Erzählungen und Jesus-Worte nach eigenem Plan und Gutdünken: Sie stellten einen bestimmten Rahmen her, so daß sich eine fortlaufende Erzählung ergab. Die Passionsgeschichte, auffällig übereinstimmend von allen vier

Evangelisten überliefert, scheint schon verhältnismäßig früh eine Erzählungseinheit gebildet zu haben. Zugleich richteten die Evangelisten, wohl auch selber in der missionarischen und katechetischen Praxis stehend, die überlieferten Texte auf die Bedürfnisse ihrer Gemeinden aus: Sie deuteten sie von Ostern her, erweiterten und paßten sie an, wo es ihnen notwendig erschien. So erhielten die verschiedenen Evangelien von dem einen Jesus bei aller Gemeinsamkeit ein sehr verschiedenes theologisches Profil.

Markus, mitten im Umbruch zwischen der ersten und der zweiten Christengeneration, war es gewesen, der kurz vor der Zerstörung Jerusalems im Jahre 70 nach heute verbreitetster Ansicht das erste Evangelium schrieb (Markus-Priorität gegenüber der traditionellen Auffassung von Mattäus als dem ältesten Evangelium). Es stellt eine höchst originelle Leistung dar: dieses »Evangelium« bildet trotz der wenig literarischen Sprache eine völlig neue literarische Gattung, eine Literaturform, wie es sie bisher in der Geschichte nicht gegeben hatte.

Mattäus (wohl Judenchrist) und *Lukas* (Hellenist für gebildetes Publikum schreibend), nach der Zerstörung Jerusalems, benutzten für ihre Großevangelien einerseits das Markus-Evangelium und andererseits eine (oder vielleicht mehr als eine?) Sammlung von Jesus-Worten, die sogenannte Logien-Quelle, in der Forschung meist einfach mit Q bezeichnet[3]. Das ist die klassische Zwei-Quellen-Theorie, wie sie bereits im 19. Jahrhundert ausgearbeitet wurde und sich inzwischen in der Einzelexegese in vielfältiger Weise bewährt hat. Sie schließt ein, daß jeder Evangelist auch noch eigenes Gut, sogenanntes Sondergut, mitverwertet hat, welches beim Vergleich der verschiedenen Evangelien klar hervortritt. Ein solcher Vergleich zeigt auch, daß Markus, Mattäus und Lukas im großen Aufbauplan, in der Auswahl und Anordnung des Stoffes und sehr oft auch im Wortlaut weithin übereinstimmen, so daß sie zum bequemeren Vergleich nebeneinander gedruckt werden können. Sie bilden eine Zusammen-Schau: eine »Syn-opse«. Sie werden deshalb die »synoptischen« Evangelien der drei »Synoptiker« genannt.

Ihnen gegenüber hat das Evangelium des im hellenistischen Raum schreibenden *Johannes* sowohl literarisch wie theologisch einen völlig anderen Charakter. Wegen der sehr verschiedenen Redeweise Jesu bei Johannes, der unjüdischen Form der langen monologischen Reden und wegen seines ganz auf die Person Jesu selber ausgerichteten Inhalts kommt das vierte Evangelium als

Quelle für die Beantwortung der Frage, wer der geschichtliche Jesus von Nazaret gewesen ist, nur sehr bedingt in Frage: zum Beispiel bezüglich der Traditionen der Leidensgeschichte und der unmittelbar vorausgehenden Ereignisse. Aufs Ganze gesehen steht es der geschichtlichen Wirklichkeit des Lebens und Wirkens Jesu offensichtlich ferner als die synoptischen Evangelien. Es ist auch zweifellos das zuletzt geschriebene Evangelium, wie schon früh im 19. Jahrhundert David Friedrich Strauss herausgefunden hatte. Es dürfte um das Jahr 100 geschrieben worden sein.

Engagierte Zeugnisse

Aus all dem wird klar: wer die Evangelien als stenografische Protokolle liest, versteht sie falsch. Die Evangelien wollen von Jesus nicht historisch berichten, wollen nicht seine »Entwicklung« beschreiben.

Von Anfang bis Ende wollen sie ihn im Licht seiner Auferweckung als den Messias, Christus, Herrn, Gottessohn verkünden. »Evangelium« meint ja ursprünglich nicht eine Evangeliumsschrift, sondern, wie bereits in den Paulusbriefen deutlich, eine mündlich proklamierte Botschaft: eine gute, erfreuliche Botschaft (euangelion). Und das zuerst von Markus geschriebene ›Evangelium Jesu Christi, des Sohnes Gottes‹ will dieselbe Glaubensbotschaft nun in schriftlicher Form weitergeben.

Die Evangelien wollen also gar keine uninteressierten objektiven Dokumentarberichte und erst recht keine neutrale wissenschaftliche Geschichtsschreibung sein. Das hat man damals auch gar nicht erwartet, da mit der Schilderung geschichtlicher Ereignisse immer auch ihre Bedeutung und Auswirkung beschrieben wurde: Berichte also, die in irgendeiner Form auch ein Zeugnis darstellten, stark eingefärbt durch die Haltung des Verfassers, die dahinterstand. Die Geschichtsschreiber Herodot und Thukydides waren ebenso von der griechischen Sache eingenommen wie Livius und Tacitus von der römischen. Sie ließen ihre Haltung klar durchscheinen und zogen sogar nicht selten Lehren aus den Ereignissen, die sie berichten: eine nicht nur erzählend-referierende, sondern lehrhaft-pragmatische Geschichtsschreibung.

Die Evangelien nun sind noch in einem sehr viel tieferen Sinne echte Zeugnisse. Sie sind, wie dies nach dem Ersten Weltkrieg die »formgeschichtliche Schule« durch Untersuchung der einzelnen

Jesus-Worte und Jesus-Geschichten bis ins kleinste Detail hinein sichtbar gemacht hat[4], bestimmt und geprägt von den verschiedenartigen Glaubenserfahrungen der Gemeinden. Sie sehen Jesus mit den Augen des Glaubens. Sie sind also *engagierte und engagierende Glaubenszeugnisse*: Dokumente nicht von Unbeteiligten, sondern von überzeugten Glaubenden, die zum Glauben an Jesus Christus aufrufen wollen und deshalb eine interpretierende, ja bekennende Form haben. Berichte, die zugleich – im weitesten Sinn des Wortes – Predigten sind. Diese Zeugen sind so von diesem Jesus ergriffen, wie man nur im Glauben ergriffen sein kann, und sie wollen diesen Glauben weitergeben. Für sie ist Jesus nicht nur eine Figur der Vergangenheit. Für sie ist er der auch heute Lebendige, dem für die Hörer dieser Botschaft eine entscheidende Bedeutung zukommt. In diesem Sinn wollen die Evangelien nicht nur berichten, sondern verkündigen, ergreifen, Glauben wecken. Sie sind engagiertes Zeugnis oder, wie es oft mit dem entsprechenden griechischen Wort gesagt wird, »Kerygma«: Verkündigung, Ankündigung, Botschaft.

Diese Zielrichtung und Eigenart der Evangelien machen nicht nur eine Biographie Jesu unmöglich. Sie erschweren überhaupt die nüchterne historische Interpretation der Texte. Freilich nimmt heute kein ernsthafter Forscher noch wie am Anfang der Evangelienkritik eine bewußte Verfälschung der Geschichte Jesu durch die Jünger an. Diese erfanden nicht willkürlich Jesus-Worte und Jesus-Taten. Man war damals einfach überzeugt, daß man jetzt besser verstand als zu Jesu Lebzeiten, wer er wirklich war und was er eigentlich bedeutete. Und so hat man, wie damals üblich, nicht gezögert, alles das, was von ihm her zu sagen war, auch unter seine persönliche Autorität zu stellen: sei es, daß man ihm bestimmte Worte in den Mund legte, sei es, daß man bestimmte Geschichten von seinem Gesamtbild her gestaltete. Aber die Frage stellt sich zumindest für unser historisches Bewußtsein sehr ernsthaft: Was ist nun in diesen Evangelien Bericht von wirklich Geschehenem und was ist Interpretation? Was ist Wort und Tat Jesu selber und was ist Deutung, Ergänzung, österliche Überhöhung oder Verklärung der Gemeinde oder des Evangelisten?

Wenn die Evangelien primär Quellen des nachösterlichen Christusglaubens der christlichen Gemeinden sind: können dann die Evangelien unter dieser Voraussetzung überhaupt noch Quellen für das sein, was der vorösterliche, irdische, geschichtliche Jesus selber gesagt und getan hat? Karl Barth[5] und mit ihm dann auch Bultmann[6] und Tillich[7] zeigten aufgrund der Ergebnisse der frühen liberalen Leben-Jesu-Forschung historische Skepsis (die A. Schweitzer keineswegs teilte) und vertraten im Anschluß an Kierkegaards Glaubensverständnis einen historisch ungesicherten (beziehungsweise gegen die Historie dogmatisch abgesicherten) Glauben als den wahren Glauben.

Heute indessen zeichnet sich aufgrund der neuen exegetischen Problemstellung eine weitgehende grundsätzliche Übereinstimmung auch zwischen der mehr progressiven deutschen und der mehr konservativen angelsächsischen und französischen Forschung ab: Die Evangelien sind zwar zweifellos Glaubenszeugnisse, Urkunden des Glaubens für den Glauben (darin hatten Barth, Bultmann und Tillich recht). Aber sie enthalten ebenso zweifellos auch historische Informationen. Jedenfalls kann man von ihnen aus auf den Jesus der Geschichte zurückfragen. Nach der Geschichte Jesu hatte ja auch der vielfach für Skepsis zu Unrecht in Anspruch genommene Albert Schweitzer – er war nur skeptisch gegenüber dem modernisierten liberalen Jesus, der jederzeit in die Debatte einer Pastorenkonferenz hätte eingreifen können – gefragt und hatte dementsprechend einen eigenen Rekonstruktionsversuch vorgelegt: den für ihn ursprünglichen Jesus der (noch zu besprechenden) »konsequenten Eschatologie«.

3. Geschichte und Glaubensgewißheit

Die Geschichten von Jesus lassen nach seiner wirklichen Geschichte fragen: zwar nicht nach einer kontinuierlichen Biographie, aber doch nach dem wirklich Geschehenen. Die Voraussetzungen für eine solche Untersuchung sind unterdessen trotz aller Schwierigkeiten besser geworden. Das ist ein Ergebnis der modernen *historisch-kritischen Methode*: Wenn das Neue Testament heute als das mit Abstand bestuntersuchte Buch der Weltliteratur – verbreitet heute in fast 1500 Sprachen – bezeichnet werden kann, so beruht dies auf der nun rund 300 Jahre umfassenden, minuziösen Arbeit ganzer Gelehrtengenerationen. Sie haben in Text- und Literaturkritik, Form- und Gattungskritik verbunden mit Begriffs-, Motiv- und Traditionsgeschichte um jede Schrift, jeden Satz, ja – wie dem Nicht-Fachmann neben den zahlreichen neutestamentlichen Kommentarreihen besonders ein Blick in das monumentale neunbändige ›Theologische Wörterbuch zum Neuen Testament‹ zeigen kann – um jedes Wort gerungen[1]:

Was hat die *Textkritik* für die Erforschung der Evangelien erreicht? Sie hat den Wortlaut der biblischen Schriften in der ältesten erreichbaren Gestalt durch äußere und innere Kritik, sprachliche und sachliche Erwägungen sowie Heranziehung der Textgeschichte mit größtmöglicher Genauigkeit und Annäherung festgestellt.

Und die *Literaturkritik*? Sie hat die literarische Integrität der Schriften untersucht. Sie hat die Differenzen in den vorausgesetzten rechtlichen, religiösen und gesellschaftlichen Zuständen, in Sprache, Chronologie und geschichtlichen Angaben, in den theologischen und moralischen Auffassungen herausgestellt. Sie hat durch Quellenunterscheidung der mündlichen und schriftlichen Traditionen die eventuellen Vorlagen unter später eingearbeitetem Material erhellt. Sie hat Alter, Herkunft, Adressatenkreis und literarische Eigenart der neutestamentlichen Schriften bestimmt. Sie hat sie in literaturvergleichenden Verfahren mit der zeitgenössischen jüdischen und hellenistischen Literatur konfrontiert und in ihrer Besonderheit beschrieben.

Und die *Form- und Gattungskritik*? Sie hat die Frage nach dem Sitz im Leben der Gemeinde und des Einzelnen, nach der literarischen Gattung, nach dem Rahmen der kleinen literarischen Einheiten, nach der ursprünglichen Form gestellt und hat so die historische Verläßlichkeit wie den Traditionsgehalt neu zu bestimmen versucht.

Und schließlich die *Traditionsgeschichte*? Sie hat den vorliterarischen Prozeß zu durchleuchten unternommen, hat die ältesten Hymnen, liturgischen Fragmente, Rechtssätze usw. analysiert, hat sie mit Gottesdienst, Predigt, Katechese und Gemeindeleben in Verbindung gebracht und so die für die Entstehung der Kirche entscheidenden Anfänge und das erste Stadium ihrer Entwicklung aufzudecken versucht.

Rückfrage nach Jesus

Mit der historisch-kritischen Methode in diesem umfassendsten Sinn ist der Theologie ein Instrument in die Hände gegeben, mit dem in einer Weise nach dem wahren, wirklichen, geschichtlichen Christus gefragt werden kann, wie dies in früheren Jahrhunderten einfach nicht möglich war.

Die Evangelien selber beanspruchen: Der von ihnen verkündigte lebendige Christus ist derselbe wie der Mensch Jesus von Nazaret, mit dem zumindest ein Teil ihrer Zeugen während seiner irdischen Wirksamkeit zusammengelebt haben. Gewiß, die Glaubenszeugnisse *sind* nicht einfach Berichte, aber sie *enthalten* Bericht und *gründen* in Berichten vom wirklichen Jesus. Aber inwiefern und inwieweit? Der Leser der Evangelien möchte ja doch gern wissen, ob und wieweit zwischen dem Jesus der Evangelien und dem Jesus der Geschichte eine Übereinstimmung besteht oder nicht: Sind es wirklich wahre Zeugnisse?

– *Die Rückfrage nach Jesus ist für den* Historiker *nicht gleichgültig: Nur von daher kann der Erforscher des Alten Orients wie des römischen Kaiserreichs, der jüdischen wie der christlichen Religion die erstaunliche Entstehung des Christentums überhaupt erklären.*
– *Sie ist aber auch für den* Glaubenden *nicht gleichgültig: Nur von daher kann der Prediger wie sein Hörer wissen, ob sein Glaube letztlich auf Geschehenem, auf Geschichte, oder auf einem Mythos, auf Legenden und Fiktionen oder vielleicht schlicht auf einem Mißverständnis beruht. Ob also sein christliches Engagement in der Welt von heute letztlich begründet und gerechtfertigt ist oder nicht.*
– *Sie ist sogar für den* Nichtglaubenden *nicht gleichgültig: Nur von daher kann der Altkommunist, kann der »neue Linke« und der liberale atheistische Humanist oder Positivist wissen, worum es letztlich geht im Streit. Ob er nicht gegen Phantome, sondern gegen den wirklichen Gegner kämpft. Ob er nicht nur politische und gesellschaftliche Auswirkungen des Christentums, nicht nur irgendein modernes, mittelalterliches oder altes Christentum trifft, sondern wahrhaft die Sache, das Herz des Christentums selbst.*

Kann in der *Theologie* die historische Wahrheitsfrage heute noch dogmatisch verdrängt, die Geschichte im Namen des Glaubens grundsätzlich diffamiert werden? Der Wind in der Forschung hat sich in den letzten Jahren gewendet, auch wenn einige ältere Kämpfer sich noch immer mit einem unbegründeten »Kerygma« und zur Not vielleicht sogar mit einem irrationalen »Credo quia absurdum« (»Ich glaube, gerade weil es unsinnig scheint«) zufriedengeben möchten. Die reine Kerygma-Theologie hat ihre Zeit gehabt. Die wissenschaftliche Beantwortung der Frage nach dem Jesus der Geschichte wird heute in neuer Form und innerhalb bestimmter Grenzen wieder als möglich angesehen: nicht nur in der angelsächsischen[2] und französischen[3] Exegese, sondern auch wieder in der deutschen, ja – nachdem im Jahre 1953 Ernst Käsemann das Signal zur Wende gegeben hatte[4] – in der Bultmannschule selbst[5]. Die berechtigte Interpretation aller neutestamentlichen Texte auf die »Geschichtlichkeit« der menschlichen Existenz (»existentiale Interpretation«) und die »Entscheidung« des Einzelnen hin darf die reale Geschichte (und damit die »Welt«, die Gesellschaft, die gesellschaftliche Relevanz der Botschaft, die Zukunft) nicht individualistisch-verinnerlicht ausblenden.

Das Kerygma der Gemeinde ist ja gar nicht verständlich ohne den ganz konkreten Ansatz beim geschichtlichen Jesus von Nazaret, wie auch Bultmanns Theologie des Neuen Testaments beweist. Die Verkündigung Jesu selbst wäre gar nicht weitergesagt und in den Evangelien schließlich aufgeschrieben worden, wenn es nicht zwischen ihr und der Verkündigung der Gemeinde eine Entsprechung gegeben hätte. Die nachösterliche Verkündigung bedeutet doch keinen absoluten Neuanfang. Zwischen dem vorösterlichen Jesus und der Verkündigung der nachösterlichen Gemeinde besteht nicht nur ein Bruch, sondern auch ein Zusammenhang: *bei aller Diskontinuität einer Kontinuität.* Die Alternative Kerygma (Verkündigung) *oder* Geschichte (Bericht) ist eine falsche Alternative. *In* der Glaubensbotschaft der Evangelien soll jene Geschichte erkannt werden, an der die Evangelisten, selber im Dienst der Verkündigung, offenkundig noch Jahrzehnte nach dem geschichtlichen Jesus und den kerygmatischen Paulusbriefen interessiert waren: und zwar nicht nur Jesu »Wort«, »Kerygma«, »Verkündigung« (Bultmann), sondern auch seine Taten, sein Kampf und sein Todesgeschick.

Freilich wäre es unbegründet, wenn ein unkritischer Leser annähme, die Zuverlässigkeit eines Überlieferungsstückes könne von uns von vornherein vorausgesetzt werden: man könne also ruhig den ganzen Inhalt der Evangelien (mit dem des Alten Testaments) pauschal als historische Tatsachen nehmen. Aber ebenfalls unbegründet wäre es, wenn ein hyperkritischer Leser meinte, die Zuverlässigkeit sei von vornherein Ausnahme: man könne also ungefähr nichts in den Evangelien als historische Tatsachen nehmen. Die Wahrheit liegt zwischen der oberflächlichen Leichtgläubigkeit, die mit dem Aberglauben eng verwandt ist, und der radikalen Skepsis, die sich öfters mit einer unkritischen Hypothesengläubigkeit verbindet. Überprüft man die neutestamentliche Quellenlage unvoreingenommen, so wird man die *Jesusüberlieferung* historisch als *relativ zuverlässig* bezeichnen. Das bedeutet für die Interpretation: Die Wandlungen, Ausgestaltungen und Gegensätzlichkeiten der neutestamentlichen Überlieferung verbieten die bequeme Annahme, Jesus selber oder der Heilige Geist hätte für ein exaktes Festhalten und Tradieren seiner Worte und Taten Sorge getragen. Mit einer Verschiebung von Perspektiven und Verlagerung von Akzenten, mit Ausbildungen und Rückbildungen, Entdeckungen und Verdeckungen innerhalb dieser Überlieferungen muß stets gerechnet werden.

Der Jesus der Geschichte ist nicht identisch, so sahen wir, mit dem Christusbild der traditionellen Dogmatik[6]. Und auch nicht mit der am Johannesevangelium orientierten spekulativen Christusidee des deutschen Idealismus[7]. Er ist aber auch nicht identisch mit den »liberalen« Jesusdarstellungen des 19. Jahrhunderts, die nun Markus bevorzugen[8]. Und wiederum nicht mit dem Jesus-Bild der »konsequenten Eschatologie«, die in Jesus einfach den Propheten des nahen Weltendes sah[9]. *Methodisch* bedeutet das: Will man heute historisch Gesichertes von Jesus aussagen, dann wird man also nicht von einem bestimmten Jesus-Bild ausgehen dürfen. Aber auch nicht von möglicherweise erst nachösterlichen Hoheitstiteln wie Messias, Christus, Herr oder Gottessohn. Man wird bescheiden bei den einzelnen sicher authentischen Sprüchen (Logien) und Taten Jesu einsetzen müssen. Methodisch hat sich dabei als kritischer Grundsatz durchgesetzt: Auf authentisch »Jesuanisches« trifft man am sichersten dort, wo etwas weder aus dem zeitgenössischen Judentum noch aus dem Urchristentum erklärt und abgeleitet werden kann. Auf diese Weise läßt sich ein Minimum an authentischem Jesus-Gut eruieren. Doch hat dieser berechtigte pragmatische Grundsatz auch seine Grenzen. Er führt zu einer minimalistischen Verengung, wenn vernachlässigt wird, daß Jesus Mensch inmitten seiner Zeit war und er ohne alle Zweifel auch viel Gemeinsames mit dem zeitgenössischen Judentum und dem Urchristentum hatte. Man wird Jesus freilich nur dann mit aller Vorsicht Gemeinsames zuschreiben dürfen, wenn es zu dem kritisch eruierten typischen Jesuanischen nicht im Widerspruch steht, sondern sich den dominanten Zügen einfügt. Dabei gibt es einen relativ breiten Grenzbereich, wo kaum je sicher auszumachen sein wird, ob hier Jesus selbst spricht oder die Gemeinde ihn interpretiert.

Und sollte auf diese Weise eine Restauration der ursprünglichen Jesus-Zeichnung durch eine vorsichtige Ablösung der verschiedenen darüber gelagerten Farbschichten nicht möglich sein? Durch eine umfassende historische Analyse der Evangelien läßt sich auf weite Strecken aufweisen, welches die *drei verschiedenen Schichten* sind: was Redaktion des *Evangelisten* (Redaktionsgeschichte), was Interpretation, Explikation und unter Umständen auch Reduktion der nachösterlichen *Gemeinde* und was schließlich vorösterliche Worte und Taten *Jesu* sind, und so, was allgemein jüdisch und was typisch für Jesus ist, was dem Gesamtkontext entspricht und was nicht.

Eine Überprüfung also Spruch um Spruch, Erzählung um Erzählung: alles in allem ein schwieriges und delikates Geschäft. Es setzt ein hohes handwerkliches Können und, wie alle historische Forschung, eine von (bekenntnismäßigen, wissenschaftsgeschichtlichen, persönlichen) Vorurteilen möglichst freie Sachlichkeit voraus. Unbezweifelbare mathematische oder naturwissenschaftliche Sicherheit wird man bei allen historischen Beweisführungen nicht erwarten dürfen. Oft kann man – bei Jesus wie bei Sokrates und in verschiedenem Ausmaß bei allen historischen Persönlichkeiten – nur mit einem mehr oder weniger hohen Grad der Wahrscheinlichkeit rechnen. Unser Wissen – angefangen bei der Frage, ob mein legitimer Vater auch der wirkliche Vater ist – baut freilich zu einem schönen Teil auf solchen Wahrscheinlichkeiten auf. Und der Glaube braucht, um vertretbar zu sein, so wenig wie die Liebe über ein garantiert unfehlbares Wissen zu verfügen. Wie jedes menschliche Wissen ist auch sein Wissen bruchstückhaft. Nur wenn er sich dessen bewußt bleibt, bleibt er frei von Überheblichkeit, Unduldsamkeit und falschem Eifer.

Trotz aller Schwierigkeiten darf somit an der historischen Möglichkeit und der theologischen Legitimität einer Rückfrage auf den Jesus der Geschichte festgehalten werden. Wenn wir die vielleicht etwas spröde Materie noch spröder zusammenfassen dürfen: Eine methodische Rückfrage von den Glaubenszeugnissen auf den Jesus der Geschichte:

Warum ist sie *möglich*? Weil zwischen der Predigt Jesu und der Predigt der Verkündiger, weil überhaupt zwischen dem Jesus der Geschichte und der urchristlichen Christus-Verkündigung bei aller Diskontinuität eine Kontinuität besteht.

Warum ist sie auch *berechtigt?* Weil nur von der Geschichte Jesu her die urchristliche Christus-Verkündigung entstehen konnte und verstanden werden kann.

Warum ist sie sogar *notwendig?* Weil nur so die urchristliche und damit auch die heutige Christus-Verkündigung gegen den Verdacht geschützt werden kann, nicht auf einer geschichtlichen Tatsache zu gründen, sondern bloß eine Behauptung, eine Projektion des Glaubens, ja ein reiner Mythos, eine Apotheose zu sein.

Damit konzentriert sich die Frage auf das *Inhaltliche:* Wenn heute eine biographische Chronologie, Topographie, Psychologie des Lebens Jesu, überhaupt ein »geschlossenes« (traditionelles, spekulatives, liberales oder konsequent-eschatologisches) Jesusbild nicht zu rekonstruieren ist, wenn es sich in den Evangelien um engagierte und engagierende Glaubenszeugnisse handelt, *was* kann dann noch durch Rückfrage wissenschaftlich rekonstruiert werden? Darauf läßt sich zunächst ganz allgemein antworten: die *charakteristischen Grundzüge und Umrisse von Jesu Verkündigung, Verhalten, Geschick!* Und gerade dies ist das für den Glaubenden Ausreichende und Entscheidende. Eine solche Rekonstruktion ist durchführbar, auch wenn nicht die sogenannte Echtheit jedes einzelnen Jesus-Wortes oder die Historizität jeder einzelnen Erzählung erwiesen wird. Ein vom Evangelisten Jesus in den Mund gelegtes, also »unechtes« Wort kann ebenso echt den echten Jesus wiedergeben wie ein von Jesus selber wirklich gesprochenes, also »echtes«. Wichtiger als die historisch erwiesene Echtheit eines bestimmten Wortes sind in diesem Zusammenhang: die bestimmenden Tendenzen, die eigentümlichen Verhaltensweisen, die typischen Grundlinien, die eindeutigen Dominanten, das nicht in Schemata und Modelle gepreßte, sondern »offene« Gesamtbild. Und hierin bleiben wir nicht ohne Antwort.

Wenigstens wenn man nicht – wie bei exegetischen Detailforschern manchmal die Gefahr – vor lauter Bäumen den Wald und vor lauter Differenzen den Konsens nicht mehr sieht! Manchmal sind diese exegetischen Detaildiskussionen so wichtig und so unwichtig wie die Frage, ob Bachs Brandenburgische Konzerte ursprünglich für den Markgrafen von Brandenburg geschrieben wurden (was sie nicht wurden) und ob das zweite in F-dur mit der Trompete oder mit dem Jagdhorn (und welchem) zu spielen sei usw. Gewichtige Unterschiede gewiß, zumindest für den Musikwissenschaftler. Aber der Name des Opus ist doch unzweideutig, und jeder erkennt, ob mit Trompete oder Jagdhorn gespielt, die Melodie. Und trotz allem Zweifel im Detail der Partitur, läßt sich an der Existenz und an der Partitur als ganzer nicht zweifeln; ja, das Brandenburgische Nr. 2 kann man sogar hören und genießen, auch wenn man die musikhistorischen Probleme nicht kennt, wiewohl einer mehr vom Hören haben dürfte, wenn er davon weiß. Ist es noch nötig, den Vergleich mit den Evangelien und ihrem Thema auszuführen?

In den Glaubenszeugnissen der Evangelien meldet sich die *Geschichte Jesu selber:* in der Gemeinde noch lebendige Erinnerungen, Erfahrungen, Eindrücke, Überlieferungen vom lebendigen Jesus von Nazaret, seinen Worten, Taten, Leiden. Nicht unmittelbar, wohl aber durch die Glaubenszeugnisse der Evangelien hindurch vermögen wir Jesus selbst zu hören. Wer nämlich angesichts dieses Zeugnisses nicht nebensächliche, sondern wesentliche Fragen stellt und sie nicht obenhin, sondern ernsthaft stellt, der erhält eigentümlich übereinstimmende, deutliche und originelle Antworten. In ihnen treffen sich nicht zufällig nur verschiedene theologische Bearbeitungen. In ihnen meldet sich – mag auch mancher Einzelzug in seiner Echtheit historisch fragwürdig bleiben – das ursprüngliche Wort Jesu, der ursprüngliche Jesus selber. Auf Überraschungen wird man dabei gefaßt sein müssen. Der ursprüngliche Jesus könnte vom traditionellen ebenso verschieden sein wie das Original des Künstlers von seinen Übermalungen. Und es könnte ans Licht kommen, was da Kirche und Theologie alles liturgisch, dogmatisch, politisch, juristisch, pädagogisch aus diesem Jesus gemacht und mit ihm angestellt haben, ohne sich dessen oft bewußt zu sein.

Restauration, Rekonstruktion sind indessen mißverständliche Worte. Nur ein positivistisches Geschichtsverständnis würde sich mit der Feststellung von Tatsachen und der Rekonstruktion von Kausalzusammenhängen zufriedengeben. Im Christentum geht es nicht nur um den »Jesus, wie er wirklich war«, nicht nur um einen in der Vergangenheit bleibenden »historischen Jesus«. Christentum ist an dem Jesus interessiert, wie er uns *hier und heute* begegnet, ist an dem interessiert, was er uns im gegenwärtigen Horizont von Mensch und Gesellschaft maßgebend zu sagen hat. Insofern lassen sich der »geschichtliche Jesus« und der »Christus des Glaubens« nicht als zwei verschiedene Größen auseinanderdividieren. Die historische Jesus-Forschung und die christologische Fragestellung ließen sich schon in der liberalen Leben-Jesu-Forschung nicht völlig trennen; aufgrund der beschriebenen neueren Problemlage ist dies noch weniger möglich. Aber es bleibt gerade für die Gegenwartsbedeutung Jesu von grundlegender Bedeutung: Wir sind heute weniger denn je auf Vermutungen und Spekulationen angewiesen. Besser als vielleicht jede frühere Christengeneration – die erste ausgenommen – vermögen wir heute wieder aufgrund der Arbeit von so vielen Exegetengenerationen und der Ergebnisse der historisch-kritischen Methode den wahren, ursprünglichen Jesus der Geschichte zu erkennen.

Allerdings: steht es deshalb schon besser um unseren *Glauben*? Was bedeutet überhaupt die historisch-kritische Jesus-Forschung für den Glauben, meinen Glauben?

Verantworteter Glaube

Kann mir die historisch-kritische Jesus-Forschung, die theologische Wissenschaft überhaupt, Glauben, Glaubensgewißheit verschaffen, wie manche hoffen? Nein, sie kann *den Glauben nicht begründen*. Ich glaube ja nicht »an« die Forschung, an die theologische Wissenschaft, an wissenschaftliche Ergebnisse, die sich oft ändern. Den Glauben kann nur die Botschaft begründen, an die ich glaube. Und auch nicht die Botschaft als solche, als menschliches Wort, sondern der, der in dieser Botschaft zu mir spricht, verkündet wird. Ich glaube – zunächst einmal ganz einfach gesagt – an Gott, wie er mich durch diesen Jesus anspricht.

Kann aber nicht umgekehrt die Jesus-Forschung, die theologische Wissenschaft überhaupt, meinen Glauben zerstören, wie andere fürchten? Nein, sie kann *den Glauben nicht zerstören*. Wie die Einbildung des theologisch Gebildeten, so ist auch die Angst des theologisch Ungebildeten nicht angebracht. Wie Theologie den Glauben nicht zu begründen vermag, so auch nicht, ihn zu zerstören. Nicht sie, Gott selbst ist der Grund des Glaubens. Und solange ich mich an diesem Grund festhalte, kann selbst tendenziöse, falsche Kritik meinen Glauben bedrohen, doch nicht zerstören. Solche Kritik wurde in der Geschichte der Exegese und der Theologie immer wieder durch echte, sachliche Kritik überwunden. Und diese wiederum kann meinem Glauben nur helfen. Inwiefern?

Theologische Wissenschaft, eine Jesus-Forschung mit Mut zum kritischen Denken und mit Respekt vor den Fakten geübt, ermöglicht es, die Glaubensüberlieferung zu überprüfen: *den*

Glauben vor sich selbst und anderen *zu verantworten.* Unkritische Gutgläubigkeit ebenso wie kritische Ungläubigkeit können durch historisch-kritische Untersuchung in ihrer falschen Sicherheit erschüttert werden. Der Glaube selber aber kann von unverschuldetem Aberglauben sowie von interessenbedingten Ideologien gereinigt werden. So lassen sich Hindernisse für den Glauben ausräumen, es läßt sich sogar Bereitschaft zum Glauben wecken. Gewiß, die historisch-kritische Forschung kann und will mir keine Glaubenbeweise liefern. Glaube setzt meine persönliche Entscheidung voraus. Ließe er sich anbeweisen, wäre er nicht mehr Glaube. Es sollte indessen eine begründete, reflektierte, verantwortete Glaubensentscheidung sein. Der Glaube soll ja auch nicht aus sich heraus historische Tatsachen statuieren wollen. Gewißheiten des Glaubens dürfen nicht als wissenschaftliche Ergebnisse präsentiert werden. Christlicher Glaube ist so zu verantworten, daß er zumutbar und gegenwärtig vollziehbar ist. Zumutbar ist nur das Verantwortbare[10].

Also: Bloß »historischer Glaube« rettet nicht; wissenschaftliche Resultate sind nicht deshalb Heilswahrheiten, weil sie historisch gesichert sind. Aber umgekehrt braucht »unhistorischer Glaube« nicht Zeichen starken Glaubens zu sein; manchmal ist er Zeichen schwachen Denkens. Der Glaube eines vernünftigen Menschen sollte zumindest nicht unvernünftiger Glaube sein. Christlicher Glaube ist nach den ursprünglichen Glaubenszeugnissen vernünftig verstehender, verantworteter Glaube. Im methodisch umsichtigen, wissenschaftlichen Verantworten jeglicher Rede von und zu Gott aber besteht die Theologie[11].

Als konkrete Aufgabe bedeutet dies: Aus der Geschichte dieses Jesus, aus seinem Wort, Verhalten und Geschick kann und soll der unverfälschte Anspruch, die wahre Bedeutung seiner Person verständlich gemacht werden. Aus der Geschichte soll erkannt werden, wie er damals| und heute den Einzelnen und die Gesellschaft in unerhört kritischer und verheißender Weise vor letzte Fragen stellt, wie er in Person Einladung, Herausforderung, Ermunterung zum Glauben ist.

Und was heißt überhaupt *glauben?* Hier genügt zunächst eine rahmenhafte Umschreibung. Dazu einige Fragen und Antworten:

– *Christlicher Glaube – eine Verstandessache?*
Den Glauben einfach als einen Akt des Verstandes zu verstehen, als eine theoretische Erkenntnis, als ein Fürwahrhalten

biblischer Texte oder kirchlicher Satzungen, gar als eine Zu-
stimmung zu mehr oder weniger unwahrscheinlichen Behaup-
tungen – das ist das intellektualistische Mißverständnis des
Glaubens.
- *Christlicher Glaube – eine Willensanstrengung?*
  Den Glauben einfach als einen Akt des Willens zu verstehen,
  als einen willentlichen Entschluß bei mangelnder Evidenz, als
  ein blindes Wagnis, als einen nicht zu begründenden Sprung,
  als ein Credo quia absurdum, gar nur als eine Pflicht des
  Gehorsams – das ist das voluntaristische Mißverständnis des
  Glaubens.
- *Christlicher Glaube – eine Gemütsbewegung?*
  Den Glauben einfach als einen Akt des Gefühls zu verstehen,
  als eine subjektive Gemütsbewegung, als einen Glaubensakt
  (fides qua creditur) ohne Glaubensinhalt (fides quae creditur),
  wo es mehr darauf ankommt, daß man glaubt als was man
  glaubt – das ist das emotionale Mißverständnis des Glaubens.
- *Christlicher Glaube ist vielmehr ein unbedingt vertrauendes*
  Sicheinlassen und Sichverlassen des ganzen Menschen mit allen
  Kräften seines Geistes auf die christliche Botschaft und auf den,
  der mit ihr angekündigt wird: also zugleich ein Akt des Erken-
  nens, Wollens und Fühlens, ein Vertrauen, das ein Fürwahrhal-
  ten einschließt.

Ich glaube also nicht einfach verschiedene Sachverhalte, Wahrheiten, Theorien, Dogmen: ich glaube nicht das oder jenes. Ich
glaube auch nicht nur der Vertrauenswürdigkeit einer Person:
ich glaube nicht einfach diesem oder jenem. Vielmehr wage
ich es, mich vertrauensvoll auf eine Botschaft, eine Wahrheit,
einen Weg, eine Hoffnung, letztlich auf jemand ganz persönlich
einzulassen: ich glaube »an« Gott und an den, den er gesandt
hat[12].
   Nun ist das Glauben in den verschiedenen christlichen Kirchen
freilich verschieden. Wo die Stärken liegen, liegen auch die
Schwächen: Die spezifische Gefahr protestantischen Glaubens
ist der Biblizismus, die Gefahr östlich-orthodoxen Glaubens der
Traditionalismus, die Gefahr römisch-katholischen Glaubens
der Autoritarismus. Dies alles sind defiziente Modi von Glauben. Dagegen ist deutlich zu sagen:

- *Der Christ (auch der protestantische) glaubt nicht an die Bibel,*
  sondern an den, den sie bezeugt.

Der Christ (auch der orthodoxe) glaubt nicht an die Tradition, sondern an den, den sie überliefert.

Der Christ (auch der katholische) glaubt nicht an die Kirche, sondern an den, den sie verkündet.

– *Das unbedingt Verläßliche, an das der Mensch sich für Zeit und Ewigkeit halten kann, sind nicht die Bibeltexte und nicht die Kirchenväter und auch nicht ein kirchliches Lehramt, sondern ist Gott selbst, wie er für die Glaubenden durch Jesus Christus gesprochen hat. Die Bibeltexte, die Aussagen der Väter und kirchlicher Autoriäten wollen – in verschiedener Gewichtigkeit – nicht mehr und nicht weniger als Ausdruck dieses Glaubens sein.*

Historische Kritik – eine Glaubenshilfe?

Kann ich meines Glaubens *sicher* sein? Nie hat ein Mensch seinen Glauben sicher, gleichsam »in der Tasche«. Wenn ich mich zum Glauben entschlossen habe – und echter Glaube bedarf einer Entscheidung –, so gilt diese Glaubensentscheidung nie ein für allemal. Und wenn ich in glaubendem Erkennen fortschreite – und echtes Glauben besagt auch immer Erkenntnis und durch die Erfahrungen des Lebens fortschreitende Erkenntis –, so folgt doch meinem Glaubenserkennen überall hin wie sein Schatten der Zweifel. Versuchungen, den Glauben aufzugeben, Herausforderung zugleich, ihn trotz allem zu bewahren und zu vertiefen, gibt es und wird es zeitlebens immer wieder geben. Und immer wieder werde ich meinen Glauben neu zu betätigen, zu verwirklichen, zu ergreifen haben: trotz aller Zweifel, Unsicherheiten, Dunkelheiten. Ergreifen, da ergriffen von einem Anderen, Umgreifenden, der nie zwingt, sondern unsichtbar in allem Sichtbaren volle Freiheit gewährt, damit der Mensch aus dem Unsichtbaren heraus zu leben und die Probleme der sichtbaren Welt zu bewältigen vermag. Diese tragende Wirklichkeit Gottes ist mir nie anschaulich, unzweideutig, zweifelsfrei, sicher gegeben. Ich kann mich immer auch anders entscheiden, kann auch leben, als gäbe es ihn nicht. Aber ich kann auch aus dem Glauben heraus leben und dann seiner zwar nicht sicher, aber ganz und gar *gewiß* sein. Wie der Liebende, so verfügt auch der Glaubende über keine zwingenden Beweise, so daß er völlig sicher sein könnte. Aber wie der Liebende, so kann auch der Glaubende des Anderen völlig gewiß sein, insofern er sich ganz auf den Anderen einläßt. Und diese Gewißheit ist stärker als alle bewiesene Sicherheit.

Wenn sich somit die letzte Wirklichkeit Gottes nur dem vertrauend sich einlassenden Glauben eröffnet, dann ist sie selbstverständlich auch der historischen Forschung nicht zugänglich. Die äußeren Wirkungen des Glaubens lassen sich in den verschiedenen Zeiten, Völkern, Kulturen historisch feststellen. Aber was solcher Glaube letztlich für ein Menschenleben und das Menschheitsleben in seiner Tiefe bedeutet, läßt sich so wenig wie die Liebe durch statistische Messungen mit wissenschaftlichen Methoden erfassen; das läßt sich nur erfahren. Doch darf dies eine klare Beantwortung der hier noch anstehenden abschließenden Fragen bezüglich historisch-kritischer Jesus-Forschung und christlichem Glauben nicht hindern.

a. Setzt historisch-kritische Jesus-Forschung Glauben voraus?
Nein. Auch der Ungläubige kann sachliche Jesus-Forschung betreiben.

Der Ungläubige wird zwar, wie auch der Glaubende, mit einem Vorverständnis an Jesus herantreten. Jesus ist ihm ja nicht einfach unbekannt. Dieses Vorverständnis darf nur nicht zu einem Vorurteil werden, wenn die Forschung objektiv betrieben werden soll:

Steht ein Forscher Jesus negativ gegenüber, dann wird er sein Nein mindestens nicht schon als Endergebnis ansehen.

Steht er ihm positiv gegenüber, dann darf sein Ja die Probleme der Forschung nicht überspielen.

Steht er ihm – wenn überhaupt möglich – indifferent gegenüber, dann darf auch diese Indifferenz nicht zum Prinzip erhoben werden.

Voraussetzung historischer Forschung ist also nicht der Glaube oder der Unglaube oder gar die Indifferenz, wohl aber eine grundsätzliche Offenheit für alles, was von dieser uns vielfach beunruhigenden Gestalt engegenkommt. Ein Vorverständnis kann man gewiß nicht einfach ablegen. Aber man kann es, sofern es einem bewußt ist, zurückstellen. Und man kann es von der zu erkennenden Gestalt her korrigieren lassen.

b. Setzt umgekehrt Glaube die historisch-kritische Jesus-Forschung voraus? Nein. Auch vor der Jesus-Forschung gab es Glauben, und auch heute glauben viele und ohne Rücksicht auf Forschungsergebnisse.

Allerdings muß solcher Glaube vom heutigen Stand des Bewußtseins aus als naiver Glaube bezeichnet werden. Naivität ist nicht schlecht, aber zumindest in Glaubensdingen gefährlich. Naiver Glaube kann am wahren Jesus vorbeiglauben und bei bester Absicht falsche Konsequenzen in Theorie und Praxis zur Folge haben. Naiver Glaube kann den Einzelnen oder eine Gemeinschaft blind, autoritär, selbstgerecht, abergläubisch werden lassen. Glaube sollte wie am Anfang so auch heute verstehender, verantworteter Glaube sein. Verstehender, verantworteter Glaube aber setzt heute – direkt oder indirekt – die historische Forschung voraus, mindestens in ihren allgemeinen Ergebnissen. Nimmt man sie nicht oder zu spät zur Kenntnis, kommt es bei unverhoffter Konfrontation zu unnötigen Glaubenskrisen. Gerne wird dann die Schuld von Kirchenleitungen, die nichts zur Aufklärung des Kirchenvolkes taten, den Theologen in die Schuhe geschoben. Die heutigen Kommunikationsmittel lassen aber ohnedies immer mehr die wichtigsten Ergebnisse der Forschung früher oder später Allgemeingut werden. Sie lassen sich, glücklicherweise, nicht mehr verheimlichen.

c. Als positive Konsequenz aus beiden Antworten ergibt sich: Christlicher Glaube und historische Forschung schließen sich in der einen und selben Person nicht aus. Die beiden Nein schließen ein Ja ein.

Christlicher Glaube kann dem wissenschaftlich Arbeitenden neue Tiefen eröffnen, vielleicht die entscheidende Tiefe. Eine absolut voraussetzungslose Geschichtswissenschaft ist von vornherein nicht möglich. Inneres Beteiligtsein aber fördert das Verstehen. Umgekehrt kann historisches Wissen dem christlich Glaubenden neue Weiten aufschließen, ihn einsichtig und damit bescheiden machen, ihn vielfältig inspirieren. Aufklärung kann – die Geschichte beweist es – dem religiösen Fanatismus und der Intoleranz wehren. Nur Glaube und Wissen zusammen, glaubendes Wissen und wissender Glaube, vermögen heute den wahren Christus in seiner Weite und in seiner Tiefe zu erfassen. Und – wäre es nach diesem langen Anmarschweg nicht an der Zeit, daß wir uns ihm in seiner ganzen Konkretheit zuwenden, in seiner Konkretheit und in seiner Fremdheit? Der nächste Abschnitt dient dem Übergang – und einer weiteren Verdeutlichung des unterscheidend Christlichen.

Jesus ist keineswegs eine nur kirchliche Figur. Manchmal ist er außerhalb sogar populärer als innerhalb der Kirche. Aber so populär Jesus ist, es zeigt sich doch sogleich – wenn man auf den wirklichen Jesus schaut – seine *Fremdheit*. Und die historische Analyse, so unbequem, mühselig oder gar überflüssig sie manchen scheinen mag, kann dazu verhelfen, daß diese Fremdheit nicht verdeckt wird: daß er nicht einfach unseren persönlichen oder gesellschaftlichen Bedürfnissen, Gewohnheiten, Wunschvorstellungen, Lieblingsbegriffen eingepaßt, daß er auch nicht in die Welt-, Moral- und Rechtsanschauungen von Kirchenbehörden und Theologen vereinnahmt und von kirchlichen Riten, Symbolen und Feiern überspielt wird. Es kommt alles darauf an, daß man Jesus uneingeschränkt sprechen läßt – sei dies bequem oder nicht. Nur so kann er selber uns in seiner Fremdheit wirklich näherkommen. Selbstverständlich ist damit nicht die mechanische Wiederholung seiner Worte, die Rezitation von möglichst vielen Bibelsprüchen, wenn möglich in alter Lutherübersetzung, gemeint. Doch setzt eine im guten Sinne aktualisierende Deutung seiner Person voraus, daß der Abstand zu ihm gewahrt wird. Im Grunde geht es dabei um einen Abstand von mir selbst: meinen eigenen Gedanken, Vorstellungen, Wertungen und Erwartungen. Nur wenn deutlich wird, was er selber wollte, welche Hoffnungen er für die Menschen seiner Zeit brachte, kann deutlich werden, was er selber für die Menschen der heutigen Zeit zu sagen hat, welche Hoffnungen er für die heutige Menschheit und eine zukünftige Welt bedeuten kann.

1. Die Leiden der Vergangenheit

Was ist uns an diesem Jesus fremd? Hier soll uns zunächst nur ein einziger, ein allerdings grundlegender Zug seines Wesens beschäftigen. Jesus war ein Mensch, das hat man in der Christenheit mehr oder weniger deutlich immer gesagt. Weniger gern aber gab man zu: Jesus war ein *jüdischer* Mensch, echter Jude. Und gerade als solcher war er nur zu oft Christen *und* Juden fremd.

Jesus war Jude: Angehöriger dieses kleinen, armen, politisch machtlosen Volkes am Rand des Imperium Romanum. Er wirkte unter Juden und für Juden. Seine Mutter Maria, sein Vater Josef, seine Familie, seine Gefolgschaft waren Juden. Sein Name war jüdisch (hebräisch »Jeschua«, Spätform von »Jehoschua« – »Jahwe ist Hilfe«). Seine Bibel, sein Gottesdienst, seine Gebete waren jüdisch. Er konnte in jener gegebenen Situation an keine Verkündigung unter den Heiden denken. Seine Botschaft galt dem jüdischen Volk, diesem allerdings in seiner Gesamtheit ohne irgendeinen Ausschluß.

Aus dieser Grundtatsache ergibt sich schlicht: ohne Judentum kein Christentum! Die Bibel der frühen Christen war das Alte Testament. Die Schriften des Neuen Testaments wurden zur Bibel durch ihre Anfügung an das Alte. Das Evangelium Jesu Christi setzt überall und durchaus bewußt Tora und Propheten voraus. In beiden Testamenten spricht auch nach der Auffassung der Christen derselbe Gott des Gerichtes und der Gnade. Und diese besondere Verwandtschaft war der Grund, weswegen wir im früheren Kapitel über die nichtchristlichen Religionen das Judentum bewußt nicht mitbehandelt haben, wiewohl alles dort positiv über die Religionen als Heilswege Gesagte in noch ganz anderem Ausmaß vom Judentum gilt. Nicht zu Buddhismus, Hinduismus und Konfuzianismus, selbst nicht zu dem von ihm beeinflußten Islam, nur zum Judentum hat das Christentum diese einzigartige Beziehung: nämlich eine Beziehung vom Ursprung her, aus welcher zahlreiche gemeinsame Strukturen und Werte resultieren. Dabei stellt sich allerdings auch sofort die Frage, warum denn trotz seines universalen Monotheismus nicht das Judentum, sondern die von Jesus ausgehende neue Bewegung, das Christentum, zu einer universalen Menschheitsreligion wurde.

Feindschaft gerade unter engsten Verwandten kann am erbittertsten sein. Eine der traurigsten Erscheinungen in der Geschichte der letzten zwei Jahrtausende: zwischen Juden und Christen herrschte beinahe von Anfang an Feindschaft. Sie war gegenseitig, wie so oft zwischen einer alten und einer neuen religiösen Bewegung. Zwar erschien die junge Christengemeinde zunächst nicht mehr als eine religiöse Sonderrichtung innerhalb des Judentums, welche eine religiöse Sonderauffassung bekannte und praktizierte, im übrigen aber die Verbindung mit dem jüdischen Volksverband aufrechterhielt. Aber der Loslösungsprozeß von der jüdischen Volksgemeinschaft war im Bekenntnis zu Jesus innerlich grundgelegt. Er wurde sehr bald durch die Bildung eines gesetzesfreien Heidenchristentums ausgelöst. Die Heidenchristen bildeten bald die überwältigende Mehrheit, und ihre Theologie verlor den aktuellen Bezug zum Judentum. Nach wenigen Jahrzehnten war der Prozeß durch die Zerstörung Jerusalems und das Aufhören des Tempelkultes abgeschlossen. In einer dramatischen Geschichte war so – quantitativ und qualitativ – die Kirche aus Juden zu einer Kirche aus Juden und Heiden und schließlich zu einer Kirche aus Heiden geworden.

Zugleich zeigten sich die Juden, die sich nicht zu Jesus bekennen wollten, feindlich gegenüber der jungen Kirche. Sie stießen ihrerseits die Christen aus der Volksgemeinschaft aus und verfolgten sie, wie insbesondere die Geschichte des Pharisäers Saulus zeigte, der allerdings auch als Apostel Paulus an der besonderen Erwählung des Volkes Israels ständig festgehalten hat. Vielleicht schon im zweiten Jahrhundert wurde die Verfluchung der »Ketzer und Nazaräer« in das täglich gebetete rabbinische Hauptgebet (»Schmone ›Esre‹«) aufgenommen. Kurz: Man lebte sich schon früh völlig auseinander und sprach aneinander vorbei. Die intellektuelle Auseinandersetzung reduzierte sich immer mehr auf ein unaufhörliches Ringen um Beweistexte für oder gegen die Erfüllung der biblischen Verheißungen in Jesus.

Eine Geschichte von Blut und Tränen

Das Weitere war vorwiegend eine Geschichte von Blut und Tränen[1]. Die Christen, später am Hebel der staatlichen Macht, vergaßen nicht so bald die über sie ergangenen jüdischen und heidnischen Verfolgungen. Die Judenfeindlichkeit der Christen war zunächst nicht rassisch, sondern religiös bedingt. Korrekter wird man überhaupt von »Anti-Judaismus« statt von »Anti-Semitismus« reden; auch die Araber sind ja Semiten. In der konstantinischen Reichskirche wird dann der vor-christliche heidnische Antijudaismus mit »christlichem« Vorzeichen aufgenommen. Und wenn es auch in der Folgezeit Beispiele fruchtbarer Zusammenarbeit zwischen Christen und Juden gab, so verschärfte sich die Lage der Juden insbesondere seit dem Hochmittelalter ungemein: Judenschlächtereien in Westeuropa während der ersten drei Kreuzzüge und Ausrottung der Juden in Palästina. Die Vernichtung von 300 jüdischen Gemeinden im Deutschen Reich 1348/49 und die Ausweisung der Juden aus England (1290), Frankreich (1394), Spanien (1492) und Portugal (1497). Später dann aber auch die greulichen antijüdischen Hetzreden des alten Luther, Judenverfolgungen nach der Reformation, Pogrome in Osteuropa ... In dieser Zeit – kann man es verschweigen? – hat die Kirche wohl mehr Märtyrer umgebracht als hervorgebracht. Alles unfaßbar für den Verstand eines heutigen Christen.

Nicht die Reformation, sondern der Humanismus (Reuchlin, Scaliger), dann der Pietismus (Zinzendorf) und besonders die Toleranz der Aufklärung (Menschenrechtserklärung in den Vereinigten Staaten und in der Französischen Revolution) haben eine Änderung vorbereitet und teilweise auch durchgesetzt. Die volle Assimilierung der europäischen Juden in der Zeit der Emanzipation allerdings gelang nur teilweise, am besten in Amerika. Es wäre vermessen, hier die vielhundertjährige entsetzliche Leidens- und Todesgeschichte des Judenvolkes nachzuzeichnen, die im nazistischen Massenwahn und Massenmord kulminierte, dem ein Drittel der gesamten Judenheit zum Opfer fiel. Das »Bedauern« in der Erklärung des Zweiten Vatikanischen Konzils – wie eine entsprechende Erklärung des Weltrates der Kirchen[2] eher ein Anfang als ein Ende – fiel angesichts dieses Grauens reichlich schwach und vage aus. Es wäre von der römischen Kurie, die sich gar sehr über Hochhuths problemgeladenen ›Stellvertreter‹ aufregte, aber nach wie vor aus politischem Opportunismus und nicht völlig überwundenen antijüdischen Affekten den Staat Israel diplomatisch nicht anerkennt, beinahe auch noch verhindert worden.

Angesichts dieser noch immer keineswegs bereinigten Lage und eines versteckten Antijudaismus in Rom und Moskau, aber leider auch in New York und anderswo muß in aller Klarheit gesagt werden: Der nazistische Antijudaismus war das Werk gottloser antichristlicher Verbrecher. Aber: ohne die fast zweitausendjährige Vorgeschichte des »christlichen« Antijudaismus, der auch die Christen in Deutschland an einem überzeugten und energischen Widerstand auf breiter Front hinderte, wäre er unmöglich gewesen!

Wenn auch manche Christen mitverfolgt wurden, und wieder andere – besonders in Holland, Frankreich und Dänemark – den Juden wirkungsvoll geholfen haben, so muß doch zur Präzisierung der Schuldfrage beachtet werden: Keine der antijüdischen

Maßnahmen des Nazismus – Kennzeichnung durch besondere Kleidung, Ausschluß von Berufen, Mischeheverbot, Plünderungen, Vertreibungen, Konzentrationslager, Hinmetzelungen, Verbrennungen – war neu. Dies alles gab es schon im genannten »christlichen« Mittelalter (das große vierte Laterankonzil 1215!) und in der »christlichen« Reformationszeit. Neu war nur die rassistische Begründung: vorbereitet vom französischen Grafen Arthur Gobineau und vom Deutsch-Engländer Houston Stewart Chamberlain, im Nazi-Deutschland dann durchgeführt in grauenvoller organisatorischer Gründlichkeit, technischer Perfektion und furchtbarer Industrialisierung des Mordens. Nach Auschwitz gibt es nichts mehr zu beschönigen: um das klare Eingeständnis ihrer Schuld kommt die Christenheit nicht herum.

2. Die Möglichkeiten der Zukunft

Aber müssen die Leiden der Vergangenheit die Leiden der Zukunft sein? Die Besinnung, die mit der Aufklärung einsetzte und sich im 19. Jahrhundert vor allem in den Vereinigten Staaten auswirkte, hat unterdessen die ganze Christenheit erfaßt.

Wachsendes Verstehen

Die jüngste furchtbarste Katastrophe des Judenvolkes und das für die Christen unerwartete Wiedererstehen des Staates Israel – das wichtigste Ereignis der jüdischen Geschichte seit der Zerstörung Jerusalems und des Tempels – hat die antijüdische »christliche« Theologie erschüttert: jene Pseudo-Theologie, welche die alttestamentliche Heilsgeschichte des jüdischen Volkes in eine neutestamentliche Fluchgeschichte uminterpretierte und die von Paulus bejahte bleibende Erwählung des Judenvolkes übersah und exklusiv auf sich als dem »neuen Israel« bezog. Mit dem Zweiten Vatikanischen Konzil hat sich die Besinnung auch in der katholischen Kirche durchgesetzt[1]:

Die Idee einer Kollektivschuld des damaligen oder gar des heutigen jüdischen Volkes am Tode Jesu wurde vom Konzil ausdrücklich abgelehnt. Die alten, weit verbreiteten Vorurteile – Juden sind »Geldmenschen«, »Brunnenvergifter«, »Christkiller«, »Gottesmörder«, »Verfluchte und zur Zerstreuung Verdammte« – wagt niemand mehr im Ernst zu vertreten.

Die im Antijudaismus wirksamen psychologischen Motive – Gruppenfeindschaft, Fremdkörperangst, Sündenbockdenken, Gegenideal, Störung der Persönlichkeitsstruktur, seelische Massenstörungen – werden jetzt immer klarer durchschaut.

Die verschämte oder unverschämte Apologetik – »Auch die Juden haben Fehler gemacht«, »Man muß alles aus der Zeit heraus verstehen«, »Das war nicht die Kirche selber«, »Man mußte das kleinere Übel wählen« – ist obsolet geworden.

Man beginnt also zu erkennen, daß die Juden eine in vielfacher Hinsicht rätselhafte Schicksalsgemeinschaft von erstaunlicher Durchhaltekraft bilden: eine Rasse und doch keine, eine Sprachgemeinschaft und doch keine, eine Religionsgemeinschaft und doch keine, ein Staat und doch keiner, ein Volk und doch keines. Eine Schicksalsgemeinschaft, deren religiöses Geheimnis für den glaubenden Juden wie für den glaubenden Christen doch eine besondere Berufung dieses »Gottesvolkes« unter den Völkern der Erde ist. Daß in dieser Perspektive die Rückkehrbewegung der Juden in ihr »verheißenes Land« – mit den grausamen Opfern für die seit Jahrhunderten dort ansässigen arabischen Palästinenser – für viele Juden auch eine religiöse Bedeutung hat, muß von den Christen zumindest zur Kenntnis genommen werden.

Wie immer man auch unter Christen arabischer Herkunft – denen man Verständnis engegenbringen wird – über den Staat Israel denkt: Eine Kirche, die, wie in der Vergangenheit so oft, Liebe predigt und Haß sät, die Leben verkündet und doch Tod verbreitet, kann sich nicht auf Jesus von Nazaret berufen. Jesus war ein Jude, und aller Antijudaismus ist Verrat an Jesus selbst. Zu oft stand die Kirche zwischen Jesus und Israel. Sie hinderte Israel, Jesus zu erkennen. Es wäre für die Christenheit an der Zeit, die »Bekehrung« nicht nur den Juden zu predigen, sondern selber »umzukehren«: zur kaum begonnenen *Begegnung* und zu einem nicht nur humanitären, sondern *theologischen Gespräch* mit den Juden, das nicht der »Mission« und der Kapitulation, sondern dem Verständnis, der gegenseitigen Hilfe und Zusammenarbeit dienen könnte. Und indirekt vielleicht sogar einem wachsenden Verstehen zwischen Juden, Christen *und* Moslems, die doch den Juden wie den Christen – wer kann das übersehen? – von ihrem eigenen Ursprung her eng verbunden sind: durch den gemeinsamen Glauben an Gott den Schöpfer und die Auferweckung der Toten in Berufung auf Abraham und Jesus, die beide im Koran einen bedeutenden Platz haben! Die Voraussetzungen für ein echtes Gespräch zwischen Christen und Juden, denen Christentum, Islam und die Menschheit überhaupt das unvergleichliche Geschenk des strengen Ein-Gott-Glaubens verdankt, sind heute nach all dem Vorausgegangenen so gut wie schon lange nicht mehr. Eine rückhaltlose Anerkennung des zweifellos rigorosen und anspruchsvollen jüdischen Partners in seiner religiösen Eigenständigkeit ist dabei Voraussetzung.

a. In der *Christenheit* und insbesondere der deutschen und angelsächsischen Exegese hatte sich schon lange vor der Hitler-Zeit eine neue Offenheit für das Alte Testament in seiner Eigenständigkeit und in seiner Übereinstimmung mit dem Neuen Testament durchgesetzt. Die Bedeutung der Rabbinen für das Verständnis des Neuen Testaments wurde ebenfalls erkannt. Und im Vergleich mit der griechisch-hellenistischen Welt war man auf die starken Seiten des hebräischen Denkens aufmerksam geworden: die größere geschichtliche Dynamik, die ganzheitliche Ausrichtung, die gläubige Welt-, Leib- und Lebensfreundlichkeit, der Hunger und Durst nach Gerechtigkeit, die Ausrichtung auf das kommende Gottesreich. Das alles hat mit zur Überwindung der neuplatonischen, neuaristotelischen, scholastischen und neuscholastischen Verkrustung des Christentums beigetragen. Für die offizielle katholische Kirche wurde die Juden-Erklärung des Vatikanum II »die Entdeckung oder Wiederentdeckung des Judentums und der Juden in ihrem Eigenwert wie in ihrer Bedeutung für die Kirche« (J. Oesterreicher[2]).

b. Die geistige Lage des *Judentums* hat sich insbesondere seit der Wiederherstellung des Staates Israel ebenfalls sehr gewandelt: Abnehmender Einfluß der kasuistischen Gesetzesfrömmigkeit besonders unter der jungen Generation und wachsende Bedeutung des Alten Testaments gegenüber der früheren Allgemeingültigkeit des Talmud. Große Geister des Judentums in unserem Jahrhundert – Frauen wie Simone Weil und Edith Stein, Männer wie Hermann Cohen, Martin Buber, Franz Rosenzweig, Leo Baeck, Max Brod, Hans Joachim Schoeps, mehr indirekt aber auch Sigmund Freud, Albert Einstein, Franz Kafka, Ernst Bloch – vermochten den Christen das Eigentümlich-Jüdische näherzubringen. Und so hat sich denn heute sogar eine gemeinsame wissenschaftliche jüdisch-christliche Erforschung des Alten Testaments sowie der Rabbinen und in Anfängen auch des Neuen Testamentes (als eines Zeugnisses auch der jüdischen Glaubensgeschichte) angebahnt, wie zugleich eine lebendigere und ursprünglichere Gestaltung des Gottesdienstes auf beiden Seiten eine Verwandtschaft sichtbar werden ließ, die weit über Literaturkritik und Philologie hinausgeht. Es ist keine Frage: Der Jude kann aus seinem Judentum heraus im Neuen Testament Aspekte entdecken, die dem Christen oft genug entgehen. Alles in allem: trotz zahlreicher Hemmungen und Schwierigkeiten ist das Bewußtsein einer gemeinsamen nicht nur humanitären, sondern *theologischen jüdisch-christlichen Basis* im Werden begriffen. Auch von jüdischer Seite wird heute »eine jüdische Theologie des Christentums und eine christliche Theologie des Judentums« gefordert (J. Petuchowski[3]).

Allerdings: das theologische Gespräch zwischen Christen und Juden erweist sich als unendlich viel *schwieriger* als das zwischen den getrennten Christen, die in der Bibel mindestens eine gemeinsame Basis haben. Der Konflikt zwischen Christen und Juden jedoch geht mitten durch die Bibel und spaltet sie in zwei Testamente, von denen die einen das erste und die anderen das zweite vorziehen. Und kann man den eigentlichen Kontroverspunkt je übersehen? Gerade der Juden und Christen zu verbinden scheint, trennt sie auch abgrundtief: der Jude Jesus von Nazaret. Ob sich über ihn Juden und Christen je verständigen können? Es scheint hier doch um mehr als nur um »zwei Glaubensweisen« (M. Buber) zu gehen. Daß die Juden ihren Unglauben gegenüber Jesus aufgeben, scheint ebenso unwahrscheinlich, wie daß die Christen von ihrem Glauben an Jesus ablassen. Dann wären ja die Juden nicht mehr Juden, und die Christen nicht mehr Christen.

Gespräch über Jesus?

Der Streit scheint ausweglos: Hat das jüdisch-christliche Gespräch über Jesus von Nazaret überhaupt einen Sinn? Man könnte aber auch die Gegenfrage stellen: Wäre nicht einiges für *beide* Seiten gewonnen, wenn sich in Gegenbewegung zur christlichen Verständigungsbereitschaft auf jüdischer Seite das Mißtrauen, die Skepsis und Gehässigkeit gegenüber der Gestalt Jesu abbauen ließen, wenn sich statt dessen eine geschichtlich-objektive Beurteilung, echtes Verständnis und vielleicht sogar Wertschätzung der Person ausbreiteten? Der Fortschritt in neuester Zeit ist unübersehbar. Lang würde die Liste von Autoren und Schriften über Jesus von Nazaret, die im Staate Israel in letzter Zeit veröffentlicht worden sind[4]. Zahlreich sind zweifellos die Juden, die zumindest den »Jesus of culture« akzeptieren möchten, auch wenn sie den »Jesus of religion«[5] ablehnen: Man bejaht also die *kulturelle* Bedeutung Jesu. Ist es doch auch recht schwierig für einen modernen Juden, an der westlichen Kultur voll teilzuhaben, ohne nicht Jesus ständig zu begegnen, sei es auch nur in den großen Werken Bachs, Händels, Mozarts, Beethovens, Bruckners und der abendländischen Kunst überhaupt.

Aber damit steht die Frage nach der *religiösen* Bedeutung Jesu noch an. Wenn heute die religiöse Bedeutung des Judentums von der Christenheit neu gewertet wird, stellt sich dann nicht umgekehrt für das Judentum die Frage nach der religiösen Bedeutung Jesu? Jesus – der letzte der jüdischen Propheten? Es gibt schon im 19. Jahrhundert eine beachtliche jüdische Tradition, die Jesus als echten Juden ernstzunehmen versucht, ja sogar als großen Glaubenszeugen. Und um die Jahrhundertwende hatte etwa Max Nordau, der treue Mitarbeiter des Gründers der zionistischen Bewegung Theodor Herzl, geschrieben: »Jesus ist die Seele unserer Seele, wie er das Fleisch unseres Fleisches ist. Wer möchte ihn also ausscheiden aus dem jüdischen Volk[6]?« In der ersten Hälfte unseres Jahrhunderts folgten dann die ersten gründlichen Untersuchungen der Gestalt Jesu von jüdischer Seite, die verschiedenen Veröffentlichungen von Claude G. Montefiore[7] und vor allem das wohl bekannteste jüdische Jesus-Buch von Joseph Klausner[8], das wegen seiner Verarbeitung des Materials aus Talmud und Midrasch als der Beginn der modernen hebräischen Leben-Jesu-Forschung bezeichnet werden kann. Der bedeutende jüdische Denker Martin Buber war es dann gewesen, der das Wort von Jesus als dem »großen Bruder« geprägt hat, dem »ein großer Platz in der Glaubensgeschichte Israels zukommt«, der »durch keine der üblichen Kategorien umschrieben werden kann«[9]. Der jüdische Jesus-Forscher David Flusser macht konkret darauf aufmerksam, daß mit Jesus ein Jude zu den Juden spricht: von ihm kann ein Jude lernen, wie er beten, fasten, den Nächsten lieben soll, was die Bedeutung des Sabbats, des Gottesreiches und des Gerichtes ist[10]. Auf dieser Linie hat Schalom Ben-Chorin sein Buch ›Bruder Jesus. Der Nazarener in jüdischer Sicht‹ geschrieben: »Jesus ist sicher eine zentrale Gestalt der jüdischen Geschichte und Glaubensgeschichte, aber er ist zugleich ein Stück unserer Gegenwart und Zukunft, nicht anders als die Propheten der hebräischen Bibel, die wir ja auch nicht nur im Lichte der Vergangenheit zu sehen vermögen[11].«

Damit wird nun allerdings auch die *Grenze* einer jüdischen Anerkennung des Juden Jesus deutlich, wie sie Schalom Ben-Chorin bei allem Verständnis gegenüber der Gestalt Jesu im gleichen Buch ausdrückt: »Ich spüre seine brüderliche Hand, die mich faßt, damit ich ihm nachfolge.« Aber dann folgt: »Es ist *nicht* die Hand des Messias, diese mit den Wundmalen gezeichnete Hand. Es ist bestimmt *keine göttliche,* sondern eine *menschliche* Hand, in deren Linien das tiefste Leid eingegraben ist ... Der Glaube Jesu einigt uns, aber der Glaube an Jesus trennt uns[12].« Wäre aber nicht gerade die mit den Wundmalen gezeichnete Hand zu deuten, tiefer zu deuten?

Es ist nicht ausgeschlossen, daß in Zukunft mehr Juden sich zur Anerkennung Jesu als eines großen Juden und Glaubenszeugen, ja eines großen Propheten oder Lehrers Israels durchringen. Die Evangelien üben auf manche Juden eine eigenartige Faszination aus. Sie zeigen dem Juden, welche Möglichkeiten im jüdischen Glauben selber liegen. Und läßt sich Jesus nicht geradezu als *personhaftes Symbol der jüdischen Geschichte* verstehen? Der Jude Marc Chagall jedenfalls hat immer wieder die Leiden seines Volkes im Bild des Gekreuzigten dargestellt. Man könnte es vielleicht auch so sehen: Kulminiert nicht die Geschichte dieses Volkes mit seinem Gott, dieses Volkes der Tränen und des Lebens, der Klage und des Vertrauens in dieser einen Figur: Jesus und seine Geschichte als sinnenfälliges Zeichen des gekreuzigten und auferstandenen Israel?

Nur – die eine erregende Frage wird in all dem bleiben: Wer ist Jesus? Mehr als ein Prophet? Mehr als das Gesetz? Gar der Messias? Ein im Namen des Gesetzes gekreuzigter Messias? Muß das Gespräch hier nicht unbedingt enden? Hier könnte vielleicht gerade der Jude dem Christen helfen: das *Gespräch* über Jesus statt »von oben« neu, wie angedeutet, *»von unten«* zu führen. Dies würde bedeuten, daß auch wir heute Jesus aus der Perspektive der jüdischen Zeitgenossen Jesu betrachten. Auch die jüdischen Jünger Jesu hatten zunächst einmal von dem jüdischen Menschen Jesus von Nazaret auszugehen und nicht von einem bereits offenkundigen Messias oder gar Gottessohn. Nur so konnten sie überhaupt die Frage nach dem Verhältnis Jesu zu Gott stellen. Und dieses Verhältnis bestand für sie auch später nicht in einer einfachen Identifikation mit Gott, als ob Jesus Gott der Vater wäre. Vielleicht könnte der Jude dem Christen sogar helfen, jene zentralen neutestamentlichen Aussagen über Jesus und insbesondere seine Ehrentitel, die einen eminent hebräischen Hintergrund haben, besser zu verstehen.

Wie immer: Wenn wir im folgenden vom jüdischen Menschen Jesus von Nazaret ausgehen, dann werden wir mit einem unvoreingenommenen Juden *ein nicht geringes Stück Weg gemeinsam* gehen können. Und mag sein, daß schließlich die endgültige Entscheidung für oder gegen Jesus doch etwas anders aussehen wird, als man dies aufgrund des langen jüdisch-christlichen Streites erwarten könnte. Hier soll zunächst nur erneut für Offenheit plädiert werden, die das unvermeidliche – christliche oder jüdische – Vor-Verständnis nicht zum Vor-Urteil werden läßt. Nicht Neutralität wird verlangt, wohl aber Objektivität im Dienst der Wahrheit. In einer Zeit der grundlegenden Neuorientierung des Verhältnisses von Christen und Juden wird man für alle Möglichkeiten der Zukunft offen bleiben müssen.

Aber damit dürfte nun vorläufig genug gesagt sein, was es ist um die *Unterscheidung* des Christlichen. Blicken wir zurück: Was macht das Christentum zum Christentum? Man mag es von den modernen Humanismen, von den Weltreligionen oder vom Judentum unterscheiden: das unterscheidend Christliche ist immer dieser Christus, der, so sahen wir, identisch ist mit dem geschichtlichen Jesus von Nazaret. Jesus von Nazaret als der Christus, als der letztlich Ausschlaggebende, Entscheidende, Maßgebende, ist das, was das Christentum zum Christentum macht.

Aber dies ist nicht nur, wie wir es bisher getan haben, formal zu umreißen. Es ist nun auch inhaltlich zu bestimmen, und damit blicken wir voraus: Jesus Christus ist selber in Person das *Programm* des Christentums. Deshalb sagten wir schon zu Beginn dieses jetzt abgeschlossenen Kapitels: Das Christentum besteht in der Aktivierung der Erinnerung an Jesus Christus in Theorie und Praxis. Zur inhaltlichen Bestimmung des christlichen Programms jedoch müssen wir wissen: Was für eine Erinnerung an ihn haben wir? »Wir müssen wieder die Frage buchstabieren lernen: Wer ist Jesus? Alles andere zerstreut. Er ist unser Maß, nicht Kirchen, Dogmen und fromme Menschen das seinige ... Sie taugen genausoviel und -wenig, wie sie von sich selbst wegweisen und in die Nachfolge Jesu als des Herrn rufen.« (E. Käsemann[13]).

C. Das Programm

I. Der gesellschaftliche Kontext

Wenn das Besondere des Christentums dieser Jesus Christus selber ist, wenn derselbe Jesus Christus zugleich das Programm des Christentums ist, dann stellt sich die Frage: Wer ist dieser Jesus? Was wollte er? Denn: Wer immer er war und was immer er wollte, das Christentum wird verschieden aussehen müssen, je nachdem er selber so oder anders war. Und nicht nur im heutigen, sondern schon im damaligen gesellschaftlichen kulturell-religiösen Gesamtzusammenhang wurde gefragt, was schließlich zu einer Lebens- und Todesfrage wurde: Jesus – was will er, wer ist er: Ein Mann des Establishments oder ein Revolutionär? Ein Wahrer von Gesetz und Ordnung oder ein Kämpfer für radikale Veränderung? Ein Vertreter der reinen Innerlichkeit oder ein Verfechter der freien Weltlichkeit[1]?

1. Establishment?

Jesus, in den Kirchen domestiziert, erschien oft geradezu als der alles rechtfertigende Repräsentant des religiös-politischen Systems, seines Dogmas, Kultes, Kirchenrechtes: das unsichtbare Haupt eines sehr sichtbaren kirchlichen Apparates, der Garant alles Gewordenen in Glaube, Sitte, Disziplin. Was mußte er in den 2000 Jahren Christenheit alles legitimieren und sanktionieren in Kirche und Gesellschaft! Wie haben sich christliche Herrscher und Kirchenfürsten, christliche Parteien, Klassen, Rassen auf ihn berufen! Wofür alles – für welche merkwürdigen Ideen, Gesetze, Traditionen, Gebräuche, Maßnahmen – mußte er herhalten! So muß denn gegen Domestizierungsversuche aller Art deutlich gemacht werden: Jesus war *kein Mann des kirchlichen und gesellschaftlichen Establishments.*

Das religiös-politische System

Eine anachronistische Fragestellung? Keineswegs. Es gab zur Zeit Jesu ein massives religiös-politisch-gesellschaftliches Establishment, eine Art theokratischer Kirchenstaat, an welchem Jesus scheitern sollte[2].

Das ganze Macht- und Herrschaftsgefüge war legitimiert von Gott als dem obersten Herrn. Religion, Rechtsprechung, Verwaltung, Politik, unlösbar ineinander verwoben. Und von denselben Männern beherrscht: Eine priesterliche Hierarchie mit höherem und niederem Klerus (Priester und Leviten), welche ihr Amt vererbte, die Liebe des Volkes nicht besaß, aber zusammen mit wenigen anderen Gruppen in der keineswegs homogenen jüdischen Gesellschaft die Herrschaft ausübte. Unter der Kontrolle allerdings der römischen Besatzungsmacht, die sich die politischen Entscheidungen, die Sorge für Ruhe und Ordnung und, wie es scheint, die Todesurteile vorbehalten hatte.

Im zentralen Regierungs-, Verwaltungs- und Gerichtskollegium, zuständig für alle religiösen und zivilrechtlichen Angelegenheiten, im Hohen Rat zu Jerusalem – griechisch Synedrion (= Versammlung, davon aramäisch Sanhedrin) genannt – waren die herrschenden Schichten vertreten: 70 Mann unter dem Vorsitz des Hohenpriesters. Dieser, obwohl von den Römern eingesetzt, war noch immer der höchste Repräsentant des jüdischen Volkes.

Und Jesus? Jesus hatte mit keiner der drei Gruppen etwas zu tun: Weder mit den »Hohenpriestern« oder Oberpriestern (der amtierende Hohepriester und, anscheinend in einer Art Konsistorium, die zurückgetretenen Hohenpriester mit einigen weiteren Inhabern hoher priesterlicher Ämter). Noch mit den »Ältesten« (die Häupter der einflußreichen nichtpriesterlichen aristokratischen Familien der Hauptstadt). Noch schließlich mit den seit einigen Jahrzehnten ebenfalls im Hohen Rat sitzenden »Schriftgelehrten« (die Juristen-Theologen meist, aber keineswegs nur pharisäischer Richtung). Alle diese Gruppen sollte Jesus bald zu Feinden haben. Er war keiner der ihren, wie sich von Anfang an zeigte.

Weder Priester noch Theologe

Der Jesus der Geschichte war – die nachträgliche, nachösterliche Interpretation des Hebräerbriefes von Jesus als dem »Ewigen Hohenpriester« darf hier nicht täuschen – *kein Priester.* Er war gewöhnlicher »Laie« und – für die Priesterschaft von vornherein verdächtig – Anführer einer Laienbewegung, von der sich die

Priester fernhielten. Seine Anhänger waren einfache Leute. Und so zahlreich auch die Gestalten sind, die in Jesu volksnahen Parabeln auftauchen: die Gestalt des Priesters taucht nur einmal auf – nicht als Vorbild, sondern zur Abschreckung, weil er anders als der ketzerische Samariter an dem unter die Räuber Gefallenen vorbeigeht. Nicht ohne Absicht nahm Jesus seinen Stoff meist aus dem alltäglichen und nicht aus dem sakralen Bereich.

Der Jesus der Geschichte war aber auch – und dies mögen Theologieprofessoren bedauern – *kein Theologe*. Die späte, in den lukanischen Kindheitsgeschichten überlieferte Legende vom Zwölfjährigen im Tempel[3] ist ein indirekter Beweis dafür. Jesus war ein Dörfler und dazu ein »Unstudierter«, wie ihm seine Gegner vorwarfen[4]. Er verfügte über keine nachweisbare theologische Bildung, hatte nicht wie üblich viele Jahre bei einem Rabbi studiert, war nicht unter Handauflegung zum Rabbi ordiniert und autorisiert worden, auch wenn er anscheinend von vielen respektvoll als »Rabbi« (so etwas wie »Herr Doktor«) angeredet wurde. Er gab sich nicht als Experte für alle möglichen Fragen der Lehre, der Moral, des Rechtes, des Gesetzes aus, sah sich nicht primär als Hüter und Interpret heiliger Überlieferungen. Bei allem Leben aus dem Alten Testament exegetisierte er es nicht schulmäßig wie die Schrifttheologen und nahm kaum Väter-Autoritäten in Anspruch, sondern trug in erstaunlicher methodischer und sachlicher Freiheit, Unmittelbarkeit und Selbstverständlichkeit Eigenes vor.

Er war, wenn man so sagen will, ein öffentlicher Geschichtenerzähler, wie man ihn noch heute etwa auf Kabuls Hauptplatz oder in Indien vor Hunderten von Menschen erleben kann. Jesus erzählte freilich keine Märchen, Sagen oder Wundergeschichten. Er schöpfte aus seinen und anderer Erfahrungen und machte sie zu Erfahrungen derer, die seine Geschichten hörten. Er hatte ein ausgesprochen praktisches Interesse und wollte den Menschen raten, helfen.

Jesu Lehrweise ist laienhaft, volkstümlich, direkt: wenn notwendig scharf argumentierend, oft bewußt grotesk und ironisch, immer aber prägnant, konkret und plastisch. Eine gezielte Sicherheit in der Aussage, in einer seltsamen Verbindung von genau beobachtender Sachlichkeit, poetischer Bildkraft und rhetorischem Pathos. Er ist nicht auf Formeln und Dogmen festgelegt. Er übt keine tiefsinnige Spekulation oder gelehrte Gesetzeskasuistik. Er spricht in allgemein verständlichen, eingängigen

Spruchworten, Kurzgeschichten, Gleichnissen, die aus dem jedermann zugänglichen, ungeschminkten Alltag genommen sind. So viele seiner Worte sind Sprichwörter der Völker geworden. Auch seine Aussagen vom Gottesreich sind keine geheimen Offenbarungen über die Beschaffenheit des Himmelreiches, keine tiefsinnigen Allegoresen mit mehreren Unbekannten, wie man sie nach ihm in der Christenheit geistreich geübt hat. Es sind scharf pointierte Gleichnisse und Parabeln, die in die nüchtern und realistisch betrachtete Wirklichkeit des Menschen die so verschiedene Wirklichkeit des Reiches Gottes hineinstellen. Bei aller Entschiedenheit seiner Auffassungen und Forderungen: besondere Voraussetzungen intellektueller, moralischer, weltanschaulicher Art werden nicht gemacht. Der Mensch soll hören, verstehen und daraus die Konsequenzen ziehen. Es wird niemand nach dem wahren Glauben, nach dem orthodoxen Bekenntnis abgefragt. Es wird keine theoretische Reflexion erwartet, sondern die sich aufdrängende praktische Entscheidung.

Nicht bei den Herrschenden

Der Jesus der Geschichte war *kein Angehöriger oder Sympathisant der liberal-konservativen Regierungspartei.* Er gehörte nicht zu den Sadduzäern. Diese Partei der sozial privilegierten Klasse – ihr Name kam entweder vom Hohenpriester Saddok (zur Zeit Salomos) oder vom Eigenschaftswort »zaduk« (= Recht übend) her – stellte regelmäßig den Hohenpriester. Als klerikal-aristokratische Partei verband sie Liberalität nach außen mit Konservativität nach innen: Man betrieb eine realistische »Außenpolitik« der Anpassung und Entspannung und respektierte die Souveränität Roms unbedingt, hatte aber im Innern die Bewahrung der eigenen Machtstellung im Auge, damit vom klerikalen Kirchenstaat gerettet werde, was zu retten war.

Jesus war aber sichtlich nicht gewillt, in scheinbarer Weltoffenheit die modernen hellenistischen Lebensformen zu übernehmen, sich für die Erhaltung des Bestehenden einzusetzen und die große Idee vom kommenden Reich Gottes hintanzustellen. Diese Art von Liberalität lehnte er ab. Aber auch diese Art von Konservativität.

Er hatte keine Sympathie für die konservative *Rechtsauffassung* der führenden Kreise: Diese sahen zwar nur das schriftliche Gesetz des Moses als verbindlich an, aber lehnten gerade deshalb die oft mildernden späteren Weiterbildungen der Pharisäer ab. Sie wollten vor allem die Tempeltradition bewahren und drangen deshalb auf kompromißlose Einhaltung des Sabbats und eine strenge Bestrafung nach dem Gesetz. In der Praxis mußten sie sich allerdings öfters der populäreren Auffassung der Pharisäer anpassen.

Und Jesus hatte auch keine Sympathie für die konservative *Theologie* des sadduzäischen Priesteradels, die beim geschriebenen Bibelwort verharrte und die altgläubige jüdische Dogmatik konservierte, nach welcher Gott die Welt und den Menschen weithin ihrem Schicksal überläßt und der Auferstehungsglaube eine Neuerung darstellt.

Radikale Veränderung

Jesus war nicht um den religiös-politischen Status quo besorgt. Er dachte ganz und gar von der besseren Zukunft, der besseren Zukunft der Welt und des Menschen her. Er erwartete eine baldige radikale Veränderung der Situation. Deshalb kritisierte er in Wort und Tat das Bestehende und stellte das kirchliche Establishment radikal in Frage. Tempelliturgie und Gesetzesfrömmigkeit – seit Israels Rückkehr aus dem babylonischen Exil im 5. Jahrhundert und der Reform des Schreibers Esra die beiden Grundpfeiler der jüdischen Religion und Volksgemeinschaft – waren für ihn nicht oberste Norm. Er lebte in einer anderen Welt als die von römischer Weltmacht und hellenistischer Weltkultur faszinierten Hierarchen und Politiker. Er glaubte nicht wie die Tempelliturgiker nur an das dauernde Herrsein Gottes über Israel, an seine immer bestehende dauernde Weltherrschaft, wie sie schon mit der Weltschöpfung gegeben ist. Er glaubte wie viele Fromme seiner Zeit an eine in naher Zukunft kommende Weltherrschaft Gottes, welche die endzeitliche und endgültige Weltvollendung bringen wird. »Dein Reich komme« – damit waren die »Eschata«, die »letzten Dinge«, war – wie man im Theologenjargon sagt – die »eschatologische« Herrschaft Gottes gemeint: *das zukünftige Reich Gottes der Endzeit*.

Jesus war also von einer intensiven *Enderwartung* getragen: Dieses System ist nicht endgültig, diese Geschichte geht dem Ende entgegen. Und zwar jetzt. Es ist soweit. Noch diese Generation wird sie erleben, die Äonenwende und endzeitliche Offenbarung (griechisch apokalypsis) Gottes[5]. Jesus steht somit unbestreitbar im Bannkreis der »apokalyptischen« Bewegung, welche weite Teile des Judentums unter dem Einfluß anonymer apokalyptischer Schriften, die Henoch, Abraham, Jakob, Mose, Baruch, Daniel, Esra zugeschrieben wurden, seit dem 2. Jahrhundert vor Christus erfaßt hat. Zwar hat Jesus kein Interesse daran, die menschliche Neugierde mit mythischen Spekulationen oder astrologischen Voraussagen zu befriedigen. Er kümmert sich nicht wie die Apokalyptiker um die genaue Datierung und Lokalisierung des Gottesreiches, er enthüllt nicht apokalyptische Ereignisse und Geheimnisse. Aber er teilt den Glauben: Gott wird in Bälde, noch zu seinen Lebzeiten, dem bisherigen Weltlauf ein Ende setzen. Das Widergöttliche, Satanische wird vernichtet werden. Not, Leid und Tod abgeschafft, Heil und Frieden, wie es die Propheten verkünden, heraufgeführt: Weltenwende und Weltgericht, Auferstehung der Toten, der neue Himmel und die neue Erde, die Welt Gottes, welche diese immer böser werdende Welt ablöst. Mit einem Wort: Gottes Reich.

Die durch einzelne prophetische Aussagen und die apokalyptischen Schriften gehegte Erwartung hatte sich im Laufe der Zeit verdichtet, und die Ungeduld hatte zugenommen. Für den, der dann später der *Vorläufer* Jesu genannt wurde, hatte die gespannte Erwartung ihren Höhepunkt erreicht. Er verkündete das nahende Reich Gottes als Gericht. Aber nicht, wie sonst bei den Apokalyptikern üblich, das Gericht über die Anderen, die Heiden, die Vernichtung der Gottesfeinde und den Endsieg Israels. Sondern das Gericht, in großer prophetischer Tradition, gerade über Israel: die Abrahamskindschaft ist keine Heilsgarantie! Die prophetische Gestalt des Johannes stellte einen lebendigen Protest gegen die Wohlstandsgesellschaft in den Städten und Dörfern, gegen die hellenistische Kultur der Residenzen dar. In selbstkritischer Weise konfrontiert er Israel mit seinem Gott und fordert im Hinblick auf Gottes Reich eine andere »Buße« als nur asketische Übungen und kultische Leistungen. Er ruft auf zur Umkehr und Hinwendung des ganzen Lebens hin zu Gott. Und deshalb tauft er. Charakteristisch ist für ihn diese nur einmal gespendete und dem ganzen Volk und nicht nur einer auserwählten Schar angebotene *Bußtaufe:* sie läßt sich weder aus den rituell wiederholten sühnenden Tauchbädern der nahe beim Jordan sich befindenden Qumrangemeinde noch aus den erst für die spätere Zeit bezeugten jüdischen Proselytentaufen – ein rechtlicher Aufnahmeritus in die Gemeinde – ableiten. Das Untertauchen im Jordan wird zum endzeitlichen Zeichen der Reinigung und Erwählung im Hinblick auf das kommende Gericht. Diese Art Taufe scheint eine originale Schöpfung des Johannes gewesen zu sein. Nicht umsonst wird das Taufen zum Bestandteil seines Namens: Johannes der Täufer.

Nach allen evangelischen Berichten fällt der *Beginn von Jesu öffentlicher Tätigkeit* in die johanneische Protest- und Erweckungsbewegung. Mit dem Täufer, den manche Kreise auch in späterer neutestamentlicher Zeit als Konkurrenten Jesu empfunden haben, setzt nach Markus der »Anfang des Evangeliums« ein, woran auch nachher durchweg festgehalten wird, wenn man vom Vorspann der mattäischen und lukanischen Kindheitsgeschichten und vom Johannesprolog absieht. Die Tatsache ist dogmatisch unbequem und wird gerade deshalb allgemein als historisch akzeptiert: auch Jesus unterzieht sich der Bußtaufe des Täufers[6]. Jesus bejaht also dessen prophetisches Wirken und knüpft in seiner Predigt – nach der Gefangensetzung des Täufers oder schon früher – an ihn an. Seinen eschatologischen Bußruf nimmt er auf und zieht radikal Konsequenzen daraus. Es ist nicht ausgeschlossen, auch wenn die Szene christologisch ausgestaltet (Himmelsstimme) und legendarisch ausgeschmückt (der Geist »wie eine Taube«)[7] ist, daß Jesus im Zusammenhang der Taufe seine eigene Berufung erfahren hat. Alle Berichte sind sich jedenfalls darin einig, daß er sich von da an als vom Geist ergriffen und von Gott bevollmächtigt erkannt hat. Die Taufbewegung, und wohl erst recht die Verhaftung des Täufers, war für Jesus ein Zeichen, daß die Zeit erfüllt sei.

Und so beginnt Jesus, die *»gute Nachricht«* im Land auf und ab zu verkünden und eigene Jünger – die ersten vielleicht aus dem Täuferkreis[8] – um sich zu sammeln: Das Reich Gottes ist nahe bevorstehend – kehret um und glaubet der guten Botschaft[9]. Aber es ist, anders als die finstere Gerichtsdrohung des Asketen Johannes, von Anfang an eine freundliche, erfreuliche Botschaft von der Güte des nahenden Gottes und einem Reich der Gerechtigkeit, der Freude und des Friedens. Das Reich Gottes nicht primär als Gericht, sondern als Gnade für alle. Nicht nur Krankheit, Leid und Tod, auch Armut und Unterdrückung werden ein Ende haben. Eine befreiende Botschaft für die Armen, Mühseligen und von Schuld Beladenen – eine Botschaft der Vergebung, Gerechtigkeit, Freiheit, Brüderlichkeit, Liebe.

Aber gerade diese für das Volk erfreuliche Botschaft zielt offensichtlich nicht auf die Einhaltung der etablierten Ordnung, wie sie durch Tempelkult und Gesetzesbeobachtung bestimmt war. Nicht nur scheint Jesus bezüglich des Opferkultes bestimmte Reserven gehabt zu haben[10]. Er hat offensichtlich mit der Zerstörung des Tempels bei der bevorstehenden Endzeit gerechnet[11], und mit dem Gesetz kam er schon bald in einer Weise in Konflikt, daß er vom jüdischen Establishment als eine ungemein gefährliche Bedrohung seiner Herrschaft angesehen wurde. Wird hier, so mußten sich die Hierarchie und ihre Hoftheologen sagen, nicht faktisch die Revolution gepredigt?

2. Revolution?

Jesu Botschaft war zweifellos revolutionär, wenn mit Revolution eine grundlegende Umgestaltung eines bestehenden Umstandes oder Zustandes gemeint ist. Man spricht ja in diesem Sinn – und nicht nur zu Reklamezwecken – sehr allgemein von Revolution (eine Revolution der Medizin, der Betriebsführung, der Pädagogik, der Damenmode usw.). Aber mit solchen wohlfeilen, schillernden allgemeinen Redensarten ist uns hier nicht geholfen. Die Frage ist präzis zu stellen: Wollte Jesus einen gewaltsamen plötzlichen Umsturz (re-volvere = umstürzen) der gesellschaftlichen Ordnung, ihrer Werte und Repräsentanten? Das ist Revolution im strengen Sinn (die Französische Revolution, die Oktoberrevolution usw.), sie komme nun von links oder rechts.

Die revolutionäre Bewegung

Auch diese Frage ist kein Anachronismus. Die »Theologie der Revolution«[1] ist nicht eine Erfindung unserer Tage. Die militanten apokalyptischen oder katharischen Bewegungen im Altertum, die radikalen Sekten des Mittelalters (besonders der politische Messianismus des Cola di Rienzo) und der linke Flügel der Reformation (besonders Thomas Münzer) repräsentieren diesen Typus in der Geschichte der Christenheit. Nach dem frühen Anreger der historisch-kritischen Evangelien-Untersuchung S. Reimarus († 1768)[2] und dem österreichischen Sozialistenführer K. Kautsky[3] bis zu Robert Eisler[4], den in unseren Tagen J. Carmichael weitgehend übernommen hat[5], und S. G. F. Brandon[6] wurde ab und zu die These vertreten, Jesus selber sei ein politisch-sozialer Revolutionär gewesen.

Nun ist kein Zweifel, daß Jesu Heimat Galiläa für revolutionäre Aufrufe besonders anfällig war und als Heimat der *zelotischen Revolutionsbewegung* (»Zeloten« = »Eiferer« mit dem Unterton des Fanatismus) galt. Weiter, daß zumindest einer seiner Anhänger Revolutionär – Simon der »Zelot«[7] und nach manchen Vermutungen vom Namen her auch Judas Ischariot und sogar die beiden »Donnersöhne« Johannes und Jakobus[8] – gewesen war. Schließlich und vor allem, daß im Prozeß vor Pontius Pilatus der Begriff des »Königs der Juden«[9] eine entscheidende Rolle spielte, daß Jesus von den Römern aus politischen Gründen hingerichtet wurde und daß er die den Sklaven und politischen Rebellen vorbehaltene Todesart zu erleiden hatte. Für diese Anklage konnten Vorgänge wie Jesu Einzug in Jerusalem und die Tempelreinigung, wenigstens so wie sie berichtet werden[10], einen gewissen Anhalt bieten.

Kein Volk hat der römischen Fremdherrschaft so ausdauernd geistigen und politischen Widerstand geleistet wie das jüdische. Für die römischen Machthaber waren die Befürchtungen eines Aufstandes nur zu real. Seit geraumer Zeit sahen sich die Römer in Palästina einer akuten revolutionären Situation gegenüber. Die revolutionäre Bewegung, die im Gegensatz zum Jerusalemer Establishment jegliche Kollaboration mit der Besatzungsmacht, ja sogar die Steuerzahlung ablehnte und zahlreiche Querverbindungen insbesondere zur pharisäischen Partei unterhielt, hatte an Einfluß gewonnen. Insbesondere in der Heimat Jesu waren zahlreiche nationalistische jüdische Partisanen tätig, gegen welche schon der vom römischen Senat zum »König der Juden« ernannte Idumäer Herodes, gegen Ende dessen Amtszeit Jesus geboren wurde, mit Todesurteilen vorgehen mußte. Und nach dem Tode des eisern und verschlagen regierenden Königs Herodes brachen wieder Unruhen aus, die durch römische Truppen des später in Germanien erfolglos tätigen syrischen Oberbefehlshabers Quintilius Varus unbarmherzig erstickt wurden. Zur eigentlichen Gründung einer Revolutionspartei kam es in Galiläa unter Judas von Gamala (meist der »Galiläer« genannt): als nicht viel später, im Jahre 6 n. Chr., der Kaiser Augustus den brutalen Herodes-Sohn Archelaos als Vasallenherrscher (nicht mehr »König«, sondern »Ethnarch«) von Judäa absetzen ließ, Judäa der direkten römischen Verwaltung unter einem Prokurator unterstellte und – wie in vager Weise auch Lukas[11] im Zusammen-

hang der Geburt Jesu erwähnt – durch den römischen Oberbe-
fehlshaber in Syrien, jetzt Sulpicius Quirinius, die ganze Bevölkerung zur besseren steuerlichen Erfassung registrieren ließ. In
Galiläa – wo man unter dem anderen Herodes-Sohn Herodes
Antipas nur indirekt betroffen war – probten die empörten Zeloten den Aufstand, bei welchem aber ihr Führer Judas umkam
und seine Anhänger zerstreut wurden.

Doch trotz der absoluten Überlegenheit der römischen Militärmacht waren die Widerstandsgruppen nicht erledigt. Besonders im wilden judäischen Gebirge hatten sie ihre Stützpunkte,
und der in römischen Diensten schreibende jüdische Geschichtsschreiber Josephus klagt über das, was er mit den Römern einfach »Räuber« oder »Banditen« nennt: »So war Judäa voll von
Räuberbanden; und wo es einem gelang, eine Gruppe von
Aufrührern um sich zu sammeln, da machte er sich zum König,
zum Verderben der Allgemeinheit. Denn während sie den Römern nur geringen Schaden zufügen konnten, wüteten sie um so
mehr mit Mord und Totschlag gegen ihre eigenen Volksgenossen[12].«

In der Art einer Stadtguerilla erledigten die Widerstandskämpfer Feinde und Kollaborateure kurzerhand mit kurzem Dolch
(lat. »sica«). Die Römer nannten sie deshalb sinnigerweise »Sikarier« (Dolchmänner). Besondere Gefahr herrschte immer an den
großen Festtagen, wenn sich ungeheure Pilgerscharen in Jerusalem einfanden. Vorsorglich zog dann meist der römische Gouverneur (Prokurator) von seiner Residenz Cäsarea am Meer hinauf in die Hauptstadt. Dies hatte auch der Gouverneur Pontius
Pilatus getan in der Zeit, als sich der Konflikt Jesu mit dem
jüdischen Establishment zugespitzt hatte. Auch ganz abgesehen
davon hatte er allen Grund dazu. Denn seit Beginn seiner Amtszeit im Jahre 26 hatte er durch ständige Provokationen die
aufrührerische Stimmung angeheizt, und ein Aufstand konnte
jederzeit ausbrechen. Hatte er doch schon damals gegen alle
heilige, auch von den Römern respektierte Tradition über Nacht
die mit dem Bild des Kaisers – der staatlichen Kultgottheit –
geschmückten Feldzeichen nach Jerusalem bringen lassen. Heftige Demonstrationen waren die Folge. Pilatus gab nach. Als er
aber für den Bau einer Wasserleitung nach Jerusalem Geld aus
dem Tempelschatz nahm, erstickte er den sich regenden Widerstand im Keime. Und nach Lukas[13] ließ er eine Anzahl Galiläer,
die in Jerusalem opfern wollten, aus irgendeinem Grund samt
ihren Opfertieren umbringen. Auch der von Pilatus statt Jesus

freigelassene Barabbas war bei einem Aufruhr mit Mord dabeigewesen[14]. Aber Pilatus war nach dem Tode Jesu im Jahre 36 wegen
seiner gewalttätigen Politik von Rom abgesetzt worden. Erst 30
Jahre später wurde aus dem Guerillakrieg schließlich der große
Volkskrieg, den das Jerusalemer Establishment nicht zu verhindern vermochte. Ein Krieg, in welchem wiederum ein Galiläer,
der Zelotenführer Johannes von Gischala, wesentlich beteiligt
war und – nach langem Streit mit anderen aufständischen Truppen – den Tempelbezirk verteidigte, bis die Römer die drei
Mauerringe durchbrachen und der Tempel in Flammen aufging.
Mit der Eroberung Jerusalems und der Liquidierung der letzten
Widerstandsgruppen, von denen sich eine noch über drei Jahre in
der herodianischen Bergfestung Masada oberhalb des Toten
Meeres gegen die römischen Belagerer zu halten vermochte,
fand die revolutionäre Bewegung ihr grausames Ende. Masada, wo sich die letzten Widerstandskämpfer schließlich
selber den Tod gaben, ist heute ein israelisches National-
heiligtum[15].

Die Hoffnung auf den Befreier

Es war keine Frage: Für die revolutionäre Bewegung spielte die
Volkserwartung eines großen Befreiers, eines kommenden »Ge-
salbten« (Messias, Christus) oder »Königs«, eines endzeitlichen
Gesandten und Bevollmächtigten Gottes eine erhebliche Rolle.
Worüber die jüdischen Machthaber am liebsten schwiegen und
auch die Theologen nicht gern sprachen, daran glaubte das Volk:
die messianische Erwartung war durch die apokalyptischen
Schriften und Ideen vielfach zum Enthusiasmus gesteigert worden. Wer immer jetzt mit einem Führungsanspruch auftrat,
weckte die Frage, ob er vielleicht der »Kommende« oder zumindest sein Vorläufer sei. Im einzelnen gingen die Erwartungen
freilich weit auseinander: erwarteten die einen den Messias als
den politischen Davidssproß, so die anderen als den apokalyptischen Menschensohn, Weltenrichter und Welterlöser. Noch 132
n. Chr., beim zweiten und letzten großen Aufstand gegen die
Römer, war der Zelotenführer Bar Kochba, der »Sternensohn«,
vom angesehensten Rabbi seiner Zeit Aqiba und vielen anderen
Schriftgelehrten als der verheißene Messias begrüßt worden, bevor er im Kampfe fiel und Jerusalem nach einer zweiten Zerstörung für die Juden auf Jahrhunderte hinaus verbotene Stadt

wurde, so daß das rabbinische Judentum in der Folge sich nur ungern des Bar Kochba erinnerte.

Und Jesus? Kam seine Botschaft nicht *der revolutionären Ideologie sehr nahe?* Sollte sie nicht auf zelotische Revolutionäre Anziehungskraft ausüben? Wie die politischen Radikalen erwartet er eine grundlegende Veränderung der Situation, den baldigen Anbruch der Gottesherrschaft anstelle der menschlichen Herrschaftsordnung. Die Welt ist nicht in Ordnung; es muß radikal anders werden. Auch er übte scharfe Kritik an den herrschenden Kreisen und den reichen Großgrundbesitzern. Er trat gegen soziale Mißstände, gegen Rechtsbeugung, Raffgier, Hartherzigkeit ein für die Armen, Unterdrückten, Verfolgten, Elenden, Vergessenen. Er polemisierte gegen die weichliche Kleider Tragenden an den Höfen der Könige[16], gestattete sich beißende ironische Bemerkungen über die Tyrannen, die sich Wohltäter des Volkes nennen lassen[17] und hieß nach der lukanischen Überlieferung Herodes Antipas respektlos einen Fuchs[18]. Auch er predigte keinen Gott der Machthaber und der Etablierten, sondern einen Gott der Befreiung und Erlösung. Auch er verschärfte das Gesetz in verschiedener Hinsicht und erwartete von seinen Nachfolgern bedingungslose Nachfolge und einen kompromißlosen Einsatz: Kein Zurückschauen, wenn man die Hand an den Pflug gelegt[19]; keine Entschuldigung wegen Handel, Heirat oder Begräbnis[20].

Ist es so erstaunlich, daß Jesus – auch ganz abgesehen vom Jesus-Look des kubanischen Guerillero Che Guevara – auf viele Revolutionäre bis zum kolumbianischen Priesterrevolutionär Camillo Torres als Revolutionär gewirkt hat? Läßt sich doch auch nicht bestreiten, daß die Evangelien keinen süßlich sanften Jesus einer alten oder neuen Romantik und keinen braven Kirchenchristus zeigen. Nichts von einem klugen Diplomaten, einem bischöflichen Mann des »Ausgleichs« und des »équilibre«. Die Evangelien zeigen einen offensichtlich sehr klarsichtigen, entschlossenen, unbeugsamen, wenn es sein mußte auch kämpferischen und streitbaren und in jedem Fall furchtlosen Jesus. Er war ja gekommen, um Feuer auf die Erde zu werfen[21]. Keine Furcht vor denen, die nur den Leib töten und darüber hinaus nichts können[22]. Eine Schwertzeit, eine Zeit größter Not und Gefahr steht bevor[23].

Und doch muß man die ganzen evangelischen Berichte verdrehen und uminterpretieren, muß man die Quellen völlig einseitig auswählen, unkontrolliert und willkürlich mit vereinzelten Jesus-Worten und Gemeindebildungen operieren und von Jesu Botschaft als ganzer weithin absehen, muß man also statt historisch-kritisch mit einer romanhaften Phantasie arbeiten, wenn man aus Jesus einen Guerillakämpfer, einen Putschisten, einen politischen Agitator und Revolutionär und seine Botschaft vom Gottesreich zu einem politisch-sozialen Aktionsprogramm machen will[24]. Auch wenn es heute ebenso populär ist, vom Rebellen, vom Revolutionär Jesus zu sprechen wie in der Hitlerzeit vom Kämpfer, Führer, Feldherrn Jesus, und in der Kriegspredigt des Ersten Weltkrieges vom Helden und Patrioten Jesus, so muß doch unbekümmert um den Zeitgeist – um Jesu willen – unmißverständlich deutlich gemacht werden: Wie kein Mann des Systems, so war er auch kein sozialpolitischer Revolutionär.

Jesus verkündet nicht wie die Revolutionäre seiner Zeit eine durch militärische oder quasi-militärische Aktion gewaltsam zu errichtende, nationale, religiös-politische Theokratie oder Demokratie. Ihm kann man nachfolgen auch ohne ein explizit politisches oder sozialkritisches Engagement. Er bläst nicht zum Sturm gegen die repressiven Strukturen, betreibt weder von links noch von rechts den Sturz der Regierung. Er wartet auf den Umsturz Gottes und verkündet die schon jetzt maßgebende, aber *gewaltlos zu erwartende uneingeschränkte, unmittelbare Weltherrschaft Gottes selbst.* Nicht ein von unten aktiv betriebener, sondern von oben verfügter Umschlag, auf den man sich freilich, die Zeichen der Zeit verstehend, ganz und gar einstellen soll. Dieses Reich Gottes gilt es zuerst zu suchen, und alles übrige, um was sich die Menschen sorgen, wird dazu gegeben werden[25].

Gegen die römische Besatzungsmacht polemisiert und agitiert er nicht. Nicht wenige Dörfer und Städte von Jesu galiläischer Wirksamkeit werden genannt, auffälligerweise aber gerade die Haupt- und Residenzstadt des Herodes, Tiberias (nach Kaiser Tiberius genannt), und das hellenistische Sepphoris überhaupt nicht. Der »Fuchs« Herodes wird in deutlicher Abwehr politischer Mißdeutung auf Jesu wahren Auftrag hingewiesen[26]. Die antirömische Stimmung anzuheizen, lehnt Jesus brüsk ab[27]. Das lukanische Bildwort vom Schwert ist in Zusammenhang mit

Jesu Ablehnung der Gewaltanwendung zu sehen[28]. Alle politisch mißdeutbaren Titel wie Messias und Davidssohn vermeidet er. Jeglicher Nationalismus und alle Ressentiments gegen die Ungläubigen fehlen in seiner Reich-Gottes-Botschaft. Nirgendwo spricht er von der Wiederherstellung des Davidreiches in Macht und Herrlichkeit. Nirgendwo zigt er ein Handeln mit dem politischen Ziel, die weltliche Herschaft zu ergreifen. Im Gegenteil: keine politischen Hoffnungen, keine revolutionäre Strategie und Taktik, keine realpolitische Ausnutzung seiner Popularität, keine taktisch kluge Koalition mit bestimmten Gruppierungen, kein strategischer langer Marsch durch die Institutionen, keine Tendenz zur Akkumulierung von Macht. Sondern im Gegenteil – was gesellschaftliche Relevanz hat! – Machtverzicht, Schonung, Gnade, Frieden: die Befreiung aus dem Teufelskreis von Gewalt und Gegengewalt, Schuld und Vergeltung.

Falls die durch biblische Symbolsprache geprägte *Versuchungsgeschichte*[29] einen geschichtlichen Kern haben sollte, dann die nur zu gut begreifliche Versuchung, auf die sich alle drei Varianten zurückführen lassen: de diabolische Versuchung eines politischen Messianismus. Eine Versuchung, der Jesus nicht nur in der Erzählung, sondern durch sein ganzes öffentliches Wirken hindurch – vielleicht auch im Satanswort an Petrus[30] – konsequent widerstanden hat. Er blieb zwischen den Fronten und ließ sich von keiner Gruppe vereinnahmen und zum »König« und Chef machen. Auf keinen Fall wollte er das Reich Gottes gewaltsam vorwegnehmen, herbeizwingen. Möglicherweise meint das dunkle Wort von »Herbeidrängen« des Himmelreiches, das vergewaltigt wird und das Gewalttätige an sich zu reißen suchen[31], eine ausdrückliche Absage an die zelotische Revolutionsbewegung. Vielleicht zeugen auch die Aufforderung zum geduldigen Warten auf Gottes Stunde im Gleichnis von der selbstwachsenden Saat[32] und die Warnung vor Falschpropheten[33] von antizelotischer Polemik, die für die Evangelisten nach dem Katastrophenjahr 70 reichlich überflüssig geworden war.

Gewiß mußte Jesus den Römern, die sich um die innerjüdischen Religionsstreitigkeiten wenig kümmerten, aber alle Volksbewegungen argwöhnisch betrachteten, als politisch verdächtig, ja schließlich als Unruhestifter und potentieller Aufrührer erscheinen. Die jüdische Anklage vor Pilatus war verständlich, scheinbar berechtigt. Und doch zutiefst tendenziös, ja letztlich – worauf die Evangelien übereinstimmend insistierten – falsch. Jesus wurde als politischer Revolutionär verurteilt – aber er war es nicht! Wehrlos hatte er sich seinen Feinden ausgeliefert. Darüber ist sich heute die ernsthafte Forschung einig: Nirgendwo erscheint Jesus als das Haupt einer politischen Verschwörung, spricht er in zelotischer Weise vom Messias-König, der die Feinde Israels zerschmettern wird, und von der Weltherrschaft des Volkes Israel. Er erscheint durch alle Evangelien hindurch als der waffenlose Wanderprediger und der charismatische Arzt, der nicht Wunden schlägt, sondern heilt. Der Not lindert und nicht für politische Zwecke nützt. Der nicht militanten Kampf, sondern Gottes Gnade und Vergebung für alle proklamiert. Selbst seine an die alttestamentlichen Propheten anklingende Sozialkritik erfolgte nicht aufgrund eines gesellschaftspolitischen Programms, sondern entscheidend aufgrund seines neuen Gottes- und Menschenverständnisses.

Revolution der Gewaltlosigkeit

Die Erzählung vom *Einzug in Jerusalem* auf einem Esel[34], ob historisch oder nicht, charakterisiert ihn richtig: nicht das weiße Pferd des Siegers, nicht das Symboltier der Herrschenden reitet er, sondern das Reittier der Armen und Machtlosen. Die von den Synoptikern anschließend berichtete *Tempelreinigung*[35] – wie die Einzugserzählung von Mattäus und Johannes im Vergleich zu Markus übersteigert und wohl schon von Markus aus Gründen erzählerischer Anschaulichkeit eher übertrieben – konnte jedenfalls nicht das Ausmaß eines Tumultes erreicht haben, welcher sofort das Eingreifen der Tempelpolizei und der römischen Kohorte in der Burg Antonia an der Nordwestecke des Tempelvorhofes zur Folge gehabt hätte. Was immer der historische Kern der Erzählung war – von einigen Exegeten wird die Historizität mit allerdings kaum genügenden Argumenten überhaupt in Frage gestellt: Nach den Quellen geht es nicht um einen typisch zelotischen Akt, nicht um einen reinen Gewaltakt oder gar offenen Aufruhr. Jesus beabsichtigte nicht die endgültige Vertreibung aller Händler, die Besitzergreifung des Tempels und eine neue Tempel- und Priesterorganisation im Sinne der Zeloten. Es ging freilich um eine bewußte Provokation, einen symbolischen Akt, eine individuelle prophetische Zeichentat, welche eine demonstrative Verurteilung dieses Treibens und der daraus Gewinn ziehenden Hierarchen darstellte: für die Heiligkeit des Ortes als eines Ortes des Gebetes. Diese Verurteilung – verbunden vielleicht mit einem Drohwort gegen den Tempel oder aber eine Verheißung für die Heiden[36] – verdient keine Bagatellisierung. Er hat damit die Hierarchie und die am Wallfahrtsrummel finanziell interessierten Kreise zweifellos in krasser Weise herausgefordert.

Dies zeigt erneut: Jesus war kein Mann des Establishments. Alles, was wir in unserem ersten Gedankengang gesehen haben, bleibt richtig. Jesus war kein Konformist, kein Apologet des Bestehenden, kein Verteidiger von Ruhe und Ordnung. Er forderte zur Entscheidung heraus. In diesem Sinne er das Schwert: nicht den Frieden, sondern den Streit, unter Umständen bis in die Familien hinein[37]. Er stellte das religiös-gesellschaftliche System, die bestehende Ordnung des jüdischen Gesetzes und Tempels grundlegend in Frage und insofern hatte seine Botschaft politische Konsequenzen. Nur ist zugleich zur Kenntnis zu nehmen: Für Jesus ist die *Alternative* zum System, zum Establishment, zur bestehenden Ordnung gerade *nicht die politisch-soziale Revolution.* Eher als Che Guevara, der romantisch die Gewalt als Hebamme der neuen Gesellschaft verherrlichte[38], und Camillo Torres konnten sich Gandhi und Martin Luther King auf ihn berufen.

Die zelotischen Revolutionäre wollten handeln, nicht nur reden. Gegenüber dem Immobilismus und der Machtbesessenheit des Establishments wollten sie die Wirklichkeit nicht nur theologisch interpretieren, sondern politisch verändern. Sie wollten sich engagieren, konsequent sein. Sein und Handeln, Theorie und Praxis sollten einander entsprechen. Konsequent, kohärent sein meint revolutionär sein[39]. »Radikal« wollten sie die Sache an der »radix«, an der Wurzel, fassen, die Verantwortung für die Welt aktiv übernehmen, so daß sie mit der Wahrheit übereinstimmt. In diesem Radikalismus erstrebten sie die endliche Realisierung des Eschaton, des Reiches Gottes – wenn in Gottes Namen notwendig: mit Waffengewalt.

Jesus billigte weder die Methoden noch die Ziele dieses revolutionären Radikalismus der Zeloten, die im Sturz der widergöttlichen Macht des römischen Staates eine göttliche Pflicht sahen und die letztlich doch restaurativ (nationalistische Wiederherstellung des davidischen Großreiches) gesinnt waren. Jesus war anders, provozierend auch nach dieser Seite. Er predigte keine Revolution, weder eine rechte noch eine linke:

– *Keine Aufforderung zur Steuerverweigerung: Gebt dem Kai-*

ser, was des Kaisers ist – gebt ihm allerdings nicht, was Gottes ist[40]!
- *Keine Proklamation eines nationalen Befreiungskrieges: Von übelsten Kollaborateuren ließ er sich zum Essen einladen, und den beinahe noch mehr als die Heiden verhaßten samaritanischen Volksfeind stellte er als Beispiel hin.*
- *Keine Propagierung des Klassenkampfes: Er teilte die Menschen nicht wie so viele Militante seiner Zeit im Freund-Feind-Schema in Kinder des Lichts und in Kinder der Finsternis ein.*
- *Kein düsterer sozialrevolutionärer Konsumverzicht: Jesus feierte in einer schlimmen Zeit politischer Knechtung und sozialer Not festliche Mähler.*
- *Keine Aufhebung des Gesetzes um der Revolution willen: Helfen, heilen, retten wollte er, keine Zwangsbeglückung des Volkes nach dem Willen Einzelner. Zuerst das Reich Gottes, und alles andere wird dazu gegeben werden*[41].

So paart sich bei Jesus die harte Kritik an den Machthabern, die ihre Macht rücksichtslos gebrauchen, mit der Aufforderung nicht zum Tyrannenmord, sondern zum Dienst[42]. Und seine Botschaft gipfelt nicht im Appell zum Erzwingen der besseren Zukunft durch Gewalt: Wer zum Schwert greift, wird durch das Schwert umkommen[43]. Sondern im Appell zum Gewaltverzicht: dem Bösen nicht zu widerstehen[44]; denen wohlzutun, die uns hassen; die zu segnen, die uns fluchen; für die zu beten, die uns verfolgen[45]. Dies alles angesichts des kommenden Reiches, von dem her alles Bestehende, alle Ordnungen, Institutionen, Strukturen, aber auch alle Unterschiede zwischen Mächtigen und Machtlosen, Reichen und Armen von vornherein relativiert erscheinen und dessen Normen schon jetzt anzuwenden sind.

Hätte Jesus in Palästina eine radikale Landreform durchgeführt, er wäre schon längst vergessen. Hätte er wie die Jerusalemer Aufständischen im Jahre 66 zuerst das Stadtarchiv samt aller Schuldverschreibungen der Bankiers in Brand gesteckt, hätte er wie zwei Jahre später der Führer der Jerusalemer Revolution, Bar Giora, die allgemeine Freilassung der jüdischen Sklaven verkündet, so wäre er – ähnlich wie auch der heroische Sklavenbefreier Spartakus mit seinen 70000 Sklaven und den 7000 Kreuzen an der Via Appia – Episode geblieben.

Jesu »Revolution« dagegen – wenn man das vieldeutige Reizwort schon gebrauchen will – war in einem echten und näher zu umschreibenden Sinn radikal und hat deshalb die Welt bleibend verändert. Er überstieg die Alternative etablierte Ordnung – sozialpolitische Revolution, Konformismus – Nonkonformismus. Man kann es auch so sagen: Jesus war revolutionärer als die Revolutionäre. Wir werden noch genauer zu sehen haben, was dies bedeutet:

– *Statt Vernichtung der Feinde: Liebe zu den Feinden!*
– *Statt Zurückschlagen: bedingungslose Vergebung!*
– *Statt Gebrauch von Gewalt: Bereitschaft zum Leiden!*
– *Statt Haß- und Rachegesänge: Seligpreisung der Friedfertigen!*

Die ersten Christen jedenfalls folgten im großen jüdischen Aufstand den Spuren Jesu. Als der Krieg ausbrach, machten sie nicht gemeinsame Sache mit den zelotischen Revolutionären, sondern flohen aus Jerusalem nach Pella auf der anderen Seite des Jordans. Und beim zweiten großen Aufstand unter Bar Kochba wurden sie fanatisch verfolgt. Die Römer aber sind bezeichnenderweise bis zur Verfolgung des Nero nicht gegen sie vorgegangen.

So hatte Jesus keine politisch-soziale Revolution gefordert oder gar in Gang gesetzt. Die von ihm in Gang gesetzte Revolution war entscheidend eine *Revolution der Gewaltlosigkeit,* eine Revolution vom Innersten und Verborgensten, von der Personmitte, vom Herzen des Menschen her auf die Gesellschaft hin. Nicht weitermachen wie bisher, sondern radikales Umdenken und Umkehren des Menschen (griechisch »metanoia«), weg von seinen Egoismen, hin zu seinem Gott und zu seinen Mitmenschen. Nicht die feindlichen Weltmächte sind die eigentlichen Fremdmächte, von denen der Mensch befreit werden muß. Sondern die Mächte des Bösen: Haß, Ungerechtigkeit, Unfrieden, Gewalt, Lebenslüge, die menschlichen Egoismen überhaupt, aber auch Leiden, Krankheit, Tod. Ein verändertes Bewußtsein, ein neues Denken, eine andere Wertskala sind deshalb erfordert. Die Überwindung des Bösen, das nicht nur im System, in den Strukturen, sondern im Menschen liegt. Die innere Freiheit, die zur Freiheit von den äußeren Mächten führt. Veränderung der Gesellschaft durch Veränderung des Einzelnen!

Wenn dem allem so ist, dann allerdings stellt sich die Frage: Ist dieser Jesus nicht letztlich doch der Vertreter eines Rückzugs oder einer Abkapselung von der Welt, einer weltabgewandten

Frömmigkeit, einer weltfernen Innerlichkeit, eines mönchischen Asketismus und Absentismus?

3. Emigration?

Es gibt den politischen Radikalismus, der aus Gründen des Glaubens auf die totale Unterwerfung der Welt, wenn nötig mit Waffengewalt, dringt: die totale Verwirklichung der Herrschaft Gottes in der Welt durch menschlichen Einsatz. Das ist der Radikalismus der Zeloten. Doch es gibt eine entgegengesetzte, ebenfalls radikale Lösung: statt des aktiven Engagements auf Leben und Tod der Widerspruch der Großen Weigerung. Nicht Aufstand, sondern Abstand. Nicht der Angriff auf die gottesfeindliche Welt, sondern die Absage an diese Welt. Nicht die Bewältigung der Geschichte, sondern der Ausstieg aus ihr.

Der apolitische Radikalismus

Das ist der apolitische (wenn auch nur scheinbar unpolitische) Radikalismus der Mönche, der »Alleinlebenden« (griechisch »monachos« = allein) oder der »Anachoreten«, der (in die Wüste) »Entwichenen«[1]. Absonderung, Auszug, Auswanderung aus der Welt also, *Emigration*: des Einzelnen oder der Gruppe, äußerlich-lokal oder innerlich-geistig, organisiert oder nicht, durch Abkapselung und Isolierung oder durch Wegzug und Neuansiedlung. Dies ist, ganz allgemein verstanden, die anachoretisch-monastische Tradition in der Geschichte der Christenheit wie auch im Buddhismus, dessen achtfacher Weg für Mönche, für eine Mönchsgemeinde bestimmt ist: die Tradition der kritischen Distanzierung und des Rückzugs von der Welt. Dazu gehören sowohl die einzelnen asketischen »Einsiedler« (Eremiten: die klassische Gestalt des ägyptischen Wüstenvaters Antonios im 3. Jahrhundert; heute noch in Griechenland auf dem Berg Athos). Dazu gehören die später kirchlich begünstigten organisierten Mönchsgemeinschaften, die ein »gemeinsames Leben« (deshalb »Koinobitentum«) führen (Begründer Pachomios im 4. Jahrhundert). Doch lebt diese Tradition des »retreatism« heute bisweilen auch in recht säkularen Formen weiter: im Hippietum und in den verschiedenen Formen von »consciousness III«, in den jugendlichen Wanderbewegungen in die Wüste, nach Indien, Nepal, Afghanistan und zum Teil im Jesus-Movement. Immer wieder neu beruft man sich dabei auf *Jesus* – zu Recht?

Jedenfalls nicht einfach zu Unrecht. Jesus war alles andere als eine gutbürgerliche Erscheinung. Sein Weg war nicht das, was man gemeinhin »Karriere« nennt. Seine Lebensführung hatte hippieartige Züge. Ob der Wüstenaufenthalt der Versuchungsgeschichte historisch ist, wissen wir nicht. Aber wir wissen: sein Lebensstil war reichlich ungewöhnlich. »Sozial angepaßt« war er zweifellos nicht. Obwohl Sohn eines Zimmermanns und anscheinend selber Zimmermann[2], übt er keinen Beruf aus. Vielmehr führt er ein unstetes Wanderleben, predigt und wirkt auf öffentlichen Plätzen, ißt, trinkt, betet und schläft des öfteren im Freien. Ein Mann, der ausgezogen ist aus seiner Heimat, der sich gelöst hat auch von seiner Familie. Wundert es noch, daß seine nächsten Angehörigen nicht zu seinen Anhängern gehören? Nach alter markinischer Überlieferung, die von Mattäus und Lukas mit Stillschweigen übergangen wird, versuchten sie sogar, ihn zurückzuholen: er sei von Sinnen, verrückt[3]. Was einige psychiatrisch Interessierte angeregt hat, für Jesu Geistesgestörtheit zu plädieren, ohne allerdings damit seine ungeheure Wirkung zu erklären. Aber wenn die Evangelien auch keine Einsicht in Jesu Psyche freigeben – ihr Interesse liegt anderswo –, so zeigen sie doch ein äußeres Verhalten, das nach damaligen Verhaltensmustern nicht gerade als »normal« bezeichnet werden kann.

Für seinen Lebensunterhalt tut Jesus nichts. Nach den evangelischen Berichten wird er von Freunden unterstützt, und ein Kreis von Frauen sorgt für ihn. Offensichtlich hat er sich um keine Familie zu kümmern. Er war, wenn wir nicht etwas in die Evangelien hineindichten[4], wie der Täufer vor ihm und Paulus nach ihm, unverheiratet. Die Ehelosigkeit eines erwachsenen Juden war in diesem Volk, für das Ehe Pflicht und Gebot Gottes war, ungewohnt, provozierend, wenn auch, wie gleich noch zu sehen sein wird, nicht unbekannt. Falls das nur bei Mattäus überlieferte Wort vom Eunuchen um des Himmelreiches willen überhaupt echt ist[5], müßte es auch als Eigenrechtfertigung verstanden werden. Ein Argument für das Zölibatsgesetz stellt Jesu Ehelosigkeit selbstverständlich nicht dar. Wird doch für seine Jünger kein Gebot ausgesprochen, sondern im Gegenteil selbst an jener einen und einzigen Mattäus-Stelle zugleich die Freiwilligkeit des Verzichtens betont: wer es fassen kann, der fasse es. Doch dürfte nicht zuletzt die Ehelosigkeit Jesu mit allem übrigen zusammen erhellen, daß man nur gegen die Texte aus Jesus einen zivilisierten pastörlichen Morallehrer machen kann, wie das liberale Exegeten im 19. Jahrhundert versucht haben. Auch in dieser Beziehung war Jesus anders. Hatte er nicht doch etwas Weltflüchtiges, Schwärmerisches, beinahe Närrisches an sich? Haben sich nicht vielleicht so manche Jesus-Käuze, Jesus-Narren in all den Jahrhunderten, haben sich nicht gerade die Mönche, die Asketen, die Ordensleute mit besonderem Recht auf ihn berufen?

Und doch muß gesagt werden: Jesus war *kein asketischer Mönch,* der in geistiger und wenn möglich auch lokaler Emigration in Abwendung von der Welt nach Vollkommenheit gestrebt hätte. Und auch dies ist keine anachronistische Feststellung.

Das Mönchtum

Es gab zur Zeit Jesu – wie man lange Zeit wenig zur Kenntnis genommen hatte – ein gut organisiertes *jüdisches Mönchtum.* Zwar wußte man schon vom jüdischen Geschichtsschreiber Josephus Flavius wie vom berühmten Zeitgenossen Jesu in Alexandrien, dem jüdischen Philosophen Philon, daß es neben den Sadduzäern, Pharisäern und Zeloten noch eine weitere Gruppierung gab: die *»Essener«* (oder »Essäer«), herkommend wohl von jenen »Frommen« (aramäisch »chasajja«, hebräisch »chasidim«), welche in der Makkabäerzeit ursprünglich hinter der makkabäischen Aufstandspartei standen, sich aber von ihnen wie dann auch von den weniger apokalyptisch und rigoristisch eingestellten Pharisäern loslösten, als die Makkabäer immer mehr politisches Machtstreben entwickelten und Jonathan, der nicht zadoqidischer Herkunft war und sich als Kriegsführer ständig rituell verunreinigen mußte, 153 das Hohepriesteramt übernahm. Nach Philon und Josephus lebten diese Essener, etwa 4000 an der Zahl, abgesondert in den Dörfern, einige auch in den Städten, zu festen Gemeinschaften zusammengeschlossen, und hatten ihr Zentrum am Toten Meer.

Hochaktuell jedoch für die Jesus-Forschung wurden die Essener erst, als 1947 ein arabischer Ziegenhirte am steilen Ostabfall der Wüste Juda zum Toten Meer hin bei der Ruine (Chirbet) *Qumran* auf eine Höhle mit Tonkrügen stieß, in denen mehrere

Schriftrollen versteckt waren. Hunderte von Höhlen wurden daraufhin untersucht und in elf Höhlen zahlreiche Texte und Textfragmente entdeckt. Darunter biblische Texte, wie besonders die zwei Rollen des Jesaja-Buches, tausend Jahre älter als die bis dahin bekannten Handschriften (heute mit anderen Qumranschriften ausgestellt im »Handschriften-Tempel« der hebräischen Universität in Jerusalem). Dann Bibelkommentare (besonders zum Buch Habakuk) und schließlich die für unsere Frage entscheidenden nichtbiblischen Texte, darunter die Gemeinderegel oder Sektenregel von Qumran (1QS) mit der kürzeren Gemeinschaftsregel (1QSa). Dies alles bildet den Rest der Bibliothek einer weitläufigen – muß man heute sagen – klösterlichen Siedlung, die denn auch 1951–56 bei der Ruine mit ihren Haupt- und Nebengebäuden, mit einem Friedhof von 1 100 Gräbern und einem raffiniert ausgebauten Wasserversorgungssystem (11 verschiedene Wasserbecken) ausgegraben wurde. Die sensationelle Entdeckung der Bibliothek und der Niederlassung der Qumrangemeinschaft, die eine wahre Literaturflut hervorrief[6], zeigt etwas höchst Bedeutungsvolles: Es gab zur Zeit Jesu eine jüdische Mönchsgemeinschaft, die bereits alle Elemente jenes christlichen Koinobitentums enthält, wie es vom Ägypter Pachomios begründet, von Basileios dem Großen theologisch untermauert, von Johannes Cassianus dem lateinischen Westen vermittelt und durch Benedikt von Nursia und die Benediktinerregel für das gesamte abendländische Mönchtum vorbildlich wurde: »1. Gemeinsamkeit des Lebensraumes in Wohnung, Arbeits- und Gebetsstätte; 2. Gleichförmigkeit in Kleidung, Nahrung und asketischer Haltung; 3. Sicherung dieser Gemeinschaft durch eine schriftlich fixierte Regel auf der Grundlage des Gehorsams[7].«

Um so dringender wird die Frage: War *Jesus* etwa Essener oder Qumranmönch? Bestehen Beziehungen zwischen Qumran und dem werdenden Christentum? Die beiden Fragen sind zu unterscheiden. Die erste wird heute, nachdem in der frühen Entdeckerfreude einzelne Forscher überall Parallelen sehen wollten[8], von allen seriösen Gelehrten verneint[9]. Die zweite Frage dürfte vorsichtig zu bejahen sein, wenn auch weniger an direkte als an indirekte Beeinflussung zu denken ist. Insbesondere mag der Täufer Johannes, welcher nach der Überlieferung in der Wüste aufwuchs und in der räumlichen Nähe von Qumran gewirkt hat, vielleicht früher eine Verbindung zur dortigen Gemeinschaft gehabt haben. Jedenfalls stehen sowohl der »Lehrer der Gerechtigkeit«, der Begründer der Qumrangemeinschaft, wie der Täufer und Jesus in Opposition zum offiziellen Judentum, zum Jerusalemer Establishment. Für sie alle geht die Scheidung mitten durch Israel. Sie alle erwarten das baldige Ende: diese letzte Generation ist böse, das Gericht bricht herein, eine Entscheidung drängt sich auf, ernste sittliche Forderungen sind unumgänglich. Aber diese Gemeinsamkeiten dürfen die Unterschiede nicht übersehen lassen. Ist doch bereits deutlich geworden, daß die wiederholten Reinigungsbäder von Qumran, die nur für die auserwählten Heiligen bestimmt sind, etwas ganz anderes sind als die einmalige und dem ganzen Volk angebotene Taufe des Johannes. Johannes stiftet nicht eine um das Gesetz gescharte und von anderen Menschen abgesonderte Gemeinschaft, sondern will durch seinen Bußruf das ganze Volk auf das Kommende ausrichten. Für Jesus aber läßt sich darüber hinaus, abgesehen von einigen gemeinsamen Begriffen, Wendungen, Vorstellungen und äußeren Ähnlichkeiten – unter Zeitgenossen nichts Erstaunliches – kaum etwas aufweisen, was auf eine direkte Verbindung Jesu mit den Essenern im allgemeinen und mit Qumran im besonderen hinwiese. Weder die Qumrangemeinde noch die Essenerbewegung werden in den neutestamentlichen Schriften auch nur erwähnt, wie sich auch umgekehrt in den Qumranschriften keine Erwähnung des Namens Jesu findet.

Kein Ordensmann

Aber diese Antwort ist zu allgemein. Im Blick auf die spätere Entwicklung des Christentums gewinnt die Frage eine hohe Wichtigkeit: Wo liegen die konkreten Unterschiede zwischen Jesus und den essenischen Ordensleuten wie den Mönchen von Qumran? Zugespitzt gefragt: Warum schickte Jesus den reichen Jüngling auf die Frage, was er tun müsse, um »vollkommen«[10] zu sein, nicht in das bekannte Kloster von Qumran? Oder wenn man das Schweigen über Qumran und die Essener im Neuen Testament mit ihrem Verschwinden nach dem jüdischen Krieg im Jahre 70 erklären will: Warum hat Jesus selber kein Kloster gegründet? Die Frage darf auch von dem nicht unterdrückt werden, der wie der Verfasser Klöster aus verschiedenen Gründen sympathisch findet, manche Ordensgemeinschaften hochschätzt und die großen Leistungen des Mönchtums für die christliche Mission, Verkündigung und Theologie, für die abendländische Kolonisation, Zivilisation und Kultur, für das Schulwesen, die Krankenpflege und Seelsorge anerkennt. Wenn man sich auch hier um unvoreingenommene Analyse bemüht, wird man sagen müssen: Zwischen Jesus und den Mönchen liegt – trotz Gemeinsamem – eine Welt. Jesu Jüngergemeinschaft trug keine eremitischen oder klösterlichen Züge:

1. Keine Absonderung von der Welt: Die *Essener* sonderten sich ab von den übrigen Menschen, um sich von aller Unreinheit fernzuhalten. Sie wollten die reine Gemeinde Israels sein. Emigration nach innen! Erst recht gilt dies für die *Qumranleute.* Nach einem harten Streit mit dem amtierenden Hohenpriester (wohl der genannte Jonathan, jetzt nur noch »Frevelpriester« genannt) war eine Schar von Priestern, Leviten und Laien aus Protest in die trostlose Wüste am Toten Meer gezogen. Also auch die äußere Emigration! Hier fern von der verdorbenen Welt wollten sie unter der Leitung eines – uns nicht mehr bekannten – »Lehrers der Gerechtigkeit« wahrhaft fromm sein: unbefleckt von allem Unreinen, abgesondert von den Sündern, bis ins kleinste sich an Gottes Gebot haltend, um so in der Wüste den Weg des Herrn zu bereiten[11]. Nicht nur die Priester, die ganze Gemeinde hielt hier die priesterlichen Reinigungsvorschriften und gewann durch tägliche Waschungen – nicht nur Händewaschen, sondern Vollbäder – die Reinheit immer wieder neu: eine wahre Gemeinde der Heiligen und der Auserwählten auf dem Weg der Vollkommenheit: »Leute vollkommenen Wandels«[12]. Ein Volk von Priestern, das ständig wie im Tempel lebt.

Jesus aber fordert weder äußere noch innere Emigration! Keine Abkehr vom Weltgetriebe, keine weltflüchtige Haltung. Kein Heil durch Abbau des Ichs und seiner Bindungen an die Welt. Fernöstliche Versenkungslehren sind Jesus fremd. Er lebt nicht in einem Kloster und auch nicht in der Wüste; diese wird übrigens an einer Stelle[13] ausdrücklich als Ort der Offenbarung abgelehnt. Er wirkt in aller Öffentlichkeit in den Dörfern und Städten, mitten unter den Menschen. Selbst mit gesellschaftlich Anrüchigen, mit den gesetzlich »Unreinen« und von Qumran Abgeschriebenen hält er Kontakt und fürchtet deshalb keine Skandale. Wichtiger als alle Reinheitsvorschriften ist ihm die Reinheit des Herzens[14]. Den bösen Mächten entweicht er nicht, er nimmt den Kampf an Ort und Stelle auf. Von seinen Gegnern setzt er sich nicht ab. Er sucht das Gespräch.

2. Keine Zweiteilung der Wirklichkeit: Über die Theologie der *Essener* berichten Philon und Josephus kurz und zum Teil in hellenisierender Weise (Unsterblichkeit der Seele). Über die Theologie der *Qumranmönche* aber wissen wir verhältnismäßig Genaues. Sie ist bei aller Bändigung durch den monotheistischen Schöpferglauben dualistisch. Wahrheit und Licht leiten die Gemeinde. Außerhalb aber, unter den Heiden und den nicht ungeteilt gesetzestreuen Israeliten, herrscht die Finsternis. Außerhalb Qumran kein Heil! Die Söhne des Lichtes, der Wahrheit und der Gerechtigkeit kämpfen gegen die Söhne der Finsternis, der Lüge und des Frevels. Die Söhne des Lichtes sollen einander lieben, die Söhne der Finsternis sollen sie hassen. Gott hat von Anfang an die Menschen zur einen oder zur anderen Bestimmung erwählt und ihnen zwei Geister zugeteilt, so daß die ganze Geschichte ein unaufhörlicher Kampf ist: zwischen dem Geist der Wahrheit oder des Lichtes und dem Geist des Frevels oder der Finsternis, welcher auch die Söhne des Lichtes verwirren kann. Erst am Ende der Tage macht Gott dem Streit ein Ende. Diese Gegenüberstellung zweier Geister ist nicht alttestamentlich, sondern dürfte eher vom persischen Dualismus beeinflußt sein, für den es zwei ewige Prinzipien, ein gutes und ein böses gibt.

Jesus aber kennt keinen solchen Dualismus: auch nicht nach dem Johannesevangelium, wo die Antithese zwischen Licht und Finsternis eine große Rolle spielt. Keine Einteilung der Menschheit in Gute und Böse von vornherein und von Anfang an: *Jeder* hat umzukehren, jeder *kann* aber auch umkehren. Jesu Bußpredigt geht nicht wie die Qumrans und auch des Täufers vom Zorne Gottes, sondern von seiner Gnade aus. Jesus predigt kein Gericht der Rache über Sünder und Gottlose. Gottes Barmherzigkeit kennt keine Grenzen. Allen wird Vergebung angeboten. Und gerade deshalb soll man auch die Feinde nicht hassen, sondern lieben.

3. Kein Gesetzeseifer: Die *Essener* übten strengsten Gesetzesgehorsam. Deswegen hatten sie sich ja auch von den für sie allzu laxen Pharisäern getrennt. Besonders zeigte sich ihr Gesetzeseifer in der strikten Beobachtung des Sabbatgebotes: Die Speisen wurden schon vorher zubereitet. Nicht die geringste Arbeit, ja nicht einmal das Verrichten der Notdurft war gestattet. Bei den *Mönchen von Qumran* findet sich eine ähnlich strenge Gesetzesobservanz. Bekehrung, Umkehr meint Rückkehr zum Gesetz des Mose. Dies ist der Heilsweg: das Gesetz zu halten. Und das heißt, das ganze Gesetz mit allen seinen Bestimmungen, ohne Kompromisse und Erleichterungen. Am Sabbat ist nichts zu tragen, auch kein Medikament, ist keinem Vieh Geburtshilfe zu leisten und auch keines, das in die Grube gefallen, herauszuholen. Aus Gesetzestreue hatten die Qumranleute gegen die Jerusalemer Priesterschaft sogar am alten Sonnenkalender festgehalten und den neu eingeführten (seleukidischen?) Mondkalender abgelehnt, was sie in Widerspruch zur Festordnung des Jerusalemer Tempels brachte. Die Sakralsprache, das reine Hebräisch als Sprache des Gesetzes, wird im Kloster gepflegt. Durch Gebet und kompromißlose Gesetzestreue wollten sie, die nicht im Tempel opfern konnten, sühnen für die Verfehlungen des Volkes.

Jesus aber ist solcher Gesetzeseifer völlig fern. Im Gegenteil: durch alle Evangelien hindurch zeigt er gegenüber dem Gesetz eine erstaunliche Freiheit. Für die essenischen Ordensleute war er – gerade in bezug auf den Sabbat – eindeutig ein strafwürdiger Gesetzesbrecher. In Qumran wäre er exkommuniziert, ausgewiesen worden.

4. Kein Asketismus: Die *Essener* übten Askese aufgrund ihres Reinheitsstrebens. Um sich nicht durch den Umgang mit einer Frau zu verunreinigen, verzichtete die Elite auf die Ehe. Allerdings gab es auch verheiratete Essener: Die Ehe war ihnen – nach dreijähriger Prüfung – gestattet: mit dem einzigen Ehezweck der Fortpflanzung, ohne ehelichen Verkehr während der Schwangerschaft. Ihr persönliches Eigentum überließen die Essener der Gemeinde, in der eine Art Kommunismus herrschte. Gegessen wurde nur, was zur Sättigung notwendig war. Auch im Kloster von *Qumran* herrschten strenge Sitten. Nur so konnte der Kampf gegen die Söhne der Finsternis geführt werden. Auch hier wurde das persönliche Eigentum beim Eintritt auf die Kommunität übertragen und von einem Aufseher verwaltet. Die Mönche der Gemeinderegel (1QS), also zumindest die im Kloster lebenden Mitglieder, mußten zölibatär sein. Nur die kürzere Gemeinschaftsregel (1QSa) – ist sie eine frühere oder spätere Phase in der Geschichte von Qumran oder eine Bestimmung für die Gemeinde Israels am Ende der Tage? – nur sie kennt auch verheiratete Mitglieder. Auch der Asketismus von Qumran war kultisch bestimmt. Ein Drittel der Nächte sollten die Vollmitglieder wachen, um im Buch der Bücher zu lesen, nach Recht zu forschen und gemeinsam Gott zu loben.

Jesus aber war kein Asket. Er forderte nie Opfer um der Opfer willen, Entsagung um der Entsagung willen. Keine zusätzlichen

ethischen Forderungen und asketische Sonderleistungen, wenn
möglich noch im Hinblick auf eine größere Seligkeit. Seine Jünger, die nicht fasten, verteidigt er[15]. Saure Frömmigkeit ist ihm
zuwider; jedes fromme Theater lehnte er ab[16]. Jesus war keine
»Opferseele« und forderte kein Martyrium. Er nahm am Leben
der Menschen teil, aß und trank und ließ sich zu Gastmählern
einladen. In diesem Sinn war er gerade kein Außenseiter. Verglichen mit dem Täufer mußte er den (zweifellos historischen)
Vorwurf hören, er sei ein Fresser und Säufer[17]. Die Ehe war für
ihn nichts Verunreinigendes, sondern der Wille des Schöpfers,
der zu respektieren ist. Er legte niemandem ein Zölibatsgesetz
auf. Eheverzicht war freiwillig: individuelle Ausnahme, nicht
Regel für die Jüngerschaft. Und auch der Verzicht auf materiellen Besitz war nicht notwendig zur Nachfolge. Gegenüber der
eher düsteren Lehre von Qumran und dem strengen Bußruf des
Johannes erschien Jesu Botschaft als eine in vielfacher Hinsicht
frohe und befreiende Botschaft.

5. *Keine hierarchische Ordnung:* Die *Essener* hatten eine strenge
Ordnung nach vier Ständen oder Klassen, die scharf untereinander geschieden waren: Priester – Leviten – Laienmitglieder –
Kandidaten. Jedes später eingetretene Mitglied war dem früher
eingetretenen auch in Kleinigkeiten nachgeordnet. Die Weisungen der Vorsteher, die die Gemeinschaft leiteten, hatte ein jeder
zu befolgen. Auch die Mönchskommunität von *Qumran* war
straff organisiert nach denselben vier Klassen. Sowohl bei Bera-
tungen, wo bei allen Gruppen ein Priester dabei sein mußte, wie
beim Essen waren die Rangstufen zu beachten. Sogar beim Mahl
mit dem Messias erscheint die Vorzugsstellung der Priesterschaft. Der Gehorsam der Geringeren gegenüber den Höheren
wurde eingeschärft und mit harten Strafen sanktioniert. Zum
Beispiel Entzug eines Viertels der Essensration: ein Jahr für
falsche Angabe des Besitzes, ein halbes Jahr für unnötiges Nackt-
gehen, drei Monate für ein törichtes Wort, dreißig Tage für
Schlaf während der Vollversammlung oder für ein dummes lau-
tes Lachen, zehn Tage für ein Ins-Wort-Fallen. Hart war insbesondere der Ausschluß aus der Gemeinde: der Exkommunizierte
mußte seinen Unterhalt, anscheinend ähnlich wie Johannes, in
der Steppe suchen.

Jesus aber kam ohne jeglichen Strafkatalog aus. Er beruft Jünger nicht in seine Nachfolge, um eine Institution zu begründen.
Gehorsam fordert er gegenüber dem Willen Gottes, und insofern

bestand Gehorsam im Freiwerden von allen anderen Bindungen. Das Streben nach den besseren Plätzen und Ehrenstellen verurteilt er verschiedentlich. Die übliche hierarchische Ordnung wird von ihm geradezu auf den Kopf gestellt: Die Niedrigen sollten die Höchsten, und die Höchsten die Diener aller sein. Unterordnung hat gegenseitig zu geschehen, im gemeinsamen Dienst.

6. *Keine Ordensregel:* Der Tageslauf der *Essener* war streng geregelt: zuerst Gebet, dann Feldarbeit, in der Mittagszeit Waschungen und gemeinsames Mahl, nachher wieder Arbeit, am Abend wieder gemeinsames Mahl. Beim Zusammensein herrschte Silentium. Bevor ein Mitglied aufgenommen wurde, hatte es zwei oder drei Jahre Noviziat (Probezeit) zu bestehen. Bei der Aufnahme wurde es feierlich auf die Satzungen verpflichtet. Es legte eine Art Gelübde ab in Form eines Eides, der im Versprechen der Treue insbesondere gegenüber dem Vorgesetzten gipfelte. Alle Mitglieder, nicht nur die Priester, mußten, insbesondere beim gemeinsamen Mahl, das weiße Gewand tragen: die Priestertracht, das Kleid der Reinen. Auch in *Qumran* verlief das ganze Leben nach einer ähnlich strengen Regel: Gebet, Essen und Beratung sollten gemeinsam sein. Die zeremoniell geregelten Mahlzeiten hatten ebenso wie die Reinigungsbäder religiöse Bedeutung. Man führte ein intensives liturgisches Leben. Opfer wurden zwar, nachdem man sich vom Tempel und seinem Kalender getrennt hatte, nicht dargebracht. Doch gab es regelmäßige Gebetsgottesdienste mit eigenen Psalmen. Ansätze für eine Art kirchlichen Stundengebetes.

Bei *Jesus* nichts von all dem: kein Noviziat, keinen Eintrittseid, kein Gelübde! Keine regelmäßigen Frömmigkeitsübungen, keine gottesdienstlichen Anweisungen, keine langen Gebete! Keine rituellen Mahle und Bäder, keine unterscheidenden Kleider! Vielmehr eine im Vergleich mit Qumran sträfliche Ungeregeltheit, Selbstverständlichkeit, Spontaneität, Freiheit! Jesus verfaßte keine Regel und keine Satzungen. Statt Regeln für eine oft geistlich verbrämte Herrschaft von Menschen über Menschen gibt er Gleichnisse von der Herrschaft Gottes. Wenn er ein ständiges unermüdliches Beten[18] fordert, so meint er damit nicht den in manchen mönchischen Gemeinschaften üblichen unaufhörlichen Gebetsgottesdienst (»ewige Anbetung«). Er meint die ständige Gebetshaltung des Menschen, der allzeit alles von Gott erwartet: Sein Anliegen darf und soll der Mensch unermüdlich

Gott vortragen. Aber er soll nicht viele Worte machen, als ob Gott nicht schon wüßte, worum es geht. Gebet soll weder eine fromme Demonstration vor anderen noch eine mühselige Leistung vor Gott werden[19].

Statt für die Elite für alle

Es dürfte deutlich geworden sein: wiederum ist Jesus anders. Er, der kein Mann des Establishments und keiner der politischen Revolution war, wollte auch kein Vertreter der Emigration, kein asketischer Mönch sein. Er entsprach offensichtlich nicht der Rollenerwartung, die manche mit einem Heiligen oder heiligmäßigen Mann oder gar einem Propheten verbinden. Dafür war er nun doch in seiner Kleidung, seinen Eßgewohnheiten, seinem allgemeinen Verhalten – zu normal. Er ragte heraus, aber nicht durch einen esoterisch-frommen Lebensstil. Er ragte heraus durch seine Botschaft. Und diese besagte gerade das Gegenteil jener exklusiven, elitären Ideologie der »Söhne des Lichtes«: Nicht die Menschen können die Scheidung vollziehen. Nur Gott, der in die Herzen sieht, kann es. Jesus verkündet nicht ein Rachegericht über die Kinder der Welt und der Finsternis, nicht ein Reich für eine Elite von Vollkommenen. Er verkündet das *Reich der grenzenlosen Güte und bedingungslosen Gnade gerade für die Verlorenen und Elenden.* Gegenüber der recht finsteren Lehre von Qumran und dem strengen Bußberuf des Täufers erscheint Jesu Botschaft als eine ungemein erfreuliche Kunde. Ob Jesus selber schon das Wort »Evangelium« gebraucht hat oder nicht, ist schwierig festzustellen[20]. Was er zu sagen hatte, war jedenfalls nicht eine Drohbotschaft, sondern, im umfassendsten Sinn des Wortes, eine »Frohbotschaft«. Vor allem für die, die nicht Elite sind und es wissen.

Imitatio Christi? Die Schlußfolgerung scheint unvermeidbar: Die spätere anachoretisch-monastische Tradition könnte sich in ihrer Loslösung von der Welt und in der Form und Organisation ihres Lebens auf die Mönchsgemeinschaft von Qumran berufen. Auf Jesus kaum. Er hat keine äußere oder innere Emigration gefordert. Die sogenannten »Evangelischen Räte« als Lebensform – Eigentumsabgabe an die Gemeinschaft (»Armut«), Zölibat (»Keuschheit«), unbedingte Unterordnung unter den Willen eines Oberen (»Gehorsam«), alles abgesichert durch Gelübde (Eide) – gab es in Qumran, nicht in Jesu Jüngerschaft. Und für jede christliche Ordensgemeinschaft wird es mehr als früher, als diese Zusammenhänge und Unterschiede noch nicht so bekannt waren, eine Frage sein müssen, ob sie sich mehr auf Qumran oder auf Jesus berufen kann. Für Gemeinschaften und Basisgruppen aller Art zum besonderen Einsatz im Geiste nicht Qumrans, sondern Jesu ist gewiß auch heute Platz in der Christenheit.

Die ernsten und frommen Asketen des Klosters von Qumran müssen von Jesus, zumindest von seiner Kreuzigung, gehört haben. Sie, die für die Endzeit nach dem ankündenden Propheten sogar zwei Messiasse erwarteten – einen priesterlichen und einen königlichen, den geistlichen und den weltlichen Leiter der Heilsgemeinde –, sie, die in ihrer Regel schon die Sitzordnung für das messianische Mahl festgelegt hatten, bereiteten vielleicht Jesus den Weg, gingen aber letztlich an ihm vorüber. Sie hielten ihr hartes Leben in der glühenden Wüste durch und gingen knapp 40 Jahre später selber in den Tod. Als der große Krieg ausbrach, da fand sich der politische Radikalismus der Zeloten und der apolitische Radikalismus der Anachoreten; entgegengesetzte Radikalismen stehen unter dem Wort »Les extrèmes se touchent«. Schon immer freilich hatten sie sich in der Einsamkeit auf den Endkampf vorbereitet; die ebenfalls aufgefundene »Kriegsrolle« (1QM) gab für den heiligen Krieg genaue Anweisungen. So nahmen auch die Mönche am Kampf der Revolutionäre teil, der für sie der endzeitliche war. Die zehnte römische Legion unter dem späteren Kaiser Vespasian rückte im Jahre 68 auf ihrem Marsch von Cäsarea bis zum Toten Meer und nach Qumran vor. Damals müssen die Mönche ihre Handschriften verpackt und in den Höhlen versteckt haben. Sie haben sie nie mehr zurückgeholt. Sie müssen damals den Tod gefunden haben. Ein Posten der zehnten Legion wurde für einige Zeit in Qumran stationiert. Im Bar Kochba-Aufstand, als sich nochmals jüdische Partisanen in den übriggebliebenen Anlagen festsetzten, wurde Qumran endgültig zerstört.

Und was bleibt übrig? Wer sich nicht bedingungslos dem Establishment verschreiben und andererseits weder den politischen Radikalismus einer gewalttätigen Revolution noch den apolitischen Radikalismus der frommen Emigration übernehmen will, scheint nur noch eine Wahl zu haben: den Kompromiß.

4. Kompromiß?

Die sozialpolitischen Revolutionäre wie die mönchischen Emigranten machen mit der Gottesherrschaft konsequent ernst. In diesem bis an die »radix«, die Wurzel gehenden rücksichtslosen Willen zur Konsequenz, zur Ganzheit und Ungeteiltheit besteht ihr Radikalismus. Also eine saubere, eindeutige Lösung, politisch oder apolitisch, eine klare Endlösung: Weltrevolution oder Weltflucht. Gegenüber solch eindeutiger Lösung scheint es in der Tat nur die Zweideutigkeit, Doppelspurigkeit, Doppelbödigkeit, Halbheit zu geben: ein taktisches Lavieren zwischen den Etablierten und den Radikalismen. Das darauf verzichtet, der Wahrheit unbedingt treu zu bleiben, das Leben nach *einem* Maßstab zu gestalten, wirklich Vollkommenheit zu erreichen.

Die Frommen

Der Weg also der glücklichen Inkonsequenz, der legalen Harmonisierung, des diplomatischen Ausgleichs, des moralischen Kompromisses. Compromittere = zusammen versprechen, übereinkommen: Muß der Mensch nicht notgedrungen einen Ausgleich versuchen zwischen dem unbedingten göttlichen Gebot und seiner konkreten Situation? Gibt es nicht einen Zwang der Verhältnisse? Ist Politik – im großen wie im kleinen – nicht die Kunst des Möglichen? Du sollst, gewiß – aber im Rahmen des Möglichen. Ist nicht das der Weg Jesu?
   Der Weg des moralischen Kompromisses: das ist der Weg des *Pharisäismus*[1]. Man hat ihn schlechter gemacht, als er war. Schon in den Evangelien, wo die Pharisäer aus späterer polemischer Sicht öfters undifferenziert als Vertreter der Hypokrisie, als »Heuchler« hingestellt werden. Das hatte seine Gründe. Als einzige Partei hatten die Pharisäer die große Revolution gegen die Römer überlebt, die das Establishment ebenso wie die Radikalen politischer und apolitischer Richtung weggefegt hat. Auf dem Pharisäismus gründet das nun folgende talmudische und auch das heutige orthodoxe Judentum. Der Pharisäismus war somit als der einzige jüdische Gegner der jungen Christenheit übriggeblieben. Und dies schlug sich in den nach 70 geschriebenen Evangelien nieder. Gelobt hingegen über die Maßen wurden die Pharisäer von Josephus Flavius – selber bis in den

Namen hinein ein lebender Kompromiß –, der mit seinem späteren projüdischen Werk über die »jüdischen Altertümer« sein prorömisches Werk über den »jüdischen Krieg« kompensieren wollte.

Die Pharisäer dürfen also nicht einfach mit den Schriftgelehrten identifiziert werden. Auch das priesterliche Establishment hatte seine theologischen und juristischen, eben sadduzäischen Experten für alle Fragen der Gesetzesauslegung, hatte seine Hoftheologen. Die »Pharisäer« sind von ihrem Namen her gerade nicht »Heuchler«, sondern die »Abgesonderten« (aramäisch »perischajja« vom hebräischen »peruschim«). Sie nannten sich auch gerne die Frommen, Gerechten, Gottesfürchtigen, Armen. Der Name »die Abgesonderten« – wohl von Außenstehenden zuerst gebraucht – hätte auch gut auf die Essener und Qumranmönche gepaßt. Vermutlich stellen diese nur so etwas wie den radikalen Flügel der pharisäischen Bewegung dar. Von der Machtpolitik und Weltlichkeit der nun etablierten makkabäischen Freiheitskämpfer, vom Haus der Makkabäer, dessen späte Nachfahrin, Mariamne, den Begründer des neuen herodianischen Herrscherhauses heiraten sollte, hatten sich, wie wir hörten, *alle* »Frommen« schon früh abgewendet. Sie wollten ihr Leben nach der Tora, nach dem Gesetz Gottes gestalten. Nur wollten die einen den Radikalismus der anderen nicht mitmachen. So spalteten sich die Frommen in Essener und Pharisäer. Nach einer blutigen Auseinandersetzung mit dem Makkabäer Alexander Jannäus (103–76), der sich als erster wieder den Königstitel zugelegt hatte, verzichteten die Pharisäer auf alle gewaltsame Änderung der Verhältnisse. Durch Gebet und frommes Leben wollten sie sich auf die Wende vorbereiten, die Gott selber herbeiführen wird. Eine Laienbewegung von etwa 6000 Mitgliedern – aber sehr einflußreich unter einer Gesamtbevölkerung von vielleicht einer halben Million –, lebten sie mitten unter den anderen, wenn auch in festen Gemeinschaften. Meist Handwerker und Kaufleute, bildeten sie unter der Leitung von Schriftgelehrten »Genossenschaften«. Politisch waren die Pharisäer aus der Zeit Jesu gemäßigt, obgleich manche mit den Zeloten sympathisierten.

Man darf nicht vergessen: Der von Jesus als Exempel herangezogene Pharisäer heuchelte nicht[2]. Er war ein ehrlicher, frommer Mann und sprach die reine Wahrheit. Er hatte alles getan, was er sagte. Die Pharisäer waren von vorbildlicher Moral und genossen entsprechendes Ansehen bei denen, die es damit nicht so weit brachten. Auf zwei Dinge kam es ihnen bei der Gesetzerfüllung vor allem an: die Reinheitsvorschriften und die Zehntpflicht.

Die für die Priester bestimmten *Reinheitsvorschriften* verlangten sie auch im Alltag von allen Mitgliedern, die ja bis auf verhältnismäßig wenige Nicht-Priester waren. Auf diese Weise gaben sie sich als priesterliches Heilsvolk der Endzeit zu erkennen[3]. Also nicht um der Hygiene und des Anstandes willen wuschen sie sich die Hände, sondern um der kultischen Reinheit willen. Bestimmte Tierarten, Blut, Berührung einer Leiche oder eines Kadavers, körperlicher Ausfluß und anderes ließen die kultische Reinheit verlieren. Durch ein Reinigungsbad oder gar eine Wartefrist mußte sie wiedergewonnen werden. Für das Beten muß man reine Hände haben. Deshalb die große Bedeutung des Händewaschens vor jeder Mahlzeit. Deshalb das bewußte Reinhalten von Bechern und Schüsseln.

Das Gebot der *Verzehntung* – von allem, was man erntet und erwirbt, zehn Prozent zum Unterhalt des priesterlichen Stammes Levi und des Tempels abzugeben – war im Volk stark vernachlässigt. Um so ernster nahmen es die Pharisäer. Von allem irgendwie möglichen, selbst von Gemüse und Küchenkräutern, wurden zehn Prozent abgesondert und den Priestern und Leviten abgeliefert.

Dies alles betrachteten die Pharisäer als Gebote. Aber über alle Gebote hinaus taten sie viel Freiwilliges. »*Werke der Übergebühr*« (Opera supererogatoria) hat dies eine spätere christliche Moral genannt, die damit pharisäische Vorstellungen wiederaufnahm: an sich nicht geforderte, sondern zusätzliche, überschüssige gute Werke, die für die große Abrechnung gegen die Verschuldungen des Menschen aufgerechnet werden konnten, damit sich die Waage der göttlichen Gerechtigkeit zum Guten hin neigt. Bußwerke, freiwilliges Fasten (zur Sühne der Sünden des Volkes zweimal in der Woche, montags und donnerstags), Almosen (Mildtätigkeit zu Gottes Wohlgefallen), pünktliches Einhalten der drei täglichen Gebetsstunden (wo man gerade stand) waren für den Ausgleich der moralischen Bilanz besonders geeignet. Und in der Tat: ist das alles so verschieden von dem, was eine spätere Christenheit (in diesem Fall besonders katholischer Prägung) als »christlich« ausgegeben hat? Jesus – zwischen dem Establishment und den Radikalismen – konnte doch wohl schlecht anders, denn sich zu dieser Partei schlagen, der Partei der wahrhaft Frommen?

Aber merkwürdig genug, mit dieser frommen Moral scheint Jesus seine Schwierigkeiten zu haben. Für sie ist der *Kompromiß* bezeichnend. An sich meint man es furchtbar ernst mit Gottes Geboten. Man tut ja mehr als das Geforderte und Gebotene. Man nimmt sie peinlich genau und baut deshalb einen ganzen Zaun von weiteren Geboten um Gottes Gebote: zur Absicherung gegen die überall drohenden Sünden, zur Anwendung auf die kleinsten Angelegenheiten des Alltags, zur Entscheidung bei allen Unsicherheiten, was Sünde ist und was nicht. Man muß doch genau wissen, woran man sich zu halten hat: wie weit man am Sabbat gehen darf, was man herumtragen, was man arbeiten darf, ob man sich verheiraten, ob man ein am Sabbat gelegtes Ei essen darf ... In eine einzige Rahmenvorschrift ließ sich ein ganzes Gewebe von Detailvorschriften einsetzen. Man denke an das Waschen der Hände: zu ganz bestimmter Zeit, bis zum Handgelenk, bei korrekter Haltung der Hände, in zwei Güssen (der erste beseitigt die Unreinheit der Hände, der zweite die unrein gewordenen Tropfen des ersten Gusses).

So lernte man Mücken seihen: eine raffinierte Technik der Frömmigkeit. Und es häufte sich Gebot an Gebot, Vorschrift an Vorschrift: ein Moralsystem, welches das ganze Leben des Einzelnen wie der Gesellschaft einzufangen vermag. Ein Eifer für das *Gesetz*, dessen Rückseite die Angst vor der überall lauernden Sünde ist. In den heiligen Schriften ist das Gesetz im engen Sinn (= die fünf Bücher Moses = der Pentateuch = ›Tora‹), bei dem ethische und rituelle Gebote als gleichwertig angesehen werden, wichtiger als die Propheten. Und zum geschriebenen Gesetz Gottes, der ›Tora‹, tritt gleichberechtigt – pari pietatis affectu anzunehmen[4] – die mündliche Überlieferung, die ›Halacha‹, die »Überlieferung der Alten«, das Werk der Schriftgelehrten. Auf diese Weise ließ sich auch eine feste Lehre von der Auferstehung der Toten gegen die Sadduzäer entwickeln. Und wichtig wird bei allem das Lehramt der Schriftgelehrten, die sich um die komplizierte Anwendung der Einzelgebote kümmern und für jeden Fall sagen können, was der einfache Mensch zu tun hat. Für jeden Fall, für jeden Kasus: »Kasuistik« hat man diese Kunst später genannt, und große Bände christlicher Moraltheologen sind voll davon. Eine Aufteilung, eine Einschachtelung des ganzen Alltags vom Morgen bis zum Abend in gesetzliche Fälle.

Eine menschenfreundliche Kunst übrigens für viele der Pharisäer: man möchte wirklich helfen. Man möchte das Gesetz *praktikabel* machen, durch geschickte Anpassung an die Gegenwart. Man möchte das Gewissen entlasten, ihm Sicherheit geben. Man möchte genau angeben, wie weit man gehen kann, ohne zu sündigen. Man möchte Auswege anbieten, wo es allzu schwierig wird. Einen Tunnel, nachdem man einen ganzen Berg von Geboten zwischen Gott und Mensch aufgeschüttet hat (nach einem Wort Johannes' XXIII. an katholische Kirchenrechtler). So ist man streng und milde zugleich, sehr traditionell und doch sehr wirklichkeitsnahe. Man insistiert auf dem Gesetz, liefert aber Entschuldigungen und Dispensen mit. Man nimmt das Gebot wörtlich, aber interpretiert das Wort elastisch. Man geht den Weg des Gesetzes, hat aber die Umwege eingeplant. So kann man das Gesetz halten, ohne zu sündigen. Am Sabbat darf man nicht arbeiten (39 am Sabbat verbotene Arbeiten hat die Schriftgelehrsamkeit zusammengetragen), aber ausnahmsweise, bei Lebensgefahr, darf man ihn entweihen. Am Sabbat darf man nichts außer Haus tragen, aber die Höfe mehrerer Häuser lassen sich als gemeinsamer Hausbezirk verstehen. Einen Ochsen, der am Sabbat in die Grube fiel, darf man – anders als in Qumran – herausholen. Kann man da nicht verstehen, daß das Volk diese Gesetzesinterpretation, die das harte sadduzäische Recht der auf dem Sabbat herumreitenden Tempelpriester erweichte, mit Dankbarkeit aufnahm? Die Pharisäer – nicht wie die sadduzäischen Hierarchen im fernen Tempel, sondern nahe dem Volk in Städten und Dörfern, nahe der Synagoge, dem Lehr- und Gebetshaus – sind so etwas wie die Führer der Volkspartei. Nicht als konservative Reaktion verstanden sie sich (die war im Tempel ansässig), sondern als moralische Erneuerungsbewegung.

Nur gegenüber denen, die das Gesetz nicht kannten oder nicht wollten, war man unerbittlich. Da war »*Absonderung*« unumgänglich. Notwendig war dies nicht nur gegenüber dem hellenisierenden Jerusalemer Establishment. Auch gegenüber dem »am-ha-arez«, den »Leuten vom Lande«, die des Gesetzes nicht kundig waren und es folglich auch nicht praktizierten, beziehungsweise als hart arbeitende Menschen sich um kultische Reinheit wenig kümmern *konnten*. »Absonderung« vor allem gegenüber allen Gattungen öffentlicher Sünder, die das Gesetz nicht halten *wollten:* natürlich die Prostituierten, aber nicht weniger die Zollpächter. Denn die Besatzungsmacht übergab die Zollstationen dem Meistbietenden, der sich dann seinerseits trotz offizieller Tarife schadlos halten durfte. »Zöllner« – gleichbedeutend mit Betrüger und Halunke: Leute, mit denen man sich unmöglich an den gleichen Tisch setzen konnte. Alle diese Gottlosen halten das Kommen des Reiches Gottes und des Messias auf. Würde das ganze Volk in Reinheit und Heiligkeit treu und genau wie die Pharisäer das Gesetz halten, dann käme der Messias, würde die zerstreuten Stämme Israels sammeln und das Reich Gottes aufrichten. Das Gesetz ist doch Zeichen der Erwählung, ist Gnade!

Kein Gesetzesfrommer

Jesus schien den Pharisäern *nahe* und war ihnen doch unendlich *fern*. Auch er verschärfte das Gesetz, wie die Antithesen der Bergpredigt beweisen: schon Zorn bedeutet Mord[5], schon ehebrecherisches Begehren Ehebruch[6]. Aber meinte er damit Kasuistik? Auf der anderen Seite war Jesus von erstaunlicher Laxheit: Es muß doch die ganze gesamte Moral untergraben, wenn der verlorene und verlotterte Sohn beim Vater schließlich besser dastehen soll als der brav daheimgebliebene[7], ja, wenn der Zollgauner bei Gott besser abschneiden soll als der pharisäische Fromme, der doch wohl wirklich nicht ist wie die anderen Menschen, diese Betrüger und Ehebrecher[8]. Solche Reden – die vom verlorenen Schaf und vom verlorenen Groschen inbegriffen[9] – sind moralisch subversiv und destruktiv und eine Beleidigung für jeden anständigen Israeliten.

Mit den Pharisäern mußte sich der Konflikt besonders zuspitzen, weil die Gemeinsamkeit besonders groß war. Wie die Pharisäer verhielt sich Jesus gegenüber dem Jerusalemer Priester-Establishment distanziert, lehnte er die zelotische Revolution ebenso ab, wie die äußere oder innere Emigration. Wie die Pharisäer wollte er fromm sein inmitten der Welt, lebte, wirkte, diskutierte er mitten unter dem Volk, lehrte er in der Synagoge. Ist er nicht doch so etwas wie ein Rabbi, der im übrigen sogar wiederholt im Haus eines Pharisäers zu Gast war[10] und gerade von Pharisäern vor Nachstellungen des Herodes gewarnt wurde[11]? Wie die Pharisäer hielt er sich grundsätzlich an das Gesetz, griff es jedenfalls nicht frontal an, indem er seine Abschaffung oder Aufhebung forderte. Nicht aufzulösen, sondern zu erfüllen war er gekommen[12]. War er nicht vielleicht doch – und einzelne jüdische Gelehrte der Gegenwart suchen ihn so zu sehen[13] – schlicht ein Pharisäer besonders liberaler Art, ein im Grund frommer, gesetzestreuer, wenn auch außerordentlich großzügiger Moralist? Gibt es nicht bei den Rabbinen Parallelen zu manchen seiner Sätze? Doch Gegenfrage: Warum kam es dann zu einer wachsenden Feindschaft auch der pharisäischen Kreise gegen Jesus?

Parallelen – im jüdischen und manchmal auch im hellenistischen Bereich – gibt es tatsächlich des öfteren. Nur, eine Schwalbe macht noch keinen Frühling, und der vereinzelte Satz eines vereinzelten Rabbinen noch keine Geschichte. Besonders wenn dem einen Satz tausend Sätze anderer entgegenstehen, wie etwa in der Sabbatfrage. Für uns hier ist nur von zweitrangiger Wichtigkeit zu wissen, wer was wo zuerst gesagt hat. Von erstrangiger Wichtigkeit ist zu wissen, von welchen Voraussetzungen her, in welchem Gesamtzusammenhang, mit welcher Radikalität, mit welchen Konsequenzen für den Verkündigenden und die Hörenden etwas gesagt wurde. Es kann ja nicht von ungefähr kommen, warum gerade dieser eine Jude Geschichte gemacht und den Lauf der Welt und die Stellung des Judentums grundlegend verändert hat.

Und da muß nun doch – in Abgrenzung gegen das Judentum und ein rejudaisiertes Christentum – unmißverständlich gesagt werden: Jesus war *kein frommer, gesetzestreuer Moralist*. Es ist unbestreitbar: sosehr der geschichtliche Jesus im ganzen durchaus gesetzestreu lebte, sowenig schreckte er dort, wo es ihm darauf ankam, vor gesetzwidrigem Verhalten zurück. Ja, er stellte sich, ohne das Gesetz aufzuheben, faktisch *über* das Gesetz. Auf drei, auch von kritischsten Exegeten anerkannte Tatbestände müssen wir unser Augenmerk heften[14].

– Keine rituelle Tabuisierung: *Nichts, was von außen in den Menschen hineinkommt, kann ihn verunreinigen, sondern was aus dem Menschen herauskommt, das verunreinigt den Menschen*[15]. *Wer so spricht, kritisiert nicht nur, wie etwa auch in Qumran, eine veräußerlichte Reinheitspraxis, der das Herz fehlt. Er verschärft nicht, wie wiederum in Qumran, die Reinheitsvorschriften. Hier war vielmehr ein im Judentum unerhörter Satz gesprochen worden, der von allen auf rituelle Korrektheit Bedachten als massiver Angriff verstanden werden mußte. Selbst wenn er vielleicht nur in einer bestimmten Situation gesprochen und nicht programmatisch (mehr gegen die mündliche Reinheitshalacha als gegen die Reinheitsbestimmungen der Tora selber) gemeint war: Er stellte doch alle*

243

Reinheitsvorschriften als bedeutungslos hin und setzte die alttestamentliche Unterscheidung von reinen und unreinen Tieren und Speisen außer Kurs. Jesus ist an kultischer Reinheit und ritueller Korrektheit nicht interessiert. Reinheit vor Gott schenkt allein die Reinheit des Herzens! Hier war letztlich jene Unterscheidung in Frage gestellt, die die Voraussetzung bildet für das alttestamentliche und überhaupt das antike Kultwesen: die Unterscheidung zwischen einem profanen und einem sakralen Bereich[16].

– Kein Fastenasketismus: *Während der Täufer nicht aß und trank, ißt und trinkt Jesus – der genannte Vorwurf des Fressens und Saufens hängt mit dem Fasten zusammen. Daß Jesus das obligatorische Fasten am Versöhnungstag und anderen Trauertagen nicht gehalten hätte, wird ihm nirgendwo vorgeworfen. Aber das freiwillige Privatfasten, wie von den Pharisäern anscheinend auch von den Johannesjüngern eingehalten, hat er nicht geübt: die Hochzeitsleute können nicht fasten, solange der Bräutigam bei ihnen ist[17]. Das Rätselwort meint: Jetzt ist Freudenzeit und nicht Fastenzeit; das Fasten wird zum Festen, weil das von der Endzeit erhoffte Fest schon beginnt. Mit solcher Lehre mußte Jesus erneut starken Anstoß erregen. Offensichtlich hielt er nichts von dieser Art Buße, Entsagung, Selbststrafe, um Gottes Huld zu gewinnen und Verdienste zu erlangen. Ein offener Angriff also auf das überschüssige gute Werk, das opus supererogatorium, welches Jesus in der Parabel vom Pharisäer und Zöllner tatsächlich als nicht rechtfertigend hinstellt[18].*

– Keine Sabbatängstlichkeit: *Mehr noch als andere Gesetzesübertretungen ist diese bezeugt. Gleichsam als klassischer Fall: Jesus hat notorisch die Sabbatruhe verletzt. Nicht nur das Ährenraufen seiner Jünger am Sabbat hat er geduldet[19], sondern auch wiederholt am Sabbat geheilt[20]. Und damit verletzte er das noch heute in der jüdischen Frömmigkeitspraxis fühlbarste und damals vom Tempel-Establishment ebenso wie von den Zeloten, den Essenern und Qumranmönchen entschieden verteidigte Gebot: das Unterscheidungsmerkmal Israels gegenüber der Heidenwelt! Und zwar tat er es nicht nur bei Lebensgefahr, sondern wo er leicht anders gekonnt hätte. Keine einzige seiner Heilungen hätte nicht ebenso am nächsten Tag erfolgen können. Auch hier interessieren Jesus nicht die einzelnen strengeren oder weicheren Interpretationen, das ganze Wenn und Aber der Kasuistik. Es werden nicht nur*

Ausnahmen von der Regel zugestanden, sondern die Regel selbst wird in Frage gestellt. Er spricht den Menschen eine grundsätzliche Freiheit gegenüber dem Sabbat zu mit dem zweifellos authentischen Wort: Der Sabbat ist um des Menschen willen da und nicht der Mensch um des Sabbats willen[21]. Für jüdische Ohren mußte eine solche Aussage in höchstem Maß skandalös klingen. Denn der Sabbat ist doch Gottesdienst par excellence: Er ist nicht für den Menschen, sondern für Gott da, der ihn nach zeitgenössischer jüdischer Auffassung in seinem Himmel mit allen Engeln zusammen mit ritueller Genauigkeit einhält. Wenn dagegen schon mal ein Rabbi irgendwo gesagt hat, der Sabbat sei den Juden und nicht die Juden dem Sabbat übergeben, so ist dies nur eine der genannten einsamen Schwalben; solchem Satz kommt keine grundsätzliche Bedeutung zu; er hatte eine andere Tendenz und zeitigte kein sabbatkritisches Verhalten. Bei Jesus aber ist der Sabbat nicht mehr religiöser Selbstzweck, sondern der Mensch ist Zweck des Sabbats. Am Sabbat soll nicht nichts, sondern das Rechte getan werden: und wenn schon Tiere gerettet werden dürfen, dann erst recht Menschen[22]. Damit ist es aber grundsätzlich dem Menschen anheimgestellt, wann er den Sabbat hält und wann nicht. Das hat Bedeutung für die Beobachtung auch der übrigen Gebote. Das Gesetz wird zweifellos nicht bekämpft, aber der Mensch faktisch zum Maß des Gesetzes gemacht. Dem orthodoxen Juden erscheinen hier die Dinge auf den Kopf gestellt.

Soviel dürfte jedenfalls zum historischen Kern der Überlieferung gehören. Wie anstößig die ganze Einstellung Jesu zur traditionellen Frömmigkeit war, ersieht man daraus, auf welche Weise die Überlieferung mit den Sabbatworten Jesu umging. Man läßt aus: Mattäus und Lukas verschweigen den obigen revolutionären Satz. Man fügt zweitrangige Begründungen hinzu: Schriftworte und Verweise auf alttestamentliche Vorbilder, die doch nicht beweisen, was zu beweisen wäre[23]. Man überhöht die Texte christologisch: Nicht einfach der Mensch, sondern der Menschensohn – so wird schon bei Markus hinzugefügt – ist der Herr des Sabbats[24].

Wieviel von den übrigen Vorwürfen an die Adresse der Pharisäer auf Jesus selber zurückgeht[25], läßt sich schwer entscheiden. Vorgeworfen wird den Pharisäern, daß sie zwar zehn Prozent der Küchenkräuter ablieferten, aber Gottes große Forderungen nach Gerechtigkeit, Barmherzigkeit und Treue ignorieren: sie seihen Mücken, aber schlucken Kamele[26]. Weiter, daß sie die Reinheitsvorschriften minuziös erfüllen, aber ihr eigenes Inneres unrein ist: schön weiß getünchte Gräber, voll von Totengebein[27]. Weiter daß sie Missionseifer an den Tag legen, aber die Menschen, die sie gewinnen, verderben: Proselyten, die zu doppelt schlimmen Höllensöhnen werden[28]. Schließlich, daß sie Geld für die Armen geben, die Gebetsstunden sorgfältig einhalten, aber daß ihre Frömmigkeit ihrem Geltungsbedürfnis und ihrer Eitelkeit dient: ein Schauspielern, das seinen Lohn bereits erhalten hat[29]. Zu einem schönen Teil gelten auch die von Jesus an die Adresse der Schriftgelehrten gerichteten Vorwürfe den Pharisäern: Sie legen den Menschen schwere Lasten auf und rühren sie selber mit keinem Finger an[30]. Sie suchen Ehren, Titel, Begrüßungen und maßen sich Gottes Stelle an[31]. Sie bauen den früheren Propheten Grabmäler und töten die gegenwärtigen[32]. Kurz: Sie haben das Wissen, aber leben nicht danach.

Wichtiger als diese Einzelvorwürfe ist das, was dahinter steckt: Was hat Jesus eigentlich gegen diese Art von Frömmigkeit? Jesus verkündet nicht ein Reich Gottes, das vom Menschen durch exakte Gesetzeserfüllung und bessere Moral errichtet, herbeigeführt, aufgebaut, ertrotzt werden könnte. Moralische Aufrüstung, welcher Art auch immer, schafft es nicht. Jesus verkündet ein *Reich, das durch Gottes befreiende und beglückende Tat geschaffen wird*. Gottes Reich ist Gottes Werk, seine Herrschaft eine befreiende und beglückende Herrschaft. Den Ernst der moralischen Bemühungen hat Jesus keineswegs nur ironisiert. Gewiß, er braucht auffällig selten die Worte »Sünde« und »sündigen«. Er ist kein pessimistischer Sündenprediger à la Abraham a Santa Clara. Aber er ist auch kein aufklärerischer Optimist à la Rousseau, der den Menschen als von Natur gut ansieht und etwas gegen Sündenbewußtsein und moralische Anstrengung hätte. Im Gegenteil: nach ihm *verharmlosen* seine Gegner *die Sünde*. In zweifacher Hinsicht[33]:

- *Durch* Kasuistik *wird die einzelne Sünde* isoliert: *Die Forderung des Gehorsams gegenüber Gott wird in detaillierte Einzelakte aufgesplittert. Statt um die falschen Grundhaltungen, Grundtendenzen, Grundgesinnungen geht es in erster Linie um die einzelnen moralischen Entgleisungen. Eine Beichtspiegelmoral! Diese Einzelakte werden registriert und katalogisiert: in jedem Gebot schwere und leichte Verfehlungen, Schwachheitssünden und Bosheitssünden. Die Tiefendimension der Sünde kommt nicht in den Blick.*
- *Von Jesus wird die Kasuistik gerade dadurch erledigt, daß er bei der Wurzel einsetzt: nicht erst beim Akt des Mordens, sondern bei der zornigen Gesinnung; nicht erst beim Akt des Ehebruchs, sondern bei der ehebrecherischen Begehrlichkeit; nicht erst beim Meineid, sondern beim unwahren Wort. Die von den Zeitgenossen bagatellisierte Zungensünde wird als das den Menschen Verunreinigende herausgestellt. Nie steckt er den Bezirk ab, innerhalb dessen Sünde ist, während außerhalb Sünde nicht mehr zu befürchten wäre. Er gibt Beispiele, aber keine Definition von Einzelfällen, in denen so oder anders verfahren werden müßte. An einer Katalogisierung der Sünden ist er nicht interessiert. Nicht einmal an der Unterscheidung von leichten und schweren, oder gar vergebbaren und unvergebbaren Sünden. Während manche Rabbinen Mord, Unzucht, Abfall, Mißachtung der Tora als unvergebbare Sünden ansehen, anerkennt Jesus nur eine einzige, die Sünde gegen den Heiligen Geist[34]: unvergebbar ist nur die Ablehnung der Vergebung[35].*
- *Durch das* Verdienstdenken *wird die Sünde* kompensiert: *Ihrem Gewicht wird das Gewicht der Verdienste entgegengesetzt, durch die sie sogar aufgehoben werden kann. Und nicht nur die eigenen Verdienste, sondern auch die anderer (der Väter, der Gemeinschaft, des ganzen Volkes) lassen sich da bequem in Anspruch nehmen. Bei diesem Verlust- und Gewinngeschäft kommt es letztlich nur darauf an, daß man nicht schließlich und endlich ein Defizit aufweist, sondern möglichst viel Verdienst für den Himmel kapitalisiert hat.*
- *Für* Jesus *gibt es überhaupt kein Verdienst[36]. Wenn Jesus vom »Lohn« spricht – er tut es, anknüpfend an die Sprechweise seiner Zeit, sehr oft –, dann meint er nicht ein »Verdienst«: nicht einen Leistungslohn, auf den der Mensch aufgrund seines Verdienstes einen Anspruch hat, sondern einen Gnadenlohn, der ihm von Gott aufgrund seines eigenen Willens ohne allen*

Anspruch geschenkt wird. Nicht die Verrechnung von Ver-
diensten gilt hier, wie die Parabel vom gleichen Lohn für alle
Weinbergarbeiter[37] drastisch zeigt. Sondern die Regel von
Gottes Barmherzigkeit, die gegen alle bürgerliche Gerechtig-
keit einem jeden – er sei Langarbeiter oder Kurzarbeiter – voll
gibt: mehr als er verdient. So soll der Mensch ruhig vergessen,
was er Gutes getan hat[38]. Auch dort, wo er meint, nichts
verdient zu haben, wird ihm vergolten[39]. Gott vergilt wirklich
– das ist mit der Rede vom Lohn gemeint. Auch jeden Becher
Wasser, den der Mensch vergessen hat. Der von Verdienst
spricht, schaut auf seine eigene Leistung; der von Vergeltung,
auf Gottes Treue.

Wer die Sünde durch Kasuistik und Verdienstdenken verharmlost, wird unkritisch gegenüber sich selbst: selbstgefällig, selbstsicher, selbstgerecht. Und das heißt zugleich: überkritisch, ungerecht, hart und lieblos gegenüber den anderen, die anders sind,
den »Sündern«. Mit ihnen vergleicht man sich. Vor ihnen will
man bestehen, von ihnen als fromm und moralisch anerkannt
werden, ihnen gegenüber setzt man sich ab. Hier und nicht nur
an der Oberfläche wurzelt der durchgängig an die Pharisäer
gerichtete Vorwurf der Heuchelei. Wer unkritisch von sich selber denkt, nimmt sich selber zu wichtig und nimmt den Mitmenschen und vor allem Gott zu wenig wichtig. So entfremdet sich
der daheimgebliebene Sohn dem Vater[40]. So weiß der Pharisäer
Simon von Vergebung und weiß doch nicht, was Vergebung ist[41].
  Was stellt sich da eigentlich zwischen Gott und den Menschen?
Paradoxerweise des Menschen eigene Moral und Frömmigkeit:
sein raffiniert ausgeklügelter Moralismus und seine hochgezüch-
tete Frömmigkeitstechnik. Es sind nicht – wie die Zeitgenossen
meinten – die Zollgauner, die es am schwersten haben, sich zu
bekehren, weil sie gar nicht wissen können, wen sie alles betrogen haben und wieviel sie zurückerstatten müßten. Nein, es sind
die Frommen, die selbstsicher der Bekehrung gar nicht zu bedürfen scheinen. Sie sind Jesu ärgste Feinde geworden. Ihnen, nicht
den großen Sündern, gelten die meisten Gerichtsworte der Evangelien. Nicht Mörder, Gauner, Betrüger und Ehebrecher, sondern die Hochmoralischen haben ihn schließlich erledigt. Sie
meinten, Gott damit einen Dienst zu erweisen.
  Der pharisäische Geist hat sich durchgehalten. Militärischer
Sieger in der großen Auseinandersetzung war Rom. Der Zelotis-
mus war gescheitert, der Essenismus ausgerottet, der Sadduzäis-

mus ohne Tempel und Tempeldienst. Der Pharisäismus aber überlebte die Katastrophe des Jahres 70. Nur die Schriftgelehrten blieben als Führer des geknechteten Volkes übrig. Und so entstand aus dem Pharisäismus das spätere normative Judentum, das sich aufgrund eines – vielfach modifizierten und akkommodierten – »Abgesondertseins« inmitten der Welt allen Anfeindungen zum Trotz am Leben erhalten und den jüdischen Staat nach beinahe 2000 Jahren wieder aufgerichtet hat. Aber auch und manchmal noch mehr im Christentum lebt der Pharisäismus weiter – im Widerspruch allerdings zu Jesus selbst.

Provokatorisch nach allen Seiten

Establishment, Revolution, Emigration, Kompromiß: Jesus in einem *Koordinatenkreuz*, dessen vier Bezugspunkte auch heute, in einer durchweg verschiedenen geschichtlichen Situation, ihren Sinn nicht verloren haben. Von gesellschaftlicher Bedingtheit darf auch der Theologe nicht nur abstrakt reden – im Zusammenhang mit Jesus oft geschehen gerade von solchen, die die gesellschaftliche Bedeutung der christlichen Botschaft betonen. Deshalb war es wichtig, Jesus von Nazaret, so konkret wie in Kürze möglich, in seinem gesellschaftlichen Kontext zu sehen: wie er wirklich war. Aber auch zugleich: wie er ist, nämlich wie er – bei aller Fremdheit – auch heute in unserem gesellschaftlichen Kontext bedeutsam werden kann. Eine solche systematische Ortsbestimmung vermeidet möglichst beides: die unaktuelle Historisierung und die unhistorische Aktualisierung. Positiv: sie berücksichtigt zugleich die *historische Distanz* und die *geschichtliche Relevanz*. So vermag sie bei allen Variablen gewichtige Konstanten zu entdecken.

War das bisherige Ergebnis nicht merkwürdig? Jesus ließ sich offensichtlich nirgendwo einordnen: weder bei den Herrschenden noch bei den Rebellierenden, weder bei den Moralisierenden noch bei den Stillen im Lande. Er erwies sich als provokatorisch – aber nach rechts und links. Von keiner Partei gedeckt, herausfordernd nach allen Seiten: »der Mann, der alle Schemen sprengt«[42]. Kein Philosoph und kein Politiker, kein Priester und kein Sozialreformer. Ein Genie, ein Held, ein Heiliger? Oder ein Reformator? Aber ist er nicht radikaler als ein Re-formator? Ein Prophet? Aber ist ein »letzter«, unüberbietbarer Prophet noch ein Prophet? Die übliche Typologie scheint zu versagen. Von verschiedensten Typen scheint er etwas zu haben (vielleicht am meisten vom Propheten und vom Reformator), um gerade keinem von ihnen zuzugehören. Er ist von anderem Rang: Gott anscheinend näher als die Priester. Der Welt gegenüber freier als die Asketen. Moralischer als die Moralisten. Revolutionärer als die Revolutionäre. So hat er Tiefen und Weiten, die anderen fehlen. Offensichtlich schwer zu verstehen und kaum ganz zu durchschauen, für Feinde und Freunde. Immer wieder neu zeigt sich: *Jesus ist anders!* Bei allen Parallelen im einzelnen erweist sich der geschichtliche Jesus als im ganzen völlig *unverwechselbar* – damals und heute.

Als Nebenergebnis dieses Kapitels verdient festgehalten zu werden, wie oberflächlich es ist, alle »*Religionsstifter*« in eine Reihe zu stellen, als ob sie im Grund nicht nur verwechselt, sondern gar ausgewechselt werden könnten. Ganz abgesehen davon, daß Jesus von Nazaret keine Religion stiften wollte – es dürfte deutlich geworden sein, daß der geschichtliche Jesus weder mit Mose noch mit Buddha, weder mit Kung-futse noch mit Mohammed verwechselt werden kann.

Um es knapp anzudeuten: Jesus war kein am Hof Gebildeter wie anscheinend Mose, war kein Königssohn wie Buddha. Aber er war auch kein Gelehrter und Politiker wie Kung-futse und kein reicher Kaufmann wie Mohammed. Gerade weil seine Herkunft so unbedeutend, ist seine bleibende Bedeutsamkeit so erstaunlich. Wie *verschieden* ist doch Jesu Botschaft

- *von der unbedingten Geltung des immer mehr ausgebauten geschriebenen Gesetzes (Mose);*
- *vom asketischen Rückzug in mönchische Versenkung innerhalb der geregelten Gemeinschaft eines Ordens (Buddha);*
- *von der gewaltsam revolutionären Welteroberung durch Kampf gegen die Ungläubigen und Errichtung theokratischer Staaten (Mohammed);*
- *von der Erneuerung der traditionellen Moral und der etablierten Gesellschaft gemäß einem ewigen Weltgesetz im Geist einer aristokratischen Ethik (Kung-futse).*

Offensichtlich geht es hier nicht nur um einige mehr oder weniger zufällige Möglichkeiten, sondern um einige höchst gewichtige *Grundoptionen* oder *Grundpositionen*: Im *zeitgeschichtlichen* Koordinatenkreuz Jesu scheinen sich einige der allgemein *religiösen* Grundpositionen zu spiegeln, die sich als solche oder in verwandelter Form als säkularisierte Grundpositionen bis heute durchgehalten haben.

Die Wahrheit der anderen Religionen ist auch im Christentum zur Geltung und sogar neu zur Geltung zu bringen. Davon ist nichts zurückzunehmen. Das Christentum hat schließlich nicht nur von Platon, Aristoteles und der Stoa, sondern auch von den hellenistischen Mysterienkulten und der römischen Staatsreligion, kaum aber etwas von Indien, China und Japan gelernt. Eine Vermischung jedoch aller Religionen läßt sich von dem, der sich auf diesen Jesus beruft, nicht rechtfertigen. Bereits Gesagtes bestätigt sich hier: Die einzelnen großen Gestalten lassen sich nicht auswechseln, ihre Wege vom einen und selben Menschen nicht zugleich gehen, Welttilgung (Buddha) und Weltwerdung (Kung-futse), Weltherrschaft (Mohammed) und Weltkrise (Jesus) nicht zugleich anvisieren[43]. Jesus von Nazaret kann nicht als Chiffre für eine Allerweltsreligion, kann nicht als Etikette für einen älteren oder neueren Synkretismus dienen.

Doch mit all dem bisher Gesagten ist die Gestalt Jesu erst in mehr negativer Abgrenzung umrissen. Die positive Frage wurde bisher mehr indirekt ausgesprochen: Was bestimmte ihn eigentlich? Was ist seine Mitte?

II. Die Sache Gottes

Nicht nach Jesu Bewußtsein, seiner Psyche wird hier gefragt; darüber verraten die Quellen nichts, wie des öfteren zu betonen war. Aber nach der Mitte seiner Verkündigung und seines Verhaltens läßt sich fragen. Wofür setzte er sich ein? Was wollte er eigentlich?

1. Die Mitte

Wie grundlegend dies ist, wird erst später deutlich werden: Nicht sich selbst verkündet Jesus. Nicht er selbst steht im Vordergrund. Er kommt nicht und sagt: »Ich bin der Gottessohn, glaubt an mich.« Wie jene noch dem Kelsos bekannten Wanderprediger und Gottesmänner, die mit dem Anspruch auftraten: »Ich bin Gott oder Gottes Sohn oder göttlicher Geist. Gekommen bin ich, denn der Weltuntergang steht vor der Tür ... Selig, der mich jetzt anbetet[1]!« Vielmehr tritt seine Person zurück hinter der Sache, die er vertritt. Und was ist diese Sache? Mit einem Satz läßt sich sagen: *Die Sache Jesu ist die Sache Gottes in der Welt.* Es ist heute Mode herauszustellen, daß es Jesus ganz und gar um den Menschen geht. Keine Frage. Aber Jesus geht es ganz und gar um den Menschen, weil es ihm zunächst ganz und gar um Gott geht.

Reich Gottes

Das meint er mit dem Wort, das in der Mitte seiner Verkündigung steht. Das er nie definiert, aber in seinen Parabeln – Urgestein der evangelischen Überlieferung – immer wieder neu und verständlich für alle beschrieben hat: das nahende *Reich Gottes* (malkut Jahwe[2])! Vom Reich Gottes, nicht von der Kirche spricht er, wie die Texte zeigen. »Reich der Himmel«, in den Evangelien (Mattäus) eine wohl sekundäre Bildung wegen der jüdischen Scheu vor dem Gottesnamen, meint dasselbe: der Himmel steht für Gott. Nicht ein Territorium, ein Herrschaftsgebiet ist mit diesem »Reich« gemeint. Sondern das Regiment

Gottes, die Herrschertätigkeit, die er ergreifen wird: die »Gottesherrschaft«. So wird Gottesreich »zum Kennwort für die Sache Gottes[3]«.

Präzisiert hat sich dieser zur Zeit Jesu äußerst populäre Ausdruck bereits in Absetzung von seinen Gegnern. Was ist das Reich Gottes für Jesus? Kurz zusammengefaßt nach dem bisher Gehörten:

- *Nicht nur die beständige, von Anfang der Schöpfung an gegebene Gottesherrschaft der Jerusalemer Hierarchen. Sondern das kommende Reich Gottes der Endzeit.*
- *Nicht die gewaltsam zu errichtende religiös-politische Theokratie oder Demokratie der zelotischen Revolutionäre. Sondern die gewaltlos zu erwartende unmittelbare, uneingeschränkte Weltherrschaft Gottes selbst.*
- *Nicht das Rachegericht zugunsten einer Elite von Vollkommenen im Sinn der Essener und Qumranmönche. Sondern die frohe Botschaft von Gottes grenzenloser Güte und unbedingter Gnade gerade für die Verlorenen und Elenden.*
- *Nicht ein von Menschen durch exakte Gesetzeserfüllung und bessere Moral aufzubauendes Reich im Geist der Pharisäer. Sondern das durch Gottes freie Tat zu schaffende Reich.*

Und was für ein Reich wird dies sein?

Ein Reich, wo nach Jesu Gebet[4] Gottes Name wirklich geheiligt wird, sein Wille auch auf Erden geschieht, die Menschen von allem die Fülle haben werden, alle Schuld vergeben und alles Böse überwunden sein wird.

Ein Reich, wo nach Jesu Verheißungen[5] endlich die Armen, die Hungernden, Weinenden, Getretenen zum Zuge kommen werden: wo Schmerz, Leid und Tod ein Ende haben werden.

Ein Reich nicht beschreibbar, aber in Bildern ankündbar: als der neue Bund, die aufgegangene Saat, die reife Ernte, das große Gastmahl, das königliche Fest.

Ein Reich also – ganz nach den prophetischen Verheißungen – der vollen Gerechtigkeit, der unüberbietbaren Freiheit, der ungebrochenen Liebe, der universalen Versöhnung, des ewigen Friedens.

In diesem Sinne also die Zeit des Heiles, der Erfüllung, der Vollendung, der Gegenwart Gottes: die absolute Zukunft.

Gott gehört diese Zukunft. Der prophetische Verheißungsglaube ist von Jesus entscheidend konkretisiert und intensiviert worden. Die Sache Gottes wird sich in der Welt durchsetzen! Von dieser Hoffnung ist die Reich-Gottes-Botschaft getragen. Im Gegensatz zur Resignation, für die Gott im Jenseits bleibt und der Lauf der Weltgeschichte unabänderlich ist. Nicht aus dem Ressentiment, das aus der Not und Verzweiflung der Gegenwart das Bild einer völlig anderen Welt in eine rosige Zukunft hineinprojiziert, stammt diese Hoffnung. Sondern aus der Gewißheit, daß Gott bereits der Schöpfer und der verborgene Herr dieser widersprüchlichen Welt ist und daß er in der Zukunft sein Wort einlösen wird.

Apokalyptischer Horizont

Sein Reich komme: Jesus hat wie die ganze apokalyptische Generation das Reich Gottes, das Reich der Gerechtigkeit, der Freiheit, der Freude und des Friedens, für die *allernächste Zeit* erwartet. Wir haben von Anfang an gesehen, wie sich seine Auffassung von Gottes Reich von der statischen Auffassung der Tempelpriester und anderer unterschied[6]: Das gegenwärtige System ist nicht endgültig, die Geschichte geht dem Ende entgegen – und zwar noch in dieser Generation, die die letzte ist, die das plötzliche und bedrohende Ende der Welt und ihr Neuwerden noch erleben wird. Aber: es sollte anders, sehr viel anders kommen.

Ob Jesus das Hereinbrechen des Reiches Gottes bei seinem Tod oder für unmittelbar nach seinem Tod erwartet hat, über solches läßt sich aufgrund der Quellen lange spekulieren, aber nichts Sicheres sagen. Daß Jesus das Reich Gottes für die unmittelbare Zukunft erwartet hat, ist eindeutig. Wir können es uns methodisch nicht erlauben, gerade die schwierigsten und unbequemsten Texte aus der Verkündigung Jesu auszuscheiden und sie kurzerhand späteren Einflüssen zuzuschreiben.

Nirgendwo meint bei Jesus das Wort Gottesreich (basileia) die dauernde Herrschaft über Israel und die Welt, vielmehr überall die zukünftige Herrschaft der Weltvollendung. Zahlreich sind die Worte, die die Nähe des (zukünftigen) Gottesreiches ausdrücklich ankünden oder voraussetzen[7]. Zwar weigert sich Jesus, einen genauen Termin anzugeben[8]. Aber kein einziges Wort Jesu schiebt das Endgeschehen in die weite Ferne. Vielmehr zeigt die älteste Schicht der synoptischen Überlieferung, daß Jesus das Gottesreich für die allernächste Zeit erwartet. Die klassischen

Texte für eine solche »Naherwartung«[9]– gerade wegen ihrer Anstößigkeit für die folgende Generation zweifellos ursprünglich – trotzen jeder verharmlosenden Interpretation: Jesus und auch die hier zum Teil schon mitsprechende Urkirche wie dann eindeutig auch der Apostel Paulus – die führenden Exegeten dürften hier größtenteils übereinstimmen – haben mit dem Kommen der Gottesherrschaft zu Lebzeiten gerechnet.

Allerdings ist mit dem Fortgang der Zeit schon im Neuen Testament ein Prozeß der *Entschärfung und Verlagerung der Aussagen* unverkennbar. In der ältesten Überlieferungsgeschichte ist es »diese Generation«[10], in einer jüngeren Schicht sind es nur noch »einige« der Hörer Jesu[11], die die Ankunft des Gottesreiches erleben werden. Beim noch späteren dritten Evangelisten wird das Auftreten Jesu selbst als die Erfüllung der Heilszeit in den Mittelpunkt gerückt[12]: im Gegensatz zu den früheren beiden Evangelisten wird nicht mehr gesagt, daß die jüdischen Richter Jesu die Ankunft des Menschensohnes noch erleben werden[13]. Die letzte Phase dieser Verschiebung der Perspektiven haben wir in den späten Schriften des Neuen Testamentes vor uns. Insbesondere im Johannesevangelium, wo das Endgeschehen – abgesehen von wenigen (manche sagen: eingeschobenen) Stellen über das Endgericht des Jüngsten Tages[14]– auf das »schon jetzt« hin verstanden wird: jetzt, beim Hören des Wortes, ergeht das Gericht, jetzt der Übergang vom Tod zum Leben. Andererseits im zweiten Petrusbrief, vielleicht der spätesten Schrift des Neuen Testaments, wo die beunruhigende Verzögerung des Tages des Herrn mit einem Psalmwort erklärt wird: daß beim Herrn ein Tag wie tausend Jahre ist und tausend Jahre wie ein Tag sind[15]. So hat schon im Neuen Testament selber ein Prozeß der Selbstinterpretation und Selbstentmythologisierung eingesetzt.

Diese Entwicklung innerhalb des Neuen Testamentes unterstreicht nur, daß Jesus selber von der Nähe der Gottesherrschaft nicht nur »in prophetischer Verschärfung« gesprochen, sondern an das unmittelbar nahe Gottesreich geglaubt hat. So viele der ungemein drängenden Worte über die Sorglosigkeit gegenüber der Sicherung des Lebens, Nahrung und Kleidung[16], über die Erhörung der Gebete[17], über den Glauben, der Berge versetzen kann[18], über die Entscheidung, die keinen Aufschub duldet[19], die Bildworte vom großen Mahl, ja auch das Vaterunser und die Seligpreisungen: sie müssen vor diesem Hintergrund gesprochen worden sein. Und die *Gleichnisse vom Gottesreich* – der größte Teil gehört nach allgemeiner Auffassung zum Grundbestand der

Jesusüberlieferung, da weder aus dem Judentum noch aus der nachösterlichen Gemeinde ableitbar – bestätigen dies. Diese Parabeln wollen nicht verhüllen, sondern auf das kommende Gottesreich vorbereiten. Das Gottesreich, für das wie für die kostbare Perle oder den Schatz im Acker alles hinzugeben sich lohnt[20], ist immer das Reich der Zukunft, wie dies im Gleichnis vom Fischnetz[21] und vom Unkraut unter dem Weizen[22] klar vorausgesetzt wird. Das Bild von der selbstwachsenden Saat[23] meint nicht einfach, daß das Reich schon da wäre und sich entwickelt, sondern daß es »von selbst« kommt. Und die beiden Bilder vom Senfkorn[24] und vom Sauerteig[25] haben ihre Pointe nicht im natürlichen Prozeß des Wachsens, sondern im gewaltigen Gegensatz von unscheinbarem Anfang und erstaunlichem Ende. Es sind also nicht Entwicklungsgleichnisse, sondern Kontrastgleichnisse[26]. Die Jesu ganze Verkündigung vom Gottesreich durchziehende Fremdheit darf nicht unterschlagen werden.

Um so dringender stellt sich die Frage: Ist diese Verkündigung des Gottesreiches nicht zu guter Letzt doch einfach eine Form spätjüdischer Apokalyptik? Ist Jesus nicht letztlich doch ein apokalyptischer Schwärmer? War er nicht in einer Illusion befangen? Kurz: hat er sich nicht geirrt? Nun, man bräuchte nicht unbedingt dogmatische Hemmungen zu haben, dies gegebenenfalls zuzugeben. Irren ist menschlich. Und wenn Jesus von Nazaret wahrhaft Mensch war, konnte er auch irren. Freilich scheinen manche Theologen den Irrtum mehr zu fürchten als Sünde, Tod und Teufel. Dies kann so weit gehen, daß man aus Angst vor dem Irrtum selbst vor einer Verfälschung der Bibel nicht zurückschreckt, und dies gerade in unserer Frage: Die theologische Vorbereitungskommission des Vatikanum II verkehrte die Aussage des Hebräerbriefes, nach welcher Jesus »in allem auf gleiche Weise versucht worden ist, doch ohne Sünde[27]« ins Gegenteil durch die Hinzufügung »doch ohne Sünde und Irrtum[28]«. Wogegen sich dann das Konzil selbst allerdings verwahrte. Wer also meint, im Zusammenhang der Naherwartung Jesu von »Irrtum« sprechen zu müssen, der tue es. Im Sinne des kosmischen Wissens war es ein Irrtum. Die Frage besteht indessen, ob der Begriff »Irrtum« in diesem Zusammenhang völlig adäquat ist[29].

Das Problem ist nicht schon damit erledigt, daß man sagt, die Ausmalung des Ablaufs der Endereignisse schon in der frühen Markusapokalypse[30] – Schändung des Tempels, Auftreten falscher Propheten, Krieg, Naturkatastrophen, Hunger, Verfolgung der Anhänger Jesu, Gericht – gehe zum größten Teil auf das Konto der Urkirche. Gewiß: Die Übernahme von apokalyptischem Traditionsgut und die Verwertung von Erfahrungen späterer Zeit (aus dem jüdischen Krieg insbesondere in der lukanischen Redaktion) ist in der »synoptischen Apokalypse« – sie fehlt bei Johannes – nicht zu übersehen. Die Tendenz, so etwas wie einen apokalyptischen Fahrplan mit möglichst genauen Zeitangaben aufzustellen, ist der von der Apokalyptik bestimmten literarischen Komposition zuzuschreiben, wie auch das Sätzchen »Der Leser möge es verstehen[31]!« verrät. Allgemein zugegeben wird, daß Jesus im Gegensatz zu den Apokalyptikern nicht interessiert war an der Befriedigung menschlicher Neugierde, an der genauen Datierung und Lokalisierung des Gottesreiches, an der Enthüllung apokalyptischer Ereignisse und Geheimnisse, an der Voraussage des genauen Ablaufs des apokalyptischen Dramas. Eine Konzentration seiner Verkündigung auf das Entscheidende ist also unverkennbar. Aber die Frage bleibt trotzdem bestehen: Hat er sich, wenn er nach zweifellos authentischem Material das baldige Ende der Welt erwartete, nicht eben doch geirrt?

Aber eine Frage zum Vergleich: Hat sich der Erzähler des Sechs-Tage-Werks und der Erschaffung des Menschen geirrt, weil er von der späteren wissenschaftlichen Beschreibung des Werdens der Welt und des Menschen desavouiert wurde – was für viele Christen der Neuzeit eine nicht geringe Enttäuschung und Anfechtung bedeutete, heute aber doch für die meisten eine Selbstverständlichkeit darstellt? Ist in diesem Prozeß der faktischen »Entmythologisierung« die *Sache,* um die es dem Verfasser ging – Gott als der Ursprung von allem, von keinem bösen Gegenprinzip konkurrenziert, die Güte alles Geschaffenen und die Größe des Menschen – nicht erhalten geblieben, ja durch das Abstreifen weltanschaulicher Hüllen sogar verdeutlicht worden?

Daß unser Planet mit unserer Menschheit einen Anfang und ein Ende hat, wird von manchen Ergebnissen der Naturwissenschaften bestätigt und ist für unser Welt- und Selbstverständnis von nicht geringer Bedeutung. Der Begriff des Irrtums erscheint also in diesem Zusammenhang des Weltanfangs als undifferenziert, gar unpassend.

Die Bibel setzt mit der Schöpfung ein und versteht das Ende als die Vollendung des Wirkens Gottes an seiner Schöpfung. Wie die »ersten Dinge«, so sind auch die »letzten Dinge«, wie die »Urzeit«, so ist auch die »Endzeit« *keiner direkten Erfahrung zugänglich*. Es gibt keine menschlichen Zeugen. Weltschöpfung und Weltvollendung sind im Grunde nur *in Bildern umschreibbar*, erzählbar: dichterische Bilder und Erzählungen für das im Grunde Unaussprechliche. Wie die biblische Protologie keine Reportage oder Historie von Anfangs-Ereignissen sein kann, so die biblische Eschatologie keine vorausgenommene Reportage oder Prognose von End-Ereignissen. Und wie die biblischen Erzählungen vom Schöpfungswerk Gottes der damaligen Umwelt entnommen wurden, so die biblischen Erzählungen von Gottes Endwerk der zeitgenössischen Apokalyptik. Und niemand dürfte wohl noch der naiven Meinung sein, daß die synoptische Schilderung des Weltendes, wo die Sterne vom Himmel fallen, die Sonne sich verfinstert und die Engel Posaune blasen, naturwissenschaftlich den Ablauf des Weltendes wiedergibt. In Bildern der damaligen Zeit wird die endzeitlich-endgültige Offenbarung der Gottesherrschaft angekündigt, die, durch Gottes Macht heraufgeführt, alle unsere Begriffe und Bilder – so wissen wir es heute nun einmal besser – übersteigt.

Eine *nicht eliminierende, sondern interpretierende Entmythologisierung* meint eine Übersetzung der Botschaft aus der damaligen Situation, dem damaligen Wirklichkeitsverständnis, dem damaligen mythologischen Weltbild in unsere heutige Situation, in das heutige Wirklichkeitsverständnis, in das moderne Weltbild hinein[32]. Sie ist nicht nur bezüglich der »ersten Dinge«, sondern auch bezüglich der »letzten Dinge« unumgänglich. Um der Menschen heute willen *und* um der Botschaft selber willen! Die schon im Neuen Testament einsetzende Selbstinterpretation und Selbstentmythologisierung ist ausdrücklich zu machen und konsequent weiterzuführen. Die Erzählungen und Bilder sind für die heutige Verkündigung – darauf ist ausdrücklich zurückzukommen – nicht etwa auszuscheiden oder auf Begriffe und Ideen zu reduzieren. Aber sie sind richtig zu verstehen. Es ist dringend zu unterscheiden zwischen dem *Verstehens- oder Vorstellungsrahmen* und der gemeinten und neu *zu verstehenden Sache*.

Jesus hat selbstverständlich im apokalyptischen Vorstellungsrahmen und in den Vorstellungsformen seiner Zeit gesprochen.

Und wenn er auch, wie angedeutet, die genauen Berechnungen der eschatologischen Vollendung ausdrücklich abgelehnt und die bildhafte Ausmalung des Gottesreiches im Vergleich mit der frühjüdischen Apokalyptik aufs äußerste beschränkt hat, so ist er doch grundsätzlich in dem uns heute befremdenden Verstehensrahmen der Naherwartung, im Horizont der Apokalyptik geblieben. Dieser Verstehensrahmen ist durch die geschichtliche Entwicklung überholt worden, der apokalyptische Horizont ist versunken – dies muß deutlich gesehen werden. Aus der heutigen Perspektive müssen wir sagen: Es handelte sich bei der Naherwartung weniger um einen Irrtum als um eine *zeitbedingte, zeitgebundene Weltanschauung,* die Jesus mit seinen Zeitgenossen teilte. Sie kann nicht künstlich wiedererweckt werden. Ja, sie sollte auch gar nicht, wie immer wieder gerade in sogenannten »apokalyptischen Zeiten« die Versuchung besteht, für unseren so verschiedenen Erfahrungshorizont wiedererweckt werden. Der damalige, uns fremdgewordene apokalyptische Vorstellungs- und Verstehensrahmen würde heute die gemeinte Sache nur verbergen und verstellen.

Es kommt heute alles darauf an, ob der Grundgedanke Jesu, ob die *Sache,* um die es Jesus mit seiner Verkündigung des kommenden Gottesreiches ging, noch einen Sinn hat: im völlig veränderten Erfahrungshorizont einer Menschheit, die sich grundsätzlich damit abgefunden hat, daß der Lauf der Weltgeschichte, vorläufig mindestens, weitergeht. Oder man kann auch mit vollem Recht positiv fragen: Wie kommt es eigentlich, daß Jesu Botschaft über seinen Tod und das nicht eingetretene Ende hinaus derart bewegend blieb, ja es überhaupt erst richtig wurde? Das hat in der Tat etwas mit seinem Tod zu tun, der ein sehr bestimmtes Ende darstellte. Aber doch auch mit seinem Leben und Lehren: eine Neudifferenzierung ist hier angebracht.

Zwischen Gegenwart und Zukunft

Die Gleichnisse, so verständlich sie ihrer Form nach sind, enthalten doch ein *Geheimnis*: »das Geheimnis des Reiches Gottes[33]«. Daß dies nur den Jüngern Jesu gesagt sein soll und dem Volk – zur Verstockung – gerade nicht, ist nachträgliche Interpretation des Evangelisten[34]. Jesu Gleichnisse selber beweisen das Gegenteil. Und auch der Evangelist sagt in der Folge ausdrücklich, daß Jesus in vielen solcher Gleichnisse zum Volk das Wort redete, wie es sie verstehen konnte[35]. Was soll trotzdem das *Geheimnis* des Gottesreiches sein, welches in den Gleichnissen angekündigt wird?

Wir haben vorhin nur die halbe Wahrheit gesagt, wenn wir bezüglich der Wachstumsgleichnisse von Kontrast sprachen. An eine organische Entwicklung des Gottesreiches, etwa gar noch identifiziert mit der Kirche, hat Jesus zweifellos nicht gedacht – das bleibt bestehen; das Reich kommt durch Gottes Tat. Aber bei allem Gegensatz von kleinem Anfang und großartigem Ende: im winzigen Senfkorn kündet sich doch schon der mächtige Baum an, im bißchen Sauerteig unter dem Mehl das Brot für viele Menschen, in der unscheinbaren Aussaat die große Ernte, im geringen Anfang schon das herrliche Ende. Und wo sollte denn schon der Anfang gemacht sein, wenn nicht eben mit Jesus? Wer ist denn der Sämann, der ausging, um zu säen, bei dem etliches auf gutes Land fiel und bereits hundertfältige Frucht bringt[36]? In Jesu unscheinbarem Reden und Tun, in seinem Wort, das den Armen, Hungernden, Weinenden, Getretenen zugerufen wird, in seinen Taten, die den Kranken, Leidenden, Besessenen, Schuldiggewordenen, Hoffungslosen aufhelfen, kündet sich schon das Reich an, wo Schuld, Schmerz, Leid und Tod ein Ende haben werden: das Reich der vollen Gerechtigkeit, Freiheit, Liebe, der Versöhnung und des ewigen Friedens, die absolute Zukunft Gottes. In ihm, Jesus, wird doch schon Gottes Name geheiligt, geschieht schon Gottes Wille auf Erden, wird alle Schuld vergeben und alles Böse überwunden, ist eben doch schon die Zeit des Heiles, der Erfüllung, der Erlösung, ja, ist schon das Reich Gottes selber – mitten unter euch[37] – angebrochen. In ihm also gründet das in den Gleichnissen angekündigte »Geheimnis des Reiches Gottes«: Er selber ist der Anfang vom Ende. Mit ihm ist die Weltvollendung, die absolute Zukunft Gottes schon im Anbruch – schon jetzt! Mit ihm ist Gott nahe!

Gerade wenn man Jesu Naherwartung ernstnimmt, muß man sagen: Anfang und Ende, Gegenwart und Zukunft lassen sich doch nicht so auseinanderreißen, wie man das tut, wenn man nur *eine* Linie in der synoptischen Verkündigung verfolgt und alles andere als unecht ausschaltet oder als unbedeutend im Schatten läßt. Weder die rein futurische »konsequente« Eschatologie (A. Schweitzer), die für die Gegenwart nichts sagt, noch die rein präsentische »realisierte« Eschatologie (C. H. Dodd), welche die ausgebliebene Zukunft übersieht, geben den *ganzen* Jesus. Jesu Verkündigung ist nicht nur eine Form spätjüdischer Apokalyptik, die *nur* um zukünftige Dinge besorgt ist und für die Gegenwart nichts fordert. Aber noch weniger ist sie eine reine Gegenwarts- und Existenzdeutung, die mit der Apokalyptik und einer absoluten Zukunft nichts zu tun hätte.

Zukunfts- *und* Gegenwartsaussagen, die sich beide in den Evangelien finden, sind ernstzunehmen und differenziert aufeinander zu beziehen. Und zwar nicht (psychologisch) als verschiedene »Stimmungen« in Jesu Psyche (W. Bousset). Auch nicht (biographisch) als verschiedene »Stadien« im Leben Jesu (P. Wernle, J. Weiss). Aber auch nicht, wir sahen es bereits, nur (traditionsgeschichtlich) als verschiedene »Schichten« in der synoptischen Überlieferung (C. H. Dodd). Will man willkürliche Postulate und Konstruktionen vermeiden, so sind Gegenwart und Zukunft in wesentlicher, nicht aufzulösender Spannung zu sehen. Gerade auf dem Hintergrund der Naherwartung gilt die *Polarität* von Noch-nicht und Doch-schon: eindeutig das Gottesreich der Zukunft, das aber durch Jesus bereits für die Gegenwart eine Macht bedeutet und eine Wirkung entfaltet. Die Zukunftsworte Jesu dürfen nicht als apokalyptische Belehrung, sie müssen als eschatologische Verheißung verstanden werden[38]. Kein Reden also vom künftigen Gottesreich ohne Konsequenzen für die gegenwärtige Gesellschaft. Aber umgekehrt auch kein Reden von der Gegenwart und ihren Problemen ohne Aussicht auf die bestimmende absolute Zukunft. Wer nach Jesus von der Zukunft reden will, muß von der Gegenwart reden und umgekehrt. Denn:

– *Die* absolute Zukunft Gottes *verweist den Menschen auf die* Gegenwart: *Keine Isolierung der Zukunft auf Kosten der Gegenwart! Das Gottesreich darf nicht eine Vertröstung auf die Zukunft sein, Befriedigung der frommen menschlichen Zukunftsneugierde, Projektion unerfüllter Wünsche und Ängste, wie Feuerbach, Marx und Freud meinten. Gerade von der Zukunft her soll der Mensch in die Gegenwart eingewiesen werden. Gerade aus der Hoffnung heraus soll die gegenwärtige Welt und Gesellschaft nicht nur interpretiert, sondern verändert werden. Nicht eine Belehrung über das Ende wollte Jesus geben, sondern einen Aufruf erlassen für die Gegenwart angesichts des Endes.*

Die Apokalyptiker fragten von der gegenwärtigen Situation des Menschen und der Welt auf das Gottesreich, die absolute Zukunft, hin. Deshalb waren sie so sehr besorgt um den genauen Termin des Eintreffens. Jesus gerade umgekehrt: Vom bald kommenden Gottesreich her fragt er auf die gegenwärtige Situation des Menschen und der Welt hin. Deshalb ist er bei aller Naherwartung gerade nicht besorgt um den genauen Tag und die Weise des Eintreffens des Gottesreiches. Wohl aber glaubt er an das absolut sichere Daß der baldigen Vollendung. Gerade der Blick auf das Ende gibt das Auge für das Zunächstliegende frei. Die Zukunft ist Gottes Anruf an die Gegenwart. Von der absoluten Zukunft her ist schon jetzt das Leben zu gestalten.

– *Die* Gegenwart *weist den Menschen auf die absolute Zukunft Gottes: keine Verabsolutierung unserer Gegenwart auf Kosten der Zukunft! Es darf nicht die ganze Zukunft des Gottesreiches in Gegenwärtigkeit aufgelöst werden. Zu traurig und zwiespältig ist und bleibt die Gegenwart, als daß sie in ihrem Elend und ihrer Schuld schon das Gottesreich sein könnte. Zu unvollkommen und unmenschlich ist diese Welt und Gesellschaft, als daß sie schon das Vollkommene und Endgültige sein könnte. Das Gottesreich bleibt nicht im Anbruch stecken, sondern soll endgültig zum Durchbruch kommen. Was mit Jesus begonnen wurde, soll auch mit Jesus vollendet werden. Die Nah-Erwartung wurde nicht erfüllt. Aber deshalb wird nicht die Erwartung überhaupt ausgeschaltet.*

Das ganze Neue Testament – und insofern wären sogar die futurischen Einschübe des Johannesevangeliums wichtig, wenn es überhaupt nur »Einschübe« sind – hält bei aller Konzentration auf die in Jesus bereits anbrechende Gottesherrschaft an der noch ausstehenden, zukünftigen Vollendung fest. Die Sache Jesu ist die Sache Gottes, und deshalb kann sie nie verloren sein. Wie von den Ur-Mythen das Ur-Geschehen der Schöpfung, so ist von den End-Mythen das End-Geschehen der Vollendung zu unterscheiden. Und wie das Alte Testament die Ur-Mythen vergeschichtlichte, an die Geschichte gebunden hat, so das Neue Testament die End-Mythen. Wenn auch die Geschichte die zeitgebundene Nah-Erwartung überholt hat, so doch damit nicht die Zukunfts-Erwartung überhaupt. Die Gegenwart ist Zeit der Entscheidung im Licht von Gottes absoluter Zukunft. Die Polarität des Noch-nicht und Doch-schon macht die Spannung des Menschenlebens und der Menschheitsgeschichte aus.

Die Botschaft Jesu vom Gottesreich behielt ihre Attraktivität.
Der Weltuntergang blieb aus. Und doch behielt die Botschaft
ihren Sinn. Der apokalyptische Horizont der Botschaft ist versunken. Aber die eschatologische Botschaft selbst, die Sache, um
die es Jesus ging, blieb auch im neuen Verstehens- und Vorstellungsrahmen aktuell. Ob es morgen kommt oder nach langen
Zeiten: das Ende wirft Licht und Schatten voraus. Können wir es
uns verhehlen? Diese Welt dauert nicht ewig! Das Menschenleben und die Menschheitsgeschichte haben ein Ende! Die Botschaft Jesu aber sagt: *An diesem Ende steht* nicht das Nichts,
sondern *Gott*. Gott, der wie der Anfang so auch das Ende ist. Die
Sache Gottes setzt sich durch, in jedem Fall. Gott gehört die
Zukunft. Mit dieser Zukunft Gottes ist zu rechnen, nicht Tage
und Stunden auszurechnen. Von dieser Zukunft Gottes her ist
die individuelle und gesellschaftliche Gegenwart zu gestalten.
Hier schon und heute.

Diese Zukunft ist also keine leere, sondern eine zu enthüllende
und zu erfüllende Zukunft. Nicht nur ein »Futurum«, ein
»Künftiges«, das die Futurologen durch Extrapolation aus der
vergangenen oder gegenwärtigen Geschichte konstruieren könnten, ohne im übrigen den Überraschungseffekt der Zukunft je
völlig ausschalten zu können. Sondern ein »Eschaton«, jenes
»Letzte« der Zukunft, das ein wirklich Anderes und ein qualitativ Neues ist, welches freilich schon jetzt in der Antizipation sein
Kommen ankündigt. Also nicht nur Futurologie, sondern
Eschatologie. Eine Eschatologie ohne wahre, noch ausstehende
absolute Zukunft wäre eine Eschatologie ohne wahre, noch zu
erfüllende Hoffnung[39].

Das bedeutet: Es gibt nicht nur vorläufige menschliche Sinn-
setzungen von Fall zu Fall. Es gibt einen *endgültigen*, dem Menschen frei angebotenen *Sinn von Mensch und Welt*. Eine Aufhebung aller Entfremdung ist möglich. Die Geschichte des Menschen und der Welt erschöpft sich nicht, wie Nietzsche meint, in
einer ewigen Wiederkehr des Gleichen, verendet aber auch nicht
schließlich in irgendeiner absurden Leere. Nein, die Zukunft ist
Gottes, und deshalb steht am Ende die Erfüllung.

Die Kategorie »Novum« (E. Bloch) erhält hier ihre Bedeutung.
Und die Hoffnung auf eine wirklich andere Zukunft ist die
Hoffnung, die nicht nur Israel und die christlichen Kirchen,
sondern auch Christen und Marxisten eint. Diese wirklich andere

absolute Zukunft läßt sich nicht, wie in einem eindimensionalen technischen Denken, identifizieren mit dem automatischen technisch-kulturellen Fortschritt der Gesellschaft oder auch mit dem organischen Fortschritt und Wachsen der Kirche. Erst recht nicht, wie in der existentialen Interpretation Heideggers und anderer, mit der Existenzmöglichkeit des Einzelnen und der je neuen Zukünftigkeit seiner personalen Entscheidung. Diese Zukunft ist etwas qualitativ Neues, das zugleich zur grundsätzlichen Veränderung der gegenwärtigen Verhältnisse anregt. Eine Zukunft freilich, die auch nicht mit einer kommenden sozialistischen Gesellschaft identifiziert werden darf.

In all diesen *falschen Identifikationen* wird übersehen, daß es um die Zukunft, um das Reich *Gottes* geht[40]. Das Reich Gottes war weder die massiv institutionalisierte Kirche des mittelalterlichen und gegenreformatorischen Katholizismus noch die Genfer Theokratie Calvins noch das apokalyptische Reich aufrührerischer apokalyptischer Schwärmer wie Thomas Münzer. Es war auch nicht das gegenwärtige Reich der Sittlichkeit und vollendeten bürgerlichen Kultur, wie theologischer Idealismus und Liberalismus dachten, und erst recht nicht das vom Nationalsozialismus propagierte tausendjährige politische Reich, basierend auf den Ideologien von Volk und Rasse. Es war schließlich auch nicht das klassenlose Reich des neuen Menschen, wie es der Kommunismus bisher zu verwirklichen trachtete.

Von Jesus her ist gegen all diese vorzeitigen Identifikationen festzustellen: Das Reich Gottes, die Vollendung, *kommt weder durch gesellschaftliche* (geistige oder technische) *Evolution noch durch gesellschaftliche* (rechte oder linke) *Revolution.* Die Vollendung kommt vielmehr durch *Gottes* nicht vorhersehbare, nicht extrapolierbare *Aktion!* Eine Aktion freilich, die des Menschen Aktion im Hier und Heute, im individuellen und gesellschaftlichen Bereich, nicht aus-, sondern einschließt. Wobei heute eine falsche »Verweltlichung« des Gottesreiches ebenso zu vermeiden ist wie früher eine falsche »Verinnerlichung«.

Es geht also um eine *wirklich andere Dimension:* die göttliche Dimension. *Transzendenz* – aber nicht mehr wie in der alten Physik und Metaphysik primär räumlich vorgestellt: Gott *über* oder *außerhalb* der Welt. Oder dann im Umschlag idealistisch oder existentialistisch verinnerlicht: Gott *in* uns. Sondern von Jesus her primär zeitlich verstanden: Gott *vor* uns[41]. Gott nicht einfach der zeitlose Ewige hinter dem einen gleichförmigen Fluß des Werdens und Vergehens von Vergangenheit, Gegenwart und Zukunft, wie er insbesondere aus der griechischen Philosophie bekannt ist, sondern *Gott als der Zukünftige, Kommende, Hoffnungstiftende,* wie er aus den Zukunftsverheißungen Israels und Jesu selbst erkannt werden kann. Seine Gottheit verstanden als die Macht der Zukunft, die unsere Gegenwart in einem neuen Licht erscheinen läßt. Gottes ist die Zukunft, das bedeutet: Wo immer der einzelne Mensch hinkommt, im Leben und Sterben, Er ist da. Wo immer die ganze Menschheit sich hinentwickelt, in Aufgang und Niedergang, Er ist da. Gott als die erste und letzte Wirklichkeit.

Was bedeutet das für den Menschen? Daß er *das Bestehende* in dieser Welt und Gesellschaft *nicht als definitiv nehmen* darf. Daß für ihn weder die Welt noch er selbst das Erste und Letzte sein können. Daß die Welt und er selbst aus sich allein vielmehr höchst relativ, fragwürdig und unbeständig sind. Daß er somit, auch wenn er es sich gern verschleiert, in einer kritischen Situation lebt. Herausgefordert ist er, sich im Letzten zu entscheiden, das Angebot anzunehmen, *sich einzulassen auf die Wirklichkeit Gottes,* die ihm voraus ist. Eine Entscheidung also, bei der um das Ganze gespielt wird: ein Entweder-Oder, für oder gegen Gott.

An der *Dringlichkeit des Appells* hat sich trotz des versunkenen apokalyptischen Horizonts nichts geändert. Eine *Umkehr* drängt sich gebieterisch auf: Ein neues Denken und Handeln ist dringend erfordert. Es geht hier um Letztes. Eine Uminterpretation des Lebens, eine neue Lebenseinstellung, ein neues Leben überhaupt. Wer fragt, wie lange er noch Zeit habe, gott-los zu leben und die Umkehr aufzuschieben, verfehlt Zukunft und Gegenwart, weil er mit Gott auch sich selbst verfehlt. Nicht erst zu einer berechenbaren oder nicht berechenbaren End-Zeit des Menschen oder der Menschheit, sondern hier und jetzt ist die Stunde der end-gültigen Entscheidung. Und zwar für einen jeden ganz persönlich. Der Einzelne kann sich nicht, wie oft in der Psychoanalyse, mit einer Erhellung seines Verhaltens ohne moralische Ansprüche begnügen. Er kann die Entscheidung und die Verantwortung auch nicht auf die Gesellschaft, ihre verfehlten Strukturen oder korrupten Institutionen abschieben. Er selber ist hier herausgefordert, zum Einsatz, zur Hingabe: Für ihn ganz persönlich geht es – bildlich – um die kostbare Perle[42], den Schatz im Acker[43]. So steht schon jetzt alles, Tod und Leben, auf dem Spiel. Schon jetzt kann er sich durch Hingabe selbst gewinnen.

Schon jetzt gilt: Wer sein Leben gewinnen will, wird es verlieren, und wer es verlieren wird, wird es gewinnen[44].

Diese Umkehr ist nur möglich im vertrauenden Sichverlassen auf die Botschaft, auf Gott selbst, in jenem Vertrauen, das sich nicht beirren läßt und das *Glaube* genannt wird. Ein Glaube, der Berge versetzen kann[45], der aber auch in der kümmerlichsten Form eines Senfkorns Anteil an der Verheißung hat, so daß der Mensch immer sagen darf: »Ich glaube, hilf meinem Unglauben[46].« Ein Glaube, der nie einfach Besitz wird, sondern Geschenk bleibt. Ein Glaube, der im Hinblick auf die Zukunft die Dimension der Hoffnung hat: in der Hoffnung kommt der Glaube zu seinem Ziel, umgekehrt hat die Hoffnung im Glauben ihren bleibenden Grund.

Aus dieser Hoffnung auf die Zukunft Gottes ist nicht nur die Welt und ihre Geschichte zu interpretieren und die Existenz des Einzelnen zu erhellen, sondern ist in Kritik des Bestehenden Welt, Gesellschaft und Existenz zu verändern. Von Jesus her ist also eine Erhaltung des Status quo auf Zeit und Ewigkeit wahrhaftig nicht zu begründen. Allerdings auch nicht die gewaltsame, totale soziale Umwälzung um jeden Preis. Im Folgenden dürfte deutlicher werden, was Umkehr aus dem Glauben einschließt. Hier genügt es, wenn auch für heute ein wenig verständlich geworden ist, was der älteste Evangelist am Anfang seines Evangeliums wohl in eigener Fomulierung als kurze Zusammenfassung der Botschaft Jesu gegeben hat: »Erfüllt ist die Zeit, und nahe gekommen das Reich Gottes! Kehret um und glaubet an die gute Botschaft[47].«

2. Wunder?

Jesus hat nicht nur geredet, er hat auch gehandelt. Herausfordernd wie seine Worte waren auch seine *Taten*. Doch gerade viele dieser Taten bereiten dem heutigen Menschen mehr Schwierigkeiten als alle seine Worte. Die Wunderüberlieferung ist weit stärker umstritten als die Wortüberlieferung. Das Wunder – nach Goethe »des Glaubens liebstes Kind« – ist im naturwissenschaftlich-technologischen Zeitalter zu des Glaubens Sorgenkind geworden. Wie sollen wir die Spannung überwinden können, die besteht zwischen dem wissenschaftlichen Weltverständnis und dem Wunderglauben, zwischen rational-technischer Weltgestaltung und Wundererfahrung? Allerdings haben schon Kirchenväter wie dann wiederum moderne Apologeten das Wunder im wesentlichen auf die Ursprungszeit der Kirche beschränkt gesehen. Heutige sprechen sogar wie schon J. S. Semler von einem merkwürdigen »Sparsamkeitsprinzip« bezüglich Wundern in der Kirchengeschichte. Gegenüber Wundern der Gegenwart scheint man schon immer mehr Hemmungen empfunden zu haben als gegenüber Wundern der Vergangenheit. Aber darin zeigt sich nur die Verlegenheit gegenüber dem Wunder überhaupt[1].

Verschleierung der Verlegenheit

Der *Begriff »Wunder«* ist beinahe so vage wie der der »Revolution«. Man kann ebenso von den Sieben Weltwundern wie vom Wirtschaftswunder, von den Wundern der Technik wie von denen des Atoms oder der Tiefsee reden: alles Wunder, die der Mensch (oder die »Natur«), aber jedenfalls nicht Gott vollbracht hat. Für Theologen hat das seine Bequemlichkeiten: Der Wunderbegriff läßt sich so weit dehnen, daß er alle harte Anstößigkeit verliert. So meinen manche, den Wunder-Knoten dadurch durchhauen zu können, daß sie überall Wunder sehen: Alles Weltgeschehen ist oder wird für sie zum Wunder, insofern alles Geschehen vom göttlichen Wirken durchwaltet ist oder als solches erkannt wird. Aber sollte etwa ein Bergsturz mit Dutzenden von Toten ebenso ein Wunder sein wie die dann oft als Wunder gepriesene Errettung verschütteter Bergleute? Oder warum sollte Gott in einer solchen Sicht mit dem zweiten Ereignis direkter zu tun haben als mit dem ersten? Mit welchem Recht bucht man nur die Glücksfälle und nicht auch die Unglücksfälle auf Gottes Konto? Hier wird der Wunderbegriff völlig entleert, indem das gesamte Weltgeschehen nachträglich religiös interpretiert wird.

Die eigentliche Problematik des neutestamentlichen Wunders aber wird auf diese Weise elegant verschleiert: ob nämlich die von Jesus berichteten Wunder, die nach dem Wortlaut gegen die Naturgesetze verstoßen, historische Tatsachen sind oder nicht. Weder ein modernes religiöses Reden vom allgegenwärtigen Wunder noch aber auch das archaisierende und ebenfalls verschleiernde Reden von »Großtaten« oder »Machttaten« Gottes, noch ein schlichtes »Erzählen« der Wundergeschichten schafft die Frage aus dem Raum, die schon D. Hume und J. St. Mill gestellt haben: Wunder nicht in einem vagen, sondern in einem strengen, neuzeitlichen Sinn, also eine Durchbrechung der Naturgesetze durch Gott – sind solche über-natürliche Eingriffe denkbar? Muß man als Christ *solche* Wunder glauben? Was sagt die kritische Geschichtswissenschaft zu dem, was für die Naturwissenschaft unmöglich scheint?

Wo man von glauben *müssen* spricht, stimmt etwas nicht. Eine *gute* Botschaft *darf* man glauben. Wie sind dann aber alle die Wundergeschichten der Evangelien zu beurteilen? Die Heilungswunder (Fieber, Lähmung, Auszehrung, Blutfluß, Taubstummheit, Blindheit, Epilepsie, Verkrümmung, Wassersucht, Schwertwunder), die Dämonenaustreibungen, die drei Totenerweckungen, die sieben Naturwunder (Seewandeln, Sturmstillung, Fischzug des Petrus, Münze im Fischmaul, Verfluchung des Feigenbaumes, Speisung in der Wüste, Verwandlung von Wasser in Wein)?

Für manche ist dies alles auch heute kein Problem. Es gibt gläubige Menschen in allen Kirchen, denen Jesus so viel und das naturwissenschaftlich-technische Weltbild und alle historischen Schwierigkeiten so wenig bedeuten, daß sie keine Hemmungen empfinden, alle Wunder wörtlich als genau so geschehen anzunehmen, wie sie beschrieben sind. Sie mögen die folgenden Seiten überschlagen und beim nächsten Kapitel weiterfahren. Es gibt aber andere, die Schwierigkeiten empfinden angesichts der neutestamentlichen Wunderberichte. Berichte von Wundern sind ja schon nach Lessing noch keine »Beweise des Geistes und der Kraft«, sind keine gegenwärtigen Wunder. Ihnen also, die nach dem wirklich Geschehenen fragen, und die man nicht als Rationalisten abqualifizieren darf, kann wohl nur restlose historische und theologische Wahrhaftigkeit nützen. Denn:

a. Kritischen Menschen werden jene Theologen kaum eine Hilfe bieten, die vielleicht noch heute die historische Tatsächlichkeit der von Jesus berichteten Wunder zwar nicht fundamentalistisch einfach zum Glauben vorschreiben, wohl aber apologetisch in allen Einzelfällen meinen beweisen zu können: Die Zeiten, da mancher sogar den Wandel Jesu über den See als möglich meinte aufweisen zu können, dürften wohl für immer vorüber sein.

b. Kritischen Menschen werden jedoch auch jene Theologen kaum voranhelfen, die nur von Jesu Botschaft reden und von seinen Wundern schweigen: Die Wundergeschichten als Ganzes (nicht jede einzelne Wundergeschichte) gehören nun einmal zu den ältesten Elementen der Überlieferung. Unter literarkritischen Gesichtspunkten ist Jesus der Wundertäter ebenso sicher bezeugt wie Jesus der Prediger. Und man kann schließlich nicht schon die Hälfte des Markus-Evangeliums aus weltanschaulicher Voreingenommenheit eliminieren, wenn man als Historiker ernstgenommen werden will.

c. Kritischen Menschen werden schließlich auch jene Theologen wenig helfen, welche die gesamte Interpretation der Wundergeschichten darauf ausrichten, daß Jesus verschiedentlich eine Beglaubigung durch Wunder abgelehnt habe[2]. Jesus übt nun einmal keine grundsätzliche Wunderkritik. Nicht weil Wunder überhaupt unmöglich wären, sondern weil sie verführerisch sind, hat er ein Zeichen verweigert. Nicht Wunderglauben lehnt er ab, sondern Wunderforderung und Wundersucht: nicht Wunder schlechthin, sondern Schauwunder. Auch ohne Wunderbeweis soll der Mensch Jesu Wort glauben.

Nun waren allerdings die Menschen der Zeit Jesu und auch die Evangelisten gerade an dem nicht interessiert, woran der heutige Mensch, der Mensch des rationalen und technologischen Zeitalters so sehr interessiert ist: an den Naturgesetzen. Man dachte *nicht naturwissenschaftlich* und verstand somit die Wunder nicht als Durchbrechung von Naturgesetzen, nicht als eine Verletzung des lückenlosen Kausalzusammenhanges. Schon im Alten Testament unterschied man nicht zwischen Wundern, die den Gesetzen der Natur entsprechen und denen, die sie sprengen; jedes Ereignis, durch welches Jahwe seine Macht offenbart, gilt als Wunder, als Zeichen, als Macht- oder Großtat Jahwes. Überall ist Gott, der Urgrund und Schöpfer der Welt, am Werk. Überall können die Menschen Wunder erfahren: von der Erschaffung und Erhaltung der Welt bis zu ihrer Vollendung, im großen wie im kleinen, in der Geschichte des Volkes wie in der Errettung des Einzelnen aus tiefer Not ...

Daß es Wunder gibt und überall Wunder geben kann, wird auch in neutestamentlicher Zeit und auch im Heidentum einfachhin vorausgesetzt: Wunder, verstanden nicht als etwas, was der naturgesetzlichen Ordnung widerspricht, sondern was ein Sich-Wundern erregt, was über das gewöhnliche menschliche Vermögen hinausgeht, für den Menschen unerklärbar ist, hinter dem sich eine andere Macht – die Macht Gottes oder aber eine böse Macht – verbirgt. Daß auch *Jesus* Wunder getan hat, ist für die Evangelisten und ihre Zeit wichtig. Aber weder das naturwissenschaftliche noch das geschichtswissenschaftliche Denken waren damals entwickelt. Und warum sollten nicht auch Darstellungsweisen und Ausdrucksmittel wie Epen und Hymnen, Mythen und Sagen geeignet sein, um das Wirken des lebendigen Gottes zu bezeugen? An eine wissenschaftliche Erklärung oder eine Nachprüfung der Wunder dachte damals niemand. Nirgendwo wird in den Evangelien beschrieben, wie sich der wunderbare Vorgang selber abgespielt hat. Keine medizinische Diagnose der Krankheit, keine Angaben bezüglich der therapeutischen Faktoren. Wozu auch? Die Evangelisten wollen nicht in das berichtete Ereignis eindringen. Sie überhöhen es. Sie erklären nicht, sondern verklären. Nicht der Beschreibung, sondern der Be-wunderung sollen die Wunder-Erzählungen dienen: so Großes hat Gott durch einen Menschen getan! Es wird kein Glaube verlangt, daß es Wunder gibt oder auch daß dieses oder jenes Geschehnis wirklich ein Wunder ist. Vielmehr wird der Glaube an Gott erwartet, der in dem Menschen, der solches tut, am Werke ist und für dessen Wirken die Wundertaten Zeichen sind.

Was wirklich geschehen ist

Ausgangspunkt für die Interpretation der evangelischen Wunderberichte muß somit sein: sie sind keine Direktreportagen, keine wissenschaftlich überprüften Dokumentationen, keine historischen, medizinischen oder psychologischen Protokolle. Sie sind vielmehr unbekümmerte volkstümliche Erzählungen, die glaubendes Staunen hervorrufen sollen. Als solche stehen sie völlig im Dienst der Christusverkündigung.

Soll aber unter diesen Voraussetzungen der Historiker zu den Wundertaten Jesu überhaupt noch etwas sagen können? Ist ihm die hinter den volkstümlichen Erzählungen verborgene Wirklichkeit überhaupt zugänglich? Die einzelne Wundergeschichte scheint einfach nicht so viel herzugeben, daß man bei ihr durch literarisch-historische Analyse auf das wirkliche »Ereignis« durchstoßen könnte. Und doch: es bleibt hier keineswegs das Alles oder Nichts – alles legendär oder nichts legendär. Man braucht keineswegs entweder in unkritischer fundamentalistischer Wundergläubigkeit *alle* Wundergeschichten als historische Tatsachen zu verstehen und ohne Rücksicht auf Widersprüche zu »glauben« oder aber in rationalistischer Engstirnigkeit überhaupt *keine* Wundergeschichte ernstzunehmen.

Der Kurzschluß resultiert daraus, daß man alle Wundergeschichten auf dieselbe Ebene stellt. Nun hat aber die neueste formgeschichtliche Forschung die literarische Gattung der Wundergeschichten eingehend untersucht. Sie hat für die Wunder im Neuen Testament festgestellt: alttestamentliche Vorbilder (besonders die Wunder beim Auszug aus Ägypten und bei den Propheten Elia und Elisa), dann bestimmte jüdischen, hellenistischen und neutestamentlichen Wundergeschichten gemeinsame Schemata in der Art des Erzählens, schließlich bestimmte Tendenzen etwa der Steigerung des Wunderhaften (besonders bei Johannes) oder auch vereinzelt der Straffung (bei Mattäus gegenüber Markus). Die neutestamentlichen Wundergeschichten selber drängen somit gebieterisch zu einer *differenzierten Betrachtungsweise,* die sich vor allem an die Einzelberichte hält und sich nicht verwirren lassen darf von den redaktionellen Zusammenfassungen (Sammelberichten) der Evangelisten[3], die den Eindruck einer beständigen, breiten Wundertätigkeit Jesu hervorrufen.

Bei aller Skepsis gegenüber der einzelnen Wundererzählung stimmen heute auch die kritischsten Exegeten darin überein, daß nicht die gesamte Berichterstattung von Wundern als ungeschichtlich abgetan werden kann. Allgemein wird trotz zahlreicher legendarischer oder legendärer Übermalungen im einzelnen angenommen:

1. Es müssen sich *Heilungen von verschiedenartigen Kranken* ereignet haben, die für die Menschen zumindest der damaligen Zeit erstaunlich waren. Zum Teil wird es sich um psychogene Leiden gehandelt haben, wobei bestimmte psychogene Hautkrankheiten in alter Zeit vermutlich unter die Rubrik »Aussatz« fielen. Der vielfach gegen Jesus erhobene und wegen seiner Anstößigkeit in den Evangelien nicht frei erfundene Vorwurf der Magie (Dämonenaustreibung durch den Erzdämonen Beelzebul) war nur denkbar aufgrund von echten Ereignissen, die ihn provozierten. Auch die historisch unbestreitbaren Sabbatkonflikte waren mit Heilungen verbunden. Das therapeutische Element würde ohne jeden Grund aus der Überlieferung gestrichen.

Nun bleiben auch heute noch manche Heilungen medizinisch unerklärbar. Und die heutige Medizin, die mehr denn je den psychosomatischen Charakter eines großen Teiles von Krankheiten erkannt hat, weiß von erstaunlichen Heilungen aufgrund von außerordentlichen psychologischen Einflüssen, aufgrund eines unendlichen Vertrauens, aufgrund von »Glauben«. Andererseits kennt die älteste Evangelientradition noch Fälle, da Jesus wie etwa in seiner Heimatstadt Nazaret keine einzige Krafttat wirken konnte, weil Glauben und Vertrauen fehlten[4]. Nur der Glaubende empfängt. Mit Magie und Zauberei, wo der Mensch gegen seinen Willen überwältigt wird, haben Jesu Heilungen nichts zu tun. Sie sind vielmehr ein Aufruf zum Glauben[5], der manchmal sogar als das eigentliche Wunder erscheint, dem gegenüber die Heilung sekundär ist[6]. Die Heilungsgeschichten des Neuen Testaments müssen als Glaubensgeschichten verstanden werden.

2. Insbesondere müssen Heilungen von »Besessenen« vorgekommen sein. Auch dieses exorzistische Element würde ohne Grund aus der Überlieferung ausgeschieden. Krankheit wurde vielfach mit der Sünde, die Sünde aber mit den Dämonen in Verbindung gebracht. Und gerade Krankheiten, die zur starken Zerrüttung der menschlichen Persönlichkeit führen, Geisteskrankheiten mit besonders auffälligen Symptomen (z. B. schäumender Mund bei Epilepsie), wurden in jener Zeit wie auch noch viele Jahrhunderte später einem Dämon zugeschrieben, der im Menschen Wohnung genommen hat. Beim Fehlen von Irrenanstalten aber wurden die Menschen auch in der Öffentlichkeit viel öfter mit Geisteskranken konfrontiert, die offensichtlich nicht mehr ihr eigener Herr waren. Die Heilung solcher Krankheiten – etwa eines tobenden Irren im Gottesdienst[7] oder eines Epileptikers[8] – wurde als Sieg über den den Kranken beherrschenden Dämon angesehen.

Nicht nur Israel, die ganze antike Welt war voll von Dämonenglauben und Dämonenfurcht. Je ferner der Gott, um so größer das Bedürfnis nach Zwischenwesen zwischen Himmel und Erde, guten und bösen. Oft spekulierte man über ganze Hierarchien von bösen Geistern unter der Anführung eines Satan, Belial oder Beelzebul. Überall in den verschiedenen Religionen bemühten sich Zauberer, Priester, Ärzte um Bannung und Vertreibung der Dämonen. Das Alte Testament war dem Dämonenglauben gegenüber recht zurückhaltend gewesen. Aber 538–331 gehörte Israel zum persischen Großreich, dessen Religion dualistisch einen guten Gott, von dem alles Gute kommt, und einen bösen Gott, von dem alles Böse kommt, annahm. Eine Beeinflussung ist unübersehbar, und deutlich erscheint so der Dämonenglaube im Jahweglaube als ein spätes, sekundäres Moment, das denn auch im späteren und besonders heutigen Judentum wiederum keine Rolle mehr spielt.

Jesus selber inmitten dieser Zeit eines massiven Dämonenglaubens zeigt nichts von einem verkappten persischen Dualismus, in welchem sich Gott und Teufel auf gleicher Ebene um Welt und Mensch streiten. Er predigt die Frohbotschaft von der Gottesherrschaft und nicht die Drohbotschaft von der Satansherrschaft. An der Figur des Satans oder Teufels, an den Spekulationen über Engelsünde und Engelsturz ist er offensichtlich nicht interessiert. Eine Dämonenlehre entwickelt er nicht. Nirgendwo findet man bei ihm aufsehenerregende Gesten, bestimmte Riten, Zaubersprüche und Manipulationen wie bei zeitgenössischen jüdischen oder hellenistischen Exorzisten. Krankheit und Besessenheit, aber nicht alle möglichen Übel und Sünden, politischen Weltmächte und ihre Herrscher werden mit Dämonen in Verbindung gebracht. Die Heilungen und Dämonenaustreibungen Jesu sind vielmehr ein Zeichen, daß die Gottesherrschaft nahegekommen ist: daß der Dämonenherrschaft eine Ende bereitet wird. Deshalb sieht Jesus nach Lukas den Satan wie einen Blitz vom Himmel fallen[9]. So verstanden bedeutet die Dämonenaustreibung, bedeutet die Befreiung des Menschen vom Dämonenbann gerade nicht irgendeinen mythologischen Akt. Sie bedeutet ein Stück Entdämonisierung und Entmythologisierung von Mensch und Welt und die Befreiung zu wahrer Geschöpflichkeit und Menschlichkeit. Gottes Reich ist heile Schöpfung. Jesus befreit die Besessenen von den psychischen Zwängen und durchbricht den Teufelskreis von seelischer Störung, Teufelsglauben und gesellschaftlicher Ächtung.

3. Schließlich können auch andere Wundergeschichten zumindest einen *geschichtlichen Anlaß* gehabt haben. Die Erzählung von der Sturmstillung etwa kann von einer Rettung aus der Seenot nach Gebet und Hilferuf ihren Anfang genommen haben. Die Erzählung von der Münze im Fischmaul kann von der Aufforderung Jesu herkommen, einen Fisch zur Bezahlung der geforderten Tempelsteuer zu fangen. Selbstverständlich sind dies nicht mehr als Vermutungen. Der eventuelle Anlaß läßt sich nicht mehr rekonstruieren, weil der Erzähler gerade daran nicht interessiert war. Ihm ging es um das Zeugnis, das möglichst eindrückliche Zeugnis für Jesus als den Christus.

Sollte es in dieser Perspektive verwunderlich sein, daß das faktisch Geschehene im Lauf von 40 bis 70 Jahren mündlicher Überlieferung, wie dies beim Weitererzählen von Geschichten nicht nur im Orient normal ist, erweitert, ausgeschmückt, gesteigert wurde?

1. *Weiterbildungen* der ursprünglichen Überlieferung sind kaum zu bestreiten: Ein Vergleich der überlieferten Texte untereinander, der hier nicht durchzuführen ist[10], zeigt, wie Berichte verdoppelt erscheinen (zwei wunderbare Fischzüge, zwei Speisungen), wie die Zahlen wachsen (ein Blinder – zwei Blinde, ein Besessener – zwei Besessene; 4000, dann 5000 Gespeiste; sieben, dann zwölf übriggebliebene Körbe), wie die Wunder vergrößert werden (der innersynoptische Vergleich, der Vergleich mit den drei johanneischen Parallelen, auch der Vergleich der drei Totenerweckungen zeigen es) und wie Jesu Wundertätigkeit schließlich verallgemeinert wird (Sammelberichte). Jesus erscheint vielfach als mit wunderbaren Kräften begabter hellenistischer »Gottesmann« (theios aner). Einiges kann auch sprachlich mißverstanden worden sein: Das aramäische »ligjona« kann »Legion« (eine Legion Dämonen) oder »Legionär« (ein Dämon mit Namen »Legionär«) heißen; für »am See« und »auf dem See« Wandeln kann im Griechischen dasselbe Wort gebraucht werden. Anderes dürfte der Freude an der Ausschmückung und Steigerung – wie etwa schon im Alten Testament bezüglich Israels Durchgang durch das Rote Meer – zuzuschreiben sein: Das Ohr des Knechtes, bei der Verhaftung Jesu nach Markus abgehauen, wird bei Lukas auch gleich wieder geheilt. Die Geschichte vom wunderbaren Fischfang könnte das Wort vom »Menschenfischer« symbolisch vorausdarstellen; sie ist jedenfalls von Lukas als Berufungsgeschichte und vom Verfasser des johanneischen Nachtragskapitels als Erscheinungsgeschichte wiedergegeben worden.

2. Natürlich kann auch nicht ausgeschlossen werden, daß die urchristlichen Gemeinden, welche die allgemeine Wunderfreudigkeit ihrer Zeitgenossen teilten, *außerchristliche Motive oder Stoffe* auf Jesus übertragen haben, um seine Größe und Vollmacht zu unterstreichen. Wie dies bei allen großen »Religionsstiftern« durch Wundergeschichten geschah! Jedenfalls kann

man nicht einfach die heidnischen und jüdischen Wundergeschichten als unhistorisch annehmen und die neutestamentlichen
als historisch. Zahlreich waren die durch (noch heute vorhande-
ne) Votivtafeln bezeugten Heilungen im Asklepios-Heiligtum
von Epidauros und anderes mehr. Rabbinische und besonders
hellenistische Wundergeschichten von Heilungen, Verwandlun-
gen, Dämonenaustreibungen, Totenerweckungen, Sturmstillun-
gen waren in nicht geringer Zahl im Umlauf.

Gewiß gibt es gewichtige Unterschiede: bei Jesus keine Selbst-
hilfewunder, Schauwunder, Strafwunder, keine Belohnungs-,
Honorar- und Profitwunder! Aber auch nicht weniger gewichtige Ähnlichkeiten: Die Münze (oder Perle) im Maul eines gefangenen Fisches ist ein im Judentum wie im Hellenismus (Ring
des Polykrates) verbreitetes Märchenmotiv. Die auffälligerweise
nur bei Johannes überlieferte Verwandlung von Wasser in Wein
stellt einen bekannten Zug des Dionysosmythos und -kultes dar.
Von Vespasian berichten Tacitus wie Sueton die Heilung eines
Blinden durch Speichel[11]. Bei Lukian hören wir von einem Geheilten, der sein Bett fortträgt[12]. Merkwürdig ist vor allem die bis
ins Detail gehende Ähnlichkeit der dem Apollonios von Tyana,
einem Zeitgenossen Jesu, zugeschriebenen Auferweckung einer
jungen Braut vor den Toren Roms[13] mit der Erweckung des
Jünglings zu Nain[14]. Die Jesus kaum glaubhaft zuschreibbare
groteske Geschichte von der Austreibung des Dämons Legion,
die den Eigentümer eine Riesenherde von 2000 (»unreine«, verbotene!) Schweine gekostet haben soll und deshalb von jedem
Juden mit Vergnügen angehört wurde, konnte von einem jüdischen Wundermann im unreinen Heidenland übernommen sein
(Motiv des betrügenden oder betrogenen Teufels).

Zu der besonders im Johannesevangelium berichteten Gabe,
den Menschen ins Herz zu sehen, gibt es eine Parallele in Qumran: Demnach wäre sie nicht Ausdruck einer mythologischen
Allwissenheit, sondern vielmehr der messianischen Vollmacht,
welche nicht für ein staunendes Publikum, sondern für die betreffenden Menschen zum »Gericht« gedacht ist[15]. Bei manchen
Wundergeschichten müßte überhaupt gefragt werden, ob nicht
mehr alttestamentliche Gestalten wie Mose und Josua, David
und Salomo, Elia und Elisa vor Augen standen als der Typus des
hellenistischen »Gottesmannes« oder »göttlichen Menschen«.

3. Aber darüber hinaus will überlegt sein, daß die Evangelien
bereits im Licht des auferstandenen, erhöhten Herrn geschrieben

sind. Es kann deshalb nicht ausgeschlossen werden, daß es sich bei einigen Wundergeschichten um *vorausgenommene Darstellungen des erhöhten Christus* handelt: Epiphaniegeschichten, die vielfach einen transparenten Sinn und eine für die Gemeinde symbolische Bedeutung haben (Rettung aus dem »Sturm« der Bedrängnis usw.). Solche Wunder nehmen die Herrlichkeit des Auferstandenen vorweg. Zu ihnen dürfte die Geschichte von der Verklärung Jesu auf dem Berg[16] ebenso gehören wie die vom Wandeln auf dem See[17] und die von der Speisung der 5000 beziehungsweise 4000[18]. Erst recht werden die Geschichten von der Totenerweckung der Jairustochter[19] und die – trotz ihres sensationellen Charakters auffälligerweise nur bei Lukas oder Johannes überlieferten – Erweckungen des Jünglings zu Nain[20] und des Lazarus[21] dazugehören. Hier überall soll Jesus als der Herr über Leben und Tod, als der Gottessohn herausgestellt werden. Christliche und nichtchristliche Motive können sich in derselben Geschichte kreuzen. Daß so vieles und insbesondere die Erzählungen vom Seesturm und Seewandel, von der Brotvermehrung und den Totenerweckungen nach alttestamentlichen Motiven (insbesondere auch aus den Psalmen) gestaltet und stilisiert worden sind, ergibt jede genaue Analyse.

Christian Science?

Mehr als alles dies gibt die historische Untersuchung nicht her, auch wenn sie keineswegs von einem apriorischen Glauben an die Unmöglichkeit von Wundern ausgeht. Es geht hier nicht um die Möglichkeit oder Unmöglichkeit von Wundern überhaupt. Nur: Wer Wunder im strengen Sinn behaupten will, hat die Beweislast. Und Wunder im streng neuzeitlichen Sinn einer Durchbrechung von Naturgesetzen sind historisch nicht zu erweisen. Folglich wird man den vieldeutigen Ausdruck »Wunder« heute meist besser vermeiden. Man befindet sich dann in merkwürdiger Übereinstimmung mit dem Neuen Testament selbst: Das seit Homer und Hesiod übliche griechische Wort für Wunder (thauma) erscheint kein einziges Mal; auch die lateinische Vulgata-Übersetzung verwendet den Begriff »miraculum« im Neuen Testament nicht. Besser wird man – wiederum im Anschluß an das Neue Testament und besonders Johannes – von »Zeichen« oder »Zeichentaten« reden. Es handelt sich um charismatische (nicht ärztliche) therapeutisch-exorzistische Taten, die zeichenhaften Charakter tragen, allerdings als solche Jesus nicht von anderen ähnlichen Charismatikern unterscheiden. Religionsgeschichtlich lassen sich diese Taten nicht als analogielos beweisen. Sie lassen sich nicht als einzigartig, unvergleichlich, unverwechselbar Jesus allein und keinem anderen zuschreiben. Aber sie waren zumindest für die Menschen seiner Zeit erstaunlich. Und zwar so erstaunlich, daß man ihm noch mehr, ja schließlich alles zutraute und ihn besonders nach seinem Tod aus der Verklärung des zeitlichen Abstandes heraus nicht genug preisen konnte.

War also Jesus so etwas wie ein *Heilpraktiker,* der eine Heil-Lehre, eine Wissenschaft des Heilens praktizierte? Die Bewegung der »Christian Science« betrachtet in der Tat Jesus von Nazaret als den ersten Lehrer und Praktiker der »christlichen Wissenschaft«: Jesus als das Vorbild einer neuartigen Heilmethode durch die Kraft des Glaubens. Überwindung also alles Unvollkommenen, alles Krankhaften und Leidvollen – letztlich als Illusion gekennzeichnet – auf geistigem, mentalem Weg, ohne alle äußeren Eingriffe?

Das wäre ein *Mißverständnis* der charismatischen Taten Jesu. Die Heilungen und Dämonenaustreibungen geschahen keinesfalls regelmäßig oder gar planmäßig. Oft entzieht sich Jesus dem Volk und gebietet den Geheilten Schweigen[22]. Jesus war nicht ein Wundermann, ein hellenistischer »Gottesmann«, der möglichst viele Kranke gesund machen wollte. Die ältere palästinische Schicht der Wundererzählungen – das zeigt die formgeschichtliche Analyse – verzichtet noch auf die hellenistische Stilisierung, wie sie die heidnischen Wunderberichte charakterisiert. Topik und Technik dieser stilisierten Wunderberichte weisen folgende stereotype Züge auf: Exposition der Schrecklichkeit der Krankheit und vergebliche Heilungsversuche, dann Schilderung der Heilung (durch Geste, Wort, Speichel usw.), schließlich Demonstration (der Lahme trägt sein Bett usw.) und Reaktion der Zeugen (Chorschluß: Ausrufe, Staunen, Furcht der Augenzeugen). Die älteren palästinischen Wundererzählungen – wie etwa die Erzählung von der Heilung der Schwiegermutter des Petrus[23] – sind kurz und literarisch anspruchslos. Sie verzichten auf Ausmalung und profane Motive. Stilgemäße Züge dringen erst zögernd ein[24].

Die ursprünglichen, schlichten Erzählungen stellen Jesu göttliche Vollmacht ins Zentrum. Jesus sah seine Berufung, seine Geisterfülltheit, seine Botschaft in seinen charismatischen Taten bestätigt und geriet darüber mit seiner Familie und den Theologen in Streit[25]. Nicht das Negative, sondern das Positive war wichtig: an einer Durchbrechung von Naturgesetzen waren die Evangelien nicht interessiert, wohl aber daran, daß in diesen Taten Gottes Macht selber durchbricht. Die charismatischen Heilungen und Dämonenaustreibungen Jesu hatten keinen Eigenzweck. Sie standen *im Dienst der Verkündigung des Gottesreiches.* Sie deuten oder bekräftigen Jesu Wort. Ein Gelähmter wird geheilt, um die Berechtigung der von Jesus zugesprochenen Sündenvergebung zu erweisen[26]. Sie geschehen nicht regelmäßig und erst recht nicht organisiert – die Umwandlung der Welt bleibt Gottes Sache. Sie geschehen beispielhaft, zeichenhaft – schon beginnt Gott, den Fluch des menschlichen Daseins in Segen zu wandeln.

Wichtiger als die Zahl und das Ausmaß der Heilungen, Dämonenaustreibungen, wunderbaren Taten ist: Jesus wendet sich all denen in Sympathie und Mitleid zu, *denen sich niemand zuwendet:* den Schwachen, Kranken, Vernachlässigten, von der Gesellschaft Ausgestoßenen. An ihnen ging man schon immer gerne vorbei. Schwache und Kranke sind lästig. Von Aussätzigen und »Besessenen« hält jedermann Abstand. Und die frommen Qumranmönche (und ähnlich zum Teil auch die Rabbinen) schlossen, getreu ihrer Regel, von vornherein bestimmte Menschengruppen aus ihrer Gemeinschaft aus:

> »Toren, Verrückte, Einfältige, Irre,
> Blinde, Lahme, Hinkende, Taube und Unmündige –
> keiner von ihnen darf in die Gemeinde aufgenommen werden;
> denn heilige Engel sind in ihrer Mitte[27].«

Von ihnen allen wendet sich Jesus nicht ab, sie alle stößt er nicht zurück. Er behandelt die Kranken nicht als Sünder, sondern zieht sie heilend heran. »Freie Bahn dem Tüchtigen, dem Gesunden, dem Jungen« – das sind nicht die Parolen Jesu. Er kennt keinen Kult der Gesundheit, der Jugend, der Leistung. Er liebt sie alle, wie sie sind, und vermag so zu helfen: den Kranken an Leib und Seele gibt er Gesundheit; den Schwachen und Altgewordenen Kraft; den Untüchtigen Tüchtigkeit; all den armen, hoffnungslosen Existenzen Hoffnung, neues Leben, Vertrauen in die Zukunft. Und sind dies alles – auch wenn sie kein einziges Naturgesetz verletzen – nicht sehr ungewöhnliche, außerordent-

liche, staunenerregende, wundersam-wunderbare Taten? Dem
Täufer im Gefängnis, der nicht weiß, was er von Jesus halten soll,
antwortet Jesus nach der Überlieferung mit einem Bild des Reiches Gottes, das in seiner poetischen Form nicht eine exakte
Wunderliste (einiges davon mag sich in Gegenwart der Boten
ereignet haben), sondern ein messianisches Lied – in erstaunlichem Kontrast zu Qumran – darstellt[28]:

> Blinde sehen und Lahme gehen,
> Aussätzige genesen und Taube hören,
> Tote werden auferweckt,
> und Arme empfangen die Frohbotschaft.

Dies will besagen: Die wunderbaren Wirkungen des kommenden Gottesreiches sind schon jetzt spürbar. Die Zukunft Gottes
wirkt schon in die Gegenwart hinein. Nicht als ob die Welt selbst
schon verwandelt wäre – das Reich Gottes wird erst kommen.
Aber in ihm, in Jesus, seinen Worten und Taten strahlt seine
Macht bereits aus, ist bereits ein Anfang gemacht. Wenn er
Kranke heilt, wenn er durch Gottes Geist Dämonen austreibt, so
ist *in ihm und mit ihm* das Reich Gottes schon gekommen[29].
Jesus hat durch seine Taten das Reich Gottes nicht schon aufgerichtet. Wohl aber hat er *Zeichen* gesetzt, in denen das kommen-
de Reich bereits aufleuchtet. Zeichenhafte, leibhafte, typische
Vorausdarstellungen jenes definitiven und umfassenden leib-gei-
stigen Wohls, welches wir das »*Heil*« des Menschen nennen!
Insofern konnte er sagen: Das Reich Gottes ist schon in eurer
Mitte[30].

Hinweise, nicht Beweise

Jesu zeichenhafte Taten sind *keine eindeutigen Argumente der
Glaubwürdigkeit,* die aus sich allein Glauben begründen könn-
ten. Wunder allein beweisen nichts. Schon für die Zeitgenossen
Jesu waren sie zweideutig: Je nachdem, wie einer zu Jesu Bot-
schaft und Person stand, war für ihn dieselbe Tat eine Machttat
Gottes oder aber ein dämonisches Blendwerk. Je nachdem ließ er
sich überzeugen oder wich er aus, betete er an oder verdammte
er. Es ist also nicht so, daß die Historizität von Wundern die
Gretchenfrage des christlichen Glaubens wäre. An sich ist die
Anerkennung der Historizität ebensowenig ein Beweis des

Glaubens wie ihre Bestreitung ein Beweis des Unglaubens. Die Gretchenfrage des *christlichen* Glaubens ist vielmehr die Frage nach diesem Christus selbst: Was haltet ihr von ihm, und was haltet ihr von Gott?

Jesu charismatische Taten sind nur Hinweise, die von ihm selber her glaubwürdig werden. Sie sind keine Beweise, die aus sich die Wirklichkeit und Wahrheit der Offenbarung sichern könnten. Jesus selber lehnt seinen Gegnern gegenüber jede Demonstration seiner Macht, jede Legitimation seiner Vollmacht ab. Solche »Zeichen«, wie die Pharisäer sie fordern und wohl auch die Apokalyptiker vom Messias erwarten, verweigert er[31]. Solche Zeichenforderung ist Herausforderung Gottes – also das Gegenteil echten Glaubens, wie es nach den synoptischen Versuchungsgeschichten besonders das Johannesevangelium deutlich herausstellt[32]. Nicht um Propaganda ging es Jesus, sondern um die Rettung des Menschen.

Das eigentliche Übel sowohl des supranaturalistischen Wunderverständnisses (Wunder als göttliche Eingriffe gegen die Naturgesetze) wie der allgemein religiösen Interpretation (alles in der Welt, in Einklang mit den Naturgesetzen, ist Wunder) ist die Ablösung der Wunderaussagen von Jesus und seinem Wort. Nicht die Durchbrechung des Naturgesetzes (welche historisch nicht zu verifizieren ist) und nicht ein allgemeines Durchwaltetsein der Welt durch Gott (was nicht bestritten werden soll), sondern er selber ist der Schlüssel zum Verständnis der neutestamentlichen Wunderberichte: Nur *von seinem Wort* her erhalten seine charismatischen Taten ihren *eindeutigen Sinn.* Deshalb gipfelt, in jener Antwort an Johannes, die Aufzählung der Zeichen des kommenden Reiches in der Predigt des Evangeliums[33] und endet mit der Seligpreisung dessen, der an seiner Person keinen Anstoß nimmt[34]. Die charismatischen Taten verdeutlichen Jesu Wort, umgekehrt bedürfen sie der Deutung durch Jesu Wort. Nur von Jesu Wort her erhalten sie die Glaubwürdigkeit.

Weder Jesu Wort noch seine Tat aber sind zu trennen von seiner Person. Wie es die so drastischen und in ihrem Sinn letztlich doch symbolhaften Wundererzählungen des Johannesevangeliums, die wohl aus einer eigenen Quelle stammen, deutlich machen: die Brotvermehrung ist Zeichen für Jesus als »das Brot des Lebens«[35], die Blindenheilung Zeichen für Jesus als »das Licht der Welt«[36], die Totenerweckung Zeichen für Jesus als die »Auferstehung und das Leben«[37]. Er selber, der das Reich Gottes in Wort und Tat ankündigt, ist im Grunde selber das einzige

Zeichen des kommenden Gottesreiches, das den Menschen gegeben wird. Ob mit dem Fortschritt der Wissenschaft das, was damals als Wunder empfunden wurde, eine wissenschaftliche Erklärung gefunden hat oder noch finden wird, ist eine ganz und gar zweitrangige Frage, die den Glauben nicht zu beunruhigen braucht. Jesus selber bleibt das Zeichen, das in Wort und Tat die Zukunft ankündet und den Glauben begründet. Nicht der Glaube an Wunder, sondern der *Glaube an Jesus* und an den, den er geoffenbart hat, ist gefordert. In diesem Sinne kann der Glaubende, wie wiederum das Johannesevangelium deutlich macht, auf Wunder überhaupt verzichten: Selig sind, die nicht sehen und doch glauben[38].

Was zeigen uns also die neutestamentlichen Wunderberichte?

- *Jesus wäre mißverstanden, wenn er als Heilpraktiker und Wunderdoktor verstanden würde, der sich methodisch um alle Gebrechlichkeiten der Menschen kümmert: Seine Tätigkeit darf nicht szientistisch mißdeutet werden.*
- *Jesus wäre aber ebenso mißverstanden, wenn er nur als Seelsorger und Beichtvater verstanden würde, dem es beim Menschen allein auf Seele und Geist ankäme: Seine Tätigkeit darf nicht spiritualistisch mißdeutet werden.*

Also: Die Botschaft vom Reich Gottes zielt auf den Menschen in allen seinen Dimensionen, nicht nur auf die Seele des Menschen, sondern auf den *ganzen* Menschen in seiner geistigen und leiblichen Existenz, in seiner ganzen konkreten leidvollen Welt. Und sie gilt *allen* Menschen: nicht nur den Starken, Jungen, Gesunden, Tüchtigen, die die Welt so gerne verherrlicht, sondern auch den Schwachen, Kranken, Alten, Untüchtigen, die die Welt so gerne vergißt, übersieht, vernachlässigt. Jesus hat nicht nur geredet, sondern auch eingegriffen in den Bereich von Krankheit und Ungerechtigkeit. Er hat nicht nur die Vollmacht des Predigens, sondern auch das Charisma des Heilens. Er ist nicht nur *Verkünder* und *Ratgeber*. Er ist zugleich *Heilender* und *Helfender*.

Und auch darin war er wieder anders als die Priester und Theologen, die Guerillakämpfer und die Mönche: Er lehrte wie einer, der Macht hat[39]. Was ist das: eine neue Lehre voll Macht? So fragt und sagt man sich nach dem ersten Wunder bei Markus[40]. Es brach in ihm etwas auf, was von den einen schärfstens abgelehnt, ja als Magie verdammt wird und was den anderen den Eindruck einer Begegnung mit der göttlichen Macht vermittelte:

das Gottesreich, das nicht nur in Vergebung und Bekehrung, sondern auch in der Erlösung und Befreiung des Leibes und in der Verwandlung und Vollendung der Welt besteht. So erscheint Jesus nicht nur als der Verkünder, sondern auch in Wort und Tat als der *Bürge* des kommenden Gottesreiches. Was aber, so muß jetzt gefragt werden, ist seine Norm?

3. Die oberste Norm

Die Frage drängt sich von allen Abgrenzungen her, die sich gezeigt haben, auf: Woran soll sich der Mensch eigentlich halten? Wenn einer sich schon nicht an das Establishment binden, wenn er sich aber auch nicht der Revolution verschreiben, wenn er sich nicht zur äußeren oder inneren Emigration entschließen und auch den moralischen Kompromiß ablehnen will: Was will er dann eigentlich? Einen fünften Bezugspunkt scheint es in diesem Koordinatenkreuz gar nicht zu geben. Woran, an welches Gesetz will er sich halten? Was soll hier überhaupt Norm, oberste Norm sein? Eine Frage von grundlegender Bedeutung damals wie heute. Was gilt für Jesus?

Kein Naturgesetz

Oberste Norm ist nicht ein natürliches Sittengesetz: *nicht ein sittliches Naturgesetz*. Dies mindestens kurz herauszustellen, dürfte nicht ganz unwichtig sein in einer Zeit, da eine wichtige päpstliche Enzyklika die Begründung für die Unsittlichkeit »künstlicher« Geburtenregelung mit Berufung auf die Autorität Jesu Christi in einem solchen Naturgesetz zu finden vorgab. Man wird es nicht nur einem Mangel an theologischer Reflexion zuschreiben dürfen, wenn Jesus zur Begründung seiner Forderungen nicht von einer angeblich sicher erkennbaren und alle Menschen verbindenden unveränderlichen Wesensnatur ausgeht. Ihm geht es eben nicht um eine abstrakte Menschennatur, sondern um den konkreten einzelnen Menschen. Ganz selbstverständlich und zugleich höchst eindrücklich spricht er von der Welt des Menschen: von den Vögeln des Himmels und den Lilien des Feldes, den Trauben und den Feigen, den Dornen und Disteln, von Saat und Ernte, Sonne und Regen, vom Wetter, vom Rost und den Motten ... Nichts wird schlecht gemacht, aber auch nichts romantisch erklärt, alles wird genommen, wie es ist. Ganz konkret spricht er auch vom Menschen in dieser Welt, wie er leibt und lebt: die Kinder auf dem Marktplatz und der Vater in der Familie, die Frau im Haus, der Arbeiter im Weinberg, der Hirte bei seinen Schafen, der Bauer auf dem Feld, der Richter und der Angeklagte, der König und der Knecht. Wiederum wird nichts angeschwärzt, aber auch nichts rosarot gefärbt, realistisch wird der Mensch gesehen, und oft nicht ohne Heiterkeit und Ironie, wie man leicht zwischen den Zeilen lesen kann.

Die Welt und der Mensch sind somit bei Jesus präsent – als Gottes Welt und Mensch. Jesus ist nicht, wie etwa Kung-futse, vom Glauben an ein ewiges Weltgesetz bestimmt, gemäß welchem der Mensch handeln soll. Auch das Wort »Schöpfung« gebraucht er kaum, und das auf griechisches Denken zurückgehende Wort »Natur« überhaupt nicht. An der Erkenntnis einer gemeinsamen, unveränderlichen Menschennatur ist ihm nicht gelegen. Er geht nicht, wie etwa die Stoiker, aus von einer Idee des Menschen, als wäre der Mensch als solcher etwas Heiliges. Vor allem denkt er nicht daran, aus irgendwelchen bleibenden und unveränderlichen Strukturen einer solchen Menschennatur allgemein verbindliche, unveränderliche Grundgesetze des Handelns abzuleiten: erste Prinzipien, aus denen dann wiederum andere Prinzipien mehr oder weniger direkt deduziert werden, und die dann alle zusammen für alle möglichen moraltheologischen Fälle (bezüglich Privateigentum, Familie, Staat, Sexualität, Ehescheidung, Todesstrafe usw.) eine eindeutige Antwort liefern.

Gewiß, Welt und Mensch besagen etwas für Jesus. Ihm kündet die Schöpfung den Schöpfer, der seine Sonne aufgehen läßt über Gute und Böse und regnen läßt über Gerechte und Ungerechte. Das Gras des Feldes und die Sperlinge künden von einer Fürsorge Gottes, die jedes ängstliche Sichsorgen des Menschen überflüssig erscheinen läßt. Saat, Wachstum und Ernte erinnern an Gottes Verheißung, Blitz, Regen und Sturm an sein Gericht. Die ganze Schöpfung liegt für Jesus im Lichte Gottes und wird zum Gleichnis, das auf den Schöpfer und Vollender zugleich verweist. Aber weder schließt Jesus von der Schöpfung durch Schlußfolgerung auf Gott, noch deduziert er durch die natürliche Vernunft von der Natur und ihren Strukturen ein ontologisch begründetes

Normen- und Lehrsystem, das für jedes andere Gesetz Fundament zu sein hätte.

Wenn Jesus so keine »Naturrechtsethik« im Sinne der an den Griechen orientierten Scholastik vertritt, so andererseits allerdings auch keine »formale Pflichtethik«, wie sie später Kant begründete. Auch die von Kant verwertete »goldene Regel« der Bergpredigt – alles, was ihr wollt, das euch die Leute tun sollen, das tut ihnen[1] – ist kein formales Prinzip, kein kategorischer Imperativ, aus welchem alle konkreten ethischen Forderungen abgeleitet werden könnten. Und schließlich vertritt Jesus auch keine »materiale Wertethik«, so wie sie dann vor allem Max Scheler entwickelt hat. Er stellt keine Wertordnung auf und begründet keine Stufung etwa von den Sachwerten über die vitalen, ästhetischen und intellektuellen zu den sittlichen und religiösen Werten. Auch der vor allem durch die Redaktion des Mattäus in der Verkündigung Jesu zur Bedeutung gekommene Begriff der Gerechtigkeit gilt nicht als Höchstwert, sondern steht neben anderen nicht weniger wichtigen allgemeinen Begriffen. Und selbst die Liebe fungiert nicht als höchster Wert, aus welchem alles übrige in Vollständigkeit abgeleitet werden könnte. An Vollständigkeit ist Jesus überhaupt nicht gelegen. Vom Staat spricht er kaum, von Wirtschaft, Kultur, Erziehung und manchem anderen überhaupt nicht. Selbstverständlich lag vieles einfach außerhalb des Horizontes seiner Zeit. Aber dies erklärt nicht alles: hier liegt nicht nur zeitbedingte Beschränktheit, sondern auch bewußte Beschränkung, Konzentration vor. Vieles, was in anderer Hinsicht wichtig sein mag, ist ihm offensichtlich nicht wichtig. Worauf also kommt es ihm an? Bevor wir positiv antworten, ist eine zweite Abgrenzung notwendig.

Kein Offenbarungsgesetz

Oberste Norm ist auch nicht ein positives Offenbarungsgesetz: *nicht ein geoffenbartes Gottesgesetz.* Jesus ist nicht, wie etwa Mose, Zarathustra und Mohammed, Vertreter einer typischen Gesetzesreligion, für welche zwar nicht ein ewiges Weltgesetz (wie im chinesischen oder stoischen Denken), sondern ein alle Lebensbereiche ordnendes Offenbarungsgesetz die bestimmende Größe im Alltagsleben ist: im Islam gar in der Form eines bei Gott präexistent vorhandenen Buches (Koran), das schon vor Mohammed durch andere Propheten den Völkern mitgeteilt, wenn auch dann verfälscht worden war, bis Mohammed als der letzte Prophet nach Jesus, als »Siegel der Propheten«, die Ur-offenbarung wiederherstellte.

Freilich hat man in der Kirchengeschichte immer wieder Jesus als »neuen Gesetzgeber« und das Evangelium als »neues Gesetz« ausgegeben. Nun hat Jesus gewiß das alttestamentliche Gesetz keineswegs als solches abgelehnt, wenn er gegen den pharisäi-schen (frühjüdischen) Legalismus anging. Und selbst für seine Zeit darf Gesetzesfrömmigkeit nicht mit dem weitverbreiteten Legalismus gleichgesetzt werden[2]. An sich bekundet das Gesetz den ordnenden Gotteswillen. An sich bekundet es Gottes Güte und Treue, ist es ein Dokument und Erweis seiner Gnade und Liebe zu seinem Volk und fordert nicht nur einzelne Handlun-gen, sondern das Herz. Jesus wollte es nicht durch seine eigene Botschaft ersetzen. Zu erfüllen, nicht aufzuheben – so sahen wir – war er gekommen. Er war kein Vertreter einer anarchistischen Gesetzlosigkeit.

Und trotzdem war für ihn das Gesetz nicht die oberste Norm, von der es keine Möglichkeit der Dispens gab. Er hätte sich sonst nicht darüber hinwegsetzen dürfen. Nun steht aber fest, wie wir ebenfalls bereits sahen: Jesus setzte sich über das Gesetz hinweg, und zwar nicht nur über die Tradition, die mündliche Überliefe-rung der Väter, die ›Halacha‹, sondern auch über die Heilige Schrift selbst, das in den fünf Büchern Moses (= Pentateuch) aufgeschriebene heilige Gesetz Gottes, die ›Tora[3]‹. Die Verbind-lichkeit der mündlichen Überlieferung lehnte er überhaupt ab: In Wort und Tat ging er sowohl gegen die kultischen Reinheitsvor-schriften wie gegen die Fastenvorschriften wie insbesondere die Sabbatvorschriften an, was, wie dargelegt, ausreichte, um ihm die erbitterte Feindschaft der Pharisäer zuzuziehen. Aber dies natür-lich auch, weil mit der Ablehnung der mündlichen Überlieferung auch die Tora selbst, das mosaische Gesetz, faktisch mitbetroffen war, welches jene Überlieferungen der Väter nur zu interpretie-ren vorgaben; man denke an die Bestimmungen der Tora über reine und unreine Nahrung[4] oder an das Sabbatgebot[5]. Direkt gegen das mosaische Gesetz aber stand Jesus im Verbot der Ehescheidung[6], im Verbot des Schwures[7], im Verbot der Vergel-tung[8], im Gebot der Feindesliebe[9].

Die Gesetzeskritik Jesu wurde noch verstärkt durch seine Kultkritik. Für Jesus ist der Tempel nicht ewig wie für die meisten seiner Volksgenossen. Er rechnet mit seinem Abbruch[10]; der neue Gottestempel stehe schon bereit, der in der Heilszeit den alten ersetzen werde[11]. In der Zwischenzeit betont Jesus nicht nur allgemein die untergeordnete Bedeutung des Opferkults[12]. Vor dem Opfer wird Versöhnung gefordert[13].

Die Kritik Jesu am alttestamentlichen Gesetz läßt sich nicht verharmlosen: Er hat das Gesetz nicht nur an bestimmten Punkten anders interpretiert; das taten auch die Pharisäer. Er hat das Gesetz auch nicht nur an bestimmten Punkten verschärft oder radikalisiert (schon Zorn ist Mord, schon ehebrecherisches Begehren Ehebruch); das tat auch der »Lehrer der Gerechtigkeit« im Qumrankloster. Nein, er hat sich in befremdender Selbständigkeit und Freiheit über das Gesetz hinweggesetzt, wann und wo es ihm richtig schien. Selbst wenn Jesus die Formeln noch nicht gebraucht hätte, was doch wohl nur eine allzu skeptische Kritik bezweifeln kann: Sowohl das »Ich aber sage euch« in den Antithesen der Bergpredigt wie das sonst von niemandem am Anfang der Sätze gebrauchte »Amen« gibt der Radikalisierung, Kritik, ja aufhebenden Reaktivierung des Gesetzes durch Jesus exakten Ausdruck und läßt zugleich die Frage nach der Autorität aufkommen, die hier in Anspruch genommen wird und die über die Autorität eines Gesetzestheologen und auch eines Propheten weit hinauszugehen scheint. Auch wer die ganze Tora als von Gott annahm, aber mit Ausnahme dieses oder jenes Verses, der nicht von Gott, sondern von Mose sei, der hatte nach dem Urteil der Zeitgenossen das Wort Jahwes verachtet. Soll es denn eine »bessere Gerechtigkeit[14]« geben können als die des Gesetzes? Schon zu Beginn des ersten Evangeliums wird berichtet, daß Jesu Zuhörer fassungslos waren, daß er anders lehrte als die Schriftgelehrten[15].

Statt Gesetzlichkeit Gottes Wille

Was also wollte Jesus? Es ist bereits deutlich geworden: Gottes Sache vertreten. Das meint er mit seiner Botschaft vom Kommen des Reiches Gottes. Daß aber Gottes Name geheiligt werde und sein Reich komme, erscheint in der Mattäusfassung des Vaterunser erweitert durch den Satz: Dein Wille geschehe! Was Gott im Himmel will, das soll auf Erden getan werden. Dies also bedeutet die Botschaft vom Kommen des Reiches Gottes, wenn sie als Forderung für den Menschen hier und jetzt verstanden wird: Es geschehe, was Gott will. Dies gilt für Jesus selbst bis in seine eigene Passion hinein: Sein Wille geschehe[16]. Gottes Wille ist der

Maßstab. Dies soll auch für seine Nachfolge gelten: Wer den Willen Gottes tut, ist ihm Bruder, Schwester, Mutter[17]. Nicht Herr, Herr sagen, sondern den Willen des Vaters tun – das führt ins Himmelreich[18]. Es ist somit unverkennbar und wird durch das ganze Neue Testament hindurch bestätigt: Oberste Norm *ist der Wille Gottes*[19].

Das Tun des Willens Gottes ist für viele Fromme eine fromme Formel geworden. Sie haben ihn mit dem Gesetz identifiziert. Daß es hier um eine sehr radikale Parole geht, erkennt man erst, wenn man sieht: Der Wille Gottes ist nicht einfach identisch mit dem geschriebenen Gesetz und erst recht nicht identisch mit der das Gesetz auslegenden Tradition. Sosehr das Gesetz den Willen Gottes künden kann, sosehr kann es auch Mittel sein, um sich hinter ihm gegen Gottes Willen zu verschanzen. So leicht führt das Gesetz zur Haltung der *Gesetzlichkeit.* Eine Haltung, die trotz rabbinischer Aussagen über das Gesetz als Ausdruck der Gnade und des Gotteswillens weit verbreitet war!

Ein Gesetz gibt Sicherheit: weil man weiß, woran man sich zu halten hat. An genau dieses nämlich: an nicht weniger (das kann manchmal lästig sein), aber auch nicht an mehr (das ist manchmal recht bequem). Nur was geboten ist, muß ich tun. Und was nicht verboten ist, das ist erlaubt. Und wieviel kann man in einzelnen Fällen tun und lassen, bevor man mit dem Gesetz in Konflikt kommt! Kein Gesetz kann alle Möglichkeiten berücksichtigen, alle Fälle einkalkulieren, alle Lücken schließen. Zwar versucht man immer wieder, frühere Gesetzesbestimmungen (für die Moral oder die Lehre), die damals einen Sinn hatten, ihn aber unterdessen verloren haben, künstlich auf die neuen Lebensbedingungen zurechtzubiegen, beziehungsweise aus ihnen künstlich etwas Entsprechendes für die veränderte Situation abzuleiten. Dies scheint der einzige Weg zu sein, wenn man den Buchstaben des Gesetzes mit dem Willen Gottes identifiziert: durch Gesetzesinterpretation und Gesetzesexplikation zur Gesetzeskumulation. Im alttestamentlichen Gesetz zählte man 613 Vorschriften (im römischen Codex Iuris Canonici zählt man 2414 Canones). Aber je feiner das Netz geknüpft ist, um so zahlreicher sind auch die Löcher. Und je mehr Gebote und Verbote man aufstellt, um so mehr verdeckt man das, worauf es entscheidend ankommt. Und vor allem ist möglich, daß man das Gesetz im ganzen oder auch einzelne Gesetze nur hält, weil es nun einmal vorgeschrieben ist und man eventuell die negativen Folgen zu fürchten hat. Wäre es nicht vorgeschrieben, würde man es nicht tun. Und umgekehrt ist möglich, daß man vieles nicht tut, was eigentlich getan werden sollte, weil es nun einmal nicht vorgeschrieben ist und einen niemand darauf festlegen kann. Wie beim Priester und Leviten in der Parabel: er sah ihn und ging vorüber. Damit erscheint die Autorität wie der Gehorsam formalisiert: man tut es, weil das Gesetz es befiehlt. Und insofern ist auch grundsätzlich jedes Gebot oder Verbot gleich wichtig. Eine Differenzierung, was wichtig ist und was nicht, ist nicht nötig.

Die *Vorteile der Gesetzlichkeit* damals wie heute sind unübersehbar. Es läßt sich leicht begreifen, warum so viele Menschen sich gegenüber anderen *Menschen* lieber an ein Gesetz halten, als sich persönlich zu entscheiden: Wie vieles müßte ich sonst tun, was nicht vorgeschrieben ist? Und wie vieles lassen, was gar nicht verboten ist? Dann doch lieber klare Grenzen. Im Einzelfall läßt sich dann noch immer diskutieren: ob wirklich eine Gesetzesübertretung vorlag, ob es wirklich schon Ehebruch war, ob direkt ein Meineid, ob geradezu Mord ...! Und wenn auch Ehebruch gesetzlich verboten ist, so doch nicht alles, was dazu führt. Und wenn schon Meineid, so doch nicht alle harmloseren Formen der Unwahrhaftigkeit. Und wenn schon Mord, so doch nicht alle böswilligen Gedanken, die bekanntlich zollfrei sind. Was ich bei mir selber, was ich in meinem Herzen denke, begehre, möchte, ist meine Sache.

Und ebenfalls läßt sich leicht begreifen, warum so viele Menschen sich auch im Blick auf *Gott* selbst lieber an ein Gesetz halten: Weiß ich auf diese Weise doch genau, wann ich meine Pflicht getan habe. Bei entsprechender Leistung darf ich auch mit entsprechender Belohnung rechnen. Und, falls ich mehr als meine Pflicht getan habe, mit einer Spezialvergütung. Auf diese Weise lassen sich meine Verdienste und Verschuldungen gerecht verrechnen, moralische Minuspunkte durch überschüssige Sonderleistungen einholen und letztlich vielleicht die Strafen durch den Lohn aufheben. Das ist eine klare Rechnung, und man weiß, woran man ist mit seinem Gott.

Aber gerade dieser gesetzlichen Haltung gibt Jesus den *Todesstoß*[20]. Nicht auf das Gesetz selbst, wohl aber auf die Gesetzlichkeit, von der das Gesetz freizuhalten ist, zielt er. Auf den *Kompromiß*, den diese Gesetzesfrömmigkeit kennzeichnet. Die den Menschen abschirmende Mauer, deren eine Seite Gottes Gesetz ist und deren andere des Menschen gesetzliche Leistungen, durchbricht er[21]. Er läßt den Menschen nicht sich hinter dem Gesetz in Gesetzlichkeit verschanzen und schlägt ihm seine Verdienste aus den Händen. Den Buchstaben des Gesetzes mißt er am Willen Gottes selbst und stellt den Menschen damit in befreiender und beglückender Weise unmittelbar vor Gott. Nicht in einem kodifizierten Rechtsverhältnis steht der Mensch zu Gott, bei dem er sein eigenes Selbst heraushalten kann. Nicht einfach dem Gesetz, sondern Gott selber soll er sich stellen: dem nämlich, was Gott ganz persönlich von ihm will.

Deshalb verzichtet Jesus darauf, gelehrt über Gott zu reden, allgemeine, allumfassende moralische Prinzipien zu proklamieren, dem Menschen ein neues System beizubringen. Er gibt nicht Anweisungen für alle Gebiete des Lebens. Jesus ist *kein Gesetzgeber* und will auch keiner sein. Er verpflichtet weder neu auf die alte Gesetzesordnung noch gibt er ein neues Gesetz, das alle Lebensbereiche umfaßt. Er verfaßt weder eine Moraltheologie noch einen Verhaltenskodex. Er erläßt weder sittliche noch rituelle Anordnungen, wie der Mensch beten, fasten, die heiligen Zeiten und Orte beachten soll. Selbst das Vaterunser, vom ältesten Evangelisten überhaupt nicht überliefert, ist nicht in einem einzigen verbindlichen Wortlaut, sondern bei Lukas (wohl ursprünglich) und Mattäus in verschiedenen Fassungen wiedergegeben; nicht auf wörtliches Nachbeten kommt es Jesus an. Und gerade das Liebesgebot soll nicht ein neues Gesetz sein.

Vielmehr: Ganz konkret zugreifend, fern aller Kasuistik und Gesetzlichkeit, unkonventionell und treffsicher ruft Jesus den Einzelnen zum *Gehorsam gegen Gott* auf, der das ganze Leben umfassen soll. Einfache, durchsichtige, befreiende Appelle, die auf Autoritäts- und Traditionsargumente verzichten, aber Beispiele, Zeichen, Symptome für das veränderte Leben angeben. Große helfende, oft überspitzt formulierte Weisungen ohne alles Wenn und Aber: Bringt dich dein Auge zu Fall, so reiße es aus! Deine Rede sei ja, ja und nein, nein! Versöhne dich zuerst mit deinem Bruder! Die Anwendung auf sein Leben hat jeder selbst zu vollziehen.

Der Sinn der Bergpredigt

Auf das radikale Ernstnehmen des Willens Gottes zielt die *Bergpredigt*[22], in der Mattäus und Lukas die ethischen Forderungen Jesu – kurze Sprüche und Spruchgruppen hauptsächlich aus der Logienquelle Q – gesammelt haben. Sie hat Christen und Nichtchristen – die Jakobiner der Revolution und den Sozialisten Kautsky ebenso wie Tolstoi und Albert Schweitzer – immer wieder neu herausgefordert. Was will die Bergpredigt?

Eines kann vorausgenommen werden: Die Bergpredigt will sicher *keine verschärfte Gesetzesethik* sein. Irreführend hat man sie bisweilen als »Gesetz Christi« bezeichnet. Doch wird in ihr gerade das angesprochen, was nicht Gegenstand einer gesetzlichen Regelung werden kann. Eine quantitative Steigerung der Forderungen ist mit der »besseren Gerechtigkeit« oder der »Vollkommenheit« nicht gemeint. Jesus verwirklicht, wie die Antithesen der Bergpredigt erkennen lassen, gerade nicht jenen Gehorsam gegenüber Jota und Häkchen des Gesetzesbuchstabens, den ein judenchristliches Logion, welches von Mattäus zitiert wird[23], fordert. Damit würde der Gehorsam – in diesem Fall nicht liberal, sondern ultrakonservativ – entschärft[24]. Seine Botschaft ist überhaupt nicht eine Summe von Geboten. Ihm nachzufolgen bedeutet nicht die Ausführung einer Anzahl von Vorschriften. Nicht umsonst stehen an der Spitze der Bergpredigt Glückverheißungen für die Unglücklichen. Das Geschenk, die Gabe, die Gnade geht der Norm, der Forderung, der Weisung voraus: Jeder ist gerufen, jedem das Heil angeboten, ohne alle Vorleistungen. Und die Weisungen selber sind Konsequenzen seiner Botschaft vom Gottesreich. Nur beispielhaft, zeichenhaft nimmt er Stellung. Aber damit ist noch keineswegs klar, was die Bergpredigt will:

– *Eine* Zwei-Klassen-Ethik? *Die minimale, normale Gerechtigkeit der Gebote für das Volk, und die »bessere Gerechtigkeit« oder »Vollkommenheit« für die Jünger oder besonders die Auserwählten? So die traditionelle katholische Lehre vor dem Vatikanum II. Doch die Bergpredigt ist keine Mönchsregel: die »Räte« (consilia evangelica) sind allen gesagt. Es kommt überhaupt nicht ins Himmelreich, wer nicht gerade die bessere Gerechtigkeit erfüllt, die somit auch nach Mattäus von jedermann gefordert ist[25].*
– *Eine unerfüllbare* Bußethik? *Ist die Bergpredigt ein einziger Bußruf und Beichtspiegel, durch den der Mensch seiner sündigen Ohnmacht zum Guten überführt werden soll? So Martin Luther. Gewiß hält die Bergpredigt dem Menschen den Spiegel vor und deckt auf, was er ist. Doch sie fordert in einer neuen Situation durchaus ein neues Tun. Keine Umkehr ohne das Tun des Willens Gottes, ohne gute Werke, ohne Taten der*

Liebe. Nirgendwo wird gesagt, daß Jesus an unserer Statt die absoluten Forderungen der Bergpredigt erfüllt.

– *Eine reine* Gesinnungsethik? *Genügt die gute Gesinnung, das gute Herz? So Kant, der philosophische Idealismus und der theologische Liberalismus des vergangenen Jahrhunderts. Gewiß: die Tat wird in der Bergpredigt relativiert, das Motiv ist letztlich ausschlaggebend, das Wie und Warum ist wichtiger als das Was. Aber es genügt nicht, das Gute gewollt zu haben. Die Bergpredigt dringt auf das Tun. Die Tat ist keineswegs belanglos. Vielmehr wird schon die Gesinnung als Tat genommen und Gehorsam bis in die konkrete Tat hinein gefordert. Herz und Handeln sind nicht zu trennen.*

– *Eine neue* Gesellschaftsethik? *Der Entwurf einer wörtlich zu befolgenden neuen Gesellschaftsordnung der Liebe und des Friedens, des Reiches Christi auf Erden, für das staatliche Gewalt und Rechtsordnung, Polizei und Armee nicht mehr notwendig sind? So im Lauf der Kirchengeschichte viele (stille und revolutionäre) Schwärmer und in unserem Jahrhundert Graf Leo Tolstoi wie auch manche Religiöse Sozialisten. Gewiß darf die Bergpredigt nicht rein privat nur für die persönlichen und familiären Beziehungen verstanden werden. Es gibt Zustände der Ungerechtigkeit, Unterdrückung und Entmenschlichung, die von der Bergpredigt her aufgedeckt und bekämpft werden müssen, wo die Liebe handeln muß. Aber trotzdem wird das Reich Gottes nicht durch die moralischen Taten der Menschen begründet. Und nirgendwo wird die Bergpredigt als das Grundgesetz einer neuen Gesellschaft vorgestellt, mit Hilfe dessen die Welt von allen Übeln befreit werden soll. Wie die Bergpredigt nicht auf die individuellen und familiären Verhältnisse beschränkt werden darf, so darf sie auch nicht einfach zu einem Sozialprogramm ausgeweitet werden.*

– *Eine kurzfristige* Interimsethik? *Eine »Ausnahmegesetzgebung« für die letzte Zeit? Radikale Forderungen, die nur für die kurze Zeit bis zum nahen Weltende überhaupt erfüllbar, jetzt jedoch sinnlos geworden sind? So J. Weiss und A. Schweitzer. Zweifellos steht die Bergpredigt im Rahmen der Botschaft vom bald kommenden Gottesreich. Aber sie erklärt sich nicht ausschließlich vom apokalyptischen Feuerschein des nahen Endes her. Jesu Forderungen, etwa die Nächstenliebe, werden nicht einfach vom nahen Weltende, sondern grundsätzlich vom Willen und Wesen Gottes her motiviert. Es werden nicht au-*

ßerodentliche, heroische Taten (Weggeben allen Besitzes, Martyrium) verlangt, sondern sehr alltägliche Liebestaten. Gerade im Tun des Willens Gottes erweist sich die ständige Bereitschaft für das nahe Reich Gottes. Allerdings: In der »letzten Zeit« tritt Gottes Wille klar und rein hervor, geschieden von allen »Menschensatzungen«. Die Nähe Gottes gibt den Forderungen Jesu außerordentliche Dringlichkeit, aber auch die frohe Gewißheit der Erfüllbarkeit.

Dies ist der Generalnenner der Bergpredigt: *Gottes Wille geschehe!* Mit der Relativierung des Willens Gottes ist es vorbei. Keine fromme Schwärmerei, keine reine Innerlichkeit, sondern den Gehorsam der Gesinnung und der Tat. Der Mensch selbst steht in Verantwortung vor dem nahen, kommenden Gott. Nur durch das entschlossene, rückhaltlose Tun des Willens Gottes wird der Mensch der Verheißungen des Reiches Gottes teilhaftig. Gottes befreiende Forderung aber ist radikal. Sie verweigert den kasuistischen Kompromiß. Sie überschreitet und durchbricht die weltlichen Begrenzungen und rechtlichen Ordnungen. Die herausfordernden Beispiele der Bergpredigt[26] wollen gerade nicht eine gesetzliche Grenze angeben: nur die linke Wange, zwei Meilen, den Mantel – dann hört die Gemütlichkeit auf. Gottes Forderung appelliert an die Großzügigkeit des Menschen, tendiert auf ein Mehr. Ja, sie geht auf das Unbedingte, das Grenzenlose, das Ganze. Kann Gott mit einem begrenzten, bedingten, formalen Gehorsam – nur weil etwas geboten oder verboten ist – zufrieden sein? Da würde ein Letztes ausgespart, was alle noch so minuziösen Rechts- und Gesetzesbestimmungen nicht fassen können und was doch über die Haltung des Menschen entscheidet. Gott will mehr: Er beansprucht nicht nur den halben, sondern den ganzen Willen. Er fordert nicht nur das kontrollierbare Äußere, sondern auch das unkontrollierbare Innere – des Menschen Herz. Er will nicht nur gute Früchte, sondern den guten Baum[27]. Nicht nur das Handeln, sondern das Sein. Nicht etwas, sondern mich selbst, und mich selbst ganz und gar.

Das meinen die verwunderlichen Antithesen der Bergpredigt, wo dem Recht der Wille Gottes gegenübergestellt wird: Nicht erst Ehebruch, Meineid, Mord, sondern auch das, was das Gesetz gar nicht zu erfassen vermag, schon die ehebrecherische Gesinnung, das unwahrhaftige Denken und Reden, die feindselige Haltung sind gegen Gottes Willen. Jegliches »Nur« in der Interpretation der Bergpredigt bedeutet eine Verkürzung und Abschwächung des unbedingten Gotteswillens: »nur« eine bessere Gesetzeserfüllung, »nur« eine neue Gesinnung, »nur« ein Sündenspiegel im Licht des einen gerechten Jesus, »nur« für die zur Vollkommenheit Berufenen, »nur« für damals, »nur« für eine kurze Zeit ...

Wie schwierig es freilich für die spätere Kirche war, Jesu radikale Forderungen durchzuhalten, zeigen ihre *Entschärfungen*[28] schon in der (palästinisch-syrischen?) Gemeinde des Mattäus: Nach Jesus soll jeglicher Zorn unterbleiben[29], nach Mattäus zumindest bestimmte Schimpfworte wie »Hohlkopf«, »Gottloser«[30]. Nach Jesus soll man das Schwören überhaupt unterlassen und mit dem einfachen Ja oder Nein durchs Leben kommen[31], nach Mattäus zumindest bestimmte Schwurformeln vermeiden[32]. Nach Jesus soll man dem Nächsten die Verfehlung vorhalten und, wenn er davon absteht, ihm vergeben[33]; nach Mattäus muß ein geregelter Instanzenweg eingehalten werden[34]. Nach Jesus soll dem Mann – zum Schutz der rechtlich empfindlich benachteiligten Frau – die Scheidung bedingungslos verboten sein[35]; nach Mattäus darf zumindest im Fall krassen Ehebruchs der Frau eine Ausnahme gemacht werden[36].

Alles nur Erweichungstendenzen? Es muß darin zumindest auch das ehrliche Bemühen um die bleibende Gültigkeit der unbedingten Forderungen Jesu in einem Alltag gesehen werden, der nicht mehr von der Naherwartung des kommenden Reiches bestimmt ist. Man denke zum Beispiel an die *Ehescheidung*[37], die Jesus ganz unjüdisch gegen das patriarchalische mosaische Gesetz[38] rigoros verboten hatte mit der apodiktischen Begründung, daß Gott die Ehen zusammenfüge und nicht wolle, daß Menschen lösen, was er vereinte. Die zwischen den Schulen der Gelehrten Schammai und Hillel heftig umstrittene Frage, ob nur eine geschlechtliche Verfehlung (Schammai) oder praktisch jegliche Sache wie selbst ein angebranntes Essen (Hillel, nach Philon und Josephus die gängige Praxis) Grund zur Entlassung der Frau sein könne, war für Jesus völlig unwichtig. Ihm ging es um das Entscheidende. Freilich: Die angesichts des sich hinauszögernden Endes drängend gewordene Frage, was zu geschehen habe, wenn trotz Gottes unbedingter Forderung Ehen zerbrechen und das Leben weitergehen soll, war von Jesus nicht beantwortet worden und mußte nun beantwortet werden. Der unbedingte Appell Jesu zur Bewahrung der Einheit der Ehe wurde nun als eine Rechtsregel verstanden, die gesetzlich immer genauer fixiert werden mußte: Dem Verbot der Entlassung und Wiederheirat der Frau wurde im Hinblick auf die hellenistische Rechtslage das Verbot der Scheidung seitens der Frau samt Ausnahmeregel für Mischehen[39] sowie das Verbot der Wiederheirat für beide Teile[40] hinzugefügt; doch mußte man so auch den Ehebruch als Ausnahmegrund für eine Ehescheidung zugestehen[41]. Ob eine andere Antwort als die wiederum kasuistische Lösung durch gesetzliche Festlegung der einzelnen Fälle möglich gewesen wäre?

Jesus selber jedenfalls, kein Jurist, ließ es mit seinen unbedingten Appellen bewenden, die in der jeweiligen Situation zu realisieren waren. Das zeigt sich am Beispiel des *Eigentums,* wo Jesus, wie noch zu sehen sein wird, weder allen den Verzicht noch auch das Gemeineigentum verordnet hat: Der eine wird den Armen alles opfern[42], ein anderer die Hälfte geben[43], wieder ein anderer durch ein Darlehen helfen[44]. Die eine gibt für Gottes Sache das Letzte[45], andere üben sich in Dienst und Fürsorge[46], eine dritte treibt scheinbar sinnlose Verschwendung[47]. Gesetzlich geregelt wird hier nichts. Und so braucht es auch keine Ausnahmen, Entschuldigungen, Privilegien und Dispensen vom Gesetz!

Die Bergpredigt zielt freilich keineswegs auf eine oberflächliche Situationsethik, als ob einfach das Gesetz der Situation dominieren dürfte. Nicht die Situation soll alles bestimmen. Vielmehr, in der betreffenden Situation, die unbedingte Forderung Gottes selbst, die den Menschen ganz in Beschlag nehmen will. Im Hinblick auf das Letzte und Endgültige, das Gottesreich, wird eine grundlegende Veränderung des Menschen erwartet.

III. Die Sache des Menschen

Ein grundlegender Wandel wird erwartet: so etwas wie eine Neugeburt des Menschen selbst, die nur der versteht, der sie selbst mitmacht. Ein Wandel also nicht nur wie bei Sokrates durch ein Fortschreiten des rechten Denkens um des rechten Tuns willen, oder wie bei Kung-futse durch Bildung des grundsätzlich guten Menschen. Ein Wandel auch nicht durch eine Erleuchtung, wie der Asket Siddharta Gautama über die Versenkung durch Erleuchtung (bodhi) zum Buddha, zum Erleuchteten, wurde, um auf diesem Weg zur Einsicht in die Ursache und die Aufhebung des Leidens und schließlich zum Erlöschen im Nirwana zu gelangen. Nach Jesus kommt es zu einem grundlegenden Wandel durch Hingabe des Menschen an Gottes Willen.

1. Humanisierung des Menschen

Jesus erwartet einen anderen, neuen Menschen: ein radikal verändertes Bewußtsein, eine grundsätzlich andere Haltung, eine völlig neue Orientierung im Denken und Handeln.

Das veränderte Bewußtsein

Jesus erwartet nicht mehr und nicht weniger als eine grundsätzliche, *ganzheitliche Ausrichtung des Menschenlebens auf Gott.* Ein ungeteiltes Herz, das im Letzten nicht zwei Herren, sondern nur einem Herrn dient. Mitten in der Welt und unter den Menschen soll der Mensch in Erwartung der Gottesherrschaft sein Herz letztlich einzig und allein an Gott hängen: weder an Geld und Eigentum[1], noch an Recht und Ehre[2], noch selbst an seine Eltern und seine Familie[3]. Hier darf man nach Jesus nicht einfach von Frieden reden, hier regiert das Schwert. Sogar die engsten Bande müssen bei dieser Grundentscheidung als zweitrangig zurückgestellt werden. Die Nachfolge auf diesem Weg geht auch den familiären Bindungen voran: Vater, Mutter und Geschwister, Frau und Kinder, ja, sogar sich selbst muß einer »hassen«, wenn er Jesu Jünger sein will. Sogar sich selbst! Der eigentliche Feind einer solchen Veränderung bin ich erfahrungsgemäß selber, ist mein eigenes Selbst. Deshalb die unmittelbare Folgerung: Wer sein Leben zu erhalten sucht, wird es verlieren; wer sein Leben verliert, wird es gewinnen[4]. Eine harte Sprache? Eine reiche Verheißung.

Damit ist nun deutlich geworden, was mit dem uns schon bekannten zentralen Begriff der »Metanoia«[5], mit der *Umkehr* oder, wie man es früher mißverständlich nannte, der »Buße« gemeint ist: Nicht ein äußeres Bußetun in Sack und Asche. Nicht ein intellektuell bestimmtes oder gefühlsbetontes religiöses Erlebnis! Sondern die entscheidende Wandlung des Willens, ein von Grund auf verändertes Bewußtsein: eine neue Grundhaltung, eine andere Wertskala. Also ein radikales Umdenken und Umkehren des ganzen Menschen, eine völlig neue Lebenseinstellung. Immerhin: Nicht Sündenbekenntnisse, nicht eine Beichte erwartet Jesus vom Menschen, der sich ändern will. Seine problematische Vergangenheit, von der er sich ja abwenden soll, interessiert ihn wenig. Nur die bessere Zukunft, der er sich allerdings unwiderruflich und vorbehaltlos – ohne mit der Hand am Pflug zurückzuschauen[6] – zuwenden soll, die Gott ihm verheißt und schenkt. Der Mensch darf von der Vergebung leben. Das ist die Umkehr aus jenem unbeirrbaren, unerschütterlichen Vertrauen auf Gott und sein Wort heraus, das man schon im Alten Testament *Glauben*[7] genannt hat. Ein gläubiges Vertrauen und ein vertrauender Glaube, der etwas sehr Verschiedenes ist von dem, was für Buddha nach indischer Philosophie die Einsicht, oder für Sokrates nach griechischem Verständnis die Dialektik des Denkens, oder für Kung-futse nach chinesischer Tradition die Pietät ist.

Gott selber macht durch sein Evangelium und seine Vergebung eine Umkehr aus dem Glauben, einen neuen Anfang möglich. Nicht Heroismus ist vom Menschen verlangt: er darf leben aus der vertrauenden *Dankbarkeit* dessen, der den Schatz im Acker gefunden, die kostbare Perle empfangen hat[8]. Er soll ja nicht unter neuen gesetzlichen Druck und Leistungszwang gestellt werden. Gewiß, er wird seine Pflicht tun und sich nichts zugute halten, wenn er nur seine Pflicht getan[9]. Aber noch mehr als der getreue Knecht wird das Kind Vorbild sein: nicht weil seine vermeintliche Unschuld romantisch zum Ideal verklärt werden soll, sondern weil es, hilflos und klein, ganz selbstverständlich bereit ist, sich helfen und beschenken zu lassen und sich ungeteilt und voll des Vertrauens hinzugeben[10]. Also die kindliche Dankbarkeit, die nicht auf einen Lohn – selbst nicht einen Gnadenlohn – schielt, wie dies der daheimgebliebene und am Ende verlorene Sohn jahrelang getan hatte[11]. Nicht wegen Lohn und Strafe soll der Mensch handeln. Lohn und Strafe sollen nicht zum Motiv des sittlichen Handelns gemacht werden; Kants Reaktion gegen den primitiven Eudaimonismus war berechtigt. Wohl aber soll der Mensch im Bewußtsein seiner Verantwortung handeln: daß er mit all seinen Gedanken, Worten und Werken der Zukunft Gottes, Gottes letzter Entscheidung entgegengeht. Und was immer der Mensch getan – es sei auch nur ein Becher Wasser für einen Durstenden[12] oder aber ein unnützes Wort[13] – bleibt für Gott, auch wenn es für den Menschen längst Vergangenheit ist, Gegenwart.

Mit der Freudlosigkeit der Frommen unter dem Gesetz hat die Übernahme dieser Verantwortung nichts zu tun. Jesu Ruf zur Umkehr ist ein Ruf zur *Freude*. Man stelle sich vor, die Bergpredigt beginne mit einem neuen Pflichtenkatalog. Nein, sie beginnt mit Seligpreisungen[14]. Ein trauriger Heiliger ist für Jesus ein trauriger Heiliger[15]. Nicht neidisch sein, weil Gott gütig ist, wird den Lohnempfängern im Weinberg gesagt[16]. Fröhlich sein und freuen soll sich der so korrekte Bruder des verlorenen Sohnes[17]. Die Abkehr von der sündigen Vergangenheit und die Heimkehr des ganzen Menschen zu Gott ist für Gott und die Menschen ein Ereignis der Freude. Und für den Betroffenen selbst eine wahre Befreiung. Denn kein neues Gesetz wird ihm auferlegt. Leicht ist das Gewicht und sanft die Bürde[18], und fröhlich darf der Mensch sie tragen, wenn er sich unter Gottes Willen stellt.

Doch damit drängt sich eine Frage neu in den Vordergrund, die bisher ständig gegenwärtig war, die aber jetzt, nachdem so viel vom Willen Gottes als der obersten Norm menschlichen Handelns und Lebens die Rede war, ausdrücklich gestellt und beantwortet werden soll: Was ist überhaupt der Wille Gottes? Was eigentlich will Gott?

Was Gott will

Der Wille Gottes ist nicht zweifelhaft. Er ist auch nicht manipulierbar. Aus all dem bisher Gesagten, aus den konkreten Forderungen Jesu selbst sollte bereits deutlich geworden sein: Gott will nichts für sich, nichts zu seinem Vorteil, nichts für seine größere Ehre. Gott will nichts anderes als den Vorteil des Menschen, seine wahre Größe, seine letzte Würde. Also das ist der Wille Gottes: *das Wohl des Menschen.*

Gottes Wille, von der ersten bis zur letzten Seite der Bibel, zielt auf das Wohl des Menschen auf allen Ebenen, zielt auf das definitive und umfassende Wohl, biblisch das »Heil« des und der Menschen. Gottes Wille ist helfender, heilender, befreiender Heilswille. Gott will das Leben, die Freude, die Freiheit, den Frieden, das Heil, das letzte große Glück des Menschen: des Einzelnen wie der Gesamtheit. Das ist es, was die absolute Zukunft, der Sieg, das Reich Gottes nach der Verkündigung Jesu meinen: umfassende Befreiung, Erlösung, Befriedung, Beglückung des Menschen. Und gerade die radikale Gleichsetzung von Wille Gottes und Wohl des Menschen, wie sie Jesus im Horizont der Nähe Gottes vorgenommen hat, macht deutlich: Hier wird nicht nur ein neuer Lappen auf ein altes Kleid genäht, hier wird nicht junger Wein in alte Schläuche gegossen. Hier geht es tatsächlich um etwas Neues, das dem Alten gefährlich wird!

Was manch einem in der Freiheit Jesu noch als selbstherrliche Willkür erscheinen mochte, wird nun deutlich als große starke Konsequenz: Gott wird nicht ohne den Menschen, der Mensch nicht ohne Gott gesehen. Man kann nicht für Gott sein und gegen den Menschen. Man kann nicht fromm sein wollen und sich unmenschlich verhalten. Ist das so selbstverständlich – damals, heute?

Gewiß wird Gott von Jesus nicht durch Mitmenschlichkeit interpretiert, auf Mitmenschlichkeit reduziert. Durch Vergötzung würde der Mensch nicht weniger entmenschlicht als durch Versklavung. Aber die Menschenfreundlichkeit des Menschen wird von der Menschenfreundlichkeit Gottes her begründet. Und deshalb soll überall der letzte Maßstab sein: Gott will das Wohl des Menschen.

So erscheint manches in einem anderen Licht. Weil *der Mensch auf dem Spiel steht:*

Deshalb schreckt Jesus, der im allgemeinen durchaus gesetzestreu lebt, vor gesetzwidrigem Verhalten nicht zurück.

Deshalb verwirft er rituelle Korrektheit und Tabuisierung und fordert statt äußerer gesetzlicher Reinheit die Reinheit des Herzens.

Deshalb verwirft er den Fastenasketismus und läßt sich als Mensch unter Menschen lieber einen Fresser und Säufer schelten.

Deshalb kennt er keine Sabbatängstlichkeit, sondern erklärt den Menschen selber zum Maß des Gesetzes[19].

Relativierte Traditionen, Institutionen, Hierarchen

Aber ist damit nicht auch das jeden frommen Juden erschreckende *Ärgernis* sichtbar geworden? Eine ungeheure Relativierung: Hier vergleichgültigt einer die heiligsten Traditionen und Institutionen des Volkes. Und ist damit nicht auch schon die Ursache des unversöhnlichen Argwohns und Hasses insbesondere der Priester und Theologen ins Blickfeld gerückt? Hier rüttelt einer, insofern er Gesetzesordnung und Kultordnung relativiert, an den Grundlagen der *Hierarchie*.

- *Jesus relativiert das Gesetz und das heißt die gesamte religiös-politisch-wirtschaftliche Ordnung, das gesamte gesellschaftliche System: Auch das Gesetz ist nicht Anfang und Ende aller Wege Gottes. Auch das Gesetz ist nicht Selbstzweck, ist nicht letzte Instanz.*
- *Also: Mit der Gesetzesfrömmigkeit alten Stils ist es aus. Der Besitz des Gesetzes und korrekte Gesetzeserfüllung garantieren nicht das Heil. Letztlich ist das Gesetz unmaßgeblich für das Heil. Solche selbstsichere Gesetzesreligion wird aufgehoben, auch wenn nicht geleugnet wird, daß das Gesetz Gottes gute Gabe ist. Aber da gilt der an sich selbstverständliche und gegenüber der traditionellen Auffassung doch revolutionäre Satz: Die Gebote sind um der Menschen willen da und nicht der Mensch um der Gebote willen[20]!*

Das bedeutet: Der *Dienst am Menschen* hat die *Priorität vor der Gesetzeserfüllung.* Keine Normen und Institutionen dürfen absolut gesetzt werden. Nie darf der Mensch einer angeblich absoluten Norm oder Institution geopfert werden. Normen und Institutionen werden nicht einfach abgeschafft oder aufgehoben. Aber alle Normen und Institutionen, alle Gesetze und Gebote, Einrichtungen und Statuten, Regeln und Ordnungen, Dogmen und Dekrete, Codices und Paragraphen stehen unter dem Kriterium, ob sie für den Menschen da sind oder nicht. Der Mensch ist das Maß des Gesetzes. Läßt sich von daher nicht kritisch unterscheiden, was richtig und was unrichtig, was wesentlich und was gleichgültig, was konstruktiv und was destrukiv, was gute oder schlechte Ordnung ist?

Die *Sache Gottes* ist nicht das Gesetz, sondern der *Mensch*. So tritt der Mensch selber an die Stelle der verabsolutierten Gesetzesordnung: *Humanität* anstelle von Legalismus, Institutionalismus, Juridismus, Dogmatismus. Zwar ersetzt der Menschenwille nicht den Gotteswillen. Aber der Gotteswille wird konkretisiert von der konkreten Situation des Menschen und des Mitmenschen her.

– *Jesus relativiert den Tempel, und das heißt die gesamte Kulturordnung, die Liturgie, den Gottesdienst im strengen Sinn des Wortes: Auch der Tempel ist nicht Anfang und Ende aller Wege Gottes. Auch der Tempel wird ein Ende haben, ist nicht ewig.*
– *Also: Mit der Tempelfrömmigkeit alten Stiles ist es aus! Der Besitz des Tempels und korrekte Durchführung des Kultes garantieren nicht das Heil. Letztlich ist der Tempel unmaßgeblich für das Heil. Solche satte Tempelreligion wird aufgehoben, auch wenn nicht geleugnet wird, daß der Tempel Gottes gute Gabe ist. Aber da gilt der an sich wiederum selbstverständliche, aber gegenüber der traditionellen Auffassung gleichfalls revolutionäre Satz: Versöhne dich zuerst mit deinem Bruder und dann komme und bringe deine Gabe dar[21]!*

Das bedeutet: *Die Versöhnung und der alltägliche Dienst am Mitmenschen* haben die *Priorität vor dem Gottesdienst* und der Einhaltung des Kulttages. Auch der Kult, die Liturgie, der Gottesdienst dürfen nicht absolut gesetzt werden. Nie darf der Mensch einem angeblich absolut verpflichtenden Ritus oder frommen Brauch geopfert werden. Kult und Liturgie werden nicht einfach abgeschafft oder aufgehoben. Aber aller Kult und alle Liturgie, Riten und Bräuche, Übungen und Zeremonien, Feste und Feiern stehen unter dem Kriterium, ob sie für den Menschen da sind oder nicht. Der Mensch ist das Maß auch des Gottesdienstes. Läßt sich von daher nicht wiederum kritisch unterscheiden, was auch in Kult und Liturgie richtig und unrichtig, was wichtig und was unwichtig, was guter und was schlechter Gottesdienst ist?

Die *Sache Gottes* ist nicht der Kult, sondern *der Mensch*! So tritt der Mensch selber an die Stelle einer verabsolutierten Liturgie: *Humanität* anstelle von Formalismus, Ritualismus, Liturgismus, Sakramentalismus. Zwar ersetzt der Menschendienst nicht den Gottesdienst. Aber der Gottesdienst entschuldigt nie vom Menschendienst: er bewährt sich im Menschendienst.

, Wenn man sagt, Gott und damit der Gottesdienst sei die entscheidende Sache für den Menschen, dann ist also sofort daran zu erinnern, daß der Mensch mit seiner Welt die entscheidende Sache für Gott selbst ist. Gottes Weisung will dem Menschen helfen und dienen. Man kann folglich nicht Gott und seinen Willen ernstnehmen, ohne nicht zugleich den Menschen und sein Wohl ernstzunehmen. Die Humanität des Menschen wird gefordert von der Humanität Gottes selbst. Die Verletzung der Humanität des Menschen versperrt den Weg zum wahren Gottesdienst. Humanisierung des Menschen ist Voraussetzung für den wahren Gottesdienst. So läßt sich zwar weder der Gottesdienst einfach auf Menschendienst und der Menschendienst einfach auf Gottesdienst reduzieren. Aber man kann und muß sagen, daß echter Gottesdienst auch schon Menschendienst und echter Menschendienst auch schon Gottesdienst ist.

Überlegt man sich alles, was hier über das veränderte Bewußtsein, den Willen Gottes und die revolutionäre Relativierung heiligster Traditionen und Institutionen zu sagen war, so versteht man, wie wesentlich – ganz auf der Linie der alttestamentlichen Propheten – das *Kämpferische*[22] zu Jesus gehört. Jesus läßt sich auf keinen Fall nur als eine weiche, milde, widerstandslose, sanftmütig und demütig duldende Gestalt verstehen. Auch das Jesusbild des Franz von Assisi hat seine Grenzen. Und erst recht das pietistische und zum Teil auch hierarchistische Jesusbild des 19. und 20. Jahrhunderts. Zu Recht hat der Pfarrerssohn Nietzsche gegen dieses schwächliche Jesusbild seiner Jugend aufbegehrt, das er mit den evangelischen Aussagen über Jesus als den aggressiven Kritiker der Hierarchen und Theologen nicht zu verbinden wußte. Er hat denn auch im ›Antichrist‹ den kämpferischen Jesus ohne allen Rückhalt in den Quellen willkürlich auf das Konto der kämpferischen Urgemeinde verbucht, die ein kämpferisches Vorbild gebraucht hätte. Aber die Quellen selber machen deutlich, wie sehr bei Jesus Selbstlosigkeit und Selbstbewußtsein, Demut und Härte, Milde und Aggressivität zusammengehören. Und dies nicht etwa im Sinne des viel empfohlenen fortiter in re – suaviter in modo. Oft war auch Jesu Ton von äußerster Schärfe. Honigsüße Rede findet man kaum in seinem Mund, bittere wohl. Wo immer Jesus gegen den Widerstand der Mächtigen – Personen, Institutionen, Traditionen, Hierarchen – für den Willen Gottes einzutreten hatte, tat er es in kämpferischer Unbedingtheit: um der Menschen willen nämlich, denen keine unnötig schweren Lasten aufgeladen werden dürfen[23]. Deshalb die Relativierung allerheiligster Institutionen und Traditionen *und ihrer Repräsentanten:* um Gottes willen, der das umfassende Wohl, das Heil der Menschen will.

Wie wenig Jesu Botschaft mit jener dekadenten Schwäche zu tun hat, die Nietzsche so sehr verabscheute, wird deutlich, wenn wir jenes für Nietzsche ebenfalls sehr verdächtige Wort einführen, mit dem wir bisher bewußt – und durchaus in Übereinstimmung mit dem Jesus der Geschichte – sehr zurückhaltend umgegangen sind, weil es christlich und unchristlich so viel mißbraucht und zur billigen Scheidemünze von Frommen und Unfrommen gemacht wurde: die Liebe.

2. Handeln

Die Worte »Liebe« und »lieben« im Sinn der Liebe zum Nächsten kommen wie das Wort »der Nächste« beim Jesus der synoptischen Evangelien – abgesehen von der aus dem Alten Testament übernommenen Formulierung des Hauptgebotes – äußerst spärlich vor. Trotzdem ist die Liebe des Mitmenschen in der Verkündigung Jesu allgegenwärtig. Offensichtlich kommt es gerade bei der Liebe mehr aufs Tun als aufs bloße Sagen an. Nicht das Reden, sondern die Tat bringt an den Tag, was Liebe ist. Kriterium ist die Praxis. Und was ist Liebe nach Jesus?

Gott und Mensch zugleich

Eine *erste* Antwort: Nach Jesus ist Liebe wesentlich *zugleich Gottes- und Menschenliebe.* Jesus kam, das Gesetz zu erfüllen, indem er den Willen Gottes, der auf das Wohl des Menschen zielt, zur Geltung brachte. Deshalb kann er sagen, daß alle Gebote im Doppelgebot der Liebe beschlossen sind. Auch schon das Judentum spricht vereinzelt von der Liebe im Doppelsinn. Jesus aber erreicht in Einfachheit und Konkretheit eine bisher nicht dagewesene *Reduktion* und *Konzentration* aller Gebote auf dieses Doppelgebot und verknüpft zugleich Gottes- und Menschenliebe zu einer unlösbaren Einheit. Seither ist es unmöglich,

Gott und Mensch gegeneinander auszuspielen. Damit wird die Liebe zu einer Forderung, die grenzenlos das ganze Leben des Menschen zu umfassen vermag und die doch zugleich auf jeden Einzelfall genau zutrifft. Das ist bezeichnend für Jesus, daß auf diese Weise die Liebe zum Kriterium der Frömmigkeit und des gesamten Verhaltens wird.

Allerdings: Gottesliebe und Menschenliebe sind für Jesus *nicht dasselbe,* weil für ihn ganz selbstverständlich Gott und Mensch nicht dasselbe sind. Eine Vermenschlichung Gottes wie eine Vergötzung des Menschen gehen auf Kosten nicht Gottes, sondern des Menschen. Gott bleibt Gott. Gott bleibt der eine Herr der Welt und des Menschen. Er kann nicht durch Mitmenschlichkeit ersetzt werden. Welcher Mensch wäre schon so ohne Grenzen und Fehler, daß er mir zum Gott, zum Gegenstand einer völlig unbedingten Liebe werden könnte. Liebesromantik oder Liebesmystik können ein idealisiertes Bild vom Anderen heraufzaubern, können Konflikte verschleiern und hinausschieben, aber nicht eliminieren. Von der unbedingten Liebe Gottes her jedoch, der alles umfaßt, läßt sich auch der Mitmensch ganz radikal so lieben, wie er ist, mit all seinen Grenzen und Fehlern. Es ist keine Frage, daß *Gott* für Jesus gerade im Interesse des Menschen *den unbedingten Primat* hat. Deshalb beansprucht er die Ganzheit des Menschen: den ganzen Willen, das Herz, den innersten Kern, den Menschen selbst. Und deshalb auch erwartet er von dem zu ihm in vertrauendem Glauben umgekehrten und heimgekehrten Menschen nicht mehr und nicht weniger als Liebe, ganze, ungeteilte Liebe: Du sollst den Herrn Deinen Gott lieben mit Deinem ganzen Herzen, mit Deiner ganzen Seele und mit Deinem ganzen Denken; dies ist das größte und erste Gebot[1].

Aber diese Liebe meint keine mystische Gottesvereinigung, in welcher der Mensch aus der Welt zu treten versucht, einsam unter den Menschen, eins mit Gott. Eine Gottesliebe ohne Menschenliebe ist letztlich lieblos. Und wenn Gott den unauswechselbaren Primat behalten muß und die Gottesliebe nie zum Mittel und zur Chiffre der Menschenliebe werden darf, so doch auch umgekehrt: Die *Menschenliebe* darf *nie* zum Mittel und zur *Chiffre der Gottesliebe* werden. Nicht nur um Gottes willen, sondern um seiner selbst willen soll ich den Mitmenschen lieben. Nicht auf Gott soll ich schielen, wenn ich mich dem Mitmenschen zuwende, nicht fromm reden, wenn ich helfen soll. Ohne alle Heranholung religiöser Gründe hilft der Samariter; die Not des unter die Räuber Gefallenen genügt ihm, und um ihn kreist in diesem Moment sein ganzes Denken[2]. Die beim Endgericht Gesegneten hatten keine Ahnung, daß sie in den von ihnen Gespeisten, Getränkten, Beherbergten, Bekleideten, Besuchten dem Herrn selber begegnet sind. Umgekehrt aber verraten die Verurteilten, daß sie bestenfalls um des Herrn willen den Mitmenschen Liebe entgegengebracht hätten[3]. Das ist nicht nur die falsche Gottesliebe, sondern auch die falsche Menschenliebe.

Doch Menschenliebe – das bleibt zu allgemein. Universale Humanität gewiß – aber wir müssen genauer reden. Von einem »Seid umschlungen, Millionen, diesen Kuß der ganzen Welt« wie in Schillers und Beethovens großer Hymne an die Freude ist bei Jesus nicht einmal andeutungsweise die Rede. Ein solcher Kuß kostet – anders als der Kuß für diesen einen Kranken, Gefangenen, Entrechteten, Hungernden – nichts. Der Humanismus ist um so billiger zu leben, je mehr er sich der ganzen Menschheit zuwendet und je weniger er den einzelnen Menschen und seine Not an sich herankommen läßt. Für den Frieden im Fernen Osten läßt sich leichter reden als für den Frieden in der eigenen Familie oder im eigenen Einflußbereich. Mit den Negern in Nordamerika oder Südafrika kann sich der humane Europäer leichter »solidarisieren« als mit den Gastarbeitern im eigenen Land. Je ferner der Mitmensch, um so leichter läßt sich die Liebe in Worten bekennen.

Der mich gerade braucht

Jesus aber ist an der allgemeinen, theoretischen oder poetischen Liebe nicht interessiert. Liebe meint für ihn nicht primär Worte, Empfindungen, Gefühle. Liebe meint für ihn primär die starke, tapfere Tat. Er will die praktische und deshalb konkrete Liebe. Und so muß denn unsere *zweite* Antwort auf die Frage nach der Liebe genauer lauten: Nach Jesus ist Liebe *nicht nur Menschenliebe, sondern wesentlich Nächstenliebe.* Liebe nicht des Menschen im allgemeinen, des Fernen, auf Abstand, sondern ganz konkret des Nahen und Nächsten. In der Nächstenliebe bewährt sich die Gottesliebe, ja die Nächstenliebe ist der exakte Gradmesser der Gottesliebe: Nur so viel liebe ich Gott, wie ich meinen Nächsten liebe.

Und *wieviel* soll ich meinen Nächsten lieben? Jesus antwortet im Anschluß an eine vereinzelte Formulierung des Alten Testaments[4] – dort allerdings nur für die Volksgenossen untereinander! – ganz lapidar und ohne jegliche Einschränkung: *wie dich selbst*[5]. Eine selbstverständliche Antwort, die im Verständnis Jesu sofort aufs Ganze geht, keine Lücken für Entschuldigungen und Ausflüchte offen läßt und der Liebe Richtung und Maß zugleich vorzeichnet. Daß der Mensch sich selber liebt, wird vorausgesetzt. Und gerade diese selbstverständliche Einstellung des Menschen zu sich selbst soll der – praktisch unüberbietbare – Maßstab der Nächstenliebe sein. Was ich mir schuldig bin, weiß ich ja nur zu gut; was mir andere schuldig sind, nicht weniger. Ganz natürlich tendieren wir in allem, was wir denken, sagen und fühlen, tun und leiden daraufhin, uns zu bewahren, zu beschützen, zu befördern, unser Selbst zu hegen und zu pflegen. Und nun wird von uns erwartet, daß wir genau die gleiche Sorge und Pflege dem Nächsten zukommen lassen. Womit jede Grenze fällt! Das bedeutet für uns Egoisten von Natur eine radikale Umkehr: den Standpunkt des Anderen einzunehmen; dem Anderen genau das zu geben, was wir uns schuldig zu sein meinen; den Mitmenschen so zu behandeln, wie wir selber von ihm behandelt zu werden wünschen[6]. Gewiß, wie Jesus selber zeigt, keine Schwächlichkeit und Weichlichkeit, kein Verzicht auf Selbstbewußtsein, kein Auslöschen seines Selbst in frommer Versenkung oder angestrengter Askese in buddhistischem oder »christlichem« Sinn. Wohl aber die Ausrichtung seines Selbst auf den Anderen: ein Wachsein, Offensein, Bereitsein für den Mitmenschen, eine schrankenlose Hilfsbereitschaft. Nicht für sich selbst, sondern für die Anderen zu leben: darin gründet, vom liebenden Menschen aus betrachtet, die unauflösliche Einheit von ungeteilter Gottesliebe und unbegrenzter Nächstenliebe.

So ist der *gemeinsame Nenner* von Gottesliebe und Nächstenliebe die *Abkehr vom Egoismus* und der *Wille zur Hingabe*. Nur wenn ich nicht für mich lebe, kann ich ganz offen sein für Gott und unbeschränkt offen für den Mitmenschen, den Gott wie mich selber bejaht. Gott geht also auch in der Liebe nicht im Mitmenschen auf. Ich bleibe Gott unmittelbar verantwortlich, und diese Verantwortung kann mir kein Mitmensch abnehmen. Aber Gott begegnet mir – nicht ausschließlich, aber weil ich selber Mensch bin, primär – im Mitmenschen und erwartet dort meine Hingabe. Er ruft mich nicht aus den Wolken, auch nicht nur unmittelbar in meinem Gewissen, sondern vor allem durch den Nächsten: ein Anruf, der nie verstummt, sondern mich alle Tage neu trifft mitten in meinem weltlichen Alltag.

Wer aber ist mein Nächster? Jesus antwortet nicht mit einer Definition, einer näheren Bestimmung, gar einem Gesetz, sondern wie so oft mit einer Geschichte, einer Beispielserzählung. Der Nächste ist danach nicht einfach der mir von vornherein Nahestehende: die Glieder meiner Familie, meines Freundeskreises, meines Standes, meiner Partei, meines Volkes. Der Nächste kann auch der Fremde und Fremdeste sein, jeder, der gerade kommt. Wer der Nächste ist, ist unberechenbar. Das sagt die Geschichte von dem unter die Räuber Gefallenen: Der Nächste ist *jeder, der mich gerade braucht*[7]. Wird am Anfang der Parabel gefragt: Wer ist mein Nächster, so am Ende in bezeichnender Umkehr der Blickrichtung: Wem bin ich der Nächste? Nicht auf die Definition des Nächsten kommt es in der Parabel an, sondern auf die Dringlichkeit, mit der gerade von mir im konkreten Fall, in der konkreten Not jenseits der konventionellen Regeln der Moral die Liebe erwartet wird. Und an Nöten fehlt es nicht. Viermal werden von Mattäus in der Gerichtsrede sechs der wichtigsten, damals wie heute aktuellen Werke der Liebe wiederholt[8]. Eine neue gesetzliche Ordnung ist damit nicht intendiert. Vielmehr wird, wie im Fall des Samariters, ein aktives schöpferisches Verhalten, produktive Phantasie und entscheidendes Handeln von Fall zu Fall je nach der Situation erwartet.

So wird in der Liebe deutlich, was Gott eigentlich will. Worum es auch in den Geboten geht: Jedenfalls nicht nur, wie im Islam, um gehorsame »Ergebenheit« (= »islam«) gegenüber dem im Gesetz geoffenbarten Willen Gottes. Von der Liebe her erhalten die *Gebote einen einheitlichen Sinn,* werden sie aber auch *begrenzt,* ja, unter Umständen sogar *aufgehoben!* Wer die Gebote gesetzlich und nicht von der Liebe her versteht, gerät immer wieder in Pflichtenkollisionen. Die Liebe aber ist das Ende der Kasuistik: Der Mensch richtet sich nicht mehr mechanisch nach dem einzelnen Gebot oder Verbot, sondern nach dem, was die Wirklichkeit selber verlangt und ermöglicht. So hat jedes Gebot oder Verbot seinen inneren Maßstab an der Liebe zum Nächsten. Das kühne augustinische »Liebe, und tue, was du willst« ist hier grundgelegt. So weit also geht die Nächstenliebe.

Auch die Feinde

Geht sie nicht vielleicht zu weit? Wenn der Nächste jeder ist, der mich gerade braucht, kann ich dann noch haltmachen? Nach

Jesus soll ich gar nicht haltmachen. Und nach unseren ersten beiden Antworten auf die Frage nach der Liebe muß jetzt mit der *dritten* Antwort eine letzte Zuspitzung gewagt werden: Nach Jesus ist Liebe nicht nur Nächstenliebe, sondern entscheidend *Feindesliebe.* Und nicht die Menschenliebe, auch nicht die Nächstenliebe, sondern die Feindesliebe ist *das für Jesus Charakteristische.*

Nur bei Jesus findet sich die programmatische Forderung der Feindesliebe. Schon Kung-futse spricht, wenn auch nicht von »Nächstenliebe«, so doch von »Menschenliebe«, meint damit aber einfach Ehrerbietung, Weitherzigkeit, Aufrichtigkeit, Fleiß, Güte. Im Alten Testament, wie bereits angemerkt, ist vereinzelt auch von der Liebe des Nächsten die Rede. Wie in den meisten großen Religionen, so kannte man auch im Judentum, vermutlich vom griechisch-römischen Heidentum her, die genannte »Goldene Regel«, und zwar in negativer und, wie in der jüdischen Diaspora, auch in positiver Formulierung: den Mitmenschen so zu behandeln, wie man selber behandelt sein will. Der große Rabbi Hillel (um 20 v. Chr.) hat diese Goldene Regel, allerdings in negativer Formulierung, geradezu als Summe des geschriebenen Gesetzes bezeichnet. Aber diese Regel ließ sich auch als egoistisch-kluge Anpassung, der Nächste auch einfach als Volks- und Parteigenosse und die Nächstenliebe als ein Gebot unter einer Unmenge anderer religiöser, sittlicher und ritueller Gebote verstehen. Schon Kung-futse kannte, in negativer Form, die Goldene Regel, lehnt aber die Feindesliebe ausdrücklich als ungerecht ab: Güte soll man mit Güte, Unrecht aber nicht mit Güte, sondern mit Gerechtigkeit vergelten. Und im Judentum galt der Haß der Feinde als relativ erlaubt; der persönliche Feind war von der Liebespflicht ausgenommen. Bei den frommen Mönchen von Qumran gar wird der Haß gegenüber den Außenstehenden, den Söhnen der Finsternis, ausdrücklich geboten. Zeigt dies nicht erneut, wie die zahlreichen Parallelen zwischen Sätzen der Verkündigung Jesu einerseits und Sprüchen der jüdischen Weisheitsliteratur und der Rabbinen andererseits im Gesamtzusammenhang des Verständnisses von Gesetz und Heil, Mensch und Mitmensch gesehen werden müssen? Die Überlegenheit Jesu wird nicht am oft durchaus vergleichbaren Einzelsatz, sondern am unverwechselbaren Ganzen sichtbar! Das programmatische »Liebet eure Feinde« gehört Jesus selbst zu und charakterisiert seine Nächstenliebe, die nun wirklich keine Grenzen mehr kennt[9].

Für Jesus ist bezeichnend, daß er die eingefleischte *Grenze und Entfremdung zwischen Genossen und Nichtgenossen nicht anerkennt.* Zwar, so hörten wir, hat er seine Sendung auf die Juden beschränkt[10]; sonst hätte es in der Urgemeinde gar keine solchen harten Auseinandersetzungen um die Heidenmission gegeben. Aber Jesus zeigt eine Offenheit, die faktisch die unverrückbaren Grenzen der Volks- und Religionszugehörigkeit sprengt. Nicht mehr der Volks- und Religionsgenosse ist für ihn ausschlaggebend. Sondern der Nächste, der uns in jedem Menschen begegnen kann: in jedem Menschen, auch im politischen und religiösen Gegner, Rivalen, Gegenspieler, Widersacher, Feind. Das ist Jesu konkreter *faktischer Universalismus.* Offenheit nicht nur für die Mitglieder der eigenen sozialen Gruppe, der eigenen Sippe, des eigenen Volkes, der eigenen Rasse, Klasse, Partei, Kirche unter Ausschluß der anderen. Sondern unbegrenzte Offenheit und Überwindung der Abgrenzungen, wo immer sie sich einstellen. Die faktische Überwindung der bestehenden Grenzen – der Grenze zwischen Juden und Nichtjuden, Nächsten und Fernsten, Guten und Bösen, Pharisäern und Zöllnern –, und nicht nur bestimmte Sonderleistungen, Liebeswerke, »Samaritertaten« sind mit jener Geschichte angestrebt, die nach dem Versagen des Priesters und Leviten, der jüdischen Oberschicht, auch nicht (wie von den Hörern Jesu erwartet) den jüdischen Laien zum Vorbild hinstellt, sondern den verhaßten samaritanischen Volksfeind, Mischling und Ketzer. Juden und Samariter verfluchten sich gegenseitig öffentlich im Gottesdienst und nahmen Hilfeleistungen voneinander nicht an[11].

In der letzten Antithese der Bergpredigt vollzieht Jesus eine ausdrückliche *Korrektur des alttestamentlichen Gebotes* »Du sollst deinen Nächsten lieben« und der Qumranvorschrift »Du sollst deinen Feind hassen«. Durch das »Ich aber sage euch«: »Liebet eure Feinde und bittet für die, die euch verfolgen«[12]. Und dies gilt nach Lukas auch für die Verfolgten und Verfluchten: »Tut Gutes denen, die euch hassen; segnet die, die euch fluchen, bittet für die, die euch beleidigen«[13]. Ist das für den Durchschnittsmenschen nicht alles übersteigert, weit überzogen? *Warum* dies alles? Etwa wegen der allen gemeinsamen Menschennatur? Aus einer Philanthropie, die auch im Elenden Göttliches findet? Aus einem universalen Mitleid gegenüber allen leidenden Wesen, welches angesichts des unendlichen Leids der Welt das eigene weiche Herz zu beschwichtigen sucht? Aus dem Ideal einer allgemeinen sittlichen Vollkommenheit?

Jesus hat ein anderes Motiv. Die vollkommene Nachahmung Gottes: weil Gott nur als der Vater richtig verstanden wird, der keine Unterschiede zwischen Freund und Feind macht, der über Gute und Böse die Sonne scheinen und regnen läßt und der seine Liebe auch den Unwürdigen – wer ist es nicht? – zuwendet! Durch die Liebe sollen sich die Menschen als dieses Vaters Söhne und Töchter erweisen[14] und aus Feinden Brüder und Schwestern werden. So ist denn Gottes Liebe zu allen Menschen für mich der Grund für die Liebe zum Menschen, den er mir schickt: der Liebe zum gerade Nächsten. Die *Feindesliebe Gottes* selbst also ist der *Grund für die Feindesliebe des Menschen.*

So läßt sich denn auch umgekehrt fragen: Wird nicht erst angesichts des Gegners die *Natur der wahren Liebe* offenbar? Wahre Liebe spekuliert nicht auf Gegenliebe, verrechnet nicht Leistung mit Gegenleistung, wartet nicht auf Lohn. Sie ist frei von Berechnung und versteckter Eigensucht: *nicht egoistisch, sondern ganz offen für den Anderen!*

Also: *nicht Eros, sondern Agape?* Nicht amor, sondern caritas? Doch so einfach ist das nicht. Beides meint Liebe. Theologen konnten zwar nicht genugtun, um den Unterschied herauszuarbeiten: zwischen dem begehrenden Eros der Griechen und der schenkenden Agape im Sinne Jesu[15]. Dabei konnten sie sich stützen auf den freilich bemerkenswerten lexikalischen Befund: Das Hauptwort »agape« kommt in der profanen griechischen Literatur kaum und das Verb »agapan« (lieben) nur am Rande vor. Umgekehrt findet sich das Wort »eros« im Neuen Testament überhaupt nicht und im griechischen Alten Testament nur zweimal – negativ – im Buch der Sprüche[16]. Offensichtlich war das Wort kompromittiert durch das, was sich mit ihm im Griechentum an morbider Erotik und rein triebhafter Sexualität bis in die Kulte hinein verbunden hatte.

Selbstverständlich gibt es den Unterschied zwischen einer begehrenden Liebe, die *nur* das Eigene sucht, und einer schenkenden Liebe, die sucht, was des Anderen ist: also den Unterschied zwischen einer egoistischen Liebe und der wahren Liebe, wie sie Jesus vor Augen hat. Trotzdem ist der *Unterschied zwischen egoistischer und wahrer Liebe nicht identisch mit dem Unterschied zwischen Eros und Agape:* als ob nur die Agape und nicht auch der Eros wahre Liebe sein könnte. Oder sollte etwa der, der den anderen Menschen begehrt, sich ihm nicht zugleich schenken können? Und sollte umgekehrt der, der sich dem anderen Menschen schenkt, diesen nicht begehren dürfen? Soll nichts

Liebenswertes und Liebenswürdiges in dem oder der Geliebten sein dürfen? Begehrt etwa der Gott des Alten Testaments nicht leidenschaftlich, »eifersüchtig« sein Volk Israel, nach dem Bild der Propheten wie der Mann seine treulose Frau? Wird so der Bund Gottes mit seinem Volk nicht in Symbolen des Eros als Ehe und der Abfall des Volkes als Ehebruch dargestellt? Ist nicht in den alttestamentlichen Kanon das Hohelied, eine Sammlung sehr sinnlicher Liebeslieder, aufgenommen worden? Und hat nicht auch die Liebe Gottes im Neuen Testament sehr menschliche Züge: die Liebe des Vaters, die den verlorenen Sohn zurückbegehrt?

Es fällt auf: Das griechische Alte Testament spricht ganz selbstverständlich vom »agapan« des Mannes zur Frau und von Mann und Frau zu ihren Kindern. Und Jesus gebraucht nach dem griechischen Neuen Testament dasselbe Verb sowohl für die Freundesliebe wie für die Feindesliebe[17]. Jesus erscheint nach den Evangelien ganz und gar als echter Mensch: der die Kinder herzt[18], sich von Frauen salben läßt[19], sich in »Liebe« verbunden weiß insbesondere mit Lazarus und seinen Schwestern[20], was offensichtlich Eros nicht ausschließt. Seine Jünger nennt Jesus »Freunde«[21]. Am Unterschied zwischen einer »himmlischen« und einer »irdischen« Liebe ist offensichtlich weder das Alte noch das Neue Testament interessiert: Von der Liebe Gottes wird erfreulich menschlich gesprochen, und die elementare menschliche Liebe in keiner Weise schlecht gemacht. Echt menschliche Gatten-, Vater-, Mutter-, Kindesliebe sind nicht im Gegensatz zur, sondern im Zusammenhang mit der Gottesliebe. Wo aber zwischen Eros und Agape nicht nur ein Unterschied gesehen, sondern ein *ausschließlicher Gegensatz* konstruiert wird, da geht dies *auf Kosten des Eros und der Agape*[22].

Dann wird der *Eros abgewertet und verteufelt*: Das leidenschaftliche Lieben, das den Anderen für sich begehrt, wird auf den Sexus beschränkt und damit Erotik und Sexualität zugleich abqualifiziert. Der Eros wird dann sogar dort verdächtigt, wo er nicht einfach als unheimliche, überwältigende, blinde, sinnliche Leidenschaft erscheint, sondern wie etwa in Platons Symposion als Drang nach dem Schönen und als schöpferische Kraft, die ein Wegweiser zum höchsten göttlichen Gut (bei Plotin ein Verlangen nach Einigung mit dem »Einen«) wird. Erosfeindliche Erziehung und überhaupt religiös begründete Eros- und Geschlechtsfeindlichkeit haben unendlich viel Unheil angerichtet. Warum aber sollen Liebesbegehren und Liebesdienst, Liebesspiel und Liebestreue sich ausschließen?

Dann wird aber zugleich die *Agape überhöht und entmenschlicht*: Sie wird dann entsinnlicht und spiritualisiert (fälschlicherweise »platonische Liebe« genannt). Das Vitale, Emotionale, Affektive wird gewaltsam ausgeschlossen: eine Liebe ohne Faszination. Wo Liebe nur ein Entschluß des Willens ist ohne ein Wagnis des Herzens, da fehlt ihr die echte Menschlichkeit. Da fehlt ihr Tiefe, Wärme, Innigkeit, Zärtlichkeit, Herzlichkeit. Christliche Caritas war oft so wenig überzeugend, weil sie so wenig menschlich war.

Sollte nicht in aller Menschenliebe, Nächstenliebe, ja sogar Feindesliebe alles Menschliche mitschwingen? Solche Liebe wird nicht zur egoistischen Liebe, die nur das Eigene sucht, wohl aber zur starken wahrhaft menschlichen Liebe, die mit Seele und Leib, Wort und Tat sucht, was des Anderen ist. In der wahren Liebe wird alles Begehren nicht zum Besitzen, sondern zum Schenken.

Die wahre Radikalität

In der Gleichsetzung der Sache Gottes und der Sache des Menschen, von Gottes Wille und Wohl des Menschen, von Gottesdienst und Menschendienst und in der daraus folgenden Relativierung von Gesetz und Kult, von heiligen Traditionen, Institutionen, Hierarchen zeigt es sich, wo genau Jesus steht im *Koordinatenkreuz* von Establishment, Revolution, Emigration und Kompromiß: warum er weder bei den Herrschenden noch bei den politischen Rebellen, weder bei den Moralisierenden noch bei den Stillen im Lande eingeordnet werden kann. Weder rechts noch links, steht er auch nicht einfach vermittelnd zwischen ihnen. Weil er nämlich *wahrhaft darüber* steht: über allen Alternativen, die er alle von der Wurzel her aufhebt. Das ist *seine Radikalität*: die Radikalität der *Liebe,* die sich in ihrer Nüchternheit und ihrem Realismus von ideologisierten *Radikalismen* gründlich unterscheidet.

Es wäre völlig falsch, bei dieser Liebe nur an große Taten, große Opfer zu denken! Etwa den in Einzelfällen notwendigen Bruch mit den Angehörigen, den unter Umständen geforderten Verzicht auf Besitz, das vielleicht abgeforderte Martyrium ... Zunächst und meist geht es um den *Alltag*: wer zuerst grüßt[23], welchen Platz man sich beim Festmahl aussucht[24], daß man nicht richtet, sondern barmherzig urteilt[25], daß man sich um unbedingte Wahrhaftigkeit bemüht[26]. Wie weit gerade im Alltag die Liebe geht, zeigen drei Stichworte, mit denen sich diese radikale Liebe sehr konkret umschreiben läßt – und zwar für den individuellen wie für den gesellschaftlichen Bereich der Beziehungen zwischen sozialen Gruppen, Nationen, Rassen, Klassen, Parteien, Kirchen.

1. *Liebe meint Vergebung:* Versöhnung mit dem Bruder kommt vor dem Gottesdienst. Es gibt keine Versöhnung mit Gott ohne Versöhnung mit dem Bruder. Deshalb die Vaterunser-Bitte: Vergib uns unsere Schuld, wie auch wir vergeben unseren Schuldigern[27]. Das heißt nicht, daß Gott vom Menschen für die Vergebung Sonderleistungen erwartet. Es genügt, daß der Mensch sich ihm vertrauend zuwendet, daß er glaubt und daß er daraus die Konsequenzen zieht. Denn wenn er schon selber auf Vergebung angewiesen ist und sie empfangen hat, soll er dieser Vergebung Zeuge sein: indem er sie weitergibt. Er kann nicht Gottes große Vergebung empfangen und seinerseits dem Mitmenschen die kleine Vergebung verweigern, wie die Parabel vom großmütigen König und seinem unbarmherzigen Knecht deutlich darlegt[28].

– *Charakteristisch für Jesus ist die* Vergebungsbereitschaft ohne Grenzen: *nicht siebenmal, sondern sieben und siebzigmal also immer wieder, endlos*[29]*! Und jedem, ohne Ausnahme! Charakteristisch für Jesus – wiederum im Widerspruch zur breiten jüdischen Theorie und Praxis – ist in diesem Zusammenhang ebenfalls die Untersagung des Richtens*[30]*: Nicht meinem Urteil untersteht der Andere. Alle unterstehen Gottes Urteil.*
– *Jesu Forderung, zu vergeben, ist nicht juristisch zu interpretieren. Jesus meint nicht ein Gesetz: 77mal soll man vergeben, aber beim 78. Mal nicht. Sondern es ist der Appell an die Liebe des Menschen: von vornherein und immer wieder neu zu vergeben.*

2. *Liebe meint Dienst:* Demut, Dien-mut ist der Weg zur wahren Größe. Dies meint das Gleichnis vom Festmahl: auf die Selbsterhöhung folgt die Erniedrigung – die Blamage der Degradierung. Auf die Selbsterniedrigung folgt die Erhöhung – die Ehre des Aufstiegs[31].

– *Charakteristisch für Jesus ist der uneigennützige* Dienst ohne Rangordnung. *Bezeichnenderweise wird derselbe Spruch Jesu vom Dienen in verschiedenen Ausprägungen (beim Jüngerstreit, beim Abendmahl, bei der Fußwaschung) überliefert: der Höchste soll der Diener (Tischdiener) aller sein*[32]*! Von daher kann es in der Jüngerschaft Jesu kein Amt geben, das einfach durch Recht und Macht konstituiert wird und dem Amt staatlicher Machthaber entspräche, noch ein Amt, das einfach durch Wissen und Würde konstituiert wird und dem Amt der Schrifttheologen entspräche.*

– *Jesu Forderung zum Dienen ist nicht zu verstehen als ein Gesetz, nach welchem es in seiner Gefolgschaft keine Über- und Unterordnung geben dürfte. Wohl aber als ein entschiedener Appell zum Dienst auch der Übergeordneten an den Untergeordneten, also zum gegenseitigen Dienst aller.*

3. *Liebe meint Verzicht:* Gewarnt wird vor der Ausbeutung der Schwachen[33]. Verlangt wird der entschlossene Verzicht auf alles, was die Bereitschaft für Gott und den Nächsten hindert. Zugespitzt gesagt: gar die Hand abzuhauen, wenn sie in Versuchung führt[34]. Aber Jesus erwartet nicht nur den Verzicht auf Negatives, auf Begierden und Sünden, sondern auch den Verzicht auf Positives, auf Recht und Macht.

– *Charakteristisch für Jesus ist der freiwillige* Verzicht ohne Gegenleistung. *Das läßt sich konkretisieren:*
Verzicht auf Rechte zugunsten des Anderen: mit dem zwei Meilen gehen, der mich gezwungen hat, eine mit ihm zu gehen[35].
Verzicht auf Macht auf eigene Kosten: dem auch noch den Mantel zu geben, der mir den Rock abgenommen hat[36].
Verzicht auf Gegengewalt: dem die linke Backe hinzuhalten, der mich auf die rechte geschlagen hat[37].

– *Gerade diese letzten Beispiele zeigen noch deutlicher als alles Frühere: Jesu Forderungen dürfen nicht als Gesetze mißverstanden werden. Jesus meint nicht: bei einem Schlag auf die linke Backe ist Vergeltung nicht erlaubt, wohl aber bei einem Schlag in den Magen. Gewiß sind diese Beispiele nicht nur symbolisch gemeint: Es sind sehr bezeichnende (und öfters in typisch orientalischer Übertreibung formulierte) Grenzfälle, die jederzeit Wirklichkeit werden können. Aber sie sind nicht gesetzlich gemeint: als ob nur dies und immer wieder dies*

geboten wäre. Verzicht auf Gegengewalt meint von vornher-
ein nicht Verzicht auf jeden Widerstand. Jesus selber hat nach
den Berichten bei einem Schlag auf die Wange vor Gericht
keineswegs die andere Wange hingehalten, sondern aufbe-
gehrt. Verzicht darf nicht mit Schwäche verwechselt werden.
Es geht bei den Forderungen Jesu nicht um ethische oder gar
asketische Leistungen, die aus sich selber einen Sinn hätten,
sondern um drastische Appelle zur radikalen Erfüllung des
Willens Gottes von Fall zu Fall zugunsten des Mitmenschen.
Aller Verzicht ist nur die negative Seite einer neuen positiven
Praxis.

In solcher Sicht erscheinen sogar die zehn Gebote des alttestamentlichen Dekalog[38] im dreifachen hegelschen Sinn des Wortes
»aufgehoben«, fallengelassen und doch bewahrt, weil auf eine
höhere Ebene gehoben durch die von Jesus verkündete radikale
»bessere Gerechtigkeit« der Bergpredigt[39]:

- *nicht nur keine anderen Götter neben ihm haben, sondern ihn*
  lieben mit ganzem Herzen, ganzer Seele und ganzem Denken,
  und den Nächsten und sogar den Feind wie sich selbst;
- *nicht nur den Namen Gottes nicht unnütz aussprechen, son-*
  dern auch bei Gott nicht schwören;
- *nicht nur den Sabbat durch Ruhe heiligen, sondern am Sabbat*
  aktiv das Gute tun;
- *nicht nur Vater und Mutter ehren, um lange zu leben auf*
  Erden, sondern, falls um des echten Lebens willen notwendig,
  ihnen sogar in der Form der Trennung Respekt erweisen;
- *nicht nur nicht töten, sondern schon zornige Gedanken und*
  Worte unterlassen;
- *nicht nur nicht ehebrechen, sondern schon ehebrecherische Ab-*
  sichten meiden;
- *nicht nur nicht stehlen, sondern sogar auf das Recht der Vergel-*
  tung für erlittenes Unrecht verzichten;
- *nicht nur kein falsches Zeugnis ablegen, sondern in uneinge-*
  schränkter Wahrhaftigkeit das Ja ein Ja und das Nein ein Nein
  sein lassen;
- *nicht nur nicht begehren seines Nächsten Haus, sondern sogar*
  Böses erdulden;
- *nicht nur nicht begehren seines Nächsten Weib, sondern schon*
  die »legale« Ehescheidung unterlassen.

War der Apostel Paulus – auch hier in auffälliger Übereinstimmung mit dem Jesus der Geschichte – nicht im Recht, wenn er dann der Überzeugung war, wer liebe, habe das Gesetz erfüllt[40]? Und nach Augustin hat man es noch zugespitzter formuliert: »Liebe, und tue, was du willst!« Kein neues Gesetz, sondern eine neue Freiheit vom Gesetz.

Aber gerade von daher drängt sich auf: Blieb es bei Jesus selbst bei Worten, bei Appellen? Eine bequeme, unverbindliche, folgenlose reine Theorie über die Praxis? Was schließlich hat Jesus getan? Wie steht es mit seiner eigenen Praxis?

3. Solidarisierung

Auch schon Jesu *Wort* war in einem eminenten Sinne *Tat*. Gerade sein Wort erforderte den ganzen Einsatz. Und durch sein Wort geschah das Entscheidende: die *Situation* wurde *grundlegend verändert*. Weder die Menschen noch die Institutionen, weder die Hierarchen noch die Normen waren nachher je wieder diejenigen, die sie vor ihm gewesen waren. Er hat mit seinem befreienden Wort die Sache Gottes und die Sache des Menschen zugleich zur Sprache gebracht. Er hat dadurch den Menschen völlig neue Möglichkeiten, *die* Möglichkeit eines neuen Lebens, einer neuen Freiheit, eines neuen *Sinnes im Leben* eröffnet: ein Leben nach Gottes Willen zum Wohl des Menschen in der Feiheit der Liebe, die alle Gesetzlichkeit hinter sich zurückläßt. Und zwar die Gesetzlichkeit der etablierten heiligen Ordnung (Law and Order) ebenso wie die Gesetzlichkeit der gewaltsam-revolutionären oder asketisch-weltflüchtigen Radikalismen und schließlich auch die Gesetzlichkeit der kasuistisch lavierenden Moral.

Jesu Wort war also keine reine »Theorie«, wie ihm überhaupt an Theorie nicht sonderlich gelegen war. Er war in seiner Verkündigung völlig praxisbezogen, praxisorientiert. Seine Forderungen schufen in aller Freiheit neue Verbindlichkeiten und hatten für ihn selber wie für andere Konsequenzen, die – wie noch zu sehen sein wird – auf Leben und Tod gingen. Aber das ist nicht alles.

Sosehr Jesu Wort in eminentem Sinn Tat war: es darf Jesu Tun nicht auf die Tat des Wortes, seine Praxis nicht auf die Praxis der Predigt, sein Leben nicht auf die Verkündigung reduziert werden. Theorie und Praxis decken sich bei Jesus in einem viel umfassenderen Sinn: seiner Verkündigung entspricht sein *ganzes Verhalten*[1]. Und während das Wort der Verkündigung sein Verhalten begründet, rechtfertigt, so macht das praktische Verhalten seine Verkündigung von der Praxis her eindeutig, unangreifbar: Er lebt, was er sagt, und das gewinnt ihm Verstand und Herz seiner Hörer.

Ein enger Ausschnitt aus diesem gelebten Verhalten hat uns dies bereits gezeigt[2]: Jesus hat sich in Wort und Tat den *Schwachen, Kranken, Vernachlässigten* zugewendet. Ein Zeichen nicht der Schwäche, sondern der Stärke. Er hat dem, was nach den Maßstäben der Gesellschaft als schwach, krank, niedrig, verachtet auszusondern ist, eine Chance des Menschseins geboten. Er hat ihnen an Seele und Leib geholfen, hat manchen physisch und psychisch Kranken Gesundheit, den vielen Schwachen Kraft und allen Untüchtigen Hoffnung geschenkt – alles Zeichen des kommenden Gottesreiches. Er war für den *ganzen* Menschen da: nicht nur für seine Geistigkeit, sondern auch für seine Leiblichkeit und Weltlichkeit. Er war für *alle* Menschen da: nicht nur für die Starken, Jungen, Gesunden, auch für die Schwachen, Altgewordenen, Kranken, Krüppel. Auf diese Weise verdeutlichen Jesu Taten sein Wort, wie umgekehrt das Wort seine Taten deutet. Aber dies allein hätte nie so viel Ärgernis hervorrufen können, wie es tatsächlich hervorgerufen hat. Es ging um mehr. Daß er sich in dieser prononcierten Art der Kranken und »Besessenen« annahm, war ungewöhnlich, konnte man ihm jedoch noch nachsehen; die Wundersucht aller Zeiten fordert schließlich auch ihre Wundermänner. Freilich war auch dies nicht unproblematisch: Kranke sind nach dem Urteil seiner Zeit selber schuld an ihrem Unglück, Krankheit ist Strafe für begangene Sünde; Besessene sind vom Teufel geritten; Aussätzige, vom erstgeborenen Sohn des Todes Befallene, verdienen keine Gemeinschaft. Sie alle sind – ob aufgrund des Schicksals, ihrer Schuld oder einfach herrschender Vorurteile ist schließlich gleichgültig – gesellschaftlich Gezeichnete. Jesus aber stellt sich grundsätzlich positiv zu ihnen allen und hat, wie wir uns hier auf Johannes verlassen können[3], die ursächliche Verknüpfung von Sünde und Krankheit und die gesellschaftliche Ächtung grundsätzlich abgelehnt.

Doch nun kam hinzu – und auch das war vielleicht das Entscheidende noch nicht, ist aber wohl zu beachten: Unbekümmert um Sitten und Gebräuche hatte er sich schon durch seine *Umgebung* verdächtig gemacht.

– *Die* Frauen, *die in der Gesellschaft von damals nicht zählten und in der Öffentlichkeit Männergesellschaft zu meiden hatten: Die zeitgenössischen jüdischen Quellen sind voll von Animosität gegen die Frau, die nach Josephus in jeder Beziehung geringeren Wertes ist als der Mann[4]. Selbst mit der eigenen Frau, so wird geraten, soll man wenig reden, erst recht nicht mit einer anderen. Die Frauen lebten möglichst zurückgezogen von der Öffentlichkeit, im Tempel hatten sie nur bis zum Frauenvorhof Zutritt, und bezüglich der Gebetsverpflichtung waren sie den Sklaven gleichgestellt. Die Evangelien aber, was immer vom biographischen Detail historisch sein mag, zeigen jedenfalls keine Hemmungen, von Jesu Beziehungen zu Frauen zu sprechen. Danach hatte sich Jesus von der Sitte gelöst, welche die Frau abschließt. Jesus zeigt nicht nur keine Frauenverachtung, sondern eine erstaunliche Unbefangenheit gegenüber Frauen: Frauen begleiteten ihn und seine Jünger von Galiläa bis Jerusalem[5]; persönliche Zuneigung zu Frauen war ihm nicht fremd[6]; Frauen sehen seinem Sterben oder seinem Begräbnis zu[7]. Die juristisch und menschlich schwache Stellung der Frau in der damaligen Gesellschaft wird durch sein Verbot der Ehescheidung durch den Mann, der allein einen Scheidebrief ausstellen konnte, erheblich aufgewertet[8].*

– *Die* Kinder, *die keine Rechte hatten: Jesus behandelt sie bevorzugt, verteidigt sie gegen seine Jünger, liebkost und segnet sie[9]. Ganz unjüdisch werden sie den Erwachsenen als Beispiele hingestellt, weil sie ohne Berechnung und Hintergedanken ein Geschenk anzunehmen bereit sind[10].*

– *Das* religiös unwissende Volk: *die zahlreichen kleinen Leute, die sich um das Gesetz nicht kümmern konnten oder wollten. Gepriesen werden die »Einfältigen«, die Ungebildeten, Rückständigen, Unreifen, Unfrommen, die so gar nicht Klugen und Weisen[11], die »Kleinen« oder »Geringen«[12], ja »Kleinsten« oder »Geringsten«[13].*

Also keine aristokratische Moral für die »Edlen«, wie sie etwa Kung-futse von den Gemeinen absetzt. Auch keine elitäre Mönchsmoral für die »Verständigen«, die für eine Ordensgemeinschaft im Sinne Buddhas in Frage kommen. Erst recht natürlich keine Moral für die oberen »Kasten« im hinduistischen Sinn, die mit allen übrigen Diskriminierungen auch noch Parias in der Gesellschaft duldet.

Welche Armen?

Die armen kleinen Leute: In provokativer Weise hat Jesus seine Botschaft als eine frohe Botschaft für die *Armen* verkündet. Den Armen galt der erste Zuruf, Zuspruch, Heilruf, seine erste Seligpreisung. Wer sind diese Armen?

Die Frage ist nicht leicht zu beantworten, da schon in den synoptischen Evangelien die erste Seligpreisung verschieden verstanden wird. Mattäus[14] versteht sie offensichtlich religiös: Die Armen »im Geist«, die *geistig* Armen, sind identisch mit den Demütigen der dritten Seligpreisung, die sich als Bettler vor Gott ihrer geistigen Armut bewußt sind. Lukas[15] aber – ohne den Zusatz des Mattäus – versteht den Ausdruck im soziologischen Sinne: die wirklich armen Leute. So dürfte ihn wohl auch Jesus selber – auf den nach der kürzeren und wohl ursprünglicheren Lukas-Fassung[16] zumindest die erste, zweite und vierte Seligpreisung der erweiterten Mattäus-Fassung[17] zurückgehen – verstanden haben: Es geht um die *wirklich* Armen, Weinenden, Hungernden, um die zu kurz Gekommenen, die am Rand Stehenden, die Zurückgesetzten, Verstoßenen, Unterdrückten dieser Erde.

Jesus selber war arm. Was immer der Historiker zum Stall von Betlehem zu sagen hat, als Symbol trifft er genau. Und vom Satz Ernst Blochs stimmt zumindest die Fortsetzung: »Der Stall, der Zimmermannssohn, der Schwärmer unter kleinen Leuten, der Galgen am Ende, das ist aus geschichtlichem Stoff, nicht aus dem goldenen, den die Sage liebt[18]«. Ein Proletarier aus der breiten untersten Schicht war Jesus freilich nicht; Handwerker waren auch damals schon etwas Besseres, Kleinbürgerliches. Aber in seiner öffentlichen Tätigkeit führte Jesus zweifellos ein freies Wanderleben in totaler Anspruchslosigkeit. Und seine Predigt ging an alle und gerade an die untersten Schichten. Seine Anhänger gehörten, wie wir hörten, zu den »Kleinen«[19] oder »Einfältigen«[20]: den Ungebildeten, Unwissenden, Rückständigen, denen das religiöse Wissen ebenso abgeht wie das moralische Verhalten und die den »Klugen und Weisen« gegenübergestellt werden. Jesu Gegner aber gehörten vor allem der schmalen kleinbürgerlichen Mittelschicht (Pharisäer) und der dünnen (vor allem sadduzäischen) Oberschicht an, die von seiner Botschaft nicht nur im religiösen, sondern auch in ihrem sozialen Gewissen beunruhigt waren[21].

Man kann es nicht wegdiskutieren: Jesus war *parteiisch für die Armen,* Weinenden, Hungernden, für die Erfolglosen, Machtlosen, Bedeutungslosen. Die Reichen, die sich Schätze anhäufen, welche Rost und Motten verzehren und Diebe stehlen können und die ihr Herz an den Reichtum hängen, stellt er bei all ihrer Sparsamkeit als abschreckendes Beispiel hin[22]. Erfolg, sozialer Aufstieg sagten ihm nichts: Wer sich selbst erhöht, wird erniedrigt werden – und umgekehrt[23]. Fremd sind Jesus jene Menschen, die sich, gesichert und geborgen, an die vergänglichen Güter dieser Welt gefesselt haben. Man muß sich entscheiden, zwei Götter kann man nicht haben: Wo immer – bei großen oder kleinen Sparern – der Besitz sich zwischen Gott und Mensch stellt, wo immer einer dem Geld dient und das Geld zum Götzen macht[24], da gilt das »Wehe den Reichen«, welches wohl Lukas selbst der Seligpreisung der Armen gegenüberstellt[25]. Jesu Warnung ist überdeutlich: Eher geht ein Kamel durch das Nadelöhr als ein Reicher ins Gottesreich[26]. Alle gekünstelten Abschwächungsversuche (statt »Nadelöhr« ein kleines Tor, statt »Kamel« ein Schiffstau) helfen nichts: Reichtum ist für das Heil äußerst gefährlich. Armut ist nichts Schlechtes. Jesus steht prinzipiell auf der Seite der Armen.

Und trotz allem: Jesus propagiert *nicht die Enteignung der Reichen,* nicht eine Art »Diktatur des Proletariats«. Nicht Rache an den Ausbeutern, nicht Expropriation der Expropriateure und Unterdrückung der Unterdrücker fordert er, sondern Frieden und Machtverzicht. Er verlangt auch nicht wie das Kloster zu Qumran die Abgabe des Besitzes an die Gemeinschaft. Wer auf Besitz verzichtet, soll ihn nicht in Gemeineigentum überführen, sondern den Armen geben. Aber er hat nicht von allen seinen Anhängern den Verzicht auf Eigentum gefordert. Auch darin, wie wir schon sahen, kein Gesetz! Verschiedene seiner Anhänger (Petrus, Levi, Maria und Marta) nannten Häuser ihr eigen. Jesus billigt es, daß Zachäus nur die Hälfte seines Besitzes verteilt[27]. Was Jesus vom reichen Jüngling[28] im Hinblick auf das

Mit-ihm-Ziehen forderte, das forderte er nicht generell und starr von jedem in jeder Situation. Gewiß, wer mit ihm ziehen wollte, mußte notwendigerweise alles hinter sich zurücklassen, konnte allerdings auch nicht von nichts leben. Wovon lebten überhaupt Jesus und seine Jünger auf ihrem Wanderleben? Die Evangelien machen kein Geheimnis daraus: durch Unterstützung der Besitzenden unter seinen Anhängern und insbesondere Anhängerinnen[29]! Manchmal ließ er sich einladen: von reichen Pharisäern wie von reichen Zöllnern. Nur Lukas idealisiert nachträglich die Verhältnisse in der Urgemeinde und begründet sie mit von ihm selber (wie der Vergleich mit Markus und Mattäus zeigt) rigoristisch verschärften Jesusworten gegen allen Besitz. In Wirklichkeit kannte auch die Urgemeinde keinen generellen Verzicht auf Besitz[30].

Jesus war also einerseits kein ökonomisch naiver Schwarmgeist, der aus der Not eine Tugend machte und die Armut religiös verbrämte: Not lehrt ja nicht nur beten, sondern auch fluchen. Jesus verklärt die Armut sowenig wie die Krankheit; er gibt kein Opium. Armut, Leid, Hunger sind Elend, nicht Seligkeit. Er verkündet keine enthusiastische Spiritualität, die das Unrecht im Geist überspringt oder billig mit einem kompensierenden Jenseits tröstet. Er war andererseits kein fanatischer Revolutionär, der gewaltsam über Nacht das Elend abschaffen will, meist um neues zu schaffen. Er zeigt keine Gehässigkeit gegen die Reichen, waren sie auch noch so brutal wie im damaligen Orient. Er war keiner jener gewaltsamen Volksbeglücker, welche die Spirale von Gewalt und Gegengewalt nur weiterdrehen statt sie zu durchbrechen. Gewiß war er keineswegs einverstanden mit den gesellschaftlichen Verhältnissen, wie sie sind. Nur: definitive Lösungen sieht er anders. Er ruft den Armen, Leidenden, Hungernden mitten in das Elend der Gegenwart hinein sein »Heil euch«, »Selig, glücklich ihr!« zu.

Ein *Glück der Armen*, ein Glück der Unglücklichen? Die Seligpreisung ist nicht zu verstehen als allgemeine Regel, jedermann einsichtig, überall und allezeit geltend: als ob jede Armut, jedes Leid, jedes Elend automatisch den Himmel und noch gar den Himmel auf Erden verbürgte! Sie ist zu verstehen als Zusage: als Verheißung, die sich für den erfüllt, der sie nicht nur neutral anhört, sondern sich vertrauensvoll zu eigen macht. Für ihn bricht Gottes Zukunft bereits in sein Leben ein, bringt sie schon jetzt Tröstung, Erbe, Sättigung. Wohin er immer kommen mag, Gott ist voraus, er ist da. Im Vertrauen auf diesen vorausseienden

Gott ändert sich schon jetzt seine Situation: Schon jetzt kann er anders leben, wird er fähig zu einer neuen Praxis, fähig zu schrankenloser Hilfsbereitschaft, ohne Prestigedenken und Neid auf diejenigen, die mehr haben. Liebe meint ja nicht rein passives Abwarten. Gerade weil der Glaubende seinen Gott voraus weiß, kann er sich aktiv engagieren und sich zugleich in aller Aktivität und allem Engagement eine erstaunliche überlegene Sorglosigkeit leisten: eine Sorglosigkeit, die sich – ähnlich den Vögeln des Himmels und den Lilien des Feldes – im Vertrauen auf den sorgenden Gott und im Ausblick auf die frohe Zukunft nicht Gedanken macht um Nahrung und Kleidung und überhaupt den morgigen Tag[31]. Dieses »einfache« Leben ist es, was an Jesus auch einem Henry Miller imponierte. Natürlich bedeutet dies etwas anderes im Land und zur Zeit Jesu, wo aufgrund der agrarischen Kultur und des Klimas der Bedarf an Kleidern gering, die Wohnungsfrage nicht dringend, die Nahrung zur Not auf dem Feld zu besorgen war. Da ließ sich geradezu von der Hand in den Mund leben und beten: Unser tägliches Brot gib uns heute[32]! Wie es Franz von Assisi und seine ersten Brüder wörtlich nachzuahmen versuchten.

Doch ausgeweitet, wie dies schon Mattäus tat, geht es um eine Forderung an *jeden* Menschen, auch wenn er nicht mit dem baldigen Weltende rechnet: Armut »im Geist« als die Grundhaltung der *genügsamen Anspruchslosigkeit* und der *vertrauenden Sorglosigkeit*! Gegen alle anspruchsvoll unbescheidene Anmaßung und kummervolle Besorgtheit, die sich auch bei ökonomisch Armen finden kann. Armut im Geist also als die *innere Freiheit vom Besitz*, die in verschiedenen Situationen verschieden zu realisieren ist. In jedem Falle aber so, daß die ökonomischen Werte nicht mehr die obersten sein können und eine neue Wertskala sich aufdrängt!

Jesus wollte nicht nur eine bestimmte Gruppe oder Schicht ansprechen und sicher nicht nur jene Gruppen, die sich den religiösen Ehrentitel »die Armen« (»die Demütigen«, nach den Propheten und Psalmen) zugelegt hatten. Mit seinen radikalen Forderungen unterläuft er jede soziale Schichtung und trifft einen jeden, die Raffgier des Reichen ebenso wie den Neid der Armen. Ihn erbarmte des Volkes, und dies nicht nur aus ökonomischen Gründen. Für jedermann ist es eine Versuchung, nur vom Brot allein zu leben. Als ob es nicht noch eine ganz andere Bedürftigkeit des Menschen gäbe. In der Sicht des Johannesevangeliums – so die Erzählung von der Brotvermehrung – entwickelt sich gerade aus dem falschen Verlangen nach Brot die große Auseinandersetzung, wonach sich die Großzahl von Jesus abwendet: nur Brot und Sattsein, nicht ihn sucht die Menge. Jesus hat wie keine Wohlstandsgesellschaft so auch keinen Gulaschkommunismus gepredigt. Nicht: »Erst kommt das Fressen, dann kommt die Moral« (B. Brecht[33]). Sondern: »Erst das Reich Gottes, und dann alles andere[34].« Auch den Verdammten dieser Erde predigt er, daß etwas anderes wichtiger ist, daß sie über die Befriedigung ökonomischer Bedürfnisse hinaus noch in sehr viel tieferem Sinn arm, elend, ausgebeutet, bedürftig sind.

Kurz: jeder Mensch steht immer wieder vor Gott und den Menschen als »armer Sünder« da: als Bettler, der der Barmherzigkeit, der Vergebung bedarf. Auch der kleine Knecht kann so hartherzig sein wie der große König[35]. Schon bei Jesaja, den Jesus in seiner Antwort an den Täufer zitiert, sind die »Armen« (anawim) die Niedergedrückten im umfassenden Sinn: die Bedrängten, Zerschlagenen, Verzagten, Verzweifelten, Elenden. Und alle Elenden und Verlorenen in äußerer Not (Lukas) oder innerer Bedrängnis (Mattäus), eben alle, die mühselig und beladen sind, auch die Schuldbeladenen, ruft Jesus zu sich. Ihr aller Anwalt ist er. Und hier allerdings liegt nun der eigentliche Skandal.

Die moralischen Versager

Was schlechthin unverzeihlich war: Nicht daß er sich um Kranke, Krüppel, Aussätzige, Besessene kümmerte, nicht daß er Frauen und Kinder um sich duldete, auch nicht nur, daß er parteiisch war für die armen, kleinen Leute. Nein, daß er sich mit *moralischen Versagern,* mit offensichtlich *Unfrommen* und *Unmoralischen* eingelassen hat: mit moralisch und politisch nicht einwandfreien Leuten, mit so manchen zweifelhaften, zwielichtigen, verlorenen, hoffnungslosen Existenzen, die es am Rande jeder Gesellschaft gibt, als unausrottbares, notwendiges Übel. Das war das eigentliche Ärgernis. Mußte man es denn gerade so weit treiben? Solch praktisches Verhalten unterscheidet sich in der Tat gar sehr vom allgemeinen religiösen Verhalten, insbesondere von der elitären (mönchischen, aristokratischen oder kastengebundenen) Ethik der östlichen Religionen und wohl am meisten von der strengen Moral der eigentlichen Gesetzesreligionen (Judentum, Mazdaismus, Islam):

Es mag vielleicht die Gemeinde gewesen sein, die es aus dem Rückblick so allgemein und programmatisch formulierte: Jesus sei gekommen, um das Verlorene zu suchen und zu retten[36], gekommen, nicht um Gerechte zu berufen, sondern Sünder[37]. Aber auch die kritischsten Exegeten bestreiten es nicht: Er hat, wie immer es historisch um die einzelnen Worte stehen mag, in provozierender Weise mit moralischen Versagern, mit Unfrommen und Unmoralischen verkehrt. Mit denen, auf die man mit Fingern zeigte, die man mit Auszeichnung und Abscheu »Sünder« nannte. Das bereits berichtete und zweifellos nicht von der Gemeinde erfundene Schimpfwort der Gegner Jesu vom »Fresser und Säufer« hat ja noch eine – um vieles schwerer wiegende – Fortsetzung: »Freund von Zöllnern und Sündern[38]!«

Zöllner – das waren die Sünder schlechthin: die traurigen Sünder par excellence. Angehörige eines verfemten Gewerbes, Verhaßte, Betrüger und Gauner, reich geworden im Dienst der Besatzungsmacht, mit permanenter Unreinheit behaftete Kollaborateure und Verräter der nationalen Sache, unfähig zur Buße, weil sie gar nicht mehr wissen können, wen sie alles um wieviel betrogen haben. Und gerade mit solchen professionellen Gaunern mußte sich Jesus einlassen. Auch hier ist nicht wichtig herauszufinden, wie weit die Erzählung vom skandalösen Festgelage beim Oberzöllner Zachäus[39] oder auch die von der Aufnahme des Zöllners Levi in Jesu Jüngerkreis[40] geschichtliche Erinnerungen wiedergeben; solche dürfen, wie nicht von vornherein angenommen, so auch nicht – gerade etwa bezüglich der schon bei Markus überlieferten Berufung des Levi, Sohn des Alfäus – von vornherein ausgeschlossen werden. Daß die Evangelien nicht weniger als drei Zöllner mit Namen kennen, die zu Jesu Anhängern gehören, ist auffällig genug. Als historisch gesichert wird jedenfalls allgemein anerkannt, was der Vorwurf der gegnerischen Kritik war: dieser nimmt Sünder an und ißt mit ihnen[41].

Er verweigerte den *Sündern*, den Gesetzlosen und Gesetzesbrechern, den Umgang nicht, wiewohl natürlich auch Gerechte zu ihm kamen. Er kehrte bei Zöllnern und notorischen Sündern ein. »Wenn dieser ein Prophet wäre, wüßte er, wer es ist und was für eine Frau, die ihn anrührt«: Es läßt sich nicht mehr überprüfen, ob jene Erzählung von der reichlich unkonventionellen Huldigung der stadtbekannten Sünderin, wohl Dirne, die seine Füße unwidersprochen mit parfümiertem Öl salbte[42], ebenso wie die in der johanneischen Überlieferung auftauchende ergreifende

Erzählung von der beim Ehebruch in flagranti Ertappten, die er vom Zugriff der Gesetzeswächter gerettet hat[43], Legenden oder Erinnerungen oder beides in einem, typisierte Erzählungen sind. Zu den sichersten Elementen der Überlieferung gehört jedenfalls: Jesus zeigte eine provokative Zuneigung zu den Sündern und solidarisierte sich mit den Unfrommen und Unmoralischen. Verkommene und Abgeschriebene hatten bei ihm eine Zukunft. Auch jene sexuell ausgenützten und dafür noch verachteten Frauen – alle Opfer einer Gesellschaft von »Gerechten«. Und die Worte aus jenen Szenen trafen: Ihre vielen Sünden sind ihr vergeben, weil sie viel geliebt hat! Wer unter euch ohne Sünde ist, werfe den ersten Stein[44]!

Es läßt sich somit nicht bestreiten: Jesus war »in schlechter Gesellschaft[45]«. Immer wieder tauchen in den Evangelien zweifelhafte Gestalten, Schuldiggewordene auf, von denen anständige Menschen besser Distanz halten. Entgegen allen Erwartungen, die seine Zeitgenossen vom Prediger des Gottesreiches hegten, hat sich Jesus geweigert, die Rolle des frommen Asketen, der Gastmählern und insbesondere bestimmten Leuten fernbleibt, zu spielen. Gewiß wäre es nicht richtig, den bei Jesus unbestreitbaren »Zug nach unten« zu romantisieren. Kein »gleich und gleich gesellt sich gern«! Jesus zeigte keine verbotene Lust an der »dolce vita«, keinen Hang zur Halbwelt. Er rechtfertigte nicht das »Milieu«. Er entschuldigte keine Schuld. Aber nach den evangelischen Berichten kann nicht bestritten werden: Entgegen allen gesellschaftlichen Vorurteilen und Schranken hat Jesus *jede soziale Disqualifizierung* bestimmter Gruppen oder unglücklicher Minderheiten *abgelehnt*.

Ob vielleicht Günter Herburger mit seinem Roman doch recht hatte, wenn er Jesus in Osaka unter Gastarbeitern sieht? Unbekümmert um alles Geschwätz hinter seinem Rücken, unbekümmert um alle offene Kritik hat sich Jesus mit Randexistenzen der Gesellschaft, mit gesellschaftlich Verfemten, religiös Ausgestoßenen, mit Diskriminierten und Deklassierten eingelassen. Er machte sich mit ihnen gemein. Er akzeptierte sie einfach. Er predigt nicht nur die Offenheit der Liebe gegenüber allen Menschen, er praktiziert sie auch. Gewiß, er biedert sich nicht an, macht das Treiben der anrüchigen Kreise keineswegs mit. Er sinkt nicht auf ihr Niveau ab, sondern zieht sie zu sich herauf. Aber er setzt sich mit diesen notorisch schlechten Menschen nicht nur auseinander, sondern *setzt sich* – ganz wörtlich – *mit ihnen zusammen*. Unmöglich, so empörte man sich.

Ob er nicht realisierte, was er tat? Ob er nicht realisierte, wie sehr ein gemeinsames Essen – damals wie heute – kompromittieren kann? Man überlegt doch, wen man einlädt, von wem man sich einladen läßt. Und wen man auf jeden Fall ausschließt! Für einen Orientalen erst recht sollte es deutlich sein: *Tischgemeinschaft* meint mehr als nur Höflichkeit und Freundlichkeit. Tischgemeinschaft bedeutet Frieden, Vertrauen, Versöhnung, Bruderschaft. Und dies sogar – würde der gläubige Jude hinzufügen – nicht nur vor den Augen der Menschen, sondern vor den Augen Gottes: Noch heute bricht in jüdischen Familien der Hausvater zu Beginn der Mahlzeit mit dem Segensspruch ein Stück Brot, damit jeder durch ein abgebrochenes Stücklein Anteil habe am herabgerufenen Segen. Tischgemeinschaft vor den Augen Gottes – mit Sündern? Genau das. Als ob das Gesetz nicht genauester Maßstab wäre, um festzustellen, mit wem man Gemeinschaft zu halten hat, wer zur Gemeinde der Frommen gehört.

Diese Mahlgemeinschaft mit den von den Frommen Abgeschriebenen war für Jesus nicht nur Ausdruck liberaler Toleranz und humanitärer Gesinnung. Sie war Ausdruck seiner Sendung und Botschaft: Friede, Versöhnung für alle ohne Ausnahme, auch für die moralischen Versager. Die Moralischen empfanden das als eine Verletzung aller konventionellen moralischen Normen, ja, als eine Zerstörung der Moral. Zu Unrecht?

Das Recht der Gnade

Auch das Judentum kannte einen Gott, der vergeben kann. Aber vergeben wem? Demjenigen, der sich geändert hat, der alles wiedergutgemacht, der Buße geleistet, der die Schuld durch Leistungen (Gesetzeserfüllung, Gelübde, Opfer, Almosen) abgetragen und einen besseren Lebenswandel an den Tag gelegt hat. Kurz: Vergeben wird dem, der aus dem Sünder zum Gerechten geworden ist. Aber doch nicht dem Sünder: den Sünder trifft Gericht, trifft Strafe. Das ist Gerechtigkeit!

Soll es also nicht mehr gelten: zuerst Leistung, Buße, dann Gnade? Soll dieses ganze System außer Kraft gesetzt sein? Muß nicht, wie im alttestamentlichen Deuteronomium und den Büchern der Chronik völlig deutlich gemacht, – Gesetzestreue von Gott belohnt und Gesetzeslosigkeit bestraft werden? Nach diesem Freund der Zöllner und Sünder soll Gott, der heilige Gott, *gerade den Sündern*, den Unheiligen, *vergeben?* Ein solcher Gott wäre doch ein Gott der Sünder! Ein Gott, der die Sünder mehr liebt als die *Gerechten!*

Hier wird eindeutig *an den Fundamenten der Religion gerüttelt:* Den Verrätern, Betrügern und Ehebrechern wird gegenüber den Frommen und Gerechten Recht gegeben[46]. Dem zu Hause hart Arbeitenden wird der heruntergekommene Gammler-Bruder vorgezogen[47]. Den Einheimischen wird ein verhaßter Ausländer und dazu noch Ketzer als Vorbild hingestellt[48]. Und am Ende werden dann alle denselben Lohn erhalten[49]!? Was sollen alle die großen Reden zugunsten des Verlorenen[50]? Sollen die Schuldiggewordenen etwa Gott näher stehen als die Gerechtgebliebenen? Skandalös, daß im Himmel mehr Freude sein soll über einen Sünder, der Buße tut, als über 99 Gerechte, die der Buße nicht bedürfen[51]! Die Gerechtigkeit scheint auf den Kopf gestellt.

Ist da nicht zu erwarten, daß ein solcher Sympathisant von Out-laws, von Gesetzlosen, auch selber das Gesetz bricht? Daß er weder die rituellen noch die disziplinären Vorschriften hält, wie es sich nach Gottes Gebot und der Väter Tradition gehört? Schöne Reinheit des Herzens! Festen statt Fasten! Der Mensch Maßstab der Gebote Gottes! Statt gestraft wird gefeiert! Daß unter solchen Umständen Prostituierte und Betrüger vor den Frommen ins Gottesreich kommen sollen[52], die Ungläubigen aus allen Richtungen vor den Kindern des Reiches[53], wen wundert's? Was für eine verrückte Gerechtigkeit, die faktisch alle geheiligten Maßstäbe aufhebt und in einer Umwertung aller Rangfolge die Ersten zu Letzten und die Letzten zu Ersten macht[54]! Was für eine naive, gefährliche Liebe, die ihre Grenzen nicht kennt: die Grenzen zwischen Volksgenossen und Nicht-Volksgenossen, Parteigenossen und Nicht-Parteigenossen, zwischen Nächsten und Fernsten, anständigen und unanständigen Berufen, Moralischen und Unmoralischen, Guten und Bösen? Als ob da Distanzierung nicht unbedingt erforderlich wäre. Als ob man da nicht richten müßte. Als ob man da je vergeben dürfte.

Ja, Jesus ging so weit: *man darf vergeben.* Endlos vergeben, siebenundsiebzigmal[55]. Und alle Sünden: außer es sündige einer gegen den Heiligen Geist, die Wirklichkeit Gottes selbst, und wolle keine Vergebung[56]. *Jedem* ist da offensichtlich *eine Chance* angeboten, unabhängig von sozialen, ethnischen, politisch-religiösen Grenzen. Und zwar ist er schon angenommen, bevor er umkehrt. Zuerst die Gnade, dann die Leistung! Der Sünder, der alle Strafe verdient hat, ist begnadigt: er braucht den Gnadenakt nur anzuerkennen. Vergebung ist ihm geschenkt: er braucht das Geschenk nur anzunehmen und umzukehren. Eine eigentliche Amnestie – umsonst: er braucht nur vertrauensvoll daraus zu leben. So gilt denn *Gnade vor Recht*. Oder besser: Es gilt das Recht der Gnade! Nur so ist die neue bessere Gerechtigkeit möglich. Aus vorbehaltloser Vergebung: einzige Vorbedingung das gläubige Vertrauen oder der vertrauende Glaube; einzige Konsequenz das großmütige Weitergeben der Vergebung. Wer aus der großen Vergebung leben darf, soll die kleine nicht verweigern[57].

Freilich: Wer seine kritische Situation erfaßt hat, der weiß auch, daß die Entscheidung keinen Aufschub duldet. Wo der moralische Ruin der Existenz droht, wo alles auf dem Spiel steht, muß kühn, entschlossen und klug gehandelt werden. Nach dem – anstößig aufreizenden – Beispiel jenes skrupellosen Verwalters, der illusionslos seine letzte Stunde nützt[58]. Es ist nicht irgendeine Chance, es ist die Chance des Lebens: Wer sein Leben gewinnen will, wird es verlieren, und wer es verliert, wird es gewinnen[59]. Eng ist die Pforte[60]. Viele sind gerufen, wenige erwählt[61]. Die Rettung des Menschen bleibt ein Gnadenwunder, möglich allein durch den Gott, bei dem freilich alles möglich ist[62].

So ist das große Festmahl bereit: bereit für alle, selbst für die Bettler und Krüppel in den Gassen und gar die draußen auf den Landstraßen[63]. Und welches Zeichen hätte deutlicher sprechen können für die allen angebotene Vergebung als jene *Mahlzeiten* Jesu mit all denen, die dabeisein wollten, unter Einschluß derer, die von anständigen Tischrunden ausgeschlossen bleiben? So empfanden es diese sonst Ausgeschlossenen mit nicht geringer Freude: hier erfährt man statt der üblichen Verurteilung Schonung. Statt des rasch gefällten Schuldspruchs erbarmenden Freispruch. Statt der allgemeinen Ungnade überraschend Gnade. Eine wahre Befreiung! Eine echte Erlösung! Hier wird Gnade ganz praktisch demonstriert. So sind diese Mahlzeiten Jesu den Gemeinden in Erinnerung geblieben und nach seinem Tod in noch ganz anderer Tiefe verstanden worden: als erstaunliches Bild, gleichsam als Vorfeier, als Vorwegnahme des in den Parabeln angekündigten endzeitlichen Heilsmahles[64].

Aber es blieb die Frage: *Wie* läßt sich *solche Gnade*, Vergebung, Befreiung und Erlösung für die Sünder *rechtfertigen?* Jesu Parabeln geben deutlich Auskunft. Seine Verteidigung besteht zunächst im Gegenangriff: Sind denn die Gerechten, die der Buße nicht bedürfen, wirklich so gerecht, die Frommen so fromm? Bilden sie sich nicht etwas ein auf ihre Moral und Frömmigkeit und werden gerade dadurch schuldig[65]? Wissen sie überhaupt, was Vergebung ist[66]? Sind sie nicht erbarmungslos gegenüber ihren versagenden Brüdern[67]? Geben sie nicht vor zu gehorchen und tun es faktisch doch nicht[68]? Verweigern sie sich nicht dem Rufe Gottes[69]? Es gibt eine Schuld der Unschuldigen: wenn sie meinen, Gott nichts schuldig geblieben zu sein. Und eine Unschuld der Schuldigen: wenn sie sich in ihrer Verlorenheit gänzlich Gott ausliefern. Das bedeutet: die Sünder sind wahrhaftiger als die Frommen, weil sie ihre Sündhaftigkeit nicht verbergen. Jesus gibt ihnen recht gegenüber denen, die ihre Sündhaftigkeit nicht wahrhaben wollen.

Doch Jesu eigentliche Rechtfertigung und Antwort ist eine andere: Warum darf man vergeben, statt zu verurteilen, warum geht Gnade vor Recht? Weil *Gott selbst* nicht verurteilt, sondern *vergibt*! Weil Gott selbst in Freiheit Gnade vor Recht gehen läßt, das Recht der Gnade übt! So erscheint Gott durch alle Parabeln hindurch in immer wieder neuen Variationen als der Generöse: als der großmütig sich erbarmende König[70], als der großzügig verzichtende Geldverleiher[71], als der suchende Hirte[72], als die nachforschende Frau[73], als der entgegenlaufende Vater[74], als der den Zöllner erhörende Richter[75]. Immer wieder neu ein Gott grenzenlosen Erbarmens und alles übersteigender Güte[76]. Der Mensch soll gleichsam Gottes Geben und Vergeben durch sein Geben und Vergeben abbilden. Nur von daher ist die Bitte des Vaterunser zu verstehen: Vergib uns unsere Schuld, wie auch wir vergeben haben unseren Schuldigern[77].

Jesus verkündet dies alles wie immer untheologisch, ohne große Gnadentheologie. Das Wort »*Gnade*« kommt bei den Synoptikern – abgesehen von Lukas in wohl meist nicht ursprünglichen Zusammenhängen – ebenso wie bei Johannes (abgesehen vom Prolog) überhaupt nicht vor. »Vergebung« erscheint meist formelhaft im Zusammenhang mit der Taufe, das Hauptwort »Barmherzigkeit« fehlt in den Evangelien überhaupt. Anders die Tätigkeitsworte »vergeben«, »erlassen«, »schenken«. Was auf das Entscheidende hinweist: Über Gnade und Vergebung spricht Jesus vor allem *im Vollzug*. Daß über den verkommenen Sohn kein Strafgericht ergeht, sondern der Vater, das Schuldbekenntnis unterbrechend, ihm um den Hals fällt, daß Festkleid, Fingerring und Sandalen gebracht, das Mastkalb geschlachtet und ein Fest gefeiert wird, das ist Gnade im Vollzug. Wie eben der Knecht, der Geldleiher, der Zöllner, das verlorene

Schaf Generösität, Vergebung, Barmherzigkeit, Gnade erfahren. Ohne Erforschung der Vergangenheit und ohne besondere Auflagen ein unbedingtes Angenommenwerden, so daß der Mensch befreit wieder leben, sich selber – und das ist nicht nur für den Zöllner das schwierigste – annehmen kann: Gnade – eine neue Lebenschance.

Die Parabeln Jesu waren also mehr als nur Gleichnisse einer zeitlosen Idee eines liebenden Vatergottes. In diesen Parabeln wurde im Wort zugesprochen, was in Jesu Tat, seiner Annahme der Sünder, geschah: Vergebung. In Tat und Wort Jesu wurde die vergebende und befreiende Liebe Gottes zu den Sündern Ereignis. *Nicht Bestrafung der Bösen, sondern* die *Rechtfertigung der Sünder:* Hier bricht Gottes Reich schon an, die kommende Gottesgerechtigkeit.

Jesus setzte durch alles, was er lehrt und praktiziert, diejenigen ins Unrecht, die, obwohl fromm, weniger großzügig, barmherzig, gut waren als er. Und so muß es denn Jesus zum großen Ärgernis dieser weniger großzügigen Frommen mit Berufung auf diesen Gott, dessen Liebe den Sündern gilt, der die Sünder den Gerechten vorzieht, auch gewagt haben, das Gottesrecht der Gnade zu antizipieren und diese Gnade, Barmherzigkeit und Vergebung Gottes nicht nur allgemein anzukünden: Er hat es gewagt, wie auch kritischste Exegeten als historisch annehmen[78], die *Vergebung direkt dem einzelnen Schuldiggewordenen zuzusprechen.*

Die erste Konfrontation, die Jesus nach dem ersten Evangelium mit seinen Gegnern hat und die einen typischen Charakter aufweist, dreht sich um einen solchen Zuspruch der Sündenvergebung: »Mein Sohn, deine Sünden sind dir vergeben[79]!« Daß Gott Sünden vergibt, glaubt auch der fromme Jude. Aber dieser Mensch hier vermißt sich, dies einem ganz Bestimmten ganz bestimmt hier und jetzt zuzusagen. Ganz persönlich gewährt und verbürgt er Sündenvergebung. Mit welchem Recht? *Mit welcher Vollmacht?* Die Reaktion erfolgt augenblicklich: »Was redet der so? Er lästert. Wer kann Sünden vergeben außer Gott allein[80]?«

Nun ist dies für Jesus zweifellos die Voraussetzung: *Gott* ist es, der vergibt. Das genau ist es, was die passive Umschreibung im überlieferten Zuspruch (»sind vergeben«) meint. Aber es ist für die Zeitgenossen offensichtlich: Hier wagt einer etwas, was bisher keiner, auch nicht Mose und die Propheten gewagt haben: Er wagt es, Gottes Vergebung nicht nur wie der Hohepriester am

Versöhnungstag im Tempel aufgrund der von Gott gesetzten höchst detaillierten Sühneordnung dem ganzen Volk anzusagen. Er wagt es, irgendwelchen moralischen Versagern die Vergebung in ihrer ganz konkreten Situation, »auf Erden«, gleichsam auf der Straße, ganz persönlich zuzusprechen und so Gnade nicht nur zu predigen, sondern hier und jetzt selber autoritativ zu üben.

Soll das also heißen: jetzt als Gegenteil einer eigenmächtigen Lynchjustiz eine eigenmächtige Gnadenjustiz? Hier nimmt doch ein Mensch Gottes Gericht vorweg. Hier tut einer gegen alle Traditionen Israels, was Gott allein vorbehalten ist: ein Eingriff und Übergriff in Gottes ureigenstes Recht! Faktisch, auch wenn der Name Gottes nicht verflucht wird, eine *Gotteslästerung*: Gotteslästerung nämlich durch Arroganz! Was maßt dieser Mann sich an? Sein sonst schon unerhörter Anspruch gipfelt in dem, was Empörung und leidenschaftlichen Protest herausfordern muß: im Anspruch, Sünden vergeben zu können. Der Konflikt – ein Konflikt auf Leben und Tod – mit all denen, die durch ihn ins Unrecht gesetzt wurden, deren Fehlverhalten er aufgedeckt hat, ist unvermeidlich geworden. Schon früh – unmittelbar nach den Berichten von der Sündenvergebung, dem Bankett mit den Zöllnern, der Vernachlässigung des Fastens, der Verletzung der Sabbatruhe – bringt das Markusevangelium[81] die Notiz von der Beratung seiner Gegner, der Vertreter von Gesetz, Recht und Moral: auf welche Weise sie ihn liquidieren können.

IV. Der Konflikt

Skandalon: ein kleiner Stein, über den man fallen kann. Jesus war in Person der Stein des Anstoßes geworden – mit allem, was er sagt und tut, ein fortgesetzter Skandal. Seine merkwürdig radikale Identifikation der Sache Gottes mit der Sache des Menschen: zu welch ungeheuerlichen Konsequenzen hatte sie ihn in Theorie und Praxis geführt! Selber streitbar nach allen Seiten, war er nun von allen Seiten umstritten. Keine der erwarteten Rollen hatte er gespielt: Für die Law-and-order-Leute erwies er sich als systemgefährdender Provokateur. Die aktivistischen Revolutionäre enttäuschte er durch seine gewaltlose Friedensliebe. Die passiv weltflüchtigen Asketen umgekehrt durch seine unbefangene Weltlichkeit. Den weltlich angepaßten Frommen schließlich war er zu kompromißlos. Den Stillen im Lande zu laut und den Lauten im Lande zu leise, den Strengen zu mild und den Milden zu streng. Als offensichtlicher Außenseiter in einem lebensgefährlichen gesellschaftlichen Konflikt: im Widerspruch zu den herrschenden Verhältnissen und im Widerspruch zu denen, die ihnen widersprechen.

1. Die Entscheidung

Ein ungeheurer Anspruch, doch so wenig dahinter: von niedriger Herkunft, ohne Unterstützung seiner Familie, ohne besondere Bildung. Ohne Geld, Amt und Würden, ohne alle Hausmacht, von keiner Partei gedeckt und von keiner Tradition legitimiert – ein machtloser Mensch beansprucht solche Vollmacht? War seine Lage nicht von vornherein aussichtslos? Wer war schon für ihn? Aber: er, der durch seine Lehre und sein ganzes Verhalten tödliche Aggressionen auf sich lenkte, fand auch spontan Vertrauen und Liebe! Kurz: an ihm schieden sich die Geister.

Die für ihn waren

Für ihn war »*das Volk*«: bekanntlich eine etwas vage und in jedem Fall recht wankelmütige Größe. Jesus hatte in seiner galiläischen Heimat eine beachtliche Bewegung ausgelöst. Auch wenn der Rahmen der einzelnen Erzählungen von den Evangelisten selber schematisch nach eigenen Intentionen gestaltet wurde: sie berichten zweifellos Historisches, wenn sie vom Zuhören, Staunen, Loben der Menge berichten. Dieses Volk, das eine Herde ohne Hirten ist, das sich weder vom Establishment noch von den Rebellen verstanden fühlt, das von den pharisäischen Frommen der Städte und Dörfer ebenso verachtet wird wie von den Asketen der Wüste, das weder zum Tempel- noch zum Waffendienst taugt, weder zur genauen Gesetzesbeobachtung noch gar zu asketischen Höchstleistungen fähig ist, dieses Volk ist es, dessen sich Jesus »erbarmt«[1]. Diese kleinen, unscheinbaren, wenig feinen Leute, arme Teufel aller Art, diese Seliggepriesenen, alle sie, die keine Stimme haben, die von den herrschenden Parteien und Machthabern jederzeit ohne Gefahr vernachlässigt und mißbraucht werden können: sie müssen sich von ihm verstanden fühlen. Sie sind für ihn – nur wie viele und wie lange?

Für ihn sind zweifellos seine *engsten Anhänger:* kleine Leute ebenfalls, Männer und Frauen, die mit ihm ziehen, die Haus und Familie, Beruf und Heimat verlassen haben und mit ihm Tage und Nächte – oft unter freiem Himmel – verbringen: die ihm also im ganz wörtlichen Sinne *»nachfolgen«*. Diesen, nicht seiner Familie, fühlte er sich verbunden, noch mehr als Buddha, Kung-futse, Sokrates und Mohammed, die verheiratet waren, wenn auch bestenfalls für Mohammeds Tätigkeit Ehe und Familie eine Rolle spielten. Jesu junge Männer, »Jünger«, »Schüler«: also nicht einfach solche, die Jesu Wort hören und annehmen oder aus Neugierde oder anderen Gründen gelegentlich hinter ihm herziehen. Die Jünger waren der engere Kreis um Jesus – bei einem ausgebildeten Lehrer in Israel keine Seltenheit. Wie aber sollte ein Unausgebildeter ausbilden? Jesus hatte – im Vergleich gerade etwa zu Buddha oder Mohammed – eine ungemein kurze Zeit, um eine Jüngergruppe zu bilden. Er bildete auf eigene Art.

Auch die bekannteren Rabbinen hatten Jünger, die ihnen nachfolgten. Die Termini »Rabbi« (Meister, Lehrer), »Jünger« (Schüler), »nachfolgen« waren im Judentum gängig[2]. Aber wie verschieden war der Kreis um Jesus. Es fehlte – wie auch bei der Gruppe um den Täufer Johannes – das Schulmäßige. Es fehlte – anders als beim Täufer Johannes, von welchem vielleicht einige der Jünger Jesu herkamen – das Asketische. Ein ungezwungenes, trotz aller Mühen freies Wanderleben, im Zeichen einer fröhlichen Botschaft. Doch der grundlegende *Unterschied* zwischen dieser Jüngergruppe und anderen lag anderswo:

Die von den Redaktoren zweifellos stark schematisierten *Berufungsgeschichten*[3] sagen nichts aus über die individualpsychologischen Voraussetzungen noch gar über einen gruppendynamischen Prozeß. Sie stellen das für Jüngerschaft überhaupt Exemplarische heraus: daß hier – anders als bei den Rabbinen-Schulen – nicht der Schüler den Meister, sondern der Meister den Schüler wählt[4]. Also nicht freier Entschluß des Schülers, sondern souveräne Berufung durch den Meister, bei welchem die Initiative liegt und bleibt. Hier wird nicht in ein Lehrverhältnis aufgenommen, sondern in eine Lebens- und Schicksalsgemeinschaft gerufen. Hier wird nicht in das Verständnis des Gesetzes eingeführt, sondern in das Tun des Willens Gottes eingeübt. Hier wird nicht auf Zeit ausgebildet, sondern auf Lebzeit gebildet. Nie wird hier aus dem Jünger ein Meister. Einer sei der Meister, alle anderen aber Brüder: mit dieser Begründung wird in der Gemeinde des Mattäus rigoros sogar das Führen des Rabbi-Titels – ebenso wie die Anrede Vater oder Lehrer – untersagt[5].

Damit ist erneut deutlich gemacht: Jesus hat *nicht* an die Bildung einer asketischen *Elite* gedacht. Bei vielen Jesusworten, etwa der Bergpredigt, läßt sich überhaupt nicht unterscheiden, ob sie an den engeren Jüngerkreis oder an alle gerichtet sind; offensichtlich war nicht nur der Evangelist, sondern waren auch Jesus und die Gemeinde an solcher Unterscheidung kaum interessiert. Warum?

– *Das Gottesreich soll für alle kommen, und die Forderungen der Umkehr, des neuen Denkens, der neuen Lebenseinstellung, des Tuns des Willen Gottes, der Liebe, Vergebung, des Dienstes, Verzichts sind grundsätzlich dieselben für alle. Und dies allein ist das Entscheidende.*

– *Jesus hat nicht von allen erwartet, daß sie Familie, Beruf und Heimat aufgeben, mit ihm ziehen und eine besondere Aufgabe übernehmen; Familie, Beruf, Heimat hat er nie grundsätzlich verworfen. Insbesondere wird Eheverzicht – falls das nur bei Mattäus[6] überlieferte Wort von den Eunuchen um des Reiches Gottes willen überhaupt auf Jesus selbst zurückgeht – nicht von allen Nachfolgern, sondern nur ausnahmsweise gefordert: um im Blick auf das baldige Ende für die besonderen Nöte und Aufgaben frei zu sein.*

– *Zugehörigkeit zum besonderen Jüngerkreis ist also keine Heilsbedingung. So viele gibt es in den Evangelien, die das Wort hören und glauben, so viele – Geheilte, Sünder, Zöllner –, die, von ihm betroffen, seine Zeugen werden, aber durchaus in ihrem Lebenskreis bleiben. Wo immer Jesus die Botschaft verkündigt, läßt er Anhänger zurück, die mit ihren Familien auf das Gottesreich warten und die ihn und seine Jünger aufnehmen. Sie alle werden nicht etwa als Halbentschlossene oder Unvollkommene getadelt oder gar vom Gottesreich ausgeschlossen. Sie alle sind für ihn.*

»Wer nicht für mich ist, ist gegen mich«[7]: Das Wort richtet sich gegen diejenigen, die es an eindeutiger Entschlossenheit für Jesus und seine Botschaft mangeln lassen und die so statt sammeln zerstreuen. Aber es richtete sich nicht gegen diejenigen, die sich dem engeren Jüngerkreis nicht anschließen. Vielmehr gilt in scheinbarer Widersprüchlichkeit:

»Wer nicht gegen uns ist, ist für uns[8].« Womit Jesus gegen allen Exklusivitätsanspruch seiner Jünger einen Mann in Schutz nimmt, der außerhalb des Jüngerkreises – quasi extra ecclesiam – im Namen Jesu charismatisch wirkt und dem das nicht verboten werden soll. Nach einer anderen Erzählung verbietet Jesus sogar einem Geheilten ausdrücklich die Nachfolge und läßt ihn in seiner Familie und Heimat die Botschaft verkünden[9].

Nachfolge Jesu ist also kein Privileg der Jüngergruppe. Das ist wichtig. Jüngersein meint keinen Elite-Status: nicht um der Askese willen müssen sie alles verlassen. Wohl aber eine besondere Aufgabe: um dieser Aufgabe willen *dürfen* sie alles verlassen. Eine besondere Aufgabe, ein besonderes Schicksal, eine besondere Verheißung: eine besondere Chance, die jener junge Reiche – durch seinen Reichtum am Mitziehen verhindert – verpaßt.

Aufgabe, Schicksal und Verheißung werden besonders deutlich bei den in allen drei synoptischen Evangelien überlieferten *Aussendungsberichten*[10]. Trotz aller nachösterlichen Bearbeitung und Anpassung müssen diese palästinisch gefärbten Berichte einen vorösterlichen Kern haben; in ihren Verkündigungsaufträgen fehlt auffälligerweise die Verkündigung des Christus. Was für die Darstellung der Jünger, ihre Aussendung, ihre pneumatischen Taten und ihre Rückkehr aus analogen Erfahrungen der Urgemeinde ergänzt wurde, läßt sich nicht mehr eruieren. Aber es dürfte nicht auszuschließen sein, daß schon der geschichtliche Jesus selbst seinen Jüngern Anteil an seiner Vollmacht des Predigens, Heilens und Helfens gegeben hat. Insofern war Jesus mehr als nur »Wegweiser« (Buddha).

Die Jünger hatten eine *besondere Aufgabe*: Menschenfischer zu sein, Menschen zu angeln, wie es drastisch deutlich im Zusammenhang mit der ersten Jüngerberufung[11] gesagt wird, womit Lukas dann die legendarische Erzählung vom wunderbaren Fischfang verbindet[12]. Menschenfangen für das kommende Reich in Vertretung Jesu selbst[13]. Also aktiv dabeisein: »um ihn« sein, die Botschaft nicht nur empfangen, sondern weitergeben, das kommende Reich und seinen Frieden mitankünden und seine heilenden Kräfte schon jetzt charismatisch wirksam werden lassen[14]. Eine frohe Botschaft, die nur dem zum Gericht wird, der sie zurückweist.

Die Jünger hatten ein *besonderes Schicksal*: Um Jesus sein, heißt alles hinter sich zurücklassen und mit ihm von Ort zu Ort ziehen. Das heißt, alte Bindungen auflösen und eine neue, eine Bindung an seine Person, eingehen. Das heißt dann auch, wie er selber nichts haben, worauf das Haupt legen[15], schutz- und wehrlos Armut und Leiden mit ihm teilen[16]. Denn der Jünger ist nicht über dem Meister, und der Knecht nicht über dem Herrn[17]. Ein solches Engagement will freilich gut überlegt sein, wie wenn einer einen Turm baut oder einen Krieg führt[18]. Unbedingter Einsatz ist erfordert, ohne Rückwärtsschauen, aus welchem Grund auch immer: Lasset die Toten die Toten begraben[19].

Die Jünger hatten eine *besondere Verheißung*: Hierarchische Ehren werden keine verheißen, keine Plätze zur Rechten und Linken[20]. Die Verheißung ist eine andere: Wer sich zu Jesus bekennt auf Erden, zu dem wird er selber sich bekennen im Gericht. Der Verheißung entspricht die Gefährdung[21].

Ist es verwunderlich, daß die *spätere Christengemeinde* in den Jüngern, die Jesus auf seinem Weg nachgefolgt sind, sich selber erkannt hat? Ist nicht jeder Glaubende auf *seine* Weise auf den Weg gerufen, Jesus nach? Hat nicht jeder seine Aufgabe der Verkündigung, sein Schicksal mit Jesus und seine Verheißung? Von daher ist verständlich, daß der Jüngername zum Namen der Glaubenden überhaupt wurde. Daß man eine Szene wie die Stillung des Sturmes schon bei Mattäus als Sinnbild für Nachfolge und Jüngerschaft versteht[22] und daß erst recht in den johanneischen Abschiedsreden die vor- und nachösterliche Situation der Jünger in einem gesehen wird[23].

Jüngerschaft ist das *Gegenteil von Hierarchie*: Hierarchie meint »heilige Herrschaft«, Jüngerschaft meint völlig unsakralen

Dienst. Das unglückliche Wort »Hierarchie« stammt von einem Anonymus, der ein gutes halbes Jahrtausend nach der neutestamentlichen Zeit unter der Maske des Paulus-Schülers Dionysios Areopagites schrieb, aber das Wort nicht nur von den Amtsträgern, sondern immerhin noch von der ganzen Kirche mit allen ihren Ständen (als einem Abbild der himmlischen Hierarchie) verstand. Die neutestamentlichen Gemeinden indessen vermeiden konsequent jegliche Ausdrücke für zivile und religiöse Behörden im Zusammenhang mit dem Jünger Jesu. Warum? Diese Ausdrücke bezeichnen alle ein Herrschaftsverhältnis. Und gerade dies ist Jüngerschaft nicht. Jüngerschaft wird nicht durch Recht und Macht konstituiert; mit dem Amt staatlicher Machthaber hat sie nichts gemein[24]. Jüngerschaft wird freilich auch nicht durch Wissen und Würde konstituiert; sie entspricht nicht dem Amt wissensbewußter Schriftgelehrter[25]. Nein, Jüngerschaft ist Ruf nicht zur Herrschaft, sondern zum *Dienst*.

Es ist somit kein Zufall, wenn die junge Gemeinde anstelle der üblichen Amtsbegriffe ein neues, völlig »unheiliges« Wort gewählt hat, um eine besondere Funktion des Einzelnen in der Gemeinde zu umschreiben: im griechischen *»diakonia«*, deutsch ganz profan »Tischdienst«. Wo kam der Unterschied zwischen Herr und Knecht bildhafter zum Ausdruck als gerade bei Tisch, wo damals die vornehmen Herren in langen Gewändern zu Tische lagen und die Diener mit gegürtetem Gewand zu bedienen hatten! Es bedeutete eine ungeheure Umstellung: »Wer unter euch groß sein will, sei euer Tischdiener; und wer unter euch der erste sein will, sei der Knecht aller[26].« Tief muß sich dieses Wort Jesu den Jüngern eingeprägt haben, denn sechsmal erscheint es in den synoptischen Evangelien, und das Johannesevangelium nimmt das Tischdienstmotiv in nachdrücklichster Weise auf in jener Erzählung, die dort anstelle der Abendmahlserzählung steht[27]: Jesus wäscht den Seinen die schmutzigen Füße – der niedrigste Dienst an einem anderen Menschen und nicht etwa ein religiös verbrämter und stilisierter, sich einmal im Jahr herablassender Kultakt eines sonst hohen Herrn.

Jüngerschaft meint also das Gegenteil einer (oft recht fromm als »Dienst« verschleierten) Herrschaft von Menschen über Menschen. Jüngerschaft meint einen in Kleinigkeiten sich bewegenden und bewährenden unprätentiösen Dienst von Menschen an Menschen im ganz gewöhnlichen banalen Alltag. Gewiß kein illusionäres Leben ohne Unterordnung und Überordnung: Sie sind in jeder Gesellschaft notwendig und hilfreich, wo immer sie statt an Titeln und Positionen an den verschiedenen Gaben und Aufgaben des Einzelnen wie am Nutzen der Gemeinschaft orientiert bleiben. Aber ein vorurteilsloses Leben ohne Herrschaft und Versklavung: ein herrschaftsfreies miteinander Reden, Handeln, auch Leiden – im Hinblick auf die Gottesherrschaft.

Ist aber die Jüngerschaft Jesu nicht mehr als lediglich ein zwangloses Miteinander aller mit allen, mehr als eine Sammlung, eine Bewegung? Hat Jesus denn nicht eine Kirche gegründet? Buddha stiftete eine Mönchsgemeinde. Kung-futse begründete eine Schule der Bildung. Mohammed errichtete einen starken expansiven islamischen Staat. Und Jesus?

Eine Kirche?

Jesus verkündete das Gottesreich, das für ihn zweifellos nicht mit einer Kirche identisch ist. Man hat sogar bestritten, daß schon Jesus selber innerhalb der Jüngergruppe eine Zahl von *Zwölfen*[28] ausgesucht hat. Doch nach dem von Paulus im Frühjahr 55 oder 56 zitierten alten Glaubensbekenntnis[29] sind die Zwölf schon für die Zeit unmittelbar nach Jesu Tod bezeugt. Die einleuchtendste Erklärung dafür ist noch immer die, welche die synoptischen Evangelien selber geben, wiewohl über den genauen Zeitpunkt und Hergang historisch kaum viel gesagt werden kann: Es war der geschichtliche Jesus selber, der die Zwölf berufen, »gemacht« hat[30]. Hätte man sonst Judas Ischariot unter die Zwölf gerechnet, was die junge Gemeinde (und Jesus, der sich in Judas folgenschwer getäuscht zu haben scheint) doch außerordentlich belasten mußte? Hätte man dem Verräter die Verheißung zuteil werden lassen, er werde auf einem der zwölf Throne sitzend die zwölf Stämme richten[31]? Hätte man für ihn die Nachwahl des Mattias vollzogen, welchem Bericht der Apostelgeschichte[32] doch kaum jeder historische Kern abgesprochen werden kann? Die unbequemen Tatsachen verbürgen die Berufung der Zwölf durch Jesus selbst. Alle anderen umständlicheren Erklärungsversuche vermögen keine überzeugende Antwort zu geben, wann, wo und wie sich sonst in so kurzer Zeit der Zwölferkreis gebildet haben könnte.

Als Einzelpersönlichkeiten sind die Zwölf für die Nachwelt freilich ohne Gesicht. Nicht einmal ihre Namen stehen einwandfrei fest; die Listen[33] weichen insbesondere bezüglich Taddäus oder Simon voneinander ab. An der Vorgeschichte und den Charakteren der Einzelnen zeigen sich die Evangelisten nicht interessiert. Offensichtlich sind kaum bedeutende Leute darunter: Fischer; ein Zöllner (Mattäus, vermutlich identisch mit Levi[34]) und ein Zelot (Simon Kananäus[35]), an sich Todfeinde; dann vielleicht einige Bauern oder Handwerker. Profiliert haben sich eigentlich – die beiden »Donnersöhne« Johannes und Jakobus bleiben umrißhafte Figuren – nur zwei: Judas Ischariot und Simon mit dem – vielleicht schon von Jesus selber gegebenen – Beinamen »Kepha« oder *»Petros«* (Fels[36]): Dieser, aus Betsaida stammende und in Kafarnaum verheiratete Fischer, von leidenschaftlicher Hingabe, aber zuletzt doch schwankend, war unbestreitbar – auch wenn seine Rolle nachträglich stilisiert wurde – Sprecher der anderen Jünger und wurde später wichtig als erster Zeuge des Auferweckten und Führer der Urgemeinde. Gerade an der ambivalenten Figur des Petrus zeigt sich deutlich, daß zumindest die ersten beiden Evangelien die Jünger keineswegs idealisieren: Sie sind normale irrende und fehlende Menschen, keine Heroen oder Genies. Ihr Unverständnis, ihr Kleinmut, ihre Unzuverlässigkeit und schließlich ihre Flucht werden ohne Beschönigung berichtet. Nur Lukas, der auch die Urgemeinde als Vorbild idealisiert, mildert oder beseitigt gar einige anstößige Züge: Er übergeht das Satanswort an Petrus nach dessen Bekenntnis, kürzt die Getsemane-Szene zugunsten der Jünger, unterschlägt dann die Notiz von der Jünger-Flucht und macht über Petrus und die Jünger erstaunlich positive Aussagen[37].

Doch wichtiger als die Frage nach einzelnen Mitgliedern ist die Frage nach dem Sinn dieses Kreises: Hatte Jesus Petrus und die Zwölf vielleicht als Fundament einer zu gründenden Kirche vorgesehen? Nun wird gewiß niemand bestreiten wollen, daß die neutestamentliche Kirche sich auf Jesus als den Christus (»Kirche Jesu Christi«) zurückführte und daß die Apostel für diese von grundlegender Bedeutung waren. Aber diese Zusammenhänge, auf die zurückzukommen sein wird, dürfen nicht simplifiziert und vor allem nicht vordatiert werden.

Der geschichtliche Jesus hat, wie wir sahen, mit der Vollendung der Welt und ihrer Geschichte zu seinen Lebzeiten gerechnet. Und für dieses Kommen des Reiches Gottes wollte er zweifellos *nicht eine von Israel unterschiedene Sondergemeinschaft* mit eigenem Glaubensbekenntnis, eigenem Kult, eigener Verfassung, eigenen Ämtern gründen. In seiner ganzen Verkündigung und Wirksamkeit hat sich Jesus nie an eine besondere Gruppe gewandt, um sie – etwa in der Art der Essener, der Qumranmönche oder der Pharisäer – aus dem Volk auszusondern. Nie hat er, wie wiederum Qumran und manche anderen Sondergruppen im Hinblick auf sich selbst, von einem »heiligen Rest« Israels gesprochen, der die reine Gottesgemeinde der Auserwählten sein würde. Jesus will keine Aussonderung und Absonderung. Nicht zur Sammlung der »Gerechten«, »Frommen«, »Reinen« weiß er sich gesandt, sondern zur Sammlung von *ganz* Israel mit betontem Einschluß der von den Restgemeinden abgeschriebenen Vernachlässigten, Minderwertigen, Armen, Sünder: eine große *endzeitliche Sammelbewegung*! Die vorzeitige Scheidung von guten und schlechten Fischen, Weizen und Unkraut lehnt er ab[38]. Trotz aller Mißerfolge wendet er sich immer wieder neu an das ganze Israel. Dieses Gesamtisrael, und nicht nur eine heilige Restgemeinde, sieht er berufen zum Gottesvolk der Endzeit.

Und genau für dieses Gottesvolk der Endzeit nun sind die Zwölf das Zeichen. Sie symbolisieren die zwölf Stämme Israels[39] und lassen die Jüngerschaft als Gottesvolk der Endzeit erscheinen. Im Hinblick auf das bald kommende Reich sind sie ausgewählt worden und repräsentieren die wiederherzustellende Vollzahl des zur Zeit so arg amputierten Israel (nur noch zweieinhalb Stämme – Juda, Benjamin und die Hälfte von Levi – bilden seit der Eroberung des Nordreichs 722 v. Chr. das Volk Israel). Weder der Jüngerkreis noch erst recht die umkehrbereiten Israeliten werden organisatorisch zusammengeschlossen. Die Zwölf werden bei ihrer Berufung im ältesten Evangelium noch nicht Apostel genannt[40]. Auch hier wieder ist es erst Lukas, der vermeldet, Jesus selber habe gerade die Zwölf »Apostel« genannt[41]. In den paulinischen Briefen werden vielmehr auch andere als die Zwölf »Apostel« genannt (Andronikos, Junias, Barnabas, vielleicht auch Silvanus und der Herrenbruder Jakobus). Die Zwölf und die Apostel dürfen also keinesfalls von vornherein identifiziert werden.

Das alles bedeutet: Jesus hat zu seinen Lebzeiten *keine Kirche gegründet*[42]. Es spricht für die Treue der von der Urkirche offenkundig nicht überspielten Überlieferung, daß die Evangelien keine an die Öffentlichkeit gerichteten Jesusworte kennen, die programmatisch zu einer Gemeinde der Auserwählten aufrufen, die Gründung einer Kirche oder eines Neuen Bundes ankünden. Die Gleichnisse vom Fischnetz und vom Sauerteig, die Saat- und Wachstumsgleichnisse beschreiben das zukünftige Gottesreich, welches nicht mit der Kirche identifiziert werden darf. Nie hat

Jesus für das Eingehen in das Gottesreich die Zugehörigkeit zu einer Kirche gefordert. Die gehorsame Annahme seiner Botschaft und das sofortige und radikale Sich-Stellen unter Gottes Willen genügte.

Überhaupt kommt das Wort »Kirche« in den Evangelien nur zweimal, und im Sinn von Gesamtkirche sogar nur einmal vor: Du bist Petrus, und auf diesen Felsen will ich meine Kirche bauen[43]. Eine der umstrittensten Stellen des Neuen Testaments! Erst heute beginnt sich ein Konsens zu bilden zwischen führenden Forschern verschiedener Kirchen. Auch katholische Exegeten geben heute zu, daß das erstaunlicherweise nur bei Mattäus zu findende (und Markus wie Lukas unbekannte) Logion Mt 16, 17–19 trotz seines semitischen Sprachcharakters nicht in die von der Naherwartung des Endes bestimmte Verkündigung Jesu hineinpaßt, sondern eine sehr alte nachösterliche Bildung schon der palästinischen Gemeinde, beziehungsweise des Mattäus ist, die eine bereits institutionell gefestigte, mit Lehr- und Rechtsvollmacht ausgestattete Kirche voraussetzt[44].

Aber wie immer dieses beinahe in jedem Wort umstrittene Logion im einzelnen zu verstehen ist: Es wurde, selbst wenn es vom geschichtlichen Jesus stammen sollte, nicht an die Öffentlichkeit gerichtet und wies das Erbauen einer Kirche eindeutig nicht der Gegenwart, sondern in allen einzelnen Formulierungen der Zukunft zu. Weder die umkehrbereiten Anhänger Jesu noch die in seine besondere Nachfolge berufenen Jünger oder die Zwölf sind von Jesus als »neues Gottesvolk« oder »Kirche« aus Israel ausgesondert und dem alten Gottesvolk gegenübergestellt worden. Erst nach Jesu Tod und Auferstehung redet die Urchristenheit von »Kirche«. Die »Kirche« im Sinne einer von Israel unterschiedenen Sondergemeinschaft ist eindeutig eine *nachösterliche Größe*.

So ist denn Jesus *nicht* das, was man gemeinhin unter einem *Religionsstifter* oder einem *Kirchengründer* versteht. Er dachte nicht an die Gründung und Organisation eines zu schaffenden religiösen Großgebildes. Er sah sich von vornherein nur zu den Söhnen Israels gesandt[45]. Er dachte weder für sich noch für die Jünger an eine Mission unter den Heidenvölkern; der Missionsbefehl ist nachösterlich[46]. Wohl aber scheint er an die von den Propheten geschilderte endzeitliche Wallfahrt der Heidenvölker zum Gottesberg gedacht zu haben[47]: In dieser Stunde der Heiden würde es dann sein, da nach jenem ebenso altertümlichen wie eigentümlichen Wort Ungenannte von Ost und West herzuströmen und im Gottesreich zu Tische liegen werden, während die Söhne des Reiches ausgestoßen sein werden[48]. Zuerst aber muß die Verheißung Gottes erfüllt und das Heil Israel angeboten werden. Mit Erfolg?

Sosehr sich Jesus an *alle* wandte, sosehr er *ganz* Israel ansprach (universal de iure) und sosehr er auch die Heiden nicht vom Reich ausschloß (universal de facto): sein ganzes Auftreten provozierte eine schmerzliche Scheidung. Die Worte, die er sprach, die Taten, die er wirkte, die Forderungen, die er erhob, stellten vor eine letzte Entscheidung. Jesus ließ niemanden neutral. Er selber – er war zur großen *Frage* geworden.

Ohne Amt und Würden

Wie soll man sich stellen zu dieser Botschaft, zu diesem Verhalten, zu diesem Anspruch, ja, schließlich und endlich zu dieser Person? Die Frage war nicht zu umgehen. Sie durchzieht als eine schon vorösterliche Frage die nachösterlichen Evangelien und ist bis heute nicht zur Ruhe gekommen: Was haltet ihr von ihm? *Wer* ist er? Einer der Propheten? Oder mehr?

Ja, was für eine »Rolle« spielt er im Zusammenhang mit seiner Botschaft? Wie verhält er sich zu seiner »Sache«? Wer ist er, der doch jedenfalls nicht ein auf Zeit menschlich verkleidetes Himmelswesen ist, sondern ein vollmenschliches, verwundbares, historisch faßbares Menschenwesen, der als Haupt einer Jüngergruppe nicht zu Unrecht mit dem Titel »Rabbi«, »Lehrer« angesprochen wird, der aber als Prediger des nahenden Gottesreiches manchen eher als ein »Prophet«, vielleicht sogar als der erwartete Prophet der Endzeit erschien, und über den die Zeitgenossen offensichtlich selber uneins waren[49]. Von einem eigentlichen prophetischen Berufungserlebnis Jesu wie bei Mose und den Propheten, auch bei Zarathustra und Mohammed, von einer Erleuchtung wie bei Buddha wird in den Evangelien auffälligerweise nichts berichtet.

Manchen Christen erscheint die Aussage »Jesus ist Gottes Sohn« als das Zentrum des christlichen Glaubens. Aber hier ist genauer zuzusehen. Jesus selber jedenfalls hat das Reich Gottes und nicht seine eigene Rolle, Person, Würde in die Mitte seiner Verkündigung gestellt. Es bestreitet niemand, daß die nachösterliche Gemeinde, an der vollen Menschlichkeit Jesu von Nazaret stets energisch festhaltend, diesen Menschen als »Christus«,

341

»Messias«, »Davidssohn«, »Gottessohn« tituliert hat. Und daß sie aus ihrer jüdischen und dann auch hellenistischen Umwelt die gewichtigsten und gefülltesten Titulaturen ausgesucht und auf Jesus übertragen hat, um auf diese Weise dessen Bedeutung für den Glauben zum Ausdruck zu bringen, läßt sich verstehen und soll später dargelegt werden. Daß sich jedoch schon Jesus selber diese Titulaturen beigelegt hat, darf aufgrund der Natur unserer Quellen nicht einfach vorausgesetzt werden. Das ist vielmehr fraglich und muß ohne Voreingenommenheit überprüft werden.

Gerade wenn es hier um das Zentrum des christlichen Glaubens geht – und darum geht es bei Jesus als dem Christus –, ist doppelte Vorsicht geboten, damit nicht Wunschdenken das kritisch verantwortete Denken überspielt. Gerade hier ist zu bedenken, daß die Evangelien nicht Dokumente der reinen Historie, sondern Schriften der praktischen Glaubensverkündigung sind; sie wollen den Glauben an Jesus als den Christus herausfordern und befestigen. Gerade hier ist die Grenze zwischen geschehener Geschichte und Interpretation der Geschichte, zwischen historischem Bericht und theologischer Reflexion, zwischen vorösterlichem Wort und nachösterlicher Erkenntnis besonders schwer zu ziehen.

Nicht nur auf die Worte des Auferstandenen und Erhöhten, sondern schon auf die Worte des irdischen Jesus, besonders die christologischen Selbstaussagen, können die jungen Christengemeinden, ihr Gottesdienst und ihre Verkündigung, ihre Disziplin und Mission, können aber auch die Redaktoren der Evangelien Einfluß gehabt haben. Das bedeutet für den Interpreten: Nicht wer möglichst *viele* Jesusworte der Evangelienüberlieferung als echt ansieht, ist der rechtgläubigste Theologe. Allerdings auch: Nicht wer möglichst *wenige* evangelische Jesusworte als echt ansieht, ist der kritischste Theologe. In dieser zentralen Frage spricht kritikloser Glaube ebenso an der Sache vorbei wie die ungläubige Kritik. Wir hörten es: Die wahre Kritik zerstört den Glauben nicht, der wahre Glaube hindert nicht die Kritik[50].

Muß nicht damit gerechnet werden, daß das Glaubensbekenntnis und die Theologie der Gemeinden in einigen *messianischen Geschichten* besonders durchgeschlagen hat?

Etwa in den bereits genannten beiden *Stammbäumen*, die Jesus als Davidssohn und Kind der Verheißung ankünden wollen, die aber im ältesten Evangelium bezeichnenderweise fehlen und die bei Mattäus und Lukas, abgesehen von ihrem Zusammentreffen bei David, so wenig übereinstimmen;

oder in den legendär ausgestalteten *Kindheitsgeschichten,* welche das Geheimnis dieser Herkunft beschreiben, die sich aber ebenfalls nur bei Mattäus und Lukas finden und dabei wenig historisch Verifizierbares bieten;

oder in den *Tauf- und Versuchungsgeschichten,* die ebenfalls einen besonderen literarischen Charakter haben und die als Lehr-Erzählungen Jesu Sendung herauszustellen trachten;

oder in der *Verklärungsgeschichte,* die schon bei Markus verschiedene Traditionsschichten umfaßt und mit verschiedenen Epiphaniemotiven Jesu endzeitliche messianische Rolle und Würde deutlich machen will?

Selbstverständlich soll nicht behauptet werden, alle diese Geschichten seien *nur* Legende oder Mythos. Knüpfen sie doch vielfach – man denke etwa an die Taufe Jesu – an historische Ereignisse an. Aber das Historische ist oft kaum auszumachen, und jedenfalls dürften die damit verbundenen messianischen Aussagen nicht einfach vorausgesetzt werden. Diese messianischen Geschichten haben ihren Sinn, aber gerade diesen Sinn verfehlt man und gerät vielfach in Widersprüche, wenn man sie Satz für Satz als historischen Rapport verstehen will.

Daß sich Glaube und Theologie der Urchristenheit besonders bei den *messianischen Titeln* ausgewirkt hat, wird heute von jedem ernsthaften Exegeten herausgestellt. Eine genauere Untersuchung – hier nur in ihren Ergebnissen wiederzugeben[51] – könnte das Folgende zeigen:

- *In der einen der beiden synoptischen Hauptquellen, in der sogenannten Reden-Quelle (Q), fehlt der Messias-Titel überhaupt.*
- *In der Erzählungsüberlieferung aber läßt sich Jesus nur von Anderen messianische Prädikationen gefallen, ohne daß er selbst ausdrücklich bejahend oder verneinend Stellung genommen hätte.*
- *Sowohl das Bekenntnis des Petrus (»Du bist der Messias«[52]) wie die Fragestellung des Hohenpriesters im Verhör Jesu (»Bist du der Messias, der Sohn des Hochgelobten[53]?«) müssen als Widerspiegelung des Christusbekenntnisses der späteren Gemeinde angesehen werden, ähnlich wie jene zwei einzigen synoptischen Stellen von »dem Sohn«[54], die in ihrer Sprache an das Johannesevangelium, aber nicht an den geschichtlichen Jesus erinnern.*
- *Nach den synoptischen Evangelien – anders natürlich das be-*

reits theologisch reflektierend vom »Sohn« und »Gottessohn« redende Johannesevangelium |– hat sich Jesus also niemals selbst die Messiasbezeichnung oder sonst einen jener messianischen Titel beigelegt.

– Noch der älteste Evangelist behandelt Jesu Messianität als Geheimnis, verborgen vor der großen Öffentlichkeit: bekannt den Über- und Unterirdischen (Dämonen), welchen aber ebenso wie den geheilten Menschen und schließlich auch dem bekennenden Jünger Petrus und den bei der »Verklärung« Jesu Anwesenden ein Stillschweigen auferlegt wird, das in Wirklichkeit selbstverständlich nicht durchzuhalten gewesen wäre; erst durch Ostern läßt sich Jesu verborgenes messianisches Wirken verstehen.

– Jesu Verkündigung und Praxis hätte den üblichen (pharisäischen, zelotischen, essenischen) Messiaserwartungen ohnehin nicht entsprochen.

Aufgrund dieses im Detail leicht zu belegenden kritischen Befundes schließen denn auch konservativere Exegeten, daß Jesus selber sich keinen einzigen messianischen Würdetitel – weder Messias noch Davidssohn, weder Sohn noch Gottessohn – zugelegt hat[55]. Vielmehr hat man nach Ostern zurückblickend die gesamte Jesusüberlieferung – und wie deutlich werden wird: nicht zu Unrecht – in einem messianischen Licht gesehen und hat von daher das Messiasbekenntnis in die Darstellung der Jesusgeschichte eingetragen. Auch die Redaktoren der Evangelien schauen zurück und reden *aus österlichem Glauben*, für den die Messianität – jetzt ganz anders verstanden – keine Frage ist. Vorher aber war sie eine Frage, eine echte Frage.

Nur bei einem einzigen Titel wird ernsthaft diskutiert, ob ihn nicht doch schon Jesus selber gebraucht hat: Der geheimnisvolle apokalyptische Titel *»Menschensohn«*, der hier entschieden mehr meint als nur »Mensch«, taucht erstmals im Danielbuch auf, in der Vision von den vier Tieren und dem, der in den Wolken des Himmels kommt und einem Menschensohn gleicht und dem Macht, Ehre und Herrschaft verliehen wird, so daß alle Völker ihm dienen in einem ewigen Reich, das niemals zerstört wird[56]. Auch in anderen apokalyptischen Schriften[57] spielt der Menschensohn, welcher nun allerdings nicht mehr wie bei Daniel als Volk Israel, sondern als Einzelgestalt verstanden wird, eine bedeutsame Rolle. Blickt man von da auf das Neue Testament, fällt ein Doppeltes auf:

Einerseits: Schon die vorpaulinische griechisch redende Kirche wie auch Paulus selbst meiden diesen Titel offensichtlich wegen seiner Mißverständlichkeit (als menschliche Abstammungsbezeichnung) und gebrauchen ihn nicht einmal in den urchristlichen Glaubensbekenntnissen.

Andererseits: Nur in den vier Evangelien selber behält der Titel seinen Platz: 82mal findet er sich hier und zwar in keiner einzigen Aussage über Jesus, sondern ausschließlich im Munde Jesu. Läßt sich dies anders erklären als dadurch, daß der Titel unantastbar in der Überlieferung der Worte Jesu von Anfang an verwurzelt war und so zumindest einige der ältesten Menschensohn-Worte – andere sind durch synoptischen Vergleich als sekundär erkennbar – in ihrem Kern auf Jesus selber zurückgehen und von ihm vermutlich im Sinn der jüdischen Apokalyptik gebraucht wurden[58]?

Dieser Befund wird freilich ungemein kompliziert dadurch, daß Jesus vom Menschensohn stets distanziert in der dritten Person spricht und daß die einen Menschensohn-Worte vom kommenden, die anderen vom leidenden, die dritten vom gegenwärtigen irdischen Menschensohn sprechen und daß die drei verschiedenen Gruppen untereinander kaum verbunden sind. Die Frage dürfte noch nicht ausdiskutiert sein[59]:

Für die einen Exegeten ist der Menschensohn-Titel schlicht Gemeinde-Theologie. Aber: Wird hier der merkwürdige Textbefund nicht zu leicht abgetan, daß Menschensohn immer Selbstbezeichnung Jesu, aber nie Anrede, Bekenntnis oder einfache Aussage ist?

Für andere umgekehrt hat Jesus selbst mit diesem geheimnisvollen Titel seinen messianischen Anspruch angemeldet. Aber: Gibt es überhaupt Texte, nach welchen Jesus mit diesem zweideutigen Geheimnamen, der auch unmessianisch einfach als »der Mensch« verstanden werden konnte, zum Nachdenken anregen wollte?

Für wieder andere hat Jesus sich nicht als gegenwärtigen, wohl aber als künftigen Menschensohn und Weltenrichter gesehen. Aber: Wo ist denn in den synoptischen Texten von solcher Bestimmung oder Designation, Entrückung oder Erhöhung zum kommenden richtenden Menschensohn die Rede?

Für die vierten schließlich spricht Jesus von einer anderen Gestalt, die er als Menschensohn erwartet; Jesus hätte sich dieser apokalyptischen Vorstellung bedient, um vom jetzigen Bekenntnis zu ihm das Urteil im kommenden Endgericht durch den vom Himmel kommenden Menschensohn abhängig zu machen[60]. Aber: Sah sich Jesus nach den Texten jemals nur als Vorläufer, und warum ist sein Verhältnis zu diesem angeblich von ihm verschiedenen Menschensohn nirgendwo bestimmt?

Sehr apodiktisch wird man hier nichts behaupten dürfen. Wahrscheinlich hat sich Jesus nicht selbst als Davidssohn, Messias (Christus), Gottessohn (Sohn) bezeichnet. Möglicherweise auch nicht – zumindest nicht in eindeutig messianischer Weise für seine Gegenwart – als Menschensohn. Sicher ist im Grunde nur: Für die nachösterliche palästinische Gemeinde ist Jesus mit dem Menschensohn zweifellos identisch; Jesus ist für sie der apokalyptische Mensch, der zum Gericht und zur Erlösung der Seinen kommen soll. Ein negativer Befund? Ja, möglicherweise ja, bezüglich der Titulaturen durch Jesus selbst. Nein, in jedem Fall nein, bezüglich des Anspruchs Jesu. Denn offensichtlich *fällt sein Anspruch nicht mit seinen Titeln*, auch nicht mit dem Titel Menschensohn. Im Gegenteil, die große Frage nach dem, was und wer er ist, wird durch diesen Befund nicht etwa erledigt, sondern in verschärfter Weise gestellt: Was und wer ist denn der, der nicht nur keine besondere Herkunft, Familie, Bildung, Hausmacht, Partei ins Feld führt, sondern der möglicherweise auch auf keine besonderen Titel und Würden Wert legt und der doch, wie bereits deutlich wurde, einen ungeheuren Anspruch erhebt?

Man darf nicht vergessen: Die hier in Frage kommenden Titel waren – ein jeder auf seine Weise – *belastet* durch die verschiedenen Traditionen und die mehr oder weniger politischen Erwartungen seiner Zeitgenossen. So wie man nun gemeinhin einen »Messias«, einen »Davidssohn«, einen »Menschensohn« erwartete, so war dieser Jesus nun einmal nicht. So wollte er allem Anschein nach auch gar nicht sein. Keiner der geläufigen Begriffe, keine der üblichen Vorstellungen, keines der traditionellen Ämter, keiner der gängigen Titel war offensichtlich geeignet, um seinem Anspruch Ausdruck zu verleihen, um seine Person und Sendung zu umschreiben, um das Geheimnis seines Wesens zu erschließen. Gerade die messianischen Hoheitstitel lassen es noch deutlicher werden als die menschlich-allzumenschlichen Rollenerwartungen der Priester und Theologen, der Revolutionäre und Asketen, der frommen oder unfrommen kleinen Leute: Dieser Jesus ist anders!

Und gerade so ließ er niemanden gleichgültig. Er war eine

öffentliche Person geworden und hatte den Konflikt mit seiner Umwelt herausgefordert. Mit ihm konfrontiert, sahen sich die Menschen und insbesondere die Hierarchie unweigerlich vor ein Letztes gestellt. Er forderte eine letzte *Entscheidung* heraus: aber aber nicht ein Ja oder Nein zu einem bestimmten Titel, zu einer bestimmten Würde, zu einem bestimmten Amt oder auch zu einem bestimmten Dogma, Ritus oder Gesetz. Seine Botschaft und Gemeinschaft warf die Frage auf, woraufhin und wonach einer sein Leben letztlich ausrichten will. Jesus forderte eine letzte Entscheidung für die Sache Gottes und des Menschen. In dieser »Sache« geht er selbst völlig auf, ohne für sich selber etwas zu fordern, ohne seine eigene »Rolle« oder Würde zum Thema seiner Botschaft zu machen. Die große *Frage* nach seiner *Person* war nur *indirekt* gestellt, und die Vermeidung aller Titel verdichtete das Rätsel.

Der Sachwalter

Man hat sich immer wieder darüber gewundert, daß die Prozeßberichte der Evangelien so wenig zur Motivierung anführen, *warum* Jesus von Nazaret zum Tode verurteilt wurde. Denn wenn etwas an diesem Leben historisch gesichert ist, dann sein gewaltsamer Tod. Aber selbst wenn einer die Frage des Hohenpriesters nach der Messianität Jesu nicht als nachösterliche Deutung ansieht: Liest er nur die Passionsgeschichte, bleibt ihm Jesu Verurteilung zum Tod weithin unverständlich. Messiasanwärter gab es einige; aber wegen messianischen Anspruchs wurde niemand zum Tode verurteilt. War es vielleicht doch nur ein tragischer Justizirrtum, rückgängig zu machen durch eine Revision des Prozesses, wie es einige gutmeinende Christen und Juden heute fordern? Oder war es doch die bewußte Bosheit eines verstockten Volkes, dessen moralische Schuld dann in den zwanzig Jahrhunderten Christenheit zahllose Juden das Leben kosten sollte? Oder war es einfach einer jener wohlbekannten Willkürakte der schließlich letztverantwortlichen römischen Autorität, wie man zur Entlastung der Juden sagen könnte? Oder aber die planmäßige Aktion der jüdischen Führer, die das harmlose Volk aufwiegelten und – wie schon die Evangelisten zur Entlastung des Vertreters Roms insinuieren – den von Jesu Unschuld überzeugten Römer als willenloses Werkzeug benutzten? Die Pilatusfrage »Was hat er denn Böses getan?« wird nach

Markus nur mit dem »überlauten« Ruf »Kreuzige ihn!« beantwortet[61].

Man kann es aber auch umgekehrt sehen und dann fragen: Was hätte er eigentlich noch Böses tun müssen, um ausreichende Gründe für seine Verurteilung zu liefern? Kann die Begründung der Verurteilung Jesu in der Passionsgeschichte nicht deshalb so kurz sein, weil die Evangelien als ganze eine umfassende und wahrhaft ausreichende Begründung für seine Verurteilung bieten? Danach, so scheint es, wäre die *Anklage* nicht schwer zu formulieren.

Oder muß denn jetzt noch einmal wiederholt werden, daß dieser Mensch sich gegen ungefähr alles vergangen hat, was diesem Volk und dieser Gesellschaft und ihren Repräsentanten heilig war: daß er sich unbekümmert um die Hierarchie in Wort und Tat über die kultischen Tabus, die Fastengewohnheiten und besonders das Sabbatgebot hinweggesetzt, daß er nicht nur gegen bestimmte Gesetzesinterpretationen (»Überlieferungen der Alten«), sondern gegen das Gesetz selbst (eindeutig im Verbot der Ehescheidung, im Verbot der Wiedervergeltung, im Gebot der Feindesliebe) angegangen ist; daß er das Gesetz nicht nur anders interpretiert, auch nicht nur an bestimmten Punkten verschärft, sondern verändert, ja, sich in befremdender Selbständigkeit und Freiheit darüber hinweggesetzt hat, wann und wo es ihm mit Rücksicht auf den Menschen richtig schien; daß er eine andere, »bessere Gerechtigkeit« als die des Gesetzes proklamiert hat, als ob es eine solche gäbe und das Gesetz Gottes nicht die letzte Instanz wäre?

Hat er also nicht faktisch, auch wenn er es nicht programmatisch ankündigte, die bestehende Ordnung des jüdischen Gesetzes und damit das gesamte gesellschaftliche System in Frage gestellt? Hat er nicht die bestehenden Normen und Institutionen, die geltenden Gebote und Dogmen, Ordnungen und Einrichtungen, auch wenn er sie gewiß nicht abschaffen wollte, doch faktisch völlig unterhöhlt, insofern er ihre unbedingte Geltung in Frage gestellt hat durch die Behauptung, sie seien um des Menschen willen da und nicht der Mensch um ihretwillen? Die Frage lag nahe: Ist dieser etwa mehr als Mose, der das Gesetz gegeben[62]?

Aber weiter: Hat er nicht, obwohl auch dies wiederum nicht programmatisch, so doch faktisch, den gesamten Kult, die Liturgie in Frage gestellt? Hat er nicht alle Riten und Bräuche, Feiern und Zeremonien, auch wenn er sie keineswegs abschaffen wollte, so doch praktisch unterlaufen, insofern er den Menschendienst dem Gottesdienst vorordnete? Die Frage ließe sich verschärfen: Ist dieser etwa mehr als Salomo, der den Tempel gebaut[63]?

Und schließlich: Hat er durch seine Identifikation der Sache Gottes mit der Sache des Menschen, des Willens Gottes mit dem Wohl des Menschen nicht den Menschen zum Maßstab der Gebote Gottes gemacht? Forciert er nicht von daher eine Menschen-, Nächsten-, Feindesliebe, welche die natürlichen Grenzen zwischen Familienangehörigen und Nicht-Familienangehörigen, zwischen Volksgenossen und Nicht-Volksgenossen, Parteigenossen und Nicht-Parteigenossen, zwischen Freunden und Feinden, Nächsten und Fernsten, Guten und Bösen nicht wahrhaben will? Relativiert er nicht die Bedeutung von Familie, Volk, Partei, ja Gesetz und Moral? Muß er so nicht die Herrschenden und die Rebellierenden, die Stillen und die Lauten im Lande gegen sich aufbringen? Werden nicht alle anerkannten Unterschiede, nützlichen Konventionen und gesellschaftlichen Schranken aufgegeben, wenn man ein Vergeben ohne Ende, ein Dienen ohne Rangordnung, ein Verzichten ohne Gegenleistung predigt? Mit der Konsequenz, daß man sich gegen alle Vernunft auf die Seite der Schwachen, Kranken, Armen, Unterprivilegierten, also gegen die Starken, Gesunden, Reichen, Privilegierten stellen muß, daß man wider die guten Sitten Frauen, Kinder, kleine Leute hätschelt, ja, daß man sich gar gegen alle Gesetze der Moral mit eigentlich Unfrommen und Unmoralischen, Gesetzlosen und Gesetzesbrechern, im Grunde Gottlosen kompromittiert und sie gegenüber den frommen, moralischen, gesetzestreuen, gottgläubigen Menschen favorisiert? Hat sich dieser Freund öffentlicher Sünder und Sünderinnen nicht auf diesem Weg so weit verstiegen, daß er statt Bestrafung des Bösen ihre Begnadigung propagiert und gar hier und jetzt in ungeheurer Vermessenheit Einzelnen Vergebung ihrer Verfehlungen direkt zusagt, wie wenn das Reich Gottes schon da und er selber der Richter, des Menschen letzter Richter wäre? Schließlich muß man sich die Frage stellen: Ist dieser etwa mehr als Jona[64], der die Buße predigte, mehr als ein Prophet?

So also hat Jesus die Grundlagen, die ganze Theologie und Ideologie der Hierarchie untergraben. Und was für ein *Kontrast*, es sei nochmals daran erinnert: Ein beliebiger Mann aus Nazaret, woher nichts Gutes kommen kann[65], von niedriger Herkunft, unbedeutender Familie, mit einer Gruppe junger Männer und ein paar Frauen, ohne Bildung, Geld, Amt und Würden, von keiner

Autorität ermächtigt, keiner Tradition legitimiert, keiner Partei gedeckt – und doch ein solch unerhörter *Anspruch*. Ein Neuerer, der sich über Gesetz und Tempel, über Mose, König und Prophet stellt und der überhaupt viel das verdächtige Wort »Ich« – nicht nur bei Johannes, sondern literarkritisch unausmerzbar schon in der synoptischen Überlieferung – im Munde führt. Dem entspricht völlig – selbst wenn es einer hyperkritisch nicht auf Jesus, sondern auf die Gemeinde zurückführen sollte – sowohl jenes »Ich aber sage euch« der Bergpredigt wie auch das merkwürdig am Anfang vieler Sätze gebrauchte »Amen«, womit eine Autorität in Anspruch genommen wird, die über die Autorität eines Rabbi oder auch eines Propheten hinausgeht.

Diesen Anspruch – in den Evangelien eine Frage sowohl bezüglich seiner Worte wie bezüglich seiner Taten – begründet er nirgendwo. Ja, in der Vollmachtsdiskussion[66] lehnt er eine Begründung ab. Er nimmt die Vollmacht einfach in Anspruch. Er hat sie und bringt sie zur Geltung, redet und handelt aus ihr, ohne sich auf eine höhere Instanz zu berufen. Er macht eine völlig unabgeleitete, höchst persönliche Autorität geltend: Nicht nur ein Sach-Kenner und Sach-Verständiger wie die Priester und Theologen. Sondern einer, der ohne alle Ableitung und ohne Begründung eigenmächtig in Wort und Tat Gottes Willen (= das Wohl des Menschen) verkündet, sich mit Gottes Sache (= die Sache des Menschen) identifiziert, ganz in dieser Sache aufgeht und so ohne allen Anspruch auf Titel und Würden zum höchstpersönlichen öffentlichen *Sach-Walter Gottes und des Menschen* wird!

Ein Sachwalter Gottes und des Menschen? »Selig, der an mir keinen Anstoß nimmt[67]!?« Muß man nicht vielmehr Anstoß nehmen?

- *Ist ein Gesetzeslehrer, der sich gegen Mose stellt, nicht ein* Irrlehrer?
- *Ist ein Prophet, der nicht mehr in der Nachfolge des Mose steht, nicht ein* Lügenprophet?
- *Ist ein über Mose und die Propheten Erhabener, der sich hinsichtlich der Sünde gar die Funktion eines letzten Richters anmaßt, der so an das rührt, was Gottes und Gottes allein ist, nicht – es muß deutlich ausgesprochen werden –* ein Gotteslästerer?
- *Ist er nicht alles andere als das unschuldige Opfer eines verstockten Volkes, vielmehr ein Schwärmer und Ketzer und als*

solcher ein höchst gefährlicher und die Position der Hierarchie
sehr real bedrohender Ordnungsstörer, Unruhestifter, Volksverführer?

Erst vor diesem Hintergrund wird deutlich: Ob sich Jesus besondere Titel zulegte oder nicht, ist völlig zweitrangig. Daß sie
ihm zumindest nachträglich zugelegt wurden, ist in seinem ganzen Wirken angelegt, wenn auch nach seinem Tod und Scheitern
keineswegs selbstverständlich. Sein ganzes Tun und Lassen hatte
einen Anspruch erhoben, der einen rabbinischen und prophetischen übersteigt und einem messianischen durchaus gleichkommt: Ob zu Recht oder Unrecht – er agiert faktisch in Wort
und Tat als der Sachwalter Gottes für den Menschen in dieser
Welt. Damit erhellt zugleich, wie falsch es wäre, Jesu Geschichte
simpel als eine unmessianische zu bezeichnen, die dann nachträglich zur messianischen gemacht wurde. Jesu Anspruch *und* Wirkung waren solcher Art, daß durch seine Verkündigung und
gesamte Tätigkeit messianische Erwartungen geweckt wurden
und auch Glauben gefunden haben, wie es im tradierten Wort der
Emmausjünger deutlich zum Ausdruck gebracht wird: »Wir
aber hofften, er sei der, der Israel erlösen sollte.«[68] Nur so läßt
sich auch der unbedingte Ruf in die Nachfolge, nur so die Berufung der Jünger und die Auswahl der Zwölf, nur so die gesamte
Volksbewegung, nur so allerdings auch die heftige Reaktion und
bleibende Unversöhnlichkeit seiner Gegner verstehen.

Als der öffentliche Sachwalter Gottes und des Menschen war
Jesus in Person zum großen Zeichen der Zeit geworden. In seiner
ganzen Existenz stellte er vor eine Entscheidung: sich für oder
gegen seine Botschaft, sein Wirken, ja seine Person zu entscheiden. Sich zu ärgern oder sich zu ändern, zu glauben oder nicht zu
glauben, weiterzumachen oder umzukehren. Und ob einer Ja
oder Nein sagte – er war gezeichnet für das nahende Reich, für
Gottes endgültiges Urteil. In seiner Person wirft die Zukunft
Gottes ihren Schatten, ihr Licht für den Menschen voraus.

Hätte er als Sachwalter Gottes und des Menschen recht, wäre
wirklich die alte Zeit abgelaufen und eine neue angebrochen.
Dann wäre eine neue, bessere Welt im Kommen. Aber wer sagt
schon, ob er recht hat? Als machtloser, armer, unbedeutender
Mensch tritt er mit solchem Anspruch, solcher Vollmacht, solcher Bedeutung auf, setzt er die Autorität Moses und der Propheten praktisch außer Kraft und beansprucht für sich die Autorität *Gottes*: wie sollte da der Vorwurf der Irrlehre, der Lügen-

prophetie, ja der Gotteslästerung und Volksverführung nicht berechtigt sein?

Gewiß, auf Gott beruft er sich für all sein Tun und Reden. Aber wiederum: Wie wäre Gott, wenn er recht hätte!? Jesu ganzes Verkündigen und Handeln stellt mit letzter Unausweichlichkeit die Frage nach Gott: wie er ist und wie er nicht ist, was er tut und was er nicht tut. Um Gott selbst geht letztlich der ganze Streit.

2. Der Streit um Gott

Der damalige Streit um Gott – dessen müssen wir uns hier erinnern[1] – muß heute unter anderen Voraussetzungen gesehen werden. Die neue wissenschaftliche Welterklärung, das andere Autoritätsverständnis, die Ideologiekritik, die Bewußtseinsverschiebung vom Jenseits zum Diesseits, die Ausrichtung des Menschen auf die Zukunft hatten ungeheure Auswirkungen auf unser Gottesverständnis und können heute nicht mit Berufung auf Jesus rückgängig gemacht werden.

Heutiges Gottesverständnis muß, wie früher ausgeführt, von einem einheitlichen Wirklichkeitsverständnis ausgehen: Gott in dieser Welt, und diese Welt in Gott. Gott nicht nur als Teil der Wirklichkeit ein (höchstes) Endliches neben Endlichem, sondern das Unendliche im Endlichen, das Absolute im Relativen, die verborgen-nahe, diesseitig-jenseitige, transzendent-immanente letzte Wirklichkeit im Herzen der Dinge, im Menschen und in der Menschheitsgeschichte. Gott wirkend nicht nur in irgendwelchen »übernatürlichen« Räumen oder exklusiv »heilsgeschichtlichen« Zeiten: in Notfällen nur als Nothelfer in der Geschichte oder Lückenbüßer im Kosmos, dort also nur, wo der Mensch mit seinen natürlichen Kräften nicht mehr hinkommt oder nichts mehr ausrichtet. Nein, Gott als die wirklichste Wirklichkeit wirkend in der ganzen Wirklichkeit: überall und jederzeit der Welt und den Menschen eine letzte Bezogenheit, Einheit, Werthaftigkeit und Sinnhaftigkeit vermittelnd. Kein Handeln Gottes *neben* der Weltgeschichte, sondern *in* der Geschichte der Welt und des handelnden Menschen.

Sollte vor einem solchen neuzeitlichen Horizont nicht auch der Gott Jesu verstanden werden können? Sollte das von Jesus her Entscheidende nicht auch vor diesem Horizont zum Tragen kommen können? Und sollte umgekehrt nicht gerade von Jesus her das beantwortet, eindeutig beantwortet werden können, was im Gottesverständnis des allgemeinen oder philosophischen Menschenverstandes, wie wir sahen, notwendig zweideutig, vage, offen bleiben mußte[2]? Wir kommen hier nicht darum herum, weiter auszuholen.

Kein neuer Gott

Freilich wollte Jesus alles andere als einen vieldeutigen Privatgott und unbestimmten Gottesglauben pseudomoderner Prägung verkünden: jenen anspruchslosen Gott einer bourgeoisen Mittelmäßigkeit, der genau unseren sehr selektiven moralischen Lieblingsideen entspricht, dem alle unangenehmen Züge ebenso fehlen wie alle unbequemen Forderungen. Der die Menschen einfach nimmt, wie sie sind, und ihren üblichen Egoismus gelten läßt. Der schon mit der Anerkennung seiner Existenz überzufrieden ist und niemandem etwas zuleide tut, weil er, alles verstehend, alles verzeiht. Kurz: ein Gott, der niemandem schadet und niemandem nützt und der doch so etwas wie eine »Religion« ermöglicht, die nichts stört und zu nichts verpflichtet[3].

Ein Gott, der unser eigener Götze ist? Nein, ein derart harmloses Produkt menschlichen Wunschdenkens, geradezu ein Exempel für die Projektionstheorie Feuerbachs und Freuds, verkündet Jesus nicht. Er verkündet keinen anderen Gott als den nicht gerade bequemen *Gott des Alten Testaments*[4]. Jesus wollte überhaupt keine neue Religion stiften, keinen neuen Gott verkünden. Schon gar nicht wie vielleicht ein Jahrhundert vor Mose, jedenfalls in der 18. Dynastie der Pharaonen, der berühmte »Ketzerkönig« Echnaton, jener idealistisch versponnene Gemahl der berühmten Schönen Nofretete, der in einer unerhört kühnen monotheistischen Revolution den höchsten ägyptischen Reichsgott Amun durch den alleinigen Gott Aton, dessen sichtbare Verkörperung die Sonne ist, ersetzen wollte, sich dabei den Haß der Priesterschaft und den Widerstand des Volkes zuzog und so scheiterte.

Wenn Jesus von Gott spricht, dann meint er den alten Gott der Väter, Abrahams, Isaaks und Jakobs, Jahwe, den Gott des Volkes Israel. Dieser ist für ihn der *eine* und *einzige* Gott, neben dem es nicht nur keine höheren, gleichhohen oder niederen, sondern –

wie schon für die Religion des Mose charakteristisch – überhaupt *keine anderen Götter* gibt. Dieser eine Gott ist nicht nur für Teilbereiche zuständig wie die Götter der Heiden: die Fruchtbarkeitsgötter für den Acker, der Kriegsgott Ares für den Sieg und die Aphrodite für die Liebe. Dieser eine Gott ist für alles zuständig: Er schenkt alles, alles Leben, alles Gute. Jesus bestätigt nach Israels erstem Gebot den strengen, bildlosen Glauben an diesen einen Gott, der des Menschen ganze Hingabe, ganze Liebe fordern darf[5].

Der Ein-Gott-Glaube ist *Juden, Christen und auch Moslems gemeinsam*: Der im Alten Testament wie im Neuen Testament wie auch im Koran für Abraham bezeugte Glaube an den einen Gott, der in der Geschichte handelt, bildet den gemeinsamen Bezugspunkt zwischen Judentum, Christentum und Islam. Er könnte die Basis bilden für ein besseres Verstehen und eine tiefere Solidarität zwischen den in der Geschichte so oft verfeindeten großen drei Glaubensgemeinschaften, die alle drei ihr eigenes Wesen nicht verstehen können ohne den Blick auf die beiden anderen: die sich deshalb nie gegenseitig als »Ungläubige« oder »Abgefallene« oder »Überholte« sehen sollten, sondern als »Väter« und »Söhne«, »Brüder« und »Schwestern« unter dem einen und selben Gott.

Dieser Ein-Gott-Glaube, obwohl kein gesellschaftliches Programm, hat einschneidende *gesellschaftliche Konsequenzen*: er entmythologisiert die göttlichen Weltmächte zugunsten des einen Gottes. Er wehrt der Vergöttlichung der politischen Mächte und Machthaber ebenso wie der Vergötzung der natürlichen Mächte und des immer wiederkehrenden kosmischen Stirb-und-Werde. Er bedeutet eine radikale Absage auch in unserem scheinbar atheistischen Zeitalter an alle die vielen Götter, die ohne Gottestitel vom Menschen angebetet werden: an alle irdischen Größen mit göttlichen Funktionen, von denen für einen Menschen alles abzuhängen scheint, auf die er hofft und die er fürchtet wie sonst nichts in der Welt. Wobei es gleichgültig ist, ob er – manchmal Monotheist, manchmal auch Polytheist – sein »Großer Gott, wir loben dich, Herr, wir preisen deine Stärke« dem großen Gott Mammon oder dem großen Gott Sexus, dem großen Gott Macht oder dem großen Gott Wissenschaft, dem großen Gott Nation oder dem großen Gott Partei singt.

So ist denn dieser eine Gott und nicht die vielen Götter für Israel und für Jesus die *eindeutige Antwort* auf jene von uns gesichteten drängenden Fragen des Menschenlebens, denen menschliches und insbesondere philosophisches Denken so schwierig ausweichen und doch auch schwierig eine eindeutige Antwort geben kann: eindeutig kein Urgrund, der letztlich vielleicht doch ein dunkler, unheilvoller Abgrund ist, wie ihn manche Gnostiker vermuteten, kein Ursinn, der letztlich vielleicht doch ein großer Unsinn ist. Sondern eindeutig ein Gott des Wohlwollens und des Heiles!

Dieser eine Gott ist für Israel bekannt aus einer langen *Geschichte*: seit nämlich unbedeutende Gruppen von Fronarbeitern, vielleicht Nomaden, die in Ägypten als billige Arbeitskräfte für die pharaonischen Bauten festgehalten wurden, an einen Gott zu glauben lernten, der ihnen Befreiung verhieß. Seiner Führung durch die Wüste hatten sie sich anvertraut, bis sie schließlich seßhaft wurden. Und immer wieder neue Generationen – Gruppen, das Volk, Einzelne – durften ihn als Befreier und Retter erfahren. So wurde dieser Gott und sein Handeln in der Geschichte ganz konkret erfahren und bezeugt: durch zahllose Erzählungen und endlich durch erstaunlich weite Zeiträume überbrückende Geschichtswerke. Man denke an den aus verschiedenen Traditionen in einem jahrhundertelangen Redaktionsprozeß hervorgegangenen »Pentateuch« (jetzt fünf nachträglich Mose zugeschriebene Bücher: Genesis, Exodus, Levitikus, Numeri, Deuteronomium), dann an das deuteronomistische Geschichtswerk (die Bücher Josua, Richter, 1-2 Samuel, 1-2 Könige) und schließlich das chronistische Geschichtswerk (die Chronikbücher, zu denen noch die Bücher Esra und Nehemia kommen)[6].

So lernte man in Israel die Geschichte als Wechselgeschehen zwischen Gott und seinem Volk verstehen. So erzählte man lobend immer wieder bestimmte Erfahrungen einzelner Menschen und Gruppen, ja des ganzen Volkes, in denen sich für die Glaubenden Gottes Wirken zeigte, im Gottesdienst wie außerhalb: die Eltern den Kindern, die Priester den Pilgern, die öffentlichen Erzähler und fahrenden Sänger ihren Zuhörern. So entwickelte sich in Israel mit der Zeit ein einzigartiges, weiträumiges, ja aufs Ganze gehendes *geschichtliches Denken*: Die Vergangenheit blieb präsent und verhalf zum Bestehen der Gegenwart wie zum Sichten der Zukunft. Israels Credo ist kein philosophisch-spekulatives, es ist ein geschichtliches Credo: zentriert auf den Gott der Befreiung, der »Israel aus Ägypten herausgeführt hat«[7], erkennbar nicht für neutrale, distanzierte Historiker, sondern für den, der in den geschichtlichen Fakten Gott am

Werk sieht. Und dieses Urbekenntnis der Glaubens- und Kultgemeinschaft von Jahweverehrern, die erst sehr viel später zu einer politischen Gemeinschaft wurde, ist ein Lobbekenntnis. Wie denn das Alte Testament überhaupt voll ist des *Lobes* Gottes und seiner Taten: angefangen von jenem wahrscheinlich ältesten Lied von Jahwe, der Roß und Wagen der Ägypter ins Meer gestürzt[8], bis zu den Lobliedern des zweiten Jesaja, der im babylonischen Exil die Befreiung ankündigt[9], und den Lobpsalmen des Volkes oder des Einzelnen wie den mächtigen Hymnen auf den Schöpfergott.

Aber ist dies nicht nur die eine Seite? Israels und Jesu Gottesverständnis darf nicht optimistisch verharmlost werden. Von eitlem Jubel ist das Alte Testament weit entfernt. Neben dem Lob steht immer wieder die *Klage*: Die Sorgen des modernen Menschen mit Gott, seiner Abwesenheit, Unbegreiflichkeit, Unwirksamkeit sind dem Alten Testament nicht fremd. Das Leid des Volkes wie des Einzelnen – jenes große Gegenargument gegen Gott und seine Güte – ist ständig gegenwärtig und schreit oft zum Himmel. Wenn Jesu letztes Wort zu seinem Gott nach dem ältesten Evangelium ein unartikulierter Schrei ist[10], so hallt in ihm das ganze Schreien der Generationen eines immer wieder leidenden und bedrückten und auch schuldig gewordenen Volkes wider. Zu Gott schrien sie schon in Ägypten, als sie ihn noch kaum kannten. Zu ihm schrie das Volk und schrien die Einzelnen, jetzt seßhaft geworden im Gelobten Land, dann im babylonischen Exil, schließlich unter der römischen Fremdherrschaft – in allen möglichen Situationen der Not und der Schuld.

Daß man zu ihm in jeder Lage schreien darf, charakterisiert diesen Gott geradezu. Und wo wird dies in alter Zeit herausfordernder getan als in jenem großen Werke der Weltliteratur aus dem 5.–2. Jahrhundert vor Jesus, wo jener völlig vereinsamte und verelendete Mensch *Hiob* – Gegenbild jenes anderen leidenden Gottesknechts Jesus – in unendlichem, grundlosem Leid zwischen Empörung und Hingabe ununterbrochen hin- und hergerissen wird? Schärfer denn irgendwo manifestiert sich in ihm die Grundhaltung des alttestamentlichen Menschen gegenüber seinem Gott: Einen letzten Halt findet dieser leidende, zweifelnde, verzweifelte Mensch – dem heutigen Menschen angesichts des Nihilismus und Atheismus so sehr verwandt – nicht mit den Schlüsseln der reinen Vernunft, die das Rätsel des Leids und des Bösen zu erschließen versucht. Nicht durch psychologische, philosophische, moralische Argumente, die das Dunkel des

Leids und des Bösen in Licht verwandeln wollen und die dann doch wieder zu abstrakt und zu allgemein sind, als daß sie im konkreten Leid viel helfen könnten. Nicht in der optimistischen Logik einer aufklärerischen Apologie und »Rechtfertigung Gottes« (seit dem großen Leibniz als »Theodizee« berühmt), die neugierig hinter Gottes Geheimnis und Weltenplan kommen möchte.

Einen letzten Halt findet der leidende, zweifelnde, verzweifelte Mensch nur im nüchternen Eingeständnis der Unfähigkeit, das Rätsel des Leids und des Bösen enträtseln zu können. Im ruhigen Verzicht auf die Anmaßung, als neutraler und angeblich unschuldiger Zensor über Gott und die Welt das Urteil sprechen zu wollen. In der entschiedenen Ablehnung eines auch nur leisen und unausgesprochenen Mißtrauens, als ob der gute Gott dem Menschen nicht wahrhaft gut sei. Positiv: In jenem gewiß ungesicherten und doch befreienden Wagnis, dem unbegreiflichen Gott in Zweifel, Leid und Schuld, in aller inneren Not und allem äußeren Schmerz, in aller Angst, Sorge, Schwäche, Versuchung, in aller Leere, Trostlosigkeit, Empörung einfach und schlicht ein *unbedingtes und restloses Vertrauen* entgegenzubringen. Ja, ihm sogar in äußerst verzweifelter Situation, wenn alles Gebet erstirbt und man zu keinem Wort fähig ist, sich einfach leer und ausgebrannt hinzuhalten: ein Grundvertrauen allerradikalster Art, das Zorn und Empörung nicht äußerlich beschwichtigt, sondern umfängt und umgreift und das auch Gottes bleibende Unbegreiflichkeit erträgt.

Nur wenn wir – trotz allem – ausgesprochen oder unausgesprochen »Amen« (»so sei es«, »so ist es recht«) sagen, läßt sich das Leid zwar nicht »erklären«, aber bestehen. »Amen-Sagen« ist die Übersetzung für das alttestamentliche Hauptwort »*Glauben*« (»heemin«)! Um Gottes Willen kann die Welt mit ihrem Rätsel, ihrem Übel und Leid bejaht werden. Sonst nicht. Das Geheimnis des Unbegreiflichen in seiner Güte umfaßt auch das Elend unseres Leidens.

Ob solch unbedingtes und unerschütterliches Vertrauen, Glauben freilich so einfach ist? Vom Neuen Testament her wird ein neues Licht darauf fallen. Und doch bleibt wahr: Das ist der eine Gott und der Glaube an ihn, wie ihn aus der dramatischen Geschichte seines Volkes zwischen Klage und Lob, Verfehlung und Verzeihung, Abfall und Neubeginn, Zorn und Gnade auch Jesus versteht. Wie er bezeugt ist in mannigfachsten Formen und Redeweisen: in Poesie und Prosa, in Selbstberichten und geschichtlichen Erzählungen, Rechtssatzungen und Kultordnungen, prophetischen Drohreden und Verheißungen, Hymnen und Klageliedern, Sagen und Legenden, Novellen und Parabeln, Orakeln, Weisheitssprüchen und theologischen Lehrsätzen. Alle diese so verschiedenen Gattungen sind selbstverständlich geprägt durch ihren ganz konkreten »Sitz im Leben« und hatten sich an einem bestimmten Ort herausgebildet: in der Großfamilie, im Kult oder in der Rechtspraxis, am Hof, im Krieg oder in den Theologenschulen. Wie auch immer und wo auch immer, immer deutlicher wird Gott bezeugt als der, der er ist: der befreiende Herr und Lenker der Geschichte, der Gesetzgeber, der Schöpfer der Welt und schließlich ihr Richter und Vollender.

Aber immer wieder bleibt dieses Volk hinter dem Anspruch seines Gottes zurück. *Mittler* treten auf zwischen Gott und seinem Volk, immer wieder von Gott berufen: Mose und die frühen charismatischen Führer (»Richter«) des Volkes. Dann in der Zeit des institutionalisierten Königtums bis zum Zusammenbruch des Nordreichs und auch des Südreichs, der Zerstörung des Tempels und des Exils in Babylon die *Propheten*: einsam, machtlos, kein Gehör findend und scheinbar erfolglos, bleiben sie ohne Gefolgschaft und mitreißende Bewegung. Die Klagen der Propheten von Elia bis Jeremia bezeugen im Übermaß die Einsamkeit, Erschöpfung, Verzweiflung der verkannten und verschlissenen Boten des einen Gottes: Die Spannungen zwischen ihrer Menschlichkeit und dem auf ihnen lastenden Auftrag, zwischen Sprachlossein und Sprechenmüssen drohen sie zu zerreißen.

In der Tradition dieser Propheten steht *Jesus*. Der Geist, der die Propheten erweckte, galt zu seiner Zeit als erloschen. Einen neuen und endgültigen Mittler erwartete man in der Gestalt des Messias oder Menschensohnes. Daneben aber gab es die erstaunlichen Lieder des zweiten Jesaja in Babylon vom »Gottesknecht«, dessen stellvertretendes Leiden für die vielen – was von keinem Propheten gesagt wird – in den Tod führen und zugleich über den Tod hinaus von Gott belohnt werden wird[11].

Jesus wollte keine neue Religion gründen: Überall knüpft er an das alttestamentliche Gottesverständnis an, wenn er von Gottes Reich und Willen spricht. Sowenig wie die Propheten beweist er den einen Gott theoretisch. Er »postuliert« ihn auch nicht moralisch. Vielmehr wird ganz praktisch mit ihm gerechnet und immer wieder neu von ihm erzählt. Ohne die Scheu vieler Juden seiner Zeit gebraucht er das Wort »Gott«, auch wenn andere

Titel wie »Höchster« oder »König« nicht vermieden werden. Wenn Jesus die Botschaft von der unwiderruflichen Nähe Gottes und seines Reiches verkündet, dann meint er keine neuen Offenbarungen über sein Wesen, keinen neuen Gottesbegriff. Über Gottes inneres Wesen reflektiert und räsoniert er nicht. Wie das Alte Testament – aber auch wie Buddha, Kung-futse, Mohammed – zeigt Jesus weder für Naturwissen noch für metaphysische Spekulationen Interesse. Um eine Lehre über Gottes An-sich-Sein, um Lehrsätze über göttliche Essenz und Attribute müht er sich nicht. Jesus spricht von Gott, wir hörten es, in Gleichnissen: Gott ist für ihn nicht »Gegenstand« des spekulativen, betrachtenden oder argumentierenden Denkens, welches nach einem einheitlichen Ursprung und Ziel fragt, sondern das konkrete Gegenüber seines glaubenden Vertrauens und hingebenden Gehorsams. Das Bekenntnis zum einen Jahwe, den der Mensch von ganzem Herzen lieben soll, wird von Jesus im Hauptgebot ausdrücklich bestätigt.

Dies freilich unterscheidet nun Jesu und Israels Gottesvorstellung grundlegend von den großen asiatischen Religionen und auch vom Griechentum. Und es dürfte sich lohnen, über diese Unterschiede etwas nachzudenken, auch wenn der religionsgeschichtlich und philosophisch weniger Interessierte den folgenden Abschnitt vielleicht lieber überschlagen wird.

Der Gott mit menschlichem Antlitz

Soviel Wahrheit in den Gottesvorstellungen des Griechentums und der orientalischen Religionen – insbesondere der des Buddhismus, darin der eigentliche religiöse Gegenpol zum Christentum – liegt und soviel von ihnen zu lernen ist, ausreichend sind sie nicht: die Unterschiede sind auch heute von Bedeutung.

Der Gott Israels und Jesu ist *anders als die unpersönliche Gottheit orientalischer Religionen.* Auch *Hinduismus* und *Buddhismus* nehmen eine höchste Wirklichkeit an. Doch sind sie, zumindest in den höher reflektierten Formen, gegenüber einem persönlichen Weltenschöpfer weithin gleichgültig. Die höchste Wirklichkeit – das Brahma – steht über dem Gott Brahma, der nach brahmanischer Theologie die Welt geschaffen hat und sich dessen rühmt.

Vielfach wird, wie in Shankaras klassischer Hindu-Philosophie, diese höchste Wirklichkeit streng monistisch verstanden:

eine absolute Einheit des Seins. Während der Atheismus nur an die Welt und nicht an Gott, und der gewöhnliche Theismus an Gott und die Welt glaubt, so der philosophisch ausgerichtete Hinduismus und Buddhismus – übertheistisch – nur an Gott. Aber dieses absolute, unpersönliche eine Sein ist auch hier keineswegs ein inhaltsloses Nichts, sondern eben reines Sein. Und die menschlichen Eigenschaften, auch die herrlichsten, sind noch allzu erbärmlich und unzulänglich, um es zu bezeichnen. So bleibt das Absolute unbestimmbar: es entzieht sich jeder Begrenzung in einem klar umrissenen anthropomorphen Begriff. Deshalb gibt es auch eine Vielzahl wahrer religiöser Standpunkte, Annäherungen an das Absolute, Weisen der Verehrung.

Wenn also Jesus das Eingehen in das Reich Gottes und damit ein persönliches und allgemeines Heil verheißt, so Hinduismus und Buddhismus das Eingehen ins Nirwana und damit das Verlöschen in einem wunschlosen, leidlosen, bewußtlosen ewigen Ruhesein. Keine auch der buddhistischen Schulen hat das Nirwana, dessen ursprünglicher Sinn nach Buddha selbst schwierig eindeutig zu bestimmen ist, schlechthin als Nichts verstanden. Im Gegensatz zum älteren Hinayana-Buddhismus, der das Nirwana mehr negativ als Aufhebung allen Leidens (und der Wiedergeburten) und als unbeschreibbaren, unerkennbaren, unwandelbaren Zustand versteht, kommt der entwickeltere Mahayana-Buddhismus zu einer sehr viel positiveren Bestimmung des Nirwana, das als Glückseligkeit und Absolutes verstanden wird. Und wenn man auch hier nicht zu einem Weltschöpfer, Weltlenker, Weltvollender gelangt, so doch zu heilbringenden Buddha-Gestalten, die Manifestationen des Urbuddha sind. Ja, im einflußreichen Amitaba-Buddhismus – in Japan als Amida-Buddhismus die verbreitetste Form des Buddhismus – spricht man sogar von einem persönlichen Seligkeitsparadies des Reinen Landes, in welches man nicht wie im älteren Buddhismus durch eigene Kraft, sondern im Vertrauen auf die Verheißung und Kraft Buddhas, des Buddhas des Lichtes und des Erbarmens, eingeht.

Auch die Geschichte des Buddhismus durchzieht also die Spannung zwischen einer mehr personal gerichteten und einer mehr apersonalen Religiosität. Aber selbst wenn das Nirwana für den Buddhismus im allgemeinen keine kosmologische Funktion hat – die Welt ist nicht Gottes Welt, sondern entstanden durch des Menschen Habgier und Dummheit –, so ist der Buddhismus andererseits doch überzeugt, »daß das Nirwana ewig sei, beständig, unvergänglich, unbeweglich, weder dem Altern noch dem Tode unterworfen, ungeboren und ungeworden, daß es Macht, Segen und Seligkeit bedeute, ein rechter Zufluchtsort sei, ein Obdach und ein Platz unangreifbarer Sicherheit; die wirkliche Wahrheit und die höchste Wirklichkeit; daß es das Gute sei, das höchste Ziel und die einzige Erfüllung unseres Lebens, ewiger, verborgener und unbegreiflicher Frieden. Damit wird der Buddha, der nichts anderes als die persönliche Verkörperung des Nirwana darstellt, Gegenstand aller Empfindungen, die wir im allgemeinen religiös nennen[12].«

Mit einem an sich verstandesmäßig begriffenen Absoluten verbindet sich denn auch ein ganzes System ritueller und religiöser Äußerungen. Was logisch kaum völlig zum Stimmen gebracht werden kann, funktioniert faktisch durch die Jahrhunderte. So duldet denn der Buddhismus wie der Hinduismus auch den Polytheismus: man betet zu allen möglichen Gottheiten. Auf diese Weise kommt das personale Moment, das in der philosophisch gerichteten Religion vernachlässigt wird, in der konkreten Religion überreich zum Ausdruck.

Auf der anderen Seite stellen sich nun aber für das *Christentum* schwerwiegende Gegenfragen: Nicht nur, ob der christliche Heiligenkult faktisch nicht doch weithin dem Polytheismus gleichkommt. Sondern vor allem, ob Gott mit Recht persönlich verstanden wird, mit Recht sogar *Person* genannt wird. Jesus gebraucht diesen Ausdruck nicht; für Gott wird er in der Bibel überhaupt nicht gebraucht. Ist er vielleicht doch allzu menschlich? Das griechische »prósopon« (= persona) meint die Maske, die der Schauspieler trägt, die Rolle, die er spielt, allgemeiner das Antlitz. So viel Bedeutung dieser Begriff für das antike Theater hatte, so wenig hatte er für die antike Philosophie. Erst die frühchristliche Trinitäts- und Inkarnationslehre gab ihm Relief. Endlos stritt man sich auf griechisch und lateinisch in einem höchst verwickelten Interpretationsprozeß, ob und inwiefern der Personbegriff (persona, prósopon, hypóstasis) – nun immer mehr als geistige Individualität verstanden – auf Gott angewendet werden könne. Nach orthodoxer Trinitätslehre, wie sie sich schließlich durchsetzte, ist Gott nicht eine Person, sondern eine Natur in drei Personen (Vater, Sohn, Geist). Umgekehrt ist Jesus Christus eine (göttliche) Person in zwei Naturen (göttliche und menschliche). Aber diese Terminologie wurde in der neueren Zeit zusehends mißverständlich bis unverständlich. Nicht zuletzt deshalb, weil Person jetzt nicht mehr ontologisch, sondern

vor allem psychologisch verstanden wird: Person als Selbstbewußtsein, und Persönlichkeit als die Gestalt der Person, welche
in der Geschichte des Individuums durch Haltung gewonnen
wird. Person, Personhaftigkeit, persönlich, Persönlichkeit erhielten von daher sehr verschiedene Sinne. Und die traditionelle
Drei-Personen-Lehre wurde vulgär weithin als Drei-Göt-
ter-Lehre (Tritheismus) verstanden, worauf zurückzukommen
sein wird.

Man sollte also nicht über das Wort streiten, weder mit Hin-
duisten und Buddhisten noch mit modernen Agnostikern oder
auch Christen. Gott ist gewiß nicht Person, wie der Mensch
Person ist: Der Allesumfassende und Allesdurchdringende ist
nie ein Gegenstand, von dem sich der Mensch distanzieren kann,
um über ihn auszusagen. Der Urgrund, Urhalt und Ursinn aller
Wirklichkeit, der jede einzelne Existenz bestimmt, ist nicht eine
Einzelperson unter anderen Personen, ist nicht einfach ein
Über-Mensch oder Über-Ich. Er ist überhaupt nicht ein Unendliches oder gar Endliches *neben* oder *über* Endlichen. Er ist das
Unendliche *in* allem Endlichen, das Sein selbst in allem Seienden.
Zu Recht betonen dies gegenüber allzu menschlichen »theisti-
schen« Gottesvorstellungen die östlichen Religionen und manche neuere Denker in Ehrfurcht vor dem göttlichen Geheimnis.
Das erkennen auch christliche Theologen, wenn sie von Gott als
von der Gottheit, dem höchsten Gut, der Wahrheit, Güte, Liebe
selbst, dem Sein selbst, der Sonne, dem Meer sprechen. Auch die
positivsten menschlichen Eigenschaften sind tatsächlich für Gott
unzulänglich. Sie bedürfen deshalb in jeder Affirmation zugleich
der Negation und der Übersetzung ins Unendliche hinein. So
sprengt Gott auch den Personbegriff: Gott ist *mehr als eine
Person.*

Aber das bedeutet zugleich: Die positiven menschlichen Eigenschaften können, wenn in ihrer Affirmation die Endlichkeit
negiert wird und sie ins Unendliche hineingehoben werden, von
Gott ausgesagt werden. Nur so bleibt für uns das Absolute nicht
doch ein inhaltsloses Nichts. Und so müssen wir denn auch
sagen: Wenn Gott mehr ist als eine Person, so ist er jedenfalls
auch *nicht weniger als eine Person.* Gott ist keine »Sache«, ist
nicht durchschaubar, verfügbar, manipulierbar, ist nicht unpersönlich, nicht unter-personal. Oder soll ein Gott ohne Geist und
Verstand, Freiheit und Liebe ein Gott sein? Sollte ein solcher
Gott in der Welt und im Menschen Geist und Verstand, Freiheit
und Liebe begründen können? Sollte ein Gott, der Personen

begründet, nicht selber personhaft sein? Heißt es nicht zu Recht in einem alten israelischen Wort: »Der das Ohr gepflanzt, sollte der nicht hören? Der das Auge gebildet, sollte der nicht sehen[13]?«

Gott ist nicht eine letzte Wirklichkeit, die sich gleichgültig verhält und uns gleichgültig läßt, sondern die uns in befreiender und beanspruchender Weise unbedingt angeht. Eine gefühllose Geometrie des Universums in naturgesetzlicher Notwendigkeit, wie sie der Physiker oder Mathematiker aufgrund seiner bestimmten und beschränkten Methode entdeckt, kann das Ganze nicht erklären. Gott ist mehr als eine universale Vernunft, mehr als ein großes anonymes Bewußtsein, mehr als ein auf sich selber bezogenes, sich selber denkendes Denken, mehr als nur die pure Wahrheit des Kosmos oder die blinde Gerechtigkeit der Geschichte. Gott ist kein Neutrum, sondern ein Gott der Menschen, der die Entscheidung von Glauben oder Unglauben herausfordert: Er ist Geist, schöpferische Freiheit, die Ur-Identität von Wahrheit und Liebe, ein alle zwischenmenschliche Personalität übergreifend-begründendes Gegenüber. Wenn man ihn schon mit den religiösen Philosophien des Ostens oder Westens das Sein selbst nennen will, dann als das Sein selbst, das sich personal manifestiert, mit unendlichem Anspruch und unendlichem Verständnis. Besser jedoch als personal oder apersonal wird man ihn – falls einem an einem Wort gelegen ist – *transpersonal, überpersönlich* nennen[14].

Welches Wort auch immer, entscheidend ist: Gott ist nicht unter unserem Niveau. Auch wenn wir von Gott nur in übertragenen Begriffen, Bildern, Vorstellungen, Symbolen reden können, so können wir ihn doch sinnvoll mit menschlichen Worten *anreden*. Wir brauchen uns die letzte Wirklichkeit nicht in Gedanken vorzustellen, aber wir sollen uns ihr selber stellen. Es soll dem Menschen nicht die Sprache verschlagen, er soll vielmehr gerade das bezeichnend Menschliche tun: das Wort ergreifen.

Von der ersten bis zur letzten Seite wird in der Bibel nicht nur von und über Gott, sondern immer auch zu und mit Gott geredet, lobend und klagend, bittend und aufbegehrend. Von der ersten bis zur letzten Seite ist Gott in der Bibel – das hat Feuerbach zweifellos richtig gesehen – Subjekt und nicht Prädikat: nicht die Liebe ist Gott, sondern Gott ist die Liebe. Von der ersten bis zur letzten Seite meint die Bibel ein echtes *Gegenüber*, das menschenfreundlich und unbedingt verläßlich ist: nicht ein Objekt, nicht ein schweigendes Unendliches, nicht ein leeres All ohne Echo, nicht eine undefinierbare gnostische Tiefe ohne Namen, nicht ein mit dem Nichts zu verwechselnder dunkler Abgrund ohne Bestimmung, erst recht nicht ein anonymes zwischenmenschliches Etwas, das mit dem Menschen und seiner (ach so gebrechlichen) Liebe verwechselt werden könnte. Nein, wo andere nur ein unendliches Schweigen vernahmen, da hörte Israel eine Stimme. Israel durfte entdecken, daß der eine Gott hörbar und anredbar ist: daß er als einer, der Ich sagt, unter die Menschen tritt und sich für sie zum Du macht: ein ansprechendes und ansprechbares *Du*! Und im Angesprochensein durch dieses Du erfährt der Mensch dann seinerseits sein eigenes Ich in einer Würde, die ihm kein säkularistischer Humanismus zu garantieren vermag: einer Würde, die es nicht zulassen kann, daß der Mensch je als Futter für Kanonen und Experimente oder als Dünger für die Evolution mißbraucht wird.

An diesem zentralen Punkt gibt es in der Bibel – trotz aller sukzessiven Berichtigung des Gottesverständnisses – keinen Entwicklungsprozeß. »Vergeistigung« wäre hier Verflüchtigung, die echtem Gebet und Gottesdienst die konkrete Basis entzöge. Wie immer in der Bibel von Gott geredet wird, ob mythologisch oder unmythologisch, ob bildlich oder begrifflich, ob prosaisch oder poetisch: das Verhältnis zu Gott als einem anredbaren Gegenüber, als einem Du – man nenne es Person oder nicht – ist eine unaufgebbare, wenn auch immer wieder neu zu interpretierende Grundkonstante des biblischen Gottesglaubens.

Der Gott mit Eigenschaften

Auch *Jesus* redet selbstverständlich von Gott und zu Gott. Und dieser Gott ist für ihn nicht vieldeutig, ein »Gott ohne Eigenschaften«: Gott ist eindeutig gut und nicht böse. Er hat auch kein böses Prinzip konkurrierend neben sich; der in frühjüdischer Zeit aus dem persischen Raum kommende Satan ist ihm eindeutig untergeordnet. Er ist nicht indifferent, sondern menschenfreundlich. Jesus nennt ihn gut, allein gut, barmherzig. Aber diese Eigenschaften spielen nicht als objektive Prädikate eine Rolle. Sondern als tätige Eigenschaften für den Menschen und die Welt: was Gott ist nicht an sich oder für sich, sondern für Mensch und Welt, wie er an Mensch und Welt handelt. Prädikate nicht eines Wesens »an sich«, sondern seines Verhältnisses zu uns. Nur im Wirken Gottes offenbart sich seine Wirklichkeit. Im

Wirken an Mensch und Welt, so daß, wenn von Gott zu reden ist, zugleich vom Menschen gesprochen werden muß.

Für Jesus wirkt Gott nicht nur in einem »übernatürlichen« Bereich, sondern er waltet mitten in der Welt und sorgt so für des Menschen große und kleine Welt. Diese Fürsorge Gottes macht jedes ängstliche Sichsorgen des Menschen überflüssig. Jesus schließt nicht von der Welt durch Schlußfolgerung auf Gott, sondern er sieht die ganze Welt im Lichte Gottes: ein Gleichnis, das auf den Schöpfer und Vollender der Welt zugleich verweist. So wird die Welt verstanden, ohne Kausalität und Naturbegriff, aber so, daß man in ihr ganz praktisch leben kann: nach der Richtschnur von Gottes Wort, wie es in der Geschichte laut geworden ist und die Welt als Gottes gute, aber vom Menschen verdorbene Welt begreifen läßt[15].

1. Der Gott Israels und Jesu ist *anders als die ferne Gottheit der klassischen griechischen Philosophie*: Gewiß ist er auch nicht nahe wie bei den früheren griechischen Denkern, wo das Göttliche als Ursprung und Formprinzip in der Welt unmittelbar anwesend ist. Oder wie später in der Stoa, wo die Gottheit pantheistisch mit der Welt identifiziert wird. Er gehört nicht einfach zur Welt, ist nicht ein Stück Welt: weder als naturhafter Weltengrund noch als Weltkraft oder als Weltgesetz. Er ist nicht nur Form, Gestalt und Ordnung der Wirklichkeit. Er ist und bleibt der ganz Andere.

Aber der Gott Israels und Jesu ist doch in aller Unterschiedenheit auch nicht getrennt von der Welt wie die Gottheit der klassischen griechischen Philosophie, die die christliche Theologie so stark prägte: Nicht wie *Platons* Idee des Guten (und Ideenwelt überhaupt), die durch eine scharfe Kluft von der erscheinenden unwahren Sinnenwelt und der schlechten Materie getrennt ist, woraus eine verhängnisvolle Materie- und Leibfeindlichkeit folgen mußte. Auch nicht wie der Gott des *Aristoteles*, der von Ewigkeit neben der Welt her lebt als ein denkendes Denken, das nur sich selber denkt, die Welt nicht kennt und nicht liebt, ohne kausales Wirken, Vorsehung, moralische Autorität. Auch nicht wie schließlich *Plotins* göttliches Eine, das getrennt von jener Welt west, die, aus seiner Einheit ausgeflossen, Abfall bedeutet: die Materie als das Schlechte, von dem der Mensch sich befreien muß.

Der *Gott Israels und Jesu* ist in aller Unterschiedenheit von Welt und Mensch nicht ferne, sondern *nahe*: Er erscheint vor allem als schöpferischer Wille. Der mächtige und dauernd wirksame Schöpfer der Welt, der nach seinem Willen die Welt – aus dem Nichts, wie das spätere Judentum konsequent weiterdenkt – als gute Welt geschaffen hat. Der souveräne Herr des Menschen, der von seinem guten, aber durch den eigenen bösen Willen verdorbenen Geschöpf Gehorsam erwartet, vom Menschen in seiner Ganzheit, ohne daß Geistiges und Sinnliches unterschieden würden. Der weise Lenker der Geschichte, der von Anbeginn die Geschichte des Volkes und der gesamten Menschheit nicht willkürlich, sondern nach seinem Plan auf ein Ziel hin lenkt, so daß alles Einzelne, auch Leid und Tod, seinen Platz und seinen Sinn bekommt in einer Geschichte des Heils, die zum Menschen spricht und ihm Weisung und Warnung zugleich bedeutet. Schließlich der gerechte Richter, der die Weltgeschichte vollendet, Gericht hält und sein Reich heraufführt. Alles dies im Alten Testament geboten nicht in der Form einer kosmologischen oder theologischen Theorie, sondern einer erzählten Geschichte, oder besser, erzählter Geschichten, die dem Menschen nicht philosophische Einsichten, vielmehr seine allseitige Abhängigkeit von Gott zum Bewußtsein bringen und den Mut zum Glauben herausfordern wollen.

So ist dieser Gott jenseitig *und* diesseitig, fern *und* nah, überweltlich *und* innerweltlich, zukünftig *und* gegenwärtig. Gott ist ausgerichtet auf die Welt: kein Gott ohne Welt! Und die Welt ganz bezogen auf Gott: keine Welt ohne Gott! Der Widerspruch besteht somit nicht wie bei den Griechen zwischen geistigem Gott und materieller Welt als solcher, sondern zwischen Gott und von ihm abgewendeter sündiger Welt. Und die Erlösung wird nicht erwartet als Überwindung des platonischen Dualismus von Gott und Welt, Geist und Materie, sondern als Befreiung der Welt von Schuld, Elend, Tod und als Gemeinschaft mit Gott.

2. Der Gott Israels und Jesu ist *anders als die apathische Gottheit der klassischen griechischen Philosophie.* Gewiß ist er nicht bewegt, wie es sich etwa der frühe griechische Denker Heraklit dachte: ein werdender Gott, der wie ein lebendig bewegtes Feuer als Weltseele und Weltvernunft das ewig fließende All, seine miteinander im Krieg liegenden Elemente und alle Erscheinungen in ihrer Rätselhaftigkeit und Doppeldeutigkeit durchwaltet. Auch nicht bewegt, wie es der Mythos darstellt: wie jene menschlich-allzumenschlichen Götter Homers, die untereinan-

der im Streite sind und die insbesondere von Xenophanes und Platon einer scharfen Kritik unterzogen werden.

Aber bei aller Beständigkeit, Stetigkeit und Identität mit sich selbst ist der Gott Israels und Jesu doch nicht unbewegt wie jener Gott der klassischen Philosophie, die gegen Mythologie und Werde-Philosophie reagiert und der christlichen Theologie oft allzusehr Vorbild war: Nicht unbewegt wie die jenseits der Geschichte seiende, außerzeitliche und außerräumliche geistige Sonne *Platons* (unter dem Einfluß von Heraklits Antipoden Parmenides), jene über der Hierarchie der ewigunveränderlichen Ideenwelt thronende höchste Idee des Guten, die sich selbst genügt als ein ewiges, absolut unbewegliches und unveränderliches Urprinzip. Oder wie der göttliche Geist des *Aristoteles,* jener unbewegte erste Beweger, der derart in seiner Unbeweglichkeit und Unveränderlichkeit erstarrt ist, daß er nur sich selbst erkennt und kein Handeln gegenüber einem anderen verträgt. Oder wie schließlich das Eine *Plotins,* welches als oberstes Prinzip des Seins in einem System auseinanderfließender Seinsstufen selber in absolut starrer Unveränderlichkeit verharrt, so daß von ihm sogar das Leben verneint werden muß. So also bei diesem klassischen Dreigestirn der Philosophie nicht nur eine Ungewordenheit und Unvergänglichkeit, sondern eine absolute Unbeweglichkeit und Unveränderlichkeit Gottes, wie sie Parmenides gegen Heraklit noch nicht Gott, wohl aber dem Sein als solchem zugeschrieben hatte.

Der *Gott Israels und Jesu* erscheint bei allem Ungewordensein und aller Unvergänglichkeit keineswegs als unbeweglicher und unveränderlicher, sondern als *lebendiger* Gott. Man lasse sich nicht täuschen durch die oft naive, mythologische, anthropomorphe, menschenförmige Redeweise der Bibel. Es geht hier nicht einfach um ein primitiveres, zurückgebliebenes Gottesverständnis. Gewiß, auch im Alten Testament gibt es eine Tendenz zur Spiritualisierung Gottes, und insbesondere die alte griechische Übersetzung der Septuaginta hat unter Umdeutung des alttestamentlichen Urtextes gewisse anthropomorphe, menschenförmige Aussagen nach Möglichkeit abzuschwächen oder gar zu eliminieren versucht. Aber jene Partien, die Anthropomorphismen enthalten, gehören keineswegs nur Schichten mit besonders niedrigem Niveau an, wie man eine Zeitlang angenommen hat. Sie finden sich auch bei den späteren Propheten. Sie sind Zeichen nicht eines unentwickelten, kindlichen, sondern eines sehr bestimmten und auf seine Weise reifen Denkens.

Dieser Gott Israels und Jesu ist weder ein naturhaftes Urprinzip noch eine metaphysische Wesenheit, ist weder eine stumme Kraft noch eine anonyme Macht. Er ist der lebendige Schöpfergott. Sicher nicht ein allzu menschlicher Gott spielerischer Launen, wohl aber ein Gott der Freiheit, welcher Welt und Geschichte möglich macht und lenkt, sie bis ins kleinste kennt, liebt, gut sein läßt.

Seine *Ewigkeit* ist nicht zu verstehen als platonische Zeitlosigkeit, sondern als machtvoll lebendige Gleichzeitigkeit zu aller Zeit;

seine *Allgegenwart* nicht als zuständliche Ausdehnung im Universum, sondern als überlegene Herrschaft über den Raum;

seine *Geistigkeit* nicht als ausschließlicher Gegensatz zu einer schlechten Materie, sondern als die allem Geschaffenen unendlich überlegene Mächtigkeit;

seine *Güte* gegenüber Welt und Menschen nicht als natürliche Ausstrahlung des Guten, sondern als frei liebende gnädige Zuwendung;

seine *Unveränderlichkeit* nicht als starre, naturhafte, tote Unbeweglichkeit, sondern als wesenhafte Treue zu sich selbst in aller lebendigen Bewegtheit;

seine *Gerechtigkeit* nicht als eine im zeitlosen Ordnungsgedanken gründende Verteilung und Vergeltung, sondern als eine in der Treue zum Bund mit den Menschen wurzelnde barmherzige, heilschaffende Gerechtigkeit;

seine *Unbegreiflichkeit* nicht als die abstrakte Eigenschaftslosigkeit eines namenlosen Woher unserer Fraglichkeit, sondern als die im Handeln sich erweisende Andersartigkeit, Unverfügbarkeit, Unvorhersehbarkeit.

Diese von den Griechen im philosophischen Rückschlußverfahren aus der vorhandenen Welt abgelesenen Prädikate werden in der Bibel also nicht kurzschlüssig negiert, wohl aber konkret überboten. Gott ist mehr als der Superlativ des menschlichen Wesens und der menschlichen Möglichkeiten.

Gott soll also nicht als abstrakte Idee aufgefaßt werden, die dem Menschen fernsteht, sondern als konkrete Wirklichkeit, die sich ihm gegenüber keineswegs gleichgültig verhält, sondern ihn unbedingt angeht und beansprucht. Nicht ein Gott, der in (oder außerhalb) einer sich bewegenden Welt unbeweglich bleibt, sondern der im Raum menschlicher Geschichte handelt, sich in menschlichen Geschehnissen zu erkennen gibt, in menschlicher Weise sich offenbart, der Begegnung, Umgang, Verkehr mit ihm ermöglicht. Nicht ein Gott also, der sich aus allem heraushält und erhaben in einer vom Leid der Welt unberührten Transzendenz verharrt, sondern der lebendig Anteil nimmt und sich in dieser dunklen Geschichte engagiert. Nicht ein Gott der Einsamkeit, sondern ein Gott der Partnerschaft, des Bundes. Nicht ein apathischer, affektloser, leidensunfähiger, sondern ein sym-pathischer, mit-leidender Gott. Kurz: *ein Gott mit menschlichem Antlitz!*

Alle im Alten Testament berichteten Worte und Taten Jahwes vom Buch Genesis an bezeugen, wie dieser Gott das Gegenteil eines apathischen Gottes ist. Er ist ein Gott, der spricht, gebietet, verheißt, zürnt, sucht, nachgibt, vergibt. Er ist ein Gott, welcher Freude und Trauer, Wohlgefallen und Abscheu kennt, Liebe und Zorn, Eifer und Haß, Rache und Reue empfindet, der fordert und Nachsicht übt, der sich gereuen lassen, aber sich auch seiner Reue gereuen lassen kann. Selbst die *negativ* besetzten Attribute sind nicht primitiv als menschlich-allzumenschliche Passionen, Gemütsbewegungen zu verstehen.

Gottes *Eifersucht* ist nicht Ausfluß von Neid und Furcht, sondern Ausdruck seiner Einzigkeit, die keine anderen Götter neben sich duldet, Konsequenz seines Willens, der zum Wohl des Menschen unbedingt auf seinen Weisungen besteht.

Gottes *Zorn* (Haß, Abscheu, Rache) meint keinen irrationalen Ausbruch, keine eigenständige Unheilsamkeit, sondern die andere Seite seiner Liebe, seines heiligen Willens, Ausdruck nämlich seines Widerwillens gegen alles Böse und seines Unwillens gegen den Sünder.

Gottes *Reue* ist nicht Folge von Ignoranz und später Einsicht, sondern Zeichen dafür, daß der Mensch keinem unabänderlichen Schicksal unterworfen ist, daß menschliche Geschichte für Gott kein leeres, gleichgültiges Schauspiel ist, daß Gott veränderten Verhältnissen gegenüber nicht unverändert verharrt und sein Wohlgefallen oder Mißfallen nicht nach blinder Willkür, sondern gerecht zuwendet.

Alle diese *Anthropomorphismen*[16] wollen Gott keineswegs einfach vermenschlichen. Gott soll Gott bleiben. Auch im Alten Testament wird betont, Gott sei kein Mensch, daß ihn gereue. Doch wollen die Anthropomorphismen Gott als Lebendigen dem Menschen nahebringen. Sie wollen echt menschliches Empfinden, Denken, Wollen Gott gegenüber ansprechen und erhalten. Sie wollen echt menschliches Hören, Antworten, Fragen, Vertrauen, Gehorchen, Beten, Loben, Danken herausfordern.

Philosophisch abstrakte Bestimmungen des göttlichen Wesens lassen den Menschen kalt. Es muß das göttliche Sein in seiner leidenschaftlichen Bewegtheit ins Bewußtsein treten, damit der Mensch seinem Gott so intensiv und konkret wie einem Menschen begegnet: einem Angesicht, das uns aufleuchtet, einer Hand, die uns führt. Welche vornehmeren, größeren, tieferen Bilder, Chiffren, Symbole, Vorstellungen, Begriffe aber hätte der Mensch zu seiner Verfügung, um sich – wie dargelegt, affirmierend, negierend, transzendierend – an Gott heranzutasten, als eben menschliche? Nur so erscheint Gott mehr denn als nur die letzte Ursache alles Geschehens, nämlich als eine Macht, die den Menschen in seiner ganzen konkreten Wirklichkeit bestimmt.

Es ist jetzt noch sehr viel deutlicher geworden[17]: Der *Gott der Philosophen* und der *Gott Israels und Jesu* lassen sich nicht oberflächlich harmonisieren. Das haben Pascal, Kierkegaard und Karl Barth gegen alle »natürliche Theologie« richtig gesehen. Freilich lassen sie sich auch nicht so einfach dissoziieren. Daran hat die große katholische Tradition gegen die »dialektische Theologie« immer zu Recht festgehalten. Das Verhältnis muß vielmehr echt dialektisch gesehen werden: Der »Gott der Philosophen« ist im »Gott Israels und Jesu« im besten Hegelschen Sinn des Wortes – positive, negative, supereminenter – *»aufgehoben«.*

Es dürfte somit beim Verständnis Jesu und seines Gottes heute darauf ankommen, zugleich die moderne Entwicklung des Gottesverständnisses und das Entscheidende des biblischen Gottesglaubens in einem neuen Verständnis der *Geschichtlichkeit Gottes* ernstzunehmen[18]. Ein Gott, der als der lebendige Gott im Gegensatz zu einem Gott in ungeschichtlicher Seinsweise, einem überirdischen Weltenlenker oder einem überzeitlichen Steuermann der Geschichte, selber eine *Geschichte hat und stiftet* und der sich für die Welt und Menschen als *Urgeschichtlichkeit* und *Geschichtsmächtigkeit* erweist. Ein Gottesverständnis also, welches die Erkenntnisse griechischer und moderner Philosophie nicht biblizistisch überspringt. Und das gleichwohl keinen abstrakten Gott postuliert, dem man mit Heidegger vorwerfen müßte: »Zu diesem Gott kann der Mensch weder beten, noch kann er ihm opfern. Vor der Causa sui kann der Mensch weder aus Scheu ins Knie fallen, noch kann er vor diesem Gott musizieren und tanzen[19].«

Der aus Israels Geschichte wohlbekannte eine und einzige Gott, sprechend in den Erfahrungen der Menschen und angesprochen in ihrem Antworten und Fragen, Beten und Fluchen: daß dieser Gott ein naher und lebendiger Gott mit menschlichem Antlitz ist, darüber war (und ist heute zwischen Christen und Juden) kein Streit notwendig. Es läßt sich sogar sagen, daß Jesus nur das Gottesverständnis Israels mit besonderer Reinheit und Konsequenz erfaßt hat. Nur?

Jesu Originalität darf in der Tat nicht übertrieben werden; das ist wichtig für das Gespräch mit den Juden heute. Oft tat und tut man so, als ob Jesus als erster Gott den *Vater* sowie die Menschen seine Kinder genannt habe. Als ob Gott nicht in verschiedensten Religionen Vater genannt würde, auch bei den eben genannten Griechen: Genealogisch schon in Homers Epen, wo Zeus, der Sohn des Chronos, als der Vater der Götterfamilie erscheint. Kosmologisch geläutert dann in der stoischen Philosophie, wo die Gottheit als der Vater des vernunftdurchwalteten Kosmos und der mit ihm verwandten und von ihm umsorgten vernunftbegabten Menschenkinder gilt.

Doch gerade angesichts des religionsgeschichtlichen Befundes wird auch schon die *Problematik der Anwendung des Vaternamens* auf Gott sichtbar, worauf im Zeitalter der Frauenemanzipation zu Recht neu aufmerksam gemacht wird. Ist es denn so selbstverständlich, daß die geschlechtliche Differenzierung auf Gott übertragen wird? Ist Gott ein Mann, maskulin, viril? Wird nicht gerade hier Gott nach dem Bild des Menschen, ja genauer, des Mannes geschaffen? Im allgemeinen treten die Götter in der Religionsgeschichte geschlechtlich differenziert auf, wiewohl es vielleicht schon am Anfang zweigeschlechtliche oder geschlechtsneutrale Wesen gegeben hat und sich auch später immer wieder doppelgeschlechtliche Züge zeigen. Es muß aber zu denken geben, daß in den mutterrechtlichen Kulturen die »große Mutter«, aus deren Schoß alle Dinge und Wesen hervorgegangen sind und in den sie zurückkehren, an der Stelle des Vatergottes steht. Sollte das Matriarchat älter sein als das Patriarchat – die Frage ist unter den Historikern nach wie vor umstritten –, so wäre der Kult der Muttergottheit, von welchem etwa in Kleinasien der spätere Marienkult gewichtige Impulse übernommen hat, dem des Vatergottes auch zeitlich vorangegangen.

Aber wie immer diese historische Frage entschieden wird: die

Vaterbezeichnung für Gott ist nicht nur von der Einzigkeit Jahwes bestimmt. Sie erscheint auch gesellschaftlich bedingt, geprägt von einer männerorientierten Gesellschaft. Gott ist jedenfalls nicht gleich Mann. Schon im Alten Testament, bei den Propheten, zeigt Gott auch weibliche, mütterliche Züge. Aus heutiger Perspektive aber muß dies noch deutlicher gesehen werden. Die Vaterbezeichnung wird nur dann nicht mißverstanden, wenn sie nicht im Gegensatz zu »Mutter«, sondern symbolisch (analog) verstanden wird: »Vater« als patriarchales Symbol – mit auch matriarchalen Zügen – für eine trans-humane, trans-sexuelle letzte Wirklichkeit. Der eine Gott darf heute weniger denn je nur durch den Raster des Männlich-Väterlichen gesehen werden, wie dies eine allzu männliche Theologie tat. Es muß an ihm auch das weiblich-mütterliche Moment erkannt werden. Eine so verstandene Vater-Anrede kann dann nicht mehr zur religiösen Begründung eines gesellschaftlichen Paternalismus auf Kosten der Frau und insbesondere zur permanenten Unterdrückung des Weiblichen in der Kirche (Amt) benützt werden[20].

Anders als in anderen Religionen erscheint Gott im *Alten Testament* nicht als der physische Vater von Göttern, Halbgöttern oder Heroen. Allerdings auch nie einfach als der Vater aller Menschen. Jahwe ist der Vater des Vokes Israel, welches Gottes erstgeborener Sohn genannt wird[21]. Er ist dann insbesondere der Vater des Königs, der in ausgezeichnetem Sinn als Gottes Sohn gilt: »Du bist mein Sohn, heute habe ich dich gezeugt«[22] – ein »Beschluß Jahwes« bei der Thronbesteigung, der nicht eine mirakulöse irdische Erzeugung, sondern die Einsetzung des Königs in die Sohnesrechte meint. Im späteren Judentum wird Gott dann auch als Vater des einzelnen Frommen[23] und des erwählten Volkes der Endzeit verheißen: »Sie werden nach meinen Geboten tun, und ich werde ihr Vater sein, und sie werden meine Kinder sein[24].« Hier überall zeigt sich das Vatersymbol jenseits aller sexuellen Bezüge und eines religiösen Paternalismus in seinen unverzichtbaren positiven Aspekten: als Ausdruck der Macht und zugleich der Nähe, des Schutzes, der Fürsorge.

Doch hierbei künden sich bei *Jesus* bedeutsame Unterschiede an. Manche überlieferten Worte Jesu könnten, für sich allein genommen, auch aus der Weisheitsliteratur stammen, wo sich Parallelen finden. Daß sie von Jesus stammen, ist wie so oft schwierig positiv aufweisbar. Aber sie erhalten ihre besondere Färbung vom gesamten Kontext, mögen sie nun immer direkt von ihm selbst stammen oder nicht. Es fällt zunächst auf, daß Jesus die Vaterschaft Gottes nie auf das Volk als solches bezieht. Wie für den Täufer Johannes so stellt auch für ihn die Zugehörigkeit zum auserwählten Volk keine Heilsgarantie dar. Noch auffälliger ist, daß Jesus ganz anders als selbst Johannes die Vaterschaft auch auf die Bösen und Ungerechten bezieht und daß er von dieser vollkommenen Vaterschaft Gottes her die für ihn so spezifische Feindesliebe begründet[25]. Was geht hier vor?

Hier überall wird mit dem Hinweis auf den »Vater« gewiß zunächst auf Gottes tätige Vorsehung und Fürsorge in allen Dingen hingewiesen: die sich um jeden Sperling und um jedes Haar kümmert[26], die um unsere Bedürfnisse weiß, bevor wir ihn bitten[27], die unsere Sorgen als überflüssig erscheinen läßt[28]. Der Vater, der um alles in dieser so gar nicht heilen Welt weiß und ohne den nichts geschieht: die faktische Antwort auf die Theodizeefrage nach den Lebensrätseln, dem Leid, der Ungerechtigkeit, dem Tod in der Welt! Ein Gott, dem man unbedingt vertrauen und auf den man sich auch in Leid, Ungerechtigkeit, Schuld und Tod ganz verlassen kann. Ein Gott nicht mehr in unheimlicher, transzendenter Ferne, sondern nahe in unbegreiflicher Güte. Ein Gott, der nicht auf ein Jenseits vertröstet und die gegenwärtige Dunkelheit, Vergeblichkeit und Sinnlosigkeit verharmlost, sondern der selbst in Dunkelheit, Vergeblichkeit und Sinnlosigkeit zum Wagnis der Hoffnung einlädt.

Aber es geht noch um mehr. Hier kommt das zum Durchbruch, was so unvergleichlich nachdrücklich vor Augen gemalt wird in jener Parabel, die eigentlich nicht den Sohn oder die Söhne, sondern den Vater zur Hauptfigur hat: jenen Vater, der den Sohn in Freiheit ziehen läßt, der ihm weder nachjagt noch nachläuft, der aber den aus dem Elend Zurückkehrenden sieht, bevor dieser ihn sieht, ihm entgegenläuft, sein Schuldbekenntnis unterbricht, ihn ohne alle Abrechnung, Probezeit, Vorbedingungen aufnimmt und ein großes Fest feiern läßt – zum Ärgernis des korrekt Daheimgebliebenen[29].

Was also wird hier mit »Vater« zum Ausdruck gebracht? Offensichtlich nicht nur, daß es ein Mißverständnis Gottes ist, wenn der Mensch meint, ihm gegenüber seine Freiheit wahren zu müssen. Nicht nur, daß Gottes Walten und des Menschen Aktivität, Theonomie und Autonomie sich nicht ausschließen. Nicht nur, daß das von Theologen vieltraktierte Problem des »Zusammenwirkens« (»concursus«) von göttlicher Vorherbestimmung und menschlicher Freiheit, von göttlichem und menschlichem

Willen kein echtes Problem ist ... Sondern genau das, was dieser »Freund von Zöllnern und Sündern«, der das Verlorene und Verkommene meint suchen und retten zu müssen, auch in anderen Parabeln zum Ausdruck brachte: wenn er sprach von Gott – wie wir schon sahen – als der Frau (!) oder dem Hirten, die sich über das wiedergefundene Verlorene freuen, als dem großmütigen König, dem großzügigen Geldverleiher, dem gnädigen Richter, und wenn er sich daraufhin auch selber mit moralischen Versagern, Unfrommen und Unmoralischen einließ, sie bevorzugt behandelte und ihnen sogar auf der Stelle Vergebung ihrer Schuld zusprach. Was bedeutet dies alles, wenn nicht: Jesus stellt Gott ganz ausdrücklich als Vater des »verlorenen Sohnes«, als den *Vater der Verlorenen* hin?

Dies also ist für Jesus der eine wahre Gott, neben dem es keine anderen auch noch so frommen Götter geben darf: der Gott des Alten Testaments – besser verstanden! Ein Gott, der offensichtlich mehr ist als der oberste Garant eines fraglos zu akzeptierenden, wenn auch vielleicht geschickt zu manipulierenden Gesetzes. Ein Gott, der mehr ist auch als jenes von oben alles diktierende und zentral lenkende, allmächtig-allwissende Wesen, das seine Planziele unerbittlich, und sei es mit »heiligen Kriegen« im großen und kleinen und ewiger Verdammung der Gegner, zu erreichen trachtet. Dieser Vater-Gott will kein Gott sein, wie ihn Marx, Nietzsche und Freud fürchteten, der dem Menschen von Kind auf Ängste und Schuldgefühle einjagt, ihn moralisierend ständig verfolgt, und der so tatsächlich nur die Projektion anerzogener Ängste, menschlicher Herrschaft, Machtgier, Rechthaberei und Rachsucht ist. Dieser Vater-Gott will kein theokratischer Gott sein, der auch nur indirekt den Repräsentanten totalitärer Systeme zur Rechtfertigung dienen könnte, die, ob fromm-kirchlich oder unfromm-atheistisch, seinen Platz einzunehmen und seine Hoheitsrechte auszuüben versuchen: als fromme oder unfromme Götter der orthodoxen Lehre und unbedingten Disziplin, des Gesetzes und der Ordnung, der menschenverachtenden Diktatur und Planung ...

Nein, dieser Vater-Gott will ein Gott sein, der den Menschen als ein Gott der rettenden Liebe begegnet. Nicht der allzumännliche Willkür- oder Gesetzesgott. Nicht der Gott geschaffen nach dem Bilde der Könige und Tyrannen, der Hierarchen und Schulmeister. Sondern der – wie schade um das so verniedlichte große Wort – *liebe Gott*, der sich mit den Menschen, ihren Nöten und Hoffnungen solidarisiert. Der nicht fordert, sondern gibt, der nicht niederdrückt, sondern aufrichtet, nicht krank macht, sondern heilt. Der diejenigen schont, die sein heiliges Gesetz und damit ihn selbst antasten. Der statt verurteilt vergibt, der statt bestraft befreit, der statt Recht vorbehaltslos Gnade walten läßt. Der Gott also, der sich nicht den Gerechten, sondern den Ungerechten zuwendet. Der die Sünder vorzieht: der den verlorenen Sohn lieber hat als den daheimgebliebenen, den Zöllner lieber als den Pharisäer, die Ketzer lieber als die Orthodoxen, die Dirnen und Ehebrecher lieber als ihre Richter, die Gesetzesbrecher oder Gesetzlosen lieber als die Gesetzeswächter!

Kann man hier noch sagen, der Vatername sei nur Echo auf innerweltliche Vatererfahrungen? Eine Projektion, die dazu dient, irdische Vater- und Herrschaftsverhältnisse zu verklären? Nein, *dieser* Vater-Gott ist anders! Nicht ein Gott des Jenseits auf Kosten des Diesseits, auf Kosten des Menschen (Feuerbach). Nicht ein Gott der Herrschenden, der Vertröstung und des deformierten Bewußtseins (Marx). Nicht ein Gott, von Ressentiments erzeugt, das Oberhaupt einer erbärmlichen Eckensteher-Moral von Gut und Böse (Nietzsche). Nicht ein tyrannisches Über-Ich, das Wunschbild illusionärer frühkindlicher Bedürfnisse, ein Gott des Zwangsrituals aus einem Schuld- und Vaterkomplex (Freud).

An einen ganz anderen Gott und Vater appelliert Jesus zur Rechtfertigung seines skandalösen Redens und Benehmens: ein wunderlicher, ja gefährlicher, ein im Grunde unmöglicher Gott. Oder sollte man das wirklich annehmen können? Daß Gott selbst die Gesetzesübertretungen rechtfertigt? Daß Gott selbst sich rücksichtslos über die Gerechtigkeit des Gesetzes hinwegsetzt und eine »bessere Gerechtigkeit« proklamieren läßt? Daß er selbst also die bestehende gesetzliche Ordnung und damit das gesamte gesellschaftliche System, ja auch den Tempel und den ganzen Gottesdienst in Frage stellen läßt? Daß er selber den Menschen zum Maßstab seiner Gebote macht, selber die natürlichen Grenzen zwischen Genossen und Nichtgenossen, Fernsten und Nächsten, Freunden und Feinden, Guten und Bösen durch Vergeben, Dienen, Verzichten, durch die Liebe aufhebt und sich so auf die Seite der Schwachen, Kranken, Armen, Unterprivilegierten, Unterdrückten, ja der Unfrommen, Unmoralischen, Gottlosen stellt? Das wäre doch ein neuer Gott: ein Gott, der sich von seinem eigenen Gesetz gelöst hat, ein Gott nicht der Gesetzesfrommen, sondern ʼder Gesetzesbrecher, ja – so zugespitzt muß es gesagt sein, um die Widersprüchlichkeit und

Anstößigkeit deutlich zu machen – ein Gott nicht der Gottes-fürchtigen, sondern ein *Gott der Gottlosen*!? Eine wahrhaft un-erhörte *Revolution im Gottesverständnis*!?

Ein »Aufstand gegen Gott« gewiß nicht im Sinn des älteren oder neueren Atheismus, wohl aber ein Aufstand gegen den Gott der Frommen: Sollte man es denn tatsächlich annehmen können, sollte man es wirklich glauben dürfen, daß Gott selbst, der wahre Gott, sich hinter einen solchen unerhörten Neuerer stellt, der sich, revolutionärer als alle Revolutionäre, über Gesetz und Tempel, über Mose, König und Propheten erhebt und sich sogar zum Richter über Sünde und Vergebung aufschwingt? Käme Gott nicht in Widerspruch zu sich selbst, wenn er einen solchen *Sach-Walter* hätte? Wenn ein solcher mit Recht Gottes Autorität und Willen gegen Gottes Gesetz und Tempel in Anspruch neh-men, mit Recht sich die Vollmacht zu solchem Reden und Han-deln zuschreiben dürfte? Ein Gott der Gottlosen, und ein Got-teslästerer als sein Prophet!?

Die nicht selbstverständliche Anrede

Unermüdlich versucht es Jesus mit allen Mitteln deutlich zu machen: Gott ist wirklich so, er ist wirklich ein Vater der Verlo-renen, wirklich ein Gott der moralischen Versager, der Gottlo-sen. Und sollte das nicht eine ungeheure Befreiung für alle sein, die mit Mühen und Schuld beladen sind? Aller Anlaß zur Freude und Hoffnung? Es ist kein neuer Gott, den er verkündigt; es ist nach wie vor der Gott des Bundes. Aber dieser alte Gott des Bundes in entschieden neuem Licht. Gott ist *kein anderer, aber* er ist *anders!* Nicht ein Gott des Gesetzes, sondern ein Gott der Gnade! Und rückwärtsblickend läßt sich vom Gott der Gnade her auch der Gott des Gesetzes besser, tiefer, eben gnädiger verstehen: das Gesetz schon als ein Ausdruck der Gnade.

Freilich, selbstverständlich ist dies alles für den Menschen nicht. Da ist ein Umdenken mit allen Konsequenzen, da ist ein wirklich neues Bewußtsein, ein eigentliches inneres Umkehren erfordert, gründend in jenem unbeirrbaren Vertrauen, das man Glaube nennt. Jesu ganze Botschaft ist ein einziger Appell, sich nicht zu ärgern, sondern sich zu ändern: sich auf sein Wort zu verlassen und dem Gott der Gnade zu trauen. Sein Wort ist die einzige Garantie, die den Menschen gegeben wird dafür, daß Gott wirklich so ist. Wer diesem Wort nicht glaubt, wird seine

Taten der Dämonie verdächtigen. Ohne sein Wort bleiben seine Taten zweideutig. Nur sein Wort macht sie eindeutig.

Aber wer immer sich auf Jesu Botschaft und Gemeinschaft einläßt, dem geht an Jesus der auf, den er mit »*mein Vater*« anredete. Mit »Vater« – Vater, wie er ihn (nicht im Gegensatz zu Mutter) verstand – war der Kern des ganzen Streits getroffen. Der sprachliche Befund gibt dafür eine merkwürdige Bestätigung[30]: Bei dem großen Reichtum an Gottesanreden, über die das antike Judentum verfügt, ist es erstaunlich, daß Jesus gerade die Anrede »Mein Vater« ausgewählt hat. Vereinzelte Aussagesätze über Gott den Vater findet man im hebräischen Alten Testament[31]. Nirgendwo jedoch ließ sich bis jetzt in der Literatur des antiken palästinischen Judentums die individuelle hebräische Gottes-Anrede »Mein Vater« nachweisen. Nur im hellenistischen Bereich gibt es, wohl unter griechischem Einfluß, einige spärliche Belege für die griechische Gottesanrede »patér«. Aber noch außergewöhnlicher ist der Befund bezüglich der aramäischen Form von Vater = »Abba«: Jesus scheint nach den vorliegenden Zeugnissen[32] Gott stets mit »Abba« angeredet zu haben. Nur so erklärt sich der nachhaltige Gebrauch dieser ungewöhnlichen aramäischen Gottesanrede selbst in griechisch sprechenden Gemeinden[33]. Denn umgekehrt gibt es in der gesamten umfangreichen sowohl liturgischen wie privaten Gebetsliteratur des antiken Judentums bis hinauf ins Mittelalter keinen einzigen Beleg für die Gottesanrede »Abba«. Wie soll man das erklären? Bisher fand man nur die eine Erklärung: »Abba« – ganz ähnlich dem deutschen »Papa« – ist seinem Ursprung nach ein Lallwort des Kindes, zur Zeit Jesu freilich auch gebraucht zur Vater-Anrede erwachsener Söhne und Töchter und als Höflichkeitsausdruck gegenüber älteren Respektspersonen. Aber diesen so gar nicht männlichen Ausdruck der Kindersprache, der Zärtlichkeit, diesen Alltags- und Höflichkeitsausdruck zur Anrede Gottes zu gebrauchen, mußte den Zeitgenossen so unehrerbietig und so ärgerlich familiär vorkommen, wie wenn wir Gott mit »Papa« oder »Väterchen« ansprächen.

Für Jesus aber ist dieser Ausdruck so wenig respektlos, wie es die vertraute Anrede des Kindes an seinen Vater ist. Vertrautheit schließt ja Respekt nicht aus. Ehrfurcht bleibt die Grundlage seines Gottesverständnisses. Aber nicht sein Zentrum: Genau wie ein Kind seinen irdischen Vater, so soll nach Jesus der Mensch seinen himmlischen Vater ansprechen – ehrerbietig und gehorsamsbereit, doch vor allem geborgen und vertrauensvoll.

Mit diesem Vertrauen, welches Ehrfurcht einschließt, lehrt Jesus auch seine Jünger Gott anreden: »Unser Vater – in den Himmeln«[34]. Gott mit »Vater« anzureden, ist der gewagteste und einfachste Ausdruck jenes unbedingten Vertrauens, das dem lieben Gott Gutes zutraut, alles Gute zutraut, das auf ihn vertraut und sich ihm anvertraut.

Das *Vaterunser:* Ohne alle Buchstabenfrömmigkeit und allen Formularzwang in zwei Fassungen – einer kürzeren[35] und einer längeren[36] – überliefert, ist es ein Bittgebet ganz aus der Gewöhnlichkeit des unsakralen Alltags heraus gesprochen. Ohne jegliche mystische Versenkung und Läuterung, allerdings auch ohne allen Anspruch auf Verdienst: nur unter der Bedingung der eigenen Bereitschaft zum Vergeben[37]. Zu den einzelnen Bitten sind leicht Parallelen in jüdischen Gebeten, etwa im Achtzehn-Bitten-Gebet, zu finden. Im ganzen aber ist das Vaterunser durchaus unverwechselbar in seiner Kürze, Präzision und Schlichtheit. Ein neues unsakrales Beten, nicht in der hebräischen Sakralsprache, sondern in der aramäischen Muttersprache, ohne die üblichen pompösen rituellen Anreden und Huldigungen Gottes. Ein sehr persönliches Beten, das doch die Beter durch die Anrede »Unser Vater« intensiv zusammenschließt. Ein sehr einfaches Bittgebet, aber ganz konzentriert auf das Wesentliche: auf die Sache Gottes (daß sein Name geheiligt werde, sein Reich komme und sein Wille geschehe), die unlöslich verbunden erscheint mit der Sache des Menschen (seine leibliche Sorge, seine Schuld, die Versuchung und Gewalt des Bösen).

Alles eine vorbildliche Realisierung dessen, was Jesus gegenüber dem wortreichen Beten gesagt hat: nicht durch Plappern vieler Worte Erhörung finden zu wollen, als ob der Vater nicht schon unsere Bedürfnisse wüßte[38]. Dies eine Aufforderung, nicht etwa das Bittgebet zu unterlassen und sich auf Lob und Preis zu beschränken, wie die Stoiker aus Gottes Allwissenheit und Allmacht folgerten. Eine Aufforderung vielmehr, im Bewußtsein von Gottes Nähe in unbeirrbarem Vertrauen ganz menschlich unermüdlich zu drängen wie der unverschämte Freund in der Nacht[39], wie die unerschrockene Witwe vor dem Richter[40]. Nirgendwo taucht die Frage der unerhörten Gebete auf; die Erhörung ist zugesichert[41]. Die Erfahrung des Nichterhörtwerdens soll nicht zum Schweigen, sondern zu erneutem Bitten führen. Immer jedoch unter der Voraussetzung, daß sein und nicht unser Wille geschehe[42]: hier liegt das Geheimnis der Gebetserhörung.

Jesus hat das Gebet fern von den Augen der Öffentlichkeit empfohlen, sogar in der Abgeschiedenheit der profanen Vorratskammer[43]. Jesus selber hat so gebetet: Sosehr die meisten Stellen in den synoptischen Evangelien redaktionelle Eintragungen des Lukas in das Markusevangelium sind[44], so berichtet doch schon das Markusevangelium vom stundenlangen Beten Jesu außerhalb der liturgischen Gebetszeiten in der Einsamkeit[45]. Jesus selber hat gedankt: Sosehr die johanneisch klingende Fortsetzung von gegenseitigem Erkennen des Vaters und des Sohnes in ihrer Authentizität umstritten ist, sowenig das unmittelbar vorausgehende Dankgebet, welches allen Mißerfolgen zum Trotz den Vater preist, daß er »solches« vor Weisen und Klugen verborgen und es Unmündigen, Ungebildeten, Geringen, Anspruchslosen geoffenbart hat[46].

Doch hier machen wir nun eine neue überraschende Feststellung. Zahlreich sind die Stellen, wo Jesus »mein Vater (im Himmel)« und dann auch »dein Vater« oder »euer Vater« sagt. Aber in allen Evangelien gibt es keine einzige Stelle, wo sich Jesus mit seinen Jüngern zu einem »Unser Vater« zusammenschließt. Ist diese grundsätzliche *Unterscheidung von »mein« und »euer« Vater* christologischer Stil der Gemeinde[47]? Man kann zumindest ebensogut der Meinung sein, daß dieser sehr bestimmte Sprachgebrauch deshalb im ganzen Neuen Testament so beständig ist, weil er, wie es die Evangelien deutlich machen, schon für Jesus selbst charakteristisch war: als Ausdruck nämlich seiner Sendung[48]. Es geht zu weit, wenn man aufgrund des einen rätselhaften johanneisch (?) klingenden Logions Mt 11, 27 par (wie dieser »Aerolith aus dem johanneischen Himmel« in die Synopse fallen konnte, hat bisher niemand erklärt) auf einen einmaligen Vorgang der Offenbarungsübermittlung (vermutlich bei der Taufe Jesu) schließt, selbst wenn man mehr als frei übersetzt: »Alles (= die volle Offenbarung) ist mir von meinem Vater überliefert. Und *wie* nur ein Vater seinen Sohn (wirklich) erkennt, *so* erkennt nur ein Sohn seinen Vater (wirklich) und wem der Sohn es offenbaren will[49].« Aber kann man andererseits leugnen, daß Jesu gesamte Botschaft von Gottes Reich und Wille orientiert ist an Gott als dem »Vater«?

Eine Überinterpretation der Gottesrede »Abba« ist auf Grund des alltäglichen Klangs des Wortes zu vermeiden. Jesus selber hat sich wohl nie einfach als »der Sohn« bezeichnet. Ja, er hat eine direkte Identifikation mit Gott, eine Vergötterung, in aller Ausdrücklichkeit abgelehnt: »Was nennst du mich gut? Niemand ist gut als Gott allein[50].« Aber andererseits sagte er nie wie die alttestamentlichen Propheten: »So spricht der Herr« oder »Spruch Jahwes«. Er spricht vielmehr – was ohne Parallele in der jüdischen Umwelt ist und zu Recht auf den vorösterlichen Jesus zurückgeführt wird – mit einem emphatischen »Ich« oder gar »Ich aber sage euch«. Kann man sich aufgrund der Quellen der Einsicht verschließen, daß dieser Künder des Vatergottes aus einer ungewöhnlichen Verbundenheit mit ihm heraus gelebt und gewirkt hat? Daß eine besondere Gotteserfahrung seine Botschaft vom Reich und Willen Gottes getragen hat? Daß sein ungeheurer Anspruch, seine souveräne Sicherheit und selbstverständliche Direktheit ohne eine sehr eigenartige Unmittelbarkeit zu Gott, seinem Vater und unserem Vater, nicht denkbar ist?

Offensichtlich ist Jesus öffentlicher *Sach-Walter Gottes* nicht nur in einem äußerlich-juristischen Sinn: nicht nur ein Beauftragter, Bevollmächtigter, Anwalt Gottes. Sondern Sach-Walter in einem zutiefst innerlich-existentiellen Sinn: ein persönlicher Botschafter, Treuhänder, Vertrauter, Freund Gottes. In ihm wurde der Mensch ohne allen Zwang, aber unausweichlich und unmittelbar mit jener letzten Wirklichkeit konfrontiert, die ihn zur Entscheidung über das letzte Wonach und Wohin herausfordert. Von dieser letzten Wirklichkeit scheint er angetrieben zu sein in all seinem Leben und Handeln: gegenüber dem religiös-politischen System und seiner Oberschicht, gegenüber Gesetz, Kult und Hierarchie, gegenüber Institution und Tradition, Familienbanden und Parteibindungen. Aber auch gegenüber den Opfern dieses Systems, den leidenden, beiseitegeschobenen, getretenen, schuldiggewordenen und gescheiterten Menschen aller Art, für die er erbarmend Partei ergreift. Von dieser letzten Wirklichkeit scheint sein Leben durchleuchtet zu sein: wenn er Gott als den Vater verkündet, wenn er die religiösen Ängste und Vorurteile seiner Zeit nicht teilt, wenn er sich mit dem religiös unwissenden Volk solidarisiert. Auch wenn er die Kranken nicht als Sünder behandelt und Gott den Vater nicht als Feind des Lebens verdächtigt sehen will, wenn er die Besessenen von den psychischen Zwängen befreit und den Teufelskreis von seelischer Störung, Teufelsglauben und gesellschaftlicher Ächtung durchbricht. Aus dieser Wirklichkeit scheint er ganz und gar zu leben: wenn er die Herrschaft dieses Gottes verkündet und die menschlichen Herrschaftsverhältnisse nicht einfach hinnimmt, wenn er die Frauen in der Ehe nicht der Willkür der Männer ausgeliefert haben will, wenn er die Kinder gegen die Erwachsenen, die Armen gegen die Reichen, überhaupt die Kleinen gegen die Großen in Schutz nimmt. Auch wenn er sich sogar für die religiös Andersgläubigen, die politisch Kompromittierten, die moralischen Versager, die sexuell Ausgenützten, die an den Rand der Gesellschaft Gedrängten einsetzt und ihnen Vergebung zusagt. Wenn er sich so für alle Gruppen offenhält und nicht einfach gelten läßt, was die Vertreter der offiziellen Religion und ihre Experten für unfehlbar wahr oder falsch, gut oder böse erklären.

In dieser letzten Wirklichkeit also, die er Gott, seinen Vater und unseren Vater nennt, wurzelt seine Grundhaltung, die sich mit einem Wort umschreiben läßt: seine *Freiheit,* die ansteckend wirkt und für den Einzelmenschen wie die Gesellschaft in ihrer Eindimensionalität eine wirklich *andere Dimension* eröffnet: eine reale Alternative mit anderen Werten, Normen und Idealen. Ein echter qualitativer Überstieg zu einem neuen Bewußtsein, einem neuen Lebensziel und Lebensweg und damit auch zu einer neuen Gesellschaft in Freiheit und Gerechtigkeit. Ein wahres Transzendieren, das eben nicht ein Transzendieren ohne Transzendenz sein kann, sondern ein *Transzendieren aus der Transzendenz in die Transzendenz.*

Wir rühren bei Jesu Bezug zum Vater an Jesu letztes Geheimnis. Die Quellen geben uns keinen Einblick in Jesu Inneres. Psychologie und Bewußtseinsphilosophie helfen uns nicht weiter. Dies aber wird man sagen dürfen: So wenig Jesus selber den prononcierten Sohnestitel in Anspruch genommen hat und so wenig eine nachösterliche Gottessohn-Christologie in die vorösterlichen Texte eingetragen werden darf, so wenig kann doch übersehen werden, wie sehr die nachösterliche Bezeichnung Jesu als »Sohn Gottes« im vorösterlichen Jesus seinen realen Anhalt hat. Jesus deutete in seinem ganzen Verkündigen und Verhalten *Gott.* Aber mußte dann von diesem anders verkündigten Gott her nicht auch *Jesus* in einem anderen Licht erscheinen? Wer immer sich auf Jesus in unbeirrbarem Vertrauen einließ, dem veränderte sich in ungeahnter, befreiender Weise das, was er bisher als »Gott« gesehen hat. Aber wenn sich einer durch Jesus auf diesen Gott und Vater einließ, mußte sich dem nicht auch umgekehrt der verändern, als den er bisher Jesus gesehen hat?

Es war ein Faktum: Die eigentümlich neue Verkündigung und Anrede Gottes als des Vaters warf ihr Licht zurück auf den, der ihn so eigentümlich neu verkündigte und anredete. Und wie man schon damals von Jesus nicht sprechen konnte, ohne von diesem Gott und Vater zu sprechen, so war es in der Folge schwierig, von diesem Gott und Vater zu sprechen, ohne von Jesus zu sprechen. Nicht bestimmten Namen und Titeln gegenüber, wohl aber diesem Jesus gegenüber fiel die Entscheidung des Glaubens, wenn es um den einen wahren Gott ging. Wie man mit Jesus umging, entschied darüber, wie man zu Gott steht, wofür man Gott hält, welchen Gott man hat. Im Namen und in der Kraft des einen Gottes Israels hat Jesus gesprochen und gehandelt. Und schließlich für ihn hat er sich umbringen lassen.

3. Das Ende

In fast allen wichtigen Fragen – Ehe, Familie, Nation, dem Verhältnis zur Autorität, dem Umgang mit anderen Menschen und Gruppen – denkt Jesus anders, als man das gewohnt ist. Der Konflikt um das System, um Gesetz und Ordnung, Kult und Bräuche, Ideologie und Praxis, um die herrschenden Normen, die zu respektierenden Grenzen und zu meidenden Leute, der Streit um den offiziellen Gott des Gesetzes, des Tempels, der Nation und Jesu Anspruch drängen dem Ende entgegen. Es sollte sichtbar werden, wer recht hat. Ein Konflikt auf Leben und Tod war es geworden. Der in seiner Großzügigkeit, Zwanglosigkeit, Freiheit so herausfordernde Kämpfer wird zum schweigenden Dulder.

Angesichts des Todes

Ein Ahnen des Todes bestimmt alle Evangelien von Anfang an: nachösterliche Tendenz, diese Geschichte als Leidensgeschichte zu schildern? Über eines hat man sich gegen die frühere phantasievoll historisierende und psychologisierende Leben-Jesu-Forschung geeinigt: Einen »galiläischen Frühling« voll des Erfolges vor der Jerusalemer Katastrophe hat Jesus nicht erlebt. Schon der nicht am Ende, sondern zu Beginn des ersten Evangeliums berichtete Todesbeschluß der Gegner[1] hätte jede Frühlingsromantik stören müssen. Aber auch die am Anfang der Evangelien berichteten Versuchungsgeschichten machen deutlich, daß Jesu

Leben und Wirken von Versuchungen, Anfechtungen, Zweifeln keineswegs frei war.

Unterdessen hat man freilich herausgefunden, daß der zeitlich-geographische *Rahmen*[2] schon des Markusevangeliums – Wirksamkeit in Galiläa mit Kafarnaum als Stammplatz, kurzer Aufenthalt in heidnischem Gebiet, Petrus-Bekenntnis und Beginn des Weges nach Jerusalem, Einzug, Aufenthalt und Passion – eine literarische Funktion hat und die Einzelheiten nicht von vornherein als historischer Bericht genommen werden dürfen. Die meisten Erzählungen ließen sich umstellen, wie denn Lukas und Mattäus teilweise anders gliedern. Sowenig wie das Petrus-Bekenntnis, so kann auch die zeitweilige Flucht vor Herodes Antipas ins Gebiet des phönizischen Tyrus nach Norden in die Gegend von Cäsarea Philippi und in das unter direkter römischer Militärverwaltung stehende »Land der zehn Städte« jenseits des Gennesaret-Sees (in der Nähe der heutigen Golan-Höhen) als historisch gesichert gelten, wenn auch ein gelegentliches Durchwandern heidnischen Gebietes nicht ausgeschlossen werden kann. Was aber fraglos feststeht: Galiläa als der Hauptwirkplatz Jesu und dann als die entscheidende Wende in seinem Leben der – nach den Synoptikern einmalige – Zug nach Jerusalem. Daß Jesus von Anfang an Zustimmung und Ablehnung, Zulauf und bittere Feindschaft erfuhr, dürfte von den Evangelien ebenfalls historisch getreu berichtet sein.

Wollte Jesus seine Botschaft dem ganzen Volk ankünden, dann mußte er sich vor allem im religiösen Zentrum stellen: in der Schicksalsstadt Israels, der heiligen Stadt Gottes und Stadt des großen Königs[3]. Hier sollte das Volk in letzter Stunde mit der Botschaft vom Reich und Willen Gottes konfrontiert werden. Die Jünger hofften, so berichtet Lukas mehrfach[4], daß mit dem Zug nach Jerusalem das Reich Gottes erscheinen werde. Hier also mußte die Entscheidung fallen.

Daß Jesus nur nach Jerusalem ging, um dort zu sterben, dürfte nachträgliche Interpretation sein. Das gilt auch von den alten palästinisch-judenchristlichen – schon bei Markus dreimal wiederholten[5] – *Leidens- und Auferstehungsankündigungen* des »Menschensohnes«, von denen die dritte geradezu ein Passions- und Auferstehungssummarium liefert. Sie sollen – mit Bedacht über die Geschichte redaktionell verteilt – Gottes geheimnisvollen Plan, auch Jesu wunderbares Vorauswissen, schließlich die Freiwilligkeit seines Leidens und seinen Gehorsam gegenüber der Schrift zum Ausdruck bringen. Im Stil der jüdischen Apokalyptik vaticinia ex eventu: Weissagungen gestaltet aufgrund des Eingetroffenseins, formuliert nach und gemäß den Ereignissen. So nennt man in der Fachsprache die schon im Alten Testament und in der antiken Literatur überhaupt häufige literarische Gattung. Diese Ankündigungen stehen im Dienst der Verkündigung, des Kerygmas, sind also nicht Weissagungen, Voraussagen im strengen Sinn. Sie sind »kerygmatische Formeln«, die Jesu Leidensweg als Erfüllung von Gottes Heilsplan und nicht als blindes Schicksal erscheinen lassen. Sie sind nicht scharfsichtige Prognosen Jesu selbst, sondern Passionsdeutungen der nachösterlichen Christenheit.

Soll das heißen, daß Jesus selbst mit seinem Tod überhaupt nicht gerechnet hat? Das ist eine andere Frage. Soll er so naiv gewesen sein, daß er gar nicht ahnte, was auf ihn zukam? Christologisches Interesse muß in den Evangelien überall einkalkuliert werden, aber historische Skepsis kann unkritisch werden. Um die *Gefahr eines gewaltsamen Endes* zu erkennen, bedurfte es keines übernatürlichen Wissens, sondern nur des nüchternen Blicks für die Realitäten.

Aufgrund seiner radikalen Botschaft, welche die frommen Selbstsicherungen des Menschen und der Gesellschaft und die gesamte überlieferte religiöse Ordnung in Frage stellte und von Anfang an auch Widerstand hervorrief, mußte Jesus mit schweren Zusammenstößen und heftigen Reaktionen der religiösen und eventuell auch politischen Machthaber unter äußersten Konsequenzen gerade im Zentrum der Macht rechnen. Vorwürfe wegen Sabbatverletzung, Gesetzesverachtung, Gotteslästerung mußten ernstgenommen werden. Der Zug des ketzerischen »Propheten«, der das gläubige Volk verwirrte und verunsicherte, aus der Provinz in die Hauptstadt bedeutete in jedem Fall eine Herausforderung der herrschenden Kreise. Noch bei Johannes kann man vernehmen: »Lies nach und erkenne, daß kein Prophet aus Galiläa kommt[6].« Wenn der bezüglich des friedlichen Reitiers symbolisch interpretierte und legendarisch umrankte Einzug in Jerusalem vermutlich nicht so triumphale Ausmaße hatte, wie nachher geschildert wurde: Wer als dämonischer Wundertäter, wer als falscher Prophet, ja als Gotteslästerer verdächtigt wurde, hatte mit der Todesstrafe zu rechnen. Es genügte schon, daß einer nach einmaliger Verwarnung vor Zeugen vorsätzlich den Sabbat brach, um des Todes schuldig zu sein (auffällig bei Markus nach dem ersten Sabbatbruch Verwarnung, nach dem zweiten sogleich Todesbeschluß[7]).

Gewiß, ein jüdisches Gericht konnte – zumindest ist dies umstritten – Todesurteile in Judäa und Samaria nicht vollstrekken; das ius gladii lag anscheinend in der Hand der römischen Besatzungsmacht. Aber abgesehen davon, daß die führenden jüdischen Kreise in bestimmten Fällen etwa gegen Volksaufrührer und Volksaufstände mit den Römern gemeinsame Interessen hatten und der Kollaboration keineswegs abgeneigt waren, so war die Situation zumindest in Galiläa verschieden: Der jüdische Landesherr dort, von Roms Gnaden, konnte Todesurteile aussprechen und vollstrecken. Die Verhaftung und Enthauptung des Täufers Johannes durch Herodes Antipas auf der Festung Machärus – entweder weil er des Herodes Heirat mit seiner Schwägerin Herodias öffentlich mißbilligt hatte[8] oder wahrscheinlicher, weil Herodes das Wirken des Johannes politisch verstand und die Möglichkeit eines Aufstandes befürchtete[9] – steht historisch fest. Sie war für Jesus, der zweifellos davon wußte und offenbar vielfach als des Johannes »Nachfolger« galt, in jedem Fall eine äußerst ernste Warnung. Auch eine nicht politische Sammelbewegung konnte den Machthabern politisch gefährlich erscheinen. Die auffälligerweise gerade Pharisäern zugeschriebene Mahnung, Herodes trachte auch ihm nach dem Leben[10], hatte einen nur zu realen Hintergrund. Jesu aufsehenerregender Einzug in Jerusalem aber besagte erhöhte Gefährdung. Und die in ihrem Kern wohl doch historische Prophetentat der Tempelreinigung bedeutete als Anmaßung im Heiligtum ebenfalls Lebensbedrohung. Das Prophetenschicksal – zumindest Jesaja, Jeremia, Amos, Micha und Sacharja galten als Märtyrer, und man baute in Jesu Tagen Grabmäler zur Sühne für ihre Ermordung – mußte Jesus zu denken geben[11]. Vielleicht auch das Schicksal des Gottesknechtes in Deuterojesaja, der für viele dahingegeben wird[12]. Wenn Jesus schon mit der Möglichkeit eines gewaltsamen Todes rechnen mußte, dann dürfte er auch eine Deutung dieses Schicksals gesucht haben. Manche halten deshalb auch ein Wort wie das vom Menschensohn, der nicht gekommen ist, bedient zu werden, sondern zu dienen und sein Leben zu geben als Lösegeld für die vielen[13], für ein im Kern ursprüngliches Wort Jesu, das darüber hinaus noch bestätigt wird durch die Abendmahlsüberlieferung[14].

Aufgrund dieser Tatsachen fällt es schwer, das gesamte Material, welches Jesu künftiges Leiden zum Gegenstand hat, kritisch zu eliminieren: also nicht nur die Leidensweissagungen, sondern auch die zahlreichen Drohworte und Anklagen gegen die Mörder der Gottesboten, gegen die Erbauer von Prophetengräbern, die den Propheten zu ermorden trachten, gegen das prophetenmordende Jerusalem, gegen den Verräter. Ebenso die Worte über das Schicksal Jesu, den Heimatlosen, die bevorstehende Trennung, das Täufer- und Prophetenschicksal, das Passalamm, den Kelch und das Verbrecherbegräbnis (was zum Teil nicht einmal eintraf). Und schließlich auch alle die Bild- und Rätselworte vom ermordeten Hirten und der zerstreuten Herde, vom entrissenen Bräutigam, vom Lösegeld, von Kelch und Taufe, vom Tempelschlußstein, von der kommenden Schwertzeit ...[15]. Auch wenn man sich kritischer Zurückhaltung befleißigt, so wird man nicht ausschließen können, daß etwa die kürzeste, unbestimmteste und sprachlich älteste Variante der Leidensweissagungen[16] einen historischen Kern hat, nämlich, daß Jesus den Menschen ausgeliefert werden wird. Auch das im Zusammenhang der Leidensankündigung ausgesprochene Satanswort an Petrus[17] dürfte nicht erfunden sein.

Wie immer man sich zur Authentizität des einen oder anderen Wortes stellt, festgehalten werden darf: Jesus, der aufgrund seines Redens und Handelns sein Leben vielfach verwirkt hatte, mußte mit einem gewaltsamen Ende rechnen. Nicht daß er den Tod direkt provoziert oder gewollt hätte. Aber er *lebte angesichts des Todes*. Und er hat den Tod frei – in jener großen Freiheit, die Treue zu sich selbst und Treue zum Auftrag, zu Selbstverantwortung und Gehorsam vereint – auf sich genommen, weil er darin den Willen Gottes erkannte: Es war nicht nur ein Erleiden des Todes, sondern eine Hergabe und Hingabe des Lebens. Dies muß man sich vor Augen halten angesichts jener Szene am Vorabend seiner Hinrichtung, auf die der spezifisch christliche Gottesdienst in den ganzen zwei Jahrtausenden zurückgeführt wird: das letzte Mahl.

Ein letztes Mahl

Daß Jesus wie zumindest einige seiner Jünger *getauft* war, aber daß er selber, und nach den synoptischen Evangelien[18] auch seine Jünger, vor Ostern nicht getauft hat und daß auch der Taufbefehl des österlichen Herrn historisch nichts Verifizierbares liefert[19]: das wird heute in der kritischen Exegese allgemein angenommen. Allgemein angenommen wird heute freilich zugleich: daß es keine tauflose Anfangszeit der Kirche gegeben und daß man schon in der Urgemeinde bald nach Ostern zu taufen begonnen hat. Ein widersprüchlicher Befund? Er findet seine Erklärung darin, daß die Gemeinde auch ohne bestimmte Weisung oder gar »Einsetzung« eines Taufritus des Glaubens sein konnte, den Willen Jesu zu erfüllen, wenn sie tauft. In Erinnerung nämlich an das von Jesus bejahte Taufen des Johannes. In Erinnerung an Jesu und der Jünger Taufe selbst. Als Antwort also zwar nicht auf bestimmte Auftragsworte Jesu, wohl aber auf seine Botschaft als ganze, die zu Umkehr und Glauben aufruft und Sündenvergebung und Heil verheißt. So tauft denn die Gemeinde im Sinn und Geist Jesu: in Erfüllung seines Willens, in Antwort auf seine Botschaft und deshalb auf seinen Namen[20].

War es vielleicht beim *Abendmahl* ähnlich: daß Jesus selber kein solches Mahl gefeiert hat, wohl aber die nachösterliche Gemeinde ein solches feierte »zu seinem Gedächtnis«, im Sinn und Geist und so im Auftrag Jesu? Die Mahlfeier der Kirche ließe sich auf diese Weise ebensogut rechtfertigen wie ihre Taufe. Doch ist der Befund hier komplexer. Taufe und Abendmahl lassen sich historisch gesehen nicht einfach auf dieselbe Stufe stellen. Freilich, daß Jesus ein Abendmahl »eingesetzt« hat, läßt sich füglich bezweifeln; der bei Paulus sich findende zweimalige Wiederholungsbefehl fehlt denn auch bei Markus. Aber daß Jesus ein Abschiedsessen, ein letztes Abendmahl mit seinen Jüngern *gefeiert* hat, läßt sich aufgrund der Quellen so leicht nicht bezweifeln.

In vier Varianten wird überliefert[21], daß Jesus vor seiner Verhaftung mit seinen Jüngern ein gemeinsames Mahl gefeiert hat. Das ist von Paulus eindeutig bezeugt für den Beginn seiner Missionstätigkeit in Korinth in den vierziger Jahren[22]. Er beruft sich aber dabei auf eine Tradition, die nach ihm selber auf den Herrn zurückgeht: die er in Damaskus, Jerusalem oder spätestens Antiochien, also direkt oder indirekt von der Urgemeinde empfangen hat und für die es noch lebende Augenzeugen gab. Der zweite Hauptstrang der Überlieferung, der Markus- und dann Mattäus-Bericht – in einzelnen semitischen Wendungen vielleicht noch ursprünglicher, aber in der Endfassung wohl jünger – weicht sprachlich zu sehr vom paulinischen Bericht ab, als daß beide eine gemeinsame griechische Quelle haben könnten. Andererseits stimmt dieser markinische Bericht in der Substanz so sehr mit dem paulinischen überein, daß beide auf eine gemeinsame aramäische oder hebräische Quelle zurückgehen müssen. Das Alter, die Breite und die Bestimmtheit der Abendmahlsüberlieferung – die lukanische Fassung ist eine Mischform aus der paulinischen und der markinischen – lassen jedenfalls kaum Raum für den Zweifel an der *Faktizität* eines letzten Mahles Jesu mit seinen Jüngern. Das eigentliche Problem – sehr erschwert durch die liturgische Überformung der Berichte – liegt in der Bestimmung der *Sinndeutung* dieses letzten Mahles.

Dies dürfte selbstverständlich sein: Man kann nicht ohne weiteres Jesus selber zuschreiben, was sich später die Urgemeinde, die hellenistischen Gemeinden oder gar die nachherige kirchliche Dogmatik unter dem Abendmahl Jesu vorgestellt haben. In den aus dem Mittelalter stammenden Abendmahlsstreitigkeiten insbesondere hat man sich das Verständnis des Abendmahles Jesu weithin dadurch verstellt, daß man sofort von den Deuteworten über Brot und Wein ausging und das letzte Mahl isoliert betrachtete. Man hat übersehen, wie grundlegend für die gesamte Verkündigung Jesu gerade die gemeinsamen Mahlzeiten waren: wie diese dadurch, daß auch Diskriminierte und Deklassierte nicht ausgeschlossen waren, eine zeichenhafte Bedeutung erhielten für das kommende Reich und die schon im voraus angebotene Gnade und Vergebung. Wenn für den Täufer die Bußtaufe die charakteristische Zeichenhandlung war, so für Jesus und seine Botschaft das in fröhlicher Stimmung gehaltene Festessen, in welchem man die gemeinsame Zugehörigkeit zum kommenden Reich feierte. Auch die Brotvermehrungsgeschichten bezeugen dies indirekt[23]. Ein letztes Mahl, ein Abschiedsessen Jesu kann sachgemäß nur auf dem Hintergrund dieser langen *Reihe von Mahlzeiten* gesehen werden, die von seinen Jüngern auch nach Ostern fortgesetzt wurden.

Von daher ist bereits zu verstehen, daß Jesus mit diesem Mahl nicht eine neue Liturgie stiften wollte. Noch einmal sollte sich die Gemeinschaft des Mahles mit denen verwirklichen, die so lange mit ihm gewandert, gegessen und getrunken haben. In der Erwartung des kommenden Reiches und seines Abschiedes wollte Jesus mit den Seinen dieses Mahl halten. Wenn ein Satz im Abendmahlsbericht auf Jesus selber zurückgeht, dann der in der späteren liturgischen Überlieferung schon bei Paulus nicht mehr übernommene Satz, daß Jesus vom Gewächs des Weinstockes nicht mehr trinken wird bis zu dem Tag, wo er es neu trinken wird im Reiche Gottes[24].

Ob dieses Mahl ein rituelles Passamahl war (so Markus allerdings nur in der Rahmenerzählung, nicht im Mahlbericht selbst) oder nicht (so Johannes), ist dagegen von zweitrangiger Bedeutung. Gründe gibt es für beides. Vor allem aber die schwache Bezeugung und die Unwahrscheinlichkeit einer Einberufung des Gerichts und der Hinrichtung Jesu am darauffolgenden Passafest machen die johanneische Datierung wahrscheinlicher und lassen die Passadatierung eher der Gemeinde zuschreiben, die das Abendmahl Jesu als Ersatz des Passamahles verstehen wollte. Im Schatten des Passagedankens stand das Mahl auch dann, wenn es eine Nacht früher gefeiert worden wäre.

Aber ob Passamahl oder nicht: Die besonderen *Worte Jesu* fielen jedenfalls nicht, wie eine isolierte Deutung voraussetzte, als heilige Einsetzungsworte gleichsam vom Himmel. Sie paßten sich leicht in den rituell geregelten – und zum Teil noch heute in jüdischen Familien üblichen – Ablauf eines festlichen jüdischen Mahles ein. Das Brotwort im Anschluß an das Tischgebet vor der Hauptmahlzeit: wo der Hausvater über dem flachen, runden Brot den Lobspruch spricht, es bricht und die Stücke des einen Brotes den Tischgenossen verteilt. Das Weinwort dann im Anschluß an das Dankgebet nach dem Mahl: wo der Hausvater den Becher mit Wein kreisen und jeden daraus trinken läßt. Eine Geste der Gemeinschaft, die jeder antike Mensch auch ohne begleitende Worte verstehen konnte.

Jesus brauchte also keinen neuen Ritus zu erfinden, sondern nur mit einem alten Ritus eine Ankündigung und neue Deutung zu verbinden: Er deutete das Brot und – zumindest nach der markinischen Fassung – auch den Wein auf sich selbst. Angesichts seines drohenden Todes deutete er Brot und Wein als gleichsam prophetische Zeichen auf seinen Tod und damit auf all das, was er war, was er getan und gewollt hat: auf das Opfer, die Hingabe seines Lebens. Wie dieses Brot so wird auch sein Leib gebrochen, wie dieser rote Wein so wird auch sein Blut vergossen: das ist mein Leib, mein Blut! Womit beidemal ganzheitlich die ganze Person und ihre Hingabe gemeint ist. Und wie der Hausvater den Essenden und Trinkenden unter Brot und Wein Anteil am Tischsegen gibt, so gibt Jesus den Seinen Anteil an seinem in den Tod gegebenen Leib (»Leib« oder »Fleisch« meinen im Hebräischen oder Aramäischen immer den ganzen Menschen) und an seinem für »viele« (einschlußweise = alle) vergossenen Blut.

So werden die Jünger in Jesu Schicksal hineingenommen. Im Zeichen des Mahles wird eine neue, bleibende Gemeinschaft Jesu mit den Seinen aufgerichtet, ja ein *»Neuer Bund«* begründet. Noch mehr als in der markinischen steht in der (ursprünglicheren?) paulinischen Fassung »Dieser Kelch ist der Neue Bund in meinem Blut«[25] der Gedanke des Neuen Bundes im Vordergrund: der Bund, der in der (durch Blutbesprengung und ein Mahl vollzogenen) Bundesschließung am Sinai vorgebildet ist[26], der von Jeremia für die Heilszeit geweissagt wurde[27] und der zur Zeit Jesu auch in Qumran, wo man ein tägliches Gemeinschaftsmahl mit Segnung von Brot und Wein kennt, eine wichtige Rolle spielte. Das vergossene Blut, der hingegebene Leib Jesu also als Zeichen des neuen Bundesschlusses zwischen Gott und seinem Volk.

Daß schon Jesus sein Sterben als sühnende *Stellvertretung* für die Vielen verstanden hat, im Sinne also des unschuldigen, geduldig getragenen, freiwilligen, von Gott gewollten und darum stellvertretenden sühnenden Leidens und Sterbens des Gottesknechtes von Jesaja 53[28], dürfte nachösterliche Deutung sein. Daß unschuldigem Sterben, unschuldig vergossenem Blut Sühnecharakter zukommt, ist dem damaligen jüdischen Denken freilich nicht unbekannt.

Sicher unsachgemäß ist jedoch die in der Reformationszeit umstrittene Frage nach der Bedeutung des »ist«, da weder die Gemeinde noch Jesus selber unseren Begriff einer Substanz hatten. Man fragte nicht, was ein Ding ist, sondern wozu es dient. Nicht woraus es besteht, sondern was seine Funktion ist. Paradoxerweise war der ursprünglich aramäische Satz aller Wahrscheinlichkeit nach überhaupt ohne dieses Wort formuliert worden, um das der jahrhundertelange Streit ging. Man sagte in der Ursprache einfach: »Dies – mein Leib[29]!«

Alte Gemeinschaft also wird durch die Handlung und das Wort des Mahles bestätigt, und zugleich *neue Gemeinschaft* verheißen: »koinonia«, »communio« mit Jesus und untereinander. Abschied vom Meister wird dem Jüngerkreis angekündigt, und doch bleibt die Gemeinschaft untereinander und mit ihm begründet: bis sich im Gottesreich die Tischgemeinschaft erneuert. Vereint sollen sie bleiben, auch in der Zeit seiner Abwesenheit. Nicht umsonst hat man später die Idee der Kirche mit Jesu Abendmahl in Verbindung gebracht[30].

Stationen

Die *Passionsgeschichte* ist hier nicht zu referieren. Leichter wird sie in einem der Evangelien, am besten zunächst nach Markus, nachgelesen[31]. In bezug auf die Reihenfolge stimmt hier sogar einmal Johannes, der einen älteren Passionsbericht benutzt haben muß, mit den drei Synoptikern überein: Verrat des Judas, letztes Mahl mit Bezeichnung des Verräters, Verhaftung und Verhör, Verhandlung vor Pilatus und Kreuzigung. Zu diesen Abschnitten, die auch bei Johannes an gleicher Stelle erscheinen, kommen noch die Gethsemane-Szene und die Verleugnung des Petrus samt ihrer Ansage.

Die Gemeinde hatte an den Begebenheiten im Zusammenhang mit Verhaftung, Prozeßverfahren und Hinrichtung verständlicherweise größtes Interesse. So ist denn die Passionsgeschichte sehr viel ausführlicher gestaltet als alles Vorausgehende. Markus verlängert sie noch in die Vorgeschichte hinein, so daß man sein Evangelium nicht ganz zu Unrecht als »Passionsgeschichte mit ausführlicher Einleitung« bezeichnet hat. Die Bedeutung der Passion tritt hier deutlich hervor und wird durch die ruhig distanzierte Erzählweise unterstrichen. Von Anfang an muß sie mit ihren einzelnen Stationen in einem geschlossenen Zusammenhang erzählt worden sein: sei es im Gottesdienst, sei es in der Unterweisung, einzelne zugewachsene Stücke vielleicht bei anderen Gelegenheiten. Während aber Markus im Kreuz und in der Übernahme der Gottverlassenheit die eigentliche Offenbarung sieht, betont Mattäus mehr Jesu Hoheit und die Vollmacht der Kirche, Lukas schließlich das Leiden des Gerechten als Vorbild für die Jünger. Bei allen Evangelisten wird dabei die Tendenz sichtbar, durch die Passionsgeschichte die Gemeinde vor Anfechtung und Abfall zu bewahren[32].

Damit ist aber auch schon deutlich gemacht: einen Polizeibericht oder ein Prozeßprotokoll wie etwa die Prozeßakten der Jeanne d'Arc haben wir nicht vor uns. Man wollte von diesem Leiden und Sterben gar nicht neutral und unbeteiligt berichten. Man glaubte an den, der diesen furchtbaren Weg gegangen war, und dieser Glaube sollte als *Appell zum Glauben* durchaus in der Erzählung durchscheinen. Geschichtliche Erinnerungen und nachösterliche Glaubenserfahrungen ließen sich nicht trennen. Man zögerte deshalb nicht, selbst Legendäres aufzunehmen, wundersame Ereignisse, Heilungen, Engelserscheinungen, sogar kosmisch-apokalyptische Wunder, kurz alles, was die Bedeutung dieser Geschichte offenbar machen konnte: daß Gott auch in diesen erschütternden Ereignissen und gerade hier seine Hand im Spiel hatte. Daß darin nicht der Zufall, sondern Gottes Plan und Vorsehung walteten. Daß die Menschen in all ihrer Eigenmächtigkeit und Schuld im Grunde doch die Werkzeuge Gottes blieben. Und vor allem, daß dieser Jesus durch diesen schändlichen letzten Weg nicht widerlegt, sondern vielmehr als Messias bestätigt wurde.

Dieser Absicht des Glaubens dient die unauffällige *Stilisierung* der Berichte mit Hilfe einer am Alten Testament orientierten eigentümlichen, erhaben-feierlichen und doch realistischen Sprache, die – ähnlich wie in musikalischer Gestaltung die Passionen J. S. Bachs – die Bedeutsamkeit des Geschehens bis in die alltäglichen, brutalen, unmenschlichen Details hinein spürbar werden läßt. Dieser Absicht des Glaubens dienen zahlreiche Anspielungen und ausdrückliche Zitate aus dem *Alten Testament,* insbesondere aus den Psalmen 22; 31; 69 und aus den Gottesknechtliedern[33]. Vom Einzug in Jerusalem, für den das Sacharja-Wort vom demütig auf einem Eselsfüllen zur Tochter Zion ziehenden König zitiert wird[34], bis zur Kleiderverlosung und Verspottung unter dem Kreuz, wofür Psalm 22 angeführt wird, soll Jesus als der erscheinen, in dem Gottes Ratschläge vollstreckt, die Schrift erfüllt wird nach dem Motto: »Der Menschensohn geht dahin, wie von ihm geschrieben steht[35].« So steht die ganze absurde Geschichte fühlbar unter dem geheimnisvollen »Muß« Gottes, wie nach Lukas der Auferweckte selbst den Emmaus-Jüngern »in allen Schriften auslegt, was über ihn handelt«: »Mußte nicht der Christus dies alles leiden, um in seine Herrlichkeit einzugehen[36]?« Den ersten Gemeinden halfen nicht zuletzt diese ständigen Verweise auf das Alte Testament, die beinahe unerträgliche Geschichte ihres Herrn und Meisters zu ertragen.

Freilich, so günstig diese stilisierende Erzählweise, die doch höchste Betroffenheit und Anteilnahme verrät und hervorruft, für den Prediger war, so schwierig macht sie es dem Historiker: wo wird rapportiert und wo interpretiert? Was ist in diesen Erzählungen *Geschichte* und was *Verkündigung,* was Historie und was Theologie? Man weiß über den so ausführlich und zusammenhängend erzählten letzten Abschnitt des Lebens Jesu weniger Sicheres, als man bei der ersten Lektüre der Evangelien annehmen möchte. Andererseits wäre es dogmatische Willkür anzunehmen, die Verkündigung habe die Geschichte völlig verdeckt und man könne nicht mehr wissen, was eigentlich geschehen sei. Auch hier kommt der ernsthafte Interpret um die freilich nicht geringe Mühe der Unterscheidung nicht herum.

In einigen Fällen macht ein einfacher Textvergleich deutlich, wie eine Erzählung ins Legendäre auswächst: Nach Markus zieht irgendeiner der Dabeistehenden das Schwert und haut dem Knecht des Hohenpriesters das Ohr ab. Nach Lukas – allgemein mehr als andere an wunderbaren Phänomenen interessiert – heilt Jesus den Verwundeten. Johannes schließlich gibt gar die Namen des Jüngers und des Knechtes an[37]. Oder: Nach Markus und Mattäus erscheint in der Gethsemane-Stunde kein Engel. Nach Lukas erscheint ein Engel, und es wird Jesu Schweiß wie Blutstropfen, die zur Erde fallen[38] usw.

Umgekehrt aber verraten kleine Belanglosigkeiten, daß die Erzählungen letztlich auf zum Teil noch bekannte Augenzeugen zurückgehen: so die sonst nicht erwähnenswerte unrühmliche Szene vom Jüngling, der bei der Verhaftung Jesu unter Zurücklassen des Mantels nackt fliehen muß[39]. Oder die Nennung der Söhne Alexander und Rufus jenes Kyrenäers Simon, der gezwungen dem Verurteilten das Kreuz (wohl den Querbalken) nachtrug[40], und die Mattäus und Lukas nicht mehr der Erwähnung wert finden[41]. Oder die Nennung der Namen der galiläischen Frauen unter dem Kreuz, bei der der Name der Mutter Jesu auffälligerweise fehlt[42]. Selbst alttestamentliche Zitationen können indirekt auf Historisches hinweisen: Die Verlosung der Kleider Jesu unter dem Kreuz las man aus Psalm 22, 19 heraus[43]; aber sie konnte auch einem bei Hinrichtung üblichen Brauch entsprechen. Die Schmach des Todes Jesu zwischen zwei Verbrechern wird mit dem Zitat Jesaja 53, 12 erträglich gemacht; aber die Erledigung mehrerer anstehender Fälle durch den für einen kurzen Aufenthalt nach Jerusalem gekommenen römischen Gouverneur ist durchaus wahrscheinlich[44]. Die vom Kopfschütteln begleitete Verspottung Jesu spielt auf Psalm 22, 8 an, aber ist psychologisch mehr als verständlich[45]. Ein Beleg aus dem Alten Testament ist also nicht von vornherein ein Argument gegen die Historizität.

Der Verweis auf diese Details soll indessen nur deutlich machen: Es ist durchaus möglich, von der verkündeten Geschichte mit Vorsicht und Scharfsicht auf die geschehene Geschichte zurückzufragen. Durch alle legendären Ausgestaltungen, Differenzen in den Berichten, alttestamentlichen Anleihen und nachträglichen christologischen Deutungen hindurch läßt sich zumindest in Umrissen – und für unsere nicht biographischen Zwecke durchaus ausreichend! – wissen, was in den verschiedenen Phasen eigentlich geschehen ist und was denn auch durch verschiedene Zeugen von den verschiedenen Konfliktsituationen zwischen

Jesus und der jüdischen und römischen Behörde und sogar zwischen Jesus und seinen Jüngern in einer oft überraschenden Übereinstimmung berichtet wird.

1. *Der Ausbruch des Konflikts:* Unmittelbarer Anlaß zur Verhaftung war nach allen Zeugnissen Jesu aufsehenerregender *Einzug in Jerusalem* kurz vor dem großen Passafest, dem Fest der Befreiung Israels aus ägyptischer Knechtschaft. Daß dieser galiläische Ketzer gerade jetzt, wo unabsehbare Pilgerscharen auch aus Galiläa – und zur Sicherheit auch der römische Gouverneur mit militärischer Verstärkung – in die Hauptstadt strömten, in Erwartung des Reiches Gottes nach Jerusalem ziehen mußte! Daß er sich gerade bei dieser Gelegenheit, wo die apokalyptischen nationalen Hoffnungen auf das Kommen des Reiches und die Befreiung von römischer Herrschaft neu aufzuleben pflegten und Zwischenfälle häufig waren, mit seiner Schar von einer bedrohlichen Anhängerschaft bejubeln lassen mußte! Daß er mit großer Wahrscheinlichkeit auch im Tempelbezirk mit Autorität aufzutreten und das Heiligtum im Hinblick auf den Anbruch des Reiches zu reinigen wagte! Daß er in Streitgesprächen – zum Teil zweifellos zeitlich und örtlich anders einzuordnen[46] – seinen Anspruch und seine Vollmacht zu verteidigen suchte[47] und dabei anscheinend auch die Zerstörung Jerusalems und des Tempels angekündigt hat[48]: das alles bedeutete doch eine offene Kampfansage an das System und seine Repräsentanten und forderte die große Kraftprobe geradezu heraus.

Was Jesus im einzelnen erwartete, wissen wir nicht. Aufgrund des Textbefundes glauben manche, er habe zwischen Kommen des Reiches (Parusie), Auferstehung und Tempelneubau nicht unterschieden; die Unterscheidung zwischen Auferstehung, Erhöhung, Wiederkunft als aufeinanderfolgenden Ereignissen sei erst nachösterliche Systematisierung[49]. Jesu ganzes Auftreten im religiösen Zentrum beweist jedenfalls, daß er in seiner Sache die Entscheidung sucht. Auf der anderen Seite mußten seine Gegner versuchen, ihn jetzt als Ketzer oder falschen Propheten, als Feind des Gesetzes, des Tempels oder auch der römischen Herrschaft zu entlarven.

2. *Der Verrat:* In der bereits zugespitzten Situation erschien den jüdischen (und vielleicht auch den römischen) Behörden schnelles Handeln angebracht. Es soll mit ihm kurzer Prozeß gemacht werden. Wegen eines möglichen Aufruhrs des Volkes müßte der

Fall noch *vor dem Fest* erledigt sein. Diese wichtige Notiz bei Markus[50] zeigt zweierlei:

a. daß die *johanneische Chronologie* wohl doch die richtige ist, da nur nach dieser der Fall vor dem Fest erledigt wird: also das letzte Abendmahl ein ganzer Tag vor dem Passavortag (= Donnerstag), dann die Hinrichtung am Passavortag, an dem im Tempel die Lämmer geschlachtet wurden, (am 14. Nisan = Freitag), schließlich das Passafest am Tag nach der Hinrichtung (= Samstag). In jedem Fall ist Jesus nach Markus und Johannes übereinstimmend am Freitag der jüdischen Passawoche im Nisan (= ungefähr unser April) – sei dieser nun der Passafesttag (15. Nisan) oder sein Vortag (14. Nisan) – hingerichtet worden[51]. Das johanneische Datum dürfte aufgrund astronomischer Berechnungen auf den 7. April des Jahres 30 fallen.

b. daß die Differenzierung zwischen *jüdischem Volk* und *Führern* ursprünglich wichtig war: Während die Synoptiker die Jesusgegner noch nach ihrer Gruppenzugehörigkeit unterscheiden, huldigt das Johannesevangelium dem verallgemeinernden und meist negativ betonten Sprachgebrauch »die Juden«. »Jude« im Johannesevangelium 71mal, in allen übrigen Evangelien zusammen nur 11mal!

Jesus »mit List«, gleichsam im Handstreich in aller Stille, zu ergreifen, ermöglichte wiederum nach übereinstimmendem Zeugnis das Angebot eines Mannes, von dem wir praktisch nichts wissen außer das eine Entscheidende, daß er Jesu Schüler, gar einer der Zwölf war. Was er genau verraten hat, insbesondere warum er eigentlich verraten hat, das wissen wir nicht. Erst Mattäus[52] gibt als Motiv des *Judas* Geldgier an und sogar, wohl von einem Sacharja-Wort inspiriert, die Summe von dreißig Silberstücken[53]. Manche meinen, »Is-kariot« meine nicht »Mann von Kariot«, sondern sei eine Verstümmelung des lateinischen »sicarius« = Dolchmann. Judas, vom zelotischen Nationalismus getrieben, habe enttäuscht mit Jesu Feinden Kontakt aufgenommen, um ihn zum Handeln zu zwingen. Aber solche Erklärungen sind reine Hypothesen, und noch andere, wie sie sich in romanhaften Leben-Jesu finden, sind reine Phantastereien. Die legendenhafte Verteufelung des Judas, den Dante zusammen mit dem Cäsar-Mörder Brutus in den untersten Kreis der Hölle verbannt, beginnt freilich schon in den späteren Evangelien[54]. Historisch könnte allerdings die Bezeichnung des Verräters beim Mahl sein[55], wobei freilich der Rahmen, Jesu Vorauswissen und das bei Markus übliche Unverständnis der Jünger, theologische Deutung sein dürften.

3. *Die Verhaftung:* Knapp vor dem Fest erfolgte die Verhaftung nach übereinstimmenden Berichten außerhalb der Stadt, jenseits des Kidrontales auf dem Ölberg in einem Garten *Gethsemane.* Von der dortigen Anfechtung und dem Gebetskampf Jesu, der keine Zeugen hatte[56], können wir nichts Historisches wissen. Für die Dogmengeschichte ist von nicht geringer Bedeutung geblieben, daß Jesu Angst und Entsetzen, ganz anders als in jüdischen oder christlichen Märtyrergeschichten, nachdrücklich geschildert werden: Nicht ein über alle menschliche Not erhabener Stoiker oder gar Übermensch leidet hier. Sondern in vollem Sinn ein Mensch, versucht und angefochten, freilich völlig unverstanden von seinen engsten Vertrauten, die eingeschlafen sind.

In einer nächtlichen Überraschungsaktion unter Führung des Judas, der mit Jesu Gewohnheiten vertraut war, wird Jesus von einer Rotte seiner Gegner verhaftet. Der Judaskuß für den in Schüler-Weise angeredeten »Rabbi«, historisch schwer erklärbar, blieb Symbol gemeinsten Verrates. Unklar bleibt, *wer* den Befehl gegeben und wer bei der Verhaftung beteiligt war. Wohl sicher ein Kommando der Tempelpriester auf Betreiben der Oberpriester im Kontakt mit dem Synedrion. Aber vielleicht hatte schon früh eine Absprache zwischen jüdischen und römischen Stellen stattgefunden. Was die Erwähnung der römischen Kohorte (wohl neben der jüdischen Tempelpolizei) durch Johannes, der sonst die römische Beteiligung zurücktreten läßt, ebenso erklären würde wie die rasche Aburteilung durch den nicht gerade als nachgiebig bekannten Pilatus. Das spätere Zusammenwirken von jüdischen und römischen Behörden kann nicht in Zweifel gezogen werden. Nach allen Berichten ist Jesus aber zunächst von den jüdischen Behörden in Gewahrsam genommen worden.

Bezeichnend ist, daß die Verhaftung *ohne jegliche Gegenwehr* Jesu und seiner Jünger erfolgte. Was ein ungeschickter, lächerlich wirkender Schwertschlag eines Unbekannten und die Legende von der Heilung des abgehauenen Ohres nur unterstreicht. Von jetzt an steht Jesus ohne jegliche Anhänger in völliger Einsamkeit da. Die *Jüngerflucht* wird wie die Verhaftung selbst knapp und ohne alle Entschuldigung berichtet; sie ist nicht zu bezweifeln. Nur Lukas versucht diese peinliche Tatsache zunächst durch Stillschweigen und nachher durch Erwähnung der von ferne zuschauenden Bekannten zu vertuschen. Johannes überhöht die Freiwilligkeit Jesu apologetisch ins Mythologische: wie vor der Erscheinung der Gottheit sinken die Häscher nieder, um ihn dann, als er seine Jünger entlassen hatte, zu ergreifen[57].

In besonders deutlichem Kontrast zu Jesu Treue (vor dem Gericht) steht die Untreue jenes Jüngers (vor einem Mädchen), der ihm in nachdrücklicher Weise Treue bis in den Tod geschworen hatte: Diese in allen vier Evangelien schlicht und glaubwürdig erzählte Geschichte von der *Verleugnung Petri* – ursprünglich wohl ein zusammenhängend für sich erzähltes Traditionsstück – konnte von Petrus selbst der Gemeinde überliefert worden sein. Jedenfalls dürfte sie – abgesehen vom wohl markinischen dramatischen Schluß mit dem zweiten Hahnenschrei (Hühner waren anscheinend in Jerusalem verboten) – den geschichtlichen Tatsachen entsprechen, da es für irgendeine Aversion gegen Petrus in der Gemeinde keine Belege gibt.

4. *Der Prozeß:* Trotz eingehendster kritischer Durchleuchtung[58] dürfte es nicht mehr möglich sein, das Prozeßverfahren Jesu, von dem wir weder Originalakten noch direkte Zeugenaussagen haben, zu rekonstruieren.

Unklar bleibt: ob nach älterem sadduzäischen oder neuerem pharisäischen Recht (wie es sich in der späteren Mischna niedergeschlagen hat) gerichtet wurde. Ob zwei Sitzungen des Hohen Rates (eine nachts und eine zweite morgens) oder nur eine am Tag (so mit größerer Wahrscheinlichkeit Lukas) stattfand. Ob die Belastungszeugen bezüglich des Tempelwortes Jesu die Wahrheit sagten oder nicht. Ob der Hohe Rat Todesurteile aussprechen und auch vollziehen durfte und ob ein solches Urteil auch in der Nacht und innerhalb eines einzigen Tages gefällt werden durfte. Ob jemand wegen messianischen Anspruchs von der jüdischen Behörde überhaupt je zum Tode verurteilt wurde und ob im Falle der Verurteilung wegen Gotteslästerung (zur Zeit Jesu sicher nicht nur Lästern des Gottesnamens) nicht Steinigung statt Kreuzigung die Strafe war. Ob ein förmliches Todesurteil ausgesprochen oder – wie wiederum Lukas insinuiert, der nichts von einem Urteil sagt – nur die Auslieferung an Pilatus beschlossen wurde. Ja, ob überhaupt ein regelrechtes Prozeßverfahren stattgefunden hat oder nur ein Verhör zur genauen Bestimmung der Anklagepunkte zu Händen des römischen Gouverneurs.

Klar ist jedenfalls, daß das ganze Inquisitionsverfahren vor dem Hohen Rat – und dann bei Johannes noch mehr das vor Pilatus – im Sinne des *Christus-Bekenntnisses der Gemeinde* gestaltet ist: nach dem Aufgebot vieler Zeugen das messianische Selbstzeugnis Jesu im Mittelpunkt und die Verurteilung zum Tode wegen Gotteslästerung als Konsequenz[59].

Das in den Evangelien vielfach betonte Schweigen Jesu will seinen Willen zum Leiden, sein Ja zum Willen des Vaters herausheben. Was hinter den »vielen« Anklagen steht, die, von einer Ausnahme abgesehen, nicht angeführt werden (was oft nicht beachtet wird!), muß, wie wir dies bereits eingehend versucht haben, aus den Evangelien als ganzen erschlossen werden. Die direkte Frage nach der *Gottessohnschaft* ist, nachdem »Gottessohn« kein messianischer Titel war, wenig wahrscheinlich. Auch erscheinen Erhöhung und Parusie außer in dieser Jesus zugeschriebenen Antwort[60] nie zusammen. Die merkwürdige Kombination von »Sitzen« (zur Rechten der Macht Gottes) und »Kommen« (mit den Wolken des Himmels) konnte aus der Verbindung zweier alttestamentlicher Sätze[61] entstanden sein. Allein wegen des Anspruchs, der Messias zu sein, wurde, soweit wir wissen, niemand verfolgt; da mußte anderes hinzukommen. – In diesem Zusammenhang kann freilich jenes Wort wohl Jesu selbst von der *Zerstörung* (und dem Aufbau) *des Tempels*[62] eine Rolle gespielt haben. Noch Josephus berichtet von einem Propheten Jesus, Sohn des Ananias, der den Untergang des Tempels angekündigt habe und deshalb von den jüdischen Autoritäten den Römern übergeben und von diesen gegeißelt und dann freigelassen worden sei[63]. Wie sehr dieses Wort Jesu der Gemeinde nachträglich Verlegenheit bereitet hat, erkennt man aus seiner Entschärfung: nach Markus ist es glatt ein Falschzeugnis, nach Mattäus ist nur ein Zerstören-Können gemeint, bei Lukas ist das Wort einfach weggelassen und bei Johannes wird es allegorisch interpretiert. Alle Evangelisten machen jedenfalls völlig deutlich, daß Jesus unschuldig verurteilt wurde. Die im Prozeßbericht an zentraler Stelle nebeneinander erscheinenden Hoheitstitel Messias, Gottessohn und Menschensohn sind das Glaubensbekenntnis der Gemeinde zu dem Verurteilten.

Klar ist darüber hinaus: Wie immer es um die Details des Inquisitionsverfahrens Jesu stehen mag, als unbestreitbare grundlegende Tatsache steht fest, daß Jesus von den jüdischen Behörden *dem römischen Gouverneur Pontius Pilatus ausgeliefert* und nicht nach jüdischer Sitte gesteinigt, sondern nach römischer gekreuzigt worden ist. Von allen Quellen wird übereinstimmend berichtet[64], daß es die jüdische Führungsschicht – Hohepriester und Älteste – war, die ihn den Römern unter politischen Verdächtigungen in die Hände gab. Im Verhör, welcher Art auch immer, waren zweifellos die Anklagepunkte zusammengesucht worden, die ein Verfahren bei der römischen Behörde auslösen konnten. Empfindlich würde diese bei der ständigen Furcht vor Massenaufständen oder -demonstrationen in jedem Fall auf die Anklage reagieren, dieser Mann sei politisch gefährlich und habe, wie etwa sein Einzug in Jerusalem und die Tempelreinigung zeigen mochten, messianische Ambitionen. Ob ein formelles Todesurteil vom Hohen Rat ausgesprochen oder nur die Auslieferung an Pilatus (mit allen Folgen) beschlossen oder gar nur Jesu Gefährlichkeit als Messiasprätendenten und damit potentiellen Aufrührers wirksam suggeriert worden war, ist relativ gleichgültig. Im Prozeß spielte nach sämtlichen Berichten der – von der Gemeinde später als messianischer Titel nie gebrauchte! – Begriff *»König der Juden«* die Hauptrolle. Was bestätigt wird durch jene in ihrer Historizität ebenfalls nicht zu bezweifelnde, bei römischen Kreuzigungen übliche Tafel (titulus) mit der Angabe der Schuld des Verbrechers: »König der Juden«[65] gibt in römisch-griechischer Formulierung wieder, was die jüdischen Ankläger vor Pilatus meinten, denn die Anklage, Messias-Ambitionen zu haben, konnte vom Römer nur politisch verstanden werden. Obwohl Jesus einen solchen politischen Anspruch nie erhoben hatte, wie wir sahen, lag es nahe, ihn von außen unter solcher Schablone zu sehen.

In Zusammenarbeit zwischen geistlichen und politischen Autoritäten wurde Jesus *zum Tode verurteilt:* Nach allen Berichten geriet der Politiker Pilatus durch die Anklage in einige Verlegenheit, weil er für Jesus, den er wohl für einen zelotischen Führer hielt, kaum einen der Anklage entsprechenden handgreiflichen Tatbestand zu finden vermochte. Auch wenn man die Tendenz der Evangelisten, den Vertreter Roms als Zeugen der Unschuld Jesu hinzustellen und zu entlasten, in Rechnung stellt: es ist doch glaubhaft, daß er Jesu Amnestierung – freilich als Einzelfall, da eine alljährliche Sitte unwahrscheinlich ist – betrieb, aber schließlich auf Wunsch des verhetzten Volkes doch dem zelotischen Revolutionär Barabbas (Sohn des Abbas) die Freiheit gab. Dies jedenfalls berichten die Quellen übereinstimmend, während die Fürsprache der Gattin des Pilatus nur von Mattäus[66], das ergebnislose Verhör vor Herodes Antipas nur von Lukas[67], das Verhör vor dem Althohepriester Annas und die ausführliche Befragung durch Pilatus nur von Johannes[68] berichtet werden. Indem aber Pilatus diesen Jesus, der nie auf messianische Titel Anspruch erhoben hatte, als »König (= Messias) der Juden« verurteilte, machte er ihn für die Öffentlichkeit paradoxerweise zum gekreuzigten Messias! Was für den nachösterlichen Glauben und sein Verständnis des vorösterlichen Jesus wichtig werden sollte. Die Ironie der Kreuzesaufschrift konnte vom Römer bewußt gewollt sein. Daß sie von den Juden – für die ein gekreuzigter Messias ein ungeheuerliches Skandalon war – so empfunden wurde, zeigt der Streit um die Formulierung[69].

5. *Die Hinrichtung:* Jesus wurde vor der Hinrichtung – auch dafür gibt es historische Parallelen – dem Hohn und Spott der römischen Soldateska überlassen. Die *Verhöhnung* Jesu als Spottkönig bestätigt die Verurteilung wegen messianischer Prätentionen. Die scheußliche Auspeitschung mit Hilfe von Lederpeitschen mit eingeflochtenen Metallstückchen, die Geißelung, war vor der Kreuzigung üblich[70]. Ein Zusammenbruch Jesu auf dem Weg unter der Last des Querholzes und die erzwungene Hilfe jenes Simon aus dem nordafrikanischen Kyrene hat – auch abgesehen von der Erwähnung von Simons Söhnen – hohe Wahrscheinlichkeit. Der Kreuzweg ist freilich nicht die heutige Via dolorosa. Vielmehr führt er vom Palast des Herodes – dieser und nicht die Burg Antonia war Residenz des Pilatus in Jerusalem – zur Hinrichtungsstätte auf einem kleinen Hügel außerhalb der damaligen Stadtmauer, der vermutlich wegen seiner Form Golgotha (= Schädel) hieß.

Knapper als vom Evangelisten kann die Hinrichtung nicht mehr beschrieben werden. »Und sie kreuzigten ihn[71].« Jedermann kannte damals nur zu gut die grauenhafte römische (aber vermutlich von den Persern erfundene) Exekutionsart für Sklaven und politische Rebellen: der Verurteilte wurde ans Querholz angenagelt und dieses auf den zuvor eingerammten Pfahl festgemacht, wobei die Füße mit Nägeln oder Stricken befestigt wurden. Die dem Verbrecher auf dem Weg zum Richtplatz umgehängte Tafel mit dem Hinrichtungsgrund wurde dann an dem Kreuz angeschlagen, für jeden sichtbar. Oft erst nach langer Zeit, machmal erst am folgenden Tage, verblutete oder erstickte der blutig Geschlagene und Gehenkte. Eine ebenso grausame wie diskriminierende Hinrichtungsart. Ein römischer Bürger durfte enthauptet, aber nicht gekreuzigt werden[72].

In den Evangelien wird *nichts ausgemalt:* Selbst die Zählung der sechs Stunden am Kreuz bei Markus (nicht übereinstimmend mit der Stundenzählung des Johannes) dürfte im Schema der dreimal drei Stunden mehr symbolisch auf die Bedeutung dieses Sterbens und den hinter allem stehenden Plan Gottes hinweisen. Dies gilt noch mehr von den beiden *apokalyptischen Zeichen,* die Markus anführt, Johannes aber nicht erwähnt: eine Sonnenfinsternis (zur Zeit des Frühlingsvollmondes unmöglich), als Zeichen auch beim Tode Cäsars und anderen großen Ereignissen der Antike vermeldet und insbesondere vom Propheten Amos im Zusammenhang mit der »Trauer um den Sohn« angekündigt[73]. Dann der zerrissene Tempelvorhang, als Zeichen wohl für das mit Jesu Tod gekommene Ende des Tempelkultes. Zeichen, die in späteren Schriften wie dem Nazoräer- und Petrusevangelium noch mirakulöser werden: Zerbrechen auch der riesigen Oberschwelle des Tempels, Finsternis wie in der Nacht, gewaltiges Beben beim Niederlegen der Leiche auf die Erde, Bekehrung Tausender von Juden, die beim Wiederscheinen der Sonne ihr Unrecht einsahen.

Das alles sind selbstverständlich keine historischen, sondern theologische Aussagen im Dienst dieser im übrigen unheimlich nüchternen, unsentimentalen Erzählung. Es werden keine Schmerzen und Qualen beschrieben, keine Emotionen und Aggressionen geweckt. Es soll überhaupt Jesu Verhalten in diesem Tod nicht beschrieben werden. Vielmehr soll mit allen Mitteln – alttestamentlichen Zitaten und Andeutungen, wunderbaren Zeichen – die Bedeutung dieses Todes herausgestellt werden: des Todes dieses Einen, der so viele Erwartungen geweckt und der nun von den Feinden liquidiert und verspottet und von den Freunden, ja von Gott selbst völlig im Stiche gelassen wird. Dabei läuft alles schon nach Markus auf die Glaubensfrage hinaus: Sieht einer in diesem furchtbaren Tod der Schande wie die Spötter das Sterben eines irregeleiteten, gescheiterten Enthusiasten, der vergebens um Rettung nach Elija schreit? Oder wie der römische Centurio – das erste Zeugnis eines Heiden – das Sterben des Gottessohnes?

Warum?

Was in der Darstellung der Evangelien als Ziel und Krönung des irdischen Weges Jesu von Nazaret erscheint, mußte den Zeitgenossen als das absolute Ende erscheinen. Hatte einer mehr den

Menschen verheißen als er? Und nun dieses völlige Fiasko in einem Tod von Schimpf und Schande!

Wer schon findet, alle Religionen und ihre »Stifter« seien gleich, der vergleiche ihren Tod, und er wird *Unterschiede* sehen: Mose, Buddha, Kung-futse, sie alle starben in hohem Alter, bei allen Enttäuschungen erfolgreich, inmitten ihrer Schüler und Anhänger, »lebenssatt« wie die Erzväter Israels. Mose starb nach der Überlieferung angesichts des verheißenen Landes inmitten seines Volkes im Alter von 120 Jahren, ohne daß seine Augen trübe geworden und seine Frische gewichen war. Buddha mit 80 Jahren friedlich im Kreis seiner Jünger, nachdem er als Wanderprediger eine große Gemeinde von Mönchen, Nonnen und Laien-Anhängern gesammelt hatte. Kung-futse, im Alter schließlich nach Lu, von wo er als Justizminister vertrieben war, zurückgekehrt, nachdem er die letzten Jahre der Heranbildung einer Gruppe meist adliger Schüler, die sein Werk bewahren und fortsetzen werden, sowie der Redaktion der alten Schriften seines Volkes, die nur in seiner Redaktionsform der Nachwelt überliefert werden sollten, gewidmet hatte. Mohammed schließlich starb, nachdem er als politischer Herr Arabiens die letzten Lebensjahre gut genossen hatte, mitten in seinem Harem in den Armen seiner Lieblingsfrau.

Und nun dagegen dieser hier: ein junger Mann von 30 Jahren nach einem Wirken von maximal 3 Jahren, vielleicht sogar nur wenigen Monaten. Ausgestoßen von der Gesellschaft, verraten und verleugnet von seinen Schülern und Anhängern, verspottet und verhöhnt von seinen Gegnern, von den Menschen und von Gott verlassen, stirbt einen Ritus, der zu den scheußlichsten und hintergründigsten gehört, die der Menschen erfinderische Grausamkeit zum Sterben erfunden hat.

Gegenüber der Sache, um die es hier letztlich geht, verblassen die ungeklärten historischen Fragen dieses Weges zum Kreuz als zweitrangig. Was immer der nähere Anlaß zum offenen Ausbruch des Konflikts war, welches immer die Motive des Verräters, wie immer die genauen Umstände der Verhaftung und Modalitäten des Verfahrens, wer auch die einzelnen Schuldigen, wo und wann genau die einzelnen Stationen dieses Weges: der Tod Jesu war kein Zufall, war kein tragischer Justizirrtum und auch kein reiner Willkürakt, sondern eine – die Schuld der Verantwortlichen einschließende – geschichtliche Notwendigkeit. Nur ein völliges Umdenken, eine wirkliche Metanoia der Betroffenen, ein neues Bewußtsein, eine Abkehr von der Verschlossenheit in ihr eigenes Tun, von aller gesetzlichen Selbstsicherung und Selbstrechtfertigung, und eine Umkehr in radikalem Vertrauen in den von Jesus verkündigten Gott der unbedingten Gnade und unbegrenzten Liebe hätte diese Not abwenden können.

Jesu gewaltsames Ende lag *in der Logik seiner Verkündigung und seines Verhaltens*. Jesu Passion war Reaktion der Hüter von Gesetz, Recht und Moral auf seine Aktion. Er hat den Tod nicht einfach passiv erlitten, sondern aktiv provoziert. Nur seine Verkündigung erklärt seine Verurteilung. Nur sein Handeln erhellt sein Leiden. Nur sein Leben und Wirken insgesamt macht deutlich, was das Kreuz dieses Einen unterscheidet von den Kreuzen jener jüdischen Widerstandskämpfer, die die Römer wenige Jahrzehnte nach Jesu Tod angesichts der Mauern der eingeschlossenen Hauptstadt massenhaft aufrichteten, aber auch von jenen 7000 Kreuzen römischer Sklaven, die man an der Via Appia nach dem gescheiterten Aufstand des (selber nicht gekreuzigten, sondern in der Schlacht gefallenen!) Spartakus aufrichtete, und überhaupt von den zahllosen großen und kleinen Kreuzen der Gequälten und Geschundenen der Weltgeschichte.

Jesu Tod war die Quittung auf sein Leben. Aber ganz anders als – nach mißglückter Königserhebung! – jener Mord am Politiker Julius Cäsar durch Brutus, wie er von Plutarch in historischer und poetischer Neugierde aufgeschrieben und von Shakespeare ins Drama gebracht wurde. Das Sterben des gewaltlosen Jesus von Nazaret, der nach keiner politischen Macht strebte, sondern nur für Gott und seinen Willen eintrat, hat einen anderen Rang. Und die evangelische Passionsgeschichte bedarf der Umsetzung ins Drama oder in Historie nicht, sondern läßt selber in ihrer nüchternen Erhabenheit die Frage aufkommen, warum man gerade diesen in dieser grenzenlosen Weise leiden ließ.

Nimmt man freilich nicht nur die Passionsgeschichte, sondern die Evangelien als ganze, auf deren Hintergrund die Passionsgeschichte überhaupt erst verständlich wird, so ist völlig klar, warum es so weit kam, warum er nicht durch einen Herzschlag oder Unfall gestorben ist, sondern gemordet wurde. Oder hätte die Hierarchie diesen Radikalen, der eigenmächtig ohne Ableitung und Begründung Gottes Willen verkündete, laufenlassen sollen?

Diesen *Irrlehrer*, der das Gesetz und die gesamte religiös-gesellschaftliche Ordnung vergleichgültigte und Verwirrung ins religiös und politisch unwissende Volk brachte?

Diesen *Lügenpropheten,* der den Untergang des Tempels prophezeite und den ganzen Kult relativierte und gerade die traditionell Frommen zutiefst verunsicherte?

Diesen *Gotteslästerer,* der in einer keine Grenzen kennenden Liebe Unfromme und moralisch Haltlose, Gesetzesbrecher und Gesetzlose in seine Gefolgschaft und Freundschaft aufgenommen hat, der so in untergründiger Gesetzes- und Tempelfeindlichkeit den hohen und gerechten Tora- und Tempelgott zu einem Gott dieser Gottlosen und Hoffnungslosen erniedrigte und in ungeheuerlicher Anmaßung sogar durch persönliche Gewährung und Verbürgung von Vergebung hier und jetzt in Gottes ureigenste souveräne Rechte eingriff?

Diesen *Volksverführer,* der in Person eine beispiellose Herausforderung des gesamten gesellschaftlichen Systems, eine Provokation der Autorität, eine Rebellion gegen die Hierarchie und ihre Theologie darstellt, was alles nicht nur Verwirrung und Verunsicherung, sondern eigentliche Unruhen, Demonstrationen, ja einen neuen Volksaufstand und den jederzeit drohenden großen Konflikt mit der Besatzungsarmee und die bewaffnete Intervention der römischen Weltmacht zur Folge haben konnte?

Der Gesetzesfeind ist – theologisch und politisch gesehen – auch ein Volksfeind! Es war durchaus nicht übertrieben, wenn nach dem oft so klarsichtigen Johannes der Hohepriester Kajefas in der entscheidenden Sitzung des Synedriums zu bedenken gab: »Ihr seid ganz ohne Einsicht und bedenkt nicht, daß es besser für euch ist, wenn ein einzelner Mensch für das Volk stirbt und nicht das ganze Volk zugrunde geht[74].«

Der politische Prozeß und die Hinrichtung Jesu als eines politischen Verbrechers durch die römische Behörde war also keineswegs nur ein Mißverständnis und ein sinnloses Schicksal, beruhend nur auf einem politischen Trick oder einer plumpen Fälschung der römischen Behörde. Ein gewisser Anlaß für die politische Anklage und Verurteilung war mit den damaligen politischen, religiösen, gesellschaftlichen Verhältnissen gegeben. Diese ließen *eine simple Trennung von Religion und Politik* nicht zu. Es gab weder eine religionslose Politik noch eine unpolitische Religion. Wer Unruhe in den religiösen Bereich brachte, brachte auch Unruhe in den politischen. Ein Sicherheitsrisiko stellte Jesus für die religiöse wie die politische Autorität dar. Und *trotzdem:* Die *politische Komponente* darf – soll Jesu Leben und Sterben nicht verzeichnet werden – *nicht als mit der religiösen gleichrangig* angesetzt werden. Der politische Konflikt mit der römischen Autorität ist nur eine (an sich nicht notwendige) Konsequenz des religiösen Konflikts mit der jüdischen Hierarchie. Hier ist genau zu unterscheiden:

Die *religiöse Anklage,* daß Jesus sich gegenüber Gesetz und Tempel eine souveräne Freiheit herausgenommen, daß er die überkommene religiöse Ordnung in Frage gestellt und mit der Verkündigung der Gnade des Vatergottes und mit der persönlichen Zusage der Sündenvergebung sich eine wahrhaft unerhörte Vollmacht zugemutet hat, war eine *wahre* Anklage. Nach allen Evangelien erscheint sie begründet: Vom Standpunkt der traditionellen Gesetzes- und Tempelreligion her mußte die jüdische Hierarchie gegen den Irrlehrer, Lügenpropheten, Gotteslästerer und religiösen Volksverführer tätig werden, außer eben sie hätte eine radikale Umkehr vollzogen und der Botschaft mit allen Konsequenzen Glauben geschenkt.

Aber die *politische Anklage,* daß Jesus nach politischer Macht gestrebt, zur Verweigerung der Steuerzahlung an die Besatzungsmacht und zum Aufruhr aufgerufen, sich als politischer Messias-König der Juden verstanden habe, war eine *falsche* Anklage. Nach allen Evangelien erscheint sie als Vorwand und Verleumdung: Wie sich schon im Abschnitt über Jesus und die Revolution in allen Details ergeben hat[75] und durch alle folgenden Kapitel hindurch bestätigt wurde, war Jesus kein aktiver Politiker, kein Agitator und Sozialrevolutionär, kein militanter Gegner der römischen Macht. Er wurde als politischer Revolutionär verurteilt, obwohl er es nicht war! Wäre Jesus politischer gewesen, hätte er eher mehr Chancen gehabt. Die politische Anklage verdeckte den religiös bedingten Haß und »Neid« der Hierarchie und ihrer Hoftheologen. Ein Messiasprätendent zu sein, war nach geltendem jüdischem Recht nicht einmal ein Verbrechen, konnte man dem Erfolg oder Mißerfolg überlassen, war aber für den Gebrauch der Römer spielend leicht in einen politischen Herrschaftsanspruch zu verdrehen. Eine solche Anklage mußte für Pilatus einleuchtend sein, war bei den damaligen Verhältnissen scheinbar berechtigt. Trotzdem war sie nicht nur zutiefst tendenziös, sondern im Kern falsch. Deshalb konnte »König der Juden« in der Gemeinde nun gerade nicht als christologischer Hoheitstitel Jesu gebraucht werden. Vom Standpunkt der römischen Macht aus mußte Pontius Pilatus gegen *diesen* »König der Juden« keineswegs tätig werden, und das vom Gouverneur allgemein berichtete Zögern bestätigt es. Nach den Quellen geht es denn auch beim politischen Konflikt keineswegs um eine ständige politische »Dimension« in der Geschichte Jesu. Offensichtlich erst in letzter Stunde und nicht aus eigener Initiative tritt die römische Behörde auf den Plan: nach allen Evangelien nur durch die Denunziation und gezielte politische Machenschaft der jüdischen Hierarchie auf den Plan gerufen.

Der religiöse Konflikt Jesu mit Gesetz, Tempel und Hierarchie (aut Christus – aut traditio legis!) darf also nicht schon vorösterlich zu einem politischen Konflikt mit dem Kaiser und der imperialistischen Pax Romana (aut Christus – aut Caesar!) emporstilisiert werden, um daraus unvermittelt und allzu direkt Folgerungen für eine »politische Theologie« ableiten zu können[76]. »Hochpolitisch« war nun gerade das Evangelium Jesu keineswegs, wiewohl es gewiß auch nicht privatreligiös »unpolitisch« war. Jesus hatte keine *direkt* politische Botschaft und Mission, sondern eine durch und durch »religiöse«, die dann freilich später einschneidende »politische« Implikationen und Konsequenzen hatte. Jesu Botschaft und Mission war, so könnte man präzisieren, *indirekt politisch,* was für eine »politische Theologie« Folgen haben dürfte.

Bestätigt wird dies durch die Wirkungsgeschichte des Gekreuzigten: Die junge Christengemeinde wurde bald aus religiösen Gründen von den jüdischen Behörden verfolgt, von den römischen aber bis in Neros Zeiten – wo andere Gründe hinzukamen – in Ruhe gelassen. Selbstverständlich gab es schon immer eine religiöse Opposition zwischen jüdischem und römischem *Glauben*. In diesem Sinn galt ein von Jesus (und den späteren Christen) selbstverständlich bejahtes »Entweder Jahwe – oder Cäsar!«. Nicht erst der Christusglaube, sondern schon der Jahweglaube stellte die römischen Staatsgötter und insbesondere den Kult vergotteter Weltherrscher religiös in Frage, was politische Verwicklungen zur Folge haben konnte. Aber wegen dieser religiösen Infragestellung sahen die Römer keinen Anlaß, der jüdischen Hierarchie den Prozeß zu machen. Die religiöse Opposition zwischen jüdischem (christlichem) und römischem Glauben mußte nicht notwendig in eine politische Opposition zwischen jüdischer und römischer *Macht* umschlagen, wie gerade Jesu Botschaft und Verhalten deutlich zeigte. Im politischen Bereich galt für Jesus nicht das zelotische »Entweder–Oder« des politischen Radikalismus, sondern ein unterscheidendes »Dem Cäsar, was des Cäsars, und Gott, was Gottes ist[77]«. Erst als der Cäsar von Christen forderte, was Gottes ist, kam es zum Konflikt mit dem römischen Staat und seinen Göttern und zum Gegensatz Christus – Kaiser, Kirche – Rom.

Wer im übrigen die größere *Schuld an Jesu Tod* hat, ist zu entscheiden wahrhaft überflüssig. Jüdische und römische Autoritäten waren darin verwickelt. Von einer Kollektivschuld des damaligen Judenvolkes (warum nicht auch Römervolkes?) hätte nie die Rede sein dürfen. Von einer Kollektivschuld des heutigen Judenvolkes (und Römervolkes?) erst recht nicht. Der globalen Rede »die Juden«, vom Johannesevangelium favorisiert, ist die präzise Rede von den wahrhaft verantwortlichen Autoritäten, Behörden, führenden Kreisen, einzelnen Gruppen im Sinne der älteren Evangelien unbedingt vorzuziehen. Die Verantwortlichen waren eine kleine Gruppe, die freilich das Volk zu repräsentieren meinten. In der gegebenen Konstellation der Verhältnisse und Mächte war der römische Gouverneur ein Werkzeug der jüdischen Hierarchie. Die jüdische Hierarchie ihrerseits, in ihrem inquisitorischen Gesetzeseifer, war ein Werkzeug des Gesetzes. Nicht einfach der einzelne Priester oder Hohepriester, Älteste oder Schriftgelehrte, sondern das Gesetz wollte seinen Tod. Sachlich, wenn vielleicht auch nicht historisch, stimmt jener Satz, den nach Johannes die Juden dem Pilatus sagten: »Wir haben ein Gesetz, und nach dem Gesetz muß er sterben[78]!« Das Gesetz also hat ihn getötet, und die Christen haben später daraus die Konsequenz gezogen. Seither freilich trennt der im Namen des Gesetzes Gekreuzigte Juden und Christen. Aber er bindet sie auch zugleich unlösbar in eine Geschichte der Solidarität, die man von beiden Seiten nie hätte verleugnen dürfen. Schuldvorwürfe wegen des Todes Jesu an die heutige jüdische Adresse sind absurd und haben unendlich viel Leid über dieses Volk gebracht. Ob die heutige Gesellschaft oder Kirche mit einer Gestalt wie Jesus leichter zurechtkäme, ja, ob sie mit ihm selbst heute leichter zurechtkommt? Doch was bleibt, ist nicht die Schuld, sondern die Verheißung der Gnade. Nicht in das jüdische Gesetz, das ihn erledigte, aber in das jüdische Volk, das auserwähltes Volk bleibt, kann der gekreuzigte Jesus jederzeit heimgeholt werden. Wer erschiene mehr als Urgestalt des in der Welt verfolgten und zum unsäglichen Leid verurteilten Judenvolkes denn der gekreuzigte Jude Jesus von Nazaret? Als schuldig am Kreuzestod Jesu heute mögen sich alle diejenigen betrachten, die, ob Juden oder Christen, den Repräsentanten der (in so vielerlei Form wirksamen) Gesetzlichkeit von damals kaum nachstehen: Sie kreuzigen Jesus wieder.

Umsonst?

Für damals bedeutete der Tod Jesu: Das Gesetz hat gesiegt! Von Jesus radikal in Frage gestellt, hat es zurückgeschlagen und ihn getötet. Sein Recht ist erneut erwiesen. Seine Macht hat sich durchgesetzt. Sein Fluch hat getroffen. »Jeder, der am Holz hängt, ist von Gott verflucht«: Dieser alttestamentliche Satz für die am Pfahl nachträglich aufgehängten Verbrecher[79] konnte auf ihn angewendet werden[80]. Als Gekreuzigter ist er ein Gottverfluchter: für jeden Juden, noch Justins Dialog mit dem Juden Tryphon zeigt es[81], ein entscheidendes Argument gegen Jesu Messianität. Sein Kreuzestod war der *Vollzug des Fluches des Gesetzes.*

Das widerspruchslose Leiden und hilflose Sterben in Fluch und Schande war für die Feinde und doch wohl auch Freunde das untrügliche Zeichen, daß es mit ihm aus war und er mit dem wahren Gott nichts zu tun hatte. Er hatte unrecht, voll und ganz: mit seiner Botschaft, seinem Benehmen, seinem ganzen Wesen. Sein *Anspruch* ist nun *widerlegt,* seine Autorität dahin, sein Weg als falsch demonstriert. Wer könnte es übersehen: Verurteilt ist der Irrlehrer, desavouiert der Prophet, entlarvt der Volksverführer, verworfen der Lästerer! Das Gesetz hat über dieses »Evangelium« triumphiert: es ist nichts mit dieser »besseren Gerechtigkeit« aufgrund eines Glaubens, der sich gegen die Gesetzesgerechtigkeit aufgrund gerechter Werke stellt. Das Gesetz, dem sich der Mensch bedingungslos zu unterziehen hat, und mit ihm der Tempel sind und bleiben die Sache Gottes.

Der Gekreuzigte zwischen den beiden gekreuzigten Verbrechern ist sichtbar die verurteilte Verkörperung der Ungesetzlichkeit, Ungerechtigkeit, Gottlosigkeit: »unter die Gottlosen gerechnet[82]«, »zur Sünde gemacht[83]«, die *personifizierte Sünde.* Buchstäblich der Stellvertreter aller Gesetzesbrecher und Gesetzlosen, für die er eingetreten ist und die im Grund dasselbe Schicksal wie er verdienen: der *Stellvertreter der Sünder* im bösesten Sinn des Wortes! Der Hohn der Feinde erscheint ebenso begründet wie die Flucht der Freunde: für diese bedeutet dieser Tod das Ende der mit ihm gegebenen Hoffnungen, die Widerlegung ihres Glaubens, den Sieg der Sinnlosigkeit.

Das Bild eines nicht zufälligen, sondern unumgänglichen Scheiterns. Die Frage läßt sich nicht unterdrücken: Ist er *nicht umsonst gestorben?* Sosehr wir annehmen können, daß Jesus mit seinem gewaltsamen Tod gerechnet hat, sowenig wissen wir darüber Bescheid, was Jesus bei diesem Tod gedacht und gefühlt hat. Nach Markus stand niemand aus der Gefolgschaft Jesu unter dem Kreuz, der Jesu letzte Worte hätte vermitteln können; nur einige galiläische Frauen, ohne die Mutter Jesu, schauten aus der Ferne zu. Die Flucht der Jünger wird hier erneut bestätigt[84]. Es hätte nahegelegen, diese Informationslücke zu schließen durch imponierende oder rührende Details in der Art jüdischer und christlicher Märtyrerlegenden. Tatsächlich hat man das später auch getan in einer im übrigen durchaus würdigen Weise: bei Lukas Bitte für die Feinde, die nicht wissen, was sie tun, und Bekehrung des einen mitgekreuzigten Verbrechers, der noch heute mit ihm im Paradiese sein wird[85]; bei Johannes in sorgender Liebe Abschied von seiner Mutter und dem geliebten Jünger[86].

Von alledem findet sich im ältesten Passionsbericht nichts. Ohne erbauliche Ausschmückungen, ohne beeindruckende Worte und Gesten, ohne Hinweis auf eine unerschütterliche innere Gelassenheit wird hier in bestürzend einfacher Weise sein Sterben kurz berichtet: »Da tat Jesus einen lauten Schrei und verschied[87].« Dieser laute, unartikulierte *Schrei* entspricht jenem übereinstimmend von den Synoptikern berichteten – und nur bei Lukas[88] durch eine Engelserscheinung, Zeichen der Nähe Gottes, gemilderten – Zittern und Zagen vor dem Tod[89]. Ist es der Schrei eines vertrauensvoll Betenden oder eines an Gott Verzweifelnden?

Es ist auffällig, wie in der späteren Überlieferung dieser schreckliche Schrei mit tröstlichen und triumphalen Worten überspielt wird. Lukas artikuliert den unartikulierten Schrei mit Hilfe des Psalmverses: »In deine Hände befehle ich meinen Geist[90].« Johannes ersetzt den Schrei durch ein Neigen des Hauptes und das große Wort: »Es ist vollbracht[91].« Diesen Abschwächungen gegenüber dürfte das von Markus und Mattäus für die Interpretation des Sterbens Jesu in Anspruch genommene und aramäisch beziehungsweise hebräisch zitierte Psalmwort der Wirklichkeit näherkommen: »Mein Gott, mein Gott, warum hast du mich verlassen[92]?« Kein »Vertrauenslied«, wie man wegen der Fortsetzung des Psalms allzu vereinfachend gemeint hat. Aber auch kein »Verzweiflungsschrei«, wie andere unter Mißachtung des Gottesanrufes interpretierten. Es ist ein Sterben, nicht einfach hingenommen in Geduld, sondern gestorben im Aufschrei zu Gott, der doch letzter Halt im Sterben bleibt, ein Halt freilich unfaßlich dem, der dem Leiden haltlos preisgegeben ist.

Das ist das Besondere dieses Sterbens: Jesus starb *nicht nur in* – bei Lukas und Johannes abgemilderter – *Menschenverlassenheit, sondern in uneingeschränkter Gottverlassenheit.* Und erst hier kommt die tiefste Tiefe dieses Sterbens zum Ausdruck, welche diesen Tod von dem so oft mit ihm verglichenen »schönen Tod« des der Gottlosigkeit und Jugendverführung angeklagten Sokrates oder mancher stoischer Weiser unterscheidet. Restlos war Jesus dem Leiden ausgesetzt. Von Heiterkeit, innerer Freiheit, Überlegenheit, Seelengröße ist in den Evangelien nicht die Rede. Kein humaner Tod nach siebzig Jahren in Reife und Ruhe, mild durch Vergiftung mit dem Schierling. Sondern ein allzu früher, alles abbrechender, total entwürdigender Tod von kaum erträglicher Not und Qual. Ein Tod, bestimmt nicht durch überlegene Gelassenheit, sondern eine nicht mehr zu überbietende allerletzte Verlassenheit! Aber gerade so: gibt es einen Tod, der die Menschheit in ihrer langen Geschichte mehr erschüttert und vielleicht auch erhoben hat als dieser in der Grenzenlosigkeit seines Leidens so unendlich menschlich-unmenschliche Tod?

Der Tod des Ketzers und Lästerers, des falschen Propheten und politisch verdächtigen Volksverführers wäre vielleicht noch in heroisch-stoischer Haltung zu sterben gewesen. Das Entscheidende – und zwar nicht als psychologisches, sondern als öffentliches Faktum – ist etwas anderes: Jesus sah sich allein gelassen nicht nur von seinem Volk, sondern von dem, auf den er sich ständig wie kein anderer vor ihm berufen hatte. Absolut allein gelassen. Nochmals, was Jesus gedacht und gefühlt hat in seinem Sterben, wissen wir nicht. Aber für alle Welt war offensichtlich: Der mit seinem Reich in Bälde kommende Gott war von ihm angekündigt worden, aber dieser Gott kam nicht. Ein menschenfreundlicher, um alle Bedürfnisse wissender, naher Gott, aber dieser Gott war abwesend. Ein schrankenlos gütiger und sich um das Geringste und die Geringsten sorgender gnädiger und zugleich mächtiger Vater, aber dieser Vater gab kein Zeichen und wirkte kein Wunder. Ja, *sein Vater,* den er vertraut anredete wie niemand sonst, mit dem er in ungewöhnlicher Weise verbunden gelebt und gewirkt hat, dessen wahren Willen er in unmittelbarer Gewißheit erfahren hatte und auf den hin er die Zusage der Sündenvergebung an Einzelne gewagt hatte: dieser sein Vater sagte kein einziges Wort. Der Zeuge Gottes von dem von ihm bezeugten Gott im Stich gelassen! Der Hohn unter dem Kreuz, in verschiedenen Varianten berichtet, unterstreicht in drastischer Weise dieses wortlose, hilflose, wunderlose, ja gott-lose Sterben.

Die einzigartige Gottesgemeinschaft, in der er sich wähnte, machte auch seine einzigartige Gottesverlassenheit aus[93]. Dieser Gott und Vater, mit dem er sich bis zum Ende völlig identifiziert hatte, identifizierte sich am Ende nicht mit ihm. Und so schien alles wie nie gewesen: umsonst. Er, der die Nähe und Ankunft Gottes, seines Vaters, öffentlich vor aller Welt angekündigt hatte, stirbt in dieser völligen Gottverlassenheit und wird so öffentlich vor aller Welt als Gottloser demonstriert: ein von Gott selbst Gerichteter, der ein für alle Male erledigt ist. Und nachdem die Sache, für die er gelebt und gekämpft hatte, so sehr an seine Person gebunden war, fiel mit seiner Person auch seine Sache. Eine von ihm unabhängige Sache gibt es nicht. Wie hätte man seinem Wort glauben können, nachdem er in dieser himmelschreienden Weise verstummte und verschied?

Vor der bei jüdischen Hingerichteten üblichen Verscharrung ist der Gekreuzigte bewahrt worden. Nach römischer Sitte konnte der Leichnam Freunden oder Verwandten überlassen werden. Kein Jünger, so wird berichtet, aber ein einzelner Sympathisant, der nur an dieser Stelle erscheinende Ratsherr Josef von Arimathia, anscheinend später nicht Glied der Gemeinde, läßt den Leichnam in seinem Privatgrab beisetzen. Nur einige Frauen sind Zeugen[94]. Schon Markus hat auf die offizielle Feststellung des Todes Gewicht gelegt[95]. Und nicht nur er, sondern auch schon das von Paulus überlieferte alte Glaubensbekenntnis[96] betonen das Faktum des Begräbnisses, das nicht zu bezweifeln ist. Aber so groß in der damaligen Zeit das religiöse Interesse an den Gräbern der jüdischen Märtyrer und Propheten war, zu einem Kult um das Grab Jesu von Nazaret ist es merkwürdigerweise nicht gekommen.

V. Das neue Leben

Wir sind am problematischsten Punkt unserer Ausführungen über Jesus von Nazaret angekommen. Wer bisher verständnisvoll folgte, könnte hier stocken. Wir empfinden dies so stark, weil dies der problematischste Punkt auch unserer eigenen Existenz ist.

1. Der Anfang

Der Punkt, wo alle Prognosen und Planungen, Sinndeutungen und Identifikationen, Aktionen und Passionen an eine unbedingte, unübersteigbare Grenze stoßen: der Tod, mit dem das alles aus ist.

Hinführung

Alles aus? Oder war etwa mit Jesu Sterben nicht alles aus? Größte Behutsamkeit ist gerade hier angebracht. Es darf nicht der Projektionsverdacht Feuerbachs bestätigt werden, für den Jesu Auferstehung nur das befriedigte Verlangen des Menschen nach unmittelbarer Vergewisserung seiner persönlichen Unsterblichkeit ist. Auch darf nicht nachträglich durch theologischen Kunstgriff rückgängig gemacht werden, daß Jesus von Nazaret überhaupt wahrhaft den Tod eines Menschen gestorben ist. Es darf sein gottverlassener *Tod nicht uminterpretiert,* mystifiziert, mythisiert werden, als ob er gleichsam nur zur Hälfte erfolgt sei: wie – mit Berufung auf Jesu unsterbliche Gottheit – die frühen Gnostiker Jesu Tod überhaupt in Zweifel gezogen, wie die mittelalterlichen Scholastiker die Gottverlassenheit des Sterbenden durch die unbiblische Behauptung einer gleichzeitigen beglückenden Gottesschau mehr oder weniger aufgehoben haben, und wie heute, wiederum aufgrund von dogmatischen Voraussetzungen, einzelne Exegeten Jesu Tod voreilig als ein

Bei-Gott-Sein und seinen Todesschrei als ein Vertrauenslied interpretieren. Da wird der Tod, diese stärkste Nicht-Utopie[1], selber zur Utopie. Doch Jesu Sterben war real, seine Menschen- und Gottverlassenheit manifest, seine Verkündigung und sein Verhalten desavouiert, sein Scheitern vollständig: ein totaler Bruch, wie ihn im Leben und Werk eines Menschen allein der Tod vollziehen kann.

Freilich wird nun auch der nichtchristliche Historiker nicht bestreiten: *Erst nach Jesu Tod* hat die auf ihn sich berufende *Bewegung ernsthaft angefangen.* Zumindest in diesem Sinn war mit seinem Tod keineswegs alles aus: seine »Sache« ging weiter! Und wer immer auch nur den Gang der Weltgeschichte verstehen, wer nur den Beginn einer neuen Weltepoche deuten, wer nur den Ursprung jener weltgeschichtlichen Bewegung, die man Christentum nennt, erklären will, sieht sich vor unausweichliche und zusammenhängende Fragen gestellt:

– *Wie kam es nach solchem katastrophalen Ende zu einem neuen Anfang? Wie nach Jesu Tod zu dieser für das weitere Geschick der Welt so folgenreichen Jesus-Bewegung? Wie zu einer Gemeinschaft, die sich gerade auf den Namen eines Gekreuzigten bezieht, zur Bildung einer Gemeinde, einer christlichen »Kirche«? Oder wenn man präziser fragen will:*
– *Wie kam es dazu, daß dieser verurteilte Irrlehrer zum Messias Israels, also zum »Christus«, daß dieser desavouierte Prophet zum »Herrn«, dieser entlarvte Volksverführer zum »Erlöser«, dieser verworfene Gotteslästerer zum »Gottessohn« wurde?*
– *Wie kam es dazu, daß die geflohenen Gefolgsleute dieses in völliger Isolierung Gestorbenen nicht etwa nur unter dem Eindruck seiner »Persönlichkeit«, seiner Worte und Taten an seiner Botschaft festhielten, einige Zeit nach der Katastrophe wieder Mut faßten und schließlich seine Botschaft vom Reich und Willen Gottes – etwa die »Bergpredigt« – weiterverkündeten, sondern daß sie sogleich ihn selber zum eigentlichen Inhalt der Botschaft machten?*
– *Wie kam es dazu, daß sie also nicht nur das Evangelium Jesu, sondern Jesus selber als das Evangelium verkündigten, so daß der Verkündiger selber unversehens zum Verkündigten, die Botschaft vom Reiche Gottes unversehens zur Botschaft von Jesus als dem Christus Gottes geworden war?*
– *Woher ist somit zu erklären, daß dieser Jesus nicht trotz seines Todes, sondern gerade wegen seines Todes, daß also gerade der*

Gehenkte zum zentralen Inhalt ihrer Verkündigung wurde? War nicht sein ganzer Anspruch durch den Tod hoffnungslos kompromittiert? Hatte er nicht Größtes gewollt und war in seinem Wollen hoffnungslos gescheitert? Und ließ sich in der damaligen religiös-politischen Situation ein größeres psychologisches und soziologisches Hindernis für das Weitergehen seiner Sache ersinnen als gerade dieses katastrophale öffentliche Ende in Schimpf und Schande?

- *Warum konnte man also gerade an ein solches hoffnungsloses Ende irgendwelche Hoffnung knüpfen, den von Gott Gerichteten als Gottes Messias proklamieren, den Galgen der Schande zum Zeichen des Heiles erklären und den offensichtlichen Bankrott der Bewegung zum Ausgang ihrer phänomenalen Neuerstehung machen? Hatten sie nicht, nachdem seine Sache mit seiner Person verbunden war, seine Sache verloren gegeben²?*
- *Woher bezogen diejenigen, die schon so bald nach solchem Fehlschlag und Mißlingen als seine Boten auftraten und keine Mühen, keine Widrigkeiten, keinen Tod scheuten, die Kraft, um diese »gute« Nachricht unter die Menschen, ja schließlich bis an die Grenzen des Imperiums zu bringen?*
- *Warum entstand jene Bindung an den Meister, die so ganz anders ist als die Bindung anderer Bewegungen an ihre Gründerpersönlichkeit, etwa der Marxisten an Marx oder enthusiastischer Freudianer an Freud: daß also Jesus nicht nur als Gründer und Lehrer, der vor Jahren gelebt hat, verehrt, studiert, befolgt, sondern – insbesondere in der gottesdienstlichen Versammlung – als Lebender verkündet und gegenwärtig Wirkender erfahren wird. Wie entstand die ungewöhnliche Vorstellung, daß er selber die Seinen, seine Gemeinde, leite durch seinen Geist?*

Also in einem Wort: das *historische Rätsel der Entstehung*, des Anfangs, des Ursprungs *des Christentums.* Wie verschieden von der allmählichen stillen Ausbreitung der Lehren der erfolgreichen Weisen Buddha und Kung-futse, wie verschieden auch von der weithin gewaltsamen Ausbreitung der Lehren des siegreichen Mohammed, alles schon zu deren Lebzeiten: diese unvermittelt nach völligem Scheitern und schändlichem Sterben erfolgte Entstehung und fast explosionsartige Ausbreitung dieser Botschaft und Gemeinschaft im Zeichen gerade eines Zu-Fall-Gekommenen! Was war denn nach dem katastrophalen Ausgang dieses Lebens die Initialzündung für jene einzigartige welthisto-

rische Entwicklung: daß vom Galgen eines in Schande Aufgehängten eine wahrhaft weltverändernde »Weltreligion« entstehen konnte?

Mit Psychologie läßt sich vieles in der Welt erklären, aber wohl
nicht alles. Und auch die herrschenden Verhältnisse erklären
nicht alles. Jedenfalls wird man, wenn man die Anfangsgeschich-
te des Christentums psychologisch deuten will, nicht nur vermuten, postulieren und neunmalklug konstruieren dürfen, sondern
man wird unvoreingenommen diejenigen fragen müssen, die die
Bewegung initiiert haben und deren gewichtigste Zeugnisse uns
erhalten geblieben sind. Und aus denen wird klar: Jene *Passionsgeschichte* mit katastrophalem Ausgang – warum hätte sie schon
in das Gedächtnis der Menschheit eingehen sollen? – wurde nur
überliefert, weil es zugleich eine *Ostergeschichte* gab, welche die
Passionsgeschichte (und die dahinter stehende Aktionsgeschich-
te) in einem völlig anderen Licht erscheinen ließ.

Aber hier hören nun freilich die *Schwierigkeiten* nicht auf, hier
beginnen sie erst. Denn wer nun diese sogenannten Auferste-
hungs- oder Ostergeschichten, statt sie psychologisch zu erklären, in schlichtem Glauben wörtlich annehmen möchte, wird,
wenn er nachdenkt und nicht alle Vernunft verliert, auf schwer
übersteigbare Hindernisse stoßen. Die Verlegenheit ist durch die
historisch-kritische Exegese eher noch vergrößert worden, nachdem vor 200 Jahren der scharfsinnigste Polemiker der klassischen deutschen Literatur, Gotthold Ephraim Lessing, jene
›Fragmente eines Ungenannten‹ (= des Hamburger Aufklärers
H. S. Reimarus † 1768) – darunter die ›Von dem Zwecke Jesu und
seiner Jünger‹ und ›Über die Auferstehungsgeschichte‹ – einer
verwirrten Öffentlichkeit preisgegeben hat. Will man als Mensch
des 20. Jahrhunderts nicht nur halbherzig und mit schlechtem
Gewissen, sondern redlich und überzeugt an so etwas wie eine
Auferweckung glauben, so müssen die Schwierigkeiten scharf
und ohne Vorurteile des Glaubens oder Unglaubens in den Blick
gefaßt werden[3]. Gerade dann zeigen sie freilich auch ihre *Kehrseite*. Es sind übersteigbare Schwierigkeiten[4].

Erste Schwierigkeit: Was von den Evangelien insgesamt gilt,
gilt von den Ostergeschichten ganz besonders: Es sind *keine
unparteiischen Berichte* von unbeteiligten Beobachtern, sondern
gläubig für Jesus Partei ergreifende Zeugnisse höchst Interessier-
ter und Engagierter. Also weniger historische als vielmehr theologische Dokumente: nicht Protokolle oder Chroniken, sondern
Glaubenszeugnisse. Der Osterglaube, der die gesamte Je-

sus-Überlieferung von Anfang an mitbestimmt hat, bestimmt selbstverständlich auch die Osterberichte selbst, was eine historische Überprüfung von vornherein ungemein erschwert. Es muß nach der Osterbotschaft *in* den Ostergeschichten gefragt werden.

Die Kehrseite dieser Schwierigkeit ist: Gerade so wird die zentrale Bedeutung des Osterglaubens für die Urchristenheit deutlich. Zumindest für die Urchristenheit gilt, daß der christliche Glaube steht und fällt mit dem Zeugnis von Jesu Auferweckung, ohne die die christliche Predigt leer und leer auch der Glaube ist. Damit erscheint Ostern – ob bequem oder unbequem – nicht nur als Keimzelle, sondern auch als bleibender konstitutiver Kern des christlichen Glaubensbekenntnisses. Schon die ältesten christologischen Kurzformeln in den Paulusbriefen sind, wenn sie mehr bieten als einen Titel, konzentriert auf Jesu Tod und Auferweckung.

Zweite Schwierigkeit: Wenn man die zahlreichen Wundergeschichten des Neuen Testamentes auch ohne die *unbeweisbare Annahme eines supranaturalistischen »Eingriffs«* in die Naturgesetze zu verstehen sucht, erscheint es als ein von vornherein verdächtiger Rückfall in überwundene Vorstellungen, wenn man für das Wunder der Auferweckung nun plötzlich doch wieder einen solch übernatürlichen »Eingriff« postuliert, der allem wissenschaftlichen Denken ebenso widerspricht wie allen alltäglichen Überzeugungen und Erfahrungen. Insofern erscheint die Auferweckung dem modernen Menschen eher als Last für den Glauben, ähnlich wie etwa Jungfrauengeburt, Höllenfahrt und Himmelfahrt.

Die Kehrseite: Es könnte sein, daß der Auferweckung doch ein besonderer Charakter eignet, der sie nicht ohne weiteres auf die gleiche Stufe stellen läßt mit anderen wundersamen oder auch legendären Elementen der urchristlichen Überlieferung. So sind zwar Jungfrauengeburt, Höllenfahrt und Himmelfahrt zusammen mit der Auferweckung im sogenannten »apostolischen« Glaubensbekenntnis aufgeführt, das aus der römischen Tradition des 4. Jahrhunderts stammt, erscheinen aber im Neuen Testament selbst im Gegensatz zur Auferweckung nur an vereinzelten Stellen und zwar ausnahmslos in späteren literarischen Schichten. Der älteste neutestamentliche Zeuge, der Apostel Paulus, sagt kein Wort von Jungfrauengeburt, Höllenfahrt und Himmelfahrt, hält aber die Auferweckung des Gekreuzigten in unerbittlicher Entschiedenheit für die Mitte der christlichen Predigt. Die Auferweckungsbotschaft ist nicht das Sondererlebnis einiger Begeisterter, die Sonderlehre einiger Apostel. Im Gegenteil: Sie gehört schon zu den ältesten Schichten des Neuen Testaments. Sie ist allen neutestamentlichen Schriften ohne Ausnahme gemeinsam. Sie erweist sich als für den christlichen Glauben zentral und zugleich als grundlegend für sämtliche weiteren Glaubensaussagen. Es ist also zumindest die Frage, ob mit der Auferweckung nicht vielleicht in anderer Weise als mit Jungfrauengeburt, Höllenfahrt und Himmelfahrt ein Allerletztes, ein Eschaton angesprochen wird, wo man sinnvollerweise nicht mehr von einem Eingriff gegen die Naturgesetze im supranaturalistischen Schema sprechen kann. Wir werden genauer zusehen müssen.

Dritte Schwierigkeit: Es gibt *keine direkten Zeugnisse* von einer Auferweckung. Im ganzen Neuen Testament behauptet niemand, Zeuge der Auferweckung gewesen zu sein. Nirgendwo wird die Auferweckung beschrieben. Nur das um 150 n.Chr. entstandene unechte (apokryphe) Petrusevangelium[5] macht eine Ausnahme und berichtet am Ende von der Auferweckung in naiver Dramatik mit Hilfe legendärer Einzelheiten, die dann freilich, wie so oft Apokryphes, Eingang gefunden haben in die kirchlichen Ostertexte, Osterfeiern, Osterlieder, Osterpredigten, Osterbilder und sich so mannigfach mit dem Volksglauben von Ostern vermischt haben. Auch einzigartige Meisterwerke der Kunst wie Grünewalds künstlerisch unübertroffene Auferweckungsdarstellung im Isenheimer Altar können da irreführen.

Die Kehrseite: Gerade die Zurückhaltung der neutestamentlichen Evangelien und Briefe gegenüber der Auferweckung weckt eher Vertrauen. Die Auferweckung wird vorausgesetzt, aber weder dargestellt noch beschrieben. Das Interesse an Übertreibungen und die Sucht des Demonstrierens, welche die Apokryphen kennzeichnet, machen diese unglaubwürdig. Die neutestamentlichen Osterzeugnisse wollen nicht Zeugnisse für die Auferweckung sein, sondern Zeugnisse für den Auferweckten und Auferstandenen.

Vierte Schwierigkeit: Eine genaue Analyse der Osterberichte zeigt nicht zu überwindende *Unstimmigkeiten und Widersprüchlichkeiten.* Zwar hat man immer wieder durch harmonisierende Kombination eine einheitliche Überlieferung zu konstruieren versucht. Aber die Übereinstimmung fehlt, zunächst kurz zusammengefaßt, 1. bezüglich der betroffenen Personen: Petrus, Maria Magdalena und die andere Maria, die Jünger, die Apostel, die Zwölf, die Emmaus-Jünger, 500 Brüder, Jakobus, Paulus; 2. bezüglich der Lokalisierung der Ereignisse: Galiläa, ein Berg dort oder der See Tiberias; Jerusalem, beim Grab Jesu oder in einem Versammlungsort; 3. überhaupt bezüglich des Ablaufs der Erscheinungen: am Morgen und Abend des Ostersonntags, acht Tage und vierzig Tage später. Überall erweist sich die Harmonisierung als unmöglich, wenn man nicht eine Veränderung der Texte und eine Bagatellisierung der Unterschiede in Kauf zu nehmen gewillt ist.

Die Kehrseite: Offensichtlich brauchte und wollte man kein einheitliches Schema und keine glatte Harmonie, erst recht nicht so etwas wie eine Biographie des Auferweckten! Daß neutestamentliche Autoren sich weder an irgendeiner Vollständigkeit noch an einer bestimmten Reihenfolge noch überhaupt an einer kritischen historischen Überprüfung der verschiedenen Nachrichten interessiert zeigen, macht deutlich, wie sehr bei den einzelnen Erzählungen anderes im Vordergrund steht: Zunächst, wie bei Paulus und Markus deutlich, die Berufung und Sendung der Jünger. Dann, bei Lukas und Johannes, immer mehr auch die Wirklichkeit der Identität des Auferweckten mit dem vorösterlichen Jesus (Identitätserfahrung, schließlich sogar Identitätsbeweis durch Demonstration der Leiblichkeit und Mahlgemeinschaft bei immer stärker betonter Überwindung des Zweifels der Jünger). Dabei wird deutlich: Jegliches Wie, Wann und Wo der Erzählungen ist zweitrangig gegenüber dem in den verschiedenen Quellen nirgendwo fraglichen Daß einer Auferweckung, die – bei allem Zusammenhang – mit Tod und Begräbnis eindeutig nicht identisch ist. Eine Konzentration auf den eigentlichen Inhalt der Botschaft legt sich nahe, die dann ein erneutes Eingehen auf die historischen Unstimmigkeiten ermöglichen wird.

Klärungen

Von den Ostergeschichten der Evangelien ist auf die Osterbotschaft zurückzufragen. Während die Geschichte vom leeren Grab sich nur in den Evangelien findet, bezeugen auch andere neutestamentliche Schriften, insbesondere die Paulusbriefe, daß Jesus den Jüngern als Lebendiger begegnet ist. Während die Ostergeschichten der Evangelisten in legendärer Weise darstellen, sprechen andere neutestamentliche Zeugnisse bekenntnismäßig. Und während die Grabesgeschichten von keinen direkten

Zeugen gedeckt sind, finden sich in den Paulusbriefen (den Evangelien um Jahrzehnte voraus) Aussagen des Paulus selbst, der von »Erscheinungen«, »Offenbarungen« des Auferweckten berichtet. Schon das bereits genannte und von Paulus ausdrücklich »übernommene« und der Gemeinde von Korinth bei ihrer Gründung »übergebene« Glaubensbekenntnis, das nach Sprache, Autorität und Personenkreis möglicherweise aus der frühen Jerusalemer Urgemeinde, jedenfalls aus der Zeit zwischen 35 und 45 stammt, da Paulus Christ und Missionar wurde, führt in seiner Erweiterung eine für die Zeitgenossen kontrollierbare Liste von Auferweckungszeugen an: denen der Auferweckte »sich sehen ließ«, »erschienen ist«, »sich geoffenbart hat«, begegnet ist, und von denen die Mehrzahl in den Jahren 55/56, als der Brief in Ephesus geschrieben wurde, noch am Leben und befragbar ist[6].

In der (die Geschichte der Urgemeinde widerspiegelnden?) Liste der maßgebenden Zeugen erscheint der auffälligerweise mit seinem aramäischen Namen »Kepha« genannte Petrus an der Spitze: Gerade als der Erstzeuge des Auferweckten dürfte er wohl auch der »Felsenmann«[7], »Bestärker der Brüder«[8] und der »Hirte der Schafe«[9] sein. Aber eine Reduktion aller Erscheinungen der Zwölf (das zentrale Führungsgremium in Jerusalem), des Jakobus (des Bruders Jesu), aller Apostel (dem größeren Kreis der Missionare), der über 500 Brüder, des Paulus selbst auf die petrinische Erscheinung, als ob jene diese nur bestätigten, ist weder von diesen noch von anderen Texten her gerechtfertigt. Zu verschieden sind Personen und Ereignisse, Ort und Zeit, zu verschieden auch die Weisen der Christusverkündigung gerade bei Petrus, Jakobus und Paulus.

Doch bevor der eigentliche Inhalt der Osterbotschaft herausgestellt werden soll, werden besser noch einige Klärungen versucht, die unnötige Mißverständnisse dieser Botschaft von vornherein verhindern können. Für das Ostergeschehen werden nämlich im Neuen Testament verschiedene Formulierungen und Vorstellungen gebraucht, die, richtig verstanden, in der Sachfrage weiterhelfen können: »Auferweckung« und »Auferstehung«, »Erhöhung« und »Verherrlichung«, »Entrückung« und »Himmelfahrt«. Wie soll das alles verstanden werden?

1. *Auferstehung oder Auferweckung?* Zu selbstverständlich spricht man heute von Auferstehung, als ob dies einfach Jesu eigenmächtige Tat gewesen wäre. Auferstehung wird jedoch nach dem Neuen Testament nur dann richtig verstanden, wenn

sie als *Auferweckung durch Gott* verstanden wird. Es geht grundlegend um ein Werk Gottes an Jesus, dem Gekreuzigten, Gestorbenen, Begrabenen. »Auferweckung« Jesu (passiv) dürfte denn auch im Neuen Testament ursprünglicher und jedenfalls allgemeiner sein als »Auferstehung« Jesu (aktiv)[10]. Bei »Auferweckung« wird ganz Gottes Tun an Jesus in den Mittelpunkt gestellt: Nur durch Gottes lebenschaffendes Handeln wird Jesu tödliche Passivität zu neu lebendiger Aktivität. Nur als der (von Gott) Auferweckte, ist er der (selber) Auferstandene. Durchweg wird im Neuen Testament Auferstehung als Tat Jesu im Sinn von Auferweckung als Werk des Vaters verstanden[11]. Wie es in altertümlicher Formulierung heißt: Gott ließ ihn auferstehen, nachdem er die Wehen des Todes gelöst hat[12]. Wenn hier bewußt meist von Auferweckung und vom Auferweckten gesprochen wird, so nicht um die anderen Ausdrücke auszuschließen, sondern um ein sich damit leicht einschleichendes mythologisches Mißverständnis zu vermeiden.

2. *Auferweckung ein historisches Ereignis?* Weil es nach neutestamentlichem Glauben in der Auferweckung um ein Handeln Gottes in den Dimensionen Gottes geht, kann es sich *nicht* um ein im strengen Sinn *historisches,* das heißt von der historischen Wissenschaft mit historischer Methode feststellbares Geschehen handeln. Auferweckung meint ja nicht ein Naturgesetze durchbrechendes, innerweltlich konstatierbares Mirakel, nicht einen lozierbaren und datierbaren supranaturalistischen Eingriff in Raum und Zeit. Zu photographieren und registrieren gab es nichts. Historisch feststellbar sind der Tod Jesu und dann wieder der Osterglaube und die Osterbotschaft der Jünger. Die Auferweckung selber aber läßt sich sowenig wie der Auferweckte mit historischer Methode dingfest machen, objektivieren. Die historische Wissenschaft – die ebenso wie die chemische, biologische, psychologische, soziologische oder theologische Wissenschaft immer nur *einen* Aspekt der vielschichtigen Wirklichkeit sieht – dürfte hier überfragt sein, weil sie aufgrund ihrer eigenen Prämissen gerade jene Wirklichkeit bewußt ausschließt, die für eine Auferweckung ebenso wie für Schöpfung und Vollendung allein in Frage kommt: die Wirklichkeit Gottes!

Aber gerade weil es nun nach neutestamentlichem Glauben in der Auferweckung um das Handeln Gottes geht, geht es um ein nicht nur fiktives oder eingebildetes, sondern um ein im tiefsten Sinne *wirkliches* Geschehen: Es ist nicht nichts geschehen. Aber was geschehen ist, sprengt und übersteigt die Grenzen der Historie. Es geht um ein transzendentes Geschehen aus dem menschlichen Tod in die umgreifende Dimension Gottes hinein. Auferweckung bezieht sich auf eine völlig neue Daseinsweise in der ganz anderen Daseinsweise Gottes, umschrieben in einer Bilderschrift, die interpretiert werden muß. Daß Gott dort eingreift, wo menschlich gesehen alles zu Ende ist, das ist – bei aller Wahrung der Naturgesetze – das wahre Wunder der Auferweckung: das Wunder des Anfangs eines neuen Lebens aus dem Tod. Nicht ein Gegenstand der historischen Erkenntnis, wohl aber ein Anruf und ein Angebot an den Glauben, der allein an die Wirklichkeit des Auferweckten herankommen kann.

3. *Auferweckung vorstellbar?* Man vergißt nur zu leicht, daß es sich sowohl bei »Auferstehung« wie bei »Auferweckung« um metaphorische, bildhafte Termini handelt. Das Bild wird übernommen vom »Aufwecken« und »Aufstehen« aus dem Schlaf. Das ist aber ein ebenso leicht verständliches wie mißverständliches Bild, Symbol, Metapher für das, was dem Toten widerfahren soll: Gerade nicht wie aus dem Schlaf die Rückkehr in den vorausgegangenen Zustand, in das vorige, irdische, sterbliche Leben! Vielmehr die radikale Verwandlung in einen ganz verschiedenen Zustand, in ein anderes, neues, unerhörtes, endgültiges, unsterbliches Leben: totaliter aliter, ganz anders!

Auf die immer wieder gern gestellte Frage, wie man sich dieses so ganz andere Leben vorstellen soll, ist schlicht zu antworten: überhaupt nicht! Hier gibt es nichts auszumalen, vorzustellen, zu objektivieren. Es wäre ja nicht ein ganz anderes Leben, wenn wir es mit den Begriffen und Vorstellungen aus unserem Leben anschaulich machen könnten! Weder unsere Augen noch unsere Phantasie können uns hier weiterhelfen, sie können uns nur irreführen. Die Wirklichkeit der Auferweckung selbst ist also völlig *unanschaulich* und *unvorstellbar.* Auferweckung und Auferstehung sind bildhaft-anschauliche Ausdrücke, sind Bilder, Metaphern, Symbole, die den Denkformen jener Zeit entsprachen und die sich natürlich vermehren lassen, für etwas, was selber unanschaulich und unvorstellbar ist und wovon wir – wie von Gott selbst – keinerlei direkte Kenntnis haben.

Gewiß können wir dieses unanschauliche und unvorstellbare neue Leben nicht nur bildhaft, sondern auch gedanklich zu umschreiben versuchen (so wie etwa die Physik die Natur des Lichts, das im atomaren Bereich zugleich Welle und Korpuskel ist und als solches nicht anschaulich und vorstellbar, mit Formeln zu umschreiben versucht). Wir stoßen da auch mit der Sprache an eine Grenze. Und es bleibt uns dann aber gar nichts anderes übrig, als in Paradoxen zu reden: daß wir für dieses ganz andere Leben Begriffe verbinden, welche in diesem Leben Gegensätze bedeuten. So geschieht es etwa in den evangelischen Erscheinungsberichten an der äußersten Grenze des Vorstellbaren: kein Phantom und doch nicht greifbar, erkennbar-unerkennbar, sichtbar-unsichtbar, faßbar-unfaßbar, materiell-immateriell, diesseits und jenseits von Raum und Zeit. »Wie die Engel im Himmel«, hatte schon Jesus selber in der Sprache der jüdischen Tradition bemerkt[13]. Oder wie es Paulus sehr zurückhaltend und diskret mit paradoxen Chiffren anzeigt, die selbst auf die Grenze des Sagbaren hinweisen: ein unvergänglicher »Geistleib«[14], ein »Leib der Herrlichkeit«[15], der durch eine radikale »Verwandlung«[16] aus dem vergänglichen Fleischesleib hervorgegangen ist. Damit meint Paulus gerade nicht in griechischer Weise eine (aus dem Kerker des Leibes befreite) Geist-Seele, wie sie von der modernen Anthropologie gar nicht mehr isoliert gedacht werden kann. Er meint in jüdischer Weise einen (von Gottes lebenschaffendem Geist umgestalteten und durchwalteten) ganz leibhaftigen Menschen, wie dies sehr viel eher der modernen ganzheitlichen Auffassung vom Menschen und der grundlegenden Bedeutung seiner Leiblichkeit entspricht. Der Mensch wird also nicht – platonisch – *aus* seiner Leiblichkeit erlöst. Er wird *mit* und *in* seiner nun verherrlichten, vergeistigten Leiblichkeit erlöst: eine Neuschöpfung, ein neuer Mensch.

4. *Leibliche Auferweckung?* Ja und Nein, wenn ich mich auf ein persönliches Gespräch mit Rudolf Bultmann beziehen darf. Nein, wenn »Leib« naiv den physiologisch identischen Körper meint. Ja, wenn »Leib« im Sinn des neutestamentlichen »Soma« die identische personale Wirklichkeit, *dasselbe Ich* mit seiner ganzen Geschichte meint. Oder anders gesagt: Keine Kontinuität des Leibes: naturwissenschaftliche Fragen wie die nach dem Verbleib der Moleküle stellen sich nicht! Sondern eine Identität der Person: es stellt sich die Frage nach der bleibenden Bedeutung ihres ganzen Lebens und Geschicks! Also in jedem Fall kein minderes, sondern ein vollendetes Wesen. Die Auffassung östlicher Denker, daß das Ich den Tod nicht überlebt und nur die Werke überleben, ist gewiß bedenkenswert, insofern ein Übergang in nicht raumzeitliche Dimensionen gemeint ist. Aber sie ist

ungenügend: Wenn die letzte Wirklichkeit Gott ist, dann ist der Tod weniger Zerstörung als eine Metamorphose – also nicht Minderung, sondern Vollendung.

Wenn es so in der Auferweckung Jesu nicht um ein Ereignis im menschlichen Raum und in der menschlichen Zeit geht[17], so doch auch nicht *nur* um den Ausdruck der Bedeutsamkeit seines Todes[18]. Vielmehr um ein zwar nicht historisches (mit Mitteln der historischen Forschung feststellbares), wohl aber (für den Glauben) wirkliches Geschehen. Es geht folglich in der Auferweckung Jesu auch nicht *nur* um die von Jesus gebrachte »Sache«[19], die weitergeht und historisch mit seinem Namen verbunden bleibt, während er selber nicht mehr ist und nicht mehr lebt, tot ist und tot bleibt. Ähnlich etwa wie die »Sache« des verstorbenen Herrn Eiffel: Der Mann ist tot, aber im Eiffelturm lebt er fort; ähnlich etwa wie Goethe, obwohl tot, in Werk und Erinnerung »auch heute spricht«. Es geht vielmehr um des lebendigen Jesu *Person* und *deshalb* Sache. Die Wirklichkeit des Auferweckten selbst läßt sich nicht ausklammern. Über Jesu Sache, die seine Jünger verlorengegeben hatten, wird von Gott selbst an Ostern entschieden: Jesu Sache hat Sinn und geht weiter, weil er selber nicht, gescheitert, im Tod geblieben ist, sondern von Gott her voll gerechtfertigt lebt.

Ostern ist somit ein Geschehen nicht *nur* für die Jünger und ihren Glauben: Jesus lebt nicht *durch* ihren Glauben. Der Osterglaube ist keine Funktion des Jüngerglaubens. Er war nicht einfach zu groß, um sterben zu können, wie manche meinten: er ist gestorben. Sondern Ostern ist ein Geschehen primär für Jesus selbst: Jesus lebt neu *durch Gott – für ihren Glauben*. Voraussetzung des neuen Lebens ist das zwar nicht zeitliche, aber sachliche Prae, Voraus des Handelns Gottes. So wird jener Glaube erst ermöglicht, gestiftet, in welchem sich der Lebendige selber als lebendig erweist. Das bedeutet im Hinblick auf die auch nach Bultmann mißverständliche Formulierung »Jesus ist auferstanden ins Kerygma (Verkündigung) hinein«[20]: Jesus lebt auch nach Bultmann nicht, weil er verkündigt wird, sondern er wird verkündigt, weil er lebt. Also ganz anders als in Rodion Stschedrins Oratorium ›Lenin im Herzen des Volkes‹, wo am Totenbett Lenins der Rotgardist singt: »Nein, nein, nein! Das kann nicht sein! Lenin lebt, lebt, lebt!« Hier geht nur »Lenins Sache« weiter.

5. *Erhöhung?* In den alten Texten des neuen Testaments ist die »Erhöhung« oder »Entrückung« Jesu einfach eine anders akzentuierte Ausdrucksweise für Jesu Auferweckung oder Auferstehung. Daß Jesus auferweckt ist, besagt im Neuen Testament nichts anderes, als daß er in der Auferweckung selbst zu Gott erhöht wurde: Erhöhung als Vollendung der Auferweckung[21].

Meint aber Erhöhung nicht Aufnahme in den *Himmel?* Bildlich gesprochen kann man in der Tat von der Aufnahme in den »Himmel« sprechen. Dabei wird man sich heute darüber im klaren sein, daß das blaue Firmament nicht mehr wie in biblischen Zeiten als die äußere Seite des Thronsaales Gottes verstanden werden kann. Wohl aber als das sichtbare Symbol oder Bild für den eigentlichen Himmel, nämlich die unsichtbare Domäne (»Lebensraum«) Gottes. Der Himmel des Glaubens ist nicht der Himmel der Astronauten, wie gerade die den biblischen Schöpfungsbericht aus dem Weltall rezitierenden Astronauten selber zum Ausdruck gebracht haben. Der Himmel des Glaubens ist der verborgene unsichtbar-unfaßbare Bereich Gottes, den keine Weltraumfahrt je erreicht. Kein Ort, sondern eine Seinsweise: freilich nicht eine, die der Erde entzieht, sondern eine, die in Gott zum Guten vollendet und Anteil gibt an der Herrschaft Gottes.

Jesus ist also aufgenommen in die Herrlichkeit des Vaters. Auferweckung und Erhöhung bedeuten im Anschluß an alttestamentliche Formulierungen[22] den *Herrschaftsantritt* (Inthronisation) dessen, der den Tod überwunden hat: daß er, in Gottes Lebensbereich aufgenommen, teilhat an Gottes Herrschaft und Herrlichkeit und so seinen universalen Herrschaftsanspruch für den Menschen geltend machen kann. Der Gekreuzigte als der *Herr*, der in die Nachfolge ruft! Eingesetzt also in seine himmlische, göttliche Würde, was traditionellerweise wiederum in einem Bild, welches an den Sohn oder Stellvertreter des Herrschers erinnert, ausgesagt wird: »Sitzet zur Rechten des Vaters.« Also seiner Macht am nächsten und sie stellvertretend ausübend in gleicher Würde und Stellung. In den ältesten christologischen Formeln, wie sie etwa in den Apostelpredigten der Apostelgeschichte verwendet werden, war Jesus zwar Mensch in Niedrigkeit, aber Gott hat ihn nach der Auferweckung zum Herrn und Messias gemacht[23]. Erst vom Erhöhten und noch nicht vom Irdischen wird Messianität und Gottessohnschaft ausgesagt[24].

Dies ist wichtig für das Verständnis der österlichen *Erscheinungen*, wie immer sie letztlich zu verstehen sind: Aus dieser

himmlischen, göttlichen Machtstellung und Herrlichkeit nämlich »erscheint« er denen, die er zu seinen »Werkzeugen« machen
will, wie es Paulus erfahren hat[25] und wie es in den Erscheinungen bei Mattäus, Johannes und im Markus-Nachtrag, wo über
das Woher und Wohin des Erscheinenden nichts bemerkt wird,
ganz selbstverständlich vorausgesetzt wird. Ostererscheinungen
sind Manifestationen des bereits Erhöhten! Immer ist es der
Erhöhte, der von Gott her erscheint: ob nun Paulus den ihn
Berufenden vom Himmel her erfährt oder ob bei Mattäus und
Johannes der Auferweckte auf Erden erscheint.

Also: Auferweckung vom Tod und Erhöhung zu Gott sind im
Neuen Testament – abgesehen von einer gleich zu besprechenden Ausnahme – eins. Wo nur vom einen die Rede ist, ist das
andere mitgedacht. Osterglaube ist Glaube an Jesus als den auferweckten = zu Gott erhöhten Herrn. Er ist zugleich der im
Geist gegenwärtige Herr seiner Kirche, ja der verborgene Herr
der Welt (Kosmokrator), mit dessen Herrschaft die definitive
Herrschaft Gottes schon begonnen hat.

6. *Eine Himmelfahrt?* In der ältesten Kirche gab es keine Tradition von einer sichtbaren Himmelfahrt Jesu vor den Augen der
Jünger[26]. Aber es gibt die eine Ausnahme: *Lukas,* von vornherein
mehr als andere an der leibhaftig erwiesenen Wirklichkeit des
Auferstandenen und der Augenzeugenschaft der Apostel interessiert, *trennt anders als die übrigen Zeugen Auferweckung und
Erhöhung zeitlich:* Einzig er kennt eine separate Himmelfahrt in
Betanien, welche die Zeit der Erscheinungen Jesu auf Erden (vor
der himmlischen bei Paulus) abschließt und die Zeit der Weltmis-
sion der Kirche bis zu Jesu Wiederkunft mit Emphase eröffnet[27].
So besonders deutlich in der auf das Lukasevangelium (nach 70)
folgenden, wohl erst zwischen 80 und 90 geschriebenen Apostelgeschichte. In dem aus dem zweiten Jahrhundert stammenden
nachträglichen Markus-Schluß wird diese separate Himmel-
fahrtsvorstellung übernommen, in Anlehnung zugleich an die
Formulierung bei der Entrückung des Elija[28] und das Psalmwort
vom Sitzen zur Rechten des Vaters[29].

Selbstverständlich hat Jesus keine Weltraumfahrt angetreten:
Himmelfahrt – wohin, wie rasch und wie lange eigentlich? Diese
für heutiges Verständnis unvollziehbare Vorstellung war damals
allerdings nicht ungewöhnlich. Nicht nur von Elija und Henoch
im Alten Testament, sondern auch von anderen Großen der
Antike wie Herakles, Empedokles, Romulus, Alexander dem

Großen und Apollonius von Tyana wird eine Himmelfahrt berichtet: eine »Entrückung«, bei der anders als bei einer »Himmelsreise« weder der Weg zum Himmel noch die Ankunft im Himmel, sondern nur das Entschwinden von der Erde geschildert wird. Die Wolke bedeutet dabei zugleich Nähe und Unnahbarkeit Gottes. Das Entrückungsschema stand Lukas somit als Vorstellungsmodell und Erzählungsform zur Verfügung.

Vermutlich hat er selbst die traditionelle Erhöhungsaussage zu einer Entrückungsgeschichte ausgestaltet, für die alle wesentlichen Bauelemente in den früheren Grabes- und Erscheinungsgeschichten bereitlagen. Warum? Es dürfte Lukas nicht allein um die Veranschaulichung der unanschaulichen Erhöhungsaussage gegangen sein. Vielmehr wie in seinem ganzen Evangelium um eine energische Korrektur der noch immer verbreiteten frühen Naherwartung der Parusie, der Wiederkunft Jesu: statt untätiges Warten die Mission der Welt! Nicht Jesus selbst, der sich in den Himmel entfernt und den Jüngern die Aufgabe überlassen hat, sondern der Heilige Geist kommt jetzt, um die Jünger für die bevorstehende Missionszeit – in Kontinuität mit der Zeit Jesu jetzt die Zeit der Kirche! – auszurüsten, bis schließlich am Ende der Zeit Jesus ebenso anschaulich wiederkommen wird. Lukas will sagen: Ostern haben nur die verstanden, die nicht zum Himmel emporstaunen, sondern in der Welt für Jesus Zeugnis ablegen[30].

So erscheint die Himmelfahrtsgeschichte – insbesondere in der nachträglichen Fassung der Apostelgeschichte mit Wolke und Engeln – geradezu als umgekehrte Parusiegeschichte. Noch im Lukasevangelium wie wieder im Markus-Nachtrag scheinen die Ostererscheinungen und Himmelfahrt am selben Ostertag erfolgt zu sein. Einzig die spätere Apostelgeschichte – in offensichtlicher Anlehnung an die heilige biblische Zahl 40 (40 Wüstenjahre Israels, Fasttage Elijas und Jesu) – erwähnt 40 Tage zwischen Ostern und Himmelfahrt: die symbolische Zahl für eine Gnadenzeit. *Nicht* als eine *zweite »Heilstatsache«* nach Ostern ist Himmelfahrt zu verstehen und zu feiern, *sondern* als ein besonders herausgehobener *Aspekt des einen Ostergeschehens.*

7. *Pfingsten?* Auch wiederum nur aus der späten lukanischen Apostelgeschichte wissen wir von einem christlichen Pfingstfest. »Pentekoste«[31] (= 50. Tag) war schon für die Juden das Erntefest. Lukas ordnet diesen Termin des jüdischen Festkalenders in

den heilsgeschichtlichen Zusammenhang von Verheißung und Erfüllung ein. Es ist für ihn offenkundig das Fest der verheißenen Mitteilung des Geistes und der Geburtsstunde der Weltkirche. Was sich historisch dahinter verbirgt, ist heute nicht mehr leicht auszumachen: Am ersten Pfingstfest nach Jesu Tod, wo zweifellos viele Festpilger nach Jerusalem kamen, konnte durchaus die erste Versammlung der (vor allem) aus Galiläa zurückgekommenen Anhänger Jesu in Jerusalem und ihre Konstitution als die endzeitliche Gemeinde (unter enthusiastisch-charismatischen Begleitumständen) stattgefunden haben. Möglicherweise hat Lukas eine Tradition vom ersten Auftreten einer geistgewirkten Massenekstase in Jerusalem am ersten Pfingstfest verwendet. Merkwürdigerweise wissen weder Paulus noch Markus noch Mattäus etwas von einem christlichen Pfingsten. Für Johannes fallen Ostern und Pfingsten (Geistmitteilung[32]) sogar ausdrücklich zusammen.

Im ganzen Neuen Testament ist die *Taufe,* die an Ostern erinnert, auch das Sakrament des Geistempfanges – mit zwei Ausnahmen wiederum bei Lukas in der Apostelgeschichte[33], die die Regel bestätigen. Aber viele Jahrhunderte später verselbständigt sich als Sonderentwicklung in der Westkirche die für Rom typische zweite Salbung nach der Taufe zu einem eigenen Ritus des Geistempfanges, weil sich im Westen die Bischöfe diese Salbung faktisch reserviert hatten: die *Firmung* (confirmatio). Zur nachträglichen Rechtfertigung dieser kirchenrechtlichen Entwicklung berief man sich nicht nur auf die beiden Texte der Apostelgeschichte (die auf die Einheit der Kirche und nicht auf ein gesondertes Sakrament zielen), sondern auch auf die lukanische Unterscheidung von Ostern und Pfingsten (obwohl auch in der Pfingsterzählung der Geistempfang der Neubekehrten an die Taufe gebunden ist). Aus heutiger Sicht wird man die Firmung nicht als ein gesondertes, autarkes und autonomes Sakrament anerkennen können. Wohl aber als die – im Zusammenhang mit der Kindertaufe sinnvolle – abschließende Phase des einen Initiationsritus (vor der Zulassung zur Eucharistie): als Entfaltung, Bestätigung und Vollendung der Taufe[34].

8. *Ein Kirchenjahr?* Während der ersten drei Jahrhunderte bezeichnete »Pentekoste« kein spezifisches Pfingstfest, sondern den ganzen 50 Tage währenden festlichen Zeitraum, der mit der Osternacht begonnen hatte: gleichsam ein andauerndes Herrenfest zur Verherrlichung des Auferstandenen, in welchem nur

stehend und nicht knieend gebetet, auch nicht gefastet, wohl in der Liturgie reichlich Halleluja gesungen wurde.

Aber jene einzige Erwähnung eines christlichen Pfingstfestes im Neuen Testament durch Lukas hat sich derart stark im Bewußtsein der Kirche durchgesetzt, daß man seit dem 5. Jahrhundert neben Ostern zunächst ein gesondertes Pfingstfest 50 Tage nach Ostern und dann auch ein gesondertes Himmelfahrtsfest 40 Tage nach Ostern zu feiern begonnen hat. Gegenüber jener 50tägigen Freudenzeit, in welcher Auferstehung, Himmelfahrt und Geistsendung in einem gefeiert wurden, setzt sich nun ein neues *historisierendes Verständnis der Feste* durch. Im Rückgriff auf biblische Zeitangaben entstand schließlich in Ausweitung der Osterfeier über das ganze Jahr hinaus das »Kirchenjahr« (ein Wort aus dem 16. Jahrhundert): ein aus Herren- und dann auch Heiligenfesten zusammengewachsener liturgischer Jahreszyklus, für den man noch im Mittelalter verschiedene Anfänge – Ostern, Mariä Verkündigung und besonders das ebenfalls seit dem 4. Jahrhundert gefeierte Weihnachtsfest – kannte und für den sich erst in neuerer Zeit der erste Adventssonntag als Anfang durchgesetzt hat.

Was aber – so läßt sich nun nach diesen Klärungen zusammenfassend fragen – ist bei all diesen Entwicklungen und zum Teil Verwicklungen der eigentliche Inhalt dieser Botschaft, welche den Glauben und den Gottesdienst von 2000 Jahren Christenheit am Leben erhalten hat, welche sowohl historischer Ursprung wie sachliches Fundament des christlichen Glaubens ist?

Die letzte Wirklichkeit

Die Botschaft mit all ihren Schwierigkeiten, ihren zeitgebundenen Konkretisierungen und Ausmalungen, situationsbedingten Erweiterungen, Ausgestaltungen und Akzentverschiebungen zielt im Grunde auf etwas Einfaches. Und darin stimmen die verschiedenen urchristlichen Zeugen, Petrus, Paulus und Jakobus, die Briefe, die Evangelien und die Apostelgeschichte durch alle Unstimmigkeiten und Widersprüchlichkeiten der verschiedenen Traditionen bezüglich Ort und Zeit, Personen und Ablauf der Ereignisse überein: *Der Gekreuzigte lebt für immer bei Gott – als Verpflichtung und Hoffnung für uns!* Die Menschen des Neuen Testaments sind getragen, ja fasziniert von der Gewißheit, daß der Getötete nicht im Tod geblieben ist, sondern lebt, und daß, wer an ihn sich hält und ihm nachfolgt, ebenfalls leben wird. Das neue, ewige Leben des Einen als Herausforderung und reale Hoffnung für alle!

Dies also sind Osterbotschaft und Osterglaube – völlig eindeutig trotz aller Vieldeutigkeit der verschiedenen Osterberichte und Ostervorstellungen. Eine wahrhaft umwälzende Botschaft, sehr leicht zurückzuweisen freilich schon damals, nicht erst heute: Darüber wollen wir dich ein ander Mal hören, sagten auf Athens Areopag nach lukanischer Darstellung einige Skeptiker schon dem Apostel Paulus[35]. Aufgehalten hat das den Siegeszug der Botschaft freilich nicht.

Sie war schon im *Judentum* vorbereitet worden: In der persischen Zeit nach dem babylonischen Exil war man dort je länger desto weniger mit der alten Antwort zufrieden, daß nach dem Grundsatz der Entsprechung oder Vergeltung, nach welchem auch die Freunde Hiobs argumentieren, im Leben zwischen Geburt und Tod alle Rechnungen aufgehen. Weder im Leben des Volkes noch in dem des Einzelnen schienen Gutes und Böses in ausreichendem Maße abgegolten. So setzte sich in den beiden Jahrhunderten vor Christus immer deutlicher – gestützt von manchen biblischen Texten über das mögliche Eingreifen Gottes in jeglicher Not und Gefahr – die Erwartung durch, daß die umfassende Erfüllung noch kommen werde: daß Gottes Gerechtigkeit in einem letzten Gericht den großen Ausgleich schaffen werde. Im Horizont dieser Erwartung war – zum erstenmal im Alten Testament wohl unter persischem Einfluß im Danielbuch um die Mitte des zweiten Jahrhunderts vor Christus[36] und dann überhaupt in der apokalyptischen Literatur, besonders im nichtkanonischen Henochbuch – der Glaube an die allgemeine Auferweckung der Toten oder zumindest der Gerechten wachgeworden: Auferweckung als die Voraussetzung für den Vollzug des Endgerichts und die Vollendung der Menschheitsgeschichte. Also weniger stand das Schicksal der Toten, über das man sehr verschieden dachte, im Vordergrund der Überlegungen. Vielmehr die Durchsetzung der Sache Gottes für das Volk und den Einzelnen in dieser so wenig gerechten Welt: Auferweckung im Dienst der Selbstrechtfertigung Gottes, der Theodizee. In diesem Sinn bekennt der gläubige Jude dreimal am Tag im zweiten Lobpreis des Achtzehn-Bitten-Gebetes: »Gepriesen bist du, Jahwe, der die Toten lebendig macht.«

Dieser jüdische Glaube ist im ganzen Neuen Testament, vor apokalyptischem Hintergrund, die selbstverständliche Voraussetzung. Der christliche Glaube dagegen, der freilich von rein zeitbedingten apokalyptischen Vorstellungselementen gelöst werden muß, faßt jenen jüdischen Glauben noch einmal in letzter Verdichtung. Juden und Christen glauben an die Auferweckung. Der Glaube der Juden und der Christen beruht darauf, daß für sie der lebendige Gott der *unerschütterlich treue Gott* ist, wie er aus der Geschichte Israels beständig entgegentritt. Er ist der Schöpfer, der seinem Geschöpf und Partner, komme, was da kommen mag, die Treue hält. Der sein Ja zum Leben nicht zurücknimmt, sondern gerade an der entscheidenden Grenze erneut Ja zu seinem Ja sagt: Treue im Tod über den Tod hinaus!

Was nun aber die Juden für alle Menschen in der Zukunft erwarten, das ist für die *Christen* in dem Einen als Zeichen der Verpflichtung und Hoffnung für alle bereits eingetreten. Der jüdische Glaube an eine allgemeine Auferweckung und der besondere Glaube an die Auferweckung Jesu stehen also in wechselseitiger Beziehung: Die ersten Christen erkennen die Auferweckung Jesu im Horizont und unter der Voraussetzung der jüdischen Hoffnung auf eine allgemeine Totenerweckung. Aber zugleich bestätigt die Auferweckung Jesu den allgemeinen jüdischen Auferweckungsglauben, wodurch die einzigartige Bedeutung dieses Jesus für die Menschen manifest wird: Die Auferweckung Jesu ist der Anfang der allgemeinen Totenerweckung, der Beginn der neuen Zeit, der Anfang vom Ende dieser Zeit[37]. Die Christen sagen also nicht nur: Weil es eine allgemeine Totenauferweckung gibt, muß gerade dieser Eine auferweckt sein. Sondern zugleich mit Paulus: Weil dieser Eine auferweckt worden ist, gibt es auch eine allgemeine Totenerweckung. Weil dieser Eine lebt und von Gott her eine solch einzigartige Bedeutung für alle hat, werden alle leben, die sich vertrauend auf ihn einlassen. Allen, die in Schicksalsgemeinschaft mit Jesus stehen, wird Anteil am Sieg Gottes über den Tod angeboten: so ist Jesus der Erstling der Toten[38], der Erstgeborene von den Toten[39].

Der Gekreuzigte *lebt?* Was heißt hier »leben«? Was verbirgt sich hinter den verschiedenen zeitgebundenen Vorstellungsmodellen und Erzählungsformen, die das Neue Testament dafür gebraucht? Wir versuchen, dieses Leben zu umschreiben mit zwei negativen Bestimmungen und einer positiven.

1. *Keine Rückkehr in dieses raumzeitliche Leben:* Der Tod wird nicht rückgängig gemacht, sondern definitiv überwunden. In Friedrich Dürrenmatts Schauspiel ›Meteor‹ kommt es zu einer

Wiederbelebung eines (freilich fingierten) Leichnams, der in ein völlig unverändertes irdisches Leben zurückkehrt – das klare Gegenteil von dem, was das Neue Testament unter Auferweckung versteht. Mit den Totenerweckungen, vereinzelt in der antiken Literatur von Wundertätern (sogar mit Arztzeugnissen beglaubigt) und in drei Fällen auch von Jesus (Tochter des Jairus[40], Jüngling von Nain[41], Lazarus[42]) berichtet, darf Jesu Auferweckung nicht verwechselt werden. Auch ganz abgesehen von der historischen Glaubwürdigkeit solcher legendärer Berichte (Markus etwa weiß nichts von der sensationellen Totenerweckung des Lazarus): gerade die vorübergehende Wiederbelebung eines Leichnams ist mit der Auferweckung Jesu nicht gemeint. Jesus ist – selbst bei Lukas – nicht einfach in das biologisch-irdische Leben zurückgekehrt, um wie die von ihrem Tod Aufgeweckten schließlich erneut zu sterben. Nein, nach neutestamentlichem Verständnis hat er den Tod, diese letzte Grenze, endgültig hinter sich. Er ist in ein ganz anderes, unvergängliches, ewiges, »himmlisches« Leben eingegangen: in das Leben Gottes, wofür, wie wir sahen, schon im Neuen Testament sehr verschiedene Formulierungen und Vorstellungen gebraucht werden.

2. *Keine Fortsetzung dieses raumzeitlichen Lebens:* Schon die Rede von »nach« dem Tod ist irreführend: Die Ewigkeit ist nicht bestimmt durch Vor und Nach. Sie meint vielmehr ein die Dimensionen von Raum und Zeit sprengendes neues Leben in Gottes unsichtbarem, unvergänglichem, unbegreiflichem Bereich: nicht einfach ein endloses »Weiter«: Weiterleben, Weitermachen, Weitergehen. Sondern ein endgültig »Neues«: Neuschöpfung, Neugeburt, neuer Mensch und neue Welt. Was die Rückkehr des ewig gleichen »Stirb und werde« endgültig durchbricht. Definitiv bei Gott sein und so das endgültige Leben haben, das ist gemeint!

3. *Vielmehr Aufnahme in die letzte Wirklichkeit:* Will man nicht bildhaft reden, so müssen Auferweckung (Auferstehung) und Erhöhung (Entrückung, Himmelfahrt, Verherrlichung) als ein identisches, einziges Geschehen gesehen werden. Und zwar als ein Geschehen in Zusammenhang mit dem Tod in der unanschaulichen Verborgenheit Gottes. Die Osterbotschaft besagt in allen so verschiedenen Varianten schlicht das eine: Jesus ist nicht ins Nichts hinein gestorben. Er ist im Tod und aus dem Tod in jene *unfaßbare und umfassende letzte Wirklichkeit hineingestor-*

ben, von ihr *aufgenommen* worden, die wir mit dem Namen *Gott* bezeichnen[43]. Wo der Mensch sein Eschaton, das Allerletzte seines Lebens erreicht, was erwartet ihn da? Nicht das Nichts, das würden auch Nirwana-Gläubige sagen. Sondern jenes Alles, das für Juden, Christen und Moslems Gott ist. Tod ist Durchgang zu Gott, ist Einkehr in Gottes Verborgenheit, ist Aufnahme in seine Herrlichkeit. Daß mit dem Tod *alles* aus sei, kann strenggenommen nur ein Gottloser sagen.

Im Tod wird der Mensch aus den ihn umgebenden und bestimmenden Verhältnissen entnommen. Von der Welt her, gleichsam von außen, bedeutet der Tod völlige Beziehungslosigkeit. Von Gott her aber, gleichsam von innen, bedeutet der Tod eine völlig neue Beziehung: zu ihm als der letzten Wirklichkeit. Im Tod wird dem Menschen, und zwar dem ganzen und ungeteilten Menschen, eine neue ewige Zukunft angeboten. Ein Leben anders als alles Erfahrbare: in Gottes unvergänglichen Dimensionen. Also nicht in unserem Raum und in unserer Zeit: »hier« und »jetzt« im »Diesseits«. Aber auch nicht einfach in einem anderen Raum und in einer anderen Zeit: ein »Drüben« oder »Droben«, ein »Außerhalb« oder »Oberhalb« ein »Jenseits«. Der letzte, entscheidende, ganz andere Weg des Menschen führt nicht hinaus ins Weltall oder über dieses hinaus. Sondern – wenn man schon in Bildern reden will – gleichsam hinein in den innersten Urgrund, Urhalt, Ursinn von Welt und Mensch: aus dem Tod ins Leben, aus dem Sichtbaren ins Unsichtbare, aus dem sterblichen Dunkel in Gottes ewiges Licht. In Gott hinein ist Jesus gestorben, zu Gott ist er gelangt: aufgenommen in jenen Bereich, der alle Vorstellungen übersteigt, den keines Menschen Auge je geschaut hat, unserem Zugreifen, Begreifen, Reflektieren und Phantasieren entzogen! Nur das weiß der Glaubende: nicht das Nichts erwartet ihn, sondern sein Vater.

Aus dieser negativen und positiven Bestimmung folgt:

Tod und *Auferweckung* bilden eine *differenzierte Einheit*. Will man die neutestamentlichen Zeugnisse nicht gegen ihre Intention interpretieren, darf man aus der Auferweckung nicht einfach ein »Interpretament«, ein Ausdrucksmittel des Glaubens für das Kreuz machen[44]:

– *Auferweckung ist Sterben in Gott hinein: Tod und Auferweckung stehen in engstem* Zusammenhang. *Die Auferweckung geschieht mit dem Tod, im Tod, aus dem Tod. Am schärfsten wird das herausgestellt in frühen vorpaulinischen Hymnen, in denen Jesu Erhöhung schon vom Kreuz aus zu erfolgen scheint[45]. Und besonders im Johannesevangelium, wo Jesu »Erhöhung« zugleich seine Kreuzigung wie seine »Verherrlichung« meint[46] und beides die eine Rückkehr zum Vater bildet[47]. Aber im übrigen Neuen Testament folgt die Erhöhung auf die Niedrigkeit des Kreuzes:*

– Das In-Gott-hinein-Sterben ist keine Selbstverständlichkeit, keine natürliche Entwicklung, kein unbedingt zu erfüllendes Desiderat der menschlichen Natur: Tod und Auferweckung müssen in ihrem nicht notwendig zeitlichen, aber sachlichen Unterschied gesehen werden. Wie das auch durch die alte, vermutlich weniger historische als theologische Angabe »auferstanden am dritten Tag« – »drei nicht als Kalenderdatum, sondern als Heilsdatum für einen Heilstag – betont wird. Der Tod ist des Menschen Sache, die Auferweckung kann nur Gottes sein: Von Gott wird der Mensch in ihn als die unfaßbare, umfassende letzte Wirklichkeit aufgenommen, gerufen, heimgeholt, also endgültig angenommen und gerettet. Im Tod, oder besser: aus dem Tod, als einem eigenen Geschehen, gründend in Gottes Tat und Treue. Die verborgene, unvorstellbare, neue Schöpfertat dessen, das, was nicht ist, ins Dasein ruft[48]. Und deshalb – und nicht als supranaturalistischer »Eingriff« gegen die Naturgesetze – ein echtes Geschenk und wahres Wunder.

Braucht man da noch eigens hervorzuheben, daß das neue Leben des Menschen, weil es um die letzte Wirklichkeit, um Gott selber geht, von vornherein eine Angelegenheit des *Glaubens* ist? Es geht um ein Geschehen der Neuschöpfung, welches den Tod als letzte Grenze und damit überhaupt unseren Welt- und Denkhorizont sprengt. Bedeutet es doch den definitiven Durchbruch in die wahrhaft andere Dimension des eindimensionalen Menschen: die offenbare Wirklichkeit Gottes und die in die Nachfolge rufende Herrschaft des Gekreuzigten. Nichts leichter, als dies zu bezweifeln! Es ist keine Frage, daß die »reine Vernunft« sich hier vor eine unübersteigbare Grenze gestellt sieht: da kann man Kant nur zustimmen. Auch durch historische Argumente läßt sich die Auferweckung nicht beweisen; da versagt die traditionelle Apologetik. Weil es der Mensch hier mit Gott, und das heißt per definitionem mit dem Unsichtbaren, Ungreifbaren, Unverfügbaren zu tun hat, ist nur eine Form des Verhaltens angemessen, herausgefordert: gläubiges Vertrauen, vertrauender

Glaube. Am Glauben vorbei führt kein Weg zum Auferweckten und zum ewigen Leben. Die Auferweckung ist kein beglaubigendes Mirakel. Sie ist selber Gegenstand des Glaubens.

Der Auferweckungsglaube ist jedoch – dies ist gegenüber allem Unglauben und Aberglauben zu sagen – nicht der Glaube an irgendeine unverifizierbare Kuriosität, die man auch noch »dazu« glauben müßte. Der Auferweckungsglaube ist auch nicht Glaube an das Faktum der Auferweckung oder an den Auferweckten isoliert genommen, sondern ist grundsätzlich Glaube an Gott, mit dem der Auferweckte nun zusammengehört[49]:

– *Der Auferweckungsglaube nicht ein Zusatz zum Gottesglauben, sondern eine* Radikalisierung *des Gottesglaubens: Ein Glaube an Gott, der nicht auf halbem Weg anhält, sondern den Weg konsequent zu Ende geht. Ein Glaube, in welchem sich der Mensch ohne strikt rationalen Beweis, wohl aber in durchaus vernünftigem Vertrauen darauf verläßt, daß der Gott des Anfangs auch der Gott des Endes ist, daß er wie der Schöpfer der Welt und des Menschen so auch ihr Vollender ist.*

– *Der Auferweckungsglaube ist also nicht nur als existentiale Verinnerlichung oder soziale Veränderung zu interpretieren, sondern als eine Radikalisierung des Glaubens an den* Schöpfergott: *Auferweckung meint die reale Überwindung des Todes durch den Schöpfergott, dem der Glaubende alles, auch das Letzte, auch die Überwindung des Todes, zutraut. Das Ende, das ein neuer Anfang ist! Wer sein Credo mit dem Glauben an »Gott den allmächtigen Schöpfer« anfängt, darf es auch ruhig mit dem Glauben an »das ewige Leben« beenden. Weil Gott das Alpha ist, ist er auch das Omega. Der allmächtige Schöpfer, der aus dem Nichtsein ins Sein ruft, vermag auch aus dem Tod ins Leben zu rufen*[50].

Gerade angesichts des Todes offenbart sich Gottes in der Welt verborgene Allmacht. Die Auferweckung aus dem Tod kann der Mensch sich nicht errechnen. Doch auf diesen Gott, der geradezu definiert werden kann als ein Gott der Lebendigen und nicht der Toten[51], *darf* der Mensch sich in jedem Fall verlassen, auf seine überlegene Schöpfermacht auch angesichts des unausweichlichen Todes unbedingt vertrauen, seinem Tod getrost entgegengehen. Dem Schöpfer und Erhalter des Alls und des Menschen ist zuzutrauen, daß er auch bei Tod und Sterben über die Grenzen alles bislang Erfahrenen hinaus noch ein Wort mehr zu sagen hat:

daß er wie das erste so auch das letzte Wort zu sagen hat. Diesem Gott gegenüber ist allein das Vertrauen, der Glaube, die der Wirklichkeit entsprechende vernünftige Haltung. Das Eingehen aus dem Tod zu Gott läßt sich nicht empirisch oder rational verifizieren. Es ist das Nicht-zu-Erwartende und Nicht-zu-Erweisende, wohl aber das im Glauben zu Erhoffende. Das Menschenunmögliche wird von Gott allein ermöglicht. Wer ernsthaft an den lebendigen Gott glaubt, glaubt also auch an die Auferweckung der Toten zum Leben, an Gottes Macht, die sich am Tode bewährt. Wie Jesus den zweifelnden Sadduzäern entgegenhielt: »Ihr kennt weder die Schriften noch die Kraft Gottes[52].«

Der christliche Glaube an den auferweckten Jesus ist sinnvoll nur als Glaube an Gott den Schöpfer und Erhalter des Lebens. Umgekehrt aber ist der christliche Glaube an den Schöpfergott entscheidend bestimmt dadurch, daß er Jesus von den Toten erweckt hat[53]. »Der Jesus von den Toten erweckt hat« wird geradezu der Beiname des christlichen Gottes[54].

Legenden?

Wer erkannt hat, worauf die Auferweckungsbotschaft zielt, für den sind einige heftig umstrittene Fragen eher peripher. Nur wer seinen Glauben an historische Details bindet, verfällt dann auch der historischen Kritik. Der Glaube aber, der auf das neue Leben des Gekreuzigten mit Gott und durch Gott ausgerichtet ist, vermag die Relativität der historischen Fragen zu erkennen. So möge denn, wer an historischen Fragen wie der Entwicklung der Osterberichte, des leeren Grabes, der Höllenfahrt und der Erscheinungen des Auferweckten nicht interessiert ist, die folgenden beiden Abschnitte überschlagen. Die historische Analyse kann den Glauben in seinem Zentrum nicht begründen, wohl aber gegenüber Unglauben und Aberglauben deuten und klären[55].

1. Die Geschichte der Auferweckungsüberlieferung läßt problematische *Erweiterungen und Ausgestaltungen,* eventuell auch Lücken sichtbar werden: Das *älteste Osterzeugnis* des Neuen Testaments – die genannte alte Glaubensformel im ersten Korintherbrief[56] – ist wie auch andere paulinische Glaubensformeln von geradezu protokollartiger Knappheit: ein Minimum an Information, ohne jegliche Beschreibung, ohne Angabe eines

Wann und Wo der Erscheinungen. Auch der älteste Osterbericht der literarisch beträchtlich jüngeren, aber sicher alte Traditionen verarbeitenden Evangelien, ist von erstaunlicher Kargheit: Dieser Bericht des *Markus*[57] – zu unterscheiden von dem (Mattäus und Lukas noch unbekannten) Markus-Nachtrag[58], der später die umlaufenden Erscheinungsüberlieferungen ebenfalls katalogartig zusammenstellt – bringt außer der (vielleicht ursprünglich selbständigen) Überlieferung vom leeren Grab und dem Hinweis (keine Erzählung!) auf Jesu Erscheinung in Galiläa nichts Neues.

Die beiden Großevangelien aber weisen – zum Teil aus apologetischen Gründen – beträchtliche Veränderungen und Erweiterungen auf. Bei *Mattäus*, der mit der Erscheinung Jesu selbst vor den Frauen erzählerisch einen Zusammenhang zwischen dem Grabgeschehen und der galiläischen Erscheinung herstellt, finden sich neu: zuerst das Erdbeben; dann die Geschichte von den Grabeswächtern und die Ausführung des Auftrages des Engels und Jesu, nach Galiläa zu gehen; schließlich die Erscheinung vor den Elf auf dem Berg in Galiläa mit dem Missions- und Taufbefehl. Bei *Lukas*, der den Auftrag, nach Galiläa zu gehen, kurzerhand streicht, die galiläische Erscheinung verschweigt und das ganze Ostergeschehen örtlich und zeitlich auf das für ihn theologisch und kirchlich wichtige Jerusalem konzentriert, werden hinzugefügt: die künstlerisch gestaltete Erzählung von den Emmaus-Jüngern, die Erscheinung vor den Elf in Jerusalem, eine kleine Abschiedsrede und ein kurzer Bericht von einer Himmelfahrt Jesu, die in der lukanischen Apostelgeschichte wieder aufgenommen und nicht unerheblich erweitert wird.

Was bereits seit langem kirchliche Praxis ist, wird in den späteren Evangelien auf Wirkung und Auftrag des Auferweckten zurückgeführt: Heidenmission und Taufe bei Mattäus, das Brotbrechen (das in der Emmaus-Szene jeden Leser an das Herrenmahl erinnern mußte) bei Lukas, die Stellung Petri und die Vollmacht der Sündenvergebung (für *jeden* Glaubenden) bei Johannes. Während im paulinischen Osterzeugnis kein Engel erwähnt wird, so bei Markus und Mattäus ein Engel, bei Lukas und Johannes gar deren zwei. Und während bei Paulus und Mattäus die Erscheinungen des Auferweckten direkt als Sendungen zur Verkündigung verstanden werden, so bei Lukas und Johannes stärker zur Beglaubigung der Auferweckung. Bei Lukas zeigt sich durchgängig eine Tendenz zur Verdinglichung. Während Paulus in paradoxer Weise von einem »geistigen«, nicht vorstellbaren Auferstehungsleib spricht, betont Lukas, wohl apologetisch gegen eine spiritistische Interpretation der Auferweckung, daß der Auferweckte kein Gespenst ist, Fleisch und Knochen hat, von gebratenem Fisch ißt. Und wie aus apologetischen Gründen die wahre Leiblichkeit des Auferweckten immer massiver betont wird, so auch das Motiv des Zweifels, der überwunden werden muß.

Das wiederum beträchtlich spätere Evangelium des *Johannes* enthält bei allen Berührungspunkten mit Lukas ebenfalls neue Elemente und Motive: das Gespräch mit Maria Magdalena, der Wettlauf Petri und des ungenannten Lieblingsjüngers, die Versammlung im Saal in Jerusalem mit der Geistmitteilung am Osterabend, die Geschichte vom ungläubigen Thomas mit dem hier am massivsten entwickelten Zweifelsmotiv. Hinzugefügt wurde später, wiederum im Dienst der Identitätserfahrung, ein Nachtragskapitel mit der Erscheinung am See Gennesaret, einem wunderbaren Fischfang mit Mahl und einem Sonderauftrag an Petrus. Hier erneut das Konkurrenzmotiv zwischen Petrus, dem Ersterscheinung und Vorrang bestätigt werden, und dem Lieblingsjünger, der im vierten Evangelium offensichtlich als der eigentliche Garant der Überlieferung dargestellt wird.

Gerade aus der Entwicklung der Ostertradition läßt sich Wichtiges ablesen: Historisch gesehen, dürfte der Osterglaube mit größter Wahrscheinlichkeit in Galiläa entstanden sein, wo sich Jesu Anhänger nach der Flucht wieder gesammelt haben, um dann in Erwartung der Wiederkunft des erhöhten Menschensohnes nach Jerusalem hinaufzuziehen. Die vielfachen Erweiterungen, Verschiebungen und Ausgestaltungen der Osterbotschaft können jedenfalls schon aufgrund der Quellenlage nicht von vornherein auf Historizität Anspruch erheben, sondern dürften weithin legendären Charakter haben. Die Verschiedenartigkeit der Berichte ergibt sich aus der Verschiedenheit der Gemeinden, Überlieferungsträger und Überlieferungssituationen (Missionspredigt, Katechese, Gottesdienst). Nicht die wechselnden Einzelzüge der verschiedenen Erzählungen, nicht die bildhaften Ausmalungen und auch nicht die verschiedenen Intentionen und Theologien der Quellen, Verfasser und Redaktoren sind das Entscheidende. Das Entscheidende ist das von allen Zeugen bejahte neue Leben Jesu aus dem Tod durch Gott und mit Gott, Gottes Leben, das alle Aussagen und Vorstellungen, Bilder, Ausmalungen und Legenden übersteigt.

2. Was ist dann aber insbesondere von der Erzählung des *leeren Grabes* zu halten? Die bereits genannte, auch bei Paulus sich findende, formelhaft wirkende Angabe »am dritten Tag« kann die Entdeckung des leeren Grabes durch die Frauen oder die erste Ostererscheinung Petri oder aber auch wie in der jüdischen Apokalyptik die Frist zwischen der Endkatastrophe und dem Anbruch des Endheils meinen, womit dann Kreuz und Auferweckung in apokalyptischer Sprache als Endereignis und der dritte Tag als Heilstag markiert würden[59]. Diese Angabe dürfte, ähnlich wie die lukanischen 40 Tage zwischen Ostern und Himmelfahrt, eine theologische Chiffre sein[60], die freilich den sachlichen (nicht notwendig zeitlichen) Unterschied zwischen Tod und Auferweckung deutlich macht. Jedenfalls wurde nun der »dritte Tag« nach dem Todesfreitag – also nicht mehr der Sabbat – zum hauptsächlichen Versammlungstag der Christen: der Sonntag als Gedenktag der Auferweckung des Herrn.

Auffällig ist nun: Das im ersten Korintherbrief wiedergegebene älteste Auferweckungszeugnis[61] sagt nichts von einem leeren Grab und nennt die Frauen – vielleicht allerdings, weil sie kein wirkliches Zeugenrecht hatten – nicht unter den Auferweckungszeugen. *Paulus* wie auch die übrigen neutestamentlichen Schriften außerhalb der vier Evangelien erwähnt in all seinen Briefen das leere Grab oder Zeugen des leeren Grabes nirgendwo. Er legt nur darauf Gewicht, daß sich Jesus den Seinen »geoffenbart« hat[62]. Paulus konnte sich Auferweckung so vorstellen, daß ein neuer Leib im Himmel zu unserer Bekleidung bereitliegt[63], so daß, ließe sich folgern, für die Auferweckung Jesu der irdische Leib im Grabe bleiben könnte. Im jüdischen Palästina stellte man sich die Auferweckung freilich ganz allgemein leiblich vor. Dem hellenistischen Judentum aber war diese Anschauung zumindest teilweise fremd und den Griechen überhaupt kaum verständlich. Aber selbst wenn sich der in Jerusalem ausgebildete hellenistische Jude Paulus bei seinem Verständnis der Einheit von Leib und lebendigmachendem Geist eine Auferweckung ohne leeres Grab nicht hätte vorstellen können: sein Auferweckungsglaube stützt sich jedenfalls weder auf das leere Grab noch auf bestimmte Vorgänge am Ostermorgen. Für die Verkündigung hat er dem leeren Grab keinerlei Bedeutung zugeschrieben: Nicht das leere Grab, sondern der Erweis Jesu als eines Lebendigen sind für seine Verkündigung entscheidend.

Die *Unterschiede* zwischen den Aussagen über die *Erscheinungen*, die nach dem ersten Korintherbrief schon in die allerälteste

Phase der Urchristenheit zurückreichen dürften und für Paulus nachprüfbar sind, und andererseits den *Grabesgeschichten,* die jedenfalls erst Jahrzehnte nach Paulus mit Markus um das Jahr 70 literarisch greifbar werden und zu dieser Zeit nicht mehr nachprüfbar sind, fallen in die Augen[64]: Die Grabesgeschichten handeln ursprünglich nur von Frauen und nicht von den Jüngern, die Erscheinungsaussagen gerade umgekehrt. Die Grabesgeschichten berichten zunächst von Engelerscheinungen und nicht von Christuserscheinungen, die Erscheinungsaussagen wiederum umgekehrt. Die Grabesgeschichten sind (zum Teil künstlerisch gestaltete) Erzählungen zum staunenden Zuhören (etwa in der gottesdienstlichen Lesung), die Erscheinungsaussagen in ihrer ältesten Form katechismusartige Zusammenfassungen zum Auswendiglernen (wohl im katechetischen Gebrauch). Die Engel, die das christliche Glaubensbekenntnis verkünden[65], fungieren als apokalyptische Deuteengel und werden in Erscheinung und Wirken nach den Vorstellungen der zeitgenössischen Apokalyptik beschrieben. Vielleicht reduziert sich die Zeugenreihe in ihrer Urform gar auf jene eine Frau, die als einzige von allen Evangelisten übereinstimmend und von Johannes sogar als ursprünglich einzige Zeugin überliefert wurde: Maria von Magdala (Maria, die Mutter Jesu, spielt in den Auferweckungszeugnissen auffälligerweise überhaupt keine Rolle).

Die Annahme also läßt sich kaum widerlegen, daß es sich bei den Grabesgeschichten, die untereinander stark abweichen und in den späteren Evangelien beträchtlich erweitert sind (Grabbewachung bei Mattäus, Lauf des Petrus zum Grab bei Lukas und Johannes, Erscheinung Jesu vor den Frauen bei Mattäus und vor Maria Magdalena bei Johannes), um *legendäre Ausgestaltungen der Botschaft von der Auferweckung* handelt, die als Botschaft des Engels deren Mittelpunkt bildet und die nach alttestamentlichen Epiphaniegeschichten gestaltet worden ist. Jedenfalls steht im Zentrum auch dieser Erzählung nicht das leere, exakter: das geöffnete Grab, sondern die Auferweckungsbotschaft. Schon beim rätselhaft kurzen ursprünglichen Markustext ist Verkündigung die Intention, die Form aber ist legendär (wunderbare Graböffnung, Flucht der Frauen infolge Engelserscheinung).

Hat jedoch nicht die Ausrichtung der Auferweckungsbotschaft in Jerusalem das Faktum des leeren Grabes vorausgesetzt? Nicht unbedingt. Die Verkündigung des Auferweckten durch die (aus Galiläa zurückgekehrten?) Jünger (auch nach eher überhöhter, idealisierender Zählung des Lukas nur 120[66]) setzte ja nicht sofort, sondern erst mehrere Wochen nach Jesu Tod (der lukanische Pfingsttermin nimmt 50 Tage an) ein, was eine Überprüfung schwierig machte, und dürfte in einer Stadt von vielleicht 25 000 bis 30 000 Einwohnern zunächst kaum viel Aufsehen gemacht und nach öffentlicher Kontrolle gerufen haben. Die Geschichte vom leeren Grab muß somit nicht als Rekognoszierung eines Faktums aufgefaßt werden. Sie läßt sich als die wohl relativ frühe erzählerische Konkretisierung und legendäre Entfaltung der vorgängigen Auferweckungskunde, wie sie in der Verkündigung des oder der Engel enthalten ist, verstehen.

Aber mag einer von der Historizität des leeren Grabes positiver denken, wie immerhin manche gewichtige Exegeten auch heute: ein juristisch ungültiges und deshalb apologetisch wertloses Zeugnis von Frauen sei kaum erfunden worden, sondern ließe wie anderes auf die – freilich nicht weiter erklärbare – Historizität des leeren Grabes schließen (leer aus welchen Gründen auch immer!). Darüber dürfte doch Übereinstimmung herrschen: Das leere Grab vermag aus sich allein auch nach den Grabesgeschichten selbst *keinen Beweis der Auferweckung* zu liefern und keine Auferweckungshoffnung zu begründen. Die Emmaus-Jünger bestätigen es nach Lukas ausdrücklich[67]. Auch wenn die Erzählung vom leeren Grab einen historischen Kern haben sollte, würde dadurch der Glaube an den Auferweckten keineswegs erleichtert, für manche heute eher erschwert. Das pure Faktum des leeren Grabes ist vieldeutig, mißdeutbar. Für ein leeres Grab gibt es viele Erklärungen, wie schon die Evangelisten, wohl in Abwehr jüdischer Tendenzgerüchte, berichteten: Jüngerbetrug, Leichendiebstahl, Verwechslung, Scheintod. Freilich hat die jüdische Polemik, soviel wir wissen, das leere Grab als solches nicht bestritten. Doch läßt sich mit dem leeren Grab als solchem die Wahrheit der Auferweckung auch nicht beweisen. Als Auferweckungsbeweis wäre es eine petitio principii. Aus sich sagt das leere Grab nur: »Er ist nicht hier[68].« Es muß schon ausdrücklich gesagt werden, was keineswegs selbstverständlich ist: »Er ist auferweckt[69].« Und gerade dies kann einem auch ohne Vorzeigen eines leeren Grabes gesagt werden. Auch die Frauen haben nicht aufgrund des leeren Grabes geglaubt. Nach dem frühesten Bericht des Markus, den die anderen Evangelisten auffällig abändern, schafft das leere Grab nicht Glauben und Verstehen, sondern Angst und Schrecken, so daß ihnen der Mund verschlossen wird[70]. Vom Werden des Glaubens wird nichts berichtet. Schon Mattäus aber fügt zur Angst der Frauen die »große Freude«

hinzu und macht aus dem Schweigen ein »Verkündigen«[71]. Jener befremdliche letzte Satz des ursprünglichen kurzen Markus-Schlusses[72] aber wurde durch die Jahrhunderte hindurch im Evangelium des Ostertags einfach nicht mit vorgelesen. Dabei kann freilich die kaum zu beweisende Vermutung mancher Exegeten auch nicht von vornherein abgewiesen werden, daß der eigentliche Schluß dieses Evangeliums, das sonst seltsam unvermittelt mit einem »nämlich« endete, verlorenging, wie solches bei den auf Papyrusblättern oder in Rollenform geschriebenen Büchern nicht allzu selten vorkam, und daß dieser Schluß ähnlich wie der Mattäus-Schluß von einer Erscheinung des Auferweckten in Galiläa berichtet hatte.

Das also ist vom leeren Grab zu halten:

– *Das leere Grab hat auch nach dem Neuen Testament niemanden zum Glauben an den Auferweckten geführt. Wie niemand behauptet, er sei bei der Auferweckung dabeigewesen oder er kenne Augenzeugen der Auferweckung, so auch niemand, der sagt, er sei durch das leere Grab zum Glauben an den Auferweckten gekommen. Nirgendwo berufen sich die Jünger auf den Befund des leeren Grabes, um den Glauben der Kirche zu bestärken oder um die Gegner zu widerlegen und zu überzeugen.*
– *Der Glaube an den Auferweckten ist also unabhängig vom leeren Grab. Das Ostergeschehen wird durch das leere Grab nicht bedingt, sondern bestenfalls erleuchtet. Das leere Grab ist kein Glaubensartikel, ist weder Grund noch Gegenstand des Osterglaubens. Nach der neutestamentlichen Botschaft selbst braucht man weder aufgrund des leeren Grabes noch erst recht an das leere Grab zu glauben. Nicht zum leeren Grab ruft der christliche Glaube, sondern zur Begegnung mit dem lebendigen Christus selbst: »Was sucht ihr den Lebendigen bei den Toten?«[73]*
– *Zumindest damals konnte die wohl ursprünglich selbständige Erzählung vom leeren Grab eine Funktion erfüllen: als verdeutlichendes und bestätigendes Zeichen dafür, daß der Auferweckte niemand anders ist als der gekreuzigte Jesus von Nazaret. Ein zumindest damals beredtes Zeichen also für die Identität: Der Auferweckte ist nicht ein anderes, etwa himmlisches Wesen, sondern jener Mensch Jesus von Nazaret, der im Grabe gelegen hat. Er wird erst recht nicht zu einem unbestimmten, mit Gott und All verschmolzenen Fluidum, sondern bleibt*

*auch in Gottes Leben dieser bestimmte, unverwechselbare Er,
der er war.*

– *Heute dagegen ist das leere Grab als Zeichen durch die historische Kritik zweifelhaft und durch die naturwissenschaftlichen
Erkenntnisse verdächtig geworden. Damit die Identität gewahrt bleibt, bedarf Gott nicht der Reliquien der irdischen
Existenz Jesu. Wir sind auf keine physiologischen Vorstellungen von Auferweckung verpflichtet. Identität der Person kann
auch ohne Kontinuität zwischen irdischem und »himmli-
schem«, »geistigem,« Leib gegeben sein. Auferweckung ist nicht
gebunden an das sich von vornherein ständig wandelnde Sub-
strat oder die Elemente dieses bestimmten Körpers. Die Leib-
haftigkeit der Auferweckung fordert nicht, daß das Grab leer
wird. Gott erweckt in neuer, anderer, nicht mehr vorstellbarer
»geistiger Leiblichkeit«. Entscheidend ist, wie dargelegt, das
neue, ewige Leben in jener letzten verborgenen Wirklichkeit,
die wir Gott nennen.*

3. »Gekreuzigt, begraben, abgestiegen zu der Hölle.« Zwischen
Kreuzestod und Auferweckung Jesu findet sich im Apostolischen Glaubensbekenntnis die Aussage von Jesu *Höllenfahrt.*
Dies freilich erst als eine sehr späte Hinzufügung aus der zweiten
Hälfte des 4. Jahrhunderts[74]. Vielleicht kann keine andere Aussage des Apostolikums so deutlich zeigen, wie wenig ein Schwören
auf vereinzelte Glaubenssätze eines Credo hilft und wieviel Vorsicht bei der Interpretation traditioneller Lehren angebracht ist.

Die Frage nach dem neutestamentlichen Befund wird oft
schon präjudiziert durch eine schiefe Fragestellung. Was heißt
»abgestiegen zu der Hölle«, »descendit ad inferna« oder »ad
inferos«? Der Wirrwarr entsteht aus einem *Doppelsinn:* »inferna« oder »Unterwelt« (wie bis ins Frühmittelalter auch das
deutsche »Hölle«) meint zunächst einfach das Totenreich (hebräisch »Scheol«, griechisch »Hades«). Seit der Scholastik aber,
wo man alle Frommen gleich nach dem Tod oder dem Fegfeuer
schon im endgültigen Zustand (Paradies, Himmel) sieht, werden
die »inferna« zum Ort der Nicht-Seligen: primär der Ort der
endgültig Verdammten (hebräisch »Gehenna«, »Hölle«) zusammen mit drei anderen unterweltlichen Bezirken: Fegfeuer (»Pur-
gatorium«), Vorhölle für die alttestamentlichen Gerechten
(»Limbus patrum«) und die ungetauften Kinder (»Limbus puer-
orum«). Von daher die Zweideutigkeit der Aussage, die sich bis
in neueste Übersetzungen des Apostolischen Credos durchhält:

früher »abgestiegen zur Hölle«, jetzt aber »abgestiegen in das Reich des Todes«! Im zweiten Sinn macht die Aussage keine Probleme, da sie über die Affirmation des Todes Jesu nicht hinausgeht. Nur fragt man sich naürlich: Warum dann noch einen eigenen Glaubensartikel nach »gestorben und begraben«? Ein solcher zielt offensichtlich nicht nur auf Jesu Tod: eine Hadesfahrt, sondern auf einen eigenen Akt *zwischen* Tod und Auferweckung: eine wie immer verstandene Höllenfahrt. Läßt sich aber eine solche vom Neuen Testament her rechtfertigen?

Nur eine einzige Stelle in dem späten, nicht authentischen ersten Petrusbrief läßt sich für eine eigentliche Wirksamkeit Jesu *zwischen* Tod und Auferweckung anführen: sie spricht vom getöteten Christus, der im Geist hingegangen ist und jenen Geistern im Gefängnis gepredigt hat, die zur Zeit der Sintflut ungehorsam waren[75]. Aber gerade die Interpretation dieser einen Stelle ist durch die ganze Kirchengeschichte hindurch widersprüchlich:

Geht es hier – wie im Gefolge Kardinal Bellarmins (aus Interesse an einem »Fegfeuer«) die katholische Theologie der Gegenreformation meinte – um die Seele (»Geist«) Jesu, die zwischen Tod und Auferweckung den Patriarchen und Gerechten des alten Bundes das Evangelium verkündete (den Limbus der Väter)? Aber die griechische Unterscheidung zwischen »Leib« und »Seele« entspricht keineswegs der neutestamentlichen Entgegensetzung von »Fleisch« und »Geist«. Und von den Vätern ist hier nicht die Rede, sondern von den Ungehorsamen zur Zeit Noahs.

Oder geht es – wie in den langen Jahrhunderten von Augustin über die mittelalterlichen Scholastiker bis zu Bellarmin in der lateinischen Theologie angenommen - um den präexistenten Christus, der nach seiner göttlichen Natur durch den Mund Noahs den Sündern vor der Sintflut predigte? Aber diese Exegese, zu weit vom Text spekulierend, findet unter den modernen Exegeten keine Gefolgschaft.

Oder geht es – wie bei den griechischen Vätern seit Clemens von Alexandrien, der als erster diesen Text mit Christi Höllenfahrt verbunden hat, und auch im Westen bis zu Augustin – um die Predigt Jesu im Totenreich, um den Toten Gelegenheit zur Bekehrung zu geben? Aber abgesehen von der unbiblischen Entgegensetzung von »Leib« und »Seele«: gerade eine vom Neuen Testament her nicht zu verantwortende Bekehrung nach Tod und Gericht wollte Augustin mit seiner Lösung ausschließen. Eine Heilsgewißheit der im Glauben entschlafenen alttestamentlichen Frommen läßt sich durchaus auch ohne eine besondere Höllenfahrt Jesu annehmen.

Oder ging es vielleicht einfach um den Tod Jesu, der nach Luther und Calvin als ein Durchgang durch die Qualen der Verdammtem verstanden werden muß: als das Erfahren von Gottes Zorn im Tod und als Anfechtung zur Verzweiflung? Aber eine solche Deutung läßt sich bestenfalls auf Texte vom Kreuzestod Jesu begründen, die jedoch nichts von einer Höllenfahrt *nach* dem Tode Jesu sagen.

Erst seitdem der protestantische Exeget F. Spitta[76] in den »Geistern«, denen Christus zu predigen hatte, rebellische Engel erkannte und der Katholik K. Gschwind[77] diese Verkündigung als die Tätigkeit des Auferweckten, war man auf der wahrscheinlich richtigen Spur: Es geht in diesem Text – wie Parallelen aus der apokryphen Literatur und besonders den beiden Fassungen des Henoch-Buches als die doch wohl überzeugendste Lösung zeigen – um den durch den Geist umgewandelten, auferweckten Christus, der wie ein neuer Henoch in seiner Himmelfahrt den gefallenen Engeln in den unteren Himmelsregionen ihre definitive Verurteilung verkündet[78]. In der christlichen Frühzeit hatte sich unter dem Einfluß hellenistischer Ideen das Weltbild zu ändern begonnen: Das Bild vom dreistöckigen Universum (Himmel, Erde, Unterwelt) wurde vielfach ersetzt durch ein Bild von einer sich frei im Raum bewegenden, von Planetensphären umgebenen Erde, wobei die Region über dem Mond den Göttern und die unter dem Mond den Geistern der Menschen und den dämonischen Mächten vorbehalten war. In diesem »zweiten Himmel« werden nach dem vermutlich christlich überarbeiteten slawischen Henoch-Buch[79] ungefähr aus der Zeit des ersten Petrusbriefes die gefallenen Engel gefangengehalten für ihre Bestrafung. Vom Kampf wider die Geisterwesen der Bosheit in den himmlischen Regionen ist im Neuen Testament auch sonst die Rede[80].

Was ist also, wenn man sich den exegetischen Befund vor Augen hält, von diesem Glaubensartikel zu halten? Mehr als Orientierungsmarken können nicht gesetzt werden:

– *Für einen Abstieg Jesu (oder seiner Seele) in die Hölle* nach *dem Tod fehlt ein eindeutiger neutestamentlicher Beleg, sofern damit mehr als die reine Aussage, daß Jesus starb und damit nach zeitgenössischer jüdischer Auffassung in den »Scheol« ging, gemeint sein soll.*

- *Das Neue Testament macht überhaupt keine Aussage über eine Tätigkeit Jesu zwischen Tod und Auferweckung: weder von einem letzten Akt der Erniedrigung nach dem Tod (Höllenfahrt als Ausdruck seines Leidens) noch von einem ersten Akt der Erhöhung vor der Auferweckung (Höllenfahrt als Ausdruck seines Triumphes). Wird der Tod als ein Hineinsterben in Gott und die Auferweckung als die Aufnahme aus dem Tod in Gottes Leben verstanden, wie oben dargelegt, wird die Frage nach einer Zwischen-»Zeit« von vornherein gegenstandslos.*

- *Die Heilsmöglichkeit der vor- und außerchristlichen Menschheit (der alttestamentlichen Frommen, der von der Verkündigung nicht Erreichten, der ungetauften Kinder) kann auch ohne die mythologische Vorstellung einer Predigt Jesu in der Vorhölle bejaht werden. Die universale Tragweite der am Kreuz geschehenen Stellvertretung hängt nicht ab von einer nicht erweisbaren Leidens- oder Triumphfahrt Jesu in eine von vornherein nicht mehr vorstellbare Unterwelt.*

- *Wenn der »Abstieg zur Hölle« aber ein wirklicher Ausdruck für die Gottverlassenheit Jesu im Tod selbst sein soll, so ist sie vom Neuen Testament gedeckt[81], bedarf aber keines eigenen Glaubensartikels neben Tod und Begräbnis. Ein psychologisierender Einblick in eine Gewissensangst Jesu, aber auch eine spekulative Interpretation seines Seelenleidens als Sieg über die Hölle vor der Auferweckung ist aufgrund der Quellen schwerlich möglich.*

- *Jesu Wirken im Neuen Testament wird ganz allgemein gesehen im mythologischen Rahmen einer siegreichen Schlacht gegen die bösen Geister[82], welche im 1. Petrusbrief gleichsam graphisch dargestellt wird, insofern der Auferweckte bei seinem Aufstieg durch die Himmel zum Vater auf die alten Feinde des Menschengeschlechts trifft. In diesen mythologischen Rahmen gehört auch die patristische Idee vom Teufelsrecht oder -betrug oder vom Loskauf der Gerechten aus der Macht des Satans.*

- *Das Böse als Macht, wie sie im Leben und Sterben Jesu in ihrer ganzen Bedrohlichkeit zum Ausdruck kommt, wird auf zwei Weisen verharmlost: Einerseits durch die Personifizierung des Bösen in einem Heer individueller Geistwesen (mythologische Vorstellungen vom Satan und von Legionen von Teufeln, die aus der babylonischen Mythologie in das frühe Judentum und von da ins Neue Testament eingedrungen sind[83]). Andererseits aber auch durch die Privatisierung des Bösen in den einzelnen Menschen. Das Böse als Macht ist sowohl vom Neuen Testa-*

ment (»Mächte und Gewalten«) wie von modernen soziologischen Erkenntnissen her (»anonyme Mächte und Systeme«) wesentlich mehr als die Summe der Bosheiten der Individuen[84].

- Die Hölle ist in jedem Fall nicht mythologisch als Ort in der Ober- oder Unterwelt zu verstehen. Sondern theologisch als ein in vielen Bildern umschriebener, aber doch unanschaulicher Ausschluß von der Gemeinschaft mit dem lebendigen Gott als extreme letzte Möglichkeit. Die neutestamentlichen Aussagen über die Hölle wollen keine Neugierde und Phantasie befriedigende Information über ein Jenseits liefern. Sie wollen gerade für das Diesseits den unbedingten Ernst des Anspruches Gottes und die Dringlichkeit der Umkehr des Menschen hier und jetzt vor Augen stellen. Die in manchen neutestamentlichen Bildworten bejahte »Ewigkeit« der Höllenstrafe (des »Feuers«) bleibt Gott und seinem Willen untergeordnet. Einzelne neutestamentliche Stellen, die mit anderen nicht ausgeglichen sind, deuten für die Vollendung eine Versöhnung aller, ein Allerbarmen an[85].

Bei diesen Orientierungsmarken wurde wohl noch deutlicher als an anderen Stellen, daß hier keine Miniaturdogmatik mit Lösungen für alle theologischen Probleme geliefert werden soll. Über Hölle, Tod und Teufel ließen sich ja nicht nur Seiten, sondern Bücher füllen[86]. Aber zu Stichworten, die der Leser in einer solchen Einführung vermissen würde und die doch nicht eingehend behandelt werden können, sollte dem Denken wenigstens eine Richtung gewiesen werden.

Entstehung des Glaubens

Wenn nun aber die Evangelienüberlieferung vom leeren Grab nicht ohne weiteres als historisch angenommen werden kann, stellt sich dann dieselbe Frage nicht auch bezüglich der *Erscheinungen*, aufgrund derer die Jünger nach den Evangelien zum Glauben an den Auferweckten gekommen sind? Dürfte es nicht schwierig sein, von den Erscheinungsgeschichten der Evangelien mit ihren zahlreichen legendären Zügen an die geschichtliche Entstehung des Osterglaubens der Jünger heranzukommen? Sind das nicht vielleicht nur Bestätigungserlebnisse? Geht es bei dem ältesten paulinischen Auferweckungszeugnis nicht um einen Legitimationsausweis? Mit der Frage nach den Erscheinungen ist freilich in sehr viel grundlegenderer Weise die Frage nach der Entstehung des christlichen Osterglaubens gestellt. Zwei grundsätzliche Möglichkeiten der Erklärung bieten sich an, wobei aber zugleich auch die Einwände zu bedenken sind.

1. *Entstehung des Glaubens durch Reflexionen der Jünger?* Seit der Aufklärung ist in verschiedenen Varianten immer wieder neu die Frage gestellt worden, ob sich der Auferweckungsglaube nicht auch ohne Annahme von Erscheinungen psychologisch und historisch plausibel machen läßt.

Neuerdings greift man besonders auf die spätjüdische Auferstehungserwartung zurück: Jüdische Traditionen über das Martyrium und die Entrückung prophetischer Figuren der Endzeit (Elija, Henoch) und deren Anwendung auf das Geschick Johannes' des Täufers könnten, so meint man, Kategorien bereitgestellt haben, die den Jüngern Jesu und Jesus selber nicht fremd waren und mit dem die Jünger nach dem Tod das Geschick ihres Meisters als Martyrium und göttliche Rechtfertigung, als Tod und Auferweckung verstehen und interpretieren konnten. Die Entstehung des Glaubens an die Auferweckung Jesu von Nazaret wäre dann vermittelt durch Reflexionen der Jünger, die gründen auf zeitgenössischem religionsgeschichtlichem Material, entscheidend aber auf Jesus selbst: seinem Wirken, seinem Geschick, seinem Tod, seiner Person, dem Glauben, den er gestiftet hat. Die Rede von seiner Auferweckung wäre Ausdruck durchgehaltenen Glaubens und glaubenden Bekenntnisses zu Jesu entscheidender Bedeutung, Sendung und Autorität trotz seines Todes[87].

Diese Erklärung der Entstehung des Auferweckungsglaubens darf nicht leichtfertig abgelehnt werden. Man bedenke:

a. Auch in dieser Sicht glaubt man an mehr als nur an Jesu weitergehende »Sache«: Man glaubt an den aus dem Tod in Gottes Leben aufgenommenen lebendigen Jesus, dessen Erhöhung mit der anderer Gerechter oder Märtyrer nicht vergleichbar ist. Die Jünger haben auch nach dieser Erklärung den Osterglauben nicht erfunden. Jesus selber hat ihn durch sein ganzes Geschick gestiftet. Das Prae, das Voraus des Handelns Gottes bleibt bei allen Reflexionen der Jünger gewahrt. Das neue Leben Jesu, auf das die Jünger reflektierten, ist bei Gott eine Wirklichkeit und nicht nur die Projektion enttäuschter Hoffnung. Es geht also nur um die Frage nach der

Entstehung des Auferweckungsglaubens: das zu beachten, ist zur Vermeidung falscher Kontroversen wichtig.

b. Gegenüber der Gewißheit der Auferweckung Jesu selbst ist letztlich nicht nur das leere Grab, sondern sind auch die Erscheinungen von zweitrangiger Wichtigkeit. Der Osterglaube richtet sich wie nicht auf das leere Grab so auch nicht auf die »Erscheinungen«, sondern auf den *lebendigen Jesus selbst*. Auch wer weder an das leere Grab noch an bestimmte Ostererfahrungen, wohl aber an Jesus als den lebenden Christus glaubt, ist als Christ zu betrachten. Dieser lebendige Christus und durch ihn der lebendige Gott, der ihn aus dem Tod zum Leben rief, sind Gegenstand des Osterglaubens. Und dieser Glaube an den Gott der Lebendigen, der Jesus nicht im Tode ließ, sondern in sein Leben aufnahm, war die Voraussetzung dafür, daß es zur Christusverkündigung, zur Gründung der Glaubensgemeinde und zur christlichen Mission gekommen ist. Aufgrund dieses Glaubens wurde aus dem, der zum Glauben rief, der Geglaubte, wurde aus der Reich-Gottes-Verkündigung Jesu die Christus-Verkündigung der Kirche. Und insofern steht und fällt nach Paulus mit dem Glauben an Jesu Auferweckung zum Leben, aber nicht einfach mit dem Glauben an bestimmte Erscheinungen, der christliche Glaube selbst.

2. *Einwände gegen eine psychologisch-religionsgeschichtliche Rekonstruktion:* Diese Einwände haben im Fall der Erscheinungen zweifellos sehr viel mehr Gewicht als im Fall des leeren Grabes[88]. Man bedenke:

a. Angesichts einer Kette von – das wird man wohl zugeben müssen – weithin hypothetischen Schlußfolgerungen im Zug einer psychologisch-historischen Ableitung des Auferweckungsglaubens kann die Frage zunächst umgedreht werden: Wäre es für die Urgemeinde nicht sehr viel einfacher gewesen, Jesus statt als einen Auferweckten einfach als einen jener *Märtyrer-Propheten* zu verkünden, die verfolgt und getötet wurden und die vor Gott doch im Recht waren, deren Gräber gerade deshalb zur Zeit Jesu ausgebaut und gepflegt und die als Fürbitter verehrt wurden[89]? Warum ist gegen diese damaligen Tendenzen um Jesus kein Grabeskult entstanden? Wäre eine solche Verkündigung von den Zeitgenossen nicht sehr viel besser verstanden worden als die Verkündigung eines bereits vor der allgemeinen Totenerweckung Auferweckten, was doch nach den vorausgegangenen Ereignissen von vornherein verdächtig erscheinen mußte?

b. Nach einzelnen alttestamentlichen Texten errettet und erhöht Gott zwar den frommen Dulder[90], aber von »Offenbarungen« solcher Erhöhter ist nichts bezeugt. Im Alten Testament ist nirgendwo die Rede von der Auferweckung eines Einzelnen aus dem Tod, die der endzeitlichen Auferweckung vorausginge. *Henoch* und *Elija* gelten zur Zeit Jesu deshalb als Zeugen der Auferweckungswirklichkeit, weil sie nach der Überlieferung[91] ohne Tod und Grablegung zu Gott entrückt wurden. Die im Alten Testament selbst nicht bezeugte spätere Erwartung, Elija werde vor der Endzeit wiederkommen, den gewaltsamen Tod der Propheten erleiden und dann auferweckt werden, erscheint in der Bezeugung zu schmal, in der Datierung zu umstritten und in der Rekonstruktion zu unsicher, als daß sie eine tragfähige Brücke zur überzeugenden Herleitung des Glaubens an die Auferweckung Jesu sein könnte. Im Neuen Testament wird denn auch kein einziges Mal mit Henoch, Elija oder auch Johannes dem Täufer für die Auferweckung Jesu argumentiert. Henoch und Elija wird auch nirgendwo die Funktion eines endzeitlichen Heilsmittlers zugeschrieben, dem man als dem Erstauferweckten zugehören müßte.

c. Die von Markus referierte, aber nicht geteilte Volksmeinung von einer angeblichen Auferweckung des *Täufers*[92] ist, gerade wenn sie dem völlig hellenisierten und in Rom erzogenen Herodes Antipas zugeschrieben wird, historisch nicht gesichert. Sie ist möglicherweise von Markus, vielleicht im Kontrast zur Auferweckung Jesu, gebildet worden. Als Erklärung reicht aus: Es geht um eine volkstümliche Meinung von der Wirksamkeit Jesu selber, in dessen Gestalt der vor kurzem getötete Täufer weiterwirkte.

d. Die Vorstellung von einer Auferweckung des *Messias* oder gar eines *gescheiterten Messias* war ein absolutes Novum in der jüdischen Tradition, das die apokalyptische Vorstellungswelt sprengt und für das Judentum bei allem Glauben an die Auferweckung der Toten bis heute unannehmbar blieb. Nach den neutestamentlichen Quellen ist nur Jesus durch Auferweckung ausdrücklich bestätigt worden, so daß seine Auferweckung und Einsetzung zum Messias, Herr, Sohn mit einer eventuellen Erhöhung auch anderer Gerechter und Märtyrer nicht verglichen werden kann. Im Judentum erscheint die Auferweckung der Gerechten als Folge ihres gerechten Tuns, im

Christentum als Folge der Auferweckung Jesu und der Zugehörigkeit zu ihm.

Als Schlußfolgerung drängt sich bezüglich dieses ersten psychologisch-historischen Erklärungsversuches der Entstehung des Osterglaubens auf: Selbstverständlich ist der ursprüngliche christliche Auferweckungsglaube durch und durch jüdisch geprägt. Selbstverständlich hat die jüdische Tradition den ersten Jüngern zahllose Verstehenshilfen geboten. Selbstverständlich ist also nichts einzuwenden gegen die Tatsache von Reflexionen der Jünger über den Tod Jesu aus jüdischem Glauben. Aber eine direkte Ableitung des Glaubens an Jesu Auferweckung aus diesem jüdischen Glauben durch Reflexionen der Jünger über Jesu Botschaft und Geschick scheint zumindest bisher nicht überzeugend bewiesen zu sein. Es stellt sich unabweislich nicht nur die Frage neuer Reflexionen, sondern auch die neuer Erfahrungen. Am gewichtigsten dürfte nämlich die weitere Frage sein: Darf sich eine historisch-psychologische Rekonstruktion der Entstehung des Auferweckungsglaubens mit historischem Recht als die »eigentliche« Meinung der neutestamentlichen Zeugnisse ausgeben, wenn diese selber konstant das Gegenteil sagen? Ist es überhaupt gestattet, sie ständig gegen ihre eigentliche Intention zu interpretieren? Allzuleicht vernachlässigt man das in allen neutestamentlichen Texten bezeugte Moment des Neuen.

3. *Entstehung des Glaubens durch neue Erfahrungen der Jünger?*
Wenn man nicht historisch spekuliert, sondern sich streng an die Zeugnisse selber hält, so läßt sich nicht bestreiten: Nach den neutestamentlichen Schriften in ihrem einhelligen Zeugnis haben die Jünger die Auferweckung Jesu nicht aus Jesu Geschick erschlossen, sondern sie haben ihn selber nach seinem Tod als den Lebendigen *erfahren*.

Hier ist zu überlegen:

a. Weder die unbestreitbare Flucht der Jünger vor Ostern[93] noch die ebenso unbestreitbare neue Qualifikation ihres Glaubens nach Ostern lassen sich hermeneutisch eskamotieren zugunsten einer durch den Tod Jesu kaum unterbrochenen Kontinuität des Glaubens. Erst jetzt bekennt ihn der Glaube als den auferweckten Messias, den erhöhten Herrn, den kommenden Menschensohn, den Gottessohn. *Keine unmittelbare Fortsetzung* der Sache Jesu nach seinem Tod ist bezeugt, *sondern* betont eine *Diskontinuität*. Die Quellen berichten nichts von einer Umkehr des weinenden Petrus vor Ostern[94], nichts von

isolierten Reflexionen der zweifellos an ihrem Meister irrege-
wordenen und geflohenen Jünger, die dann zu seinen Zeugen
und Sendboten werden.

b. Sämtliche neutestamentlichen Osterzeugnisse sind gekennzeichnet durch einen nicht eliminierbaren *Gegensatz* zwischen
dem, was die *Jünger* taten und tun, und dem, was *Gott* an und
durch Jesus getan hat. Nirgendwo verstehen sich die Jünger
gleichsam als Gottes und Jesu mehr oder weniger standhafte
Mitkämpfer, sondern als die im Glauben Gescheiterten und
von Gott durch Jesus Überwundenen. Gerade umgekehrt wie
in der Interpretation der Auferweckung in Goethes Faust: »Sie
feiern die Auferstehung des Herrn, denn sie sind selber auferstanden[95].«

c. Der Osterglaube ist ein Neuansatz, der im Neuen Testament
übereinstimmend nicht auf irgendwelche Vorbilder, nicht auf
eigene Erkenntnisse, nicht auf einen heimlich durchgehaltenen
Glauben, sondern auf – freilich zugleich gelebte und interpretierte – *neue Erfahrungen,* auf wahre Begegnungen mit dem
auferweckten Gekreuzigten zurückgeführt wird. Die Zeugen
berichten und interpretieren Widerfahrnisse mit dem auferweckten Jesus, welche die Verwirrten und Geflohenen mit
Petrus an ihrer Spitze zur Umkehr und natürlich auch zu
neuem Nachdenken gebracht haben.

d. Gedeutet wurden diese Widerfahrnisse selbstverständlich im
alttestamentlich-jüdischen Erfahrungshorizont mit Hilfe gän-
giger und zum Teil alter Begrifflichkeit: Mit »erscheinen«,
»offenbaren« etwa wird schon im griechischen Text des Alten
Testaments[96] die Erscheinung, die Offenbarung Gottes beschrieben. Paulus, der als Christenverfolger den christlichen
Auferweckungsglauben wohl gekannt, aber sicher nicht geteilt
hat, beruft sich, wie wir hörten, auf eine ihm ganz persönlich
widerfahrene Christusoffenbarung: in welcher der Auferweckte »gesehen wurde«, »sich sehen ließ«, »erschien«, »sich
offenbarte«[97], ja, in welcher Paulus den Auferweckten »sah«[98].
Dieses »Erscheinen« und das ihm entsprechende »Sehen« lassen sich nicht kritisch eliminieren oder überspielen. In der
Sprache alttestamentlicher Berufungsvisionen spricht hier
Paulus von einer Erfahrung, welche die Grundlage bildet für
die überraschende Berufung des Christenverfolgers zum
Apostel Jesu Christi und welche von ihm den Erscheinungen
der anderen Apostel gleichgeordnet wird.

e. Diese Erscheinungen geschehen – ganz anders als diejenigen in

der Kindheitsgeschichte bei Mattäus oder in der Apostelgeschichte – nie in der Nacht, im Schlaf oder im Traum, sondern
in *voller Wachheit*. Was für Paulus eine einzigartige und
grundlegende Erfahrung und Begegnung war[99] – unterschieden offensichtlich auch von sonstigen »Visionen und Offenbarungen des Herrn[100]«, die Paulus als Apostel für sich persönlich gehabt hat und die nicht Inhalt der Predigt sind[101] –, wird
von Lukas ausführlich im Stil einer Visionslegende beschrieben[102].

f. Gewiß führt jenes alte Glaubensbekenntnis im 1. Korintherbrief diese »Erscheinungen« an, um die dort genannten
Zeugen durch die Epiphanieformel »ist erschienen« als Zeugen
in ihrer Berufung zur Verkündigung zu legitimieren. Doch
nur weil ihnen Jesus »erschienen« ist, können sie als Verkündiger der Auferweckungsbotschaft legitimiert und verpflichtet
sein. Mit dieser Zeugenformel wird historisch mehr gesagt als
nur ein Legitimationsausweis. Es soll nicht nur die Geltung
bestimmter Autoritäten und ihrer Botschaft behauptet werden, sondern zugleich sollen die Erscheinungen als Anlaß der
Entstehung der Botschaft überliefert werden. Der Hinweis
des Paulus auf die Hauptzeugen, die er persönlich kennt, und
auf weitere noch lebende Zeugen bestätigt, daß es sich hier
zugleich um einen theologischen und einen historischen Sachverhalt handelt. Nach diesem Zeugnis scheint es eindeutig, daß
die Jünger nicht aufgrund eigener Reflexionen, sondern aufgrund von Erfahrungen, welcher Art auch immer, mit dem
Auferweckten zum Glauben gekommen sind. Nicht ihr
Glaube hat demnach Jesus für sie zum Leben erweckt, sondern der von Gott zum Leben Erweckte hat sie zum Glauben
und zum Bekenntnis geführt. Er lebt in keiner Weise von
seiner Jünger Gnade, sondern sie leben von ihm. Weil es also
echte *Auferweckungszeugnisse* sind, konnten sie zugleich *Le-
gitimationsausweise* sein. Die Auferweckungsbotschaft ist
zwar Glaubenszeugnis, aber nicht Glaubenserzeugnis. Wenn
wir uns also an die neutestamentlichen Zeugnisse halten wollen, so müssen wir ausgehen von Begegnungen, wie immer zu
erklären, des lebendigen Jesus mit seinen Jüngern: Wiederbe-
gegnungen und zugleich Neubegegnungen mit dem lebendigen Gekreuzigten, für welche die Initiative von Gott und nicht
von den Jüngern ausgeht und für welche die Erfahrung des
Paulus den Abschluß bildete.

4. *Einwände gegen eine Annahme neuer Erfahrungen:* Im Grunde reduzieren sich alle Einwände gegen die Annahme neuer Erfahrungen der Jünger mit Jesus, dem zum Leben Erweckten, auf den einen: Hier wird nun doch erneut ein historisch nicht zu beweisender übernatürlicher Eingriff postuliert, also gerade das, was man sowohl bezüglich der Wunder[103] wie bezüglich des leeren Grabes[104] zu vermeiden trachtete. Hier ist zu bedenken:

a. Es wäre in der Tat ein von vornherein verdächtiger Rückfall in überwundene Vorstellungen, wenn man zuerst die zahlreichen neutestamentlichen Wundergeschichten ohne die unbeweisbare Annahme eines *supranaturalistischen »Eingriffs«* in die Naturgesetze zu verstehen suchte und dann am Ende für das Wunder der Auferweckung doch wieder einen solchen übernatürlichen »Eingriff« postulierte, der allem wissenschaftlichen Denken ebenso widerspricht wie den alltäglichen Überzeugungen und Erfahrungen. Wenn man also schon von neuen Erfahrungen der Jünger nach dem Tod Jesu sprechen will, dann nicht im Sinne von supranaturalistischen, Naturgesetze aufhebenden, allgemein zugänglichen Mirakeln, bei denen die Öffentlichkeit nur zufällig abwesend ist. Auch nach den neutestamentlichen Texten selbst geht es in keiner Weise um Schauwunder, die von der Allgemeinheit bestaunt werden konnten.

b. Andererseits aber ist es bei allen unbestreitbaren legendären plastisch-dramatischen Ausmalungen und Erweiterungen, allen zeit- und umweltbedingten Interpretationen historisch-kritisch einfach nicht gerechtfertigt, die Erscheinungen *nur* als Ausdruck des Glaubens an Jesu entscheidende Bedeutung, Sendung und Autorität angesichts seines Todes anzusehen. Nicht einfach Verkündigung, Leben und Tod Jesu, sondern ganz bestimmte *Erfahrungen mit Jesus* als dem zum Leben Erweckten sind nach allen Texten dafür verantwortlich, daß aus den geflohenen und verzagten Jüngern todesmutige Bekenner geworden sind. Nicht durch den Tod Jesu, der als solcher ja gerade nicht Gottes Sieg über den Tod manifestierte, sondern durch neue Erfahrungen wurde die Verkündigung ausgelöst. Was im Neuen Testament an psychologischen Phänomenen angeführt wird, schließt eine psychologische Wende als Initialzündung jener welthistorischen Wende zum christlichen Glauben deutlich aus: ein unbestreitbares Versagen und Verzagen der Jünger, von denen ihn einer verraten, einer verleugnet und verflucht hat und ihn alle insgesamt sogleich nach der Verhaftung in schändlicher Flucht verlassen hatten, und nachher Trauer, Bestürzung, Furcht, Nichterkennen, Zweifel, Unglaube. Was berichtet wird, weist nicht auf Entwicklung, sondern auf Überraschung hin: eine Verschlossenheit, die nicht von innen durch schlußfolgernde Reflexion aufgeschlossen, sondern nur von einem anderen her durch erschließende Begegnung aufgebrochen wird. Alle noch so praktischen und dann doch wieder merkwürdig banal wirkenden psychologischen Erklärungen widersprechen dem, was die Texte selbst mit größter Hartnäckigkeit behaupten: daß der Gekreuzigte lebt und sich seinen Jüngern als Herr manifestiert hat, daß mit ihm die neue Zeit für die Welt angebrochen ist, daß seine Person und Sache nicht Vergangenheit, sondern wirkmächtige Gegenwart sind und daß deshalb die Jünger zum Glauben und Verkündigen gekommen sind. Von welchem Text man auch ausgeht, immer stößt man auf eine radikal neue Erfahrung der Jünger mit Jesus nach Jesu Tod: in diesen Erfahrungen begegnet der Gekreuzigte in seiner Lebendigkeit und in seinem einfordernden Anspruch als der Herr[105].

c. Kann aber das sich hier zeigende *Dilemma* überwunden werden? Einerseits sollen wir Erfahrungen der Jünger mit Jesus nach dem Tod annehmen, andererseits aber alle supranaturalistischen, Naturgesetze aufhebenden Eingriffe ablehnen?

5. *Die Erscheinungen meinen Berufungen:* Die »Erscheinungen« meinen gewiß ein Kundwerden der Auferweckung, des Auferweckten. Aber nicht nur: Offensichtlich gehört für Paulus und entsprechend für die anderen Apostel Erscheinung mit Berufung, gehört Begegnung mit Sendung zusammen. Wie ist das zu verstehen?

a. Es geht in den neuen Erfahrungen nicht einfach um eine Identifikation Jesu, sondern um persönliche Berufung, um Sendung zur Verkündigung, um einen Blick also nicht so sehr zurück als nach vorn: die ganz *konkrete Indienstnahme eines Menschen für diese Botschaft,* die an den glaubenden Einsatz appelliert und anscheinend auch Raum für den Zweifel läßt[106]. Die Verpflichtung von wenigen zum Dienst an den vielen. Wie das apostolische Leben des Paulus exemplarisch zeigt, hatte diese einzigartige »Offenbarung« eine auf Leben und Tod gehende totale Betroffenheit und Inanspruchnahme, Berufung und Sendung zur Folge. Was vom alten Glaubensbekenntnis und von Paulus selbst in äußerster Knappheit und verhaltenem Respekt vor dem Geheimnis zu Protokoll gegeben wird, das wird in den Auferweckungsgeschichten der Evangelien fromm legendär, widersprüchlich, aber im Vergleich etwa mit den Apokryphen noch durchaus zuchtvoll ausgemalt. Je älter der Bericht, um so nüchterner. Die Auferweckungsbotschaft weist demnach nicht in eine nebelhaft mythische Ferne, sondern an einen bestimmt umrissenen historischen Ort[107].

b. Alle *psychologisierende oder spekulierende Deutung* kommt bei solchen Berufungen rasch an ihre *Grenzen*. Das Wie ist auch nicht entscheidend. Entscheidend ist das Daß, welches von den neutestamentlichen Schriften nun freilich übereinstimmend und mit Nachdruck bejaht wird. Mit grundsätzlich beliebig zu wiederholenden Erlebnissen wie der spiritistischen Materialisation (verstorbener Geister) oder der anthroposophischen Geistesschau (einer unsichtbaren höheren Leiblichkeit Lebender) haben diese zeitlich begrenzten einmaligen Berufungen der ersten Zeugen, der Apostel, jedenfalls nichts zu tun.

c. Am ehesten wird man diese Berufungen verstehen, wenn man sie mit den *Berufungen der alttestamentlichen Propheten vergleicht,* die man ja auch nicht allesamt wie das Phänomen einer Berufung überhaupt als Halluzination abtun wird. Nach den paulinischen Aussagen wird man ähnlich wie bei den prophetischen Berufungsvisionen an Erfahrungen zu denken haben, die für den neutralen Beobachter unkontrollierbar, allein vom Zeugen verbürgt sind, dessen Zeugnis dann unter Umständen von anderen Zeugen und vor allem durch das gewandelte Leben des Betroffenen bestätigt wird, das aber allein vom Glaubenden im Glauben verifiziert werden kann. Unsere Kenntnisse bezüglich geistiger Erfahrungen, Ekstasen, Visionen, Bewußtseinserweiterungen, »mystischer« Erlebnisse sind noch immer zu beschränkt, um klären zu können, was sich an Wirklichkeit hinter den neutestamentlichen Berufungsgeschichten letztlich verbirgt. Wie wir auch nicht mehr klären können, was sich an nicht rationalistisch zu bezweifelndem prophetischem Erleben hinter den nachträglich für die Öffentlichkeit mehr oder weniger stilisierten Berufungsberichten des Alten Testaments verbirgt. Diese sprechen im 9. Jahrhundert von der Gegenwart des Geistes Jahwes und im 8. und 7. Jahrhundert von einer unmittelbaren, persönlichen Anrede von Jahwe her, welche für den betreffenden Menschen einen ganz neuen Zustand schafft und ihn völlig für einen besonderen Dienst in Anspruch nimmt: Visionen und Auditionen von einem Anderen her, unversehens und unberechenbar den Betroffenen seelisch und oft auch körperlich aufwühlend und ihn für seine Aufgabe zurüstend. Für sie ist der Ausdruck »ekstatisch« insofern mißverständlich, als Ichbewußtsein und freie Entscheidung des Propheten nicht nur nicht ausgeschaltet, sondern in einer vorher in Israel und im ganzen alten Orient nicht erlebten Weise in Anspruch genommen werden[108].

d. Alles wird davon abhängen, daß man sich Gottes Berufung nicht im supranaturalistischen Schema als ein Eingreifen Gottes von oben oder von außen vorstellt. Wenn Gott die unfaßbar umfassende letzte Wirklichkeit ist, wenn der Mensch in Gott ist und Gott im Menschen, wenn die *Geschichte des Menschen in der Geschichte Gottes aufgehoben* ist und die *Geschichte Gottes in der Geschichte des Menschen zur Auswirkung* kommt[109], dann gibt es *im Wort der Sendung oder Berufung* eine Möglichkeit der Aktion und Interaktion, ein ständiges Ineinander von Gott und Mensch, von schenkender Freiheit und geschenkter Freiheit, das die Naturgesetze in keiner Weise verletzt und das doch an Wirklichkeit nicht zu überbieten ist. Historisch, von einer Geschichtswissenschaft, die aufgrund ihrer geschichtsphilosophischen Voraussetzungen nur den Menschen als Schöpfer seiner Geschichte betrachtet und Gott von vornherein methodisch ausschaltet und ausschalten muß, läßt sich das Wirken Gottes selbstverständlich nicht feststellen. Wäre es historisch feststellbar, wäre es gar nicht das Wirken Gottes. Daß in der Geschichte der Welt und des einzelnen Menschen Gott am Werk ist, ist nicht eine historisch-kritisch abgesicherte Feststellung, sondern ist – es muß immer wieder betont werden – Sache des vertrauenden Glaubens.

6. *Berufungen zielen auf Glauben:* Berufungen appellieren nicht an ein neutrales, historisches Erkennen, sondern an das gläubige, aber Zweifel keineswegs ausschließende Vertrauen. Sie fordern im Zusammenhang mit der Auferweckung jenen Glauben, der Gott alles zutraut, auch und gerade das Letzte, nämlich den Sieg über den Tod.

a. Diese Berufungen kommen somit in ihrem ganzen Wesen als *Glaubenserfahrungen* zu ihrem Ziel. In diesen Erfahrungen lassen sich die Betroffenen frei für Nachfolge und Verkündigung dieses Gekreuzigten und doch Lebendigen in Anspruch nehmen. Es geht um ein spontanes Geschehen, das nicht zu erzwingen ist und Widerstand zu überwinden hat. Der Ruf kommt nur dann zur vollen Geltung, wenn ihn der Glaube akzeptiert. Doch geht der Glaube dem Ruf weder voraus, noch ist er mit ihm identisch. Der Ruf bedingt und ermöglicht vielmehr erst den Glauben. Die Auferweckung ist also keine rein »objektive« Tatsache, die auch ohne den Auferweckungsglauben sinnvoll gedacht werden könnte. Die Auferweckung ist nicht dinglich feststellbar, ist nicht »objektivierbar«. Ostererfahrung und Osterglaube sind nicht nur äußerlich miteinander verbunden: wie in einer Telefonverbindung, die abgebrochen werden kann, sobald die Botschaft durchgegeben ist. Ostererfahrung und Osterglaube gehören innerlich und unlöslich zusammen: sie lassen eine objektive Beobachterrolle nicht zu. Gerade das Berufungsgeschehen ist kein magisches und mechanisches Geschehen, das den Menschen vergewaltigt und jeden Zweifel automatisch ausschließt. Der Zweideutigkeit enthoben wird das Berufungsgeschehen erst im Glauben: wenn der einladende, herausfordernde Ruf angenommen ist. Nur wenn und solange sich der Jünger an den Auferweckten hält, erfährt er, daß er getragen wird: wie Petrus im Bild über das Wasser wandeln konnte, solange er nicht auf die Wogen, sondern auf den Herrn schaute[110]. Es geht also in diesen Glaubenserfahrungen um *Glaubensberufungen.* Insofern läßt sich gegenüber einer dinglich-massiv verstandenen Objektivität und Realität der Auferweckung mit Bultmann zu Recht sagen, wenn auch leicht mißverstehen, daß Jesus in den Glauben seiner Jünger, in das Wort der Verkündigung, in das Kerygma auferstanden sei[111]. Wir sind aber nicht berufen, weil wir glauben. Wir glauben, weil wir berufen sind.

b. Wiederum wie bei den alttestamentlichen Propheten hat sich Gott für sein neues Wort an sein Volk an keine der vorhandenen Institutionen gewandt, sondern dafür den Geist von *Einzelnen* angesprochen. Womit der alte und gern wiederholte Einwand, die »Erscheinungen« hätten vor neutralen Beobachtern stattfinden müssen, um historisch glaubwürdig zu sein, hinfällig wird. Diese erfolgten nicht vor Gläubigen, sondern vor »Ungläubigen«, die durch diese überraschenden Erfahrungen – ein Kennen, das ein Wiedererkennen war und insofern in Kontinuität – in Freiheit zu Glaubenden wurden: nach ihrem Zeugnis durch Gottes Tat, trotz aller ihrer Ängste und gegen alle ihre Zweifel.

c. Eine isolierte Auferweckung an sich hätte wenig Sinn, wenn es nicht eine Auferweckung *für uns* wäre. Eine Offenbarung dieses Geschehens wäre irrelevant, wenn seine Verkündigung nicht *allen* etwas zu sagen hätte. Die Auferweckung Jesu begründet die Hoffnung auf die Auferweckung aller an ihn Glaubenden: wie er, so auch sie! Weil er, deshalb auch sie! Ihre eigene Hoffnung ist begründet, verbürgt. Aber zugleich ist auch ihre Verpflichtung zur Nachfolge deutlich. Ein Sinn ist in ihr Leben und Sterben gekommen, der alle resignierende Hoffnungslosigkeit ausschließt, die in jenem nur scheinbar fröhlichen Wort liegt: »Laßt uns essen und trinken, denn morgen sind wir tot.«[112] So gehören Wirklichkeit und Bedeutsamkeit der Auferweckung zusammen. So ist der Auferweckungsglaube nicht Wissenschaft oder Weltanschauung, sondern im Blick auf den auferweckten Gekreuzigten eine Vertrauens- und Hoffnungshaltung, die sich in allen persönlichen und auch gesellschaftspolitischen Entscheidungen auszuwirken hat und die durch alle Zweifel und Verzweiflung hindurchzutragen vermag.

7. *Glauben heute:* Alle historischen Fragen nach der Historizität des leeren Grabes und der Ostererfahrung verblassen vor der Frage nach der Bedeutung der Auferweckungsbotschaft heute.

a. Uns Heutigen ist weder das leere Grab noch eine Ostererfahrung gegeben, auf denen sich unser Glaube unmittelbar begründen ließe. Diese Erfahrungen der Erstzeugen waren wie die der Propheten einmalige Berufungen. Und mit einer frommen Erleuchtung und Erweckung, in der wir diese einmaligen Erfahrungen der ersten Jünger direkt wiederholen könnten, ist nicht zu rechnen. Wir sind auf das *Zeugnis der ersten grundlegenden Zeugen angewiesen,* das uns, wie immer es sich mit Grab und Ostererfahrung verhalten mag, mit größter Eindeutigkeit sagt: Der Gekreuzigte ist nicht tot, sondern er lebt und herrscht für immer durch und mit Gott. Wir sind immer wieder neu auf das Wort der Verkündigung angewiesen. Die Ostergeschichten wollen erzählen und man soll sie auch heute erzählen lassen: Unanschauliches – und dazu gehört die Auferweckung zum Leben als Anfang der Vollendung genauso wie die Schöpfung – kann nicht in Begriffen, sondern muß in der Form zu erzählender Bilder anschaulich gemacht werden.

Neue Erfahrungen – und das sind die Berufungserfahrungen der ersten Zeugen – können nicht einfach durch Argumente, sondern müssen in der Gestalt bildhafter Erzählungen verständlich gemacht werden. Auch Begriffe wie »Auferweckung« oder »Auferstehung« sind bildhafte, metaphorische Begriffe. Auf irgendeine Anschaulichkeit und Erfahrbarkeit verzichten auch heute die meisten Menschen nur ungern. Und deshalb sind die Ostererzählungen in der Verkündigung nicht zu eliminieren, sondern differenziert kritisch zu interpretieren, und zwar so, daß sie nicht nur privat erbauen, sondern für das persönliche wie öffentliche Leben zur Nachfolge bewegen.

b. Haben wir Heutigen es in dieser Mittelbarkeit schwerer? Schon die Berufung der Erstzeugen, so sahen wir, war für Zweideutigkeit und Zweifel offen und wurde erst durch die Annahme im Glauben eindeutig. Schon die Erstzeugen kamen am Glauben nicht vorbei. Als Prediger des Glaubens waren sie vom Glauben wie am Anfang so erst recht in der Folge nicht zugunsten eines einfachen Sehens dispensiert. Von ihnen wurde kein unbeteiligtes, sondern ein glaubendes Sehen erwartet, das sich gleichzeitig in Dienst nehmen läßt. Und von uns Heutigen ist *auch nicht mehr und nicht weniger als Glauben* verlangt: unsere eigene Berufung zwar nicht zum Erstzeugnis, aber – aufgrund des Erstzeugnisses durch die Verkündigung – unsere Berufung zum Glauben anzunehmen, uns vertrauend auf Gott und die Botschaft vom lebendigen Christus einzulassen und uns zu überlegen, was das in der Praxis zu bedeuten hat. Nichts zwingt uns zum Glauben, vieles lädt uns ein: sein Wort, Verhalten und Geschick, von Gott legitimiert. Jeder Glaubende ist dabei berufen, aufgrund des apostolischen Zeugnisses auch selber in Wort und vor allem Tat Zeuge des Auferweckten zu sein.

c. Wichtiger als aller Streit um Ablauf und Erklärung der Osterereignisse ist es, aus dem neuen wirkmächtigen Leben dieses Jesus, von dem die Ostergeschichten erzählen, aus dem Glauben an ihn, sein *eigenes Leben zu gestalten*: Sollte einer mit dem Wunder der Auferweckung, des neuen Lebens noch immer nichts oder nur wenig anzufangen wissen, sollte ihm aber doch dieser Jesus für sein sterbliches Leben und endliches Sterben letztlich maßgebend und so lebendig sein, wäre ihm das Christsein nicht zu bestreiten. Anders als jenem anderen, der die Auferweckung Jesu für ein großes Wunder hält, aber daraus für sein Leben und Sterben keine Konsequenzen zieht. Ostern ist Glaubensursprung und Glaubensziel; man sollte aus ihm kein Glaubensgesetz machen. Letztes Kriterium für die Christlichkeit eines Menschen ist nicht die Theorie, sondern die Praxis: nicht wie einer über Lehren, Dogmen, Deutungen denkt, sondern wie er im Alltag handelt. Paulus hat die frühen Leugner der Auferweckung schwer getadelt und zum Umdenken aufgefordert, aber er hat sie nicht exkommuniziert[113]. Entscheidend für das Christsein ist, daß man versucht – so recht und schlecht wie Menschen möglich – Jesus alltäglich nachzufolgen und ihn als den Herrn nicht zu desavouieren[114].

d. Hier wird nochmals deutlich, wie sehr bei Jesus *Person und Sache zusammengehören:* Niemand glaubt an Jesus, der sich nicht in der Nachfolge zu seiner Sache bekennt. Umgekehrt kann man seine Sache nicht betreiben, ohne in irgendeiner Form in seine Nachfolge zu treten. Man kann also nur dann von Jesu Person und Sache glaubwürdig reden, wenn man sich in der durch den Auferweckungsglauben gewiesenen Richtung praktisch auf den Weg macht.

Damit wären nun auch die am Anfang dieses Kapitels gestellten Fragen beantwortet: Nach den übereinstimmenden neutestamentlichen Zeugnissen ist es der als lebendig erfahrene und erkannte Jesus von Nazaret selbst, sind es die neuen Glaubenserfahrungen, Glaubensberufungen, Glaubenserkenntnisse um Jesus von Nazaret, welche erklären können, warum seine Sache weiterging: warum es nach seinem Tod zu der so folgenreichen Jesus-Bewegung kam, nach Jesu Scheitern zu einem Neubeginn, nach der Jünger Flucht zu einer Gemeinschaft von Glaubenden. Von daher erklärt sich, warum dieser desavouierte und von Gott gerichtete Irrlehrer, Lügenprophet, Volksverführer und Gotteslästerer in geradezu tollkühner Weise als Messias, Christus, Herr, Erlöser, Gottessohn proklamiert wurde. Warum der Galgen der Schmach als ein Zeichen des Sieges verstanden werden konnte, warum die ersten Zeugen in einer letzten tragenden Zuversicht ohne Furcht vor Verachtung, Verfolgung und Tod eine derart skandalöse Nachricht von einem Hingerichteten als erfreuliche Kunde (»Evangelium«) unter die Menschen brachten. Warum also Jesus nicht nur als Gründer und Lehrer verehrt, studiert und befolgt, sondern als gegenwärtig Wirkender erfahren wurde, warum man mit seiner ganzen spannungsgeladenen, rätselhaften Geschichte das Geheimnis Gottes verbunden sah und somit Jesus selber der eigentliche Inhalt ihrer Verkündigung, die Zusammenfassung der Botschaft vom Gottesreich geworden ist. Das historische Rätsel der Entstehung des Christentums erscheint hier in provozierender Weise gelöst: Die Glaubenserfahrungen, Glaubensberufungen, Glaubenserkenntnisse der Jünger um den lebendigen Jesus von Nazaret bilden nach den einzigen Zeugnissen, die wir haben, die Initialzündung für jene einzigartige welthistorische Entwicklung, in der vom Galgen eines in Gott- und Menschenverlassenheit Verendeten eine »Weltreligion«, und vielleicht mehr als das, entstehen konnte. Das Christentum, insofern es Bekenntnis zu Jesus von Nazaret als dem lebendigen und wirkmächtigen Christus ist, beginnt mit Ostern. Ohne Ostern kein Evangelium, keine einzige Erzählung, kein Brief im Neuen Testament! Ohne Ostern in der Christenheit kein Glaube, keine Verkündigung, keine Kirche, kein Gottesdienst, keine Mission[115]!

2. Der Maßgebende

Die Verkündigung des auferweckten, erhöhten, lebendigen Christus bedeutete eine ungeheure Herausforderung. Aber wohlgemerkt: nicht die Verkündigung der Auferweckung an sich. Auferstanden sind in den hellenistischen wie in anderen Religionen viele: Heroen wie Herakles, die in den Olymp aufgenommen wurden. Sterbende und wiederbelebte Götter und Heilande wie Dionysos, deren Schicksal für das ihrer Gläubigen Vorbild und Urbild war und die in mystischer Partizipation immer wieder neu gefeiert wurden in jenen hellenistischen Mysterienreligionen, die umgebildete Naturkulte sind: abgelesen am natürlichen Rhythmus von Saat und Wachsen, Sonnenaufgang und Sonnenniedergang, Werden und Vergehen, projiziert von den Wünschen und Sehnsüchten der nach Unsterblichkeit verlangenden Menschen. Hier überall steht am Anfang der Mythos, der, wie etwa innerhalb des Alten Testaments, vergeschichtlicht wird. Bei Jesus ist es umgekehrt.

Bei Jesus steht am Anfang die Geschichte, die freilich oft mythologisch gedeutet wurde, für die aber das Sterben und Neuwerden des Samenkornes[1] nicht der Ausgang, sondern nur ein Bild ist. Entscheidend für den christlichen Glauben ist nicht, daß hier ein Toter auferstanden ist als Vorbild für alle Sterblichen. Entscheidend ist, daß gerade der, der gekreuzigt wurde, auferweckt worden ist! Wäre der Auferweckte nicht der Gekreuzigte, so wäre er bestenfalls ein Begriffszeichen, ein Ideogramm, ein Symbol.

Das Osterereignis darf also nicht isoliert betrachtet werden. Es zwingt vielmehr zur Rückfrage nach Jesus, seiner Botschaft, seinem Verhalten, seinem Geschick und dann natürlich zur Vorausfrage nach uns und unseren Konsequenzen. Der »Erstgeborene aus den Toten« darf den Messias der Mühseligen und Beladenen nicht verdrängen. Ostern entschärft nicht das Kreuz, sondern bestätigt es. Die Auferweckungsbotschaft ruft also nicht zur Anbetung eines himmlischen Kultgottes, der das Kreuz hinter sich gelassen hat. Sie ruft zur Nachfolge: sich in glaubendem Vertrauen auf diesen Jesus, seine Botschaft einzulassen und das eigene Leben nach dem Maßstab des Gekreuzigten zu gestalten.

Die Auferweckungsbotschaft nämlich macht es offenbar, was so gar nicht zu erwarten war: daß dieser Gekreuzigte trotz allem *recht hatte!* Gott ergriff Partei für den, der sich ganz auf ihn eingelassen hatte, der sein Leben für die Sache Gottes und der Menschen hingegeben hat. Zu ihm bekannte er sich und nicht zur jüdischen Hierarchie. Er sagte Ja zu seiner Verkündigung, seinem Verhalten, seinem Geschick.

Konkret: Jesus hatte recht, wenn er sich über bestimmte Gewohnheiten, Vorschriften, Gebote hinwegsetzte, sofern es zum allseitigen Wohl des Menschen und damit nach Gottes Willen geschah. Er hatte recht, wenn er die bestehende gesetzliche Ordnung und das gesamte religiös-gesellschaftliche System in Frage stellte und die bestehenden Normen und Institutionen, die geltenden Dogmen, Ordnungen und Einrichtungen faktisch relativierte, insofern sie dem Menschen und nicht der Mensch ihnen zu dienen hat. Er hatte ebenfalls recht, wenn er die geltende Liturgie und den gesamten Kult in Frage stellte und die bestehenden Riten und Bräuche, Feiern und Zeremonien praktisch unterlief, insofern der Menschendienst dem Gottesdienst vorgeordnet sein soll.

Richtig also war seine Identifikation der Sache Gottes mit der Sache des Menschen, des Willens Gottes mit dem allseitigen Wohl des Menschen. Richtig sein Übersteigen der Grenzen zwischen Volks- und Nichtvolksgenossen, Partei- und Nichtparteigenossen, seine Menschen-, Nächsten-, Feindesliebe. Richtig sein Eintreten für ein Vergeben ohne Ende, ein Dienen ohne Rangfolge, ein Verzichten ohne Gegenleistung. Richtig auch seine Solidarisierung mit den Schwachen, Kranken, Armen, Unterprivilegierten, ja mit den moralischen Versagern, Unfrommen und Gottlosen. Richtig sogar sein Eintreten für Begnadigung statt Bestrafung und seine Zusage der Vergebung im ganz konkreten Fall. Und richtig schließlich vor allem der Einsatz seines Lebens, sein Durchhalten und Zuendegehen seines Weges.

Das alles besagt die Auferweckungsbotschaft: Sein Anspruch, sein Mut zur Nähe Gottes, sein Gehorsam, seine Freiheit, seine Freude, sein ganzes Tun und Leiden wurden bestätigt. Der Gottverlassene wurde von Gott gerechtfertigt. Mit seiner Verkündigung und seinem ganzen Verhalten war er im Recht. Gegen alle seine höhnenden Gegner und fliehenden Freunde, gegen seine Familie, gegen das Establishment und gegen die Revolutionäre, gegen alle Parteien hat er, der bei den Menschen offensichtlich gescheitert ist, bei Gott doch recht bekommen, gesiegt. Jesu Aufnahme in Gottes Herrlichkeit bedeutet Gottes Bekenntnis zu demjenigen, dem die Welt, wie dies durchgängig das Johannesevangelium deutlich macht, das Bekenntnis versagte.

Sein ganzer Weg war richtig, auch wenn er zum Kreuzweg wurde, werden mußte. Gerade durch den Tod hindurch ist der unerhörte Anspruch dieses Menschen von niedriger Herkunft und unbedeutender Familie, der, wie wir sahen, ohne Bildung, Vermögen, Amt und Titel von keiner Autorität berufen, von keiner Tradition legitimiert, keiner Partei gestützt schien, in einer grundstürzenden Weise bestätigt, ja endgültig gerechtfertigt worden: Der Neuerer, der sich über Gesetz und Tempel, über Mose, König, Prophet stellte, der Familie, Ehe und Volk relativierte, erscheint jetzt als der große Erfüller! Der Irrlehrer als der vollmächtige und wegweisende Lehrer[2]. Der Lügenprophet als der wahre Prophet[3]. Der Gotteslästerer als der Heilige Gottes[4]. Der Volksverführer als der endzeitliche Richter des Volkes[5]. So war er definitiv als Gottes Sachwalter und als Sachwalter des Menschen legitimiert.

Die Aufnahme Jesu in das Leben Gottes bringt also nicht die

Offenbarung zusätzlicher Wahrheiten, sondern das Offenbarwerden Jesu selbst: Er erhält nun die letzte Glaubwürdigkeit. In ganz neuer Weise wird so der gerechtfertigte Jesus zum herausfordernden Zeichen der Entscheidung: Die Entscheidung für die Herrschaft Gottes, wie er sie gefordert hatte, wird zur Entscheidung für ihn selbst. Hier besteht trotz allem Bruch eine Kontinuität in der Diskontinuität. Schon während Jesu irdischer Wirksamkeit hat die *Entscheidung für oder gegen die Gottesherrschaft* mit der *Entscheidung für oder gegen ihn* zusammengehangen. Jetzt fällt sie in eins: denn in dem zu Gottes Leben erweckten Gekreuzigten ist Gottes Nähe, Herrschaft, Reich bereits verwirklicht, bereits gegenwärtig. Insofern war die *Naherwartung* in Erfüllung gegangen!

Der *zum Glauben Rufende* ist zum *Inhalt des Glaubens* geworden. Der sich mit Gott Identifizierende, mit dem hat sich Gott für immer identifiziert. An ihm hängt jetzt der Glaube an die Zukunft, an ihm die Hoffnung auf ein endgültiges Leben mit Gott. Wieder erklingt so die Botschaft vom kommenden Gottesreich, aber in neuer Gestalt: weil Jesus mit seinem Tod und neuem Leben in sie eingegangen ist und nun ihre Mitte bildet. Jesus als der zu Gott Erhöhte ist die *Personifizierung der Botschaft vom Gottesreich* geworden. Ihre zeichenhafte Abkürzung, ihre konkrete Füllung. Statt allgemein »Gottesreich verkünden« wird man jetzt immer mehr zugespitzt »Christus verkünden« sagen. Und die an ihn als den Christus Glaubenden wird man kurz die »Christen« nennen. Damit sind Botschaft und Botschafter, sind das »Evangelium Jesu« und das »Evangelium von Jesus Christus« zu einer Einheit geworden.

So erkennen die Glaubenden immer klarer, daß durch ihn Gottes in Bälde erwartete neue Welt in die von Sünde und Tod gezeichnete Welt bereits eingebrochen ist: Sein neues Leben hat die universale Herrschaft des Todes gebrochen. Seine Freiheit hat sich durchgesetzt, sein Weg sich bewährt. Und es erscheint immer deutlicher die ganze Relativität nicht nur des Todes, sondern auch des Gesetzes und des Tempels, woraus die christliche Gemeinde – zuerst die hellenistisch-jüdische und dann besonders Paulus mit den Heidenchristen – in wachsendem Ausmaß Konsequenzen ziehen wird: durch Jesus zum Leben berufen und zur Freiheit befreit[6]. Befreit von allen Mächten der Endlichkeit, von Gesetz, Schuld und Tod. Wo für die Juden Gesetz und Tempel standen, steht für die Christen immer deutlicher der Christus, der die Sache Gottes und des Menschen vertritt. Wo die Juden noch auf Erfüllung warten, ist sie in dem Einen schon da. Und was bedeutet das für diesen Einen?

Ehrentitel

Jesu Person ist nach Ostern zum konkreten Richtmaß für das Gottesreich geworden: für die Beziehung des Menschen zu den Mitmenschen, zur Gesellschaft, zu Gott. Jetzt kann Jesu Sache von seiner Person nicht mehr getrennt werden. Nicht idealistisch nur um bleibend gültige Ideen ging es im Christentum von Anfang an. Sondern ganz real um die bleibend gültige Person: um Jesus den Christus. So läßt sich sagen: Die *Sache Jesu, die weitergeht,* ist *zunächst die Person Jesu,* die für den Glaubenden in einzigartiger Weise bedeutsam, lebendig, gültig, relevant, wirkkräftig bleibt. Die selber das Geheimnis ihrer Geschichte eröffnet und so das Bekenntnis, die Homologie bei Taufe und Abendmahl, in Verkündigung und Lehre, in ihr möglich macht: die Akklamation im Gottesdienst und die Proklamation vor der Welt. Und gar bald sollte das Bekenntnis auch vor Gericht erfolgen: Wo man das Bekenntnis »Kyrios Kaisar« verlangt, werden die Gläubigen antworten mit dem Bekenntnis: »Kyrios Jesous«. Der ganze Christusglaube voll verständlich ausgedrückt in dem einen Wort: *»Herr ist Jesus!«*

Ein provoziertes und provozierendes *Bekenntnis zu Jesus als dem Maßgebenden:* Kein Ehrentitel erschien den ersten Christen zu hoch gegriffen, um die einzigartige, entscheidende, ausschlaggebende Bedeutung dessen auszudrücken, der aller Wahrscheinlichkeit nach, wie wir sahen, für sich überhaupt keine Titel in Anspruch genommen hatte. Die Aufnahme der Titel durch die Gemeinde geschieht gerade deshalb tastend und zögernd. Nicht der einzelne Titel an sich war dabei wichtig. Sondern daß durch alle diese Titel zum Ausdruck gebracht wird, daß dieser selbst, der Getötete und Lebendige, der *Maßgebende* ist und bleibt: maßgebend in seiner Verkündigung, seinem Verhalten, seinem ganzen Geschick, in seinem Leben, seinem Werk, seiner Person, maßgebend für den Menschen, seine Beziehung zu Gott, Welt und Mitmenschen, sein Denken, Handeln und Leiden, Leben und Sterben.

Die *einzelnen Titel,* so verschieden gefärbt sie auch sind, sind in bezug auf Jesus weithin austauschbar und ergänzen einander. Jede noch so kurze Formel ist nicht ein Teil des Credo, sondern das ganze Credo. *Nur in Jesus selbst* haben die verschiedenen

Titel *einen klaren gemeinsamen Bezugspunkt*[7]. Über 50 verschiedene Namen, so hat man gezählt, werden im Neuen Testament für den irdischen und auferweckten Jesus gebraucht. Die zum Teil noch heute gebrauchten Hoheitsnamen sind von den ersten Christen nicht erfunden, sondern – in der frühen palästinischen Urgemeinde, im hellenistischen Judenchristentum und dann im hellenistischen Heidenchristentum – aus der Umwelt übernommen und auf Jesus übertragen worden: Jesus als der kommende »Menschensohn«, der in Bälde erwartete »Herr« (»Mar«), der in der Endzeit eingesetzte »Messias«, der »Davidssohn« und stellvertretend leidende »Gottesknecht«, schließlich der gegenwärtige »Herr« (»Kyrios«), der »Heiland« (»Retter«), der »Gottessohn« (»Sohn«) und das »Gotteswort« (»Logos«). Das waren die wichtigsten der auf Jesus angewandten Titel. Die einen, wie etwa der geheimnisvolle apokalyptische Titel »Menschensohn« (gebraucht besonders in Q), kamen schon in den griechisch sprechenden Gemeinden vor Paulus und erst recht bei Paulus selbst wieder aus dem Gebrauch (ähnlich »Davidssohn«): weil in neuer Umgebung unverständlich oder mißverständlich. Andere, wie etwa »Gottessohn« im hellenistischen Bereich, weiteten sich in ihrer Bedeutung und erhielten ein besonders starkes Gewicht oder wuchsen sogar – wie »Messias«, übersetzt durch »Christus« – mit dem Namen »Jesus« zu einem einzigen Eigennamen zusammen: »Jesus Christus«. Während es für »Davidssohn« etwa 20, für »Gottessohn« (»Sohn«) 75, für »Menschensohn« 80 neutestamentliche Belege gibt, so wird »Herr« (»Kyrios«) etwa 350mal und Christus gar rund 500mal für Jesus gebraucht.

So entstand auf Grund des implizit (einschlußweise) christologischen Redens, Handelns und Leidens Jesu selbst die explizite (ausdrückliche) neutestamentliche »Christologie«. Oder besser: es entstanden je nach sozialem, politischem, kulturellem, geistigem Kontext, je nach dem anzusprechenden Publikum und der Eigenart des Verfassers sehr *verschiedene neutestamentliche »Christologien«.* Nicht ein einziges normatives Christusbild, sondern verschiedene, je anders akzentuierte Christusbilder! Die maßgebliche, die »christologische« Bedeutung Jesu sollte deutlich gemacht werden: was er eigentlich ist und was er entscheidend für die Menschen bedeutet. In den neutestamentlichen *Briefen* vor allem des Paulus (etwa seit 49) geschieht dies besonders mit dem Blick auf den Gekreuzigten und Auferweckten, wobei wir freilich kaum Kenntnis haben von der in diesen sehr

situationsbedingten und vielfach fragmentarischen Briefen vorausgesetzten elementaren Missionspredigt und Katechese des
Paulus, die jedenfalls eine Jesus-Tradition als festen Bestandteil
enthalten haben muß[8]. In den etwa seit 70 redigierten, aber sehr
altes Material verwendenden *Evangelien,* von deren Entstehung
wir gehört haben[9], geschieht das vorwiegend mit dem Blick auf
den irdischen Lebensweg Jesu. Dabei wird dieser irdische Jesus
im Lichte des auferweckten Jesus gesehen, so daß, wie wir ebenfalls gesehen haben[10], auch in den Evangelien der verkündigte
Jesus (= der kerygmatische Christus) nicht einfach mit dem
verkündigenden Jesus (= der historische Jesus) gleichgesetzt
werden darf. Schon das älteste Evangelium will nach der Überschrift die »Heilsbotschaft von Jesus Christus, dem Sohne Gottes«[11] ansagen. Die Evangelien wollen Jesus als den Menschen
verkünden, in dem Gott selbst am Werk ist und in dem so das
Heil der Menschen gewirkt wird.

Zugleich aber sehen die verschiedenen neutestamentlichen
Autoren aufgrund ihrer je verschiedenen Situation und theologischen Konzeption denselben Jesus in einer zum Teil recht *unter-
schiedlichen Perspektive:* Während Markus ihn als den in seiner
irdischen Lebenszeit verborgenen Gottessohn und Mattäus ihn
als den in den alttestamentlichen Schriften verheißenen, das Gesetz auslegenden und erfüllenden Messias Gottes und Israels
sehen, so Lukas vor allem als den Heiland der Armen und
Verlorenen und Johannes schließlich als das von Anfang mit
Gott seiende Wort und den im irdischen Leben offenbarten und
den Vater offenbarenden Sohn. Und während Paulus ihn etwa als
gehorsamen neuen Adam und endgültigen Menschen, der Hebräerbrief als den den alten Kult beendenden großen Hohenpriester verstehen kann, so die Apostelgeschichte als den die eine
Kirche durch den Geist regierenden erhöhten Herrn, die johanneischen Schriften als den im Fleisch Gekommenen und die
Johannesapokalypse als den Sieger Gottes[12].

Für unseren Zusammenhang dürfte es nicht notwendig sein
herauszuarbeiten, was die komplexe Geschichte und Bedeutung
eines jeden neutestamentlichen Würdetitels gewesen ist[13]. Durch
ihre Anwendung auf den einen Jesus wurden sie nicht nur letztlich auswechselbar, sondern auch zugleich *radikal verändert.*
Tastend versuchte man mit Hilfe der Titel, das in die Formen
menschlicher Sprache zu bringen, was man glaubend erkannt
hatte. Zugleich versuchte man, sich von den religiösen und politischen Mißverständnissen abzusetzen, die mit den vorgeformten

jüdisch-hellenistischen Titeln gegeben waren, wobei freilich eine Überfremdung gerade durch Heidnisches nicht von vornherein ausgeschaltet werden konnte. Aber jedenfalls sind es nicht diese vieldeutigen, mißverständlichen Titel, die Jesus Autorität gegeben haben. Er selber als der auferweckte Gekreuzigte und gekreuzigte Auferweckte gab ihnen Autorität und Eindeutigkeit. Sie wurden nicht nur übertragen, sondern umgeprägt. Nicht sie bestimmten, was er war. Er selber, seine konkrete, geschichtliche Existenz, sein Sterben und neues Leben bestimmten, wie sie neu zu verstehen sind, und gaben ihnen einen neuen Sinn:

– »Menschensohn«: Der nach frühjüdischer Erwartung in Zukunft zum Gericht kommende Menschensohn war für Jesus, der von ihm immer distanziert in der dritten Person sprach, möglicherweise nicht mit ihm (Jesus) identisch, wiewohl Jesus das Bekenntnis zu ihm selber in jedem Fall als maßgebend für das ihn bestätigende Urteil des kommenden Menschensohnes im Endgericht ansagt[14]. Für die urchristliche Gemeinde aber war Jesus nach seiner Erhöhung zur »Rechten des Vaters«, wo es keinen Platz für einen anderen neben ihm gab, ohne Zweifel mit dem Menschensohn identisch[15]. Aus dem kommenden Menschensohn des Frühjudentums war damit der bereits gekommene und in der künftigen Vollendung der Welt als Weltenrichter (in Bälde) wiederkommende Menschensohn geworden.

– »Messias-Christus«: Dieser Titel des in der Endzeit erwarteten Vollmachtträgers und Heilbringers konnte vieles besagen. Im weitestverbreiteten politischen und jüdisch-nationalen Verständnis, welches oft mit dem apokalyptischen vom Menschensohn vermischt war, meinte der »Messias Gottes« den mächtigen Kriegsheld der Endzeit und königlichen Befreier des Volkes. Doch durch Jesus erhielt der Messiastitel eine völlig neue Interpretation und meinte nun einen gewalt- und wehrlosen und so verkannten, verfolgten, verratenen und schließlich leidenden und sterbenden Messias, was für das übliche jüdische Verständnis ebenso skandalös klingen mußte wie bei der Passion der ganz entsprechende Kreuzestitulus »König der Juden«. In diesem völlig umgeprägten Sinn ist der Christustitel auch nach dem Neuen Testament für die Christenheit bis heute der häufigste Hoheitsname Jesu von Nazaret geblieben.

– »Herr«: So wurden viele angeredet, die Befehlsgewalt hatten. Jeder Übergeordnete (Arbeitgeber, Offiziere, Sklavenhalter),

*vor allem aber der Inhaber der höchsten Befehls- und Geset-
zesgewalt: im griechisch sprechenden Judentum Jahwe selbst,
im hellenistischen Heidentum der Kaiser. Wenn nun der
erhöhte Jesus mit »Herr« angeredet wurde, so sollte mit diesem
Namen die einzigartige Autorität und zugleich Nähe des
Erhöhten zum Ausdruck gebracht werden, wie er der Kommende ist und zugleich der im Gottesdienst Gegenwärtige.*
Anders aber als die anderen Herren, anders als die Pharaonen
und Cäsaren, hat sich dieser Herr zum Knecht, Diener,
Freund, Bruder *gemacht und muß jetzt, zur Rechten Gottes
erhöht, mit Gott immer zusammen gesehen werden: als der
Herr schlechthin, der keine anderen Herren, religiöse oder
politische, neben sich duldet, was mit der Zeit auch zum Konflikt mit dem immer mehr auf den Kaiserkult eingeschworenen
römischen Staat führen mußte.*

- *»Gottessohn«: So konnte im Alten Orient der König bezeichnet werden. So nannte man im Hellenismus viele Heroen und
Halbgötter. Aus dem Begriff Gottessohn als solchem ließ sich
bestimmt nicht ableiten, was Jesus war. Im Gegenteil: gegenüber allen jenen Gottessöhnen im hellenistisch-synkretistischen
Pantheon, gegenüber allen jenen gottgezeugten Königen und
Kaisern, Helden und Genies hatte der Glaubende von Jesu
Person und Geschichte abzulesen, was »Gottessohn« eigentlich, entscheidend, unvergleichbar bedeutet: der wie wir versuchte, gehorsame, gekreuzigte Gottessohn.*
- *»Logos«: Das Alte Testament spricht ebenso emphatisch vom
göttlichen »Wort« wie die griechischen Philosophen, die jü-
disch-hellenistische Weisheitsliteratur ebenso wie Philon und
das gnostische Corpus Hermeticum. Entscheidend war nicht,
daß gerade der so vieldeutige Terminus »Logos« auf Jesus
angewandt wurde – im Johannesprolog geschieht es nachdrücklich, sonst nur ausnahmsweise –, sondern daß dieser Terminus »Logos« gerade auf Jesus angewandt wurde und von
ihm her eine ganz neue Bestimmtheit und eine ganz eigene
»Logik« erhalten hat: als das fleischgewordene Wort Gottes.*

So sind verschiedene zeitgenössische Würdetitel und mythische
Symbole im Namen Jesu gleichsam getauft worden: um mit
seinem Namen bei verändertem Gehalt verbunden zu bleiben,
ihm zu Dienst zu sein und seine einzigartige maßgebliche Bedeutsamkeit für die Menschen jener Zeit und nicht nur jener Zeit
verständlich zu machen. Sie waren nicht von vornherein ver-

ständliche Ausweise, sondern auf ihn zeigende Hinweise. Nicht a priori unfehlbare Definitionen, sondern aposteriorische Explikationen dessen, was er ist und bedeutet.

Ja, sie sind, wie sich eben bei den einzelnen Titeln zeigte, noch mehr: Sie definieren und explizieren nicht nur theologisch-theoretisch Jesu Wesen, Natur, Person. Sie sind nicht nur friedlich-liturgische oder harmlos-missionarische, sie sind zugleich höchst kritische und polemische Akklamationen und Proklamationen. Stillschweigende oder gar ausdrückliche *Kampfansagen gegen alle,* die sich, ihre Macht und Weisheit absolut setzen, die fordern, was Gottes ist, *die selber die letztlich Maßgebenden sein wollen:* seien es nun die jüdischen Hierarchen, die griechischen Philosophen oder die römischen Imperatoren, seien es die großen oder kleinen Herren, Herrschenden, Machthaber, Messiasse, Göttersöhne. Ihnen allen wird die letzte Maßgeblichkeit abgesprochen und sie dafür jenem Einen, der selber nicht für sich, sondern für die Sache Gottes und des Menschen steht, zugesprochen. Insofern haben die nachösterlichen christologischen Ehrentitel eine indirekte gesellschaftliche, politische Bedeutung. Der Sturz der Götter, welcher Art auch immer, hatte eingesetzt. Und insofern gerade die Cäsaren immer mehr letzte Maßgeblichkeit beanspruchten, drohte der tödliche und in der Tat dann Jahrhunderte andauernde Konflikt mit der römischen Staatsmacht. Wo immer Cäsar forderte, was Gottes ist – aber auch nur dort –, mußte für die Christen das große Entweder-Oder gelten: »aut Christus – aut Caesar!«

Damit ist nun aber auch schon deutlich: *Nicht die Titel an sich* sind das Entscheidende. Nicht an die Titel, *sondern* an *Jesus selbst* als den definitiv Maßgebenden soll sich der Glaubende und die Glaubensgemeinschaft in Glauben und Handeln halten. Mit welchen Titeln sie dieses Maßgebende an Jesus ausdrückten, war am Anfang und ist auch heute eine zweitrangige Frage, ist wie damals so auch heute vom soziokulturellen Kontext mitbedingt. Niemand braucht alle die damaligen Titel zu repetieren und zu rezitieren. Diese sind nun einmal von einer ganz bestimmten, für uns vergangenen Welt und Gesellschaft geprägt und haben sich unterdessen – wie immer, wenn Sprache konserviert wird – verändert. Niemand braucht aus den verschiedenen Titeln und den damit verbundenen Vorstellungen eine einzige Christologie zusammenzubauen. Als ob wir statt vier Evangelisten nur einen einzigen, statt vieler apostolischer Briefe nur eine einzige neutestamentliche Dogmatik hätten. Der Glaube an Jesus läßt viele

Glaubensaussagen über ihn zu: der Christusglaube ist einer und der Christologien sind viele. So wie der Gottesglaube einer ist und der Theologien viele sind.

Zu einer Bilder- oder Titelstürmerei ist mit all dem nicht aufgerufen, wohl aber zu einer *Übersetzung* der Titel und Vorstellungen von damals in die heutige Zeit und Sprache hinein, wie es in diesem ganzen Buch versucht wird: damit der Christusglaube derselbe bleibe, damit heute unverständliche oder gar irreführende Begriffe und Vorstellungen die Annahme und das Leben der Christusbotschaft nicht erschweren oder gar verhindern. Solche Übersetzung bedeutet nicht einfach Abschaffen alter Titel und Glaubensbekenntnisse, bedeutet nicht Absehen von der langen christologischen Tradition oder gar von deren biblischem Ursprung. Im Gegenteil: Jede gute Übersetzung muß sich am Urtext orientieren und von den Fehlern und Stärken früherer Übersetzungen lernen. Jede gute Übersetzung darf aber auch nicht nur mechanisch nachreden, sondern muß schöpferisch die Möglichkeiten der neuen Sprache erspüren und ergreifen. Vor neuen Bezeichnungen Jesu braucht man ebensowenig Scheu zu haben wie vor den alten, die vielfach die schlechtesten nicht waren, sondern die Sache erstaunlich gut getroffen haben.

Wer in der nationalsozialistischen Zeit öffentlich das Bekenntnis ablegte, daß es in der Kirche nach wie vor nur einen maßgebenden »Herrn« (»Führer«) gibt, wurde – wie zwar nicht der katholische oder lutherische Episkopat, wohl aber Karl Barth, die »Bekennende Kirche« und die Synode von Barmen – ebensogut verstanden wie diejenigen Christen, die beinahe 2000 Jahre früher vor römischen Tribunalen das Bekenntnis »Herr ist Jesus« ablegten. Bezahlen, oft teuer bezahlen, muß man für solche gesprochene und gelebte Bekenntnisse nicht nur in Märtyrerzeiten, sondern auch in Wohlstandszeiten. Wo immer man mit Berufung auf Jesus die Anbetung der Götzen der Zeit – und es gibt ihrer viele – ablehnt. Nicht für christologische Titel und Prädikate, Formeln und Sätze braucht der Christ mit seinem Leiden oder gar mit seinem Leben zu bezahlen, wohl aber für diesen Jesus Christus selbst und für das, wofür er maßgebend stellvertretend gutsteht: die Sache Gottes und des Menschen.

Immer deutlicher ist man sich der ganzen Bedeutsamkeit Jesu bewußt geworden. Im frommen Gebrauch der Gemeinde haben dabei einige der alten Titel Geschichte gemacht und eine bedeutsame Eigendynamik entfaltet, was dem heutigen Verständnis nicht geringe Schwierigkeiten bereitet. Ganz besonders gilt dies vom Titel »*Gottessohn*«, der nicht erst im Hellenismus, sondern schon im Alten Testament eine Rolle gespielt hat: Im israelischen Königszeremoniell wird der König zum »Sohn Jahwes« eingesetzt, als Sohn adoptiert[16]. Und man erwartete einen Nachkommen Davids, der als »Sohn« Gottes den Thron Davids besteigen und die davidische Herrschaft über Israel für immer festigen werde[17]. Dieser Titel wird nun auf Jesus angewandt: Er wird erkannt als derjenige, der durch Auferweckung und Erhöhung – wie es im alten Glaubensbekenntnis am Anfang des Römerbriefes heißt – »eingesetzt ist zum Sohn Gottes in Macht«[18] oder, in Aufnahme des Psalmwortes, als am Ostertag »gezeugt«[19].

Doch die Frage war kaum zu vermeiden: Ist der Auferweckte nicht derselbe wie der Irdische? Muß man also das, was man vom Auferweckten aussagt, nicht schon vom Irdischen aussagen? Ist also nicht schon der Irdische der Sohn Gottes, auch wenn seine Herrschaft noch verborgen ist? So wurde der Zeitpunkt der Einsetzung in die Gottessohnschaft in anderen neutestamentlichen Schriften vorverlegt: auf die Taufe als den Beginn seiner öffentlichen Tätigkeit[20] oder auf seine Geburt[21], ja schon vor der Geburt auf Gottes Ewigkeit[22].

Ursprünglich also ging es im Titel »Gottessohn« gar *nicht um die Abkunft, sondern um die Rechts- und Machtstellung Jesu.* Weniger um das Wesen als um die Funktion. Ursprünglich meinte der Titel nicht eine leibliche Sohnschaft, sondern eine göttliche Erwählung und Bevollmächtigung: daß dieser Jesus nun anstelle Gottes über sein Volk herrscht. »Gottessohn« kennzeichnet also Jesus sowenig wie den König Israels als übermenschliches, göttliches Wesen, sondern als den durch die Erhöhung zur Rechten Gottes eingesetzten Herrscher: gleichsam als den Generalbevollmächtigten Gottes, der von allen Untertanen geehrt werden soll wie dieser selbst.

Schon der irdische, geschichtliche Jesus von Nazaret trat, indem er Gottes Reich und Willen in Wort und Tat proklamierte, als öffentlicher Sachwalter Gottes auf[23]. Und er war dabei mehr als ein im juristischen Sinn Beauftragter, Bevollmächtigter, Anwalt, Sprecher Gottes. Ohne alle Titel und Ämter erschien er in seinem ganzen Tun und Reden als ein Sachwalter im ganz existentiellen Sinn: als persönlicher Botschafter, Treuhänder, ja Vertrauter und Freund Gottes. Er lebte, litt und kämpfte aus einer letztlich unerklärlichen Gotteserfahrung, Gottesgegenwart, Gottesgewißheit, ja, aus einer eigentümlichen Einheit mit Gott heraus, die ihn Gott als seinen Vater anreden ließ. Daß man ihn in der Gemeinde wohl zunächst »den Sohn« nannte, dürfte einfach der Widerschein sein, der vom verkündeten Vater-Gott auf sein Antlitz fiel. Von da aus war der Übergang zum traditionell geprägten Titel »Sohn Gottes« verständlich.

Dieser Titel machte für die Menschen der damaligen Zeit mehr als andere deutlich, wie sehr der Mensch Jesus von Nazaret zu Gott gehört, wie sehr er an Gottes Seite steht, nun der Gemeinde und der Welt gegenüber, nur dem Vater und sonst niemand untertan. Als der endgültige zu Gott Erhöhte ist er jetzt im definitiven und umfassenden Sinn – »ein für allemal« – gegenüber den Menschen *Gottes Stellvertreter*. Titel wie »Beauftragter«, »Bevollmächtigter«, »Anwalt«, »Sprecher«, »Sachwalter«, auch »Botschafter«, »Treuhänder«, »Vertrauter«, »Freund«, ja »Repräsentant«, »Platzhalter«, »Stellvertreter« Gottes sagen heute für manche vielleicht deutlicher das aus, was die alten Namen »König«, »Hirte«, »Heiland«, »Gottessohn« oder auch die traditionelle Lehre von den drei »Ämtern« Jesu Christi (prophetisches, königliches, hohepriesterliches Amt) auszusagen versuchten.

Aber schon der irdische Jesus, für den die Sache Gottes die Sache des Menschen ist, war gerade als Sachwalter Gottes der öffentliche Sachwalter des Menschen. Mit seinem ganzen Leben und Reden, Handeln und Leiden stand er in Erfüllung des Willens Gottes für das wahre, umfassende Wohl des Menschen, stand er für des Menschen Freiheit, seine Freude, sein wahres Leben, seine Chance vor Gott, die Liebe. Er ging ganz in der Sache Gottes und so des Menschen auf. Und dies in letzter Konsequenz und Bewährung bis zum Äußersten. In seinem Tod hat er nur zu Ende gebracht, was er von Anfang an gepredigt und gelebt hat. Er starb nicht nur für seine »Überzeugung«. Auch nicht nur allgemein für eine »Sache«, sondern faktisch starb er ganz konkret für alle jene Verlorenen und Verachteten, Gesetzesbrecher, Gesetzlosen, Sünder aller Art, mit denen er sich zum Ärger seiner Gegner zusammengesetzt, solidarisiert, identifiziert hatte und die im Grunde dasselbe Schicksal verdient hätten wie er. Er hat ihr Schicksal und den Fluch, der auf ihnen lag, auf sich genommen: Er starb – nun nicht mehr im allerschlimmsten Sinn (wie seine Feinde meinten), sondern im allerbesten Sinn (wie seine Jünger im Licht der Auferweckung immer deutlicher erkannten) – als Stellvertreter der Sünder, ja, wie Paulus es nahelegt, als die personifizierte Sünde[24]. Und insofern nun in seinem Tod gerade die Frommen und Gerechten in ihrer Selbstverschlossenheit, Selbstsicherheit, Selbstgerechtigkeit als die eigentlichen Schuldigen und Sünder manifest geworden waren, starb er paradoxerweise auch für sie: starb er, wie man je länger desto klarer erkannte, »für die Vielen« ohne Unterschied des Volkes, der Klasse, der Rasse, der Kultur; starb er »für alle«, »für uns«. So erwies sich der Mensch Jesus von Nazaret, definitiv Gottes Stellvertreter, zugleich im umfassendsten und radikalsten Sinn – »ein für allemal«, Zeit und Raum übersteigend – als der Repräsentant, Platzhalter, *Stellvertreter der Menschen* vor Gott.

Aber erst nach der Katastrophe wurde Jesus als der Stellvertreter Gottes und der Menschen bestätigt und gerechtfertigt. Den Preis des Todes mußte er zuerst bezahlen, damit der radikale Durchbruch durch das Gesetz erreicht und eine neue Freiheit, eine neue Existenz, ein neuer Mensch ermöglicht wurde. Erst jetzt wurde er als der Menschen- und Gottessohn erkannt, als der Erlöser und Versöhner, als der einzige Mittler und Hohepriester des neuen Bundes zwischen Gott und den Menschen, ja, als der Weg, die Wahrheit und das Leben Gottes für die Menschen. Er ist dies alles nicht in einer magischen oder mechanischen Weise. Er ist kein Ersatzmann, der die Stelle selber besetzt statt freihält[25]. Wie er als Stellvertreter, Repräsentant, Platzhalter Gottes und des Menschen Gott nicht verdrängt, so auch nicht den Menschen. Wie er Gottes Willen respektiert, so des Menschen Verantwortung. Er ruft in die Freiheit und erwartet Zustimmung. Er geht voran, setzt sich und seinen Gott aufs Spiel und provoziert Nachfolge.

Aber auch als der zu Gott Erhöhte ist der Jesus, der nicht sich selbst, sondern das Gottesreich verkündigte, nicht zum Selbstzweck geworden. Gerade als der Gottessohn, als der Stellvertreter, Repräsentant, Platzhalter, ist er in allem der lebendige Verweis auf den Gott und Vater, der größer ist als er[26]. Er ist Gottes »Vorläufer«[27] zu den Menschen hin, bevor Gott selber sie erreicht hat. Und zugleich ist er der »Vorläufer« der Menschen auf Gott hin, der sich mit den Nachlaufenden und mit den Zurückgebliebenen identifiziert. Seine Herrschaft ist noch nicht das

Endgültige. Sie ist auf Zeit, ein Provisorium. Sie steht unter dem Zeichen des Noch-nicht und Doch-schon, zwischen Erfüllung und Vollendung, Zeit und Ewigkeit. So hat sich denn das Ziel der Geschichte, wie es von Jesus verkündigt wurde, nicht geändert dadurch, daß er aus dem Verkündiger der Verkündigte wurde: Das Ziel ist und bleibt das Gottesreich, in welchem die Sache Gottes sich durchgesetzt hat, in welchem die absolute Zukunft Gegenwart ist und der Stellvertreter seine Herrschaft dem zurückgegeben hat, den er vertritt – damit Gott nicht nur in allem, sondern alles in allem sei[28].

Der definitive Maßstab

In dieser Perspektive ist eine Vorstellung zu verstehen, die manchen Zeitgenossen, obwohl in Glaubensbekenntnissen verankert, fremd geworden ist: warum Jesus im Neuen Testament für die Vollendung der Gottesherrschaft in Gottes Reich durchgängig als der *Weltenrichter* erwartet wird, der kommt, »zu richten die Lebendigen und die Toten«.

Die schon damals weitverbreitete Vorstellung vom Totengericht hatte sich im frühen Judentum wie in der persischen Religion mit der Enderwartung verbunden: ein Gericht nicht nur über den Einzelnen unmittelbar nach seinem Tod, sondern ein Gericht über die gesamte Menschheit am Ende der Zeit. Bereits im Zusammenhang mit der Naherwartung Jesu ist uns klar geworden, wie sehr die Erwartung der Vollendung in die Formen der frühjüdischen Apokalyptik gekleidet erscheint und wie unumgänglich gerade bezüglich Anfang und Ende der Menschheitsgeschichte differenziert interpretierende Entmythologisierung ist[29]. Wir müssen hier in Kürze etwas konkreter werden[30].

Daß die Geschichte der Naherwartung eine Geschichte ihrer immer wiederholten Enttäuschung ist – auch und gerade in »apokalyptisch« genannten Zeiten –, lehrt die Kirchengeschichte vom 1. bis zum 20. Jahrhundert. Aber auch Vorstellungen wie die des (vermutlich nicht von Paulus stammenden) 2. Thessalonicherbriefes[31] von einer letzten Steigerung des Bösen, einem großen Abfall vor dem Ende und der Verkörperung der widergöttlichen und widerchristlichen Kräfte in einem endzeitlichen »Menschen der Gesetzesfeindschaft« oder in – nach den Johannesbriefen[32] – einem oder mehreren »Antichristen« (Individuum oder Kollektivum?) sind nicht, wie oft angenommen, besondere göttliche Offenbarungen über die Endzeit. Es sind Bilder aus der jüdischen Apokalyptik[33], die zum Teil alte mythologische Motive verwerten, zum Teil geschichtliche Erfahrungen (der als sichtbarer Gott kultisch zu verehrende König Antiochus IV. Epiphanes, Kaiser Caligula, Nero redivivus). Die unter sich nicht harmonisierbaren »apo-kalyptischen«, »enthüllenden« Bilder dürfen trotz ihres Namens zumindest heute nicht mehr als chronologische Enthüllung oder Information über die »letzten Dinge« am Ende der Weltgeschichte, gleichsam als ein Drehbuch für der Menschheitstragödie letzten Akt aufgefaßt werden. Hier erfährt der Mensch trotz der heute noch immer erstaunlich verbreiteten Neugierde gerade nicht, was auf ihn zukommt und wie es dann zugehen wird. Das Bild einer großen öffentlichen Gerichtsversammlung der gesamten Menschheit, also von Milliarden und Abermilliarden Menschen, ist – ein Bild.

Es gibt weder eine eindeutige wissenschaftliche Extrapolation noch eine genaue prophetische Prognose der definitiven Zukunft der Menschheit. Mit unableitbar Neuem – die Kategorie »Novum«! – ist in der Geschichte der Freiheit stets zu rechnen. Das Ende ist nicht von vornherein festgelegt. Der Mensch soll diesem Ende nicht einfach entgegenwarten, sondern soll seine Rolle in Welt und Geschichte schöpferisch wahrnehmen. Im Ineinander von schenkender Freiheit und beschenkter Freiheit ist der Mensch der unersetzliche Partner, der der unaufhaltsamen Evolution des Kosmos einen Sinn geben und seinen Stempel aufdrücken soll. Das Kommen des Reiches Gottes verurteilt den Menschen nicht zur Passivität, sondern erfordert aus dem Glauben heraus furchtlose menschenfreundliche Aktivität. Keine Flucht nach vorn, sondern – gegen allen aufkommenden Skeptizismus und Fatalismus – Taten der Hoffnung. Angesichts des kommenden Reiches der Gerechtigkeit, der Freiheit und des Friedens der unermüdliche Kampf für Gerechtigkeit, Freiheit und Frieden: gegen alle Mächte des Bösen, der Unfreiheit, des Elends, der Lieblosigkeit, des Todes. Es braucht hier nicht wiederholt zu werden, was gegen die falschen Verabsolutierungen über die Polarität von Zukunft Gottes und Gegenwart des Menschen bereits gesagt worden ist[34].

Wie der Anfang der Menschheitsgeschichte, so ist auch ihr Ende, wie ihre letzte Her-kunft, so ist auch ihre letzte Zu-kunft eine Sache des Glaubens: in der Schrift einprägsam umschrieben mit gewiß zeitbedingten dichterischen Bildern und Erzählungen, die Wachsamkeit und Zuversicht verbreiten wollen, die heute jedoch mehr als je auf das Entscheidende hin befragt werden müssen. Nicht auf die Abfolge von Endereignissen zielen sie, sondern auf das endzeitliche Handeln Gottes selbst und die Mitverantwortung des Menschen für das Ende. Dieses angekündigte *Ende* aber darf *nicht* kurzerhand mit einer kosmischen Katastrophe und einem *Abbruch* der Menschheitsgeschichte gleichgesetzt werden. Bei aller Beendigung des Alten, Bösen ist dieses Ende letzlich *doch* zu verstehen als *Voll-endung*! Als Vollendung nämlich der Menschheitsgeschichte durch den getreuen Gott, den Schöpfer und Neuschöpfer, wie dies in den Bildern des Mahles, des Festes, der Hochzeit, der neuen Erde und des neuen Himmels, einer neuen Welt also, umschrieben wird. Die weitere Zukunft der neuen Welt bleibt für den Glauben offen. Auf keinen Fall besagt sie Erstarrung, vielmehr die Dynamik ewigen Lebens: vita venturi saeculi, das Leben der zukünftigen Welt, mit welchem die Glaubensbekenntnisse triumphal enden.

Ist es erstaunlich, daß nicht die auch in den frühen christlichen Gemeinden verbreiteten *Apokalypsen,* sondern die *Evangelien* die für die junge Kirche charakteristische Literaturform geworden sind? Kleine Apokalypsen wurden in die Evangelien (und die große dem Johannes zugeschriebene Apokalypse in das Gesamt des Neuen Testaments) eingebaut, gleichsam domestiziert[35]. Was sagt das anderes als: die Apokalyptik ist vom Evangelium her zu verstehen und nicht umgekehrt[36]. Sie stellt, wie schon früher bemerkt, für eine ganz bestimmte Verstehenssituation einen Verstehens- und Vorstellungsrahmen dar, der sehr wohl von der gemeinten Sache, von der Botschaft selbst, zu unterscheiden ist. Worauf sind die Apokalypsen in den Evangelien ausgerichtet? Ganz auf das *Erscheinen Jesu,* der jetzt eindeutig mit dem Menschensohn identisch ist: Funktion und Figur des durch Vollendung der Gottesherrschaft erwarteten erhöhten Jesus haben sich spätestens hier mit Funktion und Figur des zum Endgericht erwarteten apokalyptischen Menschensohnes verschmolzen. Weltenrichter ist kein anderer als Jesus – und gerade dies ist für alle die, die sich auf Jesus eingelassen haben, das große Zeichen der Hoffnung.

Michelangelos monumentales Gemälde in der Capella Sixtina hat die Szene des ›Jüngsten Gerichts‹ der Menschheit unauslöslich eingeprägt. Aber die geniale Kunst beantwortet noch nicht die Frage eines zweifelnden Glaubens: *Was* soll denn an einer derart mythologisch ausgestalteten Szene einer Gerichtsversammlung aller Völker heute überhaupt *noch relevant* sein können? Besser wird man ohne dieses Bild von einem Versammeltwerden aller Menschen in Gott, ihrem Schöpfer und Vollender, sprechen. Am Bild vom Jüngsten Gericht bleibt relevant, wenn man es zunächst mehr *negativ* formulieren will:

daß ich mich und mein Leben letztlich nicht beurteilen und das Urteil darüber auch keinem anderen menschlichen Tribunal überlassen kann;

daß meine undurchsichtige und ambivalente Existenz wie die zutiefst zwiespältige Menschheitsgeschichte überhaupt nach einem endgültigen Durchsichtigwerden und dem Offenbarwerden eines endgültigen Sinnes verlangt;

daß alles Bestehende – die religiösen Traditionen, Institutionen, Autoritäten eingeschlossen – provisorischen Charakter hat;

daß eine wahre Vollendung und ein wahres Glück der Menschheit nur gegeben ist, wenn nicht nur die letzte Generation, sondern alle Menschen daran teilhaben werden;

daß die bessere Zukunft einer vollkommenen Gesellschaft in Frieden, Freiheit und Gerechtigkeit von den Menschen immer nur angestrebt, aber, wenn man nicht Illusionen oder gar dem Terror gewaltsamer Volksbeglücker verfallen will, nie voll realisiert werden kann.

Am Bild des Jüngsten Gerichts bleibt relevant, wenn man es mehr *positiv* ausdrücken will:

– *daß es zu einer Sinnerfüllung meines Lebens, zu einem Durchsichtigwerden der Menschheitsgeschichte, zu einer wahren Vollendung des Individuums und der menschlichen Gesellschaft erst in der Begegnung mit der offenbaren letzten Wirklichkeit Gottes kommen wird;*
– *daß auf dem Weg zur Vollendung für die tätige und leidende Verwirklichung des wahren Menschseins in der Einzelexistenz wie in der Gesellschaft jener gekreuzigte und doch lebendige Jesus letzter Richter, verläßlicher, bleibender, letzter,* definitiver Maßstab *ist*[37].

Ein Maßstab für radikales Menschsein überhaupt, ein Maßstab, an welchem alle Menschen, Christen und Nichtchristen gemessen werden und welchem Nichtchristen, die hier ebenso ernstgenommen werden, oft besser entsprechen als Christen[38]. Ein Maßstab, der sich gewiß erst in der Zukunft des Gottesreiches durchsetzen wird, der aber schon jetzt die Entscheidung herbeiführt, so daß das Johannesevangelium betonen kann, daß das Gericht schon jetzt erfolgt[39]. Die Vorstellung eines Weltgerichts weist den Christen energisch auf diesen letzten Maßstab hin: damit er sich der Vorläufigkeit der jeweiligen Gegenwart bewußt bleibe, dem Druck der herrschenden Verhältnisse und den Versuchungen des Zeitgeistes standhalte und sich nach Gottes Willen am umfassenden leib-geistigen Wohl des Menschen – die Bedeutung der leiblichen »Werke der Barmherzigkeit« in den Gerichtserzählungen[40] – orientiere.

Und wie wird das Ganze ausgehen? Um es gleich zu sagen: der *Ausgang des Ganzen* ist *nicht durchschaubar*. Nicht nur weil bei Schöpfung und Neuschöpfung alle Anschauungen und Vorstellungen versagen müssen, sondern weil die Beantwortung letzter Fragen, wie etwa, ob alle Menschen – auch die großen Verbrecher der Weltgeschichte bis Hitler und Stalin – gerettet würden, unmöglich erscheint.

Die größten Geister der Theologie – von Origenes und Augustin über Thomas, Luther und Calvin bis Barth – haben sich abgemüht mit dem dunklen Problem des letzten Schicksals, der Erwählung, Vorausbestimmung, *Prädestination* des Menschen und der Menschheit: ohne den Schleier des Geheimnisses lüften zu können! Geklärt hat sich nur, daß man dem Anfang und Ende der Wege Gottes mit einfachen Lösungen weder vom Neuen Testament noch von den Fragen der Gegenwart her gerecht wird. Weder mit der positiven Vorherbestimmung eines Teiles der Menschen zur Verdammung: Calvins Vorstellung einer »praedestinatio gemina«, einer »doppelten Vorherbestimmung«. Noch mit der positiven Vorherbestimmung aller Menschen zur Seligkeit: des Origenes »Apo-katastasis panton«, »Wieder-bringung aller«. Daß Gott alle Menschen retten (Allversöhnung) und die Möglichkeit einer endgültigen Ferne des Menschen von ihm (= Hölle) ausschließen *müsse*, widerspricht der souveränen Freiheit seiner Gnade und Barmherzigkeit. Aber ebenso, daß Gott nicht alle Menschen retten und die Hölle nicht gleichsam leer stehen lassen *dürfe*[41].

Im Neuen Testament verkünden die Gerichtserzählungen eine klare Scheidung der Menschheit. Doch andere, insbesondere paulinische Aussagen deuten ein Allerbarmen an[42]. Diese *Aussagen* sind mit jenen im Neuen Testament *nirgendwo ausgeglichen*: Die Frage kann also, wie heute viele Theologen sagen, nicht anders denn *offenbleiben*! Man sehe zu: Wer in Gefahr ist, den unendlichen Ernst seiner persönlichen Verantwortung leichtsinnig zu überspielen, wird gewarnt durch die Möglichkeit eines doppelten Ausgangs: sein Heil ist nicht von vornherein garantiert. Wer aber in Gefahr ist, am unendlichen Ernst seiner persönlichen Verantwortung zu verzweifeln, wird ermutigt durch die mögliche Errettung eines jeden Menschen: der Barmherzigkeit Gottes sind keine Grenzen gesetzt. Und daß gerade der Mensch und Mitmensch Jesus, der Freund der Bedrückten und Beladenen, auch als Richter verkündet wird, erinnert den Menschen daran: er hat nicht wie in der mittelalterlichen Totensequenz zitternd einen »Dies irae«, einen »Tag des Zornes« (dramatischer Höhepunkt in den Requiemkompositionen von Cherubini, Mozart, Berlioz, Verdi) zu erwarten, sondern darf in der Freude und Gelassenheit des altchristlichen »Maranatha« (»unser Herr komm!«) seine und aller Menschen Begegnung mit Gott erwarten.

Nicht die intellektuelle Bewältigung dieses – im spekulativen Detail höchst komplexen[43] – Problems ist von uns gefordert. Auch nicht nur das individualistisch-spiritualistische »Rette deine Seele«. Sondern mit den Anderen zusammen, im Einsatz für eine bessere Menschenwelt angesichts des kommenden Gottesreiches, ein praktisches Leben, welches sein Maß an Jesus dem Gekreuzigten nimmt. Am Gekreuzigten?

3. Das letztlich Unterscheidende

»Alexamenos betet seinen Gott an«, das ist die Unterschrift unter dem ältesten Kruzifix überhaupt: eine Spottkritzelei wohl aus dem 3. Jahrhundert, gefunden in Rom auf dem Palatin, dem kaiserlichen Bezirk, welche den Gekreuzigten mit einem Eselskopf darstellt! Deutlicher konnte man es nicht mehr machen, daß die so gar nicht erbauliche Botschaft vom Gekreuzigten ein schlechter Scherz oder, wie Paulus nach Korinth schrieb, »für die Juden ein Skandal und für die Heiden ein Unsinn« ist[1].

Umwertung

»Der Begriff *Kreuz* muß nicht nur dem Leib römischer Bürger, sondern ihren Gedanken, ihren Augen, ihren Ohren fern sein«, so hatte, hundert Jahre bevor Paulus dies schrieb, Cicero auf dem Forum Romanum in der Rede für C. Rabirius Postumus[2] erklärt, welcher nach Cicero in der Tat nicht zu verteidigen wäre, wenn er, wie angeklagt, in der Provinz römische Bürger hätte kreuzigen lassen. Der Kreuzestod ist nach ihm die schlimmste, grausamste, scheußlichste, höchste Todesstrafe[3]. Noch lange nach ihrer Abschaffung durch Kaiser Konstantin bis ins 5. Jahrhundert hinein und vielfach noch später haben sich die Christen denn auch gescheut, den leidenden Jesus am Kreuz darzustellen. In größerem Umfang ist dies erst in der mittelalterlichen Gotik Sitte geworden.

So war das Kreuz eine harte, grausame Tatsache – alles andere als ein zeitloser Mythos, gar ein religiöses Symbol oder Schmuckstück. Also gerade, was Goethe *nicht* liebte: »Ein leichtes Ehrenkreuzlein ist immer etwas Lustiges im Leben, das leidige Marterholz, das Widerwärtigste unter der Sonne, sollte kein vernünftiger Mensch auszugraben und aufzupflanzen bemüht sein[4].« Und wenn Goethe so für die säkularen Humanismen spricht, so der prominente Zen-Buddhist D. T. Suzuki für die Weltreligionen: »Wann immer ich die gekreuzigte Gestalt Christi sehe, dann kann ich nicht anders als an die Kluft denken, die zwischen Christentum und Buddhismus liegt[5]«. Kein Mensch – weder Jude noch Grieche noch Römer – hätte darauf verfallen können, mit diesem Galgen der Verfemten einen positiven, einen religiösen Sinn zu verbinden. Das *Kreuz Jesu* mußte *einem gebildeten Griechen* als *barbarische Torheit, einem römischen Bürger* als *Schande schlechthin, einem gläubigen Juden* aber als *Gottesfluch* vorkommen.

Und gerade dieser Schandpfahl erscheint jetzt in einem völlig anderen Licht. Was für jeden Menschen damals unvorstellbar war, vollbringt der Glaube an den doch lebendigen Gekreuzigten: daß dieses *Zeichen der Schmach* als ein *Zeichen des Sieges* erscheint! Daß dieser ehrenlose Tod von Sklaven und Rebellen als Heilstod der Erlösung und Befreiung verstanden werden kann! Daß das Kreuz Jesu, dieses blutige Siegel auf ein entsprechend gelebtes Leben, ein Aufruf wird zum Verzicht auf ein egoistisch geprägtes Leben. Eine Umwertung aller Werte – dies hat Nietzsche in seinen Invektiven gegen das Christliche richtig erspürt – kündigt sich hier an. Um es vorwegzunehmen: kein Weg der Verkrampfung, der schwächlichen Selbsterniedrigung ist hier gemeint, wie dies manchmal von Christen verstanden und von Nietzsche zu Recht gefürchtet wurde. Sondern – von Ungezählten gewagt – das tapfere Leben ohne Angst auch vor tödlichen Risiken: durch Kampf, Leid, Tod hindurch, im starken Vertrauen und Hoffen auf das Ziel der wahren Freiheit, Liebe, Menschlichkeit, des ewigen Lebens. Aus dem Ärgernis, dem Skandalon schlechthin war eine erstaunliche Heilserfahrung, aus dem Kreuzweg ein möglicher Lebensweg geworden[6].

Selbstverständlich ist die junge Christengemeinde mit dem ungeheuren Anstoß des gekreuzigten Messias – Jesu Legitimation war die Lebensfrage der Gemeinde – *nicht auf einen Schlag* fertiggeworden: Die Verlegenheit war durch Ostern nicht einfach beseitigt. Die verschiedenen neutestamentlichen Schriften – wir brauchen hier die Schichten nicht zu analysieren – sind von der Auseinandersetzung mit dem Kreuz durchzogen, und nicht umsonst ist die älteste zusammenhängende Jesus-Geschichte die Passionsgeschichte. Erst mit der Zeit erkannte man das Kreuz geradezu als Mitte und Summe des christlichen Glaubens und Lebens. Doch sowohl die Auseinandersetzungen im Inneren der Gemeinden wie die Apologie nach außen erzwangen eine vertiefte Reflexion, die deutlich machte, wie sehr am Kreuz Christengemeinde und Juden-, Griechen-, Römertum, ja Glaube und Unglaube sich scheiden.

An die Stelle der anfänglichen Trostlosigkeit und Sprachlosigkeit war im Licht der Ostererfahrung zunächst einfach die schlichte Überzeugung getreten, daß sich alles doch nach Gottes Ratschluß abgespielt haben muß, daß Jesus nach Gottes Willen diesen Weg gehen »mußte«. Vorbilder aus dem *Alten Testament* – der verfolgte Prophet, der für die Sünden vieler unschuldig und stellvertretend leidende Gottesknecht, das die Sünden zeichenhaft hinwegnehmende Opfertier – halfen mit, dem grausamen, sinnlosen Kreuzesgeschehen langsam einen positiven Sinn abzugewinnen. Es geschah alles »gemäß der Schrift«: so sagte man, womit man am Anfang das Alte Testament als Ganzes meinte, das überall von Jesus reden mußte, wenn dieser der Messias war. Um dies zu entdecken, war eine eigene Exegese notwendig; die jüdische Tradition hatte nicht einmal im Gottesknecht-Lied des zweiten Jesaja[7] einen leidenden oder gar gekreuzigten Messias zu Gesicht bekommen. Aber so wurde das Alte Testament nun immer mehr vom Kreuz her verstanden, und das Kreuz immer mehr vom Alten Testament her interpretiert, so daß sich klarer und klarer herausstellte: In Jesus hat Gott, der Gott des Alten Testaments, gehandelt. Im großen Stil findet sich eine solche entwickelte »Theologie des Kreuzes« einerseits im ältesten der vier Evangelien, andererseits in den paulinischen Briefen; es wird bei dieser Gelegenheit deutlich, daß auch Titel wie »Gottessohn«, die sehr oft einfach von einer »Inkarnation« her verstanden werden, nur vom Kreuz her richtig verstanden werden können.

In seinem Evangelium läßt es *Markus,* der noch keine Kindheitsgeschichte kennt, deutlich werden, daß die Passion die entsprechende Offenbarung der Gottessohnschaft ausmacht[8]. Jesus ist Sohn Gottes, wie schon die vermutlich markinische Überschrift des Evangeliums festhält. Aber das beruht nach Markus nicht auf irgendeiner wunderbaren Geburt oder Empfängnis, die gar nicht erwähnt werden. Sondern auf dem Auftrag Gottes, der ihn in der Taufe auf einen bestimmten Weg ruft[9]. Daß Jesus der Messias und Gottessohn ist, dies bleibt, nach Markus, wir sahen es schon, der Öffentlichkeit verborgen. Bekannt ist es nur den Dämonen[10] und schließlich auch Petrus, dem bekennenden Jünger, denen aber Stillschweigen auferlegt wird. Unmittelbar nach dem Messiasbekenntnis des Petrus folgt die erste Leidensankündigung: der Weg des Messias führt über das Kreuz, und wer ihm nachfolgen will, kann sein eigenes Kreuz nicht umgehen. So wird des Petrus Mißverständnis mit größter Heftigkeit – »hinweg von mir, Satan« – korrigiert[11]. Nur vom Kreuz her wird das von Markus selber in das Evangelium hineingelegte Messiasgeheimnis Jesu richtig verstanden. Erst in seinem Leiden bekennt sich Jesus nach markinischer Auffassung zum Titel Gottessohn, ohne ihn selbst zu gebrauchen. Und erst nach seinem Tod kann der erste Mensch, ein Heide, von sich aus bekennen, daß dieser Mensch Gottes Sohn gewesen ist. Erst jetzt – nach Tod (und Auferweckung) – kann Jesu Geheimnis erkannt und verkündet werden.

Aber schon lange vor Markus ist bei Paulus, bei dem eine Kindheitsgeschichte ebenfalls keine Rolle spielt, die Gottessohnschaft ganz und gar auf Jesu Kreuz und Auferweckung ausgerichtet.

Jenseits von Schwärmerei und Erstarrung

Die christliche Botschaft ist für den Apostel *Paulus*[12], der sich für die Predigt des Evangeliums unter den Heiden auserwählt sieht, wesentlich *Botschaft vom Gekreuzigten,* in welchem für ihn der ganze irdische Jesus konzentriert erscheint: Christliche Botschaft ist – abgekürzt und zugespitzt gesagt – Wort vom Kreuz[13]. Ein Wort, welches man nicht rückgängig machen oder entleeren, aber auch nicht vertuschen oder heroisieren darf. Es müssen die Gegner vor allem in Korinth und Galatien und ihre Verkürzungen und Verfälschungen des Evangeliums gewesen sein – wenn man mit dem so verschiedenen früheren ersten Brief an die Thessalonicher vergleicht –, die Paulus zu einer entschiedenen theologischen Konzentration und Zuspitzung seiner Verkündigung zwangen. Vom Gekreuzigten her bekommt die Theologie des Paulus jene kritische Schärfe, die sie vor anderen auszeichnet. Von dieser Mitte her – sie ist auch bei Paulus nicht das Ganze – geht er alle Situationen und Probleme an. Er kann deshalb zur selben Zeit sowohl nach links wie nach rechts eine erstaunlich treffende und zugleich kohärente Ideologiekritik treiben.

1. Da sind die progressiven pneumatischen *Enthusiasten* in der sprichwörtlich berüchtigten griechischen Hafenstadt *Korinth*[14]: die sich aufgrund von Taufe, Geistempfang, Liebesmahl schon gesichert, im Besitz des Heils, ja vollendet vorkommen. Die den armseligen irdischen Jesus als Angelegenheit der Vergangenheit ansehen und sich lieber auf den erhöhten Herrn und Sieger über die Schicksalsmächte berufen. Und die so aus ihrem Geistbesitz und ihren »höheren« Erkenntnissen eine selbstgewisse Freiheit ableiten, welche ihnen jegliche Selbstglorifizierung, Überheblichkeit, Lieblosigkeit, Rechthaberei, Gewalttat, auch Saufgelage und religiös gerechtfertigten Verkehr mit Prostituierten (= »korinthern«) gestattet! Diese überspannten, utopischen, libertinistischen Auferstehungsphantasten, die den Himmel auf Erden vorausnehmen wollen, verweist Paulus an den *Gekreuzigten*.

Den Gekreuzigten und nur ihn wollte er von Anfang an ihnen verkünden! Und wie sollte man angesichts dieses Gekreuzigten, der schwach für die Schwachen gestorben ist, mit religiösen Begabungen und Potenzen protzen und sich seiner überlegenen Weisheit und starken Taten rühmen dürfen? Wie sollte man rücksichtslos seine Ziele durchsetzen, seine Freiheit mißbrauchen, sich vor Gott aufspielen wollen, um sich über alles Schwache, die schwachen Menschen und die Schwäche Gottes selbst, hinwegzusetzen? Gerade in der skandalösen Schwäche und Torheit des Gekreuzigten, in welcher sich die Schwäche und Torheit Gottes selbst zu manifestieren scheint, setzt sich letztlich Gottes totenerweckende Macht und überwältigende Weisheit durch. Gerade die am Kreuz so offenkundige Schwäche Gottes erweist sich als stärker als die Macht der Menschen. Seine Torheit weiser als ihre Weisheit. Ja, das Kreuz – gesehen im Licht des neuen Lebens – bedeutet für alle, die sich vertrauend darauf einlassen, Gottes Macht und Weisheit. Im Glauben an den Gekreuzigten wird der Mensch nämlich fähig, die Freiheit nicht libertinistisch, sondern für die Anderen zu gebrauchen: die individuellen Geistesgaben zum Nutzen der Gemeinschaft einzusetzen, in allem den kühnen Weg tätiger Liebe zu gehen. So ist denn dieser gekreuzigte und lebendige Jesus Christus für die Glaubenden das Fundament, das schon gelegt ist und das durch kein anderes ersetzt werden kann. Der Gekreuzigte ist als der Lebendige der Grund des Glaubens. Er ist das Kriterium der Freiheit. Ja, er ist die Mitte und Norm des Christlichen.

Das Kreuz war die große Frage, die durch die Auferweckung beantwortet wurde. Es ist durch Paulus zur großen Antwort geworden, die ein *falsches Verständnis der Auferweckung in Frage stellt.* So bleibt das Kreuz gegenüber allem pseudoprogressiven Auferstehungs- und Freiheitsenthusiasmus das Mahnzeichen, welches den Menschen auf den Boden dieser Wirklichkeit stellt, welches ihn *in die Nachfolge des Gekreuzigten ruft.* Der Kern der christlichen Auferweckungsbotschaft, die von Paulus gegen ihre Leugner nachdrücklich verteidigt wird, ist niemand anders als der Gekreuzigte, der für die christliche Gemeinde kein Toter und Vergangener, sondern ein Lebendiger und Zukünftiger ist. Nur so weit geht die Herrschaft des Auferweckten, wie dem Gekreuzigten gedient wird! Ostern macht das Kreuz nicht rückgängig. Ostern bestätigt das Kreuz, heißt es zwar nicht gut in seinem Ärgernis, aber macht sein Ärgernis gut und sinnvoll. Keinen Moment darf also die Auferweckungsbotschaft die Kreuzesbotschaft verdunkeln[15]. Das Kreuz ist weder nur »Durchgangsstation« zur Herrlichkeit, nur der Weg für den Preis, noch auch nur eine neben anderen herlaufende »Heilstatsache«. Vielmehr ist es die bleibende Signatur des Auferweckten. Was hätte dieser für ein Gesicht, wenn er nicht der Gekreuzigte wäre? Zu Recht wird der Erhöhte immer dargestellt mit den Nägelmalen des Irdischen: Ostern wird nur dort richtig gesehen, wo der Einsatz des Karfreitags nicht vergessen wird. Gerade dann nämlich wird der Gedanke des ewigen Lebens nicht dazu verführen, über das Kreuz der Gegenwart, das Leid des Einzelnen und die Probleme der Gesellschaft hinwegzutrösten: selig von einem Leben nach dem Tod zu träumen, statt das Leben *vor* dem Tod und die sozialen Verhältnisse hier und heute zu verändern.

2. Da sind aber auch die Gegner von rechts, jene von judaisti-schen Missionaren verwirrten konservativen frommen *Morali-sten* in der kleinasiatischen Landschaft *Galatien*[16]: die nicht wie die korinthischen Enthusiasten das Ende vorausnehmen, son-dern sich wieder der Vergangenheit zuwenden. Die Freiheit vom jüdischen Gesetz sehen sie als Fehlentwicklung an. Neben Chri-stusglaube und Taufe betrachten sie wieder das jüdische Ritual, Beschneidung, Sabbat, Kalender, andere jüdische Lebensord-nungen, gar die Naturelemente als wesentlich. Und meinen nun erneut aufgrund religiöser Bräuche, moralischer Leistungen, frommer Werke mit Gott ins reine kommen zu können. Die Verheißungen Gottes machen sie zu ihrem Privileg und Gottes Gebote zum Mittel ihrer Selbstheiligung.

Auch diese wieder in die alte kultische und moralische Gesetz-lichkeit zurückgeworfenen Gesetzesfrommen, für die Jesus gar nicht hätte kommen und sterben müssen, verweist Paulus an den *Gekreuzigten:*

der nicht die Frommen frömmer machen wollte, sondern sich den Verlorenen, Unfrommen, Gesetzesbrechern, Gottlosen zugewendet hat;

der, sich selber dem Gesetz unterziehend, es doch radikal relativiert und gegen einen Gott des Gesetzes den Gott der Liebe und des Erbarmens verkündet hat;

der deshalb den Hütern von Gesetz und Ordnung als Diener der Sünde und der Sünder erschien und im Namen des Geset-zes als Verbrecher gekreuzigt wurde;

der für die Gesetz- und Gottlosen den Fluch des Gesetzes auf sich genommen hat und gerade so, vom lebendigmachenden Gott gegen das Gesetz gerechtfertigt, die Menschen endgültig vom Fluch des Gesetzes zur Freiheit und wahren Menschlich-keit befreit hat.

Mit dem Blick auf diesen Gekreuzigten, so meint Paulus, darf es keine dem jüdischen Gesetz, Ritual, überhaupt religiösen Kon-ventionen unterworfene Menschen mehr geben. Sondern nur wahrhaft *freie Christenmenschen*, die sich und ihr ganzes Ge-schick *Gott anvertrauen,* »in Christus«, das heißt »christlich« sind. Der Weg des vertrauenden Glaubens also, der gangbar ist für Juden und Heiden, Herren und Sklaven, Gebildete und Ungebildete, Männer und Frauen, ja für Fromme und Gottlose. Weil nämlich gar keine besonderen Voraussetzungen, keine be-sondere Abstammung, religiöse Tüchtigkeit, einwandfreies Le-ben, vorweisbare Frömmigkeit, rituelle Akte, moralische Leistungen als Vorausleistungen gefordert sind! Sondern nur im Blick auf Jesus dieses einfache Sich-Gott-Anvertrauen – ungeachtet aller eigenen Schwächen und Verfehlungen, ungeachtet freilich auch der eigenen Vorzüge, Verdienste, Leistungen, Ansprüche.

Wer ohne alle frommen Träume illusionslos zugibt, daß er sich bei all seinen Leistungen im letztlich Entscheidenden nicht selber helfen kann, daß er Gott gegenüber auch mit dem (nie vollkommen erfüllbaren und deshalb immer wieder neu schuldigmachenden) rituellen und moralischen Gesetz nicht vorankommt, daß er mit allen moralischen Anstrengungen und Frömmigkeitsübungen sein Verhältnis zu Gott nicht in Ordnung bringen und mit keinerlei Leistungen Gottes Liebe verdienen kann;

wer sich statt dessen völlig auf diesen Christus verläßt und glaubt, daß Gott gerade den Verlorenen, Unfrommen, Gesetzesbrechern, Gottlosen helfen will und in seiner Freundlichkeit dieses Verhältnis von sich aus in Ordnung bringt;

wer also im dunklen Geheimnis des Kreuzes den Inbegriff der Gnade und Liebe jenes Gottes erkennt, der die Menschen nicht in Menschenart nach ihren Leistungen beurteilt, sondern sie von vornherein akzeptiert, sie bejaht und liebt:

der ist nicht mehr ein vom Gesetz und Ritual und so von Menschen beherrschter Knecht und Sklave, sondern wahrhaft Gottes Kind und so wahrhaft Mensch: Als erwachsener Sohn oder Tochter dieses Vaters wird er fähig, aus dem glaubenden Vertrauen heraus ohne Gesetzeszwang und Leistungsdruck in voller Freiheit Gott gehorsam und den Menschen verpflichtet zu sein. Nicht nur in egoistischer Selbstverschließung (= Sünde) für sich, sondern für die Anderen, die um ihn sind, zu leben, um so im tätigen Dasein, in der Liebe, das Gesetz, das auf das Wohl der Menschen zielt, faktisch im Übermaß zu erfüllen.

Dies alles ist genauer nachzulesen in den Briefen des Apostels Paulus nach Korinth und Galatien über die Weisheit und Freiheit eines Christenmenschen. Aber – wird einem bei der Lektüre nicht eine ganz beträchtliche Differenz zwischen Paulus und Jesus aufgehen?

Durch den Glauben allein

Man hat manchmal *Paulus* als den eigentlichen Begründer des Christentums hingestellt. Oder – wie Nietzsche im ›Antichrist‹ Gedanken der liberalen Theologie (F. Overbecks?) ausdenkend –

als sein großer Verfälscher! Nietzsche zeigt Sympathie für Jesus: »Im Grund gab es nur einen Christen, und der *starb* am Kreuz. Das ›Evangelium‹ starb am Kreuz[17].« Paulus aber wird in grandioser Verkennung beschimpft als »Dysangelist« und »Falschmünzer aus Haß«: »der Gegensatz-Typus zum ›frohen Botschafter‹, das Genie im Haß, in der Vision des Hasses, in der unerbittlichen Logik des Hasses[18].« Und selbst christliche Theologen waren oberflächlich und töricht genug, mit dem Ruf »Zurück zu Jesus!« eine »Abkehr vom paulinischen Christentum« zu fordern.

Die *welthistorische Bedeutung des Apostels Paulus* und seiner Theologie ist unbestritten: Er hat den Nichtjuden in überlegener Freiheit praktisch und theologisch Zugang zur christlichen Botschaft verschafft. Ohne daß sie nämlich zuvor Juden, beschnittene und auf die zahllosen für Heiden befremdenden jüdischen Reinheitstabus, Speise- und Sabbatvorschriften verpflichtete Juden werden mußten! Nur durch ihn war die christliche Heidenmission im Gegensatz zur jüdisch-hellenistischen ein Erfolg geworden. Nur durch ihn war aus der Gemeinde palästinischer und hellenistischer Juden eine Gemeinde aus Juden und Heiden geworden. Nur durch ihn hat sich aus der kleinen jüdischen »Sekte« schließlich eine »Weltreligion« entwickelt. Daß zwischen der Botschaft Jesu selbst und der – im Licht von Tod und Auferweckung Jesu vorgenommenen! – jüdisch-hellenistischen Interpretation des Geschehens um Jesus ein wesentlicher Unterschied besteht, bestehen muß, ist eine – freilich noch zu bedenkende – Selbstverständlichkeit.

Trotzdem: man muß entweder blind sein für das, was Jesus selbst in der ganzen Radikalität gewollt, gelebt, erlitten hat, oder aber unter den jüdisch-hellenistischen Vorstellungsformen nicht mehr erkennen, was Paulus – wie Jesus selbst im Horizont der Naherwartung des Endes – elementar angetrieben hat, wenn man es nicht zu sehen vermag: daß gerade die paulinischen Briefe – gegen alle hellenistischen oder jüdischen Ideologisierungen der Botschaft – *ständig* »*Zurück zu Jesus*« rufen. Nicht der Mensch (Anthropologie) oder die Kirche (Ekklesiologie), aber auch nicht die Heilsgeschichte im allgemeinen, sondern der *gekreuzigte und auferweckte Christus* (die Christologie verstanden als Soteriologie) steht in der *Mitte* seines Denkens. Zugunsten des Menschen also eine Christozentrik, die in einer Theozentrik gründet und gipfelt: »Gott durch Jesus Christus« – »durch Jesus Christus zu Gott«! Aus ähnlichen binitarischen Formeln erwachsen – unter

Einbeziehung des Heiligen Geistes, in welchem Gott und Jesus Christus in der Gemeinde wie im Einzelnen gegenwärtig und wirksam sind – schon bei Paulus trinitarische Formeln: Voraussetzung für die erst später entwickelte Lehre von der Trinität, der Dreieinigkeit aus Vater, Sohn und Geist.

Des Paulus ganze Sicht der *Heilsgeschichte* von der Schöpfung über die Verheißungen an Abraham und das Gesetz des Mose bis zur Kirche und zur baldigen Vollendung der Welt hat – die Abraham-Christus-Linie[19] und die Christus-Adam-Parallele[20] zeigen es ebenso wie das Verständnis der Kirche als Gemeinde aus Juden und Heiden und als Leib Christi[21] – ihre unverrückbare kritische *Mitte* im gekreuzigten und auferweckten Jesus. Man mag diese Mitte als »Christologie«, »Kerygma«, »Theologie des Kreuzes« oder »Rechtfertigungsbotschaft« bezeichnen[22]. Des Paulus Verarbeitung der christlichen Tradition wie seine Verwendung des Alten Testaments, alle seine epochemachenden theologischen Ausführungen über Gesetz und Glaube, Zorn und Gnade Gottes, Tod und Leben, Sünde und Gottesgerechtigkeit, Geist und Buchstabe, Israel und Heidenwelt, aber auch seine Aussagen über die Verkündigung, die Kirche, die Charismen des Geistes, Taufe und Abendmahl, das neue Leben in Freiheit und Hoffnung auf Vollendung: dies alles kann nur von dieser Mitte her richtig verstanden werden[23].

Daß Paulus dabei am *geschichtlichen Jesus* nicht interessiert gewesen sei – eine nach dem Ersten Weltkrieg von einzelnen liberalen Exegeten übernommene Auffassung der dialektischen Theologie (K. Barth) und der Kerygma-Theologie (R. Bultmann) – läßt sich, das zeigt die jüngste Diskussion, nicht halten: Nirgendwo findet sich bei Paulus eine bewußte Abwertung der Jesus-Überlieferung! Aber wenn Paulus von einem *»Christus nach dem Fleisch«* nichts wissen will[24]? Dann meint er nicht den irdischen Jesus im Unterschied zum erhöhten, auch nicht den gekreuzigten im Unterschied zum auferweckten, und erst recht nicht den durch die Mittel historischer Forschung erkannten »historischen« Jesus im Gegensatz zum geglaubten Christus. Sondern er meint den damals (in seiner Verfolgungszeit) auf natürlich-ungläubige, also »fleischliche« Weise erkannten (verkannten) Jesus: Christus im Gegensatz nämlich zu dem jetzt (nach der Bekehrung) von ihm auf pneumatisch-gläubige, also »geistige« Weise erkannten (= anerkannten) Jesus Christus. Also nicht ein anderer Jesus Christus, sondern ein grundlegend verändertes Verhältnis zu ihm[25].

In seinen Briefen – wie bemerkt, meist fragmentarische Gelegenheitsschreiben, die eine elementare katechetische Einführung in den christlichen Glauben voraussetzen! – rekurriert Paulus verhältnismäßig selten auf die evangelische Jesus-Überlieferung. Aber er steht zu ihr ohne allen Zweifel positiv. Aus den authentischen paulinischen Schriften lassen sich immerhin mindestens 20 Stellen anführen, wo Paulus sich eindeutig auf die evangelische Jesus-Überlieferung stützt[26]. Was darauf schließen läßt, daß er über dieses recht zufällig Erhaltene hinaus der Gemeinde noch sehr viel mehr zu sagen wußte von dem, was er in Jerusalem, Damaskus, Antiochien oder anderswo von der Botschaft, dem Verhalten und Geschick des irdischen, des geschichtlichen Jesus gehört hatte. Paulus dürfte etwa in Korinth während anderthalb Jahren Verkündigung und Katechese kaum nur ein abstraktes »Kerygma« vom Gekreuzigten und Auferweckten immer neu wiederholt und variiert haben. Auch das Alte Testament spielt in den paulinischen Briefen teilweise eine erstaunlich geringe Rolle (im 1. Thessalonicher-, im Philipper- und in weiten Partien des 1. und 2. Korintherbriefes faktisch keine) und war dem ehemals pharisäischen Theologen Paulus doch ständig präsent. Es tritt in den Briefen eben nur dort ausdrücklich in den Vordergrund, wo dies wie etwa im Galater- oder Römerbrief die Auseinandersetzung mit Juden oder judaistischen Christen erzwingt. Wenngleich nun bei Paulus bezüglich des geschichtlichen Jesus das Wirken Gottes und deshalb Kreuz und Auferweckung im Vordergrund stehen, so hat er zweifellos auch Jesus-Traditionen gekannt und bei seinen Zuhörern vorausgesetzt, die in seinen Briefen nicht zur Sprache gebracht wurden, die freilich in ihrem tatsächlichen Umfang schwierig abzuschätzen sind. Doch geben die Quellen indirekt einige nicht unwichtige Auskünfte.

Selbstverständlich wußte der frühere *Verfolger der Christengemeinde* zu erklären, warum Jesus zum Tod am Kreuz verurteilt wurde und warum er selber meinte, die christliche Gemeinde verfolgen zu müssen: Nach eigener Aussage tut er es als ein »Pharisäer nach dem Gesetz[27]«, ein »Eiferer für die Überlieferungen meiner Väter[28]«. In Konfrontation vermutlich mit den judenchristlichen Hellenisten der Jerusalemer Gemeinde war der hellenistische Diaspora-Jude Paulus aus Tarsus auf die von Jesus her kommende Gesetzeskritik gestoßen. Er fühlte sich durch die Infragestellung des Gesetzes (der ›Tora‹ und der ›Halacha‹)[29] in seinem echt pharisäischen Eifer für Gott und sein Gesetz derart herausgefordert, daß er sich zur aktiven Bekämpfung der Gemeinde »über die Maßen«, ja zu ihrer »Vernichtung« entschloß[30]. Das Skandalon, welches mit der Behauptung eines unter dem Fluch des Gesetzes gekreuzigten Messias für jeden Juden gegeben war, konnte ihn in seinem maßlosen Verfolgungseifer nur noch bestärkt haben[31].

Dies alles erklärt jedenfalls sehr gut, wie aus dem gesetzestreuen pharisäischen Musterfrommen ein Verfolger der Christengemeinde und ihres Glaubens wurde. Wie jedoch wurde aus dem fanatischen Christenverfolger ein *Apostel des Gekreuzigten?* Das hat bisher niemand weder historisch noch psychologisch erklären können. Paulus selber führt seine radikale Wende nicht auf eine menschliche Belehrung, ein neues Selbstverständnis, eine heroische Anstrengung oder eine selbstvollzogene Bekehrung zurück. Vielmehr auf eine – von ihm nicht beschriebene und wie immer zu erklärende[32] – »Offenbarung« (ein »Sehen«) des auferweckten Gekreuzigten, die eine radikale Bekehrung zur Folge hatte[33]. Auch hier eine Berufung! Aber nur wenn seine Stellung oder sein Evangelium angefochten sind, spricht Paulus in kargsten Worten von diesem Geschehen, auf dem sein Apostolat und seine apostolische Freiheit gründen[34]. Der Mensch und nicht das Gesetz ist die Sache Gottes, auf die es Gott letztlich ankommt. Paulus versteht jetzt den Kreuzestod als eine Auswirkung des Gesetzes. Aber auch zugleich – aufgrund der Rechtfertigung Jesu gegen das Gesetz durch Gott selbst – als eine Befreiung vom Fluch des Gesetzes[35]. Käme das gute Verhältnis zwischen Gott und Mensch (= die »Gerechtigkeit«) durch das Gesetz, so wäre Jesus umsonst gestorben[36].

Was für Paulus zeitlebens *»Gnade«* als die völlig unverdiente Freundlichkeit Gottes bedeutet, gründet in dieser lebendigen Erfahrung des Gekreuzigten, der sich ihm als der Lebendige, der eigentliche Herr offenbarte. Kompromißlos – außer in Rücksicht auf das Gewissen beunruhigter Brüder[37] – verteidigt Paulus von nun an die grundlegende Bedeutung des Christusglaubens aus reiner Gnade gegen alle Tendenzen, die ein »und« behaupten: Heil durch Christus im Glauben *und* durch Werke des jüdischen (oder auch eines anderen) Gesetzes? In seinem längsten, dichtesten und umfassendsten Brief, den er an die ihm persönlich noch unbekannte Christengemeinde von *Rom*[38] schrieb, legt er dieses sein Evangelium dar. Vor dem ganzen Horizont der Heilsgeschichte zwischen Schöpfung und Vollendung führt er es, ausgehend von der allgemeinen Sündhaftigkeit der Menschen, Juden wie Heiden[39], aus: wie das definitive Wohl, das Heil des Menschen nur aufgrund des Glaubens an Jesus Christus erlangt werden kann[40], um von diesem Grunde her eindrücklich das neue Leben aus dem Geist in Freiheit und Hoffnung[41] sowie Gottes großen Heilsplan für Juden und Heiden[42] und die wichtigsten Konsequenzen für ein christliches Leben[43] zu skizzieren. Wie schon im Galaterbrief – wenn auch jetzt bezüglich des an sich guten, aber nicht zum Heil führenden Gesetzes Gottes ausgeglichener und weniger polemisch – lehnt Paulus alle zusätzlichen Bedingungen, um das Verhältnis des Menschen zu Gott in Ordnung zu bringen, mit Berufung auf den Gekreuzigten und Gottes Gnade ab. Das Heil des Menschen hängt nicht an irgendeiner Art von vorgeschriebenen Gesetzeswerken, von frommen oder moralischen Leistungen! Es hängt ausschließlich am vertrauenden Glauben an Jesus Christus. Wie Paulus das in der juridisch gefärbten jüdischen Sprache seiner Zeit ausdrückt: vor Gott (und seinem Gericht) wird der schuldige, sündige Mensch »freigesprochen«, »gerechtgesprochen«, *»gerechtfertigt«* nicht aufgrund von an sich guten Gesetzeswerken, sondern durch Gottes Gnade und Freundlichkeit allein *aufgrund des Glaubens*[44]. Oder wie man die klassische Stelle aus dem Römerbrief in moderner Sprache umschreiben kann: »Wir sind nämlich der Überzeugung, daß der Mensch zu Gott in die richtige, gute Beziehung kommen kann, ohne daß er religiösen Forderungen genügt, einfach dadurch, daß er sich ihm anvertraut und so empfängt, was Gott ihm schenken will[45].«

Keine andere Sache

So war denn der Konflikt mit dem Gesetz und dessen Gottesverständnis, der Jesus den Tod gebracht hat, auch des Paulus Konflikt und tödliche Bedrohung geworden. Seine Lehre vom Gesetz – hier zeigt sich eine grundlegende Kontinuität – stellt sich als die Fortführung der Verkündigung Jesu dar. Freilich eine vom Tod Jesu her *radikalisierte Fortführung:* insofern gibt es zwischen Jesus und Paulus keine einfache Kontinuität, sondern nur eine Kontinuität in Diskontinuität. Zwischen der Verkündigung des geschichtlichen Jesus und der Verkündigung des Paulus steht Jesu Tod: der durch Infragestellung des Gesetzes heraufgeführte, durch die Auferweckung aber in seinem Sinn geoffenbarte Tod, in welchem Paulus Gottes Handeln in Jesus erkennt. Deshalb sieht Paulus im Kreuzestod all das konzentriert, was der geschichtliche Jesus gebracht, gelebt und bis zu seinem Ende durchgehalten hat. Der Gekreuzigte ist mit dem geschichtlichen, irdischen Jesus selbstverständlich identisch und insofern ist dieser unabdingbare Voraussetzung und mitgegebener Inhalt auch des Glaubens des Paulus: er verhindert, daß der Glaube an den Gekreuzigten und Auferweckten zur Illusion oder zum geschichtslosen Mythos verblaßt. Vom Kreuz her hat Paulus Wirklichkeit und Sinn der irdischen Existenz Jesu erfaßt und ständig festgehalten.

Mit dem einen »Wort vom Kreuz« war für Paulus im Grund alles gesagt, was von Jesu Verkündigung, Verhalten und Geschick zu sagen war. Vom Kreuz des für den Glauben Lebendigen her konnte der *Theologe* Paulus nun das theologisch explizieren, was Jesus schlicht faktisch getan und oft nur implizit gesagt hatte. Nicht daß Paulus einen umfassenden theoretischen Entwurf vorlegte. Auch im Römerbrief kommt seine Theologie – gründend auf dem Gekreuzigten und Auferweckten und im Grunde nur sehr wenigen Leitideen – für die ganze konkrete Situation dieser Gemeinde zur Sprache. Aber im jeweiligen Kontext hat Paulus das, was sich in Jesu Verkündigung untheologisch und unentfaltet findet, in Konsequenz von Tod und Auferweckung ausdrücklich theologisch durchgedacht und entfaltet. Seine rabbinische Schulung und besonders Exegese nutzte er dafür ebenso wie manche Begriffe und Vorstellungen seiner hellenistischen Umwelt. Deshalb muß für den, der von der evangelischen Jesus-Überlieferung herkommt, die Botschaft Jesu bei Paulus zunächst in einem sehr verschiedenen Licht erscheinen: umgeschmolzen in ganz andere Perspektiven, Kategorien und Vorstellungen. Trotzdem ist bei näherem Zusehen nicht zu übersehen, daß von der Verkündigung Jesu sehr viel mehr zu finden ist, als einzelne Worte oder Sätze ausweisen, und daß ihre »Substanz« in die Verkündigung Pauli durchaus eingegangen ist:

– *Wie Jesus so lebt auch Paulus ganz intensiv in* Erwartung des kommenden Reiches Gottes. *Aber Jesus blickt in die Zukunft, Paulus jedoch blickt zugleich zurück auf die in Tod und Auferweckung erfolgte entscheidende Wende. Er sieht die Zwischenzeit zwischen Auferweckung und noch ausstehender Vollendung (und Auferweckung aller) unter der gegenwärtigen Herrschaft des erhöhten Christus.*
– *Wie Jesus so geht auch Paulus aus von der faktischen* Sündhaftigkeit *des Menschen, auch des gerechten, frommen, gesetzes-*

treuen Menschen. Aber Paulus entfaltet diese Einsicht theologisch: durch Verwertung alttestamentlichen Materials und vor allem durch die Adam-Christus-Entgegensetzung.

– Wie Jesus stellt auch Paulus mit seiner Botschaft den Menschen in die Krise, ruft zum Glauben, fordert Umkehr. Aber bei Paulus erscheint die Botschaft vom Gottesreich konzentriert im Wort vom Kreuz, welches ärgerniserregend die jüdische und griechische Weise der Selbstbehauptung in die Krise führt: Ende des Gesetzesgehorsams und Ende der Menschenweisheit!

– Wie Jesus sieht sich auch Paulus, ohne an einer Dämonenlehre oder Exorzistenpraxis interessiert zu sein, im Kampf mit dämonischen Unheilsmächten, deren Herrschaft dem Ende entgegengeht. Aber für Paulus sind diese Mächte wenn auch noch wirksam, so doch durch Jesu Tod und neues Leben grundsätzlich entmachtet worden.

– Wie Jesus so nimmt auch Paulus für sein Wirken Gott in Anspruch. Aber Paulus tut dies von Kreuz und Auferweckung Jesu her, wo für ihn Gottes Wirken zum definitiven Durchbruch gekommen ist: aus Jesu impliziter faktischer Christologie ist nach Tod und Auferweckung die explizite ausdrückliche Christologie der Gemeinde geworden.

– Wie Jesus hat auch Paulus das Gesetz mit all den Reinheitstabus, Speise- und Sabbatvorschriften um des Menschen willen radikal relativiert: der Glaube Israels erscheint auf seine zentralen und wesentlichen Momente konzentriert und das Gesetz auf wenige, gültige und einsichtige Grundforderungen reduziert. Aber für Paulus bedeutet Jesu Tod unter dem Gesetz das Ende des Gesetzes als Heilsweg und der Anfang des neuen Heilswegs aus dem Glauben an Jesus Christus.

– Wie Jesus so vertritt auch Paulus die Vergebung der Sünden aus reiner Gnade: die Rechtfertigung des Sünders. Aber des Paulus Botschaft von der Rechtfertigung des Sünders, des Gottlosen (Juden oder Heiden) setzt Jesu Kreuzestod voraus, der als Tod für die Sünder, die Gottlosen verstanden wird.

– Wie Jesus so hat auch Paulus ganz praktisch über die Grenzen des Gesetzes hinweg sich den Armen, Verlorenen, Bedrängten, Außenstehenden, Gesetzlosen, Gesetzesbrechern zugewendet und in Wort und Tat einen Universalismus vertreten. Aber aus Jesu grundsätzlichem Universalismus bezüglich Israel und seinem faktischen, virtuellen Universalismus bezüglich der Heidenwelt ist nun bei Paulus – im Licht des Gekreuzigten und Auferweckten – ein grundsätzlicher, formeller Universalismus

bezüglich Israel und *der Heidenwelt geworden, der die Mis-*
sion der Heiden verlangt.

– *Wie Jesus so hat auch Paulus die* Liebe Gottes und des Nächsten *als die faktische Erfüllung des Gesetzes verkündet und sie*
in unbedingtem Gehorsam gegenüber Gott und in selbstlosem
Dasein für die Mitmenschen und auch die Feinde in letzter
Radikalität gelebt. Aber Paulus erkannte gerade im Tode Jesu
die tiefste Offenbarung dieser Liebe von seiten Gottes und Jesu
selbst, welche Grund ist für der Menschen eigene Liebe zu Gott
und zum Nächsten.

So kann man denn sagen, daß diese für Paulus typische und
zentrale »Rechtfertigungsbotschaft« schon in den Parabeln Jesu
und in der Bergpredigt präsent ist, daß sie aber durch Jesu Tod
und Auferweckung in ein entscheidend anderes Licht gerückt
wird. Mit Recht bezeichnet man deshalb die paulinische Rechtfertigungsbotschaft als »angewandte Christologie«. Als solche
ist sie dann freilich auch kritische Norm für die richtige Anwendung der Christologie gegenüber allen ihren Verharmlosungen
und Entleerungen, aber auch Idealisierungen und Verklärungen.

Wann immer in der Kirchengeschichte die zentrale Bedeutung
des gekreuzigten und lebendigen Jesus als des Maßgebenden für
das Verhältnis von Mensch und Gott, Mensch und Mensch ver-
dunkelt wurde, dann ist das »gerechtfertigt allein durch den
Glauben« an Jesus Christus plötzlich neu akut geworden und hat
die Geister geschieden. Immer dann hat zusammen mit dem
Galaterbrief des Paulus Römerbrief eine geradezu explosive
Kraft entwickelt: So war es zur Zeit Augustins gegenüber dem
Pelagianismus. So erst recht zur Zeit der Reformatoren gegenüber der mittelalterlichen Werkheiligkeit und dem römischen
Amtsmißbrauch. So aber auch wieder zur Zeit Karl Barths nach
dem Ersten Weltkrieg gegenüber einem idealistisch-humani-
stisch gewordenen Kulturprotestantismus und gegenüber der
nationalsozialistischen Ideologie. Und heute, in der Zeit einer
säkularisierten Werkfrömmigkeit nach dem Leistungsprinzip?
Das »allein durch den Glauben« – ein Echo auf »allein durch
Christus« und »allein durch Gnade« – wollte gute Taten nie
ausschließen. Aber Grundlage der christlichen Existenz und Kriterium für das Bestehen vor Gott kann nicht die Berufung auf
irgendwelche gute Taten sein. Sondern nur das unbedingte Festhalten an Gott durch Jesus den Christus in einem glaubenden
Vertrauen, gegen welches weder des Menschen Versagen noch

irgendwelche guten Werke aufkommen, aus dem aber Werke der Liebe selbstverständlich folgen. Eine ungemein tröstliche Botschaft, die dem Menschenleben durch alles unvermeidbare Versagen, Irren und Verzweifeln hindurch eine solide Basis gibt. Und die es zugleich vom frommen Leistungsdruck befreit zu einer Freiheit, Weisheit, Liebe und Hoffnung, die durch schlimme und schlimmste Situationen hindurchzutragen vermag.

Eine Botschaft, über die man sich heute zwischen katholischer und evangelischer Theologie nicht mehr zu streiten braucht[46]. Nachdem das »sola fide« so lange umstritten war, geben neuere Bibelübersetzungen, wie etwa die neue ökumenische in deutscher Sprache, dem gemeinsamen Verständnis insbesondere des zentralen Textes im Römerbrief deutlich Ausdruck: »Denn wir sind der Überzeugung, daß der Mensch nur (!) durch Glauben gerecht wird, unabhängig (!) von Werken des Gesetzes[47].« Auf bestimmte Worte und Begriffe kommt es in der »Rechtfertigungslehre« freilich gerade nicht an. Paulus selber hat sie, wie wir sahen, für die Korinther ganz anders – unter den so gar nicht juristischen Stichworten »Weisheit« und »Torheit« Gottes und der Menschen – zum Ausdruck gebracht. Auf die Sache kommt es an, die jede Zeit wieder mit ihren eigenen Worten formulieren muß.

So hat Paulus – nicht ein Mann des Hasses, sondern der Liebe, ein echter »froher Botschafter« – kein neues Christentum begründet. Er hat kein neues Fundament gelegt. Er hat auf dem gebaut, welches nach seinen eigenen Worten gelegt *ist*[48]: Jesus Christus, der Ursprung, Grundlage, Inhalt und Norm der paulinischen Verkündigung, seines Kerygmas ist. Im Lichte einer grundsätzlich anderen Situation nach Jesu Tod und Auferweckung hat er doch keine andere, sondern die gleiche Sache vertreten: die *Sache Jesu*, die nichts anderes ist als die *Sache Gottes* und *Sache des Menschen* – jetzt aber nach Tod und Auferweckung verstanden als die *Sache Jesu Christi*[49]! In disziplinierter Leidenschaft, kraftvoll, selbständig und originell, in verschiedener Sprache, verschiedenen Kategorien und verschiedenen Vorstellungen hat er als bevollmächtigter Botschafter, als »Apostel« Jesu Christi, wie er sich bescheiden und stolz zugleich nannte, im Entscheidenden nichts anderes getan, als jene Linien konsequent ausgezogen, die in Verkündigung, Verhalten und Geschick Jesu vorgezeichnet waren. Er hat damit die Botschaft über Israel hinaus für die gesamte Oikumene, die damalige Welt, verständlich gemacht. Und er hat der Christenheit durch alle die Jahrhunderte hindurch wie kein zweiter nach Jesus immer wieder neue Impulse gegeben: um im Christentum – was nicht selbstverständlich ist – den wahren Christus wiederzufinden und ihm nachzufolgen.

Deutlicher als irgendeinem anderen ist es Paulus aufgrund nicht nur theologischer Reflexion, sondern konkretester, oft grausamster Erfahrung[50] in der Nachfolge Jesu, die ihn schließlich ebenfalls zum gewaltsamen Tod (unter Nero wohl 66) führte, gelungen, das zum Ausdruck zu bringen, was *das letztlich Unterscheidende* des Christentums ist. Für unsere Darstellung aber schließt sich hier der Kreis:

– *Das Unterscheidende des Christentums gegenüber den alten Weltreligionen und modernen Humanismen, so haben wir schon bei unserer ersten umrißhaften Unterscheidung festgestellt[51], ist dieser* Christus selbst. *Was aber bewahrt uns vor allen Verwechslungen dieses Christus mit anderen religiösen oder politischen Christusfiguren?*

– *Das Unterscheidende des Christentums gegenüber den alten Weltreligionen und modernen Humanismen – so haben wir dann präzisiert[52] – ist der Christus, der mit dem wirklichen, geschichtlichen Jesus von Nazaret identisch ist, ist also konkret dieser Christus* Jesus. *Was aber bewahrt uns vor allen Verwechslungen dieses geschichtlichen Jesus Christus mit falschen Jesus-Bildern?*

– *Das Unterscheidende des Christentums gegenüber den alten Weltreligionen und modernen Humanismen – wir können jetzt nach eingehender Beschäftigung mit Verkündigung, Verhalten und Geschick Jesu am Ende dieses Kapitels die Antwort geben –, das letztlich Unterscheidende des Christentums ist ganz wörtlich nach Paulus »Jesus Christus und dieser als der Gekreuzigte«[53].*

Nicht als der Auferweckte, Erhöhte, Lebendige, Göttliche, sondern als der Gekreuzigte unterscheidet sich dieser Jesus Christus unverwechselbar von den vielen auferstandenen, erhöhten, lebendigen Göttern und vergotteten Religionsstiftern, Cäsaren, Genies und Heroen der Weltgeschichte. Das Kreuz ist somit nicht nur das Beispiel und Modell, sondern Grund, Kraft und Norm des christlichen Glaubens: das große Distinktivum, das diesen Glauben und seinen Herrn auf dem Weltmarkt der religiösen und irreligiösen Weltanschauungen von anderen konkurrierenden Religionen, Ideologien und Utopien und ihren Herren radikal unterscheidet und ihn zugleich in der Wirklichkeit des konkreten Lebens mit seinen Konflikten verwurzelt. Das Kreuz trennt den christlichen Glauben vom Unglauben und vom Aberglauben. Das Kreuz gewiß im Licht der Auferweckung, aber zugleich die Auferweckung im Schatten des Kreuzes:

- *Ohne den Glauben an das Kreuz fehlt dem Glauben an den Auferweckten die Unterschiedenheit und Entschiedenheit.*
- *Ohne den Glauben an die Auferweckung fehlt dem Glauben an den Gekreuzigten die Bestätigung und Ermächtigung.*

Johannes meint dasselbe unterscheidend Christliche wie Paulus, wenn er in freilich sehr verschiedener Begrifflichkeit Jesus den Weg, die Wahrheit und das Leben[54] nennt und das mit folgenden Bildern veranschaulicht: Er ist das Brot des Lebens[55], das Licht der Welt[56], die Tür[57], der wahre Weinstock[58], der wahre Hirt, der sein Leben hingibt für die Schafe[59]. Jesus ist hier offensichtlich nicht ein Name, der ständig im Munde zu führen ist, sondern der Weg der Wahrheit des Lebens, die zu tun ist. Die Wahrheit des Christentums soll nicht »geschaut«, »theoretisiert«, sondern »getan«, »praktiziert« werden. Der christliche Wahrheitsbegriff ist nicht wie der griechische kontemplativ-theoretisch, sondern operativ-praktisch. Eine Wahrheit, die nicht nur gesucht und gefunden, sondern die befolgt und in Wahrhaftigkeit wahr gemacht, bewahrheitet und bewährt werden will. Eine Wahrheit, die auf Praxis zielt, die auf den Weg ruft, die ein neues Leben schenkt und ermöglicht.

VI. Deutungen

Im gekreuzigten und doch lebendigen Christus sind die christliche Botschaft und der christliche Glaube konkret zusammengefaßt. Er selber ist die ganz konkrete Wahrheit des Christentums. Und es war die lebendige Konkretheit seiner geschichtlichen Gestalt und seines Schicksals, die dem frühen Christentum seine Überlegenheit gab über die damaligen philosophischen Heilslehren, gnostischen Visionen, über die Mysterienkulte und ihre im Vergleich abstrakten und schicksalslosen Gestalten. »Das Bild Jesu als des Christus besiegte sie durch die Macht einer konkreten Wirklichkeit«[1]. Und die individuelle geschichtliche Konkretheit seiner Gestalt ist bis heute die Stärke des christlichen Glaubens gegenüber allgemeinen religiösen Weltanschauungen, abstrakten philosophischen Systemen und gesellschaftspolitischen Ideologien – die sich denn auch ihrerseits gerne an einen konkreten Heros in der Gestalt eines Gründers oder Führers (des Volkes, der Partei), eines Schulhauptes, Meisters, Mystagogen oder Guru gehängt haben.

Doch werden hier manche weiterfragen: Wie verhalten sich denn zu dieser einen konkreten Wahrheit des Christentums, die Jesus Christus selber ist, die verschiedenen christlichen »Wahrheiten«, Glaubenssätze, Dogmen, die anders als die konkrete Figur Jesu so schwer verstehbar und assimilierbar sind? Diese »Wahrheiten« sind zu verstehen als Deutungsversuche der einen Wahrheit.

1. Differenzierte Interpretation

Wer sich die immensen historischen wie systematischen Schwierigkeiten etwa der Geschichten vom leeren Grab, von Höllen- und Himmelfahrt, Weltgericht und Wiederkunft, aber auch, wie wir noch sehen werden, der Kindheitsgeschichten vor Augen hält, kann sehr wohl auf den Gedanken kommen: Ist hier aus der Botschaft vom wirklichen Jesus von Nazaret nicht ein Erzählen von »Göttergeschichten«, also »Mythologie« geworden? Wäre also eine radikale Entmythologisierung, eine Eliminierung alles

Mythischen und Legendären von der Wurzel her, nicht der einfachste und beste Weg, um die Evangelien für den modernen Menschen verständlich zu machen? Müßten die Evangelien nicht von all dem purifiziert und vernünftig paraphrasiert werden?

Grenzen der Entmythologisierung

Purifiziert und paraphrasiert wären die Evangelien freilich nicht mehr, was sie sind: so wenig wie Dantes Divina Commedia, das französische Rolandslied, Miltons Paradise Lost oder Goethes Faust. Nicht nur weil in den Evangelien am Anfang und Ende (Kindheits- wie Oster- und Gerichtsgeschichten) vieles ausscheiden müßte. Sondern weil auch zwischen Anfang und Ende – man denke an die Wunder- und Epiphaniegeschichten – Botschaft und Mythisch-Legendäres miteinander verwoben sind. Was wären schon die alttestamentlichen Erzählungen von der Erschaffung der Welt und des Menschen, was wären aber auch die Evangelien, wenn sie auf die »wesentlichen« Aussagen reduziert würden? Könnte man sich vorstellen, daß ein solcher Extrakt im Gottesdienst vorgelesen würde? Daß solche »Thesen zum Wesen« mehr gelesen würden als etwa die vom Mythos zum Logos fortschreitenden Sätze der Vorsokratiker?

Die Evangelien sind nun einmal in einer Zeit mythologisch denkender Menschen für mythologisch denkende Menschen geschrieben worden, auch wenn der Prozeß der Entmythologisierung und Vergeschichtlichung im Neuen Testament noch weiter fortgeschritten ist als im Alten: in Konsequenz des Ein-Gott-Glaubens gegenüber dem heidnischen Viel-Götter-Glauben. Auf den unabsehbaren Einfluß der Mythen – es seien die des alten Orients oder die der Bibel, die Indiens oder die Homers, die des alten Rom, des Mittelalters oder auch die Ersatzmythen der Neuzeit –, auf die Entwicklung der Menschheit und der einzelnen Völker können wir hier nicht eingehen. Religionswissenschaft, Anthropologie, Psychologie und Soziologie haben ihre sinnstiftende und sozialintegrierende Kraft vielfältig herausgestellt: nicht nur für religiöse Weltdeutung und Kult, sondern überhaupt für Individuation und Sozialisation des Menschen.

Sicher war damals, als die Evangelien redigiert wurden, eine bildhaft erzählende Verkündigung, die Mythen, Legenden und Symbole benützte, einfach notwendig. Wie sollen Menschen neue Erfahrungen und gerade neue Glaubenserfahrungen mitteilen, wenn nicht durch Erzählen? Daß die biblischen Weihnachts- und Ostergeschichten eingängiger und einprägsamer sind als noch so viele abstrakte Sätze über Gottessohnschaft und Durchgang durch den Tod zum Leben, leuchtet ein. Ob nicht auch heute im Zeitalter rational-kausalen und funktional-technischen Denkens eine bildhaft erzählende Verkündigung einfach notwendig ist und dafür gewisse alte im weitesten Sinn mythologische Formen nicht noch immer brauchbar sein können? Erkenntnisse der Religionswissenschaft[2] wären hier ebenso zu bedenken wie solche der Völkerpsychologie[3]. Selbst in Freuds sich so rational gebender Psychoanalyse spielt die griechische Mythologie zur Deutung der wissenschaftlichen Analysen eine nicht geringe Rolle, und C. G. Jung hat im Hinblick auf die psychische Selbstwerdung sogar eine ausgedehnte Mythenforschung betrieben. Wie immer man über Freuds Gebrauch der Mythologie etwa im Zusammenhang mit dem Ödipuskomplex oder über Jungs Theorie vom kollektiven Unbewußten, die Archetypen als Ausdruck überindividueller Lebenswahrheiten und seine psychologische Umfunktionierung von Mythen und christlichen Symbolen (selbst der marianischen Anrufungen der lauretanischen Litanei) denkt: kann man bestreiten, daß auch der moderne Mensch (und seine Massenmedien!) nicht nur von Argumenten, sondern auch von *Geschichten,* nicht nur von Begriffen, sondern auch von *Bildern,* oft uralten Bildern lebt, und daß immer wieder die Notwendigkeit gültiger Bilder und nachzuerzählender Geschichten besteht? Die Utopie des Reiches Gottes etwa hat, auch in säkularisierter Form bis zum Nazismus und – ganz anders ernsthaft – im Marxismus, eine gewaltige Strahlkraft ausgeübt. Und der messianische Erlöser in der Gestalt des Kindes, das einsam und ausgesetzt doch über seine Feinde triumphiert, hat nachweislich nicht nur Franz von Assisi und der mittelalterlichen Armutsbewegung, sondern auch modernen emanzipatorischen Bewegungen Impulse gegeben. Bilder aus der biblischen Protologie und Eschatologie haben noch heute ihre Faszination.

Aber soll nun die *Entmythologisierung,* die in diesem Buch konsequent zu geschehen hatte, etwa nachträglich rückgängig gemacht werden? Nein, sondern es sollen mit der *Notwendigkeit* nur zugleich auch die *Grenzen* der Entmythologisierung gesehen werden. Was verschiedentlich angedeutet wurde, muß hier thematisiert werden. Die christliche Botschaft ist kein Mythos, und wir leben nicht in einer mythologisch-archaischen, sondern in einer von Wissenschaft und Technik geprägten modernen Welt, nicht der Vergangenheit, sondern der Zukunft zugewendet. Es geht auf keinen Fall an, biblische Geschehnisse und Vorstellungen, die als Mythos, Sage, Legende, Symbol, Bild erwiesen worden sind, nachher in Theologie, Predigt oder Katechese wieder als historische Tatsachen auszugeben und gar noch den Glaubenden als für alle Zeiten verbindliche Glaubenswahrheiten aufzudrängen. Insofern darf die historische Kritik nicht im Turm der theologischen Wissenschaft eingeschlossen bleiben, sondern muß in die kirchliche Verkündigung und Praxis ausstrahlen und sie kritisch erhellen. Ein Dreifaches ist bezüglich *Mythen, Legenden, Bildern und Symbolen* zu beachten:

a. Mythen, Legenden, Bilder und Symbole *dürfen nicht wörtlich genommen werden:* Es war lange Zeit ein Charakteristikum *katholischer* Theologie, Kirche und Verkündigung, der Entmythologisierung geschickt oder weniger geschickt auszuweichen und, besonders im südländischen Katholizismus, den Mythos gar in allen möglichen biblischen und nachbiblischen Formen und Gestalten zu kultivieren, so daß Ignoranz und Obskurantismus im Volk und eine weitgehende Entchristlichung und Glaubenslosigkeit unter den Gebildeten die Folge war. Wird also *das Mythische einfach konserviert,* geht das auf Kosten der christlichen Botschaft, die dann mit dem Mythos verwechselt wird und den *Glauben zum Aberglauben degenerieren läßt.* Eine Entmythologisierung, so ist hier zu wiederholen, ist unumgänglich.

b. Aber umgekehrt dürfen Mythen, Legenden, Bilder und Symbole auch *nicht kritisiert werden, nur weil sie Mythen, Legenden, Bilder und Symbole sind:* War es nicht eine Gefahr der *protestantischen* Theologie, Kirche und Verkündigung, daß sie, besonders im deutschen Raum, die Entmythologisierung öfters zu unbesonnen, kurzschlüssig und willkürlich betrieben hat? Weithin wurde Bildhaftes, Mythisches, Symbolisches und Sakramentales aus der Kirche einfach ausgeschlossen. Als ob die Menschen nur Ohren und nicht auch Augen hätten. Als ob neben Intellekt und kritisch-rationalem Diskurs nicht auch Phantasie, Einbildungskraft, Emotionen, überhaupt Spontaneität, Kreativität, Innovation angesprochen werden müßten. Als ob der christliche Glaube nur eine halbe, eben nur eine Verstandessache sei, und nicht der ganze Mensch ergriffen werden müßte. Als ob das Ergriffenwerden durch das Begreifen, die Bilder durch die Begriffe, die Geschichte durch abstrakte Ideen, das Erzählen durch Proklamieren und Appellieren je ersetzt werden könnten! Eindringlich hat schon Paul Tillich den Protestantismus darauf hingewiesen, daß sein intellektualistisches Evangelium mit der Zeit nur noch die Intellektuellen anzusprechen vermag[4]. Eine – in bestimmten Gegenden bereits weit fortgeschrittene – Entvölkerung der Kirche war die Folge, verbunden oft mit einer Anfälligkeit für neue Mythologisierungen. Auch wenn also *das Mythische einfach eliminiert* wird, geht das – wie sich schon in der Theologie der Aufklärung und des Liberalismus zeigte – auf Kosten der christlichen Botschaft, die dann mit dem Mythos ausgeschüttet wird, so daß der *Glaube zur Vernunftgläubigkeit austrocknet.*

c. Echte *kritische Interpretation* verläuft zwischen Traditionalismus und Rationalismus: Sie distanziert sich von *allen* Formen des Aberglaubens, zu denen auch die Vernunftgläubigkeit gehört. Kritische Theologie heute sieht die Notwendigkeit *und* die Grenzen der Entmythologisierung: sie will – wie dies in Theorie auch Bultmann sagt – das Mythische weder konservieren noch eliminieren. Sie will, wie hier verschiedentlich betont, *das Mythische differenziert interpretieren.* Will man dabei Engführungen und ungebührliche Reduktionen der Botschaft vermeiden, darf man sich freilich keinem einseitigen Vorverständnis verschreiben: weder der Existenzphilosophie des (frühen) Heidegger noch der Kritischen Gesellschaftstheorie der Neuen Linken. Ohne dogmatische (existentialistische, sozialistische oder andere) Voreingenommenheit, ohne allen »Jargon der Eigentlichkeit« (Adorno) oder »Jargon der Uneigentlichkeit«, vielmehr von einem möglichst umfassenden Wirklichkeitsverständnis her ist die Botschaft zur Sprache zu bringen.

In einer solchen differenzierten Interpretation können dann die Mythen zweifellos nicht mehr wörtlich genommen, aber auch nicht einfach ausgeschlossen werden. Vielmehr gilt dann der Grundsatz, daß *Mythisches als Mythisches,* Legenden als Legenden, Bilder und Symbole als Bilder und Symbole *zu verstehen* sind[5]. Das heißt nicht, daß alles Mythologisch-Legendäre den heutigen Menschen noch ebenso ansprechen muß wie damals. Auch Mythen und Legenden, Bilder und Symbole können sterben und unter Umständen – freilich keineswegs beliebig – ersetzt werden: wenn sie in einer neuen Zeit nicht mehr die Macht haben, das auszudrücken, was sie ausdrücken sollen. Schon für die Menschen des Neuen Testaments spricht nicht mehr alles im Alten Testament so, wie es zu früheren Generationen in Israel gesprochen hat. Ein Bild oder Symbol für eine Sache aufgeben, heißt aber noch längst nicht, die Sache aufgeben. Sollte zum Beispiel einer die Jungfrauengeburt, worüber noch zu sprechen sein wird, als Legende für die Gottessohnschaft ansehen, so gibt er mit der Wirklichkeit der Jungfrauengeburt noch nicht notwendig die Wirklichkeit der Gottessohnschaft auf.

Wahrheit nicht gleich Faktizität

Was oft übersehen wird: nicht nur unsere Bilder, auch unsere höchst reflektierten Begriffe vermögen die letzte Wirklichkeit, die wir Gott nennen, nie direkt zu erfassen. Sie bleiben letztlich immer symbolische, ana-loge, nur hinauf-sagende, ähnlich-unähnliche Begriffe, von denen wir nur hoffen können, daß sie nicht zu eng sind, um das un-greifbare, un-begreifbare Allumfassende zu bezeichnen und einen lebendigen Zugang zu ihm zu eröffnen. Es kann durchaus nicht ausgeschlossen werden, daß je nach der Situation ein scheinbar vages Bild oder eine schlichte Erzählung mehr vom letztlich Unsagbaren auszusagen und von den Tiefenstrukturen der Wirklichkeit freizulegen vermögen als der scheinbar so präzise und gerade deshalb so fixierte, unbiegsame, beschränkte Begriff, als die so klare und bestimmte und gerade deshalb so einseitige und farblose Argumentation oder Dokumentation. Wie eben die Poesie das Geheimnis der Natur und des Menschen unter Umständen besser trifft als eine noch so exakte Beschreibung oder Photographie.

Hier ist zu bedenken: Wahrheit ist nicht gleich Faktizität, ist insbesondere nicht gleich historischer Wahrheit. Wie es *verschiedene Weisen und Schichten der Wirklichkeit* gibt, so gibt es verschiedene Weisen *der Wahrheit:* und oft in der einen und selben Erzählung verschiedene Schichten der Wahrheit. Man überlege: Kann mich nicht eine tatsächlich geschehene Geschichte völlig gleichgültig lassen? Und kann mich nicht umgekehrt eine nur fingierte (»fiktionale«) und historisch nicht geschehene Geschichte unter Umständen tief betroffen machen? Eine Zeitungsmeldung von einem auf dem Weg von Jerusalem nach Jericho überfallenen Reisenden wird mich unter Umständen völlig gleichgültig lassen: obwohl sie – leider – wahr, historisch wahr ist. Umgekehrt wird mich die erfundene Geschichte vom barmherzigen Samariter auf demselben Weg unmittelbar in Bewegung setzen: weil sie mehr Wahrheit enthält. Die erste Geschichte sagt mir eine Wahrheit, die mich nichts angeht oder zumindest nicht anzugehen scheint, die für mich nicht bedeutsam ist: ein pures Faktum, eine rein historische Wahrheit. Die andere Geschichte sagt mir eine Wahrheit, die, obwohl kein Faktum, mich zutiefst betrifft: eine für mich bedeutsame Wahrheit, eine für meine Existenz relevante (»existentiale«) Wahrheit. Gegenüber einer Geschichte wie der des barmherzigen Samariters oder des verlorenen Sohnes ist die Frage des Historikers, »wie es eigentlich gewesen ist«, fehl am Platz: die Frage nach historisch Richtig oder Falsch ist inadäquat, ohne Interesse. Die Poesie, die Parabel, die Legende hat ihre eigene Vernunft. Sie unterstreicht, setzt Akzente, hebt heraus, konkretisiert: Sie kann relevantere Wahrheit künden als der historische Bericht. Die Bibel ist primär nicht an der historischen Wahrheit, sondern an der für unser Wohl, unser Heil relevanten Wahrheit, an der »Heilswahrheit« interessiert.

Gewiß stellt sich bei allen Berichten gerade über Jesus, wie wir auf Schritt und Tritt festgestellt haben, zumindest heute unausweichlich und schon für jedes Kind die historische Frage, ob denn das Berichtete (etwa das Wandeln über den See oder die Verklärung oder die Himmelfahrt) wie berichtet geschehen, also historisch sei. Und zwar stellt sich die Frage nicht nur in der wissenschaftlichen Theologie, sondern auch in einer zeitgemäßen Verkündigung. Umgekehrt ist jedoch bereits deutlich geworden: Auch die Jesusgeschichten wollen nicht nur, was eine historisch-kritische Theologie oft allein beschäftigt hat, nach Traditionen seziert und auf ihre Aussagen über historische Tatsachen befragt werden. Selbst dort, wo einfach berichtet wird, wollen sie mehr als nur eine Wahrheit aussprechen. Es geht in diesen Geschichten nie um reine Informationen, die den Hörer oder Leser unbeteiligt lassen sollen. Es geht um *Botschaften,* die eine Verheißung oder eine Bedrohung mit sich führen. Gerade bei den Weihnachts-, Wunder-, Oster- und Gerichtsgeschichten steht im Vordergrund des Interesses weniger, was sich da eigentlich ereignet hat oder ereignen wird, worüber wir oft wenig wissen, als vielmehr die praktische Frage, *was das für uns bedeutet*: worüber sich in jeder individuellen und gesellschaftlichen Situation wieder neu kritisch nachdenken läßt. Solche Geschichten geben oft mehr Aufschluß über die Wirkung eines bestimmten Geschehens auf die Menschen als über das Geschehen selbst.

Dies gilt besonders, wenn zwischen dem Ereignis und dem überlieferten Text wie im Neuen Testament (etwa bezüglich der
Geburt Jesu, der österlichen Berufungserfahrungen) Jahrzehnte,
und im Alten Testament (etwa bezüglich des Auszugs aus Ägypten oder der Landnahme) Jahrhunderte liegen. Wissen wir dann
auch vom historischen Faktum verhältnismäßig wenig, so doch
verhältnismäßig viel, wie es gewirkt hat und wie Israel oder die
christliche Gemeinde mit ihm umgegangen sind. Die Geschichten offenbaren dann den Weg, den Israel oder die Gemeinde mit
ihren grundlegenden Geschichtserfahrungen durchschritten haben und der auch für den christlichen Weg heute von Bedeutung
ist.

Erzählende Darbietung und kritische Reflexion

Und damit sind wir wieder beim Problem der *literarischen
Form*[6]: Verkündigung, Predigt, Katechese sind etwas anderes als
Wissenschaft, als Theologie oder Historie. Wenn sie sich auch
immer wieder die wissenschaftliche Überprüfung gefallen lassen
müssen und eine solche nicht ungestraft vernachlässigen, so ist
ihr Ziel und deshalb auch ihre Sprache eine andere. Wie eben ein
Königsdrama Shakespeares ein anderes Ziel und deshalb eine
andere literarische Form hat als eine historische Darstellung etwa
Heinrichs V. Unsere Evangelien sind – selbstverständlich bei
wesentlichen Unterschieden – einem Shakespeareschen Drama
näher als einer Chronik oder einer historischen Biographie: Hier
wie dort soll nicht möglichst exakte Historie geboten und soll
trotzdem die Tradition über die zentralen Personen und Ereignisse im wesentlichen getreu wiedergegeben werden. Hier wie
dort soll so überzeugend wie möglich eine Botschaft (von einem
besseren England – von Jesus Christus und dem Gottesreich)
verkündet und ein neues Zeitalter angesprochen werden. Hier
wie dort sollen nicht nur einige wenige Gelehrte objektiv orientiert, sondern eine breite Zuhörerschaft verschiedenster Herkunft gefesselt und bewegt werden. Hier wie dort muß dies in
einer relativ kurzen Darstellung – selbst das Lukasevangelium
läßt sich in zwei Stunden lesen – geschehen. Zu diesem Ziel und
Zweck werden denn bei Shakespeare wie in den Evangelien
Chronologie und Topographie nur so weit notwendig beachtet,
werden Akzente verschoben, werden Fakten und Personen ausgewählt und, wenn nötig, auch frei erfunden. Zu diesem Ziel und

Zweck wird manchmal gerafft und ein längerer Ablauf in einen einzigen Satz zusammengefaßt und wird umgekehrt aus einem einzigen Satz eine ganze Szene gestaltet, nach dem Grundsatz: multum in parvo – viel in wenig.

Wäre es nicht lächerlich, Shakespeares Heinrich V. oder das Markusevangelium durch eine »genauere« Paraphrase ersetzen zu wollen? Wird Markus wie Shakespeare nicht noch heute wie eh und je gelesen, öffentlich (in Kirche oder Theater) zur Darstellung gebracht und von einer großen Zuhörerschaft spontan, wenn auch nicht immer richtig, verstanden, während sehr viel genauere Chroniken und Geschichtswerke bestenfalls von Spezialisten in Bibliotheken studiert werden? Es geht in den Evangelien wie bei Shakespeare nicht um eine historische, sondern um eine »*dramatische Geschichtsdarstellung*«, die über ihre eigenen Stilmittel verfügt und die wirksamer als abstrakte Ideen und Lehrsätze ihr Ziel zu erreichen vermag. In den Evangelien wie bei Shakespeare trotz aller Verschiedenheit ein komplexes, ineinander verschränktes Vielebenenspiel (in bezug auf Raum, Zeit, Zuhörerschicht) mit epischen, dramatischen und gar lyrischen Elementen, das eine Totalität plastisch vor Augen stellt.

Von daher gesehen setzt die neuerdings programmatisch herausgestellte »erzählende«, *»narrative« Theologie*[7] bei aller berechtigten Polemik gegen zuviel abstrakte Reflexion *zu eng* an. Gewiß soll eine christliche Theologie sich nie zu gut sein, von Jesus und seiner Sache zu erzählen, und gewiß hat dies nicht nur die neuscholastische, sondern auch die existentiale und die politische Theologie zuwenig getan. Aber schon literarisch sind die Evangelien keineswegs reine Erzählungen, sondern, wie dargelegt, dramatisch komponierte Geschichtsdarstellungen mit verschiedenen Erzählelementen. Gewiß wird zu Recht die Relativität der historischen Vernunft und der »argumentativen« Theologie neu betont und die Bedeutsamkeit des Erzählens neu herausgestrichen. Aber eine Theologie oder eine Verkündigung, die Geschichten, biblische oder nachbiblische, erzählt, ohne sich über die Authentizität des Geschehens selbst Rechenschaft zu geben, würde von denkenden Menschen zu Recht, und zwar sowohl literarisch wie theologisch, nicht ernstgenommen. Die Folge wäre ein »narrativer« Biblizismus oder gar ein unkontrolliertes kriterienloses Gerede. Ob der Literaturwissenschaftler und erst recht der Theologe diese Seite der Problematik genügend beachtet hat? Die Frage der historischen Authentizität ist *für den Literaturwissenschaftler* relativ unwichtig[8]. Er glaubt ja auch nicht für sein Leben und Sterben »an« Heinrich V. oder gar Heinrich VIII., an Julius Cäsar oder Wilhelm Tell; er will ihnen nicht »nachfolgen«. Ob also Wilhelm Tell in Wirklichkeit (Schiller) oder nur als Wanderlegende (Frisch) existiert, ob Cäsars Ermordung von seinen Mördern gegen seinen Willen bewerkstelligt (Shakespeare) oder von Cäsar selber zum gloriosen Abgang provoziert und inszeniert wurde (Jens), ob die heilige Johanna nach Schiller, Shaw oder Brecht zu verstehen ist, das kann dem Literaturwissenschaftler, dem es wesentlich um den Text und seine literarische Qualität und nur sekundär um die Sache des Textes geht, letztlich gleichgültig sein. Selten geht er denn auch den Weg zu den authentischen Akten.

Aber *für den glaubenden Menschen* sieht das anders aus: Für den Menschen, der an Jesus glaubt und ihn zum konkreten Maßstab seines Verhaltens macht, ist es nicht gleichgültig, ob dieser Jesus eine geschichtliche Gestalt, eine Wanderlegende oder ein Mythos ist. Ob er als Hierarch, Ordensmann oder Sozialrevolutionär gewirkt hat. Ob sein Tod zu Recht erfolgte oder nicht. Vielleicht ist ihm auch nicht gleichgültig, ob Jesus wirklich von einer Jungfrau geboren wurde, ob er Wunder gegen die Naturgesetze getan, Taufe und Abendmahl eingesetzt, das Papsttum begründet hat und buchstäblich in den Himmel aufgefahren ist. Der glaubende Mensch – und auch der Literaturwissenschaftler, sofern er glaubt – ist primär nicht am Text und seiner literarischen Qualität, sondern an der Sache selbst, an der literarisch dargestellten Person, ihrem Schicksal und ihren Konsequenzen für ihn selbst und die Gesellschaft interessiert. Er möchte wissen, ob und inwiefern sein Glaube in einer Illusion oder in der geschichtlichen Wirklichkeit gründet. Wo immer ein Glaube auf einer Illusion beruht, da geht es nicht um Glaube, sondern um Aberglaube.

Trotzdem bleibt wahr: Eine Theologie oder Verkündigung (sie sei scholastisch oder neuscholastisch, existential oder politisch orientiert), die alle tradierten Geschichten möglichst in Begriffe, Ideen, Prinzipien, Systeme umwandelte, würde ihres eigenen Ursprungs vergessen und auch die Menschen nicht wahrhaft zu ergreifen vermögen, um sie in die Nachfolge zu führen. Sie hat so oder anders einen Dogmatismus und oft auch Ritualismus zur Folge. *Erzählende Darbietung und kritische Reflexion* sind also in der christlichen Theologie und Verkündigung zu verbinden.

Entscheidend für die Theologie ist, daß es nicht bei einem vieldeutigen und dann in der Praxis mißdeuteten Schlagwort bleibt. Sondern daß dem programmatischen Ruf auch die praktisch-theologische Tat folgt. Selbstverständlich genügt es nicht, nur vom Erzählen zu erzählen und nur die Memoria zu kommemorieren. Dafür muß man sich schon die Mühe machen, zu den biblischen Erzählungen selbst zurückzukehren und durch alle historisch-kritische Forschung hindurch sich das Gedächtnis kritisch aufzufrischen. Aber wie immer man es halten wird, so rechtfertigt sich auch von dieser Seite her unser eigenes Unterfangen: daß diese Einführung ins Christsein bei aller notwendigen Systematik und kritischen Reflexion, die im folgenden weitergeführt werden soll, soviel als möglich von Jesus, seiner Leidens- und Sterbensgeschichte »erzählt« und nicht nur abstrakt über Christentum und Christsein räsoniert, argumentiert, diskutiert und theoretisiert hat. Den Verfasser würde es ermutigen, wenn möglichst viele Leser und besonders Verkündiger des Wortes sich dadurch angeregt sähen, die Texte des Neuen und Alten Testaments wieder neu zu hören, zu reflektieren und ins Leben umzusetzen. Wie denn auch dieses Buch ohne die fortlaufende Predigt (lectio et praedicatio continua) unter anderem des Markusevangeliums, der Bergpredigt und großer Teile des Alten Testaments nicht oder sicher nicht so geschrieben worden wäre.

2. Deutungen des Todes

Mythenbildung ist besonders bezüglich Ursprung und Vollendung, Geburt und Tod Jesu Christi, insofern sie ans Unanschauliche grenzen, zu erwarten. Immer wird gerade hier – bei Opfertod und Meßopfer, Präexistenz und Jungfrauengeburt – die Frage laut: Muß man das alles glauben? Aber nochmals, wo man vom Glauben-Müssen redet, stimmt etwas nicht, wie wenn einer fragt: Muß man sich freuen?

Eine kleine Vorwarnung – nicht zum Abschrecken, sondern zum Anreiz – ist vielleicht angebracht. Hier muß dem Leser, wiederum so verständlich wie möglich, etwas kompliziertere Theologie zugemutet werden, in unvermeidlicher Auseinandersetzung mit einer 2000jährigen theologischen Tradition, wie sie noch immer jede Sonntagspredigt und Religionsstunde bestimmt. Das Entscheidende ist freilich bereits gesagt. Aber verschiedene Auswirkungen sind zu bedenken. Was keineswegs – wie Theologie überhaupt – langweilig zu sein braucht.

Die Überlegungen nicht nur des Apostels Paulus, sondern der frühen Christenheit überhaupt kreisen immer wieder um Jesu Kreuzestod. Wie konnte es anders sein? Je nach der Verkündigungssituation und Eigenart der Gemeinde und Autoren werden schon vor Paulus verschiedene Deutungsversuche entwickelt: Wie kann im Licht von Jesu neuem Leben sein peinlicher, widerlicher, schändlicher Tod besser verstanden werden? Ja, wie kann er nicht als Unheilsereignis, sondern als Heilsereignis verstanden werden? Es sind begreiflicherweise sehr tastende Verstehensbemühungen. Hätte man sie je – wie in der Theologie- und Dogmengeschichte seit dem Mittelalter oft geschehen – verabsolutieren dürfen? Aus der Zeit heraus werden verschiedene Deutekategorien und oft auch mythologische Bildlichkeiten genommen, um diesen Tod und nun vor allem seine *bleibende Bedeutung und Wirkung* für die Menschen, »für uns« verständlich zu machen.

Es gibt im Neuen Testament wie auch noch in der Patristik kein exklusiv normatives Deutungsmodell. Man kennt *verschiedene, mehrschichtige und ineinander übergehende Sinndeutungen*. Da braucht man für den *Tod* Jesu juristische Deutekategorien: der Tod Jesu, wie wir gesehen haben, als Gerechtsprechung des Sünders. Aber auch kultische: der Tod Jesu als Stellvertretung, Opfer, Heiligung. Dann auch finanzielle: der Tod Jesu als Bezahlung des Lösegeldes. Schließlich sogar militärische: der Tod Jesu als Kampf mit den bösen Mächten.

Ganz entsprechend kann dann *Jesus* selber wiederum sehr verschieden gesehen werden: als der (verworfene) Lehrer, der (verkannte) Prophet, der (verratene) Zeuge, der (gerichtete) Richter, der (sich selbst opfernde) Hohepriester, der (dornengekrönte) König, der (gekreuzigte) Sieger. Auch der *Ertrag* des Kreuzesgeschehens wird entsprechend verschieden umschrieben: als Beispiel, Erlösung, Befreiung, Sündenvergebung, Reinigung, Heiligung, Versöhnung, Rechtfertigung.

Der Übergang zwischen manchen Vorstellungen – etwa der des Loskaufs, der Stellvertretung, des Opfers (Passa-, Bundes-, Sühnopfer) – ist schwebend. Die verschiedenen und verschieden geeigneten Motive wachsen jedoch im Neuen Testament nicht zusammen. Es gibt weder im Neuen Testament noch in der darauffolgenden patristischen Theologie eine einheitliche Theorie des Kreuzes oder des Todes Jesu. Eine solche hat sich erst seit dem Mittelalter, seit Anselm von Canterbury († 1274), in der katholischen und dann modifiziert auch in der evangelischen Theologie ausgebildet. Und erst seit Calvin gibt es eine systematisch entfaltete und ebenfalls nicht unproblematische Lehre von den drei Ämtern Jesu, des Propheten, Priesters und Königs[1].

Ist es eigentlich verwunderlich? *Nicht jede* dieser Begrifflichkeiten und Bildlichkeiten, die alle auf verschiedene Weise die Heilsbedeutung des Todes Jesu herausheben wollen, ist heute noch *gleich verständlich*. Manche damalige Denkmodelle sind uns fremd geworden. Einige können direkt irreführen.

Das wird nicht zuletzt zu bedenken sein im Hinblick auf jene beiden schon alten patristischen Vorstellungen vom Tode Jesu, die im lateinischen Westen vor allem durch Augustin und Papst Gregor dem Mittelalter vermittelt wurden: Einmal der Tod Jesu verstanden als »Loskauf« (= redemptio, Erlösung) durch ein an den (personhaft verstandenen) Teufel zu zahlendes Lösegeld (= Jesu Tod oder Blut). Dann der Tod Jesu verstanden als ein Gott dargebrachtes, ihn gleichsam umstimmendes »Sühnopfer« (= sacrificium, reconciliatio). Beides sind Ideen, die zur theologischen Ausgestaltung gerade im Zusammenhang mit der mittelalterlichen Ausbildung des Bußsakraments und des Meßopfers reizen mußten. Doch es stellt sich die Frage, ob hier nicht manchmal legendär-mythologische Vorstellungen oder weltanschauliche Schemata einer bestimmten Epoche mit dem Christusglauben verwechselt wurden.

Gestorben für uns

Im Gegensatz zu der mehr philosophisch-metaphysisch gerichteten östlichen Theologie war die *Theologie des lateinischen Westens* – an Rom und seiner Mentalität orientiert – mehr auf praktische Lebensgestaltung und Kirchendisziplin ausgerichtet. Schon immer hatten deshalb Juristen-Theologen und juristische Vorstellungen einen ungewöhnlich starken Einfluß: von Tertullian, dem Initiator der lateinischen Theologie angefangen. Dann über Cyprian und Gregor den Großen bis zu den Wegbereitern der Scholastik, zu Anselms Lehrer Lanfranc und Anselms Zeitgenossen Bernold von Konstanz und Ivo von Chartres, der die Verbindung von Theologie und kanonischem Recht herstellte. Solche Theologie verstand das Verhältnis von Gott und Mensch mit Vorliebe vom *Modell des Rechtsverhältnisses her*. Nach der Devise »Do ut des«: »Ich gebe, damit du gibst«! Mit klar abgegrenzten Rechten und Pflichten für beide Teile: »suum cuique«, »jedem das Seine«!

Auch das *Kreuzesgeschehen* wurde schon früh *mit Hilfe rechtlicher Denkformen gedeutet*, die eher eine Verwandtschaft mit moralistisch-legalistischen Strömungen im frühen Judentum als mit dem Rechtfertigungsverständnis des Apostels Paulus zeigten. Als juristisch gefärbte Leitbegriffe dienten: Gesetz, Schuld, Strafe, Lohn, Buße, Sühne, Loskauf, Satisfaktion, Rekonziliation, Restitution. In dieser Theologie wird nun gerade Jesus – paradox genug bei seiner Gesetzeskritik – gerne als »neuer Gesetzgeber« verstanden. Und das Evangelium als »neues Gesetz«. Kann bei dieser so moralischen, strengen und erneut auf Leistung ausgerichteten Erlösungslehre ein gewisser theoretischer wie praktischer Rejudaisierungsprozeß unter christlichem Vorzeichen in Abrede gestellt werden?

Was indessen bei den frühen lateinischen Theologen noch disparate Elemente waren, was noch bei Augustin in unsystematischer Offenheit und Vielfalt behandelt wurde, findet im 11. Jahrhundert seine erste geschlossene Gestalt: in der *Satisfaktionstheorie* des Anselm von Canterbury[2]. Sie ist für die mittelalterlich-tridentinische wie für die reformatorische Erlösungslehre faktisch normativ geworden und prägt noch heute die Katechismen der Kirchen. Aus pastoralen und apologetischen Intentionen heraus, das darf man nicht übersehen, hatte Anselm als Erzbischof von Canterbury den ersten theologischen Erlösungstraktat geschrieben[3]. Er wollte Menschwerdung, Tod und Erlösung im Geist einer neuen Zeit so rational wie irgendwie möglich erklären: als der Vernunft nicht nur angemessen, sondern notwendig. Mit einem Gespür für das, was in einer neuen Zeit nicht mehr zu verstehen war, distanzierte er sich vom patristischen Loskauf-Konzept, das dem Teufel einen Rechtsanspruch auf den sündigen Menschen und gegenüber Gott zubilligte. Statt dessen versuchte er in einer Epoche der aufblühenden Rechtswissenschaft durch ein großangelegtes, scheinbar lückenloses Beweisverfahren, die *Notwendigkeit der Menschwerdung und vor allem der Erlösung* durch den Kreuzestod *rational zu demonstrieren*. Wie läuft das Verfahren?

Anselm geht nicht vom Kreuzestod und unserer eigenen Situation aus, gleichsam von unten nach oben. Er konstruiert kühn von oben nach unten: warum gleichsam vom Standpunkt Gottes aus Menschwerdung und Kreuzestod sein mußten. Durch die Sünde – *das* Problem der anselmischen Erlösungslehre – hat der

Mensch nämlich schuldhaft Gottes gerechte und vernünftige Weltordnung gestört (der ordo universi – ein Leitgedanke von Augustin bis Thomas). Dadurch ist Gott in seiner Ehre unendlich beleidigt worden. Deshalb die unbedingte Notwendigkeit, die Ehre Gottes wiederherzustellen, zu restituieren. In rechtmäßiger Weise ist das nach Anselm nicht möglich durch bloßes Erbarmen (sola misericordia). Sondern nur durch eine entsprechende *Genugtuung (satisfactio)*. Aber kann die unendliche Schuld des Menschen gegenüber der unendlichen Majestät Gottes durch eine auch noch so große Sühneleistung eines Menschen wiedergutgemacht werden? Sie kann es nur durch den ungeschuldeten, freiwilligen, unendlich wertvollen Tod eines Gott-Menschen: durch den Tod nämlich des sich selber anbietenden Gottessohnes, der deshalb Mensch geworden ist und dessen Verdienste den Mitmenschen zugewendet werden.

Zweifellos eine für die damalige Zeit in ihrer formalen Klarheit, juristischen Konsequenz und systematischen Geschlossenheit bestechende Theorie der Erlösung! Freilich eingespannt in einen unpersönlichen juristischen Schematismus von sachhaften Äquivalenzen: Schuld und Sühne, Leistung und Gegenleistung, Schaden und Schadenersatz. Gott ist anderwärts für Anselm: »was größer nicht gedacht werden kann«[4] oder »größer als was gedacht werden kann«[5]. Aber in seiner Erlösungstheorie kommen weder Gottes Unbegreiflichkeit noch seine Freiheit (die ganz an die nun einmal etablierte Weltordnung gebunden ist) zur Geltung.

Schon Thomas von Aquin hat den rationalen Zwang, die Engführung auf den Kreuzestod und die juridisch-kultische Übersteigerung der Anselmischen Satisfaktionslehre korrigiert und umgedeutet. Statt wie Anselm apriorisch eine Vernunftnotwendigkeit zu deduzieren, wollte er aposteriorisch über eine Vernunftangemessenheit (convenientia) reflektieren. Doch von heutigen Einsichten her läßt sich die Verfremdung der biblischen Botschaft durch das juristische System Anselms noch sehr viel klarer durchschauen[6]. Was ist daran *fragwürdig*?

a. Fragwürdig ist schon die *Voraussetzung* dieser Erlösungslehre: Die *Vorstellung von einer ursprünglich paradiesisch-heilen Welt*, einer Ur-Sünde des ersten Menschenpaares und vor allem die augustinische Lehre einer durch die Zeugung übertragenen *Erb-Sünde* (gleichsam mit Sippenhaftung) erscheinen uns heute problematisch[7]. Die ersten Seiten der Bibel können und wollen doch nicht ergründen, *wie* – naturwissenschaftlich-historisch verstanden – die Welt, Mann und Frau, die Sünde wurde. Sie wollen künden, *was* in ihrem Verhältnis zu *Gott* – also theologisch verstanden – Welt, Mann und Frau, Sünde sind und sein sollen. Nicht um seiner selbst willen, sondern als Hintergrund zur Sündenfallgeschichte wird der paradiesische Urzustand geschildert: warum sind Welt und Mensch so, wie sie sind? Die ewigen Fragen nach Größe und Elend, Schicksal und Verantwortung des Menschen also. Behandelt werden – mehr volkstümlich im alten jahwistischen und mehr reflektiert im jüngeren priesterschriftlichen Schöpfungsbericht: des Menschen Umsorgtsein von Gott, seine Verfügungsgewalt über die Natur, die Macht seiner Liebe zur Frau, aber auch seine Schuld vor Gott, seine Scham vor anderen Menschen, seine mühselige tägliche Arbeit[8]. Der Traum von einem anfänglichen goldenen Zeitalter ist – ein Traum. Nicht auf ein imaginäres – und für uns im übrigen völlig uninteressantes – Urmenschenpaar vor vielleicht einer guten halben Million Jahren zielen diese Erzählungen. Sondern auf den »Adam«: das heißt »den Menschen« schlechthin. Also primär den Menschen hier und heute, auf den ja auch das Erlösungsgeschehen zielt. »Tua res agitur« – um deine, um meine Sache geht es: in Schöpfung und Erlösung.

b. Fragwürdig ist aber auch die *Zielbestimmung* dieser Erlösungslehre: Was in der Anselmischen Theorie als Ziel des Erlösungsgeschehens konsequent angestrebt wird, wird nämlich durch Jesu Tod faktisch gar nicht erreicht: Oder wird die angeblich paradiesisch-heile Weltordnung des Anfangs – wenn Leid, Tod, Begehrlichkeit, Sünde doch nicht verschwinden – etwa wiederhergestellt? Nur der durch die Sünde der Stammeltern und deren Folgen unendlich beleidigte Gott erhält *rein äußerlich* – durch die Wiederherstellung seiner »Ehre« – *Satisfaktion;* die Schuld der Menschen ist nämlich auf solider rechtlicher Grundlage durch den Gottessohn eingelöst worden. Wir sehen: nicht wie im Neuen Testament Gnade, Barmherzigkeit und Liebe, sondern wie im römischen Recht eine sehr menschlich verstandene Gerechtigkeit (iustitia commutativa), ja geradezu eine Logik des Rechts dominieren in dieser Erlösungslehre. Der Kreuzestod wird um dieser Logik willen isoliert von Jesu Botschaft und Leben und zugleich auch von seiner Auferweckung: im Grund kam Jesus, um zu sterben. Das konkrete Verkündigen, Verhalten, Erleiden und neue Leben des geschichtlichen Jesus von Nazaret spielt in dieser Theorie keine konstitutive Rolle. Dafür wird uns ein nach juristischen Gesichtspunkten ablaufendes tödliches »Schattenspiel zwischen Vater und Sohn«, ja zwischen göttlicher und menschlicher Natur im Sohn präsentiert[9]. Wobei die konkreten Menschen, denen das alles gelten soll, hinter dem Gottessohn weithin verschwinden, nicht innerlich betroffen sind und vor allem auf das jenseitige Leben vertröstet werden.

c. Also: Ob vielleicht auch wegen dieses so düsteren Erlösungs-Prozesses in der Folge die Erlösten so wenig erlöst ausschauten, wie Nietzsche kritisch bemerkte? Im Vergleich mit allem Vorausgegangenen dürfte zumindest dies offensichtlich sein: die von Anselm herkommende Satisfaktionstheorie spiegelt in ihrer spezifischen Ausformung weniger das Neue Testament als das Mittelalter und dessen juridisch-rationales Ordnungsdenken wider. Diese Theorie wurde geboren aus der voll zu bejahenden Absicht, die *alte Überlieferung einer neuen Zeit* mit einem neuen Erfahrungshorizont in einer Gläubigen und Ungläubigen gemeinsamen Denk- und Sprechweise *neu verständlich zu machen.* Aber wird man, was der mittelalterlichen Theologie gestattet war, der heutigen Theologie im Namen dieser mittelalterlichen Theologie verbieten können? Für die Deutung des vielschichtigen Erlösungsgeschehens können wir uns heute wohl sowenig wie in der neutestamentlichen oder patristischen Zeit auf eine bestimmte einschichtige Begrifflichkeit – sie sei nun juridisch, kultisch, metaphysisch oder auch naturwissenschaftlich, technisch, psychologisch, soziologisch – festlegen lassen. Das hier über Kreuz und Erlösung bereits Gesagte und im weiteren noch zu Sagende versucht, soweit in Kürze möglich, die uns durch die Jahrhunderte überkommene Tradition zu prüfen und das Beste zu bewahren, um vor einem völlig anderen Verstehenshorizont der ursprünglichen Botschaft von Kreuz und Erlösung beim heutigen Menschen neu Gehör zu verschaffen.

Opfer?

Muß dann aber zeitgemäßes Erlösungsverständnis mit dem Abbau der juristischen und kultischen Forcierungen nicht auch den Begriff des Opfers aufgeben? Läßt sich bestreiten, daß gerade der Begriff des *Sühneopfers* zumindest in populären Vorstellungen oft geradezu peinliche heidnische Mißverständnisse aufkommen ließ: als ob Gott so grausam, ja sadistisch sei, daß sein Zorn nur durch das Blut seines eigenen Sohnes besänftigt werden könne? Als ob ein Unschuldiger als Sündenbock, Prügelknabe und Ersatzmann für die eigentlichen Sünder dienen müsse?

1. Im *Neuen Testament* spielt der Begriff des »Sühnopfers« – vom Hebräerbrief abgesehen – bei weitem nicht die zentrale Rolle, die ihm theologische Systematisierungen gegeben haben. Freilich läßt sich nicht bestreiten, daß der Tod Jesu – vielleicht im Anschluß an eine Deutung des seinen Tod vorausahnenden Jesus selbst[10] und wohl im Rückgriff auf das Alte Testament[11] – in der apostolischen Verkündigung als *Sühnetod* verstanden wird: Jesus als Sühnemal der Erlösung[12], als geschlachtetes Passalamm[13], als Lamm Gottes, das die Sünden der Welt trägt[14]. Die Benützung alttestamentlicher Opferterminologie – auch im Zusammenhang mit der Kurzformel »Blut Christi« – lag natürlich nahe: Sie konnte gerade für Juden das Skandalöse des Kreuzestodes einigermaßen erträglich und verständlich machen. Doch handelt es sich mehr um formelhafte und metaphorische Einschübe. Allein im relativ späten ›Brief an die Hebräer‹ eines unbekannten hellenistischen Autors, der zum Teil paulinische Motive verwertet, wird das Opferthema in kultischer Terminologie breit entfaltet: zur radikalen Kritik des jüdischen Kultes[15]!

Das »Opfer« Jesu darf tatsächlich *nicht im alttestamentlichen oder heidnischen Sinn* verstanden werden. Im Neuen Testament besagt das Opfer keine versöhnende Beeinflussung eines zornigen Dämons, der umgestimmt werden muß. Der Mensch muß versöhnt werden, nicht Gott. Und dies durch eine Versöhnung, die ganz Gottes Initiative ist[16]: nicht indem ein persönlicher Groll Gottes, sondern indem jene reale Feindschaft zwischen Mensch und Gott beseitigt wird, die nicht aus einer Erb-Sünde, sondern aus aktueller persönlicher Schuld und dem allgemeinen Schuldverhängnis entsteht.

Jesus hat nicht wie die Tempelpriester nur äußere sachhafte Gaben (Früchte, Tiere), er hat sich selber hingegeben[17]: eine freiwillige, *personale Selbsthingabe* – in Gehorsam gegenüber Gottes Willen und in Liebe zu den Menschen. Er, der eindeutig kein Priester war, wird jetzt im übertragenen Sinn als Priester, ja als der eigentliche Hohepriester bezeichnet, der durch seine Selbsthingabe zugleich auch der Geopferte ist. Eine solche Selbsthingabe konnte im Hebräerbrief nicht nur als ein »Opfer« unter anderen, es mußte als das vollkommene »Opfer« verstanden werden, welches das *Ende aller unvollkommenen menschlichen Opfer* bedeutet. Mit dieser Selbsthingabe ist erreicht, was die Tieropfer schon immer intendierten: die Versöhnung des Menschen mit Gott. Im Hebräerbrief hat sich die Erkenntnis, die sonst im Neuen Testament nur anklingt, durchgesetzt: daß die vollkommene Selbsthingabe bleibende Gültigkeit hat und damit weitere Sühnopfer für alle Zeiten überflüssig gemacht sind. Dieses eine »Opfer« ist »ein für allemal«[18] dargebracht worden und löst die Vielheit der bisherigen Opfer ab, womit eine Entgrenzung des Geschehens in Zeit und Raum über alle Grenzen einer Generation oder eines Volkes hinaus gegeben ist. Auch der erhöhte Herr bringt nicht etwa nochmals Opfer dar. Ist doch der am Kreuz ein für allemal Hingegebene, »Geopferte« jetzt zu betrachten als der erhöhte Herr, der ewige Hohepriester, der vor Gott unablässig für die Seinen eintritt. »Hohepriester« also wird er *nicht* genannt im Sinne eines statischen *Opfer-Kultes* in einem Heiligtum. *Sondern* zunächst im Sinne eines *Opfer-Weges,* den der Sohn im Gehorsam geht: im Tod durch den Vorhang seines Fleisches hindurch ins Heiligtum, damit mit ihm auch seine Bundesgemeinde Zugang zum Throne Gottes im Heiligtum habe. Also nur von diesem geschichtlichen Weg her ist des Hohenpriesters Christus jetziges Eintreten für die Brüder zu verstehen, bis er wiederkommt – Jesus Christus gestern und heute derselbe und in Ewigkeit[19]. Soweit nach dem Hebräerbrief.

2. Doch sollte es *heute* genügen, einfach diese alten Vokabeln, Begriffe, Bilder und Vorstellungen zu wiederholen, auch wenn sich unterdessen der Erfahrungshorizont beinahe völlig verändert hat? Zum Gebrauch des Opferbegriffs heute wird man folgern dürfen:

– *Die für die Judenchristen damals so verständliche Vorstellung vom Kreuzestod als einem Sühnopfer ist nur eines und keineswegs das zentrale Interpretationsmodell des Kreuzestodes.*
– *Da in der Umwelt des modernen Menschen keine kultischen Opfer mehr dargebracht werden und auch keine Apologie gegen die Heiden (die noch zur Zeit Augustins die erste Eroberung Roms auf die ausgebliebenen Götteropfer zurückgeführt haben) das Vorweisen eines christlichen »Opfers« fordert, ist der Opferbegriff wegen des abwesenden Erfahrungskorrelats weithin mißverständlich und unverständlich geworden*[20].
– *Der kultisch verstandene Opferbegriff (»Sühnopfer«) wird*

deshalb in der heutigen Verkündigung tunlichst vermieden zugunsten verständlicherer Begriffe wie » Versöhnung«, »Stellvertretung«, »Erlösung«, »Befreiung«. Wird er trotzdem gebraucht, so sollte er personal als »Hingabe«, »Selbsthingabe[21] «, und zwar nicht nur für Jesu Sterben, sondern für seinen ganzen Lebensweg verstanden werden. Auch die kultische Opferbildlichkeit des Hebräerbriefes steht ja ganz unter dem tiefen Eindruck des einzigartig gehorsamen, Gott und den Menschen hingegebenen Lebens und Sterbens Jesu (Selbsthingabe, Lebensopfer).

– *Das »für uns« oder »zugunsten, zugute, zum besten von uns« gestorben – im Neuen Testament ausgedrückt durch verschiedene Beziehungswörter[22] – ist für den christlichen Glauben an den Gekreuzigten wesentlich: Der Kreuzestod ist gewiß ein historisches Ereignis, und ist zugleich mehr als das. Jesus ist nicht nur damals (einmal) gekreuzigt worden und lebt jetzt nur durch seine Nachwirkung, sein Beispiel und unsere Erinnerung weiter. Sondern als der zum Leben bei Gott Erweckte ist und bleibt er für uns (ein für allemal) der Gekreuzigte. So ist er für die Glaubenden lebendig präsent. Der Kreuzestod ist von daher ein historisches Faktum mit universaler Bedeutung: alle Menschen sind davon betroffen und zum Glauben berufen.*

– *Die universale Bedeutung des Kreuzestodes »für uns«, »für die vielen«, »für alle« kann jedoch auf verschiedene Weise ausgesagt werden, heute oft verständlicher, wie oben versucht, durch den Begriff der Stellvertretung[23]. In jedem Fall sollten im »für uns« nicht wie bei Anselm die Sünden, sondern die Menschen im Vordergrund stehen.*

– *Die bleibende, endgültige und unwiderrufliche Bedeutung und Wirkung von Jesu Tod muß also, wie in all den vorausgegangenen Kapiteln versucht, aus jeder schematischen Engführung hinausgeführt werden: immer betrachtet im Zusammenhang mit Verkündigung und Wirken des geschichtlichen Jesus, mit der lebendigen Präsenz des Auferweckten und selbstverständlich mit dem Erfahrungshorizont des heutigen Menschen. Nur so kann der christliche Glaube an den Gekreuzigten den Menschen und seine Welt verändern.*

3. Wenn schon der Opferbegriff heute so problematisch ist, dann erst recht der Begriff des *Meß-Opfers,* der vom Kreuzesopfer abgeleitet wird. Gerade die Ausführungen des Hebräerbriefes machen klar: das Mahl der Gemeinde, die Eucharistiefeier, darf

auf keinen Fall als Wiederholung, Ergänzung oder gar Überbietung des einmaligen »Opfers« Jesu verstanden werden. Das Abendmahl ist, wir sahen es, in erster Linie – *ein Mahl.* Der Name Meßopfer ist als irreführend zu vermeiden. Gewiß ist dieses Mahl so zu verstehen, daß mit dem (gebrochenen) Brot und dem (roten?) Wein Anteil gegeben wird an dem dahingegebenen Leib und dem vergossenen Blut Jesu. Deshalb die Opferterminologie in den Abendmahlsberichten und die hervorragende Rolle des »für uns«. Indem der Gemeinde Anteil an dieser seiner einmaligen Hingabe, seinem Lebensopfer, gegeben wird, wird sie hineingenommen in den neuen Bund, der durch sein »Opferblut« für die vielen gestiftet wurde. Und so gibt das Mahl den Glaubenden Anteil am einmaligen Kreuzesopfer Jesu. Aber gerade deshalb ist es selber *keine Wiederholung des Kreuzes-»Opfers«.* Vielmehr ist es eine anfänglich in den Häusern in großer Einfachheit und Verständlichkeit durchgeführte *Gedächtnisfeier* (Anamnese, Memoria) und *Dankesfeier* (Eucharistia): in dankbarer, glaubender Erinnerung Teilhabe an der Wirkung dieses einmaligen, bleibenden Lebensopfers Jesu.

Drei Dimensionen müssen gleichzeitig gesehen werden, wenn das Mahl der Gemeinde – das Abendmahl, das Herrenmahl[24], die Eucharistiefeier[25] – richtig verstanden werden soll:

– *Die Dimension der* Vergangenheit: *Die Eucharistiefeier war schon immer wesentlich* Gedächtnis- und Dankesmahl. *Sie soll deshalb nicht als ein steifes Trauermahl für die Gerechten, sondern darf als Freudenmahl auch für die Sünder gefeiert werden.*

– *Die Dimension der* Gegenwart: *Die Eucharistiefeier war und ist zugleich* Bundes- und Gemeinschaftsmahl. *Sie soll folglich nicht als einsames Mahl eines Einzelnen (Winkelmesse), sondern wesentlich als gemeinsames Liebesmahl (Agape) der Gemeinde zusammen mit ihrem gegenwärtigen Herrn gefeiert werden.*

– *Die Dimension der* Zukunft: *Die Eucharistiefeier war von Anfang an* Zeichen und Bild des Vollendungsmahles *im Gottesreich. Sie soll also nicht als ein rückwärts orientiertes Sättigungsmahl, sondern als ein nach vorne zeigendes und zu Taten rufendes Mahl der messianischen Hoffnung gefeiert werden*[26].

Mit diesen Präzisierungen des Opferbegriffs bezüglich Kreuzestod und Abendmahl dürfte jegliches sadistische Gottesverständnis, dem ein masochistisches Menschenverständnis entspräche – man erinnere sich an die Kritik Nietzsches und Freuds – ausgeräumt sein.

Aber damit ist jene große und schwere Menschheitsfrage, die im Hintergrund des Opferbegriffs steht, noch keineswegs beantwortet: Wie verhalten sich Gott und das Leid? Wie soll der Mensch mit der Leidensgeschichte der Menschheit und seiner eigenen Leidensgeschichte fertigwerden? Wie erst soll Gott, der von der Leidensgeschichte angeklagte allmächtige und allgütige Gott, von dieser Anklage freigesprochen werden?

Gott und das Leid

Für manche wie etwa Th. W. Adorno[27] und R. L. Rubinstein[28] genügt schon das eine Wort »Auschwitz«. Und so viele Orte rund um die Erde ließen sich hinzufügen. Das Leid der Menschheit: Wer kann diese *Leidensgeschichte der Menschheit*, der gegenüber die Jahrmillionen der vormenschlichen Naturgeschichte nun doch nicht dasselbe Gewicht haben, überschauen? Diese Geschichte mit ihren Widersprüchen und Konflikten, mit ihrer Ungerechtigkeit, Ungleichheit und sozialen Misere, all dem unheilbaren Krank- und Schuldigwerden, all dem sinnlosen Schicksal und der sinnlosen Bosheit: ein endloser Strom von Blut, Schweiß und Tränen, Schmerz, Trauer und Angst, Verlassenheit, Verzweiflung und Tod. Eine Leidensgeschichte, in der alle Identität, Sinnhaftigkeit und Werthaftigkeit der Wirklichkeit und des menschlichen Daseins immer neu durch Nicht-Identität, Sinnlosigkeit und Wertlosigkeit radikal in Frage gestellt scheint. Eine Leidensgeschichte, in der auch der Urgrund, Ursinn und Urwert der Wirklichkeit und des menschlichen Daseins immer neu durch Chaos, Absurdität, Illusion radikal fraglich wird.

Schon das Leid, das einen einzigen Menschen an einem einzigen Tag treffen kann, läßt nur zu rasch fragen: warum? Warum trifft es mich, gerade mich und jetzt? Und was soll das für einen Sinn haben? Und warum überhaupt dieses ganze furchtbare individuelle und kollektive Leiden, das zum Himmel, nein, das gegen den Himmel schreit? Das anklagt den, der der Schöpfer dieser mit Leid überladenen Menschheit ist? Gott als Inbegriff aller Sinngebung – und so viel Sinnlosigkeit in seiner Welt, so viel sinnloses Leid und sinnlose Schuld. Ist dieser Gott vielleicht doch, wie ihm nicht nur Nietzsche vorgeworfen, ein Despot,

Betrüger, Spieler, Henker? Blasphemien – oder Provokationen Gottes?

Von Epikur bis zum neuzeitlichen Rationalisten Pierre Bayle, bei dem Feuerbach lernte, hat sich die *Antwort der Skeptiker* auf die Frage, warum Gott das Übel nicht verhindert habe, kaum verändert: Entweder Gott kann nicht; ist er dann wirklich allmächtig? Oder er will nicht; ist er dann noch heilig, gerecht, gut? Oder er kann und will nicht; ist er dann nicht machtlos und mißgünstig zugleich? Oder schließlich er kann und will; warum dann aber all die Schlechtigkeit in dieser Welt?

Mythologische Lösungsversuche können uns hier nicht mehr helfen: Weder die dualistische Annahme eines guten und eines gleichrangigen bösen Urprinzips, das den guten Gott nicht mehr den einzigen Gott sein läßt (persische Religion, Markion). Noch eine Rückverschiebung der menschlichen Schuld auf den Anfang, auf von Gott abgefallene Engelmächte, die ja wiederum die Frage an Gott zurückgeben (frühjüdische Apokalyptik). An geschichtsphilosophischen Lösungsversuchen hat es ebenfalls nicht gefehlt. K. Löwith hat anhand der rückwärts geführten Linie Burckhardt – Marx – Hegel – Proudhon, Comte, Turgot, Condorcet – Voltaire – Vico – Bossuet – Joachim von Fiore – Augustin – Orosius aufgezeigt, »daß die moderne Geschichtsphilosophie dem biblischen Glauben an eine Erfüllung entspricht und daß sie mit der Säkularisierung ihres eschatologischen Vorbildes endet.«[29] In systematisch-philosophischer Weise hat in der Neuzeit der universal begabte und vielfältig tätige Philosoph und Theologe Gottfried Wilhelm Leibniz versucht, die Schwierigkeiten, die sich von der Existenz des Übels und des Bösen gegen Gottes Weltherrschaft ergeben, rational – aber letztlich doch getragen von einem unerschütterlichen Vertrauen in den guten Gott – in einer »Rechtfertigung Gottes« oder ›*Theodizee*‹ (1710) zu beantworten[30]. Aber es folgten dem Optimismus der Aufklärung 1755 das Erdbeben von Lissabon und 1789 das Menschheitsbeben der Französischen Revolution. 1791 schreibt Immanuel Kant ›Über das Mißlingen aller philosophischen Versuche in der Theodizee‹[31]. Hegel hat dann in seiner Philosophie der Weltgeschichte nochmals den großen Versuch einer Rechtfertigung Gottes gemacht. Er übersetzte Leibniz' ontologisch-statische Theodizee in eine geschichtlich-dialektische und suchte die widersprüchliche Weltgeschichte als den Gang des göttlichen Weltgeistes selbst zu verstehen: »Daß die Weltgeschichte dieser Entwicklungsgang und das wirkliche

Werden des Geistes ist, unter dem wechselnden Schauspiele ihrer Geschichten – dies ist die wahrhafte Theodizee, die Rechtfertigung Gottes in der Geschichte[32].« Die Weltgeschichte als Gottes Rechtfertigung und deshalb als Weltgericht!

Aber vermögen solche rationalen oder spekulativen Argumente, solche metaphysischen Systeme oder geschichtsphilosophischen Visionen, vermag die ganze List der Vernunft den unter dem Leid fast erdrückten Menschen wahrhaft aufzurichten? Etwa wenn ihm durch Tod oder Untreue ein geliebter Mensch für immer genommen wird oder wenn er selber unheilbar krank oder unmittelbar dem Tod ausgesetzt wird? Wird gegen all dieses existentielle Leid nicht doch nur ein zerebrales Argumentieren oder Spekulieren geboten, das dem Leidenden etwa soviel gibt wie dem Hungernden ein Vortrag über Lebensmittelchemie? Und kann solche rationale Argumentation oder Spekulation helfen, die leidvolle Welt zu verändern, die oppressiven und repressiven Strukturen zu verwandeln und das Leid wenn auch nicht abzuschaffen, so doch auf ein erträgliches Maß zu reduzieren?

Man hat lange Zeit gemeint, die Leidensgeschichte der Menschheit könne gewendet werden dadurch, daß der Mensch im *neuzeitlichen Emanzipationsprozeß* sein Geschick in eigene Verantwortung nehme. Daß an die Stelle des erlösenden Gottes nun der sich selber erlösende, sich emanzipierende Mensch trete: der Mensch statt Gott das Subjekt der Geschichte. Aber wie wir gesehen haben[33], ist es heute fraglicher denn je, daß die wissenschaftlich-technologische Evolution oder auch die politisch-soziale Revolution aus sich eine entscheidende Wende in der Leidensgeschichte der Menschheit bringen könnten. Zwar haben sich die Leiden verändert, aber weniger sind sie deshalb nicht geworden. Und statt Gott steht nun der Mensch unter Anklage, ein Täter von Untaten zu sein, und damit unter dem Zwang der Rechtfertigung: an Stelle einer Theo-dizee eine Anthropo-dizee. Im Zwang der Selbstrechtfertigung aber versucht sich der emanzipierte Mensch zu entlasten, ein *Alibi* zu finden und die Schuld durch verschiedene Entschuldigungsmechanismen von sich abzuschieben. Er übt »die Kunst, es nicht gewesen zu sein«[34]: Als sei er nur für die Erfolge und nicht für die Mißerfolge der technologischen Evolution verantwortlich. Als könnte alle Schuld und alles Versagen einem transzendentalen Ich (Idealismus) oder dem reaktionären, konterrevolutionären Klassenfeind (Marxismus) zugeschoben werden. Als sei überhaupt kein Subjekt für das Leid der Geschichte verantwortlich, sondern nur die

Umwelt des Menschen oder seine genetische Vorprogrammierung oder die Triebabläufe oder ganz allgemein die individuellen, gesellschaftlichen, sprachlichen Strukturen.

Aber ob sich der emanzipierte Mensch angesichts der zwiespältigen Ergebnisse seiner Emanzipation der *Frage seiner Schuld und damit* auch der Frage *seiner wirklichen Erlösung* – und nicht nur seiner Emanzipation – nicht doch stellen sollte? Erlösung wie Emanzipation meinen Befreiung. Aber Emanzipation meint Befreiung des Menschen durch den Menschen, meint Selbstbefreiung des Menschen. Erlösung aber meint Befreiung des Menschen durch Gott, meint keine Selbsterlösung des Menschen. Wie lange Zeit das Wort Erlösung überstrapaziert und affektiv übersetzt war, so heute das Wort Emanzipation[35].

Emanzipation läßt sich gewiß *nicht durch Erlösung ersetzen.* Allzu lange haben Christen das Leid vorschnell mit Gott versöhnt, indem sie es einfach als seinen Willen ausgaben, die Befreiung ins Jenseits verlegt und die versklavten Menschen dorthin vertröstet haben. Es wird heute vom Menschen erwartet, daß er sich selber befreit. Emanzipation als die Selbstbestimmung des Menschen gegenüber blind geglaubter Autorität und nicht legitimierter Herrschaft ist notwendig: Freiheit von Naturzwang, von gesellschaftlichem Zwang, vom Selbstzwang der mit sich selber nicht identischen Person. Emanzipation von Gruppen und Klassen, der Minderheiten, der Frauen, der Staaten. Emanzipation von Bevormundung, Unterprivilegierung und sozialer Unterdrückung.

Aber gerade deshalb gilt auch umgekehrt: *Erlösung* läßt sich nicht *durch Emanzipation ersetzen.* Allzu lange meinten Menschen in der Neuzeit, das vielfältige Leid der Menschen und der Menschheit eigenmächtig abschaffen zu können, indem sie ihm mit Wissenschaft und Technik zu Leibe rückten. Allzu lange meinten sie, die Frage nach der Identität des Menschen, nach dem Sinn des Ganzen des Menschenlebens, nach der Begründung der Moral, nach dem ungetrösteten Leid der Toten und Besiegten und auch die Frage nach der Schuld beiseitelassen zu können.

Erst die Erlösung macht den Menschen frei in einer Tiefe, in die die Emanzipation nicht hinabreicht. Erst Erlösung vermag einen von Schuld befreiten, sich für Zeit und Ewigkeit angenommen wissenden, zu einem sinnvollen Leben und zu einem vorbehaltlosen Einsatz für den Mitmenschen, die Gesellschaft, die Not in dieser Welt befreiten neuen Menschen heraufzuführen. Seiner Leidens-, Schuld- und Todesgeschichte ist ja der Mensch durch seine Emanzipation keineswegs entronnen. Und wenn er in sinnlosem Leiden und Sterben, im Leid auch der Toten und Besiegten dennoch einen Sinn finden will, so ist er auf die letzte Wirklichkeit verwiesen: *Konfrontiert mit Gott,* von dem er, selber der Rechtfertigung bedürftig, freilich nun nicht mehr wie ein Unschuldiger Rechenschaft fordern darf! An seiner wesentlichen Mitverantwortung für die Welt und die Menschheit, wie sie ist, kommt der emanzipierte Mensch nicht vorbei. Und von daher ist ihm die Selbsteinsicht heute vielleicht leichter gemacht als dem nicht emanzipierten Hiob, der sich, wie es scheint, nichts vorzuwerfen hatte. Doch in einer grundsätzlich anderen Situation als Hiob wird er mit seiner Leidensgeschichte Gott gegenüber nie sein. Mit intellektuellen Argumenten kommt er sowenig weiter wie Hiobs Freunde. Alle Ratio hat am Leid ihre Grenze.

»Warum leide ich? Das ist der Fels des Atheismus«, sagt Georg Büchner[36]. Die Einstellung zum Leid hängt zutiefst mit der Einstellung zu Gott und zur Wirklichkeit überhaupt zusammen: Im Leid kommt der Mensch an seine äußerste Grenze, zur entscheidenden Frage nach seiner Identität, nach Sinn und Unsinn seines Lebens, ja der Wirklichkeit überhaupt. Immer wieder erweist sich das *Leid als der Testfall für Gottvertrauen und Grundvertrauen,* der Entscheidungen herausfordert. Wo wird das Gottvertrauen mehr provoziert als im ganz konkreten Leid? Schon manch einem wurde konkretes Leid Anlaß zum Unglauben – manch anderem zum Glauben. Und wo wird das Grundvertrauen zur Wirklichkeit überhaupt mehr herausgefordert als angesichts allen Leids und Bösen in Welt und eigenem Leben? Schon manch einem wurde überwältigendes Leid Anstoß zum Grundmißtrauen gegenüber der Wirklichkeit überhaupt – manch anderem aber zum Grundvertrauen.

Angesichts der überwältigenden Realität des Leids in der Menschheitsgeschichte und im einzelnen Menschenleben gibt es für den leidenden, zweifelnden, verzweifelnden Menschen doch eine Alternative zur Empörung etwa eines Iwan Karamasoff gegen diese für ihn inakzeptable Gotteswelt[37], oder zur Revolte eines Albert Camus, der wie Dostojewski auf die Leiden der unschuldigen Kreatur hinweist[38]. Statt sich als emanzipierter, autonomer Prometheus trotzig gegen die Macht der Götter aufzulehnen oder dann wie Sisyphos den Felsblock vergeblich immer neu den Berg hinaufzuwälzen, von dessen Gipfel der Stein von selbst wieder hinunterrollt, kann er die Haltung des *Hiob* einnehmen: Er kann dem unbegreiflichen Gott trotz allem Leid dieser Welt ein *unbedingtes, unerschütterliches Vertrauen* entgegenbringen. Mit Resignation und Passivität hatte dies schon bei Hiob nichts zu tun. Gewiß kann einer sagen: Wenn man das unendliche Leid der Welt anschaut, kann man nicht glauben, daß es einen Gott gibt. Aber läßt sich das nicht auch umdrehen? Nur wenn es einen Gott gibt, kann man dieses unendliche Leid der Welt überhaupt anschauen! Nur im vertrauenden Glauben an den unbegreiflichen, immer größeren Gott kann der Mensch in begründeter Hoffnung jenen breiten, tiefen Fluß durchschreiten: im Bewußtsein, daß ihm über den dunklen Abgrund des Leids und des Bösen eine Hand entgegengestreckt wird.

Freilich kehrt die *Frage* immer wieder: Was ist das für ein unbegreiflicher, *teilnahmsloser Gott,* der erhaben über allem Leid den Menschen in seinem unermeßlichen Elend sitzen, kämpfen, protestieren, umkommen läßt? Aber auch diese Frage läßt sich umkehren: Ist Gott wirklich so erhaben über allem Leid, wie wir ihn uns menschlich vorstellen und bei allen unseren Protesten voraussetzen, wie ihn gerade die Philosophen denken? Erscheint Gott nicht gerade in Leiden und Sterben *Jesu* nun doch in einem anderen Licht[39]?

Für Hiob war nur die *Unbegreiflichkeit* des aus dem Leid erlösenden Gottes offenbar geworden. Auf sie soll der Mensch sein gläubiges Vertrauen setzen, auch wenn er nichts versteht und schließlich doch noch sterben muß: eine Haltung, die im konkreten Leid so schwierig durchzuhalten ist und die auch in Israel, nach dem schriftlichen Niederschlag zu schließen, wenig Gefolgschaft gefunden hat. Ist nun aber in *Jesu* Leiden und Sterben nicht über alle Unbegreiflichkeit Gottes hinaus eine *definitive Erlösung* aus dem Leid durch den unbegreiflichen Gott offenbar geworden, die Leid und Tod zum Leben und zur Erfüllung der Sehnsucht wandelt? Macht das nicht einen ganz anders verstehenden Glauben möglich, auch wenn solch verstehender Glaube immer Glaube bleibt? Das *Faktum* des Leidens jedes Menschen kann auch von Jesus her nicht rückgängig gemacht werden. Es bleibt hier immer ein Rest von Zweifel möglich. Wohl aber soll und kann das *rechte Verhältnis* des Menschen zum Leid, der *Stellenwert* und ein verborgener *Sinn* des Leids von hierher deutlich werden.

Auch Jesus hat ja das menschliche Leid nicht erklärt, sondern als der vor Gott Schuldlose *durchlitten,* durchlitten freilich – anders als Hiob – *bis zum bitteren Ende.* Seine Geschichte war anders: real, nicht fiktional. Sein Ende war anders: kein »happy end«, keine Wiedergutmachung in einem schönen Leben. Sein Leid war anders: die Quittung auf sein Leben, und definitiv bis in sein Sterben. Von Jesu definitiver Passion, seinem Leiden *und* Sterben her, könnte die Passion eines jeden Menschen, die Menschheitspassion überhaupt, einen Sinn erhalten, den die schlicht zum unbedingten Glauben und Vertrauen aufrufende Hiobserzählung nicht vermitteln kann.

Freilich darf dann das Leiden Jesu nicht nur »existential« als Chiffre (»das Faktum des Gestorbenseins«) für das private Selbstverständnis der dem Tode verfallenen Existenz genommen werden. Und auch nicht rein »futurisch« als Verheißung einer noch völlig in der Zukunft liegenden utopischen Freiheit von Leid, Schuld und Tod. Und schließlich auch nicht hoch »spekulativ« als eine sich dialektisch zwischen Gott und Gott, Gott gegen Gott abspielende innertrinitarische (ewige?) Leidensgeschichte eines gekreuzigten Gottes[40]: wo die Identifikation Jesu mit Gott direkt statt indirekt vollzogen wird und der Unterschied zwischen Vater und Sohn überspielt wird zugunsten der einen göttlichen »Natur« oder »Substanz« im Sinne der späteren hellenistischen und insbesondere lateinischen Trinitätsspekulation[41].

Das historische Leiden und Sterben Jesu darf also weder durch existentiale Reduktion noch durch utopische Futurisierung noch durch überhöhende Spekulation in argumentative Theologie aufgelöst, sondern muß als das, was es war, immer wieder neu erzählt werden[42]. Soll es aber nicht bei einem wenig hilfreichen naiven Nacherzählen der biblischen Geschichten bleiben oder gar zu einer Neuaufnahme von Mythen (wie der Höllenfahrt[43]) kommen, braucht es zugleich die mit dem Blick auf die Gegenwart vollzogene historisch-kritische Reflexion. Eine solche hat uns gezeigt[44], wie Jesu erschütternde Passion in der Konsequenz seiner ganzen Aktion lag: Die vom Standpunkt der offiziellen Religion völlig zu Recht erfolgte Verurteilung des Ketzers, Pseudopropheten, Gotteslästerers und Volksverführers zu einem Tod in Schande machte offenkundig, daß er mit dem wahren Gott nichts zu tun hatte. Sein Tod in Menschenverlassenheit, so sahen wir, war charakterisiert durch eine unvergleichliche, uneingeschränkte Gottverlassenheit: absolut allein gelassen von dem, auf dessen Nähe er alles gesetzt hatte. Alles umsonst, ein sinnloses Sterben, das sich nicht mystifizieren läßt.

Allein von der geglaubten Auferweckung Jesu zu neuem Leben mit Gott kommt ein *Sinn in dieses sinnlose Sterben:* Erst im Licht dieses neuen Lebens aus Gott wird es deutlich: daß der Tod doch nicht umsonst war. Daß der Gott, der ihn in aller Öffentlichkeit fallenzulassen schien, ihn doch durch den Tod hindurch gehalten hat. Daß Gott ihn, der wie kein anderer zuvor die Gottverlassenheit zu spüren bekam, nicht verlassen hatte. Daß Gott selbst in seiner öffentlichen Abwesenheit verborgen anwesend geblieben war. Von daher also kommt ein Sinn in dieses sinnlose menschliche Leiden und Sterben, den der Mensch, leidend und sterbend, auf keinen Fall selber produzieren, den er sich vielmehr nur von einem ganz Anderen, von Gott selbst schenken lassen kann.

Kann von dem bereits *vollendeten* Leiden und Sterben dieses Einen nicht auch ein verborgener Sinn in dem aus sich sinnlosen Leiden und Sterben der Vielen aufscheinen? Das Leiden des Menschen bleibt Leiden. Tod bleibt Tod. Vergangenes Leid wird nicht ungeschehen, gegenwärtiges nicht harmlos, zukünftiges nicht unmöglich gemacht. Leiden und Tod bleiben ein Angriff auf das Leben des Menschen. Das Leiden soll nicht umgedeutet, verniedlicht oder glorifiziert werden. Es soll auch nicht stoisch hingenommen, apathisch-affektlos ertragen werden. Es soll erst recht nicht selbstquälerisch gesucht, ihm gar asketisch Lust abgewonnen werden. Es soll vielmehr, wie später noch deutlicher werden muß, im individuellen wie im gesellschaftlichen Bereich, in den Personen wie in den Strukturen mit allen menschlichen Mitteln bekämpft werden.

Nur das eine allerdings Entscheidende läßt sich vom Leiden und Sterben dieses einen sinnlos Leidenden und Sterbenden her sagen. Auch manifest sinnloses menschliches Leiden und Sterben *kann* einen Sinn haben, kann einen Sinn *bekommen.* Einen verborgenen Sinn: Der Mensch kann ihn nicht selbst dem Leiden anheften, aber er kann ihn im Licht des vollendeten Leidens und Sterbens dieses Einen empfangen. Keine automatische Sinn-Gebung: es soll hier kein menschliches Wunschdenken befriedigt, keine Leidverklärung proklamiert, kein psychisches Beruhigungsmittel und kein billiger Trost vermittelt werden. Wohl aber ein freibleibendes *Sinn-Angebot:* Der Mensch hat zu entscheiden. Er kann diesen – verborgenen – Sinn ablehnen: in Trotz, Zynismus oder Verzweiflung. Er kann ihn auch annehmen: in glaubendem Vertrauen auf den, der dem sinnlosen Leiden und Sterben Jesu Sinn verliehen hat. Es erübrigt sich dann der Protest, die Empörung, schließlich die Frustration. Es endet die Verzweiflung.

Der Christ, der auf die Auferweckung des einen Leidenden

zum Leben sieht, hat selbst die Auferweckung nicht hinter sich, sondern noch vor sich. Das Leid bleibt ein Übel. Aber im Vertrauen auf Gott nicht mehr das unbedingte Übel, das wie im Buddhismus durch Verneinung des Lebenswillens in einem Nirwana aufzuheben wäre. Unbedingtes Übel bleibt allein die Trennung von Gott, außer dem das Übel keinen Sinn hat. Das Leiden gehört zum Menschen. Es gehört faktisch zum vollgültigen Menschsein in dieser Welt: selbst Liebe ist mit Leid verbunden. Durch Leiden soll der Mensch zum Leben gelangen. Warum das so ist, warum das für den Menschen gut und sinnvoll ist, warum es nicht ohne Leid besser ginge, das kann keine Vernunft erweisen. Das kann aber vom Leiden, Sterben und neuen Leben Jesu im Vertrauen auf Gott schon in der Gegenwart als sinnvoll angenommen werden, in der Gewißheit der Hoffnung auf ein Offenbarwerden des Sinnes in der Vollendung.

So steht denn der noch immer leidende Mensch in der Dialektik des (naturgemäß gegebenen) Leidens und der (im Glauben geschenkten) Freiheit vom Leiden. Er muß noch leiden und muß noch sterben. Aber weder Leiden noch Sterben kann ihn in Angst um die Hoffnung bringen. *In sich* ist das Leid meist sinn-los. *Im Blick auf den einen Leidenden* ist ein Sinn-Angebot gemacht, das gegen allen Wider-Sinn nur vertrauensvoll ergriffen sein will, um wissen zu können: Eine Situation mag noch so trostlos, sinnlos, verzweifelt sein – auch hier ist Gott da. Nicht nur im Licht und in der Freude, auch im Dunkel, in der Trauer, im Schmerz, in der Melancholie *kann* ich ihm begegnen. Das Leiden an sich ist kein Zeichen der Abwesenheit Gottes. Vom Leiden des Einen her ist es als Weg zu Gott offenbar geworden. Was von Leibniz behauptet und von Dostojewski dunkel erspürt, das wird dem Hiob bestätigt und vom auferweckten Gekreuzigten her definitiv offenbar und gewiß: Auch das Leiden ist von *Gott* umfangen, auch das Leid kann bei aller Gottverlassenheit Ort der Gottbegegnung *werden*! Der Glaubende weiß keinen Weg am Leid vorbei, aber er weiß einen Weg hindurch: in aktiver Indifferenz gelassen gegenüber dem Leid und gerade so zum Kampf gegen das Leid und seine Ursachen bereit. Mit dem Blick auf den einen Leidenden in glaubendem Vertrauen auf den, der auch und gerade im Leid verborgen anwesend ist und der *selbst in äußerster Bedrohung, Sinnlosigkeit, Nichtigkeit, Verlassenheit, Einsamkeit und Leere den Menschen trägt und hält:* ein Gott, der als Mit-Betroffener neben den Menschen steht, ein Gott solidarisch mit den Menschen. Kein Kreuz der Welt kann das Sinn-Angebot widerlegen, das im Kreuz des zum Leben Erweckten ergangen ist.

Nirgendwo so deutlich wie hier ist erwiesen worden, daß dieser Gott nicht nur ein Gott der Starken, Gesunden und Erfolgreichen, ein Gott der stärkeren Bataillone ist. Gerade im Leid kann sich Gott als der erweisen, als den ihn Jesus verkündigt hat, als, wie wir sahen[45], Vater der Verlorenen. Dieser selber ist die Antwort auf die Frage nach der Theodizee, nach den Lebensrätseln, dem Leid, der Ungerechtigkeit, dem Tod in der Welt. Als Vater der Verlorenen nun nicht mehr ein Gott in transzendenter Ferne, sondern ein Gott dem Menschen nahe in unbegreiflicher Güte, ihm großzügig und großmütig durch die Geschichte nachgehend, auch in der Dunkelheit, Vergeblichkeit und Sinnlosigkeit zum Wagnis der Hoffnung einladend, auch in der Gottferne ihn barmherzig auffangend.

Nirgendwo deutlicher als in Jesu Leben und Wirken, Leiden und Sterben ist es sichtbar geworden: Dieser Gott ist ein Gott für die Menschen, ein Gott, der ganz auf unserer Seite steht! Nicht ein angstmachender theokratischer Gott »von oben«, sondern ein menschenfreundlicher *mit-leidender Gott* »mit uns unten«. Wir reden hier, es braucht nicht betont zu werden, in Bildern, Symbolen, Analogien. Aber man versteht, was gemeint ist und was jetzt noch deutlicher als früher zum Ausdruck kam: Nicht ein grausamer Willkür- und Gesetzesgott hat sich in Jesus manifestiert, sondern ein dem Menschen als rettende Liebe begegnender Gott, der sich in Jesus mit dem leidenden Menschen solidarisiert hat. Wo nämlich wird das deutlicher als in dem durch die Auferweckung bestätigten und mit einem anderen Vorzeichen versehenen Kreuz? Nirgendwo deutlicher als im Kreuz wurde offenbar, daß dieser Gott tatsächlich ein Gott auf der Seite der Schwachen, Kranken, Armen, Unterprivilegierten, Unterdrückten, ja der Unfrommen, Unmoralischen und Gottlosen ist. Ein Gott, der anders als die Götter der Heiden sich nicht rächt an denen, die gegen ihn fehlen; der sich nicht bezahlen und bestechen läßt von denen, die etwas von ihm wollen; der den Menschen ihr Glück nicht neidet, der nicht ihre Liebe fordert und sie schließlich doch noch fallen läßt. Sondern ein Gott, der Gnade verschenkt an die, die sie nicht verdienen. Der neidlos gibt und nie enttäuscht. Der Liebe nicht fordert, sondern schenkt: der selber ganz Liebe ist. Und so ist denn auch das Kreuz nicht als das von einem grausamen Gott geforderte Opfer zu verstehen. Von Ostern her verstand man es gerade umgekehrt als die tiefste

Äußerung seiner Liebe. Die *Liebe,* durch die Gott – weniger in einem abstrakten »Wesen« als in seinem Wirken, seiner »Art« – definiert werden kann[46]: Liebe nicht als Affekt, sondern ein »Dasein für«, ein »Tun des Guten für andere«. Eine Liebe, die also nicht abstrakt bestimmt werden darf, sondern immer nur im Blick auf diesen Jesus.

Dieser Gott der Liebe war es nach Paulus, der nicht einmal seinen eigenen Sohn geschont, sondern ihn für uns dahingegeben hat; wie sollte er also mit ihm nicht auch uns alles schenken[47]? Und dies ist dann der Grund, weswegen dem Christen nach Paulus nichts, aber auch gar nichts gefährlich werden kann: weil ihn nichts trennen kann von dieser Liebe Gottes, wie sie in Jesus Christus manifestiert geworden ist[48]. Daß solche Theodizee nicht nur theologische Theorie ist, sondern in der Praxis gelebt und bewährt werden kann, zeigt Paulus in seinem eigenen Leben[49].

Gegen einen über allem Leid in ungestörter Glückseligkeit oder apathischer Transzendenz thronenden Gott kann der Mensch revoltieren. Aber auch gegen den Gott, der in Jesu Leid sein ganzes Mit-Leid geoffenbart hat? Gegen eine abstrakt betrachtete Gerechtigkeit Gottes und gegen eine für die Gegenwart prästabilierte oder für die Zukunft postulierte Harmonie des Universums kann der Mensch revoltieren. Aber auch gegen die in Jesus manifest gewordene Liebe des Vaters der Verlorenen, die in ihrer Voraussetzungslosigkeit und Grenzenlosigkeit auch mein Leid umfaßt, meine Empörung zum Schweigen bringt, meine Frustration überwindet und mir in allen anhaltenden Nöten ein Durchhalten und schließlich ein Obsiegen ermöglicht?

Gottes Liebe bewahrt nicht *vor* allem Leid. Sie bewahrt aber *in* allem Leid. So hebt in der Gegenwart an, was freilich erst in der Zukunft vollendet werden wird: die Rechtfertigung Gottes in der Rechtfertigung des Menschen, aller Menschen, auch der Toten und Besiegten, die Theodizee als Anthropodizee. Die Harmonie, die nicht billig ungesühnt, sondern im Kreuz aufgerichtet ist. Der definitive Sieg der Liebe eines Gottes, der nicht ein teilnahmsloses und liebloses Wesen ist, den Leid und Unrecht nicht rühren können, sondern der sich in Liebe selber des Leids der Menschen angenommen hat und annehmen wird. Der Sieg der Liebe Gottes, wie sie Jesus verkündet und manifestiert hat, als der letzten, entscheidenden Macht: das ist das Gottesreich! Denn die Sehnsucht Horkheimers und ungezählter in der Menschheitsgeschichte nach Gerechtigkeit in der Welt, nach echter Transzendenz, nach »dem ganz Anderen«, »daß der Mörder nicht über das unschuldige Opfer triumphieren möge«[50], soll in Erfüllung gehen, wie auf den letzten Seiten der Schrift jenseits aller kritischen Theorie und kritischen Theologie verheißen: »Gott selbst wird als ihr Gott bei ihnen sein. Er wird alle ihre Tränen abwischen. Es wird keinen Tod mehr geben und keine Traurigkeit, keine Klage und keine Quälerei. Was einmal war, ist für immer vorbei[51].«

Soviel zu den Deutungen des Todes Jesu. Machen aber die Deutungen seines Ursprungs nicht noch mehr Schwierigkeiten?

3. Deutungen des Ursprungs

Weihnachten gilt manchem noch heute als das Hauptfest der Christenheit, und die Menschwerdung Gottes als ihr Zentraldogma. Alles Vorausgegangene aber hat davon überzeugen können, daß nicht Jesu Geburt, sondern sein Tod und sein neues Leben mit Gott die unverwechselbare Mitte der christlichen Botschaft ausmachen.

Mensch geworden

Die drei »heiligen Nächte« der großen Weltreligionen – die Erleuchtung des Buddha, das Herabkommen des Koran und die Geburt Jesu – können gewiß nicht, wie manchmal geschehen, auf dieselbe Ebene gestellt werden. Aber läßt sich übersehen, daß *außergewöhnliche Ereignisse von der Geburt auch der großen Religionsstifter überliefert* sind und somit für eine Einzigartigkeit Jesu von Nazaret nichts hergeben? Jungfräuliche Empfängnis, wunderbare Geburt, Engelserscheinungen, Teufelsversuchungen – solches wird auch von den Religionsstiftern erzählt und ist kein Charakteristikum Jesu. Wunder umrahmen die Geburt Buddhas, Kung-futses, Zarathustras und Mohammeds. Auch die Geburt des Propheten Mohammed wird der Mutter durch einen Engel verheißen. Bei Zarathustra geschieht schon die Empfängnis unter wunderbaren Begleitumständen. Aus dem Samen Zarathustras in einer Jungfrau entsteht der persische Weltheiland Saoshyant. Auch bei Buddha geschieht eine jungfräuliche Empfängnis, da Buddha in der Gestalt eines weißen Elefanten in den Leib der Maya ein- und aus ihrer Seite wieder ausgeht. Engel erscheinen bei der Geburt Mohammeds und Kung-futses. Und allerlei wunderbare Leistungen werden nicht nur – wie nach einigen apokryphen Texten – vom Knaben Jesus, sondern auch vom jungen Prinzen Siddharta berichtet. Und wie Jesus so werden auch Buddha und Zarathustra vom bösen Geist versucht. Reduzierte sich also die Gottessohnschaft Jesu auf derartige außerordentliche Ereignisse bei der Geburt oder mirakulöse Taten im Leben, so könnte er in eine Reihe gestellt werden mit den Religionsstiftern, von anderen Heroen und mehr oder weniger dubiosen Wundertätern der Antike ganz zu schweigen.

1. Das unterscheidend Christliche ist und bleibt das Kreuz. Aber *vom Kreuz des Auferweckten schauen die ersten Zeugen zurück:* auf den Anfang des Lebens Jesu. Auch die Aussagen über die *Menschwerdung* des Gottessohnes wären eine »Göttergeschichte«, wären reine Mythologie, wenn sie nicht im Zusammenhang der Botschaft von Kreuz und Auferweckung gesehen würden. Ursprünglich wollten sie doch nur erklären, wer hier eigentlich gelitten, sich dahingegeben, solchen Gehorsam bewiesen hatte[1]. Wir sahen, wie schon die Urgemeinde Jesus den »Sohn« und den »Gottessohn« genannt hat: den Sachwalter, Bevollmächtigten und Sprecher, ja den persönlichen Botschafter, Treuhänder, Repräsentanten, Platzhalter und Stellvertreter Gottes[2]. Zunächst von der jüdischen Tradition her wird mit den Vorstellungen des Gottessohnes, dann auch des vom Geist Gezeugten, des Präexistenten und Schöpfungsmittlers Person und Sache Jesu gedeutet: Vorstellungen, welche dann in die sehr verschiedene Umgebung und Sprache der hellenistischen Welt übertragen wurden und dort dann ganz andere Assoziationen hervorrufen mußten. Diesen nicht ganz einfachen Zusammenhängen werden wir im Folgenden nachgehen.

Der Name und Begriff »in-carnatio« (»en-sarkosis«, »Fleischwerdung«, »Menschwerdung«) drängte sich vom Johannesprolog her mächtig auf. Hier und hier allein findet sich im Neuen Testament jene Idee des von Ewigkeit bei Gott und als Gott, in Gottes Wesenheit vorausexistierenden göttlichen *»Logos«* oder *»Wortes«*: das schon nach der jüdischen Weisheitsliteratur (und vorchristlichen Gnosis?) personhaft und vorzeitlich bei der Weltschöpfung zugegen war und bei den Menschen eine Stätte fand[3]. Das dann in Philons Spekulationen als Gottes erstgeborener Sohn und zweiter Gott, als Gottes Abbild und Urbild der Dinge, als Organ der Schöpfung und Offenbarung erscheint[4]. Das schließlich im Johannesprolog als göttliche Person »Fleisch« wird für die Menschen: Jesu Menschwerdung als Gottes *Offenbarung* (Leben, Licht, Wahrheit) in der Welt[5].

Aber schon in den paulinischen und deuteropaulinischen Schriften zeichnen sich nicht wenige Aussagen zur Menschwerdung des Gottessohnes ab, die bekenntnishaft[6] oder hymnisch[7] gefaßt sind und weithin auf bereits vorpaulinisches Formelgut zurückgehen dürften[8]. Die früheste Aussage ist jener von Paulus erweiterte vorpaulinische Hymnus im Philipperbrief von Jesus Christus, der in Gottes Gestalt war und es nicht für einen »Raub« hielt, mit Gott zu sein, sondern sich selbst entäußerte, indem er Knechtsgestalt annahm und den Menschen ähnlich wurde: Der Erscheinung nach wie ein Mensch erfunden, erniedrigte er sich selbst und wurde gehorsam bis zum Tod, ja, bis zum Tod am Kreuz[9]. Menschwerdung also verstanden als *Entäußerung* und *Erniedrigung*: zur Begründung christlicher Liebe und Selbstlosigkeit!

Die nachpaulinischen Pastoralbriefe nennen die Menschwerdung Jesu Christi gerne eine *»Epiphanie«*[10]. Keine harmlose liturgische Aussage, wenn man sie in ihre Zeit hineinstellt. In der hellenistischen Zeit wurde das segenbringende »Erscheinen« der Götter in den Mysterienkulten, aber auch das »Erscheinen« des Herrschers im Staatsbesuch gefeiert und in gehobener antiker Sakralsprache angekündigt. In den Christengemeinden jedoch wird nun das »Erscheinen« des »Heilandes« Jesus (griechisch »soter«: ein hellenistischer Titel für göttliche »Retter«) und seiner »Gnade«, »Menschenfreundlichkeit«, »Güte« – in seinem ganzen Leben von der Menschwerdung bis zum Tode – proklamiert! Noch am Anfang des leidvollen fünfzehnjährigen Bürgerkrieges nach Cäsars Ermordung um 42 oder 41 *vor* Jesu Geburt hatte der römische Dichter Vergil in seiner berühmten vierten Ekloge die Geburt eines Weltenheilandes angekündigt. In der Hoffnung auf Cäsars Großneffen und Adoptivsohn Oktavius und sein Haus? Jedenfalls ließ dieser, im Jahre 29 nach dem Sieg auch noch über Antonius und Kleopatra endlich als Alleinherrscher nach Rom zurückgekehrt, als erste Amtshandlung den Janustempel, den Tempel des doppelgesichtigen Kriegsgottes, schließen. Und auch weiterhin tat der »Augustus Divi Filius« – des »Göttlichen (= des zwei Jahre nach seinem Tod zum Staatsgott erhobenen Cäsar) Sohn«, im griechischen Osten mit »Gottessohn« übersetzt! – alles, um die von Vergil genährte Utopie eines anbrechenden Friedensreiches wahrzunehmen: Pax Romana, Pax Augusta, besiegelt mit der Weihe der riesigen Ara Pacis Augustae, des augusteischen Friedensaltars im Jahre 9 vor Jesu Geburt. Im selben Jahr wurde im Osten (nach der berühmten 1890 im kleinasiatischen Priene und dann auch anderswo gefundenen Inschrift) das »Evangelium« vom Geburtstag des jetzt erschienenen »Heilandes« und »Gottes« Cäsar Augustus der ganzen Welt verkündet, welcher der verdorbenen Welt neues Leben, Glück, Frieden, Erfüllung der Hoffnung der Vorfahren, Heil gebracht hat[11].

Liest man vor dem Hintergrund dieser politischen Theologie der Cäsaren die lukanische Ankündigung eines »Gottessohnes« und »Heilandes« in einem Winkel des Imperiums – von ihr wird noch die Rede sein müssen – nicht mit etwas weniger »weihnachtlichen« Augen? Und liest man nicht auch mit anderen Augen, wenn in den Pastoralbriefen in ganz ähnlich feierlichen Worten, ebenfalls in der Weihnachtsliturgie verwendet, das »Erscheinen« des »Heilandes« und »Gottes« Jesus Christus proklamiert wird[12]? Nach der Priene-Inschrift sollte mit dem *Geburtstag* des Gott-Heilands Augustus am 23. September künftig offiziell das Jahr (samt Antritt der öffentlichen Ämter) beginnen. Seit dem 4. Jahrhundert wird der Geburtstag Jesu am 25. Dezember gefeiert: »Natalis Christi« – vermutlich in bewußter Opposition gegen einen für den 25. Dezember (Wintersonnenwende) offiziell neu eingeführten römischen Reichsfeiertag »Natalis Solis Invicti« (Geburtstag des unbesiegten Sonnengottes). Und mit diesem Tag war dann, wie bemerkt, für Jahrhunderte der Jahresbeginn verbunden, bis er aus vorwiegend praktischen Gründen auf den nächstliegenden Monatsanfang, den 1. Januar, verlegt wurde. Dieses römische Weihnachtsfest setzte sich sogar im Osten durch, wo etwa in Jerusalem das Fest der »Epiphanie« (oder »Theophanie«) durchaus Jesu Geburtstag und nicht das Fest der Magier (»Dreikönigstag«) oder auch der Taufe Jesu war.

Freilich, unbedenklich ist die vom Menschwerdungsgedanken ausgehende Entwicklung keineswegs. Oder läßt sich übersehen, daß es durch eine vermehrte Konzentration auf die Menschwerdung in der christlichen Theologie und Frömmigkeit schon früh zu einer Akzentverlagerung kam? Einer Akzentverlagerung, die von der ursprünglichen Botschaft nicht gedeckt war und die auch heute ein Verständnis der christlichen Botschaft erheblich erschwert? Einer Akzentverlagerung von Tod und Auferweckung auf ewige Präexistenz und Menschwerdung: der Mensch Jesus von Nazaret im Schatten des Gottessohnes?

2. In der Tat läßt sich nicht bestreiten, daß die ursprüngliche, von unten ansetzende und in Tod und Auferweckung zentrierte *Erhöhungschristologie* (Erhöhung des menschlichen Messias zum Sohn Gottes, Zwei-Stufen-Christologie) faktisch immer mehr *überholt* wurde *durch eine oben einsetzende Inkarnationschristologie*: Menschwerdung des Gottessohnes, dessen Entäußerung und Erniedrigung freilich Voraussetzung für die Erhöhung ist. Man kann auch sagen: Die »aufsteigende« Aszendenz-Christologie, für welche die Gottessohnschaft alttestamentlich eine Erwählung und Annahme an Sohnes Statt (in Erhöhung, Taufe, Geburt) bedeutet, wurde ergänzt oder gar ersetzt durch eine »herabsteigende« *Deszendenz-Christologie*. Für sie bedeutet die Gottessohnschaft eine – immer genauer in hellenistischen Begriffen und Vorstellungen zu umschreibende – *seinshafte Zeugung* höherer Art. Es geht jetzt weniger um die alttestamentlich verstandene Rechts- und Machtstellung Jesu Christi, sondern um seine hellenistisch verstandene *Abkunft*. Es geht weniger um die Funktion als um das Wesen. Begriffe wie Wesen, Natur, Substanz, Hypothese, Person, Union sollten eine wachsende Bedeutung bekommen.

»*Gottessohn*« meint somit für die hellenistischen Hörer nicht mehr nur den Sachwalter, Bevollmächtigten, Sprecher, Platzhalter und Stellvertreter Gottes[13], sondern ganz selbstverständlich ein göttliches Wesen, das kraft seiner göttlichen Natur von der menschlichen Sphäre unterschieden ist. Ein übermenschliches Wesen göttlichen Ursprungs und göttlicher Kraft! Ein Wesen, das bei Gott von Ewigkeit vorausexistiert, aber in der Fülle der Zeit eine menschliche Gestalt annimmt und im Menschen Jesus erscheint. Zweierlei ist somit mit »Gottessohn« in einem gesagt: die *Unterscheidung von Gott*, dem Vater (Gehorsam, Unterordnung), und die Identifizierung mit Gott, dem Vater (Einheit mit Gott, Göttlichkeit).

Auf diese *Einheit mit Gott* – jetzt nicht mehr in geschichtlichen und personalen, sondern in Seinskategorien umschrieben – wird nun aber immer mehr und oft einseitig Gewicht gelegt. Freilich meint im Neuen Testament selbst der Terminus »Gott« praktisch immer den Vater. Doch sowohl die Übertragung des Gottessohnnamens wie auch schon des göttlichen Kyriosnamens (Herr Jesus) mußte im hellenistischen Raum die Übertragung göttlicher Eigenschaften auf Jesus mit sich bringen, mußte ein Nachdenken über seine göttliche Herrschaftsstellung, Würde, Wesenheit, kurz seine Göttlichkeit zur Folge haben. Jene früheste, noch sehr vage und unentwickelte Aussage über Jesu Präexistenz und Menschwerdung im Philipper-Hymnus läßt dies bereits sichtbar werden. Doch ist man hier offensichtlich weniger am Gottsein Jesu interessiert als vielmehr am Geschehen, das in Jesus von Gott her in Gang gekommen ist. Bei Paulus selber wird Jesus zur Absetzung von den vielen Herren und Göttern »der Herr« genannt und dieses Herrsein schon für sein vorweltliches Sein behauptet. Im Zusammenhang der Weltschöpfung werden an einer Stelle[14] »der Herr« (Jesus) und »Gott« (der Vater) einander sehr nahegerückt. Gott selber wird im Neuen Testament weniger »Herr« genannt, das ist nun im allgemeinen der Name für Jesus. Umgekehrt aber wird Jesus kaum einmal direkt »Gott« genannt, von Paulus selbst überhaupt nie. Bis in den Wortgebrauch hinein ist man also durchaus an einer Unterscheidung interessiert. Von einer Menschwerdung Gottes selbst ist im Neuen Testament nirgendwo die Rede. Deutlich werden erst im Johannesevangelium, im Ausruf des ungläubigen Thomas »Mein Herr und mein Gott«[15], diese beiden gewichtigsten Prädikationen zusammen auf Jesus übertragen. Außerhalb des Johannesevangeliums wird Jesus nur in wenigen, durchwegs späten, hellenistisch beeinflußten Ausnahmefällen direkt als »Gott« bezeichnet[16]. Aber dies sollte sich nun in der griechischen Theologie rasch ändern.

Vergöttlichung oder Vermenschlichung?

1. Die *griechische Theologie* der Folgezeit zog aus dem neuen hellenistischen Verständnis der Gottessohnschaft sehr weitreichende und nicht unproblematische Konsequenzen: Schon Ignatios von Antiochien um die Jahrhundertwende nennt Jesus ganz selbstverständlich »Gott«[17]. Und schon um dieselbe Zeit muß nun im hellenistischen Raum in einem verständlichen Frontwechsel nicht mehr wie im jüdischen Raum die göttliche Vollmacht und Autorität des Menschensohnes, sondern die wahre Menschlichkeit und Leidensfähigkeit des Gottessohnes (gegen gnostische Irrlehrer) verteidigt werden[18]. Den jüdischen Monotheismus wollte freilich weder Ignatios noch einer der späteren aufgeben; ein Bi-theismus oder Tri-theismus wurde grundsätz-

lich stets abgelehnt. Aber je mehr Jesus als der Sohn auf eine Seinsebene mit dem Vater gestellt wurde und je mehr man dieses Verhältnis mit naturhaften Kategorien beschrieb, um so mehr Schwierigkeiten hatte man, den *Monotheismus* und die *Gottessohnschaft*, die Unterscheidung von Gott und die Einheit mit Gott begrifflich zusammenzudenken.

So hilfreich und unvermeidlich manche hellenistischen Vorstellungen im hellenistischen Raum waren: Für die Predigt des Evangeliums von Jesus Christus unter den Juden und viele Jahrhunderte später unter den Moslems bedeutete diese Entwicklung beinahe unübersteigbare Schwierigkeiten und praktisch ein völliges Scheitern der Mission. Für die christliche Gemeinschaft selber führte sie zu ungeahnten theologischen Verwirrungen mit ständigen kirchenpolitischen Verwicklungen. An die Denk- und Lebensformen des Hellenismus, bestimmt von Philosophenschulen, Mysterienkulten und römischem Staat, hatte man sich weithin angepaßt. Immer zugespitzter wurden die philosophisch bestimmten Begriffe, immer differenzierter die Unterscheidungen zwischen den Schulen, immer komplizierter die Erklärungen, immer zahlreicher die Absicherungen der Orthodoxie durch Dogmen, die Staatsgesetze wurden. Aber auch immer zahlreicher wurden die Mißverständnisse, die Parteiungen, ja Spaltungen. Auch die großen ökumenischen Konzilien der nachkonstantinischen Ära konnten sie nur teilweise überwinden.

Anders als die des lateinischen Westens dachte die östliche[19] Erlösungslehre immer mehr von der Menschwerdung, von der Inkarnation des Logos her: Primäres Heilsereignis ist für sie weniger das Kreuz des Auferweckten als das Erscheinen eines göttlichen Wesens in menschlicher Gestalt, was verständlicherweise nicht so sehr als Skandalon, sondern als Mysterion empfunden wird. Seit dem ersten theologischen Systematiker Irenäus im 2. Jahrhundert bleibt es für die griechische Systematik entscheidend: In Jesus ging Gott selber in die Geschichte ein und wurde Mensch, damit die Menschen göttlich würden. Also: *Menschwerdung Gottes als Voraussetzung der Gottwerdung des Menschen*! Diese Vergottung des Menschen freilich nicht verstanden als eine pantheistische Identifikation mit der Gottheit, sondern als eine ontologische und durchaus dynamische Partizipation mit Gott.

Die ganze Menschheitsgeschichte wird nämlich in der griechischen Theologie in imponierender Weise als ein großer, kontinuierlicher, aufwärtsführender erzieherischer Prozeß (»paideia«)

verstanden. Das durch Schuld und Sünde verschüttete Bild Gottes wird im Menschen durch die Pädagogik Gottes selber wiederhergestellt und zur Vollendung geführt. Auf dem Höhepunkt dieser fortschreitenden Offenbarung und Erziehung des Menschengeschlechts nach einem vorauskonzipierten Plan (der Oikonomia des Heils) ereignet es sich: Gott tritt selber in seinem Sohn und Logos in die Welt ein und nimmt eine Menschennatur an. So wird der Mensch definitiv aus Finsternis, Irrtum und Tod befreit und durch Lehre und Beispiel zur Nachfolge, nämlich zur Nachahmung (»mimesis«) und Teilhabe (»methexis«) aufgefordert, um auf diese Weise zu Gott zu gelangen.

Diese großartige christliche Erlösungslehre der griechischen Theologie ist hier nicht zu würdigen. Zweifellos stellt sie eine umfassende Verchristlichung der hellenistischen (und insbesondere platonisch-stoischen) Paideia-Konzeption dar. Aber zugleich eine mit zahlreichen Negativa erkaufte Hellenisierung der christlichen Botschaft von Erlösung und Befreiung. Die Erlösungslehre des lateinischen Westens sahen wir bedroht durch eine rationalistische, juristische und moralistische Betrachtung des Gott-Mensch-Verhältnisses und eine isolierte Kreuzestheologie. Die griechische Erlösungslehre ist es auf andere Weise: Man nähert sich nicht selten einer unfruchtbaren christologischen Begriffsmystik und vernachlässigt das geschichtliche Lehren, Leben und Sterben Jesu. Man versteigt sich oft in kosmische Spekulationen und übersieht die personalen Bezüge. Man neigt in Theorie und Praxis zu einem gefährlichen Stoff-Geist-Dualismus und setzt ihn dem biblischen Sünde-Gnade-Gegensatz gleich.

Aber wichtiger ist das bereits Angedeutete: Erlösung geschieht nach dieser Konzeption grundlegend mit der Inkarnation des Logos. Neben Weihnachten und Ostern, neben der Menschwerdung und einer als Bestätigung der Menschwerdung verstandenen Auferstehung tritt Jesu Kreuzestod unangebracht zurück. Er hat mehr akzidentelle als konstitutive Bedeutung: beinahe so etwas wie ein, freilich unbegreiflich großes, Mißgeschick beim triumphalen Abstieg und Aufstieg des göttlichen Logos. Die Wirkung der Erlösung, wenn sie auch nicht direkt mit der Menschwerdung erfolgt, wird weniger personal und geschichtlich als essential und naturhaft gesehen. Sie meint – gewiß nicht einfach zu Unrecht – Unvergänglichkeit und Unsterblichkeit, Sohnschaft und Vergöttlichung des Menschen, Heimholung des ganzen Kosmos zu Gott. Aber: In Theorie wie Praxis verdrängen nicht nur Menschwerdung und Auferstehung sehr oft das Kreuz, sondern verdrängt oft das göttliche Leben das irdische, verdrängt die Vergöttlichung des Menschen seine Vermenschlichung, verdrängt die geistliche Heimholung der Welt die Veränderung der Welt und der Gesellschaft. Doch kannte die patristische Theologie noch nicht die spätere Aufteilung in Disziplinen, in Exegese, Dogmatik, Moral, Kirchenrecht. Und so verhinderte ihre Einheitlichkeit, gegenüber der die größere Differenziertheit der lateinischen Scholastik keineswegs immer ein Fortschritt war, extreme Konsequenzen.

2. Will aber *heute* noch ein vernünftiger Mensch Gott werden[20]? Damals zündende patristische Parolen wie: »Gott ist Mensch geworden, damit der Mensch Gott werde« stoßen heute auf beinahe völliges Unverständnis. Das für hellenistische Hörer hochaktuelle Thema vom Tausch zwischen Gott und Mensch (oder der beiden »Naturen«) ist für eine Zeit der so stark empfundenen Abwesenheit Gottes und »Gottesfinsternis« kein Thema mehr. Unser Problem heute ist nicht sosehr die Vergöttlichung, sondern die *Vermenschlichung des Menschen*. Das Geschehen in und mit Jesus von Nazaret wird ja auch im Neuen Testament nicht überall als Menschwerdung Gottes, genauer: des Gottessohnes oder Gotteswortes, gedeutet. Wenn diese Deutung für den heutigen Menschen überhaupt noch einen Sinn haben soll, dann nur, wenn sie etwas für die Menschwerdung des Menschen zu sagen hat.

Ist es aber, umgekehrt gesehen, bei den ungeheuren Möglichkeiten des modernen Menschen nicht eine noch ernsthaftere Versuchung, im Prozeß der Emanzipation aus eigenem Wollen »zu sein wie Gott«, wie dies schon in der biblischen Urgeschichte als Urversuchung des Menschen hingestellt wird[21]? Sind nicht gerade diejenigen »emanzipierten« Menschen, welche die Abschaffung Gottes am militantesten betreiben, nur zu oft auch diejenigen, die den scheinbar leergewordenen Platz einnehmen wollen: Platzhalter Gottes, um für sich und die Gesellschaft »zu wissen, was gut und was böse ist«? Sind nicht die anonymen Mächte und Systeme gerade in der modernen Gesellschaft zahlreich, die gerne die Rolle von Gottes Vorsehung spielen möchten? Angesichts der vielfachen individuellen und sozialen Entmenschlichung des Menschen im Zusammenhang mit der neuzeitlichen Entgottung Gottes, angesichts der den Menschen entmenschlichenden Ersatzgötter (Partei, Staat, Rasse, Wissenschaft, Geld, Personenkult, Macht) wird man sich vielleicht der alten Wahrheit wieder mehr öffnen: daß ohne Gott eine wahre Menschwerdung des Menschen im individuellen und gesellschaftlichen Bereich kaum möglich ist.

Menschwerdung des Menschen gewiß nicht durch einen, wie der Atheismus aufgrund vieler falscher Predigten immer wieder fürchtet, Gott der Über-Macht: der den Menschen klein hält und seine Freiheit erdrückt, der aber faktisch nach unserem Bild und Gleichnis geschaffen ist. Sondern wie es sich zugespitzt am Kreuz zeigt, durch einen Gott der Ohn-Macht: der den Menschen vermenschlicht und seine Freiheit ermöglicht, wie er sich schon – worauf die Weihnachtsgeschichte Gewicht legt – im Kind Jesus in seiner Menschenfreundlichkeit geoffenbart hat. In diesem Jesus, so haben es die Menschen ganz konkret erfahren und so bekennt es der Glaube, ist also Gott selbst am Werk. In ihm ist, wie wir gesehen haben, Gottes Wort und Willen offenbar, »Fleisch« geworden.

Gerade dies darf also, wenn es nicht mißverstanden werden soll, nicht nur auf das punctum mathematicum oder mysticum der Empfängnis oder Geburt Jesu bezogen werden. Nein, in Jesu *ganzem* Leben, in seinem *ganzen* Verkündigen, Verhalten und Geschick hat, wie durch alle die vorhergehenden Kapitel deutlich geworden, Gottes Wort und Wille Fleisch, eine menschliche Gestalt, angenommen: Jesus hat in seinem ganzen Reden, Tun und Leiden, hat in seiner ganzen Person Gottes Wort und Willen *verkündet, manifestiert, geoffenbart.* Ja, man kann sagen: Er, in dem sich Wort und Tat, Lehren und Leben, Sein und Handeln völlig decken, *ist* leibhaftig, *ist in menschlicher Gestalt Gottes Wort und Wille* [22].

In dieser umfassenden nicht spekulativen, sondern geschichtlichen Perspektive kann auch heute noch verstanden werden, daß Jesus schon von Paulus und dann auch in der paulinischen Tradition verstanden wird als Offenbarung von Gottes Kraft und Weisheit [23], als Haupt und Herr der Schöpfung [24], als Bild, Ebenbild Gottes [25], als Ja Gottes [26]. Und daß er von Johannes nicht nur als Wort Gottes [27], sondern indirekt als Gott gleich [28], ja als Herr und Gott [29] bezeichnet wird. In dieser Perspektive lassen sich auch so schwierige und hohe Sätze verstehen: daß Gott in Christus war und die Welt mit sich versöhnte [30], daß in Christus die ganze Fülle der Gottheit leibhaftig wohnt [31], daß Gottes Wort Fleisch geworden ist [32]. Diese Aussagen sind freilich gegen Mißverständnisse abzusichern.

Nirgendwo wird im Neuen Testament eine mythologische Zwei-Götter-Lehre entwickelt (Bi-theismus): Gott ist einer, und weder darf von Gott einfach wie vom Menschen, noch vom Menschen einfach wie von Gott geredet werden. Aber der Sohn wird auch nirgendwo mit dem Vater identifiziert (Monarchianismus, Sabellianismus): der Sohn ist nicht einfach der Vater, und der Vater ist nicht einfach der Sohn.

1. Wenn weder eine einfache Dualität noch eine einfache Identität möglich ist, wie kann dann die Beziehung Jesu zu Gott positiv ausgesagt werden? Wir können es so formulieren: Der *wahre Mensch* Jesus von Nazaret ist für den Glauben des einen *wahren Gottes* wirkliche *Offenbarung.*

So macht es vor allem das Johannesevangelium deutlich: Da der Vater den Sohn kennt und der Sohn den Vater[33], da der Vater im Sohn und der Sohn im Vater ist[34], da also der Vater und der Sohn eins sind[35], gilt: Wer den Sohn sieht, sieht auch den Vater[36]! Hier liegt weder Mythologie noch Mystik noch Metaphysik vor, sondern die nüchterne, aber grundlegende Aussage: im Wirken und in der Person Jesu begegnet Gott, manifestiert sich Gott – freilich nicht wahrnehmbar für den neutralen Beobachter, wohl aber für den sich vertrauensvoll auf Jesus einlassenden und glaubenden Menschen.

In ihm also zeigt sich Gott als der, der er ist. In ihm zeigt er gleichsam sein Gesicht. Der alttestamentliche Gott, so sahen wir früher[37], ist im Unterschied zum Gott der griechischen Metaphysik ein Gott mit Eigenschaften, mit menschlichem Antlitz. Dieses menschliche Antlitz zeigt, manifestiert, offenbart der Mensch Jesus von Nazaret in seinem ganzen Sein, Reden, Handeln und Leiden. Man kann ihn geradezu das *Antlitz* oder *Gesicht Gottes* oder wie im Neuen Testament selbst das *Bild* oder *Ebenbild Gottes* nennen[38]. Dasselbe wird auch mit anderen Begriffen ausgedrückt: wenn Jesus das *Wort Gottes* oder auch schließlich der *Sohn Gottes* genannt wird. Mit all diesen Bildbegriffen soll sowohl das einzigartige Verhältnis des Vaters zu Jesus und Jesu zum Vater ausgedrückt werden, wie dann auch das einzigartige Verhältnis Jesu zu den Menschen: sein Wirken und seine Bedeutsamkeit als Gottes Offenbarer für das Heil der Welt. Von daher versteht sich, warum die Rede *von* Jesus Christus schon immer leicht überging in die Rede *zu* Jesus Christus: warum Glaube und Bekenntnis schon immer von der Akklamation, der Anrufung, vom Gebet begleitet war.

2. Bevor wir zur Deutung des Verhältnisses von Gott und Jesus einige weitere zusammenfassende Bestimmungen wagen, scheint eine Reflexion über die Vorstellung der *Präexistenz*, also des Vorausexistierens des Gottessohnes in Gottes Ewigkeit vor seiner Menschwerdung, angebracht. Gerade dieser Gedanke ist heute schwierig zu vollziehen. Damals gerade umgekehrt – und nur so wird man diese theologische Idee überhaupt verstehen – lag der Gedanke in der Luft[39]: Nicht nur die jüdische und insbesondere Philons Spekulation über Gottes ewige Weisheit förderte ihn. Auch die apokalyptischen Vorstellungen vom kommenden, bei Gott schon verborgen existierenden Menschensohn und die rabbinischen Gedanken über die Vorausexistenz der Tora, des Paradieses, des Messiasnamens. Schließlich die gnostischen Spekulationen über die vorausexistierenden und dann in die Materie abgesunkenen Menschenseelen, die der göttliche Urmensch sammelt, aus der Materie erlöst und in die Welt Gottes zurückführt. Allerdings ist gerade in diesem letzten Punkt die Rekonstruktion möglicher gnostischer Vorstellungen schwierig, da in den gnostischen Texten ein christlicher Einfluß nicht ausgeschlossen werden kann.

Mußten in einem solchen geistigen Klima entsprechende Gedanken auch über ein Vorausexistieren Jesu, des Gottessohnes und Gotteswortes, in Gottes Ewigkeit nicht äußerst plausibel erscheinen? Irgendwelche direkten Offenbarungen darüber waren gar nicht erfordert. Die theologischen Reflexionen lagen nahe. Solche finden sich nicht nur im Prolog, sondern auch im Evangelium des Johannes[40]. Aber auch noch sehr viel früher – wohl die früheste Aussage über Jesu Präexistenz bei Gott – im genannten vorpaulinischen Christushymnus des Philipperbriefes[41], dann in Texten über die Weltschöpfung in Christus bei Paulus selbst[42] und schließlich, ein wenig mehr entfaltet, in der paulinischen Tradition[43].

Selbstverständlich ist auch hier nicht vom Anfang zum Ende, sondern *vom Ende zum Anfang hin* gedacht worden. Man sagte sich: Wenn der Gekreuzigte und zum Leben Erweckte von Gott her gesehen eine derartig einzigartige, grundlegende, maßgebende Bedeutung hat, muß er dann nicht schon immer in Gottes Gedanken gewesen sein? War also der, der Ziel der Schöpfung und der Geschichte ist, nicht schon immer in Gottes ewigem

Schöpfungs- und Heilsplan? Und war er, der jetzt als der Sohn bei Gott ist, nicht schon von Ewigkeit als Sohn und Wort bei Gott? Der Letzte ist dann auch der Erste[44]. Und der, in dem das Ende aller Dinge erschienen ist, wird erkannt als der Anfang aller Dinge, auf den hin alle Dinge schon angelegt, in dem sie geschaffen sind und Bestand haben[45]. Zeiten und Geschlechter, Lehren und Vorsteher in der Kirche wechseln, von ihm aber gilt: Jesus Christus gestern und heute derselbe auch in Ewigkeit[46].

Der Unterschied zwischen einer realen und einer idealen Präexistenz war für eine Zeit, die unter Platons Einfluß die Ideen für real hielt, nur bedingt von Interesse. Das *Denken in hellenistischen physisch-metaphysischen Kategorien* war selbstverständlich. Mit allen im damaligen Verstehenshorizont zur Verfügung stehenden Begriffen und Vorstellungen wurde versucht, die unvergleichliche Bedeutung dessen, was mit und in Jesus geschehen war, zum Ausdruck zu bringen. Mythisches hat sehr stark mitgespielt, sich indessen nie schlechthin durchgesetzt. Denn jegliche kosmische Gesetzlichkeit fand ihre Grenzen an der konkreten Geschichte dieses Menschen Jesus von Nazaret und zerbrach an seinem Kreuz.

So konnten denn auch die höchsten spekulativen oder mythologischen Aussagen über die Präexistenz des göttlichen Sohnes nie in sich selber kreisen. Immer wurden sie gleich mit der nicht wegzudiskutierenden *Wirklichkeit des Kreuzes konfrontiert*: Der hymnisch formulierte Johannesprolog vom Wort bei Gott, durch welches alles geworden ist, erreicht seine Spitze im »und das Wort ist Fleisch geworden« und damit im Nichterkannt- und Nichtangenommenwerden[47]. Der alte Hymnus des Philipperbriefes von dem, der in Gottes Gestalt war, verweilt nicht dabei, sondern schreitet bei Paulus sofort weiter zur Entäußerung, Erniedrigung und zum Gehorsam bis zum Tod am Kreuz[48]. Die hohen Worte des Kolosserbriefes über die Schöpfung in Christus führen nur über das Blut Christi zu Versöhnung und Frieden[49]. Und sogar die scheinbar idyllische Weihnachtsgeschichte und die erhabenen lukanischen Aussagen und Lieder über Maria und das Kind stehen im Schatten des Kreuzes[50].

Warum also hat man schon in neutestamentlicher Zeit theologische Folgerungen für ein Vorausexistieren des Gottessohnes in Gottes Ewigkeit gezogen? Nicht um über Gott und die Welt gescheit zu spekulieren. Sondern um den *einzigartigen Anspruch* dieses gekreuzigten und doch lebendigen Jesus sichtbar zu machen und für die christliche Praxis zu begründen. Die mythi-

schen Vorstellungen der damaligen Zeit von einer vorzeitig-jen-
seitigen himmlischen Existenz eines von Gott abgeleiteten Wesens, von einer »Göttergeschichte« zwischen zwei (oder gar drei)
Gottwesen, können nicht mehr die unseren sein. Worauf aber die
damaligen Vorstellungen eigentlich zielten, ist gewiß auch im
heutigen sehr verschiedenen Erfahrungshorizont zu beachten.

3. Was für ein Interessse steckt hinter den Präexistenzvorstellun-
gen? Es soll bildhaft zum Ausdruck gebracht werden, daß die
Beziehung zwischen Gott und Jesus nicht erst nachträglich und
gleichsam zufällig entstanden ist, sondern *von vornherein gegeben* und *in Gott selbst grundgelegt* ist. Auch wenn wir das heute
anders ausdrücken, so darf dieses Anliegen doch nicht verlorengehen[51]. Folgende Momente an der uns heute schwierig nachzu-
vollziehenden Präexistenz wären zu überlegen:
a. Es gibt *von Ewigkeit keinen anderen Gott* als den, der sich in
   Jesus manifestiert hat: Das Gesicht, das er in Jesus gezeigt hat,
   ist wirklich sein wahres und einziges Gesicht. Er ist kein Gott
   mit einem Janus-Gesicht. Er ist schon im Alten Testament
   kein anderer Gott als im Neuen. Er ist kein Gott des Rätsels,
   keine Sphinx. Es gibt hinter dem Vater der Verlorenen nicht
   noch irgendeinen unheimlichen mystischen Abgrund, wie ihn
   die Gnosis vermutete. Es gibt auch nicht den Gott eines uner-
   forschlichen dunklen Ratschlusses, wie ihn die doppelte Prädestinationslehre Calvins voraussetzte. Nein, von Anbeginn
   ist Gott so und wird auch immer so sein, wie er in Jesus
   offenbar geworden ist. Sein Sein und Handeln ist von Anfang
   an, so könnte man im nachhinein formulieren, »christologisch« geprägt.
b. Weil es keinen anderen Gott gibt als den in Jesus offenbarten,
   hat *Jesus von diesem universalen Gott her selber eine universale Bedeutung:* Wenn Gott den Menschen außerhalb der Christusverkündigung (in einer Weltreligion oder im säkularen
   Leben) begegnet, was nicht dogmatisch ausgeschlossen werden kann, begegnet ihnen der eine wahre Gott. Auch wenn die
   Menschen sein Antlitz nicht erkennen und er für sie der »unbekannte Gott«[52] ist, so ist es doch in Wirklichkeit der Gott
   mit dem Antlitz Jesu: der Gott, der ihnen im Sinn und Geiste
   Jesu begegnet. In diesem einen wahren Gott also kann auch
   der Nichtchrist, wo immer er durch das Schicksal beheimatet
   ist, sein Heil finden. Dann zwar außerhalb der Christengemeinde, außerhalb der Kirche: extra Ecclesiam. Aber nicht

außerhalb jenes Gottes, der, für Nichtchristen unerkannt, Jesu Antlitz trägt. Damit aber die Menschen dieses Antlitz auch erkennen und Gott für sie nicht der unbekannte Gott bleibt, ist die christliche Verkündigung und Mission, die Jesus als Gottes Messias, Sachwalter und Stellvertreter, als Gottes Sohn, Wort, Gesicht verkündet, eine Notwendigkeit. Nur durch das glaubende Bekenntnis zu Jesus als dem Christus Gottes wird aus dem Nicht-Christen ein Christ[53].

c. Was in und mit Jesus geschehen ist, erklärt sich für den glaubenden Menschen also nicht aus dem Lauf der Geschichte allein; in seinem *letzten Ursprung erklärt es sich* für ihn *nur von Gott her*. In Jesu Anspruch ist nach Jesus selbst Gottes Anspruch laut geworden. In seinem Wort Gottes Wort. In seinem Willen Gottes Wille. Jesu Verkündigung, Verhalten und Geschick, der Ursprung und die Bedeutung seiner Person gründen somit nicht nur im gesellschaftlichen Kontext, von dem unsere Betrachtung ausging. Vielmehr in Gottes Handeln, auf welches er in seiner Vollmacht selber verweist und auf die unsere Betrachtung hinführte: in jener zuvor-kommenden Freundlichkeit, Liebe und Treue des Schöpfers, die einen Zusammenhang zwischen Schöpfung und Erlösung sichtbar werden läßt. Der Schöpfer, der mit-leidend sein Geschöpf auch in Leid und Schuld nicht fallen läßt, sondern es in Jesus aufhebt und aufnimmt.

d. Der Mensch seinerseits ist aufgerufen, *im glaubenden Vertrauen die Welt und ihre Zeit in eine andere Dimension hinein zu übersteigen:* ein Transzendieren, nicht in ein Jenseits hinüber, wohl aber in jene letzte Wirklichkeit hinein, auf die wir uns unbedingt verlassen können und die wir Gott nennen. Nur in dieser wahrhaft anderen Dimension vermag der Mensch zu erfassen, was Jesus zutiefst ist und bedeutet: warum gerade dieser Jesus eine einzigartige und maßgebende Bedeutung für ihn und die Menschheit hat, warum gerade er und kein anderer verpflichtend in die Nachfolge zu rufen vermag. *In Jesus ruft der eine wahre Gott selbst auf den Weg!* Des Menschen definitives und umfassendes Wohl, sein Heil ist somit nicht einfach eine innerweltliche Möglichkeit, sondern immer ein Gottesgeschenk: Gnade.

4. Nach diesen Überlegungen zur Präexistenz wird man nun auch das *Verhältnis von Gott und Jesus* besser verstehen können. Im Neuen Testament, so sehen wir, wird Jesu göttliche Würde

primär funktional und nicht physisch oder metaphysisch aufgefaßt. Sie charakterisiert Jesu Person gewiß in ihrem Wesen, aber nicht im Sinn einer abstrakten Wesensaussage (»Wesenchristologie«), sondern einer Heilsaussage für uns Menschen (»funktionale Christologie«). Später freilich ist sie dann mittels zeitgenössischer philosophischer Begrifflichkeit gedeutet und als eine metaphysische erklärt worden. Eine andere Begrifflichkeit stand nicht zur Verfügung! Die hellenistischen Begriffe waren, so müssen wir aus heutiger Perspektive sagen, der ursprünglichen Botschaft zum Teil wenig angemessen[54]. Aber waren sie nicht unvermeidlich? Trotz unzulänglicher begrifflicher Mittel und Vermischung mit der kaiserlichen Politik ist es den ersten ökumenischen Konzilien – anders als spätere jedenfalls nicht mit peripheren Fragen, sondern mit dem Zentrum der christlichen Botschaft beschäftigt – gelungen, diese Mitte gegen die Mißachtung entweder des göttlichen oder des menschlichen Momentes zu schützen. Man täusche sich nicht: Nicht aus der Freude an theologischer Spekulation oder gar Dogmenentwicklung, sondern aus pastoraler Sorge haben sie definiert[55].

Das erste epochemachende ökumenische *Konzil von Nikaia* 325 hat in seiner Definition der »Wesensgleichheit« (homoousia) Jesu mit Gott seinem Vater gegen Areios dafür gesorgt, daß nicht doch verdeckt wieder ein Polytheismus ins Christentum eingeführt wurde: In Jesus ist nicht ein zweiter Gott oder Halbgott, sondern der eine wahre Gott präsent. Unsere ganze Erlösung hängt daran, daß es in Jesus um den Gott geht, der wirklich Gott ist.

Nachdem dann das vom Alexandriner Kyrill dominierte Konzil von Ephesos durch seine mißverständlichen Ausführungen die Gefahr heraufbeschwor, daß Jesu wahre Menschlichkeit von der einen alles absorbierenden Gottesnatur verschlungen wird, hat zwanzig Jahre später das *Konzil von Chalkedon* 451, unter dem Eindruck eines theologisch ausbalancierten Briefes von Papst Leo dem Großen, in einer Reihe paradoxer Formulierungen zusammen mit »dem Vater wesensgleich« das »uns wesensgleich« betont[56]. Auf diese Weise sorgte es dafür, daß die ständig bedrohte volle Menschlichkeit Jesu zumindest grundsätzlich nicht zugunsten seines göttlichen Wesens aufgegeben wurde[57].

Die gesamte Entwicklung der dogmatischen Christologie[58] bis in unsere Tage steht seit Chalkedon im Zeichen der gott-menschlichen Formel *»wahrer Gott«* (vere Deus) und *»wahrer Mensch«* (vere homo). Nach der (bedeutenden) patristischen und der (weniger bedeutenden) mittelalterlichen Entwicklung erreichte sie in der Neuzeit ihren letzten gewaltigen Höhepunkt und gleichsam ihre Rekapitulation in Hegels Religionsphilosophie[59]. Alles in allem eine wesentlich spekulative Christologie (»von oben«) mit dem Akzent auf Jesu Göttlichkeit, die nach Hegels Tod – David Friedrich Straussens ›Leben Jesu‹! – in eine geschichtliche Christologie (»von unten«) mit dem Akzent auf Jesu Menschlichkeit umschlagen mußte. Statt der »hohen« Christologie jetzt die »niedrige« Leben-Jesu-Forschung[60].

Nach dem Neuen Testament ist das eine nicht ohne das andere: Kein Jesus von Nazaret, der nicht als der Christus Gottes verkündet wird. Kein Christus, der nicht mit dem Menschen Jesus von Nazaret identisch ist. Also weder eine untheologische Jesulogie noch eine ungeschichtliche Christologie! Daß der Name Jesus mit dem Titel Christus zu einem Eigennamen zusammengewachsen ist, drückt bis in die Namensgebung hinein aus, daß für das Neue Testament der wahre Jesus der Christus Gottes, und der wahre Christus der Mensch Jesus von Nazaret ist: und beides in einer Einheit »Jesus Christus«. Daß in der Geschichte Jesu Christi wahrhaft Gott und Mensch im Spiel sind, daran muß auch heute unverrückbar im Glauben festgehalten werden. Auch wenn und gerade wenn Gottessohnschaft, Vorausexistenz, Schöpfungsmittlerschaft, Menschwerdung wieder besser – wie ursprünglich – nicht von oben her theologisch postuliert und deduziert, sondern von unten her, wie hier versucht, induziert und interpretiert werden.

Vom Neuen Testament her kann also auch heute keine Interpretation der Geschichte Jesu Christi verantwortet werden, bei der Jesus Christus »nur Gott« ist: ein der menschlichen Mängel und Schwächen enthobener, über die Erde wandelnder Gott. Oder »nur Mensch«: ein Prediger, Prophet oder Weisheitslehrer, Symbol oder Chiffre für allgemein menschliche Grunderfahrungen. Wenn man nach den negativen Abgrenzungen auf dem Hintergrund alles dessen, was in diesem dritten Hauptteil über Jesus ausgeführt wurde, in aller Fehlbarkeit eine zeitgemäße positive Umschreibung der alten Formel »wahrer Gott und wahrer Mensch« versuchen darf:

– wahrhaft Gott: *Die ganze Bedeutsamkeit des Geschehens in und mit Jesus von Nazaret hängt daran, daß in Jesus – der den Menschen als Gottes Sachwalter und Platzhalter, Repräsentant und Stellvertreter erschien und als der Gekreuzigte zum Leben erweckt von Gott bestätigt wurde – für die Glaubenden der menschenfreundliche Gott selber nahe war, am Werk war, gesprochen hat, gehandelt hat, endgültig sich geoffenbart hat. Alle oft in mythologische oder halbmythologische Formen der Zeit gekleideten Aussagen über Gottessohnschaft, Vorausexistenz, Schöpfungsmittlerschaft und Menschwerdung wollen letztlich nicht mehr und nicht weniger als das eine: die* Einzigartigkeit, Unableitbarkeit und Unüberbietbarkeit *des in und mit Jesus lautgewordenen* Anrufs, Angebots, Anspruchs *begründen, der letztlich nicht menschlichen, sondern göttlichen Ursprungs ist und deshalb, absolut verläßlich, die Menschen unbedingt angeht.*

– wahrhaft Mensch: *Daß Jesus ohne Abstriche mit allen Konsequenzen (Leidensfähigkeit, Angst, Einsamkeit, Ungesichertheit, Versuchungen, Zweifel, Irrtumsmöglichkeit) voll und ganz Mensch war, muß auch heute noch gegen alle Vergottungstendenzen immer wieder betont werden. Aber nicht ein bloßer Mensch, sondern der* wahre Mensch. *Als solcher gab er – wie hier im Zeichen der wahrzumachenden Wahrheit, der Einheit von Theorie und Praxis, Bekenntnis und Nachfolge, Glauben und Handeln zum Ausdruck gebracht – durch seine Verkündigung, sein Verhalten und Geschick ein* Modell des Menschseins, *das einem jeden, der sich vertrauensvoll darauf einläßt, ermöglicht, den Sinn des Menschseins und seiner Freiheit im Dasein für die Mitmenschen zu entdecken und zu verwirklichen. Als von Gott bestätigt, stellt er so schließlich den bleibend verläßlichen* letzten Maßstab des Menschseins *dar.*

Damit ist nun indirekt auch klar geworden: An der vom Neuen Testament wirklich gedeckten Wahrheit der alten christologischen Konzilien soll nichts abgestrichen werden, auch wenn sie aus dem soziokulturellen hellenistischen Kontext immer wieder in den Verstehenshorizont unserer Zeit hinein zu übersetzen ist.

Nach dem Neuen Testament entscheidet sich freilich das *Christsein* nicht letztlich mit der Zustimmung zu diesem oder jenem noch so hohen Dogma über Christus, *nicht* mit einer *Christologie* oder *Christus-Theorie, sondern* mit dem *Christusglauben* und der *Christusnachfolge!* Im Interesse des Christusglaubens und der Christusnachfolge darf und muß heute von Jesus wieder nüchterner und weniger im Stil antiker Festinschriften und Festansprachen und auch weniger im Stil hellenistisch-konziliärer Glaubenssymbola, sondern mehr im Stil der synoptischen Evangelien und der gegenwärtigen Sprache gesprochen werden, wie dies in den vorausgegangenen Kapiteln versucht wurde.

Enthalten nun aber gerade diese synoptischen Evangelien im Hinblick besonders auf Jesu Empfängnis und Geburt nicht so viel Mythologisches oder Halbmythologisches, so vieles im Stil antiker Legenden und Sagen, was so wenig wie die hochtheologischen hellenistischen Inkarnationsformeln für die Gegenwart einfach wiederholt werden kann?

Geboren aus der Frau

Wer sich, aus welchem Grund auch immer, an diesem Titel stoßen sollte, möge sich gleich zu Beginn daran erinnern, daß es sich hier um die älteste neutestamentliche Aussage über die Geburt Jesu aus Maria handelt[61].

1. In den *Geburtsgeschichten* von Mattäus[62] und Lukas[63] wird die Gottessohnschaft in der volkstümlichen Form einzelner Geschichten veranschaulicht. Wichtig wurden sie für die spätere Entwicklung der christlichen Frömmigkeit und des Festkalenders: von Weihnachten mit vierwöchiger Adventszeit neun Monate zurück Mariä Verkündigung (25. März), sowie im Anschluß an Weihnachten das Fest der unschuldigen Kinder (28. Dezember), der Beschneidung (1. Januar), der Erscheinung (6. Januar), der Darstellung im Tempel (2. Februar). Von Mattäus und Lukas erhält der Leser Auskunft über das, was Markus noch nicht interessiert und Johannes wieder gleichgültig sein wird, was aber von Mattäus und Lukas als wundersame Eingangshalle zu ihren Großevangelien vorangestellt wird: Jesu Stammbaum und Eltern, Geistzeugung und jungfräuliche Geburt, die Ereignisse in Betlehem und die Jugendjahre in Nazaret.

Heute wird es freilich auch von katholischen Exegeten zugegeben[64]: Es handelt sich bei diesen Geschichten um historisch weithin ungesicherte, unter sich widersprüchliche, stark legendäre und letztlich theologisch motivierte Erzählungen eigener Prägung. Ganz anders als sonst im Leben Jesu geschieht hier viel in Träumen und gehen Engel ständig ein und aus – himmlische Boten Gottes für wichtige Ereignisse in einer Zeit stärker reflektierter göttlicher Transzendenz (vgl. den alttestamentlichen »Engel des Herrn«). Die nicht harmonisierbaren Widersprüche betreffen nicht nur die beiden Stammbäume Jesu, die nur von Abraham bis David (nach jüdischen Listen) übereinstimmen[65]. Sie betreffen auch zahlreiche andere Punkte: Während Mattäus nichts von Nazaret als dem Aufenthaltsort der Mutter Jesu zu wissen scheint, so umgekehrt Lukas nichts von den doch gewiß aufsehenerregenden (aber offenkundig legendären und in keinen profanen Quellen bezeugten) Geschehnissen des Magierbesuches, des Kindermordes in Betlehem und der Flucht nach Ägypten. Die begründeten historischen Zweifel betreffen des weiteren die Verwandtschaft Jesu mit Johannes dem Täufer, die Volkszählung gerade zu dieser Zeit, Betlehem als Geburtsort.

Offensichtlich geht es hier trotz einer nicht auszuschließenden Verwertung historischen Materials nicht um historische Berichte. Es geht um mehr: um Bekenntnis- und Verkündigungsgeschichten, die aus den judenchristlichen Gemeinden stammen dürften und von Mattäus und Lukas bearbeitet und ihren Evangelien vorangestellt worden sind. Es soll hier *nachträglich* – in Rückschau aus dem Osterglauben – *Jesu Messianität verkündet und begründet werden,* und dies in doppelter Weise:

a. Jesus als der *Davidssohn:* Die providentielle Abstammung und die Berechtigung des Titels Davidssohn wird genealogisch aufgewiesen. Durch einen von David bis schließlich zum gesetzlichen Vater Josef (nicht zu Maria!) führenden Stammbaum: im symbolischen Zahlenschema 3 × 14 bei Mattäus und wohl 11 × 7 (Jesus als die 12. letzte Weltperiode?) bei Lukas.

b. Jesus als der *neue Mose*: Das providentielle Schicksal des Kleinkindes wird nach dem Vorbild frühjüdischer Mosegeschichten (sogenannten Haggaden zum Alten Testament) dargestellt. Eingeflossen ist sowohl das Motiv der Errettung des Mose vor Pharao (= Herodes) wie das Motiv der Flucht (nach Ägypten!). Zu der Herodes-Kindermord-Erzählung stellt die Geschichte vom Kommen der heidnischen Magier einen wirkungsvollen Kontrapunkt dar, die dabei einen unbestreitbaren historischen Erfahrungshorizont hat: denn Israel und die Heiden verhalten sich zu der von der Gemeinde verkündigten Botschaft vom Messias Jesus gegensätzlich. Mattäus unterstreicht das durch alttestamentliche Zitate, die den Heilscharakter der Entwicklung herausstellen: Während sich Israel dem Messias Jesus, dem ihm zugedachten zweiten Mose, versagt, kommen die Heiden zu ihm. Auch die so verschiedenen lukanischen Kindheitsgeschichten sind ganz nach alttestamentlichen Vorbildern gestaltet: die Verkündigungsszene bis in den Wortlaut hinein, auch die drei Lieder Mariens, Zacharias' und Simeons, die aus judenchristlicher Tradition stammen dürften und alttestamentlich-jüdische Poesie reflektieren. Auch wenn die Geburtsgeschichten keine Berichte eines Historikers sind, so können sie doch, wie bereits ausgeführt[66], auf ihre Weise wahr sein, eine Wahrheit kundtun[67]. Als Verkündigungs- und Bekenntnisgeschichten wollen die Geburtsgeschichten *nicht primär historische Wahrheit, sondern Heilswahrheit kundtun*: die Botschaft vom Heil der Menschen in Jesus. Und dies kann in der Form einer im einzelnen legendären Weihnachtskunde vom Krippenkind in Betlehem bildhafter und deshalb eindrücklicher geschehen als durch eine noch so einwandfrei datierende und lokalisierende Geburtsurkunde.

Nicht die historische Kritik, die auf die eigentliche Botschaft zielt, sondern die romantisch verharmlosende Idyllisierung und Privatisierung einerseits und die oberflächliche Säkularisierung und betriebsame Kommerzialisierung andererseits haben Weihnachtsbotschaft und Weihnachtsfest entleert: Als ob der »holde Knabe im lockigen Haar« – nicht bei Lukas und Mattäus, aber wie auf den Bildern – ständig gelächelt und nicht auch sehr menschlich elend (worauf ohne sozialkritischen Protest Krippe und Windeln hinweisen) geschrien hätte! Als ob der im Stall geborene Heiland der Notleidenden nicht deutlich eine Parteinahme für die Namenlosen (Hirten) gegen die mit Namen genannten Großen (Augustus, Quirinus) offenbarte! Als ob das Magnifikat der begnadeten Magd von der Erniedrigung der Mächtigen und der Erhöhung der Niedrigen, von der Sättigung der Hungrigen und der Vernachlässigung der Reichen nicht kämpferisch eine Umwertung der Rangordnung ankündete! Als ob die holdselige Nacht des Neugeborenen von seinem Wirken und Schicksal drei Jahrzehnte später absehen ließe und nicht schon das Krippenkind das Zeichen des Kreuzes auf der Stirne trüge! Als ob nicht – ähnlich wie später im Prozeß vor dem jüdischen Tribunal – schon in den Verkündigungsszenen vor Maria und den Hirten (die Mitte der Weihnachtsgeschichte) durch mehrere nebeneinander gestellte Hoheitstitel (Gottessohn, Heiland, Messias, König, Herr) das vollendete Glaubensbekenntnis der Gemeinde zum Ausdruck gebracht würde und diese Titel statt dem genannten römischen Kaiser diesem Kind zugesprochen würden! Als ob hier nicht statt der trügerischen Pax Romana – erkauft mit erhöhten Steuern, Eskalation der

Rüstung, Druck auf die Minderheiten und Wohlstands-Pessimismus – mit »großer Freude« die wahre Pax Christi angekündigt würde: gründend in einer Neuordnung der zwischenmenschlichen Beziehungen im Zeichen der Menschenfreundlichkeit Gottes und der Brüderlichkeit der Menschen!

Es ist in der Tat offensichtlich, daß selbst die scheinbar idyllische Weihnachtsgeschichte höchst reale *gesellschaftskritische* (im weitesten Sinne politische) *Implikationen und Konsequenzen* hat[68]. Dem politischen Heiland und der politischen Theologie des Imperium Romanum, welche die kaiserliche Friedenspolitik ideologisch unterstützt, wird der wahre Friede entgegengehalten, der nicht dort erwartet werden kann, wo einem Menschen und Autokraten göttliche Ehre dargebracht wird, sondern wo Gott in der Höhe zu Ehren kommt und sein Wohlgefallen auf den Menschen ruht. Man braucht das lukanische Weihnachtsevangelium nur mit dem zitierten Evangelium des Augustus von Priene zu vergleichen, um zu sehen, wie hier die Rollen vertauscht sind. Nicht mehr von den übermächtigen römischen Cäsaren, sondern von diesem ohnmächtigen, gewaltlosen Kind wird jetzt das Ende der Kriege, werden lebenswerte Verhältnisse, das gemeinsame Glück, kurz allseitiges Wohl, das »Heil« der Menschen und der Welt erwartet.

Doch diese wenigen Hinweise müssen in unserem Rahmen ausreichen, um zu bestätigen: diese Geburtsgeschichten, richtig verstanden, sind alles andere als harmlose erbauliche Geschichten vom Jesuskind. Sie sind theologisch hoch reflektierte Christusgeschichten im Dienst einer sehr gezielten Verkündigung, welche die wahre Bedeutung Jesu als des Messias zum Heil für alle Völker der Erde kunstvoll, plastisch und höchst kritisch anschaulich machen wollen: als Davidssohn und neuer Mose, als Vollender des alten Bundes und Initiator des neuen, als Heiland der Armen und als der wahre Gottessohn. Also offenkundig keine erste Phase einer Biographie Jesu oder einer trauten Familiengeschichte. Alles vielmehr ein Evangelium: eine einladende Botschaft, nach der die alttestamentlichen Verheißungen in Erfüllung gegangen sind in Jesus, dem Auserwählten Gottes, der zwar keine detaillierten politischen Rezepte und Programme, wohl aber in seinem Sein, seinem Reden, Tun und Leiden einen höchst konkreten Maßstab liefert, an den sich der Mensch in seinem individuellen und sozialen Handeln vertrauensvoll halten darf.

2. Ein besonderes und noch immer erstaunlich leidenschaftlich diskutiertes Problem stellt in diesem Zusammenhang die *Jungfrauengeburt*[69] dar. Die erst und nur bei Mattäus und Lukas in den Kindheitsgeschichten erwähnte, aber in zahlreiche alte Glaubensbekenntnisse, unter anderem das »apostolische«, aufgenommene jungfräuliche Empfängnis *Jesu* (ohne männliche Zeugung) durch die Jungfrau Maria wurde in der kirchlichen Tradition verschieden verstanden: Zunächst ganz im mattäisch-lukanischen Sinn als Jungfräulichkeit *vor* der Geburt (virginitas ante partum = jungfräuliche Empfängnis) streng christologisch. Seit dem 4./5. Jahrhundert aber wird der Sinn unter dem Einfluß wenig vertrauenerweckender Quellen (apokryphes Protevangelium des Jakobus) und einer starken asketischen Bewegung erweitert: in Richtung auf eine Jungfräulichkeit *in* der Geburt (in partu = ohne Wehen und/oder Verletzung des Hymens!), zusammen schließlich mit einer im Neuen Testament ebenfalls nicht bezeugten Jungfräulichkeit *nach* der Geburt (post partum = keine geschlechtlichen Beziehungen und keine weiteren Kinder!). Also semper virgo, allzeit, immerwährend Jungfrau! Statt der christologischen Betrachtungsweise tritt nun immer mehr die mariologische hervor, und statt von jungfräulicher Empfängnis spricht man von Jungfrauengeburt.

Trotzdem wird diese jungfräuliche Empfängnis oder Geburt *Jesu* selbst heute immer wieder verwechselt: mit der im Neuen Testament nirgendwo erwähnten, im Abendland noch von Bernhard von Clairvaux und Thomas von Aquin abgelehnten, erstmals im 12. Jahrhundert ausdrücklich ausgesprochenen und noch bis ins 16. Jahrhundert umstrittenen, aber in der Zeit der Gegenreformation immer deutlicher gelehrten und 1854 von Pius IX. unfehlbar definierten »unbefleckten Empfängnis« *Mariens* durch ihre im Neuen (und Alten) Testament nicht genannte Mutter. Daß also Maria als die Mutter Jesu von der Erbsünde nicht nur gereinigt, sondern, durch die zuvorkommende Gnade Gottes im Hinblick auf Jesu Christi Verdienste, von vornherein bewahrt wurde[70]. Welche Aussage von den orthodoxen und besonders den evangelischen Kirchen (Universalität des Sündenverhängnisses) als unbiblisch verworfen wird und seit der Kritik an der augustinischen Auffassung der Übertragung einer »Erbsünde« durch den Zeugungsakt weithin gegenstandslos geworden ist. Es ist freilich kaum zu bestreiten, daß im kirchlichen Bewußtsein beide Lehren etwas mit der von Kirchenvätern vertretenen und bis in unsere Tage hinein verbreiteten negativen

Bewertung des Geschlechtsaktes (und auch der Ehe) zu tun hatten, dessen böse Auswirkungen die (moralisch verstandene) Heiligkeit Jesu und Mariens nicht belasten durften (schon nach Papst Siricius † 398 wäre ehelicher Verkehr für Maria eine Besudelung gewesen[71]). Trifft dies aber auch die im Neuen Testament bezeugte ursprüngliche Auffassung von der Jungfrauengeburt?

Man hat über die *Herkunft* dieser Lehre bei Mattäus und Lukas viel gerätselt. Die schon im Neuen Testament zitierte Jesaja-Stelle von der »jungen Frau« (das hebräische »almah« wird im griechischen Alten Testament mit »parthenos« wiedergegeben), die empfangen und gebären wird einen Sohn mit dem Namen Immanuel[72]: Sie wird möglicherweise schon im Judentum, und jedenfalls nachträglich im Christentum auf eine »Jungfrau« hin ausgelegt. Stammt die Jungfrauengeburt (und die Übersetzung mit »parthenos«?) vielleicht aus der ägyptischen Mythologie, wo der Pharao als Gottkönig wunderbar gezeugt wird aus dem Geistgott Amon-Re in der Gestalt des regierenden Königs und der jungfräulichen Königin? Oder aus der griechischen Mythologie, wo Götter mit Menschentöchtern »heilige Ehen« eingehen, aus denen nicht nur Göttersöhne wie Perseus, Herakles und Iphikles, sondern auch geschichtliche Gestalten wie Homer, Pythagoras, Platon, Alexander, Augustus hervorgehen können? Die Gemeinsamkeiten lassen sich nicht leugnen, Unterschiede aber auch nicht übersehen: Die Ankündigung und Annahme des Empfängnisgeschehens bei Maria vollzieht sich im Wort, ohne alle Vermischung von Gott und Mensch, in einem völlig unerotischen und vergeistigten Kontext. Der Heilige Geist wird nicht als zeugender Vater, sondern als wirkende Kraft der Empfängnis Jesu verstanden. Somit kann der direkte Einfluß bestimmter Mythologien kaum bewiesen, freilich auch kaum von vornherein bestritten werden. Sicher ist nur, daß der Mythos von der Jungfrauengeburt in der ganzen Antike verbreitet war und sich sogar, wie angemerkt, in Persien, Indien und in Südamerika findet: er ist also keineswegs etwas spezifisch Christliches.

In den, wie wir sahen, nicht historisch, sondern theologisch orientierten evangelischen Geburtsgeschichten muß die Jungfrauengeburt offensichtlich *von der Gottessohnschaft her* verstanden werden und nicht umgekehrt. Der Jesus der Geschichte hatte Gott in neuer Weise als den Vater verkündigt und als seinen lieben Vater angeredet. Als der Erhöhte wurde er nach seinem Tod als der Sohn und Gottessohn tituliert, wobei man die Gottessohnschaft immer mehr von der Erhöhung auf die Taufe, ja auf den Anfang vorverlegte. Lag es da im hellenistischen Einfluß-gebiet nicht nahe, alttestamentliche Aussagen wie das »Heute habe ich dich gezeugt« (= Erwählung und Thronbesteigung des Königs)[73] in prononcierter Weise als Zeugung aus Gott und nicht durch einen menschlichen Vater zu verstehen? Konnte man durch das weitverbreitete Symbol der Jungfrauengeburt – in Alexandrien etwa wurde alljährlich am 6. Januar die Geburt des neuen Jahres (Aion) aus der Jungfrau (Kore) begangen – nicht die Gottessohnschaft Jesu sehr leicht bildhaft veranschaulichen: un-ter Benützung der doppeldeutigen griechischen Jesaja-Stelle von der »jungen Frau« oder »Jungfrau« und in (vielleicht verdeckt polemischer) Überbietung der (von Lukas mit der Jesusge-schichte verwobenen) Geburtsgeschichte des Täufers Johan-nes[74], der wie Isaak[75], Simson[76] und Samuel[77] zwar aus unfrucht-barem, aber nicht jungfräulichem Schoß ist?

Der Messias sollte nicht nur im alttestamentlichen Sinn geist-erfüllt (Geistträger wie etwa der Gottesknecht[78]), sondern vom Geist geschaffen sein. Zeugung aus schöpferischem Gottesgeist meint ursprünglich nicht einen biologischen Tatbestand, son-dern die christologische Würde des so Gezeugten. Doch hat die immer stärkere *Biologisierung* dieser Vorstellung bald eingesetzt. Die wirkliche Menschheit Jesu wird im Neuen Testament zwar durchgehend vorausgesetzt. Von gelegentlicher Korrektur[79] ab-gesehen, werden auch selbstverständlich seine Eltern genannt[80]. Von seinen »Brüdern« und »Schwestern« ist ebenfalls selbstver-ständlich die Rede[81]. Diese im Hebräischen weiteren Begriffe dürfen nicht ohne positiven Grund einfach nur auf »Vettern« und »Basen« bezogen werden. Einer von den Brüdern Jesu, Jakobus (nicht mit dem Jakobus aus dem Zwölferkreis zu ver-wechseln), hat neben und nach Petrus in der Jerusalemer Ge-meinde die Hauptrolle gespielt[82]. Hätte man so reden können, wenn man in der Frühzeit etwas von einer Jungfrauengeburt geahnt hätte? Unbefangen sagt ein frühes Glaubensbekenntnis, daß Jesus dem Fleisch nach geworden ist aus Davids Samen[83]. Für Paulus, der von einer Jungfrauengeburt nichts weiß, ist der Gottessohn, wie eingangs bemerkt, schlicht aus der Frau gebo-ren[84]. Die Vorstellung der wunderbaren Geburt – ihm von der Geburt Isaaks durch Sara her durchaus geläufig[85] – wendet er nicht auf Jesus, sondern im übertragenen, symbolischen Sinn auf die Christen als Erben der Verheißung an[86]. Auch im späten Johannesevangelium, wo erstaunlicherweise von einer Jungfrau-engeburt ebenfalls nichts verlautet, wird unmittelbar vor dem

Satz über die Menschwerdung des Logos von allen Christen insgesamt gesagt, daß sie nicht aus dem Blut, noch aus Fleischeswillen, noch aus Manneswillen, sondern aus Gott gezeugt sind[87].

In den Geburtserzählungen jedoch werden von Jesus Geistschöpfung und Jungfrauengeburt in der Form geschichtlich-leiblicher Ereignisse berichtet. Aus der Formulierung des Lukas selbst[88] geht hervor, daß mit dieser Erklärung ein Grund, eine »aitia«, für die Anwendung des bereits schon vor Lukas weitverbreiteten Titels »Gottessohn« auf Jesus angegeben werden soll. Man nennt eine solche Erzählung eine ätiologische Legende oder Sage. Das Theologumenon vom Gottessohn wird somit als Geschichte anschaulich ausgemalt: aus dem Theologumenon ist ein Mythologumenon geworden[89].

So stellt sich die Diskussionslage heute nicht nur von evangelischen, sondern auch von katholischen Theologen her dar. Offensichtlich hat das Einschreiten der römischen Glaubensbehörde[90] gegen die nur vage Ausdrucksweise des Holländischen Katechismus[91] die Debatte in der katholischen Theologie nicht nur nicht gestoppt, sondern im kritischen Sinn beeinflußt. Der Trend weg *von der biologisch-ontologischen zur christologisch-theologischen Interpretation* ist offenkundig[92]. Auch in dieser Frage kann der Theologie und der Kirche nur unbedingte Wahrhaftigkeit und nicht Verschleierung, Zweideutigkeit und Uminterpretation voranhelfen. Folgende Gesichtspunkte dürften sich in dieser freilich auch außerhalb der katholischen Kirche umstrittenen Frage durchsetzen:

– *Die nur in den mattäischen und lukanischen Vorgeschichten bezeugte Jungfrauengeburt gehört nicht zur Mitte des Evangeliums: Die christliche Botschaft kann, wie Markus, Paulus, Johannes und die übrigen neutestamentlichen Zeugen beweisen, auch ohne diese am Rand des Neuen Testaments auftauchende theologische (ätiologische) Legende verkündet werden. Jesu Gottessohnschaft hängt nicht an der Jungfrauengeburt. Er ist Gottes Sohn, nicht weil bei seiner Entstehung Gott anstelle eines Mannes wirksam war, sondern weil er von Anfang, von Ewigkeit als Sohn erwählt und bestimmt ist. Sowenig wie Gottes Vaterschaft darf Jesu Sohnschaft biologisch als Abstammung mißverstanden werden. Geburt aus Gott und menschliche Erzeugung machen sich keine Konkurrenz.*
– *Kann die Jungfrauengeburt auch nicht als historisch-biologisches Ereignis verstanden werden, so doch als zumindest da-*

mals sinnträchtiges Symbol: *daß mit Jesus, der den alten Bund abschließt und überbietet, von Gott her ein wahrhaft neuer Anfang gemacht worden ist, daß Ursprung und Bedeutung seiner Person und seines Geschicks letztlich nicht aus dem innerweltlichen Geschichtsablauf, sondern aus dem Handeln Gottes in ihm zu verstehen sind. Ein freilich schon damals mißverständliches Zeichen!* Abgelehnt zunächst von jenen, die gegen Jesu Menschheit und Menschengeburt überhaupt waren (Doketismus: menschlicher Scheinleib oder Schein-Existenz Jesu). In der Folge aber nur zu oft benützt von jenen, die in Jesus einfach einen in menschlichem Kleid erscheinenden Gott gesehen haben (Mono-physitismus: nur eine einzige, göttliche Physis oder Natur Jesu).

– *Der mit Jesus von Gott her gegebene* neue Beginn *wurde schon im Neuen Testament auch anders* als durch die Jungfrauengeburt zum Ausdruck gebracht:
durch die Zurückführung des Stammbaumes Jesu über Adam auf Gott[93];
durch die beim jüdischen Religionsphilosophen Philon (und im gnostischen Mythos vom Urmenschen?) vorbereitete Vorstellung des neuen Adam, der Anfang und Haupt der neuen Menschheit ist[94];
durch die mythologischen Bilder von der Geburt des dann erhöhten Messias-Kindes aus der vom Drachen (»Schlange« spätjüdisch = »Satan«) bedrohten, mit der Sonne, Mond und den zwölf Sternen umkleideten Frau (= Israel und vielleicht auch die Kirche), nachher oft auf Maria gedeutet[95];
durch die Idee des von Ewigkeit bei Gott vorausexistierenden göttlichen »Logos« oder »Wortes«, das Fleisch wird[96].

– *Also kann dieser* neue Beginn *auch heute anders* als mit Hilfe der Legende einer Jungfrauengeburt verkündet werden, deren Mißverständlichkeit in der modernen Zeit noch zugenommen hat. Niemand kann verpflichtet werden, an das biologische Faktum einer jungfräulichen Empfängnis oder Geburt zu glauben. Christlicher Glaube bezieht sich auf den – auch ohne Jungfrauengeburt – in seiner Unverwechselbarkeit und Unableitbarkeit zutage getretenen gekreuzigten und doch lebendigen Jesus.

– *In der gottesdienstlichen Lesung braucht die Erzählung selbstverständlich nicht verschwiegen zu werden. Sie soll nur – man erinnere sich der Notwendigkeit und der Grenzen der Entmythologisierung*[97] – *redlich und differenziert interpretiert werden.*

Die im Zusammenhang der Empfängnis und Geburt Jesu von den Theologen behandelten Fragen um Maria, die Mutter Jesu, sind zahlreich. Sieht man von der vorübergehenden Kirchenspaltung wegen der zur Freude des Volkes von Ephesos einseitig vollzogenen Definition der »Gottesmutter« ab, so sind mariologische Aussagen erst in neuester Zeit zu brennenden Streitfragen geworden: mit den dogmatischen Definitionen der unbefleckten Empfängnis (1854) und der leiblichen Aufnahme Mariens in den Himmel (1950).

1. Zu einer soliden Begründung einer Marienverehrung – auch in der katholischen Kirche verpflichtet dazu keine allgemeine Lehrentscheidung – und zu einer ökumenischen Verständigung in diesen Fragen wird es nur kommen, wenn man sich von allen Seiten an die Leitlinien des *neutestamentlichen Befundes* hält[98].

Auffälligerweise spielt Maria (gräzisierte Form von »Marjam«, der Wiedergabe des hebräischen »Mirjam«), von deren Herkunft wir nichts Sicheres wissen, in den frühen christlichen Zeugnissen überhaupt keine Rolle. Von Paulus hörten wir, wie er zwar als erster, aber nur einmal und ganz allgemein ohne Namensnennung die menschliche Geburt Jesu »aus der Frau« erwähnt[99].

Aus dem öffentlichen Leben berichten die hier maßgebenden *synoptischen Evangelien eine einzige Begegnung Jesu mit seiner Mutter*, und die steht unter eindeutig negativem Vorzeichen: Seine Verwandtschaft war entsetzt über Jesu Auftreten; man hielt ihn geradezu für verrückt und versuchte, ihn wieder einzufangen[100]. Als seine Mutter und seine Brüder zu ihm kamen, weist Jesus auf eine andere Familie. Er zeigt auf die um ihn Herumsitzenden: Sehet, das sind meine Mutter und meine Brüder. Wer den Willen des Vaters tut, der ist mir Bruder und Schwester und Mutter[101]. Im ältesten Evangelium lesen wir außer dieser Geschichte – und einer Namensnennung zusammen mit den Namen der vier Brüder und den Schwestern Jesu[102] – überhaupt nichts von Maria. Merkwürdig genug, daß dann gerade diese einzige Szene in der christlichen Verkündigung derartig in den Hintergrund gedrängt und überspielt werden konnte: Mit der Würde der Begnadeten war sie doch nur dann nicht zu vereinen, wenn man Maria als des Zweifels und des Glaubens von vornherein enthoben hielt. Dabei bestätigt jene Seligpreisung, die bei Lukas primär nicht der Mutter, sondern allen, die das Wort hören und beobachten, gilt, diese Szene[103]. Die ebenfalls lukanische Erwähnung der Mutter Jesu in der Pfingsterzählung der Apostelgeschichte stimmt damit überein: Erst nach Ostern erwartet sie gemeinsam mit Jesu Brüdern und Jüngern als Glied der glaubenden Gemeinde den Geist[104].

Im *Johannesevangelium* erscheint Maria zweimal: am Anfang des öffentlichen Lebens Jesu beim Weinwunder in Kana, wo sie wiederum deutlich als Glaubende, Bittende und nur begrenzt Verstehende erscheint, der Jesus zunächst abweisend begegnet. Und an seinem Ende unter dem Kreuz: Diese Szene, die im allgemeinen als nicht historisch gilt, weil Maria auf der Liste der Synoptiker unter dem Kreuz fehlt[105], hat doch ihre tiefe Bedeutung. Maria und der hervorragende Glaubenszeuge (der Jünger, den Jesus liebt) vertreten die Kirche, die in der Stunde des Kreuzestodes, der Mitte des johanneischen Evangeliums, zum vollen Glauben gefunden hat[106]. Wie nach den Synoptikern unter dem Kreuz, so fehlt Maria merkwürdigerweise auch in den Ostergeschichten.

So fußt denn die marianische Frömmigkeit und Theologie, die schon recht früh mit der typologischen Beziehung Eva und Maria einsetzte und deren ungeheure, wenn auch zwiespältige Bedeutung für die katholische Kirche in den vergangenen Jahrhunderten niemand bestreiten wird, im wesentlichen auf der relativ schmalen Basis der mattäischen und besonders lukanischen *Kindheitsgeschichte*. Die dortigen Aussagen geben naturgemäß für die historische Forschung wenig, aber, wie wir im weiteren Zusammenhang der Weihnachtsgeschichte gesehen haben, für die Verkündigung manches her. Maria wird hier dargestellt als die Jungfrau, die voll demütigen Glaubens unter Gottes Gnadenwahl und Segen steht, und zugleich als die prophetische Sängerin, an der sich die Großtaten Gottes im Alten Testament vollenden. Ihr kühnes Magnifikat, von dem schon die Rede war, ist gewoben aus Psalmen- und Prophetentexten und kann interpretiert werden als Lied Marias oder Israels oder der Kirche. Die Reihe der in späteren Jahrhunderten ständig gesteigerten Ehrentitel für Maria – »de Maria numquam satis«, »von Maria nie genug«, so sagte man seit dem Mittelalter – wird schon bei Lukas eröffnet[107].

Zwei Züge in ihrem Bild sind *biblisch* solide *begründet* und für die Verkündigung nicht zu vernachlässigen:

- *Maria ist die Mutter Jesu:* Sie ist ein Menschenwesen und kein Himmelswesen. Als Mensch und Mutter ist sie Zeugin seines wahren Menschseins, aber auch seines in Gott gründenden Ursprungs. Von daher ist sie später – in einer freilich, wie noch gleich zu bemerken sein wird, historisch wie sachlich sehr problematischen Entwicklung – als Christusgebärerin, ja als Gottesgebärerin (Gottesmutter) verstanden worden.
- *Maria ist Beispiel und Vorbild christlichen Glaubens:* Ihr Glaube, der das Schwert des Anstoßes, Zwiespalts und Widerspruchs erfährt und der im Blick auf das Kreuz gefordert wird[108], ist nach Lukas (für Mattäus bildet, weniger beachtet, Josefs Glaubensgehorsam das Leitmotiv!) typisch für jeden christlichen Glauben. Maria zeigt also keinen speziellen Glauben, keinen besonderen Einblick in die Geheimnisse Gottes. Vielmehr macht auch ihr Glaube eine Geschichte durch und zeichnet so den Weg des christlichen Glaubens überhaupt vor. Von daher ist sie später, in einer freilich öfters mißverstandenen Weise, als Mutter der Glaubenden (ähnlich wie für Paulus[109] Abraham als Vater der Glaubenden) und so als Bild und Typos der Kirche aufgefaßt worden.

2. Doch – darf man es verschweigen? – über die biblischen Impulse hinaus haben auf die *Marienverehrung,* die ihrerseits auf Dichtung, Kunst, Brauchtum, Feste und Feiern einen unabsehbaren Einfluß ausgeübt und von daher zurückempfangen hat, wie bei jedem gewichtigen historischen Phänomen recht *mannigfache Faktoren* eingewirkt[110]: der Kult der vorderasiatischen Muttergottheiten ebenso wie der keltischer und germanischer Göttinnen (alte Berg-, Wasser- und Baumheiligtümer, später oft verbunden mit wunderbar entstandenen Gnadenbildern), theologische Rivalitäten (alexandrinische und antiochenische Christologie), dann auch kirchenpolitische Antagonismen (zwischen den Patriarchaten von Alexandrien und Konstantinopel) und manchmal auch recht persönliche Aktionen von Kirchenmännern (Kyrills von Alexandrien großangelegte Manipulation des Konzils von Ephesos 431 und seine Definition der »Gottesgebärerin« vor der Ankunft der anderen, antiochenischen Konzilspartei).

Die Marienverehrung entstand eindeutig im *Orient,* und zwar in der Form eines Kults der »immerwährenden Jungfrau«, der »Gottesmutter« und erhabenen »Himmelskönigin«. Im Osten wurde Maria zuerst im Gebet angerufen (»Unter Deinem

Schutz« 3./4. Jahrhundert) und das Gedächtnis Marias in die Liturgie eingeführt. Im Osten wurden zuerst Marienlegenden erzählt und Marienhymnen gedichtet, wurden zuerst Kirchen nach Maria benannt (4. Jahrhundert), Marienfeste eingeführt und Marienbilder geschaffen (5. Jahrhundert). Im Osten, vor allem, kam es im 5. Jahrhundert zu der genannten Definition Marias – in der Schrift regelmäßig »Mutter Jesu« genannt – als »Mutter Gottes«[111]: ein neuer nachbiblischer Titel, erst für das vorausgehende Jahrhundert sicher bezeugt, aber nun, nach jener Aktion Kyrills, vom Volk in der Stadt der alten »Großen Mutter« (die ursprünglich jungfräuliche Göttin Artemis, Diana) mit Begeisterung aufgenommen: eine Formel (wie andere Kyrills und jenes Konzils) im Verdacht eines monophysitischen und Gott verdinglichenden Verständnisses der Gottessohnschaft und der Menschwerdung (als ab *Gott* geboren werden könnte und nicht vielmehr ein Mensch, in welchem als Gottes*sohn* Gott selbst für den Glauben *offenbar* ist).

Im *Westen* setzten sich die östlichen Frömmigkeitsformen nicht ohne Widerstand durch: Noch bei Augustin finden sich weder Hymnen noch Gebete an Maria, noch werden Marienfeste erwähnt. Erst im 5. Jahrhundert findet sich das erste Beispiel einer unmittelbaren lateinisch-hymnischen Anrede an Maria (»Salve sancta parens«, Caelius Sedulius), woraus sich dann nach Venantius Fortunatus im späten 6. Jahrhundert eine immer reichere lateinische und dann auch deutsche Mariendichtung entfaltet. In Rom wird erst im 6. Jahrhundert Marias Namen in den Kanon eingeführt (der Josefs im 20. Jahrhundert von Johannes XXIII.), werden erst im 7. Jahrhundert die östlichen Marienfeste (Verkündigung, Heimgang, Geburt, Reinigung) übernommen, gibt es erst gegen Ende des 10. Jahrhunderts jene Legenden über die wunderwirkende Kraft des Gebets zu Maria.

Das *Mittelalter* setzte diese Entwicklung fort: Seit der Definition der »Gottesgebärerin« oder »Gottesmutter« im 5. Jahrhundert bis ins 12. Jahrhundert hatte sich der Akzent immer mehr von der vergangenen Tätigkeit Marias als der Mutter Jesu auf die gegenwärtige Rolle der immer jungfräulichen Gottesmutter und Himmelskönigin für die Christen verschoben. Während ältere Kirchenväter noch von den moralischen Fehlern Marias gesprochen hatten, wird jetzt immer mehr eine vollkommene Sündenlosigkeit behauptet, ja eine Heiligkeit schon vor der Geburt durch Bewahrung vor der Erbsünde, wie man im Westen seit dem 12. Jahrhundert vereinzelt ausdrücklich zu lehren anfing.

Doch zur selben Zeit erhielt hier Maria in anderer Hinsicht, wie Jesus selber, wieder mehr menschliche Züge, vor allem unter dem Einfluß biblisch gesinnter Heiliger wie Bernhard von Clairvaux und Franz von Assisi: Sie wird jetzt mehr gesehen als Verkörperung der Barmherzigkeit und als den Menschen näherstehende allesvermögende Fürsprecherin bei ihrem Sohn (Schutzmantelmadonna). Vom Minnesang kam ein erotisches Moment in die Marien-Frömmigkeit, seit der Renaissance-Malerei greifbar auch in der bildenden Kunst. Die Scholastik versuchte eine begriffliche Klärung der Stellung Marias in der Heilsgeschichte in bezug auf die Erbsünde (Duns Skotus † 1308). Die Mystik sah in ihr vor allem das Urbild der reinen, Gott geistig empfangenden und gebärenden Seele. Die über die übliche Heiligenverehrung (doulia) hinaus gesteigerte Verehrung (hyperdoulia) war zwar theologisch von der Anbetung (latria) Gottes unterschieden. Aber in der Praxis spielte die Geschöpflichkeit und Menschlichkeit Marias oft eine geringe Rolle.

Seit dem 12. Jahrhundert ist das biblische ›Ave Maria‹ – allerdings erst seit 1500 in der heutigen Form mit der Bitte um Beistand in der Todesstunde – die verbreitetste Gebetsform und wird mit dem Vaterunser verbunden. Aus dem 13. Jahrhundert stammt das Angelusläuten, aus dem 13.–15. Jahrhundert das Rosenkranzgebet, aber erst aus dem 19. oder gar 20. Jahrhundert die Mai- und Oktoberandachten, manche Marienerscheinungen und Marienwallfahrtsorte wie Lourdes und Fatima, nationale und internationale mariologische Kongresse und Arbeitsgemeinschaften.

Die *Reformatoren* waren gegen die mittelalterliche Entwicklung auch in dieser Frage auf die biblischen Wurzeln zurückgegangen. Martin Luther ehrt Maria in seiner Auslegung des Magnifikat um Christi willen und als Vorbild des Glaubens und der Demut; Johann Sebastian Bach hat es vertont. Aber in der Aufklärung ging die evangelische Marienverehrung unter. In der Gegenreformation war die Marienverehrung vor allem von den Jesuiten antiprotestantisch propagiert worden. Nach einer zeitweisen Zurückdrängung durch die Aufklärung wird sie in der katholischen Romantik neu belebt.

Seit Pius IX., der nach der Definition der unbefleckten Empfängnis (1854) durch das Vatikanum I (1870) päpstlichen Primat und Unfehlbarkeit definieren ließ, haben die *Päpste* die Marienverehrung mit allen Mitteln gefördert. Marianismus und Papalismus gingen seit dem 19. Jahrhundert Hand in Hand und stützten sich gegenseitig. Den Höhepunkt dieses »marianischen Zeitalters« bildete das Jahr 1950 und die gegen alle protestantischen, orthodoxen und innerkatholischen Bedenken von Pius XII., dem letzten völlig absolutistisch regierenden Papst, vollzogene feierliche Dogmatisierung der leiblichen Aufnahme Mariens in die himmlische Herrlichkeit am Ende ihres Lebenslaufes. Wovon nun freilich nicht nur die Schrift, sondern auch die Tradition des ersten halben Jahrtausends nichts weiß, und zunächst nur apokryphe Quellen, Legenden, Bilder und Feste zu reden beginnen. Doch dieses Zeitalter – unterstützt durch Pius' XII. Weihe des ganzen Menschengeschlechts an das Unbefleckte Herz Mariens 1942 (Einfluß von Fatima) und das Marianische Jahr 1954 – nahm einige Jahre später ein erstaunlich rasches Ende mit dem Zweiten Vatikanischen Konzil, welches auf weitere »konsequente« marianische Dogmen (Mittlerin, Miterlöserin) bewußt verzichtete, seine (gemäßigt traditionelle) Mariologie als Schlußkapitel in seine Lehre von der Kirche integrierte und die Exzesse des Marianismus unüberhörbar tadelte. Dieser übertriebene Marienkult hat denn auch in Theologie und kirchlichem Leben seine Stoßkraft in der Zeit nach dem Konzil völlig eingebüßt[112].

3. Zu einer *ökumenischen Verständigung* in dieser Frage wird es erst kommen durch Bemühungen von beiden Seiten:

a. daß man sich auf *katholischer* Seite noch entschiedener als bisher nach den Leitlinien des biblischen Befundes richtet und auch keine Angst hat vor der redlichen kritischen Überprüfung der vier neuesten – weder in der Schrift noch in der Tradition noch durch »innere Gründe« (= theologische Postulate) allgemein überzeugend begründeten und in der »Hierarchie der Wahrheiten«[113] jedenfalls weit unten rangierenden – Marien- und Papstdogmen, die in verschiedener Hinsicht eine Einheit bilden. Bei einer solchen Überprüfung – sie kann hier nicht geschehen – wäre zwischen den möglicherweise hinter einer Definition stehenden zu bejahenden Intentionen und ihrer zu kritisierenden fragwürdigen Ausformung zu unterscheiden;

b. daß man sich auf *evangelischer* Seite nicht mit einer rein apologetischen und polemischen Haltung begnügt, sondern unvoreingenommen den biblischen Befund über Maria und überhaupt die Rolle der Frau in der Geschichte des Heils für die Verkündigung fruchtbar macht. Dabei sollte man poetischen Aussagen in der katholischen Tradition (Liedern, Hymnen,

Gebeten) und überhaupt persönlichen oder national bedingten Frömmigkeitsformen mehr Freiheit zugestehen, als man
dies bei aller Toleranz streng theologischen oder gar offiziellen
dogmatischen Äußerungen einer Kirche zugestehen kann.
Auf keinen Fall darf sich eine Kirche, wie geschehen, in Maria,
der demütigen Magd, selber glorifizieren. Wie Maria so hat eine
Kirche nur Sinn in Ein- und Unterordnung unter das Geschehen,
welches sein unverrückbares Zentrum nicht in Maria und nicht in
der Kirche, sondern allein in Jesus selber hat.

Von der Kirche muß am Schluß dieses dritten Hauptteiles
nochmals ausdrücklich die Rede sein, nachdem hinreichend klar
geworden ist, daß die Deutungsversuche des Todes Jesu seine
bleibende Bedeutung und Wirkung herausgestellt haben, die
Deutungsversuche der Empfängnis und Geburt Jesu aber seinen
einzigartigen, unableitbaren Ursprung und Anspruch. Die verschiedenen Deutungen erhellen und ergänzen sich gegenseitig.
Alle aber sind nur von der konkreten Geschichte dieses Jesus von
Nazaret her möglich, die sie auf keinen Fall im Nachhinein
verdecken dürfen. Auch die Kirche ist ja mehr als eine Deutungs-
und Argumentationsgemeinschaft, aber auch mehr als eine Er-
zählgemeinschaft: sie ist zuerst und zuletzt eine Glaubensgemeinschaft.

VII. Gemeinschaft des Glaubens

Zwei Jahrtausende ist Jesus von Nazaret für die Menschheit lebendig geblieben. Was hat ihn am Leben erhalten? Wer hat ihn der Menschheit immer neu bezeugt? Wäre er lebendig geblieben, wenn er nur in einem Buch gelebt hätte? Oder blieb er nicht lebendig, weil er während zweier Jahrtausende in den Köpfen und Herzen ungezählter Menschen lebte? In der Institution Kirche oder außerhalb ihrer oder an ihrem Rand Menschen, die bei den immensen Unterschieden der Zeit und des Ortes doch von ihm bestimmt waren: in aller Menschlichkeit und in durchaus verschiedenem Ausmaß von seinem Wort und Geist angeregt, bewegt, erfüllt und so in unterschiedlicher Weise eine Gemeinschaft des Glaubens bildend.

1. Inspiriertes und inspirierendes Wort

Ohne diese Gemeinschaft derer, die sich auf seine Sache eingelassen haben, wäre Jesus in der Menschheit nicht lebendig geblieben. Ja, ohne sie hätte es überhaupt nie jenes kleine Buch gegeben, in welchem die ältesten und besten Zeugnisse von ihm gesammelt sind.

Inspiration?

Dieses kleine Buch, das Neue Testament, fiel nicht vom Himmel. Der Koran, so sahen wir, im Himmel aufbewahrt, wurde als direktes Wort Gottes Satz um Satz für die Menschen diktiert, und ist deshalb Satz um Satz unfehlbar wahr. Also ein in jeder Hinsicht (sprachlich, stilistisch, logisch, historisch) vollkommenes, heiliges Buch, das wörtlich akzeptiert werden muß und nicht einmal interpretiert und kommentiert werden darf. Und die Bibel? Die Bibel des Neuen wie des Alten Testaments wurde, wie insbesondere die Briefe des Paulus und der Beginn des Lukasevangeliums unbefangen bezeugen – auf Erden geschrieben und gesammelt. Also eindeutig *Menschenwort*: Satz für Satz von ganz bestimmten Menschen gesammelt, niedergeschrieben, mit Akzenten versehen und in verschiedenen Richtungen weitergeführt. Und deshalb nicht ohne Mängel und Fehler, Verhüllung und Vermischung, Beschränktheit und Irrtum. So entstand eine in sich höchst vielfältige Sammlung von deutlichen und weniger deutlichen, stärkeren und schwächeren, ursprünglicheren und abgeleiteten Glaubensdokumenten[1].

Sollte aber nicht doch in diesen Schriften *Gottes Wort* niedergelegt sein? Wie so oft kommt es darauf an, eine solche Aussage recht zu verstehen: wie man nämlich die menschliche Geschichte dieser Schriften ernstnehmen und doch an Gottes Wort glauben kann. Auch hier werden wir gezwungen sein, Vorstellungen früherer Jahrhunderte zu überprüfen, ihre berechtigten Anliegen zu übernehmen und, wo nötig, ihre Sprache und Vorstellungsweisen, weil heute mißverständlich oder irreführend, kritisch in aller Behutsamkeit zu korrigieren.

Schon in der frühen hellenistischen Kirche galt die Schrift als von Gottes Geist *»inspiriert«*. Wie aber stellte man sich diese »Inspiration« vor? Unter mannigfachen außerchristlichen Einflüssen hatte sich ein Verständnis herausgebildet, das erst später von der lutherischen und reformierten Orthodoxie (und mit der beinahe üblichen Phasenverschiebung im 19. Jahrhundert auch von der römisch-katholischen Theologie) rigoros systematisiert worden war[2]. Für das hellenistische Heidentum und Judentum überkam der Geist den Menschen in der Ekstase. In der Ekstase erschien die menschliche Individualität unter der göttlichen Manie wie ausgelöscht (so die Pythia im Delphischen Orakel). Ähnlich dachten frühchristliche Theologen. Sie sahen die biblischen Autoren – ganz anders als diese sich selbst – einfach als Werkzeuge, die unter der »Inspiration«, der »Eingebung«, ja dem »Diktat« des göttlichen Geistes geschrieben haben. In der Art von Sekretären also. Oder gar wie die Flöte oder eine Harfe vom Lufthauch zum Klingen gebracht. Gott selber durch seinen Geist spielt hier die Melodie, bestimmt Inhalt und Form der Schrift, so daß die ganze Bibel um Gottes willen von Widersprüchlichkeiten, Fehlern und Irrtümern frei sein, beziehungsweise von Interpreten (durch Harmonisierung, Allegorese oder Mystifizierung) frei gehalten werden muß. Alles also inspiriert bis ins letzte Wort hinein (»Verbal-Inspiration«). Alles folglich Wort für Wort bedingungslos zu unterschreiben. Was unvermeidlich zu schwersten, aber im Grunde unnötigen Konflikten sowohl mit den Naturwissenschaften (seit der Kopernikanischen Wende) und mit der Historie (seit der Aufklärung) führen mußte.

Doch ist diese *traditionelle Auffassung* von einer gleichsam mechanischen Inspiration durch die historisch-kritische Erforschung des Alten und Neuen Testaments mehr und mehr *erschüttert* worden: In ungeahnter Weise ist in den vergangenen 200 Jahren die echte Menschlichkeit, Geschichtlichkeit und auch Irrtumsfähigkeit der Verfasser der biblischen Schriften ans Licht gekommen. Das alles kann heute vernünftigerweise niemand mehr ernsthaft bestreiten. Aber war damit die Autorität dieser Schriften zerstört, wie viele zunächst fürchteten? Oder war nicht gerade jetzt wieder eine Brücke zur ältesten Kirche geschlagen, die Gott selber in den biblischen Autoren am Werk sah und dennoch deren menschliche und geschichtliche Eigenart ganz im Sinne des Alten Testaments ernstgenommen hatte? Nicht die Unfehlbarkeit, Infallibilität oder Inerranz der Autoren stand damals im Vordergrund, sondern die Wahrheit des Inhalts, des Zeugnisses, der Botschaft selbst. Nicht als ungeschichtlich-schemenhafte Wesen, nicht als beinahe übermenschliche, aber im Grund unmenschliche, weil letzlich willen- und verantwortungslose Werkzeuge, durch die unmittelbar der Heilige Geist alles bewirkt, erscheinen hier die biblischen Verfasser. Sondern als die Glaubenszeugen, die in aller menschlichen Gebrechlichkeit, Bedingtheit und Beschränktheit, in vielfach stammelnder Sprache und höchst unzureichenden Begriffsmitteln vom eigentlichen Grund und Inhalt des Glaubens reden.

Im jüdisch-hellenistischen Raum sprach man von der ›*Heiligen Schrift*‹, von den »heiligen Schriften« und legte so die Vorstellung einer geradezu vollkommen göttlich »heiligen« Schrift nahe. Das Neue Testament dagegen vermeidet die Aussage von der Heiligkeit beinahe ganz. Nur an einer einzigen späten Stelle der bekanntlich nicht von Paulus stammenden Pastoralbriefe[3] ist in hellenistischer Weise die Rede davon, daß »jede von Gott (oder Gottes Geist) eingegebene Schrift« nützlich sei zur Belehrung, Verbesserung, Erziehung, womit jedenfalls noch längst keine mechanische Inspirationstheorie gelehrt wird[4].

Wenn heute das mißverständliche Wort von der »Inspiriertheit« der Schrift überhaupt noch gebraucht werden soll, dann jedenfalls nicht im Sinne jener späteren Inspirationslehre, die die Wirkung des göttlichen Geistes als ein Mirakel auf irgendwelche bestimmte Schreibakte eines Apostels oder biblischen Schriftstellers limitiert denkt. Nicht nur die Niederschrift, sondern die gesamte Vorgeschichte und Nachgeschichte der Schrift, der gesamte Vorgang der gläubigen Aufnahme und Weitergabe der

Botschaft hat etwas mit dem göttlichen Geist zu tun: Dieser Vorgang kann, richtig verstanden, *geistdurchwirkt* und *geisterfüllt* genannt werden. Wenn sich nämlich die ersten Zeugen vom göttlichen Geist bewegt glauben, dann bestimmt das auch ihre Schriften, ohne daß den Hörern oder Lesern gegenüber irgendwo ein anzuerkennender Inspirationsakt geltend gemacht werden muß. Es wird im Neuen Testament vielmehr schlicht vorausgesetzt, daß jedes Empfangen und Verkündigen des Evangeliums von vornherein »im Heiligen Geist« geschieht[5].

Doch schließt solch geistiges Geschehen nach dem Neuen Testament selbst durchaus die menschliche Geschichtlichkeit ein, die ihrerseits Bibelkritik nicht nur ermöglicht, sondern erfordert: Text- und Literarkritik, historische und theologische Kritik. Ernsthafte Bibelkritik – das ist hoffentlich durch alle diese Kapitel hindurch deutlich geworden – kann dazu helfen, daß die erfreuliche Botschaft nicht in einem Buch verschlossen bleibt, sondern in jeder neuen Zeit wieder neu lebendig verkündigt wird. Wie die ersten Zeugen – und als solche bleiben sie grundlegend – das Evangelium nicht als fixe Formel oder starre Doktrin diktiert bekommen und sklavisch weitergegeben haben, wie sie es vielmehr in ihrer besonderen Situation mit ihrer besonderen Eigenart aufgenommen und in eigener Interpretation und Theologie verkündigt haben, so dürfen und sollen auch die heutigen Verkünder der Botschaft an ihrem Ort zu ihrer Stunde auf ihre Weise die *alte Botschaft in neuer Gestalt* weitergeben.

Gewiß, das Neue Testament ist und bleibt der schon von der alten Kirche in einem längeren Prozeß erkannte und anerkannte Niederschlag des ursprünglichen Zeugnisses. Auch dazu bedurfte es keiner unfehlbaren Entscheidung der frühen Kirche. Im liturgischen Gebrauch vor allem hatten sich diese Schriften primär aufgrund ihres Inhalts im Gegensatz zu anderen Schriften (= Apokryphen) durchgesetzt. Man erfuhr ihre Kraft immer neu und konnte es immer neu wagen, sich ihr anzuvertrauen. Die konkrete Richtschnur (= »Kanon«) der frühen Kirche hat sich im Lauf der Jahrhunderte bewährt. Das *Neue Testament* hat seine *unersetzliche normative Autorität und Bedeutung* immer wieder neu bewiesen. Und wir bleiben an diese Norm verwiesen, solange wir im ursprünglichen Sinne Christen bleiben und nicht irgend etwas anderes werden wollen. Das Neue Testament bleibt als das ursprüngliche schriftliche christliche Zeugnis die (glücklicherweise) unveränderliche Norm auch für alle spätere kirchliche Verkündigung und Theologie, die subjektivistischer Willkür und jeder Art von Schwärmertum wehrt. Aber trotz allem: Die Freiheit und Mannigfaltigkeit der Zeugnisse im Neuen Testament, die allein durch die Botschaft vom Handeln Gottes in der Geschichte Israels und in Jesus Christus ihre Einheit und Einfalt haben, rechtfertigen die Freiheit und Mannigfaltigkeit der Zeugnisse heute. Inwiefern aber können nun diese menschlichen Zeugnisse des Neuen Testaments Wort Gottes genannt werden?

Wort Gottes?

Das Christentum, so sagten wir bereits einmal, ist keine Buch-Religion. Nicht die Schriften selber sind die göttliche Offenbarung. Diese sind nur die menschlichen Zeugnisse der göttlichen Offenbarung, in welchen die Menschlichkeit, Eigenständigkeit und Geschichtlichkeit der menschlichen Verfasser jederzeit voll gewahrt bleibt. Ich glaube nicht *zuerst* an die Schrift oder gar an die Inspiriertheit der Schrift und *dann* an die Wahrheit der von ihr überlieferten Botschaft. Ich glaube an Gott, der sich für die Glaubenden in der Geschichte Israels und schließlich in der Person Jesu befreiend kundgetan hat und der in den Schriften des Alten und Neuen Testaments ursprünglich bezeugt wird. Mein Glaube entsteht so an der Schrift: Diese zeugt mir von außen in ursprünglicher Gestalt von diesem Gott Israels und Jesu Christi. Aber mein Glaube ruht nicht auf der Schrift: Nicht das Buch als solches, sondern dieser Gott selbst in Jesus ist der Grund meines Glaubens.

So erreicht denn die *Wahrheit der Schrift* den Menschen ohne alle Vergewaltigung *durch die Menschlichkeit,* Geschichtlichkeit und Gebrechlichkeit der menschlichen Verfasser *hindurch.* Die Wahrheit der Schrift meint über alle wahren – oder naturwissenschaftlich, historisch, religiös weniger wahren – Sätze hinaus die »Wahrheit« im ursprünglich biblischen Sinn: nämlich die »Treue«, »Beständigkeit«, »Zuverlässigkeit« Gottes selbst, der zu seinem Wort und zu seinen Verheißungen steht. Keine einzige Stelle der Schrift spricht davon, daß die Schrift keinen Irrtum enthalte. Aber jede Stelle der Schrift zeugt in ihrem engeren oder weiteren Kontext von dieser unverbrüchlichen Treue Gottes zum Menschen, die Gott nie zum Lügner werden läßt.

So wird denn auch verständlich, in welchem Sinn die Schrift *Wort Gottes* genannt werden kann. »Es steht geschrieben« kann nie meinen: »Das Wort Gottes liegt geschrieben vor uns.« Also für jeden neutralen Beobachter feststellbar, dem Menschen gleichsam aufzwingbar. Will man nicht wie früher naiv, sondern will man theologisch verantwortlich reden, wird man sagen müssen[6]:

- *Die Bibel* ist *nicht einfach Gottes Wort: sie ist zunächst und in vollem Umfang Menschenwort ganz bestimmter Menschen.*
- *Die Bibel* enthält *auch nicht einfach Gottes Wort: Es sind nicht bestimmte Sätze reines Gotteswort, während die übrigen Menschenwort sind.*
- *Die Bibel* wird *zu Gottes Wort: Sie wird Wort Gottes für jeden, der sich vertrauend, glaubend auf ihr Zeugnis und damit auf den in ihr bekundeten Gott und Jesus Christus einläßt.*

Gott selber, wie er sich in der Geschichte Israels und in der Person Jesu Christi kundgetan hat, ruft durch diese Zeugnisse zum Glauben und sorgt dafür, daß die Botschaft immer wieder trotz aller Menschlichkeit und trotz aller Widerstände wahrhaft gehört, geglaubt, verstanden und verwirklicht wird. In völlig unmagischer und unverfügbarer Weise ist so das Wort wirksam. Es kann, wenn der Mensch es will, auch abgelehnt werden und bleibt trotzdem wirksam – es wirkt dann verurteilend und wird zum Gericht. Wer dieser Einladung zum Glauben nicht folgt, für den bleibt die Bibel nur reichlich problematisches Menschenwort, mag er auch noch so viel – philologisch, historisch, theologisch – von ihr wissen. Wer aber dieser Einladung zum Glauben folgt, für den bleibt die Bibel nicht Menschenwort, sondern wird bei aller Problematik zum helfenden, befreienden, rettenden Gotteswort, mag er auch von der historisch-kritischen Exegese wenig verstanden haben. Er erkennt dann durchaus klar und unzweideutig, um was es in der christlichen Botschaft entscheidend geht. Er erfaßt das Wort in allen Worten, das Evangelium in den verschiedenen Evangelien. Er läßt sich inspirieren vom Geist dieser Schrift, der in Wahrheit der Geist Gottes und der Geist Jesu Christi ist, von diesem Geist, der die Zeugnisse selber in durchaus unmechanischer Weise zu geisterfüllten und geist-durchwirkten Zeugnissen werden läßt. Und sehr viel wichtiger als die Frage, ob und wie die Bibel selber inspiriertes Wort ist, ist – auch für jene singuläre Stelle von der Inspiration in den Pastoralbriefen – die Frage, ob und wie *sich der Mensch selbst von ihrem Wort inspirieren läßt.* Denn dieses vom Geist inspirierte Wort will durch denselben Geist inspirierendes Wort sein.

Warum aber redet man dann hier so betont vom Geist? Ja, man kann die Frage verallgemeinern: Warum führt man überhaupt neben Gott, dem Vater, und Jesus Christus noch eine dritte Größe ein, so daß es schließlich zu einer Trinitätslehre gekommen ist? Waren denn die ursprünglichen Glaubensbekenntnisse, wie man im Neuen Testament leicht erkennen kann, nicht binitarisch und erst in einem späteren Stadium trinitarisch?

2. Der eine Geist

Man kann es nicht übersehen: Die Rede vom Heiligen Geist ist für viele heute derart unverständlich, daß sie nicht einmal umstritten genannt werden kann. Man sollte aber auch nicht übersehen: Schuld daran ist in einem hohen Ausmaß der Mißbrauch, dem der Begriff des Heiligen Geistes sowohl von seiten der Amtskirche wie von seiten einzelner Frommer in neuerer Zeit ausgesetzt war[1].

Unheiliger und heiliger Geist

Wenn höhere Amtsträger nicht wußten, wie sie ihren eigenen Unfehlbarkeitsanspruch begründen sollten, wiesen sie auf den Heiligen Geist. Wenn Theologen nicht wußten, wie sie eine bestimmte Lehre, ein Dogma oder Bibelwort verantworten sollten, appellierten sie an den Heiligen Geist. Wenn milde oder wilde Schwärmer nicht wußten, wie sie ihre subjektivistische Willkür rechtfertigen sollten, beriefen sie sich auf den Heiligen Geist. Der Heilige Geist zur Rechtfertigung von absoluter Lehr- und Regierungsmacht, zur Rechtfertigung von inhaltlich nicht überzeugenden Glaubensaussagen, zur Rechtfertigung von frommem Fanatismus und falscher Glaubenssicherheit? Der Heilige Geist als Ersatz für Überzeugungskraft, Legitimation, Plausibilität, innere Glaubwürdigkeit, sachliche Auseinandersetzung? In der alten Kirche und noch selbst in der mittelalterlichen war es nicht so. In dieser Zuspitzung handelt es sich um eine typisch neuzeitliche Entwicklung, entstanden einerseits aus dem reformatorischen Schwärmertum und andererseits aus der Defensivhaltung der Großkirchen, die sich gegen die Kritik der Vernunft immunisieren wollten.

Aber nun anders betrachtet: Wie sollte man denn in der Urchristenheit zum Ausdruck bringen, daß Gott, daß Jesus Christus dem Glaubenden, der Glaubensgemeinschaft wahrhaft nahe ist: ganz wirklich, gegenwärtig, wirksam? Darauf antworten die Schriften des Neuen Testaments übereinstimmend, aber ohne alle Machtansprüche für Kirche, Theologie und Frömmigkeit: Gott, Jesus Christus sind dem Glaubenden, sind der Glaubensgemeinschaft *nahe im Geist*: gegenwärtig im Geist, durch den Geist, ja, als Geist. Also nicht nur durch unsere Erinnerung, sondern durch die geistige Wirklichkeit, Gegenwärtigkeit, Wirksamkeit Gottes, Jesu Christi selbst. Was heißt hier »Geist«?

Greifbar und doch nicht greifbar, unsichtbar und doch mächtig, wirklich wie die energiegeladene Luft, der Wind, der Sturm, lebenswichtig wie die Luft, die man atmet: so haben sich die Menschen der alten Zeit vielfach den »Geist« und Gottes unsichtbares Wirken vorgestellt. »Geist«, hebräisch die »ruah« (griechisch »pneuma«), ist nach dem Anfang des Schöpfungsberichtes jener »Braus« oder »Sturm« Gottes, der sich über den Wassern bewegt[2]. Geist meint hier nicht idealistisch eine Fähigkeit des Erkennens oder eine psychologische Kraft, meint erst recht nicht ein immaterielles intellektuelles oder ethisches Prinzip, meint überhaupt nicht das im modernen Sinne Geistige im Gegensatz zum Sinnlichen, Körperlichen, zur Natur. Geist, biblisch verstanden, meint vielmehr im Gegensatz zum »Fleisch«, zur geschaffenen, vergänglichen Wirklichkeit die von Gott ausgehende Kraft oder Macht: also jene unsichtbare *Gotteskraft* und *Gottesmacht,* welche schöpferisch oder auch zerstörerisch, zum Leben oder zum Gericht, in der Schöpfung und in der Geschichte, in Israel und in der Kirche wirksam ist. Mächtig oder leise die Menschen überkommend, Einzelne oder auch Gruppen in Ekstase versetzend, wirksam oft in außerordentlichen Phänomenen, in den großen Männern und Frauen, in Mose und den »Richtern« Israels, in Kriegern und Sängern, Königen, Propheten und Prophetinnen.

Doch die Zeit der großen Propheten war in Israel längst vorbei. Im frühen Judentum zur Zeit Jesu war der Geist nach rabbinischer Lehre mit den letzten Schriftpropheten »erloschen«. Erst für die Endzeit erwartete man wieder den Geist, der dann nach der berühmten Weissagung des Joel[3] nicht nur über Einzelne, sondern über das ganze Volk »ausgegossen« werden soll. Ist es erstaunlich, daß die urchristlichen Gemeinden, die in Jesus den großen Geistträger erkannten (Taufe!), diese prophetische Erwartung nach Jesu Auferweckung in ihrer eigenen Wirklichkeit erfüllt gesehen haben? Die Austeilung des Geistes also Signal für den Beginn der Endzeit: und zwar, wie bei Joel geschrieben, nicht nur für die Privilegierten, sondern auch für die Nichtprivilegierten: nicht nur für die Söhne, sondern auch für die Töchter; nicht nur für die Alten, sondern auch für die Jungen; nicht nur für die Herren, sondern auch für die Knechte und Mägde[4].

Dieser Geist ist also nicht, wie vom Wort her durchaus möglich, der Geist des Menschen, sein wissendes und wollendes lebendiges Ich. Sondern er ist der Geist Gottes, der als *heiliger* Geist vom unheiligen Geist des Menschen und seiner Welt scharf unterschieden wird[5]. Zwar hat er, kaum klar trennbar, dynamistische und animistische Züge: Er erscheint oft mehr als unpersönliche Macht (»dynamis«), oft mehr als persönliches Wesen (»anima«). Aber er ist im Neuen Testament zweifellos nicht irgendein magisches, substanzhaftes, mysteriös-übernatürliches Fluidum dynamistischer oder auch ein Zauberwesen animistischer Art. Der Geist ist niemand anders als *Gott selbst*: sofern er nämlich den Menschen und der Welt nahe ist als die ergreifende, aber nicht ergreifbare, die schenkende, aber nicht verfügbare, die lebenschaffende, aber auch richtende Macht und Kraft. Kein Drittes, kein Ding also zwischen Gott und den Menschen, sondern die persönliche Nähe Gottes zu den Menschen. Die meisten Mißverständnisse des Heiligen Geistes stammen von daher, daß man ihn mythologisch von Gott lostrennt und verselbständigt. Dabei hat gerade das Konzil von Konstantinopel 381, dem wir die Ausweitung des nizänischen Glaubensbekenntnisses auf den Heiligen Geist verdanken, ausdrücklich betont, daß der Geist eines Wesens mit dem Vater und dem Sohn ist[6].

Die Geistauffassung der Urchristenheit ist im einzelnen freilich nicht einheitlich. Recht verschieden erscheint das Wirken des Geistes vor allem in der lukanischen Apostelgeschichte und bei Paulus[7].

Lukas ist am Wirken des Geistes gerade in seinen außerordentlichen Formen sehr interessiert und unterscheidet zeitlich, wie wir sahen[8], von Ostern ein christliches Pfingsten mit Geistempfang (erinnert der Pfingststurm an den »Gottessturm« vor aller Schöpfung?). Der Geist erscheint in der Apostelgeschichte vielfach als selbstverständliche Folge des Gläubigwerdens und der Taufe[9]. Zugleich aber auch als Ursprung der außerordentlichen charismatischen Kraftwirkung, die dem Gottesgeist in besonderen Fällen zugeschrieben wird, als besondere Gabe für bestimmte zusätzliche Taten: Der Geist ist es, der in der Kirche Auftrag, Befähigung, Vollmacht, Legitimität, Kontinuität gibt, wofür die Handauflegung Zeichen ist[10].

Paulus hat als erster über Wesen und Wirken des Geistes genauer nachgedacht. Bei ihm bestimmt der Geist nicht nur einzelne, mehr oder weniger außerordentliche Taten, sondern die Existenz des Glaubenden schlechthin[11]. Paulus versteht den Geist nämlich ganz entscheidend von jener großen Zeitwende her, die für ihn Jesu Tod und Auferweckung sind. Weil hier offenbar wurde, daß Gott selbst in Jesus gehandelt hat, kann nun der *Geist Gottes zugleich als der Geist des zu Gott erhöhten Jesus verstanden* werden. So ist Gottes Geist nicht mehr mißdeutbar als eine obskure, namenlose göttliche Kraft im Sinne der hellenistischen Gnosis, sondern ist völlig eindeutig der Geist Jesu Christi, des Sohnes[12]. Gott und der erhöhte Jesus, obwohl als »Personen« auch bei Paulus klar unterschieden, werden in bezug auf die Wirkung zusammengesehen: Gott schafft das Heil durch Jesus. Ihm ist als dem erhöhten Herrn Gottes Macht, Kraft, Geist so sehr zu eigen geworden, daß er nicht nur des Geistes mächtig ist und über ihn verfügt, sondern daß er aufgrund der Auferweckung selbst als Geist verstanden werden kann: Jesus ist zu einem lebenschaffenden Geist geworden[13]. Ja, Paulus sagt sogar: der Herr ist der Geist[14].

Was meint gerade diese rätselhafte Aussage? Das bereits Angedeutete: keine schlechthinnige Identität zweier personaler Größen. Sondern *der zu Gott erweckte Herr ist in der Existenz- und Wirkweise des Geistes.* Er erscheint als mit dem Geist identisch, sobald er nicht an sich, sondern in seinem Handeln an Gemeinde und Einzelnem betrachtet wird: Der erhöhte *Jesus handelt gegenwärtig durch den Geist, im Geist, als Geist.* Im Geist also ist der erhöhte Christus selber gegenwärtig. So können denn die Gleichsetzung des Herrn mit dem Geist und die Unterordnung des Geistes unter den Herrn nebeneinander stehen[15], können die Wendungen »im Geist« und »in Christus« oder auch »der Geist in uns« und »Christus in uns« parallel laufen und faktisch ausgewechselt werden. In der Begegnung von »Gott«, »Herr« und »Geist« mit dem Glaubenden geht es also letztlich um die eine und selbe Begegnung: »Die Gnade des Herrn Jesus Christus und die Liebe Gottes und die Gemeinschaft des Heiligen Geistes sei mit euch allen[16]!« Überall geht es um das eine Handeln Gottes selbst. Was also ist der Heilige Geist?

- *Der Heilige Geist ist Gottes Geist: Er ist Gott selber, sofern er als gnädige Macht und Kraft über das Innere, das Herz des Menschen, ja den ganzen Menschen Herrschaft gewinnt, ihm innerlich gegenwärtig wird und sich dem Menschengeist wirksam bezeugt.*
- *Als Gottes Geist ist er zugleich der Geist des zu Gott erhöhten* Jesus Christus: *dadurch ist Jesus der lebendige Herr, der Maßgebende für die Kirche und den einzelnen Christen. Weder eine Hierarchie noch eine Theologie noch ein Schwärmertum, die sich über Jesus, sein Wort, sein Verhalten und Geschick hinweg auf den »Geist« berufen wollen, können sich auf Jesu Christi Geist berufen. Deshalb sind von diesem Jesus Christus her die Geister zu prüfen und zu scheiden.*
- *Als Geist Gottes und Jesu Christi* für die Menschen *ist er nie des Menschen eigene Möglichkeit, sondern ist* Kraft, Macht, Geschenk Gottes: *Er ist kein unheiliger Menschengeist, Zeitgeist, Kirchengeist, Amtsgeist, Schwarmgeist, sondern ist und bleibt immer der heilige Gottesgeist, der weht, wo und wann er will, und der sich nicht zur Rechtfertigung absoluter Lehr- und Regierungsmacht, unbegründeter Theologie, frommen Fanatismus' und falscher Glaubenssicherheit in Anspruch nehmen läßt.*
- *Den Heiligen Geist empfängt, wer sich auf die Botschaft und damit auf Gott und seinen Christus im* Glauben *wahrhaft einläßt: Er wirkt nicht magisch-automatisch, sondern ermöglicht ein freies Ja. Sofern die Taufe Zeichen und Sakrament des des Glaubens ist, gehören Taufe und Geistempfang zusammen: Die Taufe ist ja Ausdruck der Bereitschaft, sich ganz und gar unter den Namen Jesu zu stellen, in Erfüllung des Willens Gottes zum Wohl der Mitmenschen.*
- *Als Christen glauben wir an* den Heiligen Geist (credo in Spiritum Sanctum) *in* der heiligen Kirche, *nicht aber an* die Kirche: *Die Kirche ist nicht Gott. Die Kirche sind, recht und schlecht, wir, die Gläubigen. Im strengen Sinn glauben wir nicht an uns selbst, sondern an Gott, der in seinem Geist die Gemeinschaft der Glaubenden ermöglicht. Vom heiligenden Geist her glauben wir* die heilige Kirche (credo sanctam Ecclesiam)[17].

Der Geist Gottes und Jesu Christi ist wesentlich ein *Geist der Freiheit*[18]; letztlich die Freiheit von Schuld, Gesetz, Tod, Freiheit und Mut zum Handeln, zur Liebe, zum Leben in Friede, Gerechtigkeit, Freude, Hoffnung und Dankbarkeit. Die paulinischen Briefe sind voll davon. Aber – nur eine Zwischenfrage – ist das eine Realität? Darauf läßt sich sagen: Die Freiheit der Söhne und Töchter Gottes wurde seit den Zeiten des Paulus bis auf den heutigen Tag immer wieder ganz praktisch bezeugt, erfahren, gelebt: meist unauffällig und weltgeschichtlich nur indirekt konstatierbar, mehr von den Kleinen als den Großen. Trotz aller Mängel und allen Versagens der Kirche haben ungezählte Glaubende von der apostolischen Zeit bis heute diese Freiheit immer wieder in Glauben und Gehorsam ergriffen, in Liebe und Freude gelebt, in Hoffnung und Geduld erlitten, erkämpft, erwartet. In dieser Freiheit haben ungezählte Unbekannte in ihren großen und kleinen Entscheidungen, Ängsten, Gefahren, Ahnungen und Erwartungen immer wieder neu Mut, Halt, Kraft, Trost gefunden. So weist denn der Geist der Freiheit als Geist der Zukunft die Menschen nach vorne: nicht ins Jenseits der Vertröstung, sondern in die Gegenwart der Bewährung mitten im weltlichen Alltag bis zur Vollendung, für die wir im Geist nur ein Angeld[19] haben.

Trinität

In den aufgezeigten Perspektiven läßt sich heute noch das *Verhältnis von Vater, Sohn und Geist,* lassen sich auch heute noch die zahlreichen dreigliedrigen, *triadischen Formeln* des Neuen Testaments ursprünglich unmythologisch verstehen. Die daraus entstandene theologische Lehre von der innergöttlichen Dreieinigkeit (»Trinität«), welche mit einem hellenistischen Begriffsapparat Vater, Sohn und Geist in wahrer Verschiedenheit und ungetrennter Einheit zu denken versucht, hat ihre eigenen Probleme und wird vom heutigen Menschen leider kaum noch verstanden.

Das griechische Wort »trias« findet sich zuerst beim Apologeten Theophilos von Antiochien im 2. Jahrhundert, das lateinische »trinitas« zuerst beim Afrikaner Tertullian im 3. Jahrhundert. Die *hellenistische Formel,* die sich in einem höchst komplexen, teils widersprüchlichen und jedenfalls langwierigen Denkprozeß in klassischer Weise durch die drei Kappadokier (Basileios, Gregor von Nazianz und Gregor von Nyssa) im 4. Jahrhundert herausschälte, ist bekannt: Gott ist dreifaltig in den »Personen« (»Hypostasen«, »Subsistenzen«, »Prosopa«), einfach jedoch in der »Natur« (»Physis«, »Usia«, »Wesen«, »Substanz«). Aus den ursprünglich schlichten triadischen Bekenntnisaussagen – besonders die aus der einfachen christologischen Tauformel[20] entwickelte triadische Tauformel der mattäischen Gemeindetradition[21] – baute sich nun immer mehr eine intellektuell höchst anspruchsvolle *Trinitätsspekulation* auf. Beinahe so etwas wie eine höhere trinitarische Mathematik, die freilich trotz aller Bemühung um begriffliche Klarheit kaum zu dauerhaften Lösungen gelangte. Ob diese griechische Spekulation, die sich von ihrem biblischen Boden weit entfernte und kühn in schwindelnden Höhen das Geheimnis Gottes zu erspähen versuchte, nicht vielleicht doch wie Ikaros, der Sohn des Daidalos, Ahnherr des athenischen Kunsthandwerks, mit den aus Federn und Wachs gefertigten Flügeln der Sonne zu nahe kam? Zumindest in der praktischen Verkündigung werden zwar nicht Vater, Sohn und Geist, wohl aber wird diese Trinitätslehre weithin verschwiegen. Woran auch die (gegen anhaltenden römischen Widerstand auf gallischem Boden seit dem 8. Jahrhundert propagierte) *Dreifaltigkeitsliturgie* und das erst 1334 von Papst Johannes XXII. eingeführte Dreifaltigkeitsfest wenig ändern: das erste Fest übrigens, welches nicht einem Heilsereignis, sondern einem Dogma gewidmet ist. Das Dogma wird – abgesehen vom Unitarismus – kaum bestritten, aber auch kaum mehr zur Geltung gebracht.

Das *Neue Testament* indessen bejaht in der beschriebenen Weise durchaus die Einheit von Gott, Jesus und Geist. Welchem Geist besonders nach den johanneischen Abschiedsreden[22] die personalen Züge eines »Beistandes« und »Helfers« (dies und nicht »Tröster« meint »der andere Parakletos«[23]) eigen sind: gleichsam der Stellvertreter des Erhöhten auf Erden, gesandt vom Vater in Jesu Namen, der aber nicht von sich aus redet, sondern nur an das erinnert, was Jesus gesagt hat[24]. Aber so viele triadische Aussagen es im Neuen Testament über Vater, Sohn und Geist auch gibt, eine eigentliche trinitarische Lehre von einem Gott in drei Personen (Seinsweisen) findet man auch im Johannesevangelium wie nachher im »apostolischen« Glaubensbekenntnis nicht. Das klarste Zeugnis, jenes berühmte, in seiner Authentizität von der römischen Lehrbehörde noch um die Jahrhundertwende verteidigte Comma Johanneum, ein »Einschub« im 1. Johannesbrief[25] von Vater, Wort und Geist, die eins sind, wird heute allgemein als Fälschung (im 3. oder 4. Jahrhundert in Nordafrika oder Spanien entstanden) angesehen. Der ursprüngliche Text zeugt für eine ganz andere »Trinität«, was nebenbei beweist, wie wenig aus einer Triade als solcher auf eine bestimmte Einheit geschlossen werden kann: »Drei sind, die Zeugnis geben, der Geist, das Wasser (= Taufe) und das Blut (= Herrenmahl); und diese drei gehen auf eins« (= beide Sakramente sind Zeugnisse aus der Kraft des einen Geistes)[26].

Wie die ältesten Zweierformeln von Vater und Sohn, so lassen sich gewiß auch weiterentwickelte Dreierformeln von Vater, Sohn und Geist in respektabler Zahl finden[27]: in den Briefen[28] ebenso wie in den Evangelien[29]. Aber kommt nicht alles auf die *Art der Zuordnung* dieser zwei oder drei Größen untereinander und zur einen Gottesnatur an? Oder sollte etwa das Triadische (oder Binitarische?) an sich das unterscheidend Christliche (»Zentralgeheimnis«, »Grunddogma« des Christentums) sein?

Das unterscheidend Christliche ist – so sahen wir durch dieses ganze Buch hindurch – dieser Christus selbst und er selbstverständlich in seinem entscheidenden Bezug zu Gott, seinem Vater, und damit auch zu Gottes Geist. Aber gerade die seit Urgedenken als ursprünglichste Einheit in Vielfalt faszinierende, für Religion, Mythos, Kunst und Literatur und selbst den Alltag ungemein wichtige Zahl 3 und die (von Rom und Griechenland bis Indien und China sich findende) Dreiergottheit sind offensichtlich alles andere als spezifisch christlich. Ebensowenig wie der Dreiakt des Lebens (aus der Identität mit sich ein Herausgehen und Zurückgehen zu sich selbst) oder der Dreischritt der Dialektik (Thesis – Antithesis – Synthesis). Spezifisch ist das Christologische, woher biblisch und dogmengeschichtlich alles Trinitarische abgeleitet erscheint. Freilich wird die Trinität im christlichen Volksglauben schon aufgrund des Bedeutungswandels des Begriffs weithin tri-theistisch mißverstanden: Drei »Personen« jetzt im modern-psychologischen Sinn verstanden als drei »Selbstbewußtsein«, drei »Subjekte«, also im Grunde drei Götter. Solch faktischer *Tritheismus,* wie er sich nicht nur in manchen Dreifaltigkeitsdarstellungen byzantinischer und russischer Ikonen, karolingischer Miniaturen und mittelalterlicher Bildtafeln in der Form von drei gleichgestalteten Männern (wovor 1745 Benedikt XIV. warnte), sondern auch in theologischen und liturgischen Äußerungen findet, hat mit der biblischen Einheit von Vater, Sohn und Geist wenig zu tun. Ebensowenig wie auf der anderen Seite der *Modalismus:* wo Vater, Sohn und Geist nur als drei Offenbarungs-Modi, als drei aufeinanderfolgende Erscheinungsweisen des einen Gottes verstanden werden, oder entsprechend in der Kunst der berühmte Trikephalos oder dreigesichtige Gott, wie er (trotz Warnungen von Theologen wie Antoninus von Florenz und Bellarmin) bis zum Ende des 18. Jahrhunderts immer wieder vorkam.

Gegen Tritheismus einerseits und Modalismus andererseits geht es nach dem Neuen Testament um eine *Wirk- und Offenbarungseinheit* von Vater, Sohn und Geist, welche nun eben doch, wie es gerade in den künstlerischen Darstellungen der Taufe Jesu schön zum Ausdruck kommt, *drei sehr verschiedene Größen* sind, die mit höchst analogen Begriffen bezeichnet werden. Vater, Sohn und Geist können nach dem Neuen Testament nicht so schematisch ontologisch in eine göttliche Natur eingeebnet werden (»3 Personen in einer göttlichen Wesenheit«), wie dies bei den Kappadokiern logisch-formalistisch entwickelt und dann besonders von Augustin – der Neuerung wohl bewußt[30] – anthropologisch-psychologisch durchdacht worden war. In genialer und doch fragwürdiger Analogie also zum dreidimensionalen Menschengeist (mens) – zu Gedächtnis (memoria), Erkennen (intelligentia) und Wollen (voluntas) – eine Selbstentfaltung Gottes: Der Sohn wird dem Intellekt nach (im göttlichen Denkakt) aus der Substanz des Vaters als sein Abbild »gezeugt«. Der Geist aber »geht« aus dem Vater (dem Liebenden) und dem Sohn (dem Geliebten) dem Willen nach (in einer einzigen Hauchung = spiratio) als persongewordene Liebe »hervor«. Vater, Sohn und Geist werden auf diese Weise schließlich verstanden als drei voneinander real verschiedene und doch zugleich mit der einen göttlichen Natur in eins fallende subsistierende Beziehungen (Relationen): wie dies später Thomas von Aquin, jetzt den Traktat über den dreifaltigen Gott vom Traktat über den einen Gott abspaltend, bis ins letzte mit insbesondere aristotelischen Kategorien als Notwendigkeit abgeleitet hat.

Auf diese Weise kam es auch zu einer unnötigen und bis heute offiziell nicht beigelegten *Kontroverse zwischen der lateinischen und der griechischen Kirche*: Augustin behauptete also aufgrund seiner Trinitätsvorstellung ein Hervorgehen des Geistes aus dem Vater *und* dem Sohne (filioque), was dann seit dem 6. Jahrhundert allmählich und vom Papst Benedikt VIII. 1014 endgültig in das nizäno-konstantinopolitanische Glaubensbekenntnis eingeführt wurde. Dadurch wurde für den Westen zum Dogma, was dem Osten als Fälschung des ökumenischen Glaubensbekenntnisses wie der alten Tradition und als klare Häresie erschien. Streng hielt dieser am Hervorgehen des Geistes aus dem

Vater *durch* den Sohn fest und protestierte, insbesondere seit dem 9. Jahrhundert, gegen die westliche Entwicklung, welche die Beziehungen zwischen Rom und Konstantinopel auch noch theologisch belastete. Heute wird diese Kontroverse weithin als Scheinproblem durchschaut: Westliche Interpretation stellt ja den Vater als die Quelle der innertrinitarischen Hervorgänge nicht in Frage, so daß die beiden Interpretationen sich nicht auszuschließen brauchen. Doch damit ist das Problem noch nicht erledigt.

Die eigentlichen Schwierigkeiten der spezifisch westlichen Trinitätslehre kommen von daher, daß ihr Begründer *Augustin*, Gedanken der anderen großen Afrikaner Tertullian und Cyprian nutzend, *nicht* wie die Griechen *von der Dreiheit der Personen, sondern von der Einheit der göttlichen Natur ausging*. Worin Augustin nicht nur die Griechen und im Westen etwa Hilarius von Poitiers, sondern auch das Neue Testament gegen sich hatte[31]. Für die griechischen Väter war die Quelle (»arche«) der Einheit zwischen Vater, Sohn (Wort) und Geist nicht die eine Natur. Vielmehr der eine Gott und Vater als der Ursprung, der sich durch das Wort (Sohn) im Geist offenbart. Im Bild: Nicht drei Sterne im Dreieck nebeneinander wie in der westlichen Tradition (Augustin hatte freilich gegen die trinitarische Interpretation des Dreiecks durch die Manichäer protestiert). Vielmehr drei Sterne hintereinander, wobei der erste Stern sein Licht dem zweiten und schließlich dem dritten gibt, so daß für das menschliche Auge diese drei Sterne nur als einer scheinen. Wer im Geist den Sohn sieht, sieht auch den Vater.

Im *Neuen Testament* geht es eindeutig um eine *Einheit* im *Offenbarungsgeschehen*: wobei die Verschiedenheit der »Rollen« nicht aufgehoben, die »Reihenfolge« nicht umgekehrt und insbesondere Jesu Menschlichkeit keinen Moment außer acht gelassen werden darf. Selbst im Johannesevangelium handelt es sich bei allen Aussagen über Vater, Sohn und Geist wie auch bei den Aussagen über Gott als Geist[32], Licht[33] und Liebe[34] nicht um ontologische Aussagen über Gott an sich und seine innerste Natur, über das statische, in sich ruhende Wesen eines dreieinigen Gottes. Es handelt sich im ganzen Neuen Testament um Aussagen über die Art und Weise der Offenbarung Gottes: um sein dynamisches Wirken in der Geschichte, um das Verhältnis Gottes zum Menschen und des Menschen Verhältnis zu Gott. Die triadischen Formeln des Neuen Testaments zielen nicht auf eine »immanente«, sondern eine »ökonomische« Trinitätstheologie, nicht auf eine innergöttliche (immanente) wesensmäßige Dreieinigkeit an sich, sondern auf eine heilsgeschichtliche (ökonomische) Einheit von Vater, Sohn und Geist in der Begegnung mit uns. Nicht um den Gott an sich, sondern um den Gott für uns, wie er durch Jesus selbst im Geist an uns gehandelt hat, woran die Wirklichkeit unserer Erlösung hängt[35].

Nicht zu vergessen ist in all dem: Die Trinität war ursprünglich nicht Gegenstand theoretischer Spekulation. Sie war Gegenstand des Bekenntnisses und Lobpreises (Doxologie). Das aus antiarianischer Frontstellung entstandene nebeneinanderstellende »Ehre sei dem Vater *und* dem Sohn *und* dem Heiligen Geist« ist mißverständlich. Besser wird man sich halten an die erfreulicherweise bis heute durchgehaltene klassische Form der römischen Orationen, die auch dem ursprünglichen Ansatz der griechischen Trinitätstheologie entspricht, wo immer der *Vater* selbst angeredet wird *»durch« den Sohn »im« Heiligen Geist*[36]. Dies ist durchaus die Perspektive des Neuen Testaments, die es wiederaufzunehmen und neu durchzudenken gilt. Wiederum im Bild könnte man sagen: Gott der Vater »über« mir, Jesus als der Sohn und Bruder »neben« mir, Gottes und Jesu Christi Geist »in« mir.

Das altkirchliche trinitarische Bekenntnis hat dann als theologisch immer mehr ausgebaute Trinitätslehre eine große Geschichte durchgemacht, die ihre letzten Höhepunkte im vergangenen Jahrhundert in der Religionsphilosophie Hegels[37] und im gegenwärtigen Jahrhundert in der ›Kirchlichen Dogmatik‹ Karl Barths[38] hatte. Bis in Gottesdienst und Liedgut, aber auch in die (ohne Auseinandersetzung mit Nikaia und Chalkedon angenommene) Basis-Formel des Weltrates der Kirchen hinein, welche die Unitarier ausschließt, spielt sie noch immer eine bedeutende Rolle. Jeder Versuch einer kritischen Neuinterpretation wird sich vor dieser großen Tradition zu verantworten haben[39]. Vom Neuen Testament her gesehen ist die *klassische Trinitätslehre* ebenso wie die klassische Zwei-Naturen-Lehre *weder gedankenlos zu wiederholen noch gedankenlos abzutun, sondern differenziert für die Gegenwart zu interpretieren.* Für eine Neuaussage wären folgende Gesichtspunkte zu beachten:

– *Die* Schlüsselfrage *zur Trinitätslehre ist nicht die als undurchdringliches* »Geheimnis« *deklarierte trinitarische Frage, wie drei eins sein können, sondern die* christologische *Frage, wie vernunft- und schriftgemäß das Verhältnis Jesu zu Gott zu bestimmen ist. Historisch wie sachlich war das christologische Problem Anlaß zur Entstehung des oft mißverstandenen trinitarischen Problems.*

- *Der von Israel übernommene und mit dem Islam gemeinsame Ein-Gott-Glaube darf in keiner Trinitätslehre aufgegeben werden: Es gibt außer Gott keinen anderen Gott!*
- *Über* Zuordnung *von Gott, Jesus (Wort, Sohn, Christus) und Geist nachzudenken und dabei ihre wahre* Verschiedenheit *und ungetrennte* Einheit *herauszuheben, ist vom Neuen Testament her aufgegeben. Darin liegt die legitime Grundintention der traditionellen Trinitätslehre.*
- *Die auf* hellenistischen Vorstellungen *beruhenden Deutungsversuche und die daraus hervorgegangenen dogmatischen Formulierungen dieser Zuordnung sind jedoch* zeitbedingt *und mit dieser Grundintention nicht einfach identisch: Eine Trinitätslehre darf freilich nicht deshalb abgelehnt werden, weil sie hellenistische Kategorien verwendet. Aber es darf auch nicht jede künftige Trinitätslehre auf die Verwendung solcher Kategorien verpflichtet werden. Die traditionellen Formeln der hellenistisch bestimmten Trinitätslehre, so hilfreich sie waren, können nicht als zeitlose Glaubensverpflichtung allen Gläubigen aller Zeiten auferlegt werden.*
- *Die Einheit von Vater, Sohn und Geist ist als* Offenbarungsgeschehen *und Offenbarungseinheit* zu verstehen: *In trinitarischer Betrachtungsweise muß über die christologische hinaus das Verhältnis von Gott und Jesus im Hinblick auf den* Geist *reflektiert werden; eine Christologie ohne Pneumatologie (Lehre vom Geist) wäre unvollständig. Das »wahrhaft Gott« wurde christologisch wie folgt bestimmt: der wahre Mensch Jesus von Nazaret ist des einen wahren Gottes wirkliche Offenbarung. Von daher die Frage:* wie wird er das *für uns? Antwort: nicht physisch-materiell, aber auch nicht unwirklich, sondern im Geist, in der Daseinsweise des Geistes, als geistige Wirklichkeit. Der Geist ist die Gegenwart Gottes und des erhöhten Christus für die Glaubensgemeinschaft und den einzelnen Glaubenden. In diesem Sinne ist Gott selbst durch Jesus Christus offenbar im Geist.*

In diesem kurzen Abschnitt sollte keine Trinitätslehre entwickelt, es sollte nur auf einige wichtige Gesichtspunkte zu ihrem Verständnis aufmerksam gemacht werden. Auch hier in bewußter Beschränkung. Insofern sei das Wort, das Augustin seinem

Traktat über die Dreieinigkeit vorausgeschickt hat, allen unseren zu knappen Dogmeninterpretationen nachgeschickt: »Der Leser mag dort, wo er ebenso sicher ist wie ich, mit mir weitergehen; wo er ebenso zögert, mich befragen; wo er bei sich einen Irrtum erkennt, sich an mich halten; wo er einen bei mir erkennt, mich zurückrufen[40].«

Aber vielleicht ist es jetzt doch an der Zeit, von hohen und höchsten Dogmen wieder in die »Niederungen des christlichen Alltags« hinabzusteigen, wo sich christlicher Glaube in erster Linie bewähren muß. Haben wir bisher nicht allzu selbstverständlich vorausgesetzt, was Kirche ist?

3. Die vielgestaltige Kirche

Kirche ist, kurz definiert, Gemeinschaft der an Christus Glaubenden[1]. Nicht von Jesus gegründet, sondern nach seinem Tod mit Berufung auf ihn als den Gekreuzigten und doch Lebendigen entstanden: die *Gemeinschaft derer, die sich auf die Sache Jesu Christi eingelassen haben und sie als Hoffnung für alle Menschen bezeugen.* Vor Ostern gab es nur eine endzeitliche Sammelbewegung. Erst seit Ostern gibt es eine, freilich ebenfalls endzeitlich ausgerichtete Gemeinde, Kirche: deren Grundlage zunächst nicht ein eigener Kult, eine eigene Verfassung, eine eigene Organisation mit bestimmten Ämtern, sondern einzig und allein das glaubende Bekenntnis zu diesem Jesus als dem Christus war. Die »Kirche Jesu Christi« im Sinne einer dem alten Gottesvolk gegenübergestellten Gemeinschaft ist auch nach dem Neuen Testament selbst eine nachösterliche Größe[2].

So wäre denn heute Aufgabe der Kirche das eine: der Sache Jesu Christi zu dienen, sie also zum mindesten nicht zu verstellen, sondern sie im Geiste Jesu Christi in der heutigen Gesellschaft zu vertreten, zur Geltung zu bringen, selber zu verwirklichen. Die Frage, die hier den allermeisten auf die Lippen kommen dürfte: Tut sie das? Eine Frage, die zu behandeln sein wird, die freilich jeder Christ als Glied der Kirche gleichzeitig auch sich selber stellen sollte, wenn er sie anderen, wenn er sie – zu Recht – der Institution stellt. Zunächst ist hier auch von der Kirche programmatisch zu reden.

Wie sehr die Kirche auf die Sache ihres Herrn verpflichtet wäre, verpflichtet ist, ergibt sich schon aus ihrem *Namen*[3]:Das *in den germanischen Sprachen* übliche Wort (deutsch Kirche, englisch church, schwedisch kyrka, vgl. slawisch cerkov) kommt glücklicherweise nicht von »curia«, wie Luther meinte (was nicht wenig zu seiner Abneigung gegen das Wort Kirche zugunsten von »Gemeinde« beigetragen hat). Das Wort kam nicht von Rom, sondern war aus dem Gotenreich Theoderichs des Großen donauaufwärts und rheinabwärts getragen worden. Sein Ursprung war die byzantinische Volksform »Kyrike« und meint somit »dem Herrn gehörig«, ergänzt: »Haus des Herrn«. Kurz könnte man sagen: Kyriosgemeinde, Gemeinde des Herrn. Womit also das Entscheidende gesagt ist. Im Gegensatz zu den germanischen haben die *romanischen Sprachen* auch den direkten sprachlichen Zusammenhang mit dem im Neuen Testament gebrauchten Wort bewahrt: lateinisch ecclesia, spanisch iglesia, französisch église, italienisch chiesa. Sie alle stammen vom griechischen »ekklesia« ab. Und was ist der Sinn dieses Wortes?

Im profanen Griechisch meint Ekklesia die Versammlung, die politische Volksversammlung. Doch maßgeblich für den neutestamentlichen Ekklesia-Begriff wurde der Wortgebrauch in der griechischen Übersetzung des *Alten Testaments*. Dort steht Ekklesia fast immer für den an sich profanen hebräischen Begriff »kahal« = die einberufene Versammlung. Entscheidend jedoch ist die ausgesprochene oder unausgesprochene qualifizierende Beifügung »des Herrn« oder »Jahwes«: Die Ekklesia Gottes ist mehr als das je ereignishafte Sich-Versammeln. Ekklesia ist die Versammlung der von Gott zuvor erwählten Schar, die sich um Gott als ihre Mitte versammelt. Ein religiös-kultischer Begriff, der dann immer mehr endzeitlich verstanden wird: Ekklesia als die wahre Gottesgemeinde der Endzeit. Wenn also die Urgemeinde die Bezeichnung Ekklesia übernahm, erhob sie bewußt einen großen Anspruch: die wahre Gottesversammlung, die wahre Gottesgemeinde, das wahre Gottesvolk der Endzeit zu sein, das sich im Namen und Geist Jesu Christi versammelt – also die »Ekklesia Jesu Christi«.

Ekklesia meint – wie »Versammlung« – zugleich den aktuellen *Vorgang des Versammelns* wie die *versammelte Gemeinde* selbst: Gerade das erste darf nie vergessen werden. Ekklesia ist nicht einfach dadurch, daß etwas einmal eingesetzt, gegründet wurde und dann unverändert so bleibt. Ekklesia ist nur dadurch, daß es immer wieder neu zum konkreten Ereignis des Zusammenkommens, der Versammlung und insbesondere der gottesdienstlichen Versammlung kommt. Die konkrete Versammlung ist die aktuelle Manifestation, Repräsentation, ja Realisation der neutestamentlichen Gemeinde. Umgekehrt ist die Gemeinde der bleibende Träger des immer wieder neu geschehenden Ereignisses der Versammlung.

»Versammlung«, »Gemeinde«, »Kirche« sind nicht gegeneinander auszuspielen, sondern in ihrem *Zusammenhang* zu sehen: Schon die unübersehbare Tatsache, daß das Neue Testament selbst, während wir von Versammlung oder Gemeinde oder Kirche reden, immer dasselbe Wort Ekklesia gebraucht, müßte uns davor warnen, hier Gegensätze zu konstruieren.

– *»Versammlung« drückt aus, daß die Ekklesia nie nur als eine statische Institution, sondern nur durch das immer wieder neue Ereignis der konkreten Zusammenkunft existiert.*
– *»Gemeinde« betont, daß die Ekklesia nie nur eine abstraktferne Hyperorganisation von Funktionären oberhalb der konkreten Versammlung ist, sondern immer eine sich an bestimmtem Ort zu bestimmter Zeit und zu bestimmtem Tun versammelnde Gemeinschaft.*
– *»Kirche« macht deutlich, daß die Ekklesia nie nur ein unverbundenes Nebeneinander isolierter und selbstgenügsamer religiöser Vereinigungen ist, sondern die untereinander im gegenseitigen Dienst geeinten Glieder einer umfassenden Gemeinschaft.*

Zwar betont »Versammlung« mehr das Aktuell-Ereignishafte, »Gemeinde« mehr das Orthaft-Bleibende, »Kirche« mehr das Überörtlich-Gestiftete. Und so wird man in der Übersetzung von Ekklesia manchmal lieber das eine und manchmal lieber das andere gebrauchen. Doch grundsätzlich bleiben sie auswechselbar. Und wie statt von Ortsgemeinde auch von Ortskirche, so kann man statt von Gesamtkirche auch von Gesamtgemeinde sprechen.

Wie aber verhalten sich *Ortskirche* und *Gesamtkirche*? Darauf läßt sich kurz antworten: Jede Ekklesia (= jede Einzelversammlung, -gemeinde, -kirche) *ist* zwar *nicht die* Ekklesia (= die Gesamtkirche, -gemeinde, -versammlung), aber *vergegenwärtigt* voll die Ekklesia. Dies besagt zweierlei:

Einerseits erkennen die *Katholiken* heute: Die Ortsekklesia ist nicht nur eine »Sektion« oder »Provinz« der Gesamtkirche. Sie ist keineswegs eine Unterabteilung der eigentlichen »Kirche«, die dann, weil das umfassendere Gebilde, als das rangmäßig Höhere und Primäre verstanden werden müßte. Es ist keine gute Gewohnheit, nur die Gesamtekklesia »Kirche« zu nennen – die Folge eines abstrakt-idealistischen Kirchenbegriffes. Als ob die Kirche nicht an jedem Ort *ganz* da wäre! Als ob der Ortskirche nicht die *ganze* Verheißung des Evangeliums und der *ganze* Glaube geschenkt wäre! Als ob ihr nicht die *ganze* Gnade des Vaters zugesprochen, als ob in ihr nicht der *ganze* Christus gegenwärtig sei und ihr nicht der *ganze* Heilige Geist verliehen wäre! Nein, die Ortskirche *gehört* nicht nur zur Kirche. Die Ortskirche *ist* Kirche und kann die Sache Jesu Christi voll vertreten. Nur von der Ortskirche und ihrem konkreten Vollzug her kann die Gesamtkirche verstanden werden. Die Ortskirche ist also nicht nur eine Aufbauzelle, die weder das Ganze darstellt noch einen Zweck in sich selber hat. Sondern sie ist wirklich Kirche, der an ihrem Platz alles verheißen und gegeben ist, was sie an ihrem Platz zum Heil der Menschen braucht: die Verkündigung des Evangeliums, die Taufe, das Herrenmahl, die verschiedenen Charismen und Dienste.

Andererseits anerkennen die *Protestanten* heute: Die Gesamtekklesia ist nicht nur eine »Ansammlung« oder eine »Assoziation« von Ortsekklesien. Die einzelnen Ortskirchen eint mehr als ein gemeinsamer Name, mehr als ein äußerer Zusammenschluß, mehr als eine den Einzelkirchen übergeordnete Organisation. Allen Einzelgemeinden ist die eine und selbe Sache Jesu Christi, dasselbe Evangelium, dieselbe Zusage und Verheißung gegeben. Sie alle stehen unter der Gnade des einen und selben Vaters, haben denselben Herrn, sind getrieben vom selben Geist der Charismen und Dienste. Sie alle glauben denselben Glauben, sind geheiligt durch dieselbe Taufe und sind versammelt zu demselben Mahl. Durch alles dies – und was sollte für sie wichtiger sein? – sind sie nicht nur äußerlich verbunden, sondern innerlich geeint, bilden sie alle nicht nur eine kirchliche Organisation, sondern eine Kirche Jesu Christi. Kirche ist nicht ein Dachverband von Einzelgemeinden. Nicht eine Addition der einzelnen Ekklesien ergibt die Ekklesia; die Ekklesia zerfällt nicht in die einzelnen Ekklesien. Sondern an den verschiedenen Orten ist *die* Ekklesia Gottes.

Jede Ekklesia, jede Versammlung, Gemeinde, Kirche – sei sie

noch so klein, unbedeutend, mittelmäßig, erbärmlich – vergegenwärtigt voll *die* Ekklesia, *die* Versammlung, Gemeinde, Kirche Gottes und Jesu Christi. Dies alles gilt von einer einsamen Missionsstation im afrikanischen Busch ebenso wie von einer großen wohlhabenden Gemeinde des amerikanischen Mittleren Westens oder Zentraleuropas, von einer neuen Wohnviertel-Gemeinde ebenso wie von der üblichen großen städtischen Pfarrei oder einer mehrere frühere Dorfgemeinden zusammenfassenden Regionalgemeinde. Dies darf gesagt werden nicht nur von den normalen territorialen Gemeinden oder Pfarreien, sondern auch von den funktionalen Gemeinden, also den Studenten- und Hochschulgemeinden, der Gemeinde eines Krankenhauses, eines Betriebs, eines Fremdenverkehrsortes, einer sprachlichen Minderheit; für die Gemeinden mehr in der Art einer »Service Station« (Gottesdienstgelegenheit in einer City) oder mehr in der Art einer »Effective Community« (für ein ganz bestimmtes Engagement), schließlich für Gemeinden in katholischer oder orthodoxer oder dieser oder jener protestantischen Tradition – bei wachsender Integration und hoffentlich baldiger gegenseitiger Anerkennung! Sie alle, in einer kaum vorstellbaren Pluralität und Pluriformität, sind im wahren Sinn Kirche. Und an sie alle und nicht nur an die großen diözesanen und nationalen Kirchen und auch nicht nur an die Gesamtkirche ist zu denken, wenn im folgenden von »Kirche« die Rede ist.

Alles nur Theorie? Darauf ist später zu antworten. Es mag gut sein, noch ruhig etwas weiter zu theoretisieren.

Gemeinschaft in Freiheit, Gleichheit, Brüderlichkeit

Eine Kirche, die, ob groß oder klein, Jesu Christi Sache vertritt, seinen Namen trägt, sein Wort hört und von seinem Geist getrieben wird, darf bei aller Pluriformität freilich auf keinen Fall mit einer bestimmten Klasse, Kaste, Clique oder Behörde identifiziert werden. Wie Jesus selbst richtet sich nun auch seine Kirche an das ganze Volk und gerade an die Unterprivilegierten. Und so ist Kirche die *ganze Gemeinschaft* der an Christus Glaubenden, in der sich *alle als Gottesvolk, Christusleib, Geistesbau verstehen dürfen*[4]. Entscheidender *Maßstab* dieser Gemeinschaft ist nicht ein Vorrecht der Geburt, des Standes, der Rasse oder des Amtes. Nicht ob einer in der Kirche ein »Amt« hat und was für ein »Amt« er hat, ist ausschlaggebend. Sondern ob und wieweit er schlicht und einfach ein »Gläubiger« ist: ob und wieweit er ganz konkret glaubt, dient, liebt, hofft, sich im Geiste Jesu Christi engagiert.

Anders als im heidnischen oder jüdischen Kult braucht ein Christ außer Christus keinen Priester als Mittler zum Innersten des Tempels, zu Gott selbst. Ihm ist vielmehr eine letzte Unmittelbarkeit zu Gott geschenkt, welche ihm eine kirchliche Autorität weder stören noch gar nehmen kann. Über Entscheidungen, die in diesem innersten Bereich fallen, steht niemandem Urteil, Verfügungs- und Befehlsgewalt zu. Gewiß, der christliche Glaube fällt nicht unmittelbar vom Himmel, sondern wird vermittelt in der Kirche. Aber: »Kirche« im großen oder im kleinen ist die *ganze* Glaubensgemeinschaft, die durch die Verkündigung des Evangeliums – oft mehr durch die geringen Leute als durch die Hierarchen und Theologen, mehr durch Taten als durch Worte – den Glauben an Jesus Christus weckt, Engagement in seinem Geist herausfordert, im christlichen Zeugnis des Alltags die Kirche in der Welt präsent macht und so die Sache Jesu Christi weiterträgt. Es sind ja *alle* und nicht nur einige Auserwählte, denen in all den verschiedenen Formen von Gemeinde die Verkündigung der christlichen Botschaft aufgetragen ist. Denen ein individuelles und soziales Leben aus dem Evangelium abgefordert wird. Denen die Taufe auf Jesu Namen, das Gedächtnis-, Dankes- und Bundesmahl, der Zuspruch der Sündenvergebung anvertraut sind. Denen der alltägliche Dienst und die Verantwortung für den Mitmenschen, für die Gemeinde, für Gesellschaft und Welt übertragen ist. In all diesen Grundfunktionen der Kirche eine Gemeinschaft in Freiheit, Gleichheit und Brüderlichkeit[5]!

1. *Freiheit*: Freiheit ist für die Kirche Gabe und Aufgabe zugleich. Die Kirche, im großen wie im kleinen, darf und soll eine *Gemeinschaft von Freien* sein: Wenn sie der Sache Jesu Christi dienen will, kann sie nie eine Herrschaftsinstitution oder gar eine Großinquisition sein. Zur Freiheit befreit dürfen ihre Glieder sein: befreit von der Sklaverei des Gesetzesbuchstabens, von der Last der Schuld, von der Angst vor dem Tode; befreit zum Leben, zum Sinn, zum Dienst, zur Liebe. Menschen, die Gott allein und damit weder anonymen Mächten noch anderen Menschen unterworfen zu sein haben.

Wo keine Freiheit ist, da ist der Geist des Herrn nicht. Diese Freiheit, sosehr sie sich in der Existenz des Einzelnen verwirklichen muß, darf in der Kirche nicht nur ein moralischer Appell (meist für die anderen) bleiben. Sie muß sich in der Gestaltung der kirchlichen Gemeinschaft, in ihren Institutionen und Konstitutionen auswirken, so daß diese auf keinen Fall oppressiven oder repressiven Charakter haben dürfen.

Niemand in der Kirche hat ein Recht, die grundlegende Freiheit der Kinder Gottes offen oder verdeckt zu manipulieren, zu unterdrücken, gar abzuschaffen und statt der Herrschaft Gottes eine Herrschaft von Menschen über Menschen aufzurichten. Manifestieren soll sich diese Freiheit gerade in der Kirche im freien Wort (Freimut) und in der freien Tat des Handelns und Verzichtens (Freizügigkeit und Freigebigkeit im weitesten Sinn des Wortes), aber zugleich auch in den kirchlichen Institutionen und Konstitutionen: Die Kirche soll selber *Raum der Freiheit* und zugleich *Anwalt der Freiheit in der Welt* sein!

2. *Gleichheit*: Aufgrund der geschenkten und realisierten Freiheit darf und soll die Kirche, im großen wie im kleinen, eine *Gemeinschaft von grundsätzlich Gleichen* sein: gewiß nicht im Sinne eines die Vielfalt der Gaben und Dienste einebnenden Egalismus, wohl aber im Sinne einer fundamentalen Gleichberechtigung der in sich so verschiedenen Glieder. Wenn die Kirche der Sache Jesu Christi dienen will, kann sie nie eine Klassen-, Rassen-, Kasten- oder Amtskirche sein. Durch freien Entschluß haben sich die Einzelnen der Glaubensgemeinschaft angeschlossen, oder sie bleiben in ihr. In einer Solidarität der Liebe sollen hier die Ungleichen zusammengeführt werden: Wohlhabende und Arme, Prominente und Nichtprominente, Gebildete und Ungebildete, Weiße und Farbige, Männer und Frauen. Der Glaube an den Gekreuzigten kann und will nicht alle Ungleichheit in der Gesellschaft abschaffen; das Reich der erfüllten Gleichheit steht noch aus. Aber dieser Glaube vermag in der Gemeinschaft die Ungleichheiten sozialer (»Herr und Knecht«), kultureller (»Griechen und Barbaren«), naturhafter Herkunft (»Mann und Frau«) auszugleichen, »aufzuheben«. Alle Glieder der Kirche sind grundsätzlich gleichberechtigt: sie haben grundsätzlich gleiche Rechte und gleiche Pflichten.

Im Volke Gottes soll kein Ansehen der Person den Ausschlag geben, im Leib Christi kein noch so geringes Glied Verachtung leiden. Diese fundamentale Gleichheit, sosehr sie Sache des Einzelnen ist, darf in der Kirche nicht nur eine »Gesinnung« ohne Folgen bleiben. Sie muß durch die verfaßten Strukturen der kirchlichen Gemeinschaft gewahrt und geschützt werden, so daß diese in keinem Fall der Ungerechtigkeit und Ausbeutung Vorschub leisten.

Niemand in der Kirche hat das Recht, die fundamentale Gleichheit der Glaubenden aufzuheben, zu überspielen oder in einer Herrschaft von Menschen über Menschen zu verewigen. Manifestieren soll sich solche Gleichheit gerade in der Kirche, so daß, wer groß und Erster sein will, der Knecht und Diener aller werde. Und zugleich sollen auch die kirchlichen Strukturen so verfaßt sein, daß sie von der grundlegenden Gleichheit der Glieder Zeugnis geben: Die Kirche soll selber *Stätte der Gleichberechtigung* und zugleich *Anwalt der Gleichberechtigung in der Welt* sein.

3. *Brüderlichkeit*: Aufgrund der geschenkten und realisierten Freiheit und Gleichheit darf und soll die Kirche, im großen wie im kleinen, eine *Gemeinschaft von Brüdern und Schwestern* sein: Wenn sie der Sache Jesu Christi dienen will, kann sie nie ein patriarchalisch regiertes Herrschaftsgebilde sein. Nur einer ist hier der heilige Vater, Gott selbst; alle Glieder der Kirche sind seine erwachsenen Söhne und Töchter, die nicht in die Unmündigkeit zurückversetzt werden dürfen. Menschen dürfen in dieser Gemeinschaft nur eine wahrhaft brüderliche und nicht eine paternalistische Autorität geltend machen. Nur einer ist der Herr und Meister, Jesus Christus selbst, alle Glieder der Kirche sind Brüder und Schwestern. Nicht der Patriarch also ist in dieser Gemeinschaft die oberste Norm. Sondern der Wille Gottes, der nach der Botschaft Jesu Christi auf das Wohl der Menschen, und zwar aller Menschen, zielt.

In der Freiheit der christlichen Brüderlichkeit verbinden sich Unabhängigkeit und Verpflichtetsein, Macht und Verzicht, Selbständigkeit und Dienst, Herrsein und Knechtsein – ein Rätsel, dessen Lösung die Liebe ist, in der der Herr zum Knecht und der Knecht zum Herrn, in welcher Unabhängigkeit zur Verpflichtung und Verpflichtung zur Unabhängigkeit wird. Auch die im Grunde sich widerstrebenden demokratischen Forderungen nach größtmöglicher Freiheit und bestmöglicher Gleichheit können in einer so verstandenen Brüderlichkeit ihre Versöhnung finden. Diese Brüderlichkeit, sosehr sie eine persönliche Haltung sein muß, darf in der Kirche nicht nur mit großen Worten als »Geist« der Brüderlichkeit (faktisch oft mehr ein Untertanengeist) beschworen werden. Sie muß sich gerade in den Ordnungen und den sozialen Bezügen der kirchlichen Gemeinschaft verwirklichen, so daß diese nicht zur Entfremdung des Menschen führen.

Niemand in der Kirche hat das Recht, diese Brüderlichkeit durch den Paternalismus und Personenkult eines klerikalen Systems zu ersetzen und dadurch die Herrschaft von Menschen über Menschen noch zu potenzieren. Manifestieren soll sich die Brüderlichkeit vielmehr zugleich in den kirchlichen Ordnungen und Sozialbezügen, die der Brüderlichkeit konkret Ausdruck geben sollen: Die Kirche soll selber eine *Heimat der Brüderlichkeit* und zugleich ein *Anwalt der Brüderlichkeit in der Welt* sein!

Charismen, Ämter, Dienste

So meint Kirche als Gemeinschaft in Freiheit, Gleichheit und Brüderlichkeit keine Gleichschaltung und Einförmigkeit. Im Gegenteil, sie fordert geradezu die Vielgestaltigkeit heraus.

Unterschiedliche Theologien und Lebensstile, soziale Spannungen und Probleme der Gemeindestruktur wurden von Anfang an in oft harten Konflikten ausgetragen. Immer wieder kam es zu Parteien[6]. In Jerusalem setzten sich die »Hebräer« mit den »Hellenisten« auseinander, in Antiochien die Vorkämpfer eines gesetzesfreien Christentums mit den Befürwortern der Beschneidung. Paulus beschwört die verschiedenen Gruppen von Korinth, Einmütigkeit zu bewahren, und er selbst muß sich in aller Entschiedenheit mit judaistischen Missionaren etwa in Galatien auseinandersetzen. So gab es Juden- und Heidenchristen, gab es neben Paulus die korinthischen Enthusiasten, neben bereits ausgeprägten Amtsstrukturen »frühkatholischer« Art den Kreis um den Evangelisten Johannes, der allen Ämtern zurückhaltend gegenübersteht.

So wird es auch heute eine vielfältige Kirche geben. Nicht nur eine Kirche in vielen Gemeinden, sondern auch Kirchen und Gemeinden mit vielen Gruppen und Flügeln, Richtungen und Tendenzen, Theologien und Weisen der Frömmigkeit. Entscheidend ist nur, daß keine Gruppe das Gespräch mit den anderen abbricht und zur Häresie wird, daß die Parteinahme für Jesus Christus alle Parteibildungen in der Gemeinde übersteigt[7].

Doch wollen wir hier nur einen, freilich für alle anderen entscheidenden Aspekt der Pluriformität weiterverfolgen und fragen: Wie soll eine Gemeinde strukturiert sein, damit sie in Mobilität und Flexibilität ihren Auftrag erfüllen kann?

1. *Pluriformität statt Uniformität*: Es darf vom Neuen Testament her als Selbstverständlichkeit vorausgesetzt werden: Auf der Basis der grundlegenden Freiheit, Gleichheit und Brüderlichkeit gibt es zahllose Unterschiede – Unterschiede nicht nur der Personen, sondern auch der Funktionen. Insofern eine unbestimmbare Vielfalt und Differenzierung von Funktionen, Aufgaben, Diensten gegeben ist, ist die Rede von *dem* kirchlichen Amt mißverständlich.

Es lassen sich schon im Neuen Testament unterscheiden: für die Verkündigung die Funktionen der Apostel, Propheten, Lehrer, Evangelisten, Mahner. Dann als Hilfsdienste die Funktionen der Diakone und Diakonissen, der Almosenverteiler, der Krankenpfleger, der der Gemeinde dienenden Witwen. Schließlich für die Gemeindeleitung die Funktionen der Erstlinge, Vorsteher, Episkopen, Hirten ... *Alle* diese Funktionen in der Gemeinde (und nicht nur bestimmte »Ämter«) werden von Paulus, über dessen Gemeinden wir weitaus am besten Bescheid wissen, verstanden als Gaben des Geistes, als Teilhabe an der Vollmacht des erhöhten Herrn der Kirche, als *Berufung Gottes zu einem bestimmten Dienst in der Gemeinde*, kurz als *Charisma*[8]: Charisma, das somit

a. nicht eine primär außerordentliche, sondern eine alltägliche,
b. nicht eine einförmige, sondern eine vielgestaltige,
c. nicht eine auf bestimmte Personenkreise beschränkte, sondern ganz und gar allgemeine Erscheinung in der Kirche ist.

Das heißt: *Jeder* Dienst, der faktisch (permanent oder nicht) zum Aufbau der Gemeinde geleistet wird, ist nach Paulus Charisma, ist *kirchlicher* Dienst; er verdient so Anerkennung und Unterordnung. *Jedem* Dienst, ob amtlich oder nicht, eignet also auf seine Weise *Autorität*, wenn er zum Nutzen der Gemeinde in Liebe verrichtet wird. Wie dann aber noch Einheit und Ordnung?

Einheit und *Ordnung* in der Kirche verspricht sich Paulus nicht von der Einebnung der Verschiedenheiten. Sondern vom Wirken des einen Geistes, der jedem *sein* Charisma schenkt (Regel: Jedem das Seine!), das er zum Nutzen der anderen gebrauchen (Regel: Miteinander füreinander!) und in Unterordnung unter den einen Herrn üben soll (Regel: Gehorsam dem Herrn!).

Zwei *Kriterien* insbesondere dienen *zur Unterscheidung der Geister*:

– *Echtes Charisma bindet an Jesus und seine Herrschaft: Wer den Geist von Gott hat, bekennt sich zu Jesus als dem Herrn (das unterscheidend Christliche).*

– *Echtes Charisma ist gemeindebezogen: Nicht das Wunder, sondern der Dienst zum Nutzen der Gemeinde ist das Zeichen der wahren Berufung. So ist denn jeglicher Dienst in der Kirche von vornherein auf solidarisches Verhalten, auf kollegiales Einvernehmen, auf partnerschaftliche Mitsprache, auf Kommunikation und Dialog verwiesen.*

2. *Dienst statt Amt:* Wenn auch verschiedene Funktionen im Neuen Testament erwähnt werden, so wird doch nirgendwo das Problem eines kirchlichen Amtes thematisiert. Kirchliches »Amt« ist kein biblischer, sondern ein nachträglicher und nicht unproblematischer Reflexionsbegriff. Offensichtlich mit Absicht und Konsequenz werden im Neuen Testament die weltlichen Worte für »*Amt*« im Zusammenhang mit kirchlichen Funktionen *vermieden*: sie drücken ein Herrschaftsverhältnis aus[9]!

Statt dessen wird ein anderer Oberbegriff gebraucht, der bei Paulus vielfach synonym ist mit Charisma, ein durchaus gewöhnliches, unreligiöses Wort von etwas minderwertigem Geschmack, welches somit nirgendwo Assoziationen mit irgendeiner Behörde, Obrigkeit, Herrschaft, Würde- und Machtstellung wachrufen kann: »*diakonia*«, Dienst (eigentlich Tischdienst). Hier hatte offensichtlich Jesus selbst das unverrückbare Maß gesetzt[10].

Sicher gibt es Autorität in der Kirche. Aber Autorität ist nur legitim, wo sie auf dem Dienst gründet und nicht auf brutaler oder subtiler Gewalt, auf alten oder neuen Vorrechten und Privilegien, aus denen dann erst die Verpflichtung zum Dienst entspränge. Besser als vom kirchlichen »Amt« wird man also in präziser theologischer Redeweise vom kirchlichen »Dienst« sprechen. Allerdings ist nicht das Wort entscheidend, sondern sein Verständnis; auch das Reden vom kirchlichen »Dienst« kann in falscher Demutsgestik zur Verschleierung mißbraucht werden, wenn nicht zugleich auf die Ausübung von kirchlicher Herrschaft verzichtet wird.

Aber im Gegensatz zu »Amt« ist der Begriff »Dienst«

a. im Neuen Testament terminologisch gedeckt und sachlich begründet;

b. als funktionaler Begriff nicht dem institutionalistischen Mißverständnis ausgeliefert;

c. schon in seinem Wortsinn eine Forderung zum Dienen, auf die
jeder Funktionsträger in der Praxis behaftet werden kann;
d. in seinem Mißbrauch somit durchschaubar.
In diesem Zusammenhang ist theologisch wie terminologisch auf
exakte Unterscheidung und Verschlingung der Begriffe zu
achten:

– Macht *kann gut oder schlecht gebraucht werden. Auch in der
Kirche läßt sich Macht nicht einfach abschaffen. Aber sie kann
rational in Wahrnehmung von Funktionen zum Wohl des
Ganzen ausgeübt werden.*
– *Etwas anderes als die unvermeidliche Ausübung von Macht ist
ihre Ausübung als* Herrschaft *(durch Einzelne oder Gruppen):
Hier geht es um die Erhaltung einer privilegierten Position
oder Mehrung der eigenen Macht und die Benützung (Manipulation) von Menschen zu persönlichen oder institutionellen
Zwecken.*
– *Ausübung von Macht in der Kirche ist nur vom* Dienst *her zu
verantworten und an ihrem Dienstcharakter zu messen: solche
aus dem Dienst kommende Macht ist echte (primär innere)*
Vollmacht.
– *Gegensätze sind somit nicht Macht und Dienst, sondern Ausübung von Macht als Herrschaft und Ausübung von Macht als
Dienst: Ausübung von Herrschaft (insbesondere durch äußere
Macht bis zum Grenzfall der Gewalt) ist das Gegenteil von
Dienst und ist* Machtmißbrauch.
– *In der Kirche sollte zumindest das sehr spät durch Pseudo-Dionysios eingeführte Wort von der »heiligen Herrschaft«
=* Hierarchie *als irreführend aufgegeben werden (wie man ja
auch Ausdrücke wie »Pfarrherr« und ähnliche nicht mehr
braucht). Allerdings müßte zugleich auch auf Herrschaftsstil
und Herrschaftsallüren verzichtet werden.*

3. *Leitungsdienst statt Priestertum*: Noch auffälliger ist indessen,
daß im Neuen Testament nicht nur auf die dem »Amt« entsprechenden Ausdrücke verzichtet wird. Sondern daß im Zusammenhang mit Gemeindefunktionen auch das Wort »Priester«[11]
im religionsgeschichtlichen Sinn des Opferpriesters (»hiereus«,
»sacerdos«) und überhaupt alle sakralkultischen Titulationen
zugunsten von Funktionsbezeichnungen aus dem profanen Bereich vermieden werden. Für die jüdischen und heidnischen
Würdenträger wird das Wort »Priester« gebraucht, für kirch-

liche Dienstträger nie. Erst in einer neutestamentlichen Spätphase wird, wie wir gesehen haben[12], Jesus selber, der Auferweckte und Erhöhte, als »Priester« verstanden. Aber nun in einer für das alttestamentliche Priestertum grundstürzenden Weise: als der einzige bleibende Hohepriester (Stellvertreter, Mittler), durch dessen ein für allemal geschehenes Lebensopfer alles alttestamentliche Priestertum erfüllt und abgetan ist (Hebräerbrief). Aus der Auflösung des *besonderen* Priestertums durch das Priestertum des *einen* neuen und ewigen Hohenpriesters folgt – eine weitere Reflexion der Gemeinde[13] – das *allgemeine* Priestertum *aller* Glaubenden, welches als konkreten Inhalt den unmittelbaren Zugang aller zu Gott, geistige Opfer, Verkündigung des Wortes, Vollzug von Taufe, Eucharistie und Sündenvergebung und das Füreinander-Eintreten hat.

Vom Neuen Testament her muß also, auch wenn man nicht um Worte streiten sollte, »Priester« ebenso wie »Geistliche«, »Klerus«, »Kirche« als partikulare exklusive Bezeichnung allein für kirchliche Dienstträger wegfallen, da, neutestamentlich gesehen, alle Glaubenden »Priester«, »Geistliche«, »Klerus«, »Kirche« sind. Auch der Ausdruck »priesterlicher Dienst«, wenn er dann doch wieder nicht von allen Christen, sondern nur von bestimmten kirchlichen Dienstträgern gebraucht wird, verschleiert den neutestamentlichen Sachverhalt. Wenn Paulus ein *einziges* Mal[14] im Zusammenhang der *Verkündigung* (und nicht des Kultes!) sich selber (und nicht Episkopen oder Presbyter) in *bildhafter* (und nicht wörtlicher) Weise als einen (die Heiden!) opfernden »Liturgen« bezeichnet, so läßt sich daraus für die Berechtigung eines neutestamentlichen *kultischen Priestertums* von bestimmten Amtsträgern nichts ableiten.

Statt von »Priestertum« (»Amtspriestertum«, »Weihepriestertum« u. ä.) zu reden, wären hier korrekterweise die Funktionsbezeichnungen zu wählen. Schon im Neuen Testament spricht man von Vorstehern, Episkopen, Diakonen, Ältesten, Hirten, Leitenden. Manche dieser ursprünglich betont unkultischen und unsakralen Bezeichnungen (Bischöfe, Pastoren, Presbyter, Diakone) haben sich, mit manchen späteren (Pfarrer, Parochus), zu Recht bis heute durchgehalten. Wünscht man für alle diese Dienste einen Überbegriff, dürfte sich kirchlicher *»Leitungsdienst«* oder *»Vorsteherdienst«* beziehungsweise »Leiter« oder »Vorsteher« (der Gemeinde, der Diözese oder Landeskirche usw.) empfehlen. Andere Sprachen tun sich mit den Ausdrücken »ministerium«, »ministero«, »ministerio«, »ministère«, »ministry« im Unterschied zum allgemeinen »servitium«, »servizio«, »servicio«, »service« von vornherein leichter. Andererseits braucht nicht vergessen zu werden: das deutsche Wort »Priester« (prêtre, prete, presbitero, priest) – obwohl traditionellerweise das kultisch-sakrale Sacerdotium seinen Sinngehalt ausmacht – stammt ursprünglich vom unkultischen Titel des Gemeinde-ältesten her, so daß es an sich, wie in einzelnen Kirchen üblich, sachgemäß durch »Presbyter« oder »Ältester«, beziehungsweise »Presbyter parochianus«, also »Pfarrer« ersetzt werden kann.

Die vielen Verfassungen

Sind in der Kirche alle Dienste von gleicher Wichtigkeit? Keineswegs. Eine erste Unterscheidung ergibt sich schon daraus, daß auch im Neuen Testament nicht alle Dienste oder Charismen *ständige öffentliche* Gemeindedienste sind. Die einen Charismen – bei Paulus etwa die des Ermahnens, Tröstens, der Weisheitsrede, Wissenschaft, Unterscheidung der Geister – sind offensichtlich mehr von Gott geschenkte private Begabungen und Tugenden, die in den Dienst der anderen gestellt und je nach Gelegenheit genutzt werden. Andere Charismen aber – die der Apostel, Propheten, Lehrer, Evangelisten, Diakone, Vorsteher, Episkopen, Hirten – sind von Gott gesetzte öffentliche Gemeindefunktionen, die ständig und regelmäßig ausgeübt werden. Bei den ersten wird im Neuen Testament meist die Gabe und ihre Wirkung genannt. Bei den zweiten werden die Personen bezeichnet. Die Personen können genannt werden, weil die Berufung offenkundig nicht willkürlich kommt und geht, sondern in einer bestimmten Stetigkeit mit bestimmten Personen verbunden bleibt, so daß diese Menschen in der Kirche als Apostel, Propheten usw. »gesetzt« sind.

In Zusammenhang mit dieser zweiten Art *besonderer* charismatischer Dienste, also dem Gefüge der ständigen öffentlichen Gemeindedienste, kann man von der »diakonischen Struktur« der Kirche reden, die einen bestimmten Aspekt der allgemeinen, grundlegenden charismatischen Dimension der Kirche darstellt. Doch soll auf diese terminologische Unterscheidung kein Gewicht gelegt werden, wohl aber auf die Grundlinien einer so oder anders zu bezeichnenden Struktur.

1. *Der grundlegende Apostolat*: Unter den ständigen öffentlichen Gemeindediensten hat nach dem gesamten Neuen Testament der Apostolat eine für die Kirche aller Zeiten *kirchenbegründende Funktion* und Bedeutung: Die Apostel (wie wir sahen: nicht einfach identisch mit den Zwölf) sind die Urzeugen und Urboten, die allen kirchlichen Diensten vorangehen, denen deshalb die gesamte Kirche und jedes einzelne Glied verpflichtet bleibt. Sie haben nämlich als erste Zeugen die Christusbotschaft verkündigt, die ersten Kirchen gegründet und geleitet und zugleich für die Einheit der Kirchen gesorgt. Auf sie ist somit die Kirche gebaut[15].

Die *grundlegende* »apostolische Nachfolge« ist somit nicht die bestimmter Ämter, sondern die der Kirche überhaupt und die eines jeden einzelnen Christen. Sie hat zu bestehen im je und je neu zu verwirklichenden sachlichen Zusammenhalt mit den Aposteln: Gefordert ist nämlich die bleibende Übereinstimmung mit dem *apostolischen Zeugnis* (uns überkommen im Neuen Testament) und der ständige Nachvollzug des *apostolischen Dienstes* (missionarischer Vorstoß in die Welt und Aufbau der Gemeinde). Apostolische Nachfolge ist somit primär eine Nachfolge im apostolischen Glauben und Bekennen sowie im apostolischen Dienen und Leben. Eine eventuelle *besondere* Nachfolge der Leitungsdienste wird noch zu erörtern sein.

2. *Verschiedene Lebensordnungen*: Der von Jesus selbst gesetzte Maßstab des Dienens war für die junge Glaubensgemeinschaft eindeutig bestimmt und war doch zugleich für sehr verschiedenartige Konkretisierungen offen. Nach diesem *Maßstab Jesu* und auf dem Grund der Apostel, mit denen zusammen nach Paulus die »Propheten« und »Lehrer« für die Gemeinden eine besondere Bedeutung haben, konnten sich in den verschiedenen Gemeinden je nach Zeit und Ort sehr verschiedene Lebensordnungen ausbilden[16]. Auffällig sind die Unterschiede zwischen der paulinischen und der palästinischen Gemeindeordnung.

Soweit wir feststellen können, haben sich gerade die von *Paulus* in apostolischer Vollmacht gegründeten *Gemeinden,* welche dem Apostel als dem Diener des Evangeliums frei verantwortlich blieben, jene Ordnungs- und *Leitungsdienste selber eingerichtet,* die ihnen für ihr Gemeindeleben notwendig erschienen. Diesen freiwilligen Gemeindediensten kam Autorität zu, die durchaus Unterordnung verlangen konnte. Aber nicht einfach die Faktizität des Innehabens einer bestimmten Funktion, sondern die Modalität des Dienens erweist einen Dienst als echt. Paulus, der in den unumstritten authentischen Briefen nie von Ordination und Presbytern spricht, kennt offensichtlich kein institutionalisiertes Amt, in das man eingesetzt wird und durch das man dann erst zum Dienst verpflichtet würde. Seine Kirchen sind Gemeinschaften freier charismatischer Dienste.

Auf die Dauer – und insbesondere nach dem Tod des Apostels – war eine *Institutionalisierung* auch in den paulinischen Gemeinden nicht zu vermeiden. Daß sich schon bald nach Paulus auch in der charismatischen Gemeinde von Korinth so rasch, wenn auch vermutlich nicht ohne Widerstand (1. Clemensbrief!), das System der Presbyter-Episkopen durchgesetzt hat, ist *kein Zufall und auch kein Abfall*. Nach der von der Naherwartung bestimmten Zeit der apostolischen Grundlegung mußte in der Zeit des nach-apostolischen Aufbaus und Ausbaus alles, was der Bewahrung der ursprünglichen Überlieferung helfen konnte, eine besondere Bedeutung erlangen: nicht nur die ursprünglichen Schriftzeugnisse, sondern auch die der apostolischen Überlieferung dienende Berufung in den kirchlichen Leitungsdienst unter Handauflegung (Ordination).

In der *palästinischen Tradition* hatte *die Institutionalisierung durch Übernahme des Ältestenkollegiums und der Ordination aus dem Judentum* schon sehr früh eingesetzt. Die Apostelgeschichte und die Pastoralbriefe zeigen auch für die paulinischen Gemeinden ein fortgeschrittenes Stadium der Institutionalisierung (Ordination). Andere Gemeinden (im Umkreis des Mattäus oder Johannes) weisen jedoch noch immer ausgesprochen bruderschaftliche Strukturen auf, so daß noch am Ende der neutestamentlichen Zeit die nicht harmonisierbare Vielfalt der Gemeindeverfassungen und Vielfalt der Ausprägungen der (teils charismatischen, teils schon institutionalisierten) Leitungsdienste groß ist, ohne die Einheit der Gemeinden untereinander aufzuheben. Die Frage stellt sich jedoch: Läßt sich unter solchen Umständen eine besondere »apostolische Nachfolge« der Leitungsdienste noch aufrechterhalten?

3. *Die besondere apostolische Nachfolge*: Es läßt sich historisch *nicht* halten, daß die *Bischöfe in direktem und exklusivem Sinn die Nachfolger der Apostel* (und gar noch des Zwölferkollegiums) sind. Damit ist allerdings die Frage der besonderen Nachfolge noch keineswegs erledigt. Als die unmittelbaren Erstzeugen und Erstgesandten Jesu Christi waren die Apostel von vorn-

herein durch keine Nachfolger ersetzbar und vertretbar. Aber notwendig blieb doch, wenn es auch keine neuen Apostel geben konnte, die apostolische Sendung und der apostolische Dienst. Diese werden nun allerdings, wie bereits bemerkt, primär von der ganzen Kirche wahrgenommen, die als ganze Ecclesia apostolica bleiben darf und soll.

Trotzdem ist in bezug auf die Leitungsdienste zu sagen: Insofern gerade die Leitungsdienste – Bischöfe und Presbyter oder Pfarrer können zwar rechtlich-disziplinär, aber nicht theologisch-dogmatisch unterschieden werden! – in der Kirche den *apostolischen Auftrag der Kirchengründung und Kirchenleitung,* beruhend auf Wortverkündigung, in besonderer Weise weiterführen, kann mit Recht von einer *funktional verstandenen besonderen apostolischen Nachfolge* der vielfältigen Leitungsdienste gesprochen werden. Die *besondere* »apostolische Nachfolge« der Leitungsdienste besteht somit in Kirchenleitung und -gründung, wurzelnd in der Verkündigung des Evangeliums.

Allerdings kann es exegetisch-historisch nicht auf »göttliche Einsetzung« oder »Einsetzung durch Jesus Christus«, auf ein göttliches Recht (ius divinum) zurückgeführt werden, sondern muß als eine lange *problematische geschichtliche Entwicklung*[17] angesehen werden,

a. daß die Bischöfe (Presbyter) sich gegenüber den Propheten, Lehrern und anderen charismatischen Diensten als die führenden und schließlich *alleinigen Gemeindeleiter* durchsetzten. Also: aus der »Kollegialität« *aller* Glaubenden wird immer mehr eine Kollegialität bestimmter Dienstgruppen *gegenüber* der Gemeinde, so daß sich eine Scheidung von »Klerus« und »Laien« abzeichnet;

b. daß gegenüber einer Mehrzahl von Bischöfen (Presbytern) in den Gemeinden immer mehr der monarchische Episkopat eines einzelnen Bischofs durchdringt. Also: aus der Kollegialität der verschiedenen Bischöfe oder Presbyter wird nun die Kollegialität des einen Bischofs mit seinem Presbyterium und seinen Diakonen, so daß sich die Scheidung von »Klerus« und »Laien« endgültig durchsetzt;

c. daß mit der Ausbreitung der Kirche von den Städten auch auf das Land aus dem Bischof als dem Vorsteher einer Gemeinde nun der *Vorsteher eines ganzen Kirchengebietes,* einer Diözese usw. wird: der Bischof im heutigen Sinn, für den die »apostolische Sukzession« jetzt historisiert, formalisiert und veräußerlicht wird durch das Aufzählen von Sukzessionsreihen in Sukzessionslisten. Also: neben der Kollegialität von Bischöfen und Presbyterium wird nun immer wichtiger die Kollegialität der einzelnen monarchischen Bischöfe untereinander und dann, wenn auch nur im Westen, mit dem Bischof von Rom.

Von einer solchen funktionalen und geschichtlichen Betrachtungsweise her kann eine besondere apostolische Nachfolge der Leitungsdienste für Kirchenleitung und -gründung nur unter folgenden Voraussetzungen bejaht werden:

- *Die Kirchenleiter als besondere Nachfolger der Apostel sind in der Kirche von vornherein umgeben von den anderen Gaben und Diensten: insbesondere von den Nachfolgern der neutestamentlichen Propheten und Lehrer, die im Zusammenwirken mit den Kirchenleitern eine eigene ursprüngliche Autorität haben.*
- *Die apostolische Nachfolge der Kirchenleiter unter Handauflegung erfolgt nicht automatisch oder mechanisch. Sie setzt Glauben voraus und fordert Glauben, der im apostolischen Geiste tätig ist. Sie schließt die Möglichkeit des Verfehlens und Irrens nicht aus und bedarf deshalb der Prüfung durch die Gesamtheit der Glaubenden.*
- *Die apostolische Nachfolge der Kirchenleiter hat zu geschehen in der Gemeinschaft des wechselseitigen Dienens für Kirche und Welt. Der Eintritt in die apostolische Nachfolge der Leitungsdienste sollte nach neutestamentlichem Kirchenverständnis normalerweise durch ein – auf verschiedenste Weise mögliches – Zusammenwirken von Vorstehern und Gemeinden geschehen. Der (freilich nicht exklusive) Normalfall dürfte die Berufung durch die Gemeindeleiter unter Beteiligung der Gemeinde sein. Die eigenständige Verantwortung des Gemeindeleiters im Dienst am Evangelium muß ebenso gewahrt sein wie eine Kontrollfunktion der Gemeinde dem Gemeindeleiter gegenüber*[18].
- *Von der paulinischen beziehungsweise heidenchristlichen Kirchenverfassung her müssen – insbesonders für Notfälle – auch andere Wege in Leitungsdienst und apostolischer Nachfolge der Kirchenleiter offengelassen werden: Grundsätzlich kann jemand Kirchenleiter werden auch aufgrund der Berufung durch andere Gemeindeglieder oder auch aufgrund eines frei aufbrechenden Charismas zur Gemeindeleitung oder -gründung.*
- *Die presbyterial-episkopale Kirchenverfassung, die sich in der nachapostolischen Zeit mit Recht in der Kirche faktisch durch-*

gesetzt hat, muß deshalb auch heute für andere Möglichkeiten, die in der neutestamentlichen Kirche bestanden haben, zumindest grundsätzlich offen bleiben. Diese Feststellung ist von großer Tragweite.

In missionarischer Hinsicht: eine gültige Eucharistiefeier, etwa in China oder Südamerika, ist grundsätzlich auch ohne Presbyter möglich.

In ökumenischer Hinsicht: eine Anerkennung der Gültigkeit der Dienste und Sakramente ist auch für die Kirchen gefordert, deren Vorsteher historisch nicht in der besonderen »apostolischen Sukzession« stehen.

In innerkirchlicher Hinsicht eine unvoreingenommene theologische Beurteilung von oppositionellen Gruppen, die in Konflikt mit der Kirchenleitung stehen, ist unabweisbar (Gültigkeit der Dienste und Sakramente).

4. *Konstanten und Variable*: Für die Entwicklung der kirchlichen Ämterordnung kann weder das Gefälle zum institutionellen Dienst Normativität beanspruchen, noch kann die Veränderung gegenüber dem Ursprung allein als solche schon Abfall sein. Der neutestamentliche Befund hat ergeben: Es finden sich im Neuen Testament verschiedene Modelle von Gemeindeordnung und Gemeindeleitung, die nicht aufeinander zurückgeführt werden können, wenn sie sich auch im Laufe der Zeit miteinander vermischt haben. Das Neue Testament gestattet es somit nicht, eine einzige Gemeindeverfassung zu kanonisieren. Das bedeutet für die Kirche heute keineswegs nur eine Not. Im Gegenteil: Gerade dies gibt ihr vielmehr die Freiheit, mit der Zeit zu gehen und zu neuen Entwicklungen und Ausformungen des kirchlichen Dienstes zum Wohle der Menschen und der Gemeinden fähig zu sein. Es müssen nicht die einzelnen neutestamentlichen Modelle imitiert werden. Sondern die entscheidenden neutestamentlichen Momente müssen, solange man auf Christlichkeit Anspruch erhebt, auch unter ganz veränderten Verhältnissen bewahrt und bewährt werden.

Für den Leitungsdienst in der Gemeinde erweist sich vom Neuen Testament her als entscheidend: Er muß sein

Dienst an der Gemeinde,

nach dem Maßstab Jesu, der keine Herrschaftsverhältnisse zuläßt, in Verpflichtung auf das apostolische Urzeugnis,

inmitten einer Vielfalt von verschiedenen Funktionen, Diensten, Charismen.

Aufgrund dieses neutestamentlichen Befundes lassen sich drei nicht ganz einfache Fragen beantworten[19]:

– *Welches sind die* Konstanten *des Kirchenleitungsdienstes? Neben anderen Diensten bedarf jede Gemeinde oder Kirche der Leitung, die durch Einzelne oder kollegial wahrgenommen wird. Ihre Aufgabe ist auf lokaler, regionaler oder universaler Ebene die öffentliche Wahrnehmung der gemeinsamen Sache: aufgrund einer besonderen Berufung die christliche Gemeinschaft im Geist Jesu Christi kontinuierlich zu leiten. Das heißt anzuregen, zu koordinieren, zu integrieren sowie nach außen und gegenüber den einzelnen Gliedern zu repräsentieren. Dies geschieht grundlegend durch die Verkündigung des Wortes zusammen mit dem Vollzug der Sakramente und dem tätigen Engagement in Gemeinde und Gesellschaft.*

– *Welches sind die* Variablen *des Kirchenleitungsdienstes? Die konkrete Ausgestaltung der kirchlichen Dienste muß jeweils funktionsgerecht und deshalb flexibel sein. Eine bestimmte historisch gewordene Gestalt ist zu verändern, wenn sie der Funktion des betreffenden Dienstes nicht mehr entspricht. Kirchliche Ämter können je nach den besonderen Aufgaben, Umständen und Eignungen hauptberuflich oder nebenberuflich, auf Zeit oder lebenslang, von Männern oder Frauen, von Verheirateten oder Unverheirateten, von Akademikern oder Nichtakademikern ausgeübt werden. Die gegenwärtige Auflösung des klerikalen »Standes« bedeutet nicht Auflösung des kirchlichen Leitungsdienstes überhaupt.*

– *Was ist die* Ordination? *Die Ordination ist die herkömmlicherweise unter Gebet und Handauflegung erfolgende Berufung in das Amt, das mit der Sendung der Kirche als ganzer verbunden und als Teilnahme an der Sendung Christi zu verstehen ist. Sie bevollmächtigt im Unterschied zum allgemeinen Priestertum der Gläubigen zur öffentlichen Wahrnehmung der einen Sendung Christi, zu deren zentralen Aufgaben Verkündigung und Sakramentsverwaltung gehören. Diese Vollmacht kann in verschiedenen spezialisierten Funktionen wahrgenommen werden. Im Einzelfall kann die Ordination für den Ordinierten und die Gemeinde Bestätigung eines Charismas oder Berufung mit der Verheißung des Charismas bedeuten. Ob die Ordination als Sakrament bezeichnet werden soll oder nicht, ist eine Frage der Sprachregelung.*

Eine für die Ökumene äußerst wichtige und leider mehr als alles andere belastende Frage ist freilich bisher offen geblieben: Braucht die Christenheit neben allen anderen Leitungsdiensten einen universalen Leitungsdienst, einen Papst?

Ein Petrusdienst?

Sollte es heute – 900 Jahre nach der Spaltung zwischen Ost- und Westkirche und 450 Jahre nach dem Ausbruch der protestantischen Reformation, die beide wesentlich mit dem römischen Papsttum zu tun hatten – nicht möglich, nicht notwendig sein, in unvoreingenommener Sachlichkeit auch über diese Frage zu sprechen? Blicken wir zur Klärung der Frage zunächst kurz in die Geschichte, dann in die Gegenwart und Zukunft[20].

1. *Die Ambivalenz der Geschichte*: Die Verdienste des römischen Primates um die Einheit der Kirche, ihren Glauben und das Abendland wird niemand bestreiten können[21]. Oder sollte man es nicht verstehen können, daß die jungen westlichen Völker in den Zeiten der Völkerwanderung, der allgemeinen Auflösung der staatlichen Ordnung und des Zerfalls der alten Reichshauptstadt unendlich dankbar waren für diesen Dienst der Cathedra Petri, die ungefähr das einzige war, was sich als stabiler Felsen erwies, intakt und unerschüttert? Nur ein Leo vermochte Rom vor Attila und Geiserich zu bewahren. Die römische Sedes hat den jungen Kirchen in den Wirren und stürmischen Zeiten der werdenden neuen abendländischen Völkergemeinschaft einen unermeßlichen Dienst geleistet. Und es war dies nicht nur ein kultureller Dienst bei der Erhaltung des unschätzbaren antiken Erbes, sondern auch ein echter Hirtendienst für den Aufbau und die Erhaltung dieser Kirchen: für ihre Liturgie und ihre Kirchenordnung. Dem Papsttum hat es die katholische Kirche dieser Zeit wie auch später weithin zu verdanken, daß sie nicht einfach dem Staate verfiel und daß sie ihre Freiheit gegenüber dem Cäsaropapismus der byzantinischen Kaiser wie dem Eigenkirchentum der germanischen Fürsten wie auch modernen absolutistischen und totalitären Systemen gegenüber besser als andere Kirchen bewahren konnte. Ein echter Dienst an der Einheit der Christenheit.

Wenn man so die unbestreitbaren Verdienste des römischen Primats für die Einheit der spätantiken, frühmittelalterlichen und hochmittelalterlichen Kirche des Westens auf keinen Fall übergehen darf, so wird man andererseits doch auch um die bedrückende Feststellung nicht herumkommen: Der immer mehr mit den Mitteln des Zentralismus und Absolutismus vollzogene Ausbau der Einheitskirche wurde erkauft mit der *Spaltung der Christenheit*, die sich mit diesem absolutistischen System und seinen Auswüchsen immer weniger abfinden konnte. Zuerst der orthodoxe Osten, dann auch der protestantische Norden. Wie bedauerlich wiederum, daß man diese Spaltungen nicht durch eine rechtzeitige Rückbesinnung auf den Ursprung, wie sie von so vielen gefordert wurde, vermieden hat! Doch gerade dies hat man auch in der nachtridentinischen Kirche und im gegenreformatorischen Papsttum nur in sehr beschränktem Ausmaß eingesehen. Die Bastionen der Macht wurden nicht geschleift, sondern mit allen Mitteln ausgebaut. Zwar gab es auch innerhalb der Mauern – auch in Rom, man denke an Männer wie Contarini, andere Kardinäle und den Viterbo-Kreis mit Michelangelo und Vittoria Colonna – starke Gegenströmungen. Uralte Ideen der Kirchenverfassung wirkten, wenn auch in allzu politisierten Formen, weiter bei den späteren Gallikanern, den Episkopalisten und schließlich im 19. Jahrhundert auch in der katholischen Tübinger Schule, besonders beim jungen J. A. Möhler. Aber die Versteifung wuchs, wiewohl auch in der Neuzeit die Verdienste des Papsttums um Einheit und Freiheit der katholischen Kirche, insbesondere gegenüber dem staatlichen Absolutismus, bedeutsam blieben.

Seit dem Mittelalter und nun auch die ganze Neuzeit hindurch war die offizielle katholische Ekklesiologie (Lehre von der Kirche) eine Ekklesiologie der Apologie und Reaktion gewesen. Gegen den frühen Gallikanismus und die Legisten der französischen Krone: deshalb eine Theologie der hierarchischen und besonders der päpstlichen Gewalt und das Verständnis der Kirche als eines organisierten Reiches. Gegen die konziliaren Theorien: erneut Herausstreichung des päpstlichen Primates. Gegen den wyclifitischen und hussitischen Spiritualismus: der kirchliche und soziale Charakter der christlichen Botschaft. Gegen die Reformatoren: die objektive Bedeutung der Sakramente, die Wichtigkeit der hierarchischen Gewalten, des Amtspriestertums, des Bischofsamtes und wiederum des Primates. Gegen den mit dem Gallikanismus verbündeten Jansenismus: besondere Betonung des päpstlichen Lehramtes. Gegen den Staatsabsolutismus des 18. und 19. Jahrhunderts und den Laizismus: die Kirche als die mit allen Rechten und Mitteln ausgestattete »vollkommene Gesellschaft«. Dies alles führte recht konsequent zu dem unter antigallikanischem und antiliberalem Vorzeichen stattfindenden *Ersten Vatikanischen Konzil* und seiner Definition des päpstlichen Primates und der päpstlichen Unfehlbarkeit 1870[22].

Hätte das Vatikanum II Primat und Unfehlbarkeit des Papstes definiert, wenn sie nicht schon vom Vatikanum I definiert worden wären? Johannes XXIII. war kein Pius IX. Auch hat das Vatikanum II anders als das Vatikanum I überhaupt keine neuen Dogmen gewünscht, offensichtlich aus der Einsicht heraus, die Johannes XXIII. formuliert hatte: daß neue Definitionen alter Wahrheiten der Glaubensverkündigung der Kirche in der modernen Welt nicht helfen können. Schließlich zeichnete sich das Vatikanum II durch ein waches Bewußtsein für Gemeinschaft, Kollegialität, Solidarität, Dienst aus. Dieses Bewußtsein stand im Gegensatz zur untergründigen Mentalität der Majorität des Vatikanum I, die verständlicherweise geprägt war durch die politisch-kulturell-religiöse Welt der Restaurationszeit, des romantischen Traditionalismus und des politischen Absolutismus.

2. *Die höhere Legitimität*: Es hätte nun freilich wenig Sinn, in unserem Zusammenhang alle die vielen Einwände der Reihe nach zur Sprache zu bringen, die gegen eine biblisch-historische Begründung eines Jurisdiktions- und Lehrprimats Petri und der römischen Bischöfe von evangelischer und östlich-orthodoxer Seite ins Feld geführt und von katholischer Seite kaum befriedigend beantwortet wurden. Alle Schwierigkeiten lagern sich um drei Fragen, wobei die folgende die Lösung der vorangehenden voraussetzt: Läßt sich ein Primat Petri begründen? Muß der Primat Petri fortdauern? Ist der römische Bischof der Nachfolger im petrinischen Primat?

Wenn man für die Beantwortung dieser Fragen, die nun einmal historische Fragen sind, nicht zu historisch unverantwortbaren dogmatischen Postulaten seine Zuflucht nehmen will, wird man, falls die bisherige umfangreiche Literatur nicht täuscht, bei der Entkräftung dieser Schwierigkeiten seine liebe Mühe haben[23].

Doch wie immer man sich dazu stellt, das eine wird auch der östlich-orthodoxe oder evangelische Theologe, der die katholische Argumentation keineswegs überzeugend findet, nicht bestreiten: Der Dienstprimat eines Einzelnen in der Kirche ist nicht von vornherein gegen die Schrift. Wie immer es um seine Begründung stehen mag, es gibt nichts in der Schrift, was einen solchen Dienstprimat ausschlösse. Ein solcher Primat ist also *nicht von vornherein schriftwidrig.* Ja, der orthodoxe oder evangelische Theologe wird vermutlich sogar zugeben können: Ein solcher Dienstprimat *könnte schriftgemäß sein,* jedenfalls dann, wenn er schriftgemäß begründet, geübt, vollzogen, gehandhabt wird. Das gaben die meisten Reformatoren vom jungen Luther über Melanchthon bis Calvin zu; das werden auch viele orthodoxe und evangelische Theologen heute zugeben.

Aber das Entscheidende ist nicht der historische Aufweis einer Sukzessionsreihe: bei einem Petrusdienst so wenig wie bei anderen Leitungsdiensten. Das *Entscheidende* ist die *Nachfolge im Geist*: also in der petrinischen Sendung und Aufgabe, im petrinischen Zeugnis und Dienst. Konkret gesagt: Wäre da einer, der sich einwandfrei darüber ausweisen könnte, daß sein Vorgänger und der Vorgänger seines Vorgängers und so fort schließlich der »Nachfolger« des einen Petrus ist, ja, könnte er sogar nachweisen, daß der Vorgänger seiner Vorgänger von Petrus selbst mit allen Rechten und Pflichten zu seinem Nachfolger »eingesetzt« wurde, würde er aber dieser petrinischen Sendung gar nicht nachkommen, würde er die ihm gestellte Aufgabe nicht erfüllen, würde er nicht Zeugnis geben und seinen Dienst nicht leisten – was nützte ihm, was nützte der Kirche die ganze »apostolische Sukzession«? Umgekehrt: Wäre da ein anderer, dessen Nachfolge mindestens in der Frühzeit nur schwierig nachzuprüfen, über dessen »Einsetzung« vor zweitausend Jahren nun einmal nichts protokolliert wäre, würde aber dieser andere der in der Schrift beschriebenen petrinischen Sendung nachleben, würde er Auftrag und Aufgabe erfüllen und der Kirche diesen Dienst leisten, wäre es dann nicht eine zwar noch immer wichtige, aber letztlich doch zweitrangige Frage, ob dieses echten Dieners der Kirche »Stammbaum« in Ordnung ist? Er hätte dann vielleicht nicht die einwandfreie Sukzessionsreihe, aber er hätte das Charisma, das Charisma der Leitung (Kybernese), und dies würde im Grunde ausreichen.

Also: nicht der Anspruch, nicht das »Recht«, nicht die »Sukzessionskette« als solche sind das Entscheidende, sondern *der Vollzug, die Ausübung, die Tat, der verwirklichte Dienst.* Bei den großen ökumenischen Initiativen Johannes' XXIII. für katholische Kirche, Christenheit und Welt war die Menschheit wenig daran interessiert, wie es mit der Sukzessionskette stünde, ob er sich über die Legitimität seines Amtes historisch ausweisen könne. Sie war vielmehr froh und erleichtert zu sehen: hier ist einer, der wirkt nun – trotz aller menschlichen Schwächen – als ein echter »Fels« in dieser Zeit, der der Christenheit Halt und neues Zusammenstehen zu geben vermag[24]. Hier ist einer, der aus starkem Glauben heraus »die Brüder zu stärken und zu ermutigen« vermag[25]. Hier ist einer, der »die Schafe« wie sein Herr mit uneigennütziger Liebe »hüten« möchte[26]. Die Menschen wurden deswegen nicht alle katholisch. Aber sie spürten spontan, daß dieses Tun und dieser Geist *das Evangelium Jesu Christi hinter sich* hatte und in jedem Fall von ihm gerechtfertigt war. Und diese Legitimität ist für den Petrusdienst höher als jede andere.

3. *Petrusmacht und Petrusdienst*: Damit soll die Diskussion der exegetischen und historischen Fragen nicht für überflüssig erklärt werden. Sie soll nur im richtigen Licht, in der richtigen Perspektive geschehen. Daß der Petrusdienst, dessen Felsen- und Hirtenfunktion gerade nach katholischer Auffassung die Bewahrung und Stärkung der kirchlichen Einheit sein sollte, zum übergroßen, anscheinend weder bewegbaren noch übersteigbaren noch umgehbaren Felsblock auf dem Weg zu einem gegenseitigen Verstehen der christlichen Kirchen geworden ist und es nach dem Zweiten Vatikanischen Konzil von neuem ist, dies ist eine absurde Situation, die gerade dem, der vom Nutzen eines Petrusdienstes überzeugt ist, nicht genug zu denken geben kann. Wie konnte es denn so weit kommen? Liegt das einfach an der mangelnden Kenntnis, dem unterentwickelten Verständnis oder gar der bösen Widerspenstigkeit der Gegner eines petrinischen Dienstes? Dies wird heute niemand mehr zu behaupten wagen. Auch wenn man keineswegs die Schuld an der Kirchenspaltung auf einer Seite sehen darf, so wird man doch um die Frage nicht herumkommen: Kam es zu jener faktischen Verkehrung der Funktionen des Petrusdienstes nicht auch und besonders, weil sich dieser *Petrus-Dienst* – aus sehr verschiedenen historischen Gründen und wahrhaftig nicht aus dem bösen Willen eines Einzelnen oder mehrerer Einzelner heraus – den Menschen immer mehr *als Petrus-Macht präsentiert hat?* Es war ein langer Prozeß, der das Papsttum zu einer Weltmacht und einer absolutistischen Kirchenmacht werden ließ.

Es hätte auch anders sein können! Wie immer es um die exegetische und historische Begründung, die göttliche oder menschliche Ermächtigung zu einem dauernden Petrusdienst in der Kirche stehen mochte: es wäre doch möglich gewesen – und die vorkonstantinische Zeit war für eine solche Konzeption durchaus offen –, daß sich die römische Gemeinde mit ihrem Bischof, welcher in der Tat ganz außerordentliche Gaben und Möglichkeiten des Dienstes gegeben waren, um einen wahrhaft *pastoralen Primat im Sinne geistlicher Verantwortung, innerer Führung und aktiver Sorge um das Wohlergehen der Gesamtkirche* bemüht hätte. Was sie dann auch zu einer allgemeinen kirchlichen Vermittlungsinstanz und obersten Schlichtungsinstanz befähigt hätte. Ein Primat also nicht der Herrschaft, sondern des selbstlosen Dienstes – in Verantwortung vor dem Herrn der Kirche und in bescheidener Brüderlichkeit. Ein Primat nicht im Geiste des religiös-verbrämten römischen Imperialismus, sondern im Geiste Jesu Christi.

Die Frage, die sich nun im Hinblick auf die verlorene Einheit der Kirche Christi und die vielfache Erstarrung innerhalb der katholischen Kirche aufdrängt, ist die Frage nach der Zukunft: Gibt es von diesem Herrschaftsprimat einen *Weg zurück* und gerade so *nach vorn* zum alten Dienstprimat?

Die historische Erfahrung zeigt, daß den Hochzeiten päpstlicher Machtentfaltung immer wieder Zeiten äußerer Demütigung und Machtbeschränkung folgten. Aber auch ein *freiwilliger Verzicht auf geistliche Macht* ist möglich: Was politisch, auch kirchenpolitisch, unvernünftig scheint, kann in der Kirche von Jesus her geboten sein! Und es ist erstaunlich genug und ein großes Zeichen der Hoffnung, daß dies auch wirklich geschieht. Sonst wäre – um von anderen Beispielen wie Hadrian VI. oder Marcellus II., die aufgrund der Ungunst der Zeit oder ihres baldigen Todes nicht geschichtsmächtig werden konnten, zu schweigen – nach einer Reihe von sehr herrschaftsbewußten Päpsten nicht ein Gregor der Große oder wiederum ein Johannes XXIII., und nach dem Vatikanum I kein Vatikanum II möglich gewesen.

Ohne Verzicht auf »geistliche« Macht ist eine Wiedervereinigung der getrennten christlichen Kirchen ebenso unmöglich wie eine radikale Erneuerung der katholischen Kirche nach dem Evangelium. Verzicht auf Macht ist alles andere als eine natürliche Angelegenheit. Warum sollte ein Mensch, warum sollte eine Autorität, eine Institution etwas hergeben, was sie nun einmal hat – und dies ohne sichtbare Gegenleistung? Verzicht auf Macht ist in der Tat nur dem möglich, der etwas von der Botschaft Jesu und der Bergpredigt begriffen hat. Aber auch eine kleine Besinnung auf jenen Petrus, auf dessen Nachfolge man in Rom so viel Gewicht legt, könnte helfen.

4. Drei Versuchungen[27]: Ob sich der wirkliche *Petrus* in dem Bild wiedererkannt hätte, das man in Rom von ihm gemacht hatte? Er war kein Apostel-Fürst, vielmehr bis zum Ende seines Lebens der bescheidene Fischer, jetzt Menschenfischer, der in der Nachfolge seines Herrn dienen wollte. Aber darüber hinaus hatte er nach allen Evangelien übereinstimmend eine zweite Seite, die immer wieder den Irrenden, Fehlenden, Versagenden, eben den so recht menschlichen Petrus zeigt. Es ist beinahe skandalös, wie jedem der drei klassischen Texte bei Mattäus, Lukas und Johannes für einen Vorrang Petri ein außerordentlich scharfer Kontrapunkt beigegeben ist, dessen dunkler, harter Klang die helle Oberstimme beinahe übertönt, jedenfalls im Gleichgewicht hält. Den drei hohen Verheißungen entsprechen drei tiefe Verfehlungen. Und wer die Verheißungen in Anspruch nimmt, wird nicht darum herumkommen, auch die drei Verfehlungen, die für ihn jedenfalls drei Versuchungen sind, auf sich zu beziehen. Und wenn die Verheißungen in beinahe zweimetrigen schwarzen Buchstaben auf goldenem Grund die ganze Peterskirche als Fries umziehen, dann müßten ihnen eigentlich, um nicht mißverstanden zu werden, die Gegen-Sätze in goldenen Lettern auf schwarzem Grund beigegeben sein. Hätte der große Gregor, der in dieser Kirche begraben ist, dafür nicht ebenso Sinn gehabt wie Johannes XXIII.?

Erste Versuchung nach Mattäus[28]: Sich über den Herrn zu stellen, den Meister überlegen »beiseite zu nehmen«, besser zu wissen als er, wie es nun eigentlich gemacht werden und wie es weitergehen soll: ein triumphalistischer Weg, der am Kreuz vorbeiführen soll! Und gerade diese besserwissenden Einfälle einer theologia gloriae sind eben Menschengedanken, die in geradem Gegensatz stehen zu dem, was Gott denkt und will: eine fromme theologia satanae, des Versuchers schlechthin. Wann immmer Petrus ganz selbstverständlich voraussetzt, Gottes Gedanken zu denken, wann immer er so – vielleicht ohne es zu merken – aus dem Bekennenden zum Verkennenden wird und statt für Gott für Menschliches Partei ergreift, dann dreht ihm der Herr den Rücken zu, und ihn trifft das Wort, das härter nicht sein könnte: »Hinweg von mir, Satan! Du bist mir ein Ärgernis; denn du sinnst nicht, was Gottes, sondern was menschlich ist!«

Zweite Versuchung nach Lukas[29]: Besondere Stellung und besondere Begabung bedeuten besondere Verantwortung. Aber gerade dies schließt Erprobung und Versuchung nicht aus: Auch hier erscheint der Satan, der sich ausgebeten hat, jeden Jünger

Jesu im Sieb zu schütteln wie Weizen. Des Petrus Glaube soll nicht wanken. Aber sobald er selbstbewußt meint, seine Treue sei selbstverständlich und sein Glaube sei unfehlbar fester Besitz, sobald er nicht mehr weiß, daß er am Gebet des Herrn hängt und Glaube und Treue immer wieder neu empfangen muß, sobald er seine Bereitschaft und seinen Einsatz als eigene Leistung ausgibt, sobald er also selbstsicher sich selbst überschätzt und nicht mehr auf den Herrn sein ganzes Vertrauen setzt, dann ist die Hahnenstunde der Verleugnung da, da kennt er seinen Herrn nicht mehr, da ist er fähig, ihn nicht nur einmal, sondern dreimal, und das heißt vollständig, zu verleugnen: »Ich sage dir, Petrus: Der Hahn wird heute nicht krähen, bis du dreimal geleugnet hast, mich zu kennen!«

Dritte Versuchung nach Johannes[30]: Von Petrus, der den Herrn dreimal verleugnete, ist dreimal die Liebe gefragt worden: »Liebst du mich mehr als diese?« Nur so, nur unter dieser Bedingung wird ihm die Leitung der Gemeinde übergeben; er hütet die Lämmer und weidet die Schafe, indem er Jesus in Liebe nachfolgt. Der Petrus aber, der nicht auf Jesus sieht, der sich umwendet, der sieht den, der ihn schon immer in der Liebe übertroffen hat. Und auf seine deplazierte Frage, wie es mit diesem da stehe, was mit diesem da geschehen soll, wird ihm die Antwort zuteil, die zu seinem allgemeinen Hirtenauftrag im Widerspruch zu stehen scheint: »Was geht das dich an!« Es gibt also Dinge, die Petrus nichts angehen. Wann immer Petrus sich nicht um seine eigene beschränkte Aufgabe kümmern will, wann immer er nicht sieht, daß es Schicksal gibt, über das er nicht befinden kann, wann immer er vergißt, daß es eine besondere Beziehung zu Jesus gibt, die nicht über ihn läuft, wann immer er neben seinem Weg nicht auch andere Wege gelten läßt, dann muß er das Wort hören, das ihn hart treffen muß und ihn doch wieder neu in die Nachfolge ruft: »Was geht das dich an! Du folge mir nach!«

Die Größe der Versuchung entspricht der Größe der Sendung. Und wer könnte die ungeheure Last der Verantwortung, der Sorge, des Leides und der Bedrängnis ermessen, die auf dem Petrusdienst liegt, wenn er *wirklich* Fels sein will, wirklich Schlüsselträger, wirklich Hirte im Dienst an der Gesamtkirche? Denn die Zeiten, in denen man – wie Leo X. zur Zeit Luthers gesagt haben soll – das Papsttum, da es Gott gegeben, auch genießen konnte, sind längst vorbei. Wie oft wird da bei aller mit diesem Dienste verbundenen Mühsal und Trübsal, bei allem

Unverstandensein und beim eigenen Unfähigsein der Glaube wanken wollen[31], die Liebe versagen[32], die Hoffnung, gegen die Pforten der Unterwelt anzukommen[33], verblassen wollen! Mehr als irgendein anderer Dienst ist dieser auf die Gnade des Herrn angewiesen. Dieser Dienst darf auch von seinen Brüdern viel erwarten, mehr als ihm oft gegeben wird und ihm nicht helfen kann: nicht servile Unterwürfigkeit, nicht kritiklose Devotion, nicht sentimentale Vergötterung, sondern: tägliche Fürbitte, loyale Mitarbeit, konstruktive Kritik, ungeheuchelte Liebe.

Vielleicht wird doch auch der östlich-orthodoxe und der evangelische Christ es dem Katholiken ein wenig nachfühlen können, daß nach seiner Überzeugung seiner Kirche und vielleicht auch der Christenheit etwas fehlte, wenn dieser Petrusdienst plötzlich nicht mehr da wäre; etwas, das für die Kirche nicht unwesentlich ist[34]. Was könnte er der Christenheit bedeuten, wenn er neu nüchtern und unsentimental im Lichte der Heiligen Schrift verstanden würde als das, was er sein soll: Dienst an der Gesamtkirche! Die volle biblische Kategorie des Dienstes sprengt bei weitem die juristischen Kategorien des Vatikanum I:

– *Dieser Dienstprimat ist mehr als ein Ehrenprimat (primatus honoris), den in der Kirche des Dienstes niemand zu vergeben hat und der in seiner Passivität auch niemandem helfen kann.*
– *Dieser Dienstprimat ist mehr als ein Jurisdiktionsprimat (primatus iurisdictionis), der als reine Gewalt und Macht verstanden gerade das Entscheidende, den Dienst, wenn vielleicht auch nicht verleugnet, so doch verschweigt.*
– *Petrusdienst wird biblisch richtig bezeichnet als* Dienstprimat in der Gesamtkirche, als Pastoralprimat: *primatus servitii, primatus ministerialis, primatus pastoralis im Dienst an der Kirche für die Sache Jesu Christi*[35].

5. *Keine Parteiprogramme*[36]: Wie der Petrusdienst, wie die diakonische Struktur der Kirche überhaupt, wie schließlich auch die Wiedervereinigung der getrennten christlichen Kirchen in der Zukunft aussehen wird, weiß heute niemand. Der gegenwärtigen Generation ist aufgetragen, das ihr Mögliche zu tun. Und dabei ist auf eines abschließend hinzuweisen: Jede Kirche hat aufgrund ihrer Geschichte ihre eigenen Besonderheiten, die von den anderen in dieser Weise nicht akzeptiert werden, hat gleichsam ihre »Spezialität«. »Spezialitäten« freilich von ungleichem Gewicht. Für die Katholiken ist dies nun einmal der Papst. Aber sie sind

nicht allein damit! Auch die östlichen Orthodoxen haben ihren »Papst«: die »Tradition«. Und auch die Protestanten: die »Bibel«. Und schließlich auch die Freikirchen: die »Freiheit«. Aber wie das »Papsttum« der Katholiken nicht einfach der Petrusdienst des Neuen Testamentes ist, so ist die »Tradition« der Orthodoxen nicht einfach die apostolische Überlieferung, so ist die »Bibel« der Protestanten nicht einfach das Evangelium, so ist die »Freiheit« der Freikirchen nicht einfach die Freiheit der Kinder Gottes. Auch die beste Losung wird dann mißbraucht, wenn sie zum *Parteiprogramm* wird, unter dessen Zeichen man in den Kampf um die Macht in der Kirche auszieht. Zu einem Parteiprogramm, das dann auch oft mit dem Namen eines Führers verbunden wird. Zu einem Parteiprogramm, das die Anderen aus der eigenen Kirche ausschließen muß.

Auch in Korinth gab es schon am Anfang Parteien. Sie hatten ihr Programm – wir kennen es im einzelnen nicht – an einen Führer geheftet, den sie feierten und über die Anderen erhöhten, wobei sie den Anderen die Autorität absprachen: »Denn es wurde mir über euch, meine Brüder, von den Angehörigen der Chloe mitgeteilt, daß bei euch Streitigkeiten sind. Ich spreche aber davon, daß jeder von euch sagt: ich gehöre zu Paulus; ich zu Apollos; ich zu Kephas; ich zu Christus[37].« Wenn man sich hier einen Anachronismus gestatten dürfte, so würde man die Katholiken zweifellos mit der Partei des Kephas identifizieren, der sie wegen seines Primates, seiner Schlüssel- und Hirtengewalt doch jedenfalls gegenüber allen übrigen ins Recht setzt. Und die östlichen Orthodoxen wären dann die Partei jenes Apollon, der aus der großen Tradition griechischen Denkens heraus die Offenbarung geistvoller, gedankenreicher, tiefsinniger, auch »richtiger« erklärt als alle anderen. Und die Protestanten wären gewiß die Partei des Paulus, der doch der Vater ihrer Gemeinde, der Apostel schlechthin, der einzigartige Verkünder des Kreuzes Christi ist, welcher mehr gearbeitet hat als alle übrigen Apostel. Und die Freikirchen schließlich wären vielleicht die Partei Christi selbst, die nämlich in Freiheit von allem Zwang dieser Kirchen, ihrer Autoritäten und Bekenntnisse sich allein auf Christus als den einzigen Herrn und Meister stützt und von daher das brüderliche Leben ihrer Gemeinden gestaltet.

Und für wen entschied sich Paulus? Bestimmt doch für Petrus, denn Kephas ist doch der Fels, auf den die Kirche gebaut? Aber Paulus übergeht den Namen Petri mit Schweigen, taktvoll ebenso den des Apollon. Das Erstaunliche jedoch: er desavouiert auch seine eigenen Parteigänger. Er will nicht, daß sich Gruppen an einen Menschen hängen und einen Menschen zum Programm machen, der nicht für sie gekreuzigt wurde, auf dessen Namen sie nicht getauft sind. Paulus hat den Korinthern die Taufe gebracht. Aber nicht auf seinen, sondern auf Christi, des Gekreuzigten, Namen wurden sie getauft, und auf wen sie getauft sind, dem gehören sie auch. Und deshalb darf selbst der Name des Paulus, der die Gemeinde begründete, nicht zum Parteinamen werden.

Wir sehen daraus: Der (gewichtige) Petrusdienst mag für die Kirche, ihre Einheit und ihren Zusammenhalt noch sosehr »Fels« sein; er darf doch nicht zum Kriterium schlechthin werden dafür, wo Kirche ist. Die (noch wichtigere) Tradition mag für die Kirche, ihre Kontinuität und Beständigkeit noch so gute Leitlinie sein; sie darf doch nicht zur Scheidelinie werden, jenseits derer statt »Orthodoxie« nur Heterodoxie sein kann. Die (allerwichtigste) Bibel mag für die Kirche, ihr Glauben und Bekennen noch sosehr »Fundament« sein, sie darf doch nicht zum Steinbruch werden für Steine, die nicht zum Aufbauen, sondern zum Steinigen verwendet werden. Doch nicht genug damit: Es ist auch keine Lösung, sich statt auf die Apostel auf Christus direkt zu berufen. Selbst für solche gilt: »Ist Christus zerteilt[38]?« Selbst Christus, der Herr, darf nicht dazu benützt werden, als Schild für eine Partei zu dienen, die damit gegen andere in der einen und selben Kirche Sturm laufen will!

Die Bibel als grundlegende befreiende Botschaft, die getreue Überlieferung des ursprünglichen Zeugnisses, der Petrusdienst als selbstloser Hirtendienst an der Kirche, die freie Versammlung der Brüder unter dem Geist – das alles ist gut, wenn es nicht exklusiv verstanden, wenn es nicht gegen die Anderen gewendet wird, wenn es im Dienste der Sache Jesu Christi steht, der der Herr über die Kirche und alles, was sie ausmacht, ist und bleibt. Keine Kirche kann letztlich über sich selbst urteilen. Jede ist in die Feuerprobe ihres Herrn gestellt. Da wird zum Vorschein kommen, was an ihrer Sondergestalt, ihrer Sonderüberlieferung, ihrer Sonderlehre Holz, Heu und Stroh oder aber Gold, Silber und Edelstein ist, was wertlos vergeht und was sich erhalten und bewähren wird[39].

4. Der große Auftrag

Gibt es aber, so betrachtet, überhaupt noch Unterschiede zwischen den verschiedenen Kirchen und insbesondere zwischen katholischer Kirche und evangelischen Kirchen? Was eigentlich ist heute noch »katholisch« und was ist »evangelisch«?

Katholisch – evangelisch

Alles bisher Dargelegte zeigt: Die Unterschiede liegen heute nicht mehr in einzelnen traditionellen Lehrdifferenzen etwa bezüglich Schrift und Tradition, Sünde und Gnade, Glaube und Werke, Eucharistie und Priestertum, Papst und Kirche. In all diesen einzelnen Punkten kann man sich zumindest theoretisch verständigen oder man hat sich bereits verständigt. Nur müßten die kirchlichen Apparate die theologischen Erkenntnisse mitvollziehen. Der entscheidende Unterschied liegt in traditionellen Grundhaltungen, die sich seit der Reformationszeit ausbildeten, die aber heute in ihrer Einseitigkeit überwunden und in wahre Ökumenizität integriert werden können:

- Katholisch *in der Grundhaltung ist, wem besonders an der* katholischen = ganzen, *allgemeinen, umfassenden, gesamten* Kirche gelegen ist. Konkret: an der in allen Brüchen sich durchhaltenden Kontinuität *von Glaube und Glaubensgemeinschaft in der Zeit (Tradition), und an der alle Gruppen umfassenden* Universalität *von Glaube und Glaubensgemeinschaft im Raum (gegen »protestantischen« Radikalismus und Partikularismus, die nicht zu verwechseln sind mit evangelischer Radikalität und Gemeindebezogenheit).*
- Evangelisch *in der Grundhaltung ist, wem in allen kirchlichen Traditionen, Lehren und Praktiken besonders am ständigen kritischen Rückgriff auf das* Evangelium *(Schrift) und an der* ständigen praktischen Reform *nach der Norm des Evangeliums gelegen ist (gegen »katholischen« Traditionalismus und Synkretismus, die nicht zu verwechseln sind mit katholischer Tradition und Weite).*
- *Doch, richtig verstanden, schließen sich »katholische« und »evangelische« Grundhaltung keineswegs aus: Heute kann auch der geborene Katholik wahrhaft evangelisch gesinnt und*

*auch der geborene Protestant wahrhaft katholisch gesinnt sein,
so daß bereits jetzt zahllose Christen in aller Welt – trotz der
Widerstände in den kirchlichen Apparaten – faktisch eine vom
Evangelium her zentrierte »evangelische Katholizität« oder
eine auf katholische Weite bedachte »katholische Evangelizi-
tät« leben, kurz: eine echte Ökumenizität realisieren. Auf diese
Weise kann heute ein Christ im vollen Sinn Christ sein, ohne
seine eigene konfessionelle Vergangenheit zu verleugnen, ohne
aber auch eine bessere ökumenische Zukunft zu verbauen.
Wahres Christsein bedeutet heute ökumenisches Christsein[1].*

Um was soll es der Kirche, soll es allen Kirchen gehen? Im
Grunde, so sahen wir von Anfang an, nur um dies: um die *Sache
Jesu Christi.* Und dies besagt, wie wir nun wissen, alles in einem:
die Sache Gottes und geradeso die Sache des Menschen, den
Willen Gottes und geradeso das umfassende Wohl des Men-
schen.

Die Sache Jesu Christi – das ist der große *Auftrag* der Glaubensgemeinschaft: kritisch und konstruktiv, in Theorie und Praxis, dem Einzelnen und der Gesellschaft Jesus als den Maßgebenden aufzuzeigen mit all dem, was er für Gegenwart und Zukunft
bedeutet. Indem die Kirche die Botschaft von Jesus als dem
Maßgebenden, dem Herrn, verkündigt, *nimmt sie Jesu Botschaft
von der Herrschaft Gottes in konzentrierter Form auf.* Unter
dem Programmwort »Jesus der Herr« verkündet sie – oder
verkündet sie nicht? – dieselben radikalen Forderungen Gottes,
die Jesus unter dem Programmwort »Gottes Herrschaft«
verkündet und beispielhaft bis zum letzten erfüllt hat. Die Kirche
ist nicht das Gottesreich, aber sie ist – oder ist sie es nicht?
– *Sprecherin und Zeugin* des Gottesreiches.

Glaubwürdige Sprecherin und Zeugin ist sie jedenfalls nur
dann, wenn sie Jesu Botschaft nicht in erster Linie anderen,
sondern sich selber sagt, und dabei die Forderungen Jesu nicht
nur predigt, sondern erfüllt. Man hat dem Christentum vorgeworfen, wie andere »Stifterreligionen« hätte es sich in seiner
zweiten Phase im Hinblick auf die Volksmassen dem Anspruch
der schwierigen unbedingten Nachfolge durch die weniger anspruchsvolle Vergottung des Stifters entzogen und damit zugleich sich selbst absolute Autorität verschafft: Entlastung und
Erhöhung der Kirche durch Vergottung Jesu. Es kann nicht
bestritten werden, daß es leichter ist »Herr, Herr zu sagen« als
»den Willen des Vaters zu tun«[2]. Aber nie darf kultische Vereh-

rung und Anbetung die Nachfolge in gelebter Jüngerschaft ersetzen. Kirche als Glaubensgemeinschaft ist gelebte Jüngerschaft, oder sie ist nicht Kirche Jesu Christi. Die Sache Jesu Christi ist nicht nur tragender Grund der Kirche, sie ist zugleich auch Gottes Gericht über die Kirche. Ihre ganze Glaubwürdigkeit – und was nützen Proklamieren und Organisieren, alle Rechte, Privilegien und Kirchensteuern, wenn sie nicht glaubwürdig ist? – hängt an der *Treue zu Jesus und seiner Sache.* Insofern ist keine der heutigen Kirchen – auch nicht die katholische – automatisch und in jeder Hinsicht mit der Kirche Jesu Christi identisch oder gar der »fortlebende Christus«[3]. Identisch mit der Kirche Jesu Christi ist eine Kirche nur, insofern sie Jesus und seiner Sache die Treue hält.

Die Kirche steht hier bei aller zeitlichen Distanz vor denselben religiös-gesellschaftlichen Grundpositionen und Grundoptionen: *im selben Koordinatenkreuz* zwischen Establishment, Revolution, Resignation und Kompromiß, in welchem Jesus stand. Und nach diesen Orientierungsmarken sollte sie sich ihren Weg suchen. So bleibt er in allem der Maßgebende: die christologischen Indikative werden zu ekklesiologischen Imperativen. Es lohnt sich, das kurz zu verdeutlichen[4].

Provisorische Kirche

Anders als die Vertreter des religiös-politischen Establishments seiner Zeit verkündet *Jesus* nicht nur die beständige, von Anfang der Schöpfung an gegebene Gottesherrschaft (so die Jerusalemer Hierarchen), sondern das kommende Reich Gottes der Endzeit. Wenn die *Kirche* als Glaubensgemeinschaft in der Nachfolge Jesu Christi das kommende Reich Gottes verkünden will, dann heißt dies als *Imperativ für sie selbst:*

Sie darf sich in dieser Zeit nie zum Inhalt der Verkündigung machen und sich selber propagieren. Sie hat vielmehr von sich weg auf die im lebendigen Jesus bereits angebrochene Nähe Gottes hinzuweisen, die auch sie erwartet als die kritische Vollendung ihres Auftrages. So geht sie der universalen und definitiven Offenbarung Gottes in der Welt erst entgegen. Sie darf sich also nicht als Selbstzweck hinstellen, als ob sie je eine um sich selbst kreisende Größe sein könnte. Als ob die Grundentscheidungen des Menschen sich nicht primär auf Gott und seinen Christus, sondern auf die Kirche und ihre Verlautbarungen bezögen. Als ob *sie* Ende und Vollendung der Weltgeschichte, das Definitivum wäre. Als ob *ihre* Definitionen und Deklarationen und nicht das Wort des Herrn in Ewigkeit bliebe. Als ob *ihre* Institutionen und Konstitutionen und nicht Gottes Herrschaft die Zeiten überdauerte. Als ob sie je mit allen Methoden weltlicher Machtpolitik, Strategie und Intrige arbeiten dürfte. Als ob sie als religiöses Establishment weltlichen Prunk und Aufwand treiben, Ehrentitel und Ehrenplätze zur Rechten und zur Linken vergeben, sinnlos über das Notwendige hinaus Geld und Besitz aufhäufen dürfte. Als ob die Menschen für die Kirche dazusein hätten, und nicht die Kirche für die Menschen und gerade so für die Sache Gottes dazusein hätte.

Eine Glaubensgemeinschaft, die vergißt, daß sie etwas Vorläufiges, Provisorisches, Zwischen-Zeitliches ist, die feiert Siege, die im Grunde Niederlagen sind, die ist überfordert und muß resignieren, weil sie keine echte Zukunft hat. Eine Glaubensgemeinschaft aber, die immer daran denkt, daß sie ihr Ziel nicht in sich selbst, sondern in Gottes Reich finden wird, die vermag in einer spannungsreichen Geschichte durchzuhalten: Sie weiß dann, daß sie kein endgültiges System zu erstellen, keine bleibende Heimat zu bieten braucht, daß sie gar nicht verwundert sein muß, wenn sie in ihrer Vorläufigkeit von Zweifeln angefochten, von Hindernissen blockiert, von Problemen belastet wird. Ja, wenn sie das Endgültige zu sein hätte, müßte sie verzweifeln. Wenn sie aber nur das Vorläufige ist, darf sie Hoffnung behalten. Ihr ist verheißen, daß sie die »Pforten der Hölle« nicht überwältigen werden.

Dienende Kirche

Anders als die Vertreter der politischen Revolution seiner Zeit verkündete *Jesus* nicht die gewaltsam zu errichtende religiös-politische Theokratie oder Demokratie (so die zelotischen Revolutionäre), sondern die gewaltlos, wenn auch keineswegs untätig zu erwartende unmittelbare, uneingeschränkte Weltherrschaft Gottes selbst. Wenn die *Kirche* als Glaubensgemeinschaft in der Nachfolge Jesu Christi diese gewaltlos zu erwartende, unmittelbare, uneingeschränkte Weltherrschaft Gottes selbst verkünden will, dann heißt das als *Imperativ für sie selbst*:

Sie kann in dieser Zeit weder revolutionär noch evolutionär, weder offen noch verdeckt eine religiös-politische Theokratie oder irgendeine Machtergreifung anstreben wollen. Ihre Bestimmung ist die tätige Diakonie in jeder Form. Statt ein »Imperium« geistlich-ungeistlicher Macht aufzurichten, ist ihr die Chance geboten, ein zwangsfreies und gewaltloses »Ministerium« auszuüben: indem sie sich immer wieder effektiv für die gesellschaftlich vernachlässigten oder geächteten Gruppen, für alle Verachteten, Getretenen, Verdammten dieser Erde einsetzt und doch zugleich auch unvoreingenommen die Sorgen der »Herrschenden« zur Kenntnis nimmt. Wie könnte sie also, statt Kommunikationssperren abzubauen, neue (geistige, ideologische, konfessionelle) aufrichten, statt Frieden und Gerechtigkeit, Unfrieden und ein Freund-Feind-Denken predigen dürfen? Wie sollte sie den Menschen nicht helfen, die Abwehrmechanismen zu kontrollieren, aus ihren Rollen herauszukommen, aufeinander zuzugehen, sich zu verstehen? Wie könnte sie sich mit diesen oder jenen Mächten gegen andere Menschen verbünden? Wie sich von vornherein mit irgendeiner weltlichen Gruppierung, einer politischen Partei, einem kulturellen Zweckverband, einer wirtschaftlichen und sozialen Machtgruppe identifizieren? Wie sich unkritisch und unbedingt für ein bestimmtes wirtschaftliches, soziales, kulturelles, politisches, philosophisches, weltanschauliches System einsetzen können? Wie könnte sie nicht vielmehr alle weltlichen Mächte, Parteien, Gruppierungen, Systeme mit ihrer radikalen Botschaft auch immer wieder beunruhigen, befremden, stören, in Frage stellen und gerade so dann auch ihren Widerstand und Angriff erfahren müssen? Wie könnte sie um Leiden, Verachtung, Verleumdung, gar Verfolgung herumkommen und statt des Kreuzweges einen billigen Triumphweg gehen wollen? Wie könnte sie bei all dem die Außenstehenden je als ihre zu hassenden, zu vernichtenden Feinde sehen und nicht vielmehr als ihre zu verstehenden, zu ertragenden, zu schonenden, zu ermunternden Nächsten ernstzunehmen versuchen?

Eine Glaubensgemeinschaft, die übersieht, daß sie zum selbstlosen tätigen Dienst an der Gesellschaft, an den Menschen und Gruppen und auch an ihren Gegnern da ist, verliert ihre Würde, ihren Anspruch und ihre Existenzberechtigung, weil sie die Nachfolge aufgibt. Eine Glaubensgemeinschaft aber, die sich bewußt bleibt, daß nicht sie, sondern Gottes Reich in »Macht und Herrlichkeit« kommen wird, die findet in ihrer Kleinheit ihre wahre Größe: Sie weiß dann, daß sie gerade ohne Machtentfaltung und Gewaltanwendung groß ist, daß sie nur höchst bedingt und beschränkt mit der Zustimmung und Unterstützung der Einflußreichen rechnen kann, daß ihr Dasein von der Gesellschaft immer wieder ignoriert, vernachlässigt und nur toleriert, oder aber bedauert, beklagt und weggewünscht, daß ihr Wirken immer wieder belächelt, verdächtigt, mißbilligt und unterdrückt wird, daß aber für sie über allen anderen Mächten unangreifbar Gottes Macht herrscht und sie selber unter den Völkern und in den Herzen der Menschen heilsam am Werk sein kann. Ja, wenn Weltmacht der Kirche Stärke zu sein hätte, dann würde sie sich an die Welt verlieren. Wenn aber ihre Stärke im Kreuz des Auferweckten liegt, dann ist ihre Schwäche ihre Stärke, und sie kann ohne Angst vor Identitätsverlust ihren Weg gehen. Ihr ist verheißen, daß sie, wenn sie ihr Leben hingibt, es gewinnen wird.

Schuldige Kirche

Anders als die Vertreter der frommen Emigration verkündet *Jesus* nicht das Rachegericht zugunsten einer Elite von Vollkommenen (so die Essener und Qumranmönche), sondern die frohe Botschaft von Gottes grenzenloser Güte und unbedingter Gnade für die Verlorenen und Elenden. Wenn die *Kirche* als Glaubensgemeinschaft in der Nachfolge Jesu Christi die frohe Botschaft von dieser grenzenlosen Güte und unbedingten Gnade verkünden will, dann heißt dies als *Imperativ für sie selbst*:

Sie darf in dieser Zeit bei allem Gegensatz zur Welt und ihren Mächten sich nie als drohende, einschüchternde, unheilverkündende und angstmachende Institution gebärden. Statt einer Drohbotschaft soll sie den Menschen die Frohbotschaft künden, statt Angst vor Gott Freude an Gott verbreiten. Ist doch die Kirche nicht nur für die religiös-moralisch Einwandfreien, sondern auch für die moralischen Versager, die Unfrommen und die aus verschiedenen Gründen Gottlosen da. Soll sie doch nicht verurteilen und verdammen, sondern bei allem richtenden Ernst der Botschaft heilen, verzeihen, retten und im übrigen das Gericht Gott überlassen. Sollen doch auch ihre oft unumgänglichen Mahnungen und Warnungen nicht Selbstzweck, sondern Hinweis auf Gottes erbarmende Menschenfreundlichkeit und des Menschen wahre Menschlichkeit sein. Kann sie sich doch trotz aller Verheißungen nie als selbstgerechte Kaste oder Klasse der Reinen, Heiligen, moralisch Elitären aufspielen, und nie in asketischer Aussonderung aus der Welt das Böse, Unheilige, Gottlose nur außerhalb ihrer selbst wähnen. Gibt es doch nichts an ihr, was vollkommen, was nicht gefährdet, gebrechlich, fragwürdig, was nicht immer wieder der Korrektur, Reform, Erneuerung bedürftig wäre. Geht doch die Front zwischen Welt und Gottesherrschaft, zwischen Gutem und Bösem mitten durch die Kirche, mitten durch das Herz des Einzelnen.

Eine Glaubensgemeinschaft, die nicht zur Kenntnis nehmen will, daß sie aus schuldiggewordenen Menschen bestehend für schuldiggewordene Menschen da ist, wird hartherzig, selbstgerecht, unmenschlich. Sie verdient weder das Erbarmen Gottes noch das Vertrauen der Menschen. Eine Kirche aber, die in einer Geschichte der Treue und der Untreue, der Erkenntnis und des Irrtums damit ernstmacht, daß erst Gottes Reich Weizen und Unkraut, gute und faule Fische, Böcke und Schafe getrennt haben wird, der wird aus Gnade jene Heiligkeit zuerkannt, die sie sich selber nicht verschaffen kann. Eine solche Glaubensgemeinschaft weiß dann, daß sie der Gesellschaft kein Theater hoher Moralität vorzuspielen braucht, als ob gerade bei ihr alles zum besten bestellt sei, daß ihr Glaube schwach, ihr Erkennen zwielichtig, ihr Bekennen stammelnd ist, daß es keine einzige Sünde und Verfehlung gibt, der nicht auch sie in dieser oder jener Weise schon erlegen wäre, so daß sie bei aller dauernden Distanzierung von der Sünde nie Anlaß hat, sich von irgendwelchen Sündern zu distanzieren. Ja, wenn die Glaubensgemeinschaft selbstgerecht auf die Versager, Unfrommen und Unmoralischen herabblickt, dann kann sie nicht gerechtfertigt in Gottes Reich eingehen. Wenn sie sich aber ihrer Schuld und Sünde ständig bewußt bleibt, dann darf sie fröhlich und getrost von der Vergebung leben. Ihr ist die Verheißung gegeben, daß, wer sich selbst erniedrigt, erhöht wird.

Entschiedene Kirche

Anders als die Vertreter des moralischen Kompromisses seiner Zeit verkündet *Jesus* nicht ein von Menschen durch exakte Gesetzeserfüllung und bessere Moral aufzubauendes Reich (so die Pharisäer), sondern das durch Gottes freie Tat zu schaffende Reich. Wenn die *Kirche* als Glaubensgemeinschaft in der Nachfolge Jesu Christi dieses durch Gott zu schaffende Reich verkünden will, dann heißt dies als *Imperativ für sie selbst*:

Sie darf in dieser Zeit nicht in erster Linie darum bemüht sein, daß bestimmte rituelle, disziplinäre, moralische Vorschriften eingehalten werden, sondern daß die Menschen leben können und voneinander erhalten, was sie zum Leben benötigen. Sie darf in einer Zeit allzusehr angewachsenen wirtschaftlich-gesellschaftlichen Leistungsdruckes die den verschiedenen Anforderungen nicht Gewachsenen und moralisch Versagenden erst recht nicht abschreiben, wie wenn sie gottverlassen wären, sondern muß gerade ihnen die Nähe jenes Gottes verkünden, dem es nicht in erster Linie auf Leistungen ankommt. Als Glaubensgemeinschaft darf sie selber bei allem kirchlichen und gesellschaftlichen Einsatz nicht in die Versuchung geraten, auf die eigenen Leistungen statt auf Gott zu vertrauen. Durch nichts darf sie sich von einer vertrauend glaubenden Entscheidung und Entschiedenheit für Gott und sein Reich abhalten lassen. Gerade sie selber wird sich immer wieder von ihren Egoismen in grundlegender Umkehr abzuwenden und sich angesichts des kommenden Gottesreiches in Liebe den Menschen zuzuwenden haben: nicht in Flucht vor der Welt, sondern in Arbeit an der Welt. Vor diesem radikalen Gehorsam gegenüber Gottes Willen, der auf das umfassende Wohl des Menschen zielt, kann sich die Kirche nicht drücken. Als ob sie den Gehorsam gegenüber Gott durch den Gehorsam gegen sich selbst, ihren eigenen liturgischen, dogmatischen und rechtlichen Gesetzen und Vorschriften, Überlieferungen und Gewohnheiten ablösen dürfte. Als ob sie je die zeitbedingten gesellschaftlichen Konventionen, moralischen Zwänge, sexuellen Tabus zu ewigen Normen erklären dürfte, die dann nur durch gekünstelte, gequälte Interpretationen an die je neue Zeit angepaßt werden können. Als ob sie in den großen Fragen von Krieg und Frieden und Wohlergehen der Massen, Klassen, Rassen und Geschlechter »Kamele verschlucken« und in zweitrangigen dogmatischen und moralischen (und immer wieder sexuellen) Fragen mit kleinlicher moralischer Kasuistik »Mücken seihen« dürfte. Als ob sie so die Last zahlloser Gebote und Verbote auf die Schultern der Menschen legen dürfte, die sie nicht zu tragen vermögen. Als ob sie statt eines verantworteten Gehorsams aus Liebe zu Gott einen blinden Gehorsam aus Furcht verlangen dürfte, der nicht gehorcht, weil er die Forderung versteht und bejaht, sondern nur weil es geboten ist, und der anderes täte, wenn es nicht geboten wäre. Als ob es ihr je statt um die innere Gesinnung um die äußere Legalität, statt um die »Zeichen der Zeit« um die »Überlieferung der Alten«, statt um die Lauterkeit des Herzens um den Dienst der Lippen, statt um den unbedingten und unverkürzten Gotteswillen um die »Gebote von Menschen« gehen dürfte.

Die Glaubensgemeinschaft, die vergißt, wem gerade sie selbst zu gehorchen hat, die die Herrschaft an sich selbst reißt und sich souverän macht, die wird die Gefangene ihrer selbst. Die Glaubensgemeinschaft aber, die bei allem Versagen stets auf das durch Gottes Tat kommende Reich ausgerichtet bleibt und daran denkt, wem sie gehört, für wen sie sich entschieden hat und für wen sie sich immer wieder neu kompromißlos und rückhaltlos entscheiden muß, die wird wahrhaft frei: frei in der Nachfolge Jesu Christi zum Dienst an der Welt, frei für den Menschendienst, in welchem sie Gott dient, und frei für den Gottesdienst, in welchem sie den Menschen dient. Frei sogar für die Überwindung des Leides, der Schuld und des Todes aus der Kraft des Kreuzes des lebendigen Jesus. Frei für die allumfassende schöpferische Liebe, die schon jetzt die unheile Welt nicht nur interpretiert, sondern verändert aus der unerschütterlichen Hoffnung auf das kommende Reich der vollen Gerechtigkeit, des ewigen Lebens, der wahren Freiheit, der unbegrenzten Liebe und des kommenden Friedens, auf die Aufhebung aller Entfremdung und die endgültige Versöhnung der Menschheit mit Gott. Ja, wenn die Glaubensgemeinschaft, ihrem Auftrag ungetreu, an die Welt verfällt oder sich in sich selbst verfängt, macht sie die Menschen unglücklich, elend, versklavt. Wenn sie sich aber in einer wechselvollen Geschichte immer wieder neu an Gott als ihren Ursprung, ihren Halt und ihr Ziel hält, dann macht sie in erstaunlicher Weise Unfreie frei, Trauernde fröhlich, Arme reich, Elende hoffnungsvoll, Lieblose hilfsbereit. Ihr ist verheißen, daß, wenn sie sich bereithält und bereitmacht, Gott selber *alles neu* machen wird, um alles in allem zu sein.

Damit hat der Schluß dieses dritten Hauptteils seinen Anfang eingeholt, und es dürfte auf dem langen Weg eindeutig, verständlich und anschaulich geworden sein, was im Koordinatenkreuz der damaligen und der heutigen Zeit das christliche Programm ist. Das im zweiten Hauptteil über die Unterscheidung des Christlichen mit einer Rahmenformel Angekündigte hat sich inhaltlich gefüllt: Das christliche Programm ist niemand anders als dieser Christus Jesus selbst mit all dem, was er für Leben und Handeln, Leiden und Sterben der Menschen und der Menschheit bedeutet. Der Fragen bleiben, selbstverständlich, viele. Entscheidend aber ist jetzt nur die eine: Was ist in der Praxis aus dem Programm geworden? Oder vielleicht besser: Was soll in der Praxis aus ihm werden?

D. Die Praxis

Dieser Titel könnte irreführen. Er erweckt den Eindruck, als ob es nicht bisher schon um Praxis gegangen wäre. Aber worauf ist denn das ganze christliche Programm zurückzuführen, wenn nicht auf die Praxis (des Verkündigens, Verhaltens, Erleidens, Sterbens) dieses Christus? Und worauf ist denn dieses ganze christliche Programm ausgerichtet, wenn nicht auf die Praxis (Leben, Handeln, Leiden, Sterben) des Menschen in der Nachfolge dieses Christus? So ging es also schon bisher um die »Theorie« einer bestimmten Praxis, die nun aber in ihren Konturen für den Menschen und die Gesellschaft der Gegenwart – so gut wie in Kürze möglich – expliziert, profiliert werden soll: In welcher Form soll das christliche Programm heute zur Verwirklichung und Durchführung kommen? Deshalb also der Titel ›Die Praxis‹.

Jesus von Nazaret berührt auch heute noch ganz praktisch die Erwartungen und Gewohnheiten, Einstellungen und Entscheidungen, Bedürfnisse und Finanzen eines nicht unerheblichen Teiles der Erdbevölkerung im Kleinen wie im Großen, im privaten wie im gesellschaftlichen Bereich. Jesus von Nazaret ist eine Gestalt wirksam durch alle Zeiten, Lager, Kontinente, bedeutsam für alle, die an Geschichte und Geschick der Menschheit Anteil nehmen und für eine bessere Zukunft arbeiten. Manchmal scheint Jesus außerhalb der Kirche sogar beliebter zu sein als innerhalb der Kirche und ihren Leitungsorganen, wo in der Praxis vielfach Dogmen und Kanones, Politik und Diplomatie und nochmals Politik und Diplomatie eine größere Rolle spielen als er selbst: »Man fragt nie danach, was Jesus getan und gesagt hätte; die Frage nach Jesus ist in diesem Kontext so fremd, daß sie den meisten geradezu als absurd erscheinen würde.« So urteilt über den Vatikan für viele andere ein langjähriges Mitglied der römischen Kurie[1]. Ob die Frage nach Jesus in anderen kirchlichen Macht- und manchmal auch Wissenszentren eine größere Rolle spielt? Die diplomatischen Strategen und Kirchenpolitiker, die Kirchenbürokraten und Manager, die Administratoren, Inquisitoren und systemkonformen Hoftheologen sind jedenfalls nicht nur im Vatikan, auch nicht nur in der katholischen Kirche zu suchen.

I. Die Praxis der Kirche

Schaut man vom christlichen Programm, wie es im dritten Hauptteil entwickelt wurde, auf seine Verwirklichung, auf die christliche Praxis, schaut man von der Botschaft Jesu Christi insbesondere auf die Kirchen der Gegenwart, so kommt auch der kirchlich engagierte Christ um die Frage nicht herum, ob die Kirche – und wir reden hier immer von allen Kirchen – in der Praxis nicht doch recht weit vom christlichen Programm abgekommen ist. Ist nicht dies der Grund, weswegen sich viele Menschen für Gott und Jesus entscheiden, ohne sich für die Kirche, für irgendeine Kirche entscheiden zu können?

1. Entscheidung für den Glauben

Es gibt Menschen, oft religiös erzogen, die jahrelang von Gott praktisch nichts halten, aber dann, oft auf recht merkwürdigen Wegen, zur Erfahrung kommen, daß Gott nicht erst für ihr Sterben, sondern schon für ihr Leben viel, ja Entscheidendes bedeuten könnte. Und es gibt Menschen, die, von den Dogmatismen und »Märchen« des kirchlichen Unterrichts abgestoßen oder kaltgelassen, jahrelang erst recht nichts vom mythologisch eingerahmten Jesus halten, die aber dann, wiederum auf oft merkwürdigen Wegen, zur Erfahrung kommen, daß Jesus für ihr Menschen-, Welt- und Gottesverständnis, für ihr Sein, Handeln und Leiden viel, ja Entscheidendes bedeuten könnte. Die Entscheidung für oder gegen Jesus, für oder gegen das Christ sein – sie ist hier, bevor wir uns noch einmal ganz praktisch der Kirchenfrage zuwenden, zuerst ins Auge zu fassen.

Eine persönliche Entscheidung

Wer immer sich nur ein wenig mit der Gestalt Jesu beschäftigt, sieht sich durch sie herausgefordert. Und wer sich bis hierher der langen Mühe des Mitdenkens unterzogen hat, der konnte erfahren, wie im betrachtenden Umkreisen dieser Gestalt alles Argumentative von selbst appellativen Charakter erhält und Hirn und

Herz zugleich anspricht; ein von der Sache selbst geweckter Enthusiasmus ließ sich nicht ganz verbergen. Es sind nicht nur, wie in Aussicht gestellt[1], die charakteristischen Grundzüge und Umrisse von Jesu Verkündigung, Verhalten und Geschick sichtbar geworden. Es sind auf ungefähr jeder Seite dieser nüchternen kritischen Bestandsaufnahme die sich aufdrängenden Konsequenzen für das eigene Leben greifbar geworden. Genügt dies nicht für die Praxis? Ist hier theologisch noch mehr erfordert? Im Grunde nicht. Dennoch dürfte es angesichts des gerade hier kaum übersehbaren Materials und der Schwierigkeiten der Problematik nicht überflüssig sein, die Linien des praktischen Programms auszuziehen, um für die gegenwärtige Zeit zu einer programmatischen christlichen Praxis zu kommen.

Hier zunächst zur Überleitung also einige Gedanken voraus, die Gesagtes zusammenfassen und für das Folgende Grundlage sein können. Alles über das christliche Programm Ausgeführte hat deutlich gemacht, *warum* gerade dieser Jesus für mich maßgebend sein soll. Aber *ob* er überhaupt für mich maßgebend sein soll, das ist eine ganz persönliche Frage: Das ist meine ganz persönliche Entscheidung! Und keine Kirche und kein Papst, keine Bibel und kein Dogma, aber auch keine fromme Beteuerung, kein gläubiges Bekenntnis, kein Zeugnis eines anderen und selbst keine noch so ernsthafte theologische Überlegung kann mir hier eine Antwort, eine Entscheidung aufzwingen oder auch nur abnehmen. Diese Entscheidung fällt letztlich ohne alle Zwischeninstanzen in voller Freiheit zwischen ihm und mir.

Auch die theologische Forschung – wir erinnern uns[2] – löst keine Entscheidungsfragen. Sie kann nur Raum und Grenzen abstecken, innerhalb deren eine Antwort möglich und sinnvoll ist. Sie kann Hindernisse ausräumen, Vorurteile aufklären, Unglauben und Aberglauben in die Krise führen, Bereitschaft wecken, einen – oft Zeit beanspruchenden – Entscheidungsprozeß in Gang setzen. Sie kann überprüfen, ob eine Zustimmung nicht unvernünftig, nicht unzumutbar, ob sie vielmehr überlegt und begründet ist, so, daß ich sie vor mir selber und anderen verantworten kann. Sie kann helfen, den Entscheidungsprozeß vernünftig zu steuern. Aber durch alles dies soll und kann die Freiheit der Zustimmung nicht aufgehoben, kann und soll sie vielmehr provoziert und auch etwas »kultiviert« werden.

Der Mensch kann also schließlich zu Jesus Nein sagen, und nichts in der Welt kann ihn hindern, es zu tun. Er kann das Neue Testament interessant, schön, lesenswert, erbaulich finden, kann den Mann von Nazaret sympathisch, faszinierend, bewegend, gar einen wahren Gottessohn nennen – und doch zur Tagesordnung, zur Ordnung des Tages ohne ihn übergehen. Aber er kann auch umgekehrt: die Ordnung des Tages, des Lebens unauffällig und doch entschieden nach ihm zu richten versuchen, kann ihn in all seiner allzumenschlichen Menschlichkeit als Richtlinie nehmen. Natürlich nie aufgrund eines zwingenden evidenten Beweisganges. Vielmehr aufgrund eines völlig frei geschenkten – wenn auch meist durch vertrauende und vertrauenswürdige Menschen vermittelten – Vertrauens. Warum eigentlich? Weil der Mensch in diesem Wort und Tun, Leben und Tod allmählich etwas mehr entdecken konnte als nur das durch und durch Menschliche, weil er in diesem allem ein Zeichen Gottes und eine Einladung zum Glauben erkennen und zu ihm völlig frei und doch völlig überzeugt Ja sagen kann. Ohne mathematisch sichere Beweise, aber auch nicht ohne durchaus gute Gründe. Nicht blind, aber auch nicht in Evidenz feststellend, wohl aber verstehend, unbedingt vertrauend und so unbedingt gewiß: das ist – der Liebe so ähnlich und oft in sie übergehend – der Glaube eines freien Christenmenschen.

Das Nein des Unglaubens aber ist nicht dann gegeben, wenn jemand eine oder mehrere der im Neuen Testament bezeugten »Heilstatsachen« bezweifelt, ob sie auch wirklich geschehen sind: Nicht alles ist geschehen oder so geschehen, wie es geschrieben steht. Das Nein des Unglaubens ist dann gegeben, wenn jemand sich dem schließlich klar erkannten Anspruch Gottes in Jesus entzieht, ihm und seiner Botschaft die deutlich geforderte Anerkennung verweigert und nicht bereit ist, in ihm Gottes Zeichen, Wort und Tat zu erkennen, ihn als für sein Leben maßgebend anzuerkennen. Gewiß, jeder Geldschein in der Hand erscheint wirklicher als jene wirklichste Wirklichkeit, die wir Gott nennen. Und ein Ja zu dieser wirklichsten Wirklichkeit, auf die Jesus in Person verpflichtet, wird immer vom Zweifel begleitet sein. Im ehrlichen Zweifel kann mehr Glaube sein, bedenkender Glaube, als im allsonntäglichen bedenkenlos und gedankenlos rezitierten Glaubensbekenntnis, das vor Häresien nicht bewahrt. Und an was alles glauben sie auch, die so unerschütterlich sicheren »Gläubigen«: so oft mehr an Rituale und Zeremonien, Erscheinungen und Prophezeiungen, Wunder und Geheimnisse als an den lebendigen, überraschenden, beunruhigenden Gott, der nun einmal nicht mit Tradition und Brauchtum, mit dem Gewohnten, Bequemen und Ungefährlichen identisch ist. »Christus hat nicht gesagt: ich bin die Gewohnheit (consuetudo), sondern ich bin die Wahrheit (veritas)«, so kommentierte schon im 3. Jahrhundert Tertullian mit dem Blick auf die Consuetudo Romana den Satz des Johannesevangeliums[3].

Daß auch der Glaube Gezeiten hat, seinen Tag und seine Nacht, erfahren Ungezählte. Der Glaube jedoch, der einmal lebendig war, kann nicht einfach, wie manchmal allzu naiv gesagt wird, »verlorengehen«, wie etwa eine Uhr verlorengehen kann. Aber er kann – erstickt durch Leiderfahrung oder Arbeit oder Genuß oder auch einfach Gedankenlosigkeit – einschlafen, absterben, aufhören, das Leben zu gestalten. In diesem Sinne »verliert« der Mensch, und leider besonders oft der zunächst von den neuen Möglichkeiten des Lebens (Welterfahrung, Sexualität, Geld, Karriere) faszinierte junge Mensch, seinen Glauben – ohne Ahnung, wieviel Qual es kosten kann, ihn wiederzufinden, wieder zu erwecken, wieder lebendig zu machen. Umgekehrt aber kann ein Mensch seinen Glauben auch in tiefster Finsternis bewahren. Wie ein junger Jude an die Mauer des Warschauer Gettos schrieb:

> »Ich glaube an die Sonne, auch wenn sie nicht scheint.
> Ich glaube an die Liebe, auch wenn ich sie nicht spüre.
> Ich glaube an Gott, auch wenn ich ihn nicht sehe.«

Gibt es nicht auch heute zahllose Menschen, die wie alle anderen in dieser Welt Angst und Leid, Haß und Unmenschlichkeit, Elend, Hunger, Unterdrückung und Krieg sehen? Und doch glauben sie, daß Gott die Macht hat auch über diese Mächte. Und gibt es nicht Menschen, die wie die übrigen in ihrem Leben sehen, daß andere Herren uns regieren: Aversionen und Aggressionen, Vorurteile und Sehnsüchte, Konventionen und Systeme, vor allem jede Form von Egoismus? Und doch glauben sie, daß Jesus der wahre Herr ist. Und gibt es nicht Menschen, die wie andere in ihrem Denken, Wollen und Fühlen Unsicherheit und Unzulänglichkeit, Zweifel und Rebellion, Übermut und Trägheit sehen? Und doch glauben sie, daß Gottes Geist unser Denken, Wollen und Fühlen bestimmen kann.

Zahllose Menschen suchen in ihren existentiellen Fragen und Problemen Antwort, suchen Hilfe und Halt. Dies alles *ist* angeboten! Es braucht nur ergriffen zu werden. Die ganz persönliche Entscheidung für Gott und für Jesus ist die eigentlich christliche Grundentscheidung: hier geht es um christliches Sein oder Nichtsein, Christsein oder Nichtchristsein.

Doch hier kommt für manch einen die Frage zurück: Ist diese Grundentscheidung zwischen Glauben und Unglauben von vornherein identisch mit der Entscheidung für oder gegen eine bestimmte Kirche? Es gibt heute mehr denn je Christen, oft unbestreitbar gute Christen außerhalb der Kirche, außerhalb aller Kirchen. Und – so muß jetzt etwas genauer bedacht werden – leider nicht ohne Schuld der Kirche, aller Kirchen.

Kritik an der Kirche

Gerade der kirchlich engagierte Christ hat im Blick auf die Botschaft Jesu keinen Anlaß, die Kritik an der Kirche zu scheuen und sie denen »draußen« zu überlassen. Keine noch so radikale Kritik von »draußen« kann die Kritik von »innen« ersetzen oder gar überbieten. Die schärfste Kritik an der Kirche ergibt sich nicht von den zahlreichen historischen, philosophischen, psychologischen, soziologischen Einwänden her, sondern vom Evangelium Jesu Christi selbst, auf das sich die Kirche ständig beruft. Und insofern wird man sich die Kritik an der Kirche auch nicht von »innen« – selbst nicht vom Papst und auch nicht von den vielen Päpstchen – verbieten lassen dürfen. Salva omni reverentia et caritate!

Aber noch immer wird die Kirche – und die katholische Kirche besonders – von zahllosen Menschen bewundert. Und warum nicht? Doch genauso wird sie von zahllosen Menschen getadelt und abgelehnt. Und warum nicht? Diese zwiespältige Reaktion liegt nicht nur an der verschiedenen Einstellung der Menschen, sondern an der *Ambivalenz des Phänomens Kirche selbst*.

Da bewundern die einen die in einzigartiger Weise durchgehaltene und gestaltete Geschichte von 2000 Jahren. Andere konstatieren gerade in Gestaltung und Bewältigung dieser Geschichte ein Verfallen und Kapitulieren vor der Geschichte. Die einen rühmen die weltweit verbreitete und zugleich im kleinen Raum verwurzelte wirkkräftige Organisation mit Hunderten Millionen von Mitgliedern und einer straff geordneten Hierarchie. Andere sehen in der wirkkräftigen Organisation einen mit weltlichen Mitteln arbeitenden Machtapparat; in den imposanten Zahlen von christlichen Massen ein verflachtes substanzarmes Traditionschristentum; in der wohlgeordneten Hierarchie eine herrsch- und prunksüchtige Verwaltungsbehörde. Die einen loben den traditionsreichen Kult von erhabener Feierlichkeit, das durchdachte theologische Lehrsystem, die umfassende säkulare Kulturleistung in Aufbau und Gestaltung des christlichen Abendlandes. Andere aber sehen in der kultischen Feierlichkeit einen in der mittelalterlichen, barocken Tradition steckengebliebenen unevangelisch-veräußerlichten Ritualismus; im klaren, einheitlichen Lehrsystem eine starr-autoritäre, mit überkommenen Begriffshülsen manipulierende, ungeschichtliche, unbiblische Schultheologie; in der abendländischen Kulturleistung eine Verweltlichung und ein Abweichen von der eigentlichen Aufgabe ... So werden die Bewunderer kirchlicher Weisheit, Macht und Leistung, kirchlichen Glanzes, Einflusses und Prestiges von den Gegnern der Kirche sehr deutlich erinnert an die Judenverfolgungen und Kreuzzüge, Ketzerprozesse und Hexenverbrennungen, Kolonialismus und »Religionskriege«, an die falschen Verurteilungen von Menschen und Problemlösungen, an die Verquickung der Kirche mit bestimmten Gesellschafts-, Regierungs- und Denksystemen, an ihr vielfältiges Versagen in der Sklavenfrage, in der Kriegsfrage, in der Frauenfrage, in der sozialen Frage und in wissenschaftlichen Fragen wie der Evolutionstheorie oder manchen historischen Fragen ...

Alles nur allzuviel zitierte Fehler der Vergangenheit, die man im übrigen noch »aus der Zeit heraus verstehen« muß? Aber sind das alles nur Klagen der Vergangenheit, wie sie die Nobelpreisträger Heinrich Böll an die Adresse der katholischen Kirche[4] und Alexander Solschenizyn an die Adresse der russisch-orthodoxen Kirche[5] zu richten haben? Ist solche Kritik nicht besser als das vielfach totale Desinteresse, das zahllose, insbesondere evangelische Christen, in Europa ihren evangelischen Kirchen entgegenbringen?

Was haben sie doch alles gegen die Kirche einzuwenden, die Naturwissenschaftler und die Mediziner, die Psychologen und die Soziologen, die Journalisten und die Politiker, die Arbeiter und die Intellektuellen, die kirchlich Praktizierenden und die nicht Praktizierenden, die Jungen und die Alten, die Männer und die Frauen: gegen schlechte Predigten, lahmen Gottesdienst, veräußerlichte Frömmigkeit, geistlose Tradition. Gegen autoritäre, unverständliche Dogmatik und eine lebensfremde, kleinkariert-kasuistische Moral. Gegen Opportunismus und Intoleranz, Gesetzlichkeit und Arroganz der kirchlichen Funktionäre und Theologen auf allen Stufen, gegen den Mangel an schöpferischen Menschen in der Kirche und die langweilige Mittelmäßigkeit. Gegen die vielfältige Komplizenschaft mit den Mächtigen und die Vernachlässigung der Verachteten, Getretenen, Unterdrückten, Ausgebeuteten, gegen Religion als Opium des Volkes, gegen ein nur mit sich beschäftigtes, in sich zerstrittenes Christentum, eine gespaltene Ökumene …

Sind also die Kirchen, diese institutionalisierten Trägerinnen des Christentums, in denen das ursprüngliche Feuer des Geistes erloschen scheint und die neue Experimente und Erfahrungen scheuen, nicht für viele trotz aller eingangs beschriebenen Reform- und Erneuerungsbestrebungen doch hoffnungslos zurückgebliebene Subkulturen und Organisationen des ungleichzeitigen Bewußtseins? Wer ist hier *glaubwürdig?* Etwa jene um sich selber kreisenden *Kirchenleitungen,* die Wissen und Neugierde immer wieder zu tabuisieren und das Kirchenvolk gegen Kritik von außen und innen zu immunisieren versuchen, deren Ratgeber die Angst um System, Einfluß und Macht ist und die theologisch schon längst gelöste Probleme ewig mit sich herumschleppen? Oder jene *praktizierenden Christen,* die man nie eine kritische Freiheit lehrte, die glauben, weil es der Pfarrer, der Bischof, der Papst gesagt hat, und die, auf Wandel in keiner Weise vorbereitet, bei der geringsten Änderung – des katholischen Kirchenrechts und Heiligenkalenders oder der östlich-orthodoxen Liturgie oder einer protestantischen Bibelübersetzung – fragen, was und ob man eigentlich noch glauben könne? Oder etwa jene mäßig modernen *Theologen,* denen es manchmal mehr um die Formeln und ihr eigenes kleines System, mehr um Opportunität und Anpassung als um die christliche Wahrheit zu gehen scheint? Theologen, die die Fehden des 16. Jahrhunderts noch nicht liquidiert und die Entwicklung des 18. und 19. Jahrhunderts noch nicht verdaut haben? Die sich in ihrem christlichen Glauben bedroht sehen, wenn es in der Bibel Fehler geben sollte, wenn an einem der traditionellen Sätze oder Dogmen fragend gerüttelt wird und vielleicht niemand sogleich garantiert sicher sagen kann, was man glauben »muß«? Ob solche Kirchenleitung und Theologie einladend, ob solcher Glaube ansteckend wirkt, ob solches Christsein die Neugier der Nichtchristen reizen kann? Welche Diskrepanz zwischen dem christlichen Programm und der kirchlichen Praxis!

Daß gerade die *katholische Kirche* von der Kritik besonders betroffen wird, liegt nicht nur an ihrem Alter, ihrem Einfluß, an ihrer die ganze übrige Christenheit weit übertreffenden Größe, ihrer zentralen Bedeutung für die Ökumene und ihrem Gewicht selbst bei den politischen Mächten. Vielmehr hängt dies mit der

Tatsache zusammen, daß gerade sie mit dem *Zweiten Vatikanischen Konzil* in und außerhalb der katholischen Kirche besonders große Hoffnungen geweckt, in nachkonziliarer Zeit aber besonders viele Enttäuschungen bereitet hat[6]. Das Konzil hatte ein weitreichendes Programm für eine erneuerte Kirche der Zukunft geboten. Und mit Energie war man in ungezählten Gemeinden und Diözesen auf der ganzen Welt an die Verwirklichung gegangen: In kurzer Zeit setzte sich mindestens theoretisch in der katholischen Kirche ein neues Verständnis der Kirche (als Volk Gottes) und des kirchlichen Amtes (als Dienst an diesem Volke) durch. Die Gottesdienstreform und die Einführung der Muttersprache mit neuen Perikopenordnungen bedeuteten einen kaum zu überschätzenden Fortschritt. Die ökumenische Zusammenarbeit sowohl auf Gemeindeebene (gemeinsame Aktionen und Wortgottesdienste) und auf gesamtkirchlicher Ebene (durch gegenseitige Besuche und gemischte Studienkommissionen) wurde verstärkt. Die römische Zentralverwaltung wurde von Papst Paul VI. in verschiedener Hinsicht reformiert und stärker internationalisiert. Die Reform der Priesterseminarien und Ordensgemeinschaften wurde zum Teil sehr energisch vorangetrieben. Diözesan- und Pfarräte unter starker Beteiligung der Laienschaft wurden gegründet und fingen an, aktiv zu werden. Neues Leben zeigte sich in der Theologie, und eine neue Öffnung der Kirche gegenüber den Problemen des heutigen Menschen und der Gesellschaft setzte sich offenkundig durch. Nichts war vollkommen, aber alles war grundsätzlich gut und hoffnungsvoll.

Wichtige innerkirchliche Probleme indessen waren im Konzil durch das Verhalten des Papstes und der Bischöfe, die damals nicht aufbegehrten, unerledigt geblieben. Und sie trieben die katholische Kirche mitten in eine vielschichtige Führungs- und Vertrauenskrise. Dieselbe Leitung der Kirche, die in der Konzilszeit alte und neue Fragen angepackt und in einem erstaunlichen Ausmaß der Lösung entgegengeführt hatte, scheint in unserer *nachkonziliaren Zeit* unfähig, in so dringenden Fragen wie Geburtenregelung, Gerechtigkeit und Frieden in der Welt, Bischofswahl und Krise des kirchlichen Amtes zu konstruktiven Resultaten zu kommen; das an sich periphere Zölibatsgesetz ist unverdientermaßen zu einer Testfrage der Erneuerung geworden. Aber während sich die offiziellen kirchlichen Stellen in den sehr verschiedenartigen Schwierigkeiten mit Klagen und Mahnungen begnügen oder zu willkürlichen Sanktionen greifen, geben immer mehr Priester ihren Dienst auf, und der Nachwuchs nimmt in quantitativer und qualitativer Hinsicht ab. Die Ratlosigkeit vieler Christen ist groß, und viele der besten Seelsorger haben den Eindruck, daß sie in ihren entscheidenden Sorgen von ihren Bischöfen und oft auch von den Theologen im Stich gelassen werden. Zwar haben sich einige Episkopate und einzelne Bischöfe die Sorgen ihrer Kirchen allen Ernstes zu eigen gemacht. Aber die meisten Bischofskonferenzen konnten sich nur in zweitrangigen Fragen zu konstruktiven Lösungen entschließen und haben viele Erwartungen von Klerus und Volk enttäuscht. So ist denn die Glaubwürdigkeit der katholischen Kirche, die zu Beginn des Pontifikats Paul VI. höher war als vielleicht je in den letzten 500 Jahren, in einem beunruhigenden Ausmaß abgesunken. Viele Menschen leiden an der Kirche. Resignation breitet sich aus.

Sucht man – nur summarisch ist es möglich – *Gründe für die gegenwärtige Führungs- und Vertrauenskrise,* so wird man sie nicht nur bei bestimmten Personen oder Amtsträgern, schon gar nicht bei deren bösem Willen suchen dürfen. Es ist vielmehr das kirchliche System selbst, das in seiner Entwicklung weit hinter der Zeit zurückgeblieben ist und noch immer zahlreiche Züge eines überlebten Absolutismus aufweist: Papst und Bischöfe als faktisch weithin allein herrschende Herren der Kirche, die legislative, exekutive und judikative Funktionen in ihrer Hand vereinigen. Ihre Machtausübung unterliegt trotz der inzwischen etablierten Räte noch vielerorts keiner wirksamen Kontrolle, ihre Nachfolger werden nach Kriterien der Konformität ausgewählt. Weit verbreitete Klagen in verschiedenen Gebieten der Kirche sind: Ernennung der Bischöfe in Geheimverfahren ohne Mitwirkung des betreffenden Klerus und Volkes, mangelnde Durchsichtigkeit der Entscheidungsprozesse, ständige Berufung auf die eigene Autorität und den Gehorsam der Anderen, ungenügende Motivation der Ansprüche und Anordnungen, monokratischer Amtsstil unter Mißachtung echter Kollegialität, Bevormundung der Laien und des »niederen Klerus«, welche gegen Entscheidungen der Autoritäten keinen wirksamen Einspruch einlegen können. Man fordert Freiheit für die Kirche nach außen, aber gewährt sie nicht nach innen. Man predigt Gerechtigkeit und Frieden, wo es die Kirche und ihre Führung nichts kostet. Man kämpft um Zweitrangiges und läßt ebenso große zukunftsweisende Konzeptionen wie klare Prioritäten vermissen. Selbst zaghaften Versuchen der Theologie, in dieser Situation der Kirche zu helfen, wird mit Mißtrauen und Abwehr begegnet. Passivität vieler Kirchenglieder und wachsende Apathie der großen Öffentlichkeit gegenüber den Sprechern der Kirche sind die Folgen.

Es handelt sich heute nicht nur um eine sogenannte »Demokratisierung« der Kirche. Geht man der gegenwärtigen Führungs- und Konzeptionslosigkeit der Kirche auf den Grund, stellt man immer wieder fest: die Kirche ist *nicht nur weit hinter der Zeit, sondern auch und vor allem weit hinter ihrem eigenen Auftrag zurückgeblieben.* In so vielem ist sie – nach dem Urteil von Freunden und Feinden – nicht den Spuren dessen gefolgt, auf den sie sich ständig beruft. Deshalb stellt man heute einen eigenartigen Kontrast zwischen dem Interesse an Jesus selber und dem Desinteresse an der Kirche fest. Überall wo die Kirche statt Dienst an den Menschen Macht über die Menschen ausübt, überall wo ihre Institutionen, Lehren und Gesetze Selbstzweck werden, überall wo ihre Sprecher persönliche Meinungen und Anliegen als göttliche Gebote und Anordnungen ausgeben: da wird der Auftrag der Kirche verraten, da entfernt sich die Kirche von Gott und den Menschen zugleich, da gerät sie in die Krise.

2. Entscheidung für die Kirche?

Was tun? Rebellieren? Reformieren? Resignieren? Das Versagen der Kirche wird jedem engagierten Christen von Freunden und Gegnern – wehklagend oder anklagend, niedergedrückt oder triumphierend – immer wieder vorgerechnet. Doch interessanter als die ewige Fortschreibung der kirchlichen »Chronique scandaleuse« dürfte die Frage sein, warum man denn gerade als engagierter Christ, als völlig illusionsloser »Insider«, dem man mit neuen kirchlichen Skandalgeschichten kaum noch Neues erzählen kann, dennoch in dieser, in seiner Kirche bleibt. Gefragt wird dies von beiden Seiten: Von solchen, die draußen sind und finden, man vergeude in einer erstarrten kirchlichen Institution seine Energie und könne außerhalb mehr leisten. Und von solchen, die drinnen sind und meinen, radikale Kritik an kirchlichen Zuständen und Behörden vertrage sich nicht mit einem Bleiben in der Kirche[7].

Es ist gar nicht leicht, diese Frage überzeugend zu beantworten, nachdem durch die Säkularisierung des modernen Lebens und Wissens so viele soziale Motivationen weggefallen sind und die Zeit der Staats-, Volks- und Traditionskirche zu Ende zu gehen scheint. Wie für einen Juden oder Moslem, so dürfte es freilich auch heute noch für einen Christen nicht unwichtig sein, daß er nun einmal – so war es bisher meistens – in diese Gemeinschaft hineingeboren wurde, von ihr – ob er es wollte oder nicht – in irgendeiner Form positiv oder negativ bestimmt blieb. Und es ist nicht gleichgültig, ob man mit seiner Familie Verbindung hält oder ob man sich von ihr in Zorn oder Gleichgültigkeit verabschiedet hat.

Dies ist zumindest heute für manche Christen ein Grund zum Bleiben in der Kirche und für viele Amtsträger auch zum Bleiben im kirchlichen Dienst:

Sie möchten gegen erstarrte kirchliche Tradition angehen, die das Christsein erschweren oder unmöglich machen. Aber sie möchten nicht darauf verzichten, aus der großen christlichen und eben zugleich kirchlichen Tradition von zwanzig Jahrhunderten zu leben.

Sie möchten kirchliche Institutionen und Konstitutionen der Kritik unterziehen, wo immer diesen das Glück von Personen geopfert wird. Aber sie möchten nicht verzichten auf jenes Notwendige an Institutionen und Konstitutionen, ohne das auch eine Glaubensgemeinschaft auf die Dauer nicht leben kann, ohne das allzu viele gerade in ihren persönlichsten Fragen alleingelassen würden.

Sie möchten der Anmaßung kirchlicher Autoritäten, sofern sie die Kirche statt nach dem Evangelium nach ihren eigenen Vorstellungen leiten, widerstehen. Aber sie möchten nicht verzichten auf die moralische Autorität, die die Kirche überall dort in der Gesellschaft haben kann, wo sie wirklich als Kirche Jesu Christi handelt.

Warum also bleiben? Weil man in dieser Glaubensgemeinschaft, kritisch und solidarisch zugleich, trotz allem eine große Geschichte bejahen kann, aus der man mit so vielen anderen lebt. Weil man als Glied der Glaubensgemeinschaft selber Kirche ist und Kirche nicht mit dem Apparat und den Administratoren verwechseln und ihnen gar das Gestalten der Gemeinschaft überlassen sollte. Weil man hier, bei allen heftigen Einwänden, in bezug auf die Fragen nach dem großen Woher und Wohin,

Warum und Wozu des Menschen und der Welt eine geistige Heimat gefunden hat, der man ebensowenig den Rücken zukehren möchte wie im politischen Bereich etwa der Demokratie, die auf ihre Weise nicht weniger als die Kirche mißbraucht und geschändet wird.

Selbstverständlich: es gibt auch die andere Möglichkeit. Und es sind oft nicht die schlechten Christen, die sie gewählt haben: Bruch mit dieser Kirche wegen ihres Abfalls, um höherer Werte, vielleicht um eines echten Christseins willen. Es gibt Christen – und wohl als Grenzfälle auch Christengruppen – außerhalb der Institution Kirche. Ein solcher Entscheid ist zu achten, er läßt sich sogar verstehen. In der Phase des gegenwärtigen Tiefs in der katholischen Kirche mehr denn je. Und so viele Gründe für den Exodus wie sie, die gegangen sind, könnte jeder engagierte und informierte Christ gewiß auch namhaft machen. Und doch: Der Sprung vom Boot – für jene ein Akt der Ehrlichkeit, des Mutes, des Protestes oder auch einfach der Not und des Überdrusses –, wäre er nicht letztlich doch ein Akt des Verzagens, des Versagens, der Kapitulation? Dabeigewesen in besseren Stunden, sollte man das Boot im Sturm aufgeben und das Stemmen gegen den Wind, das Wasserschöpfen und eventuell den Kampf ums Überleben den anderen überlassen, mit denen man bisher gesegelt ist? Zu viel hat man doch in dieser Glaubensgemeinschaft empfangen, als daß man hier so einfach aussteigen könnte. Zu viel hat man sich doch selber für die Veränderung und Erneuerung engagiert, als daß man je die enttäuschen dürfte, die sich mit engagiert haben. Diese Freude sollte man den Gegnern der Erneuerung nicht machen, diesen Kummer den Freunden nicht bereiten. Auf die Effizienz *in* der Kirche soll man nicht verzichten. Die Alternativen – andere Kirche, ohne Kirche – überzeugen nicht: Ausbrüche führen zur Vereinzelung des Einzelnen oder aber zu neuer Institutionalisierung. Alles Schwärmertum beweist dies. Von elitärem Christentum, das besser sein will als die vielen da, und von Kirchenutopien, die mit einer Idealgemeinschaft von reinen Gleichgesinnten rechnen, ist wenig zu halten. Sollte es da nicht *in* dieser konkreten Menschenkirche, wo man wenigstens weiß, mit wem man es zu tun hat, herausfordernder und in allem Durchleiden letztlich doch auch erfreulicher und fruchtbarer sein, den Kampf für ein »Christentum mit menschlichem Antlitz« zu kämpfen? Eine ständig neue Aufforderung zur Verantwortung, zu kritischer Solidarität, zu hartnäckiger Ausdauer, zu gelebter Freiheit, zum Widerstand in Loyalität?

Und nachdem nun heute durch offenkundiges Versagen der Leitung die Autorität, Einheit, Glaubwürdigkeit dieser Kirche vielfach erschüttert ist und sie sich immer mehr als die schwache, irrende, suchende zeigt, geht manch einem der Satz eher über die Lippen als in triumphaleren Zeiten: Wir lieben diese Kirche – so wie sie nun einmal ist und wie sie sein könnte. Nicht als »Mutter«, sondern als die Glaubensfamilie, um deretwillen die Institutionen, Konstitutionen, Autoritäten überhaupt da sind und manchmal auch einfach in Kauf genommen werden müssen. Eine Glaubensgemeinschaft, die auch heute noch trotz aller ihrer erschreckenden Mängel unter den Menschen nicht nur Wunden zu reißen, sondern noch immer Wunder zu wirken vermag: dort nämlich, wo sie »funktioniert«, wo sie nicht nur faktisch – und dies ist auch schon etwas – Ort der Erinnerung an Jesus ist, sondern wo sie wahrhaftig in Wort und Tat die Sache Jesu Christi vertritt. Und das tut sie nun doch zumindest *auch,* allerdings mehr in der kleinen als in der großen Öffentlichkeit, mehr wohl durch die geringen Leute als durch die Hierarchen und Theologen. Aber es geschieht, täglich, stündlich, durch die zahllosen Zeugen des Alltags, die als Christen die Kirche in der Welt präsent machen. Und so wäre dies die entscheidende Antwort: Bleiben in der Kirche soll man, darf man, weil die Sache Jesu Christi überzeugt und weil die Kirchengemeinschaft trotz und in allem Versagen doch im Dienst an der Sache Jesu Christi geblieben ist und es auch bleiben soll.

Die vielen, die sich Christen nennen, haben ihr Christentum nicht aus Büchern, nicht einmal aus dem »Buch der Bücher«. Sie haben es vielmehr von dieser Glaubensgemeinschaft, die sich durch zwanzig Jahrhunderte trotz aller Schwächen und Irrtümer leidlich durchgehalten hat und die immer wieder schlecht und recht Glauben an Jesus Christus geweckt und Engagement in seinem Geist herausgefordert hat. Dieser Ruf der Kirche ist weit davon entfernt, reiner Klang, reines Gotteswort zu sein. Es ist ein sehr menschliches, oft allzu menschliches Rufen. Aber was die Botschaft ist, läßt sich auch bei vielen falschen Tönen und schiefen Taten vernehmen und ist auch immer wieder vernommen worden. Was nicht zuletzt die Gegner bezeugen, die die Kirche – zu Recht – auf diese ihre Botschaft behaften, mit der sie oft so wenig übereinstimmt: Großinquisitorin, Tyrannin, Krämerin statt Sachwalterin.

Wo immer die Kirche privat und öffentlich für die Sache Jesu Christi eintritt, wo immer sie sich für seine Sache in Wort und

Tat einsetzt, da steht sie im Dienst an den Menschen und ist glaubwürdig. Da kann sie ein Ort sein, wo der Not des Einzelnen und gesellschaftlicher Not in einer anderen Tiefe begegnet werden kann, als dies die Leistungs- und Konsumgesellschaft aus sich heraus zu tun vermag. Dies alles kommt ja nicht von alleine, nicht von ungefähr. Es steht in Wechselbeziehung und Wechselwirkung zu dem, was – bescheiden genug, aber heute vielleicht doch wieder in größerer Freiheit – in der Kirche, ihrer Verkündigung und ihrem Gottesdienst geschieht. Es wird dies immer wieder neu ermöglicht dadurch, daß irgendwo ein Pfarrer auf der Kanzel, am Radio oder im kleinen Kreis diesen Jesus predigt, ein Katechet oder Eltern christlich unterrichten, ein Einzelner, eine Familie oder Gemeinde ohne Phrasen ernsthaft beten, eine Taufe in Verpflichtung auf den Namen Jesu Christi vollzogen, das Mahl des Gedenkens und Dankens in einer engagierten Gemeinschaft mit Konsequenzen für den Alltag gefeiert, aus der Kraft Gottes unbegreiflich die Vergebung der Schuld zugesprochen wird; daß also in Gottesdienst und Menschendienst, in Unterricht und Seelsorge, in Gespräch und Diakonie, in wahrhafter Weise das Evangelium verkündet, nachgelebt und vorgelebt wird, kurz: Nachfolge Christi geschieht, wo die Sache Jesu Christi ernstgenommen wird. So also kann die Kirche als Glaubensgemeinschaft – und wer sollte es ex professo tun, wenn nicht sie es tut – den Menschen helfen, Mensch, Christ, Christenmensch zu sein und es in der Tat zu bleiben.

Es liegt an der Kirche, wie sie die Krise übersteht. Am Programm fehlt es nicht. Warum also in der Kirche bleiben? Weil man aus dem Glauben *Hoffnung* schöpfen kann, daß das Programm, daß die Sache Jesu Christi selbst wie schon bisher stärker ist als aller Unfug, der in und mit der Kirche angestellt wird. Dafür lohnt sich der entschiedene Einsatz in der Kirche, dafür auch der besondere Einsatz im kirchlichen Dienst – trotz allem. Nicht *obwohl* ich Christ bin, bleibe ich in der Kirche. Ich halte mich nicht für christlicher als die Kirche. Sondern *weil* ich Christ bin, bleibe ich in der Kirche.

Praktische Impulse

Aber nochmals: was tun? Diese Frage ist mit einer grundsätzlichen theologischen Reflexion über das Bleiben in der Kirche noch nicht beantwortet. Vor allem nicht für schwierige Übergangsphasen wie die unsere. Was kann besonders in einer solchen Situation – die freilich rascher vorübergehen, aber auch rascher wiederkehren kann, als man denkt – getan werden?

Ohne lange Erklärung dürfte die Grundlinie für das praktische Verhalten klar sein: Überwunden werden kann jede Krise in der Kirche, jede Polarisierung zwischen Katholiken und Protestanten, zwischen konservativen und progressiven Christen, zwischen »vorkonziliaren« und »nachkonziliaren« Katholiken, zwischen Älteren und Jüngeren, Männern und Frauen, ja, in der katholischen Kirche zwischen Bischöfen und Klerus, Bischöfen und Volk, Papst und Kirche nur durch das eine: daß man sich erneut auf *Mitte und Fundament* besinnt – das *Evangelium Jesu Christi,* von dem die Kirche ausgegangen ist und das sie in jeder neuen Situation neu zu verstehen und zu leben hat! Was dies in den verschiedenen Kirchen, Ländern, Kulturen, Lebensbereichen, was dies für den Einzelnen und die Gemeinschaft grundsätzlich wie konkret bedeutet, kann hier nicht entwickelt werden. Nur einige unmittelbare Möglichkeiten seien angedeutet.

Für die *gesamte Ökumene,* Rom wie den Weltrat der Kirchen: nicht nur große Worte nach »außen« für die Gesellschaft und nach »innen« zwischen den Kirchen nur ewige gemischte Kommissionen, gegenseitige Höflichkeitsbesuche, endlose akademische Dialoge ohne praktische Folgen. Sondern eine echte, wachsende Integration der verschiedenen Kirchen:

- *durch Reform und gegenseitige Anerkennung der kirchlichen Ämter,*
- *durch gemeinsamen Wortgottesdienst, offene Kommunion und immer mehr auch gemeinsame Eucharistiefeiern,*
- *durch gemeinsamen Bau und gemeinsame Benützung von Kirchen und anderen Einrichtungen,*
- *durch gemeinsame Erfüllung des Dienstes an der Gesellschaft,*
- *durch zunehmende Integration auch der theologischen Fakultäten und des Religionsunterrichts,*
- *durch Erstellung konkreter Unionspläne von seiten der Kirchenleitungen auf nationaler und universaler Ebene.*

Für die *katholische Kirche* insbesondere muß das, was im Vatikanum II unerledigt blieb, immer dringender gefordert, von den Gemeinden wie ihren Vorstehern her erkämpft und endlich verwirklicht werden. Einmal mehr muß hier für die katholische

Kirche auf einigen zum Teil schon alten Reformforderungen vieler bestanden werden, die das Evangelium hinter sich haben[8]:

– *daß die* Kirchenleitungen *ihre Aufgabe ganz allgemein nicht hierarchisch, sondern kompetent, nicht bürokratisch, sondern kreativ, nicht amtsbezogen, sondern menschenbezogen wahrnehmen; daß sie den Mut aufbringen, sich mehr für die Menschen als für die Institution zu engagieren; daß sie für mehr Demokratie, Autonomie, Menschlichkeit in allen kirchlichen Rängen sorgen und nach einer besseren Zusammenarbeit zwischen Klerus und Laien trachten;*

– *daß insbesondere die* Bischöfe *nicht durch Geheimverfahren im Stil des römischen Absolutismus (mit Eiden abgesichertes »päpstliches Geheimnis«) nach Kriterien der Konformität ernannt, sondern auf eine beschränkte Zeit nach den Erfordernissen der betreffenden Diözese durch repräsentative Organe des Klerus und der Laienschaft gewählt werden;*

– *daß auch der* Papst, *wenn er mehr als der Bischof von Rom und Primas von Italien zu sein beansprucht, durch ein Organ aus Bischöfen und Laien gewählt wird, welches, anders als das einseitig vom Papst ernannte Kardinalskollegium, für die gesamte Kirche – nicht nur die verschiedenen Nationen, sondern vor allem die verschiedenen Mentalitäten und Generationen – repräsentativ ist;*

– *daß die* »Priester« *(die Vorsteher der Gemeinden wie auch die der Diözesen) gemäß der Freiheit, die das Evangelium gerade in dieser Frage gewährt, selber darüber entscheiden, ob sie je nach ihrer persönlichen Berufung verheiratet oder unverheiratet sein wollen;*

– *daß die* »Laien« *(die Gemeinden und Diözesen) das Recht haben, nicht nur mitzuberaten, sondern auch mitzuentscheiden zusammen mit ihren Vorstehern in einem gut ausgewogenen System von abgegrenzten Kompetenzen (»checks and balances«), und daß sie auch das Recht auf Widerspruch wahrnehmen, wo immer Jesus selber Widerspruch anmelden würde;*

– *daß die* Frauen *in der Kirche mindestens diejenige Würde, Freiheit und Verantwortlichkeit haben sollten, die ihnen die heutige Gesellschaft garantiert: gleiche Rechte im Kirchenrecht, in den kirchlichen Entscheidungsorganen, aber auch die praktische Möglichkeit des Theologiestudiums und der Ordination;*

– *daß in* Fragen der Moral *Freiheit und Gewissen nicht erneut durch ein Gesetz ersetzt werden und eine neue (kirchliche)*

*Sklaverei aufgerichtet wird und daß vom Evangelium her
insbesondere für eine neue Haltung gegenüber der Sexualität
Verständnis aufgebracht wird im Hinblick auf eine jüngere
Generation, die sich auch in anderen Formen ein reines Herz
bewahren kann;*
- *daß gerade die Frage der* Geburtenregelung *auch durch
»künstliche« Mittel dem Gewissensentscheid der Ehepartner
nach medizinischen, psychologischen und sozialen Kriterien
überlassen bleibt und die katholische Kirchenleitung ihre dies-
bezügliche Lehre (Enzyklika ›Humanae vitae‹) revidiert ...*

Und so weiter. Diese und ähnliche Desiderate der Kirchenre-
form sind energisch bis zur Erfüllung zu fordern und zu erkämp-
fen: um der zahllosen Menschen willen, die unter den gegenwärtigen kirchlichen Zuständen und Mißständen zu leiden haben.

Wider die Resignation

Doch sofort wird hier immer wieder die Frage laut: Verhindert
nicht die Übermacht und Geschlossenheit des kirchlichen Systems selbst eine ernsthafte Reform? Gibt es in den schwierigen
Stunden der Kirchengeschichte überhaupt einen Weg zwischen
Revolution und Resignation? Doch die Frage stellt sich auch
umgekehrt: Könnte sich die Situation gerade auch der katholischen Kirche nicht wiederum rasch wandeln, wenn das gegenwärtige »credibility gap«, wenn die Führungs- und Vertrauenskrise überwunden werden? Hier jeweils nur auf einen Wechsel
an der Spitze und eine neue Generation zu warten, wäre allerdings töricht. Deshalb seien hier einige Orientierungspunkte für
das praktische Verhalten in solchen Situationen gesetzt. Was läßt
sich gegen die Resignation tun[9]?

- Nicht schweigen: *Die Forderungen des Evangeliums und die
Nöte und Hoffnungen unserer Zeit sind in vielen anstehenden
Fragen so unzweideutig, daß Schweigen aus Opportunismus,
Mutlosigkeit oder Oberflächlichkeit ebenso schuldig machen
kann wie das Schweigen vieler Verantwortlicher in der Refor-
mationszeit.*

Deshalb: Diejenigen Bischöfe – und sie bilden innerhalb der
nationalen Bischofskonferenzen oft eine starke Minderheit oder

gar die Mehrheit –, die bestimmte Gesetze, Anordnungen und Maßnahmen für ein Unheil halten, sollten dies in aller Öffentlichkeit aussprechen und immer deutlicher nach einer Änderung verlangen. Die Mehrheitsverhältnisse bei allen Entscheidungen der Bischofskonferenzen dürfen der kirchlichen Öffentlichkeit heute nicht mehr länger vorenthalten werden. Aber auch die Theologen können sich nicht mehr unter Berufung auf die Wissenschaft aus den Fragen des kirchlichen Lebens heraushalten. Auch sie haben, wo immer wesentliche Belange der Kirche und Konsequenzen ihres Faches auf dem Spiele stehen, in geeigneter Weise Stellung zu beziehen. Jedermann in der Kirche, ob im Amt oder nicht, ob Mann oder Frau, hat das Recht und oft die Pflicht, über Kirche und Kirchenleitung zu sagen, was er denkt und was er zu tun für nötig erachtet. Gegen Tendenzen zur Auflösung soll allerdings ebenso deutlich Stellung genommen werden wie gegen Tendenzen zur Erstarrung.

– Selber handeln: *Zu viele in der katholischen Kirche klagen und murren über Rom und die Bischöfe, ohne selber etwas zu tun. Wenn heute in einer Gemeinde der Gottesdienst langweilig, die Seelsorge wirkungsarm, die Theologie steril, die Offenheit gegenüber den Nöten der Welt beschränkt, die ökumenische Zusammenarbeit mit den anderen christlichen Gemeinden minimal ist, dann kann die Schuld nicht einfach auf Papst und Episkopat abgeschoben werden.*

Deshalb: Ob Pfarrer, Kaplan oder Laie – jedes Glied tue selbst etwas zur Erneuerung der Kirche in seinem kleineren oder größeren Lebensbereich. Viel Großes in den Gemeinden und in der gesamten Kirche ist durch die Initiative Einzelner in Gang gekommen. Und gerade in der modernen Gesellschaft hat der Einzelne Möglichkeiten, das kirchliche Leben positiv zu beeinflussen. In verschiedener Weise kann er auf besseren Gottesdienst, verständlichere Predigt und zeitgemäßere Seelsorge, auf ökumenische Integration der Gemeinden und ein christliches Engagement in der Gesellschaft drängen.

– Gemeinsam vorgehen: *Ein Gemeindemitglied, das zum Pfarrer geht, zählt nicht, fünf können lästig werden, fünfzig verändern die Situation. Ein Pfarrer in der Diözese zählt nicht, fünf werden beachtet, fünfzig sind unbesiegbar.*

Deshalb: Die offiziell eingerichteten Pfarreiräte, Priesterräte, Pastoralräte können in Gemeinden, Bistümern und Nationen ein mächtiges Instrument der Erneuerung werden, wo immer sich Einzelne entscheiden und unerschrocken für bestimmte Ziele im eigenen Bereich und in der Gesamtkirche einsetzen. Zugleich sind heute aber auch die freien Gruppierungen von Priestern und Laien unumgänglich, um bestimmten Anliegen in der Kirche zum Durchbruch zu verhelfen. Die Priester- und Solidaritätsgruppen haben in den verschiedenen Ländern manches erreicht. Sie verdienen auch publizistisch eine stärkere Unterstützung. Die Zusammenarbeit der verschiedenen Gruppierungen darf nicht durch sektiererische Abkapselung gestört, sondern muß um des gemeinsamen Zieles willen verstärkt werden. Insbesondere muß der Kontakt der Priestergruppen mit den zahlreichen verheirateten Priestern ohne Amt aufrechterhalten werden im Hinblick auf deren Rückkehr in den vollen kirchlichen Dienst.

– Zwischenlösungen anstreben: *Diskussionen allein helfen nicht. Oft muß man zeigen, daß man es ernst meint. Ein Druck auf die kirchlichen Autoritäten im Geist christlicher Brüderlichkeit kann legitim dort sein, wo Amtsträger ihrem Auftrag nicht entsprechen. Die Volkssprache in der gesamten katholischen Liturgie, die Änderung der Mischehenbestimmungen, die Bejahung von Toleranz, Demokratie, Menschenrechten und so vieles in der Kirchengeschichte sind nur durch ständigen loyalen Druck von unten erreicht worden.*

Deshalb: Wo eine Maßnahme der übergeordneten kirchlichen Autorität ganz offensichtlich dem Evangelium nicht entspricht, kann Widerstand erlaubt und sogar geboten sein. Wo eine dringende Maßnahme der übergeordneten kirchlichen Autorität in unzumutbarer Weise hinausgezögert wird, können unter Wahrung der Kircheneinheit in kluger und maßvoller Weise provisorische Lösungen in Gang gesetzt werden.

– Nicht aufgeben: *Bei der Erneuerung der Kirche ist die größte Versuchung oder oft auch das bequeme Alibi jene Auskunft, daß alles keinen Sinn habe, daß man doch nicht vorankomme und sich somit besser verabschiede: Emigration nach außen oder innen. Wo indessen die Hoffnung fehlt, fehlt auch die Tat.*

Deshalb: Gerade in einer Phase der Stagnation kommt es darauf an, in vertrauendem Glauben ruhig durchzuhalten und den längeren Atem zu bewahren. Widerstände waren zu erwarten. Aber ohne Kampf keine Erneuerung. Entscheidend somit bleibt: das Ziel nicht aus den Augen zu verlieren, ruhig und entschlossen zu handeln und die Hoffnung zu bewahren auf eine Kirche, die der christlichen Botschaft mehr verpflichtet und die deshalb offener, menschenfreundlicher, glaubwürdiger, kurz: christlicher ist.

Warum besteht Grund zur Hoffnung?

Weil die Zukunft der Kirche schon begonnen hat, weil der Wille zur Erneuerung nicht auf bestimmte Gruppen beschränkt ist, weil die neuen innerkirchlichen Polarisierungen überwindbar sind, weil viele und gerade die besten Bischöfe und Pfarrer, weil besonders die Leiter und Leiterinnen der Ordensgemeinschaften einen tiefergreifenden Wandel bejahen und fördern.

Aber auch weil die Kirche die Entwicklung der Welt nicht aufhalten kann und weil auch die Geschichte der Kirche selber weitergeht.

Schließlich, nein, eigentlich zuerst: weil wir den Glauben haben, daß die Kraft des Evangeliums Jesu Christi sich in der Kirche immer wieder als stärker erweist denn alle menschliche Unfähigkeit und Oberflächlichkeit, denn unsere eigene Trägheit, Torheit, Resignation[10].

II. Menschsein und Christsein

Allzu oft – die Geschichte der christlichen Kirche, Theologie und Spiritualität beweist es – ging das Christsein auf Kosten des Menschseins. Aber ist das echtes Christsein? Für viele gab es dann nur eine einzige Alternative: Menschsein auf Kosten des Christseins. Aber ist das echtes Menschsein? Von den neuen Einsichten in die Entwicklung der menschlichen Gesellschaft und der Neubesinnung auf die christliche Botschaft her, wie wir sie kennengelernt haben, drängt sich eine Neubestimmung des Verhältnisses auf: Wie verhalten sich gerade im Hinblick auf das Handeln Menschsein und Christsein? So muß jetzt die Frage des Anfangs leitmotivisch wiederkehren.

1. Normen des Menschlichen

Vor lauter Selbst-Verleugnung und Selbst-Entäußerung, so erscheint es manchen Nichtchristen[1], vernachlässige der Christ seine *Selbst-Verwirklichung.* Der Christ wolle zwar für die Menschen da sein, sei aber zu oft selber zu wenig Mensch. Er wolle gutwillig andere retten und habe selber nie richtig schwimmen gelernt. Er verkünde die Erlösung der Welt, die Bedingtheit der Umwelt aber erkenne er nicht. Er habe große Programme der Liebe, seine eigene Vorprogrammierung aber durchschaue er nicht. Er kümmere sich um die Seele der Anderen, die Komplexe seiner eigenen Psyche aber erkenne er nicht. Solche Überbewertung und Überforderung von Nächstenliebe, Dienst, Hingabe führe denn nur zu leicht zum Scheitern, zu Resignation und Frustration.

In der Tat: Ist nicht der Mangel an Menschsein der Grund, weswegen das Christsein so oft nicht für voll genommen wird? Ist nicht der Mangel an echter, voller Menschlichkeit gerade bei offiziellen Repräsentanten und Exponenten der Kirchen der Grund, weswegen das Christsein als echte menschliche Möglichkeit mißachtet oder zurückgewiesen wird? Ist nicht eine optimale Entfaltung der einzelnen Person anzustreben: eine Humanisierung der ganzen Person in allen ihren Dimensionen, auch der Trieb- und Gefühlsschichten? Das Christsein müßte durch

Menschsein abgedeckt sein. Nicht auf Kosten, sondern zugunsten des Menschlichen muß das Christliche zur Geltung gebracht werden.

Dieses Menschliche aber ist heute mehr denn je in seinem *gesellschaftlichen Wandel* zu sehen. Früher hat die christliche Moraltheologie die Kriterien des Menschseins und die Normen des menschlichen Handelns einfach aus einer unveränderlichen allgemeinen Menschennatur scheinbar evident und stringent deduziert. Und hat sie als ewig gültig dann auch entsprechend apodiktisch vertreten. In unserer zunehmend vom Menschen selbst auf Zukunft hin geplanten und gestalteten Geschichte einer dynamisierten Gesellschaft aber, so erkennt auch immer deutlicher die theologische Ethik[2], ist das unmöglich geworden. Man kann nicht mehr von einem tradierten und einfach passiv akzeptierten System ewiger, starrer, unwandelbarer sittlicher Normen ausgehen. Vielmehr muß immer wieder neu bei der konkreten dynamischen, wandelbaren, komplexen Wirklichkeit des Menschen und der Gesellschaft eingesetzt werden. Und zwar so, wie diese vielschichtige Wirklichkeit heute nach strengen *wissenschaftlichen Methoden* möglichst vorurteilslos auf ihre Sachgesetzlichkeiten und Zukunftsmöglichkeiten hin untersucht worden ist. Zu komplex ist das moderne Leben geworden, als daß man bei der Bestimmung ethischer Normen (etwa bezüglich wirtschaftlicher Macht, Sexualität, Aggressivität) in naiver Wirklichkeitsblindheit von den wissenschaftlich gesicherten empirischen Data und Einsichten absehen dürfte. Keine Ethik also ohne engen Kontakt mit den Humanwissenschaften: mit Psychologie, Soziologie, Verhaltensforschung, Biologie, Kulturgeschichte und mit der philosophischen Anthropologie. Die Humanwissenschaften bieten eine wachsende Fülle von gesicherten anthropologischen Erkenntnissen und handlungsrelevanten Informationen: überprüfbare Entscheidungshilfen, die freilich letzte Fundierungen und Normierungen des menschlichen Ethos nicht zu ersetzen vermögen.

Autonomie des Menschen

In einem *totalitären Zwangssystem* – welcher Couleur auch immer – wird von oben, offiziell-doktrinär bestimmt, was als gesellschaftsrelevante Wahrheit zu gelten hat, was die entscheidenden Prioritäten und Werte, die eigentlichen Modelle und Normen für die Gesellschaft sind, was Selbstverwirklichung und Humanisierung für den Einzelnen. Da gibt es in weltanschaulichen Fragen klare Grenzen, an die Gewissensfreiheit und Toleranz gebunden sind. Da gibt es aber auch keine Orientierungslosigkeit: Man weiß, woran man sich zu halten hat. Kriterien für Richtig und Falsch, für Gut und Böse, für den offiziellen Way of Life sind in hohem Ausmaß verordnet. Da gilt eine Ausschließlichkeit, die keine andere Wahrheit neben sich duldet. Die Freiheit der Wahl von Werten und Normen beschränkt sich auf rein private und für die Öffentlichkeit ungefährliche Räume. Sollte aber, so fragt man sich, nicht eine Orientierung möglich sein, die doch der Freiheit des Menschen ganz anderen Raum gibt?

In einem offenen *freiheitlichen System* dagegen darf nicht offiziell-doktrinär bestimmt werden, was Wahrheit, was Lebenssinn und Lebensstil, was Selbstverwirklichung und Humanisierung, was die Werte, Prioritäten, Modelle, Ideale und Normen sind. Da gibt es die verfassungsmäßig garantierte und institutionalisierte politische Toleranz, die Freiheit des Gewissens, der Religion, der Information, der Forschung und Lehre. Dieses System baut auf die unverlierbare Würde und Freiheit des Menschen als Menschen und will die mit dem Menschsein gegebenen Menschenrechte oder demokratischen Freiheiten garantieren. Diese sollen jedoch nicht Selbstzweck sein, sondern nur die institutionellen Bedingungen dafür, daß der Mensch selber seine ganze persönliche Freiheit in Anspruch nehmen kann, um sich ohne staatlichen oder parteilichen Zwang auf ein vernünftiges Ziel, einen lebenswerten Sinn, auf Werte, Normen und Ideale auszurichten, seine Selbst-Verwirklichung und ganzheitliche Humanisierung zu betreiben[3].

Aber damit beginnt die Problematik des weltanschaulich neutralen Rechtsstaates. Er darf gerade nicht aus einer Philosophie oder Religion begründen, was er andererseits unbedingt voraussetzen muß: Würde und Freiheit des Menschen. Beläßt er also den Menschen nicht in einer völligen Orientierungslosigkeit? Droht da nicht ein Beliebigkeitspluralismus, der leicht in jenem Ordnungsnihilismus des Geltenlassens von schlechthin allem endet[4]? Kann dieses offene (lernoffene, zukunftsoffene, wahrheitsoffene) freiheitliche System ein menschliches Zusammenleben überhaupt noch ermöglichen?

Die Freiheit des Menschen läßt sich, wie die Geschichte zeigt, weder allein durch die gesellschaftlichen Verhältnisse noch allein durch die Verabsolutierung des Individuums sichern. Der

Mensch hat – bewußt oder unbewußt – ein elementares Bedürfnis nach einer grundlegenden geistigen Bindung, nach einer Bindung an Sinn, Wahrheit, Gewißheit, an Werte und Normen. Wenn dieses Bedürfnis auch im vorstaatlichen freien geistigen Kräftespiel nicht befriedigt wird, wenn also überhaupt nichts oder niemand eine Orientierung, eine Wertordnung, eine Bindung an die Wahrheit, einen Lebenssinn vermittelt oder wenn die eine letzte Sinngebung vermittelnde institutionalisierte Religion (Kirche) ihre Glaubwürdigkeit für viele verloren hat, so entsteht ein gefährliches geistiges Vakuum. Der Mensch und gerade der noch nicht festgelegte junge Mensch lebt dann vielleicht ohne letzte Bindungen: mit allen Gefahren des menschlichen Scheiterns. Oder er bindet sich an eine dann eben totalitäre Ideologie, welcher Farbe auch immer, die ihm das Gesuchte verspricht und allzu schnell vermittelt. Seine frühere Freiheit gibt er – nicht einmal ungern – auf: da er dafür Wahrheit und Sinn, Werte, Ideale und Normen erhält, an die er sich halten kann.

Sollten nun aber Wahrheit, Sinn, Werte, Ideale und Normen nicht auch in einem freiheitlichen System vermittelt werden können: ohne daß also der Einzelne die Freiheit des Denkens, Redens und Handelns einem – irreligiösen oder auch religiösen – ideologischen System opfern muß? Eine letzte Orientierung für alle die zahllosen unumgänglichen Sachentscheidungen des Lebens, die Freiheit nicht abschafft, sondern ermöglicht: weil es nämlich um eine geistige Bindung nicht an ein fixierendes Endliches, Bedingtes, eigentlich Zufälliges (= Kontingentes), sondern an ein öffnendes Unendliches, Unbedingtes, wahrhaft Notwendiges geht?

In der theologischen Ethik bemüht man sich, die frühere monistische Fixierung durch plurale Offenheit zu überwinden, ohne deshalb freilich die Suche nach dem sittlich Richtigen und Guten aufzugeben. Auf die neuestens wieder intensiv diskutierte und für Nichtfachleute schwierig zu durchschauende Fundamentalproblematik der Begründung *ethischer Normen,* also allgemein verbindlicher Regeln des menschlichen Verhaltens und Zusammenlebens und so des echten Menschseins, des Humanen, kann hier nur am Rande eingegangen werden[5]. Aus der Diskussion ist ersichtlich, wie sehr sich auch die neuere katholische Ethik vor traditionellen kategorischen Kurzformeln für das Erlaubte oder Unerlaubte und jenem primitiven apodiktischen Dogmatismus hütet, der die christliche Moral für so viele differenzierter Denkende in Verruf gebracht hat[6]. In der Tat vermögen weder naturrechtliche noch biblizistische Verabsolutierungen und Simplifizierungen eine echte Hilfe zu sein für die Lösung der beinahe unlösbar scheinenden Probleme und Konflikte der heutigen Menschheit, etwa die Fragen der Überbevölkerung und Geburtenregelung, des Wirtschaftswachstums und Umweltschutzes, der politischen Macht und ihrer Kontrolle, der Aggressivität und Sexualität usw.

In allen diesen Fragen kann der Mensch *nicht einfach fixe Lösungen aus dem Himmel* holen oder theologisch von einer unveränderlichen Wesensnatur des Menschen her deduzieren. Er muß sie erproben in Entwürfen und Modellen und sie oft durch Generationen hindurch einüben und bewähren. Historisch gesehen, haben sich die konkreten ethischen Normen und Einsichten normalerweise in einem höchst komplizierten gruppendynamischen, sozialdynamischen Prozeß gebildet: Wo Lebensbedürfnisse, denen man Rechnung tragen muß, wo menschliche Dringlichkeiten und Notwendigkeiten sich zeigten, drängten sich für das menschliche Verhalten Handlungsregulative, Prioritäten, Konventionen, Gesetze, Sitten, kurz, bestimmte Normen auf. Nach Perioden der Gewährung und Eingewöhnung kam es schließlich zur allgemeinen Anerkennung solcher eingelebter Normen und manchmal auch wieder – in einer völlig veränderten Zeit – zu ihrer Aushöhlung und Auflösung.

In all den schwierigen Problemen und Konflikten der heutigen Menschheit muß der Mensch »auf Erden«, auch dies gleichsam im Schweiße seines Angesichts, sich differenzierte *Lösungen suchen und erarbeiten*: indem er von den Erfahrungen, von der Verschiedenartigkeit und Vielschichtigkeit des Lebens ausgeht und sich an die Tatsachen hält, indem er sich gesicherte Informationen und Erkenntnisse verschafft und überall mit Sachargumenten operiert, um so zu überprüfbaren Entscheidungshilfen und schließlich praktikablen Lösungen zu kommen. Kein Appell an eine noch so hohe Autorität kann dem Menschen die innerweltliche *Autonomie*, die ethische *Selbst-Gesetzgebung* und *Selbst-Verantwortung* für die Gestaltung der Welt, wie sie ihm der neuzeitliche Säkularisierungsprozeß in Gutem wie weniger Gutem gebracht hat, abnehmen[7].

Freilich stellt sich angesichts der komplexen und teilweise widersprüchlichen wissenschaftlichen Sachproblematik und angesichts der riesenhaft angewachsenen Verantwortung des Menschen wie vielleicht noch nie zuvor die *Frage nach der letzten Fundierung und Normierung* seines Handelns. Gerade unter

Voraussetzung der diffizilen empirischen und technischen Probleme stellt sich die Frage: Woher in dieser säkularen Welt die solidarische Verantwortung begründen, die jede individuelle, soziale und erst recht globale Planung und Steuerung zur Bewältigung der Menschheitsprobleme voraussetzt? Woher in der Bevölkerungspolitik, Wirtschafts-, Sozial-, Kultur- und Außenpolitik, aber auch in der Erziehung, in Ehe und Familie, Beruf und Arbeit, im Konsumverhalten die Wert- und Zielpräferenzen bestimmen, ohne die eine operative Planung oder auch nur eine sinnvolle Gestaltung nicht auskommen? Woher überhaupt die in allen individuellen und sozialen Planungen, Steuerungen, Gestaltungen und Unternehmungen vorausgesetzte Rationalität der Wirklichkeit und den immer wieder gefragten Sinn des Ganzen begründen?

Theonomie des Menschen

Aber damit ist bereits deutlich geworden: es geht hier keineswegs um völlig neue Fragen. Im Grunde wird hier nur noch einmal die bereits behandelte Grundlagenproblematik in bezug auf das praktische Handeln neu aufgerollt. Und insofern es hier um das praktische Verhalten zur selben fraglichen Wirklichkeit geht, von der wir in einer mehr theoretischen (aber keineswegs unpraktischen) Betrachtung ausgegangen sind, können wir auch hier auf das in den Anfangskapiteln Dargelegte zurückgreifen:

a. Jegliche Annahme von Sinn, Wahrheit und Rationalität, von Werten und Idealen, Prioritäten und Präferenzen, Modellen und Normen setzt ein *Grundvertrauen zur Wirklichkeit* voraus: in welchem der Mensch im Gegensatz zum Nihilismus ein grundsätzliches Ja zur Wirklichkeit sagt und durchhält, ein Ja zu ihrer Identität, Sinnhaftigkeit und Werthaftigkeit, ein Ja auch zur grundsätzlichen Vernünftigkeit der menschlichen Vernunft[8].

b. Dieses Grundvertrauen zur Identität, Sinnhaftigkeit und Werthaftigkeit der Wirklichkeit, zur grundsätzlichen Vernünftigkeit der menschlichen Vernunft ist nur dann begründet, wenn dies alles nicht seinerseits grundlos, haltlos und ziellos bleibt, sondern in einem Ursprung, Ursinn und Urwert begründet ist: in jener wirklichsten Wirklichkeit, die wir Gott nennen. Wir sahen es: kein *begründetes* Grundvertrauen ohne Gottvertrauen, ohne *Gottesglaube*[9].

Dieser fundamentale Begründungszusammenhang gilt also auch

für die Begründung von verbindlichen normativen Regeln des menschlichen Handelns, Verhaltens und Zusammenlebens, also für die Begründung ethischer Normen. Wenn aber die Wirklichkeit und der Mensch von einer letzten Identität, Sinnhaftigkeit und Werthaftigkeit bestimmt sind, dann lassen sich sinnvollerweise einzelne Normen echt menschlichen Handelns und Seins von den wesentlichen menschlichen Bedürfnissen, Dringlichkeiten und Notwendigkeiten ablesen: wie sie im alltäglichen Leben erfahren und mit Hilfe eben der Humanwissenschaften heute auch in neuer Weise wissenschaftlich-empirisch ermittelt werden können. *Sittlich gut* ist dann, was menschlich »geht«, was das menschliche Leben in seiner individualen und sozialen Dimension auf die Dauer gelingen und glücken läßt, wo Freiheit und Liebe entbunden werden[10]. Nach dieser primären und autonomen Norm der Sittlichkeit lassen sich unterscheiden und in der Erfahrung als solche auch nachprüfen: Wege, auf denen das menschliche Dasein in seiner Identität, Sinnhaftigkeit und Werthaftigkeit gefördert wird und der Mensch eine sinnvolle und fruchtbare Existenz gewinnt; und solche, auf denen das menschliche Dasein in seiner Identität, Sinnhaftigkeit und Werthaftigkeit gehindert wird und der Mensch eine sinnvolle und fruchtbare Existenz verfehlt. Insofern sind Normen und Strukturen richtig, »wenn und solange es unter ihrer Geltung mit der Menschheit auf ihrem Weg zur vollen Entfaltung ihrer Werte und Möglichkeiten vorangeht«[11]. Hier bestätigt sich die Autonomie des Sittlichen. Der Mensch soll nicht einfach ein Prinzip oder eine allgemeine Norm, sondern sich selbst in allen seinen Dimensionen verwirklichen: Selbstverwirklichung, Humanisierung, Menschwerdung des Menschen.

Freilich, aus all diesen menschlichen Dringlichkeiten und Notwendigkeiten läßt sich kaum ein *unbedingter Anspruch* ableiten: Warum schon soll man unbedingt? Anthropologische Bestimmtheiten erweisen sich als Bedingtheiten: Abhängigkeiten aller Art. Der Mensch – der ganz konkret umweltbestimmte, vorprogrammierte, triebgesteuerte Mensch – ist ein sehr endliches, sehr bedingtes Wesen und läßt sich weder als Individuum noch als Kollektiv verabsolutieren. Und doch muß es der Ethik, darin hat Kant recht, an einem unbedingten Sollsanspruch gelegen sein: also nicht nur ein hypothetisches »Du solltest«, sondern ein absolutes »Du sollst«. Wie aber ließe sich aus lauter Endlichkeiten und Bedingtheiten des menschlichen Daseins ein solch kategorischer Anspruch ableiten?

Der unbedingte ethische Anspruch, das unbedingte Sollen, läßt sich nur von einem – freilich mit der reinen Vernunft nicht beweisbaren[12] – *Unbedingten* her begründen: von einem *Absoluten*, das einen übergreifenden Sinn zu vermitteln vermag und das nicht der Mensch als Einzelner oder als Gesellschaft sein kann. Jeglicher Anspruch, der etwa nur auf der menschlichen Kommunikations- und Argumentationsgemeinschaft begründet ist, bleibt insofern hypothetisch, als ein Teilnehmen-Wollen vorausgesetzt wird und so das menschliche Sollen letztlich von einem menschlichen Wollen abgeleitet wird: ein hypothetischer Imperativ also, der auf Interesse basiert. »Ein immanenter Humanismus kann im Prinzip logisch nur zu einer hypothetischen Forderung führen[13].«

Das einzige Absolute in allem Relativen ist jener Urgrund, Urhalt und Ursinn der Wirklichkeit, den wir *Gott* nennen: Gott ist das Unbedingte in allem Bedingten, dessen Wirklichkeit allerdings nur in einem Akt des vertrauenden Glaubens angenommen werden kann. Diese Verankerung in einem mit dem Menschen nicht identischen, sondern ihn übersteigenden letzten Grund, Halt und Sinn ermöglicht ihm ein wahres Selbstsein und Selbsthandeln, eine echte sittliche Autonomie. Und wo immer auch in einem rein immanenten Humanismus etwa von der Autonomie, der Freiheit, dem Selbstsein, der Zukunftsoffenheit des Menschen her so etwas wie Unbedingtheit postuliert wird, wird faktisch auf jene letzte Unbedingtheitsdimension als Bedingung der Möglichkeit hingewiesen, auch wenn sie nicht benannt wird[14]. An Kants Postulat der Existenz Gottes aufgrund der Moralität des Menschen ist richtig, daß Gott vorausgesetzt werden muß, sofern der Mensch letztlich sinnvoll sittlich leben will: *Theo-nomie* als die *Bedingung der Möglichkeit der sittlichen Auto-nomie des Menschen* in der säkularen Gesellschaft[15].

Nur eine theologische Legitimation vermag für einen unbedingten Anspruch in allem Bedingten eine Letztbegründung zu liefern. Es geht ja in der Problematik des Verhältnisses von Bedingtem und Unbedingtem um nicht mehr und nicht weniger als einen Aspekt der theologischen Grundproblematik von Transzendenz und Immanenz[16]. Nur die Bindung an ein Unendliches schenkt Freiheit gegenüber allem Endlichen. Nur eine solche Letztbegründung der Ethik geht hinaus über einen bloßen kritischen Vergleich von Ethik-Systemen und die damit vorausgesetzte Trennung von »objektiv-neutraler« Wissenschaft und der subjektiven Wertentscheidung. Nur eine solche Letztbegründung der Ethik läßt jene Würde und Freiheit des Menschen begründet erscheinen, die, wie wir sahen, eine freiheitliche Gesellschaft voraussetzen muß, wenn sie nicht im Nihilismus des Geltenlassens untergehen oder/und in einen Totalitarismus umschlagen will.

Das Unbedingte im Bedingten

Bedeutet nun aber diese theonome Legitimation des menschlichen Sollens nicht doch eine Absolutsetzung der *Einzelnorm,* des einzelnen (materialen, kategorialen) sittlichen Gebotes oder Verbotes? Gerade nicht: sie bedeutet keine Verabsolutierung der einzelnen sittlichen Weisung, auch wenn sie konkretes menschliches Handeln allgemein verbindlich regeln soll. Das ist doch – bei aller gefährlich abstrakten Empirie- und Geschichtsferne des rein apriorischen kategorischen Imperativs Kants – der richtige Gedanke an seiner formalen Ethik: Es lassen sich von der menschlichen Vernunft keine materialen Normen direkt theonomisch ableiten. Insofern ist der Mensch auf sich selbst gestellt: es gibt in Normfindung und Normanwendung keine (materiale) Heteronomie, sondern eine echte Autonomie des Menschen.

Gewiß: Die einzelnen zwischenmenschlichen Normen aller Art (Prioritäten, Handlungsregulative, Konventionen, Gesetze, Sitten) können intersubjektive, allgemeine Geltung beanspruchen und können in der bestimmten Situation einen letztlich theonom begründeten Anspruch verbindlich auslegen. Trotzdem können die Einzelnormen für den zwischenmenschlichen Bereich *keine absolute Geltung* beanspruchen: als ob sie in jeder Situation bedingungslos, ausnahmslos gültig seien[17]!

Zugegeben: Rein *analytisch-explikativen* (»deontologischen«) Sätzen (zum Beispiel: »Nie ungerecht handeln!« »Nie ungerecht töten!«) kann eine bedingungslose und ausnahmslose Gültigkeit zugeschrieben werden. Aber solche tautologischen Sätze taugen in der Praxis kaum. Sie sagen nicht, was nun eigentlich zu tun ist: »Du sollst nie ungerecht töten!« heißt doch im Grund nur tautologisch: »Unrecht töten ist immer ungerecht.« Auf die konkrete Frage erhält man keine Antwort: ob zum Beispiel die Tötung eines feindlichen Aggressors, eines Embryos oder seiner selbst ungerecht, widersittlich ist. Was heißt »gerecht«, »gut«, »sittlich« konkret? Die echt *synthetischen* Sätze aber, die also die konkrete Erfahrung miteinbeziehen, basieren faktisch immer (ob

653

bewußt oder nicht) auf einem Abwägen von Sachargumenten, auf einem Vorzugsurteil: daß dieses bestimmte Gut (das Leben, die Wahrheit) nun einmal wichtiger ist als ein anderes. Das gilt auch für die Lüge und die Empfängnisverhütung, deren Widernatürlichkeit die Moraltheologie lange Zeit als absolute Norm vertrat. Muß man denn unter allen Umständen die Wahrheit sagen, auch wenn man dabei einen unschuldigen Menschen um sein Leben bringt (von der Empfängnisverhütung um des Wohles der Ehe und Familie willen ganz zu schweigen)?

Daß Einzelnormen im zwischenmenschlichen Bereich keine absolute Geltung beanspruchen können, berechtigt allerdings nicht zu der Forderung nach absoluter Normfreiheit. Wenn schon keine absolute Geltung, so erst recht *keine absolute Nicht-Geltung* von Normen. Die Alternative »Leben ohne Normen« – »Leben nach Normen« und die entsprechende Klassifikation in Ethik und Moral (Ethik fordere ein verändertes Bewußtsein – Moral bedeute durch äußerliche Normen gelenkte Verhaltensregulierung) wären nicht nur falsch, sondern, wie wir sahen, gerade in der heutigen Gesellschaft auch fatal: sie führten zum nihilistischen Geltenlassen von allem und jedem.

Zwischen absoluter Geltung und absoluter Nicht-Geltung steht die *relative Geltung* von Normen. Überall im zwischenmenschlichen Bereich – anders ist es gegenüber Gott als dem »absoluten Gut« – geht es nämlich um *relative Werte,* die nicht zu einem absoluten (unbedingten) Wert deklariert werden dürfen, sondern mit anderen (relativen) Werten abgewogen werden müssen. So sind denn alle diese Gebote und Verbote gültig: aber nicht um ihrer selbst willen, sondern um der Verwirklichung des größeren Gutes willen. Sie sind der Sache nach hypothetische Imperative: nicht unfehlbar, ausnahmslos und unter allen Umständen, sondern immer nur bedingt gültige Normen (Ausdruck einer moralitas conditionata). Die »Allgemeingültigkeit« sittlicher Normen bedeutet also ein »Im-Allgemeinen-gültig-Sein«: Die Normen sind gültig, soweit sie das Allgemeine ausdrücken und soweit sie in einer bestimmten Situation die notwendigen Bedingungen und empirischen Daten umfassend und zutreffend berücksichtigen.

Relative Geltung bedeutet also nichts anderes als *situationsgerechte Geltung.* Das hat nichts mit einem prinzipienlosen *Libertinismus* zu tun, der allein aus dem Augenblick lebt und sich ausschließlich nach der *Situation* richtet (man erinnere sich an die Enthusiasten von Korinth[18]): ein Verhalten einfach nach der jeweiligen Lage, ohne alle Prinzipien und Grundsätze, Richtlinien und Markierungspunkte, Maximen und Vorschriften. Situationsgerechte Gültigkeit meint also keinen Anti-nomismus, kein »Gegen das Gesetz«: nur am Fall orientiert, rein auf den Moment bezogen, allein auf die immer ganz und gar besondere Situation gerichtet[19].

Noch weniger freilich hat situationsgerechte Geltung mit einem unfreien, heteronomen *Legalismus* zu tun, der – unbekümmert um die Situation – sich allein an das Gesetz hält (man erinnere sich an die Moralisten in Galatien[20]): der Buchstabe des Gesetzes, dem man einfach zu gehorchen hat; Paragraphen, die man unbesehen nur anwenden muß; Prinzipien und Grundsätze, Richtlinien und Markierungspunkte, Maximen und Vorschriften, die zu bedingungslos und ausnahmslos geltenden Gesetzen geworden sind. Situationsgerechte Geltung meint also keinen Nomismus, keine »Gesetzlichkeit«: keine Lösungen, die man einfach nachschlagen kann – entweder im Gesetzbuch des Naturrechts (»natürliches«, naturgemäßes Sittengesetz) rationalistisch allein mit der Vernunft, oder im Gesetzbuch der Heiligen Schrift (schriftgemäßes Sittengesetz) biblizistisch allein mit der Bibel.

Ethik ist weder Thetik noch Taktik. Weder soll allein das Gesetz noch allein die Situation herrschen. Normen ohne die Situation sind leer, die Situation ohne Norm ist blind. Die Normen sollen die Situation erhellen und die Situation die Normen bestimmen. Gut, sittlich ist nicht einfach das abstrakt Gute oder Richtige, sondern das konkret Gute oder Richtige: das Angemessene. Nur in der bestimmten Situation wird die Verpflichtung konkret, aber die Verpflichtung in einer bestimmten Situation, die freilich nur der Betroffene selbst zu beurteilen vermag, kann unbedingt werden. Unser Sollen ist situationsbezogen, aber in einer bestimmten Situation kann das Sollen absolut werden. Jede Situation ist somit gekennzeichnet durch ein Moment, das unbedingt ist, und ein anderes, das man abwägen muß: eine allgemeine normative Konstante verbunden mit einer besonderen situationsbedingten Variablen.

Es dürfte unterdessen deutlich geworden sein, daß es bei der Problematik ethischer Normenfindung und Normenbegründung um eine Anwendung der am Anfang behandelten Problematik der Gottes- und Wirklichkeitserkenntnis geht. Zurückblickend läßt sich die Parallele so formulieren:

– Die Annahme autonomer Normen des Menschlichen ist der
  ethische Ausdruck des Grundvertrauens in die Identität, Sinnhaftigkeit und vor allem Werthaftigkeit der Wirklichkeit und
  des menschlichen Daseins. Ohne dieses Grundvertrauen können autonome ethische Normen nicht sinnvoll und begründet
  angenommen werden[21].
– Die Annahme autonomer Normen des Menschlichen mit unbedingtem, also theonomem Anspruch ist der ethische Ausdruck
  des begründeten Grundvertrauens in die Wirklichkeit (und das
  menschliche Dasein), sofern dieses von einem letzten Urgrund,
  Ursinn und Urwert bestimmt ist, ist also der ethische Ausdruck
  des Gottesglaubens. Ohne dieses Vertrauen auf Gott kann ein
  unbedingter Anspruch autonomer ethischer Normen nicht
  sinnvoll und begründet angenommen werden[22].

Fraglichkeit der Normen

Wird nun aber in dieser Perspektive nicht auf der ganzen Linie
die Fraglichkeit der Normen sichtbar? Das Sittliche zeigt hier
seine plurale, aber damit doch auch fragliche Gestalt. Es läßt sich
nicht leugnen: Empirisch-rational gesehen gibt es offenkundig
nicht einen, sondern mehrere Wege sittlicher Verwirklichung des
Menschlichen, gibt es mehrere Weisen, menschenwürdig, richtig, gut, dem Gewissen entsprechend zu leben.

Oder lassen sich die Verbindlichkeiten, die sich aus dem Anspruch der Wirklichkeit ergeben, nicht sehr verschieden artikulieren? Lassen sich die menschlichen Notwendigkeiten und
Dringlichkeiten nicht sehr verschieden bestimmen? Und sind
nicht alle Erkenntnisse, auch die wissenschaftlich-»objektiven«,
von Interessen geleitet? Sehen nicht auch die vielberufenen Humanwissenschaften mit all ihren empirischen Untersuchungen
den Menschen immer nur unter einem ganz bestimmten Blickwinkel? Hat nicht auch die wissenschaftliche Ethik immer eine
beschränkte Perspektive, so daß sie kaum alle Aspekte des sittlich
Richtigen gleichzeitig oder auch nur im Nacheinander der geschichtlichen Gestaltungen zu erfassen vermag? Ist das menschliche Leben nicht gerade heute von solcher Verschiedenartigkeit und Vielschichtigkeit, daß der Pluralismus in den sittlichen Überzeugungen nur zu verständlich ist? Und stoßen im
konkreten Leben abstrakt-ideale Normen nicht überall auf
Grenzen der Realisierbarkeit? Und werden sie in ihrer Verbind-

lichkeit dem Gewissen des Einzelnen nicht sehr unterschiedlich bewußt?

Man sieht: Was wahrhaft menschlich, was human ist, läßt sich offensichtlich gar nicht so leicht ausmachen. Und wenn man sich nicht zumindest stillschweigend an christlichen Wertmaßstäben orientierte, wäre es noch sehr viel schwieriger. Warum soll eigentlich nicht Herrschen und Dominieren wahrhaft menschlich sein, wie die Herrenmenschen-Moral aller Zeiten (und des Nazismus insbesondere) meinte? Ist die herrschende Moral nicht meist die Moral der Herrschenden, wie Marx und der Marxismus kritisch gegen die Moral einer Klassengesellschaft anführen? Oder warum soll nicht Genießen und Konsumieren wahrhaft menschlich sein, wie der mehr oder weniger raffinierte Hedonismus aller Zeiten (und der der Wohlstandsgesellschaft im besonderen) meint?

Sind also die von den menschlichen Notwendigkeiten und Dringlichkeiten abgelesenen Normen wirklich so evident, daß ihnen eine zwingende innere Einsichtigkeit zukommt? Sind sie nicht mehr Wahrscheinlichkeiten als Einsichtigkeiten, auch wenn mehrere Gründe für ihre Notwendigkeit zusammentreffen, konvergieren und somit durchaus plausibel machen (Konvergenzargumentation)? Haben sich nicht auch in der christlichen Ethik – wie historische Untersuchungen zeigen – die Auffassungen im Laufe der Jahrhunderte mannigfach gewandelt: bezüglich der Erlaubtheit von Krieg, Widerstand und Revolution, bezüglich der Grenzen von Freiheit und Gehorsam, bezüglich Eigentum, Arbeit und Beruf, bezüglich Gewissensfreiheit und Toleranz, bezüglich Geschlechtsverhalten, Ehe, Ehescheidung und Zölibat? Ist etwa die von vielen Religionen und Philosophien und nicht zuletzt von Kant akzeptierte »Goldene Regel« so evident, daß sie immer einleuchtet: zum Beispiel auch dann, wenn der andere, den ich so behandeln soll, wie ich behandelt sein möchte, mir, meinen Plänen, meiner Politik, eindeutig im Wege steht? Welche Politik ist überhaupt moralisch, welche Wissenschaft ist wahrhaft menschlich, welche Kultur oder Wirtschaftsform human?

Sogar bei so elementaren Fragen wie Liebe und Haß läßt sich fragen: Ist es nicht schwierig zu begründen, warum ich nicht hassen, sondern lieben soll? Ist der Haß, wissenschaftlich betrachtet, einfach schlechter als die Liebe? »Es gibt keine logisch zwingende Begründung dafür, warum ich nicht hassen soll, wenn ich mir dadurch im gesellschaftlichen Leben keine Nachteile zuziehe.«[23] Warum sollte Krieg nicht so gut oder schlecht sein wie Frieden, Freiheit so gut oder so schlecht wie Unterdrükkung? »Denn wie läßt es sich exakt begründen, daß ich, wenn es mir Spaß macht, nicht hassen soll? Der Positivismus findet keine die Menschen transzendierende Instanz, die zwischen Hilfsbereitschaft und Profitgier, Güte und Grausamkeit, Habgier und Selbsthingabe unterschiede. Auch die Logik bleibt stumm, sie erkennt der moralischen Gesinnung keinen Vorrang zu.«[24]

Ähnlich wie das Gottesverständnis, das von der Wirklichkeit dieser Welt und des Menschen her gebildet wird, bleiben auch die von dieser Wirklichkeit abgeleiteten Normen ambivalent. Auch sie sind ja nirgendwo in unvermittelter Direktheit und gegenständlicher Ausdrücklichkeit gegeben. Und so bleiben sie für jeden Einzelnen wie für die Gemeinschaft vieldeutig, *letztlich unbestimmt*. Besonders schwierig ist zu erkennen, inwiefern in ihrer durchgängigen Bedingtheit etwas Unbedingtes zum Ausdruck kommen soll.

So läßt sich denn angesichts der Nicht-Evidenz, Fraglichkeit, Unbestimmtheit der Normen und des von daher nicht erstaunlichen Pluralismus der Ethiken schon fragen: Wo kämen wir hin, wenn jeder Mensch isoliert für sich die Normen zu finden hätte? Wenn nicht schon immer Menschen da wären, die den Sinn, die konkrete Funktion und den humanen Wert dieser Normen erprobt, durchlebt und in vielfältiger Weise erfahren hätten? Wenn nicht schon dem Kind immer wieder neu *gesagt* würde, was es zu tun hat, was wirklich menschlich ist? Wo käme die Familie, die soziale Gruppe, auch der Staat, hin, wenn nicht immer wieder – mit allen möglichen Mitteln und Medien – *gesagt* werden könnte, was man soll, woran man sich unbedingt zu halten hat, welcher Weg der richtige, der gute, der wahrhaft menschliche ist?

2. Kriterium des Christlichen

Nur relativ wenige Menschen, darin irrt man wohl nicht, sind fähig, die vielen modernen Informations- und Kommunikationsmöglichkeiten so zu nützen, daß sie zu einem völlig eigenständigen kritischen Verhalten in der Gesellschaft kommen. Und selbst der kritischste und eigenständigste Mensch richtet sich nicht einfach nach Normen, die er allein rational gefunden und begründet hat. Kein Mensch fängt ja bei Null an. Und dies nicht nur wegen seiner Umweltbestimmtheit, seinem Vorprogrammiert- und Triebgesteuertsein: Er steht in einer Gemeinschaft, in einer Tradition. Schon vor ihm versuchten Menschen, in ihren vielfältigen Verhältnissen menschenwürdig zu leben. Normatives menschliches Verhalten wird wesentlich durch Menschen vermittelt, und das geschieht in echt menschlicher Weise durch Worte, Taten, Handlungsvollzüge und Haltungen, die nicht von allgemeinen Wahrheiten abgeleitet werden können, sondern sich sehr konkret aus einer komplexen Spannung zwischen intellektueller Überlegung und unmittelbarem Engagement ergeben: immer ein riskiertes Ethos, dessen Tragfähigkeit sich an den Folgen, an den »Früchten« messen läßt. Was hier auf vielfältigste Weise expliziert und illustriert werden könnte, soll nur mit einem Satz festgehalten werden: *Das Wissen um das Gute, seine Normen, Modelle, Zeichen, wird dem Einzelnen sozial vermittelt.*

Deshalb kann denn auch weder eine philosophische noch eine theologische Ethik ein Ethos einfach schaffen und es als verpflichtend einer Allgemeinheit auferlegen. Als Wissenschaft kann die theologische Ethik – wie die theologische Wissenschaft überhaupt[1] – Raum und Grenzen abstecken, sie kann Hindernisse ausräumen, Erfahrungen aufarbeiten, Vorurteile aufklären, wahres und falsches, echtes und heuchlerisches Ethos in die Krise führen. Sie kann helfen, die Rezeption neuer ethischer Normen vernünftig zu steuern. Sie kann, indem sie die vielfältigen Erkenntnisse der Humanwissenschaften integriert, neue Impulse, Fragen und Möglichkeiten anbieten, aufgrund deren menschliches Ethos neue Dimensionen gewinnt, der Gegenwart und der heraufkommenden Zukunft besser und schneller gerecht wird. Aber durch alles dies sollen und können die Freiheit der Zustimmung, die Kraft der Erfahrung und erst recht die Macht des überzeugenden Wortes nicht ersetzt werden, vielmehr werden sie provoziert.

Sollte also ein Mensch nicht gut daran tun, die Erfahrungen und Maximen einer Gemeinschaft, der großen humanen und religiösen Traditionen, des Erfahrungsschatzes seiner eigenen Väter zu nutzen, um seine eigenen Probleme, die Fragen seiner eigenen Lebensgestaltung, Normen und Motivationen zu erhellen? Gewiß, aus der persönlichen Verantwortung für sein Tun und für seine Lebensmaximen wird er sich nie herausstehlen können. Aber gerade deshalb ist es für ihn außerordentlich wichtig zu entscheiden, *von wem* er sich etwas sagen läßt, von wem er sich *das Entscheidende* sagen läßt. Der Christ, das ist aus allem Vorausgegangenen völlig deutlich, läßt sich auch für das praktische Handeln das Entscheidende von *Christus* sagen. Aber löst das in der Praxis alle Probleme?

Spezifisch christliche Normen?

Ähnlich wie im vieldeutigen Gottesverständnis, so könnte man auch bezüglich der vieldeutigen ethischen Normen sagen: in der biblischen Verkündigung werden sie eindeutig. Man denke an das Alte Testament, insbesondere an die auch für die christliche Tradition wichtigen ›Zehn Gebote‹ (Dekalog): »Du sollst Vater und Mutter ehren, Du sollst nicht töten, nicht ehebrechen, nicht stehlen, nicht falsches Zeugnis geben ...« Aber gerade hier zeigt es sich, was mindestens kurz erläutert werden soll: Auch die biblischen Gebote und Verbote sind menschlich vermittelte Normen. Von dem allgemein über die Normen Gesagten ist nichts zurückzunehmen.

1. Das *Unterscheidende* schon *für das alttestamentliche Ethos* sind nicht die einzelnen Gebote oder Verbote, sondern ist der *Jahweglaube,* der alle die einzelnen Gebote oder Verbote dem Willen des Bundesgottes unterstellt hat.

Auch die ethischen Forderungen des Alten Testament sind – da dürfen wir uns auf die Ergebnisse der alttestamentlichen Forschung verlassen[2] – weder dem Inhalt noch der Form nach vom Himmel gefallen. Was sich für das Ethos der Propheten und das der Weisheitsliteratur entsprechend nachweisen läßt, gilt erst recht für das vorausgehende Ethos des Gesetzes. Die ganze lange Sinai-Geschichte[3] enthält ein sehr vielschichtiges Gut göttlicher Anordnungen, die verschiedene Zeitphasen widerspiegeln. Doch selbst die Zehn Gebote – »die zehn Worte«[4], die in zwei Fassungen vorliegen[5] – haben eine Geschichte durchlaufen: Die Weisungen der »zweiten Tafel« für die zwischenmenschlichen Beziehungen reichen in die sittlichen und rechtlichen Traditionen der vorisraelischen halbnomadischen Sippen zurück und haben im Vorderen Orient zahlreiche Analogien. Es hat eine lange Zeit des Einübens, Einschleifens und Bewährens gedauert, bis der Dekalog nach Inhalt und Form so universal und knapp geworden war, daß er als ein zureichender Ausdruck des Willens Jahwes gelten konnte.

Spezifisch israelisch sind also nicht diese fundamentalen Minimalforderungen, die in ihrem Ursprung dem Jahweglauben vorausliegen. Spezifisch israelisch ist erst, daß diese Forderungen der Autorität des Bundesgottes Jahwe unterstellt werden, der der »Gegenstand« der »ersten Tafel« (Pflichten gegenüber Gott) ist. Der neue Jahweglauben[6] hat Konsequenzen für das bisherige Ethos: Jetzt umreißen diese Forderungen wie im übrigen auch andere Gebotsreihen, soweit sie mit dem Jahweglauben vereinbar waren, in größtmöglicher Kürze Jahwes Willen an den Menschen. Jetzt ist es Jahwe selbst, der in den Geboten wacht über das elementare Menschsein des Menschen, wie es die »zweite Tafel« sichert in bezug auf Elternehrung, Schutz des Lebens, der Ehe, des Eigentums und der Ehre des Nächsten. Das Eigentümliche der alttestamentlichen Sittlichkeit besteht also nicht in der Findung neuer ethischer Normen, sondern in der Verankerung der überlieferten Weisungen in der legitimierenden und schützenden Autorität Jahwes und seines Bundes: in der Aufnahme des vorgefundenen Ethos in das neue Gottesverhältnis. Diese Theonomie setzt die autonome Entwicklung ethischer Normen voraus und setzt sie auch gleichzeitig neu in Gang: Es kommt zur Weiterbildung und – freilich nicht auf allen Gebieten (Ehe, Stellung der Frau) konsequenten – Korrektur der vorhandenen Normen im Lichte eben dieses Gottes und seines Bundes.

Die *Auswirkungen* der religiösen Integrierung des Dekalogs in den Bundesgedanken sind durchaus feststellbar[7]:

Es kommt zu einer *neuen Motivation des Sittlichen*: Dankbarkeit, Liebe, Gewinn des Lebens, die geschenkte Freiheit werden entscheidende Motive.

Es kommt zugleich zu einer *neuen Dynamisierung des Sittlichen:* Wachsende, aber nicht vollständige Einpassung alter vorisraelischer und neuer außerisraelischer Normen in das neue Gottesverhältnis, Entwicklung neuer sittlicher und rechtlicher Normen und eine bedeutsame Konzentration und Vereinheitlichung, insofern jetzt die »zehn Worte« aus ethischen Minimalforderungen zu lapidaren Sätzen des Gotteswillens von unbedingter Geltung werden, die für umfassendere Bereiche eine prinzipielle und repräsentative Bedeutung haben.

Es kommt schließlich zu einer *neuen Transparenz des Sittlichen*: Die Gebote und Verbote behalten gewiß ihren sozialen Sinn und bleiben unverzichtbare Postulate der Humanität. Aber zugleich werden sie in neuer Weise transparent zum Religiösen hin: Jahwe selber erscheint als der Anwalt des Menschlichen. So wird die Erfüllung des Gesetzes Ausdruck der glaubenden und liebenden Verbundenheit mit dem göttlichen Bundespartner. Und obwohl die Normen in autonomer Weise aufgrund menschlicher Erfahrungen und ihrer Auswertungen entstanden sind, gibt es nun in Israel doch kein unpersönliches Gesetz, sondern nur Forderungen des in der Geschichte sprechenden und handelnden Bundesgottes. Ganz ähnlich wie das Ethos des Gesetzes wird dann später das vorgefundene (nun israelische) Ethos von den Propheten in Erwartung der eschatologischen Gottesherrschaft und von der Weisheitsliteratur in die individualistische theologische Weisheitsvorstellung aufgenommen.

2. Das *Unterscheidende* erst recht *für das christliche Ethos* sind nicht die einzelnen Gebote oder Verbote, sondern ist der *Christusglaube*, für den alle einzelnen Gebote oder Verbote Jesus Christus und seiner Herrschaft unterstellt sind.

Auch die ethischen Forderungen des Neuen Testaments – hier können wir uns auf die Ergebnisse der neutestamentlichen Forschung verlassen[8] – sind weder der Form noch dem Inhalt nach vom Himmel gefallen. Was für das Ethos des ganzen Neuen Testaments gilt, läßt sich besonders aus den ethischen Forderungen des Apostels Paulus nachweisen. Von einer paulinischen »Ethik« sollte man eigentlich nicht reden, da Paulus kein System und keine Kasuistik der Sittlichkeit entwickelt hat. Vielmehr schöpft er – und dies ist hier wichtig – seine Ermahnung (Paränese) weithin aus hellenistischer und besonders jüdischer Tradition.

Freilich kann man ihm nicht die in der damaligen populären griechisch-römischen Ethik (Epiktet, Seneca) gängigen Haustafeln mit den Ermahnungen für die verschiedenen Stände zuschreiben, wie sie sich dann zuerst im Kolosserbrief[9] und in dem davon abhängigen Epheserbrief sowie in den Pastoralbriefen und bei den Apostolischen Vätern finden. Doch verwendet Paulus zweifellos Begriffe und Vorstellungen der damaligen hellenistischen Popularphilosophie. Und wenn er auch nur ein einziges Mal den für diese Ethik zentralen Begriff der »Tugend« gebraucht, so umgibt er ihn an dieser einen Stelle des Philipperbriefes derart mit griechischer und insbesondere stoischer ethischer Begrifflichkeit, daß man darin geradezu so etwas wie eine Zusammenfassung der landläufigen griechischen Ethik sehen wollte: »Was immer wahr, was ehrbar, was recht, was immer rein, was angenehm, was löblich, was irgend Tugend ist und Lob, das erwägt!«[10] In den anderen Tugend- und Lasterkatalogen[11] hält sich Paulus dann freilich mehr an die jüdische als an die hellenistische Tradition.

Spezifisch christlich[12] ist also gerade nicht, daß diese oder jene bestimmte ethische Forderung erwogen wird, die als einzelne unvergleichlich sein soll. Die von Paulus aus jüdischer oder hellenistischer Tradition übernommenen ethischen Forderungen ließen sich auch anders begründen. Paulus hat kein bestimmtes Prinzip der Synthese oder Auswahl, sondern benützt zur Begründung seiner ethischen Forderung verschiedene Motive: Reich Gottes, Nachfolge Christi, eschatologisches Kerygma, Leib Christi, Heiliger Geist, Liebe, Freiheit, Sein in Christus. Auch wenn er Stichworte wie Gehorsam oder Freiheit gebraucht, so meint er damit keine systematischen Leitideen, sondern einfach die Ganzheit und Unteilbarkeit der Verpflichtung des Glaubenden und der glaubenden Gemeinde gegenüber ihrem Herrn.

Spezifisch christlich also ist, daß alle ethischen Forderungen von der Herrschaft des gekreuzigten Jesus Christus her verstanden werden. Es geht also nicht nur um das Moralische. Gabe und Aufgabe fallen unter der Herrschaft Jesu Christi zusammen; der Indikativ enthält schon den Imperativ. Jesus, dem wir in der Taufe durch den Glauben ein für allemal unterstellt *sind, soll* der Herr über uns bleiben: »Es geht darum, in der Nachfolge des Gekreuzigten die Herrschaft des Erhöhten zu bekunden. Rechtfertigung und Heiligung gehören insofern zusammen, als es in beiden gilt, dem Christus gleichgestaltet zu werden. Sie unterscheiden sich, weil das nicht ein für alle Male erfolgt, sondern in wechselnden Situationen stets neu erfahren und erlitten werden muß, seit es mit der Taufe begonnen hat[13].« So ist die paulinische Ethik nichts anderes als »die anthropologische Kehrseite seiner Christologie«[14].

Und damit sind wir nun gerade in den Grundfragen des ethischen Handelns zurückverwiesen auf das Zentrum dieses Buches, das im Verkündigen und Verhalten, Erleiden, Sterben und neuen Leben dieses Christus Jesus liegt. Und es bestätigt sich nun auch von rückwärts, von der Ethik her, wie richtig es war, in der Bestimmung des Christlichen von diesem konkreten Jesus Christus auszugehen.

Nicht etwa nur historisch, sondern auch sachlich bleiben christliche Verkündigung und christliches Handeln an seine Person gebunden. Den Platonismus mag man als Lehre von Platon und seinem Leben lostrennen, den Marxismus als System von Marx und seinem Tod. Bei Jesus von Nazaret aber, so sahen wir von Anfang bis Ende, bildet die Lehre mit seinem Leben und Sterben, mit seinem Geschick derart eine Einheit, daß ein abstrahierter allgemeiner Ideengehalt nicht mehr wiedergibt, worum es wirklich ging. Schon für den irdischen Jesus und erst recht für den in Gottes Leben eingegangenen und von Gott bestätigten kommen Person und Sache voll zur Deckung. Wäre das Ende seiner Verkündigung, seines Verhaltens, seiner Person einfach das Fiasko, das Nichts und nicht Gott, so wäre sein Tod die Desavouierung seiner Sache: Es wäre dann auch nichts mit seiner Sache, die die Sache Gottes (und nur so die Sache des Menschen) zu sein beansprucht. Ist aber sein Ende das ewige Leben mit Gott, so ist und bleibt er selber in Person das lebendige Zeichen dafür, daß auch seine Sache Zukunft hat, Einsatz erwartet, Nachfolge verdient. Es kann dann niemand behaupten, er glaube an Jesus, den Lebendigen, ohne sich in Taten zu seiner Sache zu bekennen. Und es kann auch umgekehrt niemand seine Sache betreiben, ohne zu ihm faktisch in eine Beziehung der Nachfolge und Gemeinschaft zu treten.

Nachfolge unterscheidet die Christen von anderen Schülern und Anhängern großer Männer, insofern für die Christen eine letzte Verwiesenheit an diese Person, nicht nur ihre Lehre, sondern auch ihr Leben, Sterben und neues Leben gegeben ist. Kein Marxist oder Freudianer würde das für seinen Lehrer beanspruchen wollen. Obwohl Marx und Freud ihre Werke persönlich verfaßt haben, können diese auch ohne eine besondere Bindung an ihre Person studiert und befolgt werden. Ihre Werke sind, ihre Lehre ist von ihrer Person grundsätzlich ablösbar. Die Evangelien, die »Lehre« (Botschaft) Jesu aber versteht man in ihrer eigentlichen Bedeutung erst, wenn man sie im Lichte seines Lebens, Sterbens und neuen Lebens sieht: seine »Lehre« ist im ganzen Neuen Testament von seiner Person nicht ablösbar. Jesus ist so für die Christen gewiß ein Lehrer, aber auch zugleich entschieden mehr als ein Lehrer: er ist *in Person die lebendige, maßgebende Verkörperung seiner Sache.*

Insofern Jesus in Person die lebendige Verkörperung seiner

Sache bleibt, darf er nie – wie etwa Marx und Engels in totalitären Systemen – zu einem leeren, affektlosen Porträt, zur leblosen Maske, zum domestizierten Objekt eines Personenkultes werden. Dieser lebendige Christus ist und bleibt Jesus von Nazaret, wie er gelebt und gepredigt, gehandelt und gelitten hat. Dieser lebendige Christus ruft nicht zur folgenlosen Anbetung oder gar zur mystischen Einigung. Er ruft freilich auch nicht zur buchstäblichen Nachahmung. Wohl aber ruft er zur praktischen, persönlichen Nachfolge.

»Nachfolgen« – im Neuen Testament gibt es bezeichnenderweise nur das Tätigkeitswort[15] – meint ein »Hinterihmhergehen«, jetzt freilich nicht mehr äußerlich mit ihm quer durchs Land ziehen wie zu Jesu Lebzeiten, aber doch im Zeichen der gleichen Gefolgschaft und Jüngerschaft in Beziehung mit ihm treten, sich auf Dauer an ihn anschließen und sein Leben nach ihm ausrichten. Das heißt Nachfolge: *sich auf ihn und seinen Weg einlassen und nach seiner Wegweisung seinen eigenen Weg –* jeder hat seinen eigenen – *gehen.* Diese Möglichkeit wurde von Anfang an als die große Chance angesehen: kein Müssen, sondern ein Dürfen. Eine echte Berufung also zu einem solchen Lebensweg, eine wahre Gnade, die nichts voraussetzt als das eine, daß man sie vertrauend ergreift und sein *Leben* danach *einstellt.*

Auf die *Lebens-Einstellung* kommt es an: So oft hat der Mensch Schwierigkeiten, eine bestimmte Entscheidung überzeugend rational zu rechtfertigen. Warum? Weil jegliche Entscheidung sich nicht nur aus den unmittelbaren Dispositionen und Motivationen erklärt, sondern in einer bestimmten Grundeinstellung wurzelt, in einem Grundverhalten, einer Grundorientierung. Zur vollen rationalen Rechtfertigung einer Entscheidung müßte man ja nicht nur sämtliche Prinzipien, auf denen sie gründet, darstellen, sondern auch sämtliche Folgen, die sich aus ihr ergeben können. Das heißt: Man müßte eine detaillierte Beschreibung seiner Lebenseinstellung (Lebensstil, Lebensweg, way of life) geben, von der diese eine Entscheidung ein Teil ist. Aber wie soll man das praktisch machen? »Eine solche Beschreibung zu geben, ist in der Praxis unmöglich. Die Versuche, die sich einer solchen am weitesten nähern, bestehen in den großen Religionen, besonders denen, die auf historische Gestalten hinweisen können, die diese Lebensweise praktisch vorgeführt haben[16].«

Der christliche Glaube ist eine jener großen »Religionen«,

deren Stärke es ist, zur detaillierten Rechtfertigung und Begründung einer Lebenseinstellung, eines Lebensweges und Lebensstiles auf eine ganz bestimmte maßgebende historische Gestalt hinweisen zu können: mit dem Blick auf Jesus Christus lassen sich – durchaus begründet, wie wir sahen – die Grundeinstellung und die Grundorientierung eines Menschen, lassen sich Lebensform, Lebensstil und Lebensweg ebenso umfassend wie konkret umschreiben. Ja, es ist keine Frage, daß die ganze christliche Botschaft nicht nur auf bestimmte Entscheidungen, Aktionen, Motivationen, Dispositionen zielt, sondern auf eine völlig neue Lebenseinstellung: auf ein von Grund auf verändertes Bewußtsein, eine neue Grundhaltung, eine andere Wertskala, ein radikales Umdenken und Umkehren des ganzen Menschen (»Metanoia«[17]). Und da vermag nun eine historische Gestalt zweifellos ganz anders zu überzeugen als eine unpersönliche Idee, ein abstraktes Prinzip, eine allgemeine Norm, ein rein gedankliches System. Jesus von Nazaret ist selbst die *Verkörperung* dieses neuen »way of life«.

1. Als konkrete geschichtliche Person besitzt Jesus eine *Anschaulichkeit*, die einer ewigen Idee, einem abstrakten Prinzip, einer allgemeinen Norm, einem gedanklichen System abgeht.

Ideen, Prinzipien, Normen, Systemen fehlen die Bewegtheit des Lebens, die bildliche Faßbarkeit und der unerschöpfliche, nicht auszudenkende Reichtum der empirisch-konkreten Existenz. Bei aller Klarheit und Bestimmtheit, Einfachheit und Stabilität, Denkbarkeit und Aussagbarkeit erscheinen Ideen, Prinzipien, Normen, Systeme los-gelöst, abs-trahiert vom Konkret-Einzelnen und deshalb einfarbig und entrealisiert: Aus der Abstraktion folgen Undifferenziertheit, Starrheit und relative Inhaltsleere, alles angekränkelt durch die Blässe des Gedankens.

Eine konkrete Person aber regt nicht nur das Denken und den kritisch-rationalen Diskurs an, sondern immer neu auch Phantasie, Einbildungskraft und Emotionen, Spontaneität, Kreativität und Innovation, kurz, alle Schichten des Menschen. Eine Person kann man malen[18], ein Prinzip nicht. Eine Person ermöglicht, in eine unmittelbare existentielle Beziehung zu ihr zu treten: Von ihr kann man erzählen und nicht nur über sie räsonieren, argumentieren, diskutieren und theologisieren. Und wie keine Geschichte durch abstrakte Ideen ersetzt werden kann, so kein Erzählen durch Proklamieren und Appellieren, keine Bilder durch Begriffe, kein Ergriffenwerden durch Begreifen[19]. Die Person läßt sich nicht auf eine Formel bringen.

Nicht ein Prinzip, nur eine lebendige Gestalt kann *anziehend*, im tiefsten und umfassendsten Sinn des Wortes »attraktiv« sein: verba docent, exempla trahunt, Worte lehren, Beispiele reißen mit. Nicht umsonst spricht man von einem »leuchtenden« Vorbild. Die Person macht eine Idee, ein Prinzip sichtbar: sie verleiblicht, »verkörpert« diese Idee, dieses Prinzip, dieses Ideal. Der Mensch »weiß« dann nicht nur davon, er sieht es »anschaulich« vorgelebt. Es wird ihm zwar nicht eine abstrakte Norm vorgeschrieben, wohl aber ein konkretes Maß gesetzt. Es werden ihm nicht nur einzelne Richtlinien gegeben, sondern eine konkrete Zusammenschau des Ganzen seines Lebens ermöglicht. So soll er nicht nur ein allgemeines »christliches« Programm, Gesetz, Ideal übernehmen oder nur eine allgemeine »christliche« Lebensgestaltung realisieren, sondern er kann zu diesem Christus Jesus selber Vertrauen fassen und sein Leben nach seinem Maß einzurichten versuchen. Dann erweist sich Jesus, mit allem, was er maßgebend ist und bedeutet, als weit mehr denn nur als ein »leuchtendes Vorbild«[20], vielmehr als das wahre »Licht der Welt«[21].

2. Als konkrete geschichtliche Person besitzt Jesus eine *Vernehmbarkeit*, der gegenüber Ideen, Prinzipien, Normen und Systeme als stumm erscheinen.

Ideen, Prinzipien, Normen und Systeme haben weder Wort noch Stimme. Sie können nicht rufen, nicht berufen. Sie können weder ansprechen noch in Anspruch nehmen. Aus sich haben sie keine Autorität. Sie sind angewiesen auf jemanden, der ihnen Autorität verschafft. Sonst bleiben sie unbeachtet und folgenlos. Eine konkrete geschichtliche Person hat ihren unverwechselbaren Eigennamen. Und der Name Jesus – oft mit Mühe und in Scheu ausgesprochen – kann eine Macht, einen Schutz, eine Zuflucht, einen Anspruch bedeuten: weil er gegen alle Unmenschlichkeit, Unterdrückung, Unwahrhaftigkeit und Ungerechtigkeit, für Menschlichkeit, Freiheit, Gerechtigkeit, Wahrheit und Liebe steht. Eine konkrete geschichtliche Person hat Wort und Stimme. Sie kann rufen und berufen: Und die Nachfolge Jesu Christi beruht wesentlich auf einem Aufgerufensein durch seine Gestalt und ihren Weg, also auf einer – heute durch Menschenwort vermittelten – Berufung. Eine konkrete geschichtliche Person kann ansprechen und in Anspruch nehmen:

Und die Nachfolge Jesu Christi führt wesentlich zum Gefordert-sein durch seine Person und ihr Geschick, zur Verpflichtung auf einen bestimmten Weg. Durch das vermittelte Wort kann sich eine geschichtliche Person auch über den Abstand der Jahrhunderte vernehmen lassen. Und der Mensch mit seiner vernehmenden Vernunft ist aufgerufen, in verstehendem Glauben vom Wort Jesu Christi geleitet, eine Deutung des Menschenlebens zu versuchen und dieses Menschenleben zu gestalten.

Nicht ein Prinzip, nur eine lebendige Gestalt kann in umfassender Weise *fordernd* wirken: Nur sie kann einladen, auffordern, herausfordern. Die Person Jesu Christi zeichnet sich nicht nur durch Anschaulichkeit und Leuchtkraft aus, sondern auch durch praktische Richtungsweisung. Sie kann die Personmitte eines Menschen zur freien existentiellen Begegnung provozieren, sie kann jenes Grund- und Gottvertrauen aktivieren, aus welchem heraus der Mensch fähig wird, sich »von Herzen« auf Einladung und Anspruch dieser Person einzulassen. Sie weckt den Wunsch, entsprechend handeln zu können, und zeigt einen gangbaren Weg zur Verwirklichung im Alltag. Und sie verfügt über jene Autorität und jenen Vertrauensvorschuß, der auch dann noch nach ihr handeln läßt, wenn im Einzelfall nicht immer voll rational bewiesen werden kann, warum ein solches Verhalten sinnvoll und wertvoll ist. So erweist sich denn Jesus mit allem, was er ist und bedeutet, nicht nur als »das Licht«, sondern als das unter den Menschen wohnende »Wort« Gottes[22].

3. Als konkrete geschichtliche Person zeigt Jesus eine *Realisierbarkeit,* wogegen Ideen oft als unerreichbare Ideale, Normen als unrealisierbare Gesetze, Prinzipien und Systeme als wirklichkeitsferne Utopien erscheinen.

Ideen, Prinzipien, Normen und Systeme sind selber nicht die Wirklichkeit, die zu regulieren und ordnen sie da sind. Sie bieten nicht Verwirklichung, sie verlangen nach ihr. Aus sich haben sie keine Realität in der Welt, sie sind angewiesen auf jemanden, der sie realisiert.

Eine geschichtliche Person aber ist von unbestreitbarer Realität, auch wenn sie verschieden interpretiert werden kann. Daß Jesus Christus existiert hat, daß er eine sehr bestimmte Botschaft verkündet, ein sehr bestimmtes Verhalten gezeigt, daß er bestimmte Ideale verwirklicht, ein sehr bestimmtes Geschick erlitten und durchgestanden hat, läßt sich nicht bestreiten. Bei seiner Person und seinem Weg geht es nicht um eine vage Möglichkeit, sondern um eine historische Wirklichkeit. Und anders als eine Idee oder Norm kann eine historische Person nicht schlechthin »überholt« werden durch eine andere: Sie ist unersetzbar ein für allemal sie selbst. Mit dem Blick auf die historische Person Jesu darf der Mensch wissen, daß sein Weg zu gehen und durchzuhalten *ist*. Es wird hier also nicht einfach ein Imperativ auferlegt: Du sollst den Weg gehen und dich rechtfertigen, dich befreien! Es wird ein Indikativ vorausgesetzt: Er ist den Weg gegangen, und du *bist* – im Blick auf ihn – gerechtfertigt, befreit.

Nicht ein Prinzip, nur eine lebendige Gestalt kann in dieser umfassenden Weise *ermutigend* wirken. Nur sie kann in dieser Weise die Möglichkeit der Realisierung bezeugen. Nur sie kann in dieser Weise zu Befolgung anregen: indem sie das Vertrauen ermöglicht und stärkt, den Weg auch gehen zu können; indem sie den Zweifel an der eigenen Kraft zum guten Handeln zerstreut. Damit ist freilich ein neues Maß gesetzt worden: nicht nur ein äußeres Ziel, ein zeitloses Ideal, eine allgemeine Verhaltensnorm, sondern eine Wirklichkeit, eine erfüllte Verheißung, die nur vertrauensvoll angenommen werden soll. Normen haben eine Tendenz zum Minimum, Jesus zum Maximum – aber doch derart, daß der Weg zumutbar und dem Menschen gemäß bleibt. So erweist sich denn Jesus selber in allem, was er ist und bedeutet, für den Menschen nicht nur als »Licht« und »Wort«, sondern geradezu als »der Weg, die Wahrheit und das Leben«[23].

Also wirkt Jesus als die maßgebende konkrete Person: in ihrer Anschaulichkeit, Vernehmbarkeit und Realisierbarkeit, anziehend, fordernd, ermutigend. Und ist nun mit diesem »Licht« und diesem »Wort«, mit diesem »Weg«, dieser »Wahrheit« und diesem »Leben« nicht schon klar ausgesagt, was für christliches Handeln, für christliche Ethik das Entscheidende ist: das Kriterium des Christlichen, das unterscheidend Christliche, das vieldiskutierte »Proprium Christianum«[24]?

Das unterscheidend Christliche in der Ethik

Auch in der Ethik sucht man vergeblich nach dem unterscheidend Christlichen, wenn man es abstrakt in irgendeiner Idee oder einem Grundsatz, wenn man es einfach in irgendeiner Gesinnung, einem Sinnhorizont, einer neuen Disposition oder Motivation sucht. Handeln aus »Liebe« etwa oder in »Freiheit«, Handeln im Horizont einer »Schöpfung« oder »Vollendung«

– das können schließlich auch andere, Juden, Moslems, Humanisten verschiedenster Art. Das Kriterium des Christlichen, das unterscheidend Christliche – das gilt wie für die Dogmatik, so konsequenterweise auch für die Ethik – ist nicht ein abstraktes Etwas, auch nicht eine Christusidee, eine Christologie oder ein christozentrisches Gedankensystem, sondern ist *dieser konkrete Jesus als der Christus, als der Maßgebende.*

Es ist durchaus legitim, wie wir gesehen haben, der autonomen Findung oder auch Übernahme ethischer Normen nachzuspüren und die verschiedenen Bezüge zu anderen Normsystemen festzustellen. Es ist so auch legitim, im Ethos Jesu verschiedenen Traditionen nachzugehen und die Gemeinsamkeiten mit anderen jüdischen oder griechischen Lehrern zu konstatieren: Nicht nur einfache ethische Weisungen (etwa Klugheitsregeln), sondern auch bestimmte hochethische Forderungen (etwa die Goldene Regel) sind von Jesus keineswegs erstmalig vorgebracht worden, sondern finden sich auch anderswo[25]. Aber leicht wird bei diesem Bemühen der einzigartige Kontext der ethischen Forderungen Jesu übersehen, die keine einsamen Höhepunkte und Spitzensätze in einem Wust ethisch wertloser Sätze, allegorischer und mystischer Spekulationen und Spielereien, spitzfindiger Kasuistik und erstarrtem Ritualismus darstellen. Und leicht wird erst recht die Radikalität und Totalität Jesu in seinen Forderungen übersehen: die Reduktion und Konzentration der Gebote auf ein Einfaches und Letztes (Dekalog, Grundformel der Gottes- und Nächstenliebe), die Universalität und Radikalisierung der Nächstenliebe im Dienen ohne Rangordnung, Vergeben ohne Ende, Verzichten ohne Gegenleistung, in der Feindesliebe[26]. Aber entscheidend ist: Man versteht dies alles nicht in seiner vollen Bedeutung, wenn man es nicht im *Ganzen von Person und Geschick Jesu sieht.* Was heißt das?

Man kann in der Musik Wolfgang Amadeus Mozarts die Wurzeln seines Stils und alle die Abhängigkeiten von Leopold Mozart, von Schobert, Johann Christian Bach, Sammartini, Piccini, Paisiello, Haydn und wem noch alles feststellen, aber damit hat man noch nicht das Phänomen Mozart erklärt. Man kann bei ihm, der sich mit der gesamten musikalischen Umwelt und der gesamten verfügbaren musikalischen Tradition intensiv auseinandergesetzt hat, in erstaunlicher Universalität und differenziertem Gleichgewicht alle Stile und Gattungen der Musik seiner Zeit finden, man kann »deutsch« und »italienisch«, kann Homophones und Polyphones, Gelehrtes und Galantes, Fortspinnung und Kontrast analysieren, und kann sich trotzdem die Einsicht in das Neue, Einzigartige, das spezifisch Mozartsche verbauen: das Neue, Einzigartige, spezifisch Mozartsche ist das *Ganze* in seiner höheren und in der Freiheit des Geistes wurzelnden Einheit, ist *Mozart selbst* in seiner Musik.

Und so können auch in Jesu Ethos alle möglichen Traditionen und Parallelen eruiert und wieder komponiert werden, aber damit hat man noch nicht das Phänomen Jesus erklärt. Und man kann Vorrang und Universalität der Liebe bei Jesus betonen und kann im Vergleich etwa mit der jüdischen Ethik die Radikalität der Theozentrik, der Konzentration, Intensität, Verinnerlichung des Ethos Jesu herausarbeiten und zugleich den neuen Sinnhorizont und die neuen Motivationen abheben und hat damit das Neue, Einzigartige an Jesus noch immer nicht deutlich gefaßt. Das Neue, Einzigartige an Jesus ist das *Ganze* in seiner Einheit, ist dieser *Jesus selbst* in seinem Werk.

Doch ist man auch so noch erst bei der Bestimmung des »unterscheidend Jesuanischen« und noch nicht – wo die Analogie mit Mozart endet – bei der Bestimmung des »unterscheidend Christlichen«, was freilich im »unterscheidend Jesuanischen« gründet. Dieses *unterscheidend Christliche* bekommt man auch und gerade für die christliche Ethik nicht zu Gesicht, wenn man nur auf Jesu Verkündigung, die Bergpredigt (Ethos), schaut und diese dann geradewegs – als ob dazwischen nichts geschehen wäre – in die heutige Zeit übersetzt. Zwischen dem historischen Jesus der Bergpredigt und dem Christus der Christenheit aber stehen in der Dimension des Handelns Gottes Tod und Auferweckung, ohne die der verkündigende Jesus nie zum verkündigten Jesus Christus geworden wäre[27]. Gerade das unterscheidend Christliche also ist das *Ganze* in seiner Einheit, ist dieser *Christus Jesus selbst* als der Verkündigende und der Verkündigte, als der Gekreuzigte und Lebendige.

Jegliche Reduktion der Sache Jesu Christi auf eine exklusiv verstandene Sache Jesu, die auf die Dimension Gottes in diesem Geschehen verzichten zu können glaubt, verzichtet auf letzte Verbindlichkeit. Auch christliche Ethik ist dann dem ethischen Beliebigkeitspluralismus ausgesetzt. Und selbst eine »Ethik des Neuen Testaments« erreicht nur mühsam nachträglich eine Einheit[28], wenn sie Jesus, Urgemeinde, Paulus, übriges Neues Testament – gleichsam vier neue Evangelisten – nacheinander abhandelt, als ob hier von einem Nebeneinander – theologisch und historisch! – je die Rede sein dürfte. Auch jede christliche Ethik hat zu beachten, daß ihr Fundament gelegt *ist,* und das ist nicht einfach das Liebesgebot oder das kritische Verhältnis zur Welt oder die Gemeinde oder die Eschatologie, sondern allein der Christus Jesus[29].

Daß der Verweis auf diesen Namen gerade auch für die Praxis des menschlichen Handelns alles andere als eine Leerformel ist, hat sich durch dieses ganze Buch hindurch immer wieder neu erwiesen und läßt uns hier auf Konkretisierung zugunsten eines generellen und grundsätzlichen Rückverweises auf alles Vorausgegangene verzichten. Statt dessen sei das unzweideutige Wort eines Mannes zitiert, der Nachfolge nicht nur doziert, sondern bis zum Ende praktiziert hat. Er sagt vom Inhalt der Nachfolge: »Es ist abermals nichts anderes, als die Bindung an Jesus Christus allein, d. h. gerade die vollkommene Durchbrechung jeder Programmatik, jeder Idealität, jeder Gesetzlichkeit. Darum ist kein weiterer Inhalt möglich, weil Jesus der einzige Inhalt ist. Neben Jesus gibt es hier keine Inhalte mehr. Er selbst ist es.« (D. Bonhoeffer[30]).

Das Grundmodell

Zwei naheliegenden Mißverständnissen ist nun freilich sogleich vorzubeugen:

Ein Erstes: Jesus Christus wurde als historische Gestalt in ihrer Anschaulichkeit, Vernehmbarkeit, Realisierbarkeit herausgestellt. Trotz aller Anschaulichkeit, Vernehmbarkeit, Realisierbarkeit jedoch werden Jesu Person und Sache keineswegs von vornherein jedem fraglos so einsichtig und zwingend evident, daß der Mensch gar nicht mehr Nein sagen könnte. Im Gegenteil: Gerade in seiner Anschaulichkeit wirkt er derart anziehend, in seiner Vernehmbarkeit derart fordernd, in seiner Realisierbarkeit derart ermutigend, daß der Mensch sich vor eine klare und unausweichliche Entscheidung gestellt sieht, die eben nur eine *Entscheidung des Glaubens* sein kann: dieser Botschaft zu vertrauen, sich auf seine Sache einzulassen, seinem Weg nachzufolgen.

Ein Zweites: Auch für den, der sich im Glauben für ihn, seine Sache und seinen Weg entschieden hat, wird Jesus nicht zur bequemen Generalantwort auf sämtliche ethischen Fragen des alltäglichen Lebens: wie etwa Geburten geregelt, Kinder erzogen, Macht kontrolliert, die Mitbestimmung und die Fließbandarbeit organisiert oder wie die Umwelt sauber gehalten werden soll. Er ist kein beliebiges in allen Einzelheiten simpel zu kopierendes Modell, sondern ein je nach Zeit, Ort und Person in unendlich vielen Weisen zu realisierendes *Grund-Modell.* Er wird ja auch in den Evangelien nirgendwo mit Tugend-Adjektiven charakterisiert, sondern vielmehr in seinen Aktionen und Relationen beschrieben. Was er ist, zeigt sich in dem, was er tut. Dieser Jesus Christus erlaubt Nachfolge in Entsprechung, in Korrelation zu ihm selbst, aber keine Imitation, keine Kopien seiner selbst.

Läßt sich ein Mensch auf Jesus als den Maßgebenden ein, läßt er sich von der Person Jesu Christi als dem *Grundmodell einer Lebensschau und Lebenspraxis* bestimmen, so formt das allerdings den *ganzen* Menschen um. Jesus Christus ist ja nicht nur ein äußeres Ziel, eine vage Dimension, eine allgemeine Verhaltensregel, ein zeitloses Ideal. Er bestimmt und beeinflußt Leben und Verhalten des Menschen nicht nur von außen, sondern von innen her. Nachfolge Christi bedeutet nicht nur Information, sondern Formation: nicht nur eine Oberflächenänderung, sondern eine Änderung des Herzens und von daher die Änderung des ganzen Menschen. Also geradezu Formung eines *neuen Menschen*: eine Neuschöpfung im freilich je verschiedenen, individual wie sozial bedingten Kontext des eigenen Lebens in seiner Besonderheit und Eigenartigkeit, ohne alle Uniformierung.

Ja, so könnte man Jesu einzigartige Bedeutung für das menschliche Handeln zusammenfassend umschreiben: Er selbst mit seinem Wort, seinen Taten, seinem Geschick, er selbst in Anschaulichkeit, Vernehmbarkeit und Realisierbarkeit ist *in Person* die *Einladung,* der *Appell,* die *Herausforderung* für den Einzelnen und die Gesellschaft. Als das maßgebende Grundmodell einer Lebensschau und Lebenspraxis liefert er fern aller Gesetzlichkeit und Kasuistik einladende, verpflichtende und herausfordernde *Beispiele, Zeichentaten, Orientierungsmaßstäbe, Leitwerte, Musterfälle.* Und gerade so beeindruckt und beeinflußt, verändert und verwandelt er die glaubenden Menschen und damit die menschliche Gesellschaft. Dem Einzelnen wie der Gemeinschaft, die sich auf ihn einlassen, vermittelt und ermöglicht Jesus ganz konkret[31]:

– *eine neue* Grundorientierung *und* Grundhaltung, *eine neue Lebenseinstellung, zu der Jesus herausgefordert und deren Konsequenzen er aufgezeigt hat: Derjenige Mensch oder dieje-*

nige Menschengemeinschaft darf und kann anders, echter, menschlicher leben, die als konkretes Leitbild und Lebensmodell für ihr Verhältnis zu Mensch, Welt und Gott diesen Jesus Christus vor sich haben. Er ermöglicht eine Identität und innere Kohärenz im Leben.

– *neue* Motivationen, *neue Motive des Handelns, die von Jesu »Theorie« und »Praxis« abgelesen werden können*: Von ihm her ist es möglich, die Frage zu beantworten, warum der Mensch gerade so und nicht anders handeln, warum er nicht hassen, sondern lieben soll, warum er – worauf selbst Freud keine Antwort wußte[32] – auch dann noch ehrlich, schonungsbereit und womöglich gütig sein soll, wenn er dadurch zu Schaden kommt und durch die Unverläßlichkeit und Brutalität anderer zum »Amboß« wird.

– *neue* Dispositionen, *neue konsistente Einsichten, Tendenzen, Intentionen, die im Geist Jesu Christi gefaßt und durchgehalten werden*: Nicht nur für vereinzelte und vorübergehende Momente, sondern auf Dauer werden hier Bereitwilligkeit erzeugt, Haltungen geschaffen, Qualifikationen vermittelt, die das Verhalten zu steuern vermögen: Dispositionen des unprätentiösen Engagements für die Mitmenschen, der Solidarisierung mit den Benachteiligten, des Kampfes gegen ungerechte Strukturen; Dispositionen der Dankbarkeit, Freiheit, Großzügigkeit, Selbstlosigkeit, Freude, aber auch des Schonens, Verzeihens und Dienens; Dispositionen, die sich auch in Grenzsituationen bewähren, in der Opferbereitschaft aus der Fülle des Sichverschenkens, im Verzicht auch da, wo man es nicht nötig hätte, in der Leistungsbereitschaft um der größeren Sache willen.

– *neue* Aktionen, *neue Taten im Kleinen oder Großen, die in der Nachfolge Jesu Christi gerade auch dort ansetzen, wo niemand hilft*: nicht nur allgemeine gesellschaftsverändernde Programme, sondern konkrete Zeichen, Zeugnisse, Zeugen der Menschlichkeit und der Vermenschlichung des Menschen wie der menschlichen Gesellschaft.

– *einen neuen* Sinnhorizont *und eine neue* Zielbestimmung *in der letzten Wirklichkeit, in der Vollendung von Mensch und Menschheit in Gottes Reich, die nicht nur das Positive des Menschenlebens, sondern auch das Negative zu tragen vermögen*: Im Licht und in der Kraft Jesu Christi wird nicht nur für Leben und Handeln, sondern auch für Leiden und Sterben des Menschen, wird nicht nur für die Erfolgsgeschichte, sondern

*auch für die Leidensgeschichte der Menschheit dem Glauben-
den ein letzter Sinn angeboten.*

Kurz: Für den einzelnen Menschen wie für eine Gemeinschaft ist
Jesus Christus in Person mit Wort, Tat und Geschick
    Einladung (»Du darfst!«),
    Appell (»Du sollst!«),
    Herausforderung (»Du kannst!«),
    Grundmodell also eines neuen *Lebensweges, Lebensstiles, Le-
benssinnes.*

III. Christsein als radikales Menschsein

Alle theologische Rede, alle christlichen Programme von einem
»neuen Menschen«, einer »Neuschöpfung« bleiben gesellschaftlich folgenlos, ja sind oft dazu angetan, die unmenschlichen
gesellschaftlichen Verhältnisse nur noch weiter zu reproduzie-
ren, wenn die Christen heute diesen »neuen Menschen«, diese
»Neuschöpfung« nicht im Kampf gegen ungerechte Strukturen
für die Welt überzeugend sichtbar werden lassen. Wer litte nicht
täglich in irgendeiner Form unter diesen oft anonymen und
undurchschaubaren Strukturen, ob in Ehe und Familie, Betrieb
oder Ausbildung, in Wohn- oder Wirtschaftsverhältnissen, auf
dem Arbeitsmarkt, in Verbänden, Parteien, Organisationen?
»Unter bestimmten sozialen Umständen ist ein befreites und
befreiendes Verhalten so gut wie ausgeschlossen. Es gibt Unterkünfte, die die Mutter-Kind-Beziehung systematisch zerstören; es gibt Organisationsformen der Arbeit, die das Verhältnis
des Starken zum Schwachen darwinistisch definieren und also
Fähigkeiten wie Hilfsbereitschaft, Mitleid oder Fairneß als für
die Produktion unerwünscht verkümmern lassen. Werden die
Bedingungen geändert, also die Unterkünfte menschenwürdig,
die Organisationsformen kooperativ, so sind die Bedingungen
der Möglichkeit eines anderen Lebens gegeben: nicht mehr, aber
auch nicht weniger[1].«

1. Die gesellschaftliche Relevanz

Aber: Man sollte den Menschen ändern können! So grollen oder
seufzen gerade die großen Strukturveränderer, Erzieher und Politiker, Technokraten und Revolutionäre. Dennoch gelingt es
nur bedingt, ihn durch Umwelttechnologie oder Psychoanalyse
oder auch politische Revolution in seinem Inneren und Innersten, in seinem »Herzen« zu verändern. Ja, wie kann man den
Menschen in seinem Innersten verändern, ohne daß ihm durch
irgendeine Manipulation (etwa gar der Gene) Würde und Freiheit genommen wird? Wie kann man den Menschen ändern, daß
aus ihm von der Mitte her ein neuer Mensch wird? Es ist jetzt klar

geworden, daß die Botschaft von Jesus Christus genau auf diese Veränderung, auf diesen neuen Menschen zielt. Auf den Menschen in seiner Verflochtenheit in die gesellschaftlichen Strukturen, wie immer wieder betont wurde. Es ist jetzt nur noch etwas deutlicher herauszustellen, daß christliche Botschaft und gesellschaftliche Situation des Menschen in ihrer Interdependenz zu sehen sind.

Keine politischen Kurzschlüsse

Zunächst ist zu wiederholen: Jesus war bei allem furchtlosen Eintreten für eine radikale Veränderung und bei aller Kritik an den herrschenden Kreisen und den bestehenden Mißständen kein politisch-sozialer Revolutionär. Seine Botschaft vom alles verändernden Gottesreich, das von allem Bösen und für alles Gute befreit, war kein politisch-soziales Aktionsprogramm[1]. Und so wird man, wenn man ihn zum Maßstab nimmt, auch heute aus der christlichen Botschaft nicht direkt ein politisch-soziales Aktionsprogramm machen dürfen.

Aber es bleibt auch wahr: Jesus war bei aller Ablehnung von Gewalt, Haß und Rache kein Mann des Establishments und kein Apologet des Bestehenden. Von Gottes Anspruch auf den Menschen her stellte er das religiös-gesellschaftliche System grundlegend in Frage, und nur insofern hatte seine Botschaft politische Implikationen[2]. So wird man, wenn man ihn zum Maßstab nimmt, auch heute die politischen Implikationen der christlichen Botschaft ernstnehmen müssen.

Christliche Praxis darf sich also keinesfalls auf das Private und Apolitische oder auch rein Kirchliche beschränken. Sie darf keinesfalls Gesellschaft und Welt ausklammern. Schon die Trennung in der theologischen Theorie zwischen *Dogmatik* (Glaubenslehre) und *Ethik* (Sittenlehre), wie sie erst allmählich und vor allem aus technischer Nötigung zur Arbeitsteilung aufkam, ist in dieser Hinsicht nicht unproblematisch. Oft hatte sie eine praktisch folgenlose Dogmatik auf der einen und eine dogmatisch unbegründete Ethik auf der anderen Seite zur Folge. Noch die klassischen Werke der Reformationszeit, Melanchthons Loci communes und Calvins Institutio, behandeln Dogmatik und Ethik in einem, von den mittelalterlichen Summen (und der für die Systematisierung der Ethik grundlegenden Summa des Thomas von Aquin) ganz zu schweigen. Wenn nun heute aus technischen Gründen eine Arbeitsteilung zwischen Dogmatik und Ethik und sogar zwischen Individual- und Sozialethik kaum zu vermeiden ist, so sollte doch von der Dogmatik her – wie dies hier versucht wird – die Verbindung mit der Individual- und Sozialethik hergestellt werden und umgekehrt. Christlicher Glaube und christliches Handeln lassen sich nicht trennen: weder im individualen noch im sozialen Bereich.

Nun hat Jesus – ganz im Horizont der Naherwartung des Reiches Gottes – kein Programm zur Erneuerung und Veränderung der sozialen Strukturen erstellt. Weder die Sklaven- noch die Frauenfrage, noch erst recht die allgemeine Emanzipation des Menschen hat er grundsätzlich aufgerollt. Er hat auch keine Wirtschafts- oder Staats- oder Kulturethik entworfen. Um weite Bereiche des sozialen Lebens wie Recht und Politik, Wissenschaft und Kultur überhaupt kümmerte er sich in keiner Weise. Auch hat er nicht etwa die Kirche als »vollkommene Gesellschaft« (societas perfecta) eingesetzt und für sie Vollmacht (potestas directa oder indirecta) über die »zeitlichen Dinge« reklamiert. Die Bergpredigt und alle ethischen Forderungen Jesu richten sich, es läßt sich nicht übersehen, in erster Linie an den Einzelnen oder an Gruppen[3].

Aber nachdem der Horizont der apokalyptischen Naherwartung versunken war und die Christenheit sich auf längere Zeit einrichten mußte, mußten auch ganz anders als zu Anfang – im bleibenden Ausblick auf das Reich Gottes – die gesellschaftlich-politischen Implikationen der christlichen Botschaft entwickelt werden. Die Gefahr einer direkten Identifikation der christlichen Botschaft mit einem politischen Programm wurde schon in den ersten Jahrhunderten aktuell. Freilich lud erst der Machtwechsel im römischen Imperium unter Konstantin dazu ein, die Theologie unkritisch und unkontrolliert der herrschenden gesellschaftlich-politischen Ideologie auszuliefern. Der erste große Entwurf einer christlichen *»politischen Theologie«,* der des konstantinischen Hofbischofs Eusebios von Caesarea, hat als Vorbild für viele eine religiös-politische Reichstheologie nach dem Programm »ein Gott, ein Logos, ein Kaiser, ein Reich« entwickelt. Der Begriff der »theologia politika« (oder »theologia civilis«, in der Stoa unterschieden von der »mythischen« und der »natürlichen« Theologie) meint im geschichtlichen Kontext die direkte Theologisierung der bestehenden Staats- und Gesellschaftsformen und ein Ineinander von Staatlichem und Religiösem, wie es zuerst Augustin in seinem »Gottesstaat« ausführlich einer scharfen Kritik unterzogen hat. Die christliche »politische Theologie« war ja die unmittelbare Nachfolgerin der religiösen Staatsideologie des alten Rom und so selber eine reine Staatsideologie. Ihre theologische Sanktionierung des Primats der Politik und ihre Legitimierung des unbedingten Anspruchs des Staates wirken nicht nur im byzantinischen Cäsaropapismus und in der Renaissance, bei den Staats- und Gesellschaftstheoretikern Macchiavelli und Hobbes, sondern auch noch in der politischen Romantik und im französischen Traditionalismus des vergangenen Jahrhunderts (und in anderer Weise im absolutistischen religiös-politischen Papsttum) nach.

So ist der Begriff der »politischen Theologie« durch die 2000jährige Tradition einer restaurativ-integralistischen Staats- und Gesellschaftsauffassung belastet. Auch nach der Unterscheidung von Staat und Gesellschaft und dem neuen Verständnis politischer Ordnung als einer wandelbaren und veränderlichen Freiheitsordnung, wie sie durch die politische Aufklärung wirksam geworden sind, hat der Begriff seine eigene historische Schwerkraft behalten. Er läßt sich kaum ohne Mißverständnisse dekretierend in einen kritisch-revolutionären Begriff umfunktionieren: und dies besonders, nachdem er in unserem Jahrhundert seine neue zweifelhafte Bekanntheit durch den katholischen Staatsrechtler und unwillentlichen Bereiter des Nationalsozialismus Carl Schmitt[4] erlangt hat, gegen den schon der Theologe Erik Peterson in seiner bekannten Darstellung über den Monotheismus als politisches Problem »die theologische Unmöglichkeit einer ›politischen Theologie‹ zu erweisen« versuchte[5].

Alle Abgrenzungen und Distanzierungen heutiger Vertreter einer neuen »politischen Theologie«[6] konnten nicht verhindern, daß diese statt als kritisch-theologisches Bewußtsein von den gesellschaftlichen Implikationen und Aufgaben des Christentums schon vom Namen her immer wieder in Theorie *und* Praxis als direkt »politisierende Theologie« verstanden wurde. Der Begriff selber lädt dazu ein, »politische Theologie« gleichsam von rückwärts mit einer (nun freilich »linken«) politischen Ideologie aufzuladen. Jetzt nicht mehr zugunsten einer bestehenden, religiös begründeten absoluten staatlich-gesellschaftlichen Ordnung, wohl aber zugunsten der »Veränderung freiheitlicher politischer Ordnungen und Verfassungen«, der »Emanzipation«, der »Demokratie« oder des »Sozialismus« werden aus der christlichen Botschaft in politischer Parteilichkeit alle möglichen politischen Postulate direkt abgeleitet: von der Verstaatlichung der

Schlüsselindustrien bis zur jederzeitigen Abwählbarkeit sämtlicher Volksvertreter. Statt eines direkt »christlich« begründeten Anti-Kommunismus und Anti-Sozialismus jetzt eine direkt »christlich« begründete Kapitalismus-Kritik und sozialistische Gesellschaftstheorie. Bestimmte politische Denkschemata einer heutigen Gesellschaftskritik werden so zu Kategorien der christlichen Botschaft erklärt: Als Pendant zu einer reaktionären Politisierung des Glaubens von rechts (im Sinne einer Establishment-Theologie) wird hier die Gefahr einer revolutionären Neopolitisierung des Glaubens (im Extremfall eine Theologie der Revolution[7]) von links offenbar. Früher war Gott in der staatlichen Ordnung und im absolutistischen Fürsten (oder Papst) unmittelbar und unzweideutig am Werk, jetzt glaubt man seine Spuren unmittelbar in der gesellschaftlichen Freiheitsgeschichte und in der sozialistischen Revolution (aber natürlich nicht in der nationalsozialistischen Machtergreifung oder in Militärputschs) zu finden. Früher gab sich die politisierende Theologie als Bewußtsein vom ersten, jetzt vom zweiten.

Lassen es aber nicht *beide* Konzeptionen einer politisierenden Theologie an kritischer Distanz und an Respekt fehlen vor der modern-säkularen Eigengesetzlichkeit von Politik, Staat und Gesellschaft, die in die Weltlichkeit der Welt einbezogen sind und keiner neointegralistischen Theologisierung bedürfen? Verkennen nicht *beide* Konzeptionen die echte politische Relevanz der christlichen Botschaft, aus der nicht in simpler Direktheit eine bestimmte Politik und bestimmte Detaillösungen für Fragen des Rechts und der Verfassung, für Wirtschafts-, Sozial-, Kultur- und Außenpolitik abgeleitet werden können?

Aber wenn somit der historisch belastete und aktuell irreführende Begriff der »politischen Theologie« wegen terminologischer und sachlicher Bedenken besser nicht verwendet wird, so sind doch, wie schon am Anfang unseres langen Weges betont wurde[8], ihre positiven Intentionen aufzunehmen. Es bedarf in der Tat einer – so wird man besser sagen – *gesellschaftskritischen Theologie,* die sich mit der gesellschaftlichen Gegenwart, mit dem Status quo nicht einfach identifiziert, sondern dazu ein kritisch-dialektisches Verhältnis hat. Sowenig mit der christlichen Botschaft ein bestimmtes sozialpolitisches Aktionsprogramm verbunden ist, sowenig kann sich eine Verinnerlichung, Spiritualisierung und Individualisierung auf die christliche Botschaft stützen. Wo immer dies geschehen ist – und es geschieht bis in die Gegenwart hinein dauernd –, da wird die sozialethische Potenz und gesellschaftliche Relevanz des Evangeliums, da wird der primäre (und nicht erst nachträgliche) Öffentlichkeitscharakter der christlichen Botschaft, da werden auch die gesellschaftskritische Funktion und der Praxisbezug von christlicher Theologie und Kirche verkannt.

Gesellschaftliche Konsequenzen

Wenn die Christen und ihre Theologie in der Gesellschaft – in bestimmter Hinsicht und in bestimmten Grenzen – eine kritische Funktion wahrnehmen wollen, dann müssen sie wissen und verantworten können, *woher* sie kritisieren. Sagen sie in ihrer negativen wie positiven Kritik nur das, was sich die Gesellschaft auch selbst schon ständig sagt oder was eine säkulare Gesellschaftskritik der Gesellschaft sagt, so ist ihre besondere christliche Kritik überflüssig. Es reicht nicht aus, mit allen anderen nach Gerechtigkeit, Frieden und Freiheit zu rufen und dies einfach unter eine biblische Etikette wie »Reich Gottes« zu stellen. Eine Gesellschaftskritik läßt sich nach allem, was bisher entwickelt wurde, nur dann als spezifisch christlich bezeichnen, wenn sie *von diesem Christus Jesus her* ermächtigt ist.

Der Autor des besten Jesus-Buches aus marxistisch-atheistischer Sicht, der Tscheche Milan Machovec, macht zu Recht auf den charakteristischen Umstand aufmerksam, daß die gegen das Christentum sich auflehnenden »Polemiker und Kritiker eigentlich fast immer den Christen nicht vorwarfen, daß sie Anhänger Jesu sind, sondern im Gegenteil, daß sie es *nicht* sind, daß sie Jesu Sache verraten, daß für sie alle Eigenschaften des Pharisäertums zutreffen, die Jesus aufgezählt hat, besonders, daß auf sie das Wort zutrifft: ›Dieses Volk ehrt mich mit den Lippen, aber die Herzen sind ferne von mir.‹ In solchen Fällen geht es also um die Kritik des Christentums dieser oder jener Zeit, doch nicht um Kritik der eigentlichen Ideale Jesu[9].« Und er beruft sich dabei besonders auf die Vorwürfe von Karl Marx an die Adresse des verbürgerlichten Christentums unter dem Leitwort: »Straft nicht jeder Augenblick eures praktischen Lebens eure Theorie Lügen?«

Von diesem Christus Jesus her ist es bei allen berechtigten Unterscheidungen nicht möglich, Theorie und Praxis, Privat und Öffentlich, Religiös und Politisch einfach zu trennen. Oder sollte es nicht wie für den Einzelnen so auch für die säkulare Gesellschaft, sollte es nicht für den gesamten Bereich der Öffentlichkeit und des Politischen, sollte es nicht für die Personen aller Positionen, Ämter und Ränge wie für die Strukturen und Institutionen eine ungeheure Bedeutung haben, was in all den verschiedenen Kapiteln von Jesus Christus her zu sagen war:

über die Identifikation mit den Schwachen, Kranken, Armen, Unterprivilegierten, Unterdrückten und auch den moralischen Versagern?

über das Vergeben ohne Ende, den gegenseitigen Dienst ohne Rangordnung, den Verzicht ohne Gegenleistung?

über die Aufhebung der Grenzen zwischen Genossen und Nichtgenossen, Fernsten und Nächsten, Guten und Bösen in einer Liebe, die auch den Gegner und Feind aus dem Wohlwollen nicht ausschließt?

über die Normen, Gebote und Verbote, die um der Menschen, und die Menschen, die nicht um der Normen, Gebote und Verbote willen da sind?

über die Institutionen, Traditionen und Hierarchen, die um des Menschen willen zu relativieren sind?

über den Willen Gottes als oberste Norm, der auf nichts anderes als das Wohl des Menschen zielt?

über diesen Gott selbst, der sich mit den Nöten und Hoffnungen der Menschen solidarisiert, der nicht fordert, sondern gibt; der nicht unterdrückt, sondern aufrichtet; der nicht bestraft, sondern befreit; der statt Recht vorbehaltlos Gnade walten läßt?

über diesen Tod schließlich und seine Verlassenheit und über die Hoffnung des neuen Lebens und die Vollendung in Gottes Reich?

Braucht es sehr viel Phantasie, um sich vorzustellen, daß es nicht nur im Herzen der Menschen, sondern auch in der Gesellschaft, ihren Strukturen und Institutionen, anders aussähe, wenn diese Botschaft gelebt würde? Ja, daß es überall in der Gesellschaft dort wirklich anders *aussieht,* wo diese Botschaft gelebt *wird?* Es fehlt wahrhaftig nicht am grundlegenden christlichen Programm, nicht an diesem Christus Jesus selbst, es fehlt eindeutig an den Christen, wenn sich zu wenig ändert in der Welt. Das stärkste *Argument gegen das Christentum* sind die *Christen*: die Christen, die nicht christlich sind! Das stärkste *Argument für das Christentum* sind die *Christen*: die Christen, die christlich leben! Über der bekannten und oft so wenig tröstlichen Kirchengeschichte vergißt man oft die sehr viel erfreulichere Christengeschichte – leider nur äußerst beschränkt ein Gegenstand für Historiker.

Freilich kann man aus dem christlichen Programm, das Jesus Christus selber ist, *kein Gesetz* für alle machen. Und wo immer man solches auch nur in einzelnen Punkten – etwa für die Ehegesetzgebung (Ehescheidung) – versucht hat, war eine unchristliche totalitäre Vergewaltigung von Menschen durch Menschen die Folge. Und wo man solches gar konsequent und allgemein – wie etwa im religiös-politischen Schwärmerturm der wiedertäuferischen Revolutionäre von Münster (1534/35) – durchsetzen und in unbedingtem Willen zu Gerechtigkeit, Freiheit und Frieden das Reich Gottes in dieser Gesellschaft (das »Königreich Zion«) herbeizwingen wollte, endete man in der grausamen Terrorherrschaft eines christlichen Integralismus. Und wo schließlich die Kirche selber aus dem Evangelium ein unfehlbares Gesetz (der Lehre, des Dogmas, der Moral, der Disziplin) machte, da mußte anstelle der christlichen Freiheit und des geistlichen Dienstes die ungeistliche Gewalt und die Knechtschaft treten, da mußten die Scheiterhaufen (aus Holz oder anderem Material) brennen, und Menschen leiden, da mußte die Kirche zum Großinquisitor werden, von der sich Jesus selber wortlos verabschiedet.

Jesus selber, das ist überdeutlich geworden, ist nicht als neuer Gesetzgeber aufgetreten: Er hat weder ein sittliches Naturgesetz eingeschärft[10], noch ein positives Offenbarungsgesetz aufgerichtet[11]: keine Anweisungen für alle Gebiete des Lebens, keine allumfassenden moralischen Prinzipien, kein neues ethisches System. Ihm nachzufolgen meint nicht, eine Anzahl von Vorschriften auszuführen. Auch die Bergpredigt[12] – wie bekannt, eine redaktionelle Sammlung verstreuter Einzelsprüche – ist keine Summe wörtlich zu befolgender Gebote und Verbote, ist kein Verhaltenskodex, keine Moraltheologie in nucleo, ist erst recht kein Grundgesetz einer neuen Gesellschaft, in der alle Übel beseitigt und keine Staatsgewalt, Polizei, Gerichte, Armee mehr nötig wären. Die Bergpredigt steht nicht anstelle einer Rechts- und Gesetzesordnung. Sie spricht vielmehr auch das an, was nicht Gegenstand einer gesetzlichen und rechtlichen Regelung werden kann. Und sie führt zumindest indirekt zur Änderung und Vermenschlichung der Rechts- und Gesetzesordnung.

Freilich: ohne Normen, ohne einen minimalen Konsens über Normen des politischen, ökonomischen, sozialen und individuellen Verhaltens ist keine Gesellschaft lebensfähig. Doch Jesu Weisungen sind keine neuen Normen: keine abstrakten allgemein verbindlichen Regeln des menschlichen Verhaltens und Zusammenlebens, deren Grenze ja der konkrete Fall aufdeckt. Seine Weisungen sind vielmehr, wie wir sahen, Einladungen, Appelle, Herausforderungen. Und gerade das vielzitierte *»Gebot« der Liebe*[13] soll kein neues Gesetz sein: auch kein Kompendium, keine Zusammenfassung, keine Sammlung der vielen Gesetze. Man kann nicht lieben, weil man muß. Das »Gebot« der Liebe ist vielmehr die Quintessenz, die Hauptsache, der ganze Sinn, nach Paulus die »Erfüllung« des Gesetzes. Die Liebe, von Jesus her verstanden, ist nicht einfach eine Tugend neben anderen Tugenden, nicht ein Prinzip neben ähnlichen Prinzipien. Sie ist vielmehr das Grundkriterium aller Tugenden, Prinzipien, Normen, menschlichen Verhaltensweisen. Immer ist das Gebot um der Liebe willen da, und nicht die Liebe um des Gebotes willen.

Jesus hatte, so sahen wir[14], in bisher nie dagewesener Einfachheit und Konkretheit alle Gebote auf das Doppelgebot der Gottes- und Nächstenliebe konzentriert: eine Forderung, die grenzenlos das ganze Leben des Menschen zu umfassen vermag und die doch auf jeden Einzelfall ganz genau zutrifft. Liebe verstanden nicht als Empfindung und Gefühl, als Sentimentalität, sondern als die vom Willen bestimmte Haltung und Tat des Wohlwollens dem Nächsten, ja selbst dem Gegner gegenüber: ein Wachsein, Offensein, Hilfsbereitsein in schöpferischem Verhalten, in produktiver Phantasie und in entschiedenem Handeln von Fall zu Fall, je nach Situation. Frau und Mann, Freund und Freundin, Kollegen, Nachbarn, Bekannte und Fremde.

Liebe ist also nach Jesus gut *in allen Situationen*. Sie muß bei aller Güterabwägung den Ausschlag geben. Sie ist nicht auf bestimmte Handlungen festlegbar, ist aber für alle Handlungen das entscheidende Regulativ. Von der Liebe erhalten die Gebote einen einheitlichen Sinn, werden sie aber auch begrenzt und unter Umständen, wie Jesu Gesetzesübertretungen praktisch zeigen, sogar aufgehoben: um des Menschen willen. Das bedeutet keine Moral ohne Normen, bedeutet keinen Antinomismus oder Libertinismus, keinen Freipaß für die subjektivistische Willkür des eigensinnigen und oft genug uninformierten Individuums. Liebe fordert vielmehr höchste Verantwortung des Gewissens, das alle Möglichkeiten der Information und Kommunikation zu nützen hat (conscientia bene formata). Der Mensch soll sich im praktischen Leben durchaus an die Normen, Gebote und

Vorschriften halten, ohne die eine Gesellschaft oder eine bestimmte Gemeinschaft und schließlich auch der Einzelne nicht leben können: von den Verkehrsampeln angefangen bis zur Verfassung des Landes und den Zehn Geboten Gottes. Aber alle Normen – die Zehn Gebote eingeschlossen – müssen dem Menschen dienen, sind nach Jesus um des Menschen willen da, und der Mensch nicht um der Normen willen.

Dies ist der Grund, weswegen in einem jeden Fall nicht ein buchstäblich gesetzliches, sondern ein situationsgerechtes Handeln erfordert ist[15]. Und die Liebe ist es, die *für dieses situationsgerechte Handeln die Richtung* weist, die ein allumfassendes und doch konkretes letztes Kriterium bildet: Sie läßt die Pflichtenkollisionen überwinden, die bei einem buchstäblich gesetzlichen Verständnis der einzelnen Gebote unvermeidlich aufkommen. Der Mensch richtet sich so nicht mehr mechanisch nach dem einzelnen Gebot oder Verbot, sondern nach dem, was die Wirklichkeit selber verlangt und ermöglicht: jede Norm, jedes Gebot oder Verbot hat den inneren Maßstab an der Liebe zum Nächsten.

So ist denn von Jesus Christus her die Liebe, das aktive Wohlwollen zum Mitmenschen dasjenige, was die zweideutigen Normen[16] im konkreten Fall eindeutig werden läßt. Insofern kann man verstehen, wenn Paulus sagt: Die Liebe fügt dem Nächsten nichts Böses zu, und so ist nun die Liebe des Gesetzes Erfüllung[17]. Aber auch das Umgekehrte: Hätte einer alle Erkenntnis und allen Glauben und würde er selbst seinen Leib zum Verbrennen hingeben und hätte die Liebe nicht, so nützte es ihm nichts[18]. Wer aus liebendem Wohlwollen zum Nächsten handelt, erfüllt Gottes Gesetz, auch wenn er gegen ein bestimmtes Gebot handelt; denn der Sinn von Gottes Gesetz ist die Liebe. Liebe bedeutet also nicht einen Aufruf zur Anpassung oder Besitznahme, sondern zur Freiheit, die ihr Maß an der Freiheit des Anderen hat.

- *Der Mensch kann in der modernen Gesellschaft weniger denn je ohne Normen leben. Aber in der Praxis wird der Christ diese Normen im Wohlwollen der Liebe zugunsten des Nächsten auslegen und praktizieren (oder nicht praktizieren).*
- *Was also dem Anderen, der mich gerade braucht, hilft, ist in der konkreten Situation gut, was ihm schadet oder wehtut, ist schlecht.*

Was also macht in der konkreten Situation die an sich so bedrohlich vieldeutigen Normen eindeutig? Wie werden die so oft gar nicht evidenten Verbindlichkeiten, die sich aus dem Anspruch der Wirklichkeit, aus den menschlichen Dringlichkeiten und Notwendigkeiten so verschieden artikulieren und bestimmen lassen, eindeutig? Wir sahen, daß es gar nicht so leicht auszumachen ist, was echt menschlich, was human ist: warum man nicht einfach dominieren und konsumieren, warum man nicht hassen, sondern lieben soll, was ja alles rein vernünftig so gar nicht leicht zu erweisen ist. Von Jesus Christus her ist die Richtung gewiesen: Da ist es ganz eindeutig, warum der Mensch nicht hassen, sondern lieben soll, warum er nicht über die anderen Menschen dominieren, sondern ihnen dienen, warum er nicht einfach genießen, sondern auch verzichten, warum er gegen die Profitgier für die Hilfsbereitschaft, gegen die Grausamkeit für die Güte, gegen die Habgier für die Selbsthingabe optieren soll. Kurz, in welcher Situation auch immer: die *Liebe macht die Normen eindeutig!* Durch sie bleibt die oberste Norm der Wille Gottes, der das umfassende Wohl des Menschen will: Richtig ist, was dem Menschen, dem Nächsten, den Nächsten hilft.

Die Nächsten – mehr denn je ist in der modernen Massengesellschaft der Plural zu betonen: Es geht, wie heutige Gruppen-Forschung[19] vielfältig illustriert, nicht nur um das Verhältnis von Einzelnen zu Einzelnen, sondern um das Verhältnis von Einzelnen zu Gruppen, von Gruppen zu Einzelnen und besonders von *Gruppen zu Gruppen.* Man denke nur an Rassendiskriminierung, an den Nationalismus, an die soziale Unterdrückung, an die Verbands-, Standes- und Parteiegoismen. So hat die Nächstenliebe auch einen gesellschaftlichen, kollektiven Aspekt und ist besonders gefordert durch die schwächeren, benachteiligten, unterdrückten Gruppen.

Noch deutlicher als in den hochentwickelten Industriestaaten wird dies in den unterentwickelten Ländern Asiens, Afrikas und Lateinamerikas sichtbar. Auch im Großen ist die Liebe situationsbedingt, und Erfahrungen in einzelnen Ländern und Kontinenten lassen sich nur schwer verallgemeinern, wohl aber für Situationen in anderen Ländern und Kontinenten indirekt fruchtbar machen. Eine Herausforderung für den aktiv christlichen Einsatz stellt besonders das »*christliche*« *Lateinamerika* dar, wo nicht nur relativ kleine Gruppen, sondern ganze Völker, Subkulturen und Gesellschaftsklassen unter Elend und Ausbeutung leiden und von den elementarsten menschlichen Rechten kaum Gebrauch machen können. Probleme der elementaren menschlichen Selbstverwirklichung, die in Europa und Nordamerika nur mehr sehr bedingt bestehen, haben hier einen ganz anderen Grad der Dringlichkeit und bilden einen auch für Europäer und Nordamerikaner sehr ernstzunehmenden Testfall für Menschsein und Christsein.

Engagement für die Befreiung

Seit der lateinamerikanischen Bischofskonferenz von Medellin 1968 – für diesen Kontinent der Bedeutung nach dem Zweiten Vatikanischen Konzil vergleichbar – ist sich die lateinamerikanische Kirche und auch die Theologie in neuer Weise der gesellschaftlichen, politischen, kulturellen und religiösen Lage bewußt geworden: »Lateinamerika scheint noch unter dem tragischen Zeichen der Unterentwicklung zu leben, die unsere Brüder nicht nur um den Genuß der materiellen Güter bringt, sondern sogar um ihre Selbstverwirklichung als Menschen. Trotz der Anstrengungen, die unternommen werden, verbinden sich Hunger und Elend, grassierende Krankheiten und Kindersterblichkeit, Analphabetentum und Randdasein, einschneidende Einkommensunterschiede und Spannungen zwischen den Gesellschaftsklassen, Ausbrüche von Gewalttätigkeit und geringe Beteiligung des Volkes an der Verwaltung im Dienst des Gemeinwohls[20].«

Angesichts solcher *struktureller Unmenschlichkeit und »Gewalt«*, die von südamerikanischen Christen als Situation kollektiver »Sünde« und als »himmelschreiendes« Ärgernis bezeichnet werden, können die Christen, können und dürfen die Kirchen nicht schweigen, ihre Mitverantwortung verkennen und untätig bleiben[21]. Ja, sollten sie mit ihrem eigenen Programm, mit diesem Jesus Christus und den alttestamentlichen Propheten vor Augen, nicht eigentlich die ersten sein, die ihren prophetischen Protest anmelden und solidarisch sich tätig einsetzen gegen jegliche politische, wirtschaftliche, kulturelle Unterdrückung? Ein *Engagement der Befreiung* für alle, die legal um ihr Menschsein gebracht werden und für die Christsein keine reale Möglichkeit bedeutet: für die Verlassenen des Kontinents, deren Armut nicht Naturnotwendigkeit, sondern Nebenprodukt eines grausamen gesellschaftlichen Systems ist; für die offen oder versteckt ausgebeuteten Volksklassen, verachteten Kulturen, diskriminierten Rassen (Indios)! Ein Engagement der Befreiung, damit ein unterentwikkeltes Volk Grundnahrung und Grundkultur und die Benachteiligten volle Rechtsgleichheit erhalten; damit die einseitige internationale Arbeitsteilung, die stets neuen Abhängigkeiten der unterentwickelten Völker von den Industrienationen abgebaut und die ungerechten wirtschaftlichen Verhältnisse im Inneren und nach außen abgeschafft werden! Ein Engagement der Befreiung, damit in all dem eine neue Weise des Menschseins und Christseins möglich wird: nicht nur ein tatenloses Mitleid oder hochherzige Taten der Barmherzigkeit, auch nicht nur oberflächliche Reformen, sondern wirklich ein »neuer Mensch« in einer geänderten, wahrhaft gerechten, brüderlichen und freien Gesellschaftsordnung.

Die *Theologie* hat unter diesen spezifischen lateinamerikanischen Bedingungen eine besondere Funktion: Sie darf noch weniger denn anderswo nur gelehrte Beschäftigung mit der Vergangenheit sein, nur Wiederholung alter Dogmen und Lehren oder auch nur historisch-kritische Exegese der Schrift. In diesen Ländern ist der Kontrast zwischen christlichem Programm und menschlichen Möglichkeiten in breiten Volksmassen so groß, daß die Theologie nicht nur wie anderswo vor dem Problem steht, wie man vor Nicht-Christen, sondern geradezu wie man vor Nicht-Menschen oder Unter-Menschen in einer unmenschlichen Welt von Gott und seiner Menschenfreundlichkeit reden soll. Es soll in solcher Theologie nicht einfach von dem ausgegangen werden, was Theologen über die Wirklichkeit gesagt haben, sondern von dem, was heute die Wirklichkeit von Mensch und Gesellschaft unmittelbar selber sagt: nicht nur wie vor einiger Zeit in Europa eine »Theologie der irdischen Wirklichkeiten« oder eine »Theologie der Frage«, auch nicht nur eine für die Südamerikaner allzu akademische, unverbindliche, folgenlose und auf eine Weltreligion fixierte Spielart einer »politischen Theologie«, sondern programmatisch mit großer spiritueller Tiefe und evangelischer Unmittelbarkeit eine »teología de la liberación«, eine *»Theologie der Befreiung«*: Theologie als konsequente kritische Reflexion von der dort heute gelebten Erfahrung der geschichtlichen Befreiungsbewegung und Befreiungspraxis her in Konfrontation mit der sehr konkret verstandenen christlichen Botschaft[22].

Mehr als eine abstrakte Theologie der Säkularisierung wird Theologie unter solchen Umständen sich verstehen als »das Bemühen, die gegenwärtige, von Ungerechtigkeit gekennzeichnete Lage zu beseitigen und eine andere, freiere und menschlichere Gesellschaft zu schaffen«, in der »die Menschen in Würde leben und ihr Geschick in ihre eigenen Hände nehmen können«[23]. Eine Theologie also, ethisch orientiert und völlig konzentriert auf die Praxis: genauer auf die »Befreiungspraxis«. Eine Theologie, die sich in diesen Ländern gegen alle elementare Unterdrückung politisch-sozialer (Arme, Unterdrückte, Schwache), erotisch-sexueller (die Frau als Sexualobjekt) und pädagogischer (die im oligarchisch-oppressiven Bildungssystem domestizierten Kinder) Art wendet[24]. Eine Theologie, die ein geschichtliches Projekt der politischen, wirtschaftlichen, kulturellen, sexuellen Befreiung vorlegen möchte: als reales Zeichen und Vorausnahme des definitiven, eschatologischen Projekts, der vollen Freiheit im Reiche Gottes.

Aber nicht nur die Theologie, sondern auch die *Kirche,* die so oft in den Jahrhunderten einer kolonialen Christenheit bis in die Gegenwart hinein ihr eigenes Programm verriet, darf das Evangelium Jesu Christi nicht länger zur Rechtfertigung einer gesellschaftlichen Situation mißbrauchen, die den Forderungen des Evangeliums klar widerspricht: das Evangelium also denaturiert zur kirchlich sanktionierten Ideologie einer dünnen überreichen Oberschicht, zur Befriedigung der religiösen Bedürfnisse der Massen und so zur Absicherung einer Gesellschaftsordnung, die, von nur wenigen errichtet und beherrscht, auch nur wenigen wirklich dient und nützt!? Die Kirche, für die sich der universale Befreiungsanspruch in Christus nicht auf die religiöse Ebene allein beschränken darf, hat sich anders als bisher mit der elenden Lage der riesigen Massen des Volkes zu identifizieren, mit ihren Hoffnungen und Kämpfen für ein besseres Menschsein. Und so läßt sich nicht übersehen, daß sich Christen – von den Arbeitern bis zu den Priestern und Bischöfen – in wachsendem Ausmaß in den Befreiungsprozeß eingliedern: »Befreiung *von* einem ganzen System niederdrückenden und absondernden Zusammenlebens, und Befreiung *zur* Selbstverwirklichung des Volkes, das sein politisches, wirtschaftliches und kulturelles Geschick selber bestimmen kann«[25].

»Engagement für die Befreiung« also auf der ganzen Linie! Dennoch ist hier vor Schablonen zu warnen. Ist doch dieser Ausdruck und manches, was in diesem Zusammenhang gesagt und gefordert wird, eher *vage und vieldeutig.* »Noch heute läßt er sich in Lateinamerika leicht ideologisch, ja parteipolitisch ausbeuten«[26]. Kann »Theologie der Befreiung« nicht leicht zu einer Worthülse werden, die mit den gegensätzlichsten politischen Inhalten gefüllt wird: von relativ konservativen Theologen bis zu bewußt marxistisch argumentierenden Revolutionären[27]? Die meisten führenden Vertreter der »Theologie der Befreiung« sehen freilich die große Gefahr: daß die christliche Botschaft, die mit keiner bestehenden oder künftigen Gesellschaftsordnung identifiziert werden darf, auf ein politisches Programm oder eine politische Aktion verkürzt wird. Man anerkennt durchaus: Die Beteiligung der Christen am Befreiungsprozeß weist »verschiedene Radikalitätsgrade« auf und äußert sich in Sprechweisen, die, noch auf der Suche, sich »tastend und irrend« vorwärtsbewegen[28]. Man möchte sich für »mehrere Optionen« offenhalten: nicht nur für die direkt politische Betätigung, sondern auch für die erzieherische, kulturelle, wirtschaftliche, pastoral-prophetische. Das Hauptinteresse dieser Theologie ist nicht parteiegoistisch ein gesellschaftspolitisch-ökonomisches. Der Mensch soll auch hier nicht vom Brot allein leben, obwohl viele froh wären, auch nur schon von Brot leben zu können. Mit Nachdruck wird eine neue Synthese des »Militant-Engagierten« und des »Religiös-Kontemplativen«, von Aktion und Gebet, Mystik und Politik angestrebt und zu leben versucht[29]. Und gerade dem gelebten Zeugnis der Armut – als Ausdruck der Liebe zum Nächsten und Zeugnis gegen das Unrecht, nicht als aus sich wertvolles und die unmenschliche Wirklichkeit auch noch verklärendes Lebensideal – kommt unter den spezifischen gesellschaftlichen Bedingungen armer Länder besondere Bedeutung zu[30].

In der Praxis spitzt sich nun die Diskussion um die politisch-gesellschaftliche Verwirklichung des Befreiungsimpetus für die lateinamerikanischen Christen auf die Frage zu: Bedeutet das Engagement für die Befreiung nicht notwendig eine politische Option für den *Sozialismus* gegen den *Kapitalismus?* Bei den himmelschreienden Zuständen, die sich in diesem Kontinent infolge des kapitalistischen Wirtschaftssystems (aber auch anderer oft übersehener Faktoren wie Klima, kulturhistorische Entwicklung, allgemeine Mentalität, Einstellung zu Leben und Arbeit, etablierte Religion) gebildet haben und die in Europa nur mit denen des ausbeutenden Manchesterliberalismus im vergangenen Jahrhundert verglichen werden können, ist die gerade unter aktiven Christen weit verbreitete Sympathie für den Sozialismus oft der einzige politische Ausweg. Und an diesem Punkt zeigt sich auch die allgemeine Bedeutung und hohe Aktualität der lateinamerikanischen theologischen Fragestellung nicht zuletzt für Asien, Afrika und auch Nordamerika[31]. Dieselbe Frage stellt sich aber auch in Europa, selbst wenn ihr führende Vertreter der »politischen Theologie« auch weithin ausweichen und dafür von ihren lateinamerikanischen Kollegen hart kritisiert werden.

Keine unkritischen Identifikationen

Freilich müssen nun auch Theologen die hier in Frage stehenden Begriffe beim Worte nehmen, soll die Sprach- und Sachverwirrung nicht noch mehr Platz greifen: Wenn *»links«* einfach die permanente Öffnung der Gesellschaft auf ihre Zukunft hin meint und *»Sozialismus«* das Eintreten für Abschaffung der Armut, für Demokratie und eine gerechtere Gesellschaft, welcher vernünftige und anständige Mensch wäre da nicht »links« und »Sozialist«? Aber solcher Sprachgebrauch verschleiert den wahren Sachverhalt: »Sozialismus«, genau gefaßt, meint eben nicht nur irgendeine soziale Demokratie = Sozialdemokratie, gegen die selbst konservative europäische Bischofskonferenzen mittlerweile genauso wenig Ernsthaftes einwenden können wie gegen bestimmte »christliche« Parteien, die ja ebenfalls für soziale Demokratie eintreten. »Sozialismus«, genau gefaßt, meint Sozialisierung, Vergesellschaftung, faktisch Verstaatlichung der Produktionsmittel und damit die Aufhebung des Privateigentums. Und genau dieser Sozialismus ist es, den viele lateinamerikanische Christen entschieden bejahen.

Aber kann gegen einen solchen Sozialismus – mindestens solange nicht elementare menschliche Grundrechte (zum Beispiel Meinungs- und Religionsfreiheit) verletzt werden – vom Evangelium Jesu Christi selber her etwas Ernsthaftes eingewendet werden? Nein. Aber vielleicht aus anderen, aus wirtschaftlichen, sozialen und politischen Gründen: Ob die Verstaatlichung der Produktionsmittel mit allen ihren Konsequenzen – Übermacht des Staates (oder der Staatspartei) und Bedrohung der Freiheit des Individuums – das große Heilmittel für Lateinamerika ist? Das bleibt auch unter lateinamerikanischen Christen wie Nichtchristen heftig umstritten – nach so vielen Jahrzehnten unglaubwürdigen Sozialismus' in Osteuropa und den neueren sozialistischen Erfahrungen in Kuba und Chile noch mehr als zuvor. Im Ziel einer sozial gerechteren Gesellschaft ist man sich einig. Aber fraglich ist die grundsätzliche Methode, die zu einer solchen Gesellschaft führt. Auf konkrete sozialistische Gesellschaftsmodelle aber wird bei aller Betonung der Wirklichkeitsnähe von seiten der Befreiungstheologie erstaunlich wenig Bezug genommen: höchstens sehr vage und allgemein wird ein spezifisch lateinamerikanischer Weg zum Sozialismus gefordert. Dabei fordert die politisch-gesellschaftliche Wirklichkeit auch in Lateinamerika (Kuba, Chile) eine solche Konkretion gebieterisch heraus, soll nicht noch mehr gutgemeintes christliches Engagement entweder vom Kommunismus überrannt oder von Militärdiktaturen abgewürgt werden. Der programmatische Praxisbezug dieser Theologie müßte die schon in unserem Einleitungskapitel nur skizzenhaft angeführte Tatsache mitreflektieren lassen: daß sich »der Kapitalismus« (für Theologen wie »der Sozialismus« vielfach eine eher mythologische Größe) als in hohem Maß reformierbar (»soziale Marktwirtschaft« mit verstärkter staatlicher Kontrolle und Steuerung) erwiesen hat. Zugleich: daß bisher weder im Westen noch im Osten, weder in der wissenschaftlichen Theorie noch in der politischen Praxis ein anderes Wirtschafts- und Gesellschaftssystem entwickelt wurde, das die Mängel eines freiheitlichen Wirtschaftssystems beseitigte, ohne andere, schlimmere Übel zu erzeugen, und das folglich besser Freiheit und Demokratie, Gerechtigkeit und Wohlstand zu garantieren vermöchte[32].

Aber es sollen hier nicht etwa vom Evangelium her undifferenziert-unkritisch das Privateigentum oder gar das »kapitalistische System« verteidigt und Sozialisierung wie Sozialismus als unchristlich hingestellt werden. Nicht nur waren die Wahrheitsmomente und das Befreiungspotential im Sozialismus und insbesondere im marxistischen Sozialismus anzuerkennen. Es war auch von vornherein zuzugeben, daß ein Christ unter Umständen (kritischer!) »Marxist«, also auch im strengen Sinn Sozialist sein kann[33]. Nur wurde auch schon damals die Einschränkung gemacht, die jetzt zu wiederholen ist: daß man nicht nur als Marxist oder Sozialist Christ sein kann. Schon die oft als Indikativ statt als Imperativ verstandene Formel »Kein Sozialismus ohne Demokratie und keine Demokratie ohne Sozialismus« (Rosa Luxemburg gegen Lenin) läßt sich weder in ihrem ersten Teil (die sozialistischen Volksrepubliken von der DDR bis China!) noch in ihrem zweiten Teil (die nicht-sozialistischen westlichen Demokratien!) aufrechterhalten. Und erst recht läßt die Formel »Christentum = Sozialismus« übersehen, daß es auch heute überzeugte Christen gibt, die nicht Sozialisten sind, daß es folglich ein praktiziertes Christentum ohne Sozialismus gibt, wie es ja auch offensichtlich einen Sozialismus ohne Christentum gibt. So muß es denn – ungeachtet aller Unpopularität links oder rechts – dabei bleiben: Ein *Christ kann Sozialist sein* (gegen »Rechts«), aber ein *Christ muß nicht Sozialist sein* (gegen »Links«). Ein Christ kann sein Engagement für die Befreiung, wie zu Beginn dieses Abschnittes skizziert, durchaus ernstnehmen und braucht das Heilmittel doch nicht in der Sozialisierung der Industrie, der Agrarwirtschaft und womöglich auch noch der Erziehung und der Kultur zu sehen.

Warum ist diese Unterscheidung wichtig – in Europa und Nordamerika ebenso wie in Südamerika? Nicht aus irgendwelchen bürgerlichen Vorurteilen und irgendeinem Parteidenken heraus. Sondern aus sachlichen und gleich noch grundsätzlicher zu entfaltenden Gründen:

a. Nur so werden die einzelnen Christen nicht parteipolitisch – sozialistisch oder dann wieder in irgendeiner Form antisozialistisch – vergewaltigt: Favorisiert die »Hierarchie« in einem bestimmten Land ausdrücklich und stillschweigend eine Partei, wird man es Christen und auch Christen in kirchlichen Ämtern nicht verbieten können, ihre Unterstützung der Gegenpartei publik zu machen und zu organisieren.

b. Nur so wird die Polarisierung der Kirche in sozialistische und nichtsozialistische Glieder und eventuell auch Gemeinden vermieden: Parteien welcher Art auch immer sollen in der kirchlichen Gemeinschaft, die ja von ihrem christlichen Programm her bewußt auf Parteien übergreifen will, möglichst vermieden werden[34].

c. Nur so wird das Evangelium nicht von hinten theologisch aufgeladen und in ein »linkes« oder dann – je nach dem Zeitgeist – wieder »rechtes« oder auch »mittleres« parteipolitisches Programm umgedeutet: Man sucht dann vergebens nach einem unterscheidend Christlichen.

Eine generelle *Überprüfung des kirchlichen Engagements* in der Gesellschaft auf nationaler oder regionaler Ebene dürfte sich heute nicht nur in Lateinamerika aufdrängen. Dabei sollte in manchen, insbesondere »katholischen« Ländern – um von Nordirland nicht zu reden – auch der freiwillige Verzicht auf zeitbedingte und überholte Privilegien (etwa im katholischen Schulwesen) erwogen werden. Will man das richtige Engagement der Kirche in der Gesellschaft provozieren, will man ein Überengagement in den einen öffentlichen Bereichen und ein Unterengagement in anderen vermeiden, so wird man sich auf

den besonderen Auftrag der Kirche – die Sache Jesu Christi
– besinnen müssen und von dorther die *Kriterien* bestimmen:

– *Der einzelne Christ muß in allen anstehenden Fragen Stellung*
  beziehen. Die Kirche als Glaubensgemeinschaft und ihre Re-
  präsentanten aber müssen nicht, können nicht und dürfen nicht
  zu allen anstehenden Fragen Stellung beziehen.
– *Die Kirche und ihre Repräsentanten dürfen, sollen und müssen*
  auch in umstrittenen Fragen der Gesellschaft dort, *aber auch*
  nur dort *öffentlich Stellung nehmen, wo sie ihr besonderer*
  Auftrag dazu ermächtigt: wo und soweit *das Evangelium Jesu*
  Christi selbst (und nicht sonst irgendeine Theorie) unzweideu-
  tig (und nicht nur halbdeutig) dazu herausfordert.

Dieses öffentliche Engagement der Kirche hat je nach Kontinent
und Land verschieden zu erfolgen. Dafür können hier keine
allgemeinen Rezepte gegeben werden; man erinnere sich an das
Kapitel ›Fraglichkeit der Normen‹. Auch die lateinamerikanischen, asiatischen und afrikanischen Christen und Kirchen haben das Recht, in ihren eigenen Fragen eigene lateinamerikanische, asiatische, afrikanische Lösungen zu entwickeln, an denen
sie keine kirchliche Zentrale hindern sollte. Entsprechend den
obigen Grundsätzen dürfte ein gesellschaftliches Engagement
der Kirchen – etwa in Fragen wie Überbevölkerung, Friede und
Abrüstung, Rassentrennung, soziale Mißstände – vermutlich
schon öfter erfolgen, als man auf der »Rechten« wünscht! Und
etwas weniger oft, als man auf der »Linken« drängt! Vielfach
wird man bei der komplexen Sachproblematik vom Evangelium
her über die Angabe der entscheidenden Maßstäbe zum Handeln
nicht hinauskommen und auf die Angabe bestimmter fertiger
Lösungen verzichten müssen. Alle kirchlichen Proklamationen
und Aktionen sollten freilich möglichst sachbezogen, unprätentiös und realistisch sein. Bei den kirchlichen Aktionen aber wird
es heute weniger denn je darum gehen können, jegliche kirchliche Initiativen und Aktionen im gesellschaftlichen Bereich
möglichst sofort zu institutionalisieren und als Machtposition
auszubauen. Die Kirchen sollten als bewegliche »Feuerwehr«
agieren dort, wo und solange niemand anderer hilft und folglich
besonderer, möglichst unkonventioneller Einsatz nottut. Von
daher könnte ein Grundsatz der katholischen Soziallehre, das
Subsidiaritätsprinzip (»Hilfe zur Selbsthilfe«), neue Bedeutung
bekommen. Die Kirchen haben sich im Lauf der Jahrhunderte im

Gesundheitswesen, im Bildungssektor und im gesamten sozialen Bereich im Dienst der Menschen unbestreitbare und unabsehbare Verdienste erworben: Aufgaben freilich, die heute vielfach vom Staat oder von Verbänden übernommen wurden. Sollte es in irgendeiner Zeit an neuen und vielleicht zentraleren Aufgaben für die Kirche im Dienst an den Menschen mangeln?

Daß eine unkritische Identifikation der Kirchen mit politischen Parteien unbedingt zu vermeiden ist, wird auch in Lateinamerika gefordert. Es gibt mehrere Optionen. Im Entscheidenden gibt es vom Evangelium Jesu Christi her gewiß keine Neutralität: »Heute sind sich in Lateinamerika ... die Unterdrückten und Verstoßenen ihrer Nöte und Leiden bewußt geworden, und niemand kann es dulden, daß diese Verhältnisse weiterdauern, ohne daß man eifrig auf Abhilfe bedacht ist ...« Bezüglich der konkreten Lösung aber hat die Kirche sich nicht auf ein bestimmtes politisches Aktionsprogramm festzulegen, sondern muß grundsätzlich für verschiedene Optionen offen sein: »Die Kirche respektiert alle Optionen, die bei der Wahl dieser eifrigen Abhilfe möglich sind, sofern sie nur dem Ruf der Unterdrückten, Armen und Notleidenden nach Befreiung entsprechen, dem Ruf, den Jesus Christus selbst in seiner Person lebendig verkörpert[35].«

Der Ruf, den Jesus Christus selbst in seiner Person lebendig verkörpert: das unterscheidend Christliche muß überall Kriterium bleiben! Nie dürfen sich Christen mit irgendeiner Partei, Institution oder auch Kirche *total* identifizieren. Nur totalitäre Systeme verlangen totale Identifikation. Nie dürfen Christen unkritisch in jeden Ruf der Zeit einstimmen. Nur *partikulare* Identifikation ist verantwortbar: *sofern* diese Partei, Institution oder Kirche dem christlichen Kriterium entspricht oder zumindest nicht eindeutig widerspricht.

Freilich, es gibt im konkreten Leben des Individuums und der Gesellschaft, vor allem in der harten, Leben gegen Leben stellenden Konfrontation, außerordentlich schwierige, in der ganzen Problematik unentwirrbare Fälle, ausgesprochene Zwangs- und Notlagen, in denen jede allgemeine Verhaltensregel, in denen selbst eine letzte Berufung auf Jesus Christus zu versagen scheint. Was tun etwa, wenn die *Gewalt* übermächtig ist und Menschen ins Unglück stürzt? Was tun, wenn zahllose Menschen unter der »strukturellen«, »institutionalisierten« Gewalt eines äußerlich (staatspolitisch und wirtschaftlich) funktionierenden, aber eindeutig unmenschlichen grausamen Systems zu leiden haben? Konnte ein Attentat auf Hitler nicht gerade ernsthaften Christen wie Dietrich Bonhoeffer als Pflicht erscheinen? Kann nicht gewaltsame Revolution in einer bestimmten sozialen und politischen Notlage wie in einzelnen lateinamerikanischen Staaten als einziger Ausweg erscheinen? Vielleicht ja, wer will das abstrakt von vornherein entscheiden?

Gewaltherrschaft, ob willkürlich oder institutionalisiert, erzeugt früher oder später Gegengewalt. So bleibt denn in manchen Staaten aus Gründen der Vernunft und des Gemeinwohls vielleicht nur die konsequente Revolution, Entmachtung, Enteignung oder gar in Kauf genommene Tötung unmenschlicher Machthaber übrig, wenn man gerechtere, demokratischere, menschlichere Zustände erreichen oder zumindest ermöglichen will. Nach solchen Maßstäben mag Gewalt in einem Grenzfall als Notwehr, falls überhaupt sinnvoll, gerade noch zu rechtfertigen sein: für den Einzelnen, eine Gruppe oder eine Nation. Als Herausforderung allerdings für jeden, der zur Gewalt greift, bleibt festzuhalten: Auf Jesus von Nazaret wird er sich dabei nicht berufen können. Wer gewaltsam vorgeht, tritt ein in den Teufelskreis von Gewalt und Gegengewalt. Die Opfer und Risiken sind unkalkulierbar. Nicht nur werden nach fehlgeschlagenen Revolutionen Unterdrückung und Gewaltherrschaft meist nur noch härter. Selbst dann, wenn die Revolution gelingt, ändern sich oft nur die Machthaber, nicht aber die Probleme und die Unterdrückung.

Eine »Theologie der Revolution«, irgendeine theologische Verklärung der gewaltsamen Revolution wird man deshalb besser nicht propagieren. Seit Jesus ist es schwer geworden, Gott im Geschehen solcher Befreiung zu finden, die zugleich Geschehen von Gewalt ist. Gewalt mag in einem Grenzfall als Notwehr gerade noch zu rechtfertigen sein: für den Einzelnen, eine Gruppe oder eine Nation. Aber mehr Anlaß als zur Feier der Revolution wird man in solchen Fällen, wo Blut, vielleicht durchaus schuldiges Blut, fließen »mußte«, Anlaß zur Bitte um Vergebung haben. Nicht als eine positiv anzustrebende Aktion ist der allfällige Gebrauch von Gewalt zu rechtfertigen, sondern bestenfalls als eine gerade noch zu verantwortende Re-aktion im Sinne der Notwehr. Und es wird selbst dann – im »gerechten« Krieg oder in der »gerechten« Revolution – immer Christen geben, die mit Berufung auf Jesus Christus es auch da ablehnen, Gewalt zu gebrauchen: »Ich ziehe es tausendmal vor, mich töten zu lassen, als selbst zu töten« (Hélder Câmara, Erzbischof von Recife/Brasilien[36]).

Von Jesus Christus her läßt sich keine Strategie der Gewalt, sondern nur eine der Gewaltlosigkeit ableiten, wie dies nicht nur Hélder Câmara und Martin Luther King, sondern auch Mahatma Gandhi und viele andere sehr wohl verstanden und politisch wirksam gemacht haben[37]. *Gewaltlosigkeit* kann sich immer auf *Jesus Christus* berufen, *Gewaltgebrauch* vielleicht im Notfall auf die *Vernunft*. Gebrauch von Gewalt, Rache, Unterdrückung, Unversöhnlichkeit, Haß: das ist zwar nicht human, aber menschlich, allzu menschlich. Verzicht auf Gewalt, Verzicht auf den Willen zur Rache, Bereitschaft zur Schonung des Gegners, Bereitschaft zur allumfassenden Verzeihung, entschiedenes Wirken für Versöhnung und selbstloses Wohlwollen: das ist die eigentliche Herausforderung, die von Jesus Christus her ergeht. Eine Herausforderung zum wahrhaft Menschlichen, zum Humanen! Und zwar eine Herausforderung für beide Seiten: für die Garanten des Status quo repressiver »struktureller« Gewalt ebenso wie für die Aufrührer, die Gewalt als Mittel ihrer Politik einkalkulieren.

Sollte nicht gerade der Aufruf zur Gewaltlosigkeit, Schonung, ja Liebe in den großen gesellschaftlichen Auseinandersetzungen zwischen Berlin, Rio de Janeiro und Santiago de Chile noch einmal andere Möglichkeiten eröffnen? Ein letztes Mal sei eine Stimme der lateinamerikanischen »Theologie der Befreiung« zitiert: »Diese Christen sehen in ihrer Glaubenspraxis eine Garantie dafür, daß ihre Entschlüsse von der Liebe bestimmt werden, daß ihre Optionen den Sinn für die Personwürde und die ethischen Werte bewahren und daß sie selbst sich von bloß pragmatischem Denken und von macchiavellistischen politischen Methoden freihalten. Dadurch wird die Intensität ihres Einsetzens und ihre Scharfsicht keineswegs beeinträchtigt. Ihre christliche Lebensausrichtung ermöglicht es ihnen, über die Parolen der Politiker hinauszugehen und Wege zur Befreiung zu finden, die schöpferischer, menschlicher und brüderlicher sind[38].«

2. Die Bewältigung des Negativen

Die positiv aufgeladenen Reizworte der Befreiungstheologie klingen noch im Ohr: Liebe, Sinn, Personwürde, Werte, Befreiung, menschlich, schöpferisch, brüderlich. Doch: Diese Worte

sind Schall und Rauch, wenn sie nicht durchgeprüft, durchgestanden sind durch das, was man die Schattenseite des Lebens
nennt: Haß und Unsinn, Unwürde und Wertlosigkeit, Unfreiheit und Unmenschlichkeit, Erstarrung und Feindschaft in der
Banalität des öffentlichen und privaten Alltags. Hier steht nicht
mehr und nicht weniger als die Frage nach Mensch und Menschsein, Humanität und Humanismus auf dem Spiel. Hier bekommen Engagement und politischer Enthusiasmus eine Tiefen-
schärfe, die eine alltäglich-pragmatische Oberflächlichkeit nicht
hergibt. Hier steht die Frage nach Menschsein und Christsein in
ihrer ganzen Radikalität auf dem Spiel. In der Bewältigung des
Negativen haben christlicher Glaube und nichtchristliche Humanismen ihre Nagelprobe zu bestehen.

Mißbrauchtes Kreuz

Was für ein unerforschliches Rätsel für den Menschen das Leid,
die Leidensgeschichte der Menschheit und jedes Einzelnen, bedeutet, haben wir bereits betrachtet. Und ebenso die vielfältigen,
oft tiefgehenden mythologischen, philosophischen, theologischen Entwürfe, die das Rätsel aufzulösen versuchen[1]. Wie wichtig in diesem Zusammenhang der neuzeitliche Emanzipations-
oder Befreiungsprozeß ist, wurde uns eben von Lateinamerika
her noch sehr viel elementarer und konkreter vor Augen geführt:
Der Mensch muß sein Geschick in die eigene Verantwortung
nehmen und in der Umgestaltung der menschlichen Gesellschaft
sich selbst zu befreien versuchen. Emanzipation läßt sich nicht
durch Erlösung ersetzen.

Freilich auch umgekehrt: Erlösung läßt sich nicht durch
Emanzipation ersetzen. Kein Mensch kann sich der Frage des
ungetrösteten Leids der Lebenden und Toten entziehen, der
Frage seiner Schuld und seines Todes und damit einer letzten
Befreiung des Menschen: einer Befreiung durch Gott (Erlösung),
gegenüber der die Befreiung des Menschen durch den Menschen
(Emanzipation) immer nur vorläufigen Charakter haben kann.
Wie sonst soll er sich von Schuld befreit, für Zeit und Ewigkeit
angenommen, zu sinnvollem Leben und vorbehaltlosem Einsatz
für Mitmensch und Gesellschaft befreit wissen? Wie soll er in
sinnlosem Leiden und Sterben, im Leid auch der Unschuldigen
und Gescheiterten dennoch einen Sinn finden?

Was sagen wir dem gescheiterten Revolutionär, was dem Gefangenen, der sich selbst in Ketten noch seine Freiheit bewahren möchte, was dem zum Tod Verurteilten, der nach einer Hoffnung verlangt? Aber auch weniger dramatisch und vielleicht doch nicht weniger schlimm: Was sagen wir dem Menschen, der unlösbar in bestimmte gesellschaftliche Strukturen verkettet ist, in denen Revolutionen keine Aussicht auf Erfolg haben? Was dem unheilbar Kranken, was dem auf eine einmal getroffene Fehlentscheidung Festgelegten, was dem beruflichen, moralischen, menschlichen Versager?

Kann man gegen alle Versuchung der Empörung, Revolte, Resignation und des Zynismus etwas anderes sagen, als es wie Hiob zu wagen: in unerschütterlichem, unbedingtem Vertrauen trotz allem Ja zu sagen, Ja zum unbegreiflichen Gott? Und doch – man kann auch noch etwas anderes sagen:

daß alles Negative in diesem Leben einen positiven Sinn haben *kann;*

daß es keine *absolut* trostlose, sinnlose, verzweifelte Situation zu geben braucht;

daß nicht nur in Erfolg und Freude, sondern auch in Versagen, in der Melancholie, in Trauer und Schmerz Gottesbegegnung *möglich* ist.

Dies alles wage ich zu sagen im Blick auf die Passion dessen, von dem her die Passion eines jeden Menschen genauso wie die Menschheitspassion einen Sinn erhalten kann: mit dem Blick auf den Gekreuzigten glaubend vertrauend auf den, der auch und gerade – das ist das Zeugnis der Auferweckung – in äußerster Bedrohung, Sinnlosigkeit, Nichtigkeit, Verlassenheit, Einsamkeit und Leere den Menschen trägt und hält: ein Gott, der als Mit-Betroffener mit den Menschen solidarisch ist. Aber es soll hier nichts unnötig wiederholt werden, was ausführlich entwickelt worden ist[2]. Das Kreuz des Lebendigen ist es, woraufhin der Glaubende sich zum Wagnis der Hoffnung im Dunklen und Sinnlosen entschließen kann: zur Kreuzesnachfolge!

Kreuzesnachfolge: Leider ist gerade dieses Tiefste und Stärkste im Christentum in Verruf gekommen durch die »Frommen«, die, wie Nietzsche höhnte, als »Dunkler und Munkler und Ofenhocker« krumm »zum Kreuze kriechen« und alt- und kaltgeworden alle »Morgen-Tapferkeit« verloren haben[3].

Und so meint denn »zu Kreuze kriechen« im heutigen Sprachgebrauch so etwas wie klein beigeben, sich nicht trauen, nachgeben, stumm den Nacken beugen, sich ducken, unterwerfen, ergeben. Und »sein Kreuz tragen« meint dann ebenfalls: sich ergeben, sich demütigen, sich verkriechen, sich nicht mucksen, die Fäuste in die Tasche stecken ... Das Kreuz, ein Zeichen für Schwächlinge und Duckmäuser. Dies war doch wohl nicht gemeint, wenn Paulus das Kreuz zwar für die Heiden einen Unsinn und die Juden ein Skandal, für die Glaubenden aber eine »Gotteskraft« nannte[4]!

Offizielle Verkündiger des Wortes haben zu einem nicht geringen Teil die Schuld, wenn die »Frommen« das Kreuz als Entwürdigung des Menschen mißverstehen. Wie viel Schindluder hat man mit dem Kreuz getrieben! Wozu mußte das Kreuz in den Kirchen alles herhalten! Man hat sich nachgerade daran gewöhnt, daß das Kreuz nicht als Bürde auf dem Rücken, sondern als Würde auf dem Bauch (»Pectorale«: bischöfliches Brustkreuz seit dem 12. Jahrhundert nachweisbar, seit 1570 für die Messe vorgeschrieben, aber jetzt auch außerliturgisch verwendet, seit der Barockzeit immer größer und prunkvoller) getragen und dieses zentrale christliche Schand- und Siegeszeichen als serienweise verabreichter bischöflicher Segensgestus verfeierlicht und verharmlost wird. Woran man sich aber zum Beispiel nicht gewöhnen sollte: daß Hierarchen, die ihr eigenes Wort gerne mit Christi und Gottes Wort identifizieren, das Kreuz als »großen und dunklen Ratschluß Gottes« anpreisen, der zu Buße und anderen unerfindlichen Zwecken den Menschen »Schweres schickt«, und die so den »Willen zum Leiden« in Gott und Jesus hineinprojizieren. Warum und aus welchem Interesse? Um auf diese Weise moderne Werte (Lebensstandard, Mündigkeit, Strukturveränderung, Weltbejahung, intellektuelle Redlichkeit) und aktiven Einsatz für diese Werte in der Gesellschaft zu diskreditieren; um in diesem Zusammenhang die Lasten kirchlicher Traditionen wie Zölibat und anderes als gottgewollte Kreuze zu rechtfertigen; um in all dem die Gegner ihrer autoritären Kirchenleitung – die eigenen Pfarrer, Kapläne, Laien und deren »Lieblingstheologen« – der »Entleerung des Kreuzes« zu verdächtigen[5]. Das Kreuz als Holzhammer: was Paulus, freilich noch nicht Kardinal, wohl zu solcher Kreuzespredigt gesagt hätte!? Es soll hier bestimmt niemand in seiner Gesinnung gekränkt und in seinen seelsorgerlichen Intentionen angezweifelt werden. Es muß jedoch in diesem ernsten Zusammenhang, wo so viel Gedankenlosigkeit die Praxis bestimmt, doch auch sehr entschieden – opportune importune – Ehrfurcht vor dem Kreuz gefordert werden.

Aber dieses eine repräsentative Beispiel – man möge es nicht (wie so oft) dem verübeln, der davon berichtet – mag genügen: Wir möchten uns hier nicht mit den zahllosen primitiven Entstellungen der Kreuzesnachfolge aufhalten, so folgenschwer sie sich für den Einzelnen wie für ganze Kirchengebiete auswirken können. Drei sublimere Mißverständnisse der Kreuzespredigt aber, oft kritisiert[6], müssen um der echten Kreuzesnachfolge willen aufgezeigt werden.

1. Kreuzesnachfolge meint *nicht kultische Anbetung*: Wir sahen bereits: Jesu Kreuz sprengt alle Schemata von Opfertheologie und Kultpraxis[7]. Die Profanität seines Kreuzes sperrt sich gegen jede kultische Vereinnahmung und liturgische Glorifizierung des Gekreuzigten.

Freilich: man wird dem Kreuzessymbol und einer richtig verstandenen evangeliumsgemäßen Kreuzes-Verehrung zum Beispiel in der Karfreitagsliturgie seinen Respekt nicht versagen können. Und natürlich auch nicht·der großen Kunst, die um dieses zentrale christliche Thema – freilich erst nach jahrhundertelanger Scheu – mit letztem Ernst gerungen hat[8].

Aber machen wir die Probe:

Wird nicht vom Kreuz Jesu Christi her jener oft auf reinen Ritualismus zusammengeschrumpfte Gestus fragwürdig, der das Kreuz auf ein bloßes, tausendfach gedankenlos repetiertes Kreuz-Zeichen reduziert und oft zum magischen Zeichen herabwürdigt?

Wird von diesem Kreuz her nicht selbst das Kruzifix an der Wand fragwürdig, wenn daraus für die Praxis nichts folgt und man sich mit solchem Traditions- und Schmuckstück vom Kreuz Christi zu entlasten sucht?

Wird von diesem Kreuz her nicht jene clevere Devotionalienindustrie fragwürdig, die, spekulierend mit Glauben und Aberglauben, das Kreuz der billigen Kommerzialisierung ausliefert?

Es bleibt dabei: Für den, der sich ernsthaft auf Jesu Weg einläßt, kann das Kreuz Jesu nicht kultisch oder fromm für jedwede Interessen vereinnahmt werden. Jesu Kreuz bleibt das Skandalon, in dessen Zeichen die Schranken von Profan und Sakral endgültig gefallen sind. Das ist und bleibt eine Herausforderung für jeden, der in diesem Zeichen Gottesdienst feiert, Eucharistia, memoria passionis. Die liturgische Feier im Zeichen des Kreuzes darf nicht folgenlos bleiben. Dem Gedächtnis muß die praktische Nachfolge entsprechen.

2. Kreuzesnachfolge meint *nicht mystische Versenkung*: kein in Gebet und Meditation verkrampftes privatisiertes Miterleiden auf gleicher Ebene im Einswerden mit Jesu seelisch-leiblichen Schmerzen. Das wäre falsch verstandene Kreuzesmystik.

Doch auch hier: Respekt vor der großen Leidens- und Kreuzesmystik eines Franz von Assisi, Bonaventura oder eines Ignatius von Loyola, Johannes vom Kreuz, einer Teresa von Avila.

Respekt auch vor dem kritisch-emanzipatorischen Impuls, den die vom Kreuz inspirierte Laienfrömmigkeit in Kirche und Gesellschaft hineinbrachte: von den mittelalterlichen Armutsbewegungen bis zu den Negro Spirituals schwarzer Sklaven in den amerikanischen Südstaaten wurde hier der leidende, arme, schutzlose Christus gegen den himmlisch herrschenden Christus der Reichen und Mächtigen gewendet.

Respekt auch vor jenem echten religiösen Brauchtum, das etwa in den Stationen des Kreuzwegs die Erinnerung an diesen Jesus Christus in unverkrampfter, befreiender Meditation ohne alle Selbstquälerei aktiviert.

Aber machen wir auch hier die Probe:

Wird nicht von diesem Kreuz Jesu Christi her jene Mystik fragwürdig, die in frommer Verniedlichung und Verkitschung die Radikalität des Leidens Jesu, seine Gottes- und Menschenverlassenheit verharmlost?

Wird nicht von diesem Kreuz her jene Mystik fragwürdig, die in frommer Selbstbemitleidung das eigene oft selbst verschuldete Leid mit dem Leiden Christi larmoyant bedauert oder die eigenen Schmerzen mit Jesu Schmerzen heroisiert?

Wird also nicht von diesem Kreuz her jene Mystik fragwürdig, die das Gefühl für Abstand und Ehrfurcht vor dem Kreuz und dem Leid dieses Einen nicht mehr kennt, die allzu rasch die einzigartige Distanz nivelliert und aus der passiven Fügung in das Leid jegliches Tun zur Beseitigung der Ursachen des Leids im eigenen Leben und in der Gesellschaft vernachlässigt?

Es bleibt dabei: Für den, der sich ernsthaft auf Jesu Weg einläßt, läßt sich das Kreuz Jesu Christi nicht in frommer Anbiederung und Verniedlichung, nicht in Privatisierung und Nivellierung einholen. Es ist und bleibt Herausforderung zum Glauben an Gott auch in der Abwesenheit. Aber an einen Gott, der den Menschen nicht sadistisch quält, sondern mit ihm mitleidet.

Herausforderung zum Glauben an Jesus Christus, der nicht der schwächliche Dulder, sondern der mutige Bruder aller Armen, Gequälten und Geängstigten war, in dessen Gemeinschaft die Erniedrigten Erhöhung, Achtung, Anerkennung, menschliche Würde finden. Von ihm her ist das Kreuz ambivalent: Ausdruck des Elends und zugleich des Protests gegen das Elend, Zeichen des Todes und Zeichen des Sieges.

3. Kreuzesnachfolge meint *nicht ethische Nachahmung* des Lebensweges Jesu, meint nicht die getreue Kopie des Lebensmodells seines Lebens, Verkündigens und Sterbens.

Doch auch hier:

Respekt vor den großen Einzelnen, von Franz von Assisi bis Leo Tolstoi und Martin Luther King, die im Verzicht auf Besitz oder Gewalt diesem Jesus als Vorbild unmittelbar nachgegangen und unübersehbare programmatische Zeichen christlichen Handelns gesetzt haben.

Respekt vor der Tradition großer Märtyrer des Christentums, die in ihrer Selbstverleugnung, ihrem Mut und ihrer radikalen Konsequenz diesem Jesus im Leiden gleich werden wollten.

Respekt aber auch vor der großen Tradition des Mönchtums, das vor allem im Mittelalter von der Imitatio Christi her sich zu tiefgreifenden Reformen in Kirche und Gesellschaft inspirieren ließ und seine Lebensprinzipien der Heimatlosigkeit, Ehelosigkeit und Besitzlosigkeit von Christus her direkt ableitete.

Doch machen wir hier ebenfalls die Probe:

Wird nicht vom Kreuz Jesu Christi her jene Imitatio fragwürdig, mit der fromme Opferseelen das Leiden förmlich suchen bis zum Extrem der physischen Nachahmung in einem mehr als fragwürdigen Wunden- und Stigmatisierungskult (Therese von Konnersreuth[9]); mehr als fragwürdig jegliche Art von Heiligmachung zu Lebzeiten, wo man sich Verdienste im Himmel anrechnen lassen und sich vorzeitig das Heil sichern will?

Wird von diesem Kreuz her nicht jene Nachahmung fragwürdig, die anmaßend glaubt, mit Jesus als dem großen Führer sein Kreuz nachvollziehen, seinen Weg aus eigener Leistung sich zutrauen und in Bewunderung und blindem Enthusiasmus Zeit und Situation überspringend sein Leiden miterleiden zu können?

Es bleibt dabei: Für den, der sich ernsthaft auf den Weg Jesu Christi einläßt, entzieht sich das Kreuz jeder billigen Kopie, jeder heroischen Imitation, die Sicherheit verschaffen könnte. Sein Kreuz bleibt beispiellos, seine Gottes- und Menschenverlassenheit einzigartig, sein Tod unwiederholbar. Schon bei Paulus[10] bedeutet Imitatio Christi nicht einfach die »Nachahmung des irdischen Jesus in einzelnen Zügen oder nach seinem Gesamteindruck«[11], um ihm immer ähnlicher zu werden. Für Paulus meint Imitatio Christi wesentlich Gehorsam dem himmlischen Herrn gegenüber, der sich im Konkreten zu bewähren hat: ein Nachahmen, das nicht ein Imitieren, sondern ein ihm Nachfolgen bedeutet. Nachahmer sein heißt für Paulus nichts anderes als: Jünger sein. Nicht das also ist der Sinn der Nachfolge, genauso von Gott und Menschen verlassen werden, die gleichen Schmerzen erleiden, die gleichen Wunden geschlagen bekommen. Sondern im Gegenteil, gerade indem sich das Kreuz der Kopie entzieht, ist und bleibt es eine Herausforderung: das eigene Kreuz auf sich zu nehmen, im Risiko der eigenen Situation und in der Ungewißheit der Zukunft seinen eigenen Weg zu gehen.

Verstandenes Kreuz

Am Kreuz hängen viele: nicht nur gescheiterte Revolutionäre, Gefangene, zum Tod Verurteilte, nicht nur die unheilbar Kranken, die völligen Versager, die Lebensmüden und die an sich selbst und an der Welt Verzweifelten. Am Kreuz hängen viele: von Sorgen gequält und von Mitmenschen geplagt, von Ansprüchen erdrückt und von Langeweile ausgehöhlt, von Angst gepreßt und von Haß vergiftet, von Freunden vergessen und von den Medien verschwiegen ... Ja, hängt nicht jeder an seinem eigenen Kreuz?

Oft ist Schweigen angebrachter angesichts des unartikulierbaren Leidens. Wie oft einem die Antworten im Munde stecken bleiben, wie schwer der Trost zu buchstabieren ist, hat jeder in seinem eigenen Leben erfahren können angesichts von Krankheit und Tod, angesichts all der Fragen des Warum und Wozu. Doch gerade auch die Erfahrung dieser extremen menschlichen Situationen drängt zum Wort, drängt zur klärenden, tröstenden, verarbeitenden Sprache. Trauerarbeit tut not, und sie ist bei aller materiellen und seelischen Hilfe wesentlich sprachlich strukturiert. Der Christ steht vom Kreuz Christi her nicht stumm da, ohne Antwort, obwohl gerade hier vor allem Formelhaften zu warnen ist. Der Christ steht nicht stumm da, wenn er den Gekreuzigten sprechen läßt.

Was hat er zu sagen? Inwiefern soll er helfen? Wenn schon

keine kultische Adoratio, wenn schon keine mystische Unio, wenn schon keine ethische Imitatio, was soll da helfen? Wenn man es ganz nüchtern sagen will: die Nachfolge, die Nachfolge in der Weise der Correlatio, der Entsprechung? Was heißt das?

1. *Das Leid nicht suchen, sondern ertragen:* Jesus hat das Leid nicht gesucht, es wurde ihm aufgezwungen. Wer immer selbstquälerisch Schmerz und Leid geradewegs herbeisehnt oder gar sich selber zufügt, ist nicht auf der Linie der Kreuzesnachfolge Jesu. Schmerz ist und bleibt Schmerz, Leid ist und bleibt Leid: das soll man nicht umdeuten, ihm gar masochistisch Lust abgewinnen wollen. Leid und Schmerz sind und bleiben ein Angriff auf den Menschen. Der Christ aber kann kein Liebhaber der Traurigkeit sein, wie dies gerade der Genußmensch in seltsamem Umschlag seiner zur Schau getragenen Lebensgier und Lebenslust – »Bonjour tristesse«! – nur zu leicht werden kann.

Kreuzesnachfolge heißt nicht Nachahmung des Leidens Jesu, nicht Nachvollzug seines Kreuzes. Was wäre das anderes als Anmaßung! Wohl aber: ertragen des gerade *mir* in meiner unverwechselbaren Situation *widerfahrenen* Leids – in *Entsprechung* zum Leiden Christi! Wer mit Jesus gehen will, der verleugne *sich selbst* und nehme nicht Jesu Kreuz auf sich, auch nicht irgendein Kreuz, sondern *sein*, sein eigenes Kreuz auf sich und folge ihm nach[12]. Nicht in mönchischer Askese oder in romantischem Heroismus außerordentliches Leid suchen, ist christlich. Sondern – was wegen seiner öfteren Wiederkehr meist schwieriger ist als ein heroischer Akt – das gewöhnliche, das normale, das alltägliche und gerade hier dann freilich oft übergroße Leid ertragen: das ist dem an den Gekreuzigten Glaubenden aufgetragen. Also das Kreuz des Alltags[13]! Wie wenig erbaulich und selbstverständlich das gemeint ist, wird jedem klar, der erfahren hat, wie oft der Mensch sich von seinem eigenen Kreuz, all seinen täglichen Verpflichtungen, Forderungen, Ansprüchen, Versprechen in Familie und Beruf zu drücken oder sein Kreuz abzuschieben oder zu verdrängen versucht. Von daher wird das Kreuz Jesu zu einem Kriterium für selbstkritisches Erkennen und selbstkritisches Handeln.

2. *Das Leid nicht nur ertragen, sondern bekämpfen:* Eine stoische Leidensapathie, die ein möglichst affektloses Ertragen der eigenen Leiderfahrungen und das überlegene Vorbeiziehenlassen fremden Leids ohne innere Anteilnahme als Ideal verkündet,

steht ebenfalls nicht auf der Linie der Kreuzesnachfolge Jesu. Sowohl seinem eigenen wie fremdem Leid gegenüber hat Jesus seinen Schmerz nicht unterdrückt. Zeichenhaft ist er gegen die Mächte des Bösen, der Krankheit und des Todes in der so gar nicht heilen Welt angegangen[14]. Die Botschaft Jesu kulminiert in der Nächstenliebe[15], unvergeßlich eingeprägt in der Parabel von der Pflege des unter die Räuber Gefallenen[16] und im kritischen Maßstab des Endgerichts: Einsatz für die Hungernden, Dürstenden, Nackten, die Fremden, Kranken und Gefangenen[17].

Von daher hat die junge Glaubensgemeinschaft die tatkräftige Sorge um die Leidenden von Anfang an als eine besondere Aufgabe erkannt. So ist gerade die planmäßige Sorge für die Kranken eine von den Weltreligionen unterscheidende spezifisch christliche Angelegenheit geworden: von der durch Bischof und Diakone organisierten und geübten Krankenpflege der frühen Gemeinden und den im 4. Jahrhundert entstehenden Nosokomien über die mittelalterliche Krankenpflege der Klöster, insbesondere seit der clunyazensischen Reform, die ritterlichen und bürgerlichen Spitalorden bis zur modernen Krankenpflege der katholischen und evangelischen Orden und Kongregationen. Dabei lag es in der Konsequenz der historischen Entwicklung, daß der Kirche durch den Säkularisierungsprozeß viele dieser Aufgaben abgenommen wurden, die sie aus der Not heraus übernommen hatte. Um so mehr ist es Aufgabe und Pflicht der Christen und der Kirchen in der modernen Gesellschaft, an der vielschichtigen Bekämpfung des Leids, der Armut, des Hungers, der sozialen Mißstände, der Krankheit und des Todes engagiert mitzuarbeiten. Die moderne Welt hat sehr viel neues Leid gebracht, aber auch immense Möglichkeiten der Bewältigung des Leids geschaffen, wie dies die Erfolge der Medizin, der Hygiene, der Technik, der sozialen Wohlfahrt demonstrieren. Nie wird der Christ Argumente seines Glaubens dafür bemühen, um sich von der tätigen Mitarbeit in der Gesellschaft zu dispensieren und, statt die gesellschaftliche Wirklichkeit zu verändern, auf ein Jenseits zu vertrösten. Der Glaube an Gott, das Gebet, das immer Grundlage seiner Arbeit sein wird, werden nie ein Refugium sein dürfen für einen defaitistischen, dem Leid gegenüber resignierenden oder auch nur himmlisch träumenden Christen. Nüchternheit und Realistik in der Einschätzung der immer beschränkten persönlichen und gesellschaftlichen Möglichkeiten für die Änderung von Verhältnissen sind notwendig, um den Christen im

Bekämpfen des Leides vor einem leidvergessenen Pragmatismus und einem illusionären Aktionismus zu bewahren.

3. *Das Leid nicht nur bekämpfen, sondern verarbeiten:* Vom Kreuz Jesu Christi her wird den Menschen die Möglichkeit eröffnet, das Leid und seine Ursachen nicht nur punktuell aufzulösen und zu beseitigen, sondern auch positiv zu verwandeln und zu verarbeiten. Das setzt Erfahrung im Erkennen von Ursachen und Bedingungen, Zusammenhängen und Strukturen menschlichen Leidens voraus. Und Phantasie im Entwerfen von Zukunftsmöglichkeiten eines weniger leidvollen Zustandes des Menschen, im Spenden von Trost, im Eingehen auf die Bedürfnisse und die seelische Verfassung dessen, der mich gerade braucht, meines Nächsten, meiner Nächsten. Diese Phantasie verschafft sich in der Sprache Ausdruck und vermag so, die Kruste alles dumpfen, stummen, sprachlosen Leidens aufzubrechen, von der alles Leid so oft zugedeckt ist. Das auf den Anderen eingehende Gespräch ermöglicht es, alles Spontane und Elementare des Schmerzes, das Stöhnen und das Schreien, das Jammern und das Seufzen, die Resignation und die Ohnmacht bewußt zu machen, Zusammenhänge zu erkennen und Ursachen zu analysieren. Es vermag das Bewußtsein zu schaffen, daß Leid bedingt und damit auch vielfach wandelbar ist, nicht nur schicksalsverhängt oder einfach gottgegeben. Das Gespräch holt den Einzelnen heraus aus der Isolierung des privat erlebten und im Privaten steckengebliebenen Leids und macht ihn fähig zur Verarbeitung in der Gemeinschaft aller Betroffenen. Verarbeitung aber bedeutet auch positive, aktive Annahme und Integrierung des Leids in den Gesamtsinn des Lebens. »Es ist unmöglich, sich dem Leiden vollständig zu verweigern, es sei denn, man verweigere sich dem Leben überhaupt, man ginge keine Verhältnisse mehr ein, man machte aus sich einen Unverwundbaren. Schmerzen, Verluste, Amputationen sind auch im glattesten Lebenslauf, den man sich denken, nicht wünschen mag, gegeben – die Ablösung von den Eltern, das Verwelken der Jugendfreundschaften, das Absterben bestimmter Gestalten des Lebens, mit dem wir uns identifiziert haben, das Altern, das Wegsterben der Angehörigen und Freunde, schließlich der Tod. Je stärker wir die Realität bejahen, je mehr wir in sie hineingetaucht sind, desto tiefer werden wir von diesen uns umgebenden und in uns eindringenden Prozessen des Sterbens berührt[18].«

Wir haben es hier mit einem Phänomen zu tun, das eine breite

Bezeugung gefunden hat durch zahllose Christen, die so jenseits aller billigen Tröstung ihr Christsein und Menschsein gelebt haben. Zahllose unheilbar Kranke, die durch ihre Krankheit ein neues Verhältnis zu sich entdeckten. Zahllose Menschen, denen sich durch eigenes Unglück, durch den Verlust oder auch Verrat eines geliebten Menschen eine neue Erfahrungsdimension ihres Lebens eröffnete. Zahllose Menschen, die durch alle Enttäuschungen, Trennungen, Fehlschläge, Mißerfolge, Demütigungen, Zurücksetzungen und Mißachtungen ihr Leben zu einer neuen Qualität des Selbst verwandelten: die durch Leid hindurch reifer, erfahrener, bescheidener, im echten Sinn demütiger, offener für den Anderen, kurz, menschlicher wurden.

Leiden also braucht nicht und gerade für den Christen nicht ein passiv zu ertragendes Geschick zu sein, ein Fatum, ein Schicksal, in das er sich zu fügen hätte. »Leiden ist eine Art Veränderung, die der Mensch erfährt, sie ist ein Modus des Werdens[19].« Das Werden auf ein größeres, höheres, freieres Endziel hin. Woher aber hat der Christ diese ungeheuerliche Gewißheit jenseits von Vertröstung und Verharmlosung, von Ignorieren und Revoltieren?

4. *Freiheit im Leid:* Mit dem Blick auf Jesus bleibt der Mensch bei der mit allen Mitteln vollzogenen Bekämpfung des Leids realistisch. Er wird nie der Illusion verfallen, als ob es durch technologische Entwicklungen oder sozialrevolutionäre Veränderungen, durch Umweltveränderung, psychische Stabilisierung oder auch genetische Manipulation je einmal gelingen könnte, die Fraglichkeit der Wirklichkeit abzuschaffen, die Dialektik des Negativen aufzuheben, die Teufelskreise menschlicher Selbstzerstörung zu durchbrechen, die Macht des Nichtigen, des Chaos, des Sinnlosen in der Welt zu bändigen, ein Paradies auf Erden, ein goldenes Zeitalter, das Reich der Freiheit auch von allem Leid selber zu schaffen. Wir sahen: Selbst wenn der moderne Mensch mit der Welt fertig würde, mit sich selber – die Erfahrung eines jeden Einzelnen zeigt es immer wieder neu – wird er offensichtlich nicht fertig. Brauchen wir nochmals darauf hinzuweisen? Gerade der beispiellose äußere Fortschritt und Wohlstand der technologischen Gesellschaft hat den Menschen auch eine vielfach ebenso beispiellose innere Leere und Langeweile gebracht. Und die psychischen Krankheiten scheinen beinahe proportional zur Abnahme der physischen Krank-

heiten zuzunehmen. Der Mensch soll das Leid mit allen Mitteln bekämpfen. Aber es endgültig zu besiegen, ist ihm nicht gegeben.

Auch wer sich auf Jesu Weg einläßt und im Alltag sein eigenes Kreuz nüchtern auf sich nimmt, kann das Leid nicht schlechthin besiegen und beseitigen. Aber er kann es im Glauben durchstehen und bewältigen. Nie wird er dann vom Leid einfach erdrückt und im Leid verzweifelt untergehen. Wenn Jesus im äußersten Leid der Menschen- und Gottverlassenheit nicht unterging, dann wird auch der, der in vertrauendem Glauben sich an ihn hält, nicht untergehen. Denn ihm ist im Glauben Hoffnung gegeben: daß das Leid nicht einfach das Definitive, das Letzte ist. Das Letzte ist auch für ihn ein Leben ohne Leid, das freilich weder er selbst noch die menschliche Gesellschaft je verwirklichen werden, sondern das er von der Vollendung, vom geheimnisvollen ganz Anderen, von seinem Gott erwarten darf: alles Leid definitiv aufgehoben in ewigem Leben[20].

Aber die Verheißung einer leidlosen Zukunft ist keine die Neugier befriedigende Prophezeiung, um auf die Zukunft zu vertrösten. Sie ist eine Aufforderung, sich mit der Gegenwart nicht einfach resignierend abzufinden, sondern sie aktiv zu bestehen: der Ruf zum Durchhalten des Leids der Gegenwart auf eine letzte leidlose Zukunft hin, die sich dem Glaubenden bereits jetzt in den Erfahrungen der leidvollen Gegenwart eröffnet. Denn wer sich auf diesen Christus und seinen Weg eingelassen hat, in wem also Christus lebt[21], für den *ist* der alte Mensch mit seinen Egoismen bereits gekreuzigt[22], für den *ist* der neue Mensch bereits lebendige Wirklichkeit geworden: das Alte ist vergangen, Neues ist geworden[23]. Unüberwundenes Leid und immer wieder bedrohender Tod sind freilich Zeichen, daß der Mensch noch nicht vollendet ist, daß er sich letztlich nicht auf sich selbst, sondern auf Gott verlassen soll, daß er sich nie überheben, sondern auf Gottes Kraft vertrauen soll. Denn gerade in unserer Schwäche ist Gottes Kraft am Werk, gerade wenn wir schwach sind, sind wir stark[24]. Dialektische Kunstgriffe? Nein, Ausdruck einer mitten im Leid schon gelebten *Freiheit von Leid*: die Freiheit des glaubenden Menschen, der sich in aller Not und Bedrängnis nicht erdrücken läßt, der in allem Zweifel nicht verzweifelt, in aller Einsamkeit nicht verlassen, in aller Betrübnis nicht ohne Fröhlichkeit ist, in aller Niederlage nicht vernichtet wird, in aller Leere nicht ohne Erfüllung bleibt. Paulus hat nicht nur geschrieben, sondern gelebt, was jeder auf seine Weise erfahren kann:

»Von allen Seiten sind wir bedrängt, aber nicht erdrückt,
in Zweifel versetzt und doch nicht in Verzweiflung,
verfolgt und doch nicht verlassen,
zu Boden geworfen und doch nicht vernichtet ...
Sterbende, und siehe, wir leben,
Gezüchtigte und doch nicht getötet,
Betrübte, doch allzeit fröhlich,
Arme, die jedoch viele reich machen,
solche, die nichts haben und doch alles besitzen[25].«

Des Menschen Dasein, in welchem Gesellschafts- und Wirtschaftssystem auch immer, ist ein durchkreuztes, ein durch das Kreuz – durch Schmerz, Sorge, Leid und Tod – bestimmtes Geschehen. Erst vom Kreuze Jesu her aber bekommt das durchkreuzte Dasein des Menschen einen Sinn. Nachfolge ist immer, manchmal verborgen, manchmal offenkundig, leidende Nachfolge, Kreuzesnachfolge. Läßt sich der Mensch darauf ein? Unter seinem Kreuz ist er Jesus dem Gekreuzigten, seinem Herrn, am nächsten. In seiner eigenen Passion ist er in die Passion Jesu Christi gestellt[26]. Und gerade dies ermöglicht ihm in allem Leid eine letzte souveräne Überlegenheit. Denn kein Kreuz der Welt – man erinnere sich hier an all das im Zusammenhang der Theodizee-Frage Gesagte – kann das Sinn-Angebot widerlegen, das im Kreuz des zum Leben Erweckten ergangen ist: daß auch das Leid, daß auch äußerste Bedrohung, Sinnlosigkeit, Nichtigkeit, Verlassenheit, Einsamkeit und Leere von einem mit dem Menschen solidarischen Gott umfangen ist und so dem Glaubenden ein Weg zwar nicht am Leid vorbei, wohl aber durch das Leid hindurch eröffnet ist, damit er, gegenüber dem Leid in aktiver Indifferenz, gerade so bereit ist zum Kampf gegen das Leid und seine Ursachen, im Leben des Einzelnen wie in der menschlichen Gesellschaft.

Wir sprachen von der Bewältigung des Negativen als der Nagelprobe von christlichem Glauben und nichtchristlichen Humanismen. Ist nicht deutlich geworden, daß vom Gekreuzigten her das Negative in einer Weise bewältigt werden kann, wie dies für nichtchristliche Humanismen kaum möglich scheint? Nirgendwo ist die Herausforderung so unmißverständlich zurückgegeben wie an diesem Punkt.

3. Zur Freiheit befreit

Das Leid macht deutlich, wie stationär die Menschheitsgeschichte in Entscheidendem ist. Haben alle unbestreitbaren technologischen Evolutionen und politisch-sozialen Revolutionen viel daran geändert? In der Leidensgeschichte der Menschheit scheint es kaum eine ernsthafte Evolution oder Revolution zu geben. Wer hat es schwerer: ein ägyptischer Pyramidenbau-Sklave des Mittleren Reiches aus dem 2. Jahrtausend vor Christus oder ein südamerikanischer Minenarbeiter am Ende des 2. Jahrtausends nach Christus? Welches Elend war größer: das in den Proletariersiedlungen des neronianischen Rom oder das in den Slums des heutigen Rom? Was war schlimmer: die Massendeportationen ganzer Völkerschaften durch die Assyrer oder die Massenliquidationen in unserem Jahrhundert durch Deutsche, Russen, Amerikaner? Die ungeheuren modernen Möglichkeiten, Leid zu bekämpfen, scheinen den Möglichkeiten, Leid zu schaffen, ziemlich genau zu entsprechen. In dieser Hinsicht also gibt es nur bedingt »Neues unter der Sonne«. Einziger Trost, daß sich auch große Antworten und Hoffnungen durchhalten und so nicht nur die Leidensgeschichte, sondern auch die Hoffnungsgeschichte der Menschheit trotz all der ungeheuren Erschütterungen eine gewisse Stabilität aufweist. Das gilt auch und nicht zuletzt für die Frage, auf die eine heute verständliche und annehmbare Antwort noch gegeben werden muß: worauf es letztlich ankommt im Menschenleben.

Rechtfertigung oder soziale Gerechtigkeit?

Man hat nicht zu Unrecht festgestellt, daß die Hauptstreitfrage der Reformationszeit die Menschen heute in den protestantischen Kirchen ebenso kalt läßt wie in der katholischen Kirche, ganz abgesehen davon, daß sich darüber, wie wir hörten, eine Einigung erzielen läßt: Rechtfertigung durch den Glauben!? Wer fragt denn noch mit Luther: »Wie kommt es zu Gottesherrschaft im Menschen?« Wer noch mit dem Konzil von Trient: »Wie gelangt der sündige Mensch in den Gnadenstand?« Wer außer Theologen, die alle alten Fragen für ewige Fragen halten, streitet noch darüber: Ist Gnade das Wohlwollen Gottes oder eine innere Qualifikation des Menschen? Ist Rechtfertigung ein äußerlicher Richterspruch Gottes oder die innere Heiligung des Menschen? Rechtfertigung allein durch Glauben oder durch Glauben und Werke? Sind das nicht alles obsolet gewordene Fragen ohne Sitz im Leben? Sind nicht sogar die Lutheraner in ihrem »articulus stantis et cadentis Ecclesiae« – dem Glaubensartikel, mit dem die Kirche steht und fällt – nicht mehr sicher[1]?

Vor diesem zeitgeschichtlichen Hintergrund ist nicht zu verwundern, daß man heute von allen Kirchen her statt von »christlicher Rechtfertigung« von »gesellschaftlicher Gerechtigkeit« spricht[2]. Nicht, daß man das erste einfach leugnen möchte. Aber brennend interessiert ist man allein am zweiten. Und nach allem, was hier positiv über die gesellschaftliche Relevanz der christlichen Botschaft und das Engagement für die gesellschaftliche Befreiung zu sagen war, haben wir natürlich nicht den geringsten Anlaß, die hohe Wichtigkeit und Dringlichkeit der gesellschaftlichen Gerechtigkeit in Zweifel zu ziehen; von dem dort Gesagten soll hier kein Wort zurückgenommen werden. Nur das eine muß hier untersucht werden, was unmittelbar zur Beantwortung jener Frage führt, worauf es letztlich ankommt: Kann man so einfach das zweite ohne das erste haben?

Wenn man die alte und die neue Problemstellung schematisieren will, so sieht das so aus[3]:

Früher fragte man in einer großen Welt- und Seelenangst: wie bekomme ich einen gnädigen Gott?

Jetzt aber, in einer nicht kleineren Welt- und Existenzangst: wie bekommt mein Leben einen Sinn?

Früher verstand man diesen Gott als Richtergott, der den Menschen von seinen Sünden frei- und gerechtspricht.

Jetzt versteht man ihn als Partnergott, der den Menschen in die Freiheit und in Verantwortung für Welt und Geschichte ruft.

Früher ging es um die individuelle Rechtfertigung und das privatistische »Rette deine Seele!«.

Jetzt geht es um die soziale Dimension des Heiles und die allseitige Sorge um die Mitmenschen.

Früher sorgte man sich spiritualistisch um das jenseitige Heil und den Frieden mit Gott.

Jetzt sorgt man sich ganzheitlich um die gesellschaftlichen Zustände und die Reform oder gar Revolution der Strukturen.

Früher stand der Mensch vor dem Zwang, sein Leben vor Gott zu rechtfertigen.

Jetzt der Zwang, sein Leben zu rechtfertigen vor sich selbst und seinen Mitmenschen.

Aus dem ganzen Buch ist deutlich geworden, wieviel an dieser neuen Problemstellung richtig und wichtig ist; das braucht hier nicht wiederholt zu werden. Zweifellos hat Luther die gesellschaftlichen Konsequenzen aus seinem Rechtfertigungsverständnis, etwa für das Elend der Bauern, nicht gezogen. Und zu Recht hat Ernst Bloch in diesem Punkt Thomas Münzer neben und gegen ihn gestellt[4]. Luthers Zwei-Reiche-Lehre vereinfacht die Problematik entschieden und wirkte sich noch bis in die Abwehr des Nationalsozialismus hinein negativ aus. Zweifellos hat auch die katholische Tradition die Konsequenzen aus der Rechtfertigungslehre mehr im innerkirchlichen Bereich der frommen, barmherzigen Werke als in der Neugestaltung der Gesellschaft gesehen. Der päpstliche Kirchenstaat mit seiner Monsignori-Wirtschaft galt weithin als der sozial rückständigste Staat Europas, und bis zu seinem Untergang wehrte man sich in Rom mit Erfolg gegen jegliche katholische Soziallehre. Und so wäre noch vieles auch aus der Geschichte für die Wende der Kirche zu Welt und Gesellschaft zu sagen, wie sie schon in unserem einleitenden Kapitel skizziert wurde[5].

Trotzdem ist nun gegen Ende dieses Buches etwas anderes noch wichtiger, und gerade dies läßt sichtbar werden, daß die genannten Antithesen den entscheidenden Punkt nicht zur Sprache bringen.

Worauf es letztlich nicht ankommt

Im modernen Leben kommt es auf das an, was einer leistet. Man fragt weniger: »Wer ist das?«, als: »Was ist der?«, »Was macht er?« Man meint damit seinen Beruf, seine Arbeit, seine Leistungen, seine Position und sein Ansehen in der Gesellschaft. Darauf kommt es an.

Diese Fragestellung ist nicht so selbstverständlich, wie sie scheint. Sie ist typisch »westlich«, obwohl sie heute auch in den sozialistischen Ländern des Ostblocks (Zweite Welt) und in den Entwicklungsländern (Dritte Welt) zu finden ist. Ursprünglich beheimatet aber ist sie in der Ersten Welt, in Westeuropa und Nordamerika, wo sich die *moderne Industriegesellschaft* herausgebildet hat. Nur da gab es seit langem eine rational organisierte Wissenschaft mit spezialisierten Fachleuten. Nur da auch die rationale Organisation der freien Arbeit im Betrieb nach Rentabilität. Nur da ein eigentliches Bürgertum und eine spezifisch geartete Rationalisierung der Wirtschaft und schließlich der Gesellschaft überhaupt mit einer neuen Wirtschaftsgesinnung. Warum denn nur hier?

Max Weber hat in seiner bereits genannten klassischen Untersuchung ›Die protestantische Ethik und der Geist des Kapitalismus‹ (1905) diesen Vorgang genauer untersucht: Die westliche Rationalisierung wurde gewiß durch bestimmte ökonomische Bedingungen vorangetrieben (so richtig Marx). Aber andererseits kam es zur westlichen ökonomischen Rationalisierung überhaupt erst durch eine neue praktisch-rationale Wirtschaftsgesinnung, die ihren Grund in einer sehr bestimmten religiös-moralischen Lebensführung hat (so richtig Weber): Bestimmte Glaubensinhalte und Pflichtvorstellungen waren es, die diese neue Einstellung in Leben und Wirtschaft entscheidend hervorbrachten. Inwiefern? Die Wurzeln reichen, erstaunlich genug, in die angeblich heute nicht mehr aktuellen Fragen der Reformationszeit zurück: In ungewollter Folge der strengen calvinistischen Lehre von einer doppelten Erwählung (Prädestination der einen zur Seligkeit – der anderen zur Verdammung) betonte man in den von Calvin beeinflußten Kirchen die »Heiligung«, die Werke im Alltag, die Berufsarbeit als Erfüllung der Nächstenliebe und ihren Erfolg – dies alles nämlich verstanden als sichtbare Zeichen einer positiven Erwählung zur ewigen Seligkeit. Nicht aus aufklärerischen, sondern aus religiösen Motiven also war es zum Geist der rastlosen Arbeit, des Berufserfolges und des ökonomischen Fortschritts gekommen: eine höchst folgenreiche Kombination von intensiver Frömmigkeit und kapitalistischem Geschäftssinn in historisch wichtigen Kirchen und Sekten, bei den englischen, schottischen und amerikanischen Puritanern, den französischen Hugenotten, den deutschen Reformierten und Pietisten.

Je mehr nun die Säkularisierung alle Bereiche des Lebens ergriff und je mehr sich das moderne Wirtschaftssystem durchsetzte, um so mehr wurden unermüdlicher Fleiß (industria), strenge Disziplin und hohes Verantwortungsbewußtsein die Tugenden des säkularen, mündig gewordenen Menschen in der *»Industrie«-Gesellschaft*. Allseitige »Tüchtigkeit« wurde die Tugend schlechthin, der »Nutzen« die Denkweise, der »Erfolg« das Ziel, die »Leistung« das Gesetz dieser modernen *Leistungsgesellschaft*, in der ein jeder seine Rolle (Hauptrolle im Beruf und meist verschiedene Nebenrollen) zu spielen hat[6].

So versucht der Mensch nun in einer dynamisch sich entwikkelnden Welt und Gesellschaft sich selbst zu verwirklichen: anders als in der früheren statischen Welt menschliche Selbstverwirklichung, um die es ja dem Menschen in jedem Fall gehen muß[7], durch eigene Leistungen. Nur der ist etwas, der etwas leistet. Und was kann Schlimmeres von einem Menschen gesagt werden, als daß er nichts leiste? Arbeit, Karriere, Geldverdienen – was sollte wichtiger sein? Industrialisieren, Produzieren, Expandieren, Konsumieren im großen wie im kleinen, Wachstum, Fortschritt, Perfektion, Verbesserung des Lebensstandards in jeder Hinsicht: ist nicht das der Sinn des Lebens? Wie anders denn durch Leistungen soll der Mensch seine Existenz rechtfertigen? Die ökonomischen Werte rangieren zuoberst in der Wertordnung, Beruf und Tüchtigkeit bestimmen den sozialen Status, die Ausrichtung auf Wohlfahrt und Leistung lassen die Industrienationen dem Druck der Urarmut entrinnen und führen die Wohlfahrtsgesellschaft herauf.

Aber gerade dieses so erfolgreiche *Leistungsdenken* wird schließlich zu einer ernsthaften *Bedrohung für die Menschlichkeit des Menschen*: Nicht nur daß der Mensch die höheren Werte und einen umfassenden Sinn des Lebens aus den Augen verliert, sondern daß er sich zugleich an die anonymen Mechanismen, Techniken, Mächte, Organisationen dieses Systems verliert. Denn je größer Fortschritt und Perfektion, um so stärker die Einordnung des Menschen in den komplexen ökonomisch-sozialen Prozeß: Immer noch strengere Disziplin, die den Menschen gefangennimmt. Immer noch mehr Einsatz und Fleiß, der den Menschen nicht mehr zu sich selber kommen läßt. Immer noch mehr Verantwortung, die den Menschen ganz in seiner Aufgabe vereinnahmt. Immer engmaschiger das von der Gesellschaft selber geschaffene Normennetz, das den Menschen nicht nur in seinem Beruf und in seiner Arbeit, sondern auch in seiner Freizeit, seiner Unterhaltung, seinem Urlaub, seinen Reisen unbarmherzig umspannt und reglementiert. Der Straßenverkehr in jeder Stadt mit seinen Tausenden von Verboten, Geboten, Signalen, Wegweisern, die es alle früher nicht brauchte und an die man sich jetzt, will man überleben, peinlichst halten muß, ist ein Bild für das von morgens bis abends durchorganisierte, vollnormierte, bürokratisierte und bald auch komputerisierte moderne Alltagsleben. Eine neue *säkulare Gesetzlichkeit* in allen Sektoren des menschlichen Lebens von noch nie dagewesenen und auch vom einzelnen Juristen nicht mehr zu übersehenden Ausmaß, der

Opfer gebracht, sondern die Macht zum Nutzen der Menschen gebraucht wird. Die Macht kann nicht, wie es manche verlangen, einfach abgeschafft werden. Das ist illusionär. Aber die Macht kann aus dem christlichen Gewissen heraus radikal relativiert werden: zugunsten der Menschen. Macht kann statt zur Herrschaft zum Dienst gebraucht werden.

Auf diese Weise wird im Einzelfall ermöglicht, was den Menschen der kapitalistischen wie der sozialistischen Gesellschaft nicht zumutbar scheint und was doch für alles menschliche Zusammenleben der Einzelnen wie der Völker, Sprachen, Klassen und auch der Kirchen unendlich wichtig ist: statt Schuld aufzurechnen, endlos vergeben zu können; statt Positionen zu wahren, sich bedingungslos versöhnen zu können; statt des dauernden Rechtsstreites die höhere Gerechtigkeit der Liebe; statt des erbarmungslosen Machtkampfes der Friede, der alle Vernunft übersteigt. Eine solche Botschaft wird nicht zum Opium der Vertröstung. Viel radikaler als andere Programme weist sie ins Diesseits ein. Sie ist auf Veränderung aus dort, wo die Herrschenden die Beherrschten, die Institutionen die Personen, die Ordnung die Freiheit, die Macht das Recht zu erdrücken drohen.

Wo immer ein Einzelner oder eine ganze Gruppe vergessen, daß Macht nicht zur Herrschaft, sondern zum Dienst da ist, da tragen sie dazu bei, daß im gesellschaftlichen wie im individuellen Bereich Machtdenken und Machtpolitik herrschen: daß in dem nun einmal unumgänglichen Machtkampf die Entmenschlichung des Menschen betrieben wird.

Wo immer aber ein Einzelner oder eine ganze Gruppe daran denken, daß Macht statt zur Herrschaft zum Dienst da ist, da tragen sie zur Vermenschlichung des allseitigen menschlichen Konkurrenzkampfes bei und machen auch mitten im Konkurrenzkampf gegenseitigen Respekt, Achtung vor den Menschen, Vermittlung und Schonung möglich. Sie dürfen dann an die Verheißung glauben, daß alle, die barmherzig sind, auch Barmherzigkeit erfahren werden[4].

Freiheit vom Konsumdruck

Jesus lädt seine Jünger dazu ein, die innere *Freiheit von Besitz (Konsum) zu üben*[5]. Wer immer sein Verhalten letztlich von Jesus Christus inspirieren sein lassen will, dem wird zwar kein grundsätzlicher Verzicht auf Besitz und Konsum aufgezwungen.

gegenüber die alttestamentliche (religiöse) Gesetzlichkeit und die Auslegungskunst der damaligen Gesetzesgelehrten reichlich harmlos erscheinen.

Aber je mehr nun der Mensch die Forderungen dieser Gesetzlichkeit erfüllt, um so mehr verliert er seine Spontaneität, Initiative, Eigenständigkeit, um so weniger hat er Raum für sich selbst, für sein Menschsein. Oft hat der Mensch das Gefühl, er sei für die Gesetze (Paragraphen, Bestimmungen, Handlungs- und Gebrauchsanweisungen) da, nicht die Gesetze für ihn. Und je mehr er sich in diesem Netz von Erwartungen, Bestimmungen, Normen und Kontrollen verliert, desto mehr klammert er sich an sie, um in ihnen sich selbst bestätigt zu finden. Das ganze Leben ein höchst strapazierender und rasch verschleißender »Leistungssport« mit ständigen Leistungskontrollen: vom Berufs- bis zum Sexualleben nur ja kein Leistungsabfall, wo immer möglich eine Leistungssteigerung. Im Grunde ein tödlicher Regelkreis, in dem die Leistung den Menschen in Abhängigkeiten treibt, denen er nun durch neue Leistung glaubt entkommen zu können: ein großer *Verlust der Freiheit*.

So erfährt der Mensch in moderner Form das, was Paulus den *Fluch des Gesetzes* genannt hat: Das moderne Leben hält ihn unter Leistungszwang, Zugzwang, Erfolgszwang. Ständig muß er sich in seiner Existenz *selbst rechtfertigen*: nicht mehr wie früher vor dem Richterstuhl Gottes, sondern vor dem Forum seiner Umwelt, vor der Gesellschaft, vor sich selbst. Und rechtfertigen kann er sich in dieser Leistungsgesellschaft nur durch Leistung: nur durch Leistungen ist er etwas, behält er seinen Platz in der Gesellschaft, gewinnt er das Ansehen, das er braucht. Nur durch das Vorweisen von Leistungen kann er sich selbst behaupten.

Ist nun die Gefahr nicht sehr greifbar geworden, daß sich der Mensch unter diesem ungeheuren Leistungszwang, ja Leistungswahn, unter den Rollenerwartungen seiner Umgebung und der Konkurrenz von allen Seiten, die ihn zu überrollen droht, nur noch von außen leiten läßt, daß er sich an seine eigene Rolle völlig verliert: daß er nur noch Manager, Kaufmann, Wissenschaftler, Beamter, Techniker, Arbeiter, Berufsmensch ist und nicht mehr – Mensch? »Identitätsdiffusion« (E. H. Erikson) an die verschiedenen Rollen, und so Identitätskrise und Identitätsverlust: der Mensch ist nicht mehr er selbst, ist sich selber entfremdet. Er muß sich doch selber und aus eigener Kraft behaupten, gegen die Anderen und so oft auf Kosten der Anderen! Er lebt im Grunde für sich allein und versucht, alle Anderen zu seinen Zwecken zu benützen.

Die Frage ist nur: Wird der Mensch auf diesem Wege glücklich werden? Werden sich die Anderen auf diese Weise von ihm benützen und vereinnahmen lassen? Kann er selber unter dem Gesetz der Leistung alle die Forderungen, die immer wieder neu an ihn ergehen, überhaupt erfüllen? Und vor allem: Kann er durch alle seine Leistungen seine Existenz wirklich rechtfertigen? Rechtfertigt er damit im Grunde nicht doch nur seine Rolle oder seine Rollen, die er zu spielen hat, aber nicht sein Sein? Ist er denn wirklich das, was er in seinem Tun ist? Ein Mensch kann doch ein fabelhafter Manager, Wissenschaftler, Beamter oder Facharbeiter sein und seine Rolle nach allgemeinem Urteil glänzend spielen, und doch als Mensch völlig versagen: Er kreist zwar um sich, kommt aber gar nicht zu sich selbst. Er merkt nicht einmal, daß er bei allen seinen Leistungen sich selbst verloren hat, daß er sich selber wiederfinden müßte und daß er sich nicht wiederfinden wird, wenn er nicht zur Besinnung kommt. Durch alle Leistungen, durch all sein Tun gewinnt der Mensch noch keineswegs Sein, Identität, Freiheit, Personsein, gewinnt er noch keineswegs die Bestätigung seines Ich und den Sinn seiner Existenz. Wer nur sich selber bestätigen, nur sich selber rechtfertigen will, der wird sein Leben verfehlen. Man ist an das Wort erinnert: Wer sein Leben erhalten will, wird es verlieren[8]. Aber – bleibt ihm denn überhaupt etwas anderes übrig, als durch seine Leistungen sich selbst zu bestätigen, sich selbst zu rechtfertigen?

Es gibt auch einen anderen Weg: Nicht etwa nichts tun. Nicht etwa auf Leistung von vornherein verzichten. Nicht etwa die nun einmal in der Gesellschaft zu spielende Rolle plötzlich verweigern, gar den Beruf aufgeben. Aber wissen, daß der Mensch in seinem Beruf und seiner Arbeit nicht aufgeht, daß die Person mehr ist als ihre Rolle, daß die Leistungen zwar wichtig, aber nicht entscheidend sind: die guten nicht und die schlechten nicht. Kurz: daß es letztlich gerade *nicht auf die Leistungen ankommt*!

Worauf es letztlich ankommt

Wie kann man es wagen, gegen den ganzen Geist der Neuzeit angesichts der nun einmal bestehenden – und im Westen wie im Osten in verschiedener Weise solide etablierten – Leistungsgesellschaft so Ungeheuerliches zu behaupten? Nach all dem Vorausgegangenen wird man es vielleicht doch nicht so ungeheuerlich finden: Von diesem Jesus Christus her kann man es tatsächlich behaupten, daß es letztlich nicht auf die Leistungen des Menschen ankommt. *Von diesem Jesus Christus her* sollte es sogar möglich sein, *eine andere Grundhaltung einzunehmen,* ein anderes Bewußtsein zu erreichen, eine andere Lebenseinstellung zu gewinnen, um die Grenzen des Leistungsdenkens zu erkennen, um dem Leistungswahn zu entrinnen und den Leistungszwang zu durchbrechen, wirklich frei zu werden. So muß nüchtern und realistisch die Tendenz zur Entmenschlichung im Leistungsgesetz durchschaut werden, um der Menschen willen, die nun einmal nicht aus dieser Leistungsgesellschaft emigrieren können, sondern hier leben und arbeiten müssen, von ihr Bestätigung erfahren und sich doch nach einer qualitativ anderen Freiheit sehnen.

Wir erinnern uns[9]: *Jesus* verwarf nicht Leistungen an sich, gesetzliche, rituelle, moralische. Aber er wandte sich entschieden dagegen, daß gerade die Leistungen das Maß des Menschseins bestimmen sollen. Was sagte er von jenem Leistungspharisäer, der meinte, aufgrund seiner Leistungen vor Gott und den Menschen etwas zu gelten, etwas zu sein und so in seiner ganzen Existenz, in seiner Position und seinem Ansehen voll gerechtfertigt dazustehen? Jesus sagte: dieser ging nicht gerechtfertigt nach Hause. Und was sagte derselbe Jesus von jenem Leistungsversager, der keine Leistungen oder bestenfalls moralisch minderwertige aufzuweisen hatte, der aber auch gar nicht versuchte, vor Gott gerechtfertigt dazustehen, sondern sich Gott in seinem ganzen Versagen stellte und seine einzige Hoffnung auf Gottes Erbarmen setzte? Von ihm sagte Jesus: dieser ging gerechtfertigt nach Hause.

Womit noch ein Weiteres deutlich geworden ist: Es sind nicht etwa nur die positiven, schönen und guten Leistungen des Menschen, auf die es letztlich nicht ankommt. Die tröstliche Seite derselben Botschaft ist: es sind auch die negativen, bösen und häßlichen »Leistungen« des Menschen – und wieviel »leistet« sich jeder Mensch, auch wenn er nicht gerade ein sündiger Zöllner ist –, auf die es letztlich, zu unserem Glück, ebensowenig ankommt. Letztlich kommt es bei allem unumgänglichen Tun und Lassen des Menschen auf etwas anderes an: *daß der Mensch im Guten wie im Bösen auf gar keinen Fall je sein unbedingtes Vertrauen aufgibt.* Daß er also in seinen großen und guten Taten weiß, daß er nichts hat, was er nicht empfangen, und daß zur

Einbildung, zum Renommieren und Imponieren kein Anlaß besteht. Vom ersten Moment seines Lebens bis zum letzten empfängt er, ist er auf andere angewiesen, erhält er sein Leben täglich neu, verdankt er sich in allem, was er ist und hat, anderen. Es kommt aber zugleich darauf an, daß der Mensch auch in seinem Versagen, es sei so beschämend wie immer, weiß, daß er nie Anlaß zum Aufgeben und Verzweifeln hat. Daß er auch und gerade in all seiner Schuld getragen bleibt von dem, der nur als der Erbarmende richtig verstanden und ernstgenommen wird. Woher hat der Mensch diese Gewißheit? Der Gekreuzigte, der in absoluter Passivität zu keiner Leistung mehr fähig ist und der schließlich doch gegen die Vertreter der frommen Leistungen als der von Gott Gerechtfertigte dasteht, ist und bleibt das lebendige Zeichen Gottes dafür, daß das Entscheidende nun eben doch nicht vom Menschen und seinen Taten, sondern – zum Wohl des Menschen im Guten wie im Bösen – vom barmherzigen Gott abhängt, der vom Menschen in dessen eigener Passion ein unerschütterliches Vertrauen erwartet.

Vom Gekreuzigten her ist es denn, wie wir uns auch nur zu erinnern brauchen[10], gar nicht verwunderlich, wenn *Paulus* nun gerade dies als Zentralpunkt seiner Botschaft verkündigt, daß der Mensch nicht aufgrund seiner Leistungen vor Gott und Menschen gerechtfertigt dasteht. Auch Paulus verwarf nicht die Leistungen. Er konnte sich rühmen, mehr als alle anderen Apostel geleistet zu haben, und er erwartete von seinen Christen Taten, Früchte des Geistes, Äußerungen der Liebe: der Glaube ist durch die Liebe tätig[11]. Aber entscheidend sind die Leistungen nicht. Entscheidend ist der Glaube, dieses unbedingte, unerschütterliche Sich-Gott-Anvertrauen – ungeachtet aller eigenen Fehlleistungen und Schwächen, ungeachtet aber auch der eigenen positiven Leistungen, Vorzüge, Verdienste und Ansprüche. Der Mensch soll sich in *allem* Gott anvertrauen und empfangen, was Gott ihm schenken will.

Nur Theologen, die die paulinische Rechtfertigungsbotschaft nicht verstanden haben, können in der heutigen Leistungsgesellschaft, sich wieder einmal falsch anpassend, dazu auffordern, mehr auf das »Operationelle« und damit auf den Jakobusbrief und dessen »Rechtfertigung durch die Werke«[12] zu achten. Als ob Paulus das »Operationelle« nicht sehr viel besser verstanden hätte als jener uns unbekannte hellenistische Judenchrist am Ende des 1. Jahrhunderts, der sich optima fide des Namens des Herrenbruders Jakobus bediente, um nach bestem Wissen und

Können gegen faule Orthodoxie die Notwendigkeit der Orthopraxie zu verteidigen. Mit ihm verglichen – und man kommt hier um Vergleiche nicht herum – hat Paulus nicht nur die Orthopraxie besser verteidigt. Er hat auch ganz anders umfassend verstanden und begründet, worauf es im Menschsein und Christsein entscheidend ankommt.

Hier soll selbstverständlich nicht pauschal gegen Leistungen, gute Werke, Arbeit, berufliches Fortkommen polemisiert werden, als ob der Christ nicht aufgefordert sei, aus seinen »Talenten« das Beste zu machen. Christliche Rechtfertigungsbotschaft liefert nicht die Rechtfertigung für eigenes Nichtstun. Gute Taten sind wichtig. Aber Grundlage der christlichen Existenz und Kriterium für das Bestehen vor Gott kann nicht die Berufung auf irgendwelche Leistungen sein: keine Selbstbehauptung, keine Selbstrechtfertigung des Menschen. Sondern nur das unbedingte Festhalten an Gott durch Jesus in einem glaubenden Vertrauen. Eine ungemein ermutigende Botschaft ist hier verkündet, die dem Menschenleben sogar durch alles unvermeidbare Versagen, Irren und Verzweifeln hindurch eine solide Basis gibt und die es zugleich vom religiösen oder säkularen Leistungsdruck zu befreien vermag zu einer Freiheit, die auch durch schlimme und schlimmste Situationen hindurchzutragen vermag.

Wie grundlegend Vertrauen für das Menschenleben ist, wie der Mensch nur mit einem »Grundvertrauen« die Identität, Werthaftigkeit und Sinnhaftigkeit der Wirklichkeit und insbesondere seines eigenen Daseins anzunehmen vermag, wurde schon in einem sehr frühen Stadium dieser Darlegungen betont[13]. Jetzt aber ist in ganz anderer Tiefe deutlich geworden, was der Mensch, will er überhaupt zur Selbstverwirklichung kommen, will er als Person Freiheit, Identität, Sinn, Glück gewinnen, dies nur im unbedingten Vertrauen auf den tun kann, der ihm dies alles zu geben vermag. Im glaubenden Vertrauen auf Gott, wie es von Jesus Christus ermöglicht wird, erscheint das Grundvertrauen des Menschen aufs beste »aufgehoben«. Im Blick auf Jesus ein Vertrauen zu Gott, das nicht anbewiesen werden kann, das aber, wird es gewagt und vollzogen, aus sich selbst seine Sinnhaftigkeit und seine befreiende Kraft erweist.

Worin zeigt sich diese *Freiheit?* Nicht daß der Mensch in einer illusionären Weise total autonom, völlig unabhängig, absolut bindungslos wäre. Hat doch jeder Mensch seinen Gott oder seine Götter, die für ihn maßgebend sind, nach denen er sich richtet, denen er alles opfert. Sondern daß der Mensch von der Abhängigkeit und den Bindungen an die falschen Götter befreit wird, die ihn unbarmherzig zu neuen Leistungen antreiben: sei es nun das Geld oder die Karriere oder das Prestige oder die Macht oder der Genuß, oder was immer für ihn der oberste Wert ist.

Bindet der Mensch sich allein an den einen wahren Gott, der mit keiner der endlichen Wirklichkeiten identisch ist, so wird er frei gegenüber allen endlichen Werten, Gütern, Mächten. Er erkennt dann auch die Relativität seiner eigenen Leistungen und Fehlleistungen. Er steht nicht mehr unter dem unbarmherzigen Gesetz des Leisten-Müssens. Er ist zwar nicht dispensiert von aller Leistung. Wohl aber ist er befreit vom Leistungszwang und Leistungswahn. Er geht nicht mehr auf in seiner Rolle oder seinen Rollen. Er kann der sein, der er ist.

Wer so nicht für sich selber lebt, wird wahrhaft zu sich selber kommen, Mensch sein, Sinn, Identität, Freiheit gewinnen. Man ist an das Wort erinnert: Wer sein Leben verliert um meinetwillen – auf Jesu Botschaft und Person hin –, der wird es gewinnen[14]. Sinn, Freiheit, Identität, Rechtfertigung seiner Existenz kann dem Menschen nur geschenkt werden. Und ohne Empfangen, das vorausgeht, kein Handeln. Ohne Gnade, die ermöglicht, keine Leistung. Ohne wahre Demut gegenüber dem einen Gott keine wahre Überlegenheit gegenüber den vielen Pseudo-Göttern. Nur vom einen wahren Gott wird dem Menschen die große souveräne Freiheit geschenkt, die ihm neue Freiheitsräume und neue Freiheitschancen eröffnet gegenüber all dem Vielen, was ihn in dieser Welt versklaven kann.

So steht denn der Mensch nicht nur in seinen Leistungen und Rollen, sondern in seiner ganzen Existenz, in seinem Menschsein gerechtfertigt da, ganz unabhängig von seinen Leistungen. *Er weiß, daß sein Leben einen Sinn hat:* nicht nur in Erfolgen, auch in Mißerfolgen, nicht nur bei Glanzleistungen, auch bei Fehlleistungen, nicht nur bei Leistungssteigerung, sondern bei Leistungsabfall. Sein Leben hat also einen Sinn selbst dann, wenn er von seiner Umgebung oder der Gesellschaft aus irgendeinem Grund nicht mehr akzeptiert sein sollte: wenn er von den Gegnern vernichtet und den Freunden verlassen ist, wenn er sich für das Falsche eingesetzt und Mißerfolge geerntet hat, wenn seine Leistungen nachlassen und von anderen ersetzt werden, wenn er für gar niemand mehr von Nutzen ist. Selbst der bankrotte Geschäftsmann und die völlig vereinsamte Geschiedene, selbst der gestrandete und vergessene Politiker, der 50jährige Arbeitslose, die gealterte Prostituierte oder der Schwerverbrecher in der

Strafanstalt brauchen nicht zu verzweifeln. Sie alle, auch wenn sie von niemandem mehr anerkannt werden, bleiben anerkannt von dem, auf dessen Anerkennung es letztlich allein ankommt, vor dem es kein Ansehen der Person und ein Gericht nach den Maßstäben seiner Güte gibt.

Worauf also kommt es letztlich an im Menschenleben? Daß einer, ob gesund oder krank, arbeitsfähig oder arbeitsunfähig, leistungsstark oder leistungsschwach, erfolggewohnt oder erfolgverlassen, schuldig oder unschuldig, nicht nur am Ende, sondern sein ganzes Leben hindurch an jenem Vertrauen unbeirrt und unerschüttert festhält, was wir mit dem ganzen Neuen Testament den *Glauben* nennen. Wenn dann sein »Te Deum« dem einen wahren Gott und nicht den vielen falschen Göttern gilt, dann darf er es wagen, auch das Ende dieses Hymnus, in welcher Situation auch immer, als Verheißung auf sich zu beziehen: »In te Domine speravi, non confundar in aeternum«, »Auf dich, Herr, habe ich vertraut, und ich werde in Ewigkeit nicht zuschanden«[15].

4. Anregungen

Christliche Freiheit muß in jeder Situation, an jedem Ort und zu jeder Zeit wieder neu realisiert werden, individuell wie gesellschaftlich. Aus Jesus Christus als dem Grundmodell in seiner Anschaulichkeit, Vernehmbarkeit und Realisierbarkeit folgen ungezählte Möglichkeiten, das christliche Programm in die Praxis umzusetzen. Viele praktische Konsequenzen, und zwar nicht nur für die Erste und Zweite, sondern auch für die Dritte Welt, sind hier bereits sichtbar geworden. In diesem letzten Kapitel nun soll nicht etwa ein christliches Aktionsprogramm systematisch entwickelt werden. Es soll nur beispielhaft an einigen grundlegenden Problemen des heutigen Menschen und seiner Gesellschaft illustriert werden, was die Nachfolge Jesu Christi verändern kann und auch wirklich verändert hat – überall dort, wo sie ernstgenommen wird. Was dabei christliche Freiheit grundsätzlich bedeutet, ist nicht nur im vorausgegangenen Kapitel, sondern durch dieses ganze Buch hindurch entwickelt worden. Hier soll nun angedeutet werden, wie christliche Freiheit nicht nur in außerordentlichen Situationen, sondern gerade in vielen widersprüchlichen individuellen wie gesellschaftlichen Situationen des Alltags einen neuen Weg eröffnen kann, indem sie von Jesus Christus her andere Maßstäbe, Wertskalen und Sinnbezüge zur Geltung bringt. Einige knappe Anregungen also zum Weiterdenken: Denk- und Tatanstöße.

Freiheit in der Rechtsordnung

Jesus erwartet von seinen Jüngern, daß sie freiwillig *auf Rechte ohne Gegenleistung verzichten*[1]. Wer immer sich heute als Einzelner oder Gruppe in seinem Verhalten nach diesem Jesus Christus richten will, dem wird zwar kein grundsätzlicher Verzicht auf Rechte auferlegt. Aber es wird ihm im ganz konkreten Fall um des Anderen willen der mögliche Rechtsverzicht als eine Chance angeboten.

Man nehme als Beispiel das *Problem von Krieg und Frieden*: Jahrzehntelang erwies es sich als unmöglich, in bestimmten Gebieten der Erde Frieden herzustellen: im Nahen Osten, im Fernen Osten, aber auch in Europa. Warum haben wir keinen Frieden? Gewiß, weil »die andere Seite« nicht will. Aber das Problem liegt tiefer. Beide Seiten machen Ansprüche und Rechte geltend, Rechte auf dieselben Territorien, Völker, Wirtschaftsräume. Beide Seiten können ihre Ansprüche und Rechte auch begründen: historisch, ökonomisch, kulturell, politisch. Die Regierungen auf beiden Seiten haben nach ihren Staatsverfassungen die Pflicht, die Rechte des Staates zu wahren und zu verteidigen. Früher hieß es sogar noch: zu mehren.

Die Machtblöcke und politischen Lager waren und sind fixiert auf außenpolitische Feindbilder, die die eigene Position rechtfertigen sollen. Feindbilder, die individualpsychologisch von der Angst vor allem Fremden wie von Vorurteilen gegen alles Andersartige, Disparate, Ungewohnte gespeist sind. Feindbilder, die darüber hinaus gesamtgesellschaftlich eine bedeutende innenpolitische Identitäts- und Stabilisierungsfunktion haben. Solche Feindbilder und Vorurteile anderen Ländern, Völkern, Rassen gegenüber sind bequem, weil sie populär sind. Sie erweisen sich gerade wegen ihrer Verwurzelung in tiefen psychischen Schichten des Menschen als außerordentlich schwer korrigierbar. So ist die politische Lage der Machtblöcke gekennzeichnet von einer Atmosphäre des Argwohns und der kollektiven Verdächtigungen: ein Teufelskreis des Mißtrauens, der jede Friedensabsicht und jede Versöhnungsbereitschaft schon im Ansatz dadurch fragwürdig macht, daß er sie für eine Schwäche oder eine Taktik des Anderen hält.

Die Folgen sind, global gesehen, von erheblicher Relevanz: Rüstungswettlauf, gegen den selbst alle Verhandlungen und bereits geschlossenen Verträge über Rüstungsbeschränkung und Rüstungskontrolle noch kein wirksames Mittel gefunden haben. Spirale von Gewalt und Gegengewalt in internationalen Krisen, in denen sich beide Seiten machtpolitisch, wirtschaftlich, militärisch-strategisch auszumanövrieren versuchen. Und so kommt in den verschiedenen Teilen der Welt kein echter Friede zustande, weil niemand einsieht, warum gerade er und nicht der Andere auf eine Rechts- und Machtposition verzichten soll. Weil niemand einsieht, warum er nicht, wenn er die Macht dazu hat, seinen Standpunkt unter Umständen auch brutal durchsetzen soll. Weil niemand einsieht, warum er nicht dem außenpolitischen Macchiavellismus bei größtmöglicher Verminderung des eigenen Risikos huldigen soll. Was aber können Christen tun? Es sei nur kurz angedeutet:

– *Die christliche Botschaft gibt keine detaillierte Auskunft, wie etwa die Ostgrenzen Deutschlands, die Grenzen zwischen Israel und den arabischen Staaten oder die internationalen Fischereigrenzen gezogen werden sollen, wie bestimmte Konflikte in Asien, Afrika oder Südamerika, wie insbesondere der Ost-West-Konflikt geregelt werden sollen. Sie macht keine detaillierten Vorschläge zu Abrüstungskonferenzen und Friedensgesprächen. Das Evangelium ist weder eine politische Theorie noch eine bestimmte Methode der Diplomatie.*

– *Aber die christliche Botschaft sagt etwas, was grundlegend ist, was Staatsmänner ihren Völkern so leicht nicht zumuten können, was aber katholische, evangelische und orthodoxe Bischöfe, was christliche Kirchenführer, Theologen, Seelsorger und Laien in aller Welt sehr wohl sagen könnten und wohl auch sagen müßten: daß nämlich* Verzicht auf Recht ohne Gegenleistung *nicht unbedingt eine Schande sein muß, daß »Verzichtspolitiker« zumindest für Christen kein Schimpfwort sein muß. Ja, daß in ganz bestimmten Fällen – nicht als ein neues Gesetz! – ein Verzicht auf Rechte ohne Gegenleistung die große Freiheit des Christen ausmachen kann: eben zwei Meilen zu gehen mit einem, der einem eine Meile abgenötigt hat.*

Der Christ, der diese Freiheit lebt, wird kritisch gegen alle, die, auf welcher Seite auch immer, stets nur verbal ihre Friedensbereitschaft beteuern, die um der Propaganda willen Freundschaft und Versöhnung immer nur versprechen, in der politischen Praxis aber nicht bereit sind, unter Umständen obsolet gewordene Rechtspositionen um des Friedens willen aufzugeben, einen ersten Schritt auf den Anderen hin zu machen, für Freundschaft mit anderen Völkern auch dann, wenn es unpopulär ist, öffentlich zu kämpfen.

Der Christ, für den diese große Freiheit lebensbestimmend und maßgebend ist, ist darüber hinaus in seinem kleinen oder großen Einflußbereich eine Herausforderung für alle, die nicht einsehen wollen, warum es sich in bestimmten Situationen empfiehlt, um des Menschen und um des Friedens willen auf Recht und Vorteil zu verzichten. Eine Herausforderung für alle, die meinen, daß Macht und Gewalt, das Sich-Durchsetzen und Den-Anderen-Ausnützen, wo immer es bei Vermeidung des eigenen Risikos möglich ist, am vorteilhaftesten, klügsten, ja menschlich wohl am vernünftigsten sei.

Die christliche Botschaft widersetzt sich entschieden dieser Art von Herrschaftslogik, die die Menschlichkeit der Menschen um der Rechtlichkeit, Vorteilhaftigkeit und Gewalttätigkeit willen aufs Spiel setzt. Sie ist ein Angebot, im Verzichten etwas Positives, echt Menschliches zu sehen: Gewähr der eigenen Freiheit und der Freiheit des Anderen.

Wer die christliche Botschaft in diesem Punkt des naiven, wirklichkeitsblinden Neutralismus oder der rein individuell-privaten Appellation verdächtigt, hat nicht verstanden, wie groß die Sprengkraft dieser christlichen Herausforderung gerade auch für die Änderung ganzer Gesellschaftsstrukturen, ganzer Einstellungen, Haltungen und Vorurteile der Völker ist. Das gelingt aber nur, wenn es Menschen, immer mehr Menschen gibt, die sich, in welcher Partei auch immer, an dieser Forderung orientieren, wenn es Politiker, immer mehr Politiker gibt, die in dieser Forderung ihren Leitwert sehen, ohne daß sie deshalb in ihren politischen Reden und Verhandlungen, öffentlichen Auftritten und Programmen den Namen dessen ständig auf den Lippen führen müßten, der für sie in ihrer Politik letztlich maßgebend ist.

Und was gewinnt man dabei? Scheinbar nichts! Oder besser gesagt: »nur« den Frieden. Und vielleicht auf die Dauer auch den Anderen. Das ist richtig zu verstehen, nicht als simple Lösung für alle Fälle: Die christliche Botschaft, die Bergpredigt insbesondere, will die Rechtsordnung nicht abschaffen. Sie will das Recht nicht überflüssig machen. Aber sie will das Recht radikal relativieren. Warum? Damit das Recht den Menschen dient und nicht die Menschen dem Recht dienen.

Wo immer ein Einzelner oder ganze Gruppen vergessen, daß das Recht für die Menschen und nicht die Menschen für das Recht da sind, da tragen sie – die Geschichte der Staaten, aber auch der Kirchen, der Gemeinden, der Familien und des einzelnen Menschenlebens beweist es – ihren Teil dazu bei, daß im gesellschaftlichen wie im individuellen Bereich der unbarmherzige Rechtsstandpunkt durchgesetzt wird und aus dem summum ius (höchsten Recht) die summa iniuria (das höchste Unrecht) wird: daß auf diese Weise immer wieder neu zwischen den Menschen, den Gruppen, den Völkern Unmenschlichkeit verbreitet wird.

Wo immer aber ein Einzelner oder ganze Gruppen daran denken, daß in jedem Fall das Recht für den Menschen da ist, da betreiben sie die Vermenschlichung der nun einmal notwendigen Rechtsordnung und machen auch innerhalb der bestehenden Rechtsordnung in der ganz bestimmten Situation Befriedung, Vergebung, Versöhnung möglich: Sie verbreiten also gerade im Rechtsbereich Menschlichkeit zwischen den Menschen, den Gruppen und den Völkern. Sie dürfen die Verheißung auf sich beziehen, daß alle, die auf Gewalt verzichten, die Erde zum Besitz erhalten werden[2].

Freiheit im Machtkampf

Jesus appelliert an seine Jünger, daß sie freiwillig *Macht zugunsten der Anderen gebrauchen*[3]. Wer immer heute als Einzelner oder Gruppe an Jesus Christus seinen Maßstab nimmt, dem wird zwar nicht der faktisch unmögliche Verzicht auf jeden Machtgebrauch auferlegt. Aber er sieht sich in der ganz bestimmten Situation zum Machtgebrauch für andere aufgefordert.

Man denke zum Beispiel an das *Problem der wirtschaftlichen Macht*: Da hier analoge Probleme vorliegen, wie im eben behandelten Problemkreis von Krieg und Frieden, können wir uns kürzer fassen und uns auf das Allerwesentlichste beschränken. Die Fakten sind bekannt: Es scheint gegen die steigenden Preise und die Inflation kein Kraut gewachsen zu sein. Sie steigen und steigen, vor allem zuungunsten der Armen und Ärmsten. Die Arbeitgeber geben den Gewerkschaften, die Gewerkschaften den Arbeitgebern und beide zusammen der Regierung die Schuld. Ein Circulus vitiosus. Was tun? Auch hier nur knapp angedeutet:

– *Die christliche Botschaft gibt keine detaillierte Auskunft darüber, wie das Problem technisch angepackt werden soll, wie also das Rätsel des magischen Vierecks gelöst werden soll: wie gleichzeitig Vollbeschäftigung, Wirtschaftswachstum, Preisstabilität und ausgeglichene Außenhandelsbilanz erreicht werden sollen. Angebot und Nachfrage, Binnenmarkt und Außenmarkt scheinen ehernen ökonomischen Gesetzen zu gehorchen. Und ein jeder sucht sie in einem unbarmherzigen Machtkampf zu seinen Gunsten so gut als möglich auszunützen.*
– *Die christliche Botschaft sagt etwas, was normalerweise in keinem nationalökonomischen Lehrbuch, weder in einem »linken« noch in einem »rechten«, steht und was für unseren Zusammenhang so ungemein wichtig wäre: nämlich, daß es in all den unvermeidlichen Interessenkonflikten keine Schande ist, weder für den Unternehmer noch für den Gewerkschaftsführer, wenn er seine Macht gegenüber den Anderen nicht immer voll ausnützt. Daß es keine Schande ist, wenn der Unternehmer nicht jede Erhöhung der Produktionskosten auf die Konsumenten abwälzt, nur um seine Gewinnmarche konstant zu erhalten oder wenn möglich zu steigern. Daß es auch keine Schande ist, wenn der Gewerkschaftsführer einmal eine Lohnerhöhung nicht durchsetzt, obwohl er es könnte und die Mitglieder der Gewerkschaft es vielleicht erwarten. Kurz, daß es für die Machthaber keine Schande ist, wenn sie bei aller Härte der Auseinandersetzungen nicht ständig ihre gesellschaftliche Macht zu ihren Gunsten nützen, sondern in großer Freiheit bereit sind, in ganz bestimmten Situationen – wiederum nicht als allgemeines Gesetz – Macht zugunsten der Anderen zu gebrauchen; bereit, im Einzelfall auch einmal Macht, Gewinn, Einfluß zu »verschenken« und zum Rock auch noch den Mantel zu geben.*

Wozu? Nicht wegen einer verschleiernden Partnerschaftsideologie. Auch nicht, weil dadurch für die eigene Position unmittelbar etwas herausspringt. Aber um der Anderen willen: damit der Mensch (und oft sogar der Staat) nicht dem Machtkampf zum

Aber es wird ihm im ganz konkreten Fall die Realisierung dieses Verzichts um seiner und der anderen Freiheit willen als eine Chance angeboten.

Man denke an das *Problem des Wirtschaftswachstums*: Bei allen Fortschritten verwickelt sich unsere Leistungs- und Konsumgesellschaft immer mehr in Widersprüche. Gestützt auf eine allseits gepriesene Wirtschaftstheorie heißt die Devise: Immer mehr produzieren, damit man immer mehr konsumieren kann; immer mehr konsumieren, damit die Produktion nicht zusammenbricht, sondern expandiert. So wird das Anspruchsniveau immer über dem Versorgungsniveau gehalten: durch Reklame, durch Vorbilder und Leithammel des Konsums. Man will immer mehr haben. Neue Bedürfnisse werden geweckt, sobald die alten befriedigt sind. Luxusgüter werden zu notwendigen Gebrauchsgütern deklariert, um neuen Luxusgütern Platz zu machen. Die Ziele des eigenen Lebensstandards erhöhen sich mit der Verbesserung der Versorgungslage. Die Erwartungshaltung an Wohlstand und ein befriedigendes Leben hat sich dynamisiert. Die erstaunliche Folge: Auch bei ständig wachsendem Realeinkommen hat der Durchschnittsbürger den Eindruck, er habe kaum frei verfügbare Mittel, er lebe eigentlich am Existenzminimum.

Dabei gehen die industrielle Wohlstandsgesellschaft und weitgehend auch die Wirtschaftstheoretiker von der Voraussetzung aus, wachsender Wohlstand schaffe wachsendes Glück, das Vermögen zum Konsum sei der entscheidende Indikator für ein gelingendes Leben. Der Güterkonsum wird zur Demonstration des eigenen Status vor sich selbst und vor der Gesellschaft, so daß sich die Erwartungshaltungen gegenseitig nach dem Gesetz des Herdentriebs, des Prestiges und der Konkurrenz hochschaukeln. Man ist, was man verzehrt. Man ist mehr, wenn man einen höheren Standard erreicht hat. Man ist nichts, wenn man unter dem normierten Standort der Allgemeinheit bleibt. Alles in allem: Wenn wir eine bessere Zukunft erreichen wollen, müssen Produktion und Konsum immer mehr wachsen: alles muß immer größer, rascher, zahlreicher werden. Das strenge Gesetz des Wirtschaftswachstums.

Auf der anderen Seite erkennt man heute immer mehr: In den Industrienationen sind die Voraussetzungen dieses Wirtschaftsgesetzes weithin überholt. Nicht mehr die Überwindung von Armut und Güterknappheit ist unsere erste und wichtigste Sorge; denn in den hochindustrialisierten Ländern ist diese Voraussetzung für ein menschliches Leben in der Regel erfüllt. So überzeugt heute der Ruf nach dem Brot allein, allein nach Besitz und Konsum, viele nicht mehr. Einerseits sind die früheren Anstrengungen zur Behebung der Armut in eine Spirale endlos zu steigernder Bedürfniserwartung (der Konsumenten) und Bedürfnisweckung (der Produzenten) umgeschlagen. Andererseits machen bestimmte Gruppen unserer Gesellschaft immer deutlicher, daß es neben den bisher primären ökonomischen Bedürfnissen sekundäre und tertiäre Wünsche gibt, die von den Gütern der Volkswirtschaft nicht mehr befriedigt werden können. Auch die Besitzenden sind durch materiellen Wohlstand allein nicht glücklicher geworden. In wachsendem Maße macht sich gerade unter der konsumgewöhnten Jugend ein Gefühl der Langeweile und satten Orientierungslosigkeit, aber auch des Unbehagens über die einseitige Orientierung am stets wachsenden Konsum breit.

Das Gesetz des unkontrollierten Wirtschaftswachstums schafft jedoch auch eine immer größere Kluft zwischen reichen und armen Ländern und verstärkt bei den Benachteiligten der Menschheit die Gefühle des Neides, des Ressentiments, des tödlichen Hasses, aber auch der baren Verzweiflung und der Hilflosigkeit immer mehr. Und es wendet sich zuletzt gegen die Wohlhabenden selbst, wie schon eingangs dieses Buches skizziert: Immer mehr leiden wir unter den anscheinend endlos wachsenden Städten, dem auswuchernden Verkehr, dem Lärm von allen Seiten, der Verschmutzung der Flüsse und Seen und der schlechten Luft, machen uns Sorge über die Beseitigung von Butter- und Fleischbergen, werden wir vom Müll und Abfall unseres eigenen Wohlstandes erdrückt. Die Rohstoffe der Erde, rücksichtslos und immer umfassender ausgebeutet, werden knapper, das Problem einer immer weiter expandierenden Weltwirtschaft wird unübersehbar. Was aber tun? Es sei wiederum kurz umrissen:

– *Die christliche Botschaft gibt keine technischen Lösungen: zum Umweltschutz, zur Rohstoffverteilung, zur Landesplanung, zur Lärmbekämpfung, zur Müllbeseitigung; zu Strukturverbesserungen aller Art. Wir erhalten aus dem Neuen Testament auch keine Anweisungen über die Möglichkeiten, die Kluft zwischen Armen und Reichen, zwischen industrialisierten und industriell unterentwickelten Nationen abzubauen. Erst recht kann die christliche Botschaft keine Entscheidungsmodelle und Instrumentarien anbieten für die ungeheuren Probleme, die ein Kurswechsel erfordert: etwa das problematische Einfrieren*

der Volks- und Weltwirtschaft auf einem Null-Wachstum,
aber ohne Zusammenbruch von Wirtschaftszweigen, Verlust
von Arbeitsplätzen, chaotischen Folgen für die soziale Siche-
rung ganzer Bevölkerungsgruppen und die unterentwickelten
Länder.

- *Aber die christliche Botschaft vermag etwas deutlich zu ma-*
chen, was in der Wirtschaftstheorie wie in der praktischen
Wertskala der heutigen Konsum- und Leistungsgesellschaft
anscheinend gar nicht vorgesehen ist, aber vielleicht doch eine
Funktion haben könnte: gegen den Zwang zum Konsum die
Freiheit vom Konsum. Es hat auf alle Fälle einen Sinn, sein
Glück nicht auf Konsum und Wohlstand allein aufzubauen.
Von Jesus Christus her aber kann es sogar einen Sinn haben,
daß man nicht immer mehr erstrebt, daß man nicht immer alles
zu haben versucht, daß man sich nicht von den Gesetzen des
Prestiges und der Konkurrenz leiten läßt, daß man den Kult
des Überflusses nicht mitmacht, die Freiheit zum Konsumver-
zicht schon bei Kindern einübt. Also eine »Armut im Geiste«
als die innere Freiheit vom Besitz: als Grundhaltung die
genügsame Anspruchslosigkeit und vertrauende Sorglosigkeit.
Gegen alle anspruchsvoll unbescheidene Anmaßung und kum-
mervolle Besorgtheit, die sich bei ökonomisch Reichen und
Armen finden kann.

Wozu? Nicht aus Askese und Opferzwang. Nicht als ein neues,
zwingendes Gesetz. Sondern damit der konsumfreudige Nor-
malverbraucher frei bleibt, frei wird. Daß er sich nicht verkauft
an die guten Dinge dieser Welt, sei es das Geld oder das Auto,
den Alkohol oder die Zigarette, die Kosmetik oder die Sexualität.
Daß er nicht den Süchten der Wohlstandsgesellschaft verfällt.
Daß also der Mensch mitten in der Welt und ihren Gütern, die er
brauchen muß und brauchen darf, doch letztlich menschlich
bleibt. Also auch hier: Besitz, Wachstum, Konsum nicht um
seiner selbst willen. Erst recht nicht die Menschen um des Besitzes, des Wachstums, des Konsums willen. Sondern dies alles um
der Menschen willen!

Wo immer ein Einzelner oder ganze Gruppen übersehen, daß
alle guten Dinge dieser Welt um des Menschen willen da sind,
nicht der Mensch um dieser Dinge willen da ist, da beten sie nicht
den einen wahren Gott, sondern die vielen falschen Götter,
Mammon, Macht, Sexus, Arbeit, Prestige an und liefern den
Menschen diesen unbarmherzigen Göttern aus. Sie bestärken die

menschheitszerstörende Dynamik, in die unsere Wirtschaftsprozesse heute geraten sind. Sie bestärken die Gedankenlosigkeit, mit der heute auf Kosten der Zukunft gewirtschaftet wird. Sie bestärken den unmenschlichen Egoismus, mit dem heute die Kräfte der Weltwirtschaft der einen Hälfte der Menschheit zu viel geben, was die andere zu wenig erhält. Sie verbreiten in der Wohlstands- und Konsumgesellschaft, auch wenn sie es nicht erkennen, die Unmenschlichkeit.

Wo immer aber ein Einzelner oder ganze Gruppen sich daran halten, daß in jedem Fall die guten Dinge dieser Welt um des Menschen willen da sind, da helfen sie mit bei der Vermenschlichung der heute nun einmal unumgänglichen Wohlstands- und Konsumgesellschaft. Da schaffen sie die notwendige, nicht standesgebundene neue Elite, die eine neue Wertskala in dieser Gesellschaft leben lernt und auf weitere Sicht einen Prozeß des Umdenkens einzuleiten vermag. Sie ermöglichen auch in dieser neuen Zeit für sich und andere Unabhängigkeit, souveräne Anspruchslosigkeit, eine letzte sorglose Überlegenheit, die wahre Freiheit. Auch ihnen gilt dann die Verheißung, daß allen, die arm sind im Geiste, das Himmelreich gehören wird[6].

Freiheit zum Dienen

Jesus fordert von seinen Jüngern einen freiwilligen *Dienst ohne Rangordnung*[7]. Wo immer ein Einzelner oder eine Gruppe den Weg Jesu Christi einschlägt, da wird zwar nicht eine illusionäre Abschaffung aller Unter- und Überordnung in der Gesellschaft gefordert. Aber es wird der gegenseitige Dienst aller als eine neue Chance des Zusammenlebens angeboten.

Man denke an die *Probleme der Erziehung*: Erziehungsprogramme und Erziehungsmethoden, Erziehungsziele und Erziehungspersonen sind heute in eine tiefgreifende Krise geraten. Erziehungsinstanzen und Sozialisationsträger (Elternhaus, Schule, Universität, aber auch Heime und Betriebe) ebenso wie Erziehungspersonen (Vater, Mutter, Lehrer, Erzieher, Ausbilder) sehen sich massiver Kritik und ungeduldigen Vorwürfen von rechts und links ausgesetzt: den einen zu konservativ, den anderen zu progressiv, den einen zu politisch, den anderen zu unpolitisch, den einen zu autoritär, den anderen zu antiautoritär. Ratlosigkeit und Orientierungslosigkeit machen sich breit. Ursachen und Bedingungen, Symptome und Auswirkungen dieser Krise seien nur skizziert:

Im Elternhaus: Der beschleunigte soziale Wandel in der Gesellschaft bewirkt, daß Eltern nicht nur altern, sondern oft rasch veraltern. Die Maßstäbe zur Erziehung ihrer Kinder stimmen nicht mehr. Unverständnis und Unwissen sind die Folge. Eine tiefe Unsicherheit, die oft ein falsches Behauptenwollen nach sich zieht und damit katastrophale Autoritätskonflikte für Kinder und Familie heraufbeschwört.

In Schule und Universität: Die Diskrepanz zwischen Anspruch und Wirklichkeit, zwischen oft lebensfremder Theorie und gestiegenen praktischen Erwartungen und Bedürfnissen, die Rollenkonflikte zwischen Lehrern und Schülern, Professoren und Studenten machen Schule und Universität zu einem politisch-pädagogischen Streitobjekt zwischen allen gesellschaftlich relevanten Gruppen und zu einem Experimentierfeld immer neuer pädagogisch-didaktischer Entwürfe und Studienpläne. Nach der Planungseuphorie droht nun die Planungslethargie, nach der Überorganisation die Desorganisation, nach dem Zukunftsoptimismus der Chancengleichheit die Zukunftsunsicherheit durch immer mehr Studienbeschränkungen, nach der Beschwörung des Bildungsnotstands und dem Ausschöpfen letzter Bildungsreserven jetzt die Bildungsschwemme und das »akademische Proletariat«.

Und die Jugendlichen selbst? Mitten im Konfliktfeld dieser widersprüchlichen Bildungs- und Erziehungsszene reagieren sie zunehmend mit Apathie, Gleichgültigkeit und Überdruß und scheitern oft genug: Gesellschaftlich als Konsumenten ernstgenommen und als Verbraucher in ihrem Selbstbewußtsein gehätschelt, werden sie von Elternhaus und Schule oft unselbständig und abhängig gehalten. Von Erwachsenen, durch Schulbesuch und immer höheren Schulabschluß zu sozialem Prestigedenken beeinflußt, müssen sie erkennen, wie zweifelhaft die Leistungskriterien, wie lebensfremd oft die Ausbildung und wie unsicher die zukünftigen Berufschancen sind.

Und die Erwachsenen? Erziehungstugenden, gestern noch absolut tabu und fraglos, sind heute scheinbar obsolet geworden: Autorität der Erwachsenen, Gehorsam den Älteren gegenüber, Unterordnung unter den Willen der Eltern, Sicheinfügen in vorgegebene Ordnungsstrukturen. Doch nicht nur Erziehungsinhalte und -methoden, sondern Erziehung überhaupt ist für manche fragwürdig: Wer Erziehung mit Fremdbestimmung, Manipulation, Willenaufzwingen identifiziert, macht eine Wendung um 180 Grad: antiautoritäre Erziehung, absolute Selbstbestimmung, schrankenlose Freiheit, Ausleben von Aggressionen, Frustrationen, Trieben, Konflikten. Die Verhältnisse kehren sich um: nicht mehr Unterordnung der Jugendlichen unter den Willen der Erwachsenen, sondern Unterordnung der Ansprüche der Erwachsenen unter die Ansprüche, Bedürfnisse, Forderungen der Jugendlichen.

Ein signifikanter Trend zeichnet sich ab: Falsches Autoritätsverständnis auf beiden Seiten, Angst und Unsicherheit in der Reaktion auf den Anderen erzeugen eine Atmosphäre von Druck und Gegendruck, von Verweigern oder Sichbehaupten, von Verstärkung der Destruktionsneigung, von Brutalität und Aggression. Aber die Schule schiebt die Verantwortung auf Elternhaus und Gesellschaft, die Gesellschaft auf Schule und Elternhaus, das Elternhaus auf Schule und Gesellschaft: ein Circulus vitiosus. Was tun? Auch hier noch einmal knappe Anregungen:

– *Die christliche Botschaft gibt keine detaillierten Auskünfte darüber, wie das schulische und berufliche Ausbildungssystem besser und effektiver organisiert, wie Curricula erarbeitet, Bildungs- und Erziehungsprogramme durchgeführt, Bildungsfragen gelöst, Heime geleitet und Kinder erzogen werden sollen.*
– *Aber die christliche Botschaft sagt Entscheidendes über Haltung und Einstellung des Erziehers zum Kind und des Kindes zum Erzieher sowie über das Warum des Engagements auch in Enttäuschungen und Mißerfolgen: daß von der Gestalt Jesu her Erziehung nie um des eigenen Prestiges, Ansehens, Interesses willen geschehen darf, sondern immer um dessentwillen, der mir anvertraut ist. Erziehung also wesentlich nicht-repressiv verstanden: als gegenseitigen Dienst ohne Rangordnung! Das heißt: daß Kinder nie einfach um der Erzieher willen, aber auch die Erzieher nie einfach um der Kinder willen da sind; daß die Erzieher nie ihre Kinder, aber auch die Kinder nie ihre Erzieher ausnutzen; daß die Erzieher nie autoritär den Kindern ihren Willen aufzwingen, aber auch nie die Kinder antiautoritär ihren Willen den Erziehern. Gegenseitiger Dienst ohne Rangordnung in christlichem Geist meint für die Erzieher einen rational nicht erzwingbaren bedingungslosen Vorschuß des Vertrauens, der Güte, des Schenkens, des liebenden Wohlwollens, das sich nicht beirren läßt.*

Auch mit der Forderung eines Dienstes ohne Rangordnung ist keine neue Gesetzlichkeit gemeint. Vielmehr eine Einladung an beide Seiten: Dienen von seiten der Erzieher nicht zu verstehen als fromme Verschleierung einer noch immer autoritären Praxis oder auch als Schwäche der Erwachsenen den Kindern gegenüber. Dienen aber von seiten der Kinder auch nicht zu verstehen als Aufforderung, die Dienstbereitschaft des Erwachsenen als scheinbare Schwäche auszunutzen. Dienst ohne Rangordnung meint vielmehr gegenseitige Offenheit, Lern- und Korrekturbereitschaft.

Dieser von der Gestalt Jesu her motivierte Dienst ohne Rangordnung stellt jenen Pragmatismus von Erziehern in Frage, die immer nur auf Wünsche, Bedürfnisse, Forderungen der Kinder reagieren, die für die Kinder nie mehr als ihre Pflicht tun. Er stellt die Unbeweglichkeit eines erstarrenden, bequemen Lebensstils in Frage, der sich über ein von ihm selbst diktiertes Maß hinaus nicht mehr von den Erwartungen der Kinder beunruhigen läßt. Dieser Dienst stellt auch den gesellschaftlich weithin anerkannten Moralismus in Frage, der die Kinder auf seine Moralvorstellungen festlegen will und der sich auch dann noch im Recht fühlt, wenn er die Kinder fallen läßt, die dazu nicht bereit sind. Dieser Dienst stellt auch jenen scheinbar so vernünftigen Krämergeist in Frage, der Leistungen für die Kinder mindestens stillschweigend an die Bedingung knüpft, sie später gleichwertig zurückerstattet zu bekommen, und der sich bei dieser Haltung auch noch wundert, daß er brüske Ablehnung erfährt, wenn er sie moralisierend einklagt.

Christen verstehen das gegenseitige Dienen ohne Rangordnung auch im Erziehungsprozeß als einen rational nicht erzwingbaren, wohl aber von der Gestalt Jesu her zu begründenden Vorschuß des Vertrauens, der Güte, des Schenkens, des Sicheinlassens auf den Anderen: das sich auch dann nicht beirren läßt, wenn der Andere, wenn das Kind unseren Vorstellungen, Bildern, Hoffnungen nicht entspricht; wenn wir die Selbstbestätigung nicht bekommen, die wir erwarten oder brauchen; wenn wir sicher sind, daß wir im Grund mehr geben, als wir je zurückerhalten werden; wenn wir nach aller vernünftigen menschlichen Voraussicht wissen, daß alles Engagement bei einem bestimmten Kind keinen sichtbaren Erfolg zeitigen wird. Wer diesem christlichen Anspruch des Dienens ohne Rangordnung als seiner Erziehungsmaxime zu entsprechen versucht, der hat verstanden, daß hier christliche Nächstenliebe in ihrer ganzen Radikalität zur Debatte steht.

Eine neue Wertskala der Mitmenschlichkeit zeichnet sich von daher für die Erziehung ab, neue Orientierungsmarken für Erzieher und Kinder, ein neuer Sinnhorizont: auf keinen Fall eine Verabsolutierung des eigenen Selbst, sondern immer die Rücksicht auf den Anderen im Absehen von der eigenen Person, wie es sich im Teilenkönnen, im Vergebenkönnen, im Schonen, im freiwilligen Verzicht auf Rechte und Vorteile, im Schenken ohne Gegenleistung äußern kann.

Wozu also solches Dienen? Nicht aus Schwäche, sondern aus der Stärke der Überzeugung heraus, die nicht nur aus der Einsicht in die Notwendigkeit eines partnerschaftlichen, kooperativen Verhältnisses von Erzieher und zu Erziehenden resultiert, sondern aus der Selbstlosigkeit, die gerne über das hinausgeht, was Kooperation unbedingt verlangt. So ist es möglich, eine Atmosphäre des Vertrauens und Verständnisses, der echten Orientierungs- und Anleitungshilfe zu schaffen, eine nicht-repressive Erziehung jenseits von autoritär und antiautoritär. So ist es möglich, auch schon dem jungen Menschen den eigentlichen Sinn des Lebens vorzuleben: daß mein Leben nur dann einen Sinn hat, wenn ich es nicht nur für mich selbst lebe, sondern für andere, und wenn mein und der anderen Leben von einer Wirklichkeit getragen, geführt, genannt wird, die größer, dauernder, vollkommener ist als wir selbst – jene uns geheimnisvoll umfassende Wirklichkeit also, die wir Gott nennen.

Wo immer der Einzelne oder ganze Gruppen vergessen, daß Erziehung nicht zur Bestimmung über den Menschen, sondern zum gegenseitigen Dienst ohne Rangordnung da ist, da sind sie mit daran schuld, daß im gesellschaftlichen wie im individualen Bereich die Rechte des Stärkeren und Überlegeneren, die Gesetze der Fremdbestimmung und der Übermacht herrschen und daß gerade so die Voraussetzungen für Unmenschlichkeit und Würdelosigkeit geschaffen werden.

Wo immer aber ein Einzelner oder ganze Gruppen daran denken, daß Erziehung statt Bestimmung über den Menschen gegenseitiges Dienen ohne Rangordnung, über alle herrschaftsfreie Interaktion und Kooperation hinaus ein Vorschuß des Vertrauens, des Entgegenkommens, des Helfens, ja, des Wohlwollens und der Liebe ist, da tragen sie zur Vermenschlichung der menschlichen Beziehungen bei und machen dadurch auch in einer Phase der Unsicherheit und Orientierungslosigkeit ein sinnvolles und erfülltes Leben möglich. Ihnen, die in diesem Sinn die Erziehung als Dienen ohne Rangordnung verstehen, ist die

Verheißung gegeben, daß, wer ein Kind nicht nur im eigenen Namen, sondern in Jesu Namen aufnimmt, ihn aufnimmt[8]!

Doch diese Anregungen mögen genügen und das Weiterdenken provozieren: Wollte man alles aufschreiben, was Jesus getan hat, die Welt könnte »die Bücher nicht fassen, die geschrieben würden«[9]. Könnte die Welt die Bücher fassen, die geschrieben würden, wollte man aufschreiben, was in Jesu Nachfolge alles getan wurde, getan wird und vor allem – getan werden könnte?

Menschsein aufgehoben im Christsein

Ganz direkt gefragt: *Warum soll man Christ sein*? So hatten wir dieses Buch begonnen. Ebenso direkt geantwortet: *Um wahrhaft Mensch zu sein*! Was heißt das?

Kein Christsein auf Kosten des Menschseins. Aber auch umgekehrt: Kein Menschsein auf Kosten des Christseins. Kein Christsein neben, über oder unter dem Menschsein: Der Christ soll kein gespaltener Mensch sein.

Das Christliche ist also kein Überbau und kein Unterbau des Menschlichen, sondern es ist im besten Sinn des Wortes – bewahrend, verneinend und übersteigend – die *»Aufhebung« des Menschlichen*. Christsein bedeutet also eine »Aufhebung« der anderen Humanismen: Sie werden bejaht, sofern sie das Menschliche bejahen; sie werden verneint, sofern sie das Christliche, den Christus selber, verneinen; sie werden überstiegen, sofern das Christsein das Menschlich-Allzumenschliche sogar in aller Negativität voll einzubeziehen vermag.

Christen sind nicht weniger Humanisten als alle Humanisten. Aber sie sehen das Menschliche, das wahrhaft Menschliche, das Humane, sie sehen den Menschen und seinen Gott, sehen Humanität, Freiheit, Gerechtigkeit, Leben, Liebe, Frieden, Sinn von diesem Jesus her, der für sie der konkret Maßgebende, der Christus ist. Von ihm her meinen sie nicht einen beliebigen Humanismus vertreten zu können, der einfach alles Wahre, Gute, Schöne und Menschliche bejaht. Sondern einen wahrhaft *radikalen Humanismus*, der auch das Unwahre, Ungute, Unschöne und Unmenschliche zu integrieren und zu bewältigen vermag: nicht nur alles Positive, sondern auch – und hier entscheidet sich, was ein Humanismus taugt – alles Negative, selbst Leiden, Schuld, Tod, Sinnlosigkeit.

Im Blick auf ihn, den Gekreuzigten und Lebendigen, vermag

der Mensch auch in der Welt von heute nicht nur zu handeln, sondern auch zu leiden, nicht nur zu leben, sondern auch zu sterben. Und es leuchtet ihm auch dort noch Sinn auf, wo die reine Vernunft kapitulieren muß, auch in sinnloser Not und Schuld, weil er sich auch da, weil er sich im Positiven wie im Negativen von Gott gehalten weiß. So schenkt der Glaube an Jesus den Christus Frieden mit Gott und mit sich selbst, überspielt aber nicht die Probleme der Welt. Er macht den Menschen wahrhaft menschlich, weil wahrhaft mitmenschlich: bis zum Letzten offen für den Anderen, der ihn gerade braucht, den »Nächsten«.

So haben wir gefragt: Warum soll man Christ sein? Man wird es nun gut verstehen, wenn wir die Antwort auf die knappe zusammenfassende Formel bringen:

> *In der Nachfolge Jesu Christi*
> *kann der Mensch in der Welt von heute*
> *wahrhaft menschlich leben, handeln, leiden und sterben:*
> *in Glück und Unglück, Leben und Tod*
> *gehalten von Gott und hilfreich den Menschen.*

Theologische Grundliteratur

Vorbemerkung: Der theologische Laie dürfte sich kaum ein Bild davon machen, wie umfangreich und vielschichtig die theologische Literatur ist, die direkt oder indirekt ein Buch wie dieses überhaupt erst ermöglicht. Wir geben zu den einzelnen Problemkreisen die Literatur möglichst kompakt an, und zwar weitgehend nur selbständige Buchveröffentlichungen und nicht die in die Zehntausend gehenden Zeitschriftartikel.

Damit aber der Leser in der Flut der Literatur nicht ertrinkt, sei hier kurz ein Überblick über die neuere theologische Grundliteratur gegeben, die auch im Buch öfters benützt und meist abgekürzt zitiert wird.

1. Lexika

Bibellexikon. Hrsg. von *H. Haag*. Einsiedeln–Zürich–Köln 1968 (= BL).

Catholicisme. Hier – aujourd'hui – demain. Hrsg. von *G. Jaquemet*. Paris 1948 ff.

Dictionnaire de la Bible, Supplément, Bd. I–VIII. Hrsg. von *L. Pirot*, fortgesetzt von *A. Robert*. Paris 1928 ff. (= DBS).

Dictionnaire de Théologie Catholique, Bd. I– XVI. Hrsg. von *A. Vacant* und *E. Mangenot*, fortgesetzt von *E. Amann*. Paris 1903 ff.

Evangelisches Kirchenlexikon. Kirchlich-theologisches Handwörterbuch. Hrsg. von *H. Brunotte* und *O. Weber*. Göttingen 1955 ff. (= EKL).

Lexikon für Theologie und Kirche, Bd. I–X. Hrsg. von *J. Höfer* und *K. Rahner*. Freiburg ²1956 ff. (= LThK).

New Catholic Encyclopedia, Bd. I–XV. Hrsg. von der Catholic University of America, Washington. New York 1967.

Die Religion in Geschichte und Gegenwart. Handwörterbuch für Theologie und Religionswissenschaft, Bd. I–VI. Hrsg. von *K. Galling*. Tübingen ³1957 (= RGG).

Theologisches Wörterbuch zum Neuen Testament, Bd. I–VIII. Hrsg. von *G. Kittel*, fortgesetzt von *G. Friedrich*. Stuttgart 1933 ff. (= ThW).

2. Bibelkommentare

Kritisch-exegetischer Kommentar über das Neue Testament, begründet von *H. A. W. Meyer*. 16 Bde. in immer neuen Bearbeitungen. Göttingen 1932 ff. (Meyers Kommentar).

Handbuch zum Neuen Testament. Hrsg. von *H. Lietzmann*, fortgeführt von *G. Bornkamm*. 22 Abteilungen in verschiedenen Auflagen. Tübingen 1906 ff. (Lietzmanns Handbuch).

Das Neue Testament Deutsch. Neues Göttinger Bibelwerk. Hrsg. von *P. Althaus* und *J. Behm*. 12 Bde. in verschiedenen Auflagen. Göttingen 1932 ff. (NT Deutsch).

Das neue Testament. Übersetzt und kurz erklärt. Hrsg. von *A. Wikenhauser* und *O. Kuss*. 9 Bde. und Registerband in verschiedenen Auflagen. Regensburg 1938 ff. (Regensburger NT).

Herders Theologischer Kommentar zum Neuen Testament, hrsg. von *A. Wikenhauser* und *A. Vögtle*. Freiburg 1953 ff. (Herders theologischer Kommentar).

The International Critical Commentary on the Holy Scriptures of the Old and New Testament. Hrsg. von *S. R. Driver, A. Plummer* und *C. A. Briggs*. Edinburgh 1895 ff.

Etudes Bibliques. Paris 1907 ff.

Commentaire du Nouveau Testament. Hrsg. von *P. Bonnard* u. a. Neuchâtel–Paris 1949 ff.

3. Neutestamentliche Theologien und Christologien

Bultmann, R., Theologie des Neuen Testaments. Tübingen 1953. ³1958.

Konzelmann, H., Grundriß der Theologie des Neuen Testaments. München 1968.

Jeremias, J., Neutestamentliche Theologie. Erster Teil: Die Verkündigung Jesu. Gütersloh 1971.

Kümmel, W. G., Die Theologie des Neuen Testaments nach seinen Hauptzeugen Jesus, Paulus, Johannes. Göttingen 1969.

Schelkle, K. H., Theologie des Neuen Testaments, 4 Bde. Düsseldorf 1968 ff.

Cullmann, O., Die Christologie des Neuen Testaments. Tübingen 1957. ³1963.

Hahn, F., Christologische Hoheitstitel. Ihre Geschichte im frühen Christentum. Göttingen 1963.

Pannenberg, W., Grundzüge der Christologie. Gütersloh 1964.

4. Dogmatiken

Denzinger, H., Enchiridion symbolorum, definitionum et declarationum de rebus fidei et morum. Barcelona–Freiburg i. Br.–Rom ³¹1960 (= Denz).

Conciliorum Oecumenicorum Decreta. Edidit Centro di Documentazione, Istituto per le Scienze Religiose – Bologna, curantibus *J. Alberigo* etc. Freiburg 1962.

Althaus, P., Die christliche Wahrheit. Lehrbuch der Dogmatik. Gütersloh 1947. ⁶1962.

Barth, K., Die kirchliche Dogmatik, Bd. I/1–IV/4. Zürich 1932 ff.

Brunner, E., Dogmatik, Bd. I–III. Zürich 1946 ff.

Diem, H., Theologie als kirchliche Wissenschaft, Bd. I–III. München 1951 ff.

Mysterium Salutis. Grundriß heilsgeschichtlicher Dogmatik, Bd. I–V. Hrsg. von *J. Feiner* und *M. Löhrer*. Einsiedeln–Zürich–Köln 1965 ff.

Neues Glaubensbuch. Der gemeinsame christliche Glaube. Hrsg. von *J. Feiner* und *L. Vischer*. Freiburg–Zürich 1973.

Ott, H., Die Antwort des Glaubens. Stuttgart–Berlin 1972.

Rahner, K., Schriften zur Theologie, Bd. I–XI. Einsiedeln–Zürich–Köln 1962 ff.

Schmaus, M., Katholische Dogmatik, Bd. I–V. München 1956 ff.

Tillich, P., Systematische Theologie, Bd. I–III. Stuttgart ³1956ff.
Weber, O., Grundlagen der Dogmatik, Bd. I–II. Neukirchen–Moers 1959–62.

5. Einführungen ins Christentum oder ins Apostolikum

Balthasar, H.U. von, Wer ist ein Christ? Einsiedeln 1965.
Ebeling, G., Das Wesen des christlichen Glaubens. Tübingen 1963.
Glaubensverkündigung für Erwachsene (Holländischer Katechismus). Hrsg. im
   Auftrag der Bischöfe von Holland durch das Höhere Katechetische Institut in
   Nijmegen. Nijmegen–Utrecht 1968.
Harnack, A., Das Wesen des Christentums. Leipzig 1900.
Kasper, W., Einführung in den Glauben. Mainz 1972.
Barth, K., Credo. Die Hauptprobleme der Dogmatik dargestellt im Anschluß an
   das Apostolische Glaubensbekenntnis. München 1935.
Pannenberg W., Das Glaubensbekenntnis ausgelegt und verantwortet vor den
   Fragen der Gegenwart. Hamburg 1972.
Ratzinger, J., Einführung in das Christentum. Vorlesungen über das Apostolische
   Glaubensbekenntnis. München 1968.

6. Abgekürzt zitierte Werke des Verfassers

Rechtfertigung. Die Lehre Karl Barths und eine katholische Besinnung. Einsie-
   deln 1957. ⁴1964.
Strukturen der Kirche. Freiburg–Basel–Wien 1962.
Die Kirche. Freiburg–Basel–Wien 1967.
Menschwerdung Gottes. Eine Einführung in Hegels theologisches Denken als
   Prolegomena zu einer künftigen Christologie. Freiburg–Basel–Wien 1970.
Wozu Priester? Eine Hilfe. Zürich–Einsiedeln–Köln 1971.

Anmerkungen

A I: Die Herausforderung der modernen Humanismen

1. Wende zum Menschen

1 Zur Geschichte des Begriffs: *H. Lübbe*, Säkularisierung. Geschichte eines ideenpolitischen Begriffs (Freiburg–München 1965). Zur Problematik sind grundlegend: *F. Gogarten*, Verhängnis und Hoffnung der Neuzeit. Die Säkularisierung als theologisches Problem (Stuttgart 1953); *H. Cox*, The Secular City (New York 1965); dt.: Stadt ohne Gott (Stuttgart–Berlin 1966); *H. Blumenberg*, Die Legitimität der Neuzeit (Frankfurt 1966).

2 *M. Greiffenhagen*, Art. Emanzipation, in: Historisches Wörterbuch der Philosophie Bd. II (Darmstadt 1972) 448 f.; *ders.*, Ein Weg der Vernunft ohne Rückkehr. Ist die Emanzipation in eine neue Phase getreten?, in: Die Zeit vom 22. Juni 1973.

3 *M. Weber*, Die protestantische Ethik und der Geist des Kapitalismus, in: Gesammelte Aufsätze zur Religionssoziologie Bd. I (Tübingen 1920) 17–206.

4 *J. Kahl*, Das Elend des Christentums oder Plädoyer für eine Humanität ohne Gott. Mit einer Einführung v. *G. Szczesny* (Hamburg 1968); vgl. neuerdings *C. Amery*, Das Ende der Vorsehung. Die gnadenlosen Folgen des Christentums (Hamburg 1972).

5 So *F. Gogarten*, aaO, und *H. Cox*, aaO. Vgl. zur Diskussion: *D. Callahan* (Hrsg.), The Secular City Debate (New York–London 1966).

6 *H. Blumenberg*, aaO.

2. Ausverkauf des Christlichen?

1 *D. von Hildebrandt*, Das trojanische Pferd in der Stadt Gottes (Regensburg o. J.).

2 *J. Maritain*, Pensées d'un paysan de la Garonne (Paris 1966); dt.: Der Bauer von der Garonne. Ein alter Laie macht sich Gedanken (München 1969).

3 *H. U. von Balthasar*, Cordula oder der Ernstfall (Einsiedeln 1966).

4 *L. Bouyer*, La décomposition du catholicisme (Paris 1968); dt.: Der Verfall des Katholizismus (München 1970).

5 *R. Augstein*, Das große Schisma, in: Der Spiegel (1969) Nr. 18; vgl. auch: *R. Altmann*, Abschied von den Kirchen, in: Der Spiegel (1970) Nr. 28.

6 Newsweek vom 4. Okt. 1971.

7 Der Begriff wurde besonders populär durch die Veröffentlichungen von *J. B. Metz, J. Moltmann, D. Sölle* (Diskussion in: D III, 1).

8 *C. Schmitt*, Politische Theologie. Vier Kapitel zur Lehre von der Souveränität (München–Leipzig 1922, ²1934).

9 Unsere Analyse und grundsätzliche Folgerung deckt sich weithin mit dem von *Jürgen Moltmann* über Identität und Relevanz des christlichen Glaubens (»identity-involvement-dilemma«) Gesagten. Vgl. *J. Moltmann*, Der gekreuzigte Gott. Das Kreuz Christi als Grund und Kritik christlicher Theologie (München 1972) Kap. I, 1–2.

3. Keine Verabschiedung der Hoffnung

1 *A. Toffler*, The Future Shock (New York 1970) Kap. 1.
2 *D. L. Meadows*, The Limits to Growth (New York 1972); dt.: Die Grenzen des Wachstums (Stuttgart 1972).
3 *G. R. Taylor*, Das Selbstmordprogramm – Zukunft oder Untergang der Menschheit (Frankfurt 1971); *S. Kirban*, Die geplante Verwirrung (Wetzlar 1972); *G. Ehrensvärd*, Nach uns die Steinzeit. Das Ende des technischen Zeitalters (Bern 1972); *D. Widener*, Kein Platz für Menschen. Der programmierte Selbstmord (Frankfurt 1972); *E. E. Snyder*, Todeskandidat Erde. Programmierter Selbstmord durch unkontrollierten Fortschritt (München 1972); *M. Lohmann* (Hrsg.), Gefährdete Zukunft (München 1973).
4 *K. Steinbuch*, Falsch programmiert (Stuttgart 1968).
5 *K. Steinbuch*, Kurskorrektur (Stuttgart 1973) S. 9.
6 *K. Lorenz*, Die acht Todsünden der zivilisierten Menschheit (München 1973).
7 Aus dem umfangreichen Œuvre aller dieser Autoren vgl. besonders die grundlegenden Werke: *M. Horkheimer – T. W. Adorno*, Dialektik der Aufklärung. Philosophische Fragmente (Amsterdam 1947); *T. W. Adorno*, Negative Dialektik (Frankfurt 1966); *M. Horkheimer*, Zur Kritik der instrumentellen Vernunft, hrsg. v. *A. Schmidt* (Frankfurt 1967); ders., Kritische Theorie. Eine Dokumentation, hrsg. v. *A. Schmidt*, Bd. I–II (Frankfurt 1968); *H. Marcuse*, The One-Dimensional-Man. Studies in the Ideology of Advanced Industrial Society (Boston 1964); dt.: Der eindimensionale Mensch. Studien zur Ideologie der fortgeschrittenen Industriegesellschaft (Neuwied–Berlin 1967); *E. Bloch*, Das Prinzip Hoffnung (Frankfurt 1959). Eine gute Einführung bietet *A. Schmidt*, Die »Zeitschrift für Sozialforschung«. Geschichte und gegenwärtige Bedeutung. Sonderheft der Nachrichten aus dem Kösel-Verlag (München 1970).
8 Vgl. bes. *H. Marcuse*, aaO, über die eindimensionale Gesellschaft und das eindimensionale Denken.
9 Zur Auseinandersetzung mit dem Kritischen Rationalismus vgl. *H. Küng*, Existiert Gott? (München 1975).
10 Vgl. die Marx-Interpretation des französischen Strukturalisten *L. Althusser*, Pour Marx (Paris 1965); dt.: Für Marx (Frankfurt 1968); *L. Althusser – E. Balibar*, Lire le Capital Bd. I–II (Paris ²1968); dt.: Das Kapital lesen Bd. I–II (Teilausgabe Hamburg 1972).
11 *K. Marx*, Frühe Schriften Bd. I–II, hrsg. v. *H. J. Lieber – P. Furth* (Darmstadt 1962–71), bes. Thesen über Feuerbach und Die Deutsche Ideologie.
12 *K. Marx*, Das Kapital. Kritik der politischen Ökonomie Bd. I–III, hrsg. v. *H. J. Lieber – B. Kautsky* (Darmstadt 1962–64).
13 Für den orthodoxen Marxismus (Marxismus-Leninismus) grundlegend: *K. Marx – F. Engels*, Manifest der Kommunistischen Partei 1848, in: *K. Marx*, Frühe Schriften Bd. II, S. 813–858; *F. Engels*, Herrn Dührings Umwälzung der Wissenschaft (»Anti-Dühring«) 1878 (Berlin 1948); *W. I. Lenin*, Materialismus und Empiriokritizismus 1908 (Berlin 1949); *J. Stalin*, Über dialektischen und historischen Materialismus 1939, in: Fragen des Leninismus (Berlin 1950) S. 647–679.
14 Besonders aufschlußreich: *S. Stojanović*, Kritik und Zukunft des Sozialismus (Original serbokroatisch: Belgrad 1969; dt.: München 1970); *P. Vranicki*, Geschichte des Marxismus Bd. I–II (Original serbokroatisch: Zagreb 1961–71; dt.: Frankfurt 1972–74). In Ungarn wären zu nennen die verschiedenen Veröffentlichungen von *Andras Hegedüs* und *Agnes Heller*, Vertreter der dortigen Neuen Linken.

15 Vgl. *H. Pross,* Überleben des Kapitalismus? Mitwirkung der Unternehmer an der Verbesserung der Wirtschaftsverfassung, in: Sonderdruck der Arbeitsgemeinschaft Selbständiger Unternehmer e. V., unter dem Titel: Der Angriff auf den Unternehmer – Herausforderung und Chance! Jahres-Hauptversammlung 1973 vom 31. Mai – 2. Juni in München, S. 15–20.

16 So schon früh auch *H. Marcuse,* Soviet Marxism. A Critical Analysis (New York 1958); dt.: Die Gesellschaft des Sowjet-Marxismus (Neuwied–Berlin 1964). Über die Verhältnisse in der Sowjetunion, DDR, ČSSR, Kuba und Nordkorea ebenfalls von linkssozialistischer Seite die fünf Berichte von *R. Rossanda, B. Rabehl, S. Plogstedt, G. Maschke, H. Kurnitzky* und *K. D. Wolff* in dem von *H. M. Enzensberger* hrsg. Kursbuch (Berlin 1972) Heft 30.

17 *M. Djilas,* Die neue Klasse. Eine Analyse des kommunistischen Systems (München 1957); vgl. *ders.,* Die unvollkommene Gesellschaft (Wien 1969). Djilas war der langjährige Kampfgefährte Titos und 1945–54 Generalsekretär der Kommunistischen Partei Jugoslawiens, stellvertretender Ministerpräsident und maßgebender Theoretiker der Partei. Das Buch brachte ihm sechs Jahre Haft ein. Im Jahre 1962 wurde er wegen seines Buches ›Gespräche mit Stalin‹ (Frankfurt 1962) zu weiteren neun Jahren Gefängnis verurteilt.

18 Vgl. die im Westen bekanntgewordenen Veröffentlichungen prominenter russischer Regimekritiker, vor allem den Brief der Professoren *A. D. Sacharow, W. F. Turtschin* und *R. A. Medwedew* 1968 an das Zentralkomitee der KPdSU, L. I. Breschnew, abgedruckt in: Neue Zürcher Zeitung vom 22. April 1970; dann *A. D. Sacharow,* Wie ich mir die Zukunft vorstelle (Zürich 1969); *ders.,* Ein Memorandum an den Generalsekretär der KPdSU, L. I. Breschnew, 1971, abgedruckt in: Die Zeit vom 21. Juli 1972; *ders.,* Interview, in: Der Spiegel (1973) Nr. 28; *A. Amalrik,* Kann die Sowjetunion das Jahr 1984 überleben? Ein Essai (Zürich 1970); *P. I. Jakir,* Kindheit in Gefangenschaft (Frankfurt 1972); *A. Solschenizyn,* Offener Brief an die sowjetische Führung (September 1973). Lebt nicht mit der Lüge (Februar 1974) (Darmstadt–Neuwied 1974). Aufschlußreich auch die Untersuchung des früheren Moskauer Korrespondenten der Neuen Zürcher Zeitung *R. Bernheim,* Die sozialistischen Errungenschaften der Sowjetunion (Zürich 1972).

19 Vgl. von den Beteiligten *U. Bergmann, A. Dutschke, W. Lefèvre, B. Rabehl,* Rebellion der Studenten oder Die neue Opposition. Eine Analyse (Hamburg 1968). Dazu kritisch: *E. K. Scheuch* (Hrsg.), Die Wiedertäufer der Wohlstandsgesellschaft (Köln 1968); *W. Fikentscher,* Zur politischen Kritik an Marxismus und Neomarxismus als ideologische Grundlage der Studentenunruhen 1965/69 (Tübingen 1971). Zur umstrittenen Gleichsetzung von »Braun« und »Rot« vgl. *H. Grebing,* Linksradikalismus gleich Rechtsradikalismus. Eine falsche Gleichung (Stuttgart 1971); *M. Greiffenhagen, R. Kühnl, J. B. Müller,* Totalitarismus. Zur Problematik eines politischen Begriffs (München 1972).

20 *M. Horkheimer,* Vorwort zu seinem Sammelband ›Kritische Theorie‹ (Frankfurt 1968).

21 *H. Marcuse,* Der eindimensionale Mensch (nach dt. Ausg.) S. 263, 264, 266, 268.

22 *J. Habermas,* Legitimationsprobleme im Spätkapitalismus (Frankfurt 1973); vgl. *ders.,* Nachwort 1973 zu: Erkenntnis und Interesse (Frankfurt 1973).

23 Zum *Verhältnis Christentum – Marxismus* zuerst von *christlicher* Seite: *J. L. Hromádka,* Evangelium für Atheisten (Berlin 1957); *H. Gollwitzer,* Die marxistische Religionskritik und der christliche Glaube (Hamburg 1965); *E. Kellner* (Hrsg.), Christentum und Marxismus – heute. Gespräche der Paulus-Ge-

sellschaft (Wien–Frankfurt–Zürich 1966), vgl. bes. die Beiträge von *W. Dantine*, *G. Girardi*, *J. B. Metz*, *K. Rahner*, *M. Reding*, *O. Schreuder* und *G. A. Wetter*; *R. Garaudy – J. B. Metz – K. Rahner*, Der Dialog oder Ändert sich das Verhältnis zwischen Katholizismus und Marxismus (Hamburg 1966); *M. Stöhr* (Hrsg.), Disputation zwischen Christen und Marxisten (München 1966); *G. Girardi*, Marxismo e cristianesimo (Spoleto 1967); dt.: Marxismus und Christentum (Wien 1968); *F. J. Adelmann*, From Dialogue to Epilogue. Marxism and Catholicism tomorrow (The Hague 1968); *W. Post*, Kritik der Religion bei Karl Marx (München 1969); *I. Fetscher – W. Post*, Verdirbt Religion den Menschen? Marxistischer und christlicher Humanismus. Ein Interview (Düsseldorf 1969); *J. Kadenbach*, Das Religionsverständnis von Karl Marx (München–Paderborn–Wien 1970); *H. Aptheker*, The Urgency of Marxist-Christian Dialogue (New York 1970); *J. M. Lochman*, Church in a Marxist Society. A Czechoslovak View (New York 1970); *D. Sölle*, Christentum und Marxismus. Bericht über den Stand des Gesprächs, in: Das Recht, ein anderer zu werden (Neuwied–Berlin 1971); *F. v. d. Oudenrijn*, Kritische Theologie als Kritik der Theologie. Theorie und Praxis bei Karl Marx – Herausforderung der Theologie (München–Mainz 1972); *J. P. Miranda*, Marx y la Biblia. Crítica a la filosofia de la opresión (Salamanca 1972).

Zum *Verhältnis Christentum – Marxismus* dann von *marxistischer* Seite: *E. Bloch*, Das Prinzip Hoffnung Bd. I–II (1959; Frankfurt 1967); *ders.*, Thomas Münzer als Theologe der Revolution (1960; Frankfurt 1962); *ders.*, Atheismus und Christentum. Zur Religion des Exodus und des Reichs (Frankfurt 1968); *M. Machoveč*, Marxismus und dialektische Theologie. Barth, Bonhoeffer und Hromádka in atheistisch-kommunistischer Sicht (Zürich 1965); *ders.*, Jesus für Atheisten (Stuttgart 1972); *R. Garaudy*, Marxisme du XXème siècle (Paris–Genf 1966); dt.: Marxismus im 20. Jahrhundert (Hamburg 1966), bes. Kap.: Der Marxismus und die Religion S. 91–137; *V. Gardavský*, Gott ist nicht ganz tot. Betrachtungen eines Marxisten über Bibel, Religion und Atheismus (München 1968); *L. Kolakowski*, Geist und Ungeist christlicher Traditionen (Stuttgart 1971); vgl. ferner den bereits zitierten Band: Christentum und Marxismus – heute, aaO, bes. die Beiträge von *R. Garaudy*, *R. Havemann*, *L. Lombardo-Radice*.

24 *G. Mann*, Ohne Geschichte leben? Eröffnungsrede zum 29. Deutschen Historikertag vor dem Verband der Geschichtslehrer Deutschlands in Regensburg, in: Die Zeit vom 13. Oktober 1972.

25 *M. Weber*, Politik als Beruf (Oktober 1919), in: Gesammelte politische Schriften (Tübingen 1971) S. 505–560 (Zitat S. 560).

26 *R. Jungk*, Die Zukunft hat schon begonnen (Stuttgart 1952).

27 *R. Jungk*, Der Jahrtausendmensch. Bericht aus den Werkstätten der neuen Gesellschaft (München–Gütersloh–Wien 1973).

28 *H. Pross*, aaO S. 17.

29 *H. Pross*, aaO S. 19.

A II: Die andere Dimension

1. Zugang zu Gott

1 *E. Ionesco*, Die bedrohte Kultur. Rede zur Eröffnung der Salzburger Festspiele 1972. Französisches Original und deutsche Übersetzung (München 1972) S. 22 (eigene Übersetzung aus dem Französischen).

745

2 *E. Ionesco,* aaO S. 21 f.

3 Vgl. A I, 3: Humanität durch technologische Evolution?

4 Vgl. A I, 3: Humanität durch politisch-soziale Revolution?

5 Zu der hier aus Raumgründen nicht möglichen Auseinandersetzung mit dem Nihilismus vgl. *H. Küng,* Existiert Gott? (München 1975).

6 *M. Horkheimer,* Die Sehnsucht nach dem ganz Anderen. Ein Interview mit Kommentar von H. Gumnior (Hamburg 1970), bes. S. 67–69.

7 *H.F. Steiner,* Marxisten-Leninisten über den Sinn des Lebens. Eine Studie zum kommunistischen Menschenbild (Essen 1970); vgl. bes. die aus dem Russischen übersetzte Dokumentation über die Diskussion in sowjetischen Zeitschriften, S. 309–363.

8 *A. Schaff,* Marxismus und das menschliche Individuum (Wien–Frankfurt–Zürich 1965); *M. Machovec,* Jesus für Atheisten (Stuttgart–Berlin 1972) S. 15–30; vgl. *ders.,* Vom Sinn des menschlichen Lebens (tschechisch: 1965, dt: Freiburg 1971); *E. Bloch,* Religion im Erbe. Eine Auswahl aus seinen religionsphilosophischen Schriften (München–Hamburg 1967).

9 *P. Berger,* Invitation to Sociology. A. Humanistic Perspective (New York 1963); dt.: Einladung zur Soziologie. Eine humanistische Perspektive (München 1971) S. 182; *ders.,* The Rumor of Angels (New York 1969); dt.: Auf den Spuren der Engel (Frankfurt 1970), bes. Kap. 3.

10 *W. Heisenberg,* Der Teil und das Ganze. Gespräche im Umkreis der Atomphysik (München 1969) S. 116–130; vgl. ebenfalls S. 279–295; *ders.,* Naturwissenschaftliche und religiöse Wahrheit, Rede anläßlich der Guardini-Preis-Verleihung, in: Zur Debatte. Themen der Katholischen Akademie in Bayern 3 (1973) Nr. 3/4. Vgl. auch *P. Jordan,* Der Naturwissenschaftler vor der religiösen Frage. Abbruch einer Mauer (Oldenburg–Hamburg 1963).

11 Vgl. außerhalb der Freud-Schule vor allem *C. G. Jung,* Psychologie und Religion. Studienausgabe (Olten 1971). Zur Problematik: *J. Rudin,* Psychotherapie und Religion (Olten 1960). Dann der Begründer der Logotherapie *V. E. Frankl,* Ärztliche Seelsorge. Grundlagen der Logotherapie und Existenzanalyse (1946, 8. durchges. Aufl. Wien 1971); *ders.,* Der Wille zum Sinn (Bern–Stuttgart–Wien 1972); *ders.,* Der unbewußte Gott. Psychotherapie und Religion (1947, erweitert München 1974).

12 Vgl. innerhalb der Freud-Schule vor allem: *E. H. Erikson,* Identity and the Life Cycle (New York 1959); dt.: Identität und Lebenszyklus (Frankfurt 1966); Insight and Responsibility (New York 1964); dt.: Einsicht und Verantwortung. Die Rolle des Ethischen in der Psychoanalyse (Frankfurt 1971); *ders.,* Identity. Youth and Crisis (New York 1968); dt.: Jugend und Krise (Stuttgart 1970); *R. May,* The Meaning of Anxiety (New York 1950); *ders.,* Man's Search for Himself (New York 1953); *ders.,* Love and Will (New York 1969); *ders.,* Power and Innocence (New York 1972).

13 *M. Machovec,* aaO S. 25.

14 *P. Nobile* (Hrsg.), The Con III Controversy: The Critics Look at the Greening of America (New York 1971).

15 *Th. Roszak,* The Making of a Counter Culture. Reflections on the Technocratic Society and its Youthful Opposition (New York 1968).

16 *Ch. Reich,* The Greening of America (New York) S. 327.

17 *A. J. Toynbee,* Surviving the Future (London 1971) S. 44f., 66f (eigene Übersetzung aus dem Englischen). Vgl. auch *M. Mead,* Twentieth Century Faith. Hope and Survival (New York 1972) bes. S. 3; dt.: Hoffnung und Überleben der Menschheit. Glaube im 20. Jahrhundert (Stuttgart–Berlin 1972), bes. S. 8 f.

18 Vgl. die Angaben aus dem Moskauer Patriarchat nach: Der Spiegel (1974) Nr. 17.

19 Vgl. A I, 1: Säkulare Welt.

20 Vgl. zur Kritik der Säkularisationsthese und zum ganzen Komplex des Fortbestehens der Religion: *A. M. Greeley*, Religion in the Year 2000 (New York 1969); *ders.*, The Persistence of Religion (London 1974); *O. Schatz* (Hrsg.), Hat die Religion Zukunft? (Graz–Wien–Köln 1971) mit Beiträgen von *A. Toynbee, P. L. Berger, Th. Luckmann, A. Gehlen, K. Löwith, M. Horkheimer, E. Bloch, H. Cox, O. Schatz* u. a.; *G. Baum*, New Horizon (New York 1972); schließlich das von *G. Baum* und *A. M. Greeley* hrsg. Heft von Concilium 9 (1973) Nr. 1 mit Beiträgen von *M. Marty, J. Brothers, W. und N. McCready, J. Remy, E. Servais, B. van Iersel, D. Power, J. Shea, E. Kennedy, D. Tracy, R. Ruether, R. Laurentin.* Aus früheren religionssoziologischen Veröffentlichungen sind zu nennen: *E. A. Tiryakian* (Hrsg.), Sociological Theory, Values, and Sociocultural Change. Essays in Honor of P. A. Sorokin (London 1963): besonders die Beiträge von *T. Parsons* und *Th. F. O'Dea; ebenso D. R. Cutler* (Hrsg.), The Religious Situation: 1968 (Boston 1968): besonders die Beiträge von *H. Smith, J. Campbell, C. Geertz, T. Parsons, G. E. Swanson.*

21 *H. Cox,* der Autor von ›The Secular City‹, schreibt jetzt über: ›The Seduction of the Spirit. The Use and Misuse of People's Religion‹ (New York 1973). Aufschlußreich ist besonders das die Wende dokumentierende Kapitel 5 ›Beyond Bonhoeffer‹ mit dem Satz: »In short, the question of the future of religion is open again.« Die Frage war eigentlich nie geschlossen.

22 *O. F. Bollnow,* Wesen und Wandel der Tugenden (Frankfurt–Berlin 1958).

23 Vgl. *Th. Luckmann,* Verfall, Fortbestand oder Verwandlung des Religiösen in der modernen Gesellschaft?, in: *O. Schatz* (Hrsg.), aaO S. 69–82.

24 *A. M. Greeley,* Religion in the Year 2000, aaO, Kap. 3: The Data.

25 *H. Blumenberg,* Die Legitimität der Neuzeit (Frankfurt 1966) S. 41 f.

26 Zur neueren *philosophischen* Problematik der *Gottesfrage: K. Jaspers,* Der philosophische Glaube (München 1948); *W. Schulz,* Der Gott der neuzeitlichen Metaphysik (Pfullingen 1957); *M. E. Marty,* Varieties of Unbelief (New York–Chicago–San Francisco 1964); *W. Strolz,* Menschsein als Gottesfrage. Wege zur Erfahrung der Inkarnation (Pfullingen 1965); *E. Fontinell,* Toward a Reconstruction of Religion. A Philosophical Probe (New York 1970); *E. Coreth – J. B. Lotz* (Hrsg.), Atheismus kritisch betrachtet (München 1971); *W. Weischedel,* Der Gott der Philosophen. Grundlegung einer philosophischen Theologie im Zeitalter des Nihilismus Bd. I–II (Darmstadt 1971–72); *G. Hasenhüttl,* Gott ohne Gott. Ein Dialog mit J.-P. Sartre (Graz–Wien–Köln 1972); *G. D. Kaufman,* God the Problem (Cambridge 1972); *J. Splett,* Gotteserfahrung im Denken. Zur philosophischen Rechtfertigung des Redens von Gott (Freiburg–München 1973); *R. Schaeffler,* Religion und kritisches Bewußtsein (Freiburg–München 1973); *ders.*, Die Religionskritik sucht ihren Partner. Thesen zu einer erneuerten Apologetik (Freiburg–Basel–Wien 1974). – Zur Geschichte des Atheismus besonders: *F. Mauthner,* Der Atheismus und seine Geschichte im Abendland Bd. I–IV (Stuttgart 1921–23); *H. Ley,* Geschichte der Aufklärung und des Atheismus Bd. I–III (Berlin 1966–71). – Zu den *Gottesbeweisen* besonders: *W. Cramer,* Gottesbeweise und ihre Kritik. Prüfung ihrer Beweiskraft (Frankfurt 1967); *K. Riesenhuber,* Existenzerfahrung und Religion (Mainz 1968); *Q. Huonder,* Die Gottesbeweise. Geschichte und Schicksal (Stuttgart 1968; Lit.!). Vom Verfasser: Menschwerdung Gottes.

27 *K. Barth,* Nein! Antwort an Emil Brunner (München 1934); *ders.*, Kirchliche Dogmatik Bd. II, 1 (Zollikon–Zürich 1948), zum Vatikanum I bes. S. 86–92.

Vgl. *E. Brunner*, Natur und Gnade. Zum Gespräch mit Karl Barth (Zürich 1934. ²1935). Man vergleiche aber auch die Selbstkorrekturen Barths in seiner Schöpfungslehre, Kirchliche Dogmatik Bd. III, 1–3 (1947–1950), besonders Bd. III, 3 § 69, 2.

28 *R. Bultmann*, Glauben und Verstehen. Gesammelte Aufsätze Bd. I (Tübingen ²1954) S. 1–25, 26–37, 294–312.

29 Auf der Linie Barths noch neuerdings *H. Gollwitzer* in Auseinandersetzung mit *W. Weischedel*: Denken und Glauben. Ein Streitgespräch (Stuttgart 1965); *J. Moltmann*, Der gekreuzigte Gott. Das Kreuz Christi als Grund und Kritik christlicher Theologie (München 1972), bes. Kap. I, 3 und VI, 2. – Auf der Linie Bultmanns besonders *G. Ebeling*, Das Wesen des christlichen Glaubens (Tübingen 1959); *ders.*, Wort und Glaube (Tübingen 1960).

30 *Thomas von Aquin*, Summa contra gentiles I cap. 3–14; Summa theologiae I q 2.

31 *Concilium Vaticanum I*, Constitutio dogmatica de fide catholica, bes. Denz 1785. 1795–1800. 1806. Vgl. *Pius XII.*, Enzyklika ›Humani generis‹ vom 12. August 1950, in: Acta Apostolicae Sedis 42 (1950) S. 561–578.

32 *Thomas von Aquin*, Summa theologiae I q 2 ad 1–2.

33 Eine differenzierte Erneuerung der »natürlichen Theologie« findet sich bei *W. Pannenberg*, Was ist der Mensch? (Göttingen 1962); *ders.*, Offenbarung als Geschichte (Göttingen ²1963). Grundfragen systematischer Theologie. Gesammelte Aufsätze (Göttingen 1967); *ders.*, Brief an W. Weischedel, in: Philosophische Theologie im Schatten des Nihilismus, hrsg. von *J. Salaquarda* (Berlin 1971) S. 176–180, mit Antwort von *W. Weischedel* S. 180f.

34 Vgl. *H. Küng*, Existiert Gott? (München 1975).

35 *I. Kant*, Kritik der praktischen Vernunft (1788), in: Werke, hrsg. von *W. Weischedel* Bd. IV (Darmstadt 1956) S. 254–266; bes. 257.

2. *Die Wirklichkeit Gottes*

1 Aus der unabsehbaren *theologischen* Literatur zur *Gottesfrage* neben den genannten philosophischen Werken und den dogmatischen Handbüchern auf *katholischer* Seite (*M. Schmaus*, Mysterium Salutis: bes. *H. U. von Balthasar, A. Deissler, J. Pfammatter, M. Löhrer, K. Rahner*) und auf *evangelischer* Seite (*P. Althaus, K. Barth, E. Brunner, H. Diem, H. Ott, H. Thielicke, P. Tillich*) die *systematischen Monographien*: *H. U. von Balthasar*, Die Gottesfrage des heutigen Menschen (Wien–München 1956); *H. de Lubac*, Sur les chemins de Dieu (Paris 1956); *H. Gollwitzer*, Die Existenz Gottes im Bekenntnis des Glaubens (München 1963); *J. A. T. Robinson*, Honest to God (London 1963); dt.: Gott ist anders (München 1964); *J. C. Murray*, The Problem of God. Yesterday and Today (New Haven–London 1964); dt.: Das Gottesproblem gestern und heute (Freiburg–Basel–Wien 1965); *E. Jüngel*, Gottes Sein ist im Werden. Verantwortliche Rede vom Sein bei Karl Barth. Eine Paraphrase (Tübingen 1965); *Sch. M. Ogden*, The Reality of God and Other Essays (New York 1966); dt.: Die Realität Gottes (Zürich 1970); *H. Engelland*, Die Wirklichkeit Gottes und die Gewißheit des Glaubens (Göttingen 1966); *H. Zahrnt*, Die Sache mit Gott. Die protestantische Theologie im 20. Jahrhundert (München 1966; *ders.*, Gott kann nicht sterben. Wider die falschen Alternativen in Theologie und Gesellschaft (München 1970); *F. Leist*, Nicht der Gott der Philosophen (Freiburg–Basel–Wien 1966); *C. H. Ratschow*, Gott existiert. Eine dogmatische Studie (Berlin 1966); *J. Macquarrie*, God and Secularity (Philadelphia 1967); *F. Gogarten*, Die Frage nach Gott. Eine Vorlesung (Tü-

bingen 1968); *J. B. Cobb, Jr.*, God and the World (Philadelphia 1969); *G. Ebeling*, Wort und Glaube Bd. II (Tübingen 1969); *E. Schillebeeckx*, Gott – die Zukunft des Menschen (Mainz 1969); *E. R. Baltazar*, God within Process (New York 1970); *W. Kasper*, Glaube und Geschichte (Mainz 1970), bes. S. 101–143; *R. G. Smith*, The Doctrine of God (London 1970); *H. Ott*, Gott (Stuttgart–Berlin 1971); *W. Pannenberg*, Gottesgedanke und menschliche Freiheit (Göttingen 1972); *E. Biser*, Theologie und Atheismus. Anstöße zu einer theologischen Aporetik (München 1972); *J. Moltmann*, Der gekreuzigte Gott. Das Kreuz Christi als Grund und Kritik christlicher Theologie (München 1972). Vom Verfasser: Menschwerdung Gottes. Unter *sprachphilosophischem Aspekt* sind zu beachten: *F. Ferré*, Language, Logic and God (London–Glasgow 1961); *P. van Buren*, The Secular Meaning of the Gospel. Based on an Analysis of its Language (Guildford–London 1963); dt.: Reden von Gott – in der Sprache der Welt. Zur säkularen Bedeutung des Evangeliums (Zürich 1965); *L. Gilkey*, Naming the Whirlwind. The Renewal of God-Language (Indianapolis–New York 1969); *E. Castelli* (Hrsg.), L'analyse du langage théologique. Le nom de Dieu (Paris 1969).
Schließlich die *Sammelwerke* zur Gottesfrage: *A. Schaefer* (Hrsg.), Der Gottesgedanke im Abendland (Stuttgart 1964); *N. Kutschki* (Hrsg.), Gott heute. Fünfzehn Beiträge zur Gottesfrage (Mainz–München 1967); *H. Zahrnt* (Hrsg.), Gespräch über Gott. Die protestantische Theologie im 20. Jahrhundert. Ein Textbuch (München 1968); *Th. C. de Kruijf u. a.*, Zerbrochene Gottesbilder (Freiburg–Basel–Wien 1969); *H. J. Schultz* (Hrsg.), Wer ist das eigentlich – Gott? (München 1969); *A. Grabner-Haider* (Hrsg.), Gott (Mainz 1970); *J. Blank u. a.*, Gott-Frage und moderner Atheismus (Regensburg 1972); *J. Ratzinger* (Hrsg.), Die Frage nach Gott (Freiburg–Basel–Wien 1972); *J. Kopperschmidt* (Hrsg.), Der fragliche Gott. Fünf Versuche einer Antwort (Düsseldorf 1973); *K. Rahner* (Hrsg.), Ist Gott noch gefragt? Zur Funktionslosigkeit des Gottesglaubens (Düsseldorf 1973).

2 *I. Kant*, Kritik der reinen Vernunft (1781), in: Werke, hrsg. von *W. Weischedel*, Bd. II (Darmstadt 1956) S. 677.

3 Die Fundamentalproblematik der Nichtigkeit der Wirklichkeit und der damit gegebenen freien, aber nicht willkürlichen Wahl zwischen Grundmißtrauen und Grundvertrauen, zwischen Nihilismus und Seinsvertrauen, die in der Gottesfrage vorausgesetzt wird, kann hier nicht entwickelt werden. Sie wird in Auseinandersetzung vor allem mit Nietzsche entwickelt in: *H. Küng*, Existiert Gott?

4 So *W. Weischedel*, aaO Bd. II, § 127, der folgerichtig auch nur zu Gott als einem »Vonwoher der Fraglichkeit« kommt: § 128–131.

5 Es könnte hier nur das geschichtsphilosophische Argument von der notwendigen Heraufkunft des Atheismus und der Ersetzung von Religion durch Wissenschaft behandelt werden (vgl. A II, 1). Die Widerlegung der psychologischen Begründung des Atheismus – Gott als Projektion des Menschen oder Illusion der Psyche – müßte geschehen in Auseinandersetzung mit dem humanistischen Atheismus Ludwig Feuerbachs, dem sozialrevolutionären Atheismus Karl Marx', dem nihilistischen Atheismus Friedrich Nietzsches und dem psychoanalytischen Atheismus Sigmund Freuds. Dazu *H. Küng*, aaO.

6 Vgl. *H.-E. Hengstenberg*, Wahrheit, Sicherheit, Unfehlbarkeit. Zur »Problematik« unfehlbarer kirchlicher Lehrsätze, in: Fehlbar? Eine Bilanz, hrsg. von *H. Küng* (Zürich–Einsiedeln–Köln 1973) S. 217–231.

7 *M. Buber*, Betrachtungen zur Beziehung zwischen Religion und Philosophie, in: Werke Bd. I (München–Heidelberg 1962) S. 509 f.

8 W. Weischedel, aaO Bd. I.
9 W. Weischedel, aaO Bd. II, S. 494 f.
10 I. Kant, Beantwortung der Frage: Was ist Aufklärung?, in: Werke, hrsg. von
     W. Weischedel, Bd. VI (Darmstadt 1964) S. 53.
11 Über den neuzeitlichen Horizont der Gottesfrage orientieren die bereits zitier-
     ten äußerst informativen Bücher von H. Zahrnt: Die Sache mit Gott; Gott
     kann nicht sterben; sowie das Textbuch: Gespräche über Gott. Zum Folgen-
     den halten wir uns an: Gott kann nicht sterben, Kap. 1.
12 C. F. von Weizsäcker, Die Verantwortung der Wissenschaft im Atomzeitalter
     (Göttingen 1957) S. 11 f.
13 Vgl. die bibliographischen Angaben unter A II, 1: Gottesbeweise?
14 Vgl. die bibliographischen Angaben unter A II, 1: Gottesbeweise?
15 Vgl. H. Albert, Plädoyer für kritischen Rationalismus (München 1971). Zur
     Grundlagendiskussion H. Küng, Existiert Gott? (München 1975).
16 H. Albert, aaO S. 11–15.
17 W. Weischedel, Was heißt Wirklichkeit?, in: Festschrift für Ernst Fuchs, hrsg.
     von G. Ebeling – E. Jüngel – G. Schunack (Tübingen 1973) S. 337–345; Zit.
     S. 343 f.
18 Vgl. H. Küng, Unfehlbar? Eine Anfrage (Zürich–Einsiedeln–Köln 1970)
     Kap. IV, 11: Ein Lehramt?; ders. (Hrsg.), Fehlbar? Eine Bilanz, aaO Kap.
     E VII: Die Chancen eines fehlbaren Lehramts.

A III: Die Herausforderung der Weltreligionen

1. Außerhalb der Kirche Heil

1 D. Bonhoeffer, Widerstand und Ergebung (München 1951) S. 239–242.
2 K. M. Panikkar, Asien und die Herrschaft des Westens (Zürich 1955).
3 Shusaku Endo, Silence (Tokio 1969).
4 Concilium Vaticanum II, Declaratio de Ecclesiae habitudine ad Religiones
     non-christianas (1965); Declaratio de Libertate religiosa (1965).
5 Vgl. Dialog mit anderen Religionen. Material aus der ökumenischen Bewe-
     gung, hrsg. von H. J. Margull und S. J. Samartha (Frankfurt 1972). Wichtig
     besonders das Dokument von Addis Abeba 1971: Der Ökumenische Rat der
     Kirchen und der Dialog mit Menschen anderer Religionen und Ideologien.
6 Vgl. kurze Zusammenstellung der Texte bei H. Küng, Christenheit als Minder-
     heit (Einsiedeln 1965).
7 Hier bahnbrechend K. Rahner, Weltgeschichte und Heilsgeschichte. Das
     Christentum und die nichtchristlichen Religionen, in: Schriften zur Theologie
     V (Zürich–Einsiedeln–Köln 1962) S. 115–158.
8 J. Neuner, Missionstheologische Probleme in Indien, in: Gott in Welt (Fest-
     schrift K. Rahner, Freiburg-Basel-Wien 1964) Bd. II, S. 401 f.
9 H. R. Schlette, Die Religionen als Thema der Theologie. Überlegungen zu
     einer »Theologie der Religionen« (Freiburg-Basel-Wien 1963) S. 39; vgl. ders.,
     Colloquium salutis – Christen und Nichtchristen heute (Köln 1965).
10 Der Wahrheitsgehalt der Weltreligionen wird – gegen Karl Barths (auch R.
     Bultmanns und K. Heims) theologiegeschichtlich zu verstehende christliche
     Exklusivität – auch von evangelischen Theologen gesehen: einerseits aufgrund
     von religionsgeschichtlichen Einsichten besonders E. Troeltsch (und andere
     aus der Schule Ritschls stammende religionsgeschichtliche Theologen), ande-
     rerseits vom Alten und Neuen Testament her A. Schlatter (und W. Lütgert)

wie dann später P. Tillich, P. Althaus, C. H. Ratschow, W. Pannenberg. Gute Übersicht über die Problematik bei *P. Althaus,* Die christliche Wahrheit, bes. § 5 und 16. Zu neueren Tendenzen vgl. *P. Knitter,* What is German Protestant Theology Saying About the Non-Christian Religions?, in: Neue Zeitschrift für systematische Theologie und Religionsphilosophie 50 (1973) 38–64. Daß dies keine »natürliche Theologie« bedeutet, wurde bereits dargelegt: vgl. A II.

11 Zur Information über die *Weltreligionen* aus der unermeßlichen Literatur die neueren großen Sammelwerke: Histoire générale des religions, hrsg. von *M. Gorce – R. Mortier* Bd. I–V (Paris 1947–52); Die Religionen der Erde, hrsg. von *C. Clemen* (München ²1949); Christus und die Religionen der Erde. Handbuch der Religionsgeschichte, hrsg. von *F. König,* Bd. I–III (Wien 1951); Die Religionen der Menschheit, hrsg. von *Chr. M. Schröder* (Stuttgart 1960ff., auf 36 Bände geplant).

Der kurzen Orientierung dienen: *A. Bertholet–H. von Campenhausen,* Wörterbuch der Religionen (Stuttgart 1952); *H. von Glasenapp,* Die nichtchristlichen Religionen (Frankfurt 1957); *G. Günther* (Hrsg.), Die großen Religionen (Göttingen 1961); *H. Ringgren – A. V. Ström,* Die Religionen der Völker. Grundriß der allgemeinen Religionsgeschichte (Stuttgart 1959); *R. C. Zaehner,* The Concise Encyclopedia of Living Faiths (London 1959); *E. Dammann,* Grundriß der Religionsgeschichte (Stuttgart 1972); *E. Brunner-Traut* (Hrsg.), Die fünf großen Weltreligionen (Freiburg–Basel–Wien 1974). Hier überall reichlich Literaturangaben zu den einzelnen Religionen.

Ausführlicher: *P. D. Chantepie de la Saussaye,* Lehrbuch der Religionsgeschichte Bd. I–II (Tübingen ⁴1925); *G. Mensching,* Allgemeine Religionsgeschichte (Heidelberg ²1949); *J. Finegan,* The Archeology of World Religions (Princeton 1957); *H. von Glasenapp,* Die fünf großen Religionen (Düsseldorf-Köln 1951/52).

In verschiedenen Sprachen gibt es bereits Taschenbuch-Ausgaben der wichtigsten außerbiblischen religiösen Texte, insbesondere der indischen und chinesischen Weisheit.

2. Verwirrende Konsequenz

1 Zur Geschichte des Axioms »Extra Ecclesiam nulla salus« vgl. *H. Küng,* Die Kirche D II, 2; zur modernen Interpretation der Formel vgl. *ders.,* Wahrhaftigkeit (Freiburg–Basel–Wien 1968) B VIII: Manipulation der Wahrheit?

2 Denz 714, vgl. *Fulgentius von Ruspe,* De fide, ad Petrum c. 37ss, n. 78ss (Patrologia Latina 65, 703s).

3 *Concilium Vaticanum II,* Constitutio de Ecclesia (1964) Art. 16.

4 *K. Rahner,* Die anonymen Christen, in: Schriften zur Theologie Bd. VI (1965) S. 545–554. Vgl. *A. Röper,* Die anonymen Christen (Mainz 1963). Kritische Vorbehalte zu dieser heute sehr populär gewordenen Theorie wie auch zur Konzeption von *R. Panikkar,* The Unknown Christ of Hinduism (London 1964), meldet neuerdings *H. J. Margull* aufgrund konkreter, in Gesprächen mit Hindus, Buddhisten und Moslems gewonnenen Erfahrungen an (aaO S. 85).

5 *K. Barth,* Der Römerbrief (München ²1922) 7. Kap.; *ders.,* Kirchliche Dogmatik Bd. I/2 (1948) § 17; vgl. aber die Modifikationen Bd. IV/3 (1959) § 69, 2.

6 *D. Bonhoeffer,* aaO S. 178–185.

7 *F. Gogarten,* Verhängnis und Hoffnung der Neuzeit (Stuttgart ²1958).

8 *E. Brunner,* Religionsphilosophie evangelischer Theologie (München 1927); *ders.,* Die Christusbotschaft im Kampf mit den Religionen (Stuttgart–Basel 1931); *ders.,* Offenbarung und Vernunft. Die Lehre von der christlichen Glaubenserkenntnis (Zürich 1941, Neuaufl. Darmstadt 1961), bes. Kap. 14–17.

9 *H. Kraemer,* The Christian Message in a Non-Christian World; dt.: Die christliche Botschaft in einer nichtchristlichen Welt (Zürich 1940); *ders.,* Religion and
the Christian Faith (London 1956); dt.: Religion und christlicher Glaube (Göttingen 1959).

3. *Herausforderung gegenseitig*

1 Zur *Phänomenologie* der Religion: nach den frühen wichtigen Werken von *R.
Otto, H. Pinard de la Boullaye* und *N. Söderblom* vgl. *G. van der Leeuw,*
Phänomenologie der Religion (Tübingen 1933, ²1956); *ders.,* Einführung in die
Phänomenologie der Religion (Haarlem 1948, Darmstadt ²1961); *G. Men-
sching,* Vergleichende Religionswissenschaft (Heidelberg ²1949); *ders.,* Die
Religion. Erscheinungsformen, Strukturtypen und Lebensgesetze (Stuttgart
1959); *H. v. Glasenapp,* Die Religionen der Menschheit. Ihre Gegensätze und
Übereinstimmungen (Wien 1954); *M. Eliade,* Patterns of Comparative Religion (London 1958); *J. Wach,* The Comparative Study of Religions (New
York 1958); dt.: Vergleichende Religionsforschung (Stuttgart 1962); *K. Gold-
ammer,* Die Formenwelt des Religiösen (Stuttgart 1960); *F. Heiler,* Erscheinungsformen und Wesen der Religion (Stuttgart 1961); *G. Lanczkowski,*
Begegnung und Wandel der Religionen (Düsseldorf–Köln 1971).
2 *A. J. Toynbee,* An Historian's Approach to Religion (London 1956); dt.: Wie
stehen wir zur Religion? Die Antwort eines Historikers (Zürich–Stuttgart–
Wien 1958); *ders.,* Christianity among the Religions of the World (London
1958), dt.: Das Christentum und die Religionen der Welt (Gütersloh 1959).
3 *J. Ratzinger,* Der christliche Glaube und die Weltreligionen, in: Gott in Welt
(Festschrift K. Rahner. Freiburg–Basel–Wien 1964) Bd. II, S. 287–305; bes.
294 f.
4 Aufschlußreich der Roman des Afrikaners *Chinua Achebe,* Things Fall Apart
(London 1958).
5 Vgl. dazu neuestens die gewiß einseitige, aber informative Spiegel-Serie von
1973 Nr. 39–43: Asiens kranker Riese.
6 *S. Radhakrishnan,* Eastern Religions and Western Thought (London 1939)
S. 308 f. Vgl. dazu die Kritik christlicher indischer Theologen, in: *M. M.
Thomas,* The Acknowledged Christ of the Indian Renaissance (Madras 1970)
Kap. VII.
7 *G. Lanczkowski,* aaO S. 111 f., 115 f. Vgl. *G. Mensching,* Toleranz und Wahrheit in der Religion (1955, Taschenbuch-Ausgabe München–Hamburg
1966).
8 Vgl. *K. Jaspers,* Die maßgebenden Menschen (München ⁴1971) = Neudruck
aus dem Werk ›Die großen Philosophen‹ Bd. I (München 1964).
9 *K. Jaspers,* aaO S. 206.
10 Vgl. *H. Dumoulin,* Zen. Geschichte und Gestalt (Bern 1959), *ders.,* Östliche
Meditation und christliche Mystik (Freiburg–München 1966). Ein guter zu-
sammenfassender Vergleich bei *P. Kreeft,* Zen Buddhism and Christianity: An
Experiment in Comparative Religion, in: Journal of Ecumenical Studies
8 (1971) S. 513–538.
11 Vgl. die Untersuchung von *Adelheid Krämer,* Christus und Christentum im
Denken des modernen Hinduismus (Bonn 1958).
12 Ein exemplarischer Versuch ist das von christlichen und buddhistischen Fach-
spezialisten herausgegebene Werk: Buddhismus der Gegenwart, hrsg. von *H.
Dumoulin,* mit Beiträgen von *H. Bechert, E. Benz, H. Dumoulin, A. Fernan-
do, A. M. Fiske, H. Hoffmann, J. M. Kitagawa, H. Nakamura, Y. Raguin, F.*

Reynolds, *D. K. Swearer, Vu Duy-Tu, H. Welch* (Freiburg–Basel–Wien 1970). Zur fruchtbaren hinduistisch-christlichen Diskussion in Indien vgl. neben dem bereits zitierten Buch von *M. M. Thomas* besonders: *K. Baago,* Pioneers of Indigenous Christianity (Bangalore 1969); *ders.,* Bibliography of Indian Christian Theology (Madras 1969); *R. H. S. Boyd,* An Introduction to Indian Christian Theology (Madras 1969); *Robin Boyd,* What is Christianity? (Madras 1970). Unter den indischen christlichen Theologen sind zu nennen: *Joshua Marshman, Nehemiah Goreh, M. C. Parekh, C. F. Andrews, S. K. Rudra, P. D. Devanandan, P. Chenchiah, D. G. Moses, J. R. Chandran, Surjit Singh, M. Sunder Rao.*

13 Vgl. nochmals die Anmerkung A III 1, 11 zur Information über die Weltreligionen.

14 Vgl. *W. Schilling,* Einst Konfuzius – Heute Mao Tse-tung. Die Mao-Faszination und ihre Hintergründe (Weilheim/Obb. 1971).

4. Nicht Ausschließlichkeit, sondern Einzigartigkeit

1 Vgl. zum *Verhältnis Christentum – Weltreligionen* neben den bereits zitierten Werken von *K. Barth, E. Brunner* und *H. Kraemer,* sowie *K. Rahner, H. R. Schlette, H. Küng: E. Troeltsch,* Die Absolutheit des Christentums und die Religionsgeschichte (Tübingen 1929, Taschenbuch-Ausgabe München–Hamburg 1969); *O. Karrer,* Das Religiöse in der Menschheit und das Christentum (Frankfurt 1934); *F. Heiler,* Die Frage der »Absolutheit« des Christentums im Lichte der vergleichenden Religionsgeschichte, in: Eine heilige Kirche 20 (1938) 306–336; *W. Holsten,* Das Evangelium und die Völker. Beiträge zur Geschichte und Theorie der Mission (Berlin 1939); *ders.,* Das Kerygma und der Mensch (München 1953); *Th. Ohm,* Die Liebe zu Gott in den nichtchristlichen Religionen (München 1950); *ders.,* Asiens Nein und Ja zum westlichen Christentum (München ²1960); *H. H. Farmer,* Revelation and Religion. Studies in the Theological Interpretation of Religious Types (London 1954); *E. Benz,* Ideen zu einer Theologie der Religionsgeschichte (Mainz 1960); *St. Neill,* Christian Faith and other Faiths. The Christian Dialogue with Other Religions (London 1961); dt.: Gott und die Götter. Christlicher Glaube und die Weltreligionen (Gütersloh 1963); *R. C. Zaehner,* At Sundry Times. An Essay in the Comparison of Religions (London 1958); *ders.,* The Catholic Church and World Religions (London 1964); *P. Tillich,* Christianity and the Encounter of World Religions (New York 1962); dt.: Das Christentum und die Begegnung der Weltreligionen (Stuttgart 1964); *J. A. Cuttat,* Hemisphären des Geistes. Der spirituelle Dialog von Ost und West. Mit einer Einführung von Pandit Nehru (Stuttgart 1964); *ders.,* Asiatische Gottheit – Christlicher Gott. Die Spiritualität der beiden Hemisphären (neu überarbeitete Auflage Einsiedeln 1971); *R. Panikkar,* Religionen und die Religion (München 1965); *G. Thils,* Propos et problèmes de la théologie des religions non chrétiennes (Tournai 1966); *J. Heislbetz,* Theologische Gründe der nichtchristlichen Religionen (Freiburg–Basel–Wien 1967); *G. Rosenkranz,* Der christliche Glaube angesichts der Weltreligionen (Bern–München 1967); *J. Neuner* (Hrsg.), Christian Revelation and World Religions (London 1967); *O. Wolff,* Anders an Gott glauben. Die Weltreligionen als Partner des Christentums (Stuttgart 1969); *U. Mann,* Das Christentum als absolute Religion (Darmstadt 1970); *M. Seckler,* Hoffnungsversuche (Freiburg–Basel–Wien 1972) S. 13–46. *W. Kasper,* Der christliche Glaube angesichts der Religionen. Sind die nichtchristlichen Religionen heilsbedeutsam?, in: Wort Gottes in der Zeit. Festschrift für K. H. Schelkle, hrsg. von H. Feld und J. Nolte (Düsseldorf 1973) S. 347–360.

Weitere Literatur bis 1960 geben *E. Benz – M. Nambara,* Das Christentum und die nichtchristlichen Hochreligionen. Begegnung und Auseinandersetzung. Eine internationale Bibliographie (Leiden 1960). Als neuere Überblicke über die Lösungen der evangelischen und katholischen Theologie leisten nach dem bereits zitierten Werk von *G. Rosenkranz* gute Dienste *P. Beyerhaus,* Zur Theologie der Religionen im Protestantismus, und *W. Bühlmann,* Die Theologie der nichtchristlichen Religionen als ökumenisches Problem, beide in: Freiheit in der Begegnung (Festschrift O. Karrer, Frankfurt–Stuttgart 1969) S. 433–478.

2 Einen höchst aufschlußreichen kulturmorphologischen Vergleich bietet *W. S. Haas,* The Destiny of Mind (London 1956), dt. leider um wichtige Kapitel verkürzt in Rowohlts deutscher Enzyklopädie mit dem Titel ›Östliches und westliches Denken‹ (Hamburg 1967).

3 Vgl. im genannten Buch von *M. M. Thomas* die Kapitel über Rammohan Roy, Keshub Chunder Sen, P. C. Mozoomdar, Brahmobandhav Upadhyaya, Vivekananda, Radhakrishnan, Mahatma Gandhi.

4 *W. Johnston,* Einleitung zu S. Endo, Silence, aaO S. 16.

5 Gewichtige Anregungen zu diesem ganzen Kapitel verdanke ich Professor *Julia Ching* (The National University of Australia, Canberra – Columbia University New York).

B I: Das Besondere des Christentums

1. *Der Christus*

1 Apg 11, 26; vgl. 26, 28; 1 Pet 4, 16.

2 *Plinius,* Brief 96.

3 *Tacitus,* Annalen 15, 44; dieser wie die folgenden Texte finden sich in Übersetzung bei *C. K. Barrett,* The New Testament Background. Selected Documents (London 1956); dt.: Die Umwelt des Neuen Testaments. Ausgewählte Quellen (Tübingen 1959).

4 *Sueton,* Claudius 25, 4.

5 Vgl. *Josephus,* Antiquitates 20, 9, 1 mit 18, 3, 3.

6 *P. L. Berger,* Invitation to Sociology: A Humanistic Perspective (New York 1963), dt.: Einladung zur Soziologie. Eine humanistische Perspektive (München 1971) S. 97.

7 *H. Marcuse,* The One-Dimensional Man. Studies in the Ideology of Advanced Industrial Society (Boston 1964); dt.: Der eindimensionale Mensch. Studien zur fortgeschrittenen Industriegesellschaft (Neuwied–Berlin 1970) S. 117.

8 *J. B. Metz,* Zur Präsenz der Kirche in der Gesellschaft, in: Die Zukunft der Kirche. Berichtband des Concilium-Kongresses 1970 (Zürich–Einsiedeln–Köln 1971) S. 86–96. Vgl. *ders.,* Reform und Gegenreformation heute. Zwei Thesen zur ökumenischen Situation in den Kirchen (Mainz 1969) S. 40f.; *ders.,* Glaube als gefährliche Erinnerung, in: *A. Exeler, J. B. Metz, K. Rahner,* Hilfe zum Glauben (Zürich–Einsiedeln–Köln 1971) S. 23–37.

9 Vgl. A III.

10 Vgl. A I.

11 *K. Jaspers,* Die maßgebenden Menschen (München 1964, ⁴1971).

12 Nur auf diese Weise läßt sich auch die Frage nach dem »Wesen des Christentums«, wie sie sich seit der Aufklärung in neuer Form stellt, eindeutig beantworten. Sonst kann das »Wesen des Christentums«, wie indirekt aus der

Arbeit von *H. Wagenhammer*, Das Wesen des Christentums. Eine begriffsge-
schichtliche Untersuchung (Mainz 1973), hervorgeht, »nie absolut konkret
gefaßt werden« (S. 256).

2. *Welcher Christus?*

1 Vgl. zum Folgenden: *H. Küng*, Menschwerdung Gottes. Kap. II, 5: Das
 Christusbild der Modernen.
2 *H. Spaemann* (Hrsg.), Wer ist Jesus von Nazareth – für mich? 100 zeitgenössische Zeugnisse (München 1973). Als Vorlage diente: Pour vous, qui est Jésus-
 Christ? éd. A. M. Carré (Paris 1970).
3 Vgl. zum Begriff des Lehramts: *H. Küng*, Unfehlbar? Eine Anfrage (Zürich–
 Einsiedeln–Köln 1970) Kap. IV, 11.
4 Denz 54.
5 Denz 148.
6 Vgl. *H. Küng*, in: Fehlbar? Eine Bilanz (Zürich–Einsiedeln–Köln 1973) Kap. E
 VI: Die wahre Autorität der Konzilien (mit Bezug auf die Forschungen von
 H.-J. Sieben).
7 Als Einführung in die historische und theologische Problematik vgl. *H. Küng*,
 Menschwerdung Exkurse I–IV. Dazu die großen dogmengeschichtlichen
 Werke von *L.-J. Tixeront, Th. de Régnon, J. Lebreton, J. Rivière* usw. und auf
 evangelischer Seite von *A. Harnack, R. Seeberg, F. Loofs, W. Koehler, M.
 Werner, A. Adam*.
 Zur christologischen Problematik insbesondere *A. Grillmeier*, Die theologische und sprachliche Vorbereitung der christologischen Formel von Chalkedon, in: Das Konzil von Chalkedon. Geschichte und Gegenwart Bd. I (Würzburg 1951) S. 5–202; *A. Gilg*, Weg und Bedeutung der altkirchlichen Christologie (München ²1955); *B. Skard*, Die Inkarnation (Stuttgart 1958); *J. Liébaert*,
 Christologie. Von der apostolischen Zeit bis zum Konzil von Chalcedon (451)
 mit einer biblisch-christologischen Einleitung von *P. Lamarche*, in: Handbuch der Dogmengeschichte Bd. III, 1a, hrsg. von *M. Schmaus* und *A. Grillmeier* (Freiburg–Basel–Wien 1965).
8 Vgl. bes. *H. Küng*, Menschwerdung Gottes Exkurs II: Kann Gott leiden?
 Dazu: *W. Elert*, Der Ausgang der altkirchlichen Christologie. Eine Untersuchung über Theodor von Pharan und seine Zeit als Einführung in die alte
 Dogmengeschichte (Berlin 1957).
9 Vgl. *H. Küng*, aaO Exkurs V: Neuere Lösungsversuche der alten Problematik
 (bes. *K. Rahner, H. U. von Balthasar, K. Barth, E. Jüngel, D. Bonhoeffer, J.
 Moltmann*). Neuestens wichtig zur Auseinandersetzung mit der traditionellen
 Christologie *P. Schoonenberg*, Ein Gott der Menschen (Zürich–Einsiedeln–
 Köln 1969), bes. Kap. II.
10 *K. Rahner*, Probleme der Christologie von heute, in: Schriften Bd. I (1954)
 S. 169f.
11 Die klassische Formulierung der Einwände findet sich – schon vor der dogmengeschichtlichen Literatur im Gefolge A. Ritschls (bes. A. Harnack) – bei *F.
 Schleiermacher*, Der christliche Glaube (Berlin 1831) § 96. Neuerdings auf
 evangelischer Seite *W. Pannenberg*, Christologie § 8, auf katholischer *P.
 Schoonenberg*, aaO S. 52–111.
12 Vgl. z. B. *W. Pannenberg*, Christologie § 6, I.
13 Man sieht sich in dieser Forderung bestätigt durch *J. Ratzinger*, der in seiner
 ›Einführung ins Christentum‹ (1968) dogmatisch »von oben« die Ergebnisse
 der modernen Jesus-Forschung karikiert hatte (vgl. bes. S. 171–173: »Ein
 modernes Klischee des ›historischen Jesus‹«), der nun aber neuerdings sich ein

Buch wünscht, »das unseren ganzen heutigen Erkenntnisstand über Jesus von Nazareth, über die Jesus-Überlieferung des Neuen Testaments und über die Entwicklung des christologischen Dogmas aufnimmt und darin heute die Gegenwart Jesu Christi, den positiven Gehalt unseres Glaubens an ihn durchsichtig macht. Wenn ich dies sage, setze ich voraus, daß der Christus, dem die Kirche glaubt, und der Jesus der Geschichte, der heute neu entdeckte Jesus (wo immer es sich um authentische Entdeckung handelt) wirklich eins sind und daß es daher grundsätzlich möglich sein muß, diesen Zusammenhang auch darzustellen« (Im Dienst der Durchsichtigkeit des Glaubens, in: Notwendige Bücher. Heinrich Wild zum 65. Geburtstag, München 1974, S. 133–135; Zit. S. 134). Im selben Band fordert *K. Rahner* mit etwas anderer Ausrichtung einen »kleinen Katechismus für Erwachsene« (S. 129–132). Ganz identifizieren kann ich mich mit den Ausführungen von *H. R. Schlette*, der ein Buch fordert, »das auf gegenwärtigem wissenschaftlichem Niveau begründet oder motiviert, warum Jesus und gerade er im Unterschied zu anderen nach wie vor von Interesse ist« (Warum gerade Jesus, aaO S. 136–139).

14 Vgl. zum Schwärmertum historisch und grundsätzlich *H. Küng*, Die Kirche Kap. C II, 4.

15 The Jesus Revolution, in: Time vom 21. Juni 1971; Jesus Christ Superstar, in: Time vom 25. Oktober 1971; ebenfalls als Titelgeschichte ›Jesus im Schaugeschäft‹, in: Der Spiegel (1972) Nr. 8. Aus der unübersehbaren Flut verschiedensprachlicher Artikel und Schriften haben besonders dokumentarischen Wert: *H. Hoffmann*, Gott im Underground. Die religiöse Dimension der Pop-Kultur (Hamburg 1971); Jesus People Report (Wuppertal ²1972); *W. von Lojewski*, Jesus People oder Die Religion der Kinder (München ²1972); *W. Kroll* (Hrsg.), Jesus kommt! Report der »Jesus-Revolution« unter Hippies und Studenten in USA und anderswo (Wuppertal ⁵1972). Eine differenzierte Analyse versucht *G. Adler*, Die Jesus-Bewegung. Aufbruch der enttäuschten Jugend (Düsseldorf 1972).

16 Vgl. A I, 3: Humanität durch technologische Evolution?

17 *Ch. A. Reich*, The Greening of America (New York 1970); dt.: Die Welt wird jung (Hamburg 1973), bes. Kap. XI–XII.

18 *J. Frenzel*, Killer Nummer eins, in: Die Zeit vom 27. August 1971.

19 *F. J. Sheen*, Life of Christ (London 1959).

20 Dostojewskijs Briefe (in Auswahl), hrsg. von *A. Eliasberg* (München 1914) S. 61f.

21 Für entscheidende Einsichten in die Problematik dieses Kapitels und zahlreiche Anregungen im Detail danke ich meinem Tübinger Kollegen *Walter Jens*. Wichtige Informationen bekam ich auch von meinem Mitarbeiter im Institut für ökumenische Forschung *K.-J. Kuschel*, der eine Dissertation über das Jesusbild in der neueren Literatur vorbereitet; vgl. auch *P. K. Kurz*, Der zeitgenössische Jesus-Roman, in: Jesus von Nazareth, hrsg. von *F. J. Schierse* (Mainz 1972) S. 110–134. Ferner: *K. Marti*, Jesus – der Bruder. Ein Beitrag zum Christusbild in der neueren Literatur, in: Evangelische Kommentare 3 (1970) 272–276.

22 Vgl. die Gedichte ›Requiem‹ und ›Gedichte‹ von *G. Benn*, in: Gesammelte Werke, hrsg. von *Dieter Wellershoff*, Bd. 1 (Wiesbaden 1960) S. 10 und 196; *R. M. Rilke*, Der Brief des jungen Arbeiters, in: Sämtliche Werke Bd. 6 (Frankfurt 1966) S. 1111–1127.

23 *G. Papini*, Storia di Christo (1924); dt.: Lebensgeschichte Christi (München 1924).

24 *J. Dobraczyński*, Listi Nikodema (1952); dt.: Gib mir deine Sorgen. Die Briefe des Nikodemus (Freiburg 1962).

25 *P. Lagerkvist*, Barrabas (1946; Zürich 1950).

26 *M. Brod*, Der Meister (Gütersloh 1952).

27 *J. Schlaf*, Jesus und Mirjam. Der Tod des Antichrist (1901); *G. Frenssen*, Hilligenlei (1905); *G. Hauptmann*, Der Narr in Christo Emanuel Quint (Berlin 1910).

28 Vgl. *L. C. Douglas*, The Big Fisherman (1948); dt.: Der große Fischer (Stuttgart–Konstanz 1949); *R. Graves*, King Jesus (1954); dt.: König Jesus (Darmstadt–Genf 1954).

29 *G. Herburger*, Jesus in Osaka (Neuwied–Berlin 1970); *F. Andermann*, Das große Gesicht (München 1970).

30 *P. Huchel*, Dezember 1942, in: *K. Marti* (Hrsg.), Stimmen vor Tag. Gedichte aus diesem Jahrhundert (München–Hamburg 1965) S. 31; *P. Celan*, Tenebrae, in: Sprachgitter (Frankfurt 1959) S. 23.

31 *F. Dürrenmatt*, Weihnacht, in: Die Stadt 1952 (Zürich 1962) S. 11; *ders.*, Pilatus, ebd. S. 169–193; *P. Handke*, Lebensbeschreibung, in: Jesus N. Biblische Verfremdungen – Experimente junger Schriftsteller –, hrsg. von *A. Grabner-Haider* (Zürich–Einsiedeln–Köln 1972) S. 14 f.; *G. Grass*, Die Blechtrommel (Frankfurt–Hamburg 1962) bes. Kap.: Nachfolge Christi; *F. Arrabal*, Autofriedhof (Theateraufführung Tübingen 1973, Text bisher unveröffentlicht).

32 Vgl. vor allem *K. Marti* (Hrsg.), Stimmen vor Tag, aaO.; *J. Hoffmann-Herreros* (Hrsg.), Spur der Zukunft. Moderne Lyrik als Daseinsdeutung (Mainz 1973).

33 *W. Jens*, Herr Meister. Dialog über einen Roman (1963, Frankfurt–Berlin–Wien 1974) S. 58; vgl. auch S. 40, 56, 88.

34 *E. Hemingway*, Heute ist Freitag, in: Sämtliche Erzählungen (Hamburg 1966) S. 291–296, bes. S. 292 f.

35 *W. Borchert*, Jesus macht nicht mehr mit, in: Das Gesamtwerk (Hamburg 1959) S. 178–181.

36 *H. de Balzac*, Jésus Christ en Flandre (1831); dt.: Jesus Christus in Flandern (München o. J.); *F. M. Dostojewskij*, Die Brüder Karamasoff (Ausgabe Piper, ²1957) Kap. 5, 5: Der Großinquisitor; *G. Hauptmann*, Hanneles Himmelfahrt (1893), in: Das Gesammelte Werk 1. Abt. Bd. 2 (Berlin 1942), S. 253–300; *ders.*, Der Narr in Christo Emanuel Quint (Berlin 1910); *R. M. Rilke*, Christus. Elf Visionen, in: Sämtliche Werke Bd. 3, aaO S. 127–169; *R. Huch*, Der wiederkehrende Christus. Eine groteske Erzählung (1926), in: Gesammelte Werke Bd. IV, hrsg. von *W. Emrich*, S. 195–405; *G. Herburger*, Jesus in Osaka (Neuwied–Berlin 1970).

37 *H. Hesse*, Jesus und die Armen, zit. nach K. Marti, Jesus der Bruder, aaO S. 273; vgl. *R. M. Rilke*, Das Stundenbuch III, Das Buch von der Armut und vom Tode (1903), in: Sämtliche Werke Bd. I aaO S. 343–360, bes. S. 356–366; *B. Brecht*, Maria, in: Gesammelte Werke Bd. 8 (Frankfurt 1967) S. 122.

38 Vgl. *A. Holz*, der in seinem ›Buch der Zeit‹ (1885) Jesus den »ersten Sozialisten« nannte; *E. Kästner*, Dem Revolutionär Jesus zum Geburtstag, in: Das Erich Kästner Buch, hrsg. von *R. Hochhuth* (Zürich o. J.) S. 128; *C. Einstein*, Die schlimme Botschaft (1921), in: Gesammelte Werke, hrsg. von *E. Nef* (Wiesbaden 1962) S. 353–419.

39 *J. Paul*, Siebenkäs (1796/97), in: Werke Bd. 2, hrsg. von *G. Lohmann* (München 1959) S. 7–565; S. 266–271: Rede des toten Christus vom Weltgebäude herab, daß kein Gott sei.

40 Das Tagebuch der Gattin Dostojewskijs, hrsg. von *R. v. Fülöp-Miller–F. Eckstein* (München 1925) S. 506 f.

41 *F. M. Dostojewskij*, Der Idiot (Ausgabe Piper 1922) S. 380.
42 *H. Böll*, Blick zurück in Bitterkeit (zu R. Augsteins Buch ›Jesus Menschen-sohn‹), in: Der Spiegel (1973) Nr. 15.
43 Jo 12, 24.
44 Vgl. Notierte Gedanken aus den Jahren 1880 und 1881: *F. M. Dostojewskij*, Tagebuch eines Schriftstellers (München ²1972) S. 620, unmittelbar vor seinem Tod.
45 *M. L. Kaschnitz*, Auferstehung, in: Stimmen vor Tag, aaO S. 74f.; *K. Marti*, Ihr fragt, wie ist die Auferstehung der Toten, in: Leichenreden (Neuwied–Berlin 1969) S. 26, auch in: Spur der Zukunft, aaO S. 82; vgl. auch den Text von *K. Tucholsky*, abgedruckt in: Das Christentum im Urteil seiner Gegner, hrsg. von *K. H. Deschner* Bd. II (Wiesbaden 1971) S. 220.
46 *N. Kazantzakis*, Griechische Passion (Berlin 1951).

B II: Der wirkliche Christus

1 Mahatma Gandhi, Freiheit ohne Gewalt. Eingeleitet, übersetzt und hrsg. von *K. Klostermeier* (Köln 1968) S. 118.

1. Kein Mythos

1 *G. Janouch*, Gespräche mit Kafka. Aufzeichnungen und Erinnerungen (Frank-furt–Hamburg 1961) S. 111.
2 *A. Drews*, Die Christusmythe (Jena 1909, 3. verb. Aufl. 1910).
3 *J. M. Allegro*, The Sacred Mushroom and the Cross (London 1970); dt.: Der Geheimkult des heiligen Pilzes (Wien 1971).
4 Vgl. dazu die Einleitungen zum Neuen Testament von *P. Feine – J. Behm – W. Kümmel, A. Wikenhauser – A. Vögtle, K. H. Schelkle, W. Marxsen*, im angel-sächsischen Raum *R. Heard, T. Henshaw, H. F. D. Sparks*, im französischen Raum *A. Robert – A. Feuillet*.

2. Die Dokumente

1 *A. Schweitzer*, Von Reimarus zu Wrede. Eine Geschichte der Leben-Jesu-For-schung (Tübingen 1906).
2 Vgl. die angeführten Einleitungen zum Neuen Testament.
3 Der methodische Hauptmangel des Jesus-Buches von *R. Augstein* ist darin zu suchen, daß allein Markus für authentisch angenommen und damit der größte Teil des Mattäus- und Lukasevangeliums (u. a. die Bergpredigt) ohne jegliche Begründung (vgl. S. 59 f.) als nicht authentisch angesehen wird. Zur Kritik vgl. Augsteins Jesus. Eine Dokumentation, hrsg. v. *R. Pesch und G. Stachel* (Zürich 1972).
4 Vgl. *K. L. Schmidt*, Der Rahmen der Geschichte Jesu. Literarkritische Unter-suchungen zur ältesten Jesus-Überlieferung (Berlin 1919, Neudruck Darm-stadt 1964); *M. Dibelius*, Die Formgeschichte des Evangeliums (Tübingen 1919, 3. durchges. Aufl. mit einem Nachtrag von G. Iber, hrsg. von *G. Bornkamm* 1959); *R. Bultmann*, Die Geschichte der synoptischen Tradition (Göttingen 1921, ⁵1961). Zur Formkritik vgl. das allgemein verständliche Sachbuch von *G. Lohfink*, Jetzt verstehe ich die Bibel (Stuttgart 1973).
5 Vgl. vor allem den öffentlichen Briefwechsel mit *A. v. Harnack*, 1923, in: *K. Barth*, Theologische Fragen und Antworten (Zollikon–Zürich 1957) S. 7–31.

6 *R. Bultmann*, Die liberale Theologie und die jüngste theologische Bewegung, in: Glauben und Verstehen Bd. I (Tübingen 1954) S. 1–25.

7 *P. Tillich*, Systematische Theologie Bd. II (1958) Kap. II A.

3. Geschichte und Glaubensgewißheit

1 Theologisches Wörterbuch zum Neuen Testament, hrsg. von *G. Kittel* und *G. Friedrich* (Stuttgart 1933–1969); jetzt in vollständiger englischer und italienischer Übersetzung vorliegend.

2 *C. H. Dodd*, The Parables of the Kingdom (London 1935); *ders.*, The Interpretation of the Fourth Gospel (Cambridge 1953); *ders.*, The Founder of Christianity (London 1971); *W. Manson*, Jesus the Messiah (London 1943); dt.: Bist Du der da kommen soll? Das Zeugnis der drei ersten Evangelien von der Offenbarung in Christo unter Berücksichtigung der Formgeschichte (Zollikon–Zürich 1952); *T. W. Manson*, The Sayings of Jesus as Recorded in the Gospels According to St. Matthew and St. Luke. Arranged with Introduction and Commentary (London 1949); *ders.*, The Servant Messiah. A Study of the Public Ministry of Jesus (Cambridge 1953); *ders.*, The Life of Jesus: Some Tendencies in Present Day Research, in: The Background of the New Testament and its Eschatology (Festschrift C. H. Dodd, Cambridge 1956) S. 211–221; *R. H. Fuller*, The Mission and Achievement of Jesus. An Examination of the Presuppositions of New Testament Theology (London 1954); *V. Taylor*, The Life and Ministry of Jesus (London 1954); *ders.*, The Person of Christ in New Testament Teaching (London 1958); vgl. auch *ders.*, The Names of Jesus (London 1953); *ders.*, The Cross of Christ (London 1956) und *ders.*, Forgiveness and Reconciliation. A Study in New Testament Theology (London 1941); *J. L. Mc Kenzie*, The Power and the Wisdom (Milwaukee 1965); dt.: Die Botschaft des Neuen Testamentes (Luzern–Stuttgart 1968); *N. Perrin*, Rediscovering the Teaching of Jesus (London 1967), dt.: Was lehrte Jesus wirklich? Rekonstruktion und Deutung (Göttingen 1972); *A. Greeley*, The Jesus Myth (New York 1971); *J. A. T. Robinson*, The Human Face of God (London 1973).

3 *X. Léon-Dufour*, Les Évangiles et l'histoire de Jésus (Paris 1963); *L. Cerfaux*, Jésus aux origines de la tradition. Matériaux pour l'histoire évangélique (Löwen 1968). Zu Diskussionen gab Anlaß: *L. Evely*, L'Evangile sans mythes (Paris 1970).

4 *E. Käsemann*, Das Problem des historischen Jesus, in: Exegetische Versuche und Besinnungen Bd. I (Göttingen 1960) S. 187–214; vgl. aber schon *E. Fuchs*, Jesus Christus in Person (1944), veröffentlicht in der Festschrift für Rudolf Bultmann (1949) S. 48–73, jetzt in: Zur Frage nach dem historischen Jesus. Gesammelte Aufsätze Bd. II (Tübingen 1960) S. 21–54 (hier vor allem S. 37). Für die darauffolgende Entwicklung vgl. *J. M. Robinson*, A New Quest of the Historical Jesus (London 1959); dt.: Kerygma und historischer Jesus (Zürich–Stuttgart 1960); *J. Roloff*, Auf der Suche nach einem neuen Jesusbild, in: Theologische Literaturzeitung 98 (1973) 561–572 (Lit.!). Zur gesamten neueren Diskussion vgl. das umfangreiche Sammelwerk: Der historische Jesus und der kerygmatische Christus, hrsg. von *H. Ristow* und *K. Matthiae* (Berlin 1960).

Unter der neueren Literatur im angelsächsischen Raum *L. E. Keck*, A Future for the Historical Jesus (Nashville–New York 1971).

5 Nach den grundlegenden Jesusbüchern von *R. Bultmann*, Jesus (Tübingen 1926) und *M. Dibelius*, Jesus (1939, Berlin ³1960 mit einem Nachtrag von *W. G. Kümmel*), in der Bultmannschule: *G. Bornkamm*, Jesus von Nazareth

(Stuttgart 1956); *H. Conzelmann*, Art. Jesus Christus, in: RGG III (Tübingen 1959) S. 619–653; *H. Braun*, Jesus. Der Mann aus Nazareth und seine Zeit (Stuttgart–Berlin 1969); *E. Fuchs*, Jesus. Wort und Tat (Tübingen 1971).

In positivem Eingehen auf Bultmanns Fragestellung: *E. Schweizer*, Jesus im vielfältigen Zeugnis des Neuen Testaments (München–Hamburg 1968); *K. Niederwimmer*, Jesus (Göttingen 1968); *R. Schäfer*, Jesus und der Gottesglaube (Tübingen 1970).

Auf eigenen Wegen: *E. Stauffer*, Jesus – Gestalt und Geschichte (Bern 1957); *ders.*, Die Botschaft Jesu damals und heute (Bern 1959); *M. Craveri*, Das Leben des Jesus von Nazareth (Stuttgart 1970).

Neuere katholische Jesusbücher: *J. Gnilka*, Jesus Christus nach früheren Zeugnissen des Glaubens (München 1970); *G. Schneider*, Die Frage nach Jesus. Christus-Aussagen des NT (Essen 1971); *J. Blank*, Jesus von Nazareth. Geschichte und Relevanz (Freiburg–Basel–Wien 1972); *H. Zimmermann*, Jesus Christus. Geschichte und Verkündigung (Stuttgart 1973).

Auffällig im Gegensatz zu *R. Bultmann*, Theologie des Neuen Testamentes (Tübingen 1953), die breite Behandlung des synoptischen Kerygmas bei *H. Conzelmann*, Grundriß der Theologie des Neuen Testaments (München 1967); *W. G. Kümmel*, Die Theologie des Neuen Testaments nach seinen Hauptzeugen Jesus, Paulus, Johannes (Göttingen 1969); *J. Jeremias*, Neutestamentliche Theologie I. Die Verkündigung Jesu (Gütersloh 1971); *K.-H. Schelkle*, Theologie des Neuen Testaments Bd. I–III (Düsseldorf 1968 ff.).

Schließlich sind von Wichtigkeit die Christologien des Neuen Testaments von *G. Sevenster*, De Christologie van het Nieuwe Testament (Amsterdam 1946, ²1948); vgl. *ders.*, Art. Christologie im Urchristentum in RGG I (Tübingen 1957) S. 1745–1762; *O. Cullmann*, Die Christologie des Neuen Testaments (Tübingen 1957); und bes. *F. Hahn*, Christologische Hoheitstitel. Ihre Geschichte im frühen Christentum (Göttingen 1963). Mehr religionspädagogisch-pastoralen Charakter haben: Rückfrage nach der Sache Jesu (K. Schäfer), in: In Sachen Synode, hrsg. von *N. Greinacher u.a.* (Düsseldorf 1970) S. 150–169; *R. Baumann*, 2000 Jahre danach. Eine Bestandsaufnahme zur Sache Jesu (Stuttgart 1971); *M. Müssle* (Hrsg.), Die Humanität Jesu (München 1971); *N. Scholl*, Jesus – nur ein Mensch? (München 1971); *J. Schierse* (Hrsg.), Jesus von Nazareth (Mainz 1972); *A. Läpple*, Jesus von Nazaret. Kritische Reflexionen (München 1972); *F. Kerstiens*, Der Weg Jesu (Mainz 1973); *R. Schwager*, Jesus Nachfolge (Freiburg–Basel–Wien 1973); *H. Spaemann* (Hrsg.), Wer ist Jesus für mich? 100 zeitgenössische Zeugnisse (München 1973).

Von philosophischer Seite setzen sich mit der Gestalt Jesu eingehend auseinander: *K. Jaspers*, Die maßgebenden Menschen (München 1964, ⁴1971) S. 165–207; *E. Brock*, Die Grundlagen des Christentums (Bern–München 1970); *G. B. Shaw*, Die Aussichten des Christentums (Frankfurt 1971); und von marxistischer Seite: *E. Bloch*, Das Prinzip Hoffnung Bd. III (Frankfurt 1971) S. 1482–1504; *ders.*, Atheismus im Christentum (Frankfurt 1968) S. 115–243; *V. Gardavský*, Gott ist nicht ganz tot (München 1968) S. 46–64; *L. Kolakowski*, Geist und Ungeist christlicher Traditionen (Stuttgart 1971); *M. Machoveč*, Jesus für Atheisten (Stuttgart–Berlin 1972).

Aufsehen haben gemacht: *J. Lehmann*, Jesus-Report. Protokoll einer Verfälschung (Düsseldorf 1970); *A. Holl*, Jesus in schlechter Gesellschaft (Stuttgart 1971); *R. Augstein*, Jesus Menschensohn (München–Gütersloh–Wien 1972).

6 Vgl. B I, 2: Der Christus des Dogmas?

7 Vgl. *H. Küng*, Menschwerdung Gottes Kap. II, 3 (Kant), IV, 1–3 (Fichte-Schelling); zur Kritik an Hegel bes. VIII, 3: Die Geschichtlichkeit Jesu.

8 Vgl. *A. Schweitzer*, Von Reimarus zu Wrede. Eine Geschichte der Leben-Jesu-Forschung (Tübingen 1906).

9 Vgl. Zur Kritik an der »konsequenten Eschatologie« (J. Weiss, A. Schweitzer, M. Werner, F. Buri) z.B. *J. M. Robinson*, aaO sowie neuestens *W. Trilling*, Geschichte und Ergebnisse der historisch-kritischen Jesus-Forschung, in: Jesus von Nazareth, hrsg. von *F.-J. Schierse* (Mainz 1972) S. 187–213.

10 *E. Jüngel*, Thesen zur Grundlegung der Christologie, in seinem Sammelband: Unterwegs zur Sache (München 1972) S. 274–295 (Zit. S. 274).

11 *H. Ott*, Antwort des Glaubens S. 82.

12 Vgl. schon die Unterscheidung im Anschluß an *Augustin*, z.B. in Jo 29, 6; 48, 3 (Corpus Christianorum 36, 287. 413) zwischen Credere Deum, Deo, in Deum.

B III: Christentum und Judentum

1. Die Leiden der Vergangenheit

1 Das *christlich-jüdische Schrifttum* ist unübersehbar. Zu nennen sind die speziellen Schriftenreihen (Judaica, Studia Delitzschiana, Studia Judaica) und Periodika (Freiburger Rundbrief, Der Zeuge, The Bridge, The Hebrew Christian, Cahiers sioniens). Bes. wichtig sind die Sammelwerke: The Christian Approach to the Jew. Addresses delivered at the Pre-Evanston Conference at Lake Geneva, Wisconsin (New York 1954); Juden – Christen – Deutsche, hrsg. v. *H. J. Schultz* (Stuttgart–Olten–Freiburg 1961); Christen und Juden. Ihr Gegenüber vom Apostelkonzil bis heute, hrsg. v. *W.-D. Marsch und K. Thieme* (Mainz 1961); Der ungekündigte Bund. Neue Begegnung von Juden und christlicher Gemeinde, hrsg. v. *D. Goldschmidt* und *H. J. Kraus* (Stuttgart 1962); Abraham unser Vater. Juden und Christen im Gespräch über die Bibel (Festschrift O. Michel), hrsg. v. *O. Betz, M. Hengel, P. Schmidt* (Leiden–Köln 1963); Judenhaß – Schuld der Christen? Versuch eines Gesprächs, hrsg. v. *W. P. Eckert und E. L. Ehrlich* (Essen 1964); The Star and the Cross. Essays on jewish-christian relations, hrsg. v. *K. T. Hargrove* (Milwaukee 1966); Kirche und Synagoge. Handbuch zur Geschichte von Christen und Juden, Darstellung mit Quellen Bd. I–II, hrsg. v. *K. H. Rengstorf* und *S. von Kortzfleisch* (Stuttgart 1968, 1970); Jüdische Hoffnungskraft und christlicher Glaube, hrsg. v. *W. Strolz* (Freiburg–Basel–Wien 1971); Judentum und Kirche: Volk Gottes, hrsg. v. *C. Thoma* (Zürich–Einsiedeln–Köln 1974). Themenheft ›Christen und Juden‹ Concilium 10 (1974) Heft 8 mit einer Einführung von *H. Küng* und jüdisch-christlichen Parallelbeiträgen von *L. Jacobs – W. D. Davies, J. Heinemann – C. Thoma, R. Gradwohl – P. Fiedler, S. Sandmel – J. Lochman, A. Neher – A. T. Davies, J. J. Petuchowski – J. Moltmann, D. Flusser – B. Dupuy, U. Tal – K. Hruby*.
Neuere Arbeiten zur Problematik: K. Barth, Kirchliche Dogmatik, bes. Bd. II/2 § 34 (Zürich–Zollikon 1942), Bd. III/3 (1950) S. 238–256, Bd. IV/3 (1959) S. 1005–1007; *Ch. Journet*, Destinées d'Israël (Paris 1944); *H. Schmidt*, Die Judenfrage und die christliche Kirche in Deutschland (Stuttgart 1947); *J. M. Oesterreicher*, The Apostolate to the Jews (New York 1948); *J. Jocz*, The Jewish People and Jesus Christ (London 1949); A Theology of Election. Israel and the Church (London 1958); *P. Démann*, La catéchèse chrétienne et le peuple de la bible (Paris 1952); *G. Dix*, Jew and Greek (London 1953); *W. Maurer*, Kirche und Synagoge. Motive und Formen der Auseinandersetzung der Kirche mit dem Judentum im Laufe der Geschichte (Stuttgart 1953); *L. Goppelt*, Christen-

tum und Judentum im 1. und 2. Jahrhundert (Gütersloh 1954); *G. Hedenquist* u. a., The Church and the Jewish People (London–Edinburgh 1954); *F. Lovsky*, Antisémitisme et mystère d'Israël (Paris 1955); *E. Sterling*, Er ist wie Du. Aus der Frühgeschichte des Antisemitismus (München 1956); *H. U. von Balthasar*, Einsame Zwiesprache. M. Buber und das Christentum (Köln–Olten 1958); *H. Gollwitzer*, Israel – und wir (Berlin 1958); *G. Jasper*, Stimmen aus dem neureligiösen Judentum in seiner Stellung zum Christentum und zu Jesus (Hamburg 1958); *F. W. Foerster*, Die jüdische Frage (Freiburg i. Br. 1959); *W. Sulzbach*, Die zwei Wurzeln und Formen des Judenhasses (Stuttgart 1959); *E. Peterson*, Frühkirche, Judentum und Gnosis (Freiburg 1959); *M. Barth*, Israel und die Kirche im Brief des Paulus an die Epheser (München 1959); *K. Kupisch*, Das Volk der Geschichte (Berlin 1960); *H. Diem*, Das Rätsel des Antisemitismus (München 1960); *D. Judant*, Les deux Israël (Paris 1960); Israel und die Kirche. Eine Studie im Auftrag der Generalsynode der Niederländischen Reformierten Kirche (Zürich 1961; holl. Original: Israël en de Kerk. Gravenhage 1959); *G. Dellinger*, Die Juden im Catechismus Romanus (München 1963); *G. Baum*, Die Juden und das Evangelium (Einsiedeln 1963); *W. Seiferth*, Synagoge und Kirche im Mittelalter (München 1964); *Aug. Kard. Bea*, Die Kirche und das jüdische Volk (Freiburg i. Br. 1966); *F.-W. Marquardt*, Die Entdeckung des Judentums für die christliche Theologie. Israel im Denken Karl Barths (München 1967); *C. Thoma*, Kirche aus Juden und Heiden (Wien 1970); *J. Brosseder*, Luthers Stellung zu den Juden im Spiegel seiner Interpreten. Interpretation und Rezeption von Luthers Schriften und Äußerungen zum Judentum im 19. und 20. Jahrhundert, vor allem im deutschsprachigen Raum (München 1972); *P. E. Lapide*, Ökumene aus Christen und Juden (Neukirchen–Vluyn 1972). Vgl. weiter die zahlreichen Handbücher und Arbeiten zur Geschichte des Judentums und die Werke der jüdischen Autoren, die sich um die Deutung des Jüdischen bes. verdient gemacht haben *(L. Baeck, S. Ben-Chorin, M. Buber, H. Cohen, E. L. Ehrlich, A. Gilbert, J. Klausner, F. Rosenzweig, H. J. Schoeps, P. Winter)*; schließlich die Lexikonartikel zu Judentum und Judenchristentum. Zum ganzen Verhältnis Kirche – Juden vgl. schließlich vom Verfasser die eingehende Darstellung in: Die Kirche Kap. C I, 1 und 4.

2 Memorandum of the First Assembly of the World Council of Churches on the Christian Approach to the Jews (Amsterdam 1948). Auch später hat der Weltrat der Kirchen verschiedentlich zur Judenfrage Stellung bezogen.

2. *Die Möglichkeiten der Zukunft*

1 *Concilium Vaticanum II*, Declaratio de Ecclesiae habitudine ad Religiones non-christianas (1965). Sehr viel weiter geht die Erklärung des französischen bischöflichen Komitees für die Beziehungen zum Judentum über die Stellung der Christen zum Judentum (1973), veröffentlicht und von *Kurt Hruby* kommentiert in: Judaica 29 (1973) 44–70.

2 *J. Oesterreicher*, The Rediscovery of Judaism (South Orange, N. J. 1971); dt.: Die Wiederentdeckung des Judentums durch die Kirche (Meitingen–Freising 1971) S. 34.

3 *J. J. Petuchowski*, Geleitwort zu J. Oesterreicher, aaO S. 17.

4 Vgl. *Pinchas E. Lapide*, Jesus in Israel (Gladbeck 1970); *W. P. Eckert*, Jesus und das heutige Judentum, in: Jesus von Nazareth, hrsg. v. *F. J. Schierse* (Mainz 1972) S. 52–72. Ferner: das Werk von *G. Lindeskog*, Die Jesusfrage im neuzeitlichen Judentum (Neudruck Darmstadt 1974, bes. das Nachwort zum Nachdruck); *R. Gradwohl*, Das neue Jesus-Verständnis bei jüdischen Den-

kern der Gegenwart, in: Freiburger Zeitschrift für Philosophie und Theologie 20 (1973) 306–323. Einen Überblick über das Jesusbild im Judentum im Lauf der Zeiten gibt *Schalom Ben-Chorin*, Jesus im Judentum (Wuppertal 1970).

5 *S. Sandmel*, We Jews and Jesus (New York 1965) S. 112; vgl. *ders.*, A. Jewish Understanding of the New Testament (Cincinnati 1956).

6 Zit nach *S. Ben-Chorin*, Bruder Jesus. Der Nazarener in jüdischer Sicht (München 1967) S. 11.

7 *C. G. Montefiore*, The Synoptic Gospels (London 1909, ²1927).

8 *J. Klausner*, Jesus of Nazareth (ursprünglich hebräisch 1922, engl. 1925), dt.: Jesus von Nazareth. Seine Zeit, sein Leben und seine Lehre (Jerusalem 1952).

9 *M. Buber*, Zwei Glaubensweisen (Zürich 1950) S. 11.

10 *D. Flusser*, Inwiefern kann Jesus für Juden eine Frage sein?, in: Concilium 10 (1974) Heft 8; vgl. *ders.*, Jesus in Selbstzeugnissen und Bilddokumenten (Hamburg 1968).

11 *S. Ben-Chorin*, aaO S. 14.

12 *S. Ben-Chorin*, aaO S. 12.

13 *E. Käsemann*, Paulinische Perspektiven (Tübingen 1969) S. 97.

C I: Der gesellschaftliche Kontext

1. Establishment?

1 Zu den verschiedenen religiösen Bewegungen im Judentum zur Zeit Jesu vgl.: *E. Schürer*, Geschichte des jüdischen Volkes im Zeitalter Jesu Christi Bd. I–III (Leipzig ⁴1901–1911); *H. L. Strack* und *P. Billerbeck*, Kommentar zum Neuen Testament aus Talmud und Midrasch Bd. I–VI (München 1922–1961); *J. Bonsirven*, Le judaïsme palestinien au temps de Jésus-Christ (Paris 1950); *E. Stauffer*, Jerusalem und Rom im Zeitalter Jesu Christi (Bern 1957); *M. Simon*, Les sectes juives au temps de Jésus (Paris 1960); dt.: Die jüdischen Sekten zur Zeit Christi (Einsiedeln 1964); *K. Schubert*, Die jüdischen Religionsparteien im Zeitalter Jesu, in: Der historische Jesus und der Christus unseres Glaubens (Wien–Freiburg–Basel 1962) S. 15–101; *J. Jeremias*, Jerusalem zur Zeit Jesu (Göttingen ³1962); *J. Leipoldt – W. Grundmann*, Umwelt des Urchristentums Bd. I: Darstellung des neutestamentlichen Zeitalters (Berlin 1965), Bd. II: Texte zum neutestamentlichen Zeitalter 1967, Bd. III: Bilder zum neutestamentlichen Zeitalter 1966; *B. Reicke*, Neutestamentliche Zeitgeschichte (Berlin ²1968); *W. Foerster*, Neutestamentliche Zeitgeschichte (Hamburg 1968); *J. B. Bauer*, Die Zeit Jesu. Herrscher, Sekten und Parteien (Stuttgart 1969); *E. Lohse*, Umwelt des Neuen Testaments (Göttingen 1971, Lit.!); *G. Baumbach*, Jesus von Nazareth im Lichte der jüdischen Gruppenbildung (Berlin 1971).

2 Neben den genannten Werken von *G. Baumbach, J. Bonsirven, J. Jeremias, E. Lohse, E. Schürer, M. Simon* vgl. bes. *J. Wellhausen*, Die Pharisäer und die Sadduzäer (Hannover ²1924); Neudruck (Göttingen ³1967); *R. Meyer*, Art. Sadduzäer, in: ThW VII 1964, S. 35–54; *J. de Fraine*, Art. Sadduzäer, in: BL, S. 1502f.; *J. Le Moyne*, Les Sadducéens (Paris 1972); *K. Müller*, Jesus und die Sadduzäer, in: Biblische Randbemerkungen. Schülerfestschrift für R. Schnackenburg, hrsg. von *H. Merklein u. I. Lange* (Würzburg 1974) S. 3–24.

3 Lk 2, 41–52.

4 Mk 6, 2; vgl. Jo 7, 15.

5 Mk 9, 1 par; 13, 30 par; Mt 10, 23.

6 Mk 1, 9–11 par.

7 Mk 1, 10.
8 Vgl. Jo 1, 35–51.
9 Mk 1, 15 par.
10 Mk 12, 33 f.
11 Mk 13, 2 par.

2. Revolution?

1 Neben den Lexikonartikeln und den genannten Werken von *G. Baumbach, J. Bonsirven, J. Jeremias, E. Lohse, E. Schürer, M. Simon* vgl. bes. *M. Hengel*, Die Zeloten (Leiden–Köln 1961); *ders.*, War Jesus Revolutionär? (Stuttgart 1970); *S. G. F. Brandon*, Jesus and the Zealots (Manchester 1967); *O. Cullmann*, Jesus und die Revolutionäre seiner Zeit (Tübingen 1970); *G. Baumbach*, Zeloten und Sikarier, in: Theologische Literaturzeitung 90 (1965) S. 727–740; *ders.*, Die Zeloten – ihre geschichtliche und ihre religionsgeschichtliche Bedeutung, in: Bibel und Liturgie 41 (1968) S. 2–25: Baumbach will statt der von Josephus bezeugten Verbindung zwischen den »Zeloten«, die nach ihm mit den »Sikariern« nichts zu tun hätten, einen Zusammenhang zwischen priesterlichen Zeloten und den Essenern konstruieren. Dagegen *M. Hengel*, aaO S. 30. 32; vgl. *O. Cullmann*, aaO S. 15 f. Vgl. auch die Auseinandersetzung mit *S. G. F. Brandon* bei *M. Hengel* und *O. Cullmann*.
2 *H. S. Reimarus*, Vom Zwecke Jesu und seiner Jünger, hrsg. von *G. E. Lessing* (1778).
3 *K. Kautsky*, Der Ursprung des Christentums (Stuttgart 1908).
4 *R. Eisler*, Jesous basileus ou basileusas Bd. I–II (Heidelberg 1929–30).
5 *J. Carmichael*, The Death of Jesus (London 1963); dt.: Leben und Tod des Jesus von Nazareth (München 1965).
6 *S. G. F. Brandon*, aaO.
7 Lk 6, 15; Apg 1, 13.
8 Mk 3, 17; vgl. Lk 9, 51–56.
9 Vgl. Mk 15, 2. 9. 12. 18; Mt 27, 11. 29. 37; Lk 23, 3. 37. 38; Jo 18, 33. 37. 39; Jo 19, 3. 12. 14 f.
10 Mk 11, 1–11 par und Mk 11, 15–19 par; vgl. Jo 2, 12–17.
11 Lk 2, 1 f.
12 *Josephus*, Antiquitates 17, 285.
13 Lk 13, 1.
14 Mk 15, 7 par; vgl. Jo 18, 40.
15 *Y. Yadin*, Masada, Herod's Fortress and the Zealots' last stand (London 1967)
16 Mt 11, 8.
17 Lk 22, 25.
18 Lk 13, 32.
19 Lk 9, 62.
20 Lk 14, 18–20; Mt 22, 5. 8, 21 f.; Lk 9, 59 f.
21 Lk 12, 49.
22 Lk 12, 4; Mt 10, 28.
23 Lk 22, 35–38.
24 Vgl. *M. Hengel*, aaO; *O. Cullmann*, aaO.
25 Mt 6, 33; Lk 12, 31.
26 Lk 13, 31–33.
27 Lk 13, 1–5.
28 Lk 22, 35–38. 49–53; 6, 29 f.
29 Mk 1, 12 f. par. Zur Versuchungsgeschichte vgl. *P. Hoffmann*, Die Versuchungsgeschichte in der Logienquelle. Zur Auseinandersetzung der Juden-

christen mit dem politischen Messianismus, in: Biblische Zeitschrift NF 13 (1969) 207–223.

30 Mk 8, 33.
31 Mt 11, 12.
32 Mk 4, 26–29.
33 Mk 13, 22 par.
34 Mk 11, 1–10 par.
35 Mk 11, 15–19 par; vgl. Jo 2, 12–17.
36 Vgl. Jes 56, 7: ... Mein Haus soll ein Bethaus heißen für alle Völker.
37 Mt 10, 34–37; Lk 12, 51–53.
38 *Che Guevara*, Brandstiftung oder Neuer Friede (Hamburg 1969) S. 147, 160.
39 Vgl. *J. Elull*, L'autopsie de la révolution (Paris 1969) S. 325.
40 Mk 12, 13–17 par.
41 Lk 12, 31.
42 Mk 10, 42–45 par.
43 Mt 26, 52.
44 Mt 5, 39.
45 Mt 5, 44; vgl. Lk 6, 27f.

3. Emigration?

1 Gut zum politischen wie zum »unpolitischen« Radikalismus der ungarische Theologe *E. Vályi-Nagy*, Lob der Inkonsequenz. Über Glauben und Radikalismus, in: Evangelische Kommentare 4 (1971) 509–513.
2 Mk 6, 3; Mt 13, 55.
3 Mk 3, 21; vgl. Jo 10, 20.
4 So auf sage und schreibe 239 Seiten *W. E. Phipps*, Was Jesus Married? (New York 1970).
5 Mt 19, 12 kann leicht wie Apk 14, 1–5 eine Spätbildung sein.
6 Neben den genannten Werken von *G. Baumbach, J. Bonsirven, J. Jeremias, E. Lohse, E. Schürer, M. Simon* vgl. vor allem *S. Wagner*, Die Essener in der wissenschaftlichen Diskussion (Berlin 1960); *H. Kosmala*, Hebräer, Essener, Christen (Leiden 1961); *A. van den Born*, Art. Essener, in: BL, S. 439f.
Aus der uferlosen *Qumranliteratur*, für die es mehrere umfangreiche Bibliographien und Forschungsberichte und eine eigene Zeitschrift (Revue de Qumran, seit 1958) gibt, seien genannt: *H. Bardtke*, Die Handschriftenfunde am Toten Meer Bd. I–II (Berlin ²1953; 1958); *M. Burrows*, The Dead Sea Scrolls (New York 1955); dt.: Die Schriftrollen vom Toten Meer (München 1957); *ders.*, More Light on the Dead Sea Scrolls (New York 1958); dt.: Mehr Klarheit über die Schriftrollen (München 1958); *F. Bruce*, Die Handschriftenfunde am Toten Meer (München 1957); *Y. Yadin*, The Message of the Scrolls (London 1957); *K. Schubert*, Die Gemeinde vom Toten Meer (München–Basel 1958); *A. Dupont-Sommer*, Les écrits esséniens découverts près de la Mer Morte (Paris 1959); dt.: Die essenischen Schriften vom Toten Meer (Tübingen 1960); *O. Betz*, Offenbarung und Schriftforschung in der Qumransekte (Tübingen 1960); *J. Hempel*, Die Texte von Qumran in der heutigen Forschung (Göttingen 1962); *J. Jeremias*, Die theologische Bedeutung der Funde am Toten Meer (Göttingen 1962); *H. Haag*, Die Handschriftenfunde in der Wüste Juda (Stuttgart 1965); *G. R. Driver*, The Judean Scrolls (Oxford 1965); *C. Rabin and Y. Yadin*, Aspects of the Dead Sea Scrolls (Jerusalem 1965); *J. van der Ploeg*, Art. Qumran, in: BL S. 1430–1440 (hier weitere Literatur).

68 Mt 21, 28–31.
69 Lk 14, 16–24.
70 Mt 18, 23–27.
71 Lk 7, 41–43.
72 Lk 15, 1–7.
73 Lk 15, 8–10.
74 Lk 15, 11–32.
75 Lk 18, 9–14.
76 Mt 20, 1–15.
77 Mt 6, 12 par.
78 Vgl. z.B. *H. Braun*, Jesus S. 145.
79 Mk 2, 1–12 par.
80 Mk 2, 7.
81 Mk 3, 6.

C IV: Der Konflikt

1. Die Entscheidung

1 Mk 6, 34 par; vgl. Mt 14, 14; 15, 32.
2 Zur *Nachfolge* vgl. *G. Kittel*, Art. akolouthéo, in: ThW I, 210–216; *K. H. Rengstorf*, Art. mantháno, in: ThW IV, 392–465; *E. Schweizer*, Erniedrigung und Erhöhung bei Jesus und seinen Nachfolgern (Zürich 1955, ²1962); *G. Bornkamm*, Jesus S. 133–140; *M. Hengel*, Nachfolge und Charisma (Berlin 1968).
3 Mk 1, 16–20; 2, 14; Mt 4, 18–22; Lk 5, 9–11; vgl. Jo 1, 35–51.
4 Jo 15, 16.
5 Mt 23, 8–10.
6 Mt 19, 12.
7 Mt 12, 30; Lk 11, 23.
8 Mk 9, 40; vgl. Lk 9, 50.
9 Mk 5, 18–20.
10 Mk 6, 7–13; Mt 10, 1–11, 1; Lk 9, 1–6; 10, 1–16.
11 Mk 1, 17.
12 Lk 5, 10; vgl. 5, 1–9.
13 Mt 10, 40.
14 Vgl. Mk 3, 14f.
15 Mt 8, 20 par.
16 Vgl. Mt 10, 7–22.
17 Mt 10, 24f.
18 Lk 14, 28–33.
19 Lk 9, 59–62; vgl. Mt 8, 21f.
20 Mk 10, 35–40.
21 Lk 12, 8f; vgl. Mk 8, 38.
22 Vgl. Mt 8, 23–27 mit Mk 4, 35–41 par.
23 Jo 14–16.
24 Vgl. Mk 9, 33–35; 10, 42–45.
25 Vgl. Mt 23, 2–12.
26 Mk 10, 43f. par.
27 Jo 13, 1–17.
28 Vgl. zu den »Zwölf« und den »Aposteln« zunächst die Lexikonart., in: LThK (Apostel: *K. H. Schelkle*; Zwölf: *A. Vögtle*), RGG (*H. Riesenfeld*), EKL

Textausgaben: dt. von *J. Maier* oder *E. Lohse*, franz. von *A. Dupont-Sommer* oder *J. Carmignac,* engl. von *Th. Gaster* oder *G. Vermes,* holl. von *H. A. Brongers – A. S. van der Woude,* ital. von *F. M. Tocci.*

Für das Verhältnis *Qumran und Neues Testament* sind besonders wichtig: *J. Carmignac,* Le Docteur de justice et Jésus-Christ (Paris 1957); *J. Daniélou,* Les manuscrits de la Mer Morte et les origines du Christianisme (Paris 1957); dt.: Qumran und der Ursprung des Christentums (Mainz 1958); *H. Braun,* Spätjüdisch-häretischer und frühchristlicher Radikalismus. Jesus von Nazareth und die essenische Qumransekte Bd. I–II (Tübingen 1957); *ders.,* Qumran und das Neue Testament Bd. I–II (Tübingen 1966); *H. H. Rowley,* The Dead Sea Scrolls and the New Testament (London 1957); *K. Stendahl u. a.,* The Scrolls and the New Testament (New York 1957); *E. Stauffer,* Jesus und die Wüstengemeinde am Toten Meer (Stuttgart 1957); *A. Vögtle,* Das öffentliche Wirken Jesu auf dem Hintergrund der Qumranbewegung (Freiburg 1958); *J. van der Ploeg,* La secte de Qumran et les origines du Christianisme (Paris 1959); *M. Black,* The Scrolls and the Christian Origins (Edinburgh 1961); *A. Steiner,* Jesus – ein jüdischer Mönch? (Stuttgart 1971).

7 *K. Baus,* Art. Koinobitentum, in: LThK VI S. 368.

8 So *A. Dupont-Sommer,* Aperçus préliminaires sur les manuscrits de la Mer Morte (Paris 1950) S. 121.

9 Vgl. bes. *M. Burrows,* Die Schriftenrollen S. 217f., 272f.; *ders.,* Mehr Klarheit, S. 54f. *A. Dupont-Sommer* korrigierte seine früher geäußerten Ansichten: Nouveaux aperçus sur les manuscrits de la Mer Morte (Paris 1953) S. 206–209; *ders.,* Die essenischen Schriften vom Toten Meer S. 402f. Anders die Journalisten *E. Wilson,* Die Schriftrollen vom Toten Meer (München 1956), und davon abhängig *J. Lehmann,* Jesus-Report. Protokoll einer Verfälschung (Düsseldorf–Wien 1970). Zur *Kritik* an J. Lehmann: *E. Lohse,* Protokoll einer Verfälschung?, in: Evangelische Kommentare 3 (1970) 652–654; *K. Müller – R. Schnackenburg – G. Dautzenberg,* Rabbi J. Eine Auseinandersetzung mit Johannes Lehmanns Jesus-Report (Würzburg 1970). Ebenfalls das Themenheft ›Jesus von Nazaret und der Rabbi J‹ der Zeitschrift ›Bibel und Kirche‹ 26 (1971) Heft 1.

10 Mk 10, 17–22 par.

11 Jes 40, 3 wird in der Gemeinderegel 1 QS VIII, 14 zitiert.

12 1 QS IV, 22.

13 Mt 24, 26.

14 Mk 7, 14–23 par.

15 Mk 2, 18–28 par.

16 Mt 6, 16f.

17 Mt 11, 18f.

18 Lk 18, 1.

19 Mt 6, 5–8 par.

20 Vgl. Mk 1, 15.

4. Kompromiß?

1 Neben den genannten Werken zu den Sadduzäern und den Lexikonartikeln in BL *(J. de Fraine),* DBS *(A. Michel – J. Le Moyne)* und ThW *(R. Meyer – H. F. Weiss)* vgl. unter den Monographien: *R. Herford,* Die Pharisäer (Leipzig 1928); *D. C. Ridelle,* Jesus and the Pharisees (Chicago 1928); *L. Baeck,* Die Pharisäer (Berlin 1934) = Paulus, die Pharisäer und das Neue Testament (Frankfurt 1961) S. 39–98; *L. Finkelstein,* The Pharisees (Philadelphia 1938);

ders., The Pharisees and the Men of the Great Synagoge (New York 1950); *S. Zeitlin*, The Pharisees and the Gospels (New York 1938); *W. Beilner*, Christus und die Pharisäer (Wien 1959); *A. Finkel*, The Pharisees and the Teacher of Nazareth (Leiden 1964); *H. F. Weiss*, Der Pharisäismus im Lichte der Überlieferung des Neuen Testaments (Berlin 1965); *R. Meyer*, Tradition im antiken Judentum. Dargestellt an der Geschichte des Pharisäismus (Berlin 1965).

2 Vgl. Lk 18, 12.
3 Vgl. Ex 19, 6.
4 So das Konzil von Trient über Schrift und Tradition: Denz 783.
5 Mt 5, 21 f.
6 Mt 5, 27 f.
7 Lk 15, 11–32.
8 Lk 18, 10–14.
9 Lk 15, 4–6. 8–9.
10 Lk 7, 36. 11, 37. 14, 1.
11 Lk 13, 31.
12 Mt 5, 17.
13 Vgl. vor allem die Beiträge zur Jesus-Forschung von *D. Flusser*.
14 Vgl. *K. Niederwimmer*, Jesus S. 66–70; *H. Braun*, Jesus S. 72–75, 78–83.
15 Mk 7, 15; Mt 15, 11.
16 Vgl. *E. Käsemann*, Das Problem des historischen Jesus (1954), in: Exegetische Versuche und Besinnungen Bd. I (Göttingen 1960) S. 187–214, bes. S. 207.
17 Mk 2, 19 par.
18 Lk 18, 12. 14.
19 Mk 2, 23 par.
20 Mk 3, 1–6 par; Lk 13, 10–17; 14, 1–6.
21 Mk 2, 27.
22 Mk 3, 4 par; vgl. Lk 14, 5.
23 Mk 2, 25 f. par; Mt 12, 5.
24 Mk 2, 28 par.
25 Bes. in der großen Wehe-Rede Mt 23, 13–36; vgl. Lk 11, 37–52.
26 Mt 23, 23 f.
27 Mt 23, 25–28.
28 Mt 23, 15.
29 Mt 6, 1–18.
30 Mt 23, 1–4.
31 Mt 23, 5–12.
32 Mt 23, 29–36.
33 Vgl. *J. Jeremias*, Neutestamentliche Theologie Bd. I, S. 146–150.
34 Mk 3, 28 f.
35 Vgl. Mt 11, 20–24.
36 Lk 17, 10.
37 Mt 20, 1–15.
38 Mt 6, 3 f.
39 Mt 25, 37–40.
40 Lk 15, 11–32.
41 Lk 7, 36–50.
42 *E. Schweizer*, Jesus Christus S. 18.
43 Vgl. *K. Jaspers*, Die maßgebenden Menschen (München 1964) S. 203.

C II: Die Sache Gottes

1. Die Mitte

1 *Origenes,* Contra Celsum VII 9.

2 Neben den angeführten Jesusbüchern und Theologien des Neuen Testaments vgl. die Lexikonartikel zu *Reich Gottes* in: LThK *(H. Fries, R. Schnackenburg),* RGG *(H. Conzelmann, E. Wolf, G. Gloege),* EKL *(L. Goppelt, J. Moltmann),* sowie im BL *(P. van Imschoot),* und im ThW *(H. Kleinknecht, G. von Rad, K. G. Kuhn, K. L. Schmidt).* Dazu die folgenden neueren Monographien: *O. Cullmann,* Königherrschaft Christi und Kirche im NT (Zollikon–Zürich 1941); *K. Buchheim,* Das messianische Reich. Über den Ursprung der Kirche im Evangelium (München 1948); *H. Ridderbos,* De komst van het Koninkrijk (Kampen 1950); *A. N. Wilder,* Eschatology and Ethics in the Teaching of Jesus (New York ²1950); *R. Morgenthaler,* Kommendes Reich (Zürich 1952); *W. G. Kümmel,* Verheißung und Erfüllung (Zürich ²1953); *T. F. Glasson,* His Appearing and His Kingdom (London 1953); *R. H. Fuller,* The Mission and Achievement of Jesus (London 1954); *H. Roberts,* Jesus and the Kingdom of God (London 1955); *J. Bonsirven,* Le Règne de Dieu (Paris 1957); *E. Grässer,* Das Problem der Parusieverzögerung in den synoptischen Evangelien und in der Apostelgeschichte (Berlin 1957); *R. Schnackenburg,* Gottes Herrschaft und Reich (Freiburg 1959); *H. Conzelmann,* Die Mitte der Zeit (Tübingen ³1960); *Th. Blatter,* Die Macht und Herrschaft Gottes (Freiburg/Schweiz 1961); *F. Mußner,* Die Botschaft der Gleichnisse Jesu (München 1961); *W. Trilling,* Das wahre Israel (München 1964); *H. Flender,* Die Botschaft Jesu von der Herrschaft Gottes (München 1968); *R. H. Hiers,* The Kingdom of God in the Synoptic Tradition (Gainesville 1970); *A. Vögtle,* Das Neue Testament und die Zukunft des Kosmos (Düsseldorf 1970). Für die Entwicklung der Reich-Gottes-Idee in der kirchlichen Tradition s. das vielbändige Werk von *F. Staehelin,* Die Verkündigung des Reiches Gottes in der Kirche Jesu Christi (Basel 1951 ff.).

3 *Dibelius,* Jesus S. 52.

4 Mt 6, 9–13 par.

5 Lk 6, 20–22; Mt 5, 3–10.

6 Vgl. C I, 1.

7 Vgl. bes. Mk 1, 15 par.

8 Mk 13, 4–6. 32 par; Lk 17, 20f.

9 Mk 9, 1 par; 13, 30 par; Mt 10, 23.

10 Mk 13, 30 par; Mt 10, 23.

11 Mk 9, 1 par.

12 Lk 4, 18–21.

13 Vgl. Lk 22, 69 mit Mk 14, 62 und Mt 26, 64.

14 Jo 5, 25–29; 6, 39f. 44–54; 12, 48.

15 2 Pet 3, 8–10.

16 Mt 6, 25–34.

17 Mt 7, 7f. par.

18 Mt 17, 20.

19 Lk 9, 62.

20 Mt 13, 44–46.

21 Mt 13, 47–50.

22 Mt 13, 24–30; vgl. 13, 36–43.

23 Mk 4, 26–29.

24 Mk 4, 30–32.

25 Mt 13, 33.

26 Unter den Werken zu den *Gleichnissen Jesu* sind die folgenden wichtig: *A. Jülicher*, Die Gleichnisreden Jesu Bd. I (2. Aufl.) u. Bd. II (Tübingen 1910); *P. Fiebig*, Die Gleichnisreden Jesu im Lichte der rabbinischen Gleichnisse des neutestamentlichen Zeitalters (Tübingen 1912); *C. H. Dodd*, The Parables of the Kingdom (1935, verb. Aufl. London–Glasgow 1961); *T. W. Manson*, The Sayings of Jesus (1937, Neudruck London 1957); *J. Jeremias*, Die Gleichnisse Jesu (1947, 4., neubearb. Aufl. Göttingen 1957); *E. Linnemann*, Gleichnisse Jesu. Einführung und Auslegung (1961, 5., ergänzte Aufl. Göttingen 1969); *G. Eichholz*, Gleichnisse der Evangelien (Neunkirchen–Vluyn 1971).

27 Heb 4, 15.

28 »per omnia nobis assimilari voluit praeter peccatum (cf. Hebr. 4, 15) et ignorantiam«!! Schema Constitutionis Dogmaticae de Fontibus Revelationis (Vatikanstadt 1962) Cap. II, Nr. 14 (S. 14). Eine spätere Fassung enthält nur noch »›absque peccato‹ (Hebr. 4, 15)«. Eine noch spätere Fassung läßt jegliche Referenz auf Heb 4, 15 aus.

29 Vgl. *K. Rahner (–W. Thüsing)*, Christologie – systematisch und exegetisch (Freiburg–Basel–Wien 1972) S. 28–30.

30 Mk 13.

31 Mk 13, 14.

32 Zur *Entmythologisierungsdebatte* grundlegend *R. Bultmann*, Neues Testament und Mythologie. Das Problem der Entmythologisierung der neutestamentlichen Botschaft, in: Kerygma und Mythos, hrsg. von *H. W. Bartsch* (Hamburg 1948) S. 15–48. Dazu die zahlreichen Beiträge in den verschiedenen Bänden von ›Kerygma und Mythos‹, in den Sammelbänden ›Il problema della demitizzazione‹, hrsg. von *E. Castelli* und ›Kerygma and History‹, hrsg. von *C. A. Braaten* und *R. A. Harrisville*. Als Monographien sind wichtig: *K. Barth*, R. Bultmann, Ein Versuch, ihn zu verstehen (Zollikon–Zürich 1953); *E. Buess*, Die Geschichte des mythischen Erkennens. Wider sein Mißverständnis in der »Entmythologisierung« (München 1953); *F. Gogarten*, Entmythologisierung und Kirche (Stuttgart 1953); *H. Ott*, Geschichte und Heilsgeschichte in der Theologie R. Bultmanns (Tübingen 1955); *R. Marlé*, Bultmann et l'interprétation du NT (Paris 1956); *L. Bini*, L'intervento di Oscar Cullmann nelle discussione Bultmannia (Rom 1961); *G. Hasenhüttl*, Der Glaubensvollzug. Eine Begegnung mit R. Bultmann aus katholischem Glaubensverständnis (Essen 1963); *G. Greshake*, Historie wird Geschichte. Bedeutung und Sinn der Unterscheidung von Historie und Geschichte in der Theologie R. Bultmanns (Essen 1963); *E. Hohmeier*, Das Schriftverständnis in der Theologie R. Bultmanns (Berlin–Hamburg 1964); *A. Anwander*, Zum Problem des Mythos (Würzburg 1964); *F. Vonessen*, Mythos und Wahrheit. Bultmanns »Entmythologisierung« und die Philosophie der Mythologie (Einsiedeln 1964); *R. Bultmann*, Zum Problem der Entmythologisierung, in: Glauben und Verstehen Bd. IV (Tübingen 1965) S. 128–137. In der Folge erschien neben verschiedenen Aufsätzen noch *K. Prümm*, Gnosis an der Wurzel des Christentums? Grundlagenkritik der Entmythologisierung (Salzburg 1972). Dazu kritisch: *H. Häring*, Autoritativ verfaßte Kirche?, in: ThQ 154 (1974).

33 Mk 4, 11 f.

34 Vgl. zum folgenden *G. Bornkamm*, Jesus, S. 64–68.

35 Mk 4, 33.

36 Mk 4, 3–8 par.

37 Lk 17, 21.

38 Vgl. *W. G. Kümmel*, Verheißung und Erfüllung (Zürich ²1953; Lit!).

39 Nach der schockierenden Neuentdeckung des befremdlichen *eschatologischen Grundzuges* in der Verkündigung Jesu durch *J. Weiss* und *A. Schweitzer* war es *K. Barth*, der in der Theologie wieder den Sinn für das Eschatologische weckte. Nachdem dann nach dem Zweiten Weltkrieg weithin die präsentische Eschatologie im Sinne der existentialen Interpretation *R. Bultmanns* dominierte, kam es in den 60er Jahren auf den verschiedenen Gebieten zu einer mächtigen Aufwertung der Zukunft in Zukunftsdenken, Prognosen, Planungen, Futurologie. Neben *P. Teilhard de Chardin* war es – unter dem Einfluß von *E. Bloch* – vor allem *J. Moltmann*, der mit seiner »Theologie der Hoffnung« (München 1964) den theologischen Durchbruch zu einem neuen Verständnis der futurischen Eschatologie erreichte. Für die Diskussion und weitere Literaturangaben vgl. *H. Küng*, Menschwerdung Gottes Kap. VII, 6: Gott der Zukunft?

40 Zur Geschichte der verschiedenen Interpretationen des Gottesreiches in Altertum, Mittelalter und Neuzeit vgl. *H. Küng*, Die Kirche Kap. B III, 2.

41 *J. Moltmann*, Die Zukunft als neues Paradigma der Transzendenz, in: Internationale Dialog-Zeitschrift I (1969) 2–13.

42 Mt 13, 45.

43 Mt 13, 44.

44 Lk 17, 33; Mt 10, 39.

45 Mt 17, 20; vgl. Lk 17, 6.

46 Mk 9, 24.

47 Mk 1, 15.

2. Wunder?

1 Zur Problemstellung in der *Wunderfrage* vgl. *M. Seckler*, Plädoyer für Ehrlichkeit im Umgang mit Wundern, in: ThQ 151 (1971) 337–345. In diesem Artikel werden die neuesten Veröffentlichungen zur Wunderfrage besprochen, nämlich: *R. Swinburne*, The Concept of Miracle (London 1970), und *R. Pesch*, Jesu unreigene Taten? Ein Beitrag zur Wunderfrage (Freiburg–Basel–Wien 1970; Lit.!). Auf diese Problemstellung gingen ein: *R. Pesch*, Zur theologischen Bedeutung der »Machttaten« Jesu. Reflexionen eines Exegeten, in: ThQ 152 (1972) 203–213, sowie *H. Küng*, Die Gretchenfrage des christlichen Glaubens? Systematische Überlegungen zum neutestamentlichen Wunder, ebd. 214–223. Dieser Artikel diente dem folgenden Kapitel als Vorlage.
Neben den neutestamentlichen Kommentaren und den Lexikonartikeln von *A. Vögtle*, in: LThK X, 1255–1261 und *E. Käsemann*, in: RGG VI, 1835–1837 sind insbesondere die Jesusbücher wichtig, unter welchen für diese Frage herausgehoben seien die von *R. Bultmann, M. Dibelius, G. Bornkamm, E. Schweizer, K. Niederwimmer, H. Braun, E. Fuchs, C. H. Dodd, J. Blank*. Wichtig auch die Ausführungen in den neutestamentlichen Theologien von *J. Jeremias*, § 10, 1 und *K. H. Schelkle*, Bd. II § 6.
Unter den älteren Arbeiten sind noch immer unentbehrlich: *O. Weinreich*, Antike Heilungswunder (1909, Neudruck Berlin 1969) und *P. Fiebig*, Jüdische Wundergeschichten des neutestamentlichen Zeitalters (Tübingen 1911). Im weiteren neben den formgeschichtlichen Arbeiten von *M. Dibelius* und *R. Bultmann* und den Artikeln bes. im ThW (zu Wunder, Dämonen, Heilungen) die neueren Monographien von *H. R. Fuller*, Interpreting the Miracles (London 1963); dt.: Die Wunder Jesu in Exegese und Verkündigung (Düsseldorf 1967); *L. Monden*, Theologie des Wunders (Freiburg 1961); *H. van der Loos*, The Miracles of Jesus (Leiden 1965); *G. Schille*, Die urchristliche Wundertra-

dition (Berlin 1966); *K. Tagawa*, Miracles et Évangile. La pensée personnelle de l'évangéliste Marc (Paris 1966); *F. Mussner*, Die Wunder Jesu (München 1967); *K. Kertelge*, Die Wunder Jesu im Markusevangelium (München 1970); *O. Böcher*, Christus Exorcista (Stuttgart 1972); *A. Fridrichsen*, The Problem of Miracle in Primitive Christianity (Minneapolis 1972).

2 Vgl. z. B. Mk 8, 12; Lk 11, 29f.
3 Mk 1, 32–34; 3, 7–12; Mt 9, 35.
4 Mk 6, 5a; im Zusatz 6, 5b wie in der Umbildung Mt 13, 58 wird das Anstößige gemildert.
5 Vgl. Mk 5, 34; Lk 7, 50.
6 Vgl. Mk 9, 14–29.
7 Mk 1, 26 par.
8 Mk 9, 18 par.
9 Lk 10, 18.
10 Vgl. das Material bei *R. Bultmann*, Die Geschichte der synoptischen Tradition (Göttingen 1921, ⁵1961); *M. Dibelius*, Die Formgeschichte des Evangeliums (Tübingen 1919, 3. Aufl. hrsg. von *G. Bornkamm*, Tübingen 1959); *L. J. McGinley*, Form-Criticism of the Synoptic Healing Narratives (Woodstock 1944); *H. van der Loos*, aaO; *E. Käsemann*, aaO; *J. Jeremias*, Neutestamentliche Theologie Bd. I § 10, 1.
11 *Tacitus*, Historia 4, 81; *Sueton*, Vespanianus 7.
12 *Lukian*, Philopseudes 11.
13 *Philostratos*, Vita Apollonii 4, 45.
14 Lk 7, 11–17.
15 Vgl. 4 Q Mess ar; darauf wurde ich von meinem Tübinger Kollegen *O. Betz* aufmerksam gemacht.
16 Mk 9, 2–9 par.
17 Mk 6, 45–52 par.
18 Mk 6, 34–44 par; 8, 1–9 par.
19 Mk 5, 21–43 par.
20 Lk 7, 11–17.
21 Jo 11, 1–44.
22 Mk 1, 35–38. 44.
23 Mk 1, 30f.
24 Man vergleiche die topikfreie Blindenheilung von Mk 10, 46–52 mit der stilisierten von Mk 8, 22–26.
25 Mk 3, 20f. 22–30 par. 31–35 par; dazu Jo 7, 20; 8, 48. 52; 10, 21.
26 Mk 2, 1–12 par.
27 4 Q Dam b; vgl. 1 Q Sa 2, 3–9.
28 Mt 11, 5.
29 Vgl. Mt 12, 28.
30 Vgl. Lk 17, 21.
31 Mk 8, 11f. u.ö.
32 Vgl. Jo 2, 23–25; 4, 48; 20, 29.
33 Mt 11, 5.
34 Mt 11, 6.
35 Jo 6, 27. 35.
36 Jo 9, 5.
37 Jo 11, 25.
38 Jo 20, 29.
39 Mk 1, 22.
40 Mk 1, 27.

3. Die oberste Norm

1 Mt 7, 12; Lk 6, 31.
2 Vgl. *H. Limbeck*, Die Ordnung des Heils. Untersuchungen zum Gesetzesverständnis des Frühjudentums (Düsseldorf 1971); *R. J. Zwi Werblowski*, Tora als Gnade, in: Kairos (N. F.) 15 (1973) S. 156–163.
3 *J. Jeremias*, Neutestamentliche Theologie Bd. I, § 19, 1.
4 Z.B. Lev 11; Dt 14, 3–21; vgl. Mt 15, 11–20.
5 Dt 5, 12–14; vgl. Mk 2, 27 par.
6 Mk 10, 2–9. 11 f. par; vgl. Dt 24, 1–4.
7 Mt 5, 33–37.
8 Lk 6, 28.
9 Mt 5, 44 par.
10 Mk 13, 2 par.
11 Vgl. Mk 14, 58 par.
12 Mk 12, 33.
13 Mt 5, 23 f.
14 Mt 5, 20.
15 Mk 1, 22.
16 Mt 26, 42; vgl. Lk 22, 42.
17 Mk 3, 35 par.
18 Mt 7, 21; vgl. die Parabel vom gehorsamen und ungehorsamen Sohn Mt 21, 28–32.
19 Vgl. die Bibliographie zur Gottesherrschaft.
20 Interessant zum Gesetzesverständnis Jesu aus juristischer Sicht *P. Noll*, Jesus und das Gesetz. Rechtliche Analyse der Normenkritik in der Lehre Jesu (Tübingen 1968).
21 Vgl. *R. Bultmann*, Theologie des Neuen Testaments § 2; *G. Bornkamm*, Jesus S. 88–92; *K. Niederwimmer*, Jesus Kap. VII.
22 Zur *Bergpredigt* vgl. *G. Bornkamm*, Jesus S. 92–108, 201–204; *H. Conzelmann*, Theologie des Neuen Testaments § 15. Besonders half mir der neueste Kommentar zu Mt 5–7, den mir mein Zürcher Kollege *Eduard Schweizer* in großzügiger Weise als Manuskript zur Verfügung stellte (erscheint demnächst im Göttinger Bibelwerk ›Neues Testament Deutsch‹). Des weiteren vgl. neben *H.-D. Wendland*, Ethik des Neuen Testaments (Göttingen 1970) Kap. I, 4 und weiteren Arbeiten zur neutestamentlichen Ethik folgende neuere Monographien: *J. Staudinger*, Die Bergpredigt (Wien 1957); *E. Thurneysen*, Die Bergpredigt (München 1963); *W. D. Davies*, The Setting of the Sermon on the Mount (Cambridge 1964); *ders.*, Die Bergpredigt. Exegetische Untersuchungen ihrer jüdischen und frühchristlichen Elemente (München 1970); *G. Eichholz*, Auslegung der Bergpredigt (Neukirchen 1965); *H.-Th. Wrege*, Die Überlieferungsgeschichte der Bergpredigt (Tübingen 1968); *P. Pokorný*, Der Kern der Bergpredigt. Eine Auslegung (Hamburg 1969); *G. Miegge*, Il Sermone sul monte. Commentario esegetico (Torino 1970).
23 Vgl. Mt 5, 18 f.
24 Vgl. *W. Trilling*, Das wahre Israel. Studien zur Theologie des Matthäus-Evangeliums (München 1964) Kap. 9: Die Gesetzesfrage nach Mt 5, 17–20.
25 Mt 5, 17–20.
26 Mt 5, 39–41.
27 Lk 6, 43 f.; Mt 7, 16. 18.
28 Vgl. *H. Braun*, Jesus Kap. 7.
29 Mt 5, 22 a.
30 Mt 5, 22 b.

31 Mt 5, 34a. 37.
32 Mt 5, 34b–36.
33 Lk 17, 3.
34 Mt 18, 15–17.
35 Lk 16, 18; Mk 10, 11.
36 Mt 5, 32; 19, 9.
37 Vgl. *H. Braun,* Jesus Kap. 8.
38 Dt 24, 1–4; vgl. Mk 10, 9.
39 1 Kor 7, 10–16.
40 Lk 16, 18; Mk 10, 11 f.
41 Mt 5, 32; 19, 9.
42 Mk 10, 21.
43 Lk 19, 8.
44 Lk 6, 34 f.
45 Mk 12, 41–44.
46 Mk 15, 41.
47 Mk 14, 3–9 par.

C III: Die Sache des Menschen

1. Humanisierung des Menschen

1 Mt 6, 19–21. 24–34; Mk 10, 17–27.
2 Mt 5, 38–42; Mk 10, 42–44.
3 Lk 14, 26; Mt 10, 34–39.
4 Lk 17, 33; Mt 10, 39.
5 Mk 1, 15 par. Vgl. zu *Metanoia* im Neuen Testament unter den neutestamentlichen Theologien vor allem *R. Bultmann* (§ 1–2), *J. Jeremias* (§ 15), *K. H. Schelkle* (Bd. III, § 5). Unter den Jesusbüchern vor allem *G. Bornkamm* (Kap. IV, 3), *H. Braun* (§ 5), *J. Blank* (B V). Dazu *J. Schniewind,* Das biblische Wort von der Bekehrung (Berlin 1947); *A. Hulsbosch,* De bijbel over bekering (Roermond 1963); dt.: Die Bekehrung im Zeugnis der Bibel (Salzburg 1967). Unter den Lexikonartikeln vor allem *J. Behm – E. Würthwein,* Art. metanoeo, in: ThW IV, 972–1004.
6 Lk 9, 62.
7 Vgl. zu *Glaube* im Neuen Testament neben den zu Mentanoia genannten neutestamentlichen Theologien und Jesus-Büchern vor allem *A. Schlatter,* Der Glaube im Neuen Testament (Stuttgart ⁴1927, Neudruck Darmstadt 1963); *R. Bultmann – A. Weiser,* Art. pisteuo, in: ThW VI, 174–230; *E. D. O'Connor,* Faith in the Synoptic Gospels (Notre Dame/USA 1961); *H. Ljungman,* Pistis (Lund 1964).
8 Mt 13, 44–46.
9 Lk 17, 10.
10 Mk 10, 15 par.
11 Lk 15, 29.
12 Mt 10, 42.
13 Mt 12, 36.
14 Mt 5, 3–12.
15 Vgl. Mt 6, 16–18.
16 Mt 20, 15.
17 Lk 15, 32.

18 Mt 11, 30.
19 Vgl. bes. K. *Niederwimmer,* Jesus Kap. 7 und *J. Blank,* Jesus Kap. B VI.
20 Vgl. Mk 2, 27.
21 Mt 5, 23 f.
22 Vgl. *K. Jaspers,* Die maßgebenden Menschen S. 178–180.
23 Lk 11, 46.

2. *Handeln*

1 Mt 22, 37 f.
2 Lk 10, 30–35.
3 Mt 25, 31–46.
4 Lev 19, 18.
5 Mt 22, 39.
6 Mt 7, 12 par.
7 Lk 10, 29–37.
8 Mt 25, 31–46.
9 Vgl. neuestens ausführlich zur Überlieferungsgeschichte *D. Lührmann,* Liebet eure Feinde (Lk 6, 27–36/Mt 5, 39–48), in: Zeitschrift für Theologie und Kirche 69 (1972), 412–438 (Lit.!).
10 Vgl. Mt 15, 24.
11 Wie vielfältig die eine Parabel theologisch, philosophisch und literarisch anregen kann, zeigt *W. Jens* (Hrsg.), Der barmherzige Samariter (Stuttgart 1973), mit Beiträgen von *C. Amery, G. Bornkamm, H. Braun, T. Brocher, W. Dirks, I. Fetscher, W. u. R.-E. Schulz* u. a.
12 Mt 5, 43 f.
13 Lk 6, 27 f.
14 Vgl. Mt 5, 45.
15 Zu *Eros und Agape* vgl. – wenn man hier von Philosophen wie *M. Scheler* absehen will – *A. Scholz,* Eros und Caritas. Die platonische Liebe und die Liebe im Sinn des Christentums (Halle 1929), und bes. *A. Nygren,* Eros und Agape. Gestaltwandlungen der christlichen Liebe Bd. I–II (Gütersloh 1930–37), der eine intensive Diskussion und scharfe Kritik ausgelöst hat: vgl. z. B. *K. Barth,* Kirchliche Dogmatik Bd. III/2, § 45, 2; IV/2, § 68, 1; *G. Bornkamm,* Jesus S. 106–108; *K. H. Schelkle,* Theologie des Neuen Testaments Bd. III § 8–9 (dort sind auch die weiter zurückliegenden Arbeiten über Gottes- und Nächstenliebe im Alten Testament von *J. Ziegler* und *N. Lohfink,* im Neuen Testament von *K. Rahner, C. Spicq, V. Warnach* und *R. Völkl* aufgeführt). Dazu noch die entsprechenden Artikel in ThW: agapao *(G. Quell – E. Stauffer),* plesion und phileo *(H. Greeven – J. Fichtner).* Theologisch wichtig: *H. U. von Balthasar,* Glaubhaft ist nur Liebe (Einsiedeln 1963).
16 Spr 7, 18; 30, 16 (LXX).
17 Mt 5, 43–46.
18 Mk 10, 13–16.
19 Lk 7, 36–50; Mk 14, 3–9; vgl. Jo 11, 2; 12, 1–8.
20 Lk 10, 38–42; vgl. Jo 11, 3. 5. 28 f. 36; zu Johannes, der an der Brust Jesu ruhte Jo 13, 23 und den Jesus liebte Jo 19, 26; 20, 2; 21, 7. 20; synonymer Gebrauch der Wörter Agape und Philia.
21 Lk 12, 4; vgl. Jo 15, 13–15; sowie die Liebesfrage an Petrus, Jo 21, 15–17.
22 So richtig gegen allzustarke Trennung: *G. Bornkamm,* ebd.
23 Mt 5, 47.
24 Lk 14, 7–11.

25 Lk 6, 36 f; Mt 7, 1.

26 Mt 5, 37.

27 Mt 6, 12; vgl. Lk 11, 4.

28 Vgl. Mt 18, 21–35.

29 Mt 18, 22; vgl. Lk 17, 4.

30 Mt 7, 1 par.

31 Lk 14, 11 par.

32 Mk 10, 43 f. par.

33 Mt 23, 25 par; Mk 12, 40.

34 Mk 9, 43 par.

35 Mt 5, 41.

36 Mt 5, 40.

37 Mt 5, 39.

38 Ex 20, 1–17.

39 Mt 5, 20.

40 Vgl. Röm 13, 8–10.

3. Solidarisierung

1 Das *Verhalten* Jesu als der eigentliche Rahmen seiner Verkündigung bildet einen Schlüsselbegriff für das Jesusverständnis von *E. Fuchs* (gegenüber R. Bultmann): Zur Frage nach dem historischen Jesus (Tübingen 1960) S. 155 f.

2 Vgl. C II, 2: Wunder?

3 Vgl. Jo 9, 1–3.

4 Contra Apionem 2, 201; vgl. *J. Jeremias*, Neutestamentliche Theologie Bd. I, S. 217 f.

5 Mk 15, 40 f. par; Lk 8, 1–3; vgl. Apg 1, 14.

6 Lk 10, 38–42; Jo 11, 3. 5. 28 f. 36.

7 Mk 15, 40 f. par; 15, 47 par.

8 Lk 16, 18.

9 Mk 10, 13–16 par.

10 Mk 10, 15.

11 Vgl. Mt 11, 25 par; 21, 16.

12 Vgl. Mk 9, 42 par; Mt 18, 10. 14; Mt 10, 42.

13 Vgl. Mt 25, 40. 45; Mt 11, 11 par; Lk 9, 48.

14 Mt 5, 3. Das Verhältnis Jesu zu den »Armen« und zur Armut wird in allen Jesusbüchern eingehend behandelt: aufschlußreich besonders *G. Bornkamm* (Kap. IV, 2) und *H. Braun* (Kap. 9), sowie die neutestamentlichen Theologien von *J. Jeremias* (§ 12) und *K. H. Schelkle* (Bd. III, § 23).

15 Lk 6, 20.

16 Lk 6, 20–23.

17 Mt 5, 3. 4. 6.

18 *E. Bloch*, Das Prinzip Hoffnung (1959, Frankfurt 1967) S. 1482.

19 Z. B. Mk 9, 42; Mt 10, 42.

20 Mt 11, 25 par.

21 Dazu interessante Ausführungen bei *M. Weber*, Gesammelte Aufsätze zur Religionssoziologie Bd. III: Das antike Judentum (Tübingen 1920), bes. Nachtrag: Die Pharisäer S. 401–442.

22 Mt 6, 19–21 par.

23 Lk 14, 11 par.

24 Mt 6, 24.

25 Vgl. Lk 6, 24.

26 Mk 10, 25 par.

27 Lk 19, 8.

28 Mk 10, 17–22 par.

29 Lk 8, 1–3; vgl. Mk 15, 40 f. par.

30 Vgl. *H. Braun,* Jesus S. 104–113; *M. Hengel,* Eigentum und Reichtum in der frühen Kirche. Aspekte einer frühchristlichen Sozialgeschichte (Stuttgart 1973) Kap. 3: Verkündigung Jesu.

31 Mt 6, 25–34 par.

32 Mt 6, 11 par.

33 *B. Brecht,* Die Dreigroschenoper, in: Gesammelte Werke Bd. 2 (Frankfurt 1967) S. 457.

34 Vgl. Mt 6, 33.

35 Mt 18, 23–35.

36 Lk 19, 10.

37 Mk 2, 17 par.

38 Mt 11, 19. Zu *Sünde und Gnade* (Vergebung) vgl. die Jesus-Bücher und neutestamentlichen Theologien passim, bes. *H. Braun* (Kap. 11) und *K. H. Schelkle* (Bd. III, § 3; Lit.!). Zum theologischen Begriff der Gnade als Gnädigkeit vgl. *H. Küng,* Rechtfertigung. Die Lehre Karl Barths und eine katholische Besinnung (Einsiedeln 1964) Kap. 27 (Lit.!).

39 Lk 19, 1–10.

40 Mk 2, 13–17 par.

41 Lk 15, 2; vgl. Mk 2, 16 par.

42 Lk 7, 36–50, wohl identisch mit der Frau von Mk 14, 3–9 und Mt 26, 6–13, aber – trotz Jo 12, 1–8 (wo der Name Maria auftaucht) – kaum mit Maria Magdalena.

43 Jo 7, 53–8, 11.

44 Lk 7, 47; Jo 8, 7.

45 Das essayistisch gehaltene Buch von *A. Holl,* Jesus in schlechter Gesellschaft (Stuttgart 1971) stellt in aller Einseitigkeit etwas sehr Wichtiges heraus.

46 Lk 18, 10–14.

47 Lk 15, 11–32.

48 Lk 10, 30–37.

49 Mt 20, 1–16.

50 Lk 15.

51 Lk 15, 4–7; 8–10.

52 Mt 21, 31.

53 Mt 8, 11 f.

54 Mt 20, 16.

55 Mt 18, 21 f.

56 Mt 12, 31.

57 Vgl. Mt 18, 21–35.

58 Lk 16, 1–9.

59 Mt 10, 39 par; 16, 25; vgl. Jo 12. 25.

60 Mt 7, 13 f.; Lk 13, 24.

61 Mt 22, 14.

62 Mt 19, 26.

63 Lk 14, 15–24; Mt 22, 1–10.

64 Mk 2, 15–17. 19; Mt 8, 11; 22, 1–14; Lk 14, 16–24.

65 Lk 18, 9–14.

66 Lk 7, 47.

67 Lk 15, 25–32.

29 Vgl. C II, 1: Entmythologisierung unumgänglich.

30 Zur Frage von *Vollendung* und *Jüngstem Gericht* vgl. neben den Lexikonartikeln bes. *P. Althaus*, Die christliche Wahrheit § 68–70; *E. Brunner*, Dogmatik Bd. III, S. 464–497; *H. Ott*, Die Antwort des Glaubens Art. 49; *M. Schmaus*, Dogmatik Bd. IV/2; *Ch. Schütz*, Vollendung, in: Neues Glaubensbuch Kap. 22; *P. Tillich*, Systematische Theologie Bd. III, S. 446–477; *O. Weber*, Grundlagen der Dogmatik Bd. II, S. 718–759. Dazu die Auslegungen von Gericht und ewigem Leben in den Erklärungen des Apostolikum von *K. Barth*, *W. Pannenberg* und *J. Ratzinger*. Unter den neueren Monographien: *P. Schütz*, Parusia. Hoffnung und Prophetie (Heidelberg 1960); *G. C. Berkouwer*, De Wederkomst van Christus Bd. I–II (Kampen 1961–63); *A. L. Moore*, The Parusia in the New Testament (Leiden 1966).

31 2 Thess 2, 3–12.

32 1 Jo 2, 18. 22; 2 Jo 7.

33 Vgl auch Apk 13.

34 Vgl. C II, 1: Zwischen Gegenwart und Zukunft.

35 Vgl. bes. Mk 13, 24–32; Mt 24, 29–36; 25, 31–46; Lk 21, 25–33; Jo 5, 25–29; 6, 39 f. 44. 54; 11, 24; 12, 48.

36 Vgl. *Ch. Schütz*, aaO S. 533 f.

37 Vgl. *W. Pannenberg*, Das Glaubensbekenntnis S. 126–130.

38 Vgl. Mt 25, 37–40.

39 Jo 5, 24 f.

40 Nach Mt 25, 35 f.

41 Diese doppelte Abgrenzung auch sehr deutlich bei *K. Barth*, Kirchliche Dogmatik Bd. II/2, bes. S. 462.

42 1 Kor 15, 24–28; Röm 5, 18; vgl. 1 Pet 4, 6.

43 Am grandiosesten *K. Barth*, Kirchliche Dogmatik Bd. II/2, Kap. 7: Gottes Gnadenwahl (entwickelt in drei Schritten als Erwählung Jesu Christi, der Gemeinde, des Einzelnen). Für die gegenwärtige Diskussion vgl. *K. Schwarzwäller*, Das Gotteslob der angefochtenen Gemeinde. Dogmatische Grundlegung der Prädestinationslehre (Neukirchen 1970).

3. Das letztlich Unterscheidende

1 1 Kor 1, 23 f.

2 *Cicero*, Pro Rabirio 5, 16.

3 Vgl. *Cicero*, Verr V. 64, 165; V. 66, 169.

4 Vgl. zur verschiedenen Einstellung Goethes und Hegels zum Kreuz *H. Küng*, Menschwerdung Gottes S. 376–378.

5 *D. T. Suzuki*, Mysticism: Christian and Buddhist (1957); dt.: Der westliche und der östliche Weg. Essays über christliche und buddhistische Mystik (Frankfurt 1971), bes.: Kreuzigung und Erleuchtung S. 121–129 (Zit. 121).

6 Literatur zur *theologischen Deutung* des *Todes Jesu*: *G. Bornkamm*, Das Ende des Gesetzes. Paulusstudien. Gesammelte Aufsätze I (München 1958, ⁴1963); *E. Lohse*, Märtyrer und Gottesknecht. Untersuchungen zur urchristlichen Verkündigung vom Sühnetod Jesu Christi (Göttingen ²1963); *ders.*, Die Geschichte des Leidens und Sterbens Jesu Christi (Gütersloh 1964); *E. Güttgemanns*, Der leidende Apostel und sein Herr. Studien zur paulinischen Christologie (Göttingen 1966); *W. Popkes*, Christus traditus (Zürich 1967); *P. Viering* (Hrsg.), Das Kreuz Christi als Grund des Heils (Gütersloh 1967); *ders.* (Hrsg.), Zur Bedeutung des Todes Jesu (Gütersloh 1967) mit exegetischen Beiträgen von *H. Conzelmann – E. Flesseman – van Leer – E. Haenchen – E. Käsemann – E. Lohse; B. Klappert* (Hrsg.), Diskussion um Kreuz und Aufer-

(H.-D. Wendland), ThW *(K. H. Rengstorf)*. Dazu als neuere Monographien:
C. H. *Dodd,* The Apostolic Teaching and its Developments (London 1945);
H. *von Campenhausen,* Kirchliches Amt und geistliche Vollmacht in den
ersten drei Jahrhunderten (Tübingen 1953); *K. H. Schelkle,* Jüngerschaft und
Apostelamt. Eine biblische Auslegung des priesterlichen Dienstes (Freiburg i.
Br. 1957); *B. Rigaux,* Die »Zwölf« in Geschichte und Kerygma, in: Der
historische Jesus und der kerygmatische Christus, hrsg. von *H. Ristow* und *K.
Matthiae* (Berlin 1960) S. 468–486; *G. Klein,* Die zwölf Apostel. Ursprung
und Gehalt einer Idee (Göttingen 1961); *W. Schmithals,* Das kirchliche
Apostelamt. Eine historische Untersuchung (Göttingen 1961); *S. O. Barr,*
From the Apostles' faith to the Apostles' creed (New York 1964); *H. Küng,*
Die Kirche Kap. D IV; *G. W. Ittel,* Jesus und die Jünger (Gütersloh 1970); *Ch.
K. Barrett,* The Signs of an Apostle (Philadelphia 1972).

29 1 Kor 15, 5.
30 Mk 3, 14 par.
31 Mt 19, 28.
32 Apg 1, 15–26.
33 Mk 3, 16–19; Mt 10, 2–4; Lk 6, 14–16; Apg 1, 13.
34 Mk 2, 14 par.
35 Mk 3, 18.
36 Mk 3, 16.
37 Lk 22, 28. 31 f.
38 Mt 13, 47–50; 13, 24–30.
39 Mt 19, 28 par. (in der gegenwärtigen Fassung redigiert).
40 Mk 3, 14; bei Mk 6, 30 scheint Apostel noch kein dauernder Titel, sondern nur
    die zeitweise Tätigkeit eines »Abgesandten« zu sein.
41 Lk 6, 13.
42 Dies ist heute zwischen den Konfessionen nicht mehr umstritten. Vgl. zu-
    nächst von *evangelischer* Seite: *W. G. Kümmel,* Kirchenbegriff und Ge-
    schichtsbewußtsein in der Urgemeinde und bei Jesus (Uppsala 1943); Verhei-
    ßung und Erfüllung. Untersuchungen zur eschatologischen Verkündigung
    Jesu (Zürich ²1953; Lit.!); Jesus und die Anfänge der Kirche, in: Studia
    Theologica 7 (1953) 1–27; Die Naherwartung in der Verkündigung Jesu, in:
    Zeit und Geschichte (Festschrift R. Bultmann, Tübingen 1964) S. 31–46. Wei-
    ter *A. Oepke,* Der Herrenspruch über die Kirche in der neueren Forschung, in:
    Studia Theologica 2 (1948) 110–165; *P. Nepper–Christensen,* Wer hat die
    Kirche gestiftet? (Uppsala 1950); *O. Cullmann,* Petrus (Zürich–Stuttgart
    ²1960); weiter *F. G. Downing,* The Church and Jesus. A study in history,
    philosophy and theology (London 1968).
    Von *katholischer* Seite: *A. Vögtle,* Ekklesiologische Auftragsworte des Aufer-
    standenen, in: Sacra Pagina II (Paris–Gembloux 1959) 280–294; Jesus und die
    Kirche, in: Begegnung der Christen (Festschrift O. Karrer; Stuttgart–Frank-
    furt 1959) S. 54–81; Der Einzelne und die Gemeinschaft in der Stufenfolge der
    Christusoffenbarung, in: Sentire Ecclesiam (Festschrift H. Rahner; Freiburg i.
    Br. 1961) S. 50–91; Exegetische Erwägungen über das Wissen und Selbstbe-
    wußtsein Jesu, in: Gott in Welt I (Festschrift K. Rahner; Freiburg i. Br. 1964)
    S. 608–667. Weiter *J. Betz,* Die Gründung der Kirche durch den historischen
    Jesus, in: ThQ 138 (1958) 152–183; *O. Kuss,* Bemerkungen zum Fragenkreis:
    Jesus und die Kirche im NT, in: ThQ 135 (1955) 28–55; *R. Schnackenburg,*
    Gottes Herrschaft, 149–180; Art. Kirche, in: LThK VI, 167–172; *H. Riedlin-
    ger,* Geschichtlichkeit und Vollendung des Wissens Christi (Freiburg i. Br.
    1966); *H. Küng,* Die Kirche Kap. D II, 3; *F. J. Schierse* antwortet G. Dautzen-

berg, Was hat die Kirche mit Jesus zu tun? Zur gegenwärtigen Problemlage biblischer Exegese und kirchlicher Verkündigung (Düsseldorf 1970). Zur *neutestamentlichen Ekklesiologie im allgemeinen* vgl. für die vorkonziliare Literatur *H. Küng*, Die Kirche Kap. A I, 3. Als neuere Monographien sind zu erwähnen *D. M. Stanley*, The Apostolic Church in the New Testament (Westminster/Md. 1965); *N. J. Bull*, The Rise of the Church (London 1967); *B. Gherardini*, La Chiesa nella storia della teologia protestante (Torino 1969); *R. McKelvey*, The New Temple. The Church in the New Testament (London 1969); *J. Hainz*, Ekklesia. Strukturen paulinischer Gemeinde-Theologie und Gemeinde-Ordnung (Regensburg 1972).

43 Mt 16, 18.

44 Vgl. zum neuen katholischen Konsens in der *Petrusfrage* zunächst die wegweisenden Arbeiten von *A. Vögtle*, Messiasbekenntnis und Petrusverheißung. Zur Komposition Mt 16, 13–23 par (1957/58), abgedruckt in: Das Evangelium und die Evangelien. Beiträge zur Evangelienforschung (Düsseldorf 1971) S. 137–170, und *B. Rigaux*, Der Apostel Petrus in der heutigen Exegese, in: Concilium 3 (1967) 585–600. Dann insbes. die neuesten Arbeiten von *J. Blank*, Neutestamentliche Petrustypologie und Petrusamt, in: Concilium 9 (1973) 173–179; *R. Pesch*, Die Stellung und Bedeutung Petri in der Kirche des Neuen Testaments. Zur Situation der Forschung, in: Concilium 7 (1971) 240–253 (Lit.!); *W. Trilling*, Zum Petrusamt im Neuen Testament. Traditionsgeschichtliche Überlegungen anhand von Matthäus, 1 Petrus und Johannes, in: ThQ 151 (1971) 110–133. Die Übereinstimmung unter diesen drei katholischen Autoren wird herausgearbeitet von *H. Küng*, in: Fehlbar? Eine Bilanz (Zürich-Einsiedeln-Köln 1973) S. 405–414.

45 Mk 7, 27; Mt 15, 24; 10, 6.

46 Mk 16, 15; Mt 28, 18–21.

47 Jes 25, 6–9.

48 Mt 8, 11f. par; vgl. Mt 25, 32–40; 5, 14. Zur Vorstellung von der Völkerwallfahrt *J. Jeremias*, Jesu Verheißung für die Völker (Stuttgart 1956, ²1959).

49 Mk 8, 27f. par.

50 Vgl. B II, 3: Historische Kritik – eine Glaubenshilfe?

51 Zu den *messianischen Titeln* vgl. *V. Taylor*, The Names of Jesus (London 1953); *R. Fuller*, The Mission and Achievement of Jesus (London ²1955) S. 79–117; *O. Cullmann*, Die Christologie des Neuen Testaments (Tübingen 1957); *F. Hahn*, Christologische Hoheitstitel. Ihre Geschichte im frühen Christentum (Göttingen 1963); *L. Sabourin*, Les noms et titres de Jésus (Bruges 1963); *B. van Iersel*, »Der Sohn« in den synoptischen Jesusworten (Leiden 1961). Unter den Jesus-Büchern wichtig *G. Bornkamm*, S. 155–163, 204–208; *H. Conzelmann*, S. 147–159; *J. Jeremias*, S. 245–263; *J. Blank*, S. 77–86. Schließlich die Theologien zum Neuen Testament von *R. Bultmann*, § 7; 12; *H. Conzelmann*, § 10; *K. H. Schelkle*, Bd. 2, § 11 (Lit.!). Sowie die entsprechenden Artikel im Theologischen Wörterbuch zum Neuen Testament und in den theologischen Lexika.

52 Mk 8, 29 par.

53 Mk 14, 61 par.

54 Mt 11, 27; Mk 13, 32.

55 So z. B. *J. Jeremias*, aaO S. 246f.

56 Dan 7, 13f.

57 Äth. Henoch 37–71; 4 Esra 13.

58 Vgl. *J. Jeremias*, aaO § 23.

59 Zur Frage nach dem *Menschensohn* vgl. neben der zu den messianischen Titeln

angegebenen Literatur: *E. Sjöberg*, Der verborgene Menschensohn in den Evangelien (Lund 1955); *E. Schweizer*, Der Menschensohn, in: Neotestamentica (Zürich 1963) 56–84; *H. E. Tödt*, Der Menschensohn in der synoptischen Überlieferung (Gütersloh 1959); *Ph. Vielhauer*, Gottesreich und Menschensohn in der Verkündigung Jesu. Jesus und der Menschensohn, in: Aufsätze zum Neuen Testament (München 1965) 55–140. 145 f.; *C. Colpe*, Art. hyios tou anthropou, in: ThW VIII (Stuttgart 1969) 403–481.

60 Vgl. aus Q bes. Lk 12, 8 f.
61 Mk 15, 14 par.
62 Vgl. Mt 5, 21–48; vgl. Mk 10, 5 par.
63 Vgl. Mt 12, 42; vgl. 12, 6.
64 Mt 12, 41 par.
65 Jo 1, 46.
66 Mk 11, 28–33 par.
67 Mt 11, 6 par.
68 Lk 24, 21.

2. *Der Streit um Gott*

1 Vgl. A II: Die andere Dimension.
2 Vgl. neben den Theologien des Alten und Neuen Testaments (zum NT vgl. B II, zum AT siehe unten) und der einschlägigen religionswissenschaftlichen Literatur (A III) vor allem die angeführte theologische Literatur zur Gottesfrage (A II).
3 *A. Görres*, Glaube und Unglaube in psychoanalytischer Sicht, in: Internationale Katholische Zeitschrift ›Communio‹ 1 (1973) 481–504.
4 Vgl. die genaueren Darlegungen bei *H. Küng*, Menschwerdung Gottes Kap. VIII, 2: Die Geschichtlichkeit Gottes. – Zum Gottesverständnis des Alten Testaments vgl. die alttestamentlichen Theologien von *W. Eichrodt, P. Heinisch, E. Jakob, P. van Imschoot, L. Köhler, G. von Rad, Th. Vriezen, W. Zimmerli*. Wertvoller Überblick bei *C. Westermann*, Der Gott Israels, in: Neues Glaubensbuch Kap. VI.
5 Mk 12, 29–31 par.
6 Vgl. die Einleitungen zum Alten Testament, insbesondere von *J. A. Bewer, O. Eissfeldt, A. Feuillet, G. Fohrer, W. O. E. Oesterley, R. H. Pfeiffer, A. Robert, Th. H. Robinson, A. Weiser*.
7 Dt 26, 8.
8 Ex 15, 1–21.
9 Jes 40–55.
10 Mk 15, 37.
11 Jes 52, 13–53, 12.
12 Vgl. *E. Conze*, Buddhism, its Essence and Development (Oxford ²1953); dt.: Der Buddhismus. Wesen und Entwicklung (Stuttgart 1953) Zit. S. 36.
13 Ps 94, 9.
14 Eine schöne Analyse des Person-Seins (als »Gegenseitigkeit«, »Du-sagen-Können«, »Antworten-Können«, »Zwischen«) und seine Anwendung auf Gott bietet *H. Ott*, Gott (Stuttgart-Berlin 1971), bes. Kap. IV und V. Dort auch die Auseinandersetzung mit Vertretern eines »nach-theistischen« Gottesverständnisses. Vgl. in diesem Zusammenhang vom selben Verfasser: Wirklichkeit und Glaube Bd. II: Der persönliche Gott (Göttingen–Zürich 1969), bes. Kap. III–VI. Vgl. auch *P. Tillich*, Systematische Theologie Bd. I, S. 282–284.

15 Für das Folgende vgl. *H. Küng*, Menschwerdung Gottes VIII, 2: Die Geschichtlichkeit Gottes.

16 Vgl. zu den *Anthropomorphismen: P. van Imschoot*, Théologie de l'Ancien Testament Bd. I (Paris–Tournai 1954) S. 29; *W. Eichrodt*, Theologie des Alten Testaments (Stuttgart ⁵1957) Bd. I, S. 134–141; *E. Jacob*, Théologie de l'Ancien Testament (Neuchâtel 1955) S. 28–32; *Th. C. Vriezen*, Theologie des Alten Testaments in Grundzügen (Neukirchen–Moers 1956) S. 144–147; *G. von Rad*, Theologie des Alten Testaments Bd. I (München 1957) S. 217f.

17 Vgl. A II, 2: Vieldeutigkeit des Gottesbegriffs.

18 Darauf zielt die ganze Auseinandersetzung mit Hegels philosophischer Gotteslehre, wie sie entwickelt wurde, in: Menschwerdung Gottes (vgl. bes. Kap. VIII, 2).

19 *M. Heidegger*, Identität und Differenz (Pfullingen 1957) S. 70.

20 Vgl. *F. K. Mayr*, Patriarchalisches Gottesverständnis? Historische Erwägungen zur Trinitätslehre, in: ThQ 152 (1972) 224–255.

21 Ex 4, 22f.; Jer 31, 9; Jes 63, 16.

22 Ps 2, 7.

23 Sir 4, 10; Weisheit 2, 16–18.

24 Jubiläumsbuch 1, 24.

25 Mt 5, 44–48.

26 Mt 10, 29–31.

27 Mt 6, 8.

28 Mt 6, 32.

29 Lk 15, 11–32.

30 Vgl. bes. die Untersuchungen von *J. Jeremias*, Abba (Göttingen 1966) S. 15–67; *ders.*, Neutestamentliche Theologie Bd. I (Gütersloh 1971) S. 67–73.

31 Vgl. auch Ps 89, 27 (das königliche Vorrecht, Gott »mein Vater« zu sagen; vgl. Sir 51, 10), ähnlich die Verzweiflungsrufe Jes 63, 16; 64, 8; Jer 3, 4.

32 Mk 14, 36.

33 Gal 4, 6; Röm 8, 15; vgl. in diesem Zusammenhang Mt 23, 9.

34 Mt 6, 9.

35 Mt 6, 9–13.

36 Lk 11, 2–4.

37 Mk 11, 25; Mt 6, 14f.; 18, 35.

38 Mt 6, 7f.

39 Lk 11, 5–8.

40 Lk 18, 1–5.

41 Mt 7, 7–11; Lk 11, 9–13.

42 Mt 6, 10; vgl. Mk 14, 36.

43 Mt 6, 6.

44 Lk 5, 16; 6, 12; 9, 18. 28f.

45 Mk 1, 35; 6, 46 par; 14, 32–39.

46 Mt 11, 25.

47 So *H. Conzelmann*, Theologie des NT S. 121–123.

48 So *G. Bornkamm*, Jesus S. 118.

49 *J. Jeremias*, Neutestamentliche Theologie § 6.

50 Mk 10, 18 par.

3. Das Ende

1 Mk 3, 6.
2 Vgl. *K. L. Schmidt*, Der Rahmen der Geschichte Jesu. Literarkritische Untersuchungen zur ältesten Jesus-Überlieferung (Berlin 1919, Neudruck Darmstadt 1964).
3 Mt 5, 35.
4 Lk 19, 11; 24, 21; Apg 1, 6.
5 Mk 8, 31 par; 9, 31 par; 10, 33 f. par.
6 Jo 7, 52.
7 Mk 2, 24; 3, 6.
8 Mk 6, 17–29.
9 Antiquitates 18, 118f.
10 Lk 13, 31.
11 Vgl. Mt 23, 35; Lk 13, 33.
12 Jes 53, 12.
13 Mk 10, 45.
14 Mk 14, 24.
15 Mindestens soweit wird man das von *J. Jeremias*, Neutestamentliche Theologie Bd. I, S. 264–272 (Lit.!) vorgelegte Material ernstnehmen müssen.
16 Mk 9, 31.
17 Mk 8, 33.
18 Anders Jo 4, 2.
19 Mk 16, 15 gehört zum Nachtragskapitel; Jo 3, 5 ist unsicher bezeugt; der Mattäus-Schluß geht in dieser trinitarischen Form auf eine Gemeinde-Überlieferung bzw. Gemeinde-Praxis zurück.
20 Zur weiteren Deutung der *Taufe* vgl. *H. Küng*, Die Kirche Kap. C III, 1: Eingegliedert durch die Taufe (ausführliche Literatur bis 1965). Unter der neueren Literatur sind zu nennen: *G. R. Beasley-Murray*, Baptism in the New Testament (London 1962); dt.: Die christliche Taufe. Eine Untersuchung über ihr Verständnis in Geschichte und Gegenwart (Kassel 1968); *W. Bieder*, Die Verheißung der Taufe im Neuen Testament (Zürich 1966); *K. Barth*, Die kirchliche Dogmatik IV, 4: Das Christliche Leben (Fragment). Die Taufe als Begründung des christlichen Lebens (Zürich 1967); *N. Gäumann*, Taufe und Ethik. Studien zu Römer 6 (München 1967); *O. Böcher*, Christus Exorzista. Dämonismus und Taufe im Neuen Testament (Stuttgart 1972).
21 1 Kor 11, 23–25; Mk 14, 22–25; Mt 26, 26–29; Lk 22, 15–20.
22 1 Kor 11, 23–25.
23 Mk 6, 30–44; 8, 1–10 par; vgl. Mk 2, 18–20.
24 Mk 14, 25.
25 1 Kor 11, 25.
26 Ex 24, 8–11.
27 Jer 31, 31–34.
28 Vgl. bes. Jes 53, 4–10.
29 Mk 14, 22 par.
30 Zur weiteren Deutung des *Abendmahls* vgl. *H. Küng*, Die Kirche Kap. C III, 2: Geeint in der Mahlgemeinschaft (ausführliche Literatur bis 1965). Unter der neueren Literatur sind zu nennen: *J.-J. von Allmen*, Essai sur le Repas du Seigneur (Neuchâtel 1966); *C. O'Neill*, New approaches to the Eucharist (Staten Island 1967); *G. N. Lammens*, Tot Zijn Gedachtenis. Het commemoratieve Aspect van de Avondmaalsviering (Kampen 1968); *J. M. Powers*, Eucharistie in neuer Sicht (Freiburg–Basel–Wien 1968); *J. P. de Jong*, Die Eucharistie als Symbolwirklichkeit (Regensburg 1969); *B. Sandvik*, Das Kom-

men des Herrn beim Abendmahl im Neuen Testament (Zürich 1970); *H. Schürmann*, Jesu Abendmahlshandlung als Zeichen für die Welt (Leipzig 1970); *R. Feneberg*, Christliche Passafeier und Abendmahl. Eine biblisch-hermeneutische Untersuchung der ntl. Einsetzungsberichte (München 1971); *H. Fries*, Ein Glaube. Eine Taufe. Getrennt beim Abendmahl? (Graz 1971); *H. Patsch*, Abendmahl und historischer Jesus (Stuttgart 1972); *A. Gerken*, Theologie der Eucharistie (München 1973).

31 Als Kommentar sei empfohlen *E. Schweizer*, Das Evangelium nach Markus (Göttingen 1968).
32 Vgl. *G. Schneider*, Die Passion Jesu nach den drei älteren Evangelien (München 1973), wo sich die neuere Literatur zur Exegese der Passionsgeschichte zusammengefaßt findet. Davon noch immer wichtig *K. H. Schelkle*, Die Passion Jesu in der Verkündigung des Neuen Testaments (Heidelberg 1949). Zum vierten Evangelium vgl. neuerdings *A. Dauer*, Die Passionsgeschichte im Johannesevangelium (München 1972).
33 Jes 53.
34 Sach 9, 9.
35 Mk 14, 21.
36 Lk 24, 26f.
37 Mk 14, 47; Lk 22, 49–51; Jo 18, 10f.
38 Lk 22, 44 (textkritisch umstritten, vielleicht Interpolation).
39 Mk 14, 51f.
40 Mk 15, 21.
41 Vgl. Mt 27, 32; Lk 23, 26.
42 Mk 15, 40 par im Gegensatz zu Jo 19, 25.
43 Mk 15, 24 par.
44 Mk 15, 27f.
45 Mk 15, 29f.
46 So die Markus-Apokalypse Mk 13; vgl. Mt 24; Lk 21, 5–36.
47 Mk 11, 27–33 par.
48 Vgl. Mk 13, 2 mit Mk 14, 58.
49 Vgl. *C. H. Dodd*, The Parables of the Kingdom (London–Glasgow 1961) S. 100f.
50 Mk 14, 1f. par.
51 Jo 19, 42; Mk 15, 42.
52 Mt 26, 15; vgl. Jo 12, 6.
53 Mt 27, 9; vgl. Sach 11, 12f.
54 Vgl. Mk 14, 10f. mit Mt 26, 14–16; 27, 3–10.
55 Mk 14, 17–21 par.
56 Mk 14, 32–42 par.
57 Jo 18, 4–9.
58 Vgl. *H. Lietzmann*, Der Prozeß Jesu (Sitzungsbericht der Berliner Akademie 1931, XIV); *J. Blinzler*, Der Prozeß Jesu (Stuttgart 1951, 4. erneut revidierte Aufl. Regensburg 1969); *D. R. Catchpole*, The Trial of Jesus. A Study in the Gospels and Jewish Historiography from 1770 to the Present Day (Leiden 1971). Von den Jesus-Büchern vgl. vor allem *G. Bornkamm*, Jesus S. 150f.
59 Mk 14, 55–64.
60 Mk 14, 62.
61 Ps 110, 1 und Dan 7, 13.
62 Mk 14, 58 par.
63 *Josephus*, De bello Judaico 6, 301–303.
64 Bes. deutlich Lk 23, 2; Jo 19, 12. 15; aber auch Mk 15, 9f. par.

65 Vgl. Mk 15, 2. 9. 12. 18. 26. 32 und Parallelen.
66 Mt 19, 27.
67 Lk 23, 6–12.
68 Jo 18, 33–38; 19, 6–16.
69 Jo 19, 19–22.
70 Mk 15, 15–20 par.
71 Mk 15, 24 par.
72 Vgl. *J. Schneider*, Art. »stauros«, in: ThW VII, 572–584 (Lit.).
73 Mk 15, 33; vgl. Am 8, 9f.
74 Jo 11, 49f.
75 C I, 2: Revolution?
76 Dies muß bei aller weitgehenden Übereinstimmung mit *J. Moltmanns* Intentionen gegen seine Systematisierung in ›Der gekreuzigte Gott‹ S. 121–138 eingewendet werden.
77 Mk 12, 17 par.
78 Jo 19, 7.
79 Dt 21, 23 (LXX). Das Aufhängen am Holz wurde nach jüdischem Recht an gesteinigten Götzendienern und Gotteslästerern als Zusatzstrafe (also nicht als Todesstrafe) vollzogen.
80 Vgl. Gal 3, 13.
81 *Justin*, Dialog mit dem Juden Tryphon 89–90.
82 Mk 15, 28.
83 2 Kor 5, 21.
84 Vgl. Mk 15, 40f.
85 Lk 23, 39–43.
86 Jo 19, 26f.
87 Mk 15, 37; Mt 27, 50.
88 Lk 22, 43.
89 Mk 14, 34 par.
90 Lk 23, 46; vgl. Ps 31, 6.
91 Jo 19, 30.
92 Ps 22, 2; Mk 15, 34; Mt 27, 46.
93 *J. Moltmann*, aaO S. 140–142.
94 Mk 15, 42–47.
95 Mk 15, 44f.
96 1 Kor 15, 3–5.

C V: Das neue Leben

1. Der Anfang

1 *E. Bloch*, Das Prinzip Hoffnung (1959, Frankfurt 1967) S. 1297; vgl. S. 1297–1391.
2 Sogar der die Flucht der Jünger vertuschende und den Tod Jesu mit tröstlichen und erbaulichen Details mildernde Lukas spricht deutlich von der gescheiterten Hoffnung der Jünger (Lk 24, 21).
3 Die ältere Literatur zur *Auferweckung* verarbeitet gründlich *H. Grass*, Ostergeschehen und Osterberichte (Göttingen 1956, ⁴1970). Für die neuere Diskussion sind grundlegend: *K. Barth*, Die Auferstehung der Toten (München 1953); Kirchliche Dogmatik Bd. IV/1, § 59, 3; IV/2, § 64, 2–4; *R. Bultmann*, Theologie des Neuen Testaments § 7 und § 33; *ders.*, Das Verhältnis der

urchristlichen Christusbotschaft zum historischen Jesus (Heidelberger Ak. Abhandlg. 1960, Heidelberg ³1962); *W. Marxsen*, Die Auferstehung Jesu als historisches und theologisches Problem (Gütersloh 1964); *ders.*, Die Auferstehung Jesu von Nazareth (Gütersloh 1968).

Neben den betreffenden Äußerungen der Jesusbücher sind für die neuere Diskussion wichtig: *H. v. Campenhausen*, Der Ablauf der Osterereignisse und das leere Grab (Heidelberg 1952, ³1966); *G. Koch*, Die Auferstehung Jesu Christi (Tübingen 1959); *W. Künneth*, Glauben an Jesus? Die Begegnung der Christologie mit der modernen Existenz (1962, München–Hamburg ³1969); *J. Kremer*, Das älteste Zeugnis von der Auferstehung Jesu Christi. 1 Kor 15, 1–11 (Stuttgart ²1967); *ders.*, Die Osterbotschaft der vier Evangelien (Stuttgart 1967, ³1970); *Ph. Seidensticker*, Die Auferstehung Jesu in der Botschaft der Evangelisten (Stuttgart 1967); *L. Schenke*, Auferstehungsverkündigung und leeres Grab (Stuttgart 1968); *H. Schlier*, Über die Auferstehung Jesu Christi (Einsiedeln 1968, ³1970); *K. Lehmann*, Auferweckt am dritten Tag nach der Schrift (Freiburg 1968); *J. Blank*, Paulus und Jesus. Eine theologische Grundlegung (München 1968) S. 133–248; *ders.*, Der Gott der Lebenden, in: *J. Feiner – L. Vischer* (Hrsg.), Neues Glaubensbuch (Freiburg–Basel–Wien 1973) Kap. 8, bes. 173–197; *F. Mussner*, Die Auferstehung Jesu (München 1969); *G. Kegel*, Auferstehung Jesu – Auferstehung der Toten. Eine traditionsgeschichtliche Untersuchung zum Neuen Testament (Gütersloh 1970); *U. Wilckens*, Auferstehung (Stuttgart–Berlin 1970); *X. Léon-Dufour*, Résurrection de Jésus et Message pascal (Paris 1971); *K. H. Schelkle*, Theologie des Neuen Testaments Bd. II, bes. § 9: Auferweckung und Erhöhung – Geschichte und Deutung, S. 128–150 (Lit.!).

Folgende Sammelbände liefern wichtiges Material: *W. Marxsen – U. Wilckens – G. Delling – H. G. Geyer*, Die Bedeutung der Auferstehungsbotschaft für den Glauben an Jesus Christus (Gütersloh 1966, ⁷1968); Auferstehung heute gesagt. Osterpredigten der Gegenwart (Gütersloh 1970); La résurrection du Christ et l'exégèse moderne (Paris 1969) mit Beiträgen von *J. Delorme* u.a.; Dossier sur la résurrection = Lettre Nr. 163–164 (Paris 1972) mit Beiträgen von *A. Jaubert, X. Léon-Dufour, E. Floris, J. Cardonnel, M. Oraison, R. Dulong, M. de Certeau, J.-L. Afchain.*

4 Vgl. die Grundtexte der Auferweckung Jesu: Mk 16, 1–8; Mt 28; Lk 24; Jo 20f.; 1 Kor 15, 3–8.

5 Petrus-Evangelium Kap. 8, 35–44.

6 1 Kor 15, 5–8; vgl. Gal 1, 16; 1 Kor 9, 1.

7 Mt 16, 18.

8 Lk 22, 32.

9 Jo 21, 15–17.

10 Vgl. freilich schon 1 Thess 4, 14.

11 Vgl. Röm 6, 4; 8, 11. 34; 10, 9; 1 Kor 6, 4; Eph 1, 20; 2 Tim 2, 8; Apg 2, 24; 3, 15; 4, 10; 5, 30; 10, 40; 13, 30. 37.

12 Apg 2, 24.

13 Mk 12, 25; vgl. Lk 20, 36.

14 1 Kor 15, 44.

15 1 Kor 15, 43.

16 1 Kor 15, 52.

17 So *K. Barth*, Kirchliche Dogmatik Bd. IV/1, S. 364.

18 So *R. Bultmann*, Neues Testament und Mythologie. Das Problem der Entmythologisierung der neutestamentlichen Verkündigung (abgedruckt in: Kerygma und Mythos I, Hamburg 1948) S. 46.

19 So *W. Marxsen*, Die Auferstehung Jesu als historisches und theologisches Problem S. 25. Zu Marxsen vgl. *P. Schoonenberg*, Ein Gott der Menschen (Zürich–Einsiedeln–Köln 1969) S. 169–180.

20 *R. Bultmann*, Das Verhältnis der urchristlichen Christusbotschaft zum historischen Jesus (Heidelberg 1960) S. 27.

21 Vgl. *E. Schweizer*, Erniedrigung und Erhöhung bei Jesus und seinen Nachfolgern (Zürich ²1972); *W. Thüsing*, Erhöhungsvorstellung und Parusieerwartung in der ältesten nachösterlichen Christologie (Stuttgart 1969); *G. Lohfink*, Die Himmelfahrt Jesu. Untersuchungen zu den Himmelfahrts- und Erhöhungstexten bei Lukas (München 1971; Lit.!); *ders.*, Die Himmelfahrt Jesu – Erfindung oder Erfahrung (Stuttgart 1972).

22 Bes. Ps 110, 1; 68, 19.

23 Apg 2, 36.

24 Vgl. Röm 1, 3 f.

25 Gal 1, 15 f.

26 Zu dieser ganzen Frage vgl. bes. *G. Lohfink* in den beiden angegebenen Veröffentlichungen.

27 Lk 24, 50–52; Apg 1, 9–14.

28 2 Kg 2, 11.

29 Ps 110, 1.

30 Apg 1, 11.

31 Vgl. *E. Lohse*, Art. pentekoste, in ThW VI, 44–53, sowie die biblischen und theologischen Lexikonartikel zu Pfingsten. Als neueste Monographie: *J. Kremer*, Pfingstbericht und Pfingstgeschehen. Eine exegetische Untersuchung zu Apg 2, 1–13 (Stuttgart 1973).

32 Jo 20, 22.

33 Apg 8, 14–17; 19, 1–7; vgl. 10, 44–48.

34 Vgl. *H. Küng*, Die Firmung als Vollendung der Taufe, in: ThQ 154 (1974) 26–47. Die komplexe Problematik wurde exegetisch, historisch und systematisch untersucht und eingehend dargelegt von meinem Schüler *J. Amougou-Atangana*, Ein Sakrament des Geistempfangs? Zum Verhältnis von Taufe und Firmung. Ökumenische Forschungen, dritte sakramentologische Abteilung Bd. I (Freiburg–Basel–Wien 1974).

35 Apg 17, 32.

36 Dan 12, 1 f.

37 Vgl. *W. Pannenberg*, Christologie § 3; *ders.*, Das Glaubensbekenntnis S. 108–111.

38 1 Kor 15, 20.

39 Kol 1, 18; vgl. Apk 1, 5.

40 Mk 5, 21–43 par.

41 Lk 7, 11–17.

42 Jo 11.

43 Vgl. zum Hineinsterben in Gott vor allem die Ausführungen von *K. Rahner* zur Theologie des Todes, neuestens noch in: *K. Rahner (–W. Thüsing)*, Christologie – systematisch und exegetisch (Freiburg–Basel–Wien 1972) Kap. IV.

44 So *W. Marxsen*, der sich im Anschluß an R. Bultmann sehr um die verschärfte Sicht der Auferstehungsproblematik und die Bedeutung des Glaubens in diesem Zusammenhang verdient gemacht hat.

45 Vgl. *G. Bertram*, Die Himmelfahrt vom Kreuz aus und der Glaube an seine Auferstehung, in: Festgabe für A. Deissmann (Tübingen 1927) S. 187–217.

46 Jo 3, 14; 8, 28; 12, 32. 34.

47 Jo 17, 4f. Vgl. *W. Thüsing*, Die Erhöhung und Verherrlichung Jesu im Johannesevangelium (Münster ²1970).

48 Röm 4, 17.

49 Vgl. Röm 4, 24; 2 Kor 1, 9; 4, 14; Gal 1, 1; 1 Thess 1, 10; 4, 14; 1 Pet 1, 21.

50 Röm 4, 17.

51 Mk 12, 26f.; vgl. 2 Kor 1, 9.

52 Mk 12, 24.

53 Röm 4, 24.

54 Vgl. Röm 8, 11; 2 Kor 4, 14; Gal 1, 1; Eph 1, 20; Kol 2, 12.

55 Vgl. B II, 3: Historische Kritik – eine Glaubenshilfe?

56 1 Kor 15, 3–5.

57 Mk 16, 1–8.

58 Mk 16, 9–20.

59 Vgl. dazu vor allem *K. Lehmann*, der die Bedeutung der Formel aus Targum- und Midraschtexten zu erhellen versucht (bes. S. 262–290).

60 So *J. Gnilka*, Jesus Christus nach frühen Zeugnissen des Glaubens (München 1970) S. 54f.

61 1 Kor 15, 4.

62 1 Kor 15, 5–8.

63 2 Kor 5, 2–4.

64 Vgl. *G. Ebeling*, Das Wesen des christlichen Glaubens, S. 78f.

65 Mk 16, 5f.

66 Apg 1, 15.

67 Lk 24, 22–24.

68 Mk 16, 6.

69 Mk 16, 6.

70 Mk 16, 8.

71 Mt 28, 8.

72 Mk 16, 8.

73 Lk 24, 5.

74 Vgl. Denz 2–12: die Leeranzeige unter Ziffer 4 b. Dann Denz 40. 429. 462; vgl. 385. 574.

75 1 Pet 3, 18–20.

76 *F. Spitta*, Christi Predigt an die Geister (Göttingen 1890).

77 *K. Gschwind*, Die Niederfahrt Christi in die Unterwelt (Münster 1911).

78 Nach *B. Reicke*, The Disobedient Spirits and Christian Baptism (Kopenhagen 1946) und *W. Bieder*, Die Vorstellung von der Höllenfahrt Jesu Christi (Zürich 1949) vgl. vor allem die überzeugende Lösung aufgrund der Übersicht über die gesamte Forschungslage von *W. J. Dalton*, Christ's Proclamation to the Spirits (Rom 1965), Zusammenfassung im Aufsatz: Interpretation and Tradition: An Example from 1 Peter, in: Gregorianum 49 (1968) 11–37. Zu konsultieren auch die Kommentare zum ersten Petrusbrief von *U. Holzmeister, E. G. Selwyn, B. Reicke, C. Spicq* und *K. H. Schelkle* sowie den diesbezüglichen Abschnitt in den Erklärungen des Apostolikums von *K. Barth, W. Pannenberg* und *J. Ratzinger*.

79 Slaw. Henoch 7, 1–3.

80 Vgl. Eph 6, 12; 1 Kor 2, 8; Kol 2, 15; Lk 10, 18.

81 Vgl. C IV, 3: Umsonst?

82 Vgl. C II, 2: Was wirklich geschehen ist.

83 Vgl. *H. Haag*, Abschied vom Teufel (Zürich–Einsiedeln–Köln 1969).

84 *H. Haag* bereitet ein größeres Werk über den Teufel vor: Teufelsglaube (erscheint Tübingen 1974).

85 1 Kor 15, 24–28; Röm 5, 18; 1 Pet 4, 6.
86 Vgl. etwa zur Höllenfahrt Jesu das zum Nachdenken anregende Kapitel von *H. U. von Balthasar,* Der Gang zu den Toten, in: Mysterium Salutis Bd. III/2 (Einsiedeln–Zürich–Köln 1969) S. 227–255.
87 So weit über U. Wilckens hinausgehend und sich an die Hypothesen des Wilckens-Schülers K. Berger anschließend *R. Pesch,* Zur Entstehung des Glaubens an die Auferstehung Jesu, in: ThQ 153 (1973) 201–228.
88 Vgl. zum Folgenden in derselben Nummer der ThQ S. 229–269 die Antworten von *W. Kasper, K. H. Schelkle, P. Stuhlmacher* und *M. Hengel* auf die Darlegungen von *R. Pesch.* Dazu im Rückblick auf die Kontroverse *H. Küng,* Zur Entstehung des Auferstehungsglaubens. Versuch einer systematischen Klärung, in: ThQ 154 (1974) 103-117. Für den weiteren Kontext der Kontroverse: *W. Kasper,* Einführung in den Glauben (Mainz 1972), bes. S. 57–61, *K. H. Schelkle,* Theologie des Neuen Testaments Bd. II (Düsseldorf 1973), § 9; *P. Stuhlmacher,* Das Bekenntnis zur Auferweckung Jesu von den Toten und die Biblische Theologie, in: Zeitschrift für Theologie und Kirche 70 (1973) 365–403; *M. Hengel,* Nachfolge und Charisma. Eine exegetisch-religionsgeschichtliche Studie zu Mt 8, 21 f. und Jesu Ruf in die Nachfolge (Berlin 1968); *ders.,* Christologie und neutestamentliche Chronologie, in: Neues Testament und Geschichte, Festschrift O. Cullmann (Zürich–Tübingen 1972) S. 43–67; *ders.,* Die Ursprünge der christlichen Mission, in: New Testament Studies 18 (1971/72) 15–38.
89 *J. Jeremias,* Heiligengräber in Jesu Umwelt (Göttingen 1958).
90 Ps 16, 8–11; Jes 52, 13.
91 Gen 5, 24; 2 Kg 2, 11.
92 Mk 6, 14–16; vgl. Mk 9, 9–13.
93 Vgl. C IV, 3: Stationen.
94 Selbst Lk 22, 31 f. spricht von einer zukünftigen Bekehrung. Lukas schont die Jünger und verschweigt im Gegensatz zu Markus und Mattäus ihre Flucht.
95 Faust I Vers 921 f.
96 Ex 3, 2. 16; 6, 3; 1, 7.10.
97 1 Kor 15, 8; Gal 1, 16.
98 1 Kor 9, 1.
99 Gal 1, 11–17.
100 2 Kor 12, 1.
101 2 Kor 11, 17; 12, 1.
102 Apg 9, 1–9; 22, 3–11; 26, 9–20.
103 Vgl. C II, 2: Wunder?
104 Vgl. C V, 1: Legenden?
105 Vgl. *G. Bornkamm,* Jesus S. 164–170; *J. Blank,* Jesus S. 91 f.; sowie *ders.,* in: Neues Glaubensbuch S. 173–197.
106 Mt 28, 17; Jo 20, 24–29; vgl. auch Lk 24, 11.34.
107 Vgl. die scharfsinnigen Analysen *G. Ebelings,* Das Wesen des christlichen Glaubens S. 66–85.
108 Vgl. *G. von Rad,* Theologie des Alten Testaments Bd. II (München 1960) S. 62–82: Berufung und Offenbarungsempfang.
109 Vgl. C IV, 2: Revolution im Gottesverständnis.
110 Mt 14, 28–31.
111 Vgl. *K. Rahner(–W. Thüsing),* Christologie – systematisch und exegetisch S. 38, 40–42; *ders.,* Ostererfahrung, in: Schriften zur Theologie Bd. VII, S. 157–165.
112 1 Kor 15, 32.

113 Vgl. 1 Kor 15, 12. 33 f.
114 Vgl. *E. Käsemann,* Der Ruf der Freiheit (Tübingen ⁵1972) Kap. 3; *ders.,* Paulinische Perspektiven (Tübingen 1969) Kap. 2.
115 Zur systematischen Vertiefung der *Auferweckungsproblematik* vgl. *P. Althaus,* Die christliche Wahrheit § 47; *K. Barth,* Kirchliche Dogmatik, aaO; *H. U. von Balthasar,* Mysterium Pascale, in: Mysterium Salutis Bd. III/2, Kap. 9; *H. Ott,* Die Antwort des Glaubens Art. 24; *P. Tillich,* Systematische Theologie Bd. II, S. 163–178; *J. Blank,* Der Gott der Lebenden, in: Neues Glaubensbuch Kap. 8; sowie der Auferstehungsartikel in den Erklärungen des Apostolikum von *K. Barth, W. Pannenberg* und *J. Ratzinger.*

2. Der Maßgebende

1 Vgl. Jo 12, 24.
2 Vgl. Mt 23, 8.
3 Vgl. Lk 7, 39; 24, 19; Jo 1, 25.
4 Vgl. Mk 1, 24; Jo 6, 69.
5 Vgl. Mt 25, 31–45.
6 Gal 5, 13.
7 Zur dogmatischen Deutung der christologischen Titel: *Ch. Duquoc,* Christologie. Essai dogmatique (Paris 1968) S. 131–328.
8 Darauf ist zurückzukommen.
9 Vgl. B II, 2: Mehr als eine Biographie.
10 Vgl. B II, 3: Rückfrage nach Jesus.
11 Mk 1, 1.
12 Einen umfassenden Überblick über die verschiedenen neutestamentlichen Christologien gibt *E. Schweizer,* Jesus Christus im vielfältigen Zeugnis des Neuen Testaments (München–Hamburg 1968).
13 Vgl. dazu die oben angeführten Werke, insbesondere von *V. Taylor, O. Cullmann, F. Hahn, L. Sabourin,* die neutestamentlichen Theologien und die entsprechenden Artikel im ThW. Einen guten knappen historisch-kritischen Aufriß der Genese der neutestamentlichen Christologie gibt *J. Gnilka,* Jesus Christus nach frühen Zeugnissen des Glaubens (München 1970).
14 Vgl. Mk 8, 38; Lk 9, 26; 12, 8.
15 Vgl. bes. Mt 10, 32 mit Lk 12, 8: »Menschensohn« nachträglich durch »ich« ersetzt.
16 Vgl. Ps 2, 7; Ps 89, 27 f.
17 2 Sam 7, 12–16.
18 Röm 1, 3 f.
19 Apg 13, 33; vgl. Ps 2, 7.
20 Mk 1, 9–11.
21 Lk 1, 32. 35.
22 Gal 4, 4; Jo 3, 16.
23 Vgl. C IV, 1: Der Sachwalter.
24 2 Kor 5, 21.
25 Für das Verständnis der Stellvertretung wertvolle Einsichten bei *D. Sölle,* Stellvertretung. Ein Kapitel Theologie nach dem »Tod Gottes« (Stuttgart–Berlin 1965); dazu kritisch *H. Gollwitzer,* Von der Stellvertretung Gottes. Christlicher Glaube in der Erfahrung der Verborgenheit Gottes. Zum Gespräch mit Dorothee Sölle (München 1967).
26 Jo 14, 28.
27 *D. Sölle,* aaO S. 142–150.
28 1 Kor 15, 28.

stehung. Zur gegenwärtigen Auseinandersetzung in Theologie und Gemeinde (Wuppertal 1967); *A. Fohrer* – *G. Strobel* – *W. Schrage* – *P. Rieger*, Das Kreuz Jesu. Theologische Überlegungen (Göttingen 1969); *E. Käsemann*, Paulinische Perspektiven (Tübingen 1969); *H. Kessler*, Die theologische Bedeutung des Todes Jesu. Eine traditionsgeschichtliche Untersuchung (Düsseldorf 1970; Lit.!); *G. Delling*, Der Kreuzestod Jesu in der urchristlichen Verkündigung (Göttingen 1972); *J. Moltmann*, Der gekreuzigte Gott. Das Kreuz Christi als Grund und Kritik christlicher Theologie (München 1972).

7 Jes 53.

8 Es ist unnötig, überall auf die zahlreichen Bibelkommentare hinzuweisen. Nur für das grundlegende Markusevangelium seien hier die wichtigeren Kommentare vermerkt: *P. Carrington, C. E. B. Cranfield, F. C. Grant, W. Grundmann, E. Haenchen, S. E. Johnson, E. Klostermann, E. Lohmeyer, D. E. Nineham, A. Schlatter, J. Schmid, J. Schniewind, V. Taylor, M. de Tuya, F. M. Uricchio* – *G. M. Stano*. Bereits herausgehoben wurde der Kommentar von *E. Schweizer*, Das Evangelium nach Markus (Göttingen 1967), in unserem Zusammenhang wichtig der Exkurs über die Gottessohnschaft S. 206–208.

9 Mk 1, 9–11.

10 Mk 3, 11; 5, 7.

11 Mk 8, 27–33.

12 Zur *Paulusforschung* die frühen wichtigen Aufsätze u. a. von *W. Wrede, A. Schlatter, A. Schweitzer, K. Holl, R. Bultmann, R. Reitzenstein, H. Lietzmann, A. Oepke* gesammelt von *K. H. Rengstorf*, Das Paulusbild in der neueren deutschen Forschung (Darmstadt 1964). Vgl. auch den Bericht von *B. Rigaux*, St. Paul et ses lettres. État de la question (Paris–Bruges 1962); dt.: Paulus und seine Briefe. Der Stand der Forschung (München 1964). Zur Einführung in Person und Werk des Apostels Paulus vgl. unter den neueren kritischen Arbeiten bes. *M. Dibelius*, Paulus (2. Aufl. hrsg. v. *G. Kümmel*, Berlin 1956); *H. J. Schoeps*, Die Theologie des Apostels Paulus im Lichte der jüdischen Religionsgeschichte (Tübingen 1959); *Ph. Seidensticker*, Paulus, der verfolgte Apostel Jesu Christi (Stuttgart 1965); *G. Bornkamm*, Paulus (Stuttgart 1969); *O. Kuss*, Paulus. Die Rolle des Apostels in der theologischen Entwicklung der Urkirche (Regensburg 1971). Dazu die genannten neutestamentlichen Theologien von *R. Bultmann, H. Conzelmann, W. Kümmel.* Zur theologischen Problematik bedeutsam: *E. Käsemann*, Paulinische Perspektiven (Tübingen 1969).

13 1 Kor 1, 18.

14 Neben den Kommentaren zum 1. Korintherbrief – bes. wichtig die von *H. Lietzmann* (Handbuch) und *H. Conzelmann* (Meyers Kommentar) – vgl. *R. Baumann*, Mitte und Norm des Christlichen, eine Auslegung von 1 Kor 1, 1–3; 4 (Münster 1968).

15 Vgl. zu diesem Abschnitt die eindrücklichen Ausführungen von *E. Käsemann*, Der Ruf der Freiheit (Tübingen 1968) Kap. 3; *ders.*, Paulinische Perspektiven S. 97–103.

16 Unter den Kommentaren zum Galaterbrief vgl. bes. *H. Lietzmann* (Handbuch) und *H. Schlier* (Meyers Kommentar) und neuestens *F. Mussner*, Der Galaterbrief (Freiburg–Basel–Wien 1974).

17 *F. Nietzsche*, Werke, hrsg. von *K. Schlechta*, Bd. II (München 1955) S. 1200.

18 *F. Nietzsche*, Werke Bd. II, S. 1204; vgl. dazu *K. Schlechta*, Nietzsche-Index (München 1965) unter den Stichwörtern »Jesus« S. 172f.; »Paulus« S. 280f.

19 Gal 3–4; Röm 4.

20 Röm 5, 12–25; 1 Kor 15, 42–49.

21 1 Kor 1, 13; 10, 16 f.; 12, 12–31; Röm 12, 4–8; vgl. Gal 3, 26–29; Röm 1, 18–3, 28; Röm 9–11.

22 Vgl. Röm 3, 21–29 und die anthropologische Applikation in Röm 6 (Taufe); Röm 7 (Konfliktsituation des Menschen); Röm 8 (Erfahrung des Geistes) sowie die Paränese Röm 12–15.

23 Zum Verhältnis Jesus und Paulus vgl. *R. Bultmann,* Die Bedeutung des geschichtlichen Jesus für die Theologie des Paulus, in: Glauben und Verstehen Bd. I (Tübingen ²1954) S. 188–213; *E. Jüngel,* Paulus und Jesus. Eine Untersuchung zur Präzisierung der Frage nach dem Ursprung der Christologie (Tübingen 1962); und neuerdings *J. Blank,* Paulus und Jesus. Eine theologische Grundlegung (München 1968); *H.-W. Kuhn,* Der irdische Jesus bei Paulus als traditionsgeschichtliches und theologisches Problem, in: Zeitschrift für Theologie und Kirche 67 (1970) 295–320.

24 2 Kor 5, 16 für K. Barth und R. Bultmann eine Hauptbelegstelle.

25 Vgl. *J. Blank,* Paulus und Jesus Kap. 6. Dazu den bestätigenden und weiterführenden Forschungsbericht über die neueste Diskussion von *R. Pesch,* »Christus dem Fleisch nach kennen« (2 Kor 5, 16)? Zur theologischen Bedeutung der Frage nach dem historischen Jesus, in: Kontinuität in Jesus. Zugänge zu Leben, Tod und Auferstehung (Freiburg–Basel–Wien 1974) S. 9–34.

26 Vgl. *J. Blank,* aaO S. 129, 323 f.: nicht nur die zentrale Botschaft (das Kerygma) von Kreuzigung und Auferweckung (1 Kor 15, 3–8), sondern auch die Abendmahlsüberlieferung (1 Kor 11, 23–25), die Stellung zu Ehe und Ehescheidung (1 Kor 7, 10 f.), die Anweisung zum Lebensunterhalt des Verkündigers (1 Kor 9, 14), die überragende Stellung des Liebesgebots (1 Thess 4, 9; Gal 5, 13; Röm 13, 8–10; 1 Kor 13), schließlich aber auch die davidische Abstammung Jesu (Röm 1, 3), Christus dem Fleisch nach aus Israel (Röm 9, 5), die Abrahamssohnschaft (Gal 3; Röm 4), die menschliche Geburt und Unterordnung unter das Gesetz (Gal 4, 4), Menschsein, Selbsterniedrigung, Gehorsam bis zum Tod (Phil 2, 6–8), Schwachheit (2 Kor 13, 4), Armut (2 Kor 8, 9), Passion (1 Kor 11, 23); des weiteren ließen sich anfügen 1 Kor 4, 12; 13, 2; Röm 16, 19.

27 Phil 3, 5 f.

28 Gal 1, 13 f.

29 Vgl. C II, 3: Die oberste Norm.

30 Gal 1, 13 f.

31 Vgl. 1 Kor 1, 17–31; Gal 3, 1–14.

32 Vgl. C V, 1: Entstehung des Glaubens.

33 Vgl. 1 Kor 15, 8–10; 9, 1; Gal 1, 15 f.; Phil 3, 4–11. Dazu *J. Blank,* Paulus und Jesus Kap. 4.

34 Gal 1, 1. 11 f.

35 Gal 3, 13; vgl. 2, 17–19; Röm 7, 4.

36 Gal 2, 21.

37 1 Kor 10, 23–33; 8, 7–13; Röm 14.

38 Nach den Kommentaren zum Römerbrief vor allem von *O. Michel* (Meyers Kommentar) und *O. Kuss* (Regensburger NT und Monographie) erschien nun der die ganze Literatur umfassend kritisch sichtende Kommentar von *E. Käsemann,* An die Römer (Lietzmanns Handbuch, Tübingen 1973).

39 Röm 1, 18–3, 20.

40 Röm 3, 21–5, 21.

41 Röm 6–8.

42 Röm 9–11.

43 Röm 12–15.

44 Röm 3, 28; Gal 2, 16.

45 So *J. Zink* in seiner auch sonst oft sehr geglückten Übertragung des Neuen Testaments (Stuttgart 1965).

46 Diese Einsicht wurde entwickelt in meinem Buch ›Rechtfertigung. Die Lehre Karl Barths und eine katholische Besinnung‹ (Einsiedeln ⁴1964). Sie hat sich in der Zwischenzeit weithin durchgesetzt, wie neuerdings vor allem aus dem Dokument der Studienkommission zwischen dem Lutherischen Weltbund und der römisch-katholischen Kirche auf ihrer Sitzung in Malta 21.–26. Februar 1970 hervorgeht. Text in: Herder-Korrespondenz 25 (1971) 536–544. Einen kritischen Literaturbericht zur Diskussion über die Rechtfertigung gibt meine Schülerin *Ch. Hempel*, Rechtfertigung als Wirklichkeit. Ein katholisches Gespräch. Karl Barth – Hans Küng – Rudolf Bultmann und seine Schule (Essen 1974). Zur biblischen Begründung von katholischer Seite bestätigend *K. Kertelge*, Rechtfertigung bei Paulus. Studie zur Struktur und zum Bedeutungsgehalt des paulinischen Rechtfertigungsbegriffs (Münster 1967). Vgl. auch *H. Küng*, Katholische Besinnung auf Luthers Rechtfertigungslehre heute, in: Theologie im Wandel. Festschrift zum 150jährigen Bestehen der Katholisch-theologischen Fakultät an der Universität Tübingen (München–Freiburg 1967) S. 449–468.

47 Röm 3, 28.
48 1 Kor 3, 11.
49 Phil 2, 21: »Denn alle suchen das Ihre, nicht die Sache Jesu Christi«. Vgl. 1 Kor 7, 32–34: »die Sache des Herrn«.
50 Vgl. 2 Kor 10–12.
51 Vgl. B I, 1: Die Begriffe beim Wort nehmen.
52 Vgl. B II, 1: Kein Mythos.
53 1 Kor 2, 2.
54 Jo 14, 6.
55 Jo 6, 35. 48. 51.
56 Jo 8, 12.
57 Jo 10, 7.
58 Jo 15, 1. 5.
59 Jo 10, 11.

C VI: Deutungen

1. Differenzierte Interpretation

1 *P. Tillich*, Systematische Theologie Bd. II, S. 163.
2 Zu nennen bes. das Gesamtwerk von *W. F. Otto, K. Kerényi, M. Eliade, R. Pettazzoni* sowie die skandinavische »Myth and Ritual School« und die »Uppsala-Schule«.
3 Zu nennen bes. *L. Lévy-Bruhl* und *W. Wundt*.
4 *P. Tillich*, Der Protestantismus. Prinzip und Wirklichkeit (Stuttgart 1950) Kap. 15: Das Ende des protestantischen Zeitalters?, bes. S. 278f.; vgl. *ders.*, Systematische Theologie Bd. II, S. 164f., 177f.
5 Vgl. *P. Tillich*, Systematische Theologie ebd.
6 Ich verdanke diese Einsichten einem Referat des amerikanischen Literaturhistorikers *R. M. Frye,* der gewichtige Gedanken vortrug, die in der europäischen Entmythologisierungsdebatte allzusehr vernachlässigt wurden. Sie sind veröffentlicht unter dem Titel: A literary perspective for the criticism of the gospels, in: *D. G. Miller – D. Y. Hadidian,* Jesus and Man's Hope Bd. II (Pittsburgh

1971) S. 193–221. Daß mir das Pittsburgh Theological Seminary die Teilnahme an diesem sehr informativen »Congress of the Gospels« ermöglichte, sei hier dankbar vermerkt.

7 Vgl. *H. Weinrich*, Narrative Theologie, in: Concilium 9 (1973) 329–334; *J. B. Metz*, Kleine Apologie des Erzählens, ebd. S. 334–341.

8 Das gilt für Frye wie für Weinrich.

2. Deutungen des Todes

1 Die großartigste Systematik der neueren Zeit bietet *K. Barth*, Kirchliche Dogmatik Bd. IV/1–3 (1953–1959). Barth vereint nicht nur die traditionellerweise getrennten Lehren von Jesu Christi Person (Christologie) und Werk (Soteriologie), sondern auch die von den beiden Naturen (göttliche und menschliche) und den beiden Ständen (Erniedrigung und Erhöhung). So behandelt er nach dem klassischen Schema der Drei-Ämter-Lehre in drei durchgehenden Perspektiven (= Bände IV/1; IV/2; IV/3) die fünf großen Themenkreise der christlichen Versöhnungslehre:
Christologie: Jesus Christus als wahrer Gott – wahrer Mensch – Gottmensch; priesterliches – königliches – prophetisches Amt; Sündenlehre: des Menschen Hochmut – Trägheit – Lüge; Soteriologie: des Menschen Rechtfertigung – Heiligung – Berufung; Ekklesiologie: der Kirche Sammlung – Auferbauung – Sendung; Pneumatologie: Erweckung zum Glauben – Leben in Liebe – Erleuchtung zur Hoffnung.
Sehr verschieden systematisieren die Drei-Ämter-Lehre: *D. Bonhoeffer*, Wer ist und wer war Jesus Christus? (Hamburg 1962) S. 35–50; *F. Buri*, Das dreifache Heilswerk Christi und seine Aneignung im Glauben (Hamburg-Bergstedt 1962); *ders.*, Dogmatik als Selbstverständnis des christlichen Glaubens Bd. II (Bern–Tübingen 1962) S. 375–433; *W. Pannenberg*, Christologie S. 218–232; *H. Ott*, Antwort des Glaubens S. 266–275. Ein Vergleich der so verschiedenen Systematisierungen zeigt freilich auch, daß die systematisch so bequeme Drei-Ämter-Lehre nur bedingt im Neuen Testament begründet ist und nicht nur zum formalistischen Systemzwang, sondern auch zu einer gewissen Beliebigkeit und Vernachlässigung der neutestamentlichen Vielfalt Anlaß gibt.

2 *Anselm von Canterbury*, Cur Deus homo; dt.-lat. Ausgabe von *F. S. Schmitt* (Darmstadt 1956, ²1958).

3 Vgl. die die bisherige dogmengeschichtliche Arbeit zusammenfassende und weiterführende Arbeit von *H. Kessler*, Die theologische Bedeutung des Todes Jesu. Eine traditionsgeschichtliche Untersuchung (Düsseldorf 1970; Lit.!). Der Schwerpunkt dieser für die gesamte soteriologische Problematik wichtigen Arbeit liegt auf der sorgfältigen Darstellung und ausgewogenen Kritik der Satisfaktionstheorie Anselms (S. 83–165) und ihrer Weiterentwicklung bei Thomas von Aquin (S. 167–226). Vgl. zur Ergänzung *G. Greshake*, Erlösung und Freiheit. Zur Neuinterpretation der Erlösungslehre Anselms von Canterbury, in: ThQ 153 (1973) 323–345; *ders.*, Der Wandel der Erlösungsvorstellungen in der Theologiegeschichte, in: Erlösung und Emanzipation, hrsg. von *L. Scheffczyk* (Freiburg–Basel–Wien 1973) S. 69–101.

4 *Anselm von Canterbury*, Proslogion; dt.-lat. Ausgabe von *F. S. Schmitt* (Stuttgart 1962) Kap. 2 und 3 u. ö.

5 *Anselm von Canterbury*, aaO Kap. 15.

6 Der Kontrast der Konzeption Anselms zum Neuen Testament tritt deutlich zutage bei *H. Kessler*, aaO S. 227–337; vgl. die systematische Weiterführung

desselben Verfassers in: Erlösung als Befreiung (Düsseldorf 1972). Überraschend deutliche Kritik auch schon bei *J. Ratzinger*, Einführung S. 187–189, 231–233.

7 Vgl. *H. Haag*, Biblische Schöpfungslehre und kirchliche Erbsündenlehre (Stuttgart 1966); *U. Baumann*, Erbsünde? Ihr traditionelles Verständnis in der Krise heutiger Theologie (Freiburg–Basel–Wien 1970; Lit.!). Zur neuesten Diskussion vgl. *H. Haag*, Die hartnäckige Erbsünde. Überlegungen zu einigen Neuerscheinungen, in: ThQ 150 (1970) 358–366, 436–456.

8 *G. von Rad*, Theologie des Alten Testaments Bd. I (München ²1958) S. 140–168; *ders.*, Das erste Buch Mose (Göttingen 1953).

9 Vgl. schon *A. von Harnack*, Lehrbuch der Dogmengeschichte Bd. III (Freiburg–Leipzig–Tübingen ³1897) S. 373 f.

10 Vgl. Mk 10, 45 par; 14, 25 par.

11 Vgl. bes. Jes 53.

12 Vgl. bes. Röm 3, 24–26: eine vermutlich von Paulus übernommene, von alttestamentlichen Motiven durchsetzte Glaubensformel.

13 1 Kor 5, 7.

14 Jo 1, 29; vgl. Apk 5, 6 u. ö.

15 Vgl. bes. Heb 2, 17; 7–10.

16 2 Kor 5, 18.

17 Vgl. Phil 2, 7f.; Heb 9, 14.

18 Röm 6, 10; Heb 7, 27; 9, 12; 10, 10.

19 Heb 13, 8.

20 Vgl. *H. Kessler*, aaO S. 186f., 330–335.

21 Vgl. Phil 2, 7f.; Heb 9, 14.

22 Vgl. im ThW die Artikel zu den Präpositionen »anti« (F. Büchsel), »dia« (A. Oepke), »peri« und »hyper« (H. Riesenfeld).

23 Vgl. oben C V, 2: In Stellvertretung.

24 1 Kor 11, 10.

25 »Eucharistia« zuerst gebraucht in der Didache 9, 10 und bei Ignatios und Justin.

26 Vgl. Die Kirche Kap. C III, 2.

27 *Th. W. Adorno*, Negative Dialektik (Frankfurt 1966) S. 352–359.

28 *R. L. Rubenstein*, After Auschwitz (New York 1966).

29 *K. Löwith*, Weltgeschichte und Heilsgeschehen. Die theologischen Voraussetzungen der Geschichtsphilosophie (Stuttgart ³1953) S. 11 f.

30 *G. W. Leibniz*, Essais de Théodicée sur la bonté de Dieu, la liberté de l'homme et l'origine du mal, in: Werke, hrsg. von *C. J. Gerhardt*, Bd. VI (Berlin 1885) S. 3–15.

31 *I. Kant*, Über das Mißlingen aller philosophischen Versuche in der Theodizee, in: Werke, hrsg. von *W. Weischedel*, Bd. VI (Darmstadt 1964) S. 103–124.

32 *G. F. W. Hegel*, Vorlesungen über die Philosophie der Weltgeschichte, in: Kritische Gesamtausgabe, hrsg. von *Lasson–Hoffmeister*, Bd. VIII, S. 938. Vgl. *H. Küng*, Menschwerdung Gottes Kap. VII, 2: Christus in der Weltgeschichte.

33 Vgl. A I, 3: Keine Verabschiedung der Hoffnung.

34 Vgl. *O. Marquard*, Wie irrational kann Geschichtsphilosophie sein?, in: Philosophisches Jahrbuch 79 (1972) S. 241–253. Zit. S. 246, 249.

35 Zur Problematik Emanzipation – Erlösung vgl. *H. Kessler*, Erlösung als Befreiung (Düsseldorf 1972) S. 95–130; *J. B. Metz*, Zukunft aus dem Gedächtnis des Leidens. Eine gegenwärtige Gestalt der Verantwortung des Glaubens, in: Concilium 8 (1972) 399–407; *ders.*, Erlösung und Emanzipation, in: Erlösung

und Emanzipation, hrsg. von *L. Scheffczyk* (Freiburg–Basel–Wien 1973) S. 120–140.

36 *G. Büchner*, Dantons Tod III, 1, in: Werke und Briefe (München 1965) S. 40.

37 *F. M. Dostojewskij*, Die Brüder Karamasoff (Ausgabe Piper, München ²1957) Kap. 5, 4: Die Empörung.

38 Vgl. *A. Camus*, Le Mythe de Sisyphe (Paris 1942); dt.: Der Mythos von Sisyphos. Ein Versuch über das Absurde (Hamburg 1959); *ders.*, L'homme révolté (Paris 1951); dt.: Der Mensch in der Revolte (Hamburg 1953). Zum Leiden der Kinder vgl. besonders die Ausführungen *Camus'* vor den Pariser Dominikanern 1948, in: Fragen der Zeit (Hamburg 1970) S. 59.

39 Zur Theodizeefrage vgl. *H. Küng*, Gott und das Leid (Zürich–Einsiedeln–Köln 1967); *J. Moltmann*, Gott und Auferstehung. Auferstehungsglaube im Forum der Theodizeefrage, in: Perspektiven der Theologie. Gesammelte Aufsätze (München–Mainz 1968) S. 36–56; *ders.*, Der gekreuzigte Gott. Das Kreuz Christi als Grund und Kritik christlicher Theologie (München 1972), bes. Kap. VI, 3; *H. Gollwitzer*, Krummes Holz – aufrechter Gang. Zur Frage nach dem Sinn des Lebens (München 1970), bes. Kap VII und XI; *J. B. Metz*, aaO. Vgl. auch das von *J. B. Metz* hrsg. Heft von Concilium 8 (1972) Nr. 6/7 über »Wandlungen der Gottesfrage«.

40 Vgl. *J. Moltmann*, Der gekreuzigte Gott S. 144 f., 177–180, 188 f., 233 f.

41 Vgl. auch die Kritik an der trinitarischen Heilsgeschichte bei J. Moltmann durch *J. B. Metz*, Kleine Apologie des Erzählens, in: Concilium 9 (1973) 338 f.; damit weithin identisch *ders.*, Erlösung und Emanzipation S. 135–137. – Die Überleitung der spekulativen Problematik in eine andere Fragestellung in meinem Buch ›Menschwerdung Gottes‹ Kap. VIII hat Metz übersehen. Eine Verhältnisbestimmung von Gott und Jesus wird im Folgenden versucht.

42 Darin ist J. B. Metz zuzustimmen.

43 Vgl. *J. B. Metz*, Erlösung und Emanzipation S. 132 f. Dazu C V, 1: Legenden?

44 Vgl. C IV, 3: Umsonst?

45 Vgl. C IV, 2: Revolution im Gottesverständnis?

46 1 Jo 4, 8 f.

47 Röm 8, 32.

48 Röm 8, 38 f.

49 Vgl. das Autobiographische in 2 Kor 11, 16–12, 10.

50 Vgl. *M. Horkheimer*, Die Sehnsucht nach dem ganz Anderen. Ein Interview mit Kommentar von H. Gumnior (Hamburg 1970) S. 61 f.

51 Apk 21, 4.

3. Deutungen des Ursprungs

1 Vgl. Phil 2, 8; Röm 5, 19.

2 Vgl. C V, 2: In Stellvertretung.

3 Spr 8, 22–30; Sir 24, 8–12.

4 *Philon*, Landwirtschaft 51; Allegorie der Gesetze 2, 86; 3, 96; 3, 177.

5 Jo 1, 1–14.

6 Röm 1, 3 f.; vgl. 2 Tim 2, 8.

7 Phil 2, 6–11; vgl. 1 Tim 3, 16.

8 Vgl. den in der Niederschrift wohl frühesten Text über die Menschwerdung Gal 4, 4; dann 2 Kor 8, 9; Röm 8, 3 und schließlich Tit 2, 11; 2, 4. Analyse dieser Texte bei *K. H. Schelkle*, Theologie des Neuen Testaments Bd. II, S. 151–168 (Lit.!).

9 Phil 2, 5–8.

10 Vgl. 2 Tim 1, 10; Tit 2, 11; 2, 13; 3, 4.

11 Text und Kommentar bei *W. Schmithals,* Die Weihnachtsgeschichte Lk 2, 1–20, in: Festschrift für Ernst Fuchs, hrsg. von *G. Ebeling – E. Jüngel – G. Schnack* (Tübingen 1973) S. 281–297, sowie bei *K. H. Schelkle,* Theologie des Neuen Testaments Bd. II, S. 166–168.

12 Vgl. die angeführten Texte aus Tit und 2 Tim.

13 Vgl. wiederum C V, 2: In Stellvertretung.

14 1 Kor 8, 5f.

15 Jo 20, 28.

16 Jo 1, 1: der präexistente Logos, und Jo 20, 28 im Thomasbekenntnis; wahrscheinlich auch in 2 Thess 1, 12; Tit 2, 13; 2 Pet 1, 1.

17 *Ignatios,* An die Trallianer 7, 1; An die Smyrnäer 1, 1; 10, 1; An die Epheser 15, 3; 18, 2 u.ö.

18 Vgl. *H. Küng,* Menschwerdung Gottes, Exkurs II: Kann Gott leiden?

19 Neben den großen dogmengeschichtlichen Werken von *A. Harnack, R. Seeberg, J. Rivière* vgl. neuerdings *H. Kessler,* aaO § 1–2. Anders akzentuiert *G. Greshake,* Der Wandel der Erlösungsvorstellungen in der Theologiegeschichte, aaO S. 72–83.

20 Zu dieser Frage gut *F.-J. Schierse,* Niemand will mehr Gott werden. Gedanken zu Weihnachten einmal anders, in: Publik vom 25. 12. 1970.

21 Gen 3, 5.

22 Eine Christologie nach dem Modell des *Willens,* die sich von Jesu Verkündigung des Willens Gottes und vom vielfältig betonten Gehorsam Jesu aufdrängt, ist unter dem übermächtigen Einfluß der johanneischen Logos-Christologie in der Patristik kaum systematisch entwickelt worden. Doch finden sich – worauf mich mein Tübinger Kollege *H.-J. Vogt* aufmerksam macht – einige Ansätze zu einer Willenschristologie, zum Beispiel in christologischen Äußerungen Kaiser Konstantins: vgl. *H. G. Opitz* (Hrsg.), Urkunden zur Geschichte des arianischen Streites 318–328 = Athanasius Werke III, 1 (Berlin–Leipzig 1934) S. 58f., 69f. Andeutungen auch bei Irenäus, Klemens von Alexandrien und besonders Athanasios.

23 1 Kor 1, 30.

24 Vgl. 1 Kor 11, 3; 8, 6; vgl. Kol 1, 15–18; 2, 10; Eph 4, 15f.; 5, 23.

25 Vgl. 2 Kor 4, 4. 6; Röm 8, 29; vgl. Kol 1, 15.

26 2 Kor 1, 20.

27 Jo 1, 1–14.

28 Jo 5, 18f.; 10, 33–38; 19, 7.

29 Jo 20, 28; vgl. 1 Jo 5, 20.

30 2 Kor 5, 18.

31 Kol 2, 9.

32 Jo 1, 14.

33 Jo 10, 15. 38.

34 Jo 10, 38; 14, 10f. 20; 17, 21–23.

35 Jo 10, 30.

36 Jo 14, 9; 12, 45; 5, 19.

37 Vgl. C IV, 2: Kein neuer Gott.

38 2 Kor 4, 4; Kol 1, 15; vgl. auch Phil 2, 6.

39 Zur *Präexistenzvorstellung* vgl. die umfangreiche exegetische Literatur zum Begriff der Weisheit (sophia) sowie die Kommentare zum Johannesprolog. Zu Paulus vgl. *E. Schweizer,* Die Herkunft der Präexistenzvorstellung bei Paulus, in: Neotestamentica (Zürich 1963) 105–109. Zu Johannes vgl. *R. Schnackenburg,* Das Johannesevangelium Bd. 1 (Freiburg–Basel–Wien 1965)

S. 290–302: Exkurs über den (jüdischen, gnostischen, johanneischen) Präexistenzgedanken. Allgmein: *P. Benoit*, Préexistence et incarnation, in: Revue Biblique 77 (1970) 5–29; *F. Krist*, Jesus Sophia (Zürich 1970); *K. H. Schelkle*, aaO Bd II, § 10, 6. Dazu selbstverständlich die entsprechenden Abschnitte in den Dogmatiken (unter den evangelischen bes. *P. Althaus*, *K. Barth*, *W. Ott* und *O. Weber*, auf katholischer Seite bes. *M. Schmaus* und *D. Wiederkehr* in: Mysterium Salutis) sowie die Christologien *(O. Cullmann, F. Hahn, W. Pannenberg)*.

40 Vgl. Jo 1, 30; 6, 62; 8, 58; 17, 5. 24; zum Präexistenzgedanken im Johannesevangelium vgl. *R. Schnackenburg*, aaO.

41 Phil 2, 6–11.

42 1 Kor 8, 6; vgl. 10, 4.

43 Kol 1, 15; Heb 1, 2; 13, 8; zur Präexistenzidee in der paulinischen Theologie vgl. *E. Schweizer*, aaO.

44 Apk 1, 17.

45 1 Kor 8, 6; Kol 1, 15–18.

46 Heb 13, 8.

47 Jo 1, 1–14.

48 Phil 2, 5–8.

49 Kol 1, 15–20.

50 Vgl. Lk 2, 34f.

51 Vgl. hier besonders *H. Ott*, Antwort des Glaubens Art. 26.

52 Apg 17, 23.

53 Vgl. B I, 1: Die Begriffe beim Wort nehmen.

54 Vgl. B I, 2: Der Christus des Dogmas?

55 Vgl. *H. Küng*, Kirche im Konzil (Freiburg 1963) Kap. D 3: Was ist und was ist nicht die theologische Aufgabe dieses Konzils?

56 Denz 148.

57 Vgl. *A. Grillmeier – H. Bacht* (Hrsg.), Das Konzil von Chalkedon. Geschichte und Gegenwart Bd. I–III (Würzburg 1951–54, ²1959).

58 Vgl. die angegebenen dogmengeschichtlichen Werke.

59 Deshalb lohnt sich gerade die Auseinandersetzung mit der Gesamtentwicklung der Christologie Hegels: vgl. *H. Küng*, Menschwerdung Gottes. Eine Einführung in Hegels theologisches Denken als Prolegomena zu einer künftigen Christologie.

60 Vgl. *H. Küng*, aaO Kap. VIII, 3.

61 Gal 4, 4.

62 Mt 1–2.

63 Lk 1–2.

64 Vgl. *A. Vögtle*, Offene Fragen zur lukanischen Geburts- und Kindheitsgeschichte, und: Die Genealogie Mt 1, 2–16 und die mattäische Kindheitsgeschichte, in: Das Evangelium und die Evangelien. Beiträge zur Evangelienforschung (Düsseldorf 1971) S. 43–102; *ders.*, Messias und Gottessohn. Herkunft und Sinn der mattäischen Geburts- und Kindheitsgeschichte (Düsseldorf 1971); *A. Smitmans*, Maria im Neuen Testament (Stuttgart 1970), bes. S. 13–34; *K. H. Schelkle*, Theologie des Neuen Testaments II, 168–175. Zum Vergleich *H. Schürmann*, Das Lukasevangelium Bd. I (Freiburg–Basel–Wien 1969) S. 18–145; *R. Laurentin*, Struktur und Theologie der lukanischen Kindheitsgeschichte (Stuttgart 1967).

65 Vgl. Mt 1, 1–17 mit Lk 3, 23–28.

66 Vgl. C VI, 1: Wahrheit nicht gleich Faktizität.

67 Vgl. zur weiteren Interpretation gerade der Weihnachtsgeschichte *M. Dibe-*

lius, Jungfrauensohn und Krippenkind (1932), in: Botschaft und Geschichte I (Tübingen 1953) S. 1–78; *W. Schmithals,* Die Weihnachtsgeschichte Lukas 2, 1–20, in: Festschrift für Ernst Fuchs, aaO S. 281–297; *H. Schüngel-Straumann,* Politische Theologie im Weihnachtsevangelium, in: Neue Zürcher Zeitung vom 22. 12. 1973.

68 *H. Schüngel-Straumann,* aaO.

69 Zur *Jungfrauengeburt* vgl. *G. Delling,* Art. parthenos, in: ThW V, S. 824–835; *Th. Boslooper,* The Virgin Birth (London 1962); *H. von Campenhausen,* Die Jungfrauengeburt in der Theologie der alten Kirche (Heidelberg 1962); *H. J. Brosch – J. Hasenfuß* (Hrsg.), Jungfrauengeburt gestern und heute (Essen 1969); *R. Ruether,* The Collision of History and Doctrine: The Brothers of Jesus and the Virginity of Mary, in: Continuum 7 (1969) 93–105; *A. Smitmans,* aaO S. 24–34; *R. E. Brown,* The Problem of the Virginal Conception of Jesus, in: Theological Studies 33 (1972) 3–34; *ders.,* The Virginal Conception and the Bodily Resurrection of Jesus (London 1973); *W. Pannenberg,* Das Glaubensbekenntnis S. 78–85; *K. H. Schelkle,* aaO Bd. II, S. 175–182.

70 Denz 1641.

71 Denz 91.

72 Jes 7, 14.

73 Ps 2, 7.

74 Lk 1, 5–25; 57–66.

75 Vgl. Gen 17, 15–22; 18, 9–16.

76 Vgl. Ri 13, 3–5.

77 Vgl. 1 Sam 1, 4–20.

78 Jes 11, 2; 42, 1.

79 Vgl. Lk 3, 23.

80 Vgl. Lk 4, 22; Jo 6, 42.

81 Mk 3, 31–35 par.; vgl. Mk 3, 21.

82 Vgl. Mk 6, 3; Mt 13, 55; Apg 12, 17; 15, 13; 21, 18; 1 Kor 15, 7; Gal 1, 19; 2, 9. 12.

83 Röm 1, 2–4.

84 Gal 4, 4.

85 Vgl. Gen 17f.

86 Gal 3, 29.

87 Jo 1, 12f.

88 Lk 1, 34f.

89 Vgl. *K. H. Schelkle,* aaO Bd. II, S. 178, 180.

90 Vgl. Report über den holländischen Katechismus (Freiburg 1969) S. 226.

91 Vgl. Glaubensverkündigung für Erwachsene. Deutsche Ausgabe des Holländischen Katechismus (Nijmegen–Utrecht 1968) S. 85.

92 Man vgl. die zitierte neueste katholische Literatur (insbesondere *R. E. Brown* und *K. H. Schelkle*) mit der traditionellen Auffassung.

93 Vgl. Lk 3, 38.

94 Röm 5, 14–19.

95 Apk 12, 1–5.

96 Jo 1, 1–14.

97 Vgl. C VI, 1: Grenzen der Entmythologisierung.

98 Auf historisch-kritischer Grundlage von katholischer Seite *K. H. Schelkle,* Die Mutter des Erlösers (Düsseldorf ³1967); *A. Smitmans,* Maria im Neuen Testament (Stuttgart 1970).

99 Gal 4, 4.

100 Mk 3, 21.

101 Mk 3, 31–35 par.

102 Mk 6, 3; Mt 13, 55.

103 Lk 11, 27f.

104 Apg 1, 14.

105 Vgl. Mk 15, 40 par.

106 Vgl. Jo 2, 1–11 und Jo 19, 25–27.

107 Vgl. Lk 1, 28.

108 Vgl. Lk 1, 38; 2, 34f.

109 Röm 4, 11f. 16–18.

110 Zur *Geschichte der Marienverehrung* vgl. neben den Lexikonartikeln von *F. Heiler* (RGG) und *H. M. Köster* (LThK) vor allem das die Literatur umfassend behandelnde Werk von *H. Graef,* Maria. Eine Geschichte der Lehre und Verehrung (Freiburg–Basel–Wien 1964). Zu religionsgeschichtlichen Zusammenhängen in der Volksfrömmigkeit vgl. *J. Leipoldt,* Von Epidauros bis Lourdes. Bilder aus der Geschichte volkstümlicher Frömmigkeit (Hamburg 1957).

111 Denz 111a.

112 Aufschlußreich für die Wende auch in der Theologie sind neuere mariologische Veröffentlichungen wie: *K. Riesenhuber,* Maria. Im theologischen Verständnis von K. Barth und K. Rahner (Freiburg–Basel–Wien 1973); *W. Beinert,* Muß man heute von Maria reden? Kleine Einführung in die Mariologie (Freiburg–Basel–Wien 1973).

113 *Concilium Vatikanum II,* Decretum de Oecumenismo (1965) Nr. 11.

C VII: Gemeinschaft des Glaubens

1. Inspiriertes und inspirierendes Wort

1 Vgl. B II, 2: Die Dokumente.

2 Vgl. die verschiedenen Auffassungen der *Inspiration* in den Lexikonartikeln von *A. Bea,* in: LThK V, 703–711; von *G. Lanczkowski – O. Weber – W. Philipp,* in: RGG III, 773–782, ebenso wie in den verschiedenen dogmatischen Handbüchern auf katholischer Seite etwa *S. Tromp, M. Nicolau, L. Ott, M. Schmaus;* auf evangelischer *P. Althaus, K. Barth, E. Brunner, O. Weber, H. Diem.* Als neuere Veröffentlichungen sind wichtig: Unter dogmengeschichtlichem Gesichtspunkt: *J. Beumer,* Die Inspiration der Heiligen Schrift (Freiburg–Basel–Wien 1968). Unter exegetisch-systematischem Gesichtspunkt: *B. Vawter,* Biblical inspiration (Philadelphia–London 1972).

3 2 Tim 3, 16.

4 Vgl. *G. Schrenk,* Art. grapho, graphe, in: ThW I, 742–773; bes. 750–752; *E. Schweizer,* Art. pneuma, theopneustos, in: ThW VI, 394–453, bes. 452f.

5 1 Kor 7, 40; 1 Pet 1, 12.

6 *K. Barth,* Kirchliche Dogmatik I/2, § 19–21.

2. Der eine Geist

1 Vgl. *W. Pannenberg,* Glaubensbekenntnis S. 138–141.

2 Gen 1, 2.

3 Joel 2, 28–32.

4 Joel 2, 28–32 aufgenommen in der von Lukas redigierten Pfingstrede des Petrus Apg 2, 17–21.

5 Vgl. zu diesem ganzen Abschnitt *H. Küng*, Die Kirche Kap. C II, 2: Kirche des Geistes.

6 Denz 86.

7 Zum biblischen *Geistverständnis:* Unter den bibl. Lexikonartikeln vor allem *H. Kleinknecht, F. Baumgärtel, W. Bieder, E. Sjöberg* und bes. *E. Schweizer,* in: ThW VI, 330–453 (Lit.!); *E. Käsemann,* in: RGG³ II, 1272–1279; *F. Mußner,* in: LThK VIII, 572–576; unter den Theologien des NT vor allem *R. Bultmann.* Unter den neueren Monographien wichtig: *C. K. Barrett,* The Holy Spirit and the Gospel Tradition (London 1947); *E. Schweizer,* Geist und Gemeinde im NT (München 1952); *S. Zedda,* L'adozione a figli di Dio e lo Spirito Santo (Rom 1952); *H. von Campenhausen,* Kirchliches Amt und geistliche Vollmacht in den ersten drei Jahrhunderten (Tübingen 1953); *N. Q. Hamilton,* The Holy Spirit and Eschatology in Paul (London 1957); *I. Hermann,* Kyrios und Pneuma (München 1961); *K. Stalder,* Das Werk des Geistes in der Heiligung bei Paulus (Zürich 1961); *M.-A. Chevallier,* Esprit de Dieu, paroles d'hommes. Le rôle de l'esprit dans les ministères de la parole selon l'apôtre Paul (Neuchâtel 1966); *H. Küng,* Die Kirche Kap. C II, 2; *E. Brandenburger,* Fleisch und Geist. Paulus und die dualistische Weisheit (Neukirchen 1968).

8 Apg 2; vgl. C V, 1: Klärungen.

9 Vgl. Apg 2, 38 f.; 9, 17; 10, 44; 19, 6.

10 Apg 6, 6; 13, 2 f.; vgl. 15, 28; 20, 28.

11 Vgl. bes. Röm 8, 14–17.

12 2 Kor 3, 18; Gal 4, 6; Röm 8, 9; Phil 1, 19.

13 1 Kor 15, 45.

14 2 Kor 3, 17.

15 2 Kor 3, 17 f.

16 2 Kor 13, 13; vgl. 1 Kor 12, 4–6; Gal 4, 4–6; Röm 5, 1–5; Mt 28, 19.

17 Vgl. Denz 2. 6. 86 usw. Zur Entwicklung dieses Glaubensartikels vgl. *P. Nautin,* Je crois à l'Esprit Saint dans la Sainte Église pour la résurrection de la Chair. Études sur l'histoire et la théologie du symbole (Paris 1947). Literatur zum Verhältnis Geist-Kirche, in: *H. Küng,* Die Kirche S. 208, sowie die eben zitierte Literatur zum biblischen Geistverständnis.

18 2 Kor 3, 17; Röm 8, 2–11.

19 2 Kor 1, 22.

20 Apg 2, 38; 8, 16; 10, 48; vgl. 1 Kor 1, 13–15; Gal 3, 27; Röm 6, 3.

21 Mt 28, 19.

22 Jo 14–16.

23 Jo 14, 16.

24 Jo 14, 26.

25 1 Jo 5, 7.

26 1 Jo 5, 7 f. Zur Interpretation vgl. *R. Bultmann,* Die drei Johannesbriefe (Göttingen 1967) S. 83 f.

27 So *K. H. Schelkle,* Theologie des NT Bd II, § 21, 3–6.

28 Röm 1, 3; 8, 9–11; 1 Kor 12, 3–6; 2 Kor 13, 13; Gal 4, 6; Phil 3, 3; 2 Thess 2, 13 f.; Eph 1, 3; 4, 4–6; Tit 3, 5; Heb 9, 14; 1 Pet 1, 2; Jud 20 f.

29 Mk 1, 9–11 par; Mt 28, 19.

30 Vgl. die Einführung in seinen großen Traktat ›De Trinitate‹ I, 3, 5–6.

31 Vgl. *K. Rahner,* Theos im Neuen Testament, in: Schriften zur Theologie I, S. 91–167.

32 Jo 4, 24.

33 1 Jo 1, 5.

34 1 Jo 4, 8.
35 Die echten Anliegen einer »immanenten« Trinitätslehre wurden aufgenommen im Abschnitt über die ewige Präexistenz: vgl. C VI, 3: Wahrer Gott und
wahrer Mensch.
36 Vgl. zur historischen Entwicklung *J. A. Jungmann,* Die Abwehr des germanischen Arianismus und der Umbruch der religiösen Kultur im frühen Mittelalter, in: Liturgisches Erbe und pastorale Gegenwart (Innsbruck–Wien–München 1960) S. 3–86.
37 Vgl. *H. Küng,* Menschwerdung Gottes Kap. VII, 4: Christus in der Religion.
38 *K. Barth,* Kirchliche Dogmatik Bd. I/1.
39 Des weiteren die Dogmatiken von katholischer Seite *M. Schmaus, F. J. Schierse
– A. Hamman – L. Scheffczyk – K. Rahner* (in: Mysterium Salutis II), von
evangelischer Seite *P. Althaus, E. Brunner, H. Ott, P. Tillich, O. Weber.*
40 Augustin, De Trinitate I 3, 5.

3. Die vielgestaltige Kirche

1 Vgl. B I, 1: Die Begriffe beim Wort nehmen.
2 Vgl. C IV, 1: Eine Kirche? (dort Lit. zur neutestamentlichen Lehre von der
Kirche). Zur systematischen Lehre von der Kirche sind neben den neueren
fundamentaltheologischen und dogmatischen Handbüchern *(P. Althaus, K.
Barth, E. Brunner, F. Buri, H. Diem, W. Elert, Heppe-Bizer, A. Lang, L. Ott,
R. Prenter, C. H. Ratschow, J. Salaverri, M. Schmaus, F. A. Sullivan, P. Tillich,
W. Trillhaas, O. Weber, T. Zapelena)* und den Lexikonartikeln in LThK *(J.
Ratzinger, K. E. Skydsgaard),* RGG *(R. Prenter),* EKL *(J. Koukouzis, K. G.
Steck, G. F. Nuttall),* DTC *(E. Dublanchy),* Cath. *(M. J. Le Guillou),* ODCC
seit der Konzilszeit bes. folgende neuere Monographien erschienen: *H. Küng,*
Strukturen der Kirche (Freiburg i. Br. 1962); *P. Touilleux,* Réflexion sur le
Mystère de l'Église (Tournai 1962); *B. C. Butler,* The Idea of the Church
(Baltimore–London 1962); *Y. Congar,* Sainte Église. Études et approches
ecclésiologiques (Paris 1963); dt.: Heilige Kirche. Ekklesiologische Studien
und Annäherungen (Stuttgart 1966); *A. Hastings,* One and Apostolic (London
1963); *H. Fries,* Aspekte der Kirche (Stuttgart 1963); *P. Glorieux,* Nature et
mission de l'Église (Tournai 1963); *G. Wingren,* Evangelium und Kirche
(Göttingen 1963); *A. Winklhofer,* Über die Kirche (Frankfurt 1963); De
Ecclesia. Beiträge zur Konstitution »Über die Kirche« des 2. Vatikanischen
Konzils, hrsg. von *G. Baraúna,* Bd. I–II (Freiburg i. Br.–Frankfurt 1966); *H.
Fries,* Das Mysterium der Kirche (Würzburg 1966); *H. Lutz,* Die Wirklichkeit
der Kirche. Sein und Sollen (Stuttgart–Berlin 1966); *A. Dulles,* The Dimensions of the Church: A Postconciliar Reflection (Westminster/Md. 1967); *H.
Küng,* Die Kirche (1967); *ders.,* Wahrhaftigkeit. Zur Zukunft der Kirche
(Freiburg–Basel–Wien 1968); *ders.,* Was in der Kirche bleiben muß (Zürich–
Einsiedeln–Köln 1973); *G. Baum,* The Credibility of the Church Today (New
York 1968); dt.: Glaubwürdigkeit. Zum Selbstverständnis der Kirche (Freiburg–Basel–Wien 1969); *J. L. McKenzie,* The Roman Catholic Church (London 1969); *L. Bouyer,* L'Église de Dieu, corps du Christ et temple de l'Esprit
(Paris 1970); *J. Collantes,* La Iglesia de la palabra Bd. I–II (Madrid 1972); *F.
Buri – J. M. Lochman – H. Ott,* Dogmatik im Dialog Bd. I: Die Kirche und die
letzten Dinge (Gütersloh 1973).
3 Vgl. *H. Küng,* Die Kirche Kap. B III, 1. Da es sich bei der *Kirche* um einen
eigenständigen und sehr vielschichtigen Problemkreis handelt und da der
Verfasser mehrere Monographien zum Thema Kirche veröffentlicht hat, muß

hier notwendigerweise auf diese Publikationen zurückgegriffen werden. Ausführliche Belege an Schriftstellen und weitere Literaturangaben finden sich dort. Zugleich sei hingewiesen auf das Buch *H. Häring – J. Nolte* (Hrsg.), Diskussion um Hans Küng »Die Kirche« (Freiburg–Basel–Wien 1971), in dem bei allen Differenzen ein deutlich sich abzeichnender ökumenischer Konsens dokumentiert wird.

4 Für die hier nicht behandelte Grundstruktur der Kirche als Gottesvolk, Geistesgeschöpf, Christusleib vgl. *H. Küng,* Die Kirche Kap. C I–III.

5 Vgl. zum Folgenden *H. Küng,* Wozu Priester? Eine Hilfe (Zürich–Einsiedeln–Köln 1971) Kap. I.

6 Vgl. *E. Käsemann,* Einheit und Vielfalt in der neutestamentlichen Lehre von der Kirche, in: Exegetische Versuche und Besinnungen II (Göttingen 1964) 262–267; *R. Pesch,* Gibt es in der Kirche des Neuen Testaments Parteien?, in: Concilium 9 (1973) 533–538.

7 Vgl. das ganze Themenheft ›Gefahr von Parteien in der Kirche? Notwendigkeit und Grenzen des Pluralismus‹ von Concilium 9 (1973) Heft 10. (Zusammenfassende Thesen von *H. Küng.*)

8 Neben den Art. *Charisma* bzw. Geist in den bibl. und theol. Lexika vgl. vor allem *F. Grau,* Der ntl. Begriff χάρισμα. Seine Geschichte und seine Theologie (Diss. Tübingen 1946); *J. Brosch,* Charismen und Ämter in der Urkirche (Bonn 1951); *E. Lohse,* Die Ordination im Spätjudentum und im NT (Berlin 1951); *H. von Campenhausen,* Kirchliches Amt und geistliche Vollmacht in den ersten 3 Jahrhunderten (Tübingen 1953); *K. Rahner,* Das Dynamische in der Kirche (Freiburg i. Br. 1958); *E. Schweizer,* Gemeinde und Gemeindeordnung im NT (Zürich 1959); *R. Bultmann,* Theologie des NT (Tübingen ³1958); *E. Käsemann,* Amt und Gemeinde im NT, in: Exegetische Versuche und Besinnungen I (Göttingen 1960) 109–134; *G. Eichholz,* Was heißt charismatische Gemeinde? 1 Kor 12 (München 1960); *O. Perels,* Charisma im NT, in: Fuldaer Hefte 15 (Berlin 1964) 39–45; *H. Schürmann,* Die geistlichen Gnadengaben, in: De Ecclesia. Beiträge zur Konstitution »Über die Kirche« des 2. Vatikanischen Konzils, hrsg. von *G. Baraúna* (Freiburg i. Br.–Frankfurt 1966) 494–519; *H. Küng,* Die Kirche Kap. C II, 3: Die bleibende charismatische Struktur; *M. Hengel,* Nachfolge und Charisma. Eine exegetisch-religionsgeschichtliche Studie zu Mt 8, 21 f. und Jesu Ruf in die Nachfolge (Wien 1968); *G. Hasenhüttl,* Charisma. Ordnungsprinzip der Kirche (Freiburg–Basel–Wien 1969); *U. Brockhaus,* Charisma und Amt. Die paulinische Charismenlehre auf dem Hintergrund der frühchristlichen Gemeindefunktionen (Wuppertal 1972); *J. Hainz,* Ekklesia – Strukturen paulinischer Gemeinde-Theologie und Gemeinde-Ordnung (Regensburg 1972).

9 Vgl. *H. Küng,* Die Kirche Kap. E II, 1; der folgende Text hält sich an die Zusammenfassung in: Wozu Priester? Kap. II, 2–7.

10 Vgl. C III, 2: Die wahre Radikalität.

11 Neben den Abschnitten der dogmatischen Handbücher über das *Priestertum* vgl. vor allem den Art. von *G. Schrenk* in: ThW III, 221–284, sowie die diesbezüglichen Art. in den übrigen bibl. und theol. Lexika; neben den bibl. Theologien auch *O. Cullmann,* Die Christologie des NT (Tübingen 1957) 82–107; *T. F. Torrance,* Royal Priesthood (Edinburgh–London 1955); *H. Küng,* Die Kirche Kap. E I: Das allgemeine Priestertum.

12 Vgl. C VI, 2: Opfer?

13 Vgl. 1 Pet 2, 4f., 9f.; Apk 1, 5f.; 5, 10.

14 Röm 15, 16.

15 Vgl. C IV, 1: Eine Kirche?

16 Vgl. C IV, 1: Eine Kirche?
17 Vgl. *H. Küng*, Die Kirche Kap. E II, 2; *ders.*, Wozu Priester? Kap. II, 6.
18 Zur Problematik der Demokratisierung in der Kirche vgl. *H. Küng*, Wozu Priester? Kap. I, 1; IV, 6–7.
19 Die folgenden drei Texte geben die Thesen 12, 13, 15 f. des Memorandums der Arbeitsgemeinschaft Ökumenischer Universitätsinstitute wieder: Reform und Anerkennung kirchlicher Ämter (München–Mainz 1973) S. 18 f. Vgl. *H. Küng*, Wozu Priester? Kap. IV, 2–6. Zu Funktionen und Bild des Kirchenleiters heute vgl. ebd. 7–10.
20 Für die Ausführungen in *H. Küng*, Die Kirche (1967) Kap. E II, 3, an die wir uns hier halten, sind die historischen Untersuchungen von *H. Küng*, Strukturen der Kirche (1962) Kap. VII–VIII Voraussetzung.
21 Vgl. neben den Papstgeschichten *(E. Caspar, J. Haller, L. von Pastor, J. Schmidlin, F. X. Seppelt)* zur folgenden historischen Entwicklung vor allem *Y. Congar*, Geschichtliche Betrachtungen über Glaubensspaltungen und Einheitsproblematik, in: Begegnung der Christen, hrsg. v. *M. Roesle – O. Cullmann* (Stuttgart–Frankfurt/Main 1959) 405–429; dazu vom selben Verf.: Conclusion, in: Le concile et les conciles (Paris 1960) 329–334; Jalons pour une théologie du laïcat (Paris 1953); Bulletin d'ecclésiologie (1939–1946), in: Revue des sciences philosophiques et théologiques 31 (1947) 77–96, 272–296.
22 Vgl. über Vorgeschichte, Ergebnis und Problematik dieser Definition *H. Küng*, Unfehlbar? Eine Anfrage (Zürich–Einsiedeln–Köln 1970). Die »Anfrage« darf weithin als erledigt gelten: vgl. meine Bilanz der Unfehlbarkeitsdebatte in: *H. Küng* (Hrsg.), Fehlbar? Eine Bilanz (Zürich–Einsiedeln–Köln 1973). Dort eine von *B. Brooten* und *K.-J. Kuschel* zusammengestellte ausführliche Bibliographie zur Unfehlbarkeitsdebatte (S. 515–524).
23 Vgl. *H. Küng*, Die Kirche E II, 3: Petrusmacht und Petrusdienst. Ein neuer ökumenischer Konsens in der Petrusfrage, der freilich das Vatikanum I nicht bestätigt, zeichnet sich bezüglich der exegetischen Grundlagen ab: Beweis dafür sind die Arbeiten der katholischen Exegeten *A. Vögtle, J. Blank, R. Pesch, W. Trilling*, die weithin mit den Ergebnissen evangelischer Exegese (neuestens z. B. *G. Bornkamm*) übereinstimmen. Der Konsens wird herausgearbeitet in: Fehlbar? Eine Bilanz S. 405–414 (hier die genauen Literaturangaben).
24 Vgl. Mt 16, 18.
25 Vgl. Lk 22, 32.
26 Vgl. Jo 21, 15–17.
27 Vgl. *H. Küng*, Die Kirche Kap. E II, 3.
28 Nach Mt 16, 18 f. folgt Mt 16, 22 f.
29 Nach Lk 22, 32 folgt Lk 22, 34.
30 Nach Jo 21, 15 folgt Jo 21, 20.
31 Vgl. Lk 22, 32.
32 Vgl. Jo 21, 17.
33 Vgl. Mt 16, 18.
34 Vgl. das Themaheft von Concilium 7 (1971) Heft 4: ›Der Petrusdienst in der Kirche‹. Besonders die Stellungnahmen von *St. Harkianakis, P. Evdokimov, A. Allchin* und *H. Ott* zur Frage »Kann ein Petrusdienst in der Kirche einen Sinn haben?« und die katholische Antwort von *H. Häring*. Eine wichtige Bestätigung des seit ›Strukturen der Kirche‹ (1962) angestrebten ökumenischen Konsens in dieser Frage ist das Dokument der gemischten katholisch-lutherischen Theologenkommission der Vereinigten Staaten: ›Ministry and the Church Universal: Differing Attitudes Toward Papal Primacy‹ (1974). Vgl. The New York Times vom 4. März 1974.

35 Weitere Literatur zur Petrusfrage: *Ch. Journet,* Primauté de Pierre (Paris
1953); *O. Karrer,* Um die Einheit der Christen. Die Petrusfrage. Ein Gespräch
mit E. Brunner, O. Cullmann, H. von Campenhausen (Frankfurt/Main 1953);
O. Cullmann, Art. petra, petros, in: ThW VI, 99–112; Petrus. Jünger–Apostel–Märtyrer (Zürich 1952, ²1960); *P. Gaechter,* Petrus und seine Zeit (Innsbruck 1958); *J. Pérez de Urbel,* San Pedro, principe de los apóstoles (Burgos
1959); im bereits zitierten Sammelwerk: Begegnung der Christen, die Beiträge
von *J. Ringer* und *J. Schmidt.* Weitere Lit. in den wichtigen Lexikonart. über
Petrus von *A. Vögtle – O. Perler* in: LThK VIII, 334–341, und von *E. Dinkler*
in: RGG V, 247–249; ebenso in den verschiedenen Lexika die Art. über Papst
und Papsttum. Zwei sehr informative Berichte über die Forschungslage in der
Deutung von Mt 16, 18 f. mit sehr reichlichen Lit.-Angaben sind *J. Ludwig,*
Die Primatworte Mt 16, 18 f. in der altkirchlichen Exegese (Münster 1952), und
F. Obrist, Echtheitsfragen und Deutung der Primatstelle Mt 16, 18 f. in der
deutschen protestantischen Theologie der letzten dreißig Jahre (Münster
1960). Vom orthodoxen Standpunkt aus ist aufschlußreich *N. Afanassieff – N.
Koulomzien – J. Meyendorff – A. Schmemann,* Der Primat des Petrus in der
Orthodoxen Kirche (Zürich 1961).
36 Vgl. *H. Küng,* Die Kirche Kap. E II, 3.
37 1 Kor 1, 11 f.
38 1 Kor 1, 13.
39 Vgl. 1 Kor 3, 12–15; vgl. *H. Küng,* Parteien in der Kirche? Zusammenfassende
Thesen zur Diskussion, in: Concilium 9 (1973) 594–601.

4. Der große Auftrag

1 Zu den hier nicht zu behandelnden kirchlichen Unterscheidungsmerkmalen
(notae Ecclesiae) – Einheit, Heiligkeit, Katholizität, Apostolizität in katholischer Sicht, reine Lehre des Evangeliums und rechte Verwaltung der Sakramente in evangelischer Sicht – vgl. *H. Küng,* Die Kirche Kap. D I–IV: Die Dimensionen der Kirche.
2 Mt 7, 21.
3 Vgl. *H. Küng,* Die Kirche Kap. C III, Kirche als Christusleib.
4 Zum Folgenden vgl. *H. Küng,* Die Kirche Kap. B III, 3: Im Dienst an der
Gottesherrschaft.

D: Die Praxis

1 *A. Hasler,* Spiegel-Gespräch vom 10. Januar 1972. Zum besseren Verständnis
vgl. neben den großen Werken zur Papstgeschichte von *L. von Pastor, J.
Schmidlin, J. Haller, F. X. Seppelt – G. Schwaiger, C. Falconi* für die gegenwärtige Situation vor allem *F. Leist,* Der Gefangene des Vatikans. Strukturen päpstlicher Herrschaft (München 1971); *L. Waltermann,* Rom, Platz des Heiligen
Offizium Nr. 11 (Graz–Wien–Köln 1970); *A. Mühr,* Das Kabinett Gottes.
Politik in den Wandelgängen des Vatikan (Wien–Düsseldorf 1971). Mehr persönlich gefärbt *R. Raffalt,* Wohin steuert der Vatikan? Papst zwischen Religion
und Politik (München–Zürich 1973); *Hieronymus,* Vatikan intern (Stuttgart
1973).

D I: Die Praxis der Kirche

1. Entscheidung für den Glauben

1 Vgl. B II, 3: Rückfrage nach Jesus.
2 Vgl. B II, 3: Verantworteter Glaube.
3 *Tertullian,* De virginibus velandis I, 1, in: Corpus Christianorum II, 1209.
4 *H. Böll,* Brief an einen jungen Katholiken, in: Hierzulande. Aufsätze (Köln–Berlin 1963); *ders.,* Ansichten eines Clowns (Köln–Berlin 1963).
5 *A. Solschenizyn,* Fastenbrief an den Patriarchen von Moskau und ganz Rußland, Pimen, abgedruckt in: *A. Solschenizyn,* Kirche und Politik. Bericht, Dokument, Erzählung. Beiträge von *Eschlimann, Jakunin, Karelin, Scheludkow* und anderen, hrsg. von *F. Ph. Ingold* und *I. Rakusa* (Zürich 1973) S. 31–37, 42.
6 Die folgende Analyse hält sich wörtlich an die Erklärung der 33 Theologen ›Wider die Resignation in der Kirche‹, an der der Verfasser wesentlich mitgearbeitet hat. Deutsche Originalfassung in: Publik-Forum vom 24. März 1972.
7 Die folgenden Ausführungen halten sich an die Antwort, die gegeben wurde für den von *W. Dirks* und *E. Stammler* herausgegebenen Sammelband ›Warum bleibe ich in der Kirche? Zeitgenössische Antworten‹ (München 1971) S. 117–124.
8 Vgl. besonders *H. Küng,* Konzil und Wiedervereinigung. Erneuerung als Ruf in die Einheit (Wien–Freiburg–Basel 1960); *ders.,* Kirche im Konzil (Freiburg–Basel–Wien 1963); *ders.,* Wahrhaftigkeit. Zur Zukunft der Kirche (Freiburg–Basel–Wien 1968); *ders.,* Unfehlbar? Eine Anfrage (Zürich–Einsiedeln–Köln 1970); *ders.,* Wozu Priester? Eine Hilfe (Zürich–Einsiedeln–Köln 1971).
9 Auch diese Orientierungspunkte halten sich wörtlich an die genannte Erklärung ›Wider die Resignation in der Kirche‹.
10 Die Erklärung ›Wider die Resignation in der Kirche‹ ist von folgenden katholischen Theologen unterzeichnet: Jean-Paul Audet (Montreal), Alfons Auer (Tübingen), Gregory Baum (Toronto), Franz Böckle (Bonn), Günther Biemer (Freiburg), Viktor Conzemius (Luzern), Leslie Dewart (Toronto), Casiano Floristán (Madrid), Norbert Greinacher (Tübingen), Winfried Gruber (Graz), Herbert Haag (Tübingen), Frans Haarsma (Nijmegen), Bas Van Iersel (Nijmegen), Otto Karrer (Luzern), Walter Kasper (Tübingen), Ferdinand Klostermann (Wien), Hans Küng (Tübingen), Peter Lengsfeld (Münster), Juan Llopis (Barcelona), Norbert Lohfink (Frankfurt), Richard McBrien (Boston), John L. McKenzie (Chicago), Johann Baptist Metz (Münster), Johannes Neumann (Tübingen), Franz Nikolasch (Salzburg), Stephan Pfürtner (Fribourg), Edward Schillebeeckx (Nijmegen), Piet Schoonenberg (Nijmegen), Gerard S. Sloyan (Philadelphia), Leonard Swidler (Philadelphia), Evangelista Villanova (Montserrat), Hermann-Josef Vogt (Tübingen), Bonifac Willems (Nijmegen).

D II: Menschsein und Christsein

1. Die Normen der Menschlichkeit

1 So *G. Szczesny,* Worauf ist Verlaß? Referat am 15. Evangelischen Kirchentag Düsseldorf 1973, veröffentlicht (mit Kürzungen) in: Herder-Korrespondenz 27 (1973) 402–404. Vgl. *ders.,* Das sogenannte Gute. Vom Unvermögen der Ideologen (Hamburg 1971), bes. Kap. 18.

2 Vgl. zum Beispiel *A. Auer*, Die Aktualität der sittlichen Botschaft Jesu, in: Die Frage nach Jesus, hrsg. von *A. Paus* (Graz 1973) S. 273–280.

3 Zum ethischen Aspekt der Problematik von Religion und Gesellschaft vgl. *W. Korff*, Norm und Sittlichkeit. Untersuchungen zur Logik der normativen Vernunft (Mainz 1973) S. 191 f.

4 *W. Korff*, aaO S. 189–194.

5 Selbstverständlich soll hier nicht der Versuch einer Ethik oder auch nur einer Grundlegung der Ethik unternommen werden. Dazu vergleiche man die Gesamtdarstellungen christlicher Ethik.

Unter den neueren *katholischen* Ethiken seien genannt: *F. Tillmann* (Hrsg.), Handbuch der katholischen Sittenlehre (1933 ff., Düsseldorf ⁴1953); *J. Stelzenberger*, Lehrbuch der Moraltheologie. Die Sittlichkeitslehre der Königsherrschaft Gottes (Paderborn 1953, ²1965); *B. Häring*, Das Gesetz Christi. Moraltheologie (Freiburg 1954); *J. de Finance*, Ethica generalis (Rom 1959); dt.: Grundlegung der Ethik (Freiburg–Basel–Wien 1968); *J. Mausbach – G. Ermecke*, Katholische Moraltheologie Bd. I–III (Münster 1959–61); *F. Böckle*, Grundbegriffe der Moral. Gewissen und Gewissensbildung (Aschaffenburg 1967). Philosophisch: *H. E. Hengstenberg*, Grundlegung der Ethik (Stuttgart 1969).

Unter den neueren *evangelischen* Ethiken sind zu nennen: *E. Brunner*, Das Gebot und die Ordnungen. Entwurf einer protestantisch-theologischen Ethik (Tübingen 1932); *A. de Quervain*, Ethik Bd. I–II (Zollikon–Zürich 1945–1956); *D. Bonhoeffer*, Ethik, hrsg. von *E. Bethge* (München 1949, ⁶1963); *W. Elert*, Das christliche Ethos. Grundlinien der lutherischen Ethik (1949, Hamburg ²1961); *N. H. Søe*, Christliche Ethik (München 1949, ³1965); *P. Ramsey*, Basic Christian Ethics (New York 1952); *H. van Oyen*, Evangelische Ethik Bd. I–II (Basel 1952–1957); *K. Barth*, Kirchliche Dogmatik II/2 (§ 36–39), III/4; *H. Thielicke*, Theologische Ethik Bd. I–III (Tübingen 1958–1964); *W. Trillhaas*, Ethik (Berlin 1959); *P. L. Lehmann*, Ethics in a Christian Context (New York 1963); *O. A. Piper*, Christian Ethics (London 1970).

6 Vgl. zu diesem ganzen Kapitel die wichtigen Arbeiten von: *A. Auer*, Autonome Moral und christlicher Glaube (Düsseldorf 1971); *ders.*, Die Aktualität der sittlichen Botschaft Jesu, in: Die Frage nach Jesus, hrsg. von *A. Paus* (Graz 1973) S. 271–363; *F. Böckle*, Was ist das Proprium einer christlichen Ethik?, in: Zeitschrift für Evangelische Ethik 11 (1967) 148–157; *ders.*, Theonomie und Autonomie der Vernunft, in: Fortschritt wohin? Zum Problem der Normenfindung in der pluralen Gesellschaft, hrsg. von *W. Oelmüller* (Düsseldorf 1972) S. 63–86; *ders.*, Unfehlbare Normen?, in: Fehlbar? Eine Bilanz, hrsg. von *H. Küng* (Zürich–Einsiedeln–Köln 1973) S. 280–304; *J. Fuchs*, Gibt es eine spezifisch christliche Moral?, in: Stimmen der Zeit 185 (1970) 99–112; *J. Gründel – H. van Oyen*, Ethik ohne Normen? Zu den Weisungen des Evangeliums (Freiburg–Basel–Wien 1970); *W. Korff*, Norm und Sittlichkeit. Untersuchungen zur Logik der normativen Vernunft (Mainz 1973); *ders.*, Wie kann der Mensch glücken? Zur Frage einer ethischen Theorie der Gesellschaft, in: ThQ 153 (1973) 305–322; *D. Mieth*, Die Situationsanalyse aus theologischer Sicht, in: Moral, hrsg. von *A. Hertz* (Mainz 1972) S. 13–33 (Lit.!); *B. Schüller*, Zur Problematik allgemein verbindlicher ethischer Grundsätze, in: Theologie und Philosophie 45 (1970) 1–23; *ders.*, Die Begründung sittlicher Urteile. Typen ethischer Argumentation in der katholischen Moraltheologie (Düsseldorf 1973).

7 Vgl. A I, 1: Säkulare Welt.

8 Vgl. A II, 2: Die Hypothese.

9 Vgl. A II, 2: Die Wirklichkeit.

10 Vgl. *A. Auer*, Die Aktualität der sittlichen Botschaft Jesu, S. 281 (mit Berufung auf H. Rombach und G. Meyer).

11 Ebd.

12 Vgl. A II, 1: Gottesbeweise?

13 *F. Böckle*, Unfehlbare Normen? S. 291.

14 Vgl. *W. Korff*, Wie kann der Mensch glücken? S. 3.

15 Vgl. A II, 1: Mehr als reine Vernunft.

16 Vgl. A II, 2: Vieldeutigkeit des Gottesbegriffes; C IV, 2: Der Gott mit menschlichem Antlitz.

17 Vgl. *B. Schüller*, Zur Problematik allgemein verbindlicher ethischer Grundsätze, aaO.

18 Vgl. C V, 3: Jenseits von Schwärmerei und Erstarrung.

19 So ist auch die ausgesprochene Situationsethik nicht zu verstehen: vgl. *J. Fletcher*, Situation Ethics. The New Morality (Philadelphia 1966); dt.: Moral ohne Normen? (Gütersloh 1967) S. 11–30.

20 Vgl. C V, 3: Jenseits von Schwärmerei und Erstarrung.

21 Vgl. A II, 2: Die Hypothese.

22 Vgl. A II, 2: Die Wirklichkeit.

23 *M. Horkheimer*, Die Sehnsucht nach dem ganz Anderen, hrsg. von *H. Gumnior* (Hamburg 1970) S. 60.

24 *M. Horkheimer*, aaO S. 60f.

2. *Kriterium des Christlichen*

1 Vgl. B II, 3: Historische Kritik – eine Glaubenshilfe?

2 Für die alttestamentlichen Theologien vgl. besonders *W. Eichrodt*, Theologie des Alten Testaments Bd. III (Stuttgart–Göttingen ⁴1961) § 22; *G. von Rad*, Theologie des Alten Testaments (München 1958) S. 188–202; *W. Zimmerli*, Grundriß der alttestamentlichen Theologie (Stuttgart 1972) § 11. Dazu *H. van Oyen*, Ethik des Alten Testaments (Gütersloh 1967). – Zum *Dekalog* noch immer grundlegend: *A. Alt*, Die Ursprünge des israelischen Rechts (Leipzig 1934); dann neben den verschiedenen Lexikonartikeln *H. Haag*, Der Dekalog, in: Moraltheologie und Bibel, hrsg. von *J. Stelzenberger* (Paderborn 1964) S. 9–38; *G. O. Botterweck*, Form- und überlieferungsgeschichtliche Studie zum Dekalog, in: Concilium 1 (1965) S. 392–401; *N. Lohfink*, Die zehn Gebote ohne den Berg Sinai, in seinem Sammelband: Bibelauslegung im Wandel (Frankfurt 1967) S. 129–157.

3 Ex 19 – Num 10.

4 Ex 34, 28; Dt 4, 13; 10, 4.

5 Ex 20, 2–17; Dt 5, 6–21.

6 Vgl. C IV, 2: Kein neuer Gott.

7 Diese Konsequenzen aus dem alttestamentlichen Befund zieht klar *A. Auer*, Autonome Moral, aaO S. 63–68.

8 Vgl. C V, 3 die Literatur zur Paulusforschung. Zur hier behandelten Problematik sind darüber hinaus zu nennen: *L. Nieder*, Die Motive der religiös-sittlichen Paränese in den paulinischen Gemeindebriefen. Ein Beitrag zur paulinischen Ethik (München 1956); *W. Schrage*, Die konkreten Einzelgebote in der paulinischen Paränese. Ein Beitrag zur neutestamentlichen Ethik (Gütersloh 1961); *A. Grabner-Haider*, Paraklese und Eschatologie bei Paulus. Mensch und Welt im Anspruch der Zukunft Gottes (Münster 1968). Zum neutesta-

Dankeswort

Dieses in verschiedener Hinsicht außer-ordentliche Buch hat in verschiedener Hinsicht auch außerordentliche Hilfe erfahren. Zu allen Tages- und Nachtzeiten wurde daran gearbeitet, und manche Abschnitte haben nach mehreren handschriftlichen Fassungen auch mehr als ein halbes Dutzend Maschinenschrift-Fassungen erlebt. Für die mühselige Herstellung des Manuskripts und die letzte Kontrolle der Fußnoten war Dr. Margret Gentner verantwortlich, assistiert in Tübingen von Ruth Sigrist, und wenn es in meinem Schweizer Domizil Sursee nötig wurde, von Frau Marlis Abendroth-Knüsel. Dr. Christa Hempel hat die Korrekturfahnen gelesen und verschiedene bibliographische Angaben überprüft. Frau Annegret Dinkel besorgte Vervielfältigungen des Manuskripts. Neben Dr. Margret Gentner habe ich aber am meisten dem Akademischen Rat Dr. Hermann Häring und meinem Doktoranden Karl-Josef Kuschel zu danken, die in einem beispielhaften Einsatz immer wieder die verschiedenen Fassungen des Manuskripts gelesen, die ständig neu auftauchenden Probleme mit mir diskutiert und studiert und mir so mit ungezählten Anregungen und Korrekturen zur Seite gestanden haben. Ohne die generöse Hilfsbereitschaft aller meiner Mitarbeiter im Institut für ökumenische Forschung hätte das Buch nicht auf diesen Termin abgeschlossen werden können. Daß wir dabei auch physisch überlebten und in einer öfters sogar recht fröhlichen Arbeitsatmosphäre ständig mit allem Nötigen versorgt wurden, ist in meinem Hause das nicht genug zu lobende Verdienst von Frau Charlotte Renemann.

In anderer Hinsicht wurde mir die Hilfe verschiedener Kollegen in Tübingen – für Theologie, um nicht zu übertreiben, noch immer einer der besten Plätze der Welt – wichtig. Ohne das ständige Gespräch mit meinen katholischen wie evangelischen Fachkollegen und die freie Tübinger Luft wäre ein solches Buch kaum oder eben nur anders möglich geworden. Gar nicht selbstverständlich indessen ist es, daß ein Kollege der Germanistik sich um ein theologisches Buch müht: ich bin Walter Jens mehr als allen anderen dankbar, daß er das Manuskript von der ersten bis zur letzten Zeile, meist sogar mehrfach, kritisch durchgelesen hat; viele stilistische und sachliche Verbesserungen verdanke ich ihm. Wenn man sich als systematischer Theologe so detailliert aufs Neue Testament einläßt, braucht man dringend eine Kontrolle seiner Exegesen und Synthesen: Die wurde mir zuteil durch meinen Kollegen in der neutestamentlichen Exegese Gerhard Lohfink, der das ganze Manuskript gelesen hat. Ähnliches gilt für Kapitel des Hauptteiles D, in denen sich der Dogmatiker mit ethischen Fragen befassen mußte: Sie wurden gelesen von meinen Kollegen in der theologischen Ethik Alfons Auer und Wilhelm Korff. Ihnen allen danke ich für Korrekturen und Anregungen. Ebenso danke ich für die Durchsicht der Abschnitte über die Weltreligionen Professor Julia Ching (Canberra/Australien, jetzt in Tokio) und Professor Heinrich Dumoulin (Tokio).

Es sei mir gestattet, einen weiteren Kollegen hier dankbar zu erwähnen, der nur indirekt mit diesem Buch zu tun hat, ohne dessen ständige kollegiale und freundschaftliche Hilfe – öffentlich sichtbar besonders in der Antwort auf das Interview des Sekretärs der Glaubenskongregation Jérôme Hamer – ich durch die Unfehlbarkeitsdebatte noch mehr von meiner eigentlichen Arbeit abgehalten worden wäre: Johannes Neumann, der in seiner oft verborgenen Arbeit als Kirchenrechtler zeigt, wie auch in der Kirche das Recht um der Menschen willen und nicht die Menschen um des Rechtes willen da sind.

Dem Kultusministerium Baden-Württemberg danke ich für das außerordentliche Entgegenkommen eines Forschungssemesters im Winter 1973/74. Nur so wurde der Abschluß dieses Buches nicht auf unabsehbare Zeit hinausgezögert.

Tübingen, 1. August 1974

Hans Küng

Christ sein
1980. Sonderausgabe. 676 Seiten.

Die christliche Herausforderung
Kurzfassung von »Christ sein«.
1980. 361 Seiten.

Existiert Gott?
Antwort auf die Gottesfrage der Neuzeit. 1978. 878 Seiten.
»Küng gilt wie einst Luther als mutiger Katholik, der es gewagt hat, gegen den starren autoritären Führungsanspruch der Kirche aufzutreten ...«   Ivo Frenzel

Die Kirche
1980. 605 Seiten. Serie Piper 161

Weg und Werk
Herausgegeben von Hermann Häring und Karl-Josef Kuschel. Mit einer Bibliographie von Margret Gentner. 1978. 237 Seiten mit 27 Abbildungen

24 Thesen zur Gottesfrage
1980. 134 Seiten. Serie Piper 171

20 Thesen zum Christsein
1980. 75 Seiten. Serie Piper 100

Ewiges Leben?
1982. 327 Seiten.
In seinem neuen Buch setzt sich der Tübinger Theologe mit den großen letzten Fragen nach dem Sinn des menschlichen Lebens und Sterbens auseinander. Das Buch ist keine theologische Enzyklopädie von den »letzten Dingen«, sondern bietet mit wissenschaftlicher Intensität eine Fülle von Informationen und Anregungen.

Philosophie und Theologie

Erich Fromm:

**Haben oder Sein
Die seelischen
Grundlagen einer
neuen Gesellschaft
dtv 1490**

Karl Jaspers:

**Was ist Philosophie?
Ein Lesebuch
dtv 1575**

**Was ist Erziehung?
Ein Lesebuch
dtv 1617**

**Glaube und Vernunft
Texte zur
Religionsphilosophie
Hrsg. von Norbert
Hoerster
dtv 4338**

Wilhelm Weischedel:

**Die philosophische
Hintertreppe
34 große Philosophen
in Alltag und Denken
dtv 1119**

**Der Gott der
Philosophen
Grundlegung einer
philosophischen
Theologie im Zeitalter
des Nihilismus
dtv 4322 (2 Bände)**

Religion und Theologie:
Hans Küng
Heinz Zahrnt
Schalom Ben-Chorin

Hans Küng:

Christ sein
dtv 1220

Existiert Gott?
Antwort auf die Gottes-
frage der Neuzeit
dtv 1628

Hans Küng. Weg und
Werk
Chronik, Essays,
Bibliographie
Hrsg. von Hermann
Häring und Karl-Josef
Kuschel
dtv 1640

Heinz Zahrnt:

Die Sache mit Gott
Die protestantische
Theologie im
20. Jahrhundert
dtv 846

Gott kann nicht sterben
Wider die falschen
Alternativen in Theologie
und Gesellschaft
dtv 957

Warum ich glaube
Meine Sache mit Gott
dtv 1533

Wozu ist das
Christentum gut?
dtv 2506 Großdruck

Schalom Ben-Chorin:

Bruder Jesus
Der Nazarener in
jüdischer Sicht
dtv 1253

Paulus
Der Völkerapostel in
jüdischer Sicht
dtv 1550

mentlichen Ethos überhaupt unter den neutestamentlichen Theologien neuestens systematisch zusammenfassend *K. H. Schelkle*, Bd. III: Ethos. Und als repräsentative historisch-systematische Gesamtdarstellungen von katholischer Seite *R. Schnackenburg*, Die sittliche Botschaft des Neuen Testaments (München ²1962), von evangelischer Seite *H.-D. Wendland*, Ethik des Neuen Testaments. Eine Einführung (Göttingen 1970).

9 Kol 3, 18–4, 1.

10 Phil 4, 8.

11 Tugendkataloge: Gal 5, 22f.; Phil 4, 8; Lasterkataloge: Röm 1, 29–31; 1 Kor 6, 9f.; 2 Kor 12, 20f.; Gal 5, 19–21.

12 Vgl. zum folgenden *E. Käsemann*, An die Römer (Tübingen 1973).

13 *E. Käsemann*, aaO S. 166.

14 Ebd.

15 Neben der bereits in C IV, 1 genannten exegetischen Literatur *D. Bonhoeffer*, Nachfolge (München ⁷1940); *K. Barth*, Kirchliche Dogmatik IV, 2 § 66, 3; *A. Schulz*, Nachfolgen und Nachahmen (München 1962); *E. Larsson*, Christus als Vorbild (Uppsala 1962); *G. Bouwmann*, Folgen und Nachfolgen im Zeugnis der Bibel (Salzburg 1965); *H. D. Betz*, Nachfolge und Nachahmung Jesu Christi im Neuen Testament (Tübingen 1967); *M. Hengel*, Nachfolge und Charisma (Berlin 1968).

16 *R. M. Hare*, The Language of Morals (Oxford 1952); dt: Die Sprache der Moral (Frankfurt 1972) S. 96; vgl. auch *P. W. Taylor*, Normative Discourse (Englewood Cliffs, N. J. 1961) S. 151–158.

17 Vgl. C III, 1: Das veränderte Bewußtsein.

18 Vgl. B I, 2: Der Christus der Frömmigkeit?

19 Vgl. C VI, 1: Grenzen der Entmythologisierung.

20 Auch der englische Ausdruck »The Paradigmatic Individuals« übersetzt den von Karl Jaspers geprägten Begriff der »maßgebenden Menschen« nur unzureichend. Vgl. den im übrigen soliden Artikel von *A. S. Cua*, Morality and the Paradigmatic Individuals, in: American Philosophical Quarterly 6 (1969) S. 324–329.

21 Jo 8, 12.

22 Jo 1, 14.

23 Jo 14, 6.

24 Vgl. die oben zitierten Arbeiten, vor allem von *A. Auer* und *F. Böckle*.

25 Vgl. C III, 2: Auch die Feinde.

26 Vgl. C III, 2: Die wahre Radikalität.

27 Vgl. C V, 2: Der Maßgebende.

28 Dies gilt mit Einschränkung selbst für die gründliche »Einführung« in die ›Ethik des Neuen Testaments‹ von *H.-D. Wendland*.

29 1 Kor 3, 11.

30 *D. Bonhoeffer*, Nachfolge S. 14.

31 Für einzelne der folgenden Punkte erhielt ich wertvolle Anregungen aus dem Gespräch mit *J. M. Gustafson* anläßlich seines Pittsburgher Vortrags: The Relation of the Gospels to the Moral Life, in: Jesus and Man's Hope, hrsg. von *D. G. Miller* und *D. Y. Hadidian* (Pittsburgh 1971) Bd. II, S. 103–117.Vgl. *ders.*, Christ and the Moral Life (New York–London 1968).

32 »Wenn ich mich frage, warum ich immer gestrebt habe, ehrlich, für den Anderen schonungsbereit und womöglich gütig zu sein, und warum ich es nicht aufgegeben, als ich merkte, daß man dadurch zu Schaden kommt, zum Amboß wird, weil die Anderen brutal und unverläßlich sind, dann weiß ich allerdings keine Antwort.« *S. Freud*, Brief an J. J. Putnam vom 8. 7. 1915,

Sigmund Freuds Briefe 1873–1939, ausgewählt und hrsg. von *Ernst L. Freud* (Frankfurt 1960) S. 305.

D III: Christsein als radikales Menschsein

1 *D. Sölle*, Politische Theologie. Auseinandersetzung mit Rudolf Bultmann (Stuttgart–Berlin 1971) S. 78.

1. Die gesellschaftliche Relevanz

1 Vgl. C I, 2: Kein Sozialrevolutionär.
2 Vgl. C I, 2: Revolution der Gewaltlosigkeit.
3 Vgl. C II, 3: Der Sinn der Bergpredigt.
4 *C. Schmitt*, Politische Theologie. Vier Kapitel zur Lehre von der Souveränität (München–Leipzig 1922, Neuauflage 1934!), bes. S. 47–66. Ähnliches gilt auch vom Terminus »Politischer Christus«.
5 *E. Peterson*, Der Monotheismus als politisches Problem (1935), in: Theologische Traktate (München 1951) S. 45–147.
6 Die »politische Theologie« ist in neuester Zeit vor allem von *J. B. Metz* in verschiedenen Publikationen programmatisch vertreten worden: Zur Theologie der Welt (Mainz–München 1968); Das Problem einer politischen Theologie und die Bestimmung der Kirche als Institution gesellschaftskritischer Freiheit, in: Concilium 4 (1968) 403–411; Art. ›Politische Theologie‹ in: Sacramentum Mundi Bd. III (Freiburg–Basel–Wien 1968) S. 1232–1240. Dazu *J. Moltmann*, Theologische Kritik der politischen Religion, in: Kirche im Prozeß der Aufklärung. Aspekte einer neuen »politischen Theologie« (München–Mainz 1970) S. 11–51; *D. Sölle*, Politische Theologie. Auseinandersetzung mit Rudolf Bultmann (Stuttgart–Berlin 1971). Zur Diskussion vgl. *H. Peuckert* (Hrsg.), Diskussion zur »politischen Theologie« (München–Mainz 1969): zu beachten besonders die Beiträge von *H. Maier, D. A. Seeber, W. Oelmüller, H. R. Schlette, H. Schürmann, F. Böckle, K. Lehmann, T. Rendtorff, W. Pannenberg, K. Rahner*. Dann die Antwort von *J. B. Metz*, der sich erneut von der »politisierenden Theologie« abgrenzt (S. 268).
7 Vgl. *R. Shaull*, Revolutionary Change in Theological Perspective, in: Christian Ethics in a Changing World, hrsg. von J. C. Bennet (New York–London 1966) S. 23–43; *ders.*, Befreiung durch Veränderung. Herausforderung an Kirche, Theologie und Gesellschaft (München–Mainz 1970). Zur Diskussion vgl. *T. Rendtorff – H. E. Tödt*, Theologie der Revolution. Analysen und Materialien (Frankfurt 1968): hier auch der eben genannte Aufsatz von *B. Shaull* für die Vorbereitungsbände der Genfer Weltstudienkonferenz für Kirche und Gesellschaft 1966 in deutscher Sprache: Revolution in theologischer Perspektive (S. 117–139); *E. Feil – R. Weth* (Hrsg.), Diskussion zur »Theologie der Revolution« (München–Mainz 1969); *C.-H. Grenholm*, Christian Social Ethics in a Revolutionary Age. An Analysis of the Social Ethics of J. C. Bennett, H.-D. Wendland and R. Shaull (Uppsala 1973).
8 Vgl. A I, 2: Kein Zurück.
9 *M. Machoveč*, Jesus für Atheisten (Stuttgart 1972) S. 254.
10 Vgl. C II, 3: Kein Naturgesetz.
11 Vgl. C II, 3: Kein Offenbarungsgesetz.
12 Vgl. C II, 3: Der Sinn der Bergpredigt.
13 Vgl. Jo 13, 34.

14 Vgl. C III, 2: Gott und Mensch zugleich.

15 Vgl. D II, 1: Das Unbedingte im Bedingten.

16 Vgl. D II, 1: Fraglichkeit der Normen.

17 Röm 13, 10; vgl. Gal 5, 14.

18 1 Kor 13, 2f.

19 Vgl. *H. E. Richter*, Die Gruppe (Hamburg 1972); *ders.*, Lernziel Solidarität (Hamburg 1974).

20 Wir orientieren uns im folgenden weithin am höchst informativen und eindrucksvollen Heft ›Praxis der Befreiung und christlicher Glaube‹ von Concilium 10 (1974) Heft 6/7, hrsg. von *C. Geffré*, das ausschließlich Beiträge von lateinamerikanischen Theologen enthält. Dort auch S. 449f. Zitat des Dokuments von Medellin.

21 Vgl. *R. Muñoz*, Nueva Conciencia de la Iglesia en América Latina (Santiago de Chile 1973); *ders.*, Zwei typische Erfahrungen der in der Befreiungsbewegung engagierten lateinamerikanischen Christengemeinden, in: Concilium, aaO S. 449–455.

22 Grundlegend für die Theologie der Befreiung ist das ebenso engagierte wie überlegte Werk von *G. Gutiérrez*, Teología de la liberación. Perspectivas (Lima 1971); dt.: Theologie der Befreiung (München 1973). Vgl. *ders.*, Befreiungspraxis, Theologie und Verkündigung, in: Concilium, aaO S. 408–419.

23 *G. Gutiérrez*, Theologie der Befreiung S. 2, 3.

24 Vgl. *E. Dussel*, Herrschaft – Befreiung. Ein veränderter theologischer Diskurs, in: Concilium, aaO S. 396–408; *P. Freire*, Pedagogía do oprimido; dt.: Pädagogik der Unterdrückten (Stuttgart–Berlin 1972).

25 *L. Boff*, Rettung in Jesus Christus und Befreiungsprozeß, in: Concilium, aaO S. 419–426. Zit. S. 419.

26 *S. Galilea*, Die Befreiung als Begegnung zwischen Politik und Kontemplation, in: Concilium, aaO S. 388–395. Zit. S. 388.

27 Vgl. *H. Assmann*, Evaluation critique de la »Théologie de la libération«, in: Lettre (Paris) Nr. 187 (März 1974) S. 23–28. Assmann setzt sich gegen J. Moltmann und J. Alfaro ab, die er als Vertreter eines »reformistischen Progressismus« bezeichnet.

28 *G. Gutiérrez*, in: Concilium, aaO S. 408.

29 Vgl. *S. Galilea*, aaO.

30 Vgl. *G. Gutiérrez*, in: Concilium, aaO S. 411–413.

31 Vgl. *J. H. Cone*, A Black Theology of Liberation (Philadelphia–New York 1970); *R. Radford Ruether*, Liberation Theology. Human Hope Confronts Christian History and American Power (New York–Toronto 1972).

32 Vgl. A I, 3: Humanität durch politisch-soziale Revolution?

33 Ebd.

34 Vgl. Concilium 9 (1973) Heft 10: Gefahr von Parteien in der Kirche?, bes. den zusammenfassenden Beitrag von *H. Küng*, Parteien in der Kirche? (S. 594–601).

35 Die Universitätsassessoren von Sucre, Bemerkung zum Communiqué der Studentenführer (Sucre 1970, polykopiert), zit. in: Concilium, aaO S. 452.

36 Ansprache an katholische Lateinamerikaner in Paris am 25. April 1968. Vgl. *Dom Hélder Câmara*, Revolution für den Frieden (Freiburg–Basel–Wien 1969); *ders.*, Friedenspreise 1974. Zürich–Oslo–Frankfurt (Zürich 1974).

37 Vgl. *H. Goss-Mayr*, Die Macht der Gewaltlosen. Der Christ und die Revolution am Beispiel Brasiliens (Graz 1968); *H. J. Schultz* (Hrsg.), Von Gandhi bis Camara. Beispiele gewaltfreier Politik (Stuttgart–Berlin 1971).

38 *S. Galilea*, in: Concilium, aaO S. 390.

2. Die Bewältigung des Negativen

1 Vgl. C VI, 2: Gott und das Leid.
2 Vgl. ebd.
3 F. Nietzsche, Also sprach Zarathustra III: Von den Abtrünnigen; Werke, hrsg. v. K. Schlechta, Bd. II, S. 428.
4 1 Kor 1, 23 f. Vgl. C V, 3: Umwertung.
5 Auf dieser Linie bewegt sich die Verkündigung des Erzbischofs von Berlin Kardinal A. Bengsch, dessen Kreuzespredigt von einem mir als vorbildlich bekannten Pfarrer der DDR (und weiteren Confratres) ebenso wohlwollend wie kritisch untersucht wurde, mit erschütternden Ergebnissen. Vgl. K. Herbst, Zur Verkündigung von Alfred Kardinal Bengsch, in: SOG-Papiere. Mitteilungsblatt der Arbeitsgemeinschaft von Priester- und Solidaritätsgruppen in der BRD (AGP) 5 (1972) S. 81–103. Dort auch zu jener Predigt Bengschs während des Einmarsches der DDR-Truppen in der Tschechoslowakei, in der jede Stellungnahme mit der Aufforderung zum »Gebet zu Christus« überspielt wurde. Die Studie von K. Herbst wurde den Ordinarien und Seelsorgestellen in der DDR vorgelegt.
6 Vgl. neuestens J. Moltmann, Der gekreuzigte Gott Kap. II.
7 Vgl. C VI, 2: Opfer?
8 Vgl. B I, 2: Der Christus der Frömmigkeit? (vgl. C V, 3).
9 Vgl. J. Hanauer, Konnersreuth als Testfall. Kritischer Bericht über das Leben der Therese Neumann. Mit einem Anhang: Unveröffentlichte Arbeiten des bischöflichen Archivs in Regensburg (München 1972).
10 1 Kor 11, 1; 1 Thess 1, 6; Eph 5, 1.
11 Vgl. W. Michaelis, Art. mimeomai, in: ThW IV, 661–678; Zit. 676.
12 Mk 8, 34.
13 »Täglich«: so die Variante bei Lk 9, 23.
14 Vgl. C II, 2: Wunder?
15 Mk 12, 31 par.
16 Lk 10, 25–37.
17 Mt 25, 34–46.
18 D. Sölle, Leiden (Stuttgart–Berlin 1973) S. 112.
19 Ebd. S. 124.
20 Röm 6, 5–9; 1 Kor 15, 20–22.
21 Gal 2, 20.
22 Röm 6, 6; Gal 5, 24; 6, 14.
23 2 Kor 5, 17; Röm 6, 11.
24 Vgl. 2 Kor 12, 7–10.
25 2 Kor 4, 8 f.; 6, 9 f. Vgl. 2 Kor 11, 23–30; 1 Kor 4, 10–13.
26 1 Pet 2, 20 f.

3. Zur Freiheit befreit

1 Das zeigte sich auf der vierten Vollversammlung des Lutherischen Weltbundes in Helsinki 1963, wo die Botschaft von der Rechtfertigung unter dem Leitwort »Christus heute« in 26 Diskussionsgruppen diskutiert wurde, ohne daß ein gemeinsames Dokument verabschiedet werden konnte. Vgl. Rechtfertigung heute. Studien und Berichte, hrsg. von der Theologischen Kommission und Abteilung des Lutherischen Weltbundes (Stuttgart–Berlin 1965).
2 So von katholischer Seite N. Greinacher, Christliche Rechtfertigung – gesellschaftliche Gerechtigkeit (Zürich–Einsiedeln–Köln 1973). Vgl. auch C.

Mayer, Rechtfertigung durch Werke? Praxisbezug und politische Dimension des Glaubens, in: ThQ 154 (1974) 118–136.

3 Vgl. *N. Greinacher,* aaO S. 7–23.
4 Vgl. *E. Bloch,* Thomas Münzer als Theologe der Revolution (Berlin 1960).
5 Vgl. A I, 1: Öffnung der Kirchen; A I, 2: Kein Zurück.
6 Bahnbrechend für die Interpretation der Rechtfertigungsbotschaft in der säkularen Welt war *F. Gogarten,* Verhängnis und Hoffnung der Neuzeit. Die Säkularisierung als theologisches Problem (Stuttgart 1953). Neuestens zum selben Thema – mit Bezug auf Gedanken von E. H. Erikson – eindrücklich *H. Zahrnt,* Wozu ist das Christentum gut? (München 1972) Kap. 6.
7 Vgl. D II, 1: Autonomie des Menschen.
8 Mt 16, 25 par.
9 Vgl. C I, 4: Gegen Selbstgerechtigkeit; C II, 3: Die oberste Norm; C III, 3: Das Recht der Gnade.
10 Vgl. C V, 3: Durch den Glauben allein. Vgl. *H. Küng,* Rechtfertigung Kap. 31 f.
11 Gal 5, 6; vgl. 5, 22 f.
12 Vgl. Jak 2, 14–26.
13 Vgl. A II, 2: Die Hypothese.
14 Mt 16, 25 par.
15 Wie sehr Glaube und Gebet zusammengehören und wie sehr Gebet zum Christsein gehört, wird an dieser Stelle besonders deutlich. Als konsequente Fortsetzung des schon in Teil C über das Gebet Entwickelte war hier ein eigener Abschnitt über Gebet, Meditation und christlichen Gottesdienst (Sonntagsgottesdienst) geplant. Die mir erneut von Rom aufgezwungenen leidigen Auseinandersetzungen kosteten mich in der entscheidenden letzten Phase dieses Buches mindestens zwei Monate Arbeitszeit und Arbeitskraft, die ich bei der strengen Terminplanung nicht mehr einholen konnte. Der vorgesehene Abschnitt muß darum entfallen: ein Opfer der römischen Inquisitionspolitik.

4. Anregungen

1 Vgl. C III, 2: Die wahre Radikalität.
2 Mt 5, 5.
3 Vgl. C III, 2: Die wahre Radikalität.
4 Mt 5, 7.
5 Vgl. C III, 3: Welche Armen?
6 Mt 5, 3.
7 Vgl. C III, 2: Die wahre Radikalität.
8 Mk 9, 37 par.
9 Jo 21, 25.

Abkürzungen

her, but he couldn't vouch for whatever shared his
body. He searched her face, taking in her wide eyes
and tremulous mouth.

He dropped his hand and turned away. "I don't
remember much about waking now. I don't know why
I did it. I was hungry and I needed the blood . . . there
wasn't much thought past that."

Deidra folded her arms across her body, gripping
her elbows. "Is that what happens every time you grow
hungry?"

Back still to her, his shoulders hunched. "No!" He
let out a frustrated breath. "I know not. I have not
needed to . . . *feed*"—he said the word as if it were
dirty—"since that night. Hannah said I would need
to . . . feed about once a month."

"What do you do the rest of the time?"

He turned back toward her, but his expression was
obscured by the darkness. "I cannot taste anything.
Liquid sometimes quenches my thirst, but it has little
taste."

"Is everything that way?"

"What way?"

"Tasteless. Unsatisfying."

He smiled. Her heart fluttered and she nearly
smiled back.

"Oh, no." He closed the distance between them and
touched her face again, cupping it as he gazed down
at her, as if she were something precious and amazing. "Your skin . . . feels . . . unbelievable. So soft, so
fragrant . . . I can feel and smell and see things that I
never could before. This dark is nothing to me. I see

you clearly. And I am not just whole . . . I am better than whole."

She was so caught up in his words, in his touch. This time, when her eyes drifted shut, she left them that way. She wanted this to be real, for this man who stood before her, touching her, to be the same man she'd fallen in love with. It was too good to be true. There must be some consequence to this defiance of God. He had been dead. And now he stood here, touching her.

But at the moment she didn't care. She had Stephen and she was happy.

His body moved up against hers, his other hand circling her waist. "Has so much changed?" he asked softly, his breath fanning across her face.

His lips touched hers. They were cooler than she remembered but not corpse-cold, as she had expected. She sank into the kiss, her lips warming his so that there was no difference. Memories of her dream rose unbidden and sent heat down to her toes.

He kissed her cheek and pressed his mouth to her ear. "I did not choose this, Deidra. I knew it would not make you happy. But now that it's happened, I am not sorry."

She wasn't either, not now, not with his mouth pulling at her earlobe so that she thought she might melt into a heap at his feet if not for his hands supporting her. She could not be sorry when his tongue traced her jaw and licked at her neck. She could think of nothing but her own pleasure that he was alive and here with her, wanting her still.

In her mind Duke whined. He wanted to return but was afraid because of Stephen. This single thought shot through her like an arrow and she jerked, her chin bumping Stephen's head.

He bit her.

It burned across her throat like a thorn. Deidra let out a little shriek and shoved him. He held her fast, as if she weighed nothing and her strength was nothing, but he lifted his head to look down at her.

He frowned at her, confusion and alarm in his eyes. "Deidra, peace."

Her gaze moved to his mouth. Blood stained his lip, sending fear spiraling through to her belly.

"Let me go!" She struggled, her heart beating wildly, as if a bird were caught in her chest and its wings flapped frantically against her ribs. "Help!"

His hand clamped hard over her mouth. Panic shot through her. He was going to bite her in the neck and suck all of her blood out. She screamed so hard behind his hand that she went limp with the effort. Animals raced into the garden. A chicken and a goat, but they did not know what to do. Duke barked excitedly, wanting to help Deidra but deeply afraid of the Stephen-thing.

"God's blood, Deidra! Stop your damned screaming."

The blood was gone from his mouth. He seemed normal again, but she couldn't be sure of anything. She nodded shakily to indicate she wouldn't scream. He removed his hand. His arms loosened around her. She touched her neck, then looked at the blood smeared across her fingertips.

Stephen leaned back, brows furrowed, to see her neck. His head jerked up, gaze meeting hers. "You don't think . . . ?"

But he saw that she did.

His arms dropped away and he stepped back. "It's but a scratch, damn it." He bared his teeth, showing razor-sharp incisors. "I'm not yet used to these things, but I would not bite you. I would *never* hurt you." His voice was full of wounded anger, his mouth hard, jaw rigid.

Deidra worried her bottom lip, confused, frightened. She wanted to believe him, but she didn't know how much she deluded herself. Did it just *look* like Stephen? He saw her indecision, her hesitance to reassure him.

"Never," he repeated firmly. He exhaled loudly and shook his head. He seemed as if he wanted to say more, but finally he turned and left the garden.

Deidra didn't move. The darkness had lessened as morning eased away the night. Duke nuzzled at her hand. Deidra touched her neck again, tracing her finger along the tiny raw line on her neck. A scratch, not a puncture, and it had already clotted and scabbed over.

The garden was cold and empty except for herself and some animals. And that, she feared, was how it would always be. Deidra and the animals.

She had never felt more alone.

They all reconvened in the hall after the sun rose. Stephen was finding it difficult to assimilate to this life. In some instances it was the most amazing thing that had ever happened to him. He was stronger, faster, pain-free. He could see better, smell better, hear better. He even sensed the presence of other living things in a way he never had before.

And yet . . .

He couldn't sleep at night. It was impossible. Something about the moon energized him. This might not have been a problem, except everyone he wanted to talk to was asleep. And as day wore on, it became increasingly difficult for him to keep his eyes open. He was not as alert, he was not as strong. During the day all of his amazing new talents were gone. Though his back did not pain him, he still felt less than an ordinary man because he was so tired.

But he was pain-free. That was something.

He sat at the table across from Hannah. She stared at him, her face expressionless. She was an enigma. He had been afraid that she would try to enforce the deal she had initially set forward, that he would be some kind of companion-slave to her. And she was entirely capable of it—that was the frightening part. She had somehow immobilized him back in the forest after he'd awoken and controlled his will, even entering his thoughts. He suspected she could do it again if she wished.

He met her eyes, then looked away as if bored. He wanted to make sure he remained undesirable to her. Of course, in his experience, perhaps he should state his feelings and kiss her, since that seemed to have the opposite effect on the woman he did want.

But Deidra was here, too, picking at her food, as she

had begun to do of late. Already a small woman, she was growing thinner. It did not please him. She wasn't eating due to her distress, and he was the source of her distress. Though he watched her, she did not look up.

Drake was the last to the table, and he pulled out the bench beside Stephen and commenced eating.

The table was set with bread and cheese and porridge. Drake was the only one to partake, and he ate with gusto. Stephen looked at the fare longingly, but Hannah had already warned him that eating was pointless. He had not yet tested this theory because he simply didn't feel hungry. It was a bizarre feeling, as his body had been ruled by hunger for so many years.

Drake finished his bowl of porridge and had another. Everyone waited for him to finish. Silence reined except for the sounds Drake made while eating. Hannah watched Drake now, her gaze thoughtful, but he didn't so much as glance at the woman.

When finally Drake pushed the empty bowl away and leaned back in his chair with a satisfied sigh, he said, "So. What are we to do with Luthias Forsyth?"

Hannah arched a thin, elegant brow. "Dinner? Though I suppose his blood is bitter, old and thin as he is."

Drake glowered at her. "I'm not sure if you noticed or not, but we were a bit outnumbered. The entire town was there as witness. We need to get Luthias alone or with as few of his mercenaries as possible."

"First we have to find him," Stephen said.

"I sent men after him. They should be reporting back to me very soon as to his direction."

Deidra looked up finally. "So many people have seen us. I don't see how he can just die now without suspicion falling on us." She shook her head. "It's too dangerous. I think I should leave the country."

Stephen clenched his jaw and exhaled through his nose. She didn't want to leave because of Luthias. She wanted to leave because of Stephen. Because she was afraid he would attack and kill her in a weak moment.

Drake frowned at his niece. "That seems a little excessive, do ye not think? Your folks would certainly be furious to hear you've up and left the country."

Deidra met his eyes, her face rigid with anger. "It's better than them hearing that I am dead. He will *never* stop. We cannot kill him without hurting ourselves. The only answer is for me to leave."

"There has to be another way," Drake said, his brow furrowed deeply.

Stephen had an idea, he just didn't know if anyone would think it was a good one. He cleared his throat, drawing the attention of everyone at the table. "I died."

They all looked at him, waiting, though Hannah had a sly smile toying with the edges of her mouth.

"And yet, I am not dead."

"You think we should turn him into a *baobhan sith*?" Deidra asked incredulously. "How is this punishment? You are stronger than ever."

"Because he will be a *witch*," Drake answered before Stephen could say a word. He sat forward, eyes intense. "He will become everything he loathes. He will be hunted. He will know what it feels like to be the thing he devoted his life to terrorizing."

"And who will do this for you?" Hannah asked, one red brow arched.

Drake met her gaze, and Stephen could have sworn he saw Drake's jaw lock beneath his beard.

She showed no expression. "I am here because you compelled me to be. But I am not your friend or ally, and certainly not your tool."

Drake's eyes darkened, and his mouth twisted into an unpleasant smile. "Stephen will do it."

Stephen's brows shot up, but he didn't deny it. It was his idea, after all.

Hannah leaned forward, toward Stephen. "Are you ready for that, Stephen? To take a life, to bite through skin and muscle, to drink the warm blood until the body is an empty shell?"

Stephen wanted to be disgusted by her words, but he wasn't. Instead his stomach made a rumbling sound.

Deidra stood abruptly, her face pale, as if she might vomit, and left the table.

Hannah watched her go and smiled, satisfied. "Squeamish, isn't she?"

Drake pinned her with his hard stare for a long moment before he stood and left, too.

Stephen wasn't too pleased with Hannah either. What was she trying to prove? She had made it clear for all what he was. An animal. She had reminded Deidra, yet again, of how he'd attacked her. He wished *he* could remember it. He had only fleeting memories of waking as a *baobhan sith*. There had been the sensation of spiraling upward . . . no, being dragged upward through mud, fighting for each breath, and when he'd finally emerged everything had hurt. It had hurt to breath, it had hurt to see, and it had even hurt to speak. He hadn't been aware of anything when he'd woken. He'd had no memories of anything except Hannah. She'd been the only thing he'd been aware of. Her mind had been in his, talking to him, telling him that he must be calm, that he must be careful, that he must wait.

But he had not been interested in her witchery. He had refused her offer, so what had she been doing in his head? It had only made him angry and confused.

And then he had smelled it. Warm and sweet. *Blood.* And his body had ached worse. He knew then what had ailed him.

Hunger.

He'd needed blood. Once he'd realized that, the pain had centered in his gut, gnawing. The smell of the blood had only intensified the pain. And he'd heard the blood rushing. He'd thought he would die if he couldn't have it posthaste.

He remembered very little after that. A struggle. Then there had been blood and he had been better. He'd begun to come back to himself.

It had been a slow process, several nights in fact, but it had only taken him one to remember Deidra and what she was to him. That she was what had brought him to Hannah in the first place.

"Love is so fleeting," Hannah sighed. "See how strong her affection was? It died with you. It always does."

Stephen glared at her.

Hate me. But you will never be free of me.

"Get out of my head," he ground out through clenched teeth.

"Then get into mine."

He frowned at her, irritated and confused.

"You can, you know."

"Why would I want to? It would be like drowning in a cesspool of evil."

Her lips twisted into a jagged smile. "You'd better start treading water, Stephen. Because you are not one of them anymore, and I'm all you've got."

Chapter 18

———∞∞∞———

$\mathcal{I}$t took Drake's scout several days longer than expected to return with news of Luthias. And the news of his whereabouts was far worse than any of them had imagined. He had been in Sterling petitioning the kirk assembly for a warrant to arrest the Strathwick MacKays.

Deidra's knees seemed to give at this news, and she had to find a place to sit. The fireplace was behind her, and she fell heavily onto the hearth, her fingertips pressed to her lips. Her father. Rose. They had never harmed a soul, only healed others, to their own detriment. Tried. Burned. All because of her. This had gone too far. So far that Deidra didn't know if there was any way of stopping it anymore. Luthias had a warrant. The king would soon be made aware that they were witches and her whole family would be hunted—outlawed, like the MacGregors.

Stephen knelt beside her. "Nothing has happened yet. It's too soon for him to have reached Strathwick. If we leave now, there is still time."

Her throat was choked with tears; they blurred her vision. Impotent fury rose in her chest like a swarm of angry bees. The dogs in the hall stood and began to bark. She had missed so many opportunities to stop him; she'd let them pass her by.

No more.

When she could speak, she said, her voice low and shaking, "I will kill him this time. And I don't care who is watching."

They were not expecting him. They had grown complacent, wallowing in their evil ways. He was able to walk right up to William MacKay, who was in the little hamlet that crowded around the castle and loch, holding a wean, bouncing it and laughing at something someone said—until his attention was called to Luthias and his men's approach. William turned, his expression immediately transforming from magnanimous overlord to grim warlord. He handed the baby off.

Luthias had never liked William MacKay, even when he'd thought the chieftain had been doing the Lord's work. His magic gave him a brazen confidence. He believed himself beyond harm, beyond reproach. Invincible. And he had been, Luthias supposed. But not anymore.

William did not walk to meet Luthias, standing his ground instead, hands clasped behind his back, watching as Luthias and his men marched to him. His hair had gone completely gray. It was unnatural on such a youthful face.

"William MacKay," Luthias said in his loudest, clearest voice so everyone around could hear. "I hold here a warrant for you and your daughter's arrest." He held the warrant up, the yellow seal clear for everyone to see. "By order of the king."

William's gaze passed over the warrant, disinterested. "On what charges?"

"Witchcraft."

"What witchcraft? I am merely a healer."

"No," Luthias said. "You are a *baobhan sith*."

William's brows shot up. "Am I now? And where did you come by this information?" He reached for the warrant, studying it with new interest.

Luthias pulled it back, out of his reach. "Never mind that. All will be revealed during the trial."

William's eyes scanned the order from a distance. "I'm to be tried in England?"

Luthias pursed his lips, irritated that William MacKay didn't seem at all disturbed by any of this. "Aye," Luthias said reluctantly.

"Good," William said. "My son is at court, and I miss him. 'Twill be good to see him again."

"Do not start packing yet." Luthias rolled the document up and handed it to one of his men to slide into the protective leather tube. "We are not leaving for England until we have your daughter as well."

William lifted his shoulders. "I cannot help you. She has been gone a full moon without word."

Luthias smiled. "Mayhap she is on her way home."

William's jaw tightened, giving Luthias a measure of satisfaction. "Let me tell my wife." He tried to walk past Luthias, but Luthias's men stopped him.

"You stay with me," Luthias said. "I'll send someone to inform your wife and collect your things. If she wishes to visit you, she can come to us."

William shook his head, his mouth grim. "You will regret this. Mark me."

"I think not," Luthias said. "The only thing I regret is not pursuing you twelve years ago."

William stared at him defiantly, communicating with his eyes promises to kill and maim. Luthias motioned for him to be taken away, then he gave orders to shoot every animal in the village. Since they could not set up a normal camp without alerting his daughter and her cohorts the moment they arrived, he and his men would have to lodge with the villagers.

Luthias sighed, resigned to the fact that he would be sleeping on a heather-stuffed mattress crawling with lice for a while longer. He would bear it and more. The Lord had tested many men in worse ways. Job had lost far more than Luthias at Satan's hands. God would reward him tenfold, and all of this would be naught more than a bad dream.

Chapter 19

They rode without stopping, and this time Deidra didn't miss the rest. The horses couldn't move fast enough for her liking. But they understood her urgency. She communicated it to them constantly—and they pushed themselves harder. Drake had also sent word to the MacDonells. Deidra's stepmother was a Mac-Donell, so surely they would lend them aid. Unfortunately, their help might come too late.

When they were still a few miles from Strathwick, Stephen made them stop to formulate a plan. They had been riding without any idea of what they would do when they arrived at Strathwick.

"We can't just go in there, swords waving, animals snarling," Stephen said as he gave Deidra a pointed look, "else someone will end up dead."

They let their horses graze while they gathered in a small circle. Drake squatted on the ground and Deidra collapsed beside him, sitting cross-legged. Stephen and Hannah stood above them.

"It will not be me who dies," Hannah said.

"Is that so?" Drake said sarcastically, head tilted to

the side to look up at her. "If you plan to sabotage us, then think again."

"Enough!" Deidra said. She thought her head might explode if she had to listen to another moment of their bickering—or, more accurately, Hannah's baiting and Drake biting back.

They both fell silent.

Hannah folded her arms beneath her breasts. At Drake's she had managed to find more suitable clothing and now wore a wool gown suitable for travel, though a little too large for her slender frame, with an araisad wrapped around her shoulders and pinned at one side. She wore leather cork-soled boots. Yet still she looked different, more refined than any Scotswoman Deidra had ever seen.

Drake had brought a score of men, but they all seemed uneasy, watching Hannah and Stephen with wary eyes. They knew there were *baobhan siths* among them. They made signs of protection when Hannah or Stephen came near to protect themselves from evil.

"We should split up," Stephen said. "Deidra and I will see to the rescue of her father, and you two take care of Luthias."

"How are we supposed to do that?" Deidra asked, leaning back on her hands. Though she had not noticed it before, every muscle in her body ached. "We don't know where they're holding him."

"Luthias came to Strathwick for you," Stephen said. "William is merely bait."

"And that," said Drake, "is why we cannot just jig into the village and give ourselves up."

Deidra worried her bottom lip as a plan occurred to her. She didn't particularly like it, but her father and stepmother would be near, so even if one of them was harmed there was an excellent chance the damage would not be permanent.

She looked up at Stephen and then at her uncle. "I'll give myself up." Drake and Stephen immediately began to protest, but Deidra raised her voice to cut them off. "He will think I returned alone in defeat. He thinks Stephen is dead, and he doesn't know about you and Hannah. Once I am in his custody, he won't be looking for anyone else."

"How will we know where you are?" Stephen asked.

Deidra was warming to the idea. She sat up on the balls of her feet. "I'll send an animal to you. Luthias will have taken even more precautions than he did before. There will be no animals in the village." She smiled. "But even he cannot get rid of the rats. I will send you a rat."

Hannah's lips curled in disgust and she rubbed her hands over her arms.

Drake's brows drew together in confusion. "A rat will be intelligent enough to carry this out?"

Deidra nodded. "You would be surprised. They are smarter than most dogs."

"It's a sound plan," Stephen admitted reluctantly. "But I do not like the idea of Deidra going in alone. I will go with her."

Deidra shook her head. "He thinks you're dead. If he wanted to burn you before, seeing you walking and whole after he *killed* you will make him certain that you are the devil himself."

Stephen shrugged. "It will go to the grave with him, so what care I?"

Drake considered Stephen for a moment, squatting, elbows resting on his thighs. He nodded slowly. "I think you're right." He turned to Deidra. "I would feel better if he accompanied you anyway. And besides," he said with a deep breath as he stood, "it will be good to have Stephen on the inside, and it will keep Luthias busy, distracted."

Deidra looked up at Stephen, wondering what prompted him to make such an offer. Love? He looked back at her, unsmiling, and she just didn't know. Whatever it was it warmed her. She would not admit it—not after the morning in the garden—but she felt safer knowing he would be with her. It seemed ridiculous after her fear of him, but he'd had the opportunity to hurt her and he hadn't.

Her hand went to her throat, touching the place where his sharp incisor had scratched her. It was gone, not even a scab now.

Stephen's gaze dipped, registering her action, and his mouth thinned. "Let's go," he said gruffly and turned his back to her.

Luthias was washing his face in a rain barrel when she arrived. She rode into the village as if she owned it, she and her companion, and he supposed she had reason for that. Strathwick, after all, was Deidra MacKay's home.

Luthias moved surreptitiously back so that his body would be hidden behind the cottage stones. His eyes narrowed as the villagers rushed out of their homes and waved at them. One grabbed the bridle of Deidra's horse and came close, urgently speaking to her. Deidra's head shot up, a line of confusion between her eyes.

Luthias shook his head. Traitors to the king, the lot of them. He would deal with this whole community. But for now, there was only one witch he wanted. The rest could wait.

His men swarmed out of the cottages, surrounding the two riders. Luthias's eyes widened, and his heart stammered painfully against his ribs. He'd been so focused on Deidra that he had paid scant attention to her companion. But now he saw that it was none other than Stephen Ross. He had expected to see him—slung across a saddle, or dragged in a litter, not riding under his own power. And his face was completely unmarred, his hands whole and unblemished, not crippled at all.

Luthias's bowels shriveled. He had seen many wicked things, but this was true evil. He had seen this man broken beyond repair—had done the breaking himself. And now he looked fitter than he had before Luthias had even started in on him.

He found himself hesitant—nay, *afraid*—to even walk out in the open, to let Stephen Ross *see* him. Luthias swallowed hard and fisted his hands. This was another test. God had brought him this far, he would carry him the rest of the way. Luthias had faith that his fight was a good one.

He squared his shoulders and walked into the road. His men had already pulled Stephen and Deidra down from their horses. They looked to Luthias for their next orders.

There was no point in waiting. That would only give the witches time to mount a rescue, as they had twelve years ago. He would not give them the opportunity. He had also devised a way to stop Deidra MacKay from calling on her animals.

"Secure them and load them into the wagon. Load up William MacKay as well."

"What have you done to my father?" Deidra demanded, surging forward, hands balled into fists. His men held her back effortlessly.

Luthias snapped his fingers, and one of his men brought him a leather box. Luthias opened it and removed a vial, which he unstoppered.

"Drink this."

Deidra's hand swung out to knock it from his hand, but he had anticipated such defiance and pulled the vial back.

She stared at him, mouth obstinate, eyes on fire.

"I'm sure that's not necessary," Stephen said in his placating voice, a voice that Luthias now knew was false.

"You are the walking dead. You are evil incarnate. *Do not speak to me.*"

He took a threatening step closer to Deidra. "You will drink this willingly, or my men will hold you down while I pour it down your gullet then hold your nose until you swallow."

Her jaw moved as she ground her teeth, obviously searching for a response and not finding it. The only possible response was compliance. She was a fool if she didn't see that.

She looked up at her companion. His mouth was

flat and grim. He gave a single nod. Her shoulders slumped. She took the vial from Luthias.

She stared at the contents, then sighed and tossed it back. Her face twisted with disgust as she threw the vial on the ground.

"What now?" she said.

Luthias gestured to the men waiting with leather straps hanging from their hands. They came forward and secured Deidra and Stephen's wrists behind their backs, then led them to the wagon and assisted them into the back of it. Stephen walked tall and straight. No limp. Luthias's bowels shrunk again. He was no longer a cripple . . . if he'd ever been one.

As if reading his thoughts, Stephen looked back over his shoulder and smiled. It was a knowing smile, an evil smile, and Luthias fought with the urge to have him clubbed unconscious.

He scanned the area nervously. Though he'd had all of the animals except his men's horses shot and the horses secured by several men, he wouldn't put anything past Deidra. William was led to the wagon and pushed into it with his daughter.

William spoke to her in a low voice. She laid her head against his shoulder. She was already fading. The tightness in Luthias's chest eased.

He hoped—nay, he prayed—that God had guided him straight this time and he had overlooked nothing so that finally he could accomplish God's will.

Deidra's head bobbed against Stephen's shoulder in a jarring and surely painful manner. She was not yet unconscious, but she could not hold her head up. He wished he could ease her discomfort, but with his wrists tied behind his back there was nothing he could do.

The poppy juice Luthias had made her drink worked on her senses. She blinked groggily, fighting to stay lucid. Stephen only hoped it hadn't been too much for her. She was a tiny woman who did not take it with regularity, as Stephen did. He'd seen it kill people who'd taken it in excess.

William watched his daughter with a worried frown that mirrored Stephen's concern. "Did he give her too much, think you? Could it kill her?"

Stephen shrugged. "Good thing you're here, aye?"

"Aye, good thing nothing happened when I wasn't there to help."

Stephen's mouth turned down. He'd known this was coming. "I sent you word. I told you I would keep her safe."

William's shoulders thrust forward as he leaned toward Stephen. "Aye, but you didn't tell me where she was. We searched for her."

"If you were searching so desperately, what are you doing here now?"

William fell back against the wagon. His jaw shifted, and he inhaled but didn't answer. He didn't have to.

Stephen nodded. "Because Drake sent word, too, aye? Told you he had her and was protecting her. Only then did you rest easy, because Drake wasna the cripple, so he could actually protect her."

William didn't answer. The wagon hit a rut and they all banged into the wagon's sides, jarring bones.

The last time William had seen Stephen, such movement would have been excruciating to him. And William was not a man to miss much.

William's gaze traveled over Stephen, scrutinizing him. "You are not cripple any longer."

Stephen shrugged. "It appears I am not."

"*Baobhan sith,*" Deidra slurred.

William raised his brows. "You are the reason Luthias is now obsessed with the idea that we are blood witches."

Stephen nodded reluctantly.

"How did my daughter become involved in all of this?" William asked suspiciously.

Stephen's belly tightened, and he fought to maintain eye contact. He had compromised this man's daughter and not yet offered for her hand. Quite suddenly he felt his bastard heritage keenly, and he wondered if William would even consent to such a union for his daughter.

"She sought me out. She thought I was a *baobhan sith.*"

William looked at his daughter, his face creasing, as if wounded. "Why would you search out a blood witch?"

Deidra fought to keep her eyes open. She mumbled something unintelligible, then her lashes dropped heavily and she went limp against Stephen.

"What did she say?" William asked, anxious.

Stephen shrugged.

William watched his daughter, his expression full of worry. Stephen wondered which was worse—being a blood witch, a cripple, or a bastard. He was or had been all three. Not the first choice a father would make for his daughter.

Stephen leaned his head back with a sigh.

It was a long day, trapped in the back of the wagon. They stopped once and were given a cup of water and a crust of bread. Deidra was given nothing except more laudanum, which Stephen and William protested against vociferously. They were ignored. She was still unconscious while they held her mouth open and poured the stuff down her throat. She coughed a few times before going limp again. Stephen was as useless as William was during the daylight. He tugged at his bindings, but they held fast.

William scooted closer to his daughter and examined her. "Is she breathing?"

Stephen nodded. "Aye, she still breathes . . . but everything is slowing down. If it slows down too much . . . it stops."

William frowned. "How do you know this?"

"I can . . . feel it. The heart pumping blood. It is faint during the day, but at night everything is clear."

William sat back against the side of the wagon. "So the stories are true. You drink blood?"

Stephen nodded, watching William's reaction. William appeared deeply dismayed, but he said no more on the matter. Stephen guessed his chances for winning the father's approval had just diminished significantly.

Chapter 20

———⊗⊗⊗———

The entourage to England eventually stopped for the night. Stephen could tell that Luthias was unsure about where to stop, but in the end he chose a vast moorland. It was flat, so he would be able to spot trouble before it could surprise him.

He left Stephen and William tied securely in the back of the wagon so that they could not escape—at least, not if they were normal men. Their wrists were bound together behind their backs, their ankles were tied, and their mouths were gagged. Their bound wrists were tethered to the sides of the wagon. Then Luthias had a limp Deidra taken to his tent, the only one erected in the whole camp.

Night fell. The moon was high, and Stephen felt the moonlight pouring into him, giving him strength and making him more aware of everything around him. He could have broken free and killed the men around him, but instead he played along, pretending to be incapacitated by his bonds and monitoring the camp's activity. Luthias had two-thirds of his men on guard, walking the perimeter while the remainder rested. One-third was relieved every two hours.

The best time to slip away was during a change of the guards. The wait was excruciating. It was full night and the moon was high. Stephen was alive at night. His body hummed with strength and energy. He lay on his side, listening to the activity around him. He could hear everything, even the guards' conversations across camp. He knew where everyone was and what everyone said. They were afraid and hypervigilant, but their focus was outward, on the wilderness around them. They waited for animals to attack. They did not expect an attack from within. Stephen could smell their fear, sense the rapid beating of their hearts.

And he was hungry. It was not the gnawing, desperate pain of when he'd first woken as a blood witch, but he smelled their blood and he wanted to taste it.

William lay across the small expanse of the wagon, eyes wide. It was too dark for the older man to see anything, but the darkness did not hinder Stephen's vision at all. He could see William clearly, could hear the slow rubbing as William worked at the bindings on his wrists.

Stephen didn't bother working at his. He flexed and pulled his wrists apart. The rope snapped. He pulled the gag down around his neck.

He lay quietly for a moment, making certain no one was near before he rolled across the wagon. William made a soft sound of surprise, and Stephen shushed him. He reached behind William and broke the rope securing him to the wagon, then broke his bindings as well.

William quickly pulled off his gag. "Jesus God, you are strong."

"Aye," Stephen whispered as they both untied the ropes binding their ankles.

"What the hell have you been waiting for?" William hissed. "It's been hours. Luthias probably gave her more of that poison. She could be dead, and then I can do nothing at all."

"I was waiting for the guards to change. That is the best time to act."

William frowned, obviously not understanding how Stephen knew when the guard changed.

Stephen leaned back against the wagon side and listened and smelled. Nothing. He sat up and scanned the area around them. It was clear, so he climbed out of the wagon.

"Follow me and be quiet."

Her mind was a black pit of tar. She struggled to climb out of it, but the tar kept dragging her back. *Stephen.* He was near, but she could not find him, could not even call out to him. The tar covered her mouth and her eyes, hiding the world from her. It held her fast so that she could not even move. It seemed she had been mired in this pit forever when finally, its hold loosened and she climbed out.

She blinked groggily. Her head throbbed and her vision blurred, wrenching a moan from her. It felt as if a vise squeezed her head. She couldn't remember where she was supposed to be. She had been with Stephen . . . they had been going somewhere, to do something important . . . but that was all she could grasp.

She squinted this time, trying to determine where she was. A dim, firelit room. The walls . . . moved. She squeezed her eyes shut, stomach roiling. She was still trapped in the nightmare world, where everything swirled and rocked sickeningly. She tried to move her arms, but they were bound behind her.

"Ah, she's awake."

Her heart rose, trembling in her throat. *Oh God, no.* She knew that voice. Knew it only too well.

Luthias.

She opened her eyes again and saw boots. She rolled partway onto her back and raised her gaze slightly. He squatted in front of her, his head tilted to view her.

"I've been waiting for you to wake up. There is a conversation we must have that is long overdue."

Deidra shook her head, making the room spin, so she stopped. She didn't want to talk to him, didn't like his talks.

"No," she rasped. Her throat was raw and dry.

"Here," he said, grasping her by her arm and pulling her to her feet. "Let me help you up."

Her head spun again and her stomach heaved. She stumbled around, trying to get her balance and feeling as if she would die. His hold on her arm kept her from falling. He led her to a stool and forced her down on it.

She swayed woozily, then tumbled off of it, her head slamming into the ground.

Blackness overtook her again and she nearly wept

with relief, preferring the darkness to the man. But her reprieve was short-lived. Her heart seized when freezing water saturated her, flowing into her ears and mouth and nose. She gasped for air, coughing and choking.

He hauled her to her feet again, dragging her across the room. She couldn't see. Panic choked her. Water stung her eyes. Her head whirled and her stomach turned. She needed to boch, desperately, but there was nothing in her stomach to vomit up.

He pushed her to her knees.

"Now, Deidra, you and I are going to have a little talk. But first, you need to drink your medicine." The vial was pressed to her lips.

She jerked her head away, desperate. She could not drink any more. The smell made her stomach heave.

"No," she croaked. "I cannot."

"Oh, I think you can. We've been surprisingly free of vermin this whole journey. This is a very effective way to keep the animals at bay."

"But how can we talk if I'm not even awake?"

She could see again. They were in a tent. That was the reason for the fluid movement of the walls. They shuddered with the wind. A small brazier was set up across the room near a camp bed. Several candles sat on a table. A folding stool was on its side on the floor. She looked down. She knelt before a wide-mouthed bucket filled to the top with water. She see could herself in the water's reflection, face small and pale, eyes wide. Wet ringlets stuck to the sides of her face. She looked like a cornered animal.

Her head jerked up. Luthias crouched on the other side of the bucket, vial still in his hand.

"This takes a bit of time to send you to dreamland. Long enough for us to talk."

She shook her head, disgusted at the pleading that she knew entered her expression. She couldn't go back to the tar place. Something inside her told her that her body couldn't take any more. That it would kill her if he kept pouring it down her throat.

But he didn't care. "Take it or I will force it down your gullet."

"No," she whimpered. Where was Stephen? Her father? She remembered them now. That was their plan, to give themselves up, and it had been a good plan, too. It would have worked if not for the laudanum. Luthias was too clever. He would always be too clever for them.

Deidra couldn't accept that. She wanted a life, a real one, not the constant running and fear. She tried to remember what she was supposed to do, the rest of the plan. Send word to Drake via a rodent, but she didn't even know where they were now, or where Drake could be. Her mind stretched out around her, reaching for the thoughts of the surrounding animals. It was difficult and confusing, as her brain was still filled with fog, but she touched the minds of horses, and other, wild animals.

Apparently Luthias could see her mind working, because he grabbed her face in one hand and forced her mouth open, pouring the contents of the vial in it. When she would have spit it back out, he shoved upward on her jaw so that she bit her tongue, then he held her nose.

She tried to jerk away, but she was weak and sick, and he was strong. She couldn't breathe, couldn't spit the poppy juice out. Her mouth was filled with the vile, bitter liquid and the copper taste of blood. She tried to scream, but nothing came out except pathetic moans. Her vision clouded, the fog overtaking her mind. Finally, she swallowed.

He felt it and released her.

She gasped for air and sagged forward, leaning on the side of the bucket. Her belly burned, threatening to bring it all back up. She closed her eyes, hoping the world would stop swirling.

"Now, we shall talk."

Deidra didn't really know what there was to talk about or how he expected her to uphold her end of the conversation. She couldn't even raise her head, could barely keep her body balanced on the edge of the bucket. When she opened her eyes, the room spun slowly around her, making her dizzy.

"I thought . . . trial . . . England." She was dismayed by her inability to form a coherent sentence. He swam in and out of focus.

"Aye, you will be tried." He leaned close. His face blurred and doubled. "But I will not let you go to the gallows with this curse still on me."

She blinked, frowning. "Curse?"

"Aye . . . you have invaded my thoughts . . . sabotaged everything good in my life. Do you know I have never been married? No woman will have me now."

And this was her fault? Her mind struggled to understand what he was saying, but it escaped her grasp. She couldn't find the animals anymore either. Tar and fog and nausea crowded her brain. Sickness rose in her throat.

"Remove the curse."

She shook her head, trying to say that she didn't understand—what curse? But his face contorted into rage.

"Aye! You will! Before we leave here you will!"

He grasped the back of her head and shoved her forward, plunging her beneath the freezing water. She opened her mouth to scream and instead swallowed water. It choked her, burning her throat. She couldn't struggle, couldn't escape; she was too weak.

He yanked her back out. Air, like fire, burned her throat. She coughed and sputtered, sucking it greedily even as her lungs rejected it. Water poured down her face, soaking her clothes. Her body shook from the cold. Her lungs strained to suck in the air. She could no longer hold herself up, but when she fell, he caught her.

She could smell him in her face, and she heaved, water spilling down her chin.

"Remove the curse, or God help me I will drown you within an inch of your sorry life!" His breath smelled of beans and ale.

She gasped and coughed and again made the mistake of shaking her head in confusion.

He shoved her down again, plunging her head beneath the water. In her mind, she screamed. A long scream of horror and helplessness that started in the pit of her belly and encased her heart, crushing it. *Stephen, please, help me.* She was done with the fight, with the fear. She'd grown weary of this weak body.

There seemed to be no escape from this man except death.

Chapter 21

———⊗⊗⊗———

Stephen could *feel* Deidra. He could feel everyone now to some extent, but Deidra felt like no one else, as if she'd been a part of him. Her heart raced like a frantic rabbit and he followed it, his own heartbeat increasing as if to keep tempo with hers. The closer he got to her location, the stronger became the scent of her blood. It was tainted, unappetizing to him, strongly diluted with poppy juice, and thin from lack of food.

As a *baobhan sith* he was better able than a human to move about unseen. He stayed in the shadows, keeping William behind him, and the few guards who passed near simply did not see him.

His senses led him to Luthias's tent. As he and William stood outside, he became aware of Deidra's heart slowing, so slow it was about to stop.

Urgent terror sent him bursting into the tent without a thought to whom or what he might find. The only thing driving him was that Deidra's life was draining away and he could not go on without her.

Luthias hunched over a water bucket. A small figure was beneath him, her head submerged in the water. The surface of the water showed signs of calming, as if there had been a struggle, but it was over now. Luthias did not hear him enter, so intent was he on his task.

"Oh my God," William gasped behind Stephen. Then, "You bloody bastard! I'll kill you!"

Luthias whirled around, jerking Deidra's head out of the water. He grasped her by her hair and she hung there, limp, her lips blue.

Stephen's chest convulsed, his mind refusing to believe what he was seeing. Everything seemed to slow down. William rushed past him as he honed in on the man before him, whose mouth was opening, preparing to scream for help.

Fury blinded Stephen to all else but Luthias. He saw Luthias's heart pumping and squeezing with fear, the blood flowing, strong and healthy and untainted. He moved forward, so fast that Luthias didn't even have a chance to get a sound out. Stephen hit him hard enough to knock him unconscious, then yanked him back up by the front of his shirt, shoved his head to the side, and sank his teeth into his neck. Blood flowed into Stephen's mouth, quenching his thirst and quelling his hunger.

He drank until satisfied, then shoved the limp body away from him. Luthias fell to the floor. Stephen stood over him, breathing hard, strength and vitality flowing through him. And then he remembered, and grief pierced him.

He turned. William leaned over Deidra, lifting her in his arms and holding her against his chest. "Is it too late?" Stephen asked, barely able to breathe as he waited for her father's answer.

But William never had a chance to answer. Men flooded into the tent. Swiftly, Stephen drew the sword from the dead man on the ground and rushed forward to protect William and Deidra. Men attacked from both sides. Stephen swung his sword in an arc, cutting down two of them. When he turned to confront the others, sword bloodied, William slumped over Deidra's body, his back wet and glistening.

"No!" Stephen shouted, red lights exploding about his eyes. This was bad, very bad, but he couldn't grasp exactly why at the moment. The rage at what had been done engulfed him, and he flew at the rest of the men, sword slashing. The men scattered, running from the tent. The ones that weren't fast enough tasted Stephen's blade.

Luthias's sword clattered to the ground as Stephen dropped to his knees beside William and Deidra. When he rolled William off of Deidra, William gasped. Stephen leaned over Deidra to find her soaked in blood—but it wasn't her own. She was still alive and unhurt, though her pulse was weak and thready. Her father's body had protected her from harm.

"She's dying," William said, trying to sit up. There was a wet quality to his voice. Stephen smelled that he had lost a lot of blood. He placed a hand on William's shoulder, easily pinning the man to the ground.

"You cannot save her. Not now."

"If I do not, she will die."

Stephen swallowed, his gaze falling on Deidra. If left alone in his current condition, William would heal rapidly, but not so rapidly that he would be any good to his daughter. It would take him a day or more to heal from the wound that would be fatal to any other man. Deidra, however, would not last that long. Stephen could tell that by the slowing of her heart, the shallowness of her breath.

But if Stephen allowed William to heal her, William would no doubt die from it. And though William would willingly die for his daughter, Deidra and Rose might never forgive Stephen for allowing it.

Not when there was another way.

"Let me up!" William gurgled, the back of his head pressed hard against the ground, his breath sawing harshly in and out of his chest.

"You'll die, man," Stephen said gently. "I can save her . . . but she will be different."

William opened his eyes and turned his head slightly to stare at Stephen. "Like you."

Stephen nodded.

"No." William tried again to sit up, but Stephen held him down.

"Do you think she would wish to live, knowing the cost was your life?"

William's lips curled. Blood coated his teeth. "Think you she would welcome a life such as yours?"

"I love her," Stephen said.

"No—you want her, but you care nothing for her own wishes. You are selfish, to make such a decision without her consent."

Stephen's heart squeezed, the truth of William's words slipping like a blade between his ribs. His head dropped. He no longer knew what to do. He couldn't let her go . . .

he loved her ... and yet she would never forgive him if he allowed her father to kill himself healing her.

But he couldn't let her go.

He released William's shoulder. William slowly rolled onto his side, and Stephen slid his hands beneath William's arms, helping him to kneel before his daughter. Deidra coughed. Water poured from her mouth. Stephen moved around to her other side.

"No—wait," Deidra rasped. Her voice was slurred from poppy juice. She blinked, but her eyes were hazy, as if she didn't really see them.

Stephen took her cold hand in both of his, rubbing it briskly to warm it. "If he doesn't," he said, his voice thick, "you will die."

Deidra stared up at her father, a vertical frown between her brows. Her gaze traveled over his face, to the blood that covered his clothing and hers.

"You are hurt," she said.

"It's nothing," William said, then he coughed, thick and liquid. "It will heal."

Her head moved slowly from side to side. "No, it won't ... not if you do this."

William ignored his daughter, resting his hand on her chest. Deidra weakly tried to push it away.

Her desperate gaze turned to Stephen. "No," she said weakly. "I pray you, Stephen, do not let him do this."

Stephen's jaw tightened as he stared at father and daughter. It didn't have to be this way. Neither of them had to die. Deidra just had to accept a different kind of life.

He grabbed William's wrist and pulled it off Deidra.

"Damn it, Stephen, I will strike you down if you interfere."

"You cannot strike a kitten down right now."

William glared at him. He tried to pull his wrist away but slumped forward weakly.

"Do you not hear her?" Stephen said. "She doesn't wish to trade her life for yours."

"She is dying," William said. "I have lived my life. She has not yet begun hers."

"Da, Stephen can save me."

Stephen looked down at her, surprised to hear the words. Her gaze was on her father, though. "I will be like him." Her eyelids drifted closed, and Stephen felt her leaving them, felt her heart slowing. "I would be strong . . . like him."

"Deidra?" William cried, clawing his way back toward her. "Deidra!" His voice cracked and broke. He took her face between his hands and stared into it. Then he raised his gaze to Stephen's. "Do it. *Now*."

Stephen's throat felt stuffed with sand. It was what he wanted, but not this way. He didn't know why she chose it—because of her father or him. He stared down at her, wanting to do the right thing, the thing that would bring her the most happiness.

"Do it," William ordered through clenched teeth. He grabbed the front of Stephen's leather jack. With a surprising show of strength, he pulled Stephen across Deidra's body so their faces were an inch apart. "Are you deaf, man? I heard her. She wants this." He released Stephen and collapsed again. "God's blood, man—I'll kill you. I vow it."

William lay still. He was no longer of any use to either of them.

For Stephen, there was only one thing left to do. He loved her. He would do anything for her, give her anything—even his own blood. He slid his hands beneath her back and raised her, cradling her in his arms. Her skin was cold and clammy. He pressed a kiss to her blue, lifeless lips, then bit into her neck and tasted her life.

When Stephen finally emerged from the tent, the camp was deserted. All of Luthias's mercenaries had disappeared. Stephen tied William to a horse and cradled Deidra across his lap on his mount. He didn't know which way Luthias's men had escaped, but he thought it was best to lie low. He took William and Deidra deep into the wood, then laid them both in a pile of leaves to rest while he kept watch. His normally sharp senses were dulled, and he recognized the dull-ness—the poppy juice. It had been in Deidra's blood, and now her blood was a part of him. He lay beside her and gathered her close, holding her cold, lifeless body against him. She wouldn't wake until tomorrow night. He didn't know how he knew this, but he did. For tonight, she was dead and his heart grieved, even as it filled with hope and fear for what tomorrow night would bring.

After several hours William began to stir.

"Can you ride?" Stephen asked.

William lifted his shirt and twisted to look at his side. He had been run through by a sword that had stabbed deep into his side. But the wound was closed now, the flesh knitting together. He was no doubt still in great pain, but he was also well on his way to a full recovery.

William nodded wearily. His gaze moved to his daughter lying in the leaves beside Stephen. "She is . . . ?"

"Not yet, but she will be, tomorrow night."

William's mouth thinned, and he merely nodded again. They mounted and rode back toward Strathwick.

The pink light of dawn gilded the mountains when they saw a party riding toward them. Black shadows against the mountains at first, it soon became clear it was Hannah and Drake with his men.

"What the hell happened?" Drake demanded angrily when they were within shouting distance. His gaze locked on Deidra rocking with the horse against Stephen's chest, and his eye widened. "Dee-dee—is she . . . ?"

"No," Stephen said.

"Then what's wrong with her?"

Stephen didn't know how to answer. So much had happened, and right now it was impossible for Stephen to condense it down into a brief summary that would explain why Deidra was dead, but not for long.

"She did die," William said quietly. "But according to Stephen, she will be fine tonight."

Drake looked from Stephen to Deidra, then rubbed the side of his hand across his mouth. "Now it's the both of them, eh?" He looked a little uneasy, and Stephen knew it was his distrust for Hannah that made him so.

Drake's gaze darted to his brother. "You're hurt."

William shrugged. "It is nothing now. I will be fine tomorrow."

"What the hell happened?" Drake asked impatiently. "No rat ever appeared. We waited, watching for something, a bird, a titmouse, *something,* but it never came."

"He gave her poppy juice," Stephen said. "She was half dead the whole time. Such a thing had not occurred to us."

Drake's brows rose in surprise. "Why would it? Clever bastard."

"Aye, he was," Stephen said.

"So he is dead?" Hannah asked, her perceptive eyes on Stephen.

"Aye."

"Are you certain?" Drake asked.

"I saw to it myself."

Drake's eyes narrowed. "How dead is he?"

William appeared confused by the question, but Stephen knew what he was really asking. Was Luthias dead, or was he a blood witch?

"He's dead," Stephen repeated.

Drake exchanged a weighty look with Hannah and said, "I'll go and see for myself that he is truly a menace to us no longer."

William sighed, placing a hand on Stephen's shoulder, as if he expected Stephen to be insulted. "I cannot imagine he lived through that. Stephen . . . well, Stephen was not gentle." William gave Stephen a grim but apologetic sidelong look. He looked tired.

Stephen raised a hand to show he was not offended. "By all means, do whatever you feel is necessary."

Drake inclined his head and tapped his horse's sides. "We'll see you in a day or two." They rode on toward Luthias's camp. Stephen watched them go. He didn't begrudge Drake his revenge. He understood it completely. But a part of him also thought the man pursued it with too much intensity.

As they continued on toward Strathwick, William stole glances at his daughter, eyes bleak. It was true that currently Deidra was a corpse. Her dark curls covered her eyes and her lips were bluish. She *looked* dead, and, until recently, in Stephen's world the dead did not come back. It frightened him to hold her cold, dead body. He prayed that he could make it happen, just as Hannah had sired him. As soon as the sun sank, he would find out.

When Drake and Hannah finally found Luthias, it was not at all how they had expected. They had expected to infiltrate Luthias's camp and steal his body, but no clandestine schemes were necessary. They sighted the encampment from more than a mile away on the desolate moorland. It had been abandoned, leaving just an empty wagon, several smoldering fires, and a tent with a corner loose from its stake, flapping in the breeze.

They entered the encampment cautiously, but there was no sign of life. It was empty.

They dismounted and wandered about the camp, hands on sword hilts. Drake stopped outside the lone tent.

"I smell death in there," Hannah whispered.

Drake peered inside. A folding chair lay on its side, and a cold brazier was next to it. Bodies were scattered all over the floor of the tent.

Drake motioned for his men to stay outside of the tent, and he and Hannah slipped inside. They inspected the bodies until they found Luthias sprawled on the ground, his neck bent awkwardly.

Hannah circled the man on the ground and knelt beside him to examine his neck. Her hair was plaited into a thick copper rope that hung over her shoulder like a snake.

"He's dead," she said, "and he will stay dead unless he tastes a *baobhan sith*'s blood."

"As Stephen did?"

She nodded. "Aye."

Drake drew in a deep breath and ran a hand over his face, dragging his fingers through his beard. He didn't know what to do. The man was dead, no longer a threat to anyone. With his death, the hunt for the MacKays would end. Certainly there might be another, but it was doubtful. In the past decade, Luthias had been the only one to trouble them.

Trouble them. Too kind a phrase. Menace them, hunt them, terrorize them. He had been a plague. Mere death was too clean, too easy. Luthias Forsyth had spent his life murdering witches and the last twelve years making Deidra's life a living hell. Twice he'd tried to execute Drake's brother, William. Such a clean, painless death was too easy. It was unjust, unfair, a wrong not to be borne.

He turned and pinned Hannah with a hard stare. "He deserves to know what it is to be the hunted." He nodded, his decision made. "Do it."

Hannah arched that perfect brow, giving him her otherworldly ambiguous look. "You're certain? He will be powerful."

"At night."

She nodded slowly. "Aye, at night."

"Then I will make sure he is hunted during the day and when finally he is burned alive, it will be with the sun blazing overhead."

She continued to stare at him. For a moment he thought he saw a hint of doubt flit across her face, but then it was gone and he wasn't sure he had seen it at all.

"And our agreement . . . ?" she asked, her voice low and drawling.

"Aye, aye." He waved this away with irritation. He didn't want to think about that now. "I gave my word and it is good."

"Very well then. He shall not receive his heavenly reward. He will be damned." She looked up at Drake, her mouth curved into a small smile as she ran her dirk across her wrist. "Like us."

Chapter 22

———— ∞∞∞ ————

Stephen knelt beside Deidra's body, laid out in the forest her father said she had loved so much as a child. And he waited. William and Rose had wanted to accompany them and keep vigil, but Stephen hadn't allowed it. They didn't need to see her when she woke. Deidra wouldn't know them anyway.

He'd remembered his own painful awakening and had come prepared. William had sent out hunting parties and offered a reward to the first man to return with a live hart. Stephen had taken the winner's catch and Deidra into the wood as the sun had sunk low in the sky. Now he waited for her to awaken.

He watched her face as it changed from the pale marble of death. A small frown formed between her brows. He wasted no time drawing blood from the hart. As soon as her eyes fluttered open, she fell on it.

His memories of his own awakening were vague and dreamlike, but he did remember that the only person he'd recognized was Hannah, his sire. This gave him hope. He had sired Deidra, so though she would wake with few memories, she should remember him. He just didn't know how far that memory would extend. Would she remember that he loved her? Would she hate him because she now had to feed on her beloved animals?

He waited apprehensively until she raised her head and met his gaze. She stared at him for a long time, then looked around her. There was a blankness to her gaze, a confusion. He used a damp rag to clean her face. She allowed him to do this, her eyes fixing on him, a brilliant blue, like the sea.

When he stepped away from her, she looked down at the hart on the ground and a frown marred her brow. She took a step away from the corpse, hands rising to cover her mouth.

Stephen's chest tightened uneasily. "Deidra?"

She shook her head slowly, eyes still locked on the hart. "Oh God," she moaned. "I taste it . . . its blood . . . in my mouth."

Stephen approached her, hands out. "Deidra, listen to me."

She tore her gaze from the hart to look frantically around the forest. "I hear them . . . they're afraid of me." Her hands slid up into her hair and curled into fists. "Oh God—what am I? What have you done to me?"

Stephen didn't know what to say, how to respond. She was not like him, or anyone else. She'd had a special bond with the animals, and now he'd made her a predator. Perhaps it would have been better to let her die. But his heart immediately rejected that. *No.* She could learn to live with this. She *would* learn to live with it. He would help her.

"Come here, love." He touched her arm, trying to draw her close.

"No!" she screamed and fled into the woods.

He hesitated. Perhaps he should let her alone. Then he remembered how confused and disoriented he had been after he'd awakened, and he raced after her.

Deidra raced into the wood. The animals fled ahead of her, sensing her and fearing her. She wanted to scream at them not to fear her—that she would never hurt them, but that was not true. Had she not just supped on the blood of one? The thought should make her sick, but it didn't. The taste in her mouth was sweet and her belly was full, satiated. In her mind she was sick, wanting to tear out the memory, tear out her tongue.

He chased her. *Stephen.* She knew him. He was responsible for what she'd become. As she raced through the trees, she became aware of her speed. She couldn't remember much from before she woke, but she knew instinctively that this was new. She was swift and nimble, like a hare, bounding. Joy filled her heart and she ran faster.

Still he pursued. She could smell him. She could smell everything. It filled her, expanded her. The chase excited her and a smile pulled at her lips. The leaves rustled to her right and she turned. A white wolf burst from the bushes and raced beside her.

She knew the wolf, remembered the wolf. And it spoke to her, as if she were one with it, a part of it. And that was new, too.

She was so intent on the wolf that it surprised her when Stephen caught her. His arm slipped around her waist. She shrieked, but it was part laugh, part excitement because she was so *alive*. They went down, rolling onto the ground.

He was saying her name, *Deidra, Deidra*. He sounded worried, so she pulled his mouth to her and kissed him. There was no hesitation in him; he sank down into her, between her thighs, his tongue finding hers.

There was no gentleness in their kiss. It was rough and animal, and she welcomed it, tearing at his clothing. He pushed her skirts up, hands seeking and stroking, and she cried out, her body spasming even as he sank into her, stretching her and filling her, going deeper than she thought possible.

Yes, she knew this man, knew this body that rocked against hers, making her cry out and claw at him.

"You are mine," he growled against her ear. "Forever."

"Aye," she panted, hips thrusting, thighs gripping him. "Aye."

And as the climax swept over her, she knew she loved him and that all that had been done had been done for love.

Stephen lay in the leaves beside Deidra, gazing down at her. She was awake but didn't speak. She stared into the wood. Her clothing was torn. He had done that—but then she had torn his as well. The exposed skin of her shoulder was smooth and creamy and he couldn't resist; he had to lean over and kiss it.

She rolled over to look up at him. "Stephen? What happened?"

She knew his name. He pulled her close. "I believe we just made love."

She gave him a long-suffering smirk. "Not that."

"Ah, you mean before." He smiled, his heart lighter to see that she was no longer screaming, no longer miserable. "You were dead . . . but now you're alive. We're both alive and strong. No more pain. No more weakness."

Her mouth curved upwards slightly and her eyes took on a faraway quality, seeing something beyond him, inside of herself.

"Can you hear them still?" he asked softly. "The animals?"

She bit her lip and nodded. "Aye . . . but it is different now . . . I am no longer separate from them. I am one of them now."

And he could see that this was profound for her. Her eyes were wide with wonder as she took it all in. And he understood that this transformation was so much more for her than it had been for him.

She rolled onto her side, pressing her half-clad body up against his. He cupped her hips, pulling her close so she was pressed all along his body. It was heaven, having her like this.

"I remember, at the end," she said, "wanting to give up. The only thing that stopped me was the memory of you."

"You remember me? Everything?" he asked, still uncertain.

She smiled. "Aye. Not everything . . . but I know your face as I know my own heart." She touched his face with her fingertips. He turned into her caress.

"And I know that I love you and that I wanted this—to be like you. To be with you."

He covered her hand, which still touched his cheek, and pressed a kiss to the palm. "I couldn't let you go. Even if I couldn't have you forever, I will love you as long as God permits me to."

She smiled up at him, her head tilted slightly. "I think, my love, that we will have a very, very long time."

POCKET BOOKS
PROUDLY PRESENTS

My Immortal Promise

JEN HOLLING

Coming soon from
Pocket Books

Turn the page for a preview of
My Immortal Promise. . . .

Prologue

———∞∞∞———

She was twenty-seven when she first acquired a taste for blood. A grown woman, past her prime, and good for little except hard work. And she did a great deal of that. She worked all day in the fields, caring for their animals, and in the cottage cooking and washing and making certain they had light and fuel. Then she came home and was worked in bed. She usually made it through it all unscathed, providing she kept her mouth shut.

But sometimes she didn't or, more aptly, *couldn't*. Sometimes the devil in her made her say something. Like that long-ago night.

Gareth was hungry. According to him, he'd just come in from the fields and, damn it, he was hungry! Where was his dinner? Aedammair knew he'd been a few cottages down, drinking ale, but she did not comment. Not then, at least.

She'd told him dinner wasn't ready. She'd had to patch a hole in the roof, and got a late start.

It was when he said, "Damn it, woman, I am short on temper tonight," while sitting at her clean table scattering bread crumbs all over it.

Her gazed traveled downward as she said, "That isna all yer short on."

She would have slapped her hand over her mouth had she not held a ladle in one and a turnip in the other.

Never mind that she spoke the truth. Color bloomed in his cheeks, a red so deep it was almost purple. He looked as if he was ready to explode and likely he was, as there was no disputing her statement.

And so, that was how later that evening Aedammair found herself huddled on the floor of the cottage she shared with her husband. Barely able to see out of two swollen eyes. Unable to crawl to the bed because her body was so battered. She thought she had broken bones—ribs, arm, legs—but she was not sure.

She could not cry. She could do nothing but lay there and wish to die.

And then someone was there, in her cottage. A woman. Aedammair was ashamed and wished to hide, but could do nothing. The woman touched Aedammair's face. She could barely see the woman through the watery red haze. She had dark hair and pale skin, but that was all Aedammair could discern.

"It was your man, wasn't it child?"

The woman made a sound of disbelief as she pushed a lock of red hair out of Aedammair's face. "Men are worthless, disgusting vermin. We do not need them."

Aedammair wished that were true. But she would probably starve without Gareth. It was the highlands, there was no work for her. No one would take her in if she left her husband. She wished she could kill him and find another man, but who would have her now? Her bones would probably heal crooked and her face would be scarred.

"I see you do not believe me," the woman said. "Would you like me to show you?"

Show her? "I . . . do n-not . . ." She couldn't get the rest out. Her face hurt too badly. The woman swam before her as tears filled her eyes.

"I ken, child. More than you know." Her hand stroked Aedammair's hair. "You do not understand. But you will. When you wake tomorrow night, you will be a new woman, free of this pain and weakness. We will choose a new name for you. And then you will come back here and make your husband suffer as he has made you suffer. When that is over, you will come with me and we will live a new life, free of men and their base wants and needs."

It sounded heavenly. Was that what it was? A place where she was free of this pain, free of Gareth? Where justice would finally be served and Gareth would suffer all he had inflicted on her.

"Aye," she forced through her raw and bloodied lips.

"Good," the woman said, and there was a smile in her voice. "This will only hurt for a second, and then the pain will be gone forever."

Chapter 1

———⚭⚭⚭———

Drake stood in the dark alley, gaze fixed on the village center, waiting. It was full dark. The night was quiet, cool, devoid of insects. His eyes had adjusted to the darkness, but without the moon it was still difficult to make out any details.

The witch should have escaped by now. His gaze narrowed on the dark smudge of the thieves' hole, marked by a pole. Earlier that day the witch's hands had been nailed to the pole, but he'd later been ripped free and thrown down into the hole.

Drake had seen the cycle often enough in the past six months. It followed a similar pattern each time: the witch was captured, tortured into confession, and then waited in a hole or other prison to be executed. Drake observed—an interested bystander, nothing more. But he made sure to plant suggestions when he thought it prudent, not getting involved, but making certain the witch had an opportunity to escape eventually.

The escape was of vital importance since he had to be captured again in order to start the whole process all over again.

They'd been through this dance countless times. Usually the witch had escaped by now and was slinking away into the night, with the occasional stop to desperately feed on a farm animal.

But tonight deviated from the pattern. Drake continued to wait in the darkness, his lips tightening, his fists opening and closing rhythmically, battling the urge to leave the safety of the darkness. Finally, he could no longer deny that something had gone amiss.

He scanned the rest of the town square. It was empty. The windows of the houses surrounding the square stared back at him, dark eyes. He ran swiftly and quietly across the square, dropping to his knees beside the thieves' hole. He surveyed the square again.

Finding it clear, he leaned over the wood grating. "Luthias," he called in a loud whisper. "Luthias."

There was a long moment of silence. Drake sat back on his heels, listening and waiting, and wondering if the witch had finally died.

A *baobhan sith* did not die easily. Drake knew this, so the silence puzzled him. True, the cycle of abuse had been ongoing for months and any human man would have died long ago or at the very least been permanently crippled from all that Luthias had endured. But Luthias was not a human man and had been through worse than the relatively tame bit of torture he'd been subjected to in this village. A dunking. The wheel. Some rocks on the chest. Nothing a *baobhan sith* couldn't recover from in a few hours.

"Luthias," Drake called, his voice a harsh whisper. Still, nothing.

Drake's chest contracted. If Luthias was dead, then it was over. Drake could be finished with this duty he'd assigned himself. And move on to the next one.

Drake's lips pressed together. The latter held no appeal for him, and though the former once did, it no longer held the interest it once had. He was tired. His taste for vengeance had been satiated. If Luthias was not dead, he would be tomorrow when they burned him at the stake.

Drake stroked his beard thoughtfully. Though he would love to be finished with this task, he dreaded the one that followed. It had been six months. Doubtless the thing that waited for him believed he did not intend to fulfill his promise at all. And that was not true. Drake MacKay honored his promises, even the ones that caused him misery to even contemplate.

But he didn't relish the dead thing believing he'd reneged. It was time to go. He had done what was necessary to protect his family and punish the man who persecuted them.

It was over now. Justice had been served.

He secured the grate over the thieves' hole. He had unlatched it earlier so that Luthias could easily escape. Let him meet the village's sentence. He was in their hands now.

After another visual surveillance of the village, Drake returned to the safety of the dark alley. His horse was stabled close by. Now that he'd made the decision, he didn't want to waste another moment on Luthias.

He saddled his horse and led it out of the village. When he was clear of the last cottage, he mounted and road into the night, bound for the far northern highlands and destiny.

The island was exactly as Drake remembered it. Windswept, treeless, lonely. A lethargic bell clanged in the distance as a goat wandered through the tall grass. The sunlight blinded him and he squinted as he crossed the island, following the sound. He remembered the last time he had made this same journey. It had been under very different circumstances. He had come here with murder on his mind. To take revenge on the *thing* he blamed for his years of misery. Instead, the blood witch had saved the life of his friend.

But it had not been without a price.

This was not a woman who granted favors out of the kindness of her heart. In fact, technically, she wasn't a woman at all. And probably didn't have a heart. She was a *baobhan sith*. A blood-sucking witch. And he owed her a life.

His life.

It wasn't worth much these days anyway.

He waded through the tall grasses to the top of the hill. A lush green valley spread out before him dotted with white puffs of sheep. The *baobhan sith*'s house was set in a hillside, not immediately visible to the unobservant. It had a new door, no doubt thicker than the last one that he had hacked through with an ax.

The door was closed and locked from the inside, but he had expected no different. *Baobhan siths* were night creatures. They derived their power from the night or the moon—he wasn't certain which. Because of this, they often hid themselves during the daylight hours.

He pounded on the door, not really expecting any response. When none came he settled down beside the door, crossed his arms over his chest, and closed his eyes.

He slept fitfully, startling awake frequently, hand on dirk, wondering where he was. And the moment he remembered, his body would relax, his eyes turning to the door, still closed, then to the sky, gauging how long until the sun set. He shut his eyes and he slept some more.

He dreamed, too. Strange, vivid dreams that seemed real and yet couldn't be. He saw the *baobhan sith* in his dreams, walking in shadows, just out of sight. He would tell her to stop running and come out where he could see her, but she only faded further away.

The next time he woke it was in increments and with care. His eyes opened to the darkness. He didn't move, waiting for his eyes to adjust to the gloom. It was night, but no stars or moon were visible. A thick fog had moved in from the water and hung around him like a cloud. It was damp, clammy, chilly. He suppressed a shiver.

He stood, listening carefully. Sheep bleated in the distance. He felt along the grass wall until he touched the door. It was open, just a crack. She knew he was here. He pushed on it and it creaked inward.

His chest and throat tightened. His eyes narrowed and he took a step into the house. It was dark inside. Not a single candle lit. He had a vague recollection of the last time he was here and knew there was a table several feet to his right. On it had been a large squat candle. He moved toward the table, hand outstretched until he touched it. His palm skimmed over the tabletop, searching for candle and flint.

Before he encountered anything, there was a scrape and a spark. A halo of light spread across the table.

She sat at the table across from him, candle in front of her, her long slender arm lowering the flint matches to the tabletop. The candlelight lit her hair so that it burned like fire, deep auburn and copper.

The sight of her there startled him, sent a jolt of energy through him. His hands curled into fists. She was so still, so quiet. Her mood was inscrutable. He could discern nothing by her blank expression.

The silence stretched out interminably until Drake felt compelled to say, "Well. I'm here."

Her head tilted slightly to one side as she regarded him thoughtfully. Silken copper hair slid from her shoulder to fall behind her back. "It took you long enough."

"Aye, well, I'm here now."

She looked away, disinterested. "You can go."

Drake frowned at the woman before him. She seemed different. Previously she had been enigmatic, mysterious . . . but not empty.

"No," he said. "I made a promise and my word is good."

She waved a pale hand in his direction. "Obviously. You *are* here." The emotionless line of her mouth curved minutely into something resembling a smile. "Your honor is noted, Drake MacKay. No one will speak ill of the solidarity of your word. I release you from your promise."

Drake had been dreading this moment, dreading coming to this island, and most of all, dreading the fulfillment of his promise. Her words should have been welcome. And there *was* a sigh of relief in his soul. But the larger part of him was annoyed.

Released him of his promise? Why?

She stared up at him, waiting. Her eyes were large and sultry, curtained with thick auburn lashes that seemed too heavy for her to hold up consistently, so they lowered, shadowing her eyes and making her thoughts elusive.

"I came a long way," he said. What was he doing? Arguing? My God, was he insane?

Apparently he was, because rather than run to the boat and row back to the mainland, thanking God for this reprieve, he stood here arguing with her.

She seemed as puzzled by his strange behavior as he was. "I imagine you did. And if there had been some way to get word to you about this change in plans, well . . ." She lifted a palm and shrugged. "Well, I wouldn't have done it anyway, so never mind about that." The corners of her mouth pulled tight and she exhaled. "You are released. Do not be a fool and question it."

His brows drew together as he regarded her. She was right. There was no sense in questioning such a gift. He was free. He inclined his head, not willing to thank her verbally. She held his gaze for a long moment. Then her gaze drifted away, disinterested.

Drake backed out of the house and closed the door. He stood outside the door, hesitant for some inexplicable reason. She seemed so strange. Not that he had known her well, but he had spent a fortnight in her company and during that time she had been very different. Though insouciant and understated, she had still seemed *alive*. Witty and clever—conversant. He had not found her company objectionable.

The woman he walked away from was a shell.

He turned away from the door. Whatever ailed her was not his concern. He was free and that was all that mattered now.

He rowed back to the village, relief washing over him in slow waves. He had stopped thinking about a future. There had been no point. His future had been sealed when he made the promise to the *baobhan sith*. But now the future opened before him again, full of possibilities. Where did he go from here?

The thought was such a profound one that he stopped rowing. His oars trailed through the water.

Before the blood witch had saved his friend, Stephen, he had lived his life seething with anger and misery over his wife's horrible death, needing someone to blame. And that someone had been the *baobhan sith*. But then she'd helped him and though he hadn't forgiven her, he no longer felt compelled to take revenge on her.

Luthias had been punished.

The blood witch had released him from his promise.

What was left?

The sudden hollowness in his chest unnerved him. It seemed abnormal to view the years that stretched ahead of him with no interest.

There must be something. He just didn't know what yet. He was no longer young, but neither was he an old man. He would find another woman, have sons. He'd lived practically as a monk since his wife died. That needed to change.

He pulled at the oars with new vigor, letting the hard work dominate his thoughts. He kept at it until the bow hit the beach. He dragged the boat ashore and left it, trudging up the pebbled beach. No one paid much attention to him. The fishermen were farther down the shore where a narrow dock extended out into the water readying their vessels to set sail. It was very early; the sun had not yet risen.

Shops and houses clustered just past the waterline. Drake had not rented a room, so he entered the tavern and dropped wearily into a chair. The taverns never really closed since the fishermen came and went all night. The smell of bread and porridge filled the air. Within seconds, a tall, lean woman stood over him with a tankard of ale and one thick brow arched. Drake tossed his coin on the table. She exchanged the ale for the coin and left him to his drink.

Drake drained the tankard and then a second one. He wanted to drink away the troubling thoughts that plagued him about future and family. He had just started his third when he realized the men sitting at the table behind him were talking about the *baobhan sith*. He paused, then slowly brought the tankard to his lips, shifting backward slightly in his chair to eavesdrop better.

"She rejected the offering again," one of the men said, his voice deep and gruff.

"What does that mean? What does she want?" another man asked. This one sounded smaller, his voice thinner. He was frightened.

There was a brief silence. An exhalation. "Human blood," deep and gruff said ominously.

The silence drew out longer this time.

"So . . . what do we do?" a different one asked in a low harsh whisper. "Do we send her a human?"

"Mayhap we should wait," the thin voice said anxiously. "Mayhap she doesn't care about us anymore."

"The last time we waited and prayed," the gruff voice said, "bad things happened. She killed entire herds of animals. Dried up the fishing. Preyed on humans. No." Drake imagined him shaking his head decisively. "No more. We have been at her mercy too long. I say we kill her."

There was a sharp intake of breath. "It canna be done. She canna be killed."

"*Everything* can be killed," gruff man drawled.

Drake's heart beat into the silence, and he realized he had stopped drinking and sat very still, head turned toward the men, listening. He then took a drink of his ale and leaned forward on the table, rubbing the back of his head wearily.

His antics to appear as if he wasn't listening caused him to miss what was being said.

". . . told me the only way to kill one was to cut their heads off and burn them to ash."

"How do we manage that when she lives on an island? She knows who is coming and going. There is no surprising her."

"Then we have to outnumber her. And daytime is the best time."

Drake couldn't listen to anymore. He stood and left the tavern. He paced outside for a moment, his chest a knot, teeth clenched. They were going to kill her. And it sounded like maybe they knew how. He raked a hand through his hair and stopped short, staring out to sea. Her island was visible from where he stood. The fog had burned off and it looked very green in the distance. A calm place, a safe haven, not the lair of a *baobhan sith*.

But she wasn't his problem. She had released him from his promise and if he had kept walking to the stables rather than stopping to have a drink he would never have known any different.

But the problem was, he *had* stopped. He *did* know. And he couldn't just ignore what he knew. He owed her. Being released from a promise was one thing, but knowingly allowing someone who had aided him to die . . . well, that was quite another.

He headed for the beach and the skiff he'd left resting on the pebbled sand. Urgency mixed with impatience in his gut. He had thought he was finally free of everything, ready to start fresh, and here he was in the thick of it again. But no sense starting anew when there was unfinished business to resolve. And some part of him felt better with a task, a mission, something to distract him from thoughts of the future.

He shoved the skiff into the water and stepped in, rowing back toward the island.